Leslie Stephen

Dictionary of national biography

Leslie Stephen

Dictionary of national biography

ISBN/EAN: 9783742892034

Manufactured in Europe, USA, Canada, Australia, Japa

Cover: Foto ©Raphael Reischuk / pixelio.de

Manufactured and distributed by brebook publishing software
(www.brebook.com)

Leslie Stephen

Dictionary of national biography

· DICTIONARY

OF

NATIONAL BIOGRAPHY

Stanhope——Stovin

DICTIONARY

OF

NATIONAL BIOGRAPHY

EDITED BY

SIDNEY LEE

VOL. LIV.

Stanhope——Stovin

New York
THE MACMILLAN COMPANY
LONDON : SMITH, ELDER, & CO.
1898

LIST OF WRITERS

IN THE FIFTY-FOURTH VOLUME.

J. G. A. . . . J. G. ALGER.

J. A-N. . . . THE REV. JOHN ANDERSON.

W. A. J. A. . W. A. J. ARCHBOLD.

R. B-L. . . . RICHARD BAGWELL.

G. F. R. B. . G. F. RUSSELL BARKER.

T. B. . . . . THOMAS BAYNE.

T. H. B. . . PROFESSOR T. HUDSON BEARE.

H. L. B. . . THE REV. CANON LEIGH BENNETT.

H. E. D. B. THE REV. H. E. D. BLAKISTON.

G. C. B. . . THE LATE G. C. BOASE.

G. S. B. . . G. S. BOULGER.

H. B. . . . . HENRY BRADLEY.

A. B. . . . . ALEXANDER BUCHAN, M.D.

E. I. C. . . . E. IRVING CARLYLE.

E. C-E. . . . SIR ERNEST CLARKE, F.S.A.

A. M. C. . . MISS A. M. CLERKE.

S. C. . . . . SIDNEY COLVIN.

A. M. C E. . MISS A. M. COOKE.

T. C. . . . . THOMPSON COOPER, F.S.A.

J. S. C. . . . J. S. COTTON.

W. P. C. . . W. P. COURTNEY.

L. C. . . . . LIONEL CUST, F.S.A.

H. D. . . . . HENRY DAVEY.

A. D. . . . . AUSTIN DOBSON.

J. A. D. . . J. A. DOYLE.

R. D. . . . . ROBERT DUNLOP.

C. L. F. . . C. LITTON FALKINER.

C. H. F. . . C. H. FIRTH.

W. G. D. F. THE REV. W. G. D. FLETCHER.

W. F. . . . . THE REV. WILLIAM FORSYTH, D.D.

T. F. . . . . THE REV. THOMAS FOWLER, D.D., PRESIDENT OF CORPUS CHRISTI COLLEGE, OXFORD.

R. G. . . . . RICHARD GARNETT, LL.D., C.B.

A. G. . . . . THE REV. ALEXANDER GORDON.

R. E. G. . . R. E. GRAVES.

J. C. H. . . J. CUTHBERT HADDEN.

J. A. H. . . J. A. HAMILTON.

T. H. . . . . THE REV. THOMAS HAMILTON, D.D.

C. A. H. . . C. ALEXANDER HARRIS.

P. J. H. . . P. J. HARTOG.

T. F. H. . . T. F. HENDERSON

F. C. H.-R. THE REV. PREBENDARY HINGESTON-RANDOLPH.

T. E. H. . . PROFESSOR T. E. HOLLAND, D.C.L.

W. H. . . . . THE REV. WILLIAM HUNT.

W. H. H. . THE REV. W. H. HUTTON, B.D.

C. L. K. . . C. L. KINGSFORD.

J. K. . . . . JOSEPH KNIGHT, F.S.A.

J. K. L. . . PROFESSOR J. K. LAUGHTON.

T. G. L. . . T. G. LAW.

E. L. . . . . MISS ELIZABETH LEE.

S. L. . . . . SIDNEY LEE.

List of Writers.

R. H. L. . . R. H. LEGGE.

E. M. L. . . COLONEL E. M. LLOYD, R.E.

J. R. M. . . J. R. MACDONALD.

Æ. M. . . . SHERIFF MACKAY.

A. H. M. . . A. H. MILLAR.

C. M. . . . . COSMO MONKHOUSE.

N. M. . . . . NORMAN MOORE, M.D.

G. LE G. N. G. LE GRYS NORGATE.

K. N. . . . . MISS KATE NORGATE.

F. M. O'D. . F. M. O'DONOGHUE, F.S.A.

A. F. P. . . A. F. POLLARD.

B. P. . . . . MISS BERTHA PORTER.

D'A. P. . . . D'ARCY POWER, F.R.C.S.

R. E. P. . . R. E. PROTHERO.

J. M. R. . . J. M. RIGG.

G. W. E. R. G. W. E. RUSSELL.

F. S. . . . . THE REV. FRANCIS SANDERS.

T. S. . . . . THOMAS SECCOMBE.

C. F. S. . . MISS C. FELL SMITH.

L. S. . . . . LESLIE STEPHEN.

D. A. S. . . D. A. STEVENSON.

C. C. S. . . MRS. STOPES.

G. S-H. . . . GEORGE STRONACH.

C. W. S. . . C. W. SUTTON.

J. T-T. . . . JAMES TAIT.

D. LL. T. . . D. LLEUFER THOMAS.

T. F. T. . . PROFESSOR T. F. TOUT.

W. W. T. . THE REV. W. W. TULLOCH, D.D.

R. H. V. . . COLONEL R. H. VETCH, R.E., C.B.

E. T. W. . . E. T. WEDMORE.

S. W. . . . . STEPHEN WHEELER.

B. B. W. . . B. B. WOODWARD.

DICTIONARY

OF

NATIONAL BIOGRAPHY

STANHOPE, LADY, and COUNTESS OF CHESTERFIELD (d. 1667). [See KIRKHOVEN or KERCKHOVEN, CATHERINE.]

STANHOPE, CHARLES, third EARL STANHOPE (1753–1816), politician and man of science, born in London on 3 Aug. 1753, was the second but eldest surviving son of Philip, second earl Stanhope (d. 7 March 1786), who married, in 1745, Grizel (d. 1811), daughter of Charles Hamilton, (by courtesy) lord Binning [q. v.], and sister of Thomas, seventh earl of Haddington.

The father, the second earl Stanhope, was son of James Stanhope, first earl Stanhope [q. v.] Educated at Utrecht and Geneva, he acquired a love for mathematics, for the Greek language—which was as familiar to him as English—and for democratic principles. Lalande called him the best English mathematician of his day, and he was an especial friend and correspondent of Robert Simson [q. v.], the professor of mathematics at Glasgow. He paid for the posthumous impression of Simson's works and for the edition of the works of Archimedes that was printed at the Clarendon Press, and Priestley dedicated to him the third volume of his 'Experiments on Air.' In 1735 he was elected F.R.S., and at his death he left 500l. to that society (WELD, Royal Society, ii. 196). In parliament he spoke, while in England, not infrequently, and always with independence of thought. Letters of Pitt, Lord Chatham, and Franklin to him, and one from him are in the 'Chatham Correspondence' (vol. iv.) He transmitted to his son Charles his enthusiasm for science, his devotion to the cause of democracy, and his fondness for simplicity in dress (MAHON, Hist. of England, iii. 208–9).

Charles was sent to Eton at an early age. It is usually said that he went thither at the age of eight, but his name is not in the list of 1762 (Collect. Oxford Hist. Soc. iii. 367). His elder brother Philip died at Geneva on 6 July 1763 (Gent. Mag. 1763, p. 415), and Charles became Lord Mahon and the heir to the peerage. In July 1764 the whole family went to Geneva (Letters of Lady Hervey, pp. 303, 309), where the lad was instructed by G. J. Le Sage, who developed his tastes for the exacter sciences. He also spent much time in experimental philosophy. In 1765 he had the advantage for two months of the society of Adam Smith and of Henry Scott, third duke of Buccleuch [q.v.] (DUGALD STEWART, Works, x. 45). Lady Mary Coke was at Geneva in October 1769, and marvelled at the youth's 'surprising genius; his painting wou'd surprise you, and he cuts out people in paper as like as others can draw them. He has invented a mathematical instrument . . . better for the purpose it is intended than any other of the kind; yet he is but seventeen years of age' (Journal, iii. 158). Still he did not neglect the amusements of youth. He excelled in horsemanship, enrolled himself in the militia of the Genevan republic, and was an adept in shooting at a mark.

At the age of eighteen Mahon composed a paper in French on the pendulum, which the Academy of Stockholm rewarded with a prize and printed. He wrote, at Geneva in 1773, a volume, printed in 1775, of 'Considerations on the Means of preventing Fraudulent Practices on the Gold Coin.' The coin was to have very little relief, and the date was to be sunk in. The dangers to be guarded against were false coining, clipping, milling, and sweating. Very soon after its composition the Stanhopes returned to England, and Mahon threw himself with ardour into politics.

Early in September 1774 he was presented at court, and as his father would not allow him to wear powder 'because wheat is so dear,' he went in his natural 'coal-black hair' and a white feather. The wits said 'he had been tarred and feathered' (WALPOLE, *Letters,* vi. 114). A few weeks later, when only just of age, he contested the city of Westminster, but, after the poll had been open for some days, withdrew. At this time he was inspired with an ardent friendship for the second William Pitt, who was then equally ardent for reform, and their alliance was cemented by his marriage, on 19 Dec. 1774, to his friend's sister, Lady Hester Pitt, elder daughter of the first Earl of Chatham. Lady Mahon died at the family seat of Chevening, Kent, on 18 July 1780, when only twenty-five.

During the Gordon riots of June 1780 Mahon harangued the people from the balcony of a coffee-house, and urged them to retire to their homes. Walpole said that he 'chiefly contributed by his harangues to conjure down the tempest' (*Letters,* vii. 377-81). On the following 6 Sept. he was elected, through the influence of the Earl of Shelburne, member for the borough of Chipping Wycombe in Buckinghamshire, and represented it until his accession to the peerage. At the opening debate (October 1780) on the choice of speaker, he made his maiden speech, and in 1781 he was a delegate for the county of Kent to advocate the cessation of the American war and the promotion of parliamentary reform. From 1782 to 1786 he introduced into the House of Commons several bills for the prevention of bribery and corruption and for the reduction of expenses at parliamentary elections. The provisions of his bill against bribery were declared by Lord Mansfield on 23 March 1784 to be already part of the law of the land (*Gent. Mag.* 1784, i. 229). His bill for annual registration of voters, for increase in the number of polling places, and for other improvements at elections was taken charge of after he had become a peer by Wilberforce, and, with Pitt as his friend, passed the commons, but was thrown out by the lords on 5 July 1786.

Mahon had associated himself with the whigs in their opposition to the war with the American colonies, but he strongly opposed the coalition of Fox and North, and he was vehement against Fox's East India Bill. He declined office on the formation of Pitt's cabinet in 1783, but remained for a short time his strenuous supporter. At the general election in 1784 he laboured in the interest of Pitt. Walpole at the time dubbed him 'a savage, a republican, a royalist—I don't know what not' (*Letters,* viii. 469). He spoke at the meetings of the electors of Westminster in February 1784 against Fox and the coalition (cf. JEPHSON, *The Platform,* i. 155-6). His first political difference with Pitt took place on 22 July 1784 over the tax on bricks and tiles. He ridiculed the arguments of George Rose (1744-1818) [q.v.] in its favour, and Pitt rallied him ironically in return.

On 7 March 1786 he succeeded to the peerage as the third Earl Stanhope, and lost no time in attacking by speech and pamphlet Pitt's proposals for a sinking fund. His pamphlet was entitled 'Observations on Mr. Pitt's Plan for the Reduction of the National Debt,' and Pitt tried hard to dissuade him from its publication (LORD AUCKLAND, *Journal,* i. 369). Two bills were introduced by him into the House of Lords in the summer of 1789. One was for relieving members of the church of England from sundry penalties and disabilities; the other was for preventing vexatious proceedings for the recovery of tithes. Both were thrown out, the first on 18 May, the second on 3 July, and on the first date he created much amusement by informing the lord chancellor that 'on another occasion I shall teach the noble and learned lord law, as I have this day taught the bench of bishops religion.' He was accordingly represented in caricature as a schoolmaster, with a rod in his hand. His speeches abounded in pithy expressions and in illustrative anecdote, although his gesture was ungraceful.

Up to this date Stanhope had remained on friendly terms with William Pitt, but differences over the French revolution led to their permanent estrangement (STANHOPE, *Pitt,* ii. 180-1). He was chairman of the 'Revolution Society,' which was founded in 1788 to commemorate the centenary of the English revolution of 1688, and he forwarded to Paris the address of congratulation on the capture of the Bastille, which had been moved at its meeting on 4 Nov. 1789 by Dr. Price. To Rochefoucault he sent the resolution of congratulation on the establishment of liberty in France, which was proposed by Sheridan at a meeting held at the Crown and Anchor tavern in the Strand on 14 July 1790. It was read in the assembly on 21 July, and circulated in French. Letters sent by him to Condorcet were printed at Paris in 1791 and 1792, the first set arguing against the issue of false assignats, and the second relating to the treatment of negroes. He published in 1790 'A Letter to Burke, containing a Short Answer to his Late Speech on the French Revolution,' which went into a second edition and was translated into French in that year. Mrs. Macaulay addressed to Stanhope her 'Observations on the Reflections of Mr. Burke on the Revolution in France.'

Stanhope, during 1791 and 1792, supported Fox's libel bill for maintaining the rights of juries, and published his arguments with a catena of legal authorities in their support. By letter to Lord Grenville, with whom he was still on friendly terms, and by speeches in parliament, he consistently opposed the war with France. On 23 Jan. 1794 he moved to acknowledge the French republic, and on 4 April 1794 he brought forward a motion 'against any interference in the internal government of France,' which provoked his fellow-peers, at Lord Grenville's instance, to order the entry of it to be expunged from their journals. Both of these speeches were printed separately. Next month he opposed the Habeas Corpus Suspension Bill, and on 6 Jan. 1795 he introduced a second motion against interfering with the internal affairs of France. On this occasion he was 'in a minority of one,' and after entering a protest against the defeat of his motion, which he subsequently published, he withdrew from further attendance in parliament. A medal was struck in his honour with the motto 'The minority of one, 1795,' and he was long known by that title or as 'Citizen' Stanhope. From 1791 to 1808 he was a frequent figure in the caricatures of Gillray. One satiric print was entitled 'Scientific Researches, New Discoveries in Pneumatics.' When he declared himself a sans-culotte, a ballad, with a rough caricature of him by another satirist, was scattered broadcast.

Owing to his revolutionary sympathies, Stanhope's house in Mansfield Street was attacked by rioters and set on fire at different times on the night of 11–12 June 1794. He believed, and declared in an advertisement, that the mob had been paid. The Rev. Jeremiah Joyce [q. v.], his private secretary and the tutor to his sons, was on 4 May 1794 arrested at Chevening on a charge of 'treasonable practices.' To celebrate his acquittal Stanhope on 23 Dec. 1794 gave a grand entertainment at Chevening to his neighbours and tenants (Gent. Mag. 1795, i. 73). At a very large meeting at the Crown and Anchor tavern on 4 Feb. 1795, in honour of the acquittal, he was called to the chair and delivered an animated speech, which, when published, enjoyed great popularity. In this

year of 1795 Walter Savage Landor printed anonymously 'A Moral Epistle to Earl Stanhope,' a poem of twenty pages, which contrasted him with Pitt, much to the commoner's disadvantage (FOSTER, Landor, i. 68–71).

Stanhope's secession from the House of Lords lasted from 6 Jan. 1795 to 20 Feb. 1800. In the beginning of 1799 he addressed to the people of Great Britain and Ireland a pamphlet 'On the Subject of an Union,' which was reprinted and circulated by the anti-union party of Dublin. His first motion on reappearing among the peers was to propose a peace with Napoleon; but he acted without concert, and only one peer, Lord Camelford, supported him. In 1808 he took a very strong part against the Indictment Bill, as interfering with the liberty of the subject, and at all times spoke strongly against the slave trade. He advocated a reduction of fiscal duties as tending to an increase in the revenue, and was earnest for education on a comprehensive basis. On 27 June 1811 he introduced a 'gold coin and bank-note' bill, making it illegal to pay a larger sum than 21s. for a guinea, and for preventing any note issued by the Bank of England from being accepted at a discount. It passed through both houses. In the last year of his life he carried through the lords two motions for the appointment of committees—one for a revision of the statute-book, and the other for the adoption of a uniform system of weights and measures.

Throughout his life Stanhope deservedly enjoyed a great reputation for his discoveries in science, to the prosecution of which he devoted much time and money. He was elected F.R.S. on 19 Nov. 1772, but through absence from England was not admitted until 12 Jan. 1775 (Records of Royal Soc.), and he was a member of the Philadelphia Philosophical Society. It is believed that Richard Varley, father of John Varley [q. v.] the artist, was his tutor in mechanics. His principal experiments related to the safeguarding of buildings against fire by means of 'stucco,' in which he endeavoured to bring to perfection the plans of David Hartley the younger [q. v.] He took out patents for steam-vessels in March and August 1790, and in February 1807. It was announced in the 'Gentleman's Magazine' for 1792 (ii. 956) that his experiments for propelling vessels by the steam-engine without masts or sails had been so satisfactory that a ship of two hundred tons was being built under his direction on this principle. His inventions received the approval of the lords of the admiralty in 1795 and 1798. An 'ambi-navigator' ship called the Kent was constructed for him, but did not turn out a success (STANHOPE, *Pitt*, ii. 397–401). In 1795 the earl revived the project of Genevois, the pastor of Berne, for impelling boats with duck-feet oars, but the highest rate of speed attained was three miles an hour (cf. WHITAKER, *Course of Hannibal*, 1794, ii. 142; MATHIAS, *Shade of Pope*, 1799). Stanhope declared in the House of Lords on 21 May 1810 that he had invented 'a vessel 111 feet in length which drew only seven feet odd inches of water, and outsailed the swiftest vessel in the navy.' His specification 'respecting ships and vessels' was printed in 1807.

Many printing appliances devised by himself he placed at the public disposal, without any advantage to himself, and made solid contributions to the art of printing. His chief assistant in this department of mechanics was Robert Walker, an ingenious mechanician of Vine Street, Piccadilly, and Dean Street, Soho. He perfected a process of stereotyping which was acquired by the delegates of the Clarendon Press at Oxford in 1805 on the condition that they paid 4,000*l.* to the foreman and manager of his press, Andrew Wilson, of Wild Court, and stereotyping on this system became part of the general business of the press. They also acquired, but free from any payment, his iron hand-press, called the Stanhope press, and his system of logotypes and logotype cases. This system a few years later was introduced into the Oxford press; but his logotypes, like those of John Walter 'q. v.' of the 'Times,' proved a failure. The first book printed by his process was 'An Abstract of the whole Doctrine of the Christian Religion. By J. A. Freylinghausen,' 1804. Long after these dates he persevered with his experiments, either at Wilson's office or at Chevening, where he kept a foundry of his own. Another invention he called 'pantatype printing, by which one hundred thousand impressions of an engraving could be taken, all proofs; that is to say, the last impression will be as perfect as the first' (*Collectanea*, Oxford Hist. Soc. 1896, iii. 365–412; HANSARD, *Typographia*, p. 475; H. G. Bohn on *Printing*, Philobiblon Soc. iv. 90).

Stanhope published in 1806 his 'Principles of the Science of Tuning Instruments with Fixed Tones,' which was reprinted in Tilloch's 'Philosophical Magazine' (xxv. 291–312). The invention formed the subject of numerous articles by John Farey and Stanhope in that magazine, and of Dr. Callcott's 'Plain Statement of Earl Stanhope's Temperament.' In 1779 he produced his 'Principles of Electricity,' but a second volume which he promised, in refutation of the conclusions drawn from the experiments of Benjamin Wilson, was not published. In the first volume and in the 'Philosophical Transactions' (lxxvii. 130) he contended that when a large cloud is charged with electricity it drives out a considerable portion of the electricity in its neighbourhood, which often returns to its original position with such violence and in such quantity as to destroy life. In this way he explained the death of a carrier and his horses at Berwickshire in 1787, though there was no discharge of thunder nearer than some miles distance (THOMSON, *Royal Soc.* pp. 449–50). A public trial of Franklin's and Stanhope's experiments in lighting-conductors is said to have taken place at the Pantheon under the superintendence of Edward Nairne the electrician.

About 1777 Stanhope constructed two calculating machines (1) for working out with exactness complicated sums of addition and subtraction; (2) for similar sums in multiplication and division. 'The Stanhope Demonstrator, an Instrument for performing Logical Operations,' employed his thoughts at intervals for thirty years. It has been fully described by the Rev. Robert Harley, F.R.S., in an article in 'Mind' (iv. 192–210), which was reprinted separately for private circulation.

Stanhope's other inventions include a microscopic lens which, like the printing-press, bears his name; a new manner of producing cement more durable than the ordinary mortar; an improved method of 'burning chalk, marble, and limestone into lime;' an artificial slate or tile for excluding rain and snow; and a means of curing wounds made in trees. In conjunction with Robert Fulton, the American engineer, he projected a canal from his estate at Holsworthy in Devonshire to the Bristol Channel, with a novel system of inclined planes and with improved locks.

Stanhope's life was thus one of unremitting toil. He died of dropsy at Chevening, on 15 Dec. 1816, and was buried with marked simplicity in the family vault at that church on 24 Dec. In person he was tall and thin, with a high forehead and a countenance expressive of impetuosity. He was always very plain in his attire, and of late years his looks were pale and wan. A powerful voice and a vigorous gesticulation heightened the effect of his oratory. His sympathies were wide, his generosity was unbounded, and his views were much in advance of their time. In all that he did, whether it was in politics or in science, he worked for the public good. The defects of his character were an incapacity to work with others and a lack of sympathy towards his children, all of whom he disinherited after subjecting them to much ill-treatment. But Stanhope's mother left everything to her 'dearly beloved son, Charles, Earl Stanhope, from my approbation of his private and public conduct' (*Gent. Mag.* 1812, i. 673). By his will, made in 1805, Stanhope left all his disposable estate, after payment of a few legacies, among ten executors, of whom the best known were Lord Holland, Lord Grantley, Joseph Jekyll, George Dyer, and the Rev. Christopher Wyvill.

Stanhope married as his second wife, on 12 March 1781, Louisa, only daughter and sole heiress of the Hon. Henry Grenville, younger brother of Earl Temple and George Grenville. She died at Clarges Street, Piccadilly, on 7 March 1829, aged 70. By his first wife he had three daughters: (1) Hester Lucy Stanhope [q. v.]; (2) Griselda, who married at Marylebone church, on 29 Aug. 1800, John Tekell, of Hambledon, Hampshire; she died without issue, at Bagshot, on 13 Oct. 1851, aged 73 (*Gent. Mag.* 1851, ii. 667); and (3) Lucy Rachael, who eloped early in 1796 with Thomas Taylor of Sevenoaks, the family apothecary. Stanhope's resentment at this marriage exposed him to one of Gillray's most pungent satires, 'Democratic Levelling: Alliance à la Française; or the Union of the Coronet and Clyster-pipe,' 4 March 1796. Pitt requested Taylor to abandon his business, and made him controller-general of the customs. Lord Chatham made Taylor's eldest son, William Stanhope Taylor, one of his executors, and he edited with Pringle the volumes of the 'Chatham Correspondence.' Lady Lucy Taylor died at Coldharbour, Surrey, on 1 March 1814, when a pension of 100l. per annum was granted to each of her three sons and four daughters.

By his second wife Stanhope left three sons. Philip Henry, the eldest son, succeeded to the peerage [see under STANHOPE, PHILIP HENRY, fifth EARL]. Charles Banks (1785–1809), the second son, was killed at Coruña. James Hamilton (1788–1825), the third son, was captain and lieutenant-colonel of the 1st foot-guards.

A three-quarter length portrait of Stanhope by Gainsborough, left unfinished through the death of the artist, is preserved at Chevening. The first adequate reproduction is in the third volume of the 'Collectanea' of the Oxford Historical Society. A portrait of Stanhope by Opie, bequeathed to Lord Holland, is in the journal-room at Holland House (ROGERS, *Opie and his Works*, p. 165). A profile, drawn from the life and engraved by Henry Richter, was published on 4 June 1798. Another likeness, drawn and engraved by C. Warren, appeared in the 'Senator' in 1792. A number of private papers, referring chiefly to his inventions, are preserved at Chevening.

[Parliamentary History, 1780 to 1816, passim; Stanhope's William Pitt, passim; Philos. Trans. 1773, pp. 884-94, reproduced in Annual Register for 1779; Story's John Varley, pp. 200-2; Wright and Evans's Gillray Caricatures, passim; Works of Gillray, ed. Wright (really by Grego), passim, from p. 130 to p. 355; Collectanea, vol. iii. (Oxford Hist. Soc.), pp. 365-412; Nichols's Illustrations of Literature, iii. 154; Nichols's Lit. Anecdotes, ix. 669; Woodcroft's Chronological List of Patents; Notes and Queries, 1st ser. viii. 135, 2nd ser. ii. 50-1, iv. 265; Collins's Peerage, ed. Brydges, iv. 178-9; Gent. Mag. 1774 p. 598, 1780 p. 348, 1800 ii. 900, 1811 ii. 661, 1814 i. 412, 1816 ii. 563-4, 625, 1829 i. 283; Chatham Corresp. iv. 55, 373, 402, 440; Wraxall, ed. Wheatley, ii. 341, iii. 96, 295, 298, 401-2, v. 334; Annual Biogr. and Obituary, 1817, pp. 183-226; S. Fletcher's The late Earl Stanhope's Opinions, 1819.]

W. P. C.

STANHOPE, CHARLES, third EARL OF HARRINGTON (1753–1829), soldier, born on 20 March 1753, was the eldest son of William Stanhope, second earl of Harrington, and grandson of William Stanhope, first earl of Harrington [q. v.] He entered the army as an ensign in the Coldstream guards in November 1769, and in August 1773 obtained a captaincy in the 29th foot. From 1774 to 1776 he was M.P. for Thetford, and in the succeeding parliament sat for Westminster till his father's death in 1779. Meanwhile, he had exchanged his light company in the 29th for the grenadier company, his promotion being obtained, says Walpole, through the partiality of the war secretary, William Wildman Barrington, second viscount Barrington (*Journal of Reign of George III*, ii. 16). In February 1776 he embarked with the regiment for Quebec, and landed in face of an American cannonade. He was present at the subsequent successful action in the plains of Abraham. During the remainder of the year he was engaged in operations on the St. Lawrence, under Sir Guy Carleton, afterwards first lord Dorchester [q. v.] In the following year he accompanied General John Burgoyne [q. v.] as aide-de-camp on the disastrous campaign which ended with Saratoga. He was recommended by his commander to Lord George Germain [q. v.], secretary at war, as deserving of promotion on account of his excellent qualities and services during the campaign. On 24 Dec. 1777 he reached England with despatches announcing the surrender at Saratoga, the news of which had already arrived. In the following month, owing to Burgoyne's recommendation, he 'was suffered to buy' a higher commission, and obtained a captaincy in the 3rd foot-guards (ib. 17 Jan. 1778). In April 1779 he succeeded to the peerage. On 1 June of that year Harrington was examined before the select committee appointed to inquire into the management of Burgoyne's last campaign. He testified to that general's efforts to restrain the excesses of his Indian allies, and gave his opinion that a retreat after the action at Saratoga was impracticable. Walpole thought that Harrington 'did himself and Burgoyne honour' (to Conway, 5 June 1779). Having raised an infantry regiment (the 85th) at his own expense, he in 1780 embarked for Jamaica at the head of it, with the rank of brigadier. He assisted the governor (John Dalling) to put the island into an efficient state of defence in view of an expected attack by the French, but within about a year had to return home with his wife on account of bad health. The 85th suffered so much from the climate that the remnant left by the ravages of disease had to be embarked on some of Rodney's prizes and sent home.

On 26 Nov. 1782 Harrington was gazetted colonel and aide-de-camp to the king, and in the following March received the colonelcy of the 65th foot. With that regiment he first tried the new tactics introduced by Sir David Dundas (1735–1820) [q. v.] On 29 Jan. 1788 he received the command of his old regiment, the 29th. For the next three years he was in garrison with it at Windsor, and was brought much into contact with the royal family. In March 1788 he was offered the post of British resident at the court of Russia, but declined, apparently because, owing to the inferior rank of the tsarina's minister at St. James's, he could not bear the full title of ambassador (see Corresp. with Lord Carmarthen, Add. MS. 28063).

On 5 Dec. 1792 Harrington was appointed colonel of the 1st life-guards and gold stick in waiting. The latter appointment precluded him from serving (as he desired) with the Duke of York in Holland. He attained the rank of major-general in October 1793, lieutenant-general in January 1798, and general on 25 Sept. 1802; and was sworn of the privy council on 24 Oct. 1798. From July 1803 to October 1805 he acted as second in command on the staff of the London district, and on 31 Oct. of the latter year was appointed commander-in-chief in Ireland.

The latter appointment he held till January 1812. Meanwhile he had been appointed to undertake special diplomatic missions to Vienna in November 1805, and to Berlin in the following January.

On his return from Ireland he received the retiring appointment of constable and governor of Windsor Castle (14 March 1812), and in 1816 the grand cross of the Hanoverian order. At the coronation of George IV he was bearer of the great standard of England. Harrington was personally popular with both that king and his father; and his wife was a lady of the bedchamber and prime favourite of Queen Charlotte. Harrington died at Brighton on 15 Sept. 1829. Although he saw little service except in his earlier years, his military knowledge was accounted equal to that of any of his contemporaries. The new sword adopted by the army in 1792 was introduced by him.

Harrington married, in May 1779, Jane Seymour, daughter and coheiress of Sir John Fleming, bart., of Brompton Park, Middlesex. She was buried in Westminster Abbey on 12 Feb. 1824. Six sons and two daughters were issue of the marriage. The eldest son, Charles (see below), and the third son, Leicester Fitzgerald Charles Stanhope [q. v.], each succeeded to the earldom of Harrington. The second son, Major-general Lincoln Edwin Robert Stanhope, C.B., died in 1840. The fourth son, Fitzroy Henry Richard (1787–1864), was originally in the army, but afterwards took holy orders, and was father of Charles Wyndham (1809–1881), seventh earl of Harrington. Of the daughters, Anna Maria married the Marquis of Tavistock (afterwards Duke of Bedford); and Charlotte Augusta the Duke of Leinster.

A portrait of Harrington was painted by Fayram and engraved by Faber; another was engraved by Rawle. A portrait of the countess with her children was engraved by Bartolozzi from a painting by Sir J. Reynolds. Another portrait of her was painted by Reynolds and engraved by Val. Green; and one was also engraved by Cooper.

CHARLES STANHOPE, fourth EARL OF HARRINGTON (1780–1851), eldest son of the third earl, was born at Harrington House, St. James's, on 8 April 1780. He obtained an ensigncy in the Coldstream guards in December 1795, and in November 1799 became captain in the Prince of Wales's light dragoons. In February 1803 he was gazetted major in the queen's rangers, and on 25 June 1807 lieutenant-colonel of the 3rd West India regiment. He was placed on half-pay in August 1812, and on 4 June 1814 attained the rank of colonel in the army. In March

1812 he was named a lord of the bedchamber, and again held that appointment from January 1820 till November 1829. As Lord Petersham he was one of the best known figures in society during the regency and reign of George IV., and figures frequently in contemporary prints. His habits and tastes were eccentric. He never went out till 6 P.M., and his whole equipage was invariably of a certain brownish hue. He designed the Petersham overcoat and the Petersham snuff-mixture, and mixed his own blacking. In common with his family, he was a great connoisseur in tea, and his room was described by Captain Gronow as like a shop, full of tea-canisters and boxes of snuff labelled in gilt. He had a large and valuable collection of snuff-boxes. His hats were also peculiar (MELTON, *Hints on Hats*, p. 39). In person he was tall and handsome, and dressed like Henri Quatre, whom he was supposed to resemble. In spite of his affectations he was personally popular. Moore met him at dinner at Horace Twiss's chambers in Chancery Lane in June 1819 (*Diary and Corresp.* ii. 320).

Petersham was a great patron of the stage, and, after his accession to the peerage as Lord Harrington in 1829, married Maria Foote [q. v.], the actress, who survived him. Their only child, a daughter, married George, second marquis Conyngham. Harrington died on 3 March 1851. He was succeeded in the title by his brother, Leicester Fitzgerald Charles Stanhope.

[Doyle's *Official Baronage*; *Peerages* of G. E. C. and Burke; *State of the Expedition from Canada*, 1780, 2nd edit. pp. 64–81, and App.; *Gent. Mag.* 1829, ii. 365–8; *Public Characters*, 1828, ii. 306; Stanhope's *Hist. of England*, vi. 260 n., 286, 313; *Evans's Cat. Engr. Portraits*; Moore's *Diary and Corresp.* i. 110, 113, 186, ii. 32, iv. 55, viii. 62, 63. For the fourth Lord Harrington, see also Captain Gronow's *Reminiscences*, 1892, i. 284–6, where he figures in several of the coloured plates. In Ashton's *Social England under the Regency* (vol. ii.) are reproduced a portrait published in January 1812 by H. Humphrey, and a caricature of Petersham in the Cossack trousers in vogue in 1815. A drawing of Petersham as 'a noble aide-de-camp,' given in Timbs's *English Eccentrics*, probably represents his father.] G. Le G. N.

STANHOPE, SIR EDWARD (1546?–1608), chancellor of the diocese of London, born at Hull about 1546, was the fourth son of Sir Michael Stanhope [q. v.], by Anne, daughter of Nicholas Rawson of Aveley, Essex. John Stanhope, first baron Stanhope [q. v.], was his elder brother.

An elder brother, also named Edward, re-presented in parliament Nottinghamshire and Yorkshire successively, was a surveyor of the duchy of Lancaster, treasurer of Gray's Inn, recorder of Doncaster, and a member of the council of the north. He died in 1603, and was buried at Kirby Wharffe, Yorkshire.

Sir Edward the younger was scholar of Trinity College, Cambridge, from 1560 to 1563, minor fellow in 1564, and major fellow in 1569. He graduated B.A. in 1563, M.A. in 1566, and LL.D. in 1575. He was incorporated M.A. at Oxford in September 1566, 'when Queen Elizabeth was entertained by the Oxonian Muses' (WOOD, *Fasti Oxon.* i. 174). On 1 Sept. 1578 he supplicated to be incorporated D.C.L., but, though it was granted *simpliciter*, 'it appears not that he was incorporated' (*ib.* p. 211). On 25 Nov. 1572 he was appointed to the prebend of Botevant in York Cathedral. He was admitted as advocate at Doctors' Commons in 1576, and on 7 June 1577 was sworn as a master in chancery. About 1583 he was named vicar-general of the province of Canterbury, and, having meanwhile (Nov. 1584–Sept. 1585 and Oct. 1586–March 1587) served in parliament as member for Marlborough, was appointed a member of the ecclesiastical commission in 1587. Two years later he obtained, through the influence of Lord Burghley, to whose second wife he was related, the place of commissioner of the fines office. In 1589 he was also presented to the rectory of Terrington in Norfolk by his nephew William Cowper. In 1591 he resigned his stall at York on his appointment as canon and chancellor of St. Paul's Cathedral. Stanhope's name appears in the commission of March 1593 'touching jesuits and other disguised persons,' and also in that of oyer and terminer for London in February 1594. In the same year he was also a member of Whitgift's commission for the survey of ecclesiastical courts in the London diocese; and in April 1601 was a commissioner in the inquiry concerning piracies. Together with his brother Michael he received a grant from the crown in June 1600 of the manor of Hucknall Torkard, Nottinghamshire, and was knighted at Whitehall on 25 July 1603. In that year Stanhope served on the commission under which Raleigh and his associates were tried for high treason, and was appointed one of the four learned civilians who were to examine and adjudicate upon all books printed in the realm without authority.

Stanhope died on 16 March 1607–8, and was buried in St. Paul's Cathedral 'near to the great north door.' His epitaph on the monument on the eastern wall, printed in 'Monumenta Sepulchraria Sancti Pauli,'

1614, by H. H[olland], was drawn up by
William Camden [q. v.] During his lifetime he had given 100*l.* for the construction and fitting up of a library at Trinity
College, Cambridge, to which he bequeathed
700*l.* to buy lands for the maintenance of a
library-keeper and his man. He also left to
the college fifteen manuscripts and over three
hundred books, among which was his polyglot bible, known as King Philip's bible. A
small benefaction was set apart for the provision of a large vellum book ' wherein
should be fairly written and limned the
names, titles, arms, and dignities of all the
founders of the college,' and of the benefactors and masters, with a list of preferments. Benefactions were also left by Stanhope to the town of Hull and the poor of
Kentish Town and Terrington, as well as
200*l.* towards the foundation of Whitgift's
college at Croydon. Having no children, he
entailed his estates in the Isle of Axholme
and at Caldecott on his nephews.

Stanhope wrote the earlier portion of
' Memoriale Collegio [*sic*] Sanctæ et Indi-
viduæ Trinitatis in Academiâ Cantabrigiensi,'
a manuscript inscribed with his name and
left to Trinity College. It was continued, in
accordance with his wishes, up to 1700, and
was known as the Lodge Book from being
kept in the master's lodge. Several of his
letters were in the collections of Dawson
Turner and Richard Almack.

[Cooper's Athenæ Cantabr. ii. 470–3, where is
an exhaustive list of authorities.] G. Le G. N.

STANHOPE, EDWARD (1840 1893),
politician, was second son of Philip Henry,
fifth earl Stanhope [q. v.], the historian, by
Emily Harriet, second daughter of Sir Edward Kerrison, bart. He was born at his
father's house in Grosvenor Place, London, on
24 Sept. 1840. After some tuition at a private school at Brighton, he entered Harrow,
under the headmastership of Dr. Vaughan,
in September 1852. At Harrow he won
the Neeld medal for mathematics in 1859.
Though of slight physique, he more than
held his own in athletic sports and games.
Stanhope was a member of the celebrated
cricket eleven of 1859, when Harrow defeated Eton in one innings, and by his close
and masterly defence in no small degree contributed to that result. He was a first-rate
football player, fast, adroit, and indomitably
plucky. He shot extremely well, and was
fond of fishing. Stanhope left Harrow at midsummer 1859, and went up to Christ Church,
Oxford, in the following October. Pursuing his natural bent towards mathematics, he obtained a first class in mathema-

tical moderations in Michaelmas term 1861.
Being destined for the bar, he went in for a
pass in classics in Easter term 1862, and
the examiners paid him the compliment
of an 'honorary fourth.' In the following
November he was elected to a fellowship at
All Souls'. Thereupon he began his legal
studies in London, and was called to the bar
at the Inner Temple on 1 May 1865. He
joined the home circuit, but his practice was
mainly at the parliamentary bar, where his
clear elocution and power of lucid statement
soon secured him a good position. In 1868
he was appointed an assistant commissioner
to inquire into the employment of children,
young persons, and women in agriculture.
In the following year he published an exhaustive report. Some of his strictures on
the conditions of cottage life in Dorset gave
offence to the landed proprietors; but it
would seem that he was right.

James Banks Stanhope, who, as representative of Sir Joseph Banks [q. v.], had inherited Revesby Abbey, Boston, and its
estate, was first cousin to Edward Stanhope's
father, and, attracted by the character and
career of his young kinsman, he made him
heir to his property in Lincolnshire, and
brought him forward as one of the conservative candidates for Mid-Lincolnshire at
the general election of 1874. Stanhope was
returned unopposed, and again at the general election of 1880. After the redistribution of seats, consequent on the extension of
the suffrage to the agricultural labourers, he
was returned for the Horncastle division of
Lincolnshire at the general election of 1885
by a majority of 865 over a liberal candidate; at the general election of 1886 he was
returned unopposed, and at the general election of 1892 he beat his liberal opponent by
738.

At the opening of the session of 1875
Stanhope was chosen by Mr. Disraeli to
move the address to the throne; and he did
so in a speech of such sustained and stately
rhetoric that Lord Randolph Churchill (then
also a new member) likened it to 'a recita-
tion from Gibbon.' He at once gained the
ear of the house and the approbation of his
leaders, and on 18 Nov. 1875 he entered the
official hierarchy as parliamentary secretary
to the board of trade. His office had at the
moment a special importance. In the preceding July Mr. Plimsoll, M.P. for Derby,
had, by some vehement demonstrations in
the House of Commons, compelled public
attention to the scandal and dangers connected with our merchant shipping. So
much popular excitement was aroused that
the government thought it expedient to pass

the Merchant Shipping Act in 1875. It was merely temporary, and was to expire on 1 Oct. 1876. Stanhope, on his appointment to the board of trade, exerted himself to redeem the pledge made by the government to deal more thoroughly with the subject in a subsequent session, and the act of 1876, which was brought in at the beginning of that year, was drafted to a very considerable extent under Stanhope's direction and control. He made an important speech on the second reading of the bill (17 Feb. 1876), and took great interest in its further progress through the house, and in its subsequent administration by the board of trade.

On 6 April 1878 Stanhope was promoted to the more important post of under-secretary of state for India, which he held till the downfall of Lord Beaconsfield's administration at Easter 1880. At the India office he acquired the reputation of a strong and conscientious administrator. He was specially interested in questions of finance and complicated matters of exchange. He twice introduced the Indian budget into the House of Commons. On the first occasion, 13 Aug. 1878, he dealt with the new policy of a 'Famine Insurance Fund,' the abolition of the inland customs line, the equalisation of the salt duties, the abolition of the transit duties on sugar, and the amendment of the customs tariff. On the second occasion, 22 May 1879, he dealt chiefly with the measures taken to meet the large charges incurred in the Afghan war, and the loss by exchange; and he announced a determined effort to reduce Indian expenditure, in part by the employment of a larger number of natives in the civil service. On 9 Dec. 1878 he ably defended the policy of the Afghan war in the debate in the House of Commons on a vote of censure moved by Mr. Whitbread.

On Mr. Gladstone's accession to office at Easter 1880, Stanhope became a leader of the opposition, allying himself with the decorous tactics of Sir Stafford Northcote rather than with the guerilla warfare waged by Lord Randolph Churchill and the 'Fourth Party.' When Lord Salisbury became prime minister, for the first time, in the summer of 1885, Stanhope was appointed (24 June) vice-president of the committee of council on education, with a seat in the cabinet. This was the first instance in which a vice-president had been admitted to the cabinet at the time of his appointment. On the 19th of the following August he was appointed president of the board of trade, but resigned the office when Lord Salisbury made way for Mr. Gladstone's home-rule government

(3 Feb. 1886). In July 1886, after Mr. Gladstone's defeat at the general election, Lord Salisbury became prime minister for the second time, and he appointed Stanhope secretary of state for the colonies. He received the seals of office at Osborne on 3 Aug. 1886. At the colonial office he was thoroughly in his element. He was imbued with a zeal for the idea of imperial federation, and issued the invitations for the colonial conference, which was held with success in 1888. In the readjustment of offices consequent on Lord Randolph Churchill's sudden resignation at Christmas 1886, Stanhope was called, much against his wish, to succeed William Henry Smith [q. v.] at the war office. He received the seals of his new office in January 1887.

Under Stanhope's auspices the modern army system, inaugurated by Lord Cardwell, was completed. Specific spheres of action were allotted to all regular and auxiliary troops on the outbreak of war, and the volunteers for the first time took a definite place in the scheme of national defence. The process of decentralising the stores formerly concentrated at Woolwich and distributing them to the various points of mobilisation was set on foot. Sites were chosen for a line of earthworks for the defence of London in case of invasion, and negotiations for their purchase were begun. In order to supply modern guns for service by sea and land, Stanhope called the private trade of the country to his aid by the promise of continuity of demand, encouraged great firms like Armstrong & Whitworth to lay down the necessary plant and tender for orders, and thus created a valuable additional source of warlike supply. Early in 1887 Stanhope also reorganised the manufacturing departments, and the system under which warlike stores were passed into the service. He abolished the office of surveyor-general of ordnance; transferred the great departments of ordnance, works, and supply to the staff of the commander-in-chief, and placed the establishment of the ordnance factories under a single civilian head. In connection with these changes, the services of supply and transport were reorganised, and the army service corps established.

In 1888 Stanhope, turning from departmental reorganisation, introduced and passed the Imperial Defence Act. The loan of two and a half millions obtained under this act, together with more than a million borne on the annual estimates, was devoted to strengthening the defences of the coaling stations commanding the great sea routes, to improving armaments of military ports at home and abroad, and to constructing barracks at ports and coaling stations for the increased garrisons, the size of which was now for the first time determined by strategical principles.

In 1889, after a committee of the House of Commons had reported on the subject, Stanhope revised the conditions of promotion and retirement of officers. He promulgated a scheme for the reform of the general officers' list, which secured the reduction of the list by a gradual progress from 140 to 100, and the establishment of the principle that promotion to general's rank should only be by selection, and to fill actually vacant appointments allotted to that rank. At the same time he instituted a special rate of retired pay for those colonels whose prospects could be shown to be unfairly injured by the operation of the new rules.

During 1889 Stanhope made endeavours to improve the material conditions of the soldier's life. In 1890 he obtained from parliament a loan of over four millions, with which the camps at Aldershot, Shorncliffe, Strensall, and the Curragh were almost entirely rebuilt, while the barracks at Portsmouth, Plymouth, Dublin, Malta, and other large garrisons were improved and renewed. He also gave much attention to the difficult question of the employment of soldiers on return to civil life. He succeeded in persuading the great railway companies to meet him in conference, and obtained from them certain pledges as to the employment of reserve and discharged soldiers. Further, a committee appointed by him to consider the question of soldiers' diet resulted in considerable improvement. Stanhope carried forward the work of organising and developing our military resources under conditions of great difficulty. He had the ear of the House of Commons, but outside he obtained little recognition. His sagacious reforms were realised and appreciated only by the few, while his retrenchments made a bitter enemy of every officer whose interests were threatened by them. His adoption on 22 Dec. 1888, on the advice of technical experts, of a magazine rifle, though more than justified by experience, was long the subject of bitter opposition in press and parliament (*Hansard*, 3rd ser. ccexlix. 1631–83). A growing agitation against the administration of the war office under the new system of 1887 at length led to the appointment of a royal commission under Lord Hartington's presidency. The commissioners reported in 1891 that sufficient time had not elapsed to justify a verdict on the system instituted in 1887, but recommended a reconstruction of the war office on the occurrence of a vacancy in the office of commander-in-chief.

In 1891 Stanhope, to allay alarm caused by a temporary failure to meet an abnormal demand for recruits, appointed Lord Wantage's committee to inquire into the terms and conditions of service in the army. But the momentary difficulty passed away, and neither Stanhope nor his successor attempted to give effect to the far-reaching and expensive recommendations of the committee.

Lord Salisbury's second administration was overthrown by the general election of July 1892, and Stanhope surrendered the seals of the war office. His constitution, never very robust, had been completely broken by the incessant work and worry of his post. In the new parliament of 1892 he was a regular attendant and a frequent debater, and he was elected chairman of the 'church party' in the House of Commons. In this capacity, Stanhope, in the autumn session of 1893, threw himself with great ardour into the debates on such parts of the Parish Councils Bill as affected the powers or property of the establishment. He made his last speech on 9 Dec. 1893. On the same day he left London and went to Chevening to pay a visit to his brother, Lord Stanhope. There he was seized with a severe attack of gout, and, after a partial rally, he died suddenly from paralysis of the heart on 21 Dec. He was buried at Revesby.

Stanhope married, on 18 May 1870, Lucy Constance, youngest daughter of the Rev. Thomas Egerton, and niece of the first Lord Egerton of Tatton.

[Private information.]　　　　G. W. E. R.

STANHOPE, GEORGE (1660–1728), dean of Canterbury, was son of Thomas Stanhope (rector of Hertishorn or Hartshorn, Derbyshire, vicar of St. Margaret's, Leicester, and chaplain to the Earls of Chesterfield and Clare), by a lady of good family in Derbyshire, named Allestree. His grandfather, George Stanhope (*d.* 1644), was canon and precentor of York from 1631, and was rector of Wheldrake, Yorkshire, and chaplain to James I and Charles I; he was dispossessed during the Commonwealth (WALKER, *Sufferings*, p. 83).

George was born on 5 March 1660 at Hartshorn, and was successively educated at Uppingham school, Leicester, and Eton. From Eton he was elected on the foundation at King's College, Cambridge, in 1677. Graduating B.A. in 1681 and M.A. in 1685, he entered into holy orders, but remained three years longer at Cambridge. In 1688 he was appointed rector of Tewin, Hertfordshire

(*Tenin Register*), and on 3 Aug. 1689 of Lewisham, Kent, being presented to the latter by Lord Dartmouth, to whose son he was tutor, both then and apparently for five years afterwards (see dedication of CHARRON's *Wisdom* to the young earl). He proceeded D.D. in 1697, and about the same time was appointed chaplain to William and Mary. In 1701 he was appointed Boyle lecturer. In the year following he was presented to the vicarage of Deptford, was reappointed royal chaplain by Queen Anne, and on 23 March 1704 was made dean of Canterbury, still retaining Lewisham and Deptford. At this time and until 1708 he also held the Tuesday lectureship at St. Lawrence Jewry, a post which Tillotson and Sharp had made eminent.

His tenure of the Canterbury deanery brought Stanhope into the lower house of convocation at a period of bitter conflict with the upper house under Atterbury's leadership. As a man of peace, in friendship with Robert Nelson [q. v.] on one side, and with Edward Tenison [q. v.] and Burnet on the other (Burnet's son William afterwards married Stanhope's daughter Mary), Stanhope was proposed by the moderate party as prolocutor in 1705, but was defeated by the high churchman, Dr. William Binckes [q. v.] After Atterbury's elevation to the see of Rochester in 1713 he succeeded him as prolocutor, and was twice afterwards re-elected. The most prominent incident of his presidency was the censure of the Arian doctrine of Dr. Samuel Clarke (1675–1729) [q. v.] in 1714. Early in 1717 the lower house of convocation also censured a sermon by Bishop Benjamin Hoadly [q. v.] which had been preached before the king and published by royal command. To stop the matter from going to the upper house, convocation was hastily prorogued (May 1717). It was thenceforth formally summoned from time to time, only to be instantly prorogued. On the occasion of one of these prorogations Stanhope broke up the meeting (14 Feb. 1718) in order to prevent Tenison from reading a 'protestation' in favour of Hoadly. It was probably in consequence of this action that he lost the royal chaplaincy which he had held in the first year of George I. From this date convocation remained in abeyance until its revival in the province of Canterbury in 1852, and in that of York in 1861.

Stanhope was one of the great preachers of his time, and preached before Queen Anne at St. Paul's in 1706 and 1710 on two of the great services of national thanksgiving for Marlborough's victories. In 1710 he had a friendly correspondence with Atterbury, which dealt partly with the appointment of Thomas Sherlock [q. v.], afterwards bishop of London, to one of his curacies.

He died at Bath on 18 March 1728, and was buried in the church of Lewisham, where a monument with a long inscription was erected to his memory. In his will he left an exhibition of 10*l.* per annum, to be held at Cambridge by a scholar of the King's school, Canterbury. There are two portraits of him in the deanery at Canterbury.

He married, first, Olivia, daughter of Charles Cotton of Beresford, Staffordshire, and had by her a son, who predeceased him, and five daughters, of whom Mary married, in 1712, William, son of Bishop Burnet, and died two years afterwards. After his first wife's death in 1707 the dean married, secondly, Ann Parker, half-sister of Sir Charles Wager [q. v.]; she survived him two years.

Stanhope's literary works were chiefly translations or adaptations. He translated Epictetus (1694; 2nd ed. 1700, 8vo), Charron's 'Books on Wisdom' (1697, 3 vols.), and Marcus Aurelius (1697; 2nd ed. 1699, 4to). He modernised, omitting Romish passages, 'The Christian Directory' of Robert Parsons [q. v.] the jesuit (1703, 8vo; 4th ed. 1716); dedicated to Princess Anne a volume of 'Pious Meditations' (1701; 2nd ed. 1720, 8vo), drawn from St. Augustine, St. Anselm, and St. Bernard; and he translated the Greek 'Devotions' of Bishop Lancelot Andrewes [q. v.] Hutton, who edited the posthumous edition (1730, 8vo) of his translation of Andrewes, likened Stanhope's character to that of Andrewes. But the style of the translation is absolutely unlike the original. In place of the barbed point and abruptness of the Greek, the English is all smoothed out and expanded. Subsequent editions of the work appeared in 1808, 1811, 1815, 1818, 1826, and 1832. Stanhope followed the same paraphrastic system in a translation of Thomas à Kempis's 'Imitatio Christi,' which appeared in 1698 under the title 'The Christian's Pattern, or a Treatise of the Imitation of Christ,' 2 pts. London, 8vo. A fifth edition appeared in 1706, a twelfth in 1733, and new editions in 1746, 1751, 1793, 1814, and 1855. In 1886 Henry Morley [q. v.] edited it for the collection of a hundred books chosen by Sir John Lubbock. 'The pithy style of the original is lost in flowing sentences that pleased the reader in Queen Anne's reign.'

Stanhope's principal contribution to divinity is 'The Paraphrase and Comment on the Epistles and Gospels' (vols. i. and ii. 1705, vol. iii. 1706, vol. iv. 1708), dedicated originally to Queen Anne, and in a new edition to George I on his accession (1714). It was a favourite book in the eighteenth century. Its defect is the neglect of the organic relation of collect, epistle, and gospel; but it contains much that is solid, sensible, and practical in clear and easy language, quite free from controversial bitterness. In the preface Stanhope says that the work was planned for the use of the little prince George, who died in 1700.

Besides the works mentioned above Stanhope published: 1. 'Fifteen Sermons,' 1700. 2. 'The Boyle Lecture,' 1702. 3. 'Twelve Sermons,' 1726. Stanhope is credited by Todd and Chalmers with the translation of Rochefoucauld's 'Maxims,' which appeared anonymously in 1706; the book seems alien to Stanhope's mind.

[Gent. Mag. 1780, p. 463; Todd's Deans of Canterbury; Duncan's Parish Church of St. Mary, Lewisham, and Registers of Lewisham.]

H. L. B.

STANHOPE, LADY HESTER LUCY (1776–1839), eccentric, the eldest daughter of Charles, viscount Mahon (afterwards third Earl Stanhope) [q. v.], by his first wife, Hester (1755–1780), the clever sister of William Pitt and elder daughter of the great Earl of Chatham, was born at Chevening, Kent, on 12 March 1776. Hester and her sisters received a rambling kind of education. Their mother was absorbed in her coiffure and in the opera, while their father was too abstracted to take much notice of his household. Hester grew up a beauty of the brilliant rather than the handsome order. She was early distinguished by invincible cheerfulness and force of character, which enabled her to exert a complete ascendency over her sisters. Her home was not congenial to her, and from 1800 until 1803 she lived mainly with her grandmother at Burton Pynsent. Her skill in saving her brothers and sisters from the results of their father's experiments first attracted to her the attention of her uncle, William Pitt, and in August 1803 Pitt asked her to come and keep house for him. She soon became his most trusted confidant, and when in bewilderment at her dazzling indiscretions the minister's friends questioned him as to the motives of his niece's conduct, Pitt would answer, 'I let her do as she pleases; for if she were resolved to cheat the devil she could do it,' to which the lady in telling the story appended the rider, 'And so I could.' She corresponded with Pitt's friends, including Canning and Mulgrave, to whom she once retorted à propos of an unfortunate remark upon a broken spoon at the table, 'Have you not yet discovered that Mr. Pitt sometimes uses very slight and weak instruments to effect his ends?' In 1804, upon one historic occasion, she succeeded in blacking the premier's face with a burned cork, and for the next two years she arranged the treasury banquets and dispensed much official patronage. On his deathbed, in January 1806, Pitt gave her his blessing: 'Dear soul,' he said, 'I know she loves me.' His death involved the extinction of all her ambitious prospects and aspirations.

Pitt desired that 1,500l. a year should be settled upon her, but, after certain deductions, the amount of the pension was reduced to 1,200l., a sum on which Lady Hester declared her inability to maintain a carriage. Her equanimity was further sorely tried in 1808 by the death at Coruña of her favourite brother, Major Stanhope, and of Sir John Moore, for whom she is known to have cherished an affection. She retired for a time to Wales; but, becoming more and more intolerant of the restrictions of ordinary society, she left England for the Levant in 1810, and never again saw her native land. She took out with her a Welsh companion, Miss Williams, an English physician, Charles Lewis Meryon [q. v.], and a small suite, which gradually grew in numbers as she progressed eastwards. She set sail in the Jason frigate on 10 Feb. 1810. After suffering shipwreck off Rhodes, she made a stately pilgrimage to Jerusalem, traversed the desert, and presided over a vast Bedouin encampment amid the ruins of Palmyra (January 1813). She finally settled down, in the summer of 1814, among the half-savage tribes on the slopes of Mount Lebanon. The pasha of Acre ceded to her the ruins of a convent and the village of Dahar-Jûne (Djouni or Joon), situated on a conical mount and peopled by the Druses. She there built a group of houses surrounded by a garden and an outer wall, like a mediæval fortress, and occupied herself in intriguing against the authority of the British consuls in the district (for whom as commercial agents she had a supreme aristocratic contempt), in regulating and counteracting the designs of her slaves, in stimulating the Druses to rise against Ibrahim Pasha, and in endeavours to foster the declining central authority of the sultan. Though with the lapse of time and the waning of her resources her prestige suffered considerably, for a few years she exercised almost despotic power in the neighbourhood of Lebanon, and in time of panic, as after the battle of Navarino (20 Oct. 1827), Europeans fled to her from all sides for protection. Her fearlessness and her remarkable insight into character, combined with her open-handed charity in relieving the poor and distressed, caused her to be regarded with superstitious veneration as a kind of prophetess, and, if she did not share the idea, she seems to have done all in her power to encourage it.

As time went on she insensibly adopted Eastern manners and customs. Though always complaining of neglect, she had upwards of thirty personal attendants, and after Miss Williams's death, in 1828, none of these were Europeans. Her standard of demeanour was rigorous, servants not being expected 'to smile, or scratch themselves, or appear to notice anything.' Syrians were preferred because, though thievish and dirty, they were completely obsequious and required no definite or stated hours for repose. In spite, however, of much vigorous language and frequent blows from a mace, which she was in the habit of wielding, the household slaves became more and more incorrigible. Her physician, Meryon, in the course of his visits, importuned her to send 'the worst of them away, for they were only a torment to her.' 'Yes, but my rank!' was the characteristic answer. Similarly she maintained on the premises enormous numbers of cats and other animals. She had a strange regard for horses, devising a kind of superannuation scheme for those in her employ, and she was a devout believer in the transmigration of souls and in judicial astrology, which she practised upon the least provocation.

Many distinguished Europeans sought interviews with her. Lamartine visited her on 30 Sept. 1832, and described her religious belief as a clever though confused mixture of the different religions in the midst of which she had condemned herself to live. Kinglake gives a more commonplace account of her when describing his pilgrimage to Djouni in 1835. He was struck by her extraordinary appearance, her penetration and power of downright expression. Her talk was full of sparkling anecdotes of Pitt and his circle. Dr. Madden and Prince Maximilian of Bavaria were among other personages to whom she accorded interviews. Poujoulat and Michaud traversed Syria for the purpose, and were then refused admittance at Djouni upon some trivial pretext. Dr. Bowring was another traveller disappointed of an audience.

In haranguing her visitors there is no doubt that Lady Hester found the greatest happiness of her life. She frequently talked for an hour or more without stopping, and prolonged her remarks until two or three in the morning. She liked her hearer to stand, while the slaves filled the pipes or knelt around in postures of oriental humility. 'Thus she fancied herself an eastern princess.' 'I have known her,' says Meryon, 'lie for two hours at a time with a pipe in her mouth (from which the sparks fell and burned the counterpane into innumerable holes) when she was in a lecturing humour, and go on in one unbroken discourse, like a parson in his pulpit.' She harangued one unfortunate Englishman for so many hours, without respite, that he fainted away from fatigue. On summoning the servants to his assistance, she remarked quietly that he had been overpowered in listening to the state of disgrace to which his country was reduced by its ministers (this was in 1819). She could not bear to be alone, and scarce an evening passed without her summoning the worthy physician, who seems to have served her at first from self-interest, afterwards spellbound by her commanding personality, latterly from a chivalrous feeling towards an old woman in precarious health, poor, saddled with innumerable debts, and preyed on by thieves. He became, indeed, almost indispensable. She frequently abused him, and persistently refused to receive Mrs. Meryon. But he stayed with her during the spring of 1831 and the summers of 1837 and 1838, and, with an almost Boswellian power of self-effacement, he listened to and recorded her views on such themes as the superiority of the views of high-born people to the virtues of low-born ones, of the concubine to the wife, the fraudulent attempts of the middle classes to disguise their real character by education, and the proper place of doctors as the upper servants of noblemen. He himself became, indeed, little more than her apothecary. To the last she insisted on physicking and cutting out garments for all those with whom she came into close contact (a droll reference to this last peculiarity is given by Southey in the 'Doctor').

Ever since she had settled on Mount Lebanon, Lady Hester's profuse prodigality had involved her in an accumulating weight of debt. Up to 1836 it is a remarkable proof of her talents that she prevailed upon various Levantine usurers to advance her large sums upon her note of hand. But finally this resource failed her, the creditors became clamorous, and in February 1838 Lord Palmerston felt himself justified in appropriating the bulk of her pension to the settlement of their claims. Matters were not improved by abusive letters to the foreign secretary, or by a presumptuous epistle which Lady Hester thought fit to address to the queen. Some of the newspapers in

England sympathised with her 'grievances,' but she failed to obtain any redress, and in August 1838 she shut herself up in her castle with some five of her retainers, walled up the gate, and refused to see any visitors. Untamed by the miseries of her later years, she died as she had lived, in proud isolation, on 23 June 1839, with no European near her. On hearing of her illness, Niven Moore, the British consul at Beyrout, rode over the mountains to see her, accompanied by William McClure Thomson, the American missionary. They arrived just after her death, and found the place deserted. All the servants had fled as soon as the breath was out of the body, taking with them such plunder as they could secure. Not a single thing was left in the room where their mistress lay dead, except the ornaments upon her person. At midnight her countryman and the missionary carried her body by torchlight to a spot in the garden and there buried her. Sketches of her fortalice and her grave are in Thomson's 'The Land and the Book' (1886).

A portrait drawn on stone by R. J. Hamerton is bound up along with some memoranda and an autograph letter in 'Collectanea Biographica' (vol. xcv.) in the print-room at the British Museum.

[The chief authorities are Meryon's Travels of Lady Hester Stanhope (1846) and his still more entertaining Memoirs of Lady Hester Stanhope (1845), each in three volumes and illustrated by lithograph portraits of Lady Hester in costume. See also Gent. Mag. 1839, ii. 420; Stanhope's Life of Pitt; Phipps's Memoirs of Robert P. Ward, 1850, i. 143; Russell's Eccentric Personages, 1864, i. 195-15; Caroline Fox's Journals and Letters, ed. Pym, p. 54; Thomson's The Land and the Book; Lamartine's Voyage en Orient; Michaud et Poujoulat's Corresp. d'Orient, 1833, v. 530 sq.; Madden's Travels, 1829, letter xxxv.; Kinglake's Eöthen, chap. viii.; Warburton's Crescent and Cross, chap. xix.; Wolff's Travels in the East, 1860; Quarterly Review, lxxvi. 430 sq.]

T. S.

STANHOPE, JAMES, first EARL STANHOPE (1673–1721), was eldest son of Alexander Stanhope (youngest son of Philip Stanhope, first earl of Chesterfield [q. v.]), by Catharine, daughter of Arnold Burghill of Thingehill Parva, Herefordshire. His father was envoy to the States-General, and died in 1707. James was born at Paris in 1673, and was naturalised as a British subject by an act in 1696. He was educated at Eton and matriculated from Trinity College, Oxford, 'aged 14,' on 25 May 1688, but took no degree. When his father went to Madrid as British minister in 1690 he accompanied

him, and spent a year there, gaining a knowledge of the Spanish language and character which proved useful to him afterwards. In 1691 he went to Italy, and served under the Duke of Savoy. In 1694–5 he served as a volunteer in Flanders. He distinguished himself and was severely wounded in one of the assaults at Namur, and on 1 Nov. 1695 he was given a commission as captain and lieutenant-colonel in the 1st foot-guards. On 12 Feb. 1702 he obtained the colonelcy of a regiment, afterwards the 11th foot. He was elected M.P. for Newport (Isle of Wight) in 1701 and for Cockermouth in 1702. He continued to represent the latter place till 1713. He was a steady whig, and supported the act of settlement in 1701. He took part in Ormonde's expedition to Cadiz in August 1702, and acted as Spanish secretary to the duke (see his letters in *Spain under Charles II*). He was mentioned in Ormonde's despatch as having particularly distinguished himself in the storming of the south battery at Vigo on 23 Oct. He served with his regiment under Marlborough on the Meuse in 1703. He went to Portugal with it in 1704, and was sent to garrison Portalegre; but an attack of rheumatism and a Portuguese doctor, 'who, by bleeding and dieting me, had almost done my business,' obliged him to go back to Lisbon, and he escaped being made prisoner with his men in May, when Portalegre was taken by Berwick. He returned to England, and was made brigadier-general on 25 Aug. 1704.

In June 1705 he went back to the Peninsula with Peterborough's expedition [see MORDAUNT, CHARLES, third EARL OF PETERBOROUGH]. In the councils of war at Barcelona he was less averse to undertaking the siege than most of the land officers. In the attack on Fort Montjuich, on 13 Sept., he commanded the reserve, and helped to secure the possession of the captured outworks. When Barcelona itself capitulated he was sent into the town as a hostage, and his tact and knowledge of the language proved useful in appeasing the outbreak of the inhabitants, who rose against the garrison. In doing this he and Peterborough ran greater risk, as he told Burnet, than they had done during the siege. He was sent home with the despatches, charged by Peterborough to look well after his interests. The Archduke Charles, in his letter to Queen Anne, made particular mention of Stanhope's 'great zeal, attention, and most prudent conduct.'

On 29 Jan. 1706 he was appointed minister to Spain in place of (Sir) Paul Methuen [q. v.] He left England at the end of February with reinforcements, which reached

Barcelona on 8 May. The French had been besieging it for more than a month, and the breaches were ready for assault, but Tessé raised the siege, and retreated into France. This gave the allies the opportunity to get possession of Madrid, on which Galway was already advancing from Portugal [see MASSUE DE RUVIGNY, HENRI DE]. Peterborough wished to march on it from Valencia, taking the archduke Charles with him; and Stanhope, whom the archduke had welcomed as minister, did his utmost to persuade the latter to this course. But Charles, guided by his German advisers, to whom Peterborough was odious, decided to go by way of Aragon, and Stanhope went with him. On 6 Aug., a month too late, they joined Galway's army at Guadalaxara. Peterborough, who arrived at the same time from Valencia, to every one's relief soon betook himself to Italy. But by this time the Bourbon army was stronger than that of the allies, and the latter, straitened for supplies, found it necessary to fall back on Valencia. In January 1707, when the plans for the coming campaign were discussed, the majority of the officers were in favour of an advance of the whole army on Madrid before the Bourbon army should receive the reinforcements expected from France. But Noyelles, who was at the head of the Spanish contingent, the archduke Charles, and Peterborough, who had come back from Italy, recommended purely defensive action. On the other hand, Stanhope warmly declared that 'her majesty did not spend such vast sums, and send such number of forces to garrison towns in Catalonia and Valencia, but to make King Charles master of the Spanish monarchy,' and that he should protest in the queen's name against a mere defensive line of action. His course was cordially approved by the British government, but it displeased the archduke. Noyelles carried his point, and marched the Spanish troops into Catalonia, Charles and Stanhope accompanying them. Galway had only 15,500 men when, on 25 April, he encountered Berwick at Almanza, and was defeated. Peterborough, who had been peremptorily recalled, and was now on his way home, laid the blame on Stanhope. He wrote to Marlborough: 'I cannot but think Mr. Stanhope's politics have proved very fatal, having produced our misfortunes and prevented the greatest successes' (COXE, Marlborough, ii. 81). But this was mere spite. A year before he had written to Stanhope (18 Aug.): 'I see no one but yourself that can support this business;' but he had learnt that Stanhope's secretary had said things against him in England, and after his return to Spain from

Italy he and Stanhope ceased to be friends. When the House of Lords held its inquiry into the conduct of the war in Spain in January 1711, it pronounced that Peterborough had been right, and Galway and Stanhope wrong, in the discussions at Valencia; but this was a party resolution, and was really aimed at Marlborough and his colleagues.

Disgusted with the lethargy and obstructiveness he met with at Charles's court, Stanhope wished to resign, and strongly urged that Prince Eugène should be sent to Spain, or some other arrangement made which would secure unity of command. In September, at Galway's request, he joined the army, and was put in charge of what remained of the English foot. But the army was too weak to interfere with the enemy.

At the end of the year he went to England to attend parliament. It was then decided that he should succeed Galway, who wished to be relieved, in command of the English troops, retaining his post as minister with Charles. He was made major-general on 1 Jan. 1708 with the local rank of lieutenant-general, and on 26 March was appointed commander-in-chief of the British forces in Spain. He brought a bill into parliament at this time to release the highland clans from obedience to their chiefs if the latter took up arms against the queen. This was prompted by the Jacobite attempt at invasion, but was allowed to drop after the failure of that attempt.

In April 1708 Stanhope went with Marlborough to The Hague to consult Prince Eugène, and in May he rejoined the army in Catalonia. The emperor, unwilling to spare Eugène, had sent Marshal Stahrenberg to take the chief command, and the death of Noyelles removed the main cause of friction. But the allies were weak, and the Bourbons continued to gain ground throughout the campaign. The want of a port in which the British fleet could winter had been much felt, and on 15 July Marlborough wrote to Stanhope: 'I conjure you, if possible, to take Port Mahon.' In September Stanhope acted on this suggestion with skill and vigour. He landed in Minorca on the 14th with 2,600 men, and Fort St. Philip, which had a garrison of one thousand men, surrendered on the 29th. He left a garrison there consisting wholly of English troops, for, as he wrote to Sunderland, 'England ought never to part with this island, which will give the law to the Mediterranean both in time of war and peace.' Sunderland replied that his action was approved 'for the reasons you mention, though some of them must be kept very secret.'

On 2 Dec. he accompanied Stahrenberg in an attempt to surprise Tortosa, which the Bourbons had taken in July. As he wrote, 'It proved a Cremona business. We got into the old town, killed the governor and about two hundred men, brought off nine officers and fifty soldiers prisoners, but by an unlucky accident missed our aim.' In August the Duke of Orleans, with whom Stanhope had been intimate at one time in Paris, had made secret overtures to him, starting with the suggestion that he (Orleans) should be made king of Spain, instead of either Philip or Charles. Negotiations went on for some time, with the knowledge of the British government and the archduke, and probably of Louis XIV also. In Stanhope's opinion they 'very much abated the edge of the Duke of Orleans' in the campaign of 1708. But they were brought to light by the Princess Orsini in the winter, and Orleans did not return to Spain.

Stanhope was promoted lieutenant-general on 1 Jan. 1709. The campaign of that year was languid, owing to the overtures for peace made by Louis XIV and the expected withdrawal of the French troops from Spain. In April Stanhope went to the relief of Alicant, which had been besieged for more than five months. The town had been taken, but five hundred men still held out in the castle, in spite of the mine which had swallowed up the governor and all the chief officers. But it was found impracticable to land troops, and on the 18th Stanhope came to terms with the besiegers, and brought the garrison away. At the end of August he went to Gibraltar to command an expedition against Cadiz, which the British government had decided on, and for which they had sent out five thousand men. But it was found that the attempt was hopeless, and he brought the troops to Catalonia.

He spent the winter in England, and was a member of the committee which drew up articles of impeachment against Sacheverell, and one of the managers at his trial in February 1710. His speech on the 28th against the doctrine of non-resistance is said to have discomposed Sacheverell more than any of the other speeches.

At the end of May he rejoined the army in Spain. Reinforcements in July raised it to a strength of 24,500 men, of whom 4,200 were British. The Bourbon army was less in number, and consisted wholly of Spanish troops. Stahrenberg, a cautious veteran, still inclined to the defensive, and Charles also; but Stanhope pressed for a bolder course, and was supported by the other officers. On 26 July the allied army advanced towards Aragon, and Stanhope was sent forward to secure the passage of the Noguera. The enemy tried to anticipate him, and on the 27th the cavalry action of Almenara was fought, in which Stanhope, with 2,600 men, routed 4,200 supported by some battalions of foot. He killed one of the Spanish leaders in a personal encounter. The Bourbon army retired in some confusion to Lerida, and about a fortnight afterwards fell back on Saragossa.

There it offered battle on 20 Aug., and was thoroughly beaten, losing twelve thousand men out of twenty thousand. The hardest fighting was on the left of the allies, where Stanhope was in command, and opposite to which the bulk of the Bourbon cavalry was massed. General (afterwards lord) Carpenter wrote that evening to Walpole that the successes of the allies were entirely due to Stanhope, 'both for pressing in council and for the execution.' He had 'hectored the court and marshal into these marches and actions.'

He now strongly urged that the allies should march on Madrid, and be joined there by the army of Portugal. In this opinion he was supported by the majority of the officers, and it was in accordance with Marlborough's views. Stahrenberg and the archduke thought it would be better to remain in the north, to intercept communication between France and Spain, than to enter Castile, which had already shown itself so hostile. However, they gave way, and on 28 Sept. Charles entered Madrid, preceded a week before by Stanhope. The latter was sent forward to Talavera to meet the troops from Portugal.

But meanwhile the Spaniards had rallied round Philip at Valladolid with unexpected enthusiasm. Vendôme arrived from France to command his army, which by the middle of October numbered nearly twenty-four thousand men. Vendôme moved southward to Almaraz, and interposed between Madrid and the slowly advancing army of Portugal, which thereupon fell back. Noailles invaded Catalonia from Roussillon, and Charles, who had left his wife at Barcelona, quitted Madrid on 18 Nov. in order to rejoin her.

By the end of that month it had become clear that the allied army could not winter in Castile, and on 3 Dec. it began its retreat on Aragon. As Stahrenberg explained in his report, 'the late season of the year and the necessity of getting provisions and forage for the troops obliged us to march in columns and by different ways; the English troops, believing they might find some provisions in Brihuega and subsist better there, took that road' (London Gazette, 9–11 Jan.) It does not appear that he made any objection. They arrived there on the 6th, and Stanhope sent to Stahrenberg, who was at Cifuentes, seventeen miles off, for further orders. He also asked him to send some ammunition. Meanwhile the Bourbon army had marched with astonishing rapidity from Talavera (forty-five leagues in seven days), and on the morning of the 8th it appeared on the hills above Brihuega. Stanhope, who had only about 750 horse, was not able to ascertain the enemy's force, and by evening he was surrounded. He had barely time to send off an aide-de-camp to Stahrenberg; and he made such arrangements as he could to defend the town, which was enclosed by an old and unflanked wall. He had eight squadrons and eight battalions, but they were very weak. The British troops numbered little more than 2,800 officers and men, and, in addition to them, there was one Portuguese battalion of about seven hundred (Return furnished on 13 Dec. 1710, in *Foreign Office Papers*).

Having made two breaches, Vendôme assaulted them with twenty battalions at 4 p.m. on the 9th. They were vigorously defended, and the fighting was obstinate for three hours. But the streets were searched by artillery and musketry fire from the hills above; a fresh breach was made by a mine; and when six hundred of the defenders had been killed and wounded, Stanhope capitulated, seeing 'that the enemy had a considerable body of men in the town, and that in our whole garrison we had not five hundred men who had any ammunition left.' One of his officers, Pepper, wrote afterwards to Marlborough that he might have retired into the castle (Coxe, *Marlborough*, iii. 160); but the tone of the letter does not entitle it to much weight, and there seems no reason to question the stoutness of his defence, though Stanhope ought not to have let himself be surprised in so bad a post and with insufficient ammunition.

Stahrenberg was rather slow in coming to his assistance, and halted for the night about halfway between Cifuentes and Brihuega (*London Gazette*, 3-6 March). Next morning he advanced, found the enemy under Vendôme drawn up to receive him, and was defeated in the battle of Villa-Viciosa.

Stanhope's military career ended at Brihuega. He was kept a prisoner at Saragossa for more than a year and a half. He had been at once authorised to propose his exchange for the Duke of Escalona, but the exchange was not accepted so long as there was any reason to fear his influence against the conclusion of peace. He came home

through France, and met Bolingbroke at Fontainebleau, but declined to be presented by him to Louis XIV.

Stanhope arrived in England on 16 Aug. 1712 (O. S.) He was welcomed by the whigs, who were now out of favour with both court and country, and he became one of the leaders of the opposition in the House of Commons. In the election of 1710 he had been defeated for Westminster, but was again returned for Cockermouth; and when he lost that seat in 1713, he was elected for Wendover. The government bore him no good will, and sent a commission into Spain to sift the accounts of his expenditure. But instead of establishing anything against him, it turned out that a balance was due to him. His answer to the report of the commissioners was published in 1714 (40 pp.) He had been given the colonelcy of a regiment of horse in July 1710, but the regiment was disbanded at the peace.

He took an active part in the opposition to the treaty of commerce with France in May 1713, and spoke forcibly against the Schism Act in the following year. Bolingbroke has described him as 'not apt to despair, especially in the execution of his own projects' (*Letters on History*, i. 225); and he speaks of himself as 'ever inclined to bold strokes.' His sanguine and resolute character made him play a leading part in baffling the Jacobite intrigues and securing the Hanoverian succession. He made arrangements with Cadogan (acting on behalf of Marlborough, who was then at Antwerp) to bring over troops from Hanover upon the queen's death, but they proved to be needless.

On 14 Sept. 1714—four days before George I landed in England—Stanhope was appointed secretary of state for the southern department, and on the 24th he was made privy councillor. Charles Townshend, second viscount Townshend [q. v.], the principal secretary of state, being in the lords, Stanhope led the House of Commons in concert with Walpole, who was not at first in the cabinet. In the new parliament which met in March 1715 he represented Newport (I. W.) In June, after the impeachment of Bolingbroke and Oxford had been carried, he moved and carried the impeachment of Ormonde. When the Jacobite rising took place in August, he had the chief direction of the measures for its suppression; and he employed in this work the officers who had served under him in Spain—Carpenter, Wills, and Pepper. He is said to have afterwards saved the life of John Nairne, lord Nairne [q. v.], one of the six peers condemned.

He took an active part in the passing of the Septennial Act; but the sphere most

c

congenial to him was foreign affairs. He
had been sent to The Hague and to Vienna
in October 1714, to bring the Dutch and the
imperial government into agreement as to
the terms of the barrier treaty. He was
well received by the emperor, Charles VI,
with whom he had been so closely associated
in Spain; but he was not successful, and the
treaty was not signed till November 1715.

In July 1716 he accompanied George I to
Hanover, and remained there with him for
six months. During this time he was engaged in a more important negotiation—the
treaty of alliance with France, by which the
regent was to withdraw all countenance
from the Pretender in return for a guarantee
of his own succession if Louis XV died without issue. Dubois was sent by the regent to
Hanover. He and Stanhope were old acquaintances, and they arranged matters together, the many difficulties in the way being
overcome with much dexterity. The treaty
was to be signed at The Hague, and the
Dutch were to be invited to be a party to it.
Both Stanhope and the king were eager for
its completion, because troubles were brew-
ing both with Sweden and with the czar
which might cause it to fall through. They
were both much annoyed at the delays which
occurred, and which they attributed to the
ministers in England.

The king had other grievances against
Townshend, who was unwilling to let Great
Britain be dragged by Hanover into a quarrel
with the northern courts. George suspected
him of being in league with the Prince of
Wales against him. His anger was inflamed
by Sunderland, who was dissatisfied with
his own position in the ministry, and had
gone to Hanover to intrigue. The result
was that the king decided to dismiss Townshend; and Stanhope, though he tried in vain
to change his purpose, did not feel bound to
resign. On 15 Dec. he wrote to Townshend,
by the king's command, to inform him of
the decision, and to offer him the lord-
lieutenancy of Ireland. This caused a breach
not only with Townshend, but with Walpole,
and Stanhope was unjustly charged with
treachery (vide correspondence in Coxe's
Walpole, vol. ii.)

Townshend eventually accepted the lord-
lieutenancy, but he and his adherents gave
so doubtful a support to the government that
on 9 April 1717 the king deprived him of
his office. Walpole and others resigned, and
the ministry was reconstructed, Stanhope
becoming (on the 15th) first lord of the
treasury and chancellor of the exchequer.
He frankly owned his incapacity for these
duties, which were 'remote from his studies

and inclination,' and in the following year
he exchanged places with Sunderland, becoming again secretary of state for the
southern department on 21 March 1718.
He had been raised to the peerage on 12 July
1717, as Baron Stanhope of Elvaston and
Viscount Stanhope of Mahon in commemoration of his capture of Port Mahon; and on
14 April 1718 he was created Earl Stanhope.

Alberoni's preparations to recover for Spain
some of her lost possessions in Italy were
then threatening the peace of Europe. A
fleet under Byng was sent to the Mediterranean in June, and on the 14th Stanhope
set out on a special mission to Paris and
Madrid. In Paris he negotiated the quadruple alliance of England, France, Austria,
and Holland, but in spite of this powerful
combination he could not persuade Alberoni,
who had already landed thirty-five thousand
men in Sicily, to abandon his plans. The
offer to give up Gibraltar was made in vain,
and Stanhope left Madrid on 26 Aug.
But already on the 11th the Spanish fleet
had been destroyed by Byng off Cape Passaro.
The death of Charles XII a few months
later was even a heavier blow to Alberoni.
His expedition to raise the Jacobites in
Great Britain, in March 1719, miscarried;
and at the end of that year Spain purchased
peace by his dismissal and acceded to the
quadruple alliance.

Stanhope's policy was equally vigorous
and successful in behalf of Sweden, which
had made peace with England after the
death of Charles XII. Prussia and Poland
were detached from the coalition against her;
but the czar was bent on taking full advantage of her weakness, and Denmark acted
with him. So a fleet was sent to the Baltic
in 1719 under Norris, who was told by Stanhope to treat the Russian fleet as Byng had
done the Spanish. The Russian ships sought
shelter in their own ports, and Denmark
came to terms.

In domestic affairs the chief measures with
which Stanhope had to do were the repeal
of the Schism Act and the Peerage Bill.
He had strongly opposed the Schism Act
when it was passed in 1714, and he brought
in a bill to repeal it on 13 Dec. 1718. He
would have liked to repeal the Test Act
also, and he introduced clauses into his bill
cancelling some of its provisions; but the
opposition was so strong that he had to
sacrifice those clauses. The 'mischievous'
Peerage Bill was brought in on 5 March
1719, to fix the number of peers and withdraw from the crown its unlimited right of
creation. It was aimed at the Prince of
Wales, who was very hostile to the ministry,

and it was approved by the king. Sunderland has been generally regarded as mainly responsible for it, but Stanhope must at all events share the responsibility. It was dropped on 14 April, but was reintroduced in November, and passed the lords with hardly any opposition. In the commons it was rejected by a large majority on 8 Dec. This was mainly due to Walpole, who saw how good an opportunity of harassing the government was afforded by a bill which extinguished the hopes of many of its usual supporters. Stanhope's correspondence with the Abbé Vertot about the method of admission to the Roman senate (published in 1721) was no doubt prompted by this question.

In spite of the failure of the Peerage Bill, the government was strong, and it had been rejoined by Townshend and Walpole when Stanhope accompanied the king to Hanover in the summer of 1720. But the South Sea Bill had been passed in April, and the collapse of the South Sea company in the autumn brought a storm upon the ministers who had helped to inflate it. Stanhope's personal character for disinterestedness stood very high, and he had held none of the stock. But as chief minister he had to meet his share of the attacks which were made as soon as parliament met in December. On 4 Feb. 1721, in the discussion in the lords on the examination of one of the directors, Wharton compared the ministers to Sejanus. Stanhope replied, and ' with so great a vehemence that, finding himself taken suddenly with a violent headache, he went home and was cupped, which eased him a little ' (*Parl. History*). He died at 6 P.M. next day at his house in Whitehall, and was buried with military honours at Chevening on the 17th.

Stanhope was ' a handsome, dark-complexioned man,' as may be seen in Kneller's picture in the National Portrait Gallery. High-minded, liberal, and well skilled in the higher functions of statecraft, he lacked parliamentary ability, and he was ' wholly unfit to manage the finances of the country.' In debate he was impetuous and apt to lose his temper; but as a diplomatist St. Simon contrasts him with Craggs, and says that he ' ne perdait point de sang-froid, rarement la politesse, avait beaucoup d'esprit, de génie et de ressources ' (xviii. 129). He was naturally frank and open, and he used to say that he always imposed on the foreign ministers by telling them the naked truth (cf. LADY WORTLEY-MONTAGU, *Letters*, iii. 54; and LECKY, i. 320, quoting a similar saying of Lord Palmerston).

Stanhope married, on 24 Feb. 1713, Lucy, younger daughter of Thomas Pitt [q. v.], governor of Madras, and grandfather of Chatham. His widow died on 24 Feb. 1723, having made provision for the stately monument to her husband which is on the south side of the west entrance to the choir in Westminster Abbey. It was designed by Kent, and executed by Rysbrack. In the inscription the year of his death is given as 1720, according to the old style. Of his three sons and two daughters, the eldest son Philip, second earl Stanhope (1717–1786), was father of Charles Stanhope, third earl Stanhope [q. v.].

[Lord Mahon's (afterwards Earl Stanhope) War of the Succession in Spain, with an appendix of 120 pp. of extracts from Stanhope's letters in 1708–11, Histories of England, Spain under Charles II, from the correspondence of A. Stanhope, Letters from Peterborough to Stanhope in Spain (privately printed); Memoirs of the Life and Actions of James, Earl of Stanhope, published in 1721; Parnell's War of the Succession in Spain; Foreign Office Papers, Spain, 1707–10, in Public Record Office; Marlborough Despatches; Coxe's Life of Marlborough, House of Bourbon in Spain, Memoirs of Walpole (with several of Stanhope's letters in the appendix); Boyer's Annals of Queen Anne's Reign; Noble's Continuation of Granger, iii. 212; Doyle's Official Baronage.]
E. M. L.

STANHOPE, JOHN, first BARON STANHOPE OF HARRINGTON (1545?–1621), born probably about 1545, was third son of Sir Michael Stanhope [q. v.] by his wife Anne, daughter of Nicholas Rawson of Aveley-Bellhouse, Essex. His father's attainder in 1552 did not affect his estates, and John was brought up at Shelford, Nottinghamshire, where his mother's household was noted for hospitality and piety. He is probably the John Stanhope who was returned to parliament for Marlborough on 22 April 1572, for Truro in October 1586, and for Rochester on 14 Oct. 1588; but he is confused in Foster's 'Alumni Oxonienses' (1500–1714, iv. 1408) with his nephew John (1560–1611), father of Philip, first earl of Chesterfield [q. v.] On 20 June 1590 he was appointed master of the posts in succession to Thomas Randolph [q. v.] He was also a member of the council of the north and master of the posts (see *Border Papers*, 1595–1603, passim), and in 1596 he was appointed treasurer of the chamber and knighted. He appears to have had some influence at court, which Bacon sought to enlist in his favour (SPEDDING, *Letters and Life of Bacon*, ii. 50). On 16 Oct. 1597 he was elected member of parliament for Preston, and in 1600 was granted the constableship of Colchester. In

c 2

the following year he was placed on a commission to 'stay from execution all felons (except for wilful murder, rape, and burglary) and to commit them to serve in the gallies.' On 24 Sept. he was elected knight of the shire of Nottingham. His offices were regranted him on the accession of James I, and he was one of the commissioners appointed to treat of a union between England and Scotland. On 10 March 1603-4 he was returned to parliament for Newtown, Isle of Wight, and by letters patent dated 4 May 1605 he was created Baron Stanhope of Harrington. He was made member of the council of the Virginia Company on 23 May 1609, and in 1615 was one of the privy councillors who signed the warrant for the application of torture to Edmond Peacham [q.v.] He resigned the treasurership of the chamber in 1616, and died on 9 March 1620-1.

Stanhope was twice married: first to Joan, daughter of William Knollys, by whom he had no issue; and secondly, on 6 May 1589, to Margaret, daughter of Henry MacWilliams, one of the queen's gentlemen pensioners. By her he had issue one son, Charles, born in 1593, who succeeded as second baron, but died without issue in 1675, when the title became extinct, and two daughters: Elizabeth, who married Sir Lionel Talmash or Tollemache, ancestor of the earls of Dysart; and Catherine, who married Robert, viscount Cholmondeley (afterwards created Earl of Leinster). The later peers of the Stanhope family descend from the first baron's brother, Thomas.

[Cal. State Papers, Dom. 1581-1620; Hatfield MSS. pts. iv-vi.; Winwood's Memorials, ii. 57, 59; Collins's Letters and Mem. of State, vols. i. and ii. passim; Off. Ret. of Members of Parl.; Lords' and Commons' Journals; D'Ewes's Journals; Strype's Works; Spedding's Letters and Life of Bacon, vols. ii. iv. v. and vi.; Thoroton's Nottinghamshire; Alexander Brown's Genesis U.S.A.; Cornelius Brown's Nottinghamshire Worthies; Peerages by Collins (iii. 308-9) and G. E. C[okayne].] A. F. P.

STANHOPE, LEICESTER FITZGERALD CHARLES, fifth EARL OF HARRINGTON (1784-1862), born at Dublin on 2 Sept. 1784, was the third son of Charles Stanhope, third earl of Harrington [q. v.], and brother of Charles, fourth earl. He entered the army in September 1799 as a cornet in the 1st life-guards. In March 1803 he exchanged into the 9th foot. On 31 March of the same year he returned to the cavalry branch as captain in the 6th light dragoons, and exchanged into the 6th dragoon guards in November. In 1807 he

served in South America, and was present at the attack on Buenos Ayres. In July 1810 he attained the rank of major in the 47th foot, and on 24 April 1817 was appointed deputy quartermaster-general in India. During the Mahratta war of 1817-18 he took part in the action at Maheidpore and the storming of Talnier. For his services during the campaign he was created C.B. on 14 Oct. 1818. In June 1823 he was placed on half-pay with the rank of lieutenant-colonel. He became full colonel in January 1837.

Stanhope had other interests than those of his profession. He held advanced views in politics, and accepted Bentham as his master. While in India he took a prominent part in support of the Marquis of Hastings's administration, and on his return to England warmly defended him before the court of proprietors at the India House. In 1823 he justified Lord Hastings's removal of the censorship of the press in British India in 'A Sketch of the History and Influence of the Press in British India,' dedicated to Earl Grey.

In September 1823 Stanhope's offer to go to Greece as agent of the English committee in aid of the Greek cause was accepted by their secretary, John (afterwards Sir John) Bowring. On his way he succeeded in dissuading the Greek committees in Germany and Switzerland from withdrawing their help, and in Italy interviewed many persons acquainted with the condition of Greece. In November he met Byron in Cefalonia. On 12 Dec. he had a conference with Mavrocordato at Missolonghi, representing to him the fatal effects of disunion among the Greeks. At Missolonghi Stanhope set on foot a Greek newspaper, and, by means of the funds that he at once raised, prevented the Greek fleet from dispersing, formed an artillery corps, and purchased a house and grounds for a laboratory. On 5 Jan. Byron joined him, but they did not work well together. Unlike Byron, Stanhope was in favour of the establishment of a Greek republic, and, although he professed neutrality, showed more sympathy with Odysseus, the leader of the western Greeks, than with Byron's friend Mavrocordato and the eastern Greeks. To bring the two parties into closer union, Stanhope arranged a conference at Salona. It opened on the 21st, but neither Byron nor Mavrocordato attended. During Stanhope's stay at Salona Byron died, and Stanhope himself was ordered home by the English war office, owing to complaints of his conduct on the part of the Turkish government. After organising a postal service between Greece and England, he sailed in the Florida from Zante in June 1824. Byron's body and papers were placed in the same ship under Stanhope's charge, and he furnished Moore with information about Byron's career in Greece. He had been nominated a commissioner of the loan raised in England for the Greek cause, but agreed with his colleagues that, owing to the defective organisation of the Greek government, it was unadvisable to issue more money. Stanhope's services to Greece are variously estimated (cf. TRELAWNY, *Records of Byron*; FINLAY, *Hist. of Greece*, vols. vi. and vii.) Count Olerino Palma (*Greece Vindicated*, 1826) accused him of creating a third faction there, and of hindering the progress of the revolt. Personal animosities among those with whom he had to work rendered his position difficult and any conspicuous success impossible. But he was thanked by the English committee, and in April 1838 received the Greek order of the Redeemer.

Stanhope published in 1824, with a preface by Richard Ryan, his correspondence with the Greek committee in England in his 'Greece in 1823 and 1824.' Annexed to it was a 'Report on the State of Greece,' and a short life of Mustapha Ali (with coloured portrait), a young Turk he had brought over. An American edition appeared in 1825. Stanhope also contributed to the Paris edition of W. Parry's 'Last Days of Lord Byron' many letters to him from Finlay, and particulars of Byron's life and opinions, drawn from his conversations.

His elder brothers having died without children, Stanhope in March 1851 succeeded to the earldom of Harrington. He was much interested in the cause of temperance reform, and, though not himself a teetotaller, was a strong advocate of the Maine prohibition law. Harrington also advocated chancery reform and Polish independence.

He died at Harrington House, Kensington Palace Gardens, on 7 Sept. 1862. He married, in 1831, Elizabeth, daughter and heiress of William Green, esq., of Trelawney, Jamaica. The issue of the marriage was, with two daughters, a son—Sidney Seymour Hide Stanhope, sixth earl of Harrington (1845–1866), on whose death the earldom passed to his cousin Charles Wyndham Stanhope, seventh earl (1809–1881), father of the present earl. A portrait of Harrington as a child beating a drum, painted by Sir Joshua Reynolds and called 'Sprightliness,' is at Harrington House. It was engraved by Bartolozzi. Another painting by Reynolds, representing him in military uniform on horseback, is at Elvaston. There are portraits of the countess by Macpherson and F. Stone engraved by Rolls, and by A. E. Chalon engraved by H. Robinson.

[Gent. Mag. 1862, ii, 491; Doyle's Official Baronage; G. E. C.'s and Foster's Peerages; Moore's Life of Byron, pp. 601, 607, 620, 629, 632, 639, and Diary, 12 and 14 July 1824; Stanhope's Works, and a Collection of his Speeches, 1858; Trelawney's Records of Shelley, Byron, and himself, 1887, pp. 230-1; Finlay's Hist. of Greece, ed. Tozer, vi. 327-8, vii. 8-9; Waagen's Treasures of Art in Great Britain (Suppl. pp. 236, 495-6); Bone's Mod. Engl. Biogr.]   G. LE G. N.

STANHOPE, SIR MICHAEL (*d.* 1552), partisan of the Protector Somerset, second son of Sir Edward Stanhope (*d.* 1511) by his first wife, Avelina, daughter of Sir Gervase Clifton of Clifton, Nottinghamshire, was descended from an ancient Nottinghamshire family, several members of which had been knighted and had frequently represented the shire in parliament in the fourteenth and fifteenth centuries. His father was one of the leaders of the army that vanquished Simnel's adherents at Stoke in 1487; he also fought against the Cornish rebels at Blackheath in 1497, and by his second wife was father of Anne, duchess of Somerset [see SEYMOUR, EDWARD, first DUKE OF SOMERSET]. On the death of the elder son, Richard, without male issue, on 21 Jan. 1528-9, Michael succeeded to the family estates. Soon afterwards he entered the service of Henry VIII, and early in 1537 he was placed on the commission of the peace for Nottinghamshire. He benefited largely by the dissolution of the monasteries, his principal grants being Shelford priory, rectory, and manor and the priory of Lenton, both in Nottinghamshire(*Letters and Papers of Henry VIII*, vols. xii. xiii. passim). On 17 Feb. 1541-2 he was appointed lieutenant of Kingston-upon-Hull (TICKELL, pp. 186 sqq.), and from that date till the end of the reign he was actively employed in making arrangements for the wars on the border and various expeditions into Scotland (*Hamilton Papers*, vol. i. passim; *Acts P. C.* 1542-1547 passim). On 5 Jan. 1544-5 he was returned to parliament as knight of the shire of Nottingham. Soon after Edward VI's accession Stanhope was knighted and appointed chief gentleman of the privy chamber and deputy to his brother-in-law, the Protector, in the governorship of the young king. On 10 Oct. 1547 he was again elected to parliament for Nottinghamshire, and he also received a grant of the keepership of Windsor park and governorship of Hull. Two years later he lost all his appointments on the

Protector's fall, and was sent to the Tower (12 Oct. 1549). On 17 Feb. 1549-50, at a thin meeting of the council with Warwick absent, his release was ordered, but it was countermanded on the following day, and he was not set at liberty until he acknowledged a debt of 3000*l.* to the king (22 Feb.) Early in the following year he was reappointed governor of Hull, in which capacity he came into frequent collision with the mayor and townsmen (TICKELL, pp. 214 et sqq.) On 18 May 1551 he was released from his recognisances, but on 17 Oct. following he was again sent to the Tower on a charge of conspiring against Northumberland's life. He remained in prison until after Somerset's execution, and on 27 Jan. 1551-2 he was tried on a charge of felony, apparently under the act passed by Northumberland's influence in the parliament of 1549-50 (*Statutes of the Realm*, IV. i. 104). Stanhope was no doubt implicated in Somerset's endeavours to supplant Northumberland, but there is no evidence that he aimed at taking the duke's life (*Baga de Secretis*, pouch xx; cf. *Deputy-Keeper of the Records*, 4th Rep. App. ii. 230 2). He was condemned and sentenced to be hanged, but the sentence was commuted, and he was beheaded on Tower Hill, 26 Feb., stoutly maintaining his innocence. An act confirming his attainder was passed on 12 April following (*Lords' Journals*, i. 425). An anonymous three-quarter-length portrait of Stanhope belongs to Mr. Sewallis Evelyn Shirley.

Stanhope's widow, Anne, daughter of Nicholas Rawson of Aveley, Essex, was allowed to retain the priory of Shelford during life. She died on 20 Feb. 1587-8 (see *Archæologia*, xxxi. 212-4), and was buried in Shelford church, where there are monuments to her and her husband. She left, among other issue : (1) Sir Thomas Stanhope (*d.* 1596), father of Sir John Stanhope (1560-1611), who was father of Philip Stanhope, first earl of Chesterfield [q. v.]: (2) John, first baron Stanhope [q. v.], and two sons named Edward who are confused by Strype [see STANHOPE, SIR EDWARD, *d.* 1608]. From a daughter, Jane, who married Roger Townshend, were descended the viscounts Townshend.

[Authorities quoted ; Cal. State Papers, Dom.; Lit. Remains of Edward VI (Roxburghe Club); Machyn's Diary (Camden Soc.); Acts of the Privy Council, 1542-53; Cal. Hatfield MSS. vol. i.; Strype's Works; Holinshed's Chron. ed. Hooker, iii. 1081; Stow's Annals, p. 607; State Papers, Henry VIII, vols. i. v.; Off. Ret. Members of Parl.; Tytler's Edward VI and Mary, ii. 13, 19, 44, 46-7, 50, 74; Collins's Peerage, iii.

300 et sqq.; Brown's Nottinghamshire Worthies, pp. 108-9; Notes and Queries, 3rd ser. v. 516, vi. 38.]
A. F. P.

STANHOPE, PHILIP, first EARL OF CHESTERFIELD (1584-1656), son of Sir John Stanhope of Shelford, Nottinghamshire, by Cordell, daughter of Richard Allington, esq., was born in 1584, and knighted by James I on 16 Dec. 1605 (DOYLE, *Official Baronage*, i. 370; COLLINS, *Peerage*, ed. Brydges, iii. 421). On 7 Nov. 1616 he was raised to the peerage by the title of Baron Stanhope of Shelford, paying 10,000*l.* for that dignity (*Court and Times of James I*, i. 426, 436). On 4 Aug. 1628 Charles I created him Earl of Chesterfield (DOYLE).

When the civil war broke out Chesterfield and his family vigorously supported the king's cause. According to Lloyd, he refused to sit in the Long parliament after it declined to suppress the tumults raised in support of the popular party (*Memoirs of Excellent Personages*, 1668, p. 651). In November 1642 he received a commission to raise a regiment of dragoons for Charles I. About December his house at Bretby was taken and plundered by Sir John Gell (GLOVER, *Derbyshire*, App. pp. 62, 70). Chesterfield, who succeeded in escaping, established himself at Lichfield with about three hundred men, but was besieged there by Gell and Lord Brooke, and obliged to surrender (RUSHWORTH, v. 143).

The parliament ordered him to be sent to London, but allowed him to remain a prisoner on parole in his lodgings in Covent Garden, instead of committing him to the Tower (*Lords' Journals*, v. 682, vi. 17, 19, 84, 511). Chesterfield's estates were sequestrated, and in November 1645 he petitioned the House of Lords for an allowance for his maintenance, alleging that his losses amounted to 50,000*l.* (*ib.* vii. 698, ix. 43). Ultimately he was granted 5*l.* per week by parliament, and his fine for delinquency fixed at 8,698*l.* (*Calendar of Committee for Compounding*, p. 1264). Chesterfield died at London on 12 Sept. 1656, and was buried in the church of St. Giles-in-the-Fields.

Chesterfield married: first, in 1605, Catherine, daughter of Francis, lord Hastings, who died on 28 Aug. 1636. By her he had six sons. Of these John, the eldest, matriculated at Christ Church, Oxford, in November 1622, and died in July 1625 (FOSTER, *Alumni Oxon.* 1500-1714, p. 1408).

Henry, the second son, matriculated at the same time as his brother, was knighted on 2 Feb. 1626, represented Nottinghamshire in the first two parliaments of Charles I and East Retford in the third, and died on 29 Nov.

1634. His wife Catherine, eldest daughter of Thomas, lord Wotton, is noticed separately [see KIRKHOVEN, CATHERINE]; by her he left a son Philip, second earl of Chesterfield [q. v.]

Ferdinando, the fourth son, member for Tamworth in 1640, major and subsequently colonel of horse in the king's army, was killed at Bridgford, Nottinghamshire, in 1644 (FOSTER, *Alumni Oxonienses*, i. 1408; WOOD, *Fasti*, ii. 42; *Life of Colonel Hutchinson*, ii. 57, 87).

Philip, the fifth son, who matriculated at Exeter College, Oxford, on 6 Dec. 1637, was killed at the storming of Shelford House, of which garrison he was commander, on 27 Oct. 1645 (*ib.* ii. 81, 376). Arthur, the youngest son of the first marriage, represented the county of Nottingham in the Convention parliament and in the first parliament of Charles II. From him Philip, fifth earl of Chesterfield, is descended [see under STANHOPE, PHILIP DORMER, fourth EARL].

By his second wife, Anne, daughter of Sir John Pakington of Westwood, Worcestershire, and widow of Sir Humphrey Ferrars of Tamworth Castle, Warwickshire, Chesterfield had one son, Alexander, father of James, first earl Stanhope [q. v.]

The poems of Sir Aston Cokain, who was son of Chesterfield's sister, Anne Stanhope, contain a masque acted at Bretby in 1639, and verses on Ferdinando Stanhope and other members of the family (ed. 1662, pp. 118, 137, 187, 116*, 144*).

[Doyle's Official Baronage ; Collins's Peerage, ed. Brydges ; G. E. C[okayne]'s Complete Peerage.]   C. H. F.

STANHOPE, PHILIP, second EARL OF CHESTERFIELD (1633–1713), born in 1633, was the grandson of Philip, first earl of Chesterfield [q. v.], and son of Sir Henry Stanhope, by Catherine, eldest daughter of Thomas, lord Wotton [see KIRKHOVEN, CATHERINE]. His father died before he was two years old. At the age of seven he accompanied his mother to Holland, where he was educated under the tuition of Poliander, professor of divinity at the university of Leyden (whose son married his mother), spent a year at the Prince of Orange's college at Breda, and completed his education at the court of the Princess of Orange and at Paris (*Memoirs* prefixed to the *Letters of Philip, second Earl of Chesterfield*, 1835). In 1650 he travelled through Italy, and spent nine months at Rome (*ib.* p. 10; BAROHAVE, *Alexander VI and his Cardinals*, ii. 124). About 1652 Stanhope returned to England, married Anne Percy, eldest

daughter of the tenth Earl of Northumberland, and lived for some time in retirement at Petworth. On his wife's death in 1654 he left England again, and paid a second visit to Rome, returning to England about 1656. The Protector, according to Chesterfield's account, offered him a command in the army, and the hand of one of his daughters, both of which he declined. A second proposed match between Chesterfield and the daughter of Lord Fairfax was broken off after they 'had been thrice asked in St. Martin's Church' (*Letters*, p. 19; cf. *Cal. State Papers*, Dom. 1656–7, p. 349). By this time he had become notorious for drinking, gaming, and 'exceeding wildness,' and was engaged in love affairs with Barbara Villiers (afterwards Duchess of Cleveland) [q. v.] and Lady Elizabeth Howard, who subsequently married Dryden (*Letters*, pp. 86, 95, 97).

In February 1658 he was arrested for an intended duel with Lord St. John, and on 8 June the Protector committed him to the Tower for dangerously wounding Captain John Whalley in a duel (*ib.* p. 84; *Cal. State Papers*, Dom. 1657–8 p. 290, 1658–9 pp. 52, 62). At the same time he dabbled in the royalist plots against the government, and was again committed to the Tower in September 1659 on suspicion of a share in Sir George Booth's rising, but released on giving security for 10,000*l.* (*ib.* 1659–60, pp. 164, 240; *Cal. of Compounders*, p. 1265). On 17 Jan. 1660 he killed a Mr. Woolly in a duel at Kensington, fled to France, obtained a pardon from Charles II, and returned in his train to England (PEPYS, *Diary*, ed. Wheatley, i. 21; CHESTERFIELD, *Letters*, p. 110).

From 24 Feb. 1662 to July 1665 Chesterfield held the post of chamberlain to Catherine of Braganza, and he was after his resignation a member of her council (DOYLE). In 1660 he married Lady Elizabeth Butler, eldest daughter of James Butler, twelfth earl and first duke of Ormonde [q. v.] His neglect of his wife did not prevent him from being jealous, and in January 1663 he packed her off to Derbyshire, in order to put an end to the unwelcome attentions of the Duke of York (PEPYS, 19 Jan. 1663). Another of her admirers was her cousin, James Hamilton, the history of whose amour with her is detailed in the 'Memoirs' of Grammont (ed. 1853, pp. 144, 158, 173–200). The countess died in July 1665 (CHESTERFIELD, *Letters*, pp. 26, 131). On 13 June 1667 Chesterfield was appointed colonel of a foot regiment, but it was disbanded on the conclusion of peace with Holland (DALTON, *Army Lists*, i. 79;

cf. PEPYS, 9 June 1667). Towards the close of Charles II's reign he was again employed. He was a member of the new privy council appointed on 26 Jan. 1681. On 6 Nov. 1682 he became colonel of the Holland regiment of foot, but resigned his command two years later in consequence of a quarrel about precedence (DALTON, i. 298; CHESTERFIELD, *Letters*, p. 252).

On 2 Dec. 1679 Charles appointed Chesterfield warden and chief justice in eyre of the royal forests south of the Trent (DOYLE). This office had formerly been held by the Duke of Monmouth, and Chesterfield's offer to restore it to Monmouth, when the latter was restored to favour, earned him the ill will of the Duke of York. Nevertheless Chesterfield acted as lord sewer at the coronation of James II (23 April 1685), and held the post of chief justice in eyre till the following October, when he resigned on the plea of ill health (*Letters*, pp. 252, 292). He disapproved of the ecclesiastical policy of James, and placed his proxy in the hands of George Savile, marquis of Halifax [q. v.]; but Halifax found it extremely difficult to persuade him to more active measures of opposition (*ib.* pp. 297-310, 325). In like manner when the Revolution took place Chesterfield got together a hundred horse and escorted the Princess Anne from Nottingham to Warwick, but refused to take arms against James II, in spite of the solicitations of his old ally, Lord Danby (*ib.* pp. 47, 335). In the Convention he both spoke and voted against the proposal to declare the throne vacant and make the Prince of Orange king (*Memoirs of Thomas, Earl of Ailesbury*, p. 233). James sent over a commission appointing Chesterfield and three others regents of the kingdom, but he refused to accept it. He likewise refused William III's offers to make him privy councillor, gentleman of the bedchamber, and ambassador, and declined to take the association in support of William's title imposed by parliament in 1694. To William himself he explained his aversion to all such oaths, saying that if the oath of allegiance which he had taken could not bind him nothing would, and protesting his veneration for his majesty's person and his resolution not to act against the government.

Similar scruples and his increasing infirmities debarred Chesterfield from employment during the reign of Anne, at whose accession he was one of the few who refused the oath abjuring the Pretender (*Letters*, pp. 51-63; cf. SWIFT, *Works*, ed. Scott, xii. 243). He died on 28 Jan. 1713, in his eightieth year. Chesterfield was the friend of Charles Cotton and the patron of Dryden; to him Dryden dedicated his translation of the Georgics. Grammont describes Chesterfield thus: 'Il avait le visage fort agréable, la tête assez belle, peu de taille et moins d'air.'

By his second wife, Lady Elizabeth Butler, Chesterfield had a daughter Elizabeth, born in 1663, who married John Lyon, earl of Strathmore. He took for his third wife Lady Elizabeth Dormer, eldest daughter of Charles, second earl of Carnarvon. By her he had two sons and two daughters: (1) Philip, third earl of Chesterfield, who married Elizabeth Savile, daughter of the Marquis of Halifax, was father of Philip Dormer Stanhope, fourth earl [q. v.], and died in 1726: (2) Charles, who inherited the estate of the Wottons, changed his surname to Wotton, and died without issue; (3) Mary (1664-1703), wife to Thomas Coke of Melbourne, Derbyshire; (4) Catherine (1675-1728), wife to Godfrey Clarke of Chilcot, Derbyshire (COLLINS, *Peerage*, ed. Brydges, iii. 425).

Chesterfield wrote an account of his own life, portions of which are printed in the biography prefixed to the collection of his letters published in 1835. The original is now in the British Museum (Addit. MS. 19253).

[Doyle's Official Baronage, i. 371; Collins's Peerage, ed. Brydges, vol. iii.; Letters of Philip, second Earl of Chesterfield, 1835.] C. H. F.

STANHOPE, PHILIP DORMER, fourth EARL OF CHESTERFIELD (1694-1773), politician, wit, and letter-writer, was son of Philip Stanhope, third earl of Chesterfield, by his wife Elizabeth, daughter (by his second marriage) of George Savile, marquis of Halifax [q. v.]. Philip Stanhope, second earl of Chesterfield [q.v.], was his grandfather. Of his four brothers, two enjoyed much popularity in the world of fashion, viz.: William (1702-1772), who was created K.B. on 27 May 1725, and was M.P. for Lostwithiel for a few months in 1727, and for Buckinghamshire from that year until his death; and John (1705-1748), who was M.P. for Nottingham from 1727 and for Derby from 1736 till his death, and was a lord of the admiralty for the last ten months of his life. Born in London on 22 Sept. 1694, and baptised at St. James's, Piccadilly, on 9 Oct., Stanhope was educated privately. His father neglected him, but his maternal grandmother, the Marchioness of Halifax, actively interested herself in his early education. A French tutor named Jonneau perfected him in French in youth, and he spoke and wrote it with ease and correctness before he was eighteen. At that age he proceeded to Trinity Hall, Cambridge, where he developed, according to his own account, a pedantic veneration for the Latin classics, and was attracted by the mathematical lectures of the blind professor, Nicholas Saunderson [q. v.] In 1714 he left the university 'an absolute pedant' after a stay of little more than a year; but a tour in Flanders followed immediately, and transmuted him into a man of the world, whose interests were to outward appearances wholly divided between gallantry and gaming. But he found time for study, and developed an ambition to become an orator. His rank and connections secured for him a ready welcome in the best society at The Hague. At Antwerp he was the guest of the Duke and Duchess of Marlborough, and his ease of manner especially ingratiated him with the duchess. The death of Queen Anne brought his tour, which was planned to extend to Italy, to an abrupt conclusion. His kinsman, General James Stanhope, afterwards first earl Stanhope [q. v.], offered to introduce him to the new king, and a political career was thus opened to him under promising auspices.

In 1715 he was appointed gentleman of the bedchamber to the king's son, George, prince of Wales, and in the same year he entered the House of Commons as whig member for St. Germans, Cornwall. Some weeks were yet needed before he attained his legal majority. His political views embodied from the first much genuinely liberal sentiment, and he was never a staunch partisan. He supported, however, with exuberant energy the efforts of the whigs, who predominated in the new parliament, to push their advantage over their tory rivals. In his maiden speech, which he delivered on 5 Aug. in the debate on the articles of impeachment against the Duke of Ormonde, he denounced as traitors all the promoters of the peace of Utrecht. A member of the opposition privately warned him that if he voted in accordance with his speech the lawfulness of his election, owing to his being under age, would be called in question. Thereupon Stanhope discreetly retired to Paris. French manners and morals alike appealed to him, and he proved an apt pupil in the school of the fashionable demi-monde of the French capital.

Settling within a year or two again in London, he found his chances of preferment hampered by the quarrel between the prince, his master, and the king. With characteristic caution he took a middle course, and, while maintaining good relations with the prince, avoided all show of hostility to the king.

But it was obviously prudent for him to limit his political activity, and he spent his enforced leisure in the congenial society of men of letters or of fashion. With Pope he formed a close intimacy, and through Arbuthnot he came to know something of Swift. He cultivated, too, the acquaintance of Prince George's mistress, Henrietta Howard, afterwards countess of Suffolk, who was an accredited patroness of men of letters, and long maintained a lively correspondence with her. But her favour was a perilous possession. Although it helped Stanhope to maintain good relations with the court, it exposed him to the hostility of the Princess of Wales (afterwards Queen Caroline), who was an unrelenting foe. But Stanhope's tact stood him in good stead. He was elected for Lostwithiel in 1722, and in the king's interest supported a motion for augmenting the army by an addition of four thousand men. He was rewarded for his complaisance by his appointment on 26 May 1723 to the post of captain of the gentlemen-pensioners in succession to Lord Townshend. On presenting himself to his constituents for re-election he was defeated, and he did not sit in the House of Commons again. In the summer of 1725 his father's illness recalled him to the family seat of Bretby, where the rustic seclusion excited his spleen and whetted his appetite for active political work. The development of the political situation was not much to his taste. Sir Robert Walpole and Stanhope were constitutionally antipathetic, and the complete supremacy which Walpole maintained in parliament and the king's counsels from the date of his accession to power in 1721 roused Stanhope's ridicule and disgust. An open breach was not desired by Walpole. But when, in the spring of 1725, the minister offered Stanhope the ribbon of the newly revived order of the Bath, it was contemptuously rejected. Stanhope was displeased, too, with his brother William for accepting it; and in some satirical lines on the accidental loss of the badge by one of the new knights, Sir William Morgan of Tredegar, he laughed at the distinction as 'one of the toys Bob gave his boys.' Walpole resented the insult, and in May 1725 Stanhope ceased to be captain of the gentlemen-pensioners.

On 27 Jan. 1726 his father died, and he took his seat in the House of Lords. Although he cynically talked of the upper chamber as a hospital for incurables, he lost no time in manifesting a resolve to play on that platform an active part in the opposition to Walpole. His relations with the Prince of Wales, combined with his wit and eloquence—always carefully premeditated—gave him at once a commanding position. After the king's death, on 11 June 1727, he moved the address of condolence, congratulation, and thanks in reply to the speech of George II on his accession to the throne. He was confirmed in his post of lord of the bedchamber, and on 26 Feb. 1728 George II nominated him a privy councillor. But Walpole strongly deprecated the bestowal of any high office. The king insisted that something more must be done for him, and Walpole reluctantly offered him the English embassy at the Hague. It was accepted with alacrity. Chesterfield set out on 23 April 1728, and arrived on 5 May. His brother John went with him as secretary; and Richard Chenevix (1698-1779) (afterwards bishop of Waterford) was his chaplain. While attending to his official duties, and studying the constitution of the Dutch republic, he ingratiated himself with its ministers by magnificent hospitalities. At the same time he did not neglect his pleasures. 'He courted the good opinion of the Dutch people,' wrote Horace Walpole, 'by losing immense sums at play.' The intimacy he formed with a beautiful young lady named Mlle. du Bouchet had a marked influence on his life. By her he became in 1732 the father of the son whose education and progress subsequently became his main interest. He kept Mrs. Howard regularly informed of his diversions, and he well maintained himself in the king's favour.

Early in 1730 Chesterfield opened negotiations for the marriage of William, prince of Orange, with Anne, princess-royal of England, which reached a successful issue. At the end of May Boerhaave, the great physician of Leyden, attended him for a fever. He corresponded with Lord Townshend, who was involved in differences with Walpole, and canvassed the possibility of becoming Townshend's colleague as secretary of state. On 18 May 1730 he was elected a knight of the Garter, and on 18 June he came home to be installed at Windsor. Next day the staff of the lord steward of the household was given him. Walpole's magnanimity in waiving objections temporarily overcame Chesterfield's dislike. 'Lord Chesterfield,' says Lord Hervey, 'made the warmest professions to Sir Robert Walpole, acknowledging that his attachment this winter to Lord Townshend gave him no right to expect this favour, and saying, "I had lost the game, but you have taken my cards into your hand and recovered it."' The duties of the office were mainly honorary, and Chesterfield returned to The Hague, where George II visited him in

August. In October Chesterfield was again in England on leave of absence. Early next year Chesterfield was busily occupied in delicate negotiations which were needed to preserve the peace of Europe. George II was willing to join Spain and Holland in guaranteeing the pragmatic sanction, if by so doing he could prevent the emperor from disturbing the balance of European power. The States delayed their adhesion, and taught Chesterfield a lesson, he says, in the Christian virtues of patience, forbearance, and long-suffering. But at length, on 16 March 1731, Chesterfield signed at The Hague, with the pensionary and Count Zinzendorf, the second treaty of Vienna (COXE, *Memoirs of Walpole*, i. 346). Later in the year a persistent fever compelled him to apply for leave of absence. His ill-health rendered him reluctant to resume his post at The Hague, and on 26 Feb. 1732 he was formally relieved of it.

To parliament he now redirected his energies. His distrust and dislike of Walpole rapidly revived. But on 6 March 1733, in the debate on the mutiny bill, he warmly supported the government's proposal to maintain the standing army at the number of seventeen or eighteen thousand men. The unpopularity of Walpole's excise scheme, however, drew Chesterfield into the hue and cry against the minister. His three brothers voted against the bill in the House of Commons, and on 11 April Walpole, owing to the threatening decline of his majority, abandoned it before a second reading. Walpole's temper was roused. He held Chesterfield responsible for many defections in the lower house, and the king made no resistance to his proposal that Chesterfield should be dismissed from the office of lord steward. Doubtless the queen, who regarded Chesterfield with growing abhorrence as the confidant of the king's mistress, Lady Howard, silenced the king's scruples. On 13 April the dismissal was effected. Chesterfield's composure was seriously disturbed. In a letter (now lost) he protested to the king against the indignity. No reply was sent. Thenceforth Chesterfield absented himself from court, and his friendly relations with the king came to an end. Relieved of official responsibility, he vented his pique in anonymous contributions to the newspapers, and early in 1734 three amusing essays in 'Fog's Journal,' entitled respectively 'An Army in Waxwork' (17 Jan.), 'An Essay upon Ears' (24 Jan.), and 'An Essay upon Eyes' (10 April), caused Walpole and his friends much discomfort.

On 5 Sept. 1733 Chesterfield gave further

offence to the king by marrying Petronilla Melusina von der Schulenburg, the natural daughter of George I by his 'Maypole' mistress, Countess Ehrengard Melusina von der Schulenburg, duchess of Kendal [q. v.] Born in 1693, Chesterfield's bride, who was forty years old and his senior by a year, had been created Countess of Walsingham in her own right in 1722. Walpole says she had been secretly married in youth; but when Chesterfield made her acquaintance she was living with her mother, the Duchess of Kendal, in Grosvenor Square, in the house adjoining his own. In a pecuniary sense the match was desirable. The lady's portion was said to be a sum of 50,000*l.*, with 3,000*l.* per annum payable out of the civil list revenue in Ireland during her life (*Hist. Reg.*) At the same time her expectations from her mother were great. The marriage was in fact solely a political and financial arrangement. For many years after the ceremony husband and wife continued to reside next door to each other. Chesterfield seems to have celebrated the union by taking into his keeping a new mistress, Lady Frances or Fanny Shirley (1702–1778), 'a great beauty,' with whom he long maintained relations. To her he addressed much sportive verse. His friend Pope wrote poems to her, and Sir Charles Hanbury-Williams commemorated her relations with Chesterfield in his poem 'Isabella' (cf. POPE, *Works*, ed. Courthope and Elwin, iv. 402). At the same time he frequently visited his wife at the house of her mother, and 'played away all his credit' there. In December 1737 he and the countess visited Bath together. According to Horace Walpole, the countess made him 'a most exemplary wife, and he rewarded her very ungratefully.' His neglect of her was obvious and indefensible, but she does not appear to have resented it. All she expected from him was an outward show of respect, and his considerate references to her in his correspondence indicate that he did not disappoint her in that regard (ERNST, pp. 80–82). He lost no opportunity of protecting their joint pecuniary interests. When the duchess, his mother-in-law, died on 10 May 1743, George II is said to have destroyed her will to prevent Lady Chesterfield from benefiting by the dispositions of the late king in his mistress's favour (cf. WALPOLE, *Correspondence*, ed. Cunningham, vii. 141). It was believed that 40,000*l.* had been bequeathed to the duchess by George I, and had never been paid her. Chesterfield insisted that that sum should now be made over to his wife. Resistance was threatened, and an action was begun

against the crown under Chesterfield's direction; but finally Chesterfield agreed to stay proceedings on receiving payment of 20,000*l.* Elsewhere Chesterfield gave the king and Walpole as little quarter. Through the session of 1734 he supported the bill protecting military officers from deprivation of their commissions otherwise than by a court-martial or an address from both houses of parliament (13 Feb.) On 28 March he vigorously denounced a message from the king which requested parliament to give him authority to augment the naval and military forces during the parliamentary recess. In society and in the journals he made his foes (even the king and queen) feel the full force of his satiric faculty, and Walpole involuntarily offered him during the session of 1737 a singularly apt opportunity for its display. In view of the frequency of attacks in the theatres on the government, Walpole introduced a bill compelling theatrical managers to submit all plays for license to the lord chamberlain fourteen days before they were to be represented on the stage (10 Geo. II, cap. 28). When the bill was introduced into the lords, Chesterfield riddled its claim to justice or common-sense. He argued that ridicule was the natural prerogative of the theatre, and that the bill was an encroachment not merely upon liberty, but upon property, 'wit being the property of those who have it.' The speech was fully reported in 'Parliamentary History' (x. 319 sq.); an abstract appeared in 'Common Sense' (4 June 1737), and it was published as a pamphlet in 1749. Although the bill became law, Chesterfield's speech excited even the admiration of antagonists. Hervey describes it as one of the most lively and ingenious speeches that he ever heard in parliament, 'full of wit of the genteelest satire, and in the most polished classical style that the Petronius of any time ever wrote. It was extremely studied, seemingly easy, well delivered, and universally admired.' Chesterfield's unqualified assertion of the right of literary satire to immunity from police regulations roused grateful enthusiasm in the republic of letters. Pope gracefully complimented him in the 'Dunciad' (bk. 4, v. 43–4). Smollett wrote: 'The speech will ever endear his character to all the friends of genius and literature—to all those who are warmed with zeal for the liberties of their country.'

The death, on 20 Nov. 1737, of Queen Caroline, on whom Chesterfield penned a vindictive epitaph, removed a serious obstacle to his political advancement. It weakened Walpole's influence at court, and the minister's resistance of the popular cry for war with Spain during 1738 stirred all Chesterfield's energies in opposition. During the session of 1739 few speakers enunciated more bellicose sentiments. 'Let us,' he said on 31 May, 'for once speak the sense of the nation, and let us regain by our arms what we have lost by our councils.' Walpole declared war with Spain in obedience to the clamour. But the ill-success of the naval operations with which it opened gave Chesterfield and his friends new ground of attack. On 13 Feb. 1741 he signed the protest in favour of Carteret's unsuccessful motion for the removal of Sir Robert Walpole from the king's councils. But, despairing of making immediately any effective impression on Walpole's position, he afterwards set out on a seven months' visit to the continent.

There is little reason to doubt that the ostensible reason of his tour—anxiety on account of his health—was the true one. His parliamentary efforts had brought him into line with Lord Bolingbroke's following, but Horace Walpole's suggestion that he was despatched to Avignon by the enemies of the minister to obtain Jacobite support 'for Sir Robert's destruction' is unsupported. His first stopping place was Brussels, where he spent a few days with Voltaire, who read to him portions of his tragedy 'Mahomet.' After drinking the waters at Spa he passed to Paris. There Cardinal Fleury showed him 'uncommon distinctions.' He was eagerly welcomed in fashionable salons, and spent much time with men of letters, especially with Crebillon fils, with Fontenelle and Montesquieu, whom he thenceforth reckoned among his closest friends. Later, in September, he went south, and passed three days with Lord Bolingbroke, whose literary style had long excited his warmest admiration; but, according to Chesterfield's own account, they talked nothing but metaphysics. Chesterfield returned home in November 1741, and at once resumed the war on Walpole. Within a few months his triumph was assured. On 11 Feb. 1742 Walpole resigned office, and was called up to the House of Lords as the Earl of Orford.

Chesterfield's share of responsibility for Walpole's fall was very large. But his cynical temper discounted any enthusiasm for himself on the part of those with whom he had been acting, and with Pulteney and Carteret, two of his chief allies in the strife, he was wholly out of sympathy. The king was ill-disposed to him. The new ministry, of which Spencer Compton, earl of Wilmington, was the nominal head, was controlled by Carteret, whose Hanoverian leanings were repudiated by Chesterfield. Consequently he

was not invited to join the government. He professed satisfaction, and urged the new government to press their advantage over Walpole to the uttermost. When Walpole took his seat in the House of Lords, Chesterfield somewhat sardonically wished him joy, but at the same time supported the bill indemnifying witnesses who should give evidence before the committee of secrecy that had been appointed to inquire into Sir Robert Walpole's conduct in office. The bill was thrown out by the upper house.

Thenceforth Chesterfield declared himself to be 'still in opposition.' In November 1742, when he attended the king's levée, he had 'a long laughing conversation' with Orford, who was not sorry that his successors in office should feel the sting of Chesterfield's tongue. At the opening of the next session (1743) Chesterfield opposed the address to the crown. On 1 Feb. he denounced with fiery sarcasm the government's proposal to take Hanoverian troops into British pay, and talked of 'the dirty mercenary schemes of pretended patriots and avowed profligates.' He expressed himself even more bitingly in the newspapers. On 5 Feb. 1743 there appeared a new periodical, called 'Old England, or the Constitutional Journal.' To the first and third numbers Chesterfield contributed letters signed 'Geffery Broadbottom,' and effectively complained that, though the men were changed, the measures remained the same. A popular anonymous pamphlet, 'The Case of the Hanover Forces in the Pay of Great Britain examined,' which passed through three editions in 1743, was attributed to the joint pens of Chesterfield and Edmund Waller. An answer by Sir Robert Walpole's eldest brother called forth from Chesterfield and his colleague two further tracts, 'A Vindication' and 'A Further Vindication' of their position. A sequel, 'The Interest of Hanover steadily pursued since the A[ccession] ... by Broad-bottom,' was assigned to Chesterfield alone. On 15 Feb. Chesterfield attacked Carteret's 'gin' bill, which altered the duties on spirituous liquors and imposed licenses on the retailers. He argued that the proposed changes would encourage drunkenness (the report in the 'Gentleman's Magazine' for November was contributed by Johnson, who claimed to have invented it). Ten bishops joined Chesterfield in the same lobby, 'and made him fear,' he said, 'he was on the wrong side of the question. He was unaccustomed to divide with so many lawn sleeves.' But the opposition was in a minority, and the bills were carried.

On the death of Wilmington, in July

1743, Henry Pelham became prime minister; but Carteret remained in the ministry, and Chesterfield pursued him with much the same rancour as he had pursued Walpole. In the House of Lords he was now the acknowledged leader of the opposition, and played much the same rôle there that Pitt was playing in the House of Commons. In January 1744 he supported the proposal to discontinue the pay to the Hanoverian troops, 'The crown of three kingdoms,' he said, 'was shrivelled beneath an electoral cap.' To one outside observer Chesterfield's strenuous hostility to George II and his government had given unalloyed satisfaction. The Dowager Duchess of Marlborough had watched with enthusiasm the action of Chesterfield in the lords and Pitt in the commons, and when she died, on 17 Oct. 1744, she left Chesterfield a legacy of 20,000*l*. 'out of the great regard she had for his merit, and the infinite obligations she received from him on account of his opposition to the ministry.' Pitt, on the same ground, received 10,000*l*.

In the autumn of 1744 long-pending dissensions in the cabinet came to a head. Pelham and the Duke of Newcastle resolved to drive Carteret from office, and approached Chesterfield with a view to his co-operation. Although Carteret had the king's full confidence, he felt it useless to resist the combined attack, and on 24 Nov. 1744 he resigned the seals. His friends followed his example. Thereupon, in accordance with Chesterfield's known views, a new administration was formed of members drawn from both the whig and tory parties. It was at once christened, after the pseudonym that he had invented, the 'Broad-bottom administration.' Pelham retained his place as prime minister, and the king was reluctantly compelled to confer on Chesterfield the high office of lord-lieutenant of Ireland. Before he took up that post the government resolved to send him on an important diplomatic mission to The Hague, where his name was still favourably remembered. The king was with difficulty 'brought to give him a parting audience.' It did not last forty-five seconds. 'You have received your instructions, my lord,' was all that was said. Chesterfield's appointment bore date 12 Jan. 1745. His instructions were to induce the Dutch to join in the war of the Austrian succession, and to determine the number of troops they would supply. The French envoy, the Abbé de la Ville, was at The Hague before Chesterfield; but Chesterfield, while treating him with the utmost ease and politeness, successfully completed the negotiations in his country's in-

terest. Their course can be traced in detail in Chesterfield's correspondence with the Duke of Newcastle and Lord Harrington, the secretary of state, now in the British Museum (ERNST, pp. 219–39). Chesterfield returned home at the end of May, prepared to inaugurate his reign in Ireland.

Chesterfield arrived in Dublin in July, and, although his viceroyalty lasted only eight months, it proved him to be a tactful and enlightened statesman. His character had affinity to that of the Irish people, and he viewed them sympathetically. When he arrived the Scottish rebellion of 1745 was imminent; but while urging on the government in London the most rigorous measures of repression in England and Scotland, and neglecting no precaution to stay the possible spread of the contagion to Ireland, he was not surprised by panic into one needless act of coercion. With happy ridicule he discouraged the rumours of popish risings. Ireland, he said, had much more to fear from her poverty than her popery, and Miss Ambrose, the reigning beauty in Dublin society, to whom he addressed some witty flattery in verse, was the only dangerous papist he knew of [see PALMER, ELEANOR, LADY]. He firmly refused to follow the precedent of 1715, when all the catholic chapels were closed during the Jacobite outbreak, and to his prudent counsels must be attributed Ireland's tranquillity at a time when England and Scotland were torn by civil war (LECKY, *Hist. of Ireland in the Eighteenth Century*, i. 460–1). The main objects of his government were to raise the material prosperity of the country and to distribute public patronage in the public interest. 'He wished,' he wrote, 'to be remembered by the name of the Irish lord-lieutenant.' With the landlords he disavowed all sympathy, and ridiculed their improvidence and extravagant consumption of claret. He declared that 'the poor people in Ireland' were worse used than negroes by their lords and masters, 'and their deputies of deputies of deputies.' He sought to relieve public distress by undertaking public works. The planting of Phœnix Park was one of his projects.

On 23 April 1746 he left Ireland on leave of absence, and a long illness prevented his return. He had not entirely recovered in September. But the ministry stood in need of his active help, and the king was growing better disposed towards him. Chesterfield's position compelled him outwardly to support the court, and in February 1746 a caricaturist represented him along with Pitt as receiving a reprimand for his complaisance from the mouth of the Duchess of Marlborough, who reproached him with her gift of 20,000*l.* The king gave conspicuous proof of his reviving confidence by sanctioning an exchange of offices between Chesterfield and William Stanhope, first earl of Harrington [q. v.], who was vacating the post of secretary of state for the northern department. While lamenting the transference from an easy to a laborious employment, Chesterfield resigned the lord-lieutenancy of Ireland to Harrington, and entered on the duties of secretary of state on 29 Oct. 1746.

The good terms which had hitherto subsisted between Chesterfield and the Duke of Newcastle did not long survive his acceptance of the new office. The duke was almost as jealous as Walpole of brilliant colleagues, and a difference of opinion during 1747 on foreign policy led to a breach between Chesterfield and himself. Chesterfield was anxious to bring the continental war to a close, but his efforts were frustrated by the duke's secret correspondence in an opposite sense with Lord Sandwich, plenipotentiary at The Hague. Reports of Chesterfield's retirement were soon abroad. On 26 Jan. 1748 he wrote to his friend Solomon Dayrolles [q. v.], 'I can no longer continue in a post in which it is well known that I am but a *commis*, and in which I have not been able to do any one service to any one man, though ever so meritorious, lest I should be supposed to have any power, and my colleague not the whole.' He meant, he added, 'no sullen retirement from the world, but would indulge his ease and preserve his character.' His colleagues entreated him to hold on (cf. *Bedford Correspondence*, 1846, i. 206; *Marchmont Papers*, i. 262). But, ignoring their appeals, he resigned the seals in February 1748. The king parted with him reluctantly. A dukedom was offered him and was declined, but on his own initiative George II made his brother John a commissioner of the admiralty. His views of the policy of the government were set forth with some asperity in 'An Apology for a late Resignation, in a Letter from an English Gentleman to his Friend at The Hague.' The pamphlet reached a fourth edition before the end of the year (1748). According to Walpole, the tract was by Lord Marchmont writing in concert with Chesterfield. Chesterfield protested to Dayrolles, then at The Hague, that he could not so much as guess at the author; but his ignorance was perhaps assumed to anticipate inspection of the letter at the post office. There is little doubt that it was written under his inspiration. A war

of pamphlets followed, in which Chesterfield was severely handled by the partisans of the Pelhams (cf. 'An Answer from a Gentleman at The Hague ... in regard to a late Resignation;' 'The Resignation Discussed;' 'An impartial Review of two Pamphlets lately published: one intituled An Apology for a late Resignation, the other The Resignation Discussed:' and 'An Apologetical Discourse for a late celebrated Apology, shewing the real end and design of that treatise. Written by the real author of the Apology,' all 1748).

With his resignation of the secretaryship of state Chesterfield's official life came to an end. He had done, he said, with 'the hurry and plague of business, either in or out of court.' Thenceforth he rarely appeared in the political arena, and held severely aloof from party strife. But as a serene spectator he maintained a lively interest in politics, and retained much personal influence in political circles. In December 1750, according to Horace Walpole, he was offered the presidency of the council. He declined it on the score of deafness, but early next year he disinterestedly intervened in the business of parliament with marked effect. At the instance of George Parker, second earl of Macclesfield [q. v.], the virtual author of the change, he convinced himself of the need of a reformation of the calendar. Despite an appeal from the Duke of Newcastle not to stir matters that had long been quiet, he brought a bill on the subject into the House of Lords (20 Feb. 1751). He spoke by rote some astronomical jargon of which he admitted he did not understand a word, although he felt proud of its harmonious periods. On 18 March he moved the second reading, and Macclesfield explained its objects. The bill, which passed through both houses without opposition, was received in the country with a roar of disapproval. But the popular hostility was directed chiefly against Macclesfield and his family. George II continued to treat Chesterfield with consideration, and in May 1755 consulted him on the allowance to be made his grandson, Prince George, the heir-apparent. On 10 Dec. 1755 he made his last speech in the House of Lords. In accordance with the views of foreign policy he had long held, he denounced the maintenance of subsidy treaties with Prussia and Hesse-Cassel by which England's interests were, in his opinion, subordinated to those of Hanover. He spoke for nearly an hour; but the effort exhausted him, and as soon as his speech ended he left the house, never to address it again.

During the ministerial crisis of 1757 Chesterfield was called on to play a congenial part behind the scenes. The king was pronouncedly hostile to Pitt, whose presence in the ministry was inevitable. Newcastle refused to serve with Pitt, and the formation of a government that would be tolerated by the king consequently seemed impossible. Chesterfield's good offices were enlisted in bringing about a compromise. Lord Bute, at the suggestion of the court, privately invited him to overcome Newcastle's objections to take office with Pitt. The difficult task needed all Chesterfield's tact. With neither Pitt nor Newcastle had he been of late on cordial terms, but on 29 June, largely owing to his power of persuasion, the difficulties were surmounted, and Newcastle became nominal prime minister, with Pitt as the leading spirit of the government (cf. WALPOLE, *George II*, ii. 224; Newcastle Papers, *Addit. MS.* 32871). This proved Chesterfield's final incursion into practical politics, but he still corresponded with Newcastle and others on political topics. Subsequently from the vantage-ground of his retirement he viewed with all Chatham's disgust the government's attempts to tax the American colonies. He hotly condemned England's appeal to coercion. 'For my part,' he sagaciously wrote in 1765, 'I never saw a froward child mended by whipping, and I would not have the mother-country become a stepmother.'

But from the date of his resignation of office in 1748 till his death twenty-five years later, politics was the smallest of Chesterfield's interests. The same night on which he gave up his seals he resumed his practice—long interrupted by political preoccupations—of gambling at White's Club in St. James's Street, of which he and his brother William were for many years prominent members, and where his witticisms were long remembered. But he soon abandoned play; and when, about 1755, he learned that George Selwyn gave him at the club the nickname of Joe Miller he ceased to attend. In 1770 he directed his name to be struck off. His chief recreations were less exceptionable. 'My horse, my books, and my friends will divide my time pretty equally,' he told Dayrolles, when he withdrew from political office. He desired to enjoy 'the only real comforts in the latter end of life—quiet, liberty, and health.' All the happiness that wealth could bring him lay at his disposal. He spent time and money in building Chesterfield House in South Audley Street, Mayfair, which was completed in 1749 from the plans of Isaac Ware [cf. WALPOLE, *Letters*, ii. 279). The pillars for the hall

and staircase were purchased from the Duke of Chandos's mansion at Canons, and much attention was bestowed on the garden. An interesting print of the imposing exterior in Palladian style from a drawing by Eyre was published in 1750 (cf. reproduction in CHESTERFIELD, *Letters to his Godson*, 1890, ed. Carnarvon). The house is still standing, and is the residence of Lord Burton, although the streets known as Chesterfield Street and Chesterfield Gardens have been built over parts of the garden and the site of the outbuildings (cf. WHEATLEY and CUNNINGHAM's *London*). The gallery of pictures at Chesterfield House, Chesterfield wrote to Dayrolles on 4 Nov. 1748, was nearly complete; only two or three great masters were unrepresented. The death of his brother John in December 1748 meanwhile increased his resources. He received under the will 30,000l. for life and a villa at Blackheath. There, too, he built a gallery, and the fine garden, where melons and pineapples throve, inspired him with a 'furor hortensis.' Attacks of rheumatic gout rendered visits to Bath, Spa, and like resorts often necessary. In May 1752 a fall from his horse in Hyde Park temporarily crippled him. But his most serious trouble was increasing deafness. After trying every manner of remedy, he wrote on 16 Nov. 1753 to Dayrolles that cure was out of the question. The disability gradually withdrew him from society, but he bore his isolation cheerfully. 'He did not lose the power of hearing,' he wrote, 'till after he had very nearly lost the desire of it,' and he found consolation in increased devotion to literature. He wrote much on literary and social topics in the 'World' newspaper. He penned a pungent series of 'characters' of his contemporaries which was published posthumously. Walpole believed that he made some progress with some 'Memoirs of his own Time,' but burnt his notes 'a little before his death, being offended at Sir John Dalrymple's history, and saying he would leave no materials for aspersing great names.' He maintained close relations by correspondence with friends in France, including Voltaire, and leaders of intellectual society in Paris like Madame du Monconseil and Madame du Bocage. In August 1755 he was elected, much to his gratification, a member of the Academy of Inscriptions at Paris. But reading in his own library was his most satisfying resource. On 22 Nov. 1757 he wrote: 'I read with more pleasure than ever, perhaps because it is the only pleasure I have left. .... Solid folios are the people of business with whom I converse in the morning. Quartos, not quarts—pardon the quibble—are the easier mixed company with whom I sit after dinner, and I pass my evenings in the light and often frivolous chit-chat of small octavos and duodecimos.'

Patronage of literature, another of Chesterfield's diversions, involved him in greater embarrassments. The bricklayer-poet, Henry Jones (1721-1770) [q. v.], who welcomed him with a poem to Ireland in 1745, was a typical protégé. In 1748 Chesterfield invited him to London; interested himself in the collection of subscriptions for a volume of his poems; induced Colley Cibber to procure the production of Jones's 'Earl of Essex' at Covent Garden Theatre; aided Cibber in a thorough revision of the play, with a view to making its success a certainty; and finally, having rendered the poor man intolerably vain and self-indulgent, cast him off on finding him borrowing money of one of his servants. But genuine kindly sentiment underlay his relations with men of letters (cf. JAMES HAMMOND, Love Elegies, 1743, with Chesterfield's preface). He corresponded on equal terms with George Faulkner (1699?-1775) [q.v.], the Dublin bookseller; and the discredit which he incurred in the character of a patron at Dr. Johnson's vigorous hand seems ill deserved. In 1747 Johnson, at the suggestion of the publisher Dodsley, addressed to Chesterfield the prospectus of his 'Dictionary.' Apparently Chesterfield, who was secretary of state at the time, and had long been 'the butt of dedications,' made no acknowledgment beyond sending Johnson 10l. When the 'Dictionary' was on the eve of publication Chesterfield contributed anonymously to the 'World' two anticipatory eulogies (28 Nov. and 5 Dec. 1754). The story that Dr. Johnson had previously called upon Chesterfield, and had been kept waiting in the ante-chamber while Cibber was admitted without delay, was long current, but was denied by Johnson himself. Johnson had expected encouragement from Chesterfield while the heavy work was in progress, and resented conventional compliments when the labour was successfully accomplished. On 7 Feb. 1755 he addressed to the earl the famous letter in which, while expressing his resentment, he made a manly stand in behalf of literary independence. Chesterfield characteristically affected indifference to the rebuke. When Dodsley called on him soon afterwards, Johnson's epistle lay upon his table, 'where anybody might see it. He read it to me,' wrote Dodsley; 'said this man has great powers, pointed out the severest passages, and observed how well they were expressed.' Johnson, he added,

would be always more than welcome, and had he ever been denied admission, it was solely due to the ignorance of a servant. Chesterfield bore Johnson no malice, and there is little ground for identifying Johnson with the 'respectable Hottentot' described by Chesterfield in his 'Letters' (iii. 129). Chesterfield doubtless there aimed at George, first lord Lyttelton [q. v.]

Literature never wholly absorbed Chesterfield. Throughout the concluding half of his life his most serious interest was the education and the advancement in life of his natural son Philip. When the boy was barely five (in 1737) Chesterfield opened a correspondence with him, which he continued with scrupulous regularity so long as his son lived. At first he sent him elaborate essays, often both in French and English, on classical history, mythology, and composition. He never, when in office, allowed the business of state to delay the almost daily task. When he was free from political cares, and the boy had become a youth, he forwarded to him carefully considered instruction in all branches of learning on a scheme devised to make his pupil a reputable man of the world. Chesterfield wished him, he wrote (Letters, i. 108), 'as near perfection as possible. Never were so much pains taken for anybody's education, and never had anybody so many opportunities for knowledge and improvement.' Michael Maittaire [q. v.] was young Philip's Latin tutor in his early years, and Maittaire was succeeded in 1745 by Walter Harte [q. v.], who accompanied him and another youth, Edward Eliot (afterwards Lord Eliot) [q. v.], on an extended foreign tour through Holland, Germany, and Switzerland, winding up in Paris in 1751. Although Philip developed into a good-natured and sensible man, he was by nature incapable of assimilating any graces of manner. But Chesterfield's genuine affection rendered him tolerant of all defects. From August to November 1751 the young man stayed with his father, who expressed satisfaction with the extent of his knowledge and goodness of his heart. He believed that a further sojourn in Paris was all that was needed to give his deportment the polish it lacked. Chesterfield exerted all his influence to secure for the youth a promising start in the career of diplomacy which he had designed for him. Already, in 1751, he induced Lord Albemarle to give him some employment at the embassy in Paris. In the spring of 1752, when Philip left Paris for Hanover, Chesterfield wrote (15 May) to the Duke of Newcastle, secretary of state then in attendance on the king, begging, in the young man's behalf, a post as secretary of legation, even without salary. The duke was 'excessively kind and friendly,' and promised the residency at Venice. But when, in October 1752, Philip was Dayrolles's guest at Brussels, and it was arranged that he should be presented at court to Prince Charles of Lorraine, a difficulty was urged on the score of his illegitimacy. To Chesterfield's chagrin, this for a time proved a genuine bar. In the spring of 1753 Philip came to London to attend the levees, and Chesterfield's reminder to Newcastle of the promise of the post at Venice was met with the rebuff that the king objected on the ground of his birth (30 June). Some compensation was found in his election to parliament for Liskeard by the influence of his friends the Eliots in April 1754. Next year, under his father's careful coaching, he made his maiden speech on the address to the throne, but he was too shy to repeat the experience. In September 1756 he was appointed resident at Hamburg. He performed the duties of his office adequately. In February 1761 he was re-elected M.P. for St. Germans, but resigned the seat in 1765 at the earnest request of the patron, Edward Eliot, who compensated him with a money payment. Meanwhile, in June 1763, he was sent as envoy to the diet at Ratisbon, and early in 1764 he resigned his post at Hamburg to become resident minister at Dresden. He still maintained his close relations—both epistolary and personal—with his father, whose anxiety for his success was as keen as ever. But at the end of 1768 the long intercourse was closed by death. Philip had for some years suffered in health. In November 1768 he obtained leave of absence from Dresden to visit Avignon. On 16 Nov. he died there. Severely as Chesterfield must in any case have felt the blow, his sufferings were aggravated by the circumstance that the communication which brought the sad tidings revealed the fact that young Stanhope had been long secretly married, and had left on his father's hands a widow (Eugenia) and two sons. For nearly twenty years had Chesterfield plied his son with all the sagacious worldly wisdom that his own experience suggested respecting the affairs of gallantry and the dubious relations with the opposite sex which became a man of fashion. Very galling was the irony of the revelation that Philip had furtively taken refuge from the perils of polite intrigue in matrimony of no brilliant type. Chesterfield bore the shock with exemplary coolness. Despite the secret marriage with an unattractive woman of undistinguished

position, the memory of his dead son remained dear to him, and he gave proofs of the strength of his parental affection by sending his grandchildren to a good school and corresponding on amiable terms with the widow.

Happily for Chesterfield's peace of mind, he had already made himself responsible for the education of another young kinsman, also named Philip Stanhope—his godson, distant cousin, and the presumptive heir to the earldom (see ad fin.) In 1759, when this boy was four, Chesterfield told the father that he intended to treat him as a grandson. Between 28 July 1761 and 19 June 1770, while the youth was passing from his sixth to his fifteenth year, Chesterfield addressed to him a series of affectionate letters—236 are extant—in which he offered him, in much the same manner as he had written to his natural son, all the counsels likely, in his opinion, to insure his fitness for the dignities that awaited him.

Ill-health occasionally disturbed Chesterfield's equanimity during his last ten years, when, in his own words, 'he was hobbling on to his journey's end.' But his native gaiety of temperament was only at times overcast. When asked in his dying days how his friend and contemporary Lord Tyrawley did, he remarked, 'Tyrawley and I have been dead these two years, but we do not choose to have it known.' In the autumn of 1772 he completely broke down. At the end of September he left Blackheath for London so as to be near his favourite physician, Dr. Warren. During the next six months life gradually left him, and he died at Chesterfield House on 24 March 1773 in his seventy-ninth year. Within half an hour of the end his friend Dayrolles visited the sick chamber, and the earl's dying words were 'Give Dayrolles a chair.' His good breeding, remarked the physician in attendance, only quitted him with his life. His remains were removed to Audley Street chapel, and thence to Shelford for burial. His widow, with whom he had long been on merely formal terms, died on 16 Sept. 1778.

In Chesterfield's will, dated 4 June 1772, and proved April 1773, he admitted that he had had an uncommon share of the pompous follies of this life, and deprecated a pompous funeral. The expenses were not to exceed 100l., and he was to be buried in the next burying-place to where he died. He devised practically all his property to his godson Philip, and offered him characteristic warnings. He was by 'no means [to] go into Italy . . . the foul sink of illiberal manners and vices.' He was to forfeit 5l. to the dean and chapter of Westminster if he ever was

D

concerned in the keeping of any racehorse or pack of hounds, or visited Newmarket while the races were in progress there, or lost in any one day 500*l.* by gambling or betting. For Mlle. du Bouchet, the mother of his son, who survived him, he had already made ample provision, but he left her 500*l.* 'as a small reparation for the injury I did her.' To such of his servants as had lived with him for five years or upwards he left two years' full wages, remarking that he regarded them as 'unfortunate friends, my equals by nature and my inferiors only by the difference of our fortunes.' One of Chesterfield's executors was his literary protégé, Matthew Maty [q. v.], who wrote his biography.

Chesterfield incurred the dislike of three of the most influential writers of his day—Dr. Johnson, Horace Walpole, and Lord Hervey (Queen Caroline's friend). Their hostile estimates have injured his posthumous reputation, and inspired Dickens's ruthless caricature of him as Sir John Chester in 'Barnaby Rudge.' Chesterfield's achievements betray a brilliance of intellectual gifts and graces which discourages in the critic any desire to exaggerate his deficiency in moral principle. In matter and manner—in delicate raillery and in refinement of gesture—his speeches in parliament were admitted to be admirable by his foes. Horace Walpole declared on 15 Dec. 1743 that the finest speech he ever listened to was one from Chesterfield. Lord Hervey expressed himself to similar effect, although he entered the caveat: 'As Lord Chesterfield never could, or at least never did, speak, but prepared, and from dissertations he had written down in his closet and got by heart, he never made any figure in a reply, nor was his manner of speaking like debating, but declaiming' (HERVEY, ii. 341). His pointed enunciation of wise political principles made him a liberalising influence in English politics. Of his political sagacity his prophecy of the coming French revolution is a familiar example. On 15 April 1752 he wrote that he noticed a tendency in France 'to what we call here revolution principles.' At the end of 1753, after describing the condition of French society, he added : ' All the symptoms which I have ever met with in history previous to great changes and revolutions in government now exist and daily increase in France' (CHESTERFIELD, *Letters*, ii. 318, 319). Sainte-Beuve notes that Chesterfield's insight into French character has rarely been surpassed, and that he summarised the whole spirit of French political history when he told Montesquieu, ' Your parliaments can make barricades, but can never erect barriers ' (' Vos

parlements pourront bien faire encore des barricades, mais ils ne feront jamais de barrière,' Suard in *Biographie Universelle*). His apophthegms on English politics were no less to the purpose. ' If the people of England wish,' he said, ' to prevent the Pretender from obtaining the crown, they should make him elector of Hanover, for they would never fetch another king from there.' Johnson's censure of Chesterfield, that he thought him ' a lord among wits,' whereas he discovered him to be ' a wit among lords,' has no better warrant than his sneer in regard to Chesterfield's letters to his son, that ' they teach the morals of a whore and the manners of a dancing-master.'

Chesterfield embodied in rare completeness the characteristics of a shrewd man of the world—of one who had ' been behind the scenes both of pleasure and business.' He avowed no rule of conduct outside the urbane conventions of polite society. The town alone had charm for him ; the country and country pursuits were graceless superfluities. He argued that the real business of life was the subordination of natural instincts to those external refinements of manner which were recognised as good breeding in the capitals of civilised Europe, and especially in the Parisian salons. But the practice of his philosophy did not demand the repression of all individual tastes, as his confessed dislike of music, the opera, and fashionable field-sports abundantly proves. Chesterfield's worldliness was in point of fact tempered by native common-sense, by genuine parental affections, and by keen appreciation of, and capacity for, literature. Even in his unedifying treatment of the relations of the sexes his solemn warnings against acts which forfeit self-respect or provoke scandal destroyed most of the deleterious effect of the cynical principles on which he took his stand. Nowhere did Chesterfield inculcate an inconsiderate gratification of selfish desires. Very sternly did he rebuke pride of birth or insolence in the treatment of servants and dependents. His habitual text was the necessity from prudential motives of self-control and of respect for the feeling of others. As a writer he reached the highest levels of grace and perspicuity, and as a connoisseur of literature he was nearly always admirable. His critical taste was seen to best advantage in his notices of classical writers.

Despite the ' exquisitely elegant ' manner which even Johnson detected in Chesterfield, his personal appearance was not attractive. In youth he was known from his short stature as ' the little Lord Stanhope.' ' He was a stunted giant,' wrote Lord Hervey, doubtless with some spiteful exaggeration; 'he had a person as disagreeable as it was possible for a human being to be without being deformed, and a broad rough-featured ugly face with black teeth and a head big enough for a Polyphemus.'

Portraits of Chesterfield are numerous. The most interesting from an artistic point of view is that by Gainsborough, which was painted in 1769, and was presented by Chesterfield to the second Earl Stanhope, whose descendant's property it remains at Chevening. It represents him wearing the star and ribbon of the Garter. The expression is cynical. It has often been engraved—by Edward Bell, by Chambers, and by W. Greatbach, and others. A second painting, in the robes of a K.G., by William Hoare, R.A., now in the National Portrait Gallery, London, has also been frequently engraved—by Andrew Miller in 1746, by R. Houston, J. K. Sherwin, J. Brooks, and others. A third by Allan Ramsay, also in the National Portrait Gallery, was engraved by J. K. Sherwin in 1777. A fourth painting, by T. Uwins, was engraved by H. R. Cooke. A fifth portrait, by Thomas Hudson, belongs to the Duke of Fife. Bartolozzi executed an engraving ad vivum. There is a caricature by Ryall in which Diogenes shows Chesterfield 'as an honest man.' A pencil sketch by T. Worlidge of Chesterfield seated at a table with his friend, Richard Lumley, third earl of Scarborough, is reproduced in Chesterfield's 'Letters to his Godson' (1890, ed. Carnarvon). A bust by Joseph Wilton [q.v.], bequeathed by Sir Thomas Robinson [q. v.], stands in the entrance-hall of the British Museum.

In his lifetime Chesterfield authorised the publication of only the few political tracts and the contributions to the periodical press, chiefly in 'Common Sense,' 1737–9, and the 'World,' 1753–6, which have been already mentioned. But unauthorised collections of his witticisms in prose and verse were made before his death—in 'The New Foundling Hospital for Wit,' London, 1768–71, 6 pts. (3rd edit. 1771), and in 'The Humours of the Times,' 1771. Most of these reappeared in 'Lord Chesterfield's Witticisms' (with unauthentic 'memoirs of his lordship'), 12mo, London, 1773; and in 'Wit à-la-mode, or, Lord Chesterfield's Witticisms,' 12mo, London, 1778.

Chesterfield's 'Letters' to his natural son were prepared for publication by the son's widow within a year of Chesterfield's death. She sold them to Dodsley for 1,500l. The earl's surviving representatives vainly endeavoured to stop the publication by applying for an injunction. The title ran: 'Letters written by the Earl of Chesterfield to his Son, Philip Stanhope, together with several other pieces on various subjects, published by Mrs. Eugenia Stanhope,' 2 vols. 4to, London, 1774. The work attained immediate popularity. A fifth edition in four volumes (8vo) appeared within a year. An independent Dublin reprint of 1776 embodied some important additions. Dodsley issued a 'Supplement' in 1787, and the original version reached its eleventh edition in 1800. A French translation in five volumes (12mo) was issued at Paris in 1775, and a German translation by J. G. Gellius in six volumes (8vo) at Leipzig, 1774–6. An American reprint in two 16mo volumes appeared at Newbury-Port, Boston, in 1779.

Severe criticisms of Chesterfield's worldliness, of his relations with Johnson or of his opinions on the sexual relations, were issued by William Crawford and Thomas Hunter (both in 1776); by Antoine Leonard Thomas, in defence of Fénelon, in both French and English, London, 1777; and by Ann Berkeley in conjunction with Sir Adam Gordon, 2 vols. 1791. More sportive attacks figured in 'A Dialogue [in verse] between the Earl of C——d and Mr. Garrick in the Elysian Shades,' 4to, London, 1785 (in praise of Dr. Johnson and condemnatory of Chesterfield); and in 'Chesterfield Travestie, or the School for Modern Manners,' 16mo, London, 1808 (3rd edit. 12mo, London, 1811).

A collection of other portions of Chesterfield's correspondence, with authentic memoirs, some of his speeches, and contributions to the press, was prepared for publication by Maty, but his death intervened, and Maty's son-in-law, J. O. Justamond, finally issued in 2 vols. in 1777 Chesterfield's 'Miscellaneous Works, consisting of Letters to his Friends, never before printed, and various other articles. To which are prefixed Memoirs of his Life,' 2 vols. 4to, London, 1777; another edit. 3 vols. 8vo, Dublin, 1777. In the same year there also appeared 'Letters from Lord Chesterfield to Alderman G. Faulkner [of Dublin], Dr. Madden, Mr. Sexton, &c. Being a supplement to his Lordship's Letters,' 4to, London, 1777; and 'Characters of Eminent Personages of his own time [George I, Queen Caroline, Sir Robert Walpole, Mr. Pulteney, Lord Hardwicke, Mr. Fox, and Mr. Pitt], written by the late Earl of Chesterfield, and never before published,' 8vo, London, 1777; 2nd edit. same year. The Faulkner letters with ho 'characters . . . contrasted with characters of the same great personages by other respectable writers' reappeared together in a

D 2

separate volume next year. 'B. W. of the
Inner Temple' added a third volume to
Maty's 'Miscellaneous Works' in the same
year, which included his political pamphlets
and poems. All the 'Miscellaneous Works'
reappeared in 4 vols. in 1779.

A further collection of correspondence,
'Letters written by the Earl of Chesterfield
to A. C. Stanhope, Esq., relative to the Education of his Lordship's Godson Philip, the
late Earl,' appeared in London in 1817, 12mo.

Lord Mahon collected such authentic
letters and other literary pieces as were
accessible to him (including many previously
unpublished) in 5 vols. (1845–53). Another
collection of like scope was edited by John
Bradshaw (3 vols.) in 1892.

Fourteen of Chesterfield's letters to his
godson were surreptitiously printed in the
'Edinburgh Magazine and Review' in February, March, April, and May 1774. They
were copied into the Dublin edition of the
'Letters' to the earl's natural son in 1776,
and were there erroneously stated to have
been addressed to the latter. They reappeared in B. W.'s third volume of Maty's
'Miscellaneous Works,' 1778 (pp. 1–32), and
were printed separately, under the title of
'The Art of Pleasing,' in 1783 (4th edit.
same year). The originals remained at Bretby
undisturbed, with more than two hundred
other letters addressed to the godson, until
1890. In that year the whole series was
first edited for publication by Lord Carnarvon as 'Chesterfield's Letters to his Godson.'

There remains a further mass of unpub-
lished correspondence, chiefly on political
topics, among the Newcastle papers in the
British Museum. Extracts are given in
Mr. Ernst's 'Life' (1893). Others of Lord
Chesterfield's letters to Edward Eliot, the
friend of his natural son, are among Lord
St. Germans's manuscripts at Port Eliot,
Cornwall (*Hist. MSS. Comm.* 1st Rep. i. 41).

Extracts and abridgments of Chesterfield's
works, chiefly of the 'Letters' to his son,
were numerous from the first. They often
bore fanciful titles, such as 'The Principles
of Politeness,' 1775 (often reprinted—about
1830 as 'The New Chesterfield'); 'The Fine
Gentleman's Etiquette' (1776); 'Some Ad-
vices on Men and Manners' (1776); 'The
Elements of a Polite Education, by George
Gregory, D.D.' (1800); and 'Encyclopædia
of Manners and Etiquette '(1850). A useful
selection, with an admirable critical essay by
C. A. Sainte-Beuve, appeared, with the title
of 'Letters and Maxims,' in the 'Bayard
Series.' The latest selections in English are:
'The Wit and Wisdom of the Earl of Chesterfield: being Selections from his Miscel-

laneous Writings in prose and verse,' edited,
with notes, by W. Ernst Browning, London,
1875, 8vo; and 'Lord Chesterfield's Worldly
Wisdom: Selections from his Letters and
Characters. Edited by G. Birkbeck Hill,'
Oxford, 1891, 8vo. A Dutch selection appeared at Amsterdam in 1786. A German
epitome was entitled 'Quintessenz der Lebens-
weisheit und Weltkunst,' Stuttgart, 1885,
and a Spanish epitome ('cuarta edicion') was
issued at Caracas, 1841, 16mo.

The 'Economy of Human Life,' by Robert
Dodsley [q. v.], was attributed to Chesterfield in Italian translations by L. Guidelli
(4th edit. 12mo, Naples, 1780), and by A. G.
Cairoli (8vo, Milan, 1816); in a Portuguese
translation (8vo, Porto, 1777); and in a
Spanish translation by M. de Junco y Pimen-
tél (8vo, Madrid, 1755).

Chesterfield's godson and successor, PHILIP
STANHOPE, fifth EARL OF CHESTERFIELD
(1755–1815), baptised on 28 Nov. 1755, was
only surviving son of Arthur Charles Stanhope (d. 1770) of Mansfield, Nottinghamshire, by his second wife, Margaret, daughter
and coheiress of Charles Headlam of Kirby
Hall, Yorkshire (his father was son of
Dr. Michael Stanhope, a great-grandson of
Philip Stanhope, first earl of Chesterfield
q. v.) His godfather directed his education from the age of four, and took a promising view of his abilities. His tutors were
not selected with much wisdom. When about
six he went to 'Mr. Robert's boarding house
in Marylebone.' At eleven he became the
pupil of the adventurous Dr. William Dodd
q. v.) at Whitton, near Isleworth. Dodd
attracted him, and he subsequently proved
a generous patron to his tutor; but that
worthless schemer forged Chesterfield's name
in 1777 to a bond for 4,200l., and, on being
prosecuted, was convicted and hanged. Another of Chesterfield's early tutors was a hack-
writer, Cuthbert Shaw [q. v.] He came into
a little property on his father's death in March
1770, and soon set off on a foreign tour. He
was studying at Leipzig when his godfather
died in 1773, and he inherited the earldom
and the late earl's large fortune. He had
then developed characteristics diametrically
opposed to those which his godfather had
hoped to implant in him. If he might be
credited with a fair measure of shrewdness
and affability, his tastes and manners were
unaffectedly bucolic. 'How would that
quintessence of high *ton* the late Lord Chesterfield,' wrote Madame d'Arblay, 'blush to
behold his successor, who, with much share of
humour and good humour, also has as little
good breeding as any man I ever met with!'
(*Diary*, v. 92). At court he attracted the

favourable notice of George III, and afterwards spent much time with the king at Weymouth. His wealth alone and his personal relations with the king account for the occasional bestowal upon him of political office. He was appointed ambassador extraordinary and minister plenipotentiary to Madrid on 1 Jan. 1784, and was admitted to the privy council on 7 Jan. But he never went to Madrid, and resigned the nominal post in 1787 (*Cornwallis Correspondence*, i. 434). On Pitt's nomination he was master of the mint from 21 Sept. 1789 to 20 Jan. 1790, joint postmaster-general from 12 March 1790, and master of the horse from 14 Feb. 1798 to 21 July 1804. On 17 Jan. 1805 he was made K.G. He lived in London in some magnificence during the season, and had a French cook, Vincent la Chapelle, who dedicated to him two manuals of cookery. But the country chiefly attracted him. He was an enthusiast for hunting, and delighted in superintending the operations of his farms. But he showed his normal lack of taste in pulling down the old mansion of Bretby and erecting in its place a modern residence from Wyatt's plans. He died at Bretby on 29 Aug. 1815. Three interesting portraits are at Bretby, and are reproduced in Lord Carnarvon's 'Letters of the Fourth Earl to his Godson,' 1890. One by John Russell (1745-1806) [q. v.], painted in 1769, when the earl was fourteen, represents him in fancy dress; the second by Gainsborough—an admirable picture—portrays him in hunting dress with a dog; in the third, by T. Weaver, he figures in a group which consists of his son (afterwards the sixth earl), his agent, and a fine heifer. Another portrait, by Sir William Beechey, was engraved by J. R. Smith (cf. BOURKE, *Hist. of White's*, ii. 46). The fifth earl was twice married: first, on 16 Sept. 1777, to Anne, daughter of Thomas Thistlethwaite, D.D., of Norman Court; and secondly, on 2 May 1799, to Henrietta, third daughter of Thomas Thynne, first marquis of Bath [q. v.] He was succeeded as sixth Earl of Chesterfield by his son George Augustus Frederick (1805-1866); the marriage of the latter's only daughter, Evelyn (*d.* 1875), with Henry Howard Molyneux Herbert, fourth earl of Carnarvon [q. v.], brought the Bretby property on the death of her mother in 1885 into the possession of their son, the fifth and present Earl of Carnarvon. On the death of the sixth earl's only son, George Philip Cecil Arthur, seventh earl, unmarried, on 1 Dec. 1871, the earldom passed in succession to two collateral heirs, George Philip Stanhope, eighth earl (1822-1883), and Henry E. C. S. Stanhope, ninth earl (1821-1887).

The latter's son is the tenth and present earl.

[The main authority is Maty's Memoirs prefixed to Miscellaneous Works, vol. i. 1777. Some interesting marginal notes by Horace Walpole were printed privately in the Miscellanies of the Philobiblon Society, vol. x., 1866. A catchpenny 'Life' (1774, 2 vols. 12mo) and three collections of anecdotes by Samuel Jackson Pratt [q. v.], published between 1777 and 1800, are of no authenticity. The Memoirs prefixed to Lord Mahon's edition of Chesterfield's Works (5 vols. 1845-53), and to Lord Carnarvon's edition of the Letters to his godson, are of value. Some further information appears in Abraham Hayward's short biography (vol. xvii. of the Travellers' Library), London, 1854, 8vo. But the fullest biography is Mr. William Ernst's Memoirs . . . with numerous letters, now first published from the Newcastle Papers (London, 1893, 8vo). Other sources, apart from Chesterfield's voluminous correspondence enumerated above, are Horace Walpole's Memoirs of the Last Ten Years of George II, and his Letters, ed. Cunningham; Suffolk Correspondence, 1824; Papers of the Earl of Marchmont, 1831; Memoirs of George II, by Lord Hervey, ed. Croker, 1884; Pope's Works, ed. Elwin and Courthope; Ballantyne's Life of Carteret; Jesse's George Selwyn and his Contemporaries; Boswell's Life of Johnson, ed. Hill; Bedford Correspondence, 1846, ed. Lord John Russell, vol. iii. p. lxxxii; Colley Cibber's Apology; Lord Mahon's History of England; W. P. Courtney's Parliamentary Representation of Cornwall; Bourke's History of White's Club. A foolish endeavour to place the Letters of Junius to the credit of Lord Chesterfield was made by William Cramp in several pamphlets —The Author of Junius discovered in . . . Lord Chesterfield, 1821; Junius and his Works compared with the Character and Writings of Philip Dormer Stanhope, Earl of Chesterfield, 1851; Fac-simile Autograph Letters of Junius, Lord Chesterfield, and Mrs. C. Dayrolles, 1851. Cramp's theory was that Chesterfield wrote them and Dayrolles's wife copied them. But Junius's first letter is dated January 1769, when Chesterfield was in his seventy-fifth year, and his state of health and habit of mind had, as his letters show, long withdrawn him from politics (cf. Dilke's Papers of a Critic, 1875, ii. 140-54).]

S. L.

STANHOPE, PHILIP HENRY, fifth EARL STANHOPE (1805-1875), historian, born at Walmer on 30 Jan. 1805, was the elder and only surviving son of Philip Henry Stanhope, fourth earl Stanhope, by his wife Catherine Lucy, fourth daughter of Robert Smith, first baron Carrington [q. v.] Lady Hester Lucy Stanhope [q. v.] was his aunt. His father, eldest son of Charles Stanhope, third earl Stanhope [q. v.], was born on 7 Dec. 1781, sat in parliament for Wendover in 1806-7, Hull in 1807-12, and Midhurst from 1812 till his succession to the peerage on 15 Dec. 1816. He was elected F.R.S. on 8 Jan. 1807, was a president of the Medico-Botanical Society, and a vice-president of the Society of Arts; he died on 2 March 1855 (cf. *Notes and Queries*, 5th ser. vi. 229, 270, 295, 417). He inherited his father's eccentricities, and his adoption of the mysterious 'wild boy' of Bavaria, Kaspar Hauser, in 1832 gave him great notoriety (cf. DUCHESSOY CLEVELAND, *True Story of Kaspar Hauser*, 1893). His daughter, Catherine Lucy Wilhelmina, duchess of Cleveland, is mother of the present Earl of Rosebery.

The son, who was styled Viscount Mahon from 1816 till his succession to the peerage, was educated privately and at Christ Church, Oxford, matriculating on 19 April 1823, and graduating B.A. in 1827. In the same year he was elected F.R.S. On 30 Aug. 1830 he was elected M.P. for Wootton Bassett in the conservative interest; he was re-elected on 30 April 1831, but by the Reform Act of 1832 that constituency was disfranchised, and on 12 Dec. of that year he was returned for Hertford. He was, however, unseated on petition, but was again successful on 7 Jan. 1835. He sat continuously for that borough until 1852, being re-elected in 1837, 1841, and 1847. On 22 March 1831 he was appointed deputy lieutenant of Kent. On the same day he delivered his maiden speech in parliament, complaining of the misrepresentation to which the opponents of the Reform Bill were subjected, and offering a strenuous opposition to the second reading of that measure (*Hansard*, 3rd ser. iii. 719-727). Mahon continued his opposition in the new parliament which met in June; on the 21st of that month he denounced ministers for appealing to the country, and on 1 July presented a petition of 770 resident bachelors and undergraduates at Oxford against the bill. On 11 June 1834 he was created D.C.L. by the university. During Peel's brief first administration—December 1834 to April 1835—Mahon was under-secretary for foreign affairs under the Duke of Wellington, and in this capacity he had to face the attacks of Palmerston in the House of Commons. The fall of the ministry in April left Mahon once more at liberty to pursue his literary and historical work. On 28 Jan. 1841 he was elected F.S.A., of which he served as president from 23 April 1846 until his death.

When Peel returned to office in 1841 Mahon was not included in the ministry, and he now took up with energy Serjeant Talfourd's scheme for amending the law of copyright [see TALFOURD, SIR THOMAS NOON].

The law then protected an author's work either during his lifetime or during a period of twenty-eight years. In 1841 Talfourd proposed to extend the period to sixty years, but Macaulay procured the rejection of this proposal by forty-five to thirty-eight votes. After Talfourd's death Mahon, on 6 April 1842, in a speech rich in literary illustration (*Hansard*, 3rd ser. lxi. 1348-63), introduced a bill extending the period to twenty-five years after the author's death. Macaulay, who followed him, proposed a period of forty-two years, or the time of the author's life, whichever should prove the longer. Eventually a compromise was arranged, by which protection was given either for forty-two years or for seven years after the author's death, whichever period might prove the longer. With this proviso the bill became law in the same session (5 & 6 Vict. ch. xlv.; see *Annual Register*, 1842, pp. 399-404).

On 4 May 1844 Mahon was appointed a commissioner for promoting the fine arts, and on 5 Aug. 1845 he became secretary to the board of control for India. He followed Peel, with whom he was on intimate terms privately, in his conversion to free-trade principles, voted for the repeal of the corn laws, and left office on Peel's overthrow in July 1846. Nevertheless he voted with the protectionists against the repeal of the navigation laws in June 1849, and was perhaps in consequence defeated when he sought re-election for Hertford in 1852.

From this time Mahon took little part in politics. On 23 April 1846 he had been appointed a trustee of the British Museum, and from July 1850 he was occupied with Cardwell in arranging the papers of Sir Robert Peel, who had made them his literary executors. On 2 March 1855 he succeeded his father as fifth Earl Stanhope; in the same year he became honorary antiquary of the Royal Academy of Arts, acted as examiner in the new school of jurisprudence and modern history at Oxford, and founded there the Stanhope prize for undergraduates who have not completed sixteen terms from matriculation. It is of the annual value of 20*l.*, to be given in books for an essay on some point of modern history, English or foreign, within the period 1300-1815; in the award 'merit of style was to be considered, no less than the clearness of the reasoning and the accuracy of the facts' (*Oxford Univ. Cal.* 1896, p. 63).

A more important scheme occupied him during the following year. On 26 Feb. 1856 he gave notice of a motion in the House of Lords, inviting public attention to the importance of forming a British national portrait gallery. On the following day he wrote to the prince consort, who heartily endorsed the project. The motion came on on 4 March, and was carried through both houses of parliament. On 6 June following a grant of 2,000l. was voted for the purpose. On 2 Dec. a board of trustees was formed, of which Stanhope was elected chairman on 9 Feb. following. Temporary premises were provided at 29 Great George Street, Westminster, and opened on 15 Jan. 1859. In 1869, when the collection numbered 288 pictures, it was removed to the eastern portion of the long building at South Kensington. A fire in the neighbouring exhibition in 1885 caused its removal to Bethnal Green Museum on loan. In May 1889 Mr. William Alexander of Shipton, Andover, offered to build a gallery at his own expense, if the government would provide a site. This was found at the back of the National Gallery, where the present National Portrait Gallery, erected at a cost of 96,000l., was opened on 4 April 1896. Sir George Scharf [q. v.] was first keeper, and the collection now (1898) includes over a thousand pictures, exclusive of engravings (Cat. Nat. Portrait Gallery, 1897, pref. pp. iii. et seq.)

On 1 March 1858 Stanhope was elected lord rector of Marischal College, Aberdeen University, and in the same year he carried a motion through parliament removing from the prayer-book the three state services. On 3 June 1864 he was created LL.D. of Cambridge, and on 30 Oct. 1867 he was appointed first commissioner to inquire into the state of the established church in Ireland. In 1869 it was mainly due to his exertions that the historical manuscripts commission was formed, and he was one of the first commissioners. He also, at the instance of the Society of Antiquaries, proposed a parliamentary grant for excavations on the site of Troy. This laid him open to Robert Lowe's sarcasm, but Schliemann's discoveries gave Stanhope ample revenge. Another of his proposals was that an order of merit should be established for men of letters. On 11 May 1872 Stanhope was made foreign associate of the Institute of France, and on 22 Sept. 1875 he was appointed chairman of the royal copyright commission; he was also president of the royal literary fund from 1863 till his death. He died on 24 Dec. 1875 from an attack of pleurisy, at his eldest son's house, Merivale, Bournemouth. A marble bust of Stanhope was executed at Rome in 1854 by Lawrence Macdonald; the original is at the family seat, Chevening, Kent. A copy was presented to the National Portrait Gallery in 1876 by the present Earl Stanhope, and a

medallion in plaster, on a reduced scale, presented by Sir George Scharf, was placed over the entrance doorway. An engraving of a portrait painted by Lucas in 1836 is given in Doyle's 'Official Baronage.'

Stanhope married, on 10 July 1834, Emily Harriet, second daughter of General Sir Edward Kerrison, bart., and by her, who died on 31 Dec. 1873, had issue one daughter—Mary Catherine, who married, on 18 Feb. 1868, Frederick Lygon, sixth earl Beauchamp—and four sons, of whom Arthur Philip is the present Earl Stanhope; Edward Stanhope, the second son, is separately noticed.

Few men have deserved better of the world of letters and art than Stanhope. The Copyright Act, the National Portrait Gallery, and the historical manuscripts commission bear witness alike to the culture and liberality of his tastes, and to the energy and success with which he gave them effect. As a speaker he was clear, but not eloquent, and his literary and critical tastes probably militated against his success in politics. But he possessed great tact, and on committees generally got his way without provoking opposition.

As an historian—the capacity in which he was best known—he was honest and industrious, and, though without any pretensions to genius, he wrote in a clear and readable style. The value of his works consists largely in the use he made of valuable manuscript sources inaccessible to others. His first important contribution to English history was 'The History of the War of Succession in Spain, 1702–1714,' 1832, 8vo; 2nd edit. 1836. It is based largely on the papers of Mahon's ancestor, James Stanhope, first earl Stanhope [q. v.] Macaulay reviewed it in the 'Edinburgh,' lvi. 499–542, and praised Mahon's 'great diligence in examining authorities, great judgment in weighing testimony, and great impartiality in estimating characters.' This was followed by 'The History of England from the Peace of Utrecht to the Peace of Versailles, 1713–1783' (7 vols. 1836–1853; an American edition of vols. i.–iv. appeared in 1849, and the portions in the early volumes relating to India were separately issued in 1838 as 'The Rise of our Indian Empire'). The work was praised by Sismondi (Hist. des Français, xxviii. 385), and still remains the best narrative of English history during the eighteenth century. In it Mahon develops the somewhat far-fetched theory that the whigs and tories interchanged principles and policy between the eighteenth and nineteenth centuries (cf. LECKY, Hist. of England, vol. i.) Mahon's remarks on Washington involved him in a prolonged controversy with Jared Sparks, Palfrey, and other American writers (cf. his Letter to Jared Sparks, 1852, and replies to it in *Brit. Mus. Library*). Perhaps his most important work was 'The Life of the Right Hon. William Pitt, with Extracts from his unpublished Correspondence and Manuscript Papers' (4 vols. 1861-2; 2nd edit. 1862-3; 4th edit. 1867; new edit. 3 vols. 1879; translated into French 1862-3, and Italian, 1863). This still remains the standard life of Pitt, and an indispensable authority on the history of the period. Stanhope's last considerable work was 'The History of England, comprising the Reign of Queen Anne until the Peace of Utrecht' (1870; 2nd edit. same year; 4th edit. 1872). This was intended to cover the period between the close of Macaulay's 'History' and the commencement of Stanhope's own 'History of England, 1713-83.' It is careful, but its style compares unfavourably with Macaulay's.

Stanhope's other works are: 1. 'The Life of Belisarius,' 1829, 8vo, 2nd edit. 1848: one of the most noticeable contributions made by Englishmen to the history of the Byzantine Empire. 2. 'Lord John Russell and Mr. Macaulay on the French Revolution,' 1833, 8vo. 3. 'Spain under Charles II: or Extracts from the Correspondence of the Hon. Alexander Stanhope, British Minister at Madrid, 1690-1700; selected from Originals at Chevening,' 1840, 8vo; 2nd edit. 1845. 4. 'Essai sur la vie du grand Condé,' London, 1842, 8vo, written in French, and only one hundred copies printed for private circulation (cf. J. W. Croker in *Quarterly Rev.* lxxi. 100-69): an English edition was published in 1845, and reprinted in 1847 and 1848. 5. 'Historical Essays contributed to the "Quarterly Review,"' 1849. 6. 'The Forty-five; being a Narrative of the Rebellion in Scotland of 1745,' 1851, 8vo. 7. 'Essay on Joan of Arc,' 1853, 12mo. 8. 'Lord Chatham at Chevening, 1769,' 1855, 8vo. 9. 'Memoirs of Sir Robert Peel, bart., M.P.,' published by the Trustees of his Papers,' in 2 vols. and 3 parts, 1856-7, 8vo [cf. art. PEEL, SIR ROBERT, 1788-1850]. 10. 'Addresses delivered at Manchester, Leeds, and Birmingham,' 1856, 8vo. 11. 'Miscellanies,' 1863, 2nd ed. same year. 12. 'Miscellanies, 2nd ser.,' 1872. 13. 'The French Retreat from Moscow and other Historical Essays, collected from the "Quarterly Review" and "Fraser's Magazine,"' 1876, 8vo. 14. 'Notes of Conversations with Wellington,' 1888, 8vo. Stanhope also edited 'Letters to General Stanhope in Spain,' 1834; 'Correspondence between William Pitt and Charles, Duke of Rutland,' 1842; 'Extracts from Despatches

of the British Envoy at Florence, relative to the Motions and Behaviour of Charles Edward' (1843, Roxburghe Club); 'Letters of Philip Dormer, Earl of Chesterfield' (4 vols. 1845, vol. v. 1853); and 'Secret Correspondence connected with Mr. Pitt's return to office in 1804' (1852).

[Works in British Mus. Library; Hansard's Parl. Debates; Official Return of Members of Parl.; Journals of the House of Lords and Commons; Times, 25 Dec. 1875; Athenæum, 1876, i. 24; Academy, 1876, i. 9-10; Spectator, 1876, i. 3; Annual Register, 1875, pp. 156-7; Greville's Journals; Trevelyan's Life of Macaulay; Doyle, Burke, and G. E. C[okayne]'s Peerages; Allibone's Dict. of English Lit., s.vv. 'Mahon' and 'Stanhope.'] A. F. P.

STANHOPE, WILLIAM, first EARL OF HARRINGTON (1690?-1756), diplomatist and statesman, born about 1690, was the fourth son of John Stanhope of Elvaston, Derbyshire, by Dorothy, daughter and coheiress of Charles Agard of Foston in the same county. His great-grandfather, Sir John Stanhope (d. 1638), was half-brother of Philip Stanhope, first earl of Chesterfield [q. v.]

Of his three elder brothers, the third, CHARLES STANHOPE (1673-1760), succeeded to the family estates on the second brother's death in 1730. He represented Milborne Port from 1717 to 1722, Aldborough (Yorkshire) from 1722 to 1734, and Harwich from 1734 to 1741. He was under-secretary for the southern department from 1714 to 1717, and in 1720-1 was secretary to the treasury. He was charged with making use of his position to gain a profit of 250,000*l.* by dealings in South Sea stock, and, though the accusation rested on insufficient evidence, the support of the Walpoles only gained his acquittal in the House of Commons (28 Feb. 1721) by three votes. George I in 1722 made him treasurer of the chamber, but George II refused him office on account of a memorial found among his father's papers relating to himself when Prince of Wales, which was in Stanhope's writing, though its real author was Sunderland. Charles Stanhope's name is frequently mentioned in Horace Walpole's 'Correspondence.' An ode to him 'drinking tar water' is among Sir C. Hanbury-Williams's works, and he is also introduced as a character in that writer's 'Isabella, or the Morning.' He died unmarried on 17 March 1760, aged 87.

According to 'Harlequin Horace,' an anonymous satirical epistle in verse, addressed to him in 1738, William Stanhope was educated at Eton and 'half a colledge education got.' He obtained a captaincy in the 3rd footguards in 1710, and served under his kinsman,

General James Stanhope, in Spain. In 1715 he was made colonel of a dragoon regiment, and in the same year entered parliament as whig member for Derby. On 19 Aug. 1717 he was sent on a special mission to Madrid, the object of which was to arrange the differences between Philip V and the emperor Charles VI. On 1 July 1718 he announced to Alberoni the determination of England to force Spain to agree to the terms of pacification settled by the quadruple alliance, and had a very stormy interview with him. He was assiduous in urging the grievances of British merchants and gave them timely warning of the outbreak of war. On 17 Nov. 1718 he was appointed envoy at Turin, where he remained during the greater part of the war with Spain. Before returning to Madrid he saw military service as a volunteer with the French army while in Berwick's camp before Fontarabia. Stanhope concerted an attack upon some Spanish ships and stores in the port of St. Andero, and himself commanded the troops which were detached to co-operate with the English fleet. The operation was completely successful. This exploit closed his active military career, but he attained the rank of lieutenant-general in 1739 and general in 1747.

On the conclusion of peace Stanhope returned to Madrid as British ambassador. He remained there for the next seven years, and made for himself a high reputation as a diplomatist. In a series of able despatches he described the abdication of Philip V, his resumption of power after his son's death, the separation of France and Spain resulting from the failure of the match between the infanta and Louis XV, the intrigues between Spain and the emperor, and the rise and fall of their projector, the Baron Ripperda. The latter, when disgraced in 1726, fled to Stanhope's house, and was induced by him to reveal the articles of the recent secret treaty of Vienna. The information was taken down in cipher and sent by special messenger to London. During his second embassy in Spain Stanhope was also engaged in negotiations for the cession of Gibraltar. George I and some of his ministers were not averse to it, and even gave a conditional promise, but dared not propose it to parliament. In an interview with Philip V at the end of 1720, Stanhope denied the king's assertion that an absolute promise to cede Gibraltar had been given as a condition of Philip's accession to the quadruple alliance. Stanhope claimed an equivalent for the surrender of the fortress. He was persuaded that it would be to the advantage of England to yield Gibraltar in exchange for increased

facilities for commercial intercourse with Spain and her colonies. To his regret the Spaniards declined to come to terms (letter to Sir Luke Schaub, 18 Jan. 1721, in COXE, *Bourbon Kings of Spain*, iii. 22). On a fresh rupture with Spain in March 1727, Stanhope left Madrid and returned to England. On the previous 26 Sept. he had addressed a memorial to the king of Spain justifying the despatch of a British fleet to his coasts on the ground of the intrigues of his court with the emperor, Russia, and the Pretender (TINDAL, *Hist. of Engl.* iv. 608–9). His correspondence with the Marquis de la Paz was published by an opponent of the ministry to show the impolicy of the war (*Letters of the Marquis de la Paz and Colonell Stanhope … with Remarks*, 1726; *A Continuation of the Letters*, 1727). An answer entitled 'Gibraltar or the Pretender,' by Richard Newyear, appeared in 1727.

In 1727 Stanhope was named by George II vice-chamberlain and a privy councillor. He did not remain long in England, being appointed in August one of the British plenipotentiaries at the congress of Aix-la-Chapelle, which subsequently removed to Soissons. Here he seems to have been in favour of the cession of Gibraltar, then undergoing a siege (Lord Townshend to Stephen Poyntz, 14 June 1728). Newcastle, with whom he was in constant correspondence, showed some of his letters to Queen Caroline, who approved their tenor (COXE, *Mem. of Sir R. Walpole*, ii. 631). Little way being made with the negotiations at the congress, in the autumn of 1729 Stanhope was sent to negotiate directly with the court of Spain. Horatio Walpole engaged the interest of the queen in his favour, and a peerage was promised as the reward of his mission. Poyntz, one of his colleagues at Soissons, testifies to Stanhope's 'most universal and deserved credit with the whole Spanish court and nation,' and remarks that the fact of his never having taken formal leave at Madrid facilitated the English advances (*ib.* ii. 653). With the help of France the treaty of Seville was concluded on 9 Nov. 1729 between England, France, and Spain, Holland subsequently acceding. The claim to Gibraltar was passed over in silence, and important advantages were secured to British trade in return for the forwarding of Elizabeth Farnese's wishes with regard to the succession in Tuscany and Parma. Newcastle, a few days later, assured Stanhope that he had never seen the king better satisfied with any one than he was with him, and conveyed him the special thanks of Walpole and Townshend (*ib.* ii. 665). The administration was much strengthened by the settlement of Spanish affairs, which had left the emperor their single isolated opponent. On 6 Jan. 1730 Stanhope was created Baron Harrington of Harrington, Northamptonshire. On 21 Feb. he was reappointed a plenipotentiary at Soissons, where negotiations with the emperor were still going on; but in May he was declared successor to Townshend as secretary of state for the northern department. His colleague was the Duke of Newcastle, who had done much to forward his promotion. He remained secretary during the remaining years of the Walpole administration. He never cordially coalesced with Sir Robert, but made himself acceptable to George II by favouring his German interests. The British ambassador at Vienna had to officially affirm that Harrington was acting in concert with the Walpoles so early as February 1731 (Thomas Robinson to Horatio Walpole, 3 Feb. 1731). In March a treaty was signed with the emperor, who obtained a guarantee of the pragmatic sanction in exchange for his accession to the treaty of Seville; but Harrington was obliged to instruct Thomas Robinson (afterwards first Baron Grantham) [q. v.] to leave the question of Hanoverian interests for future consideration. On the outbreak of the war of the Polish succession in 1733, he was in favour of supporting the emperor against France, but was overruled by the Walpoles; and in the following year he arranged with George II the sending to England of Thomas Strickland [q. v.], bishop of Namur, as a secret envoy from Charles VI (Horatio Walpole to Sir Robert, 22 Oct. 1734). Harrington had a long and secret conference with Strickland, which gave great uneasiness to the Walpoles; but the mission was discredited by the influence of Horatio Walpole with the queen (ib. pp. 442-4).

The cabinet was much divided on questions of foreign policy, and contradictory instructions were sent to the ambassadors, according as the war policy of Harrington and the king or the peace policy of the Walpoles and the queen predominated. Harrington thought that England had no excuse for not supporting the emperor, and propounded to Horatio Walpole a plan for a joint ultimatum from England and Holland to France (ib. i. 465-6). In the end he was obliged to carry out the peace policy of the premier, and to accept as a basis of negotiation the secret arrangement between France and the emperor. The preliminaries arranged at the end of 1735 won the approbation even of Bolingbroke (ib. i. 470; cf. HERVEY, Memoirs, ii. 174).

Soon after this the king became dissatisfied with Harrington, and even proposed to dismiss him. When he went to Hanover in the summer of 1736, he insisted on taking Horatio Walpole with him to act as secretary (COXE, Walpole, i. 480). This Hervey attributes to the influence of the queen and Walpole, who had been annoyed at Harrington's conduct in the previous year, when he had sent over from Hanover despatches arraigning all the acts and measures of the queen's regency, and had even been suspected of advising the king to sign military commissions which, having delegated his powers, he was incapacitated from doing.

According to Hervey, many thought that at this time Harrington had been worked upon by Philip Dormer Stanhope, fourth earl of Chesterfield, to form a plan of becoming first minister. But George II disliked him, although not constantly, as did Queen Caroline. On 1 Aug. 1737 Harrington accompanied Sir R. Walpole to St. James's to attend the accouchement of the Princess of Wales. On this occasion the queen, who always disguised her dislike, joked with him upon his gallantry. Walpole and Harrington also had a conversation with Frederick, prince of Wales, at the bedside, of which they were requested by the king to draw up an account (see Minutes in HERVEY's Memoirs, iii. 192-4). In talking of this scandalous incident with the Prince of Wales, Alexander, lord Marchmont, described Harrington as a good-natured honest man, but not of very great reach, adding that he 'did nothing but as directed.'

In the closing years of Walpole's ministry Harrington again opposed him by acting with the party of Newcastle and Hardwicke, who were in favour of war with Spain. In 1741 he negotiated behind the premier's back a treaty with France for the neutrality of Hanover, and was careful not to commit himself to any opinion displeasing to the king (COXE, Memoirs of Lord Walpole, ii. 27, 35). Nevertheless, it was by Walpole's influence that he retained office on the rearrangement of the ministry on that minister's fall. But he had to give up the secretaryship of state to Carteret, receiving in its place the presidency of the council. He was so dependent on his official salary that in 1740 he had applied both to the king and to Walpole for a tellership of the exchequer, alleging the 'extreme straightness' of his circumstances (Hist. MSS. Comm. 10th Rep. ii. 274-5). On 9 Feb. 1742 he was advanced to an earldom. In the following year he acted as one of the lords justices. He now joined with the Pelhams in opposing Carteret's foreign policy, and in the summer of 1744 signed Hardwicke's memorial to the king, proposing that an envoy should be sent to Holland declaring that England would withdraw from the war should they refuse to enter into it. Harrington himself seems to have been asked to undertake the mission but to have declined, presumably from the fear of not being well supported (*Marchmont's Diary*, 28 Oct. 1744). On 23 Nov. the Pelhams succeeded in driving out Carteret and replacing him by Harrington.

In the summer of 1745 he accompanied George II to Hanover, but continued, in concert with the Pelhams, to oppose his desire for more extensive operations against France, and especially Carteret's project of a grand alliance. In January 1746 Harrington again urged the Dutch to declare war against France. He announced that, in consequence of the rebellion, England would have to limit her financial assistance, and would be unable to contribute to the defence of the German empire. The king now tried by means of Pulteney (Bath) to detach Harrington from the Pelhams, and on 7 Feb. 1746 had a personal interview with him. Harrington not only remained loyal to his colleagues, but took the lead in resigning office three days later. According to Chesterfield, he flung the purse and seals down upon the table and provoked the king beyond expression (*Marchmont's Diary*, 30 Aug. 1747). He had told Bath previously his opinion 'that those who dictated in private should be employed in public' (COXE, *Pelham Admin.* i. 289). When, after a few days, the king was obliged to recall Henry Pelham, 'the chief resentment was shown to Lord Harrington' (Newcastle to Chesterfield, 18 Feb. 1746; cf. *Marchmont's Diary*, 30 Aug. 1747).

Harrington had now irretrievably lost the king's favour, and retained the seals only till the following October. His wish to accept the French proposals as a basis for peace was opposed by Newcastle and Hardwicke, and a warm debate took place between him and Newcastle in the king's presence. Harrington made use of the fact of Newcastle's having carried on a separate correspondence with Lord Sandwich, British envoy at Breda, as a pretext for his resignation, which he really gave because of his treatment by the king. Hardwicke tried to avert this extreme course, and Henry Pelham greatly regretted it, and even hoped that after a time Harrington would be enabled to resume the seals. Both Pelhams concurred in urging on the king Harrington's request for the lord-lieutenancy of Ireland, which office, after

some difficulty, they obtained for him. Harrington exchanged offices with his kinsman, Lord Chesterfield. He retained the vice-royalty till 1751. In the previous year, when the Pelhams tried to get him a pension or a sinecure, the king said 'Lord Harrington deserves nothing and shall have nothing' (COXE, *Pelham Admin.* ii. 134). Harrington's viceroyalty was disturbed by the agitation headed by Charles Lucas (1731–1771) (q. v.), and saw the beginning of an organised opposition in the Irish parliament. 'Bonfires were made and a thousand insults offered him' on his departure in the spring of 1751 (Chesterfield to S. Dayrolles, 27 April 1751). Horace Walpole says that the Pelhams sacrificed him to the king. But this account is unfair, at least to Henry Pelham, who had a high regard for Harrington. In Sir Charles Hanbury-Williams's 'The Duke of Newcastle: a Fable,' Harrington is represented, with more justice, as the duke's cast-off favourite and friend. But it is difficult to see what the brothers could have done for their friend in face of the implacable resentment of the king.

Harrington took no further part in public affairs, and died on 8 Dec. 1756 at his house in the Stable Yard, St. James's.

Harrington shone rather as a diplomatist than as a statesman. Though he never spoke in debate, his advice as a strategist was listened to with respect. Horace Walpole does justice to his career, but Lord Hervey's estimate of his character was probably influenced by a private motive (*Memoirs*, i. 336, Croker's note). When he was at the court of Spain Hervey says that 'people talked, heard, and read of nothing but Lord Harrington,' who was rapidly forgotten as soon as he returned. In Hervey's 'Political Epistle to the Queen' (1736), Harrington is described as

An exile made by an uncommon doom
From foreign countries *to* his own;

and the statesman's fortune is compared to a piece of old china, bought at an enormous price, never used, and laid by and forgotten. In the satirical piece called 'The Death of Lord Hervey; or a Morning at Court,' extreme indolence is imputed to Harrington by Queen Caroline in words which she appears actually to have used (cf. *Memoirs*, ii. 42). Hervey, however, admits that he was 'well bred, a man of honour, and fortunate.' Of foreign observers Saint-Simon, who met Harrington in Spain, writes of his taciturn and somewhat repellent demeanour, but credits him with 'beaucoup d'esprit, de conduite et de sens' (*Mémoires*, xix. 419).

Campo Raso says he united the greatest vivacity with a by no means lively exterior (*Memorias Políticas y Militares*, p. 35); and Philip V of Spain asserted that he was the only minister who had never deceived him.

Two portraits of Harrington—one engraved by Ford, from a painting by Du Parc, the other painted by Fayram and engraved by Faber—are at Elvaston.

Harrington married Anne, daughter and heiress of Colonel Edward Griffiths, one of the clerk comptrollers of the Green Cloth. He was succeeded in the title by the survivor of twin sons, WILLIAM STANHOPE, second EARL OF HARRINGTON (1719–1779). Born on 18 Dec. 1719, he entered the army in 1741, and became general of the 2nd troop of horse grenadier guards in June 1745. He distinguished himself at Fontenoy, where he was slightly wounded (Walpole to Mann, 11 May 1745). He became major-general in February 1755, lieutenant-general in January 1758, and general on 30 April 1770. As Viscount Petersham he represented Bury St. Edmunds from 1747 to 1756. In 1748 he was made customer of the port of Dublin. He was a somewhat eccentric personage, and from a peculiarity in his gait was nicknamed 'Peter Shambles.' He died on 1 April 1779. He married, on 11 Aug. 1746, Caroline, eldest daughter of Charles Fitzroy, second duke of Grafton. She was one of the reigning beauties of the day. Horace Walpole, who was one of her intimates, relates many of her wild doings. She and her friend, Miss Ashe, went to comfort and weep over James Maclaine or Maclean [q. v.], the gentleman highwayman (to Mann, 2 Aug. 1750). At the coronation of George III Lady Harrington appeared 'covered with all the diamonds she could borrow, hire, or seize,' and was 'the finest figure at a distance.' Walpole's friend, Conway, had been in love with her, and a chanson by Walpole, with English translation, on the subject of their affection has been printed from the Manchester papers (in *Hist. MSS. Comm.* 8th Rep. App. ii. 111–112). One of Lady Harrington's last exploits was an application to Johnson in favour of Dr. Dodd, which produced a considerable effect upon him (BOSWELL, *Johnson*, ed. Hill, iii. 141). She died in 1784, and was buried at Kensington on 6 July. Two characteristic portraits of her are at Elvaston. One, by Hudson, depicts her in middle life; the other, by Cotes, represents her in old age with her daughter, the Duchess of Newcastle. She had five daughters and two sons. The eldest daughter, Lady Caroline, who married Kenneth Mackenzie, viscount

Fortrose, died in her twentieth year in February 1767, 'killed, like Lady Coventry and others, by white lead' (Walpole to Montagu, 12 Dec. 1766; to Mann, 13 Feb. 1767); Isabella, married Richard Molyneux, first earl of Sefton; Emilia, Richard, sixth earl of Barrymore; Henrietta, Thomas, second lord Foley (the last two inherited a full share of their mother's beauty); the youngest, Lady Anna Maria (1760–1821), married, first, Thomas Pelham-Clinton, earl of Lincoln (afterwards Duke of Newcastle), and, secondly, Colonel (afterwards Sir Charles Cregan) Craufurd, G.C.B. The second son, Henry Fitzroy, served in the army. The elder, Charles Stanhope, third earl of Harrington, is separately noticed.

[Collins's Peerage, ed. Brydges, iv. 284–90; Doyle's Official Baronage; G. E. C.'s and Burke's Peerages; Coxe's Memoirs of Sir R. Walpole, of the Pelham Administration, of Horatio Lord Walpole, his Bourbon Kings of Spain, vols. ii. iii., and House of Austria, vol. ii.; Lord Hervey's Memoirs of George II, 1884, *passim*; H. Walpole's Memoirs of George II, i. 3–5, and Letters, ed. Cunningham, *passim*; Marchmont Papers, i. 44–45, 69, 70, 88, 97 n., 124, 181–5, ii. 88, 416; Tindal's Continuation of Rapin; Ballantine's Life of Carteret, pp. 74–5, 154; Works of Sir C. Hanbury-Williams; Chesterfield's Corresp. ed. Lord Mahon; Evans's Cat. Engr. Portraits; Redford Corresp. i. 171–3, 178–9. Among Harrington's papers in the British Museum the most important are his correspondence with Sir Luke Schaub, 1721 (Addit. MSS. 22520–1), with Sir Thomas Robinson, 1730–46 (Addit. MSS. 23780–23823), with W. Titley (Egerton MSS. 2683–9), with Newcastle (Addit. MSS. 32686 et seq.), and with Newcastle, Townshend, and Alberoni (Stowe MSS. 252–6). These collections have been used by Mr. E. Armstrong in his Elizabeth Farnese, 1892. Many letters to and from him are among the Weston papers at Somerby Hall, Lincolnshire (Hist. MSS. Comm. 10th Rep. i.).]

G. LE G. N.

STANIHURST, RICHARD (1547–1618), translator of Virgil. [See STANYHURST.]

STANLEY, MRS. (1796?–1861), actress. [See FLEMING.]

STANLEY, ARTHUR PENRHYN (1815–1881), dean of Westminster, born at Alderley Rectory on 13 Dec. 1815, was the second son and third child of Edward Stanley [q. v.], bishop of Norwich, and Catherine Leycester, his wife. In September 1824 he went to a private school at Seaforth. There he was distinguished by an insatiable love of reading, and by gifts as a *raconteur* which kept his schoolfellows entranced by stories from Southey's poems and Scott's novels.

He was also a fluent writer of English verse. Already an indefatigable sightseer, he showed signs of those powers of picturesque description in which he was, in later life, unsurpassed. His diary of a visit paid to the Pyrenees in 1828 contains passages which are not only precocious in their promise, but striking in themselves.

On 31 Jan. 1829 he entered Rugby school, where Dr. Arnold had been installed as headmaster in the previous summer. His progress up the school was rapid. In August 1831 his promotion into the sixth form brought him into close contact with Dr. Arnold, whose influence was the 'lodestar of his life.' His respect for his headmaster quickly ripened into affection, and rose to veneration. 'Most sincerely,' he writes in May 1834, 'must I thank God for His goodness in placing me here to live with Arnold. Yet I always feel that the happiness is a dangerous one, and that loving him and admiring him as I do to the very verge of all love and admiration that can be paid to man, I fear I have passed the limit and made him my idol, and that in all I may be but serving God for man's sake' (PROTHERO, *Life of Dean Stanley*, i. 102). At Rugby, where Stanley won all the five school distinctions, he held a position which was almost unique at a public school. In spite of his incapacity for games, he so impressed the roughest of his contemporaries that they recognised in him a being of a higher order than themselves, not to be judged by their conventional standards (see the character of 'Arthur' in HUGHES's *Tom Brown's Schooldays*).

In November 1833 Stanley gained a scholarship at Balliol, and in the following October went into residence at Oxford. There he was plunged into the midst of influences hostile—on religious, political, and social questions—to those of his 'oracle and idol,' Dr. Arnold. Even at this stage of his career his chivalry in defending friends, detachment from party ties, and power of criticising those whom he most reverenced were conspicuous. Though the names of Faber, W. G. Ward, Marriott, and Keble often occur in his letters, and though for a time he felt 'the strong attraction of Newmanism,' he remained staunch to the views which he brought with him from Rugby. At Oxford he won the Ireland scholarship in 1837, and in the same year the Newdegate prize for English verse ('The Gypsies;' see *Letters and Verses of Dean Stanley*, pp. 29–38), and a first class in the final classical schools. In July 1838 he was elected a fellow of University College, finding that his views on church and state would probably prevent his election at Balliol. He also gained in 1839 the chancellor's Latin essay, and in 1840 the chancellor's English essay and the Ellerton theological essay.

In December 1839 he was, after prolonged hesitation, ordained by the bishop of Oxford. His reluctance to take orders proceeded not from any doubts respecting the central doctrines of Christianity, but from the stringent subscription to the damnatory clauses of the Athanasian creed which was then exacted from candidates for ordination. So great was his difficulty in this respect that he did not expect to take priest's orders. In the hope of procuring some relaxation in the stringency of the terms of subscription, he helped to promote a petition for the relief of the clergy, which was presented to the House of Lords in 1840. The petition was rejected, but Stanley adhered to his point with his usual tenacity. In 1863, when Lord Ebury's bill was before the House of Lords, his brilliant 'Letter to the Bishop of London' (published in 1863) effectively supported the proposal. The bill was lost. But a royal commission reported in favour of relaxation, and in 1865 effect was given to their recommendations by an act of parliament (28 & 29 Victoria, c. 122), and by the corresponding alterations which convocation made in the canons.

In July 1840 Stanley left England for a prolonged tour through Switzerland, Italy, Greece, and Sicily. The tour was memorable. It confirmed his love of foreign travel; it also revealed to himself and his friends his descriptive powers. Henceforward scarcely a year passed without his making some more or less lengthy tour in Europe, Asia, Africa, or America. External nature scarcely attracted him, except as the background of history or human interest. But no one ever experienced a keener delight in seeing places which were connected with famous people, striking events, impressive legends, or scenes in the works of poets and novelists. Few persons have rivalled him in his powers of communicating his own enthusiasms to his readers, of peopling every spot with living actors, of seizing the natural features which coloured local occurrences and modified events, of noting analogies in apparent opposites, or detecting resemblances beneath superficial differences. It is from the exercise of these gifts that his letters derive their charm and his historical writings their value.

After his return to England in May 1841, Stanley found Oxford divided into two hostile camps, with neither of which could he ally himself. So uncongenial was the atmosphere of religious animosity that he contemplated retiring from the university. But the appointment of Dr. Arnold in 1841 to the chair of modern history reconciled him to his position. To his lectures Stanley looked for the infusion of new life into a decaying professorial system, the restoration of a healthier tone in university life, the destruction of the barriers which then separated religious from secular learning. His hopes were disappointed by the sudden death of Arnold on 12 June 1842. The event was described by Stanley as the greatest calamity that had happened to him, and almost the greatest that could befall him. To the task of writing Arnold's life he devoted his utmost energies. His 'Life and Correspondence of Dr. Arnold' (published on 31 May 1844) was in some respects the work of Stanley's life. It gave him an assured position not only in Oxford, but in the wider world of letters.

In 1843 he had been ordained priest and appointed a college tutor. The university was still convulsed by a series of religious struggles, towards which he took up a consistent position. He advocated the toleration of divergent views, and opposed alike the degradation of W. G. Ward in 1845 and the agitation against Dr. Hampden, who was appointed to the bishopric of Hereford in 1847. Without sympathising with the views of either, he insisted on the injustice of the indiscriminating clamour with which evangelicals assailed the one and high churchmen the other. Meanwhile, in the midst of literary labours and ecclesiastical conflicts, he steadily pursued his tutorial duties. His efforts met with unprecedented success. Giving his time and his best self to the undergraduates, he fired his pupils with his own enthusiasms; his colleagues were stimulated by his example, and the college rapidly rose to a high position in the university. In October 1845 he was appointed select preacher, and preached a course of four sermons, beginning in February 1846 and ending on 31 Jan. 1847. The sermons were published in November 1847, with additions and appendices, under the title of 'Sermons on the Apostolical Age.' They were preached at a crisis in Stanley's career, and at a point of transition between the old and the new Oxford. They marked his divergence from the views of both ecclesiastical parties; they acknowledged obligations to Arnold and German theologians; they championed the cause of free inquiry as applied to Biblical studies. From this time he was an object of suspicion to both evangelicals and high churchmen, who politically identified him with the party of reform, theologically with the German rationalists. On 6 Sept. 1849 Stanley's father, the bishop of Norwich, died; on 13 Aug. of the same year his younger brother, Captain Charles Stanley, R.E., and on 13 March 1850 his elder brother, Captain Owen Stanley, R.N., also died. He was now the sole prop and stay of his mother and his two sisters, and by his succession to a small estate was obliged to resign his fellowship at the university. Immediately after his father's death he had been offered the deanery of Carlisle, vacated by the appointment of Dr. Hinds to the see of Norwich. This offer he refused; but now, deprived of his home at Oxford, and desirous of providing one for his mother and sisters, he was not prepared to refuse any independent post. In July 1851 Stanley accepted a canonry at Canterbury, and left Oxford. The five succeeding years were a period of great literary activity. Before accepting the canonry Stanley had been appointed secretary of the Oxford University commission (July 1850). The report of the commission, which was mainly his work, was issued in May 1852. Thereupon he started on a tour in Egypt and the Holy Land, which produced his 'Sinai and Palestine' (published March 1856), perhaps the most widely popular of his writings. His 'Commentary on the Epistles to the Corinthians' (published June 1855) was a companion work to Jowett's 'Commentary on the Epistles to the Thessalonians, Galatians, and Romans.' On the picturesque, historical, and personal side it is valuable; but doctrinally it is weak, and in scholarship and accuracy it is deficient. Stanley wisely accepted the criticism of Dr. Lightfoot, afterwards bishop of Durham, in the 'Journal of Classical and Sacred Philology' (iii. 81-121), that critical notes were not his vocation. In his 'Memorials of Canterbury' (published December 1854) he found full scope for his gifts of dramatic, pictorial narrative. To make others share in his enthusiasms for the historical associations of the cathedral and the city was one side of his ideal of the duties of a canon. Another side of that ideal is illustrated in his 'Canterbury Sermons' (published March 1859), in which he endeavours to enforce the practical side of religion; to make it a life rather than a creed; to set forth its truths, not to attack its errors.

In December 1856 Stanley was appointed professor of ecclesiastical history at Oxford. To the chair was attached a canonry at Christ Church; the appointment, therefore, though he was not installed as canon till March 1858, required his removal from Canterbury and return to the university. At the same time he accepted the post of examining chaplain to Dr. Archibald Campbell (afterwards archbishop) Tait [q. v.], who in September 1856 had been appointed bishop of London. His 'Three Introductory Lectures on the Study of Ecclesiastical History' (published in 1857) were delivered in February 1857. His 'Lectures on the History of the Eastern Church (published in 1861) and his 'Lectures on the History of the Jewish Church' (part i. 1863; part ii. 1865; part iii. 1876) were also based upon lectures delivered as professor of ecclesiastical history. Through the lecture-room, the pulpit, and social life, he exercised a remarkable influence over young men at Oxford. To Stanley, for example, John Richard Green attributed his devotion to historical studies; from him also he learned the 'principle of fairness' (PROTHERO, *Life of Dean Stanley*, ii. 13-15). Among older men he was not an intellectual leader, though always a stimulating force. He could not join himself unreservedly to any party, and hated the spirit of combination for party purposes. His passion for justice plunged him continually into ecclesiastical conflicts. It was this feeling, even more than personal friendship, which stirred him to support Professor Jowett's claims to the endowments of the Greek chair against those who, on theological grounds, withheld his salary while they accepted his services. Though he regretted the publication of the first volume of Dr. Colenso's work on the Pentateuch (October 1862), he championed the writer's cause, because he could not 'join in the indiscriminate outcry against an evidently honest and single-minded religious man.' He disapproved of some of the contents of 'Essays and Reviews' (1860); but he pleaded that each essay should be judged by itself, and urged the unfairness of involving the different writers in the same sweeping censure (see his article on 'Essays and Reviews' in the *Edinburgh Review* for April 1861).

In January 1862 he was asked to accompany the Prince of Wales on a tour in the east. Leaving England in February, he returned home in the following June. The 'Sermons in the East' (published in 1863) were preached on this tour. During his absence abroad his mother died (Ash-Wednesday, 7 March 1862). This second tour in the Holy Land produced two results which were important in his career: it connected him closely with the court; it also made him better known to Lady Augusta Bruce (1822-1876), fifth daughter of the seventh Earl of Elgin, whom he had first met in

Paris in 1857, and whose brother, General Bruce, his fellow-traveller throughout the prince's tour, died in 1862 of a fever caught in the marshes of the Upper Jordan.

On 23 Dec. 1863 he was married to Lady Augusta in Westminster Abbey, and on 9 Jan. 1864 was installed as dean of the abbey in succession to Richard Chenevix Trench [q. v.], who was promoted to the archbishopric of Dublin.

Stanley at once made his mark in his new position. In convocation, in literature, in society, in his official duties as dean, and in the pulpit, his work was rich in results and his influence grew in extent. By the ancient instrument to which he declared his assent at his installation as dean, he held his office for 'the enlargement of the Christian church.' To obtain recognition for the comprehensiveness which was, in his opinion, secured to the church by its union with the state, and, within the limits of the law, to widen its borders so that it might more worthily fulfil its mission as a national church, were the objects to which he devoted himself. In this double meaning of the enlargement of the church lies the key to his sermons, speeches, and writings. The sacrifices which he was prepared to make for the attainment of his ideal repelled numbers of the best men in his own church, whether their views were high or low. On the other hand, the breadth of his charity attracted thousands of the members of other communions. Outside the pale of his own church no ecclesiastic commanded more respect or personal affection. Within its limits no one was more fiercely assailed. In the controversies in which he took part or provoked, such as those which centred round Dr. John William Colenso [q. v.] or Dr. Vance Smith, his attitude was at least consistent. He opposed every effort to loosen the tie between church and state, to resist or evade the existing law, or to contract the freedom which the widest interpretation of the formularies of the church would permit. In his 'Essays, chiefly on Questions of Church and State, from 1850 to 1870' (published in 1870), as well as in the 'Journals of Convocation,' are preserved the memories of many forgotten controversies.

In Westminster Abbey he found the material embodiment of his ideal of a comprehensive national church, an outward symbol of harmonious unity in diversity, a temple of silence and reconciliation which gathered under one consecrated roof every variety of creed and every form of national activity, whether lay or ecclesiastical, religious or secular. It was one of the objects of his life to open the abbey pulpit to churchmen of every shade of opinion, to give to laymen and ministers of other communions opportunities of speaking witin its walls, to make its services attractive to all classes and all ages, to communicate to the public generally his own enthusiasm for its historical associations by conducting parties over the building, as well as by compiling his 'Memorials of Westminster Abbey' (published in 1868).

As a preacher he pursued the same objects. He insisted that the essence of Christianity lay not in doctrine, but in a Christian character. He tried to penetrate to the moral and spiritual substance, which gave vitality to forms, institutions, and dogmas, and underlay different and apparently hostile views of religion. On this bed-rock, as it were, of Christianity he founded his teaching, because here he found the common ground on which Anglican, Roman catholic, presbyterian, and nonconformist might meet (see his *Lectures on the Church of Scotland*, 1872; *Addresses and Sermons delivered at St. Andrews*, 1877; *Addresses and Sermons delivered in the United States and Canada*, 1879; *Christian Institutions*, 1881.

In the midst of multifarious activities, social, political, literary, and official, he continued his annual tours, on the continent, in Scotland, or in America, the record of which is preserved in some of his published letters. In January 1874 he performed at St. Petersburg the marriage service between the Duke of Edinburgh and the Grand Duchess Marie of Russia. Later in the same year Lady Augusta Stanley, who had represented the queen at the wedding, fell ill, and, after months of suffering, died on Ash Wednesday, 1 March 1876. Her portrait, painted by George Richmond, R.A., belongs to the Lady Frances Baillie. By her bedside the third part of her husband's 'Lectures on the Jewish Church' was mainly written (1876). Stanley never recovered the shock of his wife's death, though his life to the last was full of activity. In the summer of 1881 he was preaching a course of sermons on the Beatitudes on Saturday afternoons in Westminster. At the service on Saturday, 9 July 1881, he spoke his last words in the abbey. He left the pulpit for his bed. His illness proved to be erysipelas, of which he died on Monday, 18 July 1881. On Monday, 25 July, he was buried in Westminster Abbey by the side of his wife.

Stanley's principal works have been already mentioned. None of them, with the possible exception of the 'Life of Dr. Arnold,' belong to the highest or most permanent class of literature. His personal charm was a stronger influence than his books. Of the fascination that he exercised over his friends, a vivid picture will be found in Dean Bradley's 'Recollections of Arthur Penrhyn Stanley' (1883).

A full-length recumbent figure of Stanley, modelled by Sir Edgar Boehm, is in the National Portrait Gallery, London, of which Stanley had been appointed a trustee in 1866. A portrait by G. F. Watts is in the Bodleian Library, Oxford.

[Prothero's Life and Correspondence of Dean Stanley (1893) and Letters and Verses of Dean Stanley (1895) contain the fullest information respecting the life and works of Stanley. Other books which also illustrate the subject are Dean Bradley's Recollections (1883), My Confidences, by F. Locker-Lampson (1896), and the Life and Letters of Benjamin Jowett, by Messrs. Campbell and Abbott, 1897.] R. E. P.

STANLEY, CHARLOTTE, Countess of Derby (1599–1664), born at Thouars early in December 1599 (LOUISE DE COLIGNY, *Corresp.* ed. 1887, p. 166), was the second child but eldest daughter of Claude de la Trémoille, duc de Thouars, by his wife Charlotte (1580–1626), third daughter of William the Silent, prince of Orange, by his third wife, Charlotte de Bourbon ('Chartrier de Thouars,' 1877, pp. 153, 162, 272–9, apud *Documents Historiques et Généalogiques*; SAINT-MARTHE, *Hist. Généalogique de la Maison de la Trémoille*, 1668, p. 260; *Les La Trémoille pendant Cinq Siècles*, Nantes, 1890–6). Louisa, wife of the elector palatine Frederick IV, was her aunt; the Duc de Bouillon, head of the French protestants, and Prince Maurice of Nassau were her uncles. Her father died in 1604, and Charlotte spent most of her early days at Thouars, occasionally paying visits to her relatives at The Hague. Her mother came to England in 1625 in the train of Charles I's queen, Henrietta Maria, and during her visit arranged a marriage between Charlotte and James Stanley, lord Strange (afterwards seventh Earl of Derby) [q. v.] Charlotte was then staying at The Hague with Elizabeth, the daughter of James I and fugitive queen of Bohemia, whose husband, Frederick V, was Charlotte's cousin. There the marriage took place on 26 June 1626 (BELLI, *Osservazion*, p. 95), the ceremony being disturbed by a contest for precedence between the English and French ambassadors. The statement that she was of the same age as her husband was a polite fiction to cover the fact that she was seven years his senior.

For sixteen years after her marriage Lady Strange lived quietly with her husband at Knowsley or Lathom House, and during this period she bore him nine children (*Stanley Papers*, III. ii. pp. cclxxxviii–ccxcii). She remained at Lathom House when, on the outbreak of the civil war, her husband joined the king. Lancashire, however, favoured the parliamentary cause, and by May 1643 Lathom House was the only place held by the king's adherents. No serious steps, however, were taken for its reduction until February 1643–4. On the 25th of that month Sir William Fairfax [q. v.] encamped between Wigan and Bolton, and on the 28th Lathom House was invested. The garrison consisted of three hundred men under six captains and six lieutenants (*ib.* pp. xciii–iv), but the Countess of Derby (as she had become in the preceding year) reserved all important decisions to herself. A week was occupied in parleys, but the countess rejected with scorn all proposals for surrender, declaring that she and her children would fire the castle and perish in the flames rather than yield. These words were backed by spirited sorties of the garrison on 17–18 and 20 March. On the latter occasion two messengers broke through the enemy's lines, conveying urgent appeals for aid to Prince Rupert and the Earl of Derby. Fairfax now left the command to Alexander Rigby [q. v.] On 10 April the parliamentarians opened a destructive fire with a new mortar, which threatened to put a speedy end to the defence; but about four A.M. on 26 April the garrison made a brilliant sortie and captured the mortar. This exploit disheartened the besiegers, and on 26 May they received news of Rupert's approach from Newark. They retired to Bolton, which Rupert stormed on the 28th, sending the countess as a present twenty-two banners that had lately waved over the heads of her besiegers. The parliamentarians spread a report that the countess, being a better soldier than her husband, dressed herself in man's clothes and in this disguise conducted the defence of Lathom House.

The respite was not of long duration. The battle of Marston Moor (2 July) ruined the royalist cause in Lancashire, and before the end of the month Lathom House was again besieged. The earl, however, had removed with his wife and children to the Isle of Man, and on 8 Dec. following Lathom House surrendered. The countess remained in the Isle of Man until after her husband's execution in 1651. The island was then surrendered by William Christian [q. v.], the deputy-governor, to the parliamentarians,

and the countess removed to Knowsley, where she lived until the Restoration, occasionally visiting London. On 9 June 1660 she petitioned that her husband's 'murderers might be brought to condign punishment.' But the obloquy cast upon her because of her alleged persecution of Christian is said to have been unmerited (*Stanley Papers*, III. ii. pp. cclxxiv et seq.) She died at Knowsley on 21 March 1663–4, and was buried near her husband in Ormskirk church.

Vandyck's group of the Earl and Countess of Derby and child in the Clarendon Gallery is one of his finest pictures. The sketch of Lady Derby's figure for this picture is among the original Vandyck drawings in the British Museum (LADY THERESA LEWIS, *Friends of Clarendon*, iii. 338). A portrait by Janssen formerly belonged to the Earl of Liverpool, and two others belong to Earl Fitzwilliam. A portrait belonging to the Earl of Derby, engraved by C. H. Jeens, is prefixed to Madame de Witt's 'Lady of Latham.'

[The large collection of letters from the Countess of Derby to her French relatives, in the possession of the Duc de la Trémoille, were used by Madame de Witt in her Lady of Latham, London, 1869, 8vo, and by M. Marlet in his Charlotte de la Trémoille, Paris, 1895. The latter is the best biography of the countess. Other lives of her are given in Cummings's The Great Stanley, 1847, and the Stanley Papers (Chetham Soc.) For the siege of Lathom House are two anonymous manuscripts, one of which, extant in Ashmolean MS. A. Wood, D. 16, is printed as a sequel to the Memoirs of Colonel Hutchinson, 1846; the other, extant in Harl. MS. 2043, was published in 1823, 12mo, and in Ormerod's Civil War Tracts in Lancashire (Chetham Soc.), 1844. The countess is portrayed in Scott's Peveril of the Peak and in Harrison Ainsworth's Leaguer of Lathom. See also Correspondance de Louise de Coligny, ed. MM. Marchegay et Marlet, 1887, passim; Chartrier de Thouars, 1877; Warburton's Prince Rupert; Thurloe and Rushworth's Collections; Gardiner's Civil War; Collins's and G. E. C.'s Peerages; Intermédiaire des Chercheurs et Curieux, xxiv. 588; authorities quoted in Marlet's Charlotte de la Trémoille, pp. xiv–xv, and in art. STANLEY, JAMES, seventh EARL OF DERBY.]

A. F. P.

STANLEY, EDWARD, first BARON MONTEAGLE (1460?–1523), born probably about 1460, was fifth son of Thomas Stanley, first earl of Derby [q. v.], by his first wife Eleanor, daughter of Richard Neville, earl of Salisbury (1400–1460) [q. v.], and sister of the 'king-maker.' He was knighted during Edward IV's reign, and on 17 April 1483 officiated as one of the pall-bearers at that king's funeral. His father's marriage with

E

Henry of Richmond's mother and services at Bosworth secured Henry's favour for the family when he became king. Edward became sheriff of Lancashire in the autumn of 1485; on 15 Oct. he was directed to provide for the safety of the shire against Scottish attacks, and on 1 Dec. he was granted the office of keeper of New Park, Langley; he also became knight of the body to the king. On 4 March 1488–9 he was granted the manors of Farleton in Lonsdale, Farleton in Westmoreland, and Brierley in Yorkshire. He took part in the ceremonies at the creation of Prince Henry as Duke of York in November 1494, and at the reception of Catherine of Arragon in October 1501. On 5 Nov. 1509 he was granted a license to import seventy tuns of Burgundy wine, and in 1511 he served as commissioner of array in Yorkshire and Westmoreland. He received further grants of land in June 1513, and on 9 Sept. following he took a prominent part in the battle of Flodden Field. Popular ballads (see *Flodden Field*, ed. Weber, pp. 37–40, 50–9 et seq.) represent the English army as begging Surrey to put Stanley in command of the van; Surrey, out of jealousy, placed him in the rear, where nevertheless he greatly distinguished himself, forcing the Scots to evacuate their position of vantage on the hill, and killing James IV of Scotland with his own hand (his name occurs in the well-known line of Scott's 'Marmion,' 'Charge, Chester, charge—on, Stanley, on'). These details receive no confirmation from the official version (*Letters and Papers*, i. 1441); but Thomas Ruthall [q. v.], bishop of Durham, reported that Stanley behaved well, and recommended his elevation to the peerage for his services. On 8 May 1514 he was installed K.G., and six days later he is said to have landed at Calais with Sir Thomas Lovell [q. v.] Various deeds of valour during the French war are assigned to him by the peerage historians. On 9 Oct. in the same year he was present at the marriage of the princess Mary to Louis XII of France, and on 23 Nov. he was summoned to the House of Lords as Baron Monteagle (cf. *ib.* ii. 1464). He was present at the Field of the Cloth of Gold in June 1520. He died on 6 April 1523, and was buried at Hornby, Lancashire, where he had commenced a religious foundation in commemoration of his success at Flodden (cf. *Letters and Papers*, iii. 2834). Monteagle married, first, Elizabeth, daughter of Sir Thomas Vaughan of Tretower, Brecknockshire, and widow of John, lord Grey de Wilton, by whom he had no issue; and secondly, Anne, daughter of Sir John Harrington, by whom he had apparently two sons, both named Thomas. The elder succeeded to the peerage, and died in 1560; his son William, third baron Monteagle, died without male issue in 1581, leaving a daughter Elizabeth, who married Edward Parker, tenth baron Morley, and was mother of William Parker [q. v.], who succeeded as fourth baron Monteagle and eleventh baron Morley.

THOMAS STANLEY (d. 1570), bishop of Sodor and Man, the first lord Monteagle's second son, was educated at Oxford, and then became rector of Winwick and Wigan, Lancashire, and Bardsworth, Yorkshire. In 1530 he was appointed bishop of Sodor and Man, but was deprived by Henry VIII in 1545. He was restored by Queen Mary in 1556, and died in 1570. He was author of a metrical chronicle of the Stanleys of Lathom, several copies of which are extant in manuscript (cf. *Stanley Papers*, i. 16–17). It was printed in Halliwell's 'Palatine Anthology' [1850], but is of little authority (WOOD, *Athenæ Oxon.* ii. 807; LE NEVE, *Fasti*, iii. 326).

[Campbell's Materials for the Reign of Henry VII, and Gairdner's Letters and Papers of Henry VII (Rolls Ser.); Brewer's Letters and Papers of Henry VIII, vols. i–iii.; Stanley Papers (Chetham Soc.), vol. i.; Stanley's Metrical Chron. in Halliwell's Palatine Anthology; Weber's Flodden Field, pp. 2, 5, 37–40, 50–7, 72, 112, 116, 118, 132–3, 263–4; La Rotta de Scozese (Roxburghe Club); Seacome's Mem. of the Stanleys, ed. 1840, pp. 93–4; Pollard's Stanleys of Knowsley, pp. 31–2; Baines's Lancashire; Gregson's Portfolio of Fragments; Peerages by Collins, Burke (Extinct), and G. E. C.]

A. F. P.

STANLEY, EDWARD, third EARL OF DERBY (1508–1572), second but eldest surviving son of Thomas Stanley, second earl of Derby, by his wife Anne, daughter of Thomas, lord Hungerford, was born in 1508 (*Letters and Papers of Henry VIII*, iii. 2820). His father, eldest son of George, lord Strange (d. 1497), and grandson of Thomas, first earl of Derby [q. v.], born before 1485, was made K.B. on 31 Oct. 1494, succeeded his grandfather as second Earl of Derby on 29 July 1504, and his mother in the barony of Strange on 20 March 1513–14. He attended Henry VIII on the French expedition in 1513, and was present at the battle of Spurs (18 Aug.) In 1520 he was in attendance on Charles V at Dover, and in the same year he was sworn of the privy council. He died on 23 May 1521, and was buried at Sion monastery, Middlesex. An anonymous portrait belongs to the present Earl of Derby (*Cat. First Loan Exhib.* No. 70).

The third earl was a minor at his father's death, and became a ward of Cardinal Wolsey. He took his seat in the House of Lords in the parliament that met on 3 Nov. 1529, and on 13 July 1530 he was one of the peers who signed the letter to the pope petitioning him to grant Henry VIII's divorce. In 1532 he was present with Henry at his interview with Francis I at Boulogne. He was made a knight of the Bath on 30 May 1533, and on 1 June following he officiated as cupbearer at the coronation of Anne Boleyn. He took a prominent part in suppressing the northern rebellions in 1536 and 1537 (*Letters and Papers of Henry VIII*, ed. Gairdner, vols. xi. and xii. passim). In 1542 he accompanied Thomas Howard, third duke of Norfolk, on his raid into Scotland. He was elected K.G. on 17 Feb. 1546-7, and three days later bore the sword 'curtana' at the coronation of Edward VI. He was, however, strongly opposed to religious change, and protested in the House of Lords against the bills confirming the new liturgy (10 Dec. 1548), for the destruction of the old service books (December 1549), compelling attendance at divine service (January 1552-3), and legalising the marriage of priests (March 1552-3). In June 1551 it was reported that he had been commanded to 'renounce his title of the Isle of Man,' but refused, and was preparing to resist by force (*Cal. State Papers*, For. i. 119-20). Nevertheless, he was on 9 Aug. 1551 sworn a privy councillor on condition of attending only when specially summoned, and in the same year he was one of the parties to the peace with Scotland. He took little part in the proceedings of the council, but in December 1551 he was one of the peers who tried Somerset, while his eldest son was one of the principal witnesses against the duke. On 16 May 1552 he was appointed lord lieutenant of Lancashire.

Derby naturally welcomed the accession of Queen Mary, and was one of her earliest adherents. On 17 Aug. 1553 he was made a regular member of the privy council, which he frequently attended, and in the same month was placed on a commission to investigate Bonner's deprivation of the bishopric of London. He was created lord high steward for the coronation of Mary on 1 Oct. and bore the sword 'curtana' at that ceremony. On 11 Nov. following he was made a special commissioner for the trial of Lady Jane Grey and others, and during Mary's reign he frequently took part in the proceedings against heretics, John Bradford (1510?-1555) [q. v.] being one of the victims of his activity (FOXE, *Actes and Mon.* vol. vii. passim;

MAITLAND, *Essays on the Reformation*). He attended Philip of Spain at his landing on 19 July 1554, and on 30 May 1557 he was appointed captain of the vanguard to serve against the Scots. He was one of those summoned to attend Queen Elizabeth on her entry into London in November 1558, and before the end of the year became a member of Gray's Inn. He was retained as a member of the privy council, was appointed chamberlain of Chester on 16 April 1559, visitor of the churches in the province of York on 24 June 1559, commissioner for ecclesiastical causes in the diocese of Chester on 20 July 1562, and lord lieutenant of Cheshire and Lancashire on 18 Nov. 1569. But though he often took part in proceedings against recusants and gave the government timely warning of the insurrection of 1569, his sympathies and connections rendered him an object of suspicion to Elizabeth. The queen's enemies counted on his support (cf. *Cal. State Papers*, Dom. Addenda, 1566-79, pp. 371-2), and his sons, Edward and Thomas, were in 1571 implicated in an attempt to release Mary Queen of Scots from Tutbury (*Hatfield MSS.* i. 505-76). Derby died at Lathom House on 24 Oct. 1572; he had been noted for his splendid hospitality, and his funeral at Ormskirk on 4 Dec. 1572 was one of the most magnificent on record (cf. *The Derby Household Books*, Chetham Soc.; *Cal. State Papers*, Dom. 1547-81, p. 455; COLLINS, *Peerage*, iii. 65-62). His will, dated 24 Aug., was proved on 21 Nov. 1572. An engraving of an anonymous portrait of Derby belonging to the present Earl Derby is given by Doyle.

Derby was thrice married. His first wife was Katherine (her name is given in the peerage as Dorothy), daughter of Thomas Howard I, second duke of Norfolk, who on 21 Feb. 1529-30 received a pardon 'for the abduction of Edward, earl of Derby, and marriage of the said Edward to Katherine, daughter of the said Thomas, without royal license' (*Letters and Papers*, iv. 6248, art. 21). By her Derby had issue Henry Stanley, fourth earl [q. v.], Sir Thomas Stanley (d. 1576), and Sir Edward (d. 1609); and four daughters. His second wife was Margaret, daughter of Ellis Barlow of Barlow, Essex, by whom he had one son and two daughters. She died on 23 Feb. 1558-9, and an epilogue on her death, by Richard Sheale, is printed in the 'British Bibliographer,' vol. iv. (cf. *Stanley Papers*, i. 14). His third wife was Mary, daughter of Sir George Cotton of Combermere Abbey, Cheshire, who afterwards married Henry Grey, earl of Kent, and died without issue on 16 Nov. 1580.

[Letters and Papers of Henry VIII, ed. Brewer and Gairdner, vols. iv-xv. passim; Cal. State Papers, Dom. 1547-81, and Addenda, 1547-65, 1565-79; Stanley Papers, (5 pts.) and Lancashire Lieutenancy under the Tudors (Chetham Soc.); Cal. Hatfield MSS. pt. i.; Acts of the Privy Council, 1542-75; Lit. Remains of Edward VI (Roxburghe Club); Machyn's Diary, Chron. of Queen Jane, and Narr. of the Reformation (Camden Soc.); Corr. Pol. de Odet de Selve; Camden's Elizabeth; Foxe's Actes and Mon.; Burnet's Hist. Reformation, ed. Pocock; Strype's Works; Lords' Journals; Froude's Hist.; Baines's Lancashire; Hibbert Ware's Manchester; Collins's, Doyle's, and G. E. C[okayne]'s Peerages.]   A. F. P.

STANLEY, EDWARD (1779-1849), bishop of Norwich, second son and seventh child of Sir John Thomas Stanley, sixth baronet, of Alderley Park, Cheshire, and of Margaret Owen, of Penrhos, Anglesey, was born in London on 1 Jan. 1779. His elder brother, John Thomas, was first Baron Stanley of Alderley, and father of Edward John Stanley, second baron Stanley of Alderley [q. v.] Edward's natural inclination was for the sea; but he was not allowed to enter the navy. Educated partly at private schools, partly by tutors, he was sent in 1798 to St. John's College, Cambridge, knowing nothing of Greek, almost equally ignorant of Latin, and possessing only a smattering of mathematics. His industry to some extent remedied these deficiencies. In 1802 his name appears in the mathematical tripos as sixteenth wrangler.

Ordained in 1802, he was for three years curate of Windlesham in Surrey. In 1805 he was presented by his father to the family living of Alderley, where he remained for thirty-two years. An excellent parish priest at a time when the standard of parochial duty was low, he devoted himself earnestly to his work. In education he was keenly interested, introducing into his schools gymnastic exercises, and such subjects as elementary botany, English history, and geography. Infant schools, temperance societies, mechanics' institutes, and statistical societies found in him a zealous patron. He was also instrumental in founding a clerical society among the neighbouring clergy. A natural aptitude for science, and a conviction of its intimate connection with religion, made him a student of such subjects as ornithology, entomology, mineralogy, and geology. His ornithological observations were embodied in his 'Familiar History of Birds, their Nature, Habits, and Instincts' (2 vols. published in 1836). He was one of the first clergymen who ventured to lecture on the then suspected science of geology. A whig in politics, and by nature a reformer, he took up a position towards questions of the day which was rare in his profession. He endeavoured by pamphlets, published in 1829 and 1836, to allay the animosities between Roman catholics and protestants. In 1831, in the midst of the Reform Bill agitation, he promoted a petition for church reform. When the new and unpopular poor law came into operation in 1834, he offered his services as chairman of the board of guardians called on to administer the act in his union.

In 1837 Dr. Bathurst, bishop of Norwich, died at the age of ninety-three. The vacant see was offered by Lord Melbourne to Stanley, and was accepted by him. He had previously declined overtures of a similar kind with regard to the bishopric of Manchester, the immediate creation of which was then contemplated. He now entered upon episcopal work in a diocese which was a by-word for laxity and irregularity. Non-residence, pluralities, scarcity of services, neglect of schools, carelessness in admission to holy orders, were some of the abuses by which he was confronted. By vigorous enforcement of the Plurality and Non-residence Act, he added during his episcopate 173 parsonage-houses. During the same period he increased the number of Sunday services by 347. He doubled the number of schools and rendered them more efficient. The examinations for ordination were carefully conducted, and the bishop made himself personally acquainted with the previous career of every candidate. At great personal expense he prosecuted and removed those clergymen whose lives had brought them within the reach of the law. By the appointment of seventy rural deans, each of whom was every year entertained at the palace, he made himself acquainted with what passed in every part of his diocese. Instead of the old septennial confirmations at a few large centres, he confirmed annually at convenient stations. He assisted all the charitable institutions of the county, especially in Norwich, interested himself in the working of the poor laws, and personally inspected the efficiency of the local schools. In the House of Lords he was a regular attendant, and a staunch supporter of whig principles. His most telling speeches were delivered in defence of the government scheme of education in 1839, on behalf of relaxing the stringent terms of clerical subscription in 1840, and on the endowment of Maynooth in 1842. He took part, with especial pleasure, in such movements as bible societies, city missions, British and foreign schools, which brought together on neutral ground churchmen and nonconformists. The same feeling led him to support in the National Society in 1839 such changes as would open the doors of schools to the children of nonconformists. He was also the first bishop who interested himself in the movement for ragged schools. Always an eager advocate of temperance, he appeared on the platform with Father Mathew, who in 1843 was his guest at Norwich.

Stanley's liberal views, fearlessness of obloquy, and vigorous reforms at first created ill-feeling in the diocese. Before the close of his episcopate, however, he not only changed the whole atmosphere of religious life throughout his see, but won the affectionate esteem of all classes, whether lay or clerical. In August 1849 he started for a tour in Scotland with his wife and daughters. At Brahan Castle in Ross-shire he was taken ill, and, after a few days, died from congestion of the brain on 6 Sept. 1849. His body was brought by sea from Invergordon to Yarmouth, and on 21 Sept. was buried in the centre of the nave of Norwich Cathedral.

By his wife Catherine (1792–1862), daughter of the Rev. Oswald Leycester, rector of Stoke-upon-Terne, whom he married in 1810, Stanley had, besides other issue, Arthur Penrhyn Stanley [q. v.] and a daughter Mary (1813–1879), who in 1854 was entrusted by Sydney Herbert, secretary of state for war, with the charge of fifty nurses during the Crimean war. Subsequently she assisted her brother in charitable work at Westminster, and in 1861 was active in relieving the distress in Lancashire due to the cotton famine. She became a Roman catholic in 1856, and died on 26 Nov. 1879. She was author of 'True to Life: a simple Story,' 1873, 8vo.

[Addresses and Charges of Edward Stanley, D.D., late bishop of Norwich, with a Memoir by his son, Arthur Penrhyn Stanley, London, 1851. The Memoir is reprinted, with some additions, in the Memoirs of Edward and Catherine Stanley, by Arthur Penrhyn Stanley, London, 1879.]   R. E. P.

STANLEY, EDWARD (1793–1862), surgeon, son of Edward Stanley, who was in business in the city of London, was born on 3 July 1793, his mother being the sister of Thomas Blizard [q. v.], surgeon to the London Hospital. He was entered at Merchant Taylors' School in April 1802, and remained there until 1808, when he was apprenticed to Thomas Ramsden, one of the surgeons at St. Bartholomew's Hospital. Ramsden died

in 1810, and Stanley was turned over to John Abernethy to serve the remainder of his time. He was admitted a member of the College of Surgeons in 1814, and gained the Jacksonian prize in 1815. He was elected assistant surgeon to St. Bartholomew's Hospital on 29 Jan. 1816, at the early age of 24. Even during his apprenticeship he had rendered important services to the medical school of the hospital, for his love of morbid anatomy led him, with Abernethy's assistance and approval, to enlarge the museum so greatly that he practically created it. He acted for a time as demonstrator of anatomy, but in 1826 he was appointed to lecture upon this subject on Abernethy's resignation. He continued to lecture until 1848, when he was succeeded by Frederic Carpenter Skey [q. v.] Stanley was elected to the post of full surgeon in 1838, and he then rapidly became famous as a clinical teacher of great power. He was elected a fellow of the Royal Society in 1830.

At the Royal College of Surgeons he held in succession the most important offices. He was elected a life member of the council in 1832, Arris and Gale professor of human anatomy and physiology in 1835, Hunterian orator in 1839, a member of the court of examiners in 1844, and president in 1848 and again in 1857. He was appointed surgeon-extraordinary to the queen in 1858, and he was president of the Royal Medical and Chirurgical Society as early as 1843.

Stanley resigned his post of surgeon to St. Bartholomew's Hospital in 1861, but he regularly attended the weekly operations on Saturdays until 24 May 1862, when he was attacked by cerebral hæmorrhage while watching an operation, and died an hour later. Stanley was one of the most sagacious teachers and judicious practitioners of his day. He was a blunt, kindly, humorous, straightforward, and honest man.

He published: 1. 'Illustrations of the Effects of Disease and Injury of the Bones,' with descriptive and explanatory statements, plates, London, folio, 1849. A series of coloured plates splendidly executed, drawn from original preparations, most of which are still extant. 2. 'A Treatise on Diseases of the Bones,' 8vo, London, 1849. An edition was also published in the same year at Philadelphia. These two classical works represented for many years all that was known of the pathology of the subject of bone disease. 3. 'A Manual of Practical Anatomy,' London, 12mo, 1818; 2nd edit. 1822; 3rd edit. 1826. 4. 'An Account of the Mode of performing the Lateral Operation of Lithotomy,' plates, 4to, 1829. 5. 'Hunterian Oration,' London, 1839.

[Alfred Willett's account of Edward Stanley, St. Bartholomew's Hospital Journal, 1894, i. 147; Robinson's Register of Merchant Taylors' School.]

D'A. P.

STANLEY, EDWARD GEORGE GEOFFREY SMITH, fourteenth EARL OF DERBY (1799–1869), son of Edward Smith Stanley, thirteenth earl [q. v.], by Charlotte Margaret, his cousin, second daughter of the Rev. Geoffrey Hornby, was born at Knowsley Park, Lancashire, on 29 March 1799. He was sent to Eton, where he was in the fifth form in lower division in 1811 and upper division in 1814 (*Eton School Lists*, pp. 69, 77). Proceeding to Christ Church, Oxford, and matriculating on 17 Oct. 1817, he won the Chancellor's Latin verse prize in 1819 with a spirited poem on 'Syracuse;' he took no degree, but on 19 Oct. 1852 was created D.C.L. On leaving Oxford he was brought into parliament for Stockbridge in the whig interest on 6 March 1820. The borough had been in the hands of a tory, a West Indian proprietor named Joseph Foster Barham, who, being in difficulties, sold it to a whig peer, and, on a successor being found by the purchaser in the person of young Stanley, at once vacated the seat himself, introducing him to the electors. Stanley made no speech in the House of Commons till 30 March 1824, when he spoke with considerable success on the Manchester Gas-light Bill, having in the previous year been appointed a member of the committee on the subject. On 6 May he answered Joseph Hume in the debate on the latter's motion for an inquiry into the Irish church establishment. He opposed any design to interfere with church property, and proved himself to be by instinct a powerful debater. He did not, however, follow up this success for some time. In the autumn of 1824 he travelled in Canada and the United States, and, in May 1825, married Emma Caroline, second daughter of Edward Bootle Wilbraham (afterwards Lord Skelmersdale). During that session he was silent in the House of Commons, and hardly spoke at all in 1826. He ceased to be member for Stockbridge, and was elected for Preston on 26 June 1826, where the local franchise was a popular one, and the representation had long been divided between a nominee of the Derby family and a nominee of the corporation. Though opposed by Cobbett and others, he was returned at the head of the poll by a very large majority.

The views of Canning approximated so closely to the opinions that Stanley then held that he, with other whigs, gave his support to Canning's ministry in 1827, and accepted the under-secretaryship of the colonies. He retained it under Lord Goderich, [see ROBINSON, FREDERICK JOHN, first EARL OF RIPON], but declined to be a member of the Duke of Wellington's administration, pointing to the divergence of the old tories from the freer spirit of the Canningites, and hinting that the older toryism was a thing of the past. Still he foresaw as little as others the near triumph of the whigs. In 1828 he supported the transference to Birmingham of the East Retford seat, in opposition to the government; he voted in silence for the Catholic Emancipation Bill in 1829, and spoke guardedly in favour of parliamentary reform in 1830. At the general election on the death of George IV he was re-elected for Preston on 30 July, but, having accepted office in Lord Grey's administration as chief secretary for Ireland and having been sworn of the privy council, he was defeated in August by 'Orator' Hunt at the by-election for Preston in December, and was mobbed and ran some risk of his life [see HUNT, HENRY, 1773–1835]. Eventually a vacancy was made at Windsor, and Stanley was elected there on 10 Feb. 1831.

O'Connell's indignation when the new ministry refused the silk gown he had had reason to expect at their hands vented itself particularly in attacks on the new chief secretary. Stanley was not slow to retaliate, and eventually allowed himself to be irritated into challenging O'Connell; the challenge was refused, but the attacks continued. O'Connell was then prosecuted in January 1831 for a breach of the Association Act; he pleaded guilty, and was bound over to come up for judgment in the following term; but before he was in fact required to come up parliament was dissolved. The Association Act expired with the dissolution, and further proceedings were impossible. It was currently believed that the ministry had arranged for this abortive result in order to secure O'Connell's support at the approaching election, and that Stanley had been active in carrying out the plan. Fortunate, however, as the issue was for the ministry at the moment, it seems that the result was purely accidental (see *State Trials*, new ser. ii. 629–58); at any rate, Stanley point blank denied that there had been any arrangement (HANSARD, 13 Feb. 1831, p. 610), and O'Connell's antagonism towards him continued unabated.

During the reform struggle Stanley's speeches, though brilliant (RUSSELL, *Recollections*, p. 92), showed that he scarcely appreciated how great a constitutional change the ministerial proposals made. At heart he was no friend to extreme reform; he vigorously supported the bill in debate, answering Peel, for example, on 4 March 1831 very effectively; but when attempts at compromise were made, after the House of Lords had rejected the bill in October, and riots had occurred in various parts of the country, he was among the most active in promoting an agreement. With Lord Grey's approval, he visited Lord Sandon [see RYDER, DUDLEY, second EARL OF HARROWBY], to discuss terms of compromise, and was regarded as the leader of the moderate reformers in the cabinet. Thus, on the one hand, he delivered a brilliant and crushing speech in reply to Croker during the second reading debate of the third bill on 17 Dec. 1831 (HANSARD, 3rd ser. ix. 521), and, on the other, was pressing Lord Grey for concessions with regard to duplicate voting and to the number of the proposed metropolitan constituencies. By May 1832 these concessions had almost been obtained, when the ministry was compelled to resign by the lords' acceptance of Lyndhurst's motion to postpone consideration of the disfranchising clauses to that of the enfranchising clauses. The failure of negotiations so nearly completed was keenly resented by Stanley, and in an after-supper speech at Brooke's he used language of extreme bitterness towards the Duke of Wellington. From this time he vigorously supported the full reform scheme, and no doubt the success of the bill was materially aided by his speeches. On 19 Jan. 1832 he also introduced the ministerial Reform Bill for Ireland; but it excited little interest, though he proposed an increase in the number of Irish members. He succeeded his father as member for North Lancashire on 17 Dec. 1832, and held the seat till he was raised to the peerage.

During the debates and dissolutions on reform, Stanley had been incessantly occupied not only with the fortunes of the bill, but with the administrative duties of his office. He had to 'adjust the state of Ireland to that first retreat from the Ascendency position which was involved in the granting of catholic emancipation.' He instituted the Irish board of works and the Shannon navigation improvements. In 1831 he brought in the Irish Education Act, which was remarkable for the creation of the Irish board of national education and for the compromise by which, while children of all denominations were to be admitted to the schools receiving the government grant, the education given was not to be wholly secular, but was to include religious teaching of an undogmatic and

neutral character. The bill was favoured by the Roman catholic priesthood, and was probably as successful as any measure on such a subject could be in Ireland. In December of the same year he was chairman of a committee on Irish tithes, and in the following spring, in spite of the most determined and violent opposition from the Irish Roman catholic members, he passed a temporary palliative act, followed in July by the first of three bills to apply a more permanent remedy by making tithe composition compulsory. The act, with the addition of Littleton's Tithe Act in the following year, continued in force till 1838. During these debates Stanley's relations with O'Connell and his followers had become gravely embittered. Matters became worse in November, after he had declared in the strongest terms in an election speech in North Lancashire that he would resist repeal to the death. His measures in 1833 were a very strong Peace Preservation Act and an Irish Church Temporalities Act, and his first battle on the former was in the cabinet. Althorp wished to resign rather than be responsible for such a proposal. Stanley insisted; and as it was apparent that the resignation of either must break up the ministry, Lord Althorp gave way. The conduct of the bill was placed in Althorp's hands, but he introduced it in a speech so half-hearted that many of the ministerialists wavered, and a defeat became dangerously probable. Stanley took the papers, shut himself up for a couple of hours, mastered the complicated facts and figures, and, returning, made a speech so convincing, so uncompromising, and so hostile to the Irish party that he silenced O'Connell, and, thanks to his sole exertions, passed the bill by huge majorities (for the description of this incident see RUSSELL, Recollections, pp. 112, 113; LE MARCHANT, Life of Lord Althorp, p. 455). The Church Temporalities Bill also, though introduced by Althorp, was Stanley's bill.

Having achieved so much Irish legislation during a comparatively short tenure of the chief secretaryship and shown himself a masterful and drastic administrator, he was on 28 March transferred to the colonial office. Greville states (Memoirs, 1st ser. ii. 366) that a positive promise of a secretaryship of state had been made him in 1832, and that it was only on his threats of resignation and the strongest pressure on Goderich that room was made for him in the latter's place. In his new office he attacked the question of the abolition of slavery, at first by resolutions (HANSARD, Parl. Deb. 3rd ser.

xvii. 1230), proposing a limited period of apprenticeship for the slave and compensation for the owners, and afterwards by bill, which reduced the apprenticeship and increased the compensation. His introductory speech of 14 May was published. In the conduct of this bill he showed himself less the orator of the Irish debates than a hardheaded man of business. The bill became law in August 1833, but before it came into force in 1834 Stanley had resigned. On 6 May 1834 Russell, speaking on Littleton's Tithe Bill, declared in favour of the alienation to secular purposes of a portion of the Irish church revenues. The question was one on which two parties existed in the cabinet, and no collective declaration had been hitherto made by the ministry. Stanley has been accused of having actually introduced an appropriation clause into the Church Temporalities Bill in 1833; but his speeches during its progress show that he was opposed to any secularisation of church property, and did not think or desire, that by Clause 147 any such object would be effected. At any rate he saw that Russell's declaration meant the break up of the ministry. 'Johnny has upset the coach,' he whispered to his neighbour Graham. Henry George Ward [q. v.], member for St. Albans, followed up Russell's announcement with his 'Appropriation Resolution' for the redistribution of the Irish church revenues; it was to come on on 27 May, and the ministry, hesitating between their radical and whig followers, resolved to meet it with a proposal for a commission of inquiry. Stanley instantly tendered his resignation, and had ceased to be a minister before Ward had finished introducing his motion. He never afterwards rejoined the whigs; for a time he spoke and voted as an independent member, but he inevitably drifted towards the conservative party. In him the whigs lost one of their ablest men of business, and incomparably their best debater. Earl Russell (*Recollections*, p. 114) speaks of 1833 as the most distinguished and memorable of Derby's whole career, and says that, had Althorp then resigned, Stanley's 'infinite skill, readiness, and ability' would have qualified him for the succession to the leadership of the House of Commons.

During the rest of the session of 1834 Stanley spoke sometimes for and sometimes against the government: for them on the bill to admit dissenters to the universities and on Althorp's plan for the abolition of church rates; against them in the speech on 2 July, in which he compared their conduct on the Tithe Bill to the sleight of hand of thimbleriggers at a fair. In general his speeches at this time were too full of bitterness and invective against his former colleagues. When Melbourne was dismissed, and Peel's return from Rome was anxiously awaited, his position was commanding. United with Stanley, Peel might well form and maintain an administration. Opposed by him, his premiership must be short-lived. Stanley, while willing to serve under Peel as far as personal feeling was concerned, thought it best to decline to take office. He had too frequently been Peel's antagonist while in office himself to become so soon afterwards his colleague. He promised, however, an independent support, and no doubt his decision was wise. Between Peel's conservatism and the opinions of Stanley and his friends, nominally some fifty strong, there was perhaps no great discrepancy; but until Peel had asserted himself over the older section of the tory party, Stanley could not tell, if he joined such a ministry, how soon he might not be compelled to leave it. Whether he hoped to form and keep alive a party of his own cannot now be determined. He certainly spoke in a very whiggish tone at Glasgow in December. He assembled his followers when parliament met, and O'Connell, quoting from Canning's 'Loves of the Triangles,' nicknamed them the 'Derby Dilly, carrying six insides.' The idea of an independent party was soon abandoned, for Peel's administration, short-lived as it was, soon proved that he might well now unite himself with so progressive a party. On 1 July 1835 he, Graham, and others formally took their seats with the followers of Peel, and in 1838, at the banquet to Peel in the Merchant Taylors' Hall, he figured as one of Peel's chief lieutenants.

Stanley was now, by his grandfather's death on 21 Oct. 1834, Lord Stanley. Till 1841 he remained in vigorous opposition, criticising especially the government's Irish and ecclesiastical proposals, its Jamaica Bill, and its policy with regard to Canada; and his continual attacks on the whig tithe settlement at length compelled the government seriously to modify the disendowment portion of their proposals. He joined Peel's administration in 1841 as colonial secretary, and in 1843 supported the Canadian Corn Bill. His language with regard to it showed that he was for free trade, or practically for free trade with the colonies generally, but did not propose to apply the same rule to foreign powers. He demonstrated his great value to the government in the House of Commons by the part which he took in defending its Irish policy; but it was in urgent need of debating assistance in the

House of Lords, and he was accordingly in October 1844 called up by the title of Lord Stanley of Bickerstaffe. He explained that he was tired of the life of the House of Commons, and was afraid that his health was breaking down; but the change was probably due to the fact that he did not get on well with Peel. At any rate dissensions between them became visible. Stanley combated the arguments in favour of immediate free trade, which Peel drew from the condition of Ireland, and though he eventually agreed to the suspension of the corn laws, still, on Peel's declaration in favour of their complete and immediate repeal, he resigned. Even if Peel's course had seemed sound to him as a stroke of policy, which it did not, it involved in his eyes an intolerable sacrifice of personal consistency and principle. When Peel resigned in December 1845 and Russell failed to form a ministry, Stanley was applied to and declined, after such a break-up of his party, to attempt the task of carrying on the government as a protectionist. As he put it himself, if he took office he would have no colleagues. To protection as an economic system he was by no means indissolubly wedded, but, as he declared in a speech, which is perhaps his best, (see GREVILLE, 2nd ser. ii. 395) on 25 May 1846 in the House of Lords, protection was, in his opinion, necessary for the maintenance of the landed interest and the colonial system, the two pillars on which he conceived the British empire to rest. Naturally, therefore, it was round Stanley that there gathered that body of conservatives which revolted from Peel after the fall of his administration. Lord George Bentinck was Stanley's intimate friend, and Disraeli now entered into close relations with him; but Stanley accepted the leadership of the Protectionist party with reluctance, and for a while seems to have thought now of forming a new party by a union with the Palmerstonian whigs, and now of shaking himself free of all party ties and in a great measure withdrawing from public life. He spoke frequently and brilliantly in the House of Lords, particularly on the conduct of the Spanish government in summarily directing Sir Henry Bulwer, the British ambassador, to quit Madrid in 1848; on his amendment to the address in 1849; on the Navigation Bill, on Lord Roden's removal from the commission of the peace, for his conduct in regard to the Dolly's Brae affair (18 Feb. 1850); and on the question of Don Pacifico, when he obtained a majority of 37 against the ministry on 17 June 1850.

When Russell resigned in 1851, Stanley was sent for by the queen on 22 Feb. and gave a qualified refusal to form a ministry, first recommending that Lord John Russell should again make an attempt. Russell failed, and Stanley was sent for again on the 25th; he now endeavoured to obtain the adhesion of the Peelites, but without success. He then applied to his own supporters, but eventually, according to Lord Malmesbury (*Memoirs*, i. 278), he was baulked by the hostility of Henley and Herries, and resigned his commission again to the queen on the 27th. He explained his position in the House of Lords on 28 Feb., not without expressing some bitterness at his followers' want of courage. As yet, however, his party had hardly a sufficiently definite policy to have justified their taking office. Stanley himself was still in favour of moderate protection, though prepared to abandon any return to it, if the next verdict of the constituencies should prove to be unmistakably against it. In June his father died, and he succeeded to the earldom. On 21 Feb. 1852 Russell again resigned, and Lord Derby formed a ministry; but it was untried, and some of the members of it were not even personally known to their chief. He made his first declaration of policy on 27 Feb., carried on the government till the beginning of July, and then dissolved. In spite of the speech when he declared in the House of Lords that the mission of a conservative government was 'to stem the tide of democracy,' Lord Derby was not now himself disposed to reaction, but he was compelled to come before the country as advocating protection, without the power or perhaps the wish to restore it, and in the result was outnumbered, though not very heavily, by a combination of all the parties opposed to him. The general election of July resulted in the return of 299 conservatives, 315 liberals, and 40 Peelites. Negotiations began for the admission of Palmerston and some of the Peelites to the ministry, but they came to nothing. Instead of accepting the position frankly, Derby continued in office; the inevitable defeat came on the budget on the night of 16 Dec., and next day he resigned, Lord Aberdeen forming a ministry. Whether he gained anything by not resigning upon the conclusion of the general election may well be doubted, but he was bitterly accused of having betrayed the protectionists in not attempting the impossible on their behalf during this brief prolongation of office. In opposition he continued to follow in the House of Lords the same course as in 1850 and 1851. He opposed the policy of the government with regard to the Canada clergy reserves, and in 1853 came into acute collision with Bishop Wilberforce upon this subject (see LORD ALBEMARLE, *Fifty Years of my Life*; *Life of Bishop Wilberforce*, ed. 1888, p. 142).

When, in January 1854, parliament reassembled on the eve of the Crimean war, Derby criticised Lord Aberdeen's policy in regard to the eastern question. As it was his government which had recognised Louis Napoleon as emperor in December 1852, he might well claim, as he did, that in the government's place he would have shown such unquestionable cordiality towards France as would have persuaded the Emperor Nicholas of the unanimity of Great Britain and France while there was yet time for him to draw back. Disraeli used to declare that he knew of his own knowledge there would have been no Crimean war if Derby had been in office. Later on, however, when war appeared to be inevitable, Lord Derby gave the ministry an assurance of his general support.

When Aberdeen's government was defeated on Roebuck's motion for an inquiry into the conduct of the war, on 29 Jan. 1855, and resigned, Derby was sent for and endeavoured to form a ministry; but he told the queen that the assistance both of Palmerston and of the Peelites would be indispensable to him; and when, for reasons still obscure, he failed to secure them, he resigned the attempt. Russell was equally unsuccessful, and accordingly Palmerston became prime minister. Had Derby formed an administration exclusively among his own supporters, he would, as he explained to the House of Lords on 7 Feb. 1855, have found himself overthrown by the coalition against him of the divided sections of radicals, whigs, Palmerstonians, and Peelites. He forgot, however, or so conservatives have since maintained, that in that case he had still the resource of a dissolution, with the high probability of wide electoral support as the minister who was seeking to repair the blunders of the Aberdeen government. He attributed undue importance to the Peelites, and he thought the rout of the protectionists more complete than it really was; perhaps, too, he was personally not very anxious to again assume the burden of office. But though he was content with opposition his party was not, and it was greatly disheartened and disorganised for some years. Lord Derby resumed his old attitude towards the government in the House of Lords. He supported Lord Ellenborough's resolutions condemnatory of the conduct of the war; he attacked the terms of the peace of Paris in the debate on the address in 1856; he opposed the life peerage of Lord Wensleydale; he criticised severely Lord Palmerston's management of the lorcha Arrow question, and the government's conduct of the war of the mutiny in 1857; but during a great part of the year he appeared little in parliament. His health was impaired, his party was insubordinate, and on the whole he kept to his sports and his private life as much as he could.

When Lord Palmerston resigned in 1858, the queen again sent for Lord Derby on 21 Feb., who, after another ineffectual application to the Peelites, formed, with Mr. Disraeli, a purely conservative administration. ' No one,' says Count Vitzthum von Eckstädt (*Residence at St. Petersburg*, p. 276), ' entertained fewer illusions than Lord Derby himself as to the possibility of forming a lasting government with the forces at his disposal,' though Lord John Russell's support was secretly assured to him; but he saw that he could now do his party a service by accustoming its leading members to official business, and the nation to seeing once more an actual conservative ministry. He promised some kind of franchise measure, but he found himself in the first instance confronted with the disputes with France arising out of the Orsini plot; with Naples regarding the seizure of the Cagliari; with the United States in connection with the right of search in the course of the suppression of the slave trade; and with the difficulties connected with the Indian mutiny and the government of India. These questions were fairly satisfactorily concluded. Lord Derby's eldest son, Lord Stanley, succeeded to the India office when Lord Ellenborough resigned. The India Bill was passed. The disabilities of Jews in regard to the parliamentary oath were removed [see ROTHSCHILD, LIONEL NATHAN DE], the various international disputes adjusted, and the colony of British Columbia founded. In 1859 Lord Derby introduced a Reform Bill, since the question of reform had already been mooted by Lord John Russell, and he did not wish the conservative party to appear as stubborn opponents of all reform. Accordingly he introduced a bill to equalise the town and county franchise, but on the clause disfranchising the forty-shilling freeholders his ministry was in March placed by Russell in a minority of thirty-nine, and accordingly he dissolved parliament (April). Though he gained seats, he was still in a minority when the new parliament met. He was much attacked for his supposed support of Austria against France on the eve of the war of 1859: though the complaint of Count Beust, the Austrian ambassador, was (*Memoirs*, i. 178) that he had been too loth to commit himself, had even tried to go beyond the popular anti-Austrian feeling, and at the Guildhall banquet on 25 April had spoken of the 'criminal step which had been taken by Austria.' A vote of want of confidence was carried on the motion of the Marquis of Hartington (the present Duke of Devonshire) in June, and Lord Derby gladly resigned, Palmerston once more becoming prime minister. The queen thereupon made him an extra knight of the Garter. He was also a G.C.M.G.

He had now to consider how best to deal with the existing political situation. The attempt to reunite the party which had followed Peel had been tried and had failed. A union with Lord Palmerston had been suggested and had failed also. His own followers were numerous, but insufficient in themselves to support a stable ministry. He therefore endeavoured to come to an understanding with Palmerston by which, in return for support against the radicals, the whig government was to promise the conservatives to govern on substantially conservative lines. In the main this understanding was successful; Lord Derby, as he put it, 'kept the cripples on their legs.' Accordingly, except for criticism on Lord John Russell's foreign policy, he had little to say to the ministerial policy for several years. This state of peace was grateful to him. His health was failing and he was more and more incapacitated by gout. Knowing that, although he might upset the liberal government, he was not strong enough to take and keep their place, he was content to exercise occasional authority through the House of Lords, and to leave to Disraeli the task of maturing combinations for the next election. One of these, the understanding with the Roman catholics, he himself imperilled by one of his characteristically rash pleasantries in a speech on the Roman Catholic Oaths Bill on 26 June 1865. On the other hand, in 1864, when leading liberals and many conservatives were strongly for intervention in the German-Danish war, it was due to Lord Derby's influence, and to a great speech, lasting three hours, which he delivered in the House of Lords on 4 Feb., that the government took no active step.

When he was sent for by the queen on the resignation of Russell's administration in June 1866, Derby exchanged a position of power without office for one in which he was much less able to support the causes with which his career had identified him. He again endeavoured to obtain the support of others than his own regular followers, notably of Robert Lowe (afterwards Lord Sherbrooke) [q. v.], but failed, and took office as before as the head of a purely conservative ministry. But in his impaired state of health most of the impulse of legislation lay with Disraeli. Derby spoke on the Parliamentary Oaths Bill, and though he described the ministerial reform bill in his speech on the third reading as a 'leap in the dark,' 6 Aug. 1867, and would have preferred, if he could, to let the question alone, he felt that something must be done, and nothing better was open than household suffrage. To this view he had been steadily coming for some time, and the bill was probably quite as much his own measure as Disraeli's. Whatever else may be said of it, two things are true—that it changed the current of English history quite as much as the Reform Bill of 1832, and that its consequences were probably as little desired as foreseen by one half of those who voted for it.

Almost his last appearance in parliament was in the debate on the address at the beginning of the autumn session of 1867. In January 1868 he was again attacked by gout; in February his life was in danger, and on 24 Feb. he retired, and Disraeli became prime minister. He at the same time gave up the formal leadership of his party in the House of Lords, though he continued to take part in debate. He spoke repeatedly and with great force against the disestablishment of the Irish church, both before and after the general election. His last speech was on 17 June 1869. At the end of the session he returned to Knowsley, was again attacked by gout, and, after a lingering and hopeless illness, died on 23 Oct., and was buried in the Knowsley village church. He left three children: Edward Henry, fifteenth earl of Derby [q. v.]; Frederick, afterwards baron Stanley of Preston and sixteenth and present earl of Derby; and Emma Charlotte, who married the Hon. W. Talbot.

There are several portraits of Derby at Knowsley: one, by Harlowe, representing him as a boy of eighteen, of which a replica is at Eton and an engraving was published in Baines's 'History of Lancashire,' vol. iv. A full-length by W. Derby was painted about 1841, and another by Sir F. Grant, P.R.A., engraved and published in 1860. There is a statue of him in Miller Square, Preston; and another, in Parliament Square, Westminster, was unveiled by Disraeli in July 1874, when he summed up Derby's achievements in the sentence, 'He abolished slavery, he educated Ireland, he reformed parliament.'

Derby's reputation as a statesman suffers from the fact that he changed front so often. A whig, a Canningite, a strenuous whig leader, a strenuous conservative leader, the head of the protectionists, the opponent of democracy, and the author of the change which upset his own policy of 1832 and committed power to democracy in 1867, all these parts he filled in turn. He was not a statesman of profoundly settled convictions or of widely constructive views. He was a man rather of intense vitality than of great intellect, a brilliant combatant rather than a cautious or philosophic statesman. The work with which he was most identified, the re-creation of the conservative party after its disintegration on the fall of Peel, was Disraeli's rather than his own; and the charge of a timid reluctance to assume the responsibilities and toil of office is one that may fairly be made against him.

Derby's personality was full of charm. He was handsome in person, with striking aquiline features; in manner he was somewhat familiar and off-hand, but beneath this facility lay an aloofness from all but social equals and intimates which stood considerably in his way as a party leader. This disadvantage operated less in his earlier years. 'Although he gave offence now and then,' says Stratford Canning in 1835 (POOLE, *Life of Stratford Canning*, ii. 37), 'by a sort of schoolboy recklessness of expression, sometimes even of conduct, his cheerful temper bore him out and made him more popular than others who were always considerate but less frank.' Twenty years later, however, there is no doubt that his party had reason to complain of the way in which their leader stood apart from their rank and file. He had a beautiful tenor voice, though he knew and cared nothing about music; his delivery was stately and animated, and he was always a luminous and impressive speaker. He was one of those orators who feel most nervous when about to be most successful. 'My throat and lips,' he told Macaulay, 'when I am going to speak are as dry as those of a man who is going to be hanged.' 'Nothing can be more composed and cool,' adds Macaulay, 'than Stanley's manner; his fault is on that side. Stanley speaks like a man who never knew what fear or even modesty was' (TREVELYAN, *Life of Macaulay*, i. 242). Bulwer-Lytton, in the 'New Timon' (1845), described him as 'frank, haughty, rash, the Rupert of debate.'

Derby was a rapid and shrewd man of business and a great Lancashire magnate. In 1862 he succeeded the Earl of Ellesmere as chairman of the central relief committee at Manchester during the cotton famine, and it was to the impetus which he gave to the movement both before and after this change,

especially by his great speeches at Bridgewater House and at the county meeting on 2 Dec. 1862 (separately published), and to his conduct of its business, that the success of the relief movement was due (see A. ARNOLD, *History of the Cotton Famine*).

All his life he was keenly interested in scholarship and passionately devoted to sport. His latinity was easy and excellent, and as chancellor of the university of Oxford, in which office he succeeded the Duke of Wellington in 1852, he made Latin speeches, especially in 1853 at his installation, and in 1863, when the Prince and Princess of Wales visited Oxford, which were the envy of many professional scholars (for the latter speech see *Ann. Reg.* cv. 98). The Derby (classical) scholarship, tenable for a year, and of the annual value of about 150*l.*, was founded in 1870 to commemorate his connection with Oxford University. His blank-verse translation of the 'Iliad,' which had occupied him for some years, appeared first privately in 1862, then was formally published in 1864, and had reached a sixth edition by 1867, to which were added other translations of miscellaneous poetry, classical, French, and German, chiefly written before he was thirty. His 'Iliad' is spirited and polished, and, though often rather a paraphrase than a translation, is always more truly poetic than most of the best translations. He had a strong literary faculty, and his English prose—for example, in his report on the cotton famine in 1862—was nervous and admirable. He also wrote some 'Conversations on the Parables for the Use of Children,' 1837; other editions 1849 and 1868. To shooting and racing he was equally devoted. He constantly said, perhaps with some affectation, that he had been too busy with pheasants to attend to politics, and his ready indulgence in sporting slang, even on the gravest occasions, occasioned some misgiving to his respectable middle-class supporters. Greville, who knew him well on the turf, but neither liked nor trusted him, dwells on his boisterous and undignified manners and on the sharpness of his practices (e.g. *Memoirs*, 1st ser. ii. 374, iii. 35; 2nd ser. iii. 403, 463). He never won the Derby, Oaks, or St. Leger, though he had begun training when, as quite a young man, he managed his grandfather's racing stud, and made many efforts with many racehorses. He owned Toxopholite, which was favourite for the Derby in 1858; Ithuriel, which was got at and lamed; Dervish, and Canezou. He trained with John Scott (1794–1871) [q. v.], and would often leave the House of Lords to catch the night mail train and see his horses' gallops next morning. Still he was not unsuccessful on the turf. In the twenty-two years of his racing career, down to 1863, when he sold his stud and quitted the turf, he won in stakes alone 94,000l., and the letter which he wrote to the Jockey Club in 1857, giving notice of a resolution that a sharper named Adkins should be warned off Newmarket Heath, has always been considered a compendium of the principles that should guide the conduct of race meetings.

[Two lives of Lord Derby have appeared, by T. E. Kebbel and G. Saintsbury. Derby is also elaborately criticised in Kebbel's History of Toryism. See, too, Greville Memoirs; Malmesbury's Memoirs of an ex-Minister; Disraeli's Lord George Bentinck; Walpole's Life of Lord John Russell; Dalling and Ashley's Life of Palmerston; Martin's Life of the Prince Consort; Memoirs of J. C. Herries; McCullagh Torrens's Lord Melbourne; Roebuck's History of the Whig Ministry; Scharf's Catalogue of Pictures at Knowsley; Trevelyan's Life of Lord Macaulay; Walpole's History of England; Count Vitzthum von Eckstädt's A Residence at the Courts of St. Petersburg and London; Fitzpatrick's Correspondence of O'Connell; Hansard's Parliamentary Debates.] J. A. H.

STANLEY, EDWARD HENRY, fifteenth EARL OF DERBY (1826–1893), eldest son of Edward George Geoffrey Smith, fourteenth earl of Derby [q. v.], by his wife, Emma Caroline, second daughter of Edward, first lord Skelmersdale, was born on 21 July 1826. He was at school at Rugby, under Arnold, though not much influenced by him, and then went to Trinity College, Cambridge, where, besides taking college prizes, he was tenth in the first class of the classical tripos, and fourteenth junior optime in the mathematical tripos of 1848. Down to the time of his leaving Cambridge, he was a member of the undergraduate society known as 'The Apostles,' most of whose members became eminent in after life (LESLIE STEPHEN, *Life of Sir James Stephen*, p. 102). He graduated M.A. in 1848, and was made LL.D. on 9 June 1862, and D.C.L. of Oxford on 7 June 1853. In March 1848 he contested the borough of Lancaster as a protectionist, but was beaten by six votes, and then made a prolonged tour in the West Indies, Canada, and the United States. During his absence he was elected, on 22 Dec. 1848, to fill the vacancy at King's Lynn caused by the death of Lord George Bentinck. Often afterwards he was asked to contest other seats—for example, Edinburgh in 1868—but only once, in 1850, when he stood for Marylebone, without success, against Edwin James and Sir

Benjamin Brodie, was he tempted to leave King's Lynn. He represented the constituency continuously till he succeeded his father in the earldom in October 1869.

As the result of his tour he published a pamphlet on the West Indian colonies in 1849, followed by a second in 1851, which stated the planters' case very clearly and to their entire satisfaction. His maiden speech, too, in the House of Commons, which Peel praised highly and Greville (*Memoirs*, 2nd ser. iii. 337) mentions as giving promise of great debating power, was made, on 31 May 1850, on Buxton's motion on the sugar duties. He took his place in the ranks of the conservatives, now led by his father; but he was not naturally a party man, and in opinion approximated to the moderate whigs. He travelled widely, and was when young an ardent mountaineer. He again visited Jamaica and Ecuador in the winter of 1849 and 1850, publishing privately on his return a book called 'Six Weeks in America,' and it was while absent on a tour in Bengal in March 1852 that he received the post of under-secretary for foreign affairs in his father's first administration. He held office till its fall in December, when he went with his party into opposition. In 1855, on the death of Sir William Molesworth [q.v.], Lord Palmerston, knowing him to be at heart more of a liberal than anything else, and struck by the ability displayed in his speech on the Government of India Bill in 1853, made him the offer of the colonial secretaryship. But this proposal Stanley, at his father's instance, declined. He spoke during these years principally on Indian and colonial questions, and on such social matters as education, factory legislation, and competitive examinations. In 1855 he was 'suspected of coquetting with the Manchester party;' and, with an antagonism to war which clung to him through life, he joined Bright and Cobden in 1854 in resisting the policy of drifting into war, and supported 'The Press,' a weekly journal which was energetically anti-ministerial. He served on the commission on purchase in the army, which he strongly condemned, and supported such movements as those in favour of mechanics' institutes and free libraries, the amendment of the law as to the property of married women, the removal of Jewish disabilities, the abolition of church rates, and the creation of the divorce court.

When the second Derby administration was formed in February 1858, Stanley joined it as colonial secretary, and subsequently, on the resignation of Lord Ellenborough, took his place as president of the board of control. The conduct of the India Bill was accordingly in his hands, and when it passed he became the first secretary of state for India. In this office he came on several occasions into collision with the policy of the governor-general, Lord Canning; in parliament, though not a prominent debater, he showed talents for business, and the general success of his Indian administration added to the reputation of the government. In the discussions in the cabinet on the Reform Bill of 1859 Stanley supported the disfranchising clauses, even threatening resignation unless the measures were made more liberal (MALMESBURY, *Memoirs of an ex-Minister*, ii. 157). Going out of office again in June, he continued active in support of reforms of a moderate liberal character. He served on the Cambridge University commission, and supported the admission of nonconformists to fellowships. He presided over commissions on the sanitary state of the Indian army and on patent law.

A curious episode followed in 1862-3. On the revolution which expelled King Otho, the throne of Greece was offered to and refused by Queen Victoria's second son, Prince Alfred (afterwards Duke of Saxe-Coburg and Gotha). Thereupon the idea was seriously entertained by the authorities in Greece of making the offer to Stanley. 'The Greeks really want to make our friend Lord Stanley their king,' wrote Disraeli on 7 Feb. 1863. Stanley declined the suggestion (FROUDE, *Earl of Beaconsfield*, p. 184). He increased his reputation in the House of Commons when he seconded Lord Grosvenor's amendment to the Reform Bill of 1866, which proposed the postponement of the discussion of any reduction of the franchise until the whole of the government scheme had been placed before the House of Commons; this speech was considered 'the finest and most statesmanlike he had ever made.' Just before and at the time of the fall of Lord John Russell's ministry (June 1866), serious suggestions were made that he should form the succeeding administration; it was anticipated that he would command the support of the Adullamites [see LOWE, ROBERT, and HORSMAN, EDWARD]. Such a plan, though supported by so shrewd an observer as Delane, proved impracticable, and Stanley's father was again sent for on Lord John's resignation. In Lord Derby's third administration Stanley took the foreign office. Here his policy was as far as possible to maintain neutrality with regard to continental disputes, and by all means to avoid war. In spite of the Abyssinian expedition in 1868 he was fairly successful; he avoided war without too great concessions, and although, especially at that juncture, he, as

an untried man, found it a difficult task to follow a statesman of Lord Clarendon's experience, he filled the office of foreign minister in the main with credit. He held aloof from the war of Prussia, Italy, and Austria, mediated between France and Prussia on the Luxemburg question, and postponed a Franco-German war for a time by devising the 'collective guarantee' of Luxemburg's neutrality at the conference of London in May 1867. Somewhat, as was thought, at the cost of his reputation for humanity, he avoided interfering in the Cretan rebellion, and refused to take sides in the disputes between Turkey and Greece. He declined the Emperor Napoleon's proposal for a conference on the Roman question, and of his attitude when the French troops occupied Rome Lord Augustus Loftus says (*Diplomatic Reminiscences*, 2nd ser. i. 203): 'I cannot sufficiently extol the wise statesmanship and prudent course taken by Lord Stanley during this critical time. He was calm in judgment and free from any enthusiastic impulse, and when his opinion was formed he never deviated from it.' With regard to the disputes with the United States arising out of the depredations of the Alabama, he admitted the principle of referring the question to arbitration which Russell had declined to recognise (RUSSELL, *Speeches and Despatches*, ii. 259), and he negotiated a convention which the United States refused to ratify. In domestic affairs he was not prominent. What share he had in the Reform Bill of 1867 is uncertain. Lord Malmesbury attributes to him the form into which the bill was hastily recast on 25 Feb., just before the introduction in the House of Commons, when the tender of Lord Cranborne's resignation involved alterations in it. At any rate he cannot be altogether acquitted of inconsistency in supporting the bill after the declarations unfavourable to democracy which he had made in previous years. Stanley continued at the foreign office when Disraeli succeeded, on Lord Derby's retirement, to the post of prime minister in February 1868. He resigned with the rest of the ministry after the general election (November 1868).

Stanley was selected to lead the opposition to Mr. Gladstone's Irish church resolutions in 1869. Throughout his life, however, his leanings towards liberalism had been more marked on ecclesiastical matters than elsewhere. He had published a pamphlet as early as 1853 in favour of exempting nonconformists from the payment of church rates, and accordingly the defence he made on this occasion was somewhat ambiguous. A little later he incurred the suspicion of his party by declining to vote against the Irish Land Bill of 1870. In fact his general tendency at this time was towards projects of administrative reform. He thought that, until it had a substantial majority, the conservative party should avoid office, and seek to check the extremer measures of its opponents and support their moderate bills. He had long been conspicuous for his knowledge of and interest in such non-party matters as sanitary reform, technical education, the regulation of mines, the acquisition of people's parks, and the growth of co-operative societies, and he was surpassed only by Lord Shaftesbury in the time, thought, and trouble that he gave to them. His influence in the country generally was in consequence perhaps higher than in his own party, though even there he was much esteemed, and, had he chosen, might have led his party in the House of Lords from 1869, when his father's death conferred on him the earldom of Derby.

Disraeli took office in February 1874, and Derby again became foreign secretary. The eastern question was once more the disturbing factor in European politics. Between his conviction that the integrity of Turkey was a most important British interest and his passion for peace Lord Derby soon found himself in a position of perplexity from which it was difficult for him in office to emerge satisfactorily. At first he was sanguine of success in his efforts to preserve England from the risk of war, and, ignoring the possibilities of failure, was perhaps more tolerant of diplomatic rebuffs than the situation warranted. He was a party, but not very willingly, to the purchase of the Suez Canal shares; he accepted the Andrassy note urging reforms on the sultan of Turkey, but only after considerable delay. Count Beust, the Austrian ambassador to the court of St. James, pursued him to Knowsley, and there and in London spent three weeks in a siege of persuasion before obtaining the despatch of 25 Jan. 1876 to Sir Henry Elliot, the British ambassador to Vienna, which secured the adhesion of Great Britain to the Austrian proposals for the reorganisation of the Turkish government. Suspecting secret arrangements between Russia and Austria, he declined to join in May 1876 in the Berlin memorandum, which urged upon Turkey the necessity of fulfilling her promises of reform. In September he wrote to Elliot, then ambassador at Constantinople, ordering him to demand of the Porte the punishment of those responsible for the Bulgarian atrocities. The Constantinople conference of December 1876, which was intended to

compel reforms in the government of the Porte, was due to his initiative, and he sought in general to assist and encourage the Porte to carry out reforms, while giving it warning that military protection from England was not to be looked for should Turkey be attacked by other powers. In April 1877 Russia invaded Turkey. Public opinion was divided as to the part that England should play in the struggle. The Bulgarian outrages, on the one hand, excited in one half of the population an hostility to Turkey which diplomacy could not control, while, on the other hand, an equally large party in England, suspicious of Russia, urged an armed defence of Turkey, and was the more powerful in the ministry and among the influential classes of society. Derby's efforts to bring the Russo-Turkish war to a close failed, and in a despatch of 6 May 1877 he defined the conditions in which England must intervene and take the offensive against the enemies of Turkey. Russia's continued successes seemed to make war for England inevitable, and Derby, unready to face that possibility, found himself increasingly in disagreement with the prime minister. The result was the appearance of vacillation in the government policy. When the order was given, at the prime minister's instance, for the fleet to pass the Dardanelles on 23 Jan. 1878, Derby felt that the die had been cast for war, and tendered his resignation; but when this advance was countermanded, he returned to office. He concurred in the policy of refusing to recognise the treaty of San Stefano, by which Russia imposed her own terms on Turkey (March 1878), but disapproved of the vigorous menaces of war with Russia which Beaconsfield made thereon. Accordingly, having reluctantly supported the credit of 6,000,000*l.*, he suddenly resigned again on 28 March 1878, ostensibly, but far from solely, upon the policy of calling out the reserves (HANSARD, cxli. 1703). It was asked why, if he was only to resign at last, he had consented to resume office after his recent resignation. His attitude failed to become clearer when on 11 July his statements, in announcing his resignation in the House of Lords, and those of Lord Salisbury, who succeeded him at the foreign office, were in flat contradiction of each other. His actions certainly bore an appearance of indecision, owing doubtless to his natural disposition, in matters of emergency, to temporise rather than to strike. But his main object was at all hazards to keep England out of a European war, and it was at any rate in part owing to his efforts that that result was achieved. After quitting office, he drifted further and further from his old party ties; he opposed the acquisition of Cyprus and the first Afghan war (1879), and eventually, in a letter to Lord Sefton, 12 March 1880, he announced his severance from the conservative party, avowedly in consequence of its foreign policy.

Derby was soon accepted as a leader of the liberal party. From December 1882 to 1885 he was colonial secretary in Mr. Gladstone's second administration, and in 1884 he was made a knight of the Garter. His policy as colonial secretary was sensible, but not impressive. 'We don't want any more black men,' was one of his favourite expressions, and he therefore resisted further annexation of tropical colonies. He favoured withdrawal from the Soudan; he declined to seize New Guinea, and he supported the policy of contraction in South Africa by concluding the convention with the Boers of 1884. Though he accepted Australian aid for the Soudan, he discouraged any plan of Australian federation. He left the colonial office in the summer of 1885, when Mr. Gladstone and his colleagues resigned.

In 1886 the home-rule question led to a further change in Derby's political allegiance. From the first he disapproved of Mr. Gladstone's policy of giving home rule to Ireland, and he joined the new party of liberal unionists on its formation early in 1886. Until the Marquis of Hartington succeeded to his father's peerage in 1891 he led the liberal unionist peers in the House of Lords. Thenceforward he retired practically from active public life, and occupied himself with social questions. His last public speech was on the occasion of the unveiling of the statue of John Bright at Manchester in October 1891. In 1892 he presided over the labour commission. In the previous year, when he was severely attacked by influenza, his usually robust health had broken down, and he died at Knowsley of an affection of the heart on 21 April 1893. He was buried at Knowsley church on 27 April.

Derby held many dignified offices outside politics. He was chancellor of the university of London from 1891 till his death, was lord rector of the university of Glasgow from 1868 to 1871, and of Edinburgh from 1875 to 1880, and was a trustee of the British Museum. He was for eighteen years—from 1875 to 1893—an active president of the Royal Literary Fund, and was one of the founders of University College, Liverpool.

In his habits Derby was simple and unassuming, in manner somewhat awkward and shy. In character he was singularly cool, fair, and critical, but he was too diffident of his own powers, and perhaps too undecided,

to become a great man of action. He was unambitious and disinterested, as indeed he conclusively showed when, by leaving Lord Beaconsfield in 1878, he sacrificed the almost certain reversion of the leadership of the conservative party. His memory and his reading were alike great. He was unrhetorical in mind or speech. Though his enunciation was imperfect, he spoke impressively, and had a great gift 'of making speeches with which every one must agree, and which at the same time were never commonplace.' He was an industrious and excellent man of business, and managed his great estates very successfully. For years he showed himself in Lancashire a model chairman of quarter sessions, an active and a hopeful agriculturist, and a benevolent promoter of institutions for the benefit of the working classes. On such matters his opinions were almost those of an old-fashioned radical, for he strongly believed in self-help, and was continuously active in attacking fads and urging the views of J. S. Mill, whom he greatly admired. He lived much in his own county, spoke, like his father, with a Lancashire accent, and was on the whole popular among Lancashire men.

He married, on 5 July 1870, Mary Catherine, second daughter of George, fifth earl De La Warr, and widow of James, second marquis of Salisbury, but had no issue, and was succeeded in the title by his brother Frederick, baron Stanley of Preston. There are at Knowsley pictures of him by W. Derby as a boy, by George Richmond in 1864, and by Sir Francis Grant. The photograph prefixed to the edition of his speeches, which was taken in 1894 by Messrs. Sanderson and Roscoe, is a very good likeness.

[Mr. W. E. H. Lecky's Prefatory Memoir to Speeches of Lord Derby, ed. Sanderson and Roscoe, 1894; Times, 22 April 1893; Macmillan's Mag. xl. 180; Westminster Review, lxxvii. 493; Martin's Life of Lord Sherbrooke, ii. 51, 281; Malmesbury's Memoirs; Life of Sir S. Northcote; Memoirs of Count Beust; Pollard's Stanleys of Knowsley; Scharf's Cat. of Pictures at Knowsley. See, too, Lord Derby's Address to the Co-operative Congress at Leeds, 1881; Speech on the Irish Question, 29 June 1886; Speech on Indian Finance, 13 Feb. 1859.] J. A. H.

STANLEY, EDWARD JOHN, second BARON STANLEY OF ALDERLEY (1802–1869), was the son of Sir John Thomas Stanley, seventh baronet, and nephew of Edward Stanley [q. v.], bishop of Norwich. Sir John, born in 1766, was a considerable magnate in Cheshire, where he was for more than twenty years chairman of quarter sessions. He was elected F.R.S. on 29 April 1790, and in the following year, having paid a visit to Iceland, wrote a short 'Account of the Hot Spring' (Edinburgh, 1791, 8vo). His only other literary effort was a translation of Bürger's 'Leonora' (1796). On 9 May 1839 he was created Baron Stanley of Alderley. Lord Stanley died at Alderley Park, Cheshire, on 23 Oct. 1850. He married, on 11 Oct. 1796, at Fletching, Sussex, Maria Josepha (1771–1863), daughter of John Baker Holroyd, first earl of Sheffield [q. v.], the friend and correspondent of Gibbon. Her early letters, some of them addressed from abroad, to her girlish friends and her aunt, 'Serena' Holroyd, were printed in 1896, under the editorship of Miss J. H. Adeane (London, 8vo, with portraits of her and her husband). They refer to the period 1786–96, and contain some highly interesting glimpses of Gibbon, the Comte Lally Tollendal, and the French exiles. Several of Lady Maria's vivacious letters to the great historian are printed in Gibbon's 'Correspondence' (ed. 1896, vol. ii. passim). After his death, of which in her 'Letters' she gives graphic details, she assisted her father and William Hayley in editing Gibbon's 'Synoptic Memoirs' for publication in 1796 (*Autobiographies of Edward Gibbon*, 1896, Introduction).

Edward John, the eldest son, born on 13, and baptised 14, Nov. 1802, at Alderley, was educated at Eton and Christ Church, Oxford, where he matriculated on 18 Jan. 1822, and graduated B.A. in 1825. He entered parliament as whig member for Hindon, Wiltshire, in 1831, and, when that borough was disfranchised, he represented North Cheshire from 1832 until 1841, when he lost the seat, to regain it in 1847. For a short time Stanley held the post of secretary to Lord Durham, one of the drafters of the Reform Bill; and he was under-secretary for the colonies 1833–4, and to the home department from July to November 1834. In Lord Melbourne's second administration he was patronage secretary to the treasury from 1835 to 1841, when he was admitted to the privy council; and from June to September held the lucrative office of paymaster-general. During this period 'Mr. E. J. Stanley' was best known as the principal whip of the whig party, or, if we may believe Lord Palmerston, 'joint-whip with Mrs. Stanley.' Palmerston indeed gave the lady priority when he described her to Guizot as 'notre chef-d'état major.' There is no doubt, however, that Stanley was a most efficient whip, warmly liked by his friends, in spite of the caustic tongue which gained from some of his opponents the sobriquet of 'Ben'[jamin Backbite'. Mel-

bourne handed over the seals to Sir Robert Peel at the close of 1841, but on the return of the whigs to office in 1846 Stanley was under-secretary for foreign affairs from that year to 1852, when Palmerston was his chief. On 12 May 1848 he was created Baron Eddisbury of Winnington; two years later he succeeded to the barony of Stanley. He was president of the board of trade 1855 to 1858, and Palmerston appointed him postmaster-general in 1860. He was subsequently offered a seat in the cabinet by Mr. Gladstone on the formation of his first ministry (December 1868), but refused it on the score of health. He died at his London house, 40 Dover Street, on 16 June 1869.

Stanley married, at Florence, on 7 Oct. 1826, Henrietta Maria, eldest daughter of Henry Augustus Dillon-Lee, thirteenth viscount Dillon.

HENRIETTA MARIA STANLEY, LADY STANLEY OF ALDERLEY (1807–1895), born at Halifax, Nova Scotia, on 21 Dec. 1807, first came to England in 1814, and soon proceeded with her family to Florence, where she attended the weekly receptions of the Countess of Albany, widow of the young Pretender. She obtained popularity with the natives by refusing to dance with the Austrian officers, 'though they danced much better than the Italians;' but she admits that her own native Jacobinism was in some danger from the violent republicanism of her gouvernante. After her marriage in 1826 'Mrs. Stanley' soon became a personage. In conversation she invariably expressed herself with uncompromising frankness, but, gifted with rare social qualities, and possessed with an ardent faith in the doctrines of liberalism as then understood, she rendered very real service to her husband's party. Though a warm admirer of Mr. Gladstone, she was unable to follow him in 1886 on the question of home rule, and was the moving spirit of the Woman's Liberal Unionist Association.

A friend of Carlyle from 1839, of F. Denison Maurice, and in later years of Jowett (who paid his first visit to Alderley in 1861), Lady Stanley of Alderley, as she was known from 1850, was no less prominent as a promoter of women's education. She was one of the original 'lady visitors' of Queen's College, London, in 1848; she was an active member of the committee for obtaining the admission of girls to the university local examinations, founded in October 1862; she was a promoter of Girton College in 1865, and was an active supporter of the Girls' Public Day-school Company, originated in the summer of 1872; she was, finally, a promoter of the 'Medical College for Women,' which was initiated in October 1874, to promote the opening of the medical profession to women (see Lady Stanley's 'Personal Recollections of Women's Education' in *Nineteenth Century*, August 1879).

Lady Stanley retained her faculties until her death, at the age of eighty-seven, at Dover Street on 16 Feb. 1895.

She left issue: Henry Edward John, the present peer; John Constantine, colonel of the grenadier guards, who died in 1878; Mr. Edward Lyulph Stanley; and the Rev. Algernon Charles, domestic prelate to the pope. Of her six daughters, Henrietta Blanche married, in 1851, the Earl of Airlie; Katharine Louisa married, in 1864, Viscount Amberley; and Rosalind Frances married, in 1864, George James Howard, ninth earl of Carlisle.

[G. E. Cokayne's Peerage; Burke's Peerage; Foster's Alumni Oxon. 1715-1886; Ann. Reg. 1869 and 1895; Greville's Diary, iii. 112; Cooper's Register and Mag. of Biography, 1869; Abbott and Campbell's Life of Jowett; Times, 19 Feb. 1895; Guardian, 20 Feb. 1895; Spectator, 20 Feb. 1895.]   T. S.

STANLEY, EDWARD SMITH, thirteenth EARL OF DERBY (1775-1851), eldest son of Edward, twelfth earl of Derby, by his first wife, Lady Elizabeth Hamilton, only daughter of James, sixth duke of Hamilton, was born on 21 April 1775. His great-grandfather, Edward, eleventh earl of Derby, was descended from a brother of Thomas, second earl of Derby, and succeeded to the earldom on the extinction of the direct line in 1736 [see under STANLEY, JAMES, seventh EARL OF DERBY]. His grandfather, James, lord Strange, took the additional name of Smith in accordance with the will of his wife's father, Hugh Smith (d. 1745) of Weald Hall, Essex.

The thirteenth earl, after spending some years at Eton, went to Trinity College, Cambridge, where he graduated M.A. in 1795. He was at once brought into parliament for one of the two Preston seats at the general election of 1796 as a member of the whig party. For the previous half-century a standing dispute had existed between the earls of Derby and the corporation of Preston as to the right to nominate the representatives of the borough. From 1768 to 1795 nominees of the Derby family had held both seats. In 1796 local feeling ran high. The corporation prepared to make a vigorous effort to secure one seat, and nominated, in the growing manufacturing interest, John Horrocks, head of the well-known Lancashire firm of Horrocks, Miller, & Co., local mill-owners. The poll was kept open for eleven days, and eventually Stanley and Horrocks were elected, the former leading by a majority of thirty. Scarlett (afterwards Lord Abinger) acted on this occasion as 'assistant' to the mayor, and received a fee of two hundred guineas (WILLIAM DOBSON, *History of the Parliamentary Representation of Preston*). At the next election in 1802 a compromise, much attacked at the time, was negotiated by T. B. Bayley of Hope, by which each party obtained one seat. Stanley and Horrocks were elected, and in 1806 Stanley and Horrocks the younger. In 1807, though opposed in politics, they had a joint committee, made a joint canvas, and were elected together. In spite of opposition by other candidates, this arrangement lasted even after Stanley had ceased to sit for Preston, and down to 1826, when his son successfully contested the seat. In 1812 Stanley ceased to sit for Preston, and was elected one of the members for the county of Lancaster. He continued to hold that seat till the passing of the Reform Bill in 1832. Throughout his parliamentary career he supported the whig party without ever taking a prominent place in it, and in the House of Commons spoke little.

In 1832 Lord Grey's ministry required further strength in the House of Lords, and Stanley was called up in his father's lifetime by the title of Baron Stanley of Bickerstaffe. Two years afterwards, on the death of his father on 21 Oct. 1834, he succeeded to the earldom, and on 17 April 1839 was created a knight of the Garter. From this time forward he made no figure in public life.

Lord Stanley early displayed great interest in the science of zoology. From 1828 to 1833 he was president of the Linnæan Society, and at the time of his death had for some years been president of the Zoological Society. Between 1834 and 1847 he contributed many papers to its proceedings and many specimens to its collections. He formed at Knowsley a private menagerie of a very extensive kind, and had also a fine museum of various classes of specimens. The maintenance of the menagerie alone cost 10,000l. to 15,000l. per annum; it occupied one hundred acres of land and seventy of water, and his agents collected specimens all over the world. He gave his own daily care to it, made copious notes and observations, and successfully crossed Brahmin with shorthorn cattle. The graceful *Scops Paradisea* was named by Dr. Latham the 'Stanley Crane' after him. He had at his death 94 species and 345 head of mammalia, principally antelopes, 318 species and 1272 head of birds, not counting poultry, and his museum contained twenty thou-

and specimens of quadrupeds, birds, eggs, reptiles, and fishes. The collection was dispersed on his death; the museum was given to the city of Liverpool, where the corporation now maintains it as the Derby Museum. Some of the living animals were given to the Zoological Society in Regent's Park, and the remainder were sold in October 1851, but realised over 7,000*l.*

Lord Derby was lord lieutenant of Lancashire, and passed much of his time at Knowsley, where he devoted himself to public charity and to private hospitality. He died there on 30 June 1851, and was buried in the family vault at Ormskirk on 8 July. He married, on 30 June 1798, his cousin, Charlotte Margaret, second daughter of his aunt, the Hon. Lucy Stanley, by her marriage with the Rev. Geoffrey Hornby. She predeceased him on 16 June 1817. By her he had a family of three sons and four daughters, the eldest of whom, Edward George Geoffrey Smith Stanley [q.v.], succeeded him in the title. There are portraits of him at Knowsley, viz. by Romney as a boy, by Sir Thomas Lawrence, and by William Derby.

[Gent. Mag. 1851, ii. 190, 644; Pollard's Stanleys of Knowsley; Times, 3 July 1851; Gray's Gleanings from the Menagerie at Knowsley; Scharf's Cat. of Pictures at Knowsley; Baines's Hist. of Lancashire; Eton School Lists; Grad. Cantabr. 1656–1823.]   J. A. H.

STANLEY, FERDINANDO, fifth EARL OF DERBY (1559?–1594), son of Henry, fourth earl [q. v.], was born in London about 1559. He matriculated in 1572, at the age of twelve, at St. John's College, Oxford, and graduated M.A. on 17 Sept. 1589. As a boy of fourteen he was called to Windsor by Queen Elizabeth, though he does not appear to have held any office. In 1585 and afterwards he acted as deputy lieutenant of Lancashire and Cheshire on behalf of his father, and during the time of the alarm of the Spanish invasion in 1588 he was mayor of Liverpool, and raised a troop of horsemen. He was summoned to parliament as Lord Strange on 28 Jan. 1588–9. He was a patron and friend of many of the poets of the time, and was himself a writer of verses. Some of his pieces are contained in 'Belvedere, or the Garden of the Muses,' edited by John Bodenham, 1600, but they are without signature and difficult to identify. The only piece with which his name is positively associated is a pastoral poem, of no great merit, contributed by Sir John Hawkins to Grose's 'Antiquarian Repertory,' and reprinted in Walpole's 'Royal and Noble Authors' (ed. Park, 1806, ii. 45). Spenser celebrates him, under the name of 'Amyntas,' in 'Colin Clout's come Home again:'

He, whilst he lived, was the noblest swain
That ever piped upon an oaten quill.
Both did he other, which could pipe, maintain,
And eke could pipe himself with passing skill.

Robert Greene dedicated his 'Ciceronis Amor,' 1589, to Stanley; Nash, in his 'Piers Pennilesse,' 1592, has a panegyric on him, and Chapman in 1594, in the dedication of the 'Shadow of the Night,' speaks of 'that most ingenious Darbie.' For several years, from 1589 to 1594, he was patron of the company of actors which had formerly been under the patronage of the Earl of Leicester. While Stanley was its patron it was known as 'Lord Strange's company.' After his death it passed to the patronage of Henry Carey, first lord Hunsdon, the lord chamberlain, and became known as the 'Lord Chamberlain's company' (cf. FLEAY, *History of the Stage*, p. 41).

On the death of his father, on 25 Sept. 1593, he succeeded to the earldom of Derby and the sovereignty of the Isle of Man, with other titles and dignities, including the lieutenancy of Lancashire and Cheshire. From 1591 some of the catholics cast their eyes on him as successor to the crown in right of his mother, Margaret Clifford [see STANLEY, SIR WILLIAM, 1548–1630]. In 1593 catholic conspirators abroad sent Richard Hesketh [q. v.] to persuade him to set up his claim, promising Spanish assistance, and threatening him with death if the design was divulged. Stanley, however, delivered Hesketh to justice, and he was executed at St. Albans on 29 Nov. 1593.

Stanley died on 16 April 1594 at Lathom House, Lancashire, and was buried at the neighbouring church of Ormskirk. He had been ill for sixteen days. He appears to have died from natural causes, though there were rumours afloat that he met his end by witchcraft (STOW, *Chronicle*, pp. 767–8, giving a curious account of his illness and death). A ballad in his memory is entered in the 'Stationers' Register' (ARBER, ii. 619).

He married, in 1579, Alice, daughter of Sir John Spencer of Althorp, Northamptonshire, and left three daughters: Anne, who married in succession Grey, baron Chandos, and the notorious Earl of Castlehaven; Frances, countess of Bridgewater; and Elizabeth, countess of Huntingdon. In default of male issue he was succeeded in the earldom by his brother William [see under STANLEY, JAMES, seventh EARL].

His widow married secondly, in 1600, Thomas Egerton, viscount Brackley, better known as Lord-chancellor Ellesmere [q. v.]

F 2

She, like her husband, patronised and was praised by the poets of her day. Milton's 'Arcades' was written in compliment to her. She died at Harefield, Middlesex, on 26 Jan. 1636-7.

There are portraits of Lord and Lady Derby at Knowsley Hall (SCHARF, *Catalogue*, 1875, p. 79), and of the former in the possession of Lord Gerard and at Worden Hall, the residence of the ffaringtons. The last named is engraved in the 'Derby Household Books' (Chetham Soc.)

[The best account of Stanley is that by Canon Raines in Lancashire Funeral Certificates, p. 63. Heywood's Earls of Derby and the Verse Writers. Allen's Defence of Sir W. Stanley, ed. T. Heywood, p. xlii, Derby Household Books, ed. Raines, passim, Farington Papers, pp. 130, 136, Lancashire Lieutenancy, Corser's Collectanea Anglo-Poetica (the foregoing are all published by the Chetham Soc.); Camden's Hist. of Elizabeth, 4th edit. 1688, p. 491 ; Lodge's Illustr. of British Hist. 1791, iii. 47 ; Sir R. Sadler's State Papers, iii. 20 ; Calendars of State Papers, Dom. 1591-1594, 1595-7; Masson's Life of Milton, i. (1881 edit.) 590; Manchester Court Leet Records, ed. Earwaker, ii. 92; Collins's Peerage, ed. Brydges, iii. 80 ; Cokayne's Complete Peerage, iii. 72; Doyle's Official Peerage, i. 557, with portrait; Wood's Fasti Oxon. (Bliss) i. 250 ; Register of Univ. of Oxford (Oxford Hist. Soc.); Brydges's British Bibliographer, i. 281 ; Evans's Cat. of Portraits, i. 96, mentions a portrait engraved by Stow; Cat. of Exhibition of National Portraits, 1866, p. 51; Collier's Mem. of Edward Alleyn; Henslowe's Diary; Simpson's School of Shakespeare; Manchester Quarterly, April 1896, p. 113.]   C. W. S.

STANLEY, HANS (1720?–1780), politician, was the only son of George Stanley of Paultons, near Ower, in the new parish of Copythorne, formerly North Eling, and close to Romsey in Hampshire. His father married in 1719 Sarah, elder daughter and coheiress of Sir Hans Sloane [q. v.]; he committed suicide on 31 Jan. 1733-4; his wife survived until 19 April 1764. A monument by Rysbrach, 'in the bad taste of the time, with weeping Cupid, urn, and inverted torch,' was erected by her in the chancel of Holy Rood church, Southampton, to her daughter, Elizabeth Stanley (d. 1738, aged 18), who is panegyrised in Thomson's 'Seasons' (Summer, ll. 564 sq.)

Hans Stanley is believed to have been born in 1720, and to have been baptised at St. George's, Hanover Square, London. He was returned as member for St. Albans at a by-election on 11 Feb. 1742-3, and sat for it until the dissolution in 1747. He had no place in the next parliament, and for a time meditated abandoning parliamentary life for diplomacy. He travelled frequently in France, resided for two years at Paris, and studied the law of nations. At the general election of 1754 he was elected in the tory interest by the borough of Southampton, and represented it continuously until his death (cf. *Hist. MSS. Comm.* 11th Rep. App. pt. v. pp. 364-5; OLDFIELD, *Representative Hist.* iii. 551; cf. DAVIES, *Hist. of Southampton*, pp. 113, 203).

From 13 Sept. 1757 to August 1765 Stanley was a lord of the admiralty (cf. *Letters of Lady Hervey*, p. 265). Hearing from Lord Temple of Pitt's good opinion of him, he recounted in a letter to Pitt, 18 April 1761, his claims to employment should it be desired to open negotiations with France (*Chatham Correspondence*, ii. 116-19). He was at that time a follower of the Duke of Newcastle, but Pitt enlisted his services, 'from opinion of his abilities.' Stanley set out for Calais to meet the French agent on 24 May 1761, and early in the next month arrived at Paris as chargé d'affaires. There he remained until 20 Sept., when it became clear that the mission had ended in failure, and he demanded his passports (cf. *Chatham Correspondence*, ii. 124-42; THACKERAY, *Life of the Earl of Chatham*, i. 505-79, ii. 519-620; *Grenville Papers*, i. 362-85; and *Bedford Correspondence*, iii. 11-46). Though his despatches did not please Charles Jenkinson, first earl of Liverpool [q. v.], they are described by Carlyle as 'the liveliest reading one almost anywhere meets with in that kind.' Stanley, adds Carlyle, was 'a lively, clear-sighted person, of whom I could never hear elsewhere' (*Frederick the Great*, vi. 204). He was disappointed at not being trusted with the conduct of the negotiations when they were renewed in 1762, but he wrote the Duke of Bedford a handsome letter on their success, and, though numbered at this time among Pitt's followers, defended the peace in the House of Commons with 'spirit, sense, and cleverness' (9 Dec. 1762). Pitt paid him 'the highest compliments imaginable' (*Bedford Correspondence*, iii. 150-68).

Stanley was created a privy councillor on 26 Nov. 1762. On 7 April 1763 he sent a spirited letter to George Grenville, who was then in office, and to whom he was then attached, declining a seat at the treasury, and setting out how his claims had been neglected. Next August he was at Compiègne. He solicited and obtained in July 1764 the post of governor of the Isle of Wight and constable of Carisbrook Castle. Lady Hervey described the governorship as 'a very honourable, very convenient employment for him, and also very lucrative.'

Steephill Cottage, on the site of the present castle, near Ventnor, was built by him in 1770 at considerable expense, and he entertained there several foreign ambassadors (HASSELL, *Isle of Wight*, i. 212-19; *Guide to Southampton*, 4th edit. p. 87).

In July 1766 Pitt made Stanley ambassador-extraordinary to Russia. He was instructed to proceed to St. Petersburg by way of Berlin, with credentials to the king of Prussia. The object of the mission was to make a 'triple defensive alliance' of Great Britain, Russia, and Prussia. The appointment was hastily made without the knowledge of Conway, then leading the House of Commons, without any intimation to Macartney, our ambassador at St. Petersburg, and without consultation with Sir Andrew Mitchell, the British representative at Berlin. Stanley himself said that he had been offered the choice of embassies to Madrid or St. Petersburg, and that he had accepted the latter 'as a temporary retreat from the present confusion.' Before Stanley left England the government's overtures were coldly received by Frederick of Prussia, and Stanley never took up the appointment (*Chatham Corresp.* iii. 15-174). On 24 March 1767 Grenville made a severe attack on Chatham for his magnificent plans for special embassies, and mentioned this case. Stanley, 'a very warm man, retorted with vigour,' as he had acted 'with singular honour' in waiving his right to the appointment (WALPOLE, *George III*, ii. 438-439).

On 4 Dec. 1766 Stanley was appointed cofferer of the household, an office which he temporarily vacated in 1774, but resumed in 1776 and held till his death. He had meanwhile resigned his post of governor of the Isle of Wight, but was reappointed to that office also in 1776. Afterwards the post was conferred upon him for life, an act without precedent at the time, and 'it was said with an additional pension' (WALPOLE, *Last Journals*, i. 327, ii. 362). In November 1768 he seconded the address to the king (cf. CAVENDISH, *Debates*).

Early in January 1780 Stanley paid a visit to Earl Spencer at Althorp. On the morning of 13 Jan. he cut his throat with a penknife in the woods, and died before assistance could be obtained.

Stanley's abilities were unquestioned, and his character stood high. Lady Hervey, who knew him well, called him 'a very ingenious, sensible, knowing, conversable, and, what is still better, a worthy, honest, valuable man' (*Letters*, 1821, pp. 204-332). He was awkward in appearance, ungracious in manners, and eccentric in his habits. He never laughed,

and his speech is described by Madame Du Deffand as slow and cold without action, and as pompous without weight (*Letters*, 1810 edit. ii. 244-5). A bachelor, with 'a large house in Privy Gardens, joining to Lord Loudoun's,' and with the country residences of Paultons, which he inherited from his father, and Steephill, which he built at Ventnor, he spent most of his time away from them, 'and when at home in town commonly dined at an hotel.' He left a natural son at Winchester school. From his mother he inherited her share in the Sloane property at Chelsea. Paultons Square and Paultons Terrace at Chelsea perpetuate his connection with the parish. The estate of Paultons passed, subject to the life interest of Stanley's sisters, to a cousin, Hans Sloane, nephew of Sir Hans Sloane. Stanley was one of the trustees for the collection of Sir Hans, and was until death a family trustee of the British Museum.

Stanley left in manuscript various works, including a defence, written in Ciceronian Latin, of the English seizure of the French ships previous to the declaration of war. A poem of his in three cantos was imitated from Dryden's 'Fables,' and at the time of his death he was engaged in translating Pindar. Dr. Joseph Warton praised his knowledge of modern and ancient Greek (POPE, *Works*, 1797, ed. ii. 58-9), stating that he maintained a learned correspondence with the Abbé Barthélemy of Paris on the origin of Chaucer's 'Palamon and Arcite.' Many of his manuscript letters are in the British Museum Additional MSS. (22359 and 32734-33008), and most of his correspondence with Chatham is preserved at Paultons. Printed communications are in Belsham's 'Life of Theophilus Lindsey' (pp. 497-500) and 'Life of Viscount Keppel' (ii. 237). He was an intimate friend of Helvetius, much to the discontent of Gibbon, who complained in February 1763 of the excessive admiration enjoyed by Stanley in French society; and he was a pall-bearer at Garrick's funeral (LESLIE and TAYLOR, *Sir Joshua Reynolds*, ii. 247).

His portrait as a young man, with long face and dark hair, was painted by Sir Joshua Reynolds, and is at Paultons. In 1765 there was published a profile engraving of 'Hans de Stanley, dessiné par C. N. Cochin, le fils, gravé par S. C. Miger.'

[*Gent. Mag.* 1761 pp. 236, 475, 1764 p. 109, 1780 p.51; *Corresp. of George III and North*, i. 213; Thomas Hutchinson's *Diary*, ii. 325-9; Albemarle's *Rockingham*, i. 21-76; *Walpole's George III* (ed. Le Marchant), i. 58-9, ii. 363-5; Walpole's *Letters*, ii. 443, iv. 352, 361-2, vi. 113,

vii. 312-21 ; Grenville Papers, passim ; Barrow's Earl Macartney, i. 31-3, 413-27 ; Gibbon's Letters, ed. 1896, i. 29 ; Faulkner's Chelsea, i. 368, 373-4 ; James's Letters on Isle of Wight, ii. 531-9.]

W. P. C.

STANLEY, HENRY, fourth EARL OF DERBY (1531-1593), eldest son of Edward Stanley, third earl of Derby [q. v.], by his first wife, Katherine, daughter of Thomas Howard I, second duke of Norfolk [q. v.], was born in September 1531, and was christened on 4 Oct. (*Letters and Papers of Henry VIII*, v. 576). He was styled Lord Strange until his succession to the peerage. He was knighted on 20 Feb. 1546-7, at the coronation of Edward VI, to whom he became gentleman of the privy chamber. In April 1550 he was sent as a hostage to France, in company with the Earl of Hertford and other noblemen's sons, and about the same time a project was formed for marrying him to Margaret, daughter of the Duke of Somerset. According to his own statement, he was employed by Somerset to induce Edward VI to marry the duke's third daughter (Jane), to keep a watch on the young king's words and deeds, and to report any secret conferences he might have with his councillors. These proceedings formed one of the principal charges on which Somerset was condemned, though he denied them on oath at his trial (TYTLER, *England under Edward VI and Mary*, ii. 15-25). In July 1554 Strange was appointed gentleman of the privy chamber to Philip of Spain, and on 7 Feb. following he married at the royal chapel, Whitehall, Margaret, eldest daughter of Henry de Clifford, second earl of Cumberland [q. v.] The ceremony was marked by the introduction of a Spanish game, 'Juego de cañas,' which has been misinterpreted as a masque, with the title 'Jube the Cane' or 'Jube the Sane' (cf. COLLIER, i. 146; *Stanley Papers*, i. 12; MACHYN, *Diary*, pp. 82, 312). His wife was granddaughter of Henry VIII's younger sister, Mary, duchess of Brandon, and thus had some claim to the crown (BAILEY, *Succession to the English Crown*, pp. 171 et seq.; cf. art. CLIFFORD, HENRY, second EARL OF CUMBERLAND). But Strange himself kept these claims in the background, and never suffered any molestation on their account.

Soon after Elizabeth's accession he was, on 23 Jan. 1558-9, summoned to parliament as Baron Strange. In 1562 he became a member of Gray's Inn, and on 6 Sept. 1569 he was created M.A. of Oxford. On 26 Oct. 1572 he succeeded his father as fourth Earl of Derby and lord lieutenant of Lancashire. He frequently served as commissioner for ecclesiastical causes, and was an active member of the council of the north. He did not share his father's Roman catholic tendencies, and was a vigorous enemy to recusants in Lancashire. On 24 April 1574 he was elected K.G., and on 20 Jan. 1579-80 he was appointed ambassador-extraordinary to confer the insignia of the order of the Garter on Henry III of France (*Cal. Hatfield MSS.* iii. 39, 75, 90, 94, 96; *Tanner MSS.* lxxviii. ff. 22-36, 78-9, 234). On 20 May 1585 he was sworn of the privy council, and on 6 Oct. 1586 he was appointed one of the commissioners to try Mary Queen of Scots. In January 1587-8 he was made chief commissioner to treat for peace with Spain at Ostend, and on 23 March 1588-9 he was appointed lord high steward. On 14 April following he was lord high steward for the trial of Philip Howard, first earl of Arundel [q. v.] He died on 25 Sept. 1593, and was buried at Ormskirk. An engraving of an anonymous portrait of Derby, belonging to the present Earl Derby, is given in Doyle. He was patron of a company of actors who performed before the queen on 14 Feb. 1579-1580; it became more famous under the patronage of his son Ferdinando.

By his wife Margaret (1540-1596), with whom he had frequent quarrels, leading to their separation (cf. *Cal. State Papers*, Dom. Addenda, 1566-79, pp. 33-4, 42-3), he had four sons—Edward, who died young; Ferdinando Stanley, fifth earl of Derby [q. v.]; William, sixth earl [see under STANLEY, JAMES, seventh EARL OF DERBY]; and Francis, who died young.

[Cal. State Papers, Dom. 1547-93, and Addenda, passim; Hatfield MSS. pts. i.-iv.; Acts of the Privy Council, 1550-88; Stanley Papers and Lancashire Lieutenancy (Chetham Soc.); Machyn's Diary (Camden Soc.); Lit. Remains of Edward VI (Roxburghe Club); Lords' Journals; Strype's Works, passim; Foster's Alumni Oxon. 1500-1714; Froude's History; Collins's, Doyle's, and G. E. C[okayne]'s Peerages.]

A. F. P.

STANLEY, JAMES (1465?-1515), bishop of Ely, born probably about 1465, was sixth son of Thomas Stanley, first earl Derby [q. v.] by his first wife, Eleanor, daughter of Richard Neville, earl of Salisbury [q. v.] Edward Stanley, first baron Monteagle [q. v.], was his brother. He is said to have studied both at Oxford and Cambridge, and to have graduated at the latter university, but he was certainly M.A. of Oxford (*Reg. Univ. Oxon.* i. 46). He has been confused by Newcourt, Le Neve, and Cooper with his uncle James, who became prebendary of Holywell, London, on 26 Aug.

1458, prebendary of Driffield on 11 Nov. 1400, archdeacon of Chester in 1478, prebendary of Dunham in Southwell Cathedral, warden of the collegiate church of Manchester in 1481, and died in 1485 or 1486. The nephew's first preferment was the deanery of St. Martin-le-Grand, London, which he was given on 20 Sept. 1485, probably through the influence of his father's second wife, Margaret Beaufort, countess of Richmond and Derby [q. v.], the mother of Henry VII (CAMPBELL, *Materials*, i. 19, 125–6). In the same year he succeeded his uncle as warden of the collegiate church of Manchester, the buildings of which were considerably extended during his tenure of office (HIBBERT-WARE, *Hist. Collegiate Church Manchester*, i. 48–55). In June 1492 he received a dispensation from the pope to study at Oxford, although he held a benefice with cure of souls. In 1496 he was at Paris, and is stated to have been the rich young priest who had declined a bishopric and was living in Erasmus's house at Paris. He made tempting offers to Erasmus to induce him to become his tutor, but Erasmus refused (KNIGHT, *Erasmus*, p. 19; BUDINSKY, *Die Universität Paris*, p. 85). On 19 Nov. 1500 he became archdeacon of Richmond, and on 10 Sept. 1505 he was collated to a prebend in Salisbury Cathedral (LE NEVE, ii. 643). Early in the following year he was appointed by papal bull to the bishopric of Ely, and the temporalities were restored to him on 5 Nov. following. On 18 June in the same year the university of Oxford conferred on him the degree of D.Can.L. During his tenure of the see he took part in his stepmother's foundation of St. John's and Christ's colleges, Cambridge (BAKER, *Hist. St. John's College*, i. 66, 68, 71; WILLIS AND CLARK, *Architectural Hist. of Cambridge*, ii. 194, iii. 301, 516). He also compiled statutes for Jesus College, Cambridge, to which he appropriated the rectory of Great Shelford, and improved his episcopal residence at Somersham. He resigned the wardenship of Manchester in 1509, and died on 22 March 1514–15. He was buried in the collegiate church at Manchester, where there is an inscription to his memory. His will, dated 20 March and proved 23 May 1515, is printed in Nicolas's 'Testamenta Vetusta,' ii. 535–6. Stanley's loose morals afforded an easy mark for protestant invective (cf. GODWIN, *De Præsulibus*, ed. Richardson, p. 271). By a lady who shared his episcopal residence at Somersham he had at least two sons, John and Thomas, and a daughter, Margaret, who married Sir Henry Halsall of Halsall. The elder son, John, fought at Flodden Field on 9 Sept.

1513, was knighted, and founded the family of Stanleys of Hanford, Cheshire.

[Authorities quoted; Campbell's Materials for the Reign of Henry VII (Rolls Ser.); Andreas's Historia, pp. 108, 125 (Rolls Ser.); Letters and Papers of Henry VIII, ed. Brewer, vols. i. and ii.; Rymer's Fœdera; Le Neve's Fasti, ed. Hardy, passim; Collins's Peerage, iii. 48; Fuller's Worthies; Wood's Athenæ Oxon. ii. 704–5; Dodd's Church Hist.; Hibbert-Ware's Collegiate Church of Manchester, i. 48–64; Hollingworth's Mancuniensis; Churton's Lives of W. Smyth, &c., pp. 13, 548–9; Seacome's Memoirs of the House of Stanley, edit. 1840, pp. 70–1; Ormerod's Cheshire; Bentham's Ely; Cooper's Athenæ Cantabr. i. 16, 525; Foster's Alumni Oxon. 1500–1714; Chambers's Book of Days.] A. F. P.

STANLEY, JAMES, seventh EARL OF DERBY (1607–1651), born at Knowsley on 31 Jan. 1606-7, was the eldest son of William, sixth earl of Derby, by his wife, Elizabeth (1575–1627), daughter of Edward de Vere, seventeenth earl of Oxford [q. v.] The father, younger son of Henry Stanley, fourth earl of Derby [q. v.], passed much of the early part of his life abroad (*Stanley Papers*, III. i. 47), succeeded as sixth earl on the death of his brother Ferdinando, fifth earl of Derby [q. v.], on 16 April 1594, was elected K.G. on 23 April 1601, and served as privy councillor extraordinary from March to May 1603. For many years he was involved in ruinous litigation over his estates with his nieces, the coheiresses of his brother. On 22 Dec. 1607 he was appointed lord lieutenant of Lancashire and Cheshire, and died on 29 Sept. 1642. His portrait, engraved from a drawing in the Sutherland collection, is given by Doyle; another, also anonymous, belongs to the present Earl of Derby (*Cat. First Loan Exhib.* No. 497).

His son, who was styled Lord Strange during his father's lifetime, is erroneously said to have been educated at Bolton grammar school and at Oxford. After some private education he was sent abroad, visiting France and Italy, and learning the languages of those countries. In 1625 he was returned to parliament as member for Liverpool, where the Stanley interest had completely superseded that of the earls of Sefton. He was created K.B. at the coronation of Charles I on 1 Feb. 1625-6, and on 26 June following married, at The Hague, Charlotte de la Trémoille, daughter of Claude, duc de Thouars [see STANLEY, CHARLOTTE, COUNTESS OF DERBY]. On 27 Dec. following he was associated with his father in the lieutenancy of Lancashire and Cheshire, and on 23 Oct. in the chamberlainship of Chester. He also took part in the government of the Isle of Man, of which the earls of Derby were hereditary sovereign lords. On 7 March 1627–1628 he was summoned as Baron Strange to the House of Lords, and about the same time he was made lord lieutenant of North Wales.

Lord Strange's tastes were those of a gentleman farmer; but he was fond of the good library he possessed, and gave encouragement to minor authors. He made Peter du Moulin (1601–1684) [q. v.], who had been introduced to him through his wife's family, his chaplain, and was patron of a company of players. He was a constitutional royalist and moderate Anglican, but his aversion to court life and nonattendance at parliament occasioned some ill-founded aspersions on his loyalty. When war broke out with the Scots in 1639, he joined Charles at York; he was again at York in 1640, but saw no active service against the Scots. He took no part in the proceedings of the Long parliament, and vainly endeavoured to arrange a compromise between the two parties in Lancashire (*Stanley Papers*, vol. i. p. lxix; *ffarington Papers*, pp. 80, 85). But when war was inevitable he threw himself ardently into the royalist cause, and urged that the king's standard should first be raised in Lancashire. Warrington was selected as the rendezvous, and Strange is said to have mustered over sixty thousand men in Lancashire and Cheshire. Charles unwisely vetoed his plan, and summoned Strange to join him at Nottingham. His first commission was to recover Manchester, which was strongly fortified and favoured the parliamentary cause [cf. art. ROSWORME or ROSWORM, JOHN]. He began by utilising his friendly relations with the leading citizens, and attended a banquet in Manchester on 15 July. The roundheads, however, suspected his intentions, and he narrowly escaped being shot in retiring to Ordsall (*Manchesters Resolution against Lord Strange*, 1642, 4to; POINTZ, *A True Relation ... of the sudden rising of the Lord Strange in Lankashire*, 1642, 4to; JESLAND, *A Full and True Relation of the Troubles in Lancashire between the Lord Strange ... and the well affected of that countie*, 1642, 4to). He succeeded, however, in seizing magazines in several towns, which he was ordered to restore by parliament. He was deprived of his lord-lieutenancy, and on 16 Sept. was impeached of high treason and proclaimed a traitor by the House of Commons. On 24 Sept. he laid siege, with four thousand troops, to Manchester, but the vigorous defence compelled him to raise it on 1 Oct. By his father's death on 29 Sept. he succeeded as seventh Earl of Derby. He now entrenched himself at Warrington, but towards the end of November his troops suffered two defeats at Chowbent and Lowton Moor (ORMEROD, *Civil War Tracts in Lancashire*). On 16 Feb. 1642-3 Derby, having taken Preston, made an unsuccessful assault on Bolton. He then (18 Feb.) went on to Lancaster, which he occupied and set fire to, but he failed to capture the castle, and similar ill-success attended a second attempt to capture Bolton on his return. Early in April he repelled an attack on Warrington by Sir William Brereton, but a fortnight later he was defeated at Whalley by Captain Ashton, and retreated to York. Warrington surrendered in consequence (cf. *Manchesters Joy for Derbies Overthrow*, 1643, 4to).

Meanwhile disturbances had broken out in the Isle of Man, and Derby arrived there on 15 June to restore order. He remained till November (*Stanley Papers*, vol. i. pp. lxxxviii-xciii), but is said to have attended the parliament at Oxford during the winter. In February 1643-4 he was with Rupert in Cheshire, and he also accompanied Rupert in the following May when he beat the roundheads at Stockport, relieved Lathom House, and captured Bolton, where Derby is said to have led the last assault, and otherwise distinguished himself [see STANLEY, CHARLOTTE]. Thence he accompanied Rupert to Marston Moor (2 July), and after the ruin of the royalist cause in the north he withdrew (30 July) with his family to the Isle of Man. He was present, however, during part of the second siege of Lathom House in the autumn.

In the Isle of Man Derby established himself at Castle Rushen, and there he remained six years, entertaining fugitive royalists and resolutely refusing to make his peace with parliament. He was summoned to surrender a second time in July 1649, and was offered terms which he rejected in an indignant letter to Cromwell (printed in COLLINS, *Peerage*, iii. 67; cf. *A Declaration of the ... Earl of Derby ... concerning his resolution to keep the Isle of Man for his Majesties service against all force whatsoever*, 1649, 4to). On 12 Jan. 1649-50 he was elected K.G. at Jersey, and in the same year he was selected by Charles II to command the forces of Cheshire and Lancashire in the projected royalist insurrection. In August 1651, though he disliked Charles II's agreement with the Scots, he made preparations for joining him on his march through England. He landed at Wyre Water in Lancashire on 15 Aug. with 250 foot and 60 horse, and had an interview with Charles II on the 17th (GARDINER, *Commonwealth*, i. 434). He then proceeded to Warrington, where his endeavour to enlist presbyterian support failed through his refusal to take the covenant (*ib.* pp. 435–6). On the 25th he was routed by Robert Lilburne [q. v.] at Wigan (CARY, *Memorials*, ii. 338; LILBURNE, *Two Letters . . . containing particulars of the totall rout and overthrow of the Earl of Derby*, 1651, 4to). He had two horses shot under him and was severely wounded, but he escaped and joined Charles at Worcester on 2 Sept. After the battle (3 Sept.) he conducted Charles to Boscobel, but then proceeding northward alone he was captured near Nantwich, being given quarter by Captain Oliver Edge. He was arraigned on 29 Sept. at Chester before a court-martial, commissioned by Cromwell on the authority of an act of parliament passed in the previous August, declaring all who corresponded with Charles guilty of high treason. Colonel Humphry Mackworth presided. Derby pleaded the quarter granted him, but it was overruled on the ground that he was not a prisoner of war but a traitor, and he was condemned to death (*The Perfect Tryall and Confession of the Earl of Derby*, 1651). His petition to parliament, which was strongly supported by Cromwell ((GARDINER, *Commonwealth*, i. 402), and his open recommendation to the countess to surrender Man, proved of no avail. He then attempted to escape from Chester Castle, but was recaptured on Dee bank. On 13 Oct. he was removed to Bolton, where he was executed on the 15th. ‘Among the sufferers for King Charles the First none cast greater lustre on the cause’ (WALPOLE, *Royal and Noble Authors*, iii. 37). He was buried in Ormskirk church, and became known as the ‘ martyr Earl of Derby.’

Two portraits of Derby, painted by Vandyck, belong to the present Earl of Derby (*Cat. First Loan Exhib.* 1866, Nos. 689, 691). A copy of the first, painted while he was Lord Strange, was presented in 1860 to the National Portrait Gallery, London, by the fourteenth Earl of Derby. They were engraved by Loggan and Vertue, and copies are given in Walpole's ‘ Royal and Noble Authors’ (iii. 37) and in the ‘ Stanley Papers’ (Chetham Soc.) (BROMLEY, *Cat. Engr. Portraits*).

By his wife, Charlotte, Derby had issue five sons and four daughters (*Stanley Papers*, vol. ii. pp. cclxxxviii–ccxcii). Charles, the eldest, born 19 Jan. 1627–8, took part in Sir George Booth's abortive rising in 1658, and was restored as eighth Earl of Derby on the reversal of his father's attainder at the Re-

storation. He was author of ‘The Protestant Religion is a sure Foundation of a True Christian,’ 1668, 4to (2nd ed. 1671), and ‘ Truth Triumphant,’ 1669, 4to. He died in December 1672, and was buried at Ormskirk, being succeeded as ninth and tenth earls by his sons, William George Richard (1655 ?–1702) and James (*d.* 1736). On the death of the latter, in 1736, the earldom passed to a distant cousin, Edward Stanley (1689–1776), whose great-grandson was Edward Smith Stanley, thirteenth earl of Derby [q. v.] At the same time the sovereignty of the Isle of Man and the barony of Strange passed to James Murray, second duke of Atholl [q. v.], whose grandfather, John Murray, second earl and first marquis of Atholl [q.v.], had married the seventh Earl of Derby's third daughter, Amelia Anna Sophia.

The seventh earl was author of several works extant in manuscript at Knowsley, comprising three books of devotions, printed in ‘ Stanley Papers’ (Chetham Soc.), pt. iii. vol. iii.; ‘ A Discourse concerning the Government of the Isle of Man,’ printed in Peck's ‘ Desiderata Curiosa,’ 1732, vol. ii., in the ‘ Stanley Papers,’ pt. iii. vol. iii., and by the Manx Society, vol. iii. 1859; a book of observations, a commonplace book, a book of prayers, and a volume of historical collections (*Stanley Papers*, pt. iii. vol. ii. pp. cccvii–cccxi). Some of his correspondence is among the Tanner MSS. in the Bodleian Library.

[The elaborate memoir of Derby prefixed by Francis Robert Raines [q. v.] to his edition of Derby's Devotions (Chetham Soc.) is based on the earl's manuscripts, but is biassed and glosses over his defeats and military incompetence; other memoirs of him are contained in Seacome's House of Stanley; The Earl of Derby and his Family, 1843; Cummings's The Great Stanley, 1847, and in the Lives of his wife [see art. STANLEY, CHARLOTTE, COUNTESS OF DERBY]. See also the numerous tracts catalogued under his name in the Brit. Mus. Cat., and those printed in Ormerod's Civil War Tracts in Lancashire (Chetham Soc. vol. ii.); The First Blood drawn in the Civil War, Manchester, 1878; Cal. State Papers, Dom.; Clarendon State Papers; Journals of the Lords and Commons; Whitelocke's Memorials; Nalson's, Rushworth's, and Thurloe's Collections; Cobbett's State Trials, v. 293–324; Dugdale's Baronage, Collins's, Doyle's, and G. E. C[okayne]'s Peerages; Clarendon's Great Rebellion, ed. Macray, Heath's Royal Martyrs; Lloyd's Loyalist; Walpole's Royal and Noble Authors; Warburton's Prince Rupert, i. 299 et passim; Lady Theresa Lewis's Friends of Clarendon, iii. 338; Cary's Memorials of the Civil War; Gardiner's Civil War and Hist. of Commonwealth and Protectorate.]   A. F. P.

STANLEY, JOHN (1714–1786), musician, was born in London on 17 Jan. 1713–14. When two years old he was completely blinded by falling on a marble hearth while holding a china basin in his hand. Soon afterwards his musical tastes attracted notice. At the age of seven he was placed under John Reading (1677–1764) [see under READING, JOHN, d. 1692], and some time later under Maurice Greene. In November 1723 the boy of eleven was entrusted with the post of organist of All Hallows, Bread Street. This post he left in 1726 for St. Andrew's, Holborn, where Daniel Purcell and John Isham had recently officiated, and where counsel's opinion was taken at the time regarding the right of electing an organist (*Hist. MSS. Comm.* 7th Rep. p. 689 *b*): in 1734 he was also elected organist to the Society of the Inner Temple. He held both posts till his death, and at the Temple it was not uncommon to see forty or fifty other organists, with Handel himself, assembled to hear the last voluntary. Stanley had graduated Mus. Bac. Oxon. on 19 July 1729, at the age of sixteen; this is the youngest recorded age for an Oxford musical graduate, and has been surpassed at Cambridge only by Thomas Ravenscroft. Stanley married the daughter of Captain Arlond, in the East India Company's service, but had no issue.

Despite the loss of his sight, Stanley was a good player at skittles, shovel-board, and billiards, and also of whist, using perforated cards. He invented an apparatus for teaching music to the blind, and his own ear and memory were trained to an extent quite incredible except to those familiar with the powers of blind musicians. He could remember and perform any piece after hearing it once; even when he had to accompany a new oratorio, his sister-in-law, Miss Arlond, played it through to him once only. Musicians at this period were unaccustomed to the extreme keys; but Stanley, having once to accompany a Te Deum of Handel's in D (probably the Dettingen), and finding the organ a semitone above concert pitch, immediately transposed the entire composition without hesitation, a feat which seems to have specially impressed his contemporaries. He was usually engaged (BURNEY) to perform whenever a charity sermon was preached or a new organ was opened. He frequently played organ concertos at Vauxhall, and was also in much request as a teacher, among his earliest pupils being John Alcock, only two years his junior. He led the subscription concerts at the Swan tavern in Cornhill and the Castle in Paternoster Row, using a Stainer violin for orchestral playing, and a Cremona for solos; both were lost when the Swan was burnt. In 1752, when Handel became blind and could not accompany his oratorio performances, Stanley was recommended to him as a substitute; but Handel preferred John Christopher Smith [q. v.], objecting, he said, to the blind leading the blind. An oratorio by Stanley, entitled 'Jephthah,' was performed in 1757.

After Handel's death in 1760 Smith and Stanley entered into partnership, and continued the Lenten oratorio performances at Covent Garden. For their first season (1760) Stanley composed 'Zimri;' this was published in full score, but without the choruses. He played a concerto in the interval of every oratorio performance, and accompanied throughout. In the same year he set an ode, performed at Drury Lane, intended as an elegy on George II and a homage to George III. On the occasion of the royal wedding, in 1762, he composed a dramatic pastoral, 'Arcadia.' From 1769 to 1777 he gave annual performances in aid of the Foundling Hospital. In 1774 Smith retired. Stanley then associated the elder Linley with himself in the speculation, and produced another oratorio, 'The Fall of Egypt' (the manuscripts of this and of 'Jephthah' are at the Royal College of Music; see *Catalogue of Sacred Harmonic Society's Library*, Nos. 1833–4). In February 1779, on the death of Dr. Boyce, Stanley was appointed master of the king's band; and after Weideman's sudden death, in 1782, he led it himself. His last composition was probably the ode written by Warton for the king's birthday, 4 June 1786. It was duly performed, but Stanley had died at his house in Hatton Garden on 19 May. He was buried on the evening of the 27th in the new ground attached to St. Andrew's, Holborn. On the following Sunday an appropriate selection was performed 'on that organ on which Mr. Stanley had with much eminence displayed his musical abilities near sixty years.'

Stanley published a set of six cantatas in 1742, to words mostly by Sir John Hawkins (1719–1789) [q. v.]; they were so well received that a second set followed in the same year. He also published, besides 'Zimri,' three sets of organ voluntaries, and concertos for organ or strings, with the direction that the same accompaniments would serve for either. They are among the best English instrumental compositions of the eighteenth century. His works are occasionally represented in the programmes of organ recitals, and three of the voluntaries, arranged for the modern instrument with pedal keyboard, were reprinted in A. H. Brown's 'Organ Arrangements,' 1886. Six of Stanley's preludes and fugues are included in Pittman's 'Progressive Studies for Pianoforte, Organ, or Harmonium,' 1882. One hymn tune is used in the Temple church.

Stanley's portrait by Gainsborough, a half-length, was finely engraved by Mary Ann Rigg (Scott), and published in 1781. Another portrait, representing him at the organ, was engraved by Mac Ardell, and appeared in the 'European Magazine.'

[European Mag. 1784, ii. 171; Gent. Mag. 1760 p. 218, 1779 pp. 103, 317, 1780 p. 37, 1786 pp. 442, 512; Georgian Era, iv. 313; C. F. Pohl's Mozart in London, p. 179; Morning Post, June 22, 1786; Courtney's English Whist, p. 313; Marpurg's Traité de la Fugue et du Contrepoint, Berlin, 1756, § 2, p. xxv; Burney's General Hist. of Music, iii. 621, iv. 587, 654, 663; Grove's Dict. of Music and Musicians, iii. 690; C. F. Abdy Williams's Degrees in Music, p. 85; Ouseley's Contributions to Naumann's Illustrirte Geschichte der Musik, English edit. p. 920; Musical News, 16 Oct. 1897.]

H. D.

STANLEY, MONTAGUE (1809–1844), actor and painter, was born at Dundee on 5 Jan. 1809. His father, who was in the royal navy, was ordered to New York in March 1810, and took his family thither. By the death of his father in 1812 Stanley was left entirely to the care of his mother. She married again in 1816, and removed with her son to Halifax, Nova Scotia. In 1817 the family went to Kingston, Jamaica. Two years afterwards Stanley sailed for England with his mother and a young brother and sister, and settled with friends in Lancashire. It was about this time that he first evinced a taste for drawing, but he had already shown a predilection for the stage, and in 1824 he took a theatrical engagement at York, under the assumed name of Manby. In the summer season of 1826, resuming his own name, he joined W. H. Murray's company at Edinburgh. 'He was a very handsome young man, well suited for the parts he played, and was useful as well as a singer, being often cast for vocal parts such as Don Ferdinand in "The Duenna"' (DIBDIN, Annals of the Edinburgh Stage, p. 319). Although he acted at Dublin in 1830 and London in 1832–3, he remained at Edinburgh twelve years, taking his farewell benefit on 26 Feb. 1838, when he played Richard III. He appeared for the last time on 28 April, when he played Laertes to Charles Kean's Hamlet. 'One of his best parts was Robert Macaire, in which the mixture of broad farce and melodrama seemed

to suit him exactly' (ib. p. 373). His withdrawal from the stage was due to religious scruples.

On quitting the stage in 1838 he mainly devoted himself to painting, which he had practised while an actor. At the same time he taught drawing, elocution, and fencing, in which he was an expert, and wrote serious verse, some of which was printed in the 'Christian Treasury.' There is no record of his having had any regular art education. It is stated that he took lessons from John W. Ewbank [q. v.] in Edinburgh at a comparatively late period in his career. When not confined by theatrical or tutorial duties to Edinburgh, he visited Wales, England, and the west of Scotland, making sketches, which he afterwards completed as pictures for the Scottish Academy. From 1828 till 1844 (save in 1831-32-33) he was a regular exhibitor there, mainly of Scottish landscapes. The only picture shown by Stanley in the Royal Academy of London, 'Wreck on the Lancashire Sands,' was exhibited in 1833, while he was in London. He was elected an associate of the Royal Scottish Academy in 1839.

He secured a house at Ascog in Bute early in 1844, but died there on 4 May in that year, being buried in the churchyard. He married in 1833 an Edinburgh lady of good position; she survived him with seven children.

Stanley made his reputation as a landscape-painter, and many of his pictures have been engraved as book illustrations. Sir T. Dick Lauder's edition of Uvedale Price's 'On the Picturesque' (1842) was illustrated by sixty wood engravings from Stanley's designs. Others were engraved for his published biography by the Rev. D. T. K. Drummond. Many of them were burnt while being conveyed by railway to Edinburgh to be sold by auction, a spark from the engine having ignited the truck in which they were packed.

[Brydall's Art in Scotland, p. 469; Drummond's Memoir of Montague Stanley, Edinburgh, 1848; Redgrave's Dict. of Artists; Dibdin's Annals of the Edinburgh Stage, passim; Catalogues of the Royal Academy and Royal Scottish Academy.]

A. H. M.

STANLEY, THOMAS, first EARL OF DERBY (1435?–1504), was son of Thomas Stanley, first lord Stanley (1406?–1459), and his wife, Joan, daughter and coheiress of Sir Robert Goushill of Hoveringham, Nottinghamshire, by Elizabeth Fitzalan, dowager duchess of Norfolk (d. 1425).

SIR JOHN STANLEY, K.G. (1350?–1414), the founder of the family fortunes, was his great-grandfather. He came of a younger branch of a famous Staffordshire house, the Audleys of Healey, near Newcastle-under-Lyme; the cadet line took its name from the manor of Stanlegh, close to Cheddleton, but settled in Cheshire under Edward II on acquiring, by marriage, the manor of Storeton and the hereditary forestership of Wirral. The nephew of Sir John (who was a younger son) removed the chief seat of the elder line of Stanley to Hooton in Wirral by marriage with its heiress (DUGDALE, ii. 247; ORMEROD, ii. 411). A still more fortunate alliance (before October 1385) with Isabel, daughter of Sir Thomas Latham, made Sir John Stanley himself lord of great part of the hundred of West Derby in south-west Lancashire, including Knowsley and Lathom (Rot. Parl. iii. 205; cf. WYLIE, ii. 280). The famous Stanley crest of the eagle and child, which gave rise to a family legend, no doubt came from the Lathams (BAINES, i. 49, iv. 248; SEACOME, p. 22; GREGSON, pp. 244, 250). Their badge in the fifteenth century was an eagle's (or griffin's) leg (DOYLE, Official Baronage, i. 553; GAIRDNER, p. 412; ORMEROD, iii. 641). Sir John, who in his youth had served in Aquitaine, went to Ireland as deputy for Richard II's favourite, De Vere, in 1386, and subsequently held important posts both there (lieutenant, 1389-91) and on the Welsh and Scottish borders. Henry IV rewarded his speedy adhesion with Hope and Mold castles and a regrant (10 Dec. 1399) of his old office in Ireland. But he became officially bankrupt, and in 1401 was superseded. Steward of the household to Henry, prince of Wales, from 1403, he entered the order of the Garter in 1405. The king rewarded his services during the northern revolt of that year by a grant, first for life and then in perpetuity, by the service of a cast of falcons at coronations, of the Isle of Man, which had been forfeited by the rebellion of the Earl of Northumberland (Fœdera, viii. 419; BAINES, i. 370). In 1409 Stanley was made constable of Windsor. Henry V once more sent him to govern Ireland, and it was at Ardee, in that island, that he died on 18 Jan. 1414 (DUGDALE, ii. 248; SEACOME, p. 20). The Irish writers ascribed his death to irritation caused by the virulent lampoons of the plundered bard Niall O'Higgin (GILBERT, Viceroys, p. 301). Stanley built the tower in Water Street, Liverpool, which survived till 1821 (GREGSON, p. 172). His third son, Thomas, was the ancestor of the Stanleys of Aldford and Elford. The eldest, John, the Manx legislator, married Isabel, sister of Sir William and daughter of Sir John Harrington of Hornby Castle, Lancashire, and died in 1437

(ORMEROD, ii. 412; cf. COLLINS, ed. Brydges, iii. 54).

Their eldest son, THOMAS STANLEY (1406?-1459), born about 1406, first appears in 1424, when an armed affray between 'Thomas Stanley, the younger of the Tower, esquire,' and Sir Richard Molyneux (d. 1439) [see under MOLYNEUX, SIR RICHARD, d. 1459], constable of Liverpool Castle, at the opposite end of the town, was prevented only by the arrest of both (GREGSON, p. 171). He was knighted before 1431, when Henry VI made him lieutenant-governor of Ireland for six years. In 1446 Eleanor Cobham [see under HUMPHREY, DUKE OF GLOUCESTER] was entrusted to his keeping in the Isle of Man. From that year to 1455 Stanley represented Lancashire in parliament; he took part in more than one negotiation with Scotland, and by March 1447 became comptroller of the royal household (Fœdera, xi. 169). The parliament of 1450-1 demanded his dismissal from court with others of Suffolk's party (Rot. Parl. v. 216), but on the triumph of the Yorkists in 1455 he was made, or remained, lord-chamberlain and a privy councillor, and 15 Jan. 1456 received a summons to the house of peers as Lord Stanley. He became K.G. before May 1457, and died on 20 Feb. 1459 (Complete Peerage, iii. 68; cf. ORMEROD, iii. 337). By his wife, Joan Goushill, he had four sons and three daughters; the second son, Sir William Stanley of Holt (d. 1495), is separately noticed; the third, John, was the ancestor of the Stanleys of Alderley; the fourth, James, was archdeacon of Carlisle [see under STANLEY, JAMES, 1465?-1515].

The eldest, Thomas, who succeeded as second Baron Stanley, was born about 1435, and in 1454 had been one of Henry VI's esquires (Ord. Privy Council, vi. 223). His political attitude was from the first ambiguous. When Richard Neville, earl of Salisbury [q. v.], who was perhaps already his father-in-law, encountered the royal forces at Blore Heath in August 1459, Stanley, though not more than six miles away, kept the two thousand men he had raised at the queen's call out of the fight. His brother William fought openly on the Yorkist side, and was attainted in the subsequent parliament. Stanley himself, though he came in and took the oath of allegiance, was impeached as a traitor by the commons, who alleged that he had given Salisbury a conditional promise of support. The queen, however, thought it better to overlook his suspicious conduct (Rot. Parl. v. 348, 369). He was with Henry at the battle of Northampton in the following summer, but the triumphant Yorkists made him (January 1461) chief justice of Chester and Flint (DOYLE). Edward IV's accession was the signal for the reassertion of the Scrope claim to the lordship of Man, which William le Scrope, earl of Wiltshire [q. v.], had held under Richard II, and Stanley's title was still disputed in 1475. When his brother-in-law, Warwick, fleeing before Edward IV in 1470, made his way to Manchester in the hope of support from him, Stanley cautiously held aloof, but on the king-maker's succeeding in restoring Henry VI, he turned to the rising sun, and in March 1471 we find him besieging Hornby Castle on behalf of the Lancastrian government (*Paston Letters*, ii. 396; *Fœdera*, xi. 699). Nevertheless, after Warwick's defeat and death, Edward made Stanley lord steward of his household and privy councillor. He took part in the king's French expedition of 1475, when he characteristically seized a private opportunity of recommending himself to the favour of Louis XI (COMINES, i. 340, 347), and held a high command in Gloucester's invasion of Scotland seven years later. His services there were specially brought to the attention of parliament (*Rot. Parl.* vi. 197). Polydore Vergil credits him, perhaps rather partially, with the capture of Berwick. Not long after he married Margaret Beaufort, countess of Richmond, whose second husband, Henry Stafford, younger son of the second Duke of Buckingham, died in the same year.

After Edward's death Stanley remained loyal to his son, but though wounded in the head with a halbert during the scuffle in the council chamber (13 June 1483), when Gloucester arrested Hastings, his good fortune did not desert him, and he escaped with a short imprisonment. Gloucester is said to have feared that Stanley's son would raise Lancashire and Cheshire (FABYAN, p. 668; MORE, pp. 45-8; POLYDORE VERGIL, p. 689). With his accustomed pliancy he carried the mace at Richard's coronation, and his wife bearing the queen's train (*Excerpta Historica*, pp. 380, 384). He remained steward of the household, and succeeded Hastings as knight of the Garter. His wife was deeply engaged in Buckingham's rising [see STAFFORD, HENRY, second DUKE OF BUCKINGHAM] on behalf of her son, Henry Tudor, earl of Richmond; but the wary Stanley avoided committing himself, and actually improved his position by the collapse of the revolt. Richard must 'have known him well enough to feel sure that he would not turn traitor until he could do so with the minimum of risk. He accepted his assurances of loyalty, and ap-

pointed him (16 Dec. 1483) constable of England in Buckingham's place. Stanley undertook to put a stop to his wife's intrigues, 'keeping her in some secret place at home, without having any servant or company,' and her estates were transferred to him for life (HALL, p. 398; *Rot. Parl.* vi. 250). In 1484 Richard employed him in a Scottish mission. No one except the Dukes of Norfolk and Northumberland profited more by Richard's bounty (RAMSAY, ii. 534). But Stanley could not but feel that Richard's throne was insecure, and that in any case his own position would be much safer with his stepson wearing the crown. Not long before Richmond's landing, the 'wily fox' (HALL) asked and obtained leave to go home to Lancashire on private affairs. Richard apparently suspected nothing at first, for on hearing that Richmond was likely to land in Wales, he ordered Stanley and his brother to be prepared to take the field against the rebels (GAIRDNER, p. 287). But his prolonged absence at last roused suspicion, and he received peremptory orders either to come to the king at Nottingham himself or send his son, Lord Strange. He sent his son, but when news reached Richard that Richmond was marching unhindered through North Wales, of which Sir William Stanley (d. 1495) [q. v.] was justiciar, he ordered the father imperatively to join him at once. Stanley excused himself, however, on the plea that he was ill of the sweating sickness. Strange's futile attempt to escape from court, and his admission that he and his uncle were in league with Richmond, made Stanley's position still more delicate, though his son offered to guarantee his fidelity if his own life were spared (*Cont. Croyl. Chron.* p. 573). Richmond reckoned on the support of both Stanleys, but the elder was obliged to temporise, if only to save his son. The two brothers were playing much the same game as they had done at Blore Heath a quarter of a century before. Richmond was pretty sure of Sir William, who had been proclaimed a traitor. But Lord Stanley, who had thrown himself with five thousand men between the two approaching armies, evacuated Lichfield before Henry, and after a secret interview with him at Atherstone (20 Aug.) he marched on ahead to Bosworth. He selected an ambiguous position and returned an evasive answer when Richmond begged him to join forces before the battle began. He took no part in the action, hanging between the two armies, and it was his brother's intervention which gave Henry the victory. It was he, however, who placed the crown, taken from Richard's corpse, upon the victor's head. Richard had given orders for his son's execution, but they had been ignored (POLYDORE VERGIL, p. 563; cf. BAINES, i. 436).

Stanley's services were duly rewarded. The forfeited estates of the Pilkingtons (between Manchester and Bury) and several other Lancashire families swelled his possessions, and on 27 Oct. following he was created Earl of Derby; the title was taken from the county in which he had no lands, and not from the hundred of West Derby, in which the bulk of his estates lay (Complete Peerage, iii. 69). He purchased the Yorkshire and Axholme estates of the Mowbrays from William, marquis of Berkeley, for whose soul he provided for prayers at Burscough Priory in his will (STONEHOUSE, Isle of Axholme, p. 140; DUGDALE, ii. 249).

Stanley figured in the coronations of Henry and Elizabeth of York as one of the commissioners for executing the office of lord high steward (LELAND, Collectanea, iv. 225). Henry confirmed him in his posts of constable of England (5 March 1486), high steward of the duchy of Lancaster, and high forester north of Trent, adding the constableship of Halton Castle, Cheshire, the receivership of the county palatine of Lancaster, and other lucrative positions (Rot. Parl. vi. 373). He was godfather to Prince Arthur, and in July 1495 the king and queen paid him a visit of nearly a month's duration at Knowsley and Lathom (Excerpta Historica, p. 104). He enlarged Knowsley House and built a bridge at Warrington for the occasion (GREGSON, p. 230). Henry probably intended the honour as an assurance that he dissociated Derby from the treason of his brother, who had perished on the scaffold in the previous February. He died at Lathom on 29 July 1504, and was buried with his ancestors in the neighbouring priory of Burscough.

His portrait at Knowsley, engraved in Baines's 'History of Lancashire,' shows a long thin face, with a full beard.

Derby married twice: his first wife was Eleanor Neville, daughter of Richard Neville, earl of Salisbury [q. v.]; they were married before 1460, and she died between 1464 and 1473 (Rot. Parl. v. 545, vi. 46). By her he had six sons, several of whom died young, and four daughters. George, the eldest surviving son, married Joan, only child of Lord Strange (d. 1477) of Knockin in the march of Wales, and in her right was summoned to the House of Lords under that title from 1482; Henry VII made him a knight of the Garter (1487) and a privy councillor. He died on 5 Dec. 1497 ('at an

ungodly banquet, alas! he was poisoned,' SEACOME, p. 36) at Derby House, St. Paul's Wharf, London, whose site is now occupied by the Heralds' College, and was buried with his mother at St. James's, Garlickhithe. His widow died on 20 March 1514. Thomas, eldest of four sons, became second earl of Derby [see under STANLEY, EDWARD, third EARL OF DERBY]. Two younger sons of Derby—Edward, lord Monteagle, and James, bishop of Ely—are separately noticed.

Derby's second wife (c. 1482) was Margaret Beaufort, countess of Richmond [q. v.], then widow of Sir Henry Stafford (d. 1481).

Derby was a benefactor of Burscough priory, in which he erected a tomb with effigies of himself and his two wives, and placed images of his ancestors up to his great-grandfather in the arches of the chancel (DUGDALE, ii. 249).

[The early history of the Stanleys received a romantic colouring in the 'Song of the Lady Bessy' by Humphrey Brereton, a retainer of the first Earl of Derby, and the metrical family chronicle said to have been written about 1562 by Thomas Stanley, bishop of Sodor and Man [see under STANLEY, EDWARD, 1460?–1523]. The metrical history supplied Seacome (Memoirs of the House of Stanley, 1741; 7th ed. 1840) with the romantic details in the early life of the first Sir John Stanley which passed into the short histories of the family by Ross (1848), Draper (1864), and others. See also Rotuli Parliamentorum; Ordinances of the Privy Council, ed. Nicolas; Rymer's Fœdera, orig. edit.; Polydore Vergil's Anglica Historia; More's Richard III, ed. Lumby; Fabyan and Hall's Chronicles, ed. Ellis; Continuation of the Croyland Chronicle, ed. Gale, 1691; Paston Letters, ed. Gairdner; Comines's Memoirs, ed. Dupont; Dugdale's Baronage; G. E. C[okayne]'s Complete Peerage; Ormerod's History of Cheshire, ed. Helsby; Baines's History of Lancashire; Gregson's Portfolio of Fragments relating to the History of Lancashire, 1817; Leland's Collectanea, ed. Hearne; Bentley's Excerpta Historica, 1831; Gairdner's Richard III; Ramsay's Lancaster and York; Wylie's History of Henry IV; Palatine Note Book, iii. 161; Stanley Papers (Chetham Soc.); Hutton's Bosworth Field, 1813.] J. T-T.

STANLEY, THOMAS (1625–1678), author, born at Cumberlow, Hertfordshire, in 1625, was only son of Sir Thomas Stanley, knt., of that place, and of Leytonstone, Essex, by his second wife, Mary, daughter of Sir William Hammond of St. Albans, near Dover (cf. CARTER, Analysis of Honour, 1660; Visitation of Essex, 1634, Harl. Soc. p. 493). His father was grandson of Thomas Stanley, a natural son of Edward Stanley, third earl of Derby [q. v.] His mother's family brought him into lineal relations with many accomplished writers of verse. Her brother was William Hammond [q. v.], and through her grandmother, Elizabeth Aucher of Bishopsbourne, Kent, she was cousin to the poet Richard Lovelace [q.v.] William Fairfax, son of Edward Fairfax, the translator of Tasso, directed his early education in his father's house, and he soon became not merely an excellent classical scholar, but an enthusiastic student of French, Spanish, and Italian poetry. On 22 June 1639, at the age of thirteen, he entered Pembroke Hall, Cambridge, as a gentleman commoner (*College Reg.*), matriculating 13 Dec. He graduated M.A. in 1641, and was incorporated in the same degree at Oxford on 14 July 1640. An early and prosperous marriage did not interrupt his devotion to study. After some years spent in foreign travel (mainly in France), he retired, towards the close of the civil war, to lodgings in the Middle Temple, and engaged in literary work. He cultivated literary society, and his wealth enabled him to aid many less fortunate men of letters. His closest literary friends were Sir Edward Sherburne [q. v.], John Hall (1627–1656) [q. v.] of Durham, and James Shirley [q. v.], the dramatist, all of whom he relieved in their necessity. Sherburne dedicated to him his 'Salmacis' (1651). To him and Sherburne conjointly, Edward Phillips (1630–1696?) [q.v.] dedicated his 'Theatrum Poetarum' (1675). Hall dedicated to him as 'his dearest friend' his 'Poems' in 1646, and inserted in the volume three pieces addressed to his friend and patron. Other intimate associates were his mother's brother William Hammond [q. v.] and his cousins Richard Lovelace [q. v.] and Dudley Posthumus Lovelace, the latter's brother; Hammond and Richard Lovelace each wrote a poem in honour of his wedding, while another appeared in Jordan's 'Forest of Fancie' (cf. GAMBLE, *Second Book of Ayres*, 1659).

Stanley's linguistic faculty and lyric gifts were shown to advantage in his initial volume, 'Poems' by Thomas Stanley, esq., 1647, dedicated to Love. Many of the verses celebrate Chariessa, Celia, Doris, and other imaginary mistresses. Succeeding pieces eulogise Hammond, Shirley the dramatist, and Sir Edward Sherburne. Among the foreign writers, translations of whose verse were included in the volume, are Guarini, Marino, Tasso, Lope de Vega, and Petrarch. One poem (p. 42) is in the metre of Tennyson's 'In Memoriam.' There followed in 1649 another volume of translations, entitled 'Europa: Cupid Crucified (by Ausonius): Venus Vigils' (London, by W. W., for Humphrey Moseley, 1649). At the same date there

appeared in yet a third volume two translations in prose interspersed with verse: 'Aurora, Ismenia, and the Prince,' by Don Juan Perez de Montalvan, and 'Oronta, the Cyprian Virgin,' by Signor Girolamo Preti; a second edition, with additions, was dated 1650. Finally, in 1651, Stanley reissued, in a fourth volume, all his previously published verse, with the addition of his classical rendering of Anacreon's odes and other translations. This charming volume was divided into five sections, each introduced by a new title-page. It opens with the title 'Poems, by Thomas Stanley, esq.: printed in the year 1651'—a reprint of the volume of 1647. The second title-page runs: 'Anacreon; Bion; Moschus; Kisses by Johannes Secundus; Cupid Crucified by Ausonius; Venus' Vigil Incerto Authore.' The third title-page introduces 'Excitations,' a learned appendix of notes, chiefly textual, on the preceding translations, which Stanley avers 'were never further intended but as private exercises of the languages from which they are deduced.' The fourth title-page runs: 'Sylvia's Park, by Theophil; Acanthus Complaint by Tristran; Oronta by Preti; Echo by Marino; Love's Embassy by Boscan; The Solitude by Gongara.' The fifth and last title-page introduces 'A Platonick Discourse upon Love written in Italian by John Picus Mirandola in explanation of a Sonnet by Hieronimo Benivieni.' To some copies is appended a sixth title-page, introducing the prose novel of Montalvan which had been already published with Preti's 'Oronta' in 1649 and 1650.

Stanley subsequently wrote verses which were set to music by John Gamble (*d.* 1687), and published by him in his 'Ayres and Dialogues' (1656). A commendatory poem by Richard Lovelace was there inscribed to 'My noble kinsman, Thomas Stanley, esq., on his lyrick poems,' and another poem by Dudley Lovelace, Richard's youngest brother, 'to my much honoured cozen Mr. Stanley.' A song by Stanley, 'O turn away those cruel eyes,' figures in 'The Second Book of Ayres' by Henry Lawes, 1655. In 1657 Stanley prepared for publication extracts from the Εἰκὼν Βασιλικὴ, under the title of 'Psalterium Carolinum: the Devotions of his Sacred Majestie in his Solitude and Sufferings, rendered in Verse.'

Stanley's original poems and translations from the Latin and Greek were collected and edited by Sir Samuel Egerton Brydges in two volumes, published respectively in 1814 and 1815. His translations of 'Venus' Vigil' and Johannes Secundus's 'Kisses' were reissued in Bohn's 'Classical Library.' Stanley's translation of 'Anacreon' with the Greek text, was reprinted by Mr. A. H. Bullen in 1893.

But Stanley soon turned from poetry to a serious study of Greek philosophy. At the suggestion of Sir John Marsham [q. v.], the chronologer, who married his mother's sister, he produced his 'History of Philosophy,' of which the first volume appeared in 1655 (dedicated to Marsham), the second in 1656, a third in 1660, and a fourth, entitled 'The History of Chaldaick Philosophy,' in 1662. The work consisted of a long series of biographies, chiefly of the Greek philosophers from Thales to Carneades. The greater part was derived from Diogenes Laertius; but the analysis of the Platonic philosophy was from Alcinous, and the account of the Peripatetic system was derived directly from Aristotle. The doctrine of the Stoics was elaborately worked up from various authorities. Stanley on the whole brought a good deal from an almost untrodden field; but he was an historian rather than a critic of philosophy (HALLAM). The compilation long ranked as a standard authority. It was republished in one volume in 1687 (3rd ed. 1700, and 4th ed. with memoir of author, 1743). Portions of the work were printed in French at Paris in 1660. Vols. i-iii. of the first edition were translated into Latin with additions, by Godfrey Olearius (Leipzig, 1711, 4to). Vol. iv. was rendered into Latin by John Le Clerc and issued at Amsterdam, with Le Clerc's notes and a dedication to Bishop Burnet (1680, 8vo); it reappeared in Le Clerc's 'Opera Philosophica,' vol. ii.

Stanley, after completing his 'History of Philosophy,' worked with no less success on an edition of Æschylus. This appeared in 1663 in folio with Latin translation and notes, and was dedicated to Sir Henry Newton [q. v.] The date 1664 appears in some copies. Stanley's edition of Æschylus was superior to any that had preceded it; it was long regarded at home and abroad as the standard edition, and remains 'a great monument of critical learning.' It was republished in De Pauw's edition (2 vols. 4to, 1745). The text and Latin translation reappeared at Glasgow in 1746, and the text was twice corrected by Porson, for reissue in 1795 and 1806 respectively. The Latin version was reissued separately in 1819. The whole edition was revised and enlarged (1809-16 in 4 vols.) by Samuel Butler (1774-1839) [q. v.], and elicited some adverse criticism from Charles James Blomfield [q. v.], who charged Stanley with borrowing at least three hundred of his many emendations of the text from notes

which he had derived from Casaubon, Dorat, and Scaliger. A controversy followed on this and other points connected with Butler's revision of Stanley's text, and in it J. H. Monk, as well as Blomfield and Butler, took part (cf. Blomfield in *Edinburgh Review*, 1809, 1812, and in *Museum Criticum*, ii. 498; Monk's letter to the Rev. S. Butler; *Quarterly Review*, 1821). Stanley's reputation was not appreciably injured.

Stanley died at his lodgings in Suffolk Street, Strand, on 12 April 1678, and was buried in the church of St. Martin-in-the-Fields. His wife Dorothy was daughter and coheiress of Sir James Envon, baronet, of Flower, Northamptonshire. By her he had a son Thomas, born in 1650, who was admitted a fellow-commoner at Pembroke College, Cambridge, on 6 April 1665, and published in the same year a translation of 'Claudius Ælianus Various Histories,' London, 1665, 8vo; this was dedicated, like his father's edition of Æschylus, to Sir Henry (Puckering) Newton [q. v.] Sir Edward Sherburne prefixed verses.

Stanley's genuine literary gifts and his versatile employment of them procured him a wide contemporary reputation. Winstanley calls him 'the glory and admiration of his time.' Pope invariably spoke of him with respect (SPENCE, *Anecdotes*, p. 198). William Wotton [q. v.] eulogised him at the end of his edition of Scævola St. Marthe's 'Elogia Gallorum' (1722). His classical scholarship was of a high order. His translation of 'Anacreon' satisfies almost every requirement. It is as agreeable reading as the version of Thomas Moore, and adheres far more closely to the original.

Stanley left in manuscript many volumes of notes on classical authors, which were acquired by Bishop Moore, and are now in the University Library at Cambridge. These include eight folio volumes of 'Commentaries on Æschylus;' adversaria on passages in Sophocles, Euripides, Callimachus, Hesychius, Juvenal, Persius, and others; prelections in Theophrastus's characters, and an essay on the first-fruits and tenths of the spoil said in the Epistle to the Hebrews to have been given by Abraham to Melchisedek. He obviously was especially interested in Callimachus. In the British Museum there is a copy of Callimachus's 'Cyrenæi Hymni' (1577), with manuscript notes by Stanley. Bentley was accused of using without acknowledgment Stanley's comments on Callimachus (see *A Short Account of Dr. Bentley's Humanity and Justice to those Authors who have written before him, with an honest Vindication of Thomas Stanley, Esq., and his*

Notes on Callimachos, London, 1699, 8vo; addressed to Boyle).

Stanley's portrait, painted by Sir Peter Lely, is in the National Portrait Gallery, and an engraving by William Faithorne forms the frontispiece of the 'History of Philosophy.'

[Sir S. E. Brydges's Memoir prefixed to his reprint of Stanley's Poems and Translations in 1814; Memoir prefixed to Stanley's History of Philosophy, 1743; Anacreon, with Thomas Stanley's translation edited by Mr. A. H. Bullen, 1893; Park's British Bibliographer, iii. 360 seq.; Lovelace's Poems, ed. W. C. Hazlitt, pp. 227, 247; Hallam's Literature of Europe, iii. 250, 304.]   S. L.

STANLEY, VENETIA (1600–1633), afterwards wife of Sir Kenelm Digby. [See under DIGBY, SIR KENELM.]

STANLEY, SIR WILLIAM (d. 1495), lord chamberlain to Henry VII, was the second son of Thomas Stanley, first lord Stanley, by Joan, daughter of Sir Robert Goushill of Hoveringham, Nottinghamshire, and his wife, Elizabeth Fitzalan, dowager duchess of Norfolk. Thomas Stanley, first Earl of Derby [q. v.], was his elder brother. Stanley was born after 1435, and made his first known public appearance while still a squire in 1459 as a Yorkist partisan, taking part in 'the distressing of King Henry's true liege people at Bloreheath,' where two of his brothers-in-law, Sir William Troutbeck and Sir Richard Molyneux [q. v.] of Sefton, fell on the opposite side. In the ensuing parliament Stanley was attainted with other Yorkists (*Rot. Parl.* v. 348, 369). As he did not fall into the hands of the government, we may perhaps assume that he escaped abroad, like the rest, after the rout of Ludford. The accession of Edward IV brought him his reward; the office of chamberlain of Chester was at once conferred upon him, and he apparently retained it until his death (ORMEROD, i. 60). At York, after the battle of Hexham in 1464, the king made him a further grant under the great seal, and in November 1465 bestowed upon him the castle and lordship of Skipton and other lands in Craven forfeited by Lord Clifford, who fell on the Lancastrian side at Towton (*Rot. Parl.* v. 530, 582). When Edward returned from his temporary exile in 1471, Stanley joined him with three hundred men at Nottingham (WARKWORTH, p. 14, but cf. *Arrival of Edward IV*, p. 7). He was subsequently steward of the Prince of Wales's household (RAMSAY, ii. 482). Richard III did his best to retain Stanley's support; he gave him Buckingham's for-

feited office of justiciar of North Wales (the 'Croyland Continuator' says chamberlain) and a great landed position there by the grant of the castle and lordship of 'Lione otherwise called the Holte,' i.e. Holt Castle on the Dee, with a moiety of Bromfield, Yale, and four other marcher lordships, three whole manors, and a moiety of seventeen others, among them Wrexham and Ruabon (*Rot. Parl.* vi. 316). He seems also to have had an interest in the lordship of Chirk, whose castle he repaired (LELAND, *Itinerary*, v. 36; GAIRDNER, p. 402). These lands, which comprised a great part of what is now East Denbighshire, he claimed in the next reign to have obtained by exchange for others of 'great value.' This vagueness and the obvious motive for such a statement render it rather doubtful, but he may possibly have surrendered Skipton in return for these Welsh grants. Henry VII, as soon as he gained the throne, certainly restored Skipton to Lord Clifford, 'the shepherd lord.' At Ridley, a few miles north, under the shadow of the Peckforton Hills, Stanley built himself 'the fairest gentleman's house in al Chesttreshyre' (LELAND, v. 81, vol. vii. pt. i. p. 43). From here one September he wrote to his 'cousin' Piers Warburton of Arley, excusing himself from a promise to kill a buck in his park, 'beyng so besy with olde Dyk I can have no layf thereunto' (ORMEROD, ii. 301). He did not hesitate to betray 'olde Dyk' when the time came. Early in August 1485 Henry of Richmond crossed a corner of North Wales unmolested, and at Stafford Stanley, who had three thousand 'red coats' with his livery of the hart's head not far away, came to an understanding with the invader. Henry had a further interview with him and his brother, Lord Stanley, at Atherstone two days before the decisive battle of Bosworth (POLYDORE VERGIL, p. 224; GAIRDNER, p. 414). Though already denounced to Richard by his nephew, Lord Strange, and proclaimed a traitor at Coventry and elsewhere, Stanley would not unite his force with Richmond's, and on 22 Aug. pitched his camp on Hanging Hill, between Bosworth and Shenton, some distance from both the main bodies (HUTTON, App. p. 245; cf. HALL, p. 414). Yet he can hardly have hoped to recover Richard's favour had the day gone against Henry, and it was when the king's desperate charge seemed to make this likely that Stanley brought his three thousand men into action and so decided the battle (*ib.* pp. 418–19). If his real object was to place Henry more clearly and deeply in his debt, it was certainly attained. He became lord chamberlain and knight of the Garter, and was confirmed in possession of his Welsh estates.

Stanley's fall ten years after came no doubt as a surprise to most people, but Henry long before entertained suspicions of the man who had in turn betrayed Lancaster and York (BREWER, *Letters and Papers*, iii. 490). It is a curious coincidence, if no more, that the informer who denounced him at the end of 1494 as an accomplice of Perkin Warbeck should have been Sir Robert Clifford, uncle of the young lord whose property at Skipton he had for a time usurped (DUGDALE, i. 342). How deeply he involved himself with Warbeck we do not know; he must surely have done more than declare that 'if he knew certainly that the young man [Warbeck] was the undoubted heir of King Edward IV, he would never fight or bear armour against him.' On 6 Feb. 1495 he was 'found guilty of treason by a quest of divers knights and worshipful gentlemen,' and on the 16th beheaded on Tower Hill (*Cott. MS.* Vitellius, A. xvi. 152-3; FABYAN, p. 685; POLYDORE VERGIL; HALL, p. 469; BUSCH, p. 95). The more cruel part of an execution for treason was dispensed with. Henry defrayed the cost of his burial at Sion (*Excerpta Historica*, pp. 101-2). It was afterwards believed that forty thousand marks in ready money, plate, and jewels were found in Holt Castle, and Bacon, in his 'Life of Henry VII,' estimates Stanley's income at three thousand a year.

Stanley was at least twice married. In 1465 he married Joan, daughter of the first Viscount Beaumont, and widow of John, lord Lovel (*Rot. Parl.* v. 582; *Complete Peerage*, v. 165). He subsequently (after 1470) married Elizabeth, daughter of Thomas Hopton of Hopton, Shropshire, who had already survived two husbands, Sir Roger Corbet of Moreton-Corbet, Shropshire, and John Tiptoft, earl of Worcester [q. v.] (*ib.* vii. 402). The pedigrees following Sir Peter Leycester are in error respecting his marriage (cf. BAINES, *Hist. of Lancashire*, iv. 10; ORMEROD, i. 412). Stanley left three children—a son and two daughters. The son, Sir William Stanley, married Joan, heiress of the Masseys of Tatton in Cheshire, and died in or about 1498; one daughter, Joan, married Sir John Warburton of Arley, and the other, Catherine, Thomas Coeat of Holt.

A three-quarter-length portrait of Stanley in richly ornamented armour is preserved at Wentworth House, Yorkshire, and was engraved in Baines's 'Lancashire' (iv. 19). He is represented with a thinnish face and short beard.

[See Rot. Parl.; Hall and Fabyan's Chronicles, ed. Ellis; Polydore Vergil, Warkworth's Chronicle and Arrival of Edward IV (Camden Soc.); Bentley's Excerpta Historica, 1831; Stanley Papers (Chetham Soc.' vol. xxix.); Ormerod's Hist. of Cheshire, 1876; Dugdale's Baronage; Complete Peerage by G. E. C[okayne]; Gairdner's Richard III; Ramsay's Lancaster and York; Busch's England under the Tudors, Engl. tr.; other authorities in the text. Stanley is one of the heroes of the contemporary 'Song of Lady Bessy' (Elizabeth of York) written by a Stanley retainer, Humphrey Brereton, and edited by Halliwell for the Percy Society in 1847.]

J. T-T.

STANLEY, SIR WILLIAM (1548-1630), adventurer, was eldest son of Sir Rowland Stanley of Hooton and Storeton, Cheshire, the head of the senior branch of the house of Stanley. Sir Rowland for many years took a prominent place in his native county, of which he was sheriff in 1576; he died in 1612, aged 96, the oldest knight in England. William Stanley, born in 1548, in all probability at Hooton, was brought up as a Roman catholic. At the age of twelve he was married to Ann Dutton, a bride of ten, but the union was dissolved in 1565 (FURNIVALL, *Child Marriages in the Diocese of Chester*, pp. 47-9). After this marriage the youth was sent to school with 'Dr. Standish at Lathom,' whence he entered the 'service' of his kinsman, Edward Stanley, third earl of Derby [q. v.]. Soon afterwards he crossed to the Netherlands and embarked on his adventurous career. He took service as a volunteer under Alva, the Spanish general, in 1567. Stanley quitted the Spanish service about 1570, and joined Elizabeth's forces in Ireland, where he served for fifteen years (cf. *Cal. Hatfield MSS.* i. 567). In 1579, as one of Sir William Drury's captains in the campaign against the followers of the Earl of Desmond, he assisted in an inroad into Limerick, and for his gallantry was knighted by Drury at Waterford. He took part in the battle of Monasternenagh, and distinguished himself in the defence of Adare. In 1580 he was sent to England to enlist troops, which he led to Munster; but he was speedily recalled by Lord-deputy Grey to assist in putting down the rebellion which had broken out in the Pale [see GREY, ARTHUR, fourteenth LORD GREY DE WILTON]. Through the greater part of 1581 he was engaged in Wicklow, doing great execution against the O'Tooles and the Kavanaghs. Stanley received a commission from Grey, 30 Aug. 1581, to follow the latter, and his 'courage and toilsome travail' throughout the whole campaign won the highest commendation (*ib.* ii. 427). On the discharge of his troops at the end of the year, he repaired to England, and prayed Burghley for fresh employment. At the beginning of 1583 he was sent back to Ireland, where the Geraldines were again giving trouble. He was appointed by Ormonde to the command of a garrison at Lismore, and at the same time made constable of Castlemaine, which he intended 'to make a town of English.' He took part in hunting down Desmond and Fitzgerald of Imokelly and in thoroughly subduing Munster. As a reward for his services he supplicated Burghley and Walsingham (15 March 1584) to make him president of Connaught. This request was refused; but in August he was appointed sheriff of Cork, and the government of Munster was left in his hands during the absence of the president, Sir John Norris (1547?–1597) [q. v.] In a letter to Walsingham he reported that he had hanged three hundred rebels, and so terrified the rest that 'a man might now travel the whole country and none molest him.' Towards the end of the year he was sent northward with Bagenal by Lord-deputy Perrot to act against the Ulster chiefs and their allies, the Scottish highlanders (see PERROT, SIR JOHN). In this campaign he showed his customary vigour, receiving some severe wounds, which invalided him several months. In October 1585 he returned to England.

Stanley's service in Ireland had been long and brilliant. Though the war, as Burghley admitted, was a religious one, and Sir William was a Roman catholic, he had served with fidelity. 'Qui singulari fide et fortitudine in Hibernico bello meruerat' is Camden's testimony (Annals, p. 471). But there can be no doubt that he left Ireland a disappointed man. In the partition of the great Desmond estates, which he had contributed to win, he had been passed over, while others, who had done little or nothing, received enormous grants. His resentment at his treatment, together with strong religious feelings, explains his future treachery. In December 1585 Stanley accompanied Leicester in the expedition sent by Elizabeth to the assistance of the united provinces against Spain. The need of more troops was speedily felt, and Sir William was despatched to Ireland to levy recruits among the disbanded troops and native kernes. He raised about fourteen hundred men, the greater part of whom were Irish. While in England, on his way back to the Netherlands, he was probably guilty of traitorous conduct. 'While in London he was in the confidence of the jesuits. He knew part, if not the whole, of the Babington conspiracy. He corresponded with Mendoza, and con-

trived to communicate with Lord Arundel in the Tower. When ordered to the Low Countries he made pretexts for delaying in London, in the hope that the queen might be killed, or that the Spanish fleet might arrive from Cadiz. When excuses would serve no longer and he was obliged to sail, he undertook to watch his moment, and, when he could do most injury, revolt with his regiment to Parma' (FROUDE, Hist. of Engl. chap. 68; cf. Cal. Simancas MSS. iii. 604, 607).

Stanley's forces joined Leicester on 12 Aug. 1586, and in September he assisted Sir John Norris in taking possession of Doesborg, where his men 'committed frightful disorders and thoroughly rifled the town' (Norris to Wilkes in MOTLEY, United Netherlands, ii. 44). At the action by Zutphen on 22 Sept., in which Philip Sidney received his death wound, Stanley displayed great prowess, and was declared by Leicester to be worth his weight in pearl. He assisted at the capture of the Zutphen sconce, which was committed by Leicester to the charge of Sir Rowland York [q. v.] In October Sir William Pelham [q. v.] and Stanley took possession of the important city of Deventer, deposed the magistracy, which inclined to the Spanish side, and installed a patriotic body in its place. In spite of the remonstrances of the States-General (ib. ii. 155–8), Stanley was appointed governor of the city, with a garrison of twelve hundred men, mostly Irish catholics; and, to give him additional authority, he was commissioned by Leicester to act independently of Norris (his bitter enemy), who, on the earl's departure to England, held the chief command. Stanley saw that his opportunity was come. Having acquired a full mastery of the city and made all the necessary arrangements, he put himself into communication, by means of his fellow-traitor York, with Tassis, the Spanish governor of Zutphen. To him he surrendered the place on 29 Jan. 1587. The garrison, with a few exceptions, entered the Spanish service (ib. ii. 159–64, 169–77).

From his new master Stanley received but slight rewards for his action, nor does he appear to have sought them. Parma declared his conduct to have been 'singularly disinterested.' There can be no doubt that at this period of his life he was almost entirely under the influence of the jesuits, of which order his brother John was a member. His conduct was loudly applauded by his jesuit friends. The society urged his claims for reward and countenance on the pope, Philip, and Parma, while Cardinal Allen published a letter at Antwerp in which he laboured to justify the treason. Almost at the moment of the surrender of Deventer, Elizabeth had it in contemplation to reward Stanley's services by honours and titles, and by appointing him viceroy of Ireland (cf. *Acts P. C.* 1586-7, p. 62).

Soon after leaving Deventer, Stanley, upon whose head the States-General had put a price of three thousand florins, proceeded to Spain to advise on the proposed invasion of England. He recommended that Ireland should be made the basis of operations, and that the troops should disembark at Milford Haven rather than at Portsmouth. Sir William was disappointed at his reception and entertainment, 'which was far colder than he expected;' but the Spanish government awarded him a pension (*Cal. Hatfield MSS.* ii. 335). Returning to the Netherlands, he was at Nieuwport in July 1588, at the head of seven hundred men, called the English legion, ready to join the armada. But on the overthrow of that expedition he withdrew to Antwerp. In 1590 he was again at Madrid, urging a design for the invasion of England, inspecting the seaports, and perhaps taking part in the preparations to resist Drake. He was now thoroughly identified with the jesuits and their adherents (cf. *Sadler Papers,* ii. 569), and eager to embark in any scheme against Elizabeth. He paid a visit to Rome in 1591 to consult with Allen and other enemies of the queen. In the event of her death he urged that the Lady Arabella Stuart or Lord Strange [see STANLEY, FERDINANDO, fifth EARL OF DERBY] should be recognised as her successor. While keeping his regiment in the Netherlands, Stanley made almost yearly journeys to Spain. In 1595 he was described as half desperate, and was reproved by a Spanish governor for his violent language against the queen. In 1596 he took part in the invasion of France by the Spaniards, and appears to have been in Amiens at its recapture by the French in 1597. In 1598 he engaged in the attempt to raise the siege of Geldern, besieged by Maurice of Nassau, and in 1600 he was with the Spaniards when that prince defeated them at Nieuwport.

On Elizabeth's death Stanley, who had previously sent Thomas Wright to Madrid, now despatched his subaltern officer, Guy Fawkes, with an emissary of Catesby, to warn Philip against James, and again to recommend Milford Haven for disembarkation of a Spanish army. Soon afterwards Sir William appears to have been negotiating with the English government for his own pardon. There is no evidence to connect him with complicity in the gunpowder plot, though he, together with Hugh Owen and Baldwin, was placed under arrest at Brussels on suspicion

of having been concerned in it. Cecil, however (30 Jan. 1606), altogether exonerated him from the charge.

The remainder of Stanley's life was spent in comparative obscurity. He took a great interest in the establishment of a jesuit novitiate at Liège in 1614, and contributed largely to it. He appears to have been appointed governor of Mechlin. James Wadsworth, the author of 'The English Spanish Pilgrim,' met him at Madrid in 1624, when he complained of being compelled at his advanced age to go to seek the pension which had not been paid him for six years. He quarrelled with the jesuits, and spent much of his time latterly with the English Carthusians near Ostend, having sought in vain for permission to return to England. He died at Ghent on 3 March 1630, and was honoured with a magnificent public funeral in the church of Our Lady over the Dyle at Mechlin. By his wife, Elizabeth, daughter of John Egerton of Egerton, who was buried in Mechlin Cathedral in 1614, Stanley left two sons and three daughters. His grandson William succeeded to the family estates, and his son, of the same name, was created a baronet in 1661. The male line of the Stanleys of Hooton became extinct by the death of the twelfth baronet, Sir John Stanley-Errington, in 1893.

[Ormerod's Cheshire; Meteren's Historia Belgica; Strada's De Bello Belgico; Cal. Papers preserved at Simancas, vol. iii.; Whitney's Choice of Emblems; Murdin's Burghley Papers; Acts of the Privy Council, ed. Dasent, vols. xii-xiv.; Cal. Hatfield MSS. vols. i-vi.; Motley's United Netherlands, vol. ii.; Leycester Correspondence (Camden Soc.); Irish State Papers; Hardwick State Papers; Cabala; Stow's Chronicle; Allen's Defence of Stanley, ed. Heywood; Tierney's Dodd; Strype's Annals; Winwood's Memorials; information supplied by W. H. J. Weale and by the Rev. Ethelred L. Taunton.] F. S.

STANLEY, WILLIAM, D.D. (1647-1731), dean of St. Asaph, son of William Stanley, gentleman, of Hinckley, Leicestershire, by his wife Lucy, daughter of William Beveridge, D.D., vicar of Barrow-upon-Soar, and sister to Bishop William Beveridge [q. v.], was born at Hinckley in 1647, and baptised there on 22 Aug. the same year. He was educated in a school kept at Ashley, Lancashire, by Jeremy Crompton, and was on 4 July 1663 admitted a sizar of St. John's College, Cambridge, where he graduated B.A. in 1666 (MAYOR, *Admissions to St. John's College,* i. 160). He was elected a fellow of Corpus Christi College in 1669, and commenced M.A. in 1670. After being ordained priest in 1672, he became a university preacher in 1676, and graduated B.D. in 1678. He became curate of Hadham Magna, Hertfordshire, and chaplain to the Earl of Essex, who presented him to the rectory of Raine Parva, Essex, on 20 Oct. 1681. This he voided by cession for the rectory of St. Mary Magdalen in Old Fish Street, London. He was preferred to the prebend of Codington Major in the church of St. Paul, 18 Sept. 1684. At this time he was engaged in a scheme for printing an edition of the English bible, with a plain practical and protestant commentary, the portion assigned to him being the minor prophets; but the design was eventually abandoned.

He was appointed chaplain to the Princess of Orange on the dismissal of Dr. John Covel [q. v.] in 1685, and before he proceeded to Holland the archbishop of Canterbury conferred upon him the Lambeth degree of D.D., 12 Nov. 1685 (*Gent. Mag.* May 1864, p. 636). As soon as Mary was seated upon the throne of England, he was advanced to the post of clerk of the closet with a salary of 200*l*. a year settled upon him for life. In 1689 he became canon residentiary of St. Paul's; on 13 Aug. 1690 he was collated by Bishop Compton to the rectory of Hadham Magna; and on 5 March 1691-2 he was appointed archdeacon of London. The natural tone of his voice was so loud that when taking part in the cathedral services he was heard above all the other singers. A humorous account was given of him by Sir Richard Steele in the 'Tatler,' under the name and character of Stentor. He was unanimously chosen master of Corpus Christi College, Cambridge, 13 July 1693, in succession to Dr. John Spencer [q. v.], and served the office of vice-chancellor of the university in the same year. On 18 Jan. 1694 he was created D.D. at Cambridge. He resigned the mastership in 1698, and he accepted the deanery of St. Asaph on 7 Dec. 1706, at the request of Bishop Beveridge. He defrayed the whole cost of procuring the act of parliament which annexed prebends and sinecures to the four Welsh sees in order to relieve the widows and children of the Welsh clergy from the distress of paying mortuaries to the bishops upon the death of every incumbent. He died on 9 Oct. 1731, and was buried in St. Paul's Cathedral.

He married Mary, second daughter of Sir Francis Pemberton [q. v.], lord chief justice of England, and had three sons—Thomas, William, and Francis. His widow died on 28 April 1758, aged 85 (CLUTTERBUCK, *Hertfordshire*, iii. 403).

Besides some occasional sermons, Stanley published: 1. 'A Discourse concerning the Devotions of the Church of Rome, especially as compared with those of the Church of England' (anon.), London, 1685, 4to; reprinted in Gibson's 'Preservative against Popery' (1738), vol. ii., and in Cardwell's 'Enchiridion Theologicum' (1837), vol. iii. 2. 'The Faith and Practice of a Church of England-Man' (anon.), London (3 editions), 1688, 12mo; 1700, 12mo; 1702, 8vo; 1707, 12mo; Boston, U.S. 1815, 12mo; 1841, 12mo; 1848, 8vo; reprinted in the 'Churchman's Remembrancer' (1807), vol. ii. and in 'Tractarianism no Novelty,' 1854. 3. 'Catalogus Librorum Manuscriptorum in Bibliotheca Collegii Corporis Christi in Cantabrigiâ, quos legavit Matthæus Parkerus Archiepiscopus Cantuariensis,' London, 1722, fol.

[Addit. MSS. 5807 p. 40, 5880 f. 27; Clutterbuck's Hertfordshire, iii. 402; Graduati Cantabr.; Granger's Biogr. Hist. of England, iii. 368 n.; Gutch's Collect. Curiosa (1781), vol. i. p. lxiv, contents, pp. x, xi, 299, 300, 302; Jones's Popery Tracts, i. 11, ii. 327; Masters's Hist. of C.C.C.C. p. 171, and Lamb's edit. p. 292; Nichols's Lit. Anecd. i. 243; Nichols's Leicestershire, iv. 742-4; Richardson's manuscript Athenæ Cantabr. p. 318; Salmon's Hertfordshire, p. 279; Memoirs of Dr. Stukeley (Surtees Soc.), i. 60; Willis's Survey of Cathedrals.]

T. C.

STANNARD, JOSEPH (1797-1830), painter, was born at Norwich on 13 Sept. 1797. He was for a short time a pupil of Robert Ladbrooke [q. v.], and became an eminent member of the Norwich school. He painted chiefly river and coast scenes and shipping with much of the feeling of the Dutch artists, whose works he studied and copied during a visit to Holland in 1821. Stannard first exhibited with the Norwich Society in 1811, and he was one of the members who seceded from it in 1816; he contributed to the Royal Academy and British Institution between 1820 and 1829. His best known picture is the 'Water Frolic at Thorpe,' now in the Norwich Castle museum. He practised etching, and published a set of plates of Norfolk scenery. He had always delicate health, and died at Norwich on 7 Dec. 1830. A portrait of him, painted by George Clint, is in the Norwich Museum, and another, by Sir W. Beechey, belongs to Mr. J. J. Colman. Stannard married Emily Coppin, an excellent painter of fruit, flowers, and still-life, for works of which class she received three gold medals from the Society of Arts; she died at Norwich on 6 Jan. 1885, at the age of eighty-two.

ALFRED STANNARD (1806-1889), younger brother of Joseph, painted landscapes in the style characteristic of the Norwich school.

A ' River Scene with Mill ' by him is in the
Norwich Museum. He died in 1880. He had
a son, Alfred George, who painted landscapes,
and died in 1885; and a daughter, who was
a painter of fruit and flowers.

[Redgrave's Dict. of Artists; Catalogue of the
Norwich Castle Museum; Wodderspoon's John
Crome and his Works; Norfolk Chronicle, 1830
and 1885; information from Mr. James Reeve.]

F. M. O'D.

STANNUS, Sir EPHRAIM GERRISH
(1784–1850), major-general, born in 1784,
was second son of Ephraim Stannus of
Comus, co. Tyrone, by Susannah, daughter
of Joseph Gerrish of Halifax, Nova Scotia.
He went out to India as a cadet in 1799,
was commissioned as an ensign in the Bombay army on 6 March 1800, became lieutenant on 26 May, and was appointed to the
European regiment (now 2nd battalion royal
Dublin fusiliers) in 1803. He served in the
Kathiawar campaign in 1807, and became
captain on 6 July 1811.

He distinguished himself in the Pindari
war of 1817–18, was promoted major on
8 Oct. 1818, and was private secretary to
Mountstuart Elphinstone while governor
of Madras (1819–27). He was made lieutenant-colonel of the 9th native infantry on
31 Oct. 1822, C.B. on 23 July 1823, and
colonel of the 10th native infantry on 5 June
1829. From 1823 to 1826 he was first
British resident in the Persian Gulf. From
this he was transferred to the 2nd European
regiment (now 2nd battalion Durham light
infantry). On 13 March 1834 he was appointed lieutenant-governor of the East India
College, Addiscombe, and he was knighted
in 1837. He was promoted major-general
(local) on 28 June 1838. Though just and
kindly, he was no administrator, and was
systematically irritated by the cadets into
extraordinary explosions of wrath and violent
language. During the latter years of his
rule at Addiscombe the discipline seems to
have got very slack (cf. ' Addiscombe ' in
Blackwood's Mag. May 1893); he remained
there until his death on 21 Oct. 1850. On
16 Oct. 1829 he married Mary Louisa, widow
of James Gordon. He had no children.

[Gent. Mag. 1850, ii. 659; Vibart's Addis-
combe, 1894, chap. iv. (with portrait); Burke's
Landed Gentry; Royal Engineers' Journal,
January 1893.]

E. M. L.

STANWIX, JOHN (1690?–1766), lieutenant-general, born about 1690, was nephew
and heir to Brigadier-general Thomas Stanwix. Thomas Stanwix was a captain in
Colonel Tidcomb's foot in 1693, served in
Flanders under Marlborough, and in Spain,

and was appointed governor of Gibraltar on
13 Jan. 1711. He was colonel of the 12th
foot from 25 Aug. 1717 until his death; he
was also governor of Kingston-upon-Hull,
and sat in parliament as member for Carlisle from 1705 to 1715; for Newport, Isle
of Wight, in 1721; and for Yarmouth, Isle
of Wight, in 1722; he died on 14 March
1724–5.

The nephew, John, entered the army in
1706, became adjutant of his regiment, and
captain of the grenadier company, and in
January 1741 he was given a majority in one
of the new marine regiments. On 4 Oct.
1745 he was made lieutenant-colonel of a
regiment raised by Lord Granby on account
of the Jacobite insurrection, and disbanded
in 1746. In 1749 he was appointed equerry
to the Prince of Wales, in 1752 governor of
Carlisle (for which city he had been elected
M.P. in December 1746), and in 1754 deputy
quartermaster-general.

At the beginning of 1756, in consequence
of Braddock's defeat, the royal American regiment (62nd foot, afterwards 60th, and now
the king's royal rifle corps) was raised, and
Stanwix was made colonel-commandant of
the 1st battalion from 1 Jan. and was sent
to America. In 1757 he was employed in
Pennsylvania. In January 1758 he was
made brigadier, and was sent up the Hudson
to Albany, and thence to Oneida portage,
where he built Fort Stanwix. A plan of this
fort is given in vol. iv. of the ' Documentary
History of New York.' In 1759, while
Wolfe was taking Quebec, Stanwix was
guarding the western border of Pennsylvania, and repairing Fort Duquesne, re-
named Pittsburg. He was promoted major-
general on 25 June 1759.

He returned to England in August 1760.
On 19 Jan. 1761 he became lieutenant-
general, and on 14 Dec. he was made colonel
of the 49th foot, from which he was transferred on 11 April 1764 to the 8th foot.
He was appointed governor of the Isle of
Wight in 1763. His first wife having
died in 1754, Stanwix married, on 20 April
1763, a daughter of Marmaduke Sowle, commissioner of appeals in the excise in Dublin,
but had no children by her. On 29 Oct. 1766,
after making some military inspections in
Ireland, he left Dublin for Holyhead with
his wife and daughter. The vessel, the
Eagle, was leaky when she started, and was
lost at sea. He was on his way to London
to attend parliament, having been elected
M.P. for Appleby on 8 April 1761.

[Dalton's English Army Lists, iii. 195; Hist.
Reg. 1725 (Chron. Diary), p. 13; Beatson's
Political Index, ii. 212; Gent. Mag. 1767, p.

164; Appleton's Cyclopædia of American Biography; Parkman's Montcalm and Wolfe; Wallace's Chronicle and Hist. of the 60th or King's Royal Rifle Corps.] E. M. L.

STANWIX, RICHARD (1608–1656), divine, born in 1608, was son of James Stanwix of Carlisle, who was fourth son of James Stanwix, head of an ancient family which had their origin at Stanwix, near Carlisle. Richard was educated at the free school in Carlisle under Thomas Robson, formerly of Queen's College, Oxford. He was admitted a servitor of the college under the tuition of Charles Robson [q. v.], son of his old schoolmaster, and matriculated on 21 Nov. 1628, according to Foster. He afterwards became a tabarder, graduating B.A. on 12 May 1629, and proceeding M.A. on 24 Jan. 1631–2. He was made a fellow about the same time, and on 4 July 1639 obtained the degree of B.D. In 1640 he was incorporated at Cambridge. Entering into holy orders, he was appointed chaplain to the lord keeper, Thomas Coventry [q. v.], through the recommendation of the provost, Christopher Potter [q. v.], and, after Coventry's death, to his successor, Sir John Finch, baron Finch of Fordwich [q. v.] When Finch was impeached by the Long parliament in 1640, and took refuge in Holland, Stanwix returned to Oxford, and was appointed rector of Chipping Warden, Northamptonshire, in 1643, by Sir Richard Saltonstall, of Queen's College. He remained undisturbed in his living during the Commonwealth, and died at Chipping Warden on 8 April 1656.

He was the author of ' A Holy Life here the only Way to Eternal Life hereafter. Wherein this truth is especially asserted, that a Holy Life, or the Habitual Observing of the Laws of Christ, is indispensably necessary to Salvation,' London, 1652, 8vo.

[Wood's Athenæ Oxon. ed. Bliss, iii. 427; Foster's Alumni Oxon. 1500–1714; Bridges's Northamptonshire, ed. Whalley. i. 116; Foster's Visitations of Cumberland and Westmoreland, p. 128.] E. I. C.

STANYAN, ABRAHAM (1669?–1732), diplomatist, elder son of Laurence Stanyan of Headley, Middlesex, was born about 1669, and entered as a student of the Middle Temple in 1680. He is to be distinguished from the Abraham Stanyan (probably a cousin) who was admitted from Winchester as a scholar of New College, Oxford, on 14 July 1691, and who died of smallpox when a fellow of New College in 1696. Stanyan's ability met with early recognition, and in 1698 he was offered the post of secretary to Sir William Norris [q. v.], who was

despatched in that year as king's commissioner to obtain certain privileges from the Mogul emperor, Aurangzib. After much hesitation he declined the offer, and his refusal was justified in the following year, when he was appointed one of the clerks to the council extraordinary. Some four years later, on 6 Jan. 1702, he was appointed secretary to the Earl of Manchester at Paris, a post which had been recently held by Matthew Prior. He cannot have remained there long, as the war broke out almost immediately; but he was despatched on 8 May 1705, in the place of ' Mr. Aglionby,' as envoy to the Swiss cantons, taking with him bills of exchange upon the bankers of Genoa for the allied forces in Italy. His instructions were also to detect and neutralise the artifices of the French minister at Geneva, and to endeavour to obtain a free passage for the allied troops through the Swiss mountain passes. With these objects he caused to be published in 1707, ' Mémoire de M. de Stanian, envoyé extraordinaire de S. M. la Reine de la Grande Bretagne vers les Louables Cantons Réformés, presenté 25 Juillet.' Another ' Mémoire ' printed by Stanyan about the same time had an object of more immediate importance. On 16 June 1707 died at Paris the Duchesse de Nemours, princess of Neufchatel and Valangin. No less than thirteen competitors laid claim to the principality, to rescue which from French influence became a paramount object with the allies. Stanyan at once hastened to Neufchatel, and, joining his influence to that of the Dutch envoy (Runkel), succeeded in obtaining the investiture for the king of Prussia. Louis XIV moved a large force up to the frontier as if with the purpose of invading the territory, but Stanyan's vigilance obtained from the sovereign council at Berne a prompt resolution to defend the principality with all their forces, ' whereupon the French thought it advisable to lie quiet under their disappointment ' (BOYER, pp. 306–7; State Papers, Dutch, in Add. MS. 5132). In 1708 he found it necessary to issue a letter contradicting a rumour which had been circulated by Louis to the effect that in North Britain the natives were ready to sacrifice everything for ' James VIII.' Stanyan returned home in February 1709, but was soon back again in Switzerland, and was in February 1710 entrusted with a secret mission to Piedmont. During the summer of 1712 he was very busy at Milan endeavouring to adjust the differences between the emperor and the Duke of Savoy, and to obtain the adherence of both to the proposed terms of the treaty of Utrecht, upon the conclusion of which in the following year Stanyan returned to England (cf. *Stowe MS.* 246, ff. 25–8). He now compiled his brochure entitled 'An Account of Switzerland written in the year 1714,' destined to enlighten the profound darkness which he found prevailing as to the constitution, religion, and manners of the federated cantons (the original edition, London, 1714, 8vo, with a dedication to Somers, is extremely rare; it bears no name, and the copy at the Bodleian Library is wrongly attributed to Temple Stanyan; 2nd ed. 1756; in French, Amsterdam, 1714 and 1757, 8vo; and translated by Besset de la Chapelle, Fribourg and Paris, 1766, 12mo. A paraphrase entitled 'L'État de la Suisse' was added, as a supplementary dissertation, to the second and later editions of Ruchat's well-known 'Délices de la Suisse' (ed. 1730, vol. ii.) Stanyan's book was used by William Coxe in his 'Sketches of the Natural, Civil, and Political State of Swisserland' (1779). It was commended by Lord Chesterfield to his son (*Letters*, ed. Mahon, i. 68). The Swiss bibliographer G. E. von Haller describes its information as astonishingly accurate (*Bibliothek der Schweizer-Geschichte*, 1785).

After the accession of George I, Stanyan was on 16 July 1716 appointed envoy extraordinary to the emperor. To enable him to support his diplomatic expenses he was added to the admiralty board, and held office there until April 1717. He had been returned to parliament for Buckingham in 1715, and on his return from Vienna he was in November 1717 appointed one of the clerks in ordinary to the privy council, a post which he resigned in 1719 upon his appointment as ambassador extraordinary to the Porte. At Constantinople he succeeded Edward Wortley Montagu [see MONTAGU, LADY MARY WORTLEY]. He seems to have returned to England early in 1720, when he was succeeded by Sir Everard Fawkener [q.v.], and was soon appointed to one of the clerkships in the privy seal office. Though a whig of old standing and a member of the Kit-Cat Club, Stanyan was on friendly terms with Pope and his circle. He was a subscriber to Pope's 'Iliad,' and when he went out to Vienna in the autumn of 1716 he bore a letter from the poet to Lady Mary Wortley Montagu. He died at his seat near Buckingham on 11 Sept. 1732. The fine Kit-Cat by Kneller was engraved by Faber in 1733 and by Cook in 1786 (prefixed to vol. v. of the 'Tatler,' ed. Nichols).

Abraham's younger brother, TEMPLE STANYAN (*d.* 1752), entered Westminster School as a queen's scholar in 1691, and was elected in 1695 to Christ Church, Oxford, where he matriculated on 18 June, aged eighteen, but, like his brother, he does not appear to have taken a degree. He was appointed secretary under Viscount Townshend 'in the room of Horace Walpole, esq.,' on 15 Oct. 1715, and continued in his under-secretaryship by Addison on 20 April 1717. On 5 Feb. 1719 he was appointed clerk in ordinary to the privy council in the room of his brother (*Hist. Reg.* Chronol. Diary, p. 8). Numerous diplomatic letters addressed to him from Paris during the embassy of Sir Luke Schaub [q. v.] are in Add. MS. 22521 *passim.* He was a good scholar, and in 1735 wrote the Latin inscriptions for the statue of George II at Greenwich Hospital (LYSONS, *Environs*, iv. 441); but he is best known for 'The Grecian History' down to the death of Philip of Macedon (London, 1739, 2 vols. 8vo; several editions, and a French translation by Diderot, Paris, 1743, 3 vols. 12mo), a compilation which held the field for educational purposes until the appearance of the much larger history by William Mitford the younger [q. v.] Temple Stanyan died at his seat of Rawlins, Oxfordshire, on 25 March 1752. He married as his second wife, on 28 April 1726, a 'Mrs. Pauncefort.' He left an only daughter Catherine (she died on 19 Feb. 1801, aged 75), who married Admiral Sir Charles Hardy the younger [q. v.]

[Foster's *Alumni Oxon.* 1500–1714 (the two Abraham Stanyans are here confused); note from the Warden of New College, Oxford; *Gent. Mag.* 1732 p. 979, 1752 p. 144; Hist. Reg. 1732, Chronol. Diary, p. 37; Welch's *Alumni Westmon.* p. 229; Luttrell's Brief Hist. Relation, iv. 454, 518, 524; Boyer's Queen Anne, 1735, pp. 179, 306, 336, 400, 602; Add. MSS. 31130, 31134 (letters to Lord Raby, 1700–1706); Memoirs of Celebrated Persons composing the Kit-Cat Club, 1821, p. 207; Marlborough's Despatches, ed. Murray, vol. iv.; Noble's Contin. of Granger, iii. 180–1; Lady M. W. Montagu's Works; Coolidge's Swiss Travel and Guide Books, 1889, pp. 169–71; Pope's Works, ed. Elwin, iv. 488, ix. 357, 364; Quérard's France Littéraire, ix. 256; Notes and Queries, 1st ser. vol. i. passim; Nichols's Lit. Anecd. i. 299.]

T. S.

STANYHURST, RICHARD (1547–1618), translator of Virgil, was born in Dublin in 1547. From the fourteenth to the eighteenth century his family was settled at Corduff, co. Dublin. In 1489 one Richard Stanyhurst was lord mayor of Dublin. Nicholas Stanyhurst (*d.* 1554), the translator's grandfather, held the same office in 1542; he was interested in medicine, wrote in Latin ' Dicta Medicorum, lib. i.,' and was reputed ' a great and good householder.'

JAMES STANYHURST (d. 1573), the translator's father, long held a prominent position in Dublin. He was recorder of the city and speaker of the Irish House of Commons in the parliaments of 1557, 1560, and 1568. At the opening of each session he delivered an oration. Although he presided over a parliament in Queen Mary's reign, he proved himself a zealous supporter of protestantism under Elizabeth, and contrived to secure the passing through the house of the statute of uniformity in 1560, by putting the question when its chief opponents were absent from the chamber. In 1570 he recommended to parliament, in a speech which he delivered at the prorogation, a system of national education for Ireland, proposing the establishment of grammar schools throughout the country. At the same time he suggested the formation of a university at Dublin such as was inaugurated a few years later. The speech is said to have been printed. Stanyhurst's educational policy was not accepted by the government, although Sir Henry Sidney, with whom he was on intimate terms, strongly supported it. Edmund Campion [q. v. was also a close friend, and often enjoyed his hospitality. From the elder Stanyhurst's conversation, and from his collection of books and manuscripts, Campion acknowledged much assistance in writing his history of Ireland. His son Richard, while crediting his father with an exact knowledge of the common law, described him as 'a good orator and proper divine,' and attributed to him, besides parliamentary ' orations,' a series of ' Piæ orationes' and several letters to Thomas O'Heirnan or O'Hifferuan, dean of Cork. James Stanyhurst died at Dublin on 27 Dec. 1573, aged 61. A Latin elegy by his son Richard was printed in the latter's description of Ireland, as well as in the appendix to his translation of Virgil. Besides Richard, James Stanyhurst left another son, Walter, who translated into English 'Innocent. de Contemptu Mundi.' A daughter Margaret married Arnold Ussher, one of the six clerks of the Irish court of chancery, and was mother of Archbishop James Ussher [q. v.] The latter was thus Richard Stanyhurst's nephew (cf. Stanyhurst's ' Description of Ireland' in HOLINSHED's *Chronicles*, 1577, cap. vii. p. 27; W. B. WRIGHT, *The Ussher Memoirs*, 1889).

Richard was first educated under Peter White, who kept a school at Waterford, and proceeded in 1563 to University College, Oxford. He was admitted B.A. in 1568. While an undergraduate he came to know Edmund Campion. He gave notable proofs of his precocity by writing Latin commentaries on Porphyry which amazed Campion by their learning. They were published in 1570 as ' Harmonia sive Catena Dialectica in Porphyrianas Constitutiones.' After graduating, Stanyhurst studied law first at Furnivall's Inn, and afterwards at Lincoln's Inn. But history and literature diverted his attention, and, accompanied by Campion as his tutor, he returned to Ireland, where the combined influence of his father and of Campion led him to devote himself to Irish history and geography. Campion had undertaken to contribute the history of Ireland to the great collection of chronicles which Raphael Holinshed was preparing between 1573 and 1577. Under Campion's guidance, Stanyhurst contributed to the same work a general description of Ireland, after the manner of Harrison's ' Description of England.' For Holinshed's undertaking Stanyhurst also compiled a history of Ireland during Henry VIII's reign, in continuation of Campion's work on earlier periods. Stanyhurst's ' Description of Ireland,' and his share in the ' History of Ireland ' forming the third book, both appeared in the first volume of Holinshed's ' Chronicles,' 1577. The 'Description' was dedicated to Sir Henry Sidney, the lord deputy, his father's friend. Stanyhurst's English prose is remarkable for its bombastic redundancy and unintentional burlesque effects.

Meanwhile Stanyhurst had married, and had removed to Knightsbridge. His wife, Janet, daughter of Sir Christopher Barnewall, died there in childbed on 26 Aug. 1579, aged 19. She was buried at Chelsea. A Latin elegy on her by Stanyhurst is appended to his translation of Virgil. After his wife's death Stanyhurst left England for the Low Countries, and he never returned to England or his native country. There can be little doubt that under Campion's influence his religious views had undergone a change. Although the date of his conversion to Roman catholicism is undetermined, it probably took place soon after he arrived on the continent. At first he resided at Leyden, and there he worked at a translation of Virgil's ' Æneid ' into English. It was originally published at Leyden in 1582, with the title ' The first foure Bookes of Virgil his Æneis, intoo English Heroicall Verse, by Richard Stanyhurst. Wyth oother Poëticall deuises theretoo annexed.' Imprinted at Leiden in Holland by John Pates, Anno MDLXXXII.' Only two copies of the Leyden edition are known. One is the property of Mr. Christy Miller at Britwell, the other belonged to the Earl of Ashburnham. Both are slightly imperfect.

The work was dedicated from Leyden on 30 June 1582 to Stanyhurst's brother-in-law, Patrick Plunket, lord Dunsany, who had married a sister of his late wife. In the dedication he warmly deprecates the suspicion that he had plagiarised the work of Thomas Phaer [q. v.], whose translation of nine books of the 'Æneid' appeared in 1562. The first three books, he affirms, he compiled at his leisure; the fourth he 'huddled up' in ten days. In an address to the learned reader he developed that theory of English prosody of which Gabriel Harvey was the champion, maintaining that quantity rather than accent ought to be the guiding principle of English as of Latin metre. Stanyhurst rendered 'Virgil' into hexameters by way of proving that position. The result was a literary monstrosity. The Latin was recklessly paraphrased in a grotesquely prosaic vocabulary, which abounded in barely intelligible words invented by the translator to meet metrical exigencies. Frequent inversions of phrase heightened the ludicrous effect. Gabriel Harvey, who proudly boasted that he was the inventor of the English hexameter, wrote of Stanyhurst as a worthy disciple (*Four Letters*, 1592, pp. 19, 48). But, at the hands of all other critics of his own and later days, Stanyhurst has been deservedly ridiculed. In his preface to Greene's 'Arcadia' (1589), Nash justly parodied his effort when he wrote of him:

Then did he make heaven's vault to rebound
   with rounce, robble, hobble,
Of ruff, raffe, roaring, with thwicke, thwack,
   thurlerie, bouncing.

Subsequently Nash wrote: 'Master Stanyhurst (though otherwise learned) trod a foule, lumbering, boystrous, wallowing measure in his translation of "Virgil." He had never been praised by Gabriel for his labour if therein he had not bin so famously absurd' (NASH, *Pierce Pennilesse*, 1593). The translation could 'hardly be digested' by Puttenham. Bishop Hall was equally contemptuous. More recently Southey, in 'Omniana, or Horæ Otiosiores' (i. 193, ed. 1812), wrote in reference to 'the incomparable oddity' of Stanyhurst's translation: 'As Chaucer has been called the well of English undefiled, so might Stanyhurst be denominated the common sewer of the language. He is, however, a very entertaining and, to a philologist, a very instructive writer.... It seems impossible that a man could have written in such a style without intending to burlesque what he was about, and yet it is certain that Stanyhurst seriously meant to write heroic poetry.'

Stanyhurst appended to the translation of Virgil a rendering into English of certain psalms of David, i-iv., in classical metres, with a few lumbering original poems and epitaphs, some in Latin, others in English. The Leyden version was reissued, with a slight revision, in London in 1583, by Henry Bynneman, and this was reprinted in an edition limited to fifty copies at Edinburgh in 1836, under the direction of James Maidment. The Leyden edition was reprinted by Mr. Arber in his 'English Scholars' Library' in 1880 (with new title-page, 1895). A careful philological study of Stanyhurst's 'Virgil' was the subject of a thesis by Heinrich Schmidt, issued at Breslau in 1887.

Stanyhurst was not encouraged to repeat his incursion into pure literature, or indeed to publish anything further in English. He thenceforth wrote solely in Latin prose, and confined himself to historical or theological topics. Removing to Antwerp, he published there in 1584, at the press of Christopher Plantin, a treatise on the early history of Ireland down to the time of Henry II, with an annotated appendix of extracts by Giraldus Cambrensis. The title of the volume ran 'De rebus in Hibernia gestis' (in four books), and it was dedicated, like the 'Virgil,' to his brother-in-law, Baron Dunsany. Combining legendary history with theology in a very credulous spirit, Stanyhurst produced in 1587, again with Plantin at Antwerp, a life of St. Patrick. This was entitled 'De Vita S. Patricii Hyberniæ Apostoli,' and was dedicated to Alexander Farnese, archduke of Parma and Placentia. The volume marked the close of Stanyhurst's researches in Irish history and legend.

In all his works on Ireland Stanyhurst wrote from an English point of view. Barnaby Rich, who often met him at Antwerp, criticised adversely, in his 'New Description of Ireland' (1610, p. 2), his want of sympathy with the native Irish and his prejudiced misrepresentations. Keating, in his 'General History of Ireland' (1723, p. xii), condemns Stanyhurst on the three grounds that he was too young when he wrote, that he was ignorant of the Irish language, and that he was bribed by large gifts and promises of advancement to blacken the character of the Irish nation. The last charge is unsubstantiated. Keating adds, on equally doubtful authority, that Stanyhurst lived to repent of 'the injustice he had been guilty of,' and, after formally promising to revoke all his falsehoods, prepared a paper in that sense to be printed in Ireland; of this nothing further is known. Sir James Ware likewise asserts that Stanyhurst's books on

Irish history abound in 'malicious representations.'

According to Barnaby Rich, Stanyhurst, while pursuing his historical researches at Antwerp, also 'professed alchemy, and took upon him to make gold' (RICH, *Irish Hubbub*). At the same time politics attracted his attention. Under the influence of the jesuits he embarked in conspiracy with other catholic exiles in Flanders against the English government, and he became an object of suspicion to English spies. His relations with the catholics grew more equivocal after a second marriage (before 1585) with Helen, daughter of William Copley of Gatton, Surrey, and granddaughter of Sir Thomas Copley [q. v.] (cf. COPLEY, *Letters*, ed. Christie, Roxburghe Club, 1897, p. xlviii). Like other members of her family, she was a fervent Roman catholic, and her sister Mary became in 1637 superioress of the abbey of Louvain. About 1590 Stanyhurst visited Spain and, it was stated, professed medicine there; but his chief occupation was the offering of political advice to the Spanish government in regard to the position of affairs in England. He was at Toledo in 1591. Writing from Madrid to Justus Lipsius on 1 Feb. 1592, he refers to an interview with Philip II, and speaks with enthusiasm of the king's kindness and affability. About 1595 it was reported that he had left the Spanish 'court with a good provision in Flanders, and is not likely to deal more in matters of state or physic' (*Cal. State Papers*, Dom. 1595-7, p. 157; cf. *Cal. State Papers*, Dom. Eliz. cclvii. 3, 44). His (second) wife died about 1602, soon after the birth of a second son. Thereupon Stanyhurst took holy orders. Rich asserts that he became 'a massing priest.' Archduke Albert, the ruler of the Netherlands, appointed him chaplain to himself and to his wife Isabella (Philip II's daughter), and to these patrons Stanyhurst dedicated a devotional treatise: 'Hebdomada Mariana ex Orthodoxis Romanae Ecclesiae Patribus collecta: in memoriam septem festorum Beatissimae Virginis Mariae,' Antwerp, 1609, 8vo. He also appears to have acted as chaplain to the English Benedictine convent at Brussels. In 1605 he wrote commendatory verses for his friend and co-religionist Richard Verstegan's 'Restitution of Decayed Intelligence,' which was published at Antwerp in 1605 [see ROWLANDS, RICHARD]. In 1614 he brought out another devotional treatise, 'Hebdomada Eucharistica,' Douay, 1614, 8vo.

Despite differences in religion, Stanyhurst seems to have maintained an affectionate correspondence with his kinsfolk in Ireland. His nephew, James Ussher, writing to him 'at the English College in Louvain' about 1610, asked for a copy of his 'Margarita,' 'presuming on that natural bond of love which is knit betwixt us.' Ussher sent his mother's 'most kind remembrance,' and signed himself 'your most loving nephew.' Ussher's biographers represent Stanyhurst as making vain efforts to convert his nephew to his own faith, but there is no hint of this in the many respectful references which Ussher made in his published works to Stanyhurst's 'Life of St. Patrick' and others of his uncle's writings (cf. USSHER, *Works*, ed. Elrington, iv. 550, 562, vi. 374, 380, 447). When Ussher brought out in 1613 his treatise 'De Successione et Statu Christianae Ecclesiae,' in which he attempted to identify the pope with Antichrist, Stanyhurst replied in 'Brevis praemunitio pro futura concertatione cum Jacobo Usserio Hiberno Dublinensi,' Douay, 1615, 8vo. According to Wood, Stanyhurst died at Brussels in 1618. His nephew wrote at the time to Lydiat that 'my late uncle's answer' was to come out at Paris (*ib.* xv. 148).

Two of Stanyhurst's sons by his second wife became jesuits. The elder, Peter, born in the Netherlands, studied humanities under the jesuit fathers at Brussels, entered the society at Mechlin on 18 Sept. 1610, and died in Spain on 27 May 1627 (FOLEY, *Records*, vii. 731, *Chron. Cat.* p. 26). The younger son, WILLIAM STANYHURST (1602-1663), born at Brussels in 1602, after studying there, entered the Society of Jesus at Malines on 25 Sept. 1617 (DE BACKER). He chiefly resided at Brussels, and preached in both English and Flemish. Wood describes him as 'a comely person endowed with rare parts.' He died in Belgium on 10 Jan. 1663. He was a voluminous writer of religious works, many of which enjoyed a European vogue. His 'Dei Immortalis in corpore mortali patientis Historia,' which appeared at Antwerp in 1660, has been repeatedly reprinted down to the present day, both in the original Latin and in French, Spanish, Flemish, Dutch, German, Polish, and Hungarian translations. His 'Veteris Hominis . . . quatuor novissima metamorphosis et novi genesis,' dedicated to James van Baerlant, Antwerp, 1661 (Prague, 1700; Vienna, 1766), was translated into French, German, Italian, and Spanish. Others of his works, all of which passed through many editions, are: 1. 'Album Marianum,' describing God's beneficence to Austria (Louvain, 1641, fol.) 2. 'Regio mortis sive Domus infelicis aeternitatis,' Antwerp, 1652,

12mo. 3. 'Quotidiana Christiani Militis tessora,' Antwerp, 1661, 4to (portions of this reappeared in 'Selectissima moralis Christianæ præcepta harmonicis metris ac rythmis expressa,' Antwerp, 1662, 8vo). 4. 'Ecclesia Militans,' Antwerp, 4to (FOLEY; DE BACKER, *Biblioth. des Ecrivains S. J.*, 1876, iii. 880; SOUTHWELL, *Bib. Soc. Jesu*, 1676, p. 320).

[Arber's admirable introduction to his reprint of Stanyhurst's Translation of Virgil, 1895; Wood's Athenæ Oxon. ed. Bliss, ii. 252-8; Foley's Records, vii. 732; Simpson's Life of Campion, chap. ii.; Wright's Ussher Memoirs, 1889; information kindly supplied by the Rev. Ethelbert Taunton.] S. L.

STAPELDON, WALTER DE (1261-1326), bishop of Exeter, and virtual founder of Exeter College, Oxford, a younger son of William and Mabilla de Stapeldon, was born at Annery in the parish of Monkleigh, Devonshire, on 1 Feb. 1260-1. His eldest brother, Sir Richard, was a puisne judge of the king's bench, and resided at Stapeldon, near Holsworthy. Walter was a man of learning, and a distinguished member of the university of Oxford, where he became professor of canon law. Before 1294 he was parson of Aveton Gifford, Devonshire (*Cal. Patent Rolls*, 1292-1301, pp. 93, 271). He was also chaplain to Clement V and precentor of Exeter. The king's license to elect a successor to Thomas de Bytton, bishop of Exeter, was granted on 6 Oct. 1307, and Stapeldon was unanimously chosen on 13 Nov., all the canons but one being present or represented. Much delay arose through the vexatious opposition of Richard de Plympstoke, rector of Exminster and Uffculme, who in an appeal to the pope contested the right of nine of the canons to vote. The king's assent to Stapeldon's election was notified on 3 Dec. (*ib.* 1307-13, p. 20), but the archbishop, Robert Winchelsey [q. v.], also raised difficulties which can only be described as frivolous. The election was confirmed at last on 13 March, and three days later the temporalities were restored (cf. RYMER, *Fœdera*, iii. 36-7). Plympstoke, however, renewed his vindictive persecution of Stapeldon; the result being a further postponement of his consecration, which took place at Canterbury on 13 Oct. 1308, nearly a year after his election. The cost of these proceedings was very heavy, and the revenues of the see were appropriated by the king during the long vacancy. Stapeldon tells us in pathetic terms that he was penniless, and was even compelled to ask Walter Reynolds [q. v.], the elect of Worcester, who was consecrated with him, to pay their joint expenses. He entered, however, with undaunted spirit on his episcopal duties; and his register shows that he was indefatigable in fulfilling them. His cathedral, the rebuilding of which had been but half accomplished, became the object of his special care, and as soon as money came in he spent it lavishly on internal decorations and improvements, and on the accumulation of materials for the rebuilding of the nave, which were utilised after his death by Bishop Grandisson. The fabrick-rolls show that he contributed no less than 1,800l., an immense sum for those days, equivalent, according to the calculations of Hallam and other competent authorities, to 40,000l. of our money. He was a generous patron of learning, and in 1314, in conjunction with his brother, Sir Richard, he founded Stapeldon Hall in Oxford (now known as Exeter College) for poor scholars from his diocese, and established there four scholarships for natives of Cornwall.

Stapeldon's political career had begun in 1306 with a mission to France. He was summoned to serve against the Scots on 22 Aug. 1308, and to a council held at Westminster in the following February. From that time he was summoned to all the councils and parliaments held in Edward II's reign (*Parl. Writs*, Alphabetical Digest of Persons, pp. 828-31). In March 1310 Stapeldon joined the lords ordainers against Gaveston, though he protested that the ordainers' proceedings should not prejudice the royal authority (*Chron. of Edw. I and Edw. II*, Rolls Ser. i. 170). In February 1312-13 he was sent on a mission to the king of France with Aymer de Valence, earl of Pembroke [q. v.] (RYMER, iii. 381-2), and in May 1313 he was again sent to do homage for Aquitaine (*ib.* iii. 772-3). In 1314 he was accused in parliament of maintenance (*Rot. Parl.* i. 292 a), but in the following year he was sworn of the privy council (*ib.* i. 350 b) and appointed to hold a parliament in Edward's absence. On 18 Feb. 1319-20 he was appointed lord high treasurer of England (*ib.* i. 287), and in the following June accompanied Edward to Amiens, where he did homage to the French king for Ponthieu. In July 1321 he vainly attempted to mediate between Edward II and Thomas of Lancaster. In 1325 he was sent to aid Queen Isabella and the young Prince Edward in Gascony. But he was one of the four who were described as especially unpopular there because of their being Edward II's favourites, and he was forced to flee to England by night in disguise (*ib.* ii. 285-6, 307; cf. RYMER, iv. 62, 69, 77, 79, 90, 117, 161, 180-2). On 2 May 1326 he was directed to prepare for the defence of the realm against Isabella's threatened invasion. Stapeldon had been closely identified with the later policy of Edward II, and was therefore exceedingly obnoxious to the people (see RYMER, *Fœdera*, Record ed., vol. ii. pt. i. passim). On the king's flight he was left in charge of London, and was murdered by the mob in Cheapside on 15 Oct. 1326. His remains were buried in St. Clement Danes (*Chron. Edw. I and Edw. II*, Rolls Ser. i. 316–17; MURIMUTH, pp. 44–8, 59, 282); but on 28 March 1327 they were transferred to Exeter, where they rest under a beautiful tomb on the north side of the high altar. His head was sent to Queen Isabella at Gloucester (MATT. WEST. *Flores Hist.* iii. 234), and his murderers were excommunicated. In the parliament that met at the end of the year the 'forcible acts done by him as an adherent of the Spencers were annulled' (*Rot. Parl.* ii. 56).

[Cal. Patent and Close Rolls, Edw. I and Edw. II, ed. 1890–6, passim; Parl. Writs; Rotuli Parliamentorum, vols. i. and ii.; Rymer's Fœdera, original and Record editions, vol. ii. pt. i.; Matthew of Westminster's Flores Historiarum, Chronicles of Edw. I and Edw. II, Murimuth's and Walsingham's Hist. Angl. (all in Rolls Ser.); Le Neve's Fasti Eccl. Angl. ed. Hardy; Dublin Review, July 1895; Godwin, De Præsulibus, ed. Richardson; Stubbs's Const. Hist. ii. 375, 383, &c.; Boase and Courtney's Bibl. Cornub. ii. 684; Prince's Worthies of Devon, pp. 722–6; Oliver's Lives of the Bishops of Exeter, pp. 55–61; Register of Bishop Stapeldon, ed. Hingeston-Randolph, pp. viii–xxxiv; Boase's Hist. of Exeter College, pp. iii–v.] F. C. H. R.

STAPLES or **STAPLE**, EDWARD (1490?–1560?), bishop of Meath, born probably about 1490, is said to have been a native of Lincolnshire or Lancashire. He was educated first at Oxford and then at Cambridge, where he graduated B.A. in 1511, and M.A. in 1514. In 1525 he was made canon of Cardinal College, Oxford, and on 9 March 1525–6 he supplicated for incorporation in Oxford University, and for the degrees B.D. and D.D. (*Reg. Univ. Oxon.* i. 142). About the same time he was appointed chaplain to Henry VIII. On 7 March 1527–8 he was presented to the prebend of Wigginton in the collegiate church of Tamworth, but resigned it in the following July, and was appointed master of St. Bartholomew's Hospital, London (*Letters and Papers of Henry VIII*, iv. 4124, 4489, 4594). He resigned the latter post in July 1532 on being instituted to the vicarage of Thaxted, Essex.

Meanwhile, in 1530, at Henry's request,

the pope provided Staples to the bishopric of Meath. In that capacity he took a prominent part in the government of Ireland, and in the strife between the various factions of the official class. In 1534 he was compelled to flee to England before the rebellion of Thomas Fitzgerald, tenth earl of Kildare [q. v.] He returned in the following year, when he and Archbishop George Browne (d. 1556) [q. v.] became Henry VIII's principal instruments in introducing the Reformation into Ireland. His relations with Browne, however, were always hostile. Staples was not so advanced as the archbishop, and clung to the mass, though he was 'as zealous as any' for the royal supremacy, and it was partly owing to his urgent advice that Henry assumed the title of king of Ireland. His quarrel with Browne became such a scandal that on 31 July 1537 Henry wrote to Browne threatening to remove him for his lightness of behaviour and pride, and to Staples censuring his neglect of his ecclesiastical duties (*Cal. State Papers*, Irish, 1509–71, p. 28). Little effect seems to have been produced, and on one occasion in 1538, while preaching before Browne in Kilmainham church, Staples denounced him as a heretic. This sermon was examined by the Irish council, and both Staples and Browne complained to Cromwell, but the quarrel was patched up. In 1544, as a reward for his zeal, Staples was allowed to annex the archdeaconry of Kells.

After Edward VI's accession Staples's protestant opinions became more pronounced. On 7 April 1547 he was granted the parsonage of Ardbraccan, and soon after was made judge of faculties. About this time he married, and preached a strong sermon against the mass, which rendered him intensely unpopular in his diocese. In June 1552, in a discussion at St. Mary's Abbey, Dublin, he maintained the protestant cause against George Dowdall [q. v.], archbishop of Armagh (MANT, *Hist. of the Church of Ireland*, i. 207–11). In August 1553 he took part in the proclamation of Queen Mary, but on 29 June 1554 he was deprived on account of his marriage. He remained in his diocese, destitute and disliked, and on 16 Dec. 1558, after Elizabeth's accession, he wrote to Cecil relating his woes and seeking preferment. He was not, however, restored to his see, and, as no subsequent mention of him occurs, he is believed to have died soon after.

[State Papers, Henry VIII, vols. i.–iii. passim; Cal. Letters and Papers of Henry VIII, ed. Brewer and Gairdner; Cal. State Papers, Irish Ser.; Cal. Carew MSS.; Cotton's Fasti Eccl. Hib. iii. 115, 131, v. 221; Lascelles's Liber

Munerum Hib.; Wood's Athenæ Oxon.; Cooper's Athenæ Cantabr. i. 190; Ware's Bishops of Ireland, ed. Harris; Mant's Hist. Church of Ireland, i. 127, 149, 198, 206, 208, 234-5; Dixon's Hist. Church of England; Cogan's Diocese of Meath, i. 81-104, ii. 258; Bagwell's Ireland under the Tudors, vols. i-ii. passim; Foster's Alumni Oxon. 1500-1714.] A. F. P.

STAPLETON, AUGUSTUS GRAN-VILLE (1800-1880), biographer of George Canning and political pamphleteer, was born in 1800. He was entered on 18 Sept. 1814 in the register of Rugby school as 'son of John Stapleton, esq., and ward of the Rev. T. Yeoman, Barnstaple, Devon, aged 13' (Register, i. 120). It has, however, been said that he was 'a natural son of Lord Morley' (JEKYLL, Letters, p. 226), i.e. of the first Earl Morley, the intimate friend of Canning. He was entered at Trinity Hall, Cambridge, on 22 Feb. 1817, but did not take up his residence there, and on 14 Oct. 1818 he was admitted pensioner at St. John's College. He graduated B.A. in 1823.

On leaving the university Stapleton became the private secretary of Canning, and was admitted into his closest confidence. He walked side by side with his chief at the funeral of the Duke of York in St. George's Chapel at Windsor, when Canning caught his fatal cold, and was with him at Chiswick shortly before his death. By the special desire of George IV, and as a tribute to Canning's memory, he was appointed a commissioner of customs on 31 Aug. 1827. This appointment he vacated in a few years, and in 1837, at the request of his political leaders, he contested Birmingham in the conservative interest, and, though possessed of much oratorical power, was badly beaten.

In 1830 Stapleton caused to be printed two volumes of his 'Political Life of George Canning, 1822-1827.' But at the instance of the Duke of Wellington, intimations induced him to defer their publication (JEKYLL, Letters, p. 226). When tracts appeared with reflections on Canning, Stapleton issued the work in 1831 (3 vols.) A second edition, which came out in the same year, included additional matter. In 1859 he published 'George Canning and his Time,' which was deficient in system, but, like the previous work, contained much information. In continuance of the subject, Stapleton subsequently contributed to 'Macmillan's Magazine' (xxvi. 25-32) an article on 'A Month at Seaford in 1825 with Canning and Hookham Frere,' and three more of his papers appeared in the same periodical (vol. xxxi.), including one entitled 'Political Reminiscences.' Stapleton died at Warbrook, Evers-

ley, near Winchfield, Hampshire, on 26 Feb. 1880. He married, in 1825, Catherine, second daughter of John Bulteel of Flete, Devonshire. She died at Kensington on 18 June 1856, having had issue three sons and two daughters. His youngest son, Edward J. Stapleton, of the home office (d. 27 Jan. 1896, aged 56), edited in 1887 two volumes of 'Official Correspondence of George Canning,' the second of which contained numerous letters to and from his father in 1826 and 1827.

From 1836 Stapleton was a constant contributor to the newspapers and a prolific pamphleteer. The chief of these were: 1. 'Observations on the Report of the Bullion Committee in 1810,' 1837. 2. 'The Real Monster Evil of Ireland,' 1843. 3. 'Sequel to the real Monster Evil of Ireland,' 1843; the evil was over-population, and he advocated a large expenditure, say 10,000,000l., in that country on works of public improvement. 4. 'The Claims of the Irish Priest. The Duty of the British People,' 1847; against the endowment of 'popery.' 5. 'Suggestions for a Conservative and Popular Reform in the Commons,' 1850; a plea for a direct representation of the professional classes and of the arts and sciences. A petition to this effect drawn up by Stapleton and George Harris, LL.D., F.S.A., was presented by Lord Harrowby to the House of Lords on 27 May 1852, and produced a long speech from Lord Derby (HANSARD, cxxi. 1181-92; cf. HARRIS, Autobiogr. pp. 184-91). 6. 'The Irish Education Question: a Letter to the Earl of Eglinton,' 1853. 7. 'Oath of Supremacy and the "Oaths Bill,"' 1854; in favour of the maintenance of the oath of supremacy. 8. 'Hostilities at Canton,' 1857; against the proceedings of Sir John Bowring and Admiral Sir Michael Seymour over the Arrow lorcha; a concentrated statement of the case against Lord Palmerston's government, which led, in the author's opinion, to the defeat of the ministry. 9. 'A Letter to the Bradford Foreign Affairs Committee,' also on the China question. 10. 'Affair at Greytown,' 1857, arguing that England should have demanded satisfaction from the American government for the outrages at Grey Town, Nicaragua. 11. 'Intervention and Non-intervention; or the Foreign Policy of Great Britain, 1790-1865' (1866), a volume summing up his arguments in former pamphlets on foreign affairs, and the substance of his letters in the 'Morning Herald' (1850-5), signed 'Lex Publica.' 12. 'Origin of Fenianism,' 1868. 13. 'The French Case truly stated,' 1871, an argument that France was not the aggressor in the Franco-Prussian war; a translation was published at Brussels.

[Men of the Time, 10th ed.; Burke's Landed Gentry, 6th ed. p. 1513; Academy, 6 March 1880; Standard, 30 Jan. 1896; Morning Post, 12 April 1880; Gent. Mag. 1856, ii. 127; information from Mr. R. F. Scott of St. John's College, Cambridge.]   W. P. C.

STAPLETON, BRIAN DE (1321?–1394) of Wighill, knight, was the second son of Sir Gilbert de Stapleton, and younger brother of Miles de Stapleton (*d.* 1364) [q. v.] His father died in 1321, and the length of his life makes it unlikely that he was born much earlier. In 1385 he describes himself as 'sixty years of age and more' and 'fifty years in arms' (*Scrope and Grosvenor Roll*). This would make his active career begin with Edward III's first wars against France, in which he won considerable distinction. He was at the siege of Tournay in 1340, and again in 1347 at the siege of Calais, having probably therefore served in the Crecy campaign. He attached himself to William de Montacute, second earl of Salisbury [q. v.], serving under him for example in the campaign of 1359, and for many subsequent years. In 1369 he was one of the knights sent to help the Black Prince in Aquitaine, under Edmund, earl of Cambridge. In 1373 he served under Salisbury at sea, and again when Salisbury had custody of Calais, where he did him such faithful service that he received two manors from him as a reward. In 1378 he was exempted from serving on juries or being forced to hold offices against his will (*Cal. Rot. Pat.* 1377–81, p. 288). The subsidy roll of 1378–9 gives an interesting list of his household at Helaugh (*Yorkshire Arch. Journ.* vii. 176, 181). On 20 Feb. 1380 Stapleton was himself made captain and warden of the castle of Calais (*Fœdera*, iv. 77), and a little later of Guisnes. On 11 March 1381 he was also warden of the castle of Guisnes (*ib.* iv. 107). In April 1380 he was associated with others in negotiations with the French. In 1382 he became knight of the Garter, remaining in office at Guisnes till 1383, and holding in that year a muster of Bishop Despenser's crusading force (*ib.* iv. 70). He was employed in various negotiations with France and Flanders, including those which led to the truce of Leulinghen (*ib.* iv. 122, 172). In 1386 and 1388 he was similarly employed in Scotland (*ib.* old edit. vii. 572). He gave evidence in the Scrope-Grosvenor controversy, and was one of the commissioners appointed to examine witnesses. As late as 1390 he appeared in arms among the knights of the Garter at a tournament at Smithfield. He is the hero of several famous legends of the later genealogists. There is a sixteenth-century story of his slaying a Moor in single combat, and therefore bearing as his crest a Saracen's head. He is also said to have brought from France the right hand of St. Mary Magdalen, which he placed in the house of the friars preachers at York, and where, according to the legend, he himself was buried.

Before 1360 Stapleton married Alice, widow of Sir Stephen Waleys of Helaugh and daughter and coheiress of Sir John de St. Philibert. He inherited Carlton and Kentmere from a cousin, and in 1376 bought Wighill, where he died on 25 July 1394. His will, written in French, was dated 16 May the same year, and is published in 'Testamenta Eboracensia' (i. 198 sq.) He directed that his body should be buried at Helaugh priory, beside his wife, who had died before him; he left directions for a sumptuous burial, and made many legacies to friends and kinsfolk. He left two sons, of whom, the elder, Brian, who married Elizabeth, daughter of Sir William Aldeburgh, and was the ancestor of the Stapletons of Carlton (now represented by Lord Beaumont), died before him; the younger, Sir Miles (*d.* 1400), was the ancestor of the Stapletons of Wighill.

[Chetwynd-Stapylton's Stapeltons of Yorkshire, pp. 110–38, collects practically all that is known; other authorities quoted in the text.]   T. F. T.

STAPLETON, GREGORY, D.D. (1748–1802), catholic prelate, born at Carlton, Yorkshire, in 1748, was seventh son of Nicholas Stapleton, by his third wife, Winifred, daughter of John White of Dover Street, London. He proceeded to the English College, Douay, in 1762. Ten years later, being then a deacon, he was appointed professor of music. On his ordination, a year later, he became procurator of the college, and he retained that post for more than twelve years. After this he travelled abroad with a pupil; and on his return from Italy, in 1787, he was appointed president of the English College at St. Omer, in succession to Alban Butler [q. v.] Some three years after the outbreak of the French revolution he and the students of the English colleges at St. Omer and Douay were imprisoned in the citadel of Dourlens. In 1795 he obtained leave to go to Paris, and after many repulses he procured from the directory an order for the release of all the students, ninety-four in number, who were conveyed to England in an American vessel, and landed at Dover on 2 March 1795. Soon afterwards Stapleton, in company with Bishop Douglass, waited upon the Duke of Portland and Mr. Pitt to solicit their approval of a plan for converting the school at Old Hall Green, near Ware, Hertfordshire, into a catholic college. The duke had previously known Stapleton, and he and Pitt gave them encouragement. Stapleton accordingly conducted his students to Old Hall Green, and on 19 Aug. 1795 the first stone was laid of the college of St. Edmund. Stapleton presided over it till the autumn of 1800, when, having accompanied the Rev. John Nassau to Rome on an important secret mission, he was raised to the episcopate. His appointment to be bishop of Hierocæsarea *in partibus* and vicar-apostolic of the Midland district, in succession to Dr. Charles Berington [q. v.], was approved by the pope on 29 May 1800, and he was consecrated on 8 March 1801. He took up his residence at Long Birch, near Wolverhampton, and employed Dr. John Milner [q. v.] as his secretary. He died at St. Omer on 23 May 1802, and was succeeded in his vicariate by Dr. Milner.

[Brady's Episcopal Succession; Evans's Cat. of Engraved Portraits, No. 21652; Husenbeth's Colleges on the Continent, pp. 15–16; Husenbeth's Life of Milner, p. 84; Michel, Les Écossais en France, ii. 330; Notes and Queries, 3rd ser. x. 43; Smith's Brewood, 2nd edit. 1874, p. 49; Ward's Hist. of St. Edmund's College, Old Hall, 1893, p. 343, with portrait.] T. C.

STAPLETON, MILES DE (*d.* 1314), baron, was the son of Nicholas de Stapleton (III) and his wife Margaret, daughter of Miles Basset. Nicholas belonged to a Richmondshire family that took its name from the township of Stapleton, on the south bank of the Tees, about two miles south-west of Darlington, in which it possessed a small estate. The first member of the family to attain any position was Nicholas de Stapleton I, who was custos of Middleham Castle in the reign of King John, and was the father of Nicholas de Stapleton II, the father of the first-mentioned Nicholas (III). Nicholas III served as a judge of the king's bench between 1272 and 1290, held sixteen carucates of land scattered throughout Yorkshire, besides some Berkshire lands that he obtained from his wife, and died in 1290.

Miles de Stapleton was the eldest surviving son, and at his father's death was already married to Sybil (also called Isabel), daughter and coheiress to John de Bellew. Through her mother Laderana, Sybil inherited a share of the possessions of the elder line of the Bruces, which were divided among four sisters and coheiresses at the death of her uncle, Peter de Bruce of Skelton, in 1271. In memory of this connection with a great house, Miles de Stapleton assumed the lion rampant of the Bruces as his arms. Miles served in the Gascon and Scottish wars of Edward I. In 1291 he was engaged on the king's business, under Roger de Mowbray, in Scotland (*Cal. Patent Rolls*, 1281–92, p. 434). In 1295 he was in Gascony. In 1298 he was in the Falkirk campaign, serving under his patron Henry de Lacy, third earl of Lincoln [q. v.] (GOUGH, *Scotland in 1298*, p. 43). In 1300 he was summoned to the siege of Carlaverock, but he was not mentioned in the famous French poem on the siege. In the same year he accompanied the Earl of Lincoln, on a mission to the court of Rome, receiving on 9 Oct. letters of protection for one year (*Cal. Patent Rolls*, 1292–1301, p. 538). He was entrusted by the king with the direction of the household of Edward, prince of Wales, served in the siege of Stirling, in attendance on the prince (PALGRAVE, *Doc. illustrative of Scottish History*, p. 271); and in October 1305, when the Earl of Lincoln wished to appoint Stapleton to manage his household during his absence at the papal court, the prince informed the earl that he had no power to give Stapleton leave to hold this post without the express command of the king (*Deputy-Keeper Public Rec.* 9th Rep. p. 249). Stapleton was one of the experienced men of affairs to whom Edward I entrusted the difficult task of bringing up his son in businesslike and soldierly ways. Meanwhile his estates and influence in Yorkshire were steadily increasing. The betrothal of his eldest son to a daughter of John of Brittany, earl of Richmond, and a grand-niece of the king, and his second son's betrothal to one of the daughters of Brian Fitzalan, lord of Bedale [q. v.], connected him with two branches of the greatest family of his district, and increased the importance of the house. After the death of Edmund of Cornwall had led to the lapse of his vast property to the crown, Edward I made Stapleton seneschal of Knaresborough Castle, and steward and joint constable of Knaresborough forest. In 1305 he was, jointly with John de Byron, appointed commissioner to suppress the clubmen or trail-bastons of Lancashire, but they were shortly afterwards superseded.

With Edward II's accession Stapleton's importance was for the moment increased. He became steward to the king's household, and went abroad in January 1308 on the occasion of the king's marriage at Boulogne. In a few months, however, he lost his stewardship, and was forced to surrender the royal manor of Brustwick in Holderness, of which he had had custody, to Gaveston (*Fœdera*, ii. 48). In 1311 he was summoned to serve against the Scots (*ib.* ii. 139). His losses in the interests of the Gascon favourite made Stapleton hostile to his old master Edward, and attached him to Earl Thomas of Lancaster. He was in October 1313 included, with his wife and three sons, in a long list of adherents of Lancaster, who were then pardoned for the murder of Gaveston (*ib.* ii. 230). Previously to this, however, he had received back the custody of Brustwick, and in the same year he was thrice summoned as a baron to parliament. In 1314 he obeyed the summons to muster for the relief of Stirling. On 24 June he was slain, along with two of his sons, at Bannockburn.

By his first wife, Sybil, Stapleton left several children. The eldest, Nicholas, born in 1286 (ROBERTS, *Cal. Genealogicum*, p. 608), was also summoned to parliament, and died in 1343. His son and successor, Miles, died in 1372. Miles's only son, Thomas, died in 1373, whereupon the barony fell into abeyance, and the estates of the elder branch passed to his sister Elizabeth, and remained with the Metham family, her husband's kin. A younger son of Miles and Sybil, Gilbert (*d.* 1321), became royal escheator beyond Trent, and by his wife Agnes, daughter of Brian Fitzalan, lord of Bedale, was the father of Miles de Stapleton (*d.* 1364) [q. v.] and Brian de Stapleton (*d.* 1394) [q. v.] After Sybil's death Stapleton married, as his second wife, Joan (wrongly called Cecily), daughter of Peter of Tynedale, who survived him (*Cal. Close Rolls*, 1313-18, p. 231); by her he had a daughter named Joan.

Among Stapleton's pious benefactions the most important was the establishment of a chapel dedicated to St. Nicholas in North Moreton church, near Wallingford in Berkshire, where he had an outlying estate. This building, described as a 'gem of decorated architecture,' still survives, with the contemporary stained glass in the east window, now much spoilt through successive stages of neglect and restoration. The license to alienate lands in mortmain to endow two chaplains to celebrate divine service in the chapel is dated 28 March 1299 (*Cal. Patent Rolls*, 1292-1301, p. 401).

[Roberts's Calendarium Genealogicum; Cal. of Patent Rolls, 1282-91 and 1292-1301; Cal. of Close Rolls 1307-13 and 1318; Ann. London. in Stubbs's Chron. Edw. I and Edw. II (Rolls Ser.); Parl. Writs; Rymer's Fœdera; Dugdale's Baronage, ii. 70; Foss's Judges of England and Biographia Juridica, p. 629. Chetwynd-Stapyl-

ton's Stapletons of Yorkshire (a very careful family history) collects on pp. 1-52 nearly all that is known of Stapleton and his ancestors.]

T. F. T.

STAPLETON, MILES DE (*d.* 1364), of Bedale and Ingham, knight of the Garter, was the eldest son of Gilbert de Stapleton, knt. (*d.* 1321), and the grandson of Miles de Stapleton (*d.* 1314) [q. v.] His mother was Matilda (*b.* 1298), also called Agnes, elder daughter and coheiress of Brian Fitzalan, lord of Bedale [q. v.], from whom he inherited a moiety of Fitzalan's estates, including half Bedale, Askham Brian, and Cotherstone in Yorkshire. Brian de Stapleton [q. v.] was his younger brother. At his father's death Stapleton was only a child. In early life he is often called Miles de Stapleton of Cotherstone. He afterwards obtained considerable fame as a warrior during the French wars of Edward III. It is, however, very difficult to distinguish him from his cousin and namesake, Sir Miles de Stapleton of Hathelsay (*d.* 1373), who was sheriff of Yorkshire in 1353, served in the French and Scottish wars from 1355 to 1360, and in 1356 conducted the captive David Bruce from Newcastle to London; was summoned to parliament in 1358, but never received a subsequent writ, and died in 1373, leaving a son and heir Thomas, whose widow ultimately took the estate to her near kin the Fitzwilliams. Dugdale in his 'Baronage' (ii. 70) has woven the exploits of Miles of Bedale into the history of Miles of Hathelsay. He was probably in the Breton expedition of 1342, and at the siege of Calais in 1347. Either he or his cousin was the Miles de Stapleton who on 19 Jan. 1344 obtained the chief credit on the first day of a famous Windsor tournament, and afterwards took part in the foundation of a 'round table' (MURIMUTH, p. 155). In June 1345 he received, as Miles de Stapleton of Cotherstone, letters of protection on going beyond sea with the king (*Fœdera*, iii. 48, cf. p. 39). In 1347 and 1348 he was again prominent in the tournaments that preceded the foundation of the order of the Garter, becoming one of the original knights of the Garter, standing seventeenth in the list, and occupying the ninth stall in St. George's Chapel on the 'king's side.' In 1349 and 1354 he was again serving in France, and in the latter year was one of the magnates who signed a procuration referring the disputes of England and France to the pope (*ib.* iii. 285). He took part in the raid of Lancaster towards Paris in 1356 (G. LE BAKER, p. 139, cf. p. 298). In January 1358 he went on a mission from Edward III to Philip of Navarre, receiving 50*l.* as his wages as king's messenger (*Fœdera*, iii. 387). In July 1359 he was again going abroad on the king's service (*ib.* iii. 439), and was one of the negotiators of the treaty of Bretigny in 1360 (*ib.* iii. 494), being afterwards ordered with two others to see to its faithful execution. In June 1361 he received an annuity of 100*l.* from the exchequer for his 'unwearied labours and laudable services.' In January 1364 he again obtained letters of attorney for three years, and went to France to support John de Montfort's candidature for the Breton succession. He died in December of the same year, possibly, as the family historian conjectures, of wounds received in the battle of Auray.

Stapleton is celebrated by Geoffrey le Baker (p. 139) as a good and experienced soldier, a man of great probity and singular devotion to the Blessed Virgin. He was twice married. By his first wife he had a son John, who died in 1355. He married his second wife in 1350. This lady was Joan, daughter and coheiress of Oliver de Ingham, baron of Ingham [q. v.] in Norfolk, and widow of Roger Lestrange of Knockin. Henceforward Stapleton is as often described as 'of Ingham' as of 'Bedale,' and became a considerable proprietor in Norfolk. In 1360 he obtained royal license to dispense with the statute of mortmain, and, in conjunction with his wife, began to found a college of Mathurius or Trinitarians at Ingham, an order of canons established to pray for and redeem Christian captives from the Turks. He rebuilt the parish church of Ingham on a grand scale, and obtained from Bishop Thomas Percy of Norwich an ordinance for a foundation for a prior (or warden), sacrist, and six canons (*Monasticon*, vi. 1454–9), in which the rectory of the parish was absorbed. At first only the warden and two chaplains were appointed. The building is still the parish church, and parts are of this date. Stapleton was buried at Ingham; a sumptuous brass placed over his tomb is engraved in Gough's 'Sepulchral Monuments' (vol. i. pt. ii. p. 120), and in Mr. Chetwynd-Stapylton's 'Stapeltons of Yorkshire' (p. 100), who also gives the inscription from Blomefield's 'Norfolk' (ix. 324, 8vo). The brass was dilapidated in Blomefield's time, and has since disappeared. Stapleton's eldest son John died before him, and he was succeeded at Ingham as well as Bedale by Miles, his son by the heiress of Ingham. Their only other issue was a daughter Joan, married to Sir John Plays. Another three generations in the male line succeeded Stapleton at Ingham, after which the property was divided among coheiresses. A remarkable series of brasses, also destroyed, preserved their memory in Ingham church.

[Rymer's Fœdera; Geoffrey le Baker, ed. E. M. Thompson; Dugdale's Monasticon, vol. vi.; Dugdale's Baronage, vol. ii.; Blomefield's Norfolk, ix. 320–9, 8vo; Norfolk Archæological Journal, 1878; Chetwynd-Stapylton's Stapeltons of Yorkshire, pp. 87–101, and for Miles of Hathelsay, pp. 71–3.] T. F. T.

STAPLETON or **STAPILTON**, Sir PHILIP (1603–1647), soldier, born in 1603, was the second son of Henry Stapleton of Wighill, Yorkshire, and Mary, daughter of Sir John Foster of Bamborough. Stapleton was admitted a fellow-commoner of Queens' College, Cambridge, on 16 May 1617. In 1627 he married the widow of John Gee of Bishop Burton (eldest daughter of Sir John Hotham), and shortly after bought the estate of Warter Priory in Yorkshire (CHETWYND-STAPYLTON, *The Stapletons of Yorkshire*, p. 253). He was knighted on 25 May 1630 (METCALFE, *Book of Knights*, p. 190). Clarendon describes Stapleton as 'a proper man of fair extraction; but being a branch of a younger family inherited but a moderate estate, about five hundred pounds the year in Yorkshire, and, according to the education of that country, spent his time in those delights which horses and dogs administer' (*Rebellion*, iv. 19). In June 1640 Stapleton was one of the signatories of the petition of the Yorkshire gentlemen against free quarter (RUSHWORTH, iii. 1214). In November he was returned to the Long parliament as member for Boroughbridge, and joined Sir John Hotham [q. v.] and other 'northern men' in the prosecution of Strafford (*ib.*; *Trial of Strafford*, pp. 14, 33, 601, 604). The popular leaders noted him as 'a man of vigour in body and mind,' and he 'quickly outgrew his friends and countrymen in the confidence of those who governed.' On 20 Aug. 1641 he was selected as one of the two commissioners whom the House of Commons appointed to attend the king to Scotland, and was joined with John Hampden that he might be 'initiated under so great a master' (CLARENDON, iv. 19; *Lords' Journals*, iv. 372, 401, v. 398).

In the second session of the Long parliament Stapleton was one of the four persons selected by the commons to bear their answer to the king's demand for the arrest of the five members (3 Jan. 1642), and one of the committee of twenty-five appointed to sit in the Guildhall during the adjournment of the house (FORSTER, *Arrest of the Five Members*, ed. 1860, pp. 126, 280). A week later he made a vigorous speech against Colonel Thomas Lunsford [q. v.], Lord Digby, and other delinquents (*Old Parliamentary History*, x. 210). When Charles went to York and attempted to possess himself of Hull, Stapleton was one of the five parliamentary commissioners sent down to report and resist his movements—a difficult task, and one which exposed the commissioners to many insults from the king's followers (*ib.* x. 493, 511, 518; RUSHWORTH, iv. 620).

At the opening of the civil war Stapleton became commander of the hundred gentlemen who formed Essex's life-guard and colonel of his regiment of horse (LUDLOW, *Memoirs*, ed. 1894, p. 39). At Edgehill he did excellent service, and the rout of the king's foot was due specially to him and to Sir William Balfour (*ib.* p. 42 ; RUSHWORTH, v. 36). At Chalgrove Field he rallied the defeated parliamentary horse (*A Letter from His Excellency the Earl of Essex,* 19 June 1643, p. 3). In the march to Gloucester and in the first battle of Newbury no man's services were more conspicuous (*Bibliotheca Gloucestrensis,* pp. 237–44; MAY, *History of the Long Parliament,* p. 348). Whitelocke quotes from the newspapers of the day anecdotes of his courage (*Memorials,* i. 217).

Stapleton marched with Essex on his western campaign, but was not with it at the disaster in Cornwall; for Essex, about the end of July, sent him to London to give an account of the state of his army and of the condition of the western counties (DEVEREUX, *Lives of the Earls of Essex,* p. 423; *Tanner MSS.* lxi. 32). It was to Stapleton that Essex addressed his narrative of the defeat, and his complaints of the government which had left them unsuccoured (RUSHWORTH, vi. 701). As the bosom friend of Essex, Stapleton enjoyed considerable influence in the House of Commons, where he was held to represent the general's opinions on questions of war and negotiations (SANFORD, *Studies and Illustrations of the Great Rebellion,* pp. 541–4, 571). He was also a member of the committee of safety (4 July 1642) and of the committee of both kingdoms (16 Feb. 1644). The self-denying ordinance, which deprived him of his military position, he strongly opposed, and he was one of the originators of the plan for accusing Cromwell as an incendiary which the partisans of Essex projected (WHITELOCKE, *Memorials,* i. 349). He was generally coupled with Denzil Holles as a leader of the English presbyterians. 'What a sway,' said Cromwell in 1647, 'Stapleton and Holles had heretofore in the kingdom,' adding, according to Major Huntington, that 'he was as able to govern the kingdom as either of

them' (MASERES, *Select Tracts,* i. 405). The value at which the parliament estimated his services was shown by their vote on 1 Dec. 1645, when they asked the king to make Stapleton a baron and endow him with 2,000*l.* a year (*Commons' Journals,* iv. 361).

As a staunch presbyterian Stapleton enjoyed great influence with the Scottish commissioners. They relied upon him and his friends to counterwork the independents and the army. 'Stapleton and Holles, and some others of the eleven members,' wrote Baillie in September 1647, 'had been the main persuaders of us to remove out of England and leave the king to them, upon assurance, which was most likely, that this was the only means to get the evil army disbanded, the king and peace settled according to our minds' (*Letters,* iii. 16). Just before the disbanding of the army was attempted, Stapleton incurred the special animosity of the soldiers by assaulting a certain Major Tulidah, who was one of the presenters of a petition the circulation of which parliament wished to prevent. Tulidah was imprisoned for a week by order of the commons, and Stapleton was denounced as seeking to destroy the right of petition. When the eleven presbyterian leaders in the commons were impeached by the army (16 June 1647), he was accused, like the rest, of endeavouring to overthrow the liberties of the subject and to cause another civil war, to which the charge of obstructing the relief of Ireland was added (GARDINER, *Great Civil War,* iii. 256, 298; LILBURNE, *Rash Oaths Unwarrantable,* 1647, pp. 36–42). On 6 July more detailed articles were presented, to which a lengthy answer was drawn up by William Prynne on behalf of the eleven (*Old Parliamentary History,* xvi. 69, 116). The accused members preferred to withdraw from the house rather than to let the impeachment take its course, and on 20 July the house gave them leave to absent themselves and passes to go beyond seas if they desired (*Commons' Journals,* v. 251). After the riots of 26 July, however, Stapleton and the accused members returned to the house, and he was one of the committee of safety originally appointed on 11 June, and revived 30 July 1647 (RUSHWORTH, vi. 653). When the resistance of the city collapsed, he and five others of the accused obtained passes from the speaker and took ship off Essex for Calais (14 Aug.) The partisans of the army were eager to prevent their escape, and a certain Captain Lamming overtook the fugitives a few miles from Calais, and forced them to return. Vice-admiral Batten, commander of the fleet in the Downs, at once dismissed them (RUSHWORTH, vii. 785), and they landed at Calais on 17 Aug. Stapleton was ill, and the hardships of the journey increased his fever to such an extent that he died on the following day, at an inn called the Three Silver Lions, and, as his illness was suspected to be the plague, he was buried immediately in the protestant burying-ground at Calais (*A True Relation of Captain Batten*, &c., 1647, 4to: *A Short and True Narrative of the Sickness and Death of Sir Philip Stapleton*, 1647, 4to).

A friendly biographer, supposed to be Denzil Holles, describes Stapleton as a man 'of a thin body and a weak constitution, but full of spirit,' adding that he was 'quick of apprehension, sound of judgment, of clear and good elocution' (*ib.* pp. 3, 5). Robert Baillie styles him, 'after Holles, the second gentleman for all gallantry in England' (*Letters*, iii. 19). The Sutherland Clarendon in the Bodleian Library contains four engraved portraits of Stapleton.

Stapleton married twice: first, the widow of John Gee, of Bishop Burton, Yorkshire, 1627. By her he left four children: (1) John Stapleton of Warter; (2) Robert Stapleton of Wighill (*d.* 1675); (3) Katherine, married George Leeson of Dublin; (4) Mary, married first one Bigges of Gray's Inn; secondly, Thomas, fourth viscount Fitzwilliam, of Merrion in Ireland. By his second wife, Barbara, daughter of Henry Lennard, twelfth lord Dacre of Hurstmonceaux, whom he married at St. Anne's, Blackfriars, 6 Feb. 1638 (MALCOLM, *Londinium Redivivum*, ii. 370), he had two sons—Henry and Philip—and a daughter Frances, who married Sir Nathaniel Powell of Ewhurst Place, Sussex, besides other children who died young.

[The only biography of Stapleton is contained in a series of articles by H. E. Chetwynd-Stapylton, printed in the Journal of the Yorkshire Archæological Society, 1883–4, vol. viii, and reprinted in 1896 under the title of The Stapeltons of Yorkshire.] C. H. F.

STAPLETON or **STAPYLTON**, Sir ROBERT (*d.* 1669), dramatic poet and translator, was the third son of Richard Stapleton of Carlton by Snaith, Yorkshire, by Elizabeth, daughter of Sir Henry Pierrepoint of Holm Pierrepoint (DUGDALE, *Visitation of Yorkshire*, ed. Davies, p. 205). He was educated in the Benedictine convent of St. Gregory at Douay, where he became a professed monk of the order on 30 March 1625 (WELDON, *Chronicle*, Appendix, p. 9). But being, as Wood observes, 'too gay and poetical to be confined within a cloyster,' he left the Benedictines, turned protestant, and

was appointed one of the gentlemen in ordinary of the privy chamber to Prince Charles. He followed the king when his majesty left London, and was knighted at Nottingham on 13 Sept. 1642 (METCALFE, *Book of Knights*, p. 199). After the battle of Edgehill he accompanied the king to Oxford, where he was created D.C.L. in November 1642. He remained at Oxford until its surrender to Fairfax in May 1645. Under the Commonwealth he lived a studious life, and at the Restoration he was made one of the gentlemen ushers to the privy chamber.

Stapleton died on 10 or 11 July 1669, and was buried on the 15th near the vestry door of Westminster Abbey (CHESTER, *Registers of Westminster Abbey*, p. 170). His will, dated 11 June 1669, was proved on 29 July by Elizabeth Simpson of Westminster, widow, to whom he left the bulk of his estate (although he had a wife living, whom he barely mentioned) in consideration, as he alleged, of the great care she had taken of him during his long illness. His wife was a Mrs. Hammond, widow (born Mainwaring).

For the stage he wrote: 1. 'The Royal Choice,' a play entered in the register of the Stationers' Company, 29 Nov. 1653. No copy of this appears to have been preserved. 2. 'The Slighted Maid,' London, 1663, 4to, a comedy, in five acts and in verse, which Pepys saw acted at the Duke's House, Lincoln's Inn Fields, on coronation day, 20 May 1663. The cast included the Bettertons, Cave Underhill [q. v.], and other well-known actors. Genest styles it 'a pretty good comedy' (*History of the Stage*, i. 46). 3. 'The Step-Mother,' London, 1664, a tragi-comedy, in five acts and in verse, acted at Lincoln's Inn Fields by the Duke of York's servants on 28 May 1663. The cast was much the same as for the preceding play, but Genest says 'the serious scenes of it are bad' (*ib.* i. 46–7). 4. 'The Tragedie of Hero and Leander,' London, 1669, 8vo, in five acts and in verse. 'This is an indifferent tragedy—it is founded on the poem of Musæus—the original story being very simple, Stapylton was obliged to make large additions to it in order to form 5 acts—he has not been happy in these additions' (*ib.* x. 142). It was never acted.

Stapleton published the following translations: 5. 'Pliny's Panegyricke: a Speech in the Senate, wherein publick Thanks are presented to the Emperor Trajan,' Oxford, 1644, 4to, from the Latin of Pliny the younger, illustrated with annotations. 6. 'The first Six Satyrs of Juvenal ... with annotations clearing the obscure places out of History, Laws, and Ceremonies of the Romans,'

Oxford, 1644, 8vo. Dr. Bartholomew Holyday used to say that Stapleton made use of his translation of Juvenal, having borrowed it in manuscript. 7. 'The Loves of Hero and Leander: a Greek poem [by Musæus] translated into English verse, with annotations upon the original,' Oxford, 1645, 4to; London, 1647, 8vo. 8. 'Juvenal's Sixteen Satyrs [translated in verse]. Or, a Survey of the Manners and Actions of Mankind. With arguments, marginall notes, and annotations,' London, 1647, 8vo; 1660, fol. 1673, 8vo. 9. Translation of Faminius Strada's 'De Bello Belgico,' or 'The History of the Low-Countrey Warres,' London, 1650 and 1667, fol.

He has verses (a) before Harding's 'Sicily and Naples,' a play, 1640; (b) before the Earl of Monmouth's 'Romulus and Tarquine,' 1648; (c) before Cartwright's 'Comedies,' 1651; (d) before Gayton's 'Case of Longevity,' 1659; (e) in Ashmolean MS. 36.

Langbaine states that Stapleton executed the translations of De Marmet's 'Entertainments of the Cours; or Academical Conversations,' 1658, and of Cyrano de Bergerac's 'Σεληναρχία, or the Government of the World in the Moon,' 1659, both published under the name of Thomas Saint Serf. It appears, however, that the real translator was Thomas Sydserf or Saint Serfe, son of Thomas Sydserf [q. v.], bishop of Galloway and afterwards of Orkney (Miscellany of the Abbotsford Club, i. 85).

There are three engraved portraits of Stapleton. One is by William Marshall.

SIR MILES STAPLETON (1628–1707), third son of Sir Robert's eldest brother Gilbert (d. 1634), by his wife Eleanor, daughter of Sir John Gascoigne of Barnbow, first baronet, was born in 1628, and created a baronet on 20 March 1661–2. Being charged by the informer Bolron with being concerned in the plot of Sir Thomas Gascoigne [q. v.], in June 1680 he was sent from London to be tried at York (LUTTRELL, Historical Relation of State Affairs, i. 48). He was brought up to the bar in the following month, but he challenged so many jurors that the trial was postponed. It came off on 18 July 1681, and there were three witnesses against him, viz. Bolron, Mowbray, and John Smith of Walworth, Durham. Sir Miles defended himself energetically, and brought many persons to throw discredit on the testimony of the informers. The jury immediately acquitted him; but, as Dodd observes, it is very surprising that when Thomas Thwing was afterwards tried upon the same evidence, he was condemned and executed (Church Hist. iii. 254). Sir Miles was a gentleman of great honour, position, and ability. On his death in 1707 the baronetcy became extinct. His first wife was Elizabeth, daughter of Robert Bertie, earl of Lindsey [q. v.], by whom he had three sons, all dying in infancy; his second wife was Elizabeth, daughter of Sir Thomas Langueville.

[Chetwynd-Stapylton's Stapyltons of Yorkshire, 1897, pp. 165, 169; Addit. MS. 24489, pp. 81, 366; Ashmolean MS. 788, art. 27; Baker's Biogr. Dramatica, 1812, i. 682, ii. 298, iii. 228, 283, 300; Brüggemann's English Editions of Greek and Latin Authors, pp. 13, 679, 699; Burke's Extinct Baronetage, p. 506; Cibber's Lives of the Poets, ii. 102; Courthope's Synopsis, p. 188; Dodd's Church Hist. iii. 252, 253; Foster's Alumni Oxon. (1500–1714), iv. 1413; Granger's Biogr. Hist. of England, 5th edit. iii. 134, iv. 53; Hazlitt's Manual of Old English Plays; Langbaine's Dramatick Poets, p. 491; Lowndes's Bibl. Man. ed. Bohn, p. 2495; Wood's Fasti Oxon. ed. Bliss, ii. 39; Depositions from the Castle of York, 1861.] T. C.

STAPLETON, THEOBALD (fl. 1636), Irish writer, who called himself in Irish Teaboid Gáilduf, was a native of Kilkenny of English descent, but does not seem to have been related to the Stapletons of Yorkshire (CHETWYND-STAPYLTON, Stapyltons of Yorkshire, 1897). He was ordained priest and lived for some time in Flanders. In 1639 he published in Brussels, 'Catechismus seu Doctrina Christiana Latino-Hibernica,' dedicated to Ferdinand, infant of Spain. He says that his motive in making the translation was that Irish was too much considered the exclusive property of poets and secular authors, so that the Irish themselves often said prayers in Latin, though knowing no language but Irish. The book, which is a quarto, was printed by Hubert Anthony Velpius at the Golden Eagle near the palace in Brussels, and is remarkable as the first book in which the Irish language was printed in Roman type. The title-page has a vignette copied with slight differences from that of the Sgathan an Chrabhaidh printed at Louvain in 1616. At the end is printed 'Modh ro vras na teanghan Ghaoilaige do bagh,' directions for reading Irish. The Irish letters, diphthongs, triphthongs, aspiration, eclipsis, and some contractions are explained in nineteen sections.

[Works; Anderson's Historical Sketches of the Native Irish, 2nd ed. 1830; Rev. C. P. Meehan's Rise and Fall of the Irish Franciscan Monasteries, 6th ed.] N. M.

STAPLETON, THOMAS, D.D. (1535–1598), catholic controversialist, born at Henfield, Sussex, in July 1535, was son of

William Stapleton, steward to the bishop of Winchester, and a member of the Carlton family of Stapleton (CHETWYND-STAPYL-TON, *Stapeltons of Yorkshire*, 1897, p. 161). Thomas acquired the rudiments of grammar in the free school at Canterbury under John Twyne [q. v.] In 1550 he was admitted a scholar at Winchester, where the entry in the register states that he was then twelve years of age and that he was a native of, or a resident at, Oving, Sussex (KIRBY, *Winchester Scholars*, p. 129). He was elected to a fellowship at New College, Oxford, 18 Jan. 1552-3, and graduated B.A. on 2 Dec. 1556 (*Oxford Univ. Register*, i. 233). Shortly before the death of Queen Mary he was collated by Bishop Christopherson to the prebend of Woodhorne in Chichester Cathedral. Being attached to the ancient form of religion, he left the country soon after Queen Elizabeth's accession, and settled at Louvain, where he applied himself to the study of theology. Subsequently he proceeded to the university of Paris in order to complete his knowledge of the sacred tongues, and then 'for devotion sake' paid a visit to Rome. On his return to Louvain he found letters from his father desiring his immediate attendance in England. He complied with the request, and was required by his diocesan Bishop Barlow to abjure the authority of the pope, and to acknowledge the spiritual supremacy of the queen. In consequence of his refusal he was deprived of his prebend early in 1563, and he again retired to Louvain, taking with him his father and some other members of his family (*Records of the English Catholics*, i. 306; CARTWRIGHT, *Rape of Bramber*, p. 275).

In 1569 William (afterwards Cardinal) Allen [q. v.] invited him to the newly founded English College in the university of Douay, where he rendered signal service both as a teacher and a benefactor; he was appointed lecturer in divinity at Anchin College with a considerable salary. One of his pupils was Douay was John Pits [q. v.] When the university of Douay became aware of his extraordinary qualifications, he was unanimously chosen public professor of divinity, and he and Allen completed the degree of D.D. on 10 July 1571. He also obtained a canonry in the collegiate church of St. Amatus at Douay. In consequence of the political disturbances in Belgium, Stapleton, Gregory Martin [q. v.], and Dr. Richard White [q. v.] proceeded to Rome on 9 Nov. 1576. Stapleton returned to the college on 14 June 1577.

Having resolved to join a religious order, he resigned his canonry and professorship,

and entered the Society of Jesus in the Belgian province in 1584, but he left the noviciate before pronouncing the vows (MORE, *Hist. Prov. Anglicanæ Soc. Jesu*, p. 29). Dodd says it was by Allen's persuasion that he forsook the noviceship, but the 'Douay Diary' and Stapleton's metrical autobiography concur in stating that ill-health was the cause of his not continuing in it (CONSTABLE, *Specimen of Amendments to Dodd's Church Hist.* pp. 119-22; DODD, *Apology for the Church Hist.* p. 129). Stapleton now returned to his canonry of St. Amatus, which he retained until 1590. Philip II, by letters patent dated 13 July 1590, conferred upon him the chair of holy scripture at Louvain, vacant by the death of Michael Bains, together with the canonry of St. Peter, which was annexed to the professorship. Shortly afterwards the king presented him to the deanery of Hilverenbeeck, in the diocese of Bois-le-Duc. The latter benefice was worth a thousand florins a year, and that sum, added to what he already possessed, and to the fees which he obtained as a private tutor to youths of good family, enabled him to render pecuniary assistance to his exiled fellow-countrymen (PAQUOT, *Hist. Littéraire des Pays-Bas*, ii. 526).

Stapleton's fame as a controversialist had spread all over Europe, and Pope Clement VIII esteemed his writings so highly that he ordered portions of them to be read publicly at his table. In 1596 the pontiff twice invited him to Rome: first, with an offer of residence in the household of Cardinal Aldobrandino, the pope's nephew; and the second time with the promise of a chair in the Sapienza. Stapleton declined both invitations; but in January 1596-7 he accepted from his holiness a third offer of an appointment as prothonotary apostolic. His friends believed that he would be created a cardinal. Father Agazzari, rector of the English College at Rome, was alarmed at the prospect of Stapleton's promotion to the purple, and suggested on 25 Sept. 1596 to Parsons, who was at Madrid, the promotion of an ecclesiastic whose fidelity to the crown of Spain there could be no doubt. Stapleton wrote from Louvain to Parsons at Madrid in 1597 that he was, and sincerely intended to remain, a true and trusty servant to the king of Spain 'though I hap to live, and perhaps to continue, in the court of Rome.' Stapleton intended to set out for Rome in August 1597, but, either from illness or some other cause, remained at Louvain. Dr. Humphrey Ely implies that there was some other reason, for he writes: 'The first man you [i.e. Father Parsons] name is M. D. Stapleton "whom his Holiness purposed to prefer to higher dignity." If he were now alive, he would tell another tale against those that hindered him from that higher dignity, and that told him a tale in his ear when he was ready to put his foot into his litter, and made him stay at home and lose that "higher dignity"' (ELY, *Certaine Briefe Notes*, &c., 1603, p. 254). Stapleton died at Louvain on 12 Oct. (N.S.) 1598, and was buried in the church of St. Peter, where a monument was erected to his memory with a long Latin inscription, which has been printed by Pits (*De Angliæ Scriptoribus*, p. 797). He left all his books and manuscripts to the English College at Douay; but Dodd, after a diligent search, was unable to find any of the manuscripts.

Wood calls Stapleton 'the most learned Roman catholic of all his time,' and it is generally admitted that he was a most skilful controversialist. Even his chief adversary, William Whitaker [q.v.], paid a willing tribute to his powers and erudition. Stapleton attempted to introduce some moderation at least into the theory of the relations between the papal authority and civil governments. He disclaimed any suzerainty of the pope over princes, and he denied that the pope had any right to dethrone them for any merely civil cause. At the same time he held that the pope could justly interfere with temporal governments when they were hostile or detrimental to the catholic religion, and that the pope might excite the people to throw off the authority of their prince and to dethrone him; and if this did not succeed, the prince might give the throne to some catholic prince. Stapleton was one of the English writers on whose information Pius V mainly relied when he issued his famous bull against Queen Elizabeth. His principal polemical opponents were Dr. William Fulke, Dr. William Whitaker, Dr. John Rainolds, Bishop Jewell, and Dr. John Bridges, bishop of Oxford.

His portrait, engraved by L. Gaultier and representing him in a doctor of divinity's habit, forms the frontispiece of his collected works (GRANGER, *Biogr. Hist.* i. 224). It is reproduced in Richardson's collection of 'Engravings illustrating Granger's Biographical History of England' (vol. iii.)

Stapleton's principal works are: 1. 'The History of the Church of Englande. Compiled by Venerable Bede, Englishman. Translated out of Latin into English,' Antwerp, 1565, 4to; St. Omer, 1622, 8vo. 2. A translation from the Latin of Frederic Staphylus's 'Apologie, intreating of the true and right

vnderstanding of holy Scripture,' Antwerp, 1565, 4to. To this is appended a 'Discours of the Translatour vppon the doctrine of the protestants, which he trieth by the three first founders and fathers thereof, Martin Luther, Philip Melancthon, and especially Iohn Caluin.' 3. 'A Fortresse of the Faith first planted amonge vs englishmen, and continued hitherto in the vniuersall Church of Christ. The faith of which time Protestants call Papistry,' Antwerp, 1565, 4to. 4. 'A returne of vntruthes vpon M. Iewels Replie,' Antwerp, 1566, 4to. 5. 'A Counterblast to M. Hornes vayne blaste against M. Fekenham,' Louvain, 1567, 4to. The substance of the 'Counterblast' was in reality penned by Fekenham, who was in custody in England, and who requested Stapleton to revise the manuscript and to publish the work in his own name. 6. 'Of the express Word of God,' Louvain, 1567, from the Latin of Cardinal Hosius. 7. 'In Laudem Franc. Richardoti Atrebat. Episc. Oratio Funebris. Duaci habita MDLXXIIII mense Augusto,' Douay, 1608, 4to. 8. 'Orationes Funebres,' Antwerp, 1577. 9. 'Principiorum Fidei doctrinalium Demonstratio methodica, per controuersias septem in libris duodecim tradita,' Paris, 1578, 1579, and 1582, with a thirteenth book. 10. 'Speculum pravitatis hæreticæ per orationes quasi ad oculum demonstratæ,' Douay, 1580. 11. 'De Universa Justificationis Doctrina, hodie controversa, lib. xii.,' Paris, 1581. 12. 'Tres Thomæ; seu res gestæ S. Thomæ apostoli, S. Thomæ archiepisc. Cantuar. et martyris, et Thomæ Mori Angliæ quondam cancellarii,' Douay, 1588, 8vo; Cologne, 1612, 8vo. The 'Life of More' was in 1689 printed both separately (Gratz [1689], 12mo), and as a preface to More's collected Latin works (see under MORE, SIR THOMAS); and a French translation, by A. Martin, appeared at Paris (1849, 8vo), 'avec une introduction, des notes et commentaires par M. Audin.' 13. 'Promptuarium Morale super Evangelia Dominicalia totius anni. Pars Hyemalis,' Antwerp, 1591; Cologne, 1615; Paris, 1617, 8vo. 'Pars Æstivalis,' Venice, 1593, 1594; Mayence, 1610; Cologne, 1620; both parts, 2 vols. Antwerp, 1613, 8vo; Paris, 1 vol. 1627, 8vo. 14. 'Promptuarium Catholicum in Evangelia Dominicalia totius Anni,' Cologne, 1592, 1602; Paris, 1617, 8vo. 15. 'Promptuarium Catholicum in Evangelia Ferialia totius Quadragesimæ,' reprinted Paris, 1617, 8vo. 16. 'Promptuarium Catholicum in Evangelia Festorum totius Anni,' Cologne, 1592; Antwerp, 1608. 17. 'Relectio Scholastica et Compendiaria Principiorum Fidei Doctrinalium,' Antwerp, 1592;

Louvain, 1596. 18. 'Authoritatis Ecclesiasticæ circa S. Scripturarum approbationem ... Defensio ... contra Disputationem de Scriptura Sacra G. Whitakeri,' Antwerp, 1592, 8vo (cf. Lambeth MS. 182: 'De ecclesiæ autoritate ex dictatis eximii viri Thomæ Stapletoni'). 19. 'Apologia pro rege catholico Philippo II Hispaniæ rege, contra varias et falsas accusationes Elizabethæ Angliæ reginæ, per edictum suum publicatas et excusas, authore Didymo Veridico Henfildano,' Constance, 1592, 8vo (*Letters and Memorials of Cardinal Allen*, p. 339). The quaint pseudonym, being interpreted, seems to mean 'Thomas the Stable-toned (or truth-speaking) Henfieldite.' 20. 'Antidota Evangelica in quatuor Evangelia,' Antwerp, 1595. 21. 'Antidota Apostolica in Acta Apostolorum,' Antwerp, 1595. 22. 'Antidota Apostolica in Epist. Pauli ad Romanos,' Antwerp, 1595. 23. 'Antidota Apostolica in duas Epistolas ad Corinthios,' Antwerp, 1598, 1600. 24. 'Orationes Catecheticæ, sive Manuale Peccatorum, de Septem Peccatis Capitalibus,' Antwerp, 1598; Lyons, 1599. 25. 'Verè admiranda: seu de Magnitudine Romanæ Ecclesiæ Libri duo' (edited by Christopher ab Assonvilla, lord of Alteville), Antwerp, 1599, 4to; Rome, 1600, 8vo; Bruges, 1881, 8vo. 26. 'Orationes Academicæ Miscellaneæ;' some of these were published in 1602. 27. 'Oratio Academica; an politici horum temporum in numero Christianorum sint habendi?' Munich, 1608, 8vo.

His collected writings were published in four huge folio volumes under the title of 'Opera omnia; nonnulla auctius et emendatius, quædam jam antea Anglice scripta, nunc primum studio et diligentia doctorum virorum Anglorum Latine reddita' (Paris, 1620). Prefixed to the first volume is a curious autobiography of Stapleton in Latin hexameter verse, and a brief sketch of his life by Henry Holland, licentiate of theology at Douay.

[Metrical autobiography; Life by Holland; Ames's Typogr. Antiq. ed. Herbert; Dodd's Church Hist. ii. 84; Douay Diaries, pp. lxxiii, civ, 441; Duthilloeul's Bibl. Douaisienne, 2nd edit. pp. 36, 371; Foster's Alumni Oxon. 1500-1714, iv. 1413; Fuller's Worthies; Laity's Directory, 1812, with portrait; Lansdowne MS. 982, f. 209; Lower's Worthies of Sussex, p. 275; Lowndes's Bibl. Man. ed. Bohn; Molanus, Hist. de Louvain, 1861, i. 481; Parker Society Publications (Gough's gen. index); Simpson's Biography of Campion, pp. 59, 368; Cal. State Papers, Dom. Eliz. 1547-80 p. 150, 1598-1601 p. 488; Strype's Works (gen. index); Tablet, 1888, pt. ii. pp. 657, 705, 745, 785, 826; Tanner's Bibl. Brit.; Wood's Athenæ Oxon. ed. Bliss, i. 669.]   T. C.

STAPLETON, THOMAS (1805–1849), antiquary, born in 1805, was the second son of Thomas Stapleton of Carlton Hall, Yorkshire, by his first wife, Maria Juliana, daughter of Sir Robert Gerard, bart. On the death of his father in 1839 he succeeded to some landed property near Richmond, Yorkshire. He was elected a fellow of the Society of Antiquaries on 15 Jan. 1839, and, being the intimate friend of John Gage Rokewode [q. v.], the director of that body, he took a zealous interest in its operations. He was appointed one of its vice-presidents in 1846. His most valuable literary production was the prefatory exposition of the rolls of the Norman exchequer, printed at the expense of the Society of Antiquaries under the title of 'Magni Rotuli Scaccarii Normanniæ sub Regibus Angliæ,' 2 vols. 1841–4. He also contributed several learned papers to the 'Archæologia.' At the meeting of the Archæological Institute at York in 1846 he read a long memoir (pp. 230) entitled 'Historical Details of the Ancient Religious Community of Secular Canons in York prior to the Conquest of England, having the name of the Church of the Holy Trinity, otherwise Christ Church, showing its subsequent conversion into a Priory of Benedictine Monks . . . with Biographical Notices of the Founder, Ralph Paynell, and of his Descendants.' Stapleton became a fellow of the Royal Society. He was also one of the founders of the Camden Society, and undertook one of its earliest works, 'The Plumpton Correspondence,' 1839, which, as a collection of fifteenth-century letters, is inferior only to that of the Pastons. He afterwards edited, for the same society in 1846, the chronicle of London, extending from 1178 to 1274, entitled 'De Antiquis Legibus Liber.' His last work for the Camden Society was the edition of the 'Chronicon Petroburgense,' 1849. He died at Cromwell Cottage, Old Brompton, on 4 Dec. 1849. His 'Historical Memoirs of the House of Vernon' (pp. 115), an incomplete work, was privately printed in London about 1855, 4to.

[Index to the Archæologia; Bruce's Pref. to Chronicon Petroburgense, 1849; Gent. Mag. 1850, i. 180, 322; Lowndes's Bibl. Man. (Bohn), Suppl. pp. 39, 42, 43; H. E. Chetwynd-Stapylton's Stapeltons of Yorkshire, p. 105 n.; Nichols's Cat. of the Works of the Camden Soc. pp. 3, 27, 37.]   T. C.

STAPLEY, ANTHONY (1590–1655), regicide, baptised at Framfield on 30 Aug. 1590, was the son of Anthony Stapley of Framfield, Sussex, by his third wife, Ann, daughter of John Thatcher of Priesthawes,

Sussex. The Stapley family removed about 1615 from Framfield to Patcham. Anthony represented the borough of New Shoreham in the parliaments of 1624 (elected 21 Jan. 1623–4) and of 1625 (elected 2 May), and the borough of Lewes in that of 1628 (elected 26 Feb. 1627–8), having unseated Sir George Rivers by petition. He was returned both for the county of Sussex and for the borough of Lewes to the Short parliament in March 1639–40, when he elected to sit for the county. He was again chosen by the county on 22 Oct. 1640 (Long parliament), and continued to represent it in the parliaments of 1653 and of 1654.

In January 1639–40 Stapley, then a justice of the peace, was reported to Dr. William Bray (d. 1644) [q. v.], Laud's chaplain, as causing trouble to the churches by his puritan leanings. On the outbreak of the civil war he received a colonel's commission in the parliamentary army, and was present at the siege of Chichester in December 1642 under Sir William Waller [q. v.] He was left as governor of the town and garrison when Waller moved on to the siege of Arundel. On 22 Sept. 1643 he took the covenant. At the beginning of 1644 he raised objections to the quartering in the town of some of Waller's horse. The dispute was referred to a committee of the House of Commons, and finally to the committee of both kingdoms on 20 Feb. He was ordered by both bodies to observe Waller's commands. While detained in London he was exonerated from all blame in the event of disaster at Chichester. He resumed the command of the town and garrison at the termination of the proceedings early in March. He retained his governorship till 1645, when he was succeeded by Colonel Algernon Sidney [q. v.] In January 1644 he was deputy lieutenant of the county of Sussex.

Stapley was one of the judges of Charles I. He was present at Westminster Hall on 27 Jan. 1648–9 when sentence was pronounced, and signed the death-warrant on 29 Jan. He was elected a member of the first council of state of the Commonwealth on 17 Feb. 1648–9 (when he signed the engagement), and re-elected on 17 Feb. 1649–1650, 25 Nov. 1651, 30 Nov. 1652, and 9 July 1653. He was one of Cromwell's interim council of thirteen (29 April to 14 July 1653), and of the supreme assembly called on 6 June 1653. He had joined the admiralty committee or the committee of both kingdoms on 6 June 1649, was nominated vice-admiral for the county of Sussex on 22 Feb. 1650, and took the oath of secrecy the following day. He died early

in 1655, and was buried at Patcham on 31 Jan. At the Restoration he was one of the regicides notified as dead, and excepted from the act of pardon and oblivion of 6 June 1660.

Stapley married Ann, daughter of George Goring of Danny, and sister of George, lord Goring [q. v.] She was buried at Patcham on 11 Nov. 1637. By her Stapley had three sons and one daughter. Stapley married a second wife, 'Dame Anne Clarke,' who predeceased him on 15 Jan. 1654.

SIR JOHN STAPLEY (1628–1701), the second but eldest surviving son, was baptised at Patcham on 29 June 1628. He represented the county of Sussex in the parliaments of 1654 and 1656 (elected 20 Aug.), and the borough of Lewes in the first Restoration parliament of 1661 (elected 23 March 1660–1). In January 1655–6 he was appointed deputy lieutenant of the county. In 1657 Stapley, abandoning the political views of his father, became entangled in a plot for the return of Charles II. At the house of his grandmother, Lady Champion, he had come under the influence of Dr. John Hewit [q. v.] and John Mordaunt, baron Mordaunt (1627–1675) [q. v.] Ostensibly with a view to 'the expiation of his father's crime,' he professed himself anxious to 'venture his life and his fortune for his majesty's restoration.' In June 1657, through the instrumentality of Hewit, he had received from the exiled king a commission for the raising of a troop of horse and six colonels' commissions, to be distributed at his discretion. His interest in the county was considered to be great, and his promises of support to the royalist party were confident. Doubts were, however, thrown upon his ability to carry out all his plans (CARTE, Collections, ii. 123, 130). Through the treachery of a subordinate he fell into the hands of Cromwell in the spring of 1658, when he disclosed such particulars of the plot as led to the arrest of Hewit, Mordaunt, and Sir Henry Slingsby [q. v.] Cromwell, however, dismissed him with a reproof, presumably on account of his friendship with his father. Stapley appeared as a witness against Mordaunt at his trial on 2 July 1658, but, according to Clarendon, answered 'in so disorderly and confused a manner that it appeared that he had much rather not have said it.' His younger brother Anthony was also concerned in the plot, and made full disclosures when examined by Colonel William Goffe [q. v.] and Henry Scobell [q. v.] in April 1658. Many of the informations are among the Rawlinson MSS. in the Bodleian Library.

At the Restoration Stapley contrived to

win the king's favour, and was created a baronet on 28 July 1660. Subsequently he appears to have retired into private life in Sussex. He died in 1701, when the baronetcy became extinct. He married Mary (b. 1634), eldest daughter and coheiress of Sir Herbert Springett of Broyle Place, Ringwood, Sussex, by whom he had two sons, who predeceased him, and several daughters. His widow lived till 1708.

[Berry's County Genealogy—Sussex, p. 85; Sussex Archæological Collections, i. 36, iv. 300, v. 88–91, xvi. 78, 108–9, 113, 116, 119–20; Masson's Milton, iv. 13, 224, 354, 446, 501, 505, 523; Commons' Journals, i. 878, iii. 362, 401, 403, 616, vi. 146, vii. 37, 42, 303, viii. 61; Official List of Members of Parliament; Cal. of State Papers, Dom. 1639 to 1654 passim; Vicars's Jehorah-Jireh, pp. 234–40; Dallaway's Western Sussex, vol. i. pp. 14, 20, vol. ii. pt. i. p. 23; Rushworth's Memorials, iii. ii. 480; Nalson's Trial of Charles I; Noble's Lives of the Regicides, pp. 240–6; Horsfield's Sussex, ii. app. pp. 49, 55; Thurlow State Papers (Birch), passim; Macrae's Cal. of Clarendon State Papers, iii. 281, 312, 358, 374, 388–9, 405; Clarendon's Hist. of the Rebellion (Macrae), vi. 58–9, 63; Burke's Extinct Baronetage; P. C. C. 189 (Aylett); Registers of Patcham, Addit. MS. 5698. f. 118.]

R. P.

STARK, ADAM (1784–1867), antiquary, was born in Edinburgh on 24 Feb. 1784. In 1804, in connection with his cousin, John Stark, he became a printer, but the partnership was dissolved in 1810. In conjunction with J. Richardson he published the 'Hull and Lincoln Chronicle' for some time; it afterwards was known as the 'Lincoln and Hull Chronicle.' In 1810 he became a bookseller at Gainsborough, and continued that business until his retirement in 1844. He died at Gainsborough on 31 Dec. 1867, having married, first, Ann Trotter of Lincoln; secondly, Harriet, daughter of Henry Mozley of Gainsborough, and sister of Anne Mozley [q. v.], James Bowling Mozley [q. v.], and of Thomas Mozley [q. v.]; and, thirdly, Sarah Wooton of Newington, near Ramsgate.

Stark was the author of: 1. 'The History and Antiquities of Gainsborough, with a Topographical and Descriptive Account of Stow,' 1817; another edit. 1841. 2. 'An Account of the Parish of Lea, Lincolnshire,' 1841. 3. 'The Visitors' Pocket Guide to Gainsborough and its Neighbourhood,' 1840. 4. 'History of the Bishopric of Lincoln,' 1852. 5. 'Printing: its Antecedents, Origin, History, and Results,' 1855.

[The Travellers' Library, No. 82 in vol. xxv.; Gent. Mag. 1868, ii. 250.]   G. C. B.

STARK, JAMES (1794–1859), landscape-painter, was the son of Michael Stark, a native of Scotland, who settled as a dyer in Norwich, where his son was born on 19 Nov. 1794. The boy showed an early fondness for drawing, and in 1811 was articled for three years to John Crome [q. v.], the landscape-painter, whose son, the younger Crome, had been his schoolfellow and companion. In the same year he sent five landscapes to the exhibition of the Norwich Society of Artists, of which he was elected a member in 1812. In 1811 he also exhibited for the first time in London, sending to the Royal Academy a 'View on King-Street River, Norwich.' In 1814 he came to London, and sent to the British Institution a 'Village Scene near Norwich,' and in 1815 'The Bathing Place: Morning.' These were followed in 1817 by 'Fishing,' and in 1818 by 'Penning the Flock' and 'Lambeth, looking towards Westminster Bridge,' and he was awarded by the directors a premium of 50l. In 1817 he was admitted a student of the Royal Academy. He began to receive commissions from several leading connoisseurs, but before long he was compelled by illness to return home, and for three years he did no work. In 1830, after an absence of twelve years, he came back to London, and took up his residence in Chelsea, sending his works to the exhibitions of the Royal Academy and the Society of British Artists, and still more frequently to that of the British Institution. In 1834 was completed the 'Scenery of the Rivers of Norfolk,' engraved from Stark's pictures by Edward Goodall, William Miller, George Cooke, and others, with text by J. W. Robberds. The publication of this fine and costly work had been commenced in 1827, and the artist narrowly escaped serious pecuniary loss. About 1839 he removed to Windsor, where he painted many pictures of the scenery of the Thames, but in 1849 he returned again to London, for the sake of his son's education in art.

Stark's style was based on that of Crome, but it was much influenced by study of the Dutch masters. It was very truthful and thoroughly English, but it lacked the richness and power of his master. An exhibition of his works was held by the Norwich Art Circle in 1887. The National Gallery possesses his 'Valley of the Yare, near Thorpe,' of which there is an etching by Francis S. Walker, and the National Gallery of Scotland a view in 'Gowbarrow Park.' Three views at Hastings, a distant view of Windsor, and two other landscapes are in the Sheepshanks collection in the South Kensington Museum, and a 'Landscape with

Cattle' is in the Mappin Art Gallery at Sheffield. His picture of 'Sheep-washing, Postwick Grove, Norwich,' has been engraved in mezzotint by Alfred Skrimshire.

Stark died at Mornington Place, Hampstead Road, London, on 24 March 1859. His son, Arthur James Stark, is a landscape-painter of merit, who has exhibited at the Royal Academy and elsewhere since 1848.

[Art Journal, 1850 p. 182 with portrait, 1859 p. 135; Redgrave's Century of Painters of the English School, 1866, ii. 372-4; Bryan's Dictionary of Painters and Engravers, ed. Graves and Armstrong, 1886-9, ii. 526; Redgrave's Dict. of Artists of the English School, 1878; Exhibition Catalogues of the Royal Academy, British Institution (Living Artists), and Society of British Artists, 1811-59; Exhibition Catalogues of the Norwich Society of Artists, 1811-25.]

R. E. G.

STARK, WILLIAM (1740-1770), physician, born in Birmingham in July 1740, was of Irish parentage on his father's side, though his mother was a native of Scotland. He studied philosophy at Glasgow University, and then proceeded to Edinburgh, where he acquired the friendship of William Cullen [q. v.] Thence he came to London in 1765, and devoted himself to the pursuit of medicine, entering as a pupil at St. George's Hospital. He studied anatomy under John Hunter (1728-1773) [q. v.], and employed himself in making experiments on the blood and other animal fluids. On 2 Sept. 1766 he graduated M.D. at Leyden, publishing his thesis, 'Specimen Med. Inaug. septem Historias et Dissectiones Dysentericorum exhibens,' Leyden, 1766, 4to. In June 1769 he began a series of experiments on diet, in which he was greatly encouraged by Sir John Pringle [q. v.] The zeal with which he tried these experiments on his own person ruined his health, and on 23 Feb. 1770 he fell a victim to his enthusiasm.

'The Works of the late William Stark . . . consisting of clinical and anatomical observations, with experiments dietetical and statical,' were edited by James Carmichael Smyth [q. v.], London, 1788, 4to.

[Smyth's Introduction to Stark's Works; account of Stark's illness and death appended to his Works; Georgian Era, iii. 491; Allibone's Dict. of Engl. Lit.]

E. I. C.

STARKE, MARIANA (1762?-1838), writer of guide-books, born about 1762, was daughter of Richard Starke by his wife Mary, daughter of Isaac Hughes of Banstead, Surrey. The father was for some time governor of Fort St. George in Madras, and later a resident at Epsom, Surrey. Mariana's early years were passed in India, where her keen observation of Anglo-Indian life afterwards afforded material for 'The Sword of Peace, or a Voyage of Love,' a comedy which was acted at the Haymarket Theatre on 9 Aug. 1788, with Miss Farren in the cast. It was published, Dublin, 1789, 8vo, and it was again played at Bath on 23 March 1800. Indian colour is also introduced into 'The Widow of Malabar,' a tragedy in three acts (Dublin, 1791, 8vo; London, 1791, 8vo; 3rd edit. 1791, 8vo). The epilogue was written by Miss Starke's nephew, R. J. Hughes Starke (d. at Dinard, Brittany, 1838). The tragedy was produced at Mrs. Crespigny's private theatre, Camberwell, and at Covent Garden Theatre in 1798. A third dramatic effort was 'The Tournament,' a tragedy, London, 1800. All were of slight interest.

A seven years' residence in Italy in attendance on a consumptive relative led Miss Starke to write 'Letters from Italy' (2 vols. London, 1800; 2nd edit. 1815; translated into German, 1802). While in Italy she became acquainted with the Dowager-countess Spencer, at whose suggestion she published 'The Beauties of Carlo Maria Maggi Paraphrased,' with sonnets of her own, Exeter, 1811, 8vo. Miss Starke had by that date removed to Exmouth, but she revisited Italy in 1817-19, and published 'Travels on the Continent,' London, 1820, 8vo, which was followed by her 'Information and Directions for Travellers on the Continent' (5th edit. London, 1824, 8vo; 6th edit. 1828; 7th edit. 1829; translated into French, Paris, 1826, 8vo). It was enlarged and republished as 'Travels in Europe for the use of Travellers on the Continent and likewise in the Island of Sicily, to which is added an account of the Remains of Ancient Italy' (8th edit. London, 1832, 8vo). These guide-books are carefully compiled, and proved useful forerunners of the labours of Murray and Baedeker. Miss Starke died at Milan, on a journey from Naples to England, in the spring of 1838, aged 76.

[Genest's Hist. of the Stage, vi. 510, vii. 369, viii. 157, x 219; Baker's Biogr. Dramatica, ii. 345, 405, 813; Gent. Mag. 1838, ii. 111; Lit. Mem. of Living Authors, ii. 276; Reuss's Reg. of Living Authors, p. 350; Notes and Queries, 2nd ser. iii. 87; Querard's La France Littéraire, ix. 257.]

C. F. S.

STARKEY, GEOFFREY (fl. 1440), compiler of the 'Promptorium Parvulorum.' [See GEOFFREY THE GRAMMARIAN.]

STARKEY, GEORGE (d. 1665), empiric, may be identical with George Starkey, born in 1606, son of John Starkey of Leicestershire by his wife Katherine, daughter of John Dartneill of Rutland (NICHOLS, *Leicestershire*, iii. 728).

Starkey asserts that he obtained a medical degree after a regular course at a university. Crossing to America, he practised as a doctor in the English settlements. There he met the mysterious 'Eirenæus Philalethes' (see below), who initiated him into some of the secret methods of transmuting the precious metals. In 1646 Starkey returned to England, and from 1650 onwards he rendered himself conspicuous by vending quack medicines, styling himself 'a Philosopher made by the fire, and a Professor of that Medicine that is real, not Histrionical.' On the Restoration he posed as an enthusiastic royalist, and addressed a fervent memorial to Charles II and the Duke of York, entitled 'Royal and other Innocent Bloud crying aloud to Heaven for due vengeance. By George Starkey, a true honourer and faithfull friend of his country,' London, 1660, 4to, in which he urged the necessity of retaliation on the puritan party. In 1666 he ventured to dissect a plague patient, and fell a victim to his zeal.

He was the author of: 1. 'Nature's Explication and Helmont's Vindication; or a short and sure Way to a long and sound life,' London, 1657, 8vo. 2. 'Pyrotechny asserted and illustrated,' London, 1658, 8vo; 1696, 8vo. 3. 'The admirable efficacy of oyl which is made of Sulphur-Vive,' 1660, 12mo. 4. 'George Starkey's Pill vindicated,' 4to. 5. 'A brief Examination and Censure of several Medicines,' London, 1664, 12mo. 6. 'A smart Scourge for a silly, sawcy Fool, an answer to letter at the end of a pamphlet of Lionell Lockyer,' London, 1665, 4to. 7. 'An Epistolar Discourse to the author of Galeno-Pale' [George Thomson (*fl.* 1620–1680), q.v.], London, 1665, 8vo. 8. 'Liquor Alchahest, or a Discourse of that Immortal Dissolvent of Paracelsus and Helmont,' London, 1675, 8vo. He has some verses in Heydon's 'Idea of the Law,' London, 1660, 8vo, and in his 'Theomagia,' London, 1664, 8vo, and wrote two prefaces for 'The Marrow of Alchemy, by Eirenæus Philoponus Philalethes,' London, 1654, 8vo.

Starkey has been erroneously confused with the last-named writer, whose identity has not been determined, although it has been suggested that his real name was Childe. He is at any rate to be distinguished not merely from Starkey, his disciple, but from both 'Alazonomastix Philalethes,' a pseudonym adopted by Henry More (1614–1687) (q.v.], and from 'Eugenius Philalethes,' the customary signature of Thomas Vaughan

(q.v.], but, in one case at least, adopted also by Eirenæus Philalethes. Born in England of good family about 1622, 'Eirenæus' led a mysterious life, wandering under various names from country to country. According to his own statements and those of Starkey, he discovered the philosopher's stone in 1645, in his twenty-third year, and was a friend of Robert Boyle. He was author of: 1. 'The Marrow of Alchemy, being an Experimental Treatise discovering the secret and most hidden mystery of the Philosophers Elixer,' London, 1654, 8vo. 2. 'Introitus apertus ad occlusum Regis Palatium,' Amsterdam, 1667, 8vo (Brit. Mus. Libr.), a treatise on practical alchemy which had a European reputation, being translated into English, French, and Spanish. 3. 'Tractatus tres: (i.) Metallorum Metamorphosis; (ii.) Brevis Manuductio ad Rubinum Coelestem; (iii.) Fons Chymicæ Veritatis,' Amsterdam, 1668, 8vo; reprinted in the 'Musæum Hermeticum,' Frankfort, 1678, 4to; translated into English 'by a Lover of Art and Them,' London, 1694, 8vo. 4. 'Ripley Reviv'd; or an Exposition upon Sir George Ripley's Hermetico-Poetical Works,' in five parts, London, 1677–8, 8vo. 5. 'Opus Tripartitum de Philosophorum Arcanis. Videlicet: (i.) Enarratio methodica trium Gebri medicinarum; (ii.) Experimenta de præparatione Mercurii Sophici; (iii.) Vade Mecum philosophicum, sive breve manuductorium ad Campum Sophiæ,' London, 1678, 8vo; Amsterdam, 1678, 8vo. 6. 'The Secret of the Immortal Liquor Alchahest, or Ignis-Aqua,' published in 'Collectanea Chymica,' London, 1684, 8vo; reprinted in 'Collectanea Chemica,' London, 1893, 8vo. This tract is distinct from Starkey's 'Liquor Alchahest,' though probably Starkey possessed 'Philalethes' manuscript when he wrote his treatise (*Works of Philalethes and Starkey*; WAITE, *Lives of Alchemical Philosophers*, 1888, pp. 187–200; WAITE, *Real Hist. of the Rosicrucians*, 1887, pp. 308–14; *Lives of Alchemystical Philosophers*, 1815, pp. 88–94, 160–75).

[Starkey's Works; Lenglet du Fresnoy's Histoire de la Philosophie Hermétique, i. 404, 480, iii. 302; Gray's Index to Hazlitt.]   E. I. C.

STARKEY, Sir HUMPHREY (*d.* 1486), chief baron of the exchequer, was descended from the Starkeys of Oulton and Wrenbury, Cheshire. He was a member of the Inner Temple, and is first mentioned as a lawyer in the year-books in Hilary term 1454. There are references to him as counsel for John Paston in lawsuits in 1464 and 1466 (*Paston Letters*, ii. 144, 258). In 1471 he was elected recorder of London, and in Trinity term 1478 became a serjeant. He resigned the recordership on being appointed chief baron of the exchequer during the short reign of Edward V, on 15 June 1483. On the accession of Richard III he was knighted, and was continued in his office. He also acted as a justice of the common pleas during the reign of Richard III (*Rot. Parl.* vi. 332, 341), and was continued in both his offices by Henry VII. The last fine levied before him was at midsummer 1486, and he died before 29 Oct. of that year. He was buried at St. Leonard's, Shoreditch, with his wife Isabella, by whom he left four daughters. Starkey purchased the manor of Littlehall in Woldham, Kent, to which he gave his own name, and where he built a house.

[Hasted's Kent, iv. 404; Foss's Judges of England; Dugdale's Orig. Jurid. et Chron. Series; Archæologia Cantiana, x. 256; authorities quoted.] C. L. K.

STARKEY, RALPH (*d.* 1628), archivist, was the second but eldest surviving son of John Starkey (*d.* 1613?) of Darley Hall, Cheshire, by his wife Alice (*d.* 1620), daughter of Ralph Dutton. His family was distantly related to that of Thomas Starkey [q. v.] On his father's death, about 1613, Ralph is said to have been defrauded of his estates by his younger brother Henry (*d.* 1653), who destroyed their father's will (*Cal. State Papers*, Dom. 1623-5, p. 313), and Ralph became a merchant in London. His energies were, however, chiefly devoted to the collection and transcription of state papers and other manuscripts. Before 1619 he had acquired many important and confidential papers that had formerly belonged to William Davison [q. v.], Queen Elizabeth's secretary of state. The government obviously had reason for keeping these papers secret, and on 10 Aug. 1619 a warrant was issued to Sir Thomas Wilson authorising him to search Starkey's house and seize all Davison's papers. This was done on the 14th, and Wilson delivered to the government a sack of papers containing forty-five parcels (*Harl. MS.* 286, f. 286). Starkey died in October 1628 at his residence in Bloomsbury. He married Winifred, daughter of Richard Poynter of Whitchurch, Shropshire, and had issue one son and two daughters. D'Ewes describes him as 'an ignorant, mercenary, indigent man. . . . He had gathered together many old deeds and some old manuscripts and coins. But he had great plenty of new written collections and divers original letters of great moment, and other autographs of later time, besides divers old parchments and other particulars' (*Autobigr.* i. 391-2). There was some competition for the purchase of these documents, and finally D'Ewes secured the best part for 140*l.*, to be paid in five years (*ib.* pp. 392-3, 399). The agreement made on 22 Oct. 1628 between Arthur Barnardiston, Sir Simonds D'Ewes [q. v.], Ambrose Scudamore, and Nicholas Bragge is in Harleian MS. 97, art. 14. D'Ewes's grandson sold them to Sir Robert Harley, and they are now in the Harleian collection in the British Museum.

The following are the more important: collections relative to the laws, customs, and constitution of England in Harleian MSS. 88, 90, 168, 169, 250; collections and lists of papers relative to British history in Harleian MSS. 286, 298, 352, 353. Of these, vol. 286 contains many valuable letters from Robert Dudley, earl of Leicester, Sir Philip Sidney, and Sir Francis Walsingham; and vol. 353 is an equally important collection of state papers relating to the reign of Edward VI, which are not included among those calendared in the various calendars of state papers. Harleian MS. 253 is a volume devoted to ships and shipbuilding in the time of Elizabeth; No. 90 in the same collection comprises the 'contents' of the patent rolls of Edward III, and No. 81 the acts of the privy council, 20-24 Henry VI. Another work of Starkey relating to the privy council is a transcript of the council's letter-book for 1547-8; the original is lost, and Starkey's transcript is printed as an appendix to the second volume of the 'Acts of the Privy Council,' ed. Dasent.

Starkey was an author as well as a transcriber and collector. A poem entitled 'Infortunio,' consisting of 581 stanzas, said to be written in imitation of Edmund Spenser, is extant in Harleian MS. 558. A treatise on the 'Privilege and Practice of the High Court of Parliament' is extant in Harleian MS. 37, and a collection made by Starkey of the pedigrees of the Starkey family formerly belonged to William Radclyffe, rouge croix.

[Harl. MSS. 306 art. 22, 506 arts. 44, 104-112, 2012 art. 13; Acts of the Privy Council, ed. Dasent, vol. ii. pref. pp. x-xii; Ormerod's Cheshire, ii. 103-4.] A. F. P.

STARKEY, THOMAS (1499?-1538), writer, born about 1499, was the elder son of Thomas Starkey (*d.* 3 May 1529) of Wrenbury, Cheshire, by his wife Maud, daughter of Sir John Mainwaring of Peover in the same county. He was educated at Magdalen College, Oxford, graduating B.A. on 30 June 1516, and proceeding M.A. on 18 March

1520-1. At Oxford he learnt both Latin and Greek, and after graduating was lecturer in natural philosophy at Magdalen. From May to Michaelmas 1522 he served as proctor on Wolsey's nomination. He was also fellow of Magdalen from 1522 to 1524. On 31 July 1530 Warham, on the resignation of Thomas Lupset [q. v.], presented Starkey to the living of Great Mongeham, Kent. He was in London in November 1531, but soon afterwards appears to have accepted some office in Reginald Pole's household at Venice and Padua. While abroad he graduated LL.D., possibly at the latter city. In 1533 he wrote to the king, suggesting that the divorce should be referred to a general council. He returned to London at the end of 1534, when he became chaplain to Pole's mother, the Countess of Salisbury, and was made, no doubt by the intervention of Cromwell, to whom he had written (*Harl. MS.* 283, art. 60), one of the king's chaplains. He was sent to visit the Carthusian Richard Reynolds (d. 1535) [q. v.] before his execution. That Henry thought well of him may be gathered from the fact that he commissioned him to write to Pole and get his opinion on the divorce and the pope's authority. This he did on 15 Feb. 1535 (*ib.* art. 61). Pole replied shortly, and important correspondence followed, with the result that Pole sent to Henry his 'Pro Ecclesiasticæ Unitatis Defensione' in 1536 (cf. Dixon, *History of the Church of England*, i. 433, 434, 442, 482). Starkey was now in some danger. He had raised hopes which were not satisfied, and he seems to have incurred suspicion through his somewhat wavering attitude towards the question of the royal supremacy. In a letter to the king, written in 1536, he gives a very fair statement of the wishes of the sincere but moderate reformers of the day.

In his troubles in 1536 he retired to Bosham, a little benefice which he held near Chichester; but there, owing to the neighbourhood of the Poles, he had no peace. He remained, however, chaplain to the king, who, on 14 Dec. 1536, appointed him master of the college of Corpus Christi, connected with the church of St. Lawrence, Candlewick Street, London, He was formally instituted on 26 Jan. 1536-7. On 24 March following the king summoned him to a conference with the bishops on the invocation of saints, purgatory, and other burning questions. On 7 Jan. 1537-8 he was placed on a commission to inquire into a case of witchcraft, and on 24 March preached for the last time before the king. He died in the last week in August 1538, his will being dated the 25th of that month, but not proved until

2 May 1544 (printed with his works, E. E. T. S. 1878).

Starkey wrote in 1535 'An Essay on Preaching,' which is in manuscript in the Record Office. But his fame rests on two other works. His 'Exhortation to Christian Unity,' otherwise called 'A Treatise against the Papal Supremacy,' was written about 1534, and published by Berthelet (n. d.); it is extremely rare, but a copy was sold at Sotheby's on 1 July 1885. More celebrated is his 'Dialogue between Pole and Lupset,' which was found in manuscript by J. M. Brewer, and edited with notes by J. M. Cowper for the Early English Text Society in 1871. This dialogue gives a detailed account of many evils from which England suffered at the time it was written, and compares with the 'Commonweal of this Realm of England' (see under STAFFORD, WILLIAM, 1554-1612). But Starkey's 'Dialogue' also has an important place in the history of the science of politics as an attempt to define the conditions of a true commonwealth. Many of Starkey's letters were edited by S. J. Herrtage in 1878 for the same society. Further letters are described in Macray's 'Register of Magdalen College' (i. 159-63).

[Edition of the Dialogue, by Cowper; Zimmermann's Kardinal Pole, sein Leben und seine Schriften, pp. 72, &c.; Ormerod's Cheshire, iii. 205; Macray's Reg. Magdalen Coll. i. 156-63; Registers of the Univ. of Oxford (Oxford Hist. Soc.), i. 99; Ellis's Original Letters, 2nd ser. vol. ii. passim; Strype's Memorials, i. i. 266, &c., ii. 279, &c.; Letters and Papers, Henry VIII; Cunningham's Growth of English Industry and Commerce, ii. 526; art. POLE, REGINALD; The Commonweal of this Realm of England, ed. Lamond, 1893, pp. xxiv, &c.] W. A. J. A.

STARKIE, THOMAS (1782-1849), legal writer, eldest son of the Rev. Thomas Starkie, vicar of Blackburn, Lancashire, was born at Blackburn vicarage on 12 April 1782, and educated at Clitheroe grammar school and St. John's College, Cambridge, where he was entered as a pensioner on 2 Jan. 1799. He was senior wrangler and first Smith's prizeman in 1803, in which year he graduated B.A., proceeding M.A. in 1806. He was called to the bar at Lincoln's Inn on 23 May 1810, and immediately joined the northern circuit. He also practised as a special pleader as well as in the common-law courts, and was K.C. at Lancaster previously to his obtaining the rank of Q.C. at Westminster Hall. As a member of the commission for the amendment of the law he rendered most important services, but was less successful as a lecturer on common law and equity in the Inner Temple. In

1823 he was elected Downing professor of law at Cambridge. Originally a tory in politics, Starkie afterwards became a liberal, and in that interest unsuccessfully contested the representation of the borough of Cambridge in 1840. In 1847 he became judge of the Clerkenwell county court, which had jurisdiction over the greater part of Middlesex. He died at his rooms in Downing College, Cambridge, on 15 April 1849.

He married Lucy, daughter of the Rev. Thomas Dunham Whitaker [q. v.], the historian of Whalley, and had five children, of whom two daughters survived him.

Starkie was author of : 1. 'Practical Treatise on the Law of Slander, Libel, and incidentally of Malicious Prosecutions,' 1812. Later editions were published in 1827, 1830, and 1869, and American editions were brought out in 1832, 1843, 1852, and 1853, edited by T. Huntington and J. L. Wendell. 2. 'Treatise on Special Pleading, with Precedents of Indictments,' 1814, 2 vols.; later editions 1819, 1822, 1828, and an American edition, 1824. 3. 'Reports at Nisi Prius, K.B. and C.P.,' 1817-23, 3 vols. 4. 'Practical Treatise on the Law of Evidence,' 1824, 3 vols. Of this, Starkie's chief work, revised editions were issued in 1833, 1842, and 1853. It was often reprinted in America.

[Law Review, May 1849, p. 201 ; Gent. Mag. 1849, ii. 208 ; Graduati Cantabr.]   C. W. S.

STARLEY, JAMES (1831-1881), improver of bicycles and inventor of the Coventry tricycle, born at Albourne, Sussex, on 21 April 1831, was son of Daniel Starley (d. 1858), a farmer. At the age of nine he commenced working on his father's farm; but, not liking the place, about 1846 he walked to London and became gardener to John Penn at Lewisham in Kent. While there he invented the adjustable candlestick, the one-stringed window blind, and the mechanical bassinette. About 1855 he entered the employment of Newton Wilson, 144 High Holborn, London, and made improvements in sewing machines. In 1857 he went to Coventry, bringing with him a sewing machine of his own invention, which he called 'The European.' The Coventry Machinists' Company was formed for manufacturing this machine, and Starley was engaged as managing foreman. In the succeeding years he invented and patented many kinds of sewing machines, and most of the modern machines now embody the results of his inventions. After seeing a French bicycle, in 1868, he immediately turned his attention to improving these vehicles. His first invention was the

bicycle known as 'The C spring and step machine, or the Coventry Model.' The superiority of this was at once evident, the curved spring, the small hind wheel, and the step for mounting being the principal improvements. The 'Ariel' bicycle, which became widely popular, speedily followed. This machine was fitted with pivot-centre steering, being the first bicycle to which this improvement was applied. From that time his inventions and improvements followed each other in rapid succession. He left the Machinists' Company and started for himself in St. John Street, where he made 'Ariel' bicycles and sewing machines, and brought out the well-known 'Europa' sewing machine. Subsequently he went into partnership with Borthwick Smith, and the firm of Smith, Starley, & Co. commenced business at the St. Agnes Works, St. Agnes Lane, Coventry. Later on they sold the 'Ariel' patents. Starley dissolved the partnership with Smith after five years.

Still endeavouring to improve the bicycle, he finally introduced the 'Tangent' bicycle, and was fully employed in making 'Tangent' wheels. In 1876 he brought out the 'Coventry' tricycle. No similar machine is known to have existed before, and Starley may be regarded as its inventor. He invented the double-throw crank and the chain and chain-wheels to obtain rotary motion in tricycles, and the rack, and he first applied the pinion steering-gear to the same machine. Subsequently he produced his masterpiece, the 'Salvo' quadricycle.

Starley, by his many improvements, rendered bicycles and tricycles machines capable of general use. To his perseverance and energy Coventry owes its position as the centre of industry for the manufacture of cycles. Starley's ingenuity was as remarkably displayed in inventions which he failed to patent. These included the chain-wheels of the tricycle.

He died at Upper Well Street, Coventry, on 17 June 1881, and was buried in Coventry cemetery on 21 June. On 8 Nov. 1884 a granite memorial monument, having on it a portrait in profile of Starley, and on the sides representations of the 'Rotatory' tricycle and the 'Royal Salvo,' was unveiled in the Queen's Road, Coventry.

Starley married, on 22 Sept. 1853, Jane, daughter of William Todd. His three sons —James, John Marshall, and William—are members of the firm of Starley Brothers, cycle manufacturers, Coventry.

[Pall Mall Gazette, 23 June 1881, p. 10; Coventry Standard, 24 June 1881 pp. 3, 5, 1 July p. 5, 8 July p. 5, 14 Nov. 1884 p. 3;

Cycling (Badminton Library), 1887, pp. 67, 492; Cyclist, 24 Jan. 1883; information from Messrs. Starley Brothers.] G. C. B.

STATHAM, NICHOLAS (*fl.* 1467), lawyer, is stated to have been born at Morley, Derbyshire (*Ashmolean MS.* 816, where he is called John). He was reader of Lincoln's Inn in Lent term 1471. On 30 Oct. 1467 he received a patent for the reversion as second baron of the exchequer on the death of John Clerke. Clerke was certainly alive in 1471, but there is no mention of either him or Statham between that date and 3 Feb. 1481, when Thomas Whittington was made second baron. Consequently it is not known whether Statham ever obtained the office. Statham's name is never mentioned in the year-books, but he is credited with an abridgment of the cases reported in them in the reign of Henry VI, which is the earliest work of the kind now extant. Statham's abridgment was printed by R. Pynson as 'Epitome Annalium Librorum tempore Henrici Sexti,' London [1495?], 4to; other editions appeared in 1585 and 1679 (*Brit. Mus. Cat.*)

[Dugdale's Orig. pp. 68, 247, 257; Fuller's Worthies; Tanner's Bibl. Brit.-Hib. p. 690; Foss's Judges of England.] C. L. K.

STAUNFORD, SIR WILLIAM (1509–1558), judge. [See STANFORD.]

STAUNTON, EDMUND (1600–1671), president of Corpus Christi College, Oxford, a younger son of Francis (afterwards Sir Francis) Staunton, was born at Woburn, Bedfordshire, on 20 Oct. 1600. He matriculated from Wadham College, Oxford, on 9 June 1615, and on 4 Oct. following was admitted scholar of Corpus Christi. While still an undergraduate, on 22 March 1616-17, he was transferred from the Bedfordshire scholarship to the Bedfordshire fellowship. After a dangerous illness when he was about eighteen, and a narrow escape from drowning in the river, whither he had repaired 'alone, to wash himself,' he had, about 1620, to use his own words, 'many sad and serious thoughts concerning my spiritual and eternal state.' On proceeding M.A. in 1623, he selected the ministry as his profession, and commenced his clerical life as afternoon lecturer at Witney, where he was very acceptable to the people, but obnoxious to the rector of the parish. But he soon left Witney for the valuable living of Bushey in Hertfordshire, and this living he shortly afterwards exchanged for that of Kingston-on-Thames, where he remained for about twenty years, being known by the name of 'the searching preacher.' There he devoted himself to constant preaching and catechising, taught from house to house, and set up a weekly lecture, supplied, in turn, by the most eminent preachers in that part of England. While at Kingston he proceeded B.D. and D.D. at Oxford in 1634, and he was chosen to be not only one of the assembly of divines which met at Westminster in 1643, but also one of the six preachers in the abbey.

When Dr. Robert Newlyn was ejected from the presidency of Corpus by the 'committee of Lords and Commons for Reformation of the University of Oxford' (22 May 1648), Staunton, a former fellow and a leading puritan divine, was appointed in his place. But the actual ejection of Dr. Newlyn and assumption of the office by Dr. Staunton did not take place till 11 July following. Staunton was a great improvement upon his predecessor, who was remarkable solely for the extreme old age to which he lived, and for the shameless nepotism which he practised after his restitution at the Restoration. Staunton was a good disciplinarian, and as a presbyterian divine was earnest in preaching, prayer, and catechising. He thereby incurred the ridicule of the royalist party (for some macaronic verses on his style of preaching, see FOWLER, *History of Corpus Christi College*, pp. 221–2).

On 15 June 1652 Staunton, who had submitted to the 'engagement,' was nominated by the committee of parliament to be on the new board of visitors, which was limited to ten. On the third board, nominated by the lord protector about two years afterwards, Staunton's name does not appear.

Staunton was, in his turn, ejected from the president's lodgings on 3 Aug. 1660, his predecessor, Newlyn, having been already reinstated in his office. Withdrawing from Oxford, he retired, in the first instance, to Rickmansworth in Hertfordshire, whence he ministered in various parishes around. On St. Bartholomew's day 1662 he was silenced, like other nonconformists, but he seems, after remaining at Rickmansworth about two years longer, to have lived in various private families, and to have exercised his ministerial functions in a private manner possibly, but in defiance of the law. 'His great sufferings and often imprisonments,' alluded to by the author of the 'Brief Relation' (see below), may probably be referred to this period of his life. According to the Rev. Robert Watts (*d.* 1726), 'after preaching in several conventicles at London, Staunton became pastor of a celebrated meeting-house at Salters' Hall, which was built on purpose for him' (WOOD, *Athenæ*, ed. Bliss).

His last remove was to Bovingdon, Hertfordshire, where, and at the neighbouring towns, such as St. Albans, 'seeing he could not preach in a church to many, he would preach in a chamber to a few.' He died at Bovingdon on 14 July 1671, and was buried in the parish church, where there still exists 'a fair stone' bearing an inscription with a quaint Latin epitaph to his memory. Ten of Staunton's children lie buried in Kingston church, where a brass over their grave commemorates the fact in doggerel rhyme.

Though so constant a preacher, and occupying so prominent a position among those of his own beliefs, Staunton wrote only a few occasional sermons and two puritanic tracts, entitled respectively 'A Dialogue between a Minister and a Stranger about Soul Affairs,' and 'A Treatise of Christian Conference.' These were published at the end of Mayo's biography in 1671. Staunton's literary unproductiveness affords a confirmation of the character given of him by a junior contemporary: namely, that he was reckoned by his friends 'a man that had parts, but idle, and would instruct but not study for what he did.'

[Fowler's Hist. of Corpus Christi College, pp. 208-9, 211-12, 217-25, 363; Wood's Athenæ Oxon., University and Coll. Registers; The Life and Death of Edmund Staunton, D.D., published by Richard Mayo (or Mayow), of Kingston, London, 1671, to which is added A Brief Relation, &c., by Mr. J. M. A short Appendix to the life of Edmund Staunton, D.D., London, 1673, published anonymously, but written by Fulman, was a series of sarcastic strictures on the former book.] T. F.

STAUNTON, FRANCIS FRENCH (1779?-1825), lieutenant-colonel, born about 1779, went to India as a cadet in 1797, and was commissioned as ensign in the Bombay army on 21 Sept. 1798. He became lieutenant on 6 March 1800, and captain on 18 June 1807. He served in the Mysore war, including the storming of Seringapatam, and in the campaign of 1801 in Egypt, receiving medals for both. But his claim to remembrance is his conduct in the action of Korigaum, against the army of the peshwa, Baji Rao, on 1 Jan. 1818. He was ordered from Seroor to Poona to reinforce Colonel Burr with five hundred men of the 2nd battalion 1st Bombay native infantry—his own regiment—three hundred irregular horse, and twenty-four men of the Madras artillery, with two 6-pounders. After a night march of twenty-seven miles he reached the Bhima at 10 A.M., and found the army of the peshwa drawn up on the opposite side. It consisted of five thousand

foot and twenty-five thousand horse. He threw his men into the village of Korigaum, and there they fought all day without food or water. Many of the houses were set on fire by the enemy, who had guns and rockets, and succeeded in gaining possession of part of the village. The British troops (all native except the artillery) lost nearly two hundred men in killed and wounded, including six out of the seven English officers, but they held out till night. Next morning they found that the peshwa had retreated upon news of the approach of reinforcements. A stone obelisk still marks the spot. The battalion was made a grenadier battalion, and Staunton was nominated C.B. and aide-de-camp to the governor-general. He was promoted major on 15 April 1819, and lieutenant-colonel on 28 Sept. 1823. He died on board the Florentia on 25 June 1825.

[Grant Duff's History of the Mahrattas, iii. 432; Colebrooke's Life of Mountstuart Elphinstone, iii. 17; Gent. Mag. 1825, ii. 286; Georgian Era, vol. ii.] E. M. L.

STAUNTON, Sir GEORGE LEONARD (1737-1801), diplomatist, born at Cargin, co. Galway, on 19 April 1737, was the son of George Staunton (1700-1780), colonel of militia, of Cargin, and Margaret (d. 1784), daughter of John Leonard of Carra, co. Galway. In 1753 he was sent to France to complete his education. After studying about a twelvemonth at the Jesuit College, Toulouse, he joined the school of medicine at Montpellier, where he graduated M.D. in 1758. In October 1759 he arrived in London, and he attained some reputation as a writer on medical subjects. Among his friends at this time was Dr. Johnson, one of whose letters to him is quoted by Boswell. In 1762 he went to the West Indies, where he practised as a physician and held several official appointments, being at one time secretary to the governor of Dominica. Having acquired a large fortune, he purchased an estate in Grenada, and in 1770 returned to England. His interests being neglected by agents, he was obliged in 1772 to proceed again to the West Indies, where he remained till 1779, being for some time member of the legislative council and attorney-general for Grenada. In 1774 began his life-long friendship with George Macartney (afterwards Earl Macartney) [q. v.], appointed in that year governor of the Caribee Islands. When Grenada was attacked by the French in 1779, Staunton, as colonel of militia and aide-de-camp to the governor, took an active part in the defence, and after the capitulation was one of the hostages sent to Paris.

His plantations had been pillaged by the enemy, and he left the West Indies a ruined man. During his detention in France he negotiated an exchange of prisoners which released Lord Macartney from his parole; and when in 1781 that nobleman went out to Madras as governor, Staunton accompanied him as secretary.

The first important service he performed in India was a mission in 1782 to Calcutta, to confer with Warren Hastings, whose temper he found 'somewhat affected by the long opposition he had met in council.' In the following year, private information having been received from England of the near conclusion of peace with France, he was appointed to negotiate with the Marquis de Bussy and Admiral Suffren for a suspension of hostilities. In September 1783 he was charged with the duty of arresting General James Stuart [q. v.] in command of the Madras troops, who had defied the governor's authority (THORNTON, India, ii. 279). Later in the year he was appointed, with two other envoys, to treat with Tippu Sultan. After protracted negotiations, a treaty of peace with the ruler of Mysore was signed on 11 March 1784 (THORNTON, ii. 285). Lord Macartney's appreciation of his secretary's services was conveyed in a letter to the court of directors dated Fort St. George, 28 July 1784, and in a private letter of the same date to Charles James Fox, in which the governor wrote: 'His sagacity and singular talents for public business, his extensive knowledge of most parts of the world, his spirit, integrity, and fidelity, so fully experienced by myself, give me a right to speak of him in high terms.'

In 1784 Staunton returned to England with despatches. The court of directors on 11 April 1785 awarded him a pension of 500l. a year for life, while from the crown he received the honour of an Irish baronetcy (created 31 Oct. 1785). In the same year he entered into possession of his father's estate at Cargin, on paying the balance of the sum for which it had been conveyed for a term of years to Robert French.

Sir George Staunton remained in England without public employment till 1792. He was intimate with Edmund Burke, who sought his advice when threatened, as he wrote, by the malice of 'the villains who in the India Office and in India have been labouring for the destruction of so large a part of mankind' (Burke to Staunton, June 1785). In February 1787 Staunton was elected a fellow of the Royal Society, and on 16 June 1790 was made an honorary D.C.L. at Oxford.

In 1792 he was sent with Lord Macartney on a mission to China, being appointed secretary to the embassy and, provisionally, minister plenipotentiary in the event of the ambassador's death. It was also intended that he should eventually take up his residence at Pekin as British minister, but ill-health, on his return to England, prevented his acceptance of the post. In 1797 he published 'An authentic account of the Earl of Macartney's Embassy from the King of Great Britain to the Emperor of China,' London, 8vo.

The remainder of his life was saddened by prolonged ill-health, and he died at his London house in Devonshire Street, Portman Square, on 14 Jan. 1801. He was buried in Westminster Abbey, where a monument by Chantrey is erected to his memory. He married, 22 July 1771, Jane, daughter of Benjamin Collins, banker of Salisbury, and M.P. for that city. By her he had two sons: George, born 1775, died in infancy; and Sir George Thomas Staunton [q.v.]

A portrait of Staunton in conference with his chief, Macartney, by Lemuel Abbott [q.v.], is in the National Portrait Gallery, London; an engraving from Engleheart's portrait painted in 1792 appears in the 'Memoir' mentioned below.

[Memoir of the Life and Family of the late Sir George Leonard Staunton, bart., edited by his son, Havant, 1823 (for private circulation); Gent. Mag. 1801, i. 183, 189.]   S. W.

STAUNTON, SIR GEORGE THOMAS (1781–1859), writer on China, only surviving child of Sir George Leonard Staunton [q. v.], Indian administrator, was born at Milford House, near Salisbury, on 26 May 1781. He was educated privately, and became a good classical scholar. In 1792 he accompanied his father to China, under the nominal designation of page to the ambassador. Before embarking, and during the voyage, he studied Chinese under two native Chinese missionaries from the Propaganda College at Naples, and was soon able to speak with fluency and to write in the native character. In an interview with the emperor of China he was the only member of the embassy able to converse in Chinese. During a visit to England in 1797 he kept two terms as a fellow-commoner at Trinity College, Cambridge. On 10 April 1798 he was appointed a writer in the East India Company's factory at Canton. On 14 Jan. 1801 he succeeded his father as second baronet. In 1804 he was promoted to be a supercargo, and in the following year he was the means of introducing vaccination into China by making a translation of George Pearson's treatise on that subject. In 1808 he was appointed interpreter to the factory, and in January 1816 became chief of the factory. In July 1816, in conjunction with William, earl Amherst [q. v.], and Sir Henry Ellis (1777–1855) [q. v.], he was appointed a 'king's commissioner of embassy' to proceed to Pekin to make representations on the conduct of the mandarins towards the merchants at Canton. The exaction of the ceremony of the 'Kotoo' was, after much discussion, waived, chiefly through objections made by Staunton; but other complications arose, and the embassy returned to Canton in January 1817 without obtaining an interview with the emperor. This was only the second time that any party of Englishmen had been permitted to advance so far into the interior of China (SIR HENRY ELLIS, *Journal of the late Embassy to China*, 1817, pp. 38 et seq.)

In the same year Staunton returned to England, and did not again hold any public appointment, but his advice was often sought privately by the East India Company and by the government. As a 'liberal tory' he sat for the borough of St. Michael's in Cornwall from 1818 to 1820; for Heytesbury, Wiltshire, from 1830 to 1831; and for South Hampshire from 1832 to 1835. He unsuccessfully contested the last-named constituency in 1835 and 1837, and finally sat for Portsmouth from 1838 to 1852. In 1829 he gave evidence before a committee upon Chinese affairs, and in 1830 he became a member of the East India committee and a strong supporter of the East India Company. In the commons he was a frequent speaker on colonial subjects, and his opinions carried some weight.

In 1823 he co-operated with Henry Thomas Colebrooke [q. v.] in founding the Royal Asiatic Society, and, as a commencement for the library, gave three thousand volumes of Chinese works. He became F.R.S. on 28 April 1803, and D.C.L. of Oxford in 1818.

He died, unmarried, at 17 Devonshire Street, Portland Place, London, on 10 Aug. 1859.

Staunton published: 1. 'Miscellaneous Notices relating to China and our Commercial Intercourse with that Country,' 1822; 2nd edit., two parts, 1822–8; 3rd edit. 1850. 2. 'Memoirs of the Life and Family of the late Sir G. L. Staunton,' 1823. 3. 'Notes of Proceedings and Occurrences during the British Embassy to Pekin,' 1824. 4. 'The Lamentation of Sir G. Stan-Ching-quot, Mandarin of the Celestial Empire' [i.e. Sir G. T. Staunton], in verse, 1834, 4to. 5. 'Remarks on the British Relations with China and the proposed Plan for removing them,' 1836. 6. 'An Inquiry into the proper Mode of rendering the word God in translating the Sacred Scriptures into the Chinese Language,' 1849. 7. 'Observations on our Chinese Commerce,' 1850. 8. 'Memoir of Sir J. Barrow, Bart.,' 1852. For the Hakluyt Society he edited 'The History of the Great and Mighty Kingdom of China,' by J. Gonzalez de Mendoza; reprinted from the translation of R. Parke, 1853. He translated from the Chinese 'Ta Tsing leu lee, being the Fundamental Laws of China,' 1810; this was the first book translated from Chinese into English, and is useful as a law-book. Staunton also translated from the Chinese the 'Narrative of the Chinese Embassy to the Khan of the Tourgouth Tartars,' by Too-le-Shin, 1821, and revised 'The Life of Taou-Kwang,' by C. F. A. Guetzlaff, 1852.

[Memoirs of Sir G. T. Staunton, bart., 1856, with a portrait; Select Letters written on the occasion of the publication of the Memoirs of Sir G. T. Staunton, 1857; Proceedings of the Royal Society, 1860, x. pp. xxvi–xxix; Foreign Office List, 1860, p. 140; Dodd's Peerage, 1859 p. 518.] G. C. B.

STAUNTON, HERVEY DE (d. 1327), judge, was son of Sir William de Staunton of Staunton, Nottinghamshire, by Athelina, daughter and coheiress of John de Masters of Bosingham, Lincolnshire (THOROTON, *Nottinghamshire*, i. 305). He seems to have held the living of Soham, Norfolk, as early as 1289; afterwards he held the livings of Thurston and Werbeton, and about 1300, on being ordained priest, received the living of East Derham (BLISS, *Cal. Pap. Reg.* ii. 19). In November 1300 there is mention of him as going to the court of Rome (*Cal. Pat. Rolls*, Edward I, 1292–1301, p. 556). He was a justice itinerant in Cornwall in 1302 and in Durham in 1303. In the parliament of September 1305 he was a receiver of petitions from Ireland and Guernsey (*Rolls of Parliament*, i. 159), and on 20 April 1306 was appointed one of the judges of the common pleas. On the accession of Edward II, Staunton was reappointed to the common pleas, and is frequently mentioned in judicial commissions (*Calendars of Close Rolls* and *Patent Rolls*). On 28 Sept. 1314 he was appointed one of the barons of the exchequer, and on 22 June 1316 chancellor of the exchequer, but continued to act as a judge, and was regularly summoned to parliament with the other judges (*Parl. Writs*, ii. 1157). In 1323 he was made chief justice of the king's bench, and directed to discharge his duties

I 2

at the exchequer by a substitute (DUGDALE, *Orig.* p. 38; MADOX, *Hist. Exchequer*, ii. 53). On 27 March 1324 Staunton resigned the chief-justiceship, and on 26 March was reappointed chancellor of the exchequer. He resigned the latter post on 18 July 1326, when he was appointed chief justice of the common pleas (*Parl. Writs*, ii. pp. ii, 1458). Staunton seems to have sided with Edward II, and in September Queen Isabella seized eight hundred marks which he had deposited at Bury St. Edmunds (*Chr. Edw. I and Edw. II*, i. 314). He was not reappointed on the accession of Edward III, and the proceedings of an *iter* he had held at London were reversed (*ib.* i. 328; *Cal. Pat. Rolls*, Edward III, i. 2). As prebend of Husthwaite, York, and parson of East Derham, he is mentioned as receiving protection on 30 Jan. and 11 Feb. 1327 (*ib.* i. 1, 10). On 2 March he had license to alienate in mortmain the manor and advowson of Barenton to the masters and scholars of St. Michael, Cambridge (*ib.* i. 25). Staunton died in 1327, before he could give effect to his foundation, and the license was renewed to his executors (*ib.* i. 232, 319, 395, ii. 146). He was buried in the church of St. Michael, Cambridge. His foundation of Michael House was eventually absorbed in Trinity College, where Staunton is still commemorated as a benefactor.

[*Chronicles of Edward I and Edward II* (Rolls Ser.); *Calendars of Close and Patent Rolls*, Edward II and Edward III; Foss's *Judges of England*; Mullinger's *Hist. University of Cambridge*, i. 234–6.]   C. L. K.

STAUNTON, HOWARD (1810–1874), chess-player and editor of Shakespeare, born in 1810, was reputed to be the natural son of Frederick Howard, fifth earl of Carlisle [q. v.]. He was neglected in youth, and received little or no education. He is said to have spent some time at Oxford, but was never a member of the university. On coming of age he received a few thousand pounds under his father's will. This money he rapidly spent. He was devoted to the stage, and claimed to have acted in his early days Lorenzo to the Shylock of Edmund Kean. When thrown upon his own resources, he sought a livelihood from his pen. The main subjects of his literary labours were chess and the Shakespearean drama.

Staunton played chess from an early age, and soon acquired a skill in the game which has not been equalled by any British-born player. Alexander Macdonnell (1798–1835) [q. v.], who could alone be regarded as his rival, is now regarded as his inferior by competent critics. For some twenty years a great part of Staunton's time was spent in playing the game and in writing upon it. From 1836 he frequented the Divan, Huttmann's, and other public chess resorts. Four years later he first became known as a player of distinction, and between 1840 and 1851 he made his reputation. During 1841 and 1842 he engaged in a long series of matches with Cochrane, and in the majority was victorious. A match at Paris with the champion of Europe, St. Amant, followed in 1843, and Staunton's victory gave him a world-wide fame as a chess-player. Carl Meier, among others, published an account of this engagement (Zurich, 1843). In 1846 Staunton defeated the German players Horwitz and Harrwitz. An account of his match with Mr. Lowe in 1848 was published by T. Beeby. In 1851 his powers showed signs of decay, and in the great international tournament of that year he was beaten by Anderssen and by Williams; to the latter he had given odds not long before. In 1852 he met one of the greatest players of any period, Baron von Heydebrand und der Lasa of Berlin, and was defeated by a small number of games. He rarely played in public matches again. George Walker, a rigorous critic, credited Staunton's play with 'brilliancy of imagination, thirst for invention, judgment for position, eminent view of the board, and untiring patience.'

Meanwhile Staunton was energetically turning his knowledge of the game to account as a journalist. In 1840, the year in which his supremacy as a player was first recognised, he projected the monthly periodical, 'The Chess Player's Chronicle,' which he owned and edited till he sold it in August 1854. About 1844 he took charge of the chess column in the 'Illustrated London News,' which had been commenced two years earlier, and he conducted it till his death. For some time he also edited a chess column in the 'Era' newspaper.

Staunton compiled for Bohn's 'Scientific Series' some valuable manuals on the game. Of these 'The Chess Player's Handbook' (1847; 2nd edit. 1848) long deserved, and still longer retained, the reputation of being the best English treatise on its subject. 'The Chess Player's Companion' (1849) included a treatise on games at odds, and so far was supplementary to the 'Handbook,' but it was mainly devoted to the record of his own games. 'This still remains a work of the highest interest, and a noble monument for any chess-player to have raised for himself. The notes are in general as much distinguished by their good taste as by their literary talent and critical value.' 'The Chess Tournament' (1852) contains the games of the international tournament of 1851 and some others; of this a German rendering appeared at Berlin. A defence of the London Chess Club (by 'a member') from the strictures passed on it by Staunton in this volume was issued in 1852. 'The Chess Praxis' (1860) was another supplement to the 'Handbook,' carrying on chess theory for some twelve years later, and containing many well-selected games.

Staunton's name was conferred on the set of chessmen which are recognised as the standard type among English-speaking peoples. His 'Chess Player's Text-book' was issued in 1849, without date, to be sold with the Staunton chessmen.

Staunton's 'Chess: Theory and Practice' was left in manuscript at his death, and was edited in 1876 by R. B. Wormald, who succeeded him as editor of the chess column of the 'Illustrated London News.'

From 1854 Staunton largely devoted his attention to the study of Shakespeare, of whose works he had been from youth an enthusiastic admirer. Between November 1857 and May 1860 he issued, with Messrs. Routledge, a new edition of Shakespeare in monthly parts, with 824 illustrations by Sir John Gilbert. The parts were bound up in three volumes. A reissue without the illustrations followed in 1864 in 4 vols. Staunton's text was based on a collation of the folio editions with the early quartos and with the texts of modern editors from Rowe to Dyce. The conjectural emendations, which were usually sensible, were kept within narrow limits, and showed much familiarity with Elizabethan literature and modes of speech. The general notes combined common-sense with exhaustive research. In 1864 Staunton issued a photo-lithographic facsimile of the 1600 quarto of 'Much Ado about Nothing' from the copy in the Ellesmere collection. In 1866 he edited a photo-lithographic facsimile of the first folio edition of Shakespeare's works of 1623. Subsequently, between October 1872 and his death, he contributed a series of nineteen articles on 'Unsuspected Corruptions of Shakespeare's Text' to the 'Athenæum' (cf. Notes and Queries, 6th ser. iv. 264). His only other literary undertaking was a carefully compiled account of the 'Great Schools of England' (1865; 2nd edit. 1869).

Staunton was a brilliant talker in congenial society, prolific in anecdote and in apt quotation from Shakespeare. He died suddenly from heart disease at his house in London on 22 June 1874. He married, about 1854, Frances, widow of W. D. Nethersole, a solicitor, who was some years his senior. She died about 1882.

The St. George's Chess Club possesses a medallion-portrait, as well as a lithograph depicting the match in 1843 between Staunton and St. Amant.

[Information kindly furnished by the Rev. W. Wayte; Chess Player's Chronicle, 1874-5, pp. 117, 161-2; Athenæum, 1874, i. 862; Illustrated London News, 4 July 1874, with portrait.] S. L.

STAVELEY, Sir CHARLES WILLIAM DUNBAR (1817-1896), general, was the eldest son of Lieutenant-general William Staveley [q. v.], by Sarah, daughter of Thomas Mather. He was born at Boulogne on 18 Dec. 1817, was educated at the Scottish military and naval academy, Edinburgh, and was commissioned as second lieutenant in the 87th (royal Irish fusiliers) on 6 March 1835. He became lieutenant on 4 Oct. 1839, and captain on 6 Sept. 1844. From July 1840 till June 1843 he was aide-de-camp to the governor of Mauritius, where his regiment was stationed, and where his father was acting-governor for part of the time. On his return home he was quartered at Glasgow, and saved a boy from drowning in the Clyde at imminent risk of his own life, as he was not fully recovered from a severe attack of measles.

He exchanged to the 18th foot on 31 Jan. 1845, and to the 44th on 9 May. From 15 June to 11 May 1847 he was aide-de-camp to the governor-general of British North America. An admirable draughtsman, his sketches proved very useful during the settlement of the Oregon boundary question in 1846. He was assistant military secretary at Hongkong, where his father was in command, from 20 March 1848 to 27 Feb. 1851.

He had become major in the 44th on 7 Dec. 1850, and went with it to Turkey in 1854. When the regiment embarked for the Crimea he was to have been left behind on account of illness, but he hid himself on board till the vessel sailed. He was present at Alma and at Balaclava, where he acted as aide-de-camp to the Duke of Cambridge. On 12 Dec. 1854 he became lieutenant-colonel in his regiment. The 44th belonged to Sir William Eyre's brigade of the third division, and took part in the attempt on the dockyard creek on 18 June 1855, and in the capture of the cemetery—the sole success achieved. Staveley was mentioned in despatches (London Gazette, 4 July) and was made C.B. He also received the Crimean medal with three clasps, the Sardinian and Turkish medals, and the Medjidie (fifth class).

He commanded the regiment from 30 June 1855. It returned to England in July 1856, embarked for Madras in August 1857, and went on to China in March 1860. He had become colonel in the army on 9 March 1858, and on 28 April 1860 he was made brigadier-general, and was given command of a brigade in Michel's division during the Anglo-French expedition to Peking. He was present at the capture of the Taku forts, was mentioned in despatches (*ib.* 4 Nov. 1860), and received the medal with clasp. On 18 Jan. 1861 he was given one of the rewards for distinguished service.

He was left in command of the British troops remaining in China in 1862. The Taeping insurrection was then in full career. The rebels had broken their promise not to come within thirty miles of Shanghai, and were threatening that city itself. In April Staveley marched against them with a force of about two thousand men, of which about one-third consisted of French and English seamen and marines. He shelled them out of their entrenched camp at Wongkadze, and stormed Tsipu, Kahding, Tsingpu, Nanjao, and Cholin in the course of April and May. But the Chinese imperial troops were unable to hold all the towns recovered, and he had to withdraw the British garrison from Kahding (*ib.* 18 July and 5 Aug. 1862). In the autumn Kahding and Tsingpu were again taken, and the thirty-mile radius cleared of the rebels.

In December he was asked by Li Hung Chang to name a British officer to replace the American Burgevine as commander of the disciplined Chinese force which had been formed by Frederick Townsend Ward. Staveley named Charles George Gordon [q. v.], who had been chief engineer under him in the recent operations, and had surveyed all the country round Shanghai. They had served together before Sebastopol, and Staveley's sister was the wife of Gordon's brother. The appointment had to be approved from England, and was not taken up till the end of March 1863. At that time ill-health obliged Staveley to resign his command and go home.

In March 1865 he was made K.C.B. and was appointed to the command of the first division of the Bombay army. On 25 Sept. 1867 he was promoted major-general, and in November, by Sir Robert Napier's desire, he was given command of the first division of the force sent to Abyssinia. He showed his energy to good purpose in the organisation of the base at Annesley Bay, and he conducted the fight on the Arogye plain, which immediately preceded the capture of Magdala. Napier said in his despatch that Staveley had afforded him most valuable support and assistance throughout the campaign (*ib.* 16 and 30 June 1868). He received the thanks of parliament and the medal.

Staveley commanded the troops in the western district for five years from 1 Jan. 1869, and in the autumn manœuvres of 1871 round Aldershot one of the three divisions was under him. He was commander-in-chief at Bombay from 7 Oct. 1874 to 7 Oct. 1878, with the local rank of lieutenant-general, which became his substantive rank on 29 April 1875. On 1 Oct. 1877 he became general. He was given the colonelcy of the 30th foot on 2 Feb. 1876, and transferred to his old regiment, the 44th (which had become the first battalion of the Essex regiment), on 25 July 1883. He received the G.C.B. on 24 May 1884. He had been placed on the retired list on 8 Oct. in the previous year.

He died at Aban Court, Cheltenham, on 23 Nov. 1896, and was buried at Brompton cemetery on the 27th. In 1864 he married Susan Millicent, daughter of Charles William Minet of Baldwyns, Kent. She survived him with several children.

[Times, 24 Nov. 1896; Carter's Historical Record of 44th Regt.; Royal Engineers' Papers, new ser. xix. 109; Boulger's Life of Gordon; Markham's History of the Abyssinian Expedition.]   E. M. L.

STAVELEY, THOMAS (1626–1684), antiquary, son of William Staveley, rector of Cossington, Leicestershire, by his wife Anne, daughter of Thomas Babington of Rothley, was born at East Langton, Leicestershire, in 1626. He was educated at Peterhouse, Cambridge, admitted of the Inner Temple on 2 July 1647, and called to the bar on 12 June 1654. He resided the greatest part of his life at Belgrave, but a few years before his death removed to Leicester; he there held the office of steward of the court of records, to which he was appointed in 1672, probably by the Earl of Huntingdon. The stimulus given to protestant opinion by the conversion of James, duke of York, to Romanism (avowed in 1669), the Declaration of Indulgence (1672), and the countermove of the Test Act of 1673, elicited from Staveley in 1674 the work by which he is best known, 'The Romish Horseleech: or an Impartial Account of the Intolerable Charge of Popery to this Nation' (London, 8vo). To the 1769 edition of this work is annexed an essay by Staveley 'of the supremacy of the king of England.'

During the later years of his life Staveley studied English history and the antiquities of his native county. He left some valuable collections for the history and antiquities of Leicester, which were printed by Nichols, first in his 'Bibliotheca Topographica Britannica,' and afterwards, with a curious historical pedigree of Staveley's family drawn up in 1682, in his 'History of Leicestershire.' He was a justice of the peace for Leicestershire, and was reputed to be 'strictly just, abhorring bribery.'

Staveley died at Leicester on 2 Jan. 1683–4, at the age of fifty-seven, and was buried in St. Mary's Church, Leicester, on the 8th. His monumental inscription is given in Nichols's 'History' (i. 318), as well as an engraved portrait (ii. 678). He married, at Cossington, Leicestershire, on 31 Dec. 1656, Mary, daughter of John Onebye of Hinckley, by whom he had three sons and four daughters. His wife died on 12 Oct. 1669.

After his death were published: 1. 'Three Historical Essays,' published by his youngest son in 1703. 2. 'The History of Churches in England; wherein is shown the time, means, and manner of founding, building, and endowing of churches, both cathedral and rural, with their furniture and appendages,' 1712 (a second edition, with improvements, in 1773); a work of research and learning. Manuscript copies of 'The History and Antiquities of the Ancient Town, and once City, of Leicester,' are in the British Museum (Addit. MS. 15917) and in the Leicester Free Library.

[Nichols's Leicestershire, i. 3, 318, 469, &c.; ii. 677, 685, &c; Hill's History of Langton, p. 23; Chalmers's Biographical Dictionary, xxviii. 350.]   W. G. D. F.

STAVELEY, WILLIAM (1784–1854), lieutenant-general, born at York on 29 July 1784, was the son of William Staveley of York, by Henrietta, born Henderson, a native of Caithness. He was commissioned as ensign in the Caithness legion in 1798, served with it in Ireland during the rebellion of that year, and when it was disbanded obtained a commission in the royal staff corps on 14 July 1804. He became lieutenant on 21 April 1808, and joined Wellesley's army at Oporto in May 1809. He served on the staff of the quartermaster-general throughout the Peninsular war, and was present at Talavera, Fuentes de Oñoro, Vittoria, the battle of the Pyrenees, and Toulouse, besides the sieges of Ciudad Rodrigo and Badajos, and many minor actions.

At Ciudad Rodrigo he volunteered to act as guide to the stormers of the light division, and was one of the first men to reach the top of the smaller breach. He was stunned by the explosion which took place as the troops made their way along the ramparts, and he was picked up for dead. On 6 May 1813 he was given a company in the royal African corps, and on 15 Dec. 1814 a brevet majority.

He returned to the royal staff corps on 12 Jan. 1815, and went with a detachment of it to the Netherlands in April. He was on the headquarter staff at Waterloo. In a letter of 22 June he wrote: 'Blucher sent word at one o'clock that he would attack in half an hour. At four Lord Wellington sent me to him to see what he was about, and tell him how well we were getting on. I rode all along our line at full gallop, and, after crossing the country about two miles to our left, found him. He told me to tell Lord Wellington that he would attack as soon as he could form his men, which would probably be in an hour or less, but he did not come up with the enemy until they were fairly driven from the field.' He was made brevet lieutenant-colonel and C.B., and subsequently received the Peninsular war medal with eight clasps, the Waterloo medal, and one of the rewards for distinguished service.

He was one of two officers sent into Paris to carry out the terms of the convention of 3 July, and was severely wounded by some French soldiers in the suburbs of the city. He remained in France during the occupation of the allies, returned to England in 1818, and was sent with his company to Mauritius in 1821. He remained there twenty-six years, being appointed deputy quartermaster-general and commandant of Port Louis on 29 Sept. 1825, and acting as governor for several months in 1842. When he left the colony he received an address from the inhabitants, to whom he had always shown himself 'juste, impartial, affable, bienveillant envers chacun.'

Staveley was promoted colonel on 10 Jan. 1837, and major-general on 9 Nov. 1846. A year afterwards he left Mauritius for Hongkong, where he commanded the troops for three years. In March 1851 he took up the command of a division of the Bombay army, and in the following year held the command-in-chief for several months. In August 1853 he was given the colonelcy of the 99th foot, and was appointed commander-in-chief at Madras with the local rank of lieutenant-general. He took up this command on 27 Oct. He died suddenly on 4 April 1854 on his way to the Nilgiri Hills, and was buried at Utakamand. He married, on 23 Jan. 1817, Sarah, daughter of Thomas Mather, and left, with other issue, Sir Charles William Dunbar Staveley [q. v.] The inhabitants of Mauritius put up a tablet to his memory in the protestant church at Port Louis, and a duplicate was erected in the cathedral at Madras.

[Gent. Mag. 1854, ii. 390; Reminiscences of Lieutenant-general Staveley, printed for private circulation in 1866; private information.]

E. M. L.

STAWELL or STOWELL, Sir JOHN (1599-1662), royalist, born between February and October 1599, was second but eldest surviving son of Sir John Stawell of Cothelstone, Somerset, by his wife Elizabeth, daughter of George Touchet, earl of Castlehaven, who afterwards married Sir Thomas Griffin of Dingley, Northamptonshire. The family had long been settled in Somerset, and the elder Sir John had been created K.B. at the coronation of James I. A relative, Sir Edward Stawell, distinguished himself at the battle of Cheriton Wood on 29 March 1644 (GARDINER, Civil War, i. 325-6).

The royalist matriculated as a gentleman-commoner from Queen's College, Oxford, on 25 Oct. 1616, aged 17, but left the university without a degree. He was elected knight of the shire for Somerset to the parliament which met on 17 May 1625, and on 2 Feb. following he was made K.B. at the coronation of Charles I. In 1628 he served as sheriff of Somerset, and on 12 Oct. 1640 he was again returned to the Long parliament for Somerset. He 'was a gentleman of very great estate in those parts, and who from the beginning had heartily and personally engaged himself and his children for the king, and was in the first form of those who had made themselves obnoxious to parliament' (CLARENDON, Rebellion, vii. 98).

On the outbreak of the civil war Stawell 'raised three regiments of horse and two of dragoons and of foot upon his sole charge' for the king's service. He was in consequence, on 8 Aug. 1642, disabled from sitting in parliament. In the autumn of that and spring of the following year he accompanied Hertford through his successful campaign in the west [see SEYMOUR, WILLIAM, first MARQUIS OF HERTFORD and second DUKE OF SOMERSET], during which Taunton was captured. Being a man 'of notorious courage and fidelity,' Stawell was appointed governor of that town. On 16 Jan. 1642-3 he was created M.A., and on the 31st M.D., as a member of Wadham

College, by the university of Oxford. In 1645 he was one of the chief advocates of the scheme for associating the four western counties under Prince Charles, and in the same year he took part against Goring by supporting the petitions of the Somerset men against the depredations of Goring's army. At the same time his personal differences with Coventry 'drew the whole country into factions' (CLARENDON, vii. 177, ix. 59).

Stawell continued fighting in the west till the close of the war. He was at Exeter when it surrendered to Fairfax on 9 April 1646 upon the 'Exeter articles.' These stipulated that the prisoners should be allowed to compound on promising not to bear arms against parliament, and on 15 July Stawell came to London to arrange his composition. On 4 Aug. he was brought before the committee for compounding; but on his refusal to take the national covenant and negative oath he was committed a prisoner to Ely House. On 18 Aug. he was brought before the House of Commons. He declined to kneel when ordered to do so, and again refused the covenant. He was accordingly committed to Newgate for high treason in levying war on parliament, and a committee of the house was appointed to draw up the indictment for his trial before the next Somerset assizes. The order for his trial was repeated on various occasions, but nothing was done; on 14 March 1648-9 it was resolved to proceed against him before the upper bench. On 28 June 1650 he was selected as one of the six prisoners of war who were to be tried on a capital charge, and in the following month, by order of the high court, he was removed from Newgate to the Tower. Finally, on 17 Dec. 1650, he was brought to trial; but the high court preferred not to sentence him, and referred him to parliament. There his case was much discussed but not determined (BURTON, Parl. Diary, vol. i. pp. lxi, 165, 202, iii. 41).

Meanwhile his estates had been sold, and various judgments given against him for actions during the war, involving the payment of 7,000l. damages. His wife and children were allowed a fifth of his estate, amounting to 500l. a year, for their support, and Stawell himself received a pension of 6l. a week. He frequently petitioned against the illegality of these proceedings, but no attention was paid to them, and parliament passed an act confirming the purchasers of his estates in their possession. Stawell remained in the Tower until May 1660, but in March his pension, which had been discontinued, was renewed, and after the Restoration he received back his estates in full. He was returned to parliament as knight of the shire for Somerset on 1 April 1661, and died, aged 62, at Nether Ham, Somerset, on 21 Feb. 1681-2. He was buried on 23 April in Cotholstone parish church.

By his wife Elizabeth, daughter of Sir Edward Hext (d. 1624), and widow of Sir Joseph Killigrew, whom he married before 1623, he had, besides other issue, a son Ralph, who, in consideration of his father's services, was on 15 Jan. 1682-3 created Baron Stawell of Somerton, Somerset. The barony became extinct on the death of Ralph's grandson Edward, fourth baron, in 1735.

[Many of Stawell's petitions were printed at the time—see Brit. Mus. Cat., s.v. 'Stawell, Sir John;' Lords' Journals, xi. 23, 137; Commons' Journals, vols. iv-vii. passim; Cal. Committee for Compounding, pp. 1425-30, 3280; Cal. State Papers, Dom.; Cal. Clarendon State Papers, ed. Macray; Hist. MSS. Comm. 5th Rep. App. and 7th Rep. App. passim; Official Returns of Members of Parliament; Clarendon's Hist. of the Rebellion, ed. Macray; S. R. Gardiner's Commonwealth and Protectorate, vol. i. (s.v. 'Stowell'); Wood's Fasti Oxon. ii. 48; Visitations of Somerset (Harl. Soc.); Collinson's Somerset, vol. i. pp. xxxii, xxxviii, vol. iii. pp. 251, 431, 445; Foster's Alumni Oxon. 1500-1714; R. B. Gardiner's Reg. Wadham Coll. Oxford, i. 153; Reg. Univ. Oxon. II. ii. 354; Burke's Extinct and G. E. C[okayne]'s Peerages.]   A. F. P.

STAWELL, Sir WILLIAM FOSTER (1815-1889), first chief justice of Victoria, son of Jonas Stawell of Old Court, Cork, and Anna, daughter of William Foster, bishop of Clogher, was born on 27 June 1815. Educated at Trinity College, Dublin, he graduated B.A. in 1837. After studying law both at King's Inn, Dublin, and Lincoln's Inn, he was called to the Irish bar in 1839.

In 1842 Stawell emigrated to Melbourne, and was admitted to practice at the bar; but for a time gave almost as much attention to squatting, in which he joined a cousin, Foster Fitzgerald. His reputation in the courts, however, rapidly grew, and he was drawn into active political life, becoming one of the great advocates for the separation of Port Phillip from New South Wales. In 1851 he became the first attorney-general of the newly erected colony and held this office till 28 Nov. 1855, drafting and conducting through the council the early laws of the colony. He also took an active part in the preparation of the new Constitution Act in 1854-5. To him are due the names 'House of Representatives' and 'Legislative Assembly' for the two chambers. He met with much opposition and obloquy, but great re-

serve force and patience triumphed over attacks. Henry Samuel Chapman [q. v.] called him 'almost the only efficient man connected with the government.'

When in November 1855 the new constitution came into operation, Stawell was elected for Melbourne to the House of Representatives. He took office at once as attorney-general; but on 25 Feb. 1857 retired from political life on becoming chief justice of Victoria. In 1858 he was knighted. Apart from his judicial duties, his time was chiefly devoted during the following years to furthering the progress of the church of England and of education in the colony. He was a staunch supporter of Bishop Charles Perry [q. v.], and framed the act establishing the synod of the church. In 1873 he went on leave to England for nearly two years. In 1875, and again in 1877, he acted as governor of the colony, on the second occasion bearing the brunt of the crisis which arose on the defeat of Graham Berry's ministry and the accession to power of Sir James McCulloch [q. v.] He again acted as governor from March to July 1881. In August 1886 he resigned his office as chief justice, and in the following year was appointed lieutenant-governor of Victoria. In January 1889 he left for Europe in order to recruit his health, and died at Naples on 12 March.

Stawell was a masterful but an upright and strong judge; for many years he was one of the most prominent figures in the political life of Victoria. He was an enthusiastic promoter of exploration. He was president of the Philosophical Institute (afterwards the Royal Society) of Victoria in 1858-9, and later was chancellor of Melbourne University, trustee of the public library, and president of the Melbourne hospital. He became LL.D. of Dublin in 1874 and K.C.M.G. in 1886.

Stawell married, in 1856, Mary Frances Elizabeth, daughter of William Pomeroy Greene, R.N., of Woodlands, Victoria (Burke, Colonial Gentry, i. 42), and left six sons and four daughters.

[Melbourne Argus, 14 March 1889; Mennell's Dict. of Australian Biography.]   C. A. H.

STAYLEY, GEORGE (1727-1779?), actor and playwright, was born at Burton-on-Trent on 1 March 1727. In 1745 he was adopted by his mother's brother, an attorney named Monk, who wished him to study law; but after five years his kinsman, perceiving he had no aptitude in that direction, left him to his own devices. After two years of idleness he landed in Ireland on 29 May 1752, and obtained employment at the theatre in Smock Alley as an actor. In 1760 Henry

Mossop [q. v.] discharged him for giving political toasts while acting the part of Lovel in the farce of 'High Life.' The remainder of his life was spent in broils with theatrical managers and fellow-actors. Though a good actor he was inordinately vain, and had an unfortunate knack of irritating those with whom he came in contact. In the beginning of 1766 he proceeded to Edinburgh and appeared at the Canongate Music Hall, afterwards the Canongate Theatre Royal. Next year he was not re-engaged, but he was more appreciated by the public than by the management. A riot ensued in consequence on 24 Jan., and the theatre was wrecked. Stayley afterwards taught elocution, and died in obscurity before 1780.

Stayley published: 1. 'The Court of Nassau,' a comedy, Dublin, 1753, 4to. 2. 'The Rival Theatres,' a farce, Dublin, 1759, 12mo, a skit on the rivalry between Sheridan at Smock Alley and Barry and Woodward at Crow Street. 3. 'The Chocolate Makers, or Mimickry Exposed,' printed with the preceding. 4. 'The Life and Opinions of an Actor,' Dublin, 1762, 12mo, which contains also a number of short pieces in prose and verse. 5. 'An Enquiry into the Natural Worth and Dignity of Man,' Edinburgh, 1766, 12mo.

[Stayley's Life and Opinions of an Actor; Baker's Biogr. Dramatics, i. 683; Lowe's English Theatrical Literature, p. 321; Dibdin's Annals of the Edinburgh Stage, 1888, pp. 135–43; Hitchcock's History of the Irish Stage, 1788–94, passim; Jackson's History of the Scottish Stage, 1793, pp. 60–6.] E. I. C.

STAYLEY, WILLIAM (d. 1678), victim of the popish plot. [See STALEY.]

STAYNER, SIR RICHARD (d. 1662), admiral, described by Le Neve (*Pedigrees of the Knights*, p. 112) as 'of Greenwich'—which may, however, only mean that he was living there in 1660—had probably served in a subordinate rank in the parliamentary navy during the civil war (*Cal. State Papers*, Dom. 21 Dec. 1653). On 22 June 1649 he was appointed commander of the Elizabeth prize, 'now a State's ship,' though a very small one, her principal armament being two sakers, that is, six-pounders. She was specially fitted out 'for surprising small pickaroons that lurk among the sands' on the Essex coast, and for convoy service in the North Sea. In August he captured the Robert, a small frigate, apparently one of Prince Rupert's vessels, for which and other good services he was awarded 20l. and 5l. for a gold medal (ib. 13 April 1650). In November 1652 he commanded the Mermaid, fitting out

at Chatham; but seems to have been moved from her in January to command the Foresight, which was one of the fleet with Blake in the battle off Portland on 18 Feb. 1652–3. He was certainly with the fleet in the following April, when he signed the declaration of the sea-officers on the dissolution of the parliament by Cromwell, which was, in fact, a resolution 'not to meddle with state affairs, but to keep foreigners from fooling us' (cf. GARDINER, *Hist. of the Commonwealth and Protectorate*, ii. 218).

In the battle off the Gabbard on 2–3 June 1653, Stayner commanded the Foresight in the white squadron under the immediate command of Penn, and was afterwards sent into the river in convoy of twelve disabled ships, eleven Dutch prizes, with 1,350 prisoners, and the body of Admiral Richard Deane [q. v.], which he was ordered to take to Woolwich (*Cal. State Papers*, Dom. 9 June 1653). He rejoined the fleet in time to take part in the decisive battle of 29–31 July, and continued with it till the end of the season. In December he was strongly recommended by Monck for a larger ship, and in the following January was appointed to the Plymouth, in which during the spring, till the peace with the Dutch, he was employed in active cruising in the North Sea, during which he made several captures, including one rich East Indiaman. In July he was appointed by Blake to the Catherine, and in September sailed for the Mediterranean with Blake, returning to England with him in October 1655 [see BLAKE, ROBERT]. In the following February he was in command of the Bridgwater and sailed again with Blake for Cadiz, which was kept closely blockaded.

In September, when the generals with the greater part of the fleet went to Aveiro, Stayner, then in the Speaker, was left off Cadiz in command of a small squadron of some six or seven ships. On 8 Sept. he fell in with the Spanish treasure fleet which, having information from a prize that the English had left the coast, was pushing on for Cadiz in such perfect confidence that, it is said, the Spaniards supposed Stayner's ships to be fishing-vessels; yet three of Stayner's ships at least, the Speaker, Bridgwater, and Plymouth, were each of more than nine hundred tons. Nothing could be done that night, and the next morning several of Stayner's ships had fallen to leeward. He had only three with him, but these were the powerful ships just named; and as they were now within twelve miles of Cadiz, he judged that delay was unadvisable, and attacked the Spaniards about nine o'clock in the forenoon. Of the four capital ships in the Spanish fleet, one escaped and ran for Cadiz, but struck on a rock and went to the bottom. The three others were captured, but two of them caught fire and were burnt with all their cargo and a great part of their men. The fourth remained in the possession of the English ; some of the other ships also were taken. The value of the prize to the captors was estimated at about 600,000*l.* ; but it was stated by the Spaniards that their loss was not less than nine million dollars, or nearly two millions sterling. The news of this tremendous blow reached England early in October. An official narrative of it was published on 4 Oct., and a thanksgiving service ordered to be held on the 8th in all the churches in London and Westminster (*A true Narrative of the late Success . . . against the King of Spain's West India Fleet in its Return to Cadiz*).

Shortly after this Stayner returned to England with Mountagu [see Montagu, Edward, first Earl of Sandwich]; but rejoined Blake early the next year, and took a brilliant part in the destruction of the Spanish ships at Santa Cruz on 20 April. For his conduct on this occasion he was knighted by Cromwell on his return to England in the following August. During the rest of the year and during 1658 he commanded in the Downs, nominally as second to Mountagu, who was most of the time in London, and really as commander-in-chief, with his flag as rear-admiral sometimes in the Essex, sometimes in the London, and towards the end of the time in the Speaker. His work was entirely administrative, and he had no active share in the operations against Mardyke and Dunkirk, though he was in constant communication with Goodsonn, by whom they were entirely conducted. In the summer of 1659 he was rear-admiral of the fleet with Mountagu in the Sound, and on 16 April 1660 was appointed by Mountagu to be rear-admiral of the fleet which went over to bring the king to England. For this service he was knighted on 24 Sept., his earlier knighthood, conferred by Cromwell, not being recognised by the royalists.

In the early summer of 1661 Stayner was again commander-in-chief in the Downs, and in June sailed for Lisbon and the Mediterranean as rear-admiral of the fleet under the Earl of Sandwich. When Sandwich went home in April 1662, Stayner, with his flag in the Mary, remained as vice-admiral of the fleet, under Sir John Lawson [q. v.] On 2 July it was reported from Lisbon that he had just arrived from Tangiers; on 20 July that he was dangerously ill; on 9 Oct. that

he had died—apparently a few days before. In pursuance of his wish to be buried beside his wife, who seems to have died in 1658, his body was embalmed and brought home in the Mary, which arrived at Spithead on 3 Nov. He left a son Richard, who on 30 May 1663 was petitioning for repayment of 300*l.* which his father had advanced for the king's service. The claim was approved by Sandwich, but there is no mention of the money having been paid.

[Cal. State Papers, Dom. 1649–63 ; Charnock's Biogr. Nav. i. 45.] J. K. L.

STEARNE. [See also Stern and Sterne.]

STEBBING, HENRY (1687–1763), divine, baptised at Malton in Suffolk on 19 Aug. 1687, was the fourth son of John Stebbing, (1647–1728), a grocer of Malton by his wife Mary (*d.* 1821), daughter and coheiress of Richard Kenington. Henry entered St. Catharine Hall, Cambridge, as a sizar on 24 Feb. 1704–5, graduating B.A. in 1708, M.A. in 1712, and D.D. in 1730. On 19 Oct. 1710 he was elected a fellow, and on 27 June 1738 was incorporated at Oxford. On Lady-day 1713 he resigned his fellowship on being presented to the parish of Lower Rickinghall in Suffolk, and on 31 May 1726 he was instituted rector of Garboldisham in Norfolk. On 14 July 1731 he was elected preacher to the Society of Gray's Inn, and in the following year was appointed chaplain in ordinary to the king. On 19 July 1735 he was installed archdeacon of Wiltshire, and in 1739 became chancellor of Sarum. In 1748 he became rector of Redenhall in Norfolk, and retained the charge for the rest of his life. He died at Gray's Inn on 2 Jan. 1763, and was buried in Salisbury Cathedral, where a monument was erected to his memory. His portrait, painted in 1757 by Joseph Highmore, hangs in the National Portrait Gallery, London. An engraving by James Roberts is prefixed to the edition of his 'Tracts' published in 1763.

Stebbing was well known among his contemporaries as a controversial champion of Church of England orthodoxy. Among others he wrote against George Whitefield [q. v.] and Benjamin Hoadly [q. v.], bishop of Bangor. His chief antagonist, however, was Warburton, with whom he carried on a voluminous warfare for many years. Its origin was Stebbing's attack on Warburton's 'Divine Legation of Moses.' Stebbing's most important works were : 1. 'A Rational Enquiry into the proper methods of supporting Christianity, so far as it concerns the Governors of the Church,' London, 1720, 8vo. 2. 'An

Essay concerning Civil Government, considered as it stands related to Religion,' London, 1724, 8vo; reprinted in 'The Churchman armed against the Errors of the Times,' vol. iii., London, 1814, 8vo. 3. 'An Apology for the Clergy of the Church of England,' London, 1731, 8vo. 4. 'A Brief Account of Prayer and the Sacrament of the Lord's Supper, and other religious duties appertaining to Christian Worship,' London, 1739, 8vo; 4th edit. 1771, 12mo. 5. 'A Caution against Religious Delusion,' London, 1739, 8vo; this work, directed against the methodists, ran through six editions within a year. 6. 'Christianity justified upon the Scripture Foundation,' London, 1750, 8vo. 7. 'Sermons on Practical Christianity,' London, 1759-60, 8vo. A collected edition of his earlier writings appeared in 1737, entitled 'The Works of Henry Stebbing,' London, fol. He has also been credited with an anonymous satire entitled 'The Fragment,' published at Cambridge in 1751, which assailed several leading statesmen and ecclesiastics of the time.

By his wife, a daughter of Robert Camel of Eye, Suffolk, Stebbing had a son, HENRY STEBBING (1716-1787), a fellow of St. Catharine Hall, who became in 1749 rector of Gimingham and Trunch in Norfolk, and, on the resignation of his father in 1750, was appointed preacher to the Society of Gray's Inn. He died at Gray's Inn on 13 Nov. 1787. He was the author of a collection of 'Sermons on Practical Subjects,' London, 1788-90, 8vo, published by his son, Henry Stebbing, a barrister, with a memoir (*Brit. Mus. Addit. MS.* 19170, f. 196; *Gent. Mag.* 1787, ii. 1032).

[*Brit. Mus. Addit. MSS.* 5880 ff. 144, 167, 19160 f. 100, 19166 ff. 283-93, 19169 f. 17, 19174 f. 650; Foster's Register of Gray's Inn; Nichols's Lit. Anecd. *passim*; Gent. Mag. 1731 p. 309, 1735 *passim*, 1737 pp. 82, 208, 210, 1739 pp. 384, 415, 554, 1748 p. 240, 1763 p. 46, 1802 ii. 631; information kindly given by the master of St. Catharine College, Cambridge.]

E. I. C.

STEBBING, HENRY (1799-1883), poet, preacher, and historian, born at Great Yarmouth, Norfolk, on 26 Aug. 1799, was the son of John Stebbing (d. 11 Dec. 1826), who married Mary Rede (d. 24 May 1843) of the Suffolk family of that name, both of whom were buried in the cemetery of St. James, Piccadilly. He 'penned a stanza' when he was a schoolboy, and his first poem, 'The Wanderers,' was printed at the close of 1817 and circulated among his friends. In the following August he published 'Minstrel of the Glen and other Poems,' which included

'The Wanderers,' and in October 1818 he proceeded to St. John's College, Cambridge, where he had been admitted a sizar on 4 July 1818. He graduated B.A. 1823, M.A. 1827, and D.D. 1839, and on 3 July 1857 was admitted *ad eundem* at Oxford. On 3 April 1845 he was elected F.R.S.

Stebbing was ordained deacon by Bishop Bathurst of Norwich in 1822, and priest in 1823. Within a few months he was in charge of three parishes for absentee incumbents, and rode forty miles each Sunday to do the duty. In 1825 he was appointed evening lecturer at St. Mary's, Bungay, and about 1824 he became perpetual curate of Ilketshall St. Lawrence, Norfolk. He married, at Calton church, near Norwich, on 21 Dec. 1824, Mary, daughter of William Griffin of Norwich, and sister of Vice-admiral William Griffin, and in order to increase his income he became, in January 1826, second master, under Dr. Valpy, of Norwich grammar school. Henry Reeve (1813-1895) [q. v.] was one of his pupils there.

In 1827 Stebbing moved to London, and was soon 'working for the booksellers from morning to night and sometimes from night to morning.' His connection with the 'Athenæum' from its foundation was what he most valued. He was engaged by Silk Buckingham 'in the very first planning of the new journal, and in shaping the mode of its publication.' A notice by him of Dr. Hampden's work on 'Butler's Analogy, or Philosophical Evidences of Christianity,' was the opening review in the first number of 2 Jan. 1828, and his article on Whately's 'Rhetoric' led the second number. After three or four issues he became the working editor (cf. his letter on *The Athenæum in 1828-30*, which appeared in that paper on 19 Jan. 1878).

From 1834 to 1836 he edited, with the Rev. R. Cattermole, thirty volumes of the 'Sacred Classics' of England. He was editor of the 'Diamond Bible' (1834, 1840, and 1857), 'Diamond New Testament' (1835), 'Charles Knight's Pictorial Edition of the Book of Common Prayer' (1838-1840), Tate and Brady's 'Psalms' (1840), 'Psalms and Hymns, with some original Hymns' (1841), and many modern theological works. He also edited the works of Josephus (1842) and of Bunyan, Milton's 'Poems' (1839 and 1851), Defoe's 'Plague' (1830), and 'Robinson Crusoe' (1850).

Stebbing wrote a continuation to the 'Death of William IV,' of Hume and Smollett's 'History of England.' His 'Essay on the Study of History,' which appeared as an addition to Hume, was published separately in 1841. In 1848 he owned and edited the 'Christian Enquirer and the Literary Companion,' but only seven numbers of it were published.

A life of literary activity brought Stebbing the acquaintance of many distinguished men. He breakfasted with Rogers, and was introduced by Basil Montagu to Coleridge's set at Highgate. He conversed with Scott, corresponded with Southey, heard Tom Moore sing his Irish ballads, and knew Thomas Campbell and Charles Dickens.

With his literary drudgery Stebbing combined much clerical work. From 1829 he was alternate morning preacher, and from 1836 to 1857 perpetual curate, of St. James, Hampstead Road, London. He officiated during the same period at the large cemetery of St. James, Piccadilly, which was situated behind his church, and from 1834 to December 1879 he acted as chaplain to University College hospital. For a few months, from 21 Nov. 1835 to the following spring, he held, on the presentation of John Norris, the vicarage of Hughenden in Buckinghamshire. In 1841 he was chaplain to the lord mayor, Thomas Johnson.

These appointments brought with them small pecuniary reward; but in 1857 Dr. Tait, then bishop of London, conferred upon him the more lucrative rectory of St. Mary Somerset, with St. Mary Mounthaw in the city of London. Under the Union of Benefices Act the parishes of St. Nicholas Cole-Abbey and St. Nicholas Olave were united with them in November 1866, and those of St. Benet and St. Peter, Paul's Wharf, in June 1879. At this composite living Dr. Stebbing did duty for the rest of his days. He was a moderate churchman, inclining to evangelicalism. In 1847 he published 'A Letter to Lord John Russell on the Established Church,' in which he argued for a reform of the system of patronage. He died at St. James's parsonage, Hampstead Road, London, on 22 Sept. 1883, and was buried on 27 Sept. in Kensal Green cemetery.

His wife (born at Norwich on 22 Feb. 1805) died on 3 Feb. 1882, and was buried in the same cemetery. Five sons and four daughters survived. Two of his sons, Mr. William Stebbing and Mr. Thomas Roscoe Rede Stebbing, F.R.S., have distinguished themselves respectively in literature and science; while two daughters, Beatrice (now Mrs. Batty) and Miss Grace Stebbing, are also well known as authors. The eldest son, John (d. 1885), translated Humboldt's 'Letters to a Lady' and Thiers' 'History of France under Napoleon.'

Stebbing's portrait was painted at least four times, the artists being Harland, Wivell, Baugniet, and Rivière. There were published an engraving by S. W. Reynolds of the portrait by T. W. Harland, and a large lithograph by C. Baugniet. A portrait, from a photograph, appeared in the 'Illustrated London News' (6 Oct. 1883).

Stebbing's chief works, excluding sermons and those already noticed, were: 1. 'History of Chivalry and the Crusades' in Constable's 'Miscellany,' vols. l. and li., 1830; much praised by Professor Wilson for its clearness of style and picturesque descriptions. 2. 'Lives of the Italian Poets,' 1831, 3 vols.; 2nd edit. with numerous additions, 1832, 3 vols.; new edition in one volume, with omissions and alterations, 1860. 3. 'History of the Christian Church' in Lardner's 'Cabinet Cyclopædia,' 1833, 2 vols. 4. 'History of the Reformation' in Lardner's 'Cabinet Cyclopædia,' 1836, 2 vols. 5. 'History of Church of Christ from Diet of Augsburg, 1530, to the Eighteenth Century;' originally intended as a continuation of Milner's 'History,' 1842, 3 vols. 6. 'The Church and its Ministers,' 1844. 7. 'History of the Universal Church in Primitive Times,' 1845; prefixed is his portrait with autograph signature. 8. 'The Christian in Palestine, or Scenes of Sacred History;' to illustrate sketches on the spot by W. H. Bartlett, 1847. 9. 'Short Readings on Subjects for Long Reflection,' 1849. 10. 'History of Christ's Universal Church prior to the Reformation,' 1850, 2 vols. 11. 'The long Railway Journey and other Poems,' 1851. 12. 'Jesus: a poem in six Books,' 1851. 13. 'Christian Graces in Olden Time: Poetical Illustrations,' 1852. 14. 'Near the Cloisters,' 1868, 2 vols.; descriptive of life at Norwich early in this century.

[Foster's Alumni Oxon.; Lipscomb's Buckinghamshire, iii. 587; Notes and Queries, 8th ser. v. 424-5, vi. 11; Athenæum, 29 Sept. 1883, pp. 400-1; Academy, 29 Sept 1883, p. 214; Annual Reg. 1883, p. 171; Men of the Time, 9th ed.; Times, 7 Feb. 1882, p. 1, 24 Sept. 1883, p. 7; information from Mr. R. F. Scott, St. John's College, Cambridge, and Mr. William Stebbing.] W. P. C.

STEDMAN, CHARLES (1753-1812), military historian, was of a family that claims descent from Andrew Barton [q. v.] According to the Stedman tradition, Andrew Barton left an only son, Charles, who married Susan Stedman of Leith and took his wife's name. His descendants acquired land in Kinross-shire, and supplied many ministers to the kirk. Alexander (1703-1794), the father of the military historian, became an advocate and a Jacobite, but was compelled to fly the country after Culloden, together with two of his brothers. He found refuge at Philadelphia, where he was ultimately appointed a judge of the supreme court. On the declaration of independence he withdrew to England and died at Swansea in 1794 (cf. APPLETON, *American Biogr.*) He married Elizabeth Chancellor, the daughter of an immigrant to America from Somerset, who had been captured during the Spanish war and brought up in a convent.

Charles, their second son, was born at Philadelphia in 1753, and educated for the law at William and Mary College in Virginia. Like his father, he remained loyal to the British crown, and, on the outbreak of hostilities, he was appointed commissary to the troops under the command of Sir William Howe. His knowledge of the German language, presumably acquired from early intercourse with the numerous German settlers in Pennsylvania, stood him in good stead, both as interpreter with the Hessian auxiliaries, and afterwards as commander of a rifle corps of colonists from the Palatinate. He was twice taken prisoner, and sentenced to be hanged as a rebel; but on each occasion he managed to escape, once from the same prison that held the ill-fated Major André. He was also twice severely wounded. On the conclusion of peace in 1783 he retired to England on the half-pay of a colonel. He was one of those appointed to examine and settle the claims of the American loyalists. In 1794 appeared his ‘History of the Origin, Progress, and Termination of the American War’ (2 vols. London, 4to, with folding maps and plans; and in the same year 2 vols., Dublin, 8vo), which still remains the standard work on the subject. It is dedicated to Lord Rawdon, earl of Moira, his former commander-in-chief. Shortly after it appeared Sir Henry Clinton printed ‘Some Observations upon Mr. Stedman's History’ (4to, 1794), which impugn the author's accuracy on minor points; but these strictures appear to have been prompted mainly by personal feeling. Through the influence of the Marquis of Cornwallis, Lord Rawdon's predecessor in the command, Stedman was in 1797 appointed to the office of deputy controller and accountant-general of the revenue of stamps, with reversion to the chief controllership, which, however, never fell in. He died on 26 June 1812, and was buried at Paddington. He married Mary Bowen, by whom he had one son, John, who became judge of the court of admiralty at Gibraltar, and compiled a genealogical memoir of the family (1857).

[John Stedman's Memoir of the Family of Barton, continued through that of Stedman, privately printed, 1857; Gent. Mag. 1812, ii. 91.]   J. S. C.

STEDMAN, JOHN ANDREW (1778–1833), general in the Dutch army, was the son of William George Stedman. Both his father and grandfather, who belonged to the same family as Charles Stedman [q. v.] and John Gabriel Stedman [q. v.], were officers in the Scots brigade in the service of the States-General of Holland—a corps whose history extends from 1570 to 1783. Both of them married Dutch wives of noble blood. In 1783, when the Scots brigade was formed into Dutch regiments, and most of the officers resigned their commissions, Captain William George Stedman elected to be naturalised in the country of his adoption. John Andrew, his only son, was born at Zutphen in 1778, and received a commission in the Dutch army when only a child. At the early age of sixteen he first saw service with the allied forces, under the Duke of York and the Prince of Orange, which were employed in 1794 on the northern frontier of France. His next service was in 1799, when the Batavian republic was in alliance with France, and the Duke of York commanded the opposing army at Bergen. At a later date he again served against the English at Walcheren. Meanwhile he had held important staff appointments, and, on the incorporation of Holland with France, he became general of brigade in the French army. In this capacity he served for two years in Italy, and was present at the battles of Bautzen and Dresden. In 1814 he attached himself to the Prince of Orange, afterwards King William of Holland, and commanded the Dutch troops in reserve at Waterloo, with the rank of lieutenant-general. He died at Nimeguen in 1833. He married Nicola Gertrude van de Poll, granddaughter of the last reigning burgomaster of Amsterdam. Their only son, Charles John William Stedman, became a Prussian subject, settling at Besselich Abbey, near Coblentz. He was a member of the national assemblies of Frankfort and Erfurt, and received the title of freiherr or baron. He had a large family, of which nearly all the sons entered the Queen Augusta regiment of guards; they have reverted to the original family name of Barton.

[John Stedman's Memoir of the Family of Barton, 1857.]   J. S. C.

STEDMAN, JOHN GABRIEL (1744–1797), lieutenant-colonel and author, was grandson of John Stedman (1678–1713), minister of Dalmeny and afterwards of the Tron Church, Edinburgh (cf. HEW SCOTT, *Fasti*, I. i. 59, 182), who was a great-uncle of Charles Stedman [q. v.] His father, Robert, was an officer in the Scots brigade in the service of the States-General of Holland, and fought at Fontenoy and Bergen-op-Zoom. He died at Breda in 1770.

John Gabriel, the elder son of Robert by his wife, Antoinetta Christina van Coulen, was born in Holland in 1744. According to his own account, his ambition was to enter the British navy, to which he was well recommended. But, the paternal estate having been lost by accidental misfortunes, he was glad to accept a commission in General John Stuart's regiment in the Scots brigade in 1760, as a preliminary to which he had to take the oaths of abjuration and allegiance to King George. In 1772 he volunteered to accompany an expedition sent out by the States-General to subdue the revolted negroes in Surinam, or Dutch Guiana. This service, in which he was employed for five years, gave him the opportunity of his life. His narrative of it is a model of what such a book should be. Its rules for marching and fighting amid tropical swamps anticipate those laid down for the Ashanti expedition. The field of his curiosity embraced not only all branches of natural history, but also economical and social conditions. His description of the cruelties practised on the negroes, and of the moral deterioration resulting to their masters, forms one of the most vivid indictments of slavery that have been penned. While he did his duty as a soldier in the pay of Holland, he does not disguise his sympathy with the rebels. Not the least curious thing in the book is the story of his relations with Joanna, a beautiful mulatto, who nursed him when sick, and bore him a son. The freedom of the son was granted to the father by the government of Surinam in recognition of 'his humanity and gallantry;' but the boy died at sea as a midshipman in the British navy.

Stedman, immediately on his return to Holland, although Joanna was still alive (she died in November 1782), married a Dutch wife, Adriana Wiertz van Coehorn, a granddaughter of the famous military engineer. He was restored to his rank in Stuart's regiment, with which he continued to serve until the Scots brigade ceased to exist in 1783. On the outbreak of war with England in that year the privates, who now belonged to all nationalities, were naturalised as Dutchmen, while the great majority of the officers resigned their commissions and came over to England. Parliament forthwith voted to them the half-pay of their rank, and later on they were re-embodied under General Francis Dundas, and sent to garrison Gibraltar. Stedman's commission as major in the second battalion of the Scots brigade is dated 5 July 1793, and on 3 May 1796 he was promoted lieutenant-colonel. Oddly enough, on the title-page of his book, dated 1796, he uses the style of captain; and, still more oddly, his name continues to appear in the 'Army List' until 1805, when he had been eight years dead. He seems to have lived latterly at Tiverton in Devonshire. This is the place from which the dedication of his book to the Prince of Wales is dated, 1 Jan. 1796; and according to family tradition, he retired here on meeting with a severe accident which prevented him from taking up the command of his regiment at Gibraltar. At Tiverton he died on 7 March 1797. He had left instructions to be buried in the neighbouring parish of Bickleigh, at midnight and by torchlight, by the side of Bamfylde Moore Carew [q. v.], the king of the gipsies, whom he apparently regarded as a kindred spirit. As a matter of fact, the two lie on opposite sides of the church, Stedman directly in front of the vestry door. By his wife Adriana he left three sons, two of whom were killed in action, while the third died at sea, after forty years' service in India, a lieutenant-colonel in the Bengal cavalry and C.B. The male line is now extinct.

The full title of Stedman's book is 'Narrative of a Five Years' Expedition against the Revolted Negroes of Surinam, in Guiana, on the Wild Coast of South America, from the year 1772 to 1777 : elucidating the History of that Country, and describing its Productions, viz. Quadrupeds, Birds, Fishes, Reptiles, Trees, Shrubs, Fruits and Roots; with an Account of the Indians of Guiana and Negroes of Guinea,' London, 1796. It is in 2 vols. 4to, illustrated with eighty plates from drawings by the author, many of which are engraved by Bartolozzi and Blake. Large-paper copies have the plates handsomely coloured by hand. A second edition 'with an Account of the Indians of Guiana and Negroes of Guinea,' appeared in 1806 (London, 2 vols. 4to; reprinted 1813). A French translation by P. F. Henry appeared in 1799, and a German translation by Sprengel shortly afterwards. A romance founded upon Stedman's narrative, and called 'Joanna,' was issued in 1824 (London, 12mo).

[Stedman's Memoir, 1857; Stedman's Narrative; Appleton's Cyclop. of American Biogr. v. 656; European Mag. 1797, i. passim.] J. S. C.

STEDMAN, ROWLAND (1630?–1673), nonconformist divine, son of Henry and Mary Stedman, was born about 1630 at Corfton, in the parish of Diddlebury in Shropshire (there is a gap in the registers from 1598 until 1683). He matriculated at Balliol College, Oxford, as 'plebeian,' on 12 March 1648–9, but migrated to University College on obtaining a scholarship there in 1649. He graduated B.A. on 16 Oct. 1651, and proceeded M.A. on 22 March 1655–6.

Stedman was appointed to the rectory of Hanwell, Middlesex, in 1657, and remained there for three years. In 1660 he was made rector of Wokingham in Berkshire, and held that living until 1662, when he refused episcopal ordination and was ejected for nonconformity. After his ejection Stedman resided at Neasdon in the parish of Willesden in Middlesex, but presently became chaplain at Wooburn in Buckinghamshire to Philip, fourth lord Wharton [q. v.], who, dying on 5 Feb. 1694–5, was described in his monument in Wooburn church as opening his mansions for 'an asylum for the suffering ministers of the word of God.' Stedman remained at Wooburn until his death, on 14 Sept. 1673, and was buried on the 16th at Wooburn church, 'leaving behind him the character of a zealous nonconformist' (Wood). His will, dated 24 Oct. 1667, was proved 8 Oct. 1673 (P.C.C., 132 Pye). He married Margaret, daughter of William and Anne Jemmatt, who survived him.

His works are: 1. 'The Sure Way to Salvation; or, a Treatise of the Mystical Union of Believers with Christ; wherein that great mystery and privilege of the Saints' union with the Son of God is opened in the nature, property, and necessity of it,' 1668. 2. 'Sober Singularity, or an Antidote against Infection by the example of a multitude; being practical reflections on Exod. xxiii. verse 2,' 1668.

[Wood's Athenæ Oxon. iii. 993; Calamy's Nonconformist's Memorial, ed. Palmer, i. 291; Burrows's Register of Visitors of the University of Oxford in 1647–8, pp. 480, 558; Foster's Alumni Oxon. 1500–1714; and private information.] W. G. D. F.

STEEL, Sir SCUDAMORE WINDE (1789–1865), lieutenant-general, born in 1789, was appointed a cadet in the East India Company's service in 1805, and became lieutenant in the Madras army on 11 Sept. 1806. In 1808–9 he served under Colonel Doveton in Berar against the Pindaris. He took part in the Mahratta war of 1817–18 as assistant quartermaster, and was slightly wounded in the capture of one of the hill forts. He became captain in the army on 27 March 1821, and in the 51st native infantry on 1 May 1824. He was employed on the quartermaster-general's staff at Nagpur, and in the first Burmese war in 1826. He was promoted major in his regiment on 15 Dec. 1832, and was secretary in the military department at Madras from 1832 to 1845. He planned and took part in the operations for the reduction of Coorg in 1834. He was made lieutenant-colonel in the army on 28 July 1835, and of the 24th native infantry on 9 April 1838. On 20 July in that year he was made C.B.

In 1845 he was appointed military auditor-general; on 13 Sept. 1847 colonel of the Madras fusiliers; and on 8 March 1849 colonel of the 18th native infantry. He commanded the Madras division of the army engaged in the second Burmese war in 1852–1853, was mentioned in General Godwin's despatch of 24 Dec. 1852, and directed the column sent to Martaban in January to operate on the Salwin. He was made K.C.B. on 9 Dec. 1853, and was appointed to the command of the Pegu division and the Martaban provinces, being promoted major-general on 28 Nov. 1854. Steel returned to England in 1856, became lieutenant-general on 2 Sept. 1861, and died at Gloucester Terrace, Hyde Park, London, on 11 March 1865.

[Gent. Mag. 1865, i. 533; Times, 13 March 1865; Blacker's Operations during the Mahratta War of 1817–19; Laurie's Pegu: a Narrative of the second Burmese War; East India Registers.] E. M. L.

STEELE, ANNE (1717–1778), hymn-writer, daughter of William Steele (1689–1769), timber merchant and lay baptist preacher, was born at Broughton, Hampshire, in 1717. Her otherwise uneventful life was deeply affected by the drowning of her affianced lover a few hours before the time fixed for the wedding. She died on 11 Nov. 1778, 'aged 61 years and 6 months' (inscription on tombstone at Broughton).

Miss Steele wrote very many original hymns. In 1760 she published 'Poems on Subjects chiefly devotional,' under the signature of 'Theodosia,' and after her death this was reissued in three volumes (Bristol, 1780), with numerous additions and with a preface by Dr. Caleb Evans. Her complete works were published in one volume by Daniel Sedgwick [q. v.] (London, 1863), under the title of 'Hymns, Psalms, and Poems by Anne Steele, with memoir by John Sheppard.' They include 144 hymns, 34 metrical psalms, and about 50 poems on moral subjects. Few of the hymns can be placed in the first rank, but one or two, such as 'Father, whate'er of earthly bliss,' ' Dear Refuge of my weary soul,' and ' Far from these narrow scenes of night,' are constantly sung. Miss Steele's personal sufferings are reflected in her verse. Her manuscripts, including many unpublished pieces, are in the hands of a collateral descendant, Miss Bompas, at Broughton. Her poems were reprinted in America in 1808. Her hymns enjoy an extended vogue in America and among the baptists elsewhere.

[Memoir by Caleb Evans as above; Miller's Our Hymns, their Authors and Origin; Julian's Dict. of Hymnology; Christophers's Hymn Writers and their Hymns; Quiver, June 1879 (with facsimiles of handwriting); information from Miss Bompas.]   J. C. H.

STEELE, CHRISTOPHER (fl. 1756), portrait-painter, was born at Egremont, Cumberland, about 1730. He resided for a year in Paris, where he was instructed by 'Carle' Vanloo, and on his return practised portrait-painting in the north of England with some success. By his foreign manners and expensive tastes he acquired the title of 'Count' Steele. In 1755, while residing at Kendal, he received George Romney [q. v.] as a pupil, and shortly afterwards, with Romney's assistance, he eloped with and married a young lady of some fortune. He then removed to York, where he had Laurence Sterne among his sitters. In 1757 Steele went to Ireland, where he is supposed to have died.

[Redgrave's Dict. of Artists; Hayley's Life of Romney, 1809; J. Romney's Memoirs of G. Romney, 1820.]   F. M. O'D.

STEELE, JOSHUA (1700–1791), writer on prosody, was born in Ireland in 1700. He resided many years in London, and in 1756 was elected a member of the Society of Arts. He possessed great knowledge of the theory of music, and in 1775 published ' An Essay towards establishing the Melody and Measure of Speech to be expressed and perpetuated by certain Symbols,' London, 4to, in which he proposed to extend to speech the symbolic method by which the modulations of musical sounds are expressed. His essay excited considerable interest, and was discussed, among others, by James Burnett, lord Monboddo [q. v.], author of the ' Origin and Progress of Language,' and by David Garrick. A second edition, entitled ' Prosodia Rationalis,' appeared in 1779. He also contributed two papers on musical instruments to the ' Philosophical Transactions' in 1775.

Steele possessed estates in Barbados, and, being dissatisfied with their management,

he resolved in 1780 to look after them himself. In the following year he founded a society in Bridgetown similar to the London Society of Arts, with a view to amending the government of the slave population, and soon after became a member of his majesty's council for the island. On his own estates he abolished arbitrary punishment, and erected courts among the negroes themselves for the punishment of offences. He also promoted voluntary labour by offering small wages, and succeeded in this manner in obtaining much better work from his slaves. In 1789 he proceeded further, by erecting his estates into manors, and making his negroes copyholders bound to their tenements, and owing rent and personal service which they paid in labour on the demesne lands. Steele encountered considerable opposition, and the Bridgetown Society of Arts was broken up by his opponents; but on his own estates his system was completely successful, and furnished a strong argument in favour of liberal treatment of slaves. He was also indefatigable in his efforts to employ the poor white population, encouraging native industries and introducing several new manufactures from England. He died in the beginning of 1791. His letters to Thomas Clarkson [q. v.], describing the management of his estates, were published in 1814 in Dickson's ' Mitigation of Slavery.' Rich attributes to Steele a pamphlet entitled ' An Account of a late Conference on the Occurrences in America,' published at London in 1766 (Bibl. Amer. Nova, i. 154).

[Dickson's Mitigation of Slavery; Clarkson's Thoughts on the Necessity of improving the Condition of Slaves, 1823, pp. 31–44; Aitken's Life of Richard Steele, ii. 355; Boswell's Johnson, ed. Croker, p. 439; Nichols's Lit. Anecd. ii. 358, iii 208–9, 670.]   E. I. C.

STEELE or STEEL, RICHARD (1629–1692), nonconformist divine, son of Robert Steele, farmer, was born at Barthomley, Cheshire, on 10 May 1629. He was educated at Northwich grammar school, admitted sizar at St. John's College, Cambridge, on 1 April 1642, and incorporated M.A. at Oxford on 5 July 1656. He succeeded Thomas Porter as rector of Hanmer, Flintshire, probably in 1650. Henry Newcome [q. v.] visited him there on 10 June 1654. He was a member of the fourth Shropshire classis (constituted by parliament in April 1647), and, as such, was one of the ordainers of Philip Henry [q. v.] on 16 Sept. 1657. Thirty years later (9 May 1687) he was one of the ordainers, at his own house in London, of Philip Henry's son, Matthew Henry [q. v.] In September 1660 he was presented

K

at Flint assizes for not reading the common prayer; the prosecution fell through, owing to Charles II's declaration in October. He was again presented at the spring assizes on 28 March 1661 at Hawarden. He resigned his living in consequence of the Uniformity Act of 1662, preaching a farewell sermon (17 Aug.), in which he said he was ejected for not subscribing his assent to the new prayer-book, which he had not yet seen. He continued to communicate at Hanmer, where he received 'sitting' on 19 April 1663. On 25 July he was presented for baptising his own children, and in October was arrested on suspicion of treason. Early in 1665 he was made collector for Hanmer of the 'royal aid,' the point being to treat him as a layman. In April 1665 he was again arrested, as he was setting out for London; his pocket diary was taken from him, and passages were misconstrued. An entry of an appointment 'on a carnal account' was 'interpreted to be some woman design.' Philip Henry records 'a great noise in the country concerning Mr. Steel's almanack.' The Five Miles Act, coming into force on 25 March 1666, compelled him to leave Hanmer, and he took up his residence in London. Urwick conjectures (*Nonconformity in Cheshire*, 1864, p. xlix) that his was the license granted on 10 June 1672 for presbyterian preaching in 'the house of Rob. Steele' at Barthomley, Cheshire; he certainly contributed to the building of a school at Barthomley in 1675. Though he may have made occasional visits to the north, Philip Henry's diary shows that he was constantly exercising his ministry in London from 1671. He gathered a morning congregation at Armourers' Hall, Coleman Street; in the afternoon he preached at Hoxton. He died on 16 Nov. 1692. George Hamond [q. v.], his colleague and successor, preached his funeral sermon. He had ten sons, five of whom were dead in 1672. His portrait is in Dr. Williams's Library; an engraving from it by Hopwood is given in Wilson.

Steele published: 1. 'An Antidote against Distractions . . . in the Worship of God,' 1667, 8vo; 3rd edit. 1673, 8vo; 4th edit. 1695, 12mo; last edit. 1834, 12mo. 2. 'The Husbandman's Calling,' 1668, 8vo; 1670, 8vo. 3. 'A Plain Discourse upon Uprightness,' 1670, 8vo; 1671, 8vo. 4. 'The Tradesman's Calling,' 1684, 8vo; a revision of this by Isaac Watts passed through many editions with title 'The Religious Tradesman;' last edit. Edinburgh, 1821, 12mo. 5. 'A Discourse concerning Old Age,' 1688, 8vo. Also four sermons in the 'Morning Exercises,' 1660–90, and a biographical preface to the

posthumous sermons (1678) of Thomas Froysell (1622–1672).

[Funeral Sermon by Hamond, 1693; Calamy's Account, 1713, p. 708; Calamy's Continuation, 1727, ii. 835; Wilson's Dissenting Churches of London, 1808, ii. 448 sq.; Williams's Life of Philip Henry, 1825, passim; Lee's Diaries and Letters of Philip Henry, 1882, passim; Mayor's Admissions to St. John's, Cambridge, 1882, i. 63.] A. G.

STEELE, SIR RICHARD (1672–1729), essayist, dramatist, and politician, was born in Dublin in March 1672 (N. S.), and was baptised at St. Bridget's Church on the 12th of that month. He was consequently some weeks older than Joseph Addison [q. v.], who was born on 1 May following. Steele's father, also Richard Steele, was a well-to-do Dublin attorney, who had a country house at Mountain (Monkstown), and was at one time sub-sheriff of Tipperary. He married, in 1670, an Irish widow named Elinor Symes (or Sims), born Sheyles. When his son was 'not quite five years of age' (*Tatler*, No. 181), the elder Steele died, and of Mrs. Steele we know nothing but what the same authority tells us, namely, that she was 'a very beautiful woman, of a noble spirit.' She cannot have long survived her husband, since Steele seems to have passed early into the care of an uncle, Henry Gascoigne, private secretary to James Butler, first duke of Ormonde [q. v.], by whose influence the boy in November 1684 obtained a nomination to the Charterhouse, of which the duke was a governor. Two years later Addison entered the same school, and a lifelong friendship began between the pair.

In November 1689 Steele was 'elected to the university' of Oxford, whither Addison had already preceded him. On 13 March 1690 he matriculated at Christ Church, and on 27 Aug. 1691 he became a postmaster of Merton, his college tutor being Dr. Welbore Ellis [q. v.], afterwards mentioned in the 'Christian Hero.' He continued his friendship with Addison, then a demy at Magdalen, and appears to have visited him in his home at Lichfield (Preface to the *Drummer*, 1722, and *Tatler*, No. 235). While at college he enjoyed some reputation as a scholar. He dabbled also in letters, composing a comedy which, by the advice of a friend, Mr. Parker of Merton, he burned. Then suddenly, in 1694, much to the regret of 'the whole Society,' he left Merton without taking a degree, and entered the army as a cadet or gentleman-volunteer in the second troop of life-guards, at that time under the command of the second Duke of Ormonde, thereby losing, as he tells us in the 'Theatre,' No. 11, 'the succession to a very good estate in the county of Wexford in Ireland.' What this estate was his biographers have failed to discover, although it has been conjectured that, if it existed at all, it belonged to a relative of his mother.

On 28 Dec. 1694 Queen Mary died, and among the mourning bards who, in black-framed folio, celebrated her funeral was Steele, whose verses, described as 'by a Gentleman of the Army,' and entitled 'The Procession,' were, doubtless from motives of policy, dedicated to John, lord Cutts [q. v.], who had just become colonel of the 2nd or Coldstream regiment of foot-guards. Lord Cutts took Steele into his household, and in 1696-7 employed him as his confidential agent or secretary (cf. CARLETON, Memoirs, 1728, ch. iii.) Ultimately he gave him a standard in his own regiment. By 1700 Steele is referred to as 'Captain,' and there is also evidence that he was in friendly relations with Sedley, Congreve, Vanbrugh, Garth, and other contemporary wits. In the same year (16 June), 'one or two of his acquaintance' having 'thought fit to misuse him and try their valour upon him ' (Apology for himself and his Writings, 1714, p. 80), he fought a duel in Hyde Park with a Captain Kelly, whom he wounded dangerously, but not mortally (LUTTRELL, Diary, iv. 657). This occurrence made a serious impression upon him, and laid the foundation of that dislike of duelling which he ever afterwards exhibited. In all probability it is connected with his next literary effort, the treatise called 'The Christian Hero: an Argument proving that no Principles but those of Religion are sufficient to make a great Man.' This (which was also dedicated to Lord Cutts) was published by Tonson in April 1701, a second and enlarged edition following on 19 July. Steele's own account of this work in his 'Apology,' p. 80, is that, finding the military life 'exposed to much irregularity,' he wrote it 'to fix upon his own mind a strong impression of virtue and religion, in opposition to a stronger propensity towards unwarrantable pleasures,' which admission has probably been construed too literally (cf. Biogr. Brit. 1763, vol. vi. pt. i. p. 3823). The 'Christian Hero' was at first designed solely for his private use, but finding 'that this secret admonition was too weak,' he ultimately 'printed the book with his name,' as a 'standing testimony against himself.' It differs considerably both in style and teaching from the ordinary devotional manual, and without much straining may be said to exhibit definite indications of that faculty for essay-writing which was to be so signally

developed in the 'Spectator,' in which indeed certain portions of it were afterwards embodied. Upon his colleagues at the Tower Guard (whence its Preface is dated) its effect was what might have been anticipated. 'From being thought no undelightful companion, he was soon reckoned a disagreeable fellow. . . . Thus he found himself slighted, instead of being encouraged, for his declarations as to Religion, and it was now incumbent upon him to enliven his character, for which reason he writ the comedy called "The Funeral," in which (tho' full of incidents that move laughter) virtue and vice appear as they ought to do ' (Apology, p. 80).

'The Funeral; or, Grief a-la-Mode,' was acted at Drury Lane late in 1701, and was published in book form in December of that year, with a dedication to the Countess of Albemarle. The principal parts were taken by Cibber, Wilks, and Mrs. Verbruggen, and the championship of the author's military friends helped to secure its success. 'With some particulars enlarged upon to his advantage' (by which must probably be understood certain politic references to William III in the 'Christian Hero'), it also obtained for him the notice of the king. 'His [Steele's] name, to be provided for, was in the last table-book ever worn by the glorious and immortal William the Third ' (ib. p. 81). His majesty, however, died on 9 March 1702, and Steele's fortunes were yet to make. In the preceding month he had become a captain in Lord Lucas's newly formed regiment of foot (AITKEN, Life, i. 79); and in December 1703 he produced at Drury Lane a second comedy, 'The Lying Lover; or, the Ladies Friendship,' which was published on 26 Jan. 1704. This piece was based upon the 'Menteur' of Corneille, and differed from its predecessor, 'The Funeral,' in that it was a more deliberate attempt to carry out upon the stage those precepts which, a few years earlier, Jeremy Collier [q. v.] had advocated in his 'Short View of the Profaneness and Immorality of the English Stage.' Among other things it contained an indictment of duelling. Upon its first appearance it ran but six nights. Its author described it years afterwards as 'damned for its piety' (Apology, p. 48), but it was also inferior to its predecessor. Steele nevertheless set to work upon a third effort, 'The Tender Husband; or, the Accomplished Fools.' This, a frank imitation of Molière's 'Sicilien,' was brought out at Drury Lane in April 1703. It was better than the 'Lying Lover,' but scarcely more successful, though Addison (now back from Italy) wrote its prologue, and added 'many applauded [though now undistinguishable] strokes' to the piece itself (*Spectator*, No. 555). In May, when the play was printed, it was dedicated to Addison 'as no improper memorial of an inviolable friendship.'

Soon after the production of the 'Tender Husband,' which, for several years, closed Steele's career as a playwright, he married. His wife (for particulars respecting whom we are indebted to the researches of Mr. Aitken) was a widow named Margaret Stretch, née Ford, the possessor of more or less extensive estates in Barbadoes, which she had inherited from a brother then recently dead. It has been also hinted that she was elderly, and that her fortune was the main attraction to her suitor, whose indefinite means had about this time been impaired by futile researches for the philosopher's stone (*New Atalantis* and *Town Talk*, No. 4). The marriage must have taken place not long after March 1705, when Mrs. Stretch took out letters of administration to her West Indian property, which is said to have been worth 850*l.* per annum. It was, however, encumbered with a debt of 3,000*l.*, besides legacies, &c. In December 1706 Mrs. Steele died, and Steele, in his turn, administered to her estate in January 1707. During the brief period of his married life—in August 1706—he had become a gentleman waiter to Prince George of Denmark (salary 100*l.* yearly, 'not subject to taxes'), and in April or May 1707, on the recommendation of Arthur Mainwaring [q. v.], he was appointed by Harley gazetteer, at a further annual salary of 300*l.*, which was, however, liable to a tax of 45*l.* 'The writer of the "Gazette" now,' says Hearne in May 1707, 'is Captain Steel, who is the author of several romantic things, and is accounted an ingenious man.' Steele seems to have honestly endeavoured to comply with 'the rule observed by all ministries, to keep the paper very innocent and very insipid' (*Apology*, p. 81); but the rule was by no means an easy one to abide by. His inclinations still leaned towards the stage. Already, in March 1703, he had received from Rich of Drury Lane part payment for an unfinished comedy called 'The Election of Goatham' (AITKEN, i. 112), a subject also essayed by Gay and Mrs. Centlivre; and in January 1707 he was evidently meditating the completion of this or some other piece when his wife's death interrupted his work (*Muses Mercury*, January 1707). But his only definite literary production between May 1705 and 1707 was a 'Prologue' to the university of Oxford, published in July 1706.

Before he had held the post of gazetteer many months he married again. The lady, whose acquaintance he had made at his first wife's funeral, was a Miss, or Mistress, Mary Scurlock, the daughter and heiress of Jonathan Scurlock, deceased, of Llangunnor in Carmarthen, and, according to Mrs. Manley (*New Atalantis*, 6th ed. vol. iv.), 'a cry'd up beauty.' For reasons now obscure, the marriage was kept a secret, but it is supposed to have taken place on 9 Sept. 1707, soon after which time Steele set up house in Bury Street, or (as his letters give it) 'third door, right hand, turning out of Jermyn Street.' This was a locality described by contemporary advertisements as in convenient proximity 'to St. James's Church, Chapel, Park, Palace, Coffee and Chocolate Houses,' and was obviously within easy distance of the court and Steele's office, the Cockpit at Whitehall. Both before and after marriage Steele kept up an active correspondence with his 'Charmer' and 'Inspirer,' names which, later on, are exchanged, not inappropriately, for 'Ruler' and 'Absolute Governess.' Mrs. Steele preserved all her husband's letters, over four hundred of which John Nichols the antiquary presented in 1787 to the British Museum (Add. MSS. 5145, A, B, and C), where they afford a curious and an instructive study to the inquirer. The lady, though genuinely attached to her husband, was imperious and exacting; the gentleman ardent and devoted, but incurably erratic and impulsive. His correspondence reflects these characteristics in all their variations, and, if it often does credit to his heart and understanding, it as often suggests that his easy geniality and irregular good nature must have made him 'gey ill to live with.' It was a part of his sanguine temperament to overestimate his means (AITKEN, passim). Hence he is perpetually in debt and difficulties (he borrowed 1,000*l.* of Addison, which he repaid; letter of 20 Aug. 1708); hence always (like Gay) on the alert for advancement. In October 1708 the death of Prince George deprived him of his post as gentleman waiter, and, though he had previously been seeking an appointment as usher of the privy chamber, and almost immediately afterwards tried for the under-secretaryship rendered vacant by Addison's departure for Ireland as secretary of state to Lord Wharton, the lord-lieutenant, he was successful in neither attempt. All these things were but unpromising accompaniments to a chariot and pair for his 'dear Prue,' with a country box (in the shadow of the palace) at Hampton Wick; and it seems certain that towards the close of 1708 an execution for arrears of rent was put into the Bury Street house. In the following March his daughter Elizabeth was born, having for godfathers Addison and Wortley Montagu. A month later, without premonition of any kind, Steele inaugurated his career as an essayist by establishing the 'Tatler.'

The first number of the 'Tatler,' a single folio sheet, was issued on 12 April 1709, and it came out three times a week. The first four numbers were given away gratis; after this the price was a penny. The supposed author was one 'Isaac Bickerstaff,' the pseudonym borrowed by Swift from a shopdoor to demolish John Partridge [q. v.] the astrologer. The paper's name, said Steele ironically, was invented in honour of the fair sex (No. 1), and it professed in general to treat, as its motto for many numbers indicated, of 'Quicquid agunt homines,' dating its accounts of gallantry, pleasure, and entertainment from White's coffee-house, its poetry from Wills's, its learning from the Grecian, and its foreign and domestic intelligence (which Steele hoped to supplement out of his own official gazette) from the St. James's. Whatever came under none of these heads was dated from 'My own apartment.' As time went on the project developed, and when the first volume was dedicated to Mainwaring (who, as already stated, had helped Steele to his gazetteership), it was already claimed for the new venture that it had aimed at 'exposing the false arts of life, pulling off the disguises of cunning, vanity, and affectation, and recommending a general simplicity in our dress, our discourse, and our behaviour' (see also *Tatler*, No. 89). In this larger task Steele was no doubt aided by Addison, who, playing but an inconspicuous part in the first volume (his earliest contribution was to No. 18), gave very substantial aid in its successors; and from a hotch-pot of news and town gossip the 'Tatler' became a collection of individual essays on social and general topics. In the preface to the fourth and final volume, Steele, with a generosity which never failed him, rendered grateful testimony to his anonymous coadjutor's assistance. In thanking Addison for his services as 'a gentleman who will be nameless,' he goes on to say: 'This good office [of contributing] he performed with such force of genius, humour, wit, and learning, that I fared like a distressed Prince who calls in a powerful neighbour to his aid; I was undone by my auxiliary; when I had once called him in, I could not subsist without dependence on him.'

After a career, prolonged to 271 numbers, about 188 of which were from Steele's own pen, the 'Tatler' came to a sudden end on 2 Jan. 1711. The ostensible reason for this was that the public had penetrated the editor's disguise, and that the edifying precepts of the fictitious 'Mr. Bickerstaff' were less efficacious when they came to be habitually identified in the public mind with the fallible personality of Steele himself (*Tatler*, No. 271). But it has been shrewdly surmised that there were other and more pressing reasons (which Steele also hints at) for its abrupt cessation. In addition to his office of gazetteer, he had been made in January 1710 a commissioner of stamps, an office which increased his income by 300*l.* per annum. When in August of the same year Harley became head of the government, certain papers satirising him had recently made their appearance in the 'Tatler;' and in the following October Steele lost his gazetteership. That he was not deprived of his commissionership of stamps as well has been ascribed to the intervention of Swift, whose friends were in power (*Journal to Stella*, 15 Dec. 1710), and with this forbearance of the ministry the termination of the 'Tatler' is also supposed to be obscurely connected. 'What I find is the least excusable part of this work,' says Steele in the final number quoted above, 'is that I have in some places in it touched upon matters which concern both the church and state.' But however this may be, the 'Tatler' was not long without a successor. Two months later (1 March) began the 'Spectator,' professing in its first number 'an exact neutrality between the whigs and tories,' and setting in motion almost from the first that famous club of which Sir Roger de Coverley is the most prominent member. The first sketch (in No. 2) of this immortal friendly gathering was undoubtedly due to Steele's inventive alertness. But Addison, working at leisure upon his friend's rapid and hasty outline, gradually filled in the features of the figure whose fortunes to-day constitute the chief interest of the periodical. Diversified in addition by the critical essays of Addison and the domestic sketches of Steele, the 'Spectator' proceeded with unabated vivacity to its five hundred and fifty-fifth number and seventh volume, surviving even that baleful Stamp Act of August 1712 (10 Aune, cap. 19) which nipped so many of its contemporaries. Out of the whole of the papers Addison wrote 274 and Steele 236. As before, no satisfactory explanation is forthcoming for the termination of the enterprise, the success of which is admitted. Towards the end of its career, the 'Spectator' was selling ten thousand per week, and Steele himself says that the first four volumes had obtained it a further sale of nine thousand copies in book form (No. 555). What is clear is that Addison's assistance was still anonymous, and Steele's gratitude to him as strong as ever. 'I am indeed,' he wrote, 'much more proud of his long-continued friendship than I should be of the fame of being thought the author of any writings he is capable of producing. . . . I heartily wish that what I have done here were as honorary to that sacred name [of friendship] as learning, wit, and humanity render those pieces which I have taught the reader now to distinguish for his '—i.e. by the letters C, L, I, O.

During the progress of the 'Spectator,' Steele had made his first definite plunge as a politician by 'The Englishman's Thanks to the Duke of Marlborough.' This appeared in January 1712, just after the duke had been deprived of all his offices, a catastrophe which also prompted Swift's opposition 'Fable of Midas.' There were other signs of political disquiet in some of Steele's subsequent contributions to the 'Spectator' ('he has been mighty impertinent of late,' wrote Swift to Stella in July 1712); and although in the new periodical, which he began in March 1713, he made profession of abstinence from matters of state, only seven days before he had put forth a 'Letter to Sir Miles Wharton concerning Occasional Peers.' In the 'Guardian' he philosophically declared himself to be, with regard to government of the church, a tory; and with regard to the state, a whig. But he was, in Johnson's phrase, 'too hot for neutral topics;' and before the middle of 1713 he was actively embroiled with the 'Examiner,' the *casus belli* being an attack that tory paper (behind which was the formidable figure of Swift) had made in its No. 41 upon Lord Nottingham's daughter, Lady Charlotte Finch, the Nottinghams having deserted to the whigs. On 4 June he resigned his commissionership of stamps, and his pension as Prince George's gentleman-in-waiting, and entered the lists of faction with an indictment of the government upon the vexed question of the postponed demolition, under the treaty of Utrecht, of the Dunkirk fortifications. 'The British nation,' he declared, 'expects the demolition of Dunkirk' (*Guardian*, No. 128). The 'Examiner' retorted by charging him with disloyalty. Steele rejoined (22 Sept.) by a pamphlet entitled 'The Importance of Dunkirk consider'd,' addressed to the bailiff of Stockbridge, Hampshire, for which town in August he had been elected M.P. Swift answered by a bitterly contemptuous 'Importance of the Guardian consider'd.' Before this came out, however, on 31 Oct. the 'Guardian' had been dead for a month, and had been succeeded on 6 Oct. by the 'Englishman,' 'a sequel' of freer political scope.

By this time Steele was in the thick of party strife. In November a scurrilous 'Character' of him 'by Toby Abel's kinsman' (i.e. Edward King, nephew of Abel Roper of the 'Postboy') was issued by some of Swift's 'under spur-leathers,' and early in January 1714 Swift himself followed suit with a paraphrase of Horace (ii. 1), in which it was suggested that when he (Steele) had settled the affairs of Europe, he might find time to finish his long-threatened (but unidentified) play. Shortly afterwards (19 Jan.) Steele put forth another widely circulated pamphlet, 'The Crisis,' in which, aided by the counsels of Addison, Hoadly, William Moore of the Inner Temple, and others, he reviewed the whole question of the Hanoverian succession. Swift was promptly in the field (23 Feb.) with the 'Public Spirit of the Whigs,' one of his most masterly efforts in this way; and when Steele took his seat in parliament he found that his doom was sealed, and on 12 March he was formally accused of uttering seditious libels. Supported by Walpole, Addison, General Stanhope, and others of his party, he spoke in his own defence for some three hours, and spoke well; but what he afterwards called, with pardonable energy, 'the insolent and unmanly sanction of a majority' (*Apology*, p. xvi) prevailed, and on 18 March 1714 he was expelled the House of Commons.

In these circumstances he turned once more to his proper vocation—letters. Even at the end of 1714 he had contrived to issue a volume of 'Poetical Miscellanies,' dedicated to Congreve, and numbering Pope, Gay, and Parnell among its contributors. In this he reprinted his own 'Procession' of 1695. The short-lived 'Englishman' came to an end in February 1714, and was immediately succeeded by the 'Lover' (25 Feb.) In April came the 'Reader.' Both of these were dropped in May. In No. 6 of the latter Steele announced that he was preparing a 'History of the War in Flanders,' a subject for which he was not without qualifications. But the project came to nothing. He produced, however, several pamphlets: the 'Romish Ecclesiastical History of late Years' (25 May), a 'Letter concerning the Bill for preventing the Growth of Schism' (3 June), and another on Dunkirk (2 July). Then, on 1 Aug., Queen Anne died. On 18 Sept.

George I landed at Greenwich, and the tide turned. The champion of the Hanoverian succession was speedily appointed J.P., deputy-lieutenant for the county of Middlesex, and surveyor of the royal stables at Hampton Court. What was better still (and more definitely lucrative), he obtained the position of supervisor of the Theatre Royal of Drury Lane, the license of which had expired with the queen's death. The license was shortly afterwards converted into a patent, and Steele in this manner came into receipt of 1,000*l.* per annum.

Henceforward his life grows more and more barren of notable incident. In the same month in which his honours came upon him he published the compilation known as 'The Ladies' Library,' volume iii. of which was dedicated, with much grace and tenderness, to his wife. He also vindicated his past proceedings with considerable spirit in the pamphlet entitled 'Mr. Steele's Apology for himself and his Writings' (22 Oct.), citations from which have already been made. On 2 Feb. 1715 he was elected M.P. for Boroughbridge, Yorkshire, and two months later (8 April) the presentation of an address to the king procured him a knighthood. During the next few years he continued as of old to busy himself with projects, literary and otherwise. He established in Villiers Street, York Buildings, Strand, a kind of periodical conversazione called the 'Censorium,' which he inaugurated on his majesty's birthday (28 May) by a grand banquet and entertainment, to which Tickell supplied the prologue and Addison the epilogue (*Town Talk*, No. 4). He wrote another overgrown pamphlet on the Roman catholic religion (13 May), began a new volume of the 'Englishman' (11 July to 21 Nov.), and established and abandoned three more periodicals, 'Town Talk' (17 Dec.), 'The Tea-Table' (2 Feb. 1716), and 'Chit Chat' (6 March). In June he was appointed one of the thirteen commissioners for forfeited estates in Scotland, the salary being 1,000*l.* per annum. Two years later, in June 1718, he obtained a patent for a project called the 'Fish pool,' a plan (which proved unsuccessful) for bringing salmon alive from Ireland in a well-boat. Then, in December 1718, he lost his 'dear and honoured wife.' Lady Steele died on the 26th, and was buried in Westminster Abbey. Early in the succeeding year Steele's evil star involved him in a painful controversy with his lifelong friend Addison. He started a periodical called the 'Plebeian' (14 March) to denounce Lord Sunderland's bill for limiting the power of creating new peers. Addison

replied acrimoniously in the 'Old Whig,' and, what was worse, died so soon afterwards (17 June) that the breach thus created was never healed, while Steele's opposition to the measure (which was dropped) led indirectly to the withdrawal by the Duke of Newcastle in January 1720 of the Drury Lane patent. With this last occurrence is connected the establishment of another, and perhaps the most interesting, of his later periodical efforts, as it was also the last, 'The Theatre' (2 Jan. to April 1720).

His next publications were two pamphlets, 'The Crisis of Property' (1 Feb.) and its sequel 'A Nation a Family' (27 Feb.), in which he warmly combated the South Sea mania. In 1721 his former ally, Walpole, became chancellor of the exchequer, and the Drury Lane patent was restored (2 May). In December of the same year he published a second edition of Addison's 'Drummer,' in the preface to which, addressed to Congreve, he vindicated himself against the aspersions cast upon him in the edition of Addison's works, which Tickell had put forth in the preceding October. In March 1722 he became member for Wendover, Buckinghamshire. Then, in November of the same year, he produced at Drury Lane his last comedy, 'The Conscious Lovers,' which, notwithstanding that (in Parson Adams's words) it contained 'some things almost solemn enough for a sermon,' proved a hit, and brought its writer five hundred guineas from George I, to whom it was dedicated. Its groundwork was the 'Andria' of Terence, and it attacked duelling. Besides the 'Conscious Lovers,' Steele began, but did not finish, two other pieces, 'The School of Action' and 'The Gentleman,' fragments of which were printed by Nichols in 1809. Lawsuits and money difficulties thickened upon him in his later days, and in 1724, in pursuance of an honourable arrangement with his creditors, and not, as Swift wrote, 'from perils of a hundred gaols,' he retired first to Hereford, and finally to Carmarthen, where he lived chiefly at Tygwyn, a farmhouse overlooking the Towy. In Victor's 'Original Letters' (1776, i. 330) there is a pretty picture of his still unabated kindliness of nature. Broken and paralytic, he is shown delightedly watching from his invalid's chair the country folk at their sports on a summer evening, and writing an order upon his agent for a prize of a new gown to the best dancer. He died at a house in King Street, Carmarthen, on 1 Sept. 1729, aged 58, and was buried in St. Peter's Church, where in 1876 a mural tablet was erected to him. There is also an earlier memorial to him at his old estate of Llangunnor. Two only of his four children survived him: Mary, who died in the year following his death; and Elizabeth, the eldest daughter, who ultimately married a Welsh judge (afterwards the third Lord Trevor of Bromham). His two sons, Richard and Eugene, died in 1716 and 1723 respectively. He had also a natural daughter, known as Miss Ousley, who married a Welsh gentleman named Stynaton. About 1718 it seems to have been proposed to marry her to Richard Savage [q. v.] the poet.

There are three principal portraits of Steele, all mentioned by himself (*Theatre*, No. 2) in answer to an attack made upon him by John Dennis the critic. The first, by Jonathan Richardson, now in the National Portrait Gallery, was executed in 1712, and gives us the Steele of the 'Spectator.' It was engraved in the following year by J. Smith, and later by Bartolozzi and Meadows. The second, by Sir Godfrey Kneller, was painted shortly afterwards for the Kit-Cat Club (of which Steele was among the earlier members), and exhibits him in one of the fine full-bottomed black periwigs he wore when he rode abroad (DRAKE, *Essays*, 1814, i. 179). This belongs to Mr. Baker of Bayfordbury, and has been engraved by Vertue, Simon, Faber, Houbraken, and others. The third, by Thornhill, is at Cobham Hall, and was reproduced in copper by Vertue in 1713, and by James Basire. In this Steele appears in a dressing-gown and a tasselled cap. The Richardson, he tells us, makes him 'indolent,' the Kneller 'resolute,' the Thornhill 'thoughtful.' There is another reputed Kneller at Stationers' Hall; and there is said to be a portrait of him when he was a commissioner in Scotland, by Michael Dahl. The Thornhill is the best known; the Kneller Kit-Cat is probably the best likeness. Sir Godfrey also executed a picture of Lady Steele, which does full justice to her good looks. It belongs to Mrs. Thomas of Moreb, Llandilo, Carmarthenshire, and figures as the frontispiece to vol. ii. of Mr. Aitken's 'Life.'

As regards the written portraits of his character, Macaulay in his famous essay on Addison sought by deeply drawn lines to heighten the contrast between Steele and his colleague. Thackeray softened the asperity of the likeness in his lecture (in the 'English Humorists'). Forster's vindicatory study in the 'Quarterly' is not entirely sympathetic. That Steele was an undetected hypocrite and a sentimental debauchee is now no longer maintained, although it cannot be

denied that his will was often weaker than his purpose; that he was constitutionally improvident and impecunious; and that, like many of his contemporaries in that hard-drinking century, he was far too easily seduced by his compliant good-fellowship into excess in wine. 'I shall not carry my humility so far as to call myself a vicious man,' he wrote in 'Tatler' No. 271, 'but must confess my life is at best but pardonable.' When so much is admitted, it is needless to charge the picture, though it may be added that, with all his faults, allowed and imputed, there is abundant evidence to prove that he was not only a doting husband and an affectionate father, but also a loyal friend and an earnest and unselfish patriot. As a literary man his claim upon posterity is readily stated. As a poet—even in that indulgent age of Anne—he cannot be classed; as a pamphleteer he is plain-spoken and well-meaning, but straggling and ineffectual; as a dramatist, despite his shrewd perceptive faculty and his laudable desire to purify the stage, his success is no more than respectable. In the brief species of essay, however, which he originated and developed—the essay of the 'Tatler' and its immediate successors—he is at home. Without ranking as a great stylist—his hand was too hasty for laboured form or finish, and he claimed and freely used the license of 'common speech'—he was a master of that unembarrassed manner which (it has been well said) is the outcome of unembarrassed matter. He writes, as a rule, less from his head than from his heart, to the warmth of which organ his rapid pen gives eager and emphatic expression. His humour is delightfully kindly and genial, his sympathies quick-springing and compassionate, his instincts uniformly on the side of what is generous, honest, manly, and of good report. 'He had a love and reverence of virtue,' said Pope; and many of his lay sermons are unrivalled in their kind. As the first painter of domesticity the modern novel owes him much, but the women of his own day owe him more. Not only did he pay them collectively a magnificent compliment when he wrote of Lady Elizabeth Hastings, that 'to love her was a liberal education' (*Tatler* No. 49); but in a time when they were treated by the wits with contemptuous flattery or cynical irreverence, he sought to offer them a reasonable service of genuine respect which was immeasurably superior to those 'fulsome raptures, guilty impressions, senseless deifications and pretended deaths' with which (as he himself wrote in the

'Christian Hero') it was the custom of his contemporaries to insult their understandings.

[Biographia Britannica; Drake's Essays, 1805; Hazlitt's English Comic Writers, 1819; Macaulay's Essay upon Addison, 1843; Leigh Hunt's Book for a Corner, 1849; Thackeray's English Humorists, 1853; Forster's Essay on Steele, 1855; Montgomery's Memoirs of Steele, 1865; All the Year Round, 5 Dec. 1868; Clarendon Press Selections from Steele, 1885, 1896; Richard Steele (English Worthies), 1886; Aitken's Life of Richard Steele, 1889 (a work, of extraordinary patience in research, which practically exhausts the facts of the subject, besides including an elaborate bibliography); Contemporary Review, October 1889; Aitken's Steele's Plays, 1894, and contributions to the Athenæum, 27 Dec. 1890, 16 June 1891, 5 Dec. 1891, and 19 Nov. 1892; an excellent selection from Steele's entire works has also been published (1897) by Prof. Carpenter of Columbia University.]

A. D.

STEELE, THOMAS (1788–1848), Irish politician, was born at Derrymore, co. Clare, 3 Nov. 1788. He belonged to an old Somerset family which had settled in Ireland in the seventeenth century. His father, William Steele, who died while he was an infant, was the younger brother of Thomas Steele of Cullane, the owner of a very considerable property in co. Clare, to which Steele succeeded at an early age. He was educated at Trinity College, Dublin, where he graduated B.A. in 1810, and subsequently at Magdalene College, Cambridge, where he graduated M.A. in 1820, after being incorporated B.A. in the same year. A man of ardent and even quixotic disposition, his whole life was one of action and adventure. In the Spanish war of 1823 against Ferdinand VII, he joined the patriot army, and impoverished his estate by raising 10,000l. on mortgages to provide military stores for the insurgents. He was present at the battle of the Trocadero, and it was not until the evacuation of Cadiz by the French that he abandoned a hopeless contest. In 1824 he published an account of his share in the struggle entitled 'Notes of the War in Spain' (London, 8vo).

On his return to Ireland Steele threw himself with fervour into the agitation for catholic emancipation. Although a protestant, he was one of the earliest members of the revived Catholic Association. He seconded O'Connell's nomination for Clare in 1828, and it was largely by his advice that the great agitator was induced to stand on that occasion (WYSE, History of the Catholic Association, i. 373). Steele opened the electoral campaign in Clare by expressing his readiness to fight any landlord who should

conceive himself aggrieved by his interference with his tenants. His position as a protestant landlord made him peculiarly valuable to O'Connell, and Sheil considered that he contributed more largely than any other individual to the return of O'Connell on 5 July (SHEIL, Sketches, ii. 108). He was appointed by his leader to the position of 'head pacificator,' an odd post for a man of his character; and was often instrumental in preventing outrages among his followers. John O'Connell, being asked ' Why did Dan make a semi-lunatic his head pacificator?' is said to have replied ' Why, indeed! Pray, who the devil else would take such a position?' (DUFFY, Four Years of Irish History, p. 399). At O'Connell's second election for Clare, Steele challenged and fought William Smith O'Brien [q. v.], who had not then embraced popular principles, for asserting that O'Connell was not supported by any of the gentry of Clare.

After the passing of catholic emancipation Steele took a less prominent part in politics, though he remained a staunch adherent of O'Connell, to whom he was personally devoted, declaring that if the latter ordered him to sit on a mine he would obey the mandate. He was one of those arrested and tried with O'Connell in 1843. In the dissensions between O'Connell and the Young Irelanders, he took the side of his old chief. Shortly after O'Connell's death Steele, who was much distressed by that event, and whose fortune had been completely wasted by his sacrifices for the causes with which he was associated, attempted suicide by throwing himself into the Thames off Waterloo Bridge. Though rescued from drowning, he died at Peele's coffee-house, Fleet Street, a few days later, on 15 June 1848. Lord Brougham was among those who attended his deathbed. His remains were brought to Ireland, and buried beside O'Connell's in Glasnevin cemetery.

Steele's is one of the most picturesque figures in the history of Irish popular movements. Though his actions were often wild and his principles extreme, he appears to have been a man of absolute sincerity, and was known through his career as 'Honest Tom Steele.' He took much interest in his property and in the condition of the people, and in 1828 published a book entitled 'Practical Suggestions for the Improvement of the Navigation of the Shannon,' in which there are passages of vivid, if florid, description. It marks the oddity of Steele's character that in the same volume he published an animated essay on the widely different subject of the treatment of the Irish catholics after the treaty of Limerick. He was also the author of 'An Analytical Exposition of the Absurdity and Iniquity of the Oaths, when taken by Protestants, that the Sacrifice of the Mass and the Invocation of Saints are superstitious, idolatrous, and damnable,' London, 1829, 8vo.

[O'Neill Daunt's Ireland and her Agitators; Fitzpatrick's Correspondence of Daniel O'Connell; Torrens's Memoirs of Sheil; Webb's Compendium of Irish Biography; Gent. Mag. 1846, ii. 207.] C. L. F.

STEELE, SIR THOMAS MONTAGUE (1820-1890), general, born on 11 May 1820, was eldest son of Major-general Thomas Steele of Guilsborough, Northamptonshire, by Elizabeth, second daughter of the fifth Duke of Manchester. After passing through Sandhurst he was commissioned as ensign in the 64th foot on 10 Jan. 1838. He exchanged into the Coldstream guards on 20 July, became lieutenant and captain on 29 March 1844, and captain and lieutenant-colonel on 31 Oct. 1851. From 25 July 1842 to 23 Feb. 1848 he was aide-de-camp to the governor of Madras. He was appointed military secretary to Lord Raglan on 23 Feb. 1854, and (with the exception of one month, 5 July to 6 Aug. 1855, during which he was assistant adjutant-general) he occupied that position under Raglan and his successor up to 16 Nov. 1855. He was at the Alma, Balaclava, Inkerman, and at the fall of Sebastopol, and was specially mentioned in Raglan's despatches of 23 Sept. (for Alma) and 11 Nov. (for Inkerman). At the Alma he took a message from Sir De Lacy Evans to the Duke of Cambridge, urging the immediate advance of the 1st division to support the light division; and this was fortunately acted upon at once, the duke inferring from the messenger that it was Raglan's order. Steele accompanied his own regiment, the Coldstreams, in their advance. He was made brevet colonel on 28 Nov. 1854, and C.B. on 5 July 1855; and he received the Crimean medal with four clasps, the Turkish medal, the Medjidie (third class), the Legion of Honour (fifth class), and the order of St. Maurice and St. Lazarus (second class). He was also made aide-de-camp to the queen 29 June 1855.

He became major in his regiment on 13 Dec. 1860, and lieutenant-colonel on 8 Nov. 1862. He retired from it to half-pay on 24 Nov. 1863, and was promoted major-general on 17 Aug. 1865. He commanded the troops in the Dublin district from 1 April 1872 to 31 March 1874. On 7 Jan. 1874 he became lieutenant-general, and on 23 Sept.

he was given the colonelcy of the Gloucestershire regiment. He commanded the division at Aldershot from 14 April 1875 to 30 June 1880, becoming full general on 1 Oct. 1877; and from 1 Oct. 1880 he held the command of the forces in Ireland for five years. On 11 May 1887 he was placed on the retired list. He had been made K.C.B. on 20 May 1871, and received the G.C.B. on 21 June 1887. He was made colonel of his old regiment, the Coldstream guards, on 7 Aug. 1884. Steele died at Farnborough, Hampshire, on 25 Feb. 1890. He was twice married: first, in 1856, to Isabel, daughter of E. M. Fitzgerald, who died in 1858; and secondly, in 1865, to Rosalie, daughter of T. M'Carthy of New York.

[Times, 26 Feb. 1890; Kinglake's Invasion of the Crimea; official despatches.] E. M. L.

STEELE, WILLIAM (d. 1680), lord chancellor of Ireland, son of Richard Steele of Sandbach, Cheshire, was admitted to Gray's Inn on 13 June 1631, and was called to the bar on 23 June 1637 (Foss, Judges, vi. 490). On 17 Aug. 1644 he was one of the commissioners appointed by parliament for the execution of martial law, and in January 1647 he conducted the prosecution of Captain Burley for his attempt to rescue Charles I in the Isle of Wight (HUSBANDS, Ordinances, folio, 1646, p. 535; HILLIER, King Charles in the Isle of Wight, 1852, p. 67). On 29 Jan. 1648 the House of Commons recommended him to the lords to succeed Serjeant Glynne as recorder of London, but he did not obtain the post till 25 Aug. 1649 (Foss, vi. 490; Commons' Journals, v. 450). On 10 Jan. 1649 the court which tried Charles I appointed four counsel to manage the case on behalf of the Commonwealth, one of them being Steele, who was selected to act as attorney. Steele was ill and could not act. 'The said Mr. Steele,' ran the report, 'no way declineth the service of the said court out of any disaffection to it, but professeth himself to be so clear in the business that if it should please God to restore him, he should manifest his good affection to the said cause, and that it is an addition to his affliction that he cannot attend this court to do that service that they have expected from him, and as he desires to perform' (NALSON, Trial of Charles I, pp. 9, 21). On 9 Feb. following he was sufficiently recovered to take the leading part in the prosecution of the Duke of Hamilton, the Earl of Holland, and other royalists before another high court of justice (State Trials, iv. 1064, 1167, 1209). He published his argument on Hamilton's case under the title of 'Duke

Hamilton, Earl of Cambridge, his Case' (4to, 1649).

As recorder of London, Steele took part in the trial of John Lilburne [q. v.] in July 1653, and in May 1654 he was one of the commissioners for the trial of Don Pantaleon Sa for murder. On 17 Jan. 1652 he was appointed one of the committee for the reformation of the law (*Commons' Journals*, vii. 74). He became serjeant-at-law on 25 Jan. 1654, and on 8 Feb. 1654, when Cromwell was entertained by the city, welcomed him with a long speech on the origin of government and the duties of rulers (*Mercurius Politicus*, 9–16 Feb. 1654; Foss, vi. 491). In the parliament of 1654 he was one of the members for London. He was sent on circuit as commissioner with Judge Aske in March 1655, and on 28 May of the same year was made chief baron of the exchequer (*Mercurius Politicus*, 24–31 May 1655; THURLOE, iii. 244, 305, 540).

Steele had been appointed a member of the council for the government of Ireland on 27 Aug. 1654, but he had never entered on the duties of his office; on 26 Aug. 1656 he was promoted to the post of lord chancellor of Ireland, and in September following he landed at Dublin (*Deputy Keeper of Irish Records*, 14th Rep. p. 28; Foss, vi. 491; THURLOE, i. 731, v. 215, 398, 405, 558; SHARPE, *London and the Kingdom*, ii. 348). His letters to Thurloe on the offer of the crown to Cromwell and the proclamation of the second protectorate in Ireland breathed great devotion to the Protector, and in December 1657 he received a summons to Cromwell's House of Lords (*ib.* vi. 294, 416). As he could not be spared from Ireland, this was a mere compliment.

When Cromwell died, Steele took part in the proclamation of Richard Cromwell in Ireland, and, while lamenting the old Protector, wrote cheerfully of the prospects of the cause (*ib.* vii. 383, 388). Meanwhile, however, he had quarrelled with Henry Cromwell, who complained that Steele, while professing the greatest desire to be serviceable to him, was secretly intriguing to gain partisans among the opponents of the lord deputy in the hope of ruling the roast himself (*ib.* vii. 199). Thurloe, however, disbelieved this account of Steele's intrigues, thinking it not in accordance with his character to endeavour to set up for himself (*ib.* vii. 243, 269). After the fall of Richard Cromwell and the recall of Henry, Steele was one of the five commissioners appointed by the restored Long parliament to govern Ireland on 7 June 1659 (*Commons' Journals*, vii. 674. The instructions of the commissioners are Carte MS. lxvii. 307). On 26 Oct. 1659 the army in England, having a second time expelled the Long parliament, erected a committee of safety, of which body they named Steele a member. Steele took the opportunity to return to England, 'by whose departure,' comments Ludlow, 'the affairs of Ireland suffered much, he being generally esteemed to be a man of great prudence and uncorrupted integrity.' When he came to London, however, he refused to act on the committee of safety, and advised Fleetwood and the officers to leave constitutional questions to the parliament (LUDLOW, *Memoirs*, ii. 125, 131, 153). At the Restoration, thanks to the fact that he had no hand in the king's death, Steele was not in any way excluded from the act of indemnity. It has been said that he 'secured his personal safety . . . by betraying the secrets of Henry Cromwell to Clarendon and Ormonde,' but the statement rests on no evidence and is opposed to probability (DUHIGG, *History of the King's Inns*, 1806, p. 190). Steele took shelter in Holland for some time after the Restoration (*Cal. State Papers*, Dom. 1663–4, pp. 498, 505, 507). He returned to England later, and died in 1680. His will, proved on 19 Oct. 1680, describes him as of Hatton Garden, Middlesex.

Steele married first, on 15 March 1638, Elizabeth, daughter of Richard Godfrey of Wye, Kent; secondly, Mary Mellish, widow of Michael Harvey. He left three sons: Richard, William, and Benjamin (AITKEN, *Life of Richard Steele*, ii. 350–3).

[Noble's House of Cromwell, ed. 1787, i. 396; Foss's Judges of England, vi. 489–92; Aitken's Life of Richard Steele, ii. 349–53, gives a pedigree of this branch of the Steele family. O'Flanagan's Lives of the Lord Chancellors and Keepers of the Great Seal of Ireland, 1870, i. 351–7; Burke's History of the Lord Chancellors of Ireland, 1879, pp. 86–7.] C. H. F.

STEELL, GOURLAY (1819–1894), animal-painter, son of John Steell, a well-known wood-carver, by his wife, Margaret Gourlay of Dundee, was born in Edinburgh on 22 March 1819. Like his elder brother, Sir John Steell [q. v.], the sculptor, he began his art studies under the guidance of his father, and continued them in the school of the board of manufactures under Sir William Allan [q. v.], and in the studio of Robert Scott Lauder [q. v.] At the early age of thirteen, in 1832, he exhibited at the Royal Scottish Academy a model of a greyhound, and in 1835 a life-sized study of a bloodhound, and from that time forward works by him were seldom, if ever, absent from the annual exhibitions of that body, of which he was elected an associate in 1846 and an academician in 1859. In his earlier years he was much employed as a draughtsman on wood for book illustration, and he devoted himself a good deal to modelling, of which he was for some years teacher in the Watt Institute, Adam Square, in succession to his father. He also modelled many groups of horses, dogs, and cattle, which were afterwards cast in silver. In 1857 he exhibited at the Royal Scottish Academy 'Llewellyn and Gelert,' a picture which attracted much attention, as did also, a few years later, a 'Highland Raid,' representing the Macgregors defending the cattle which they had raided against an attack of the royal troops. The latter was purchased for their prize distribution by the Royal Association for the Promotion of the Fine Arts, and a replica of the former was painted for the queen, who possesses also 'The Pass of Leny : Cattle going to Falkirk Tryst.' In 1865 he exhibited 'A Cottage Bedside at Osborne,' the queen reading the Bible to a sick fisherman, which became very popular through the engraving of it by William Henry Simmons [q. v.] 'A Challenge,' exhibited at the Royal Scottish Academy, and also at the Royal Academy in London in 1877, still further increased his reputation. 'Dandie Dinmont and his Terriers,' engraved by James Stephenson, was one of many pictures suggested by incidents in the 'Waverley Novels.'

Steell painted two large hunt pictures: one, in 1863, of the Earl of Wemyss, and another, in 1871, of Colonel Carrick Buchanan of Drumpellier. The latter was exhibited at the Royal Academy in London, and both have been engraved. He painted also several equestrian portraits, including those of the Earl of Eglinton and Winton and of Andrew Gillon of Wallhouse, and in 1868 that of the Lord-president Inglis with a shooting party at Glencorse. Many of his later works were large studies of animals executed in oil, tempera, and charcoal, chiefly for the decoration of highland mansions. His last picture, entitled 'Lochaber no more,' which he left nearly finished, was rendered doubly pathetic by the artist's death. In 1872 he was appointed animal-painter to the queen for Scotland, and he held a similar office in connection with the Highland and Agricultural Society. He succeeded Sir William Fettes Douglas, P.R.S.A., as curator of the National Gallery of Scotland in 1882.

Steell died at 23 Minto Street, Edinburgh, on 31 Jan. 1894, and was interred in the cemetery at Morningside. He was an admirable draughtsman of horses and dogs, and

especially of highland cattle. He was a good shot and a keen angler, and throughout his life was fond of outdoor amusements. One of his sons, David George Steell, A.R.S.A., is a painter of animals and sporting subjects.

[Scotsman, 1 Feb. 1894; Academy, 1894, i. 133 ; Art Journal, 1894, p. 125 ; Annual Report of the Royal Scottish Academy, 1894 ; Exhibition Catalogues of the Royal Scottish Academy, 1832–1894 ; Royal Academy Exhibition Catalogues, 1855–80.]   R. E. G.

STEELL, SIR JOHN (1804–1891), sculptor, son of John Steell, a carver and gilder, by his wife, Margaret Gourlay of Dundee, and elder brother of Gourlay Steell [q. v.], was born at Aberdeen on 18 Sept. 1804. When he was about a year old his father removed to Edinburgh, and he was in due course apprenticed to him as a wood-carver, and placed also under the tuition of John Graham in the Trustees' Academy. On the expiration of his apprenticeship he adopted the profession of sculpture, studying at Rome for several years. On his return to Edinburgh in 1833 he modelled the group of 'Alexander taming Bucephalus,' which has since been cast in bronze and placed in St. Andrew Square. This work, which was often reproduced, brought him at once into notice, and he received from the board of manufactures a special reward of 50l. Sir Francis Legatt Chantrey [q. v.] urged the rising artist to remove his studio to London, but his desire to devote himself to the improvement of art in his native country led him to decline the prospects of fame and fortune offered to him. His success, however, led to a commission for the colossal statue of the queen which surmounts the Royal Institution, and this was followed by the competition for the statue of Sir Walter Scott which adorns Kemp's Gothic monument in Prince's Street, in which Steell won the first place. This seated figure of Sir Walter Scott is stated to have been the first marble statue commissioned in Scotland from a native artist, although that by Steell of Professor Blaikie at Aberdeen was the first finished. It has frequently been reproduced in various sizes and materials. Among other commissions which followed was that for the colossal equestrian statue in bronze of the Duke of Wellington which stands in front of the General Register House in Edinburgh.

Steell's principal work, however, is the Scottish memorial to the prince consort erected in Charlotte Square, which was inaugurated by the queen in August 1876, when the sculptor was knighted.

Other notable statues by him are those of

Lord De Saumarez for Greenwich Hospital, Lord Jeffrey, Lord Melville, Lord-president Boyle, Allan Ramsay, George Kinloch of Dundee, Dr. Chalmers, the Earl of Shrewsbury, and that in bronze of Professor Wilson ('Christopher North') in Prince's Street Gardens, Edinburgh. He also executed statues of Lord Dalhousie and of James Wilson for Calcutta, of the Countess of Elgin for Jamaica, and a colossal statue of Burns for New York, for which city he made also a replica of that of Sir Walter Scott. Many of his busts are distinguished by great dignity and refinement, and among them may be especially named those of the queen, the Prince of Wales, the Duke of Edinburgh, Sir Robert Peel, Thomas De Quincey, Florence Nightingale, Professor Edward Forbes, Lord Cockburn, Lord Fullerton, Lord Colonsay, David Scott, R.S.A., and a bust in bronze of Dr. Guthrie. He executed likewise several regimental and other monuments, as well as the figures illustrating the parable of the ten virgins which decorate the Standard Assurance office; these he repeated and enlarged for the office in Dublin. He prepared for the bank at Montreal figures descriptive of the history of commerce.

In 1829 Steell became a Royal Scottish academician, and in 1838 he was appointed sculptor to the queen for Scotland. He first introduced artistic bronze casting into Scotland, and built at his own expense a foundry in which not only his own works but also those of other artists could be reproduced in metal.

Steell, who on account of ill-health had lived for several years in complete retirement, died at 24 Greenhill Gardens, Edinburgh, on 15 Sept. 1891, and was interred in the Old Calton burying-ground. On 30 Nov. 1826 he married Elizabeth, daughter of John Graham, a merchant of Edinburgh. She died in 1885. Latterly he was in receipt of a civil list pension of 100l. Busts by him of David Scott, R.S.A., James Wilson, the Duke of Wellington, and others, are in the National Gallery of Scotland. A plaster bust of Thomas De Quincey is in the National Portrait Gallery, London.

[Scotsman, 16 Sept. 1891; Academy, 1891, ii. 270; Annual Report of the Royal Scottish Academy, 1891; Exhibition Catalogues of the Royal Scottish Academy, 1830-89; Royal Academy Exhibition Catalogues, 1837-76; Men and Women of the Time, 1891.] R. E. G.

STEERE, EDWARD (1828-1882), missionary bishop in Africa, son of William Steere of the chancery bar, and Esther (Ball) his wife, was born in London on 4 May 1828, and educated, first under Alexander Allen, at Hackney, then at University College school, London. Proceeding to University College, he graduated B.A. of the university of London in 1847, LL.B. in 1848, and LL.D., with gold medal for law, in 1850. The same year he was called to the bar at the Inner Temple, but showed a preference for philosophy and theology, and came under the influence of the tractarian revival. Living chiefly in London, Steere was deeply impressed by the need of earnest work among the poor, and in May 1854 joined a small society, known as the Guild of St. Alban. He had already learned the art of printing, and set up a private press, from which he issued the monthly magazine of the guild. Before the end of the year, on receiving a small legacy from an uncle, he gave up his chambers, and in May 1855 he founded in connection with the guild a sort of brotherhood at 'The Spital,' near Tamworth. The scheme did not answer his expectations, and in response to the appeals of friends to carry out an earlier intention, he was ordained at Exeter Cathedral on 21 Sept. 1856.

Steere's first curacy was at King's Kerswell, Newton Abbot, Devonshire. In the summer of 1858 he was invited to undertake the sole charge of Skegness and curacy of Winthorpe, Lincolnshire, by the vicar of Burgh-cum-Winthorpe, William George Tozer. He was admitted priest at Lincoln Cathedral. Skegness was then a straggling village which had long been without parochial care, but Steere made his reputation among the fishermen as a 'downright shirt-sleeve man and a real Bible parson;' while the Wesleyans 'came to church in the morning to please him.' In the autumn of 1859 he became rector of Little Steeping, at the foot of the Wolds. Towards the close of 1862 he obtained leave of absence in order to accompany his friend Tozer, the new missionary bishop of the universities mission to Central Africa, to the Shiré. On 19 May 1863, after narrowly escaping being drowned in a storm, he landed at the mouth of the Zambesi. For many months the newcomers failed to make much progress, until in August 1864 they fixed their headquarters at Zanzibar, then the centre of the slave traffic. Here the missionary work was begun with a few slave boys, and by the middle of 1866 had so well advanced that Steere was about to return home, when the bishop fell ill, and was ordered to England, leaving him in charge of the mission. Steere had already compiled a handbook to the Swahili language, reduced to writing the dialect of the Usambara country, and produced a Shambala grammar, which he printed with the aid of native boys. Having thus overcome the linguistic difficulties, Steere inaugurated a mission on the mainland, arriving in August 1867 at Vuga, the capital of the Usambara country. A year later he set sail for England.

On settling down again in Lincolnshire his spare time was at first entirely occupied with the Swahili translations for the Bible Society. At the church congress at Nottingham in 1871 he delivered an important address upon the duty of the country as regards the slave trade. When news came in 1872 of Bishop Tozer's ill-health, he volunteered to return to Zanzibar. He went out in the same ship as the Livingstone search expedition, the members of which he instructed in the native language on the voyage. By April 1872 he was left almost alone to face the work of the mission. Yet before the end of 1873 he had made good progress towards erecting an English cathedral on the site of what had formerly been the Zanzibar slave-market.

Only after several refusals did Steere accept the nomination as bishop of Central Africa: returning to England, he was consecrated at Westminster Abbey on 24 Aug. 1874. The rest of the year was spent in gathering new workers and rousing fresh interest; his headquarters were in Euston Square, but he constantly lectured or preached in provincial towns. He left England on 11 Feb. 1875. One of his earliest efforts was to bring the Nyassa district within his scope; he started with a party, but was compelled to continue his journey alone from the coast inland to Mwembe, the residence of the chief Mataka. The journey occupied him from August 1875 to February 1876. Later in this year he visited one of the mainland missions, and towards its close started on the expedition for founding the Masasi station, from which he returned in ill-health in January 1877. In February he sailed for England, and, as soon as he was recovered, devoted himself to preaching and lecturing for the mission. At Oxford he was made D.D.; at Cambridge he was appointed Ramsden preacher. Returning to Zanzibar in November, he found the mission work steadily growing; but his own health was impaired, and he was worried by pecuniary difficulties. In 1879 he issued his complete translation of the New Testament and prayer-book in Swahili, while on Christmas day of the same year he presided at the opening of the cathedral church at Zanzibar. In 1880 and 1881 he pressed on, though not in person, the establishment of the mission settlement towards Lake Nyassa. Early in 1882 his

health obliged him to return to England. He got back to work in August, but died at Zanzibar on 28 Aug. He was buried in Christ Church, Zanzibar. Steere married, in 1858, Mary Bridget, daughter of Henry Langford Brown of Barton Hall, King's Kerswell. She died in 1883, leaving no issue.

Steere was a consistent high churchman, but by his width of view he won the esteem of men of every persuasion. His manner and appearance did not suggest the typical divine, nor was the work he was called upon to do purely spiritual. His success as a missionary was due in great measure to his versatility in throwing himself into all kinds of occupation, manual or mental, the 'architect' bishop scorning none of the industrial occupations he was anxious to teach the Africans. His linguistic power was great; he carefully studied the Swahili and Yao dialects, each of which he first made practicable as a written language, and devoted much attention to other native dialects (see below); he spoke French, German, and Portuguese, and had some acquaintance with Italian, Spanish, Arabic, and Hebrew, besides Latin and Greek.

Besides editing Bishop Butler's 'Analogy' (1857) and 'Sermons and Remains' (1862), Steere published an 'Essay on the Existence and Attributes of God' (1856), written originally for the Burnett treatise competition; an 'Historical Sketch of English Brotherhoods' (1856); and an 'Account of the Persecutions of the Church under the Roman Empire' (1859; 2nd edit. 1880). Steere's works relating to the mission in Central Africa include an 'Account of Zanzibar' (1870), a sketch of the 'Central African Mission' in 1873, 'Walks in the Nyassa Country' (1876), and 'Walks in the Zaramo Country' (1880). His laborious study of East African dialects resulted in 'Vocabularies of Gindo, Zaramo, and Angazidja' (1869), 'Collections for Handbooks' to the Shambala language (1867), to the Yao language (1871), to Nyamwezi (1871), and to Makonde (1876). But his chief attention was directed to the Swahili language. His 'Handbook of Swahili' (1870; 3rd ed. rev. by A. C. Madan, 1884) was followed by 'Swahili Tales' (1871, 2nd ed. 1889), and he also translated or revised the translation into this tongue of the New Testament, a large portion of the Old Testament, the prayer-book, and a number of hymns and primers.

[Heanley's Memoir of Bishop Steere, 1888, 2nd ed. 1891; Brit. Mus. Cat.; notes kindly supplied by the bishop's brother, Francis W. Steere, esq.]

C. A. H.

STEEVENS. [See also STEPHENS and STEVENS.]

STEEVENS, CHARLES (d. 1761), rear-admiral, was promoted to be a lieutenant in the navy on 19 March 1729. For the next two years he was on half-pay, and in February 1730-1 he was appointed to the Salisbury, in which he served for upwards of five years, part of the time on the home station with Captain the Hon. George Clinton, and afterwards in the Mediterranean with Captain Edward Falkingham, afterwards comptroller of the navy. In December 1737 Steevens was appointed first lieutenant of the Falmouth, commanded by Captain William Douglas, which sailed for the coast of Guinea with Captain George (afterwards Lord) Anson [q. v.] At St. Iago of the Cape Verd Islands, on 28 May 1738, the Falmouth was detached to go to Jamaica, Anson, for some reason never explained, giving Steevens a copy of Douglas's orders. The next day Steevens, after holding a council of the commissioned and warrant officers of the ship, and in 'conjunction' with them, confined Captain Douglas in his cabin 'for the preservation of their lives,' he being 'disordered in his senses' (Log of the Falmouth, 29 May). On arriving at Jamaica on 20 June Steevens reported the circumstance to Commodore Brown, the commander-in-chief. The next day Brown went on board the Falmouth, and, judging that Douglas was not mad, released him from confinement. Douglas then demanded that Steevens and the other officers should be tried for mutiny; but there were many difficulties in the way of holding a court-martial, and especially the absence of Anson. Brown, too, was convinced that Steevens had acted in good faith; and finally Douglas consented to receive an apology, which was formally given on 6 July on the Falmouth's quarterdeck, in presence of Brown and all the captains then in port (Brown to Burchett, 8 July; *Admirals' Despatches*, Jamaica). The next day Steevens was moved into the Sheerness, and within a few days all the other officers, some of the midshipmen, and even of the seamen, were moved into other ships (*Paybook of the Falmouth*), Douglas remaining in command of the Falmouth till his death in May 1741.

In May 1740 Steevens was moved into the Princess Louisa, and on 25 March 1741 he was promoted by the admiral, Edward Vernon [q. v.], to the command of the Cumberland fireship, in which he was present at the unsuccessful attack on Cartagena. On 12 June he was moved into the Phaeton fireship, and on 14 Oct. received an order to command the Ludlow Castle, to which he was formally commissioned on 11 Jan. 1741-2. He returned to England in the spring of 1744, and in October was appointed to the 50-gun ship Portland, in which, on 9 Feb. 1745-6, he captured the French 50-gun ship Auguste, in the entrance of the Channel; on 14 Oct. 1747 took part, under Hawke, in the defeat of M. de l'Etenduère, and on 31 Jan. 1747-8, in company with Captain (afterwards Sir Robert) Harland [q.v.], captured the very fine 74-gun ship Magnanime. After the peace he commanded the Tiger guardship for three years; and in January 1755 he was appointed to the Lichfield, in which in March he was sent out to the Leeward Islands as commodore and commander-in-chief. It was only for a short time, and, on his return, he was appointed to the Oxford, one of the Channel squadron under the command of Vice-admiral John Byng, and on 14 Nov. captured the French Espérance, a 74-gun ship, but old and worn out, so that Byng ordered her to destroyed.

In January 1757 Steevens was appointed to the Elizabeth, in which he went out to the East Indies with a commodore's broad pennant, in command of a small reinforcement. Having gone in the first instance to Bombay, he did not join Vice-admiral (afterwards Sir) George Pocock [q. v.] at Madras till the end of March 1758. In the actions of 29 April and 3 Aug. Steevens commanded in the second post; in the latter, he was wounded by a musket-ball in the shoulder. On 6 July he was promoted to be rear-admiral of the blue, but he did not receive the news till the end of the year. In the spring of 1759 he moved his flag into the Grafton, having as his flag-captain Richard Kempenfelt [q. v.], and in her commanded in the second post, under Pocock, in the action of 10 Sept. When, early in the following year, Pocock left the station, Steevens remained as commander-in-chief, and in September undertook the blockade of Pondicherry, in co-operation with the land forces under the command of Colonel (afterwards Sir) Eyre Coote (1726-1783) [q. v.] On 15 Jan. 1761 the place surrendered. A few months later, being, it is said, extremely corpulent, he died from the effects of the heat on 17 May 1761. He seems to have been unmarried. A brother George, an attorney, was probably the Mr. Stevens, whose death is recorded on 19 May 1762 (*Gent. Mag.* 1762, p. 242), mentioned in the several paybooks as receiving his pay.

[Charnock's Biogr. Nav. v. 229; official documents in the Public Record Office.] J. K. L.

STEEVENS, GEORGE (1736-1800), commentator on Shakespeare, was born at Poplar on 10 May 1736, and was baptised at Stepney parish church nine days later. He was only son of George Steevens and his wife Mary. The father, although he was described as 'mariner' in the baptismal register, was a well-to-do captain in the East India Company's fleet, who on retirement from active service occupied a substantial residence at Poplar, was elected a vestryman in 1746, obtained a seat as director of the East India Company, and died in January 1768 (cf. *Gent. Mag.* 1768, p. 93, where he apparently figures in the obituary as '*Thomas* Stevens, esq., formerly an East India captain'). In early years George attended a school at Kingston-on-Thames, whence he passed to Eton. He was admitted a fellow-commoner of King's College, Cambridge, on 29 March 1753, matriculating on 14 April following. He resided in the college till the summer of 1756. Although he read the classics and English literature assiduously, he left the university without a degree. He showed some interest in his college at later periods, and paid a visit to friends at Cambridge almost every autumn until his death. But his perversity of temper never rendered him a very welcome guest.

Steevens inherited from his father a competence and some real property in the neighbourhood of Poplar. When his student days closed he settled in London, at first apparently in chambers in the Temple. But he soon secured a house (formerly a tavern) at Hampstead, called the Upper Flask, near the summit of the Heath. A cousin, Mrs. Mary Collinson (born Steevens), with her daughters, kept house for him there for the rest of his life. Very methodical in his habits, he walked into London before seven each morning and paid visits to literary friends, bookshops, and publishing offices, returning on foot early in the afternoon. At his Hampstead residence he brought together a valuable library, mainly consisting of Elizabethan literature, and a fine collection of the engravings of Hogarth. 'Mr. Steevens,' wrote Malone to Lord Charlemont on 18 June 1781, 'has gone so far as not only to collect a complete set of the first and best impressions of all his [i.e. Hogarth's] plates, but also the last and worst of the retouched ones, by way of contrast, to show at the same time all the varieties, and to set the value of the former in a more conspicuous light' (*Hist. MSS. Comm.* 12th Rep. App. x. 383). In June 1781 he 'ransacked' Mrs. Hogarth's house for obsolete and unfinished plates (WALPOLE, *Corresp.* viii. 55). In the same

year he made contributions to Nichols's 'Biographical Anecdotes of Mr. Hogarth,' and his accumulated notes on the subject were incorporated after his death in 'The Genuine Works of Hogarth' (1808-17): on the title-page his name figured in conjunction with Nichols's. Steevens was himself a capable draughtsman, and he made many clever sketches of churches or copies of old pictures and engravings. An etching by him of an old woman named Mary Keighley is in the print-room of the British Museum.

But the main business of Steevens's life was the systematic study and annotation of Shakespeare's works. With a view to the formation on sound principles of a correct text, he directed his earliest labours to a careful reprint of twenty of the quarto editions of Shakespeare's plays, many of which he borrowed for the purpose from Garrick's library. Steevens inaccurately claimed that this reprint, which appeared in four octavo volumes in 1766 and included the sonnets, dealt with 'the whole number' of Shakespeare's plays 'printed in quarto in his lifetime.' Dr. Johnson, whose edition of Shakespeare had appeared a year earlier, was impressed by the intelligence that Steevens's useful venture displayed. The two men met in the Temple, and Johnson readily accepted Steevens's offer to prepare a more fully annotated version of his edition of Shakespeare. Steevens sent to the newspapers a prospectus describing his design, and appealed to the reading public for suggestions. He promised that his publisher (Tonson) should make payment on his behalf to 'those whose situation in life will not admit of their making presents of their labours,' and he undertook to treat respectfully the efforts of earlier commentators. But that counsel of perfection he was constitutionally incapable of observing. Johnson's share in the enterprise was confined to advice. On 21 March 1770 he invited his friend Farmer to supplement 'an account of all the translations that Shakespeare might have seen, by Mr. Steevens, a very ingenious gentleman, lately of King's College.' The edition appeared, with both Johnson's and Steevens's names on the title-page, in ten volumes in 1773. The younger man brought to his task exceptional diligence, method, and antiquarian knowledge of literature. His illustrative quotations from rare contemporary literature were apter and more abundant than any to be met with elsewhere. But his achievement exhibited ingrained defects of taste and temper. He spoke scornfully of the labours of many predecessors, and especially of those of Edward Capell, one of the most capable. In Capell's defence a clergyman, John Collins (1741-1797) [q.v.], charged Steevens with plagiarism in 'A Letter...to George Hardinge' (1777), which Steevens never forgave. Another commentator, Charles Jennens [q.v.], whom Steevens ridiculed with better justification, also retaliated in like fashion. Despite controversy, Steevens's edition was well received, and he 'revised and augmented' a reissue in 1778. Next year he prepared for the printer, John Nichols, a useful volume called 'Six Old Plays on which Shakespeare founded his "Measure for Measure," "Comedy of Errors," "Taming the Shrew," "King John," "Henry IV," "Henry V," and "King Lear."' In 1783 Joseph Ritson [q.v.], who proved Steevens's match in the employment of virulent abuse, opened attack on his edition of Shakespeare in a pamphlet of 'Remarks.' About the same date a third issue of the Shakespeare was called for, but Steevens declared that he had joined the ranks of 'dowager-editors' and committed the task to a friend, Isaac Reed [q.v.] To Reed's revised edition of Baker's 'Biographia Dramatica' (1782) Steevens had already made valuable contributions. Reed completed his editorial labours on Steevens's 'Shakespeare,' in 1785. Two years later Steevens was induced to act as literary adviser in Boydell's scheme of a fully illustrated edition of the plays (Charlemont MSS., *Hist. MSS. Comm.* 12th Rep. App. x. 383). But he affected to regard his labours in Shakespearean exegesis as at an end.

Steevens obtained admission to much literary society, and was rarely unready to aid others in literary research, although he was more at home in adverse criticism of their work. He sedulously cultivated his intimacy with Dr. Johnson, attending his morning levees and delighting 'in the roarings of the old lion.' In 1781 he supplied the doctor with anecdotes and quotations for the 'Lives of the Poets,' and bowdlerised for the work Rochester's poems; he contributed to Hawkins's edition of Johnson's 'Works' in 1787 a not very trustworthy collection of anecdotes. Johnson was not blind to his congenital faults, but took so charitable a view of them as to nominate him for membership of 'The Club' in February 1774, and of the Essex Head Club in 1783. Steevens had already joined both the Society of Antiquaries and the Royal Society in 1767. With a few of the men of letters whose acquaintance he thus had opportunities of making—with John Nichols, Bishop Percy, Dr. Parr, Isaac Reed, Thomas Tyrwhitt, and Dr. Farmer—he lived in amity. On occasion, too, he

was amiable to strangers. William Cole, no lenient judge, met him at dinner at Dr. Lort's rooms in Trinity College, Cambridge, on 9 Aug. 1780, and found him 'much of a gentleman, well bred, civil, and obliging' (NICHOLS, *Lit. Anecdotes,* ix. 803). When Cole introduced him to Horace Walpole, he made a similar impression (WALPOLE, viii. 146, 157). That he was generous in relief of genuine distress is well attested, and he heartily joined Johnson and others in making provision for an impoverished relative of Oliver Goldsmith.

But Steevens's irrepressible saturnine humour overshadowed his virtues. In conversation, even with intimates, he recklessly sacrificed truth to cynicism. Dr. Parr, who was well disposed towards him, said he was one of the wisest, most learned, but most spiteful of men (JOHNSTONE, *Parr,* viii. 128). Johnson, the most indulgent of his friends, admitted that he was mischievous, but argued that he would do no man an essential injury. When Lord Mansfield remarked that one could only believe half of what Steevens said, the doctor sagely retorted that no one could tell which half deserved credence. The main motive of his sarcasms was doubtless, as Johnson suggested, a love of making 'sport of people by vexing their vanity.' Broils with literary associates were consequently the chief result of the widening of his social circle. 'He came to live,' wrote Dr. Johnson, 'the life of an outlaw. The warmth of his temper put him at variance with so many of his acquaintance and he wished to avoid them' (BOSWELL, ii. 375). The sentiment was doubtless reciprocal.

Throughout the controversy over the authenticity of the poems which Chatterton pretended to have derived from the manuscripts of the supposititious monk Rowley, Steevens's acrid taunts embittered the fray. He gave some assistance to Tyrwhitt in preparing his edition of the so-called Rowley poems in 1777, and had not then detected that they were forgeries; but as soon as he reached that conclusion he directed all his armoury against the champions of Chatterton's honesty. To the 'Gentleman's Magazine' (1782, pp. 276, 288) he contributed humorous drawings, with appropriately satirical letterpress, of the supposititious poets, Chedder and Turgot, to whom Chatterton's dupes claimed that the fictitious Rowley stood indebted. Dean Milles and Dr. Robert Glynn (afterwards Clobery), two of the most strenuous advocates of the Rowley myth, were assailed by Steevens with so much rancour that Glynn invited a heated personal altercation with him when they chanced to meet at Cambridge in the autumn of 1785 (*Notes and Queries*, 2nd ser. ix. 282-3).

Some of the uses to which he was charged with putting his satiric talents entitled him to no quarter if the facts alleged against him can be proved. He received much attention from Garrick, who aided him in his Shakespearean researches. Garrick showed his confidence in Steevens in 1770 by adopting his barbarous proposal to play 'Hamlet' with 'all the rubbish of the fifth act omitted.' Steevens somewhat ironically suggested at the time that the omitted scenes might follow the tragedy in the guise of a farce, to be entitled 'The Gravediggers, with the pleasant humours of Osric the Danish macaroni' (*Garrick Correspondence*, i. 451). A little later, according to Garrick, Steevens slandered him in the press, and, when taxed with the offence, denied it on his word of honour, but afterwards bragged that 'it was fun to vex Garrick.' Garrick declined further intercourse with him, and denounced him to common acquaintances as 'a pest to society' (*ib.* ii. 361). Johnson's friend Beauclerk, Topham, whose hospitality Steevens often enjoyed, similarly represented to Johnson that Steevens deserved 'to be kicked' for attacking him in the newspapers' those with whom he lives on the best terms,' Another of Johnson's friends, Sir John Hawkins—of whose 'History of Music' he always spoke with bitter scorn—thoroughly mistrusted him (BOSWELL, iv. 408). One of the Chatterton advocates, Jacob Bryant [q. v.], sent to Horace Walpole some ironical verses in the same sense in 1789:

His slaver so subtle no med'cine allays,
It kills by kind paragraphs, poisons with praise.
Thy 'Chronicle,' James, but too truly can tell
How the malice of man can fetch poison from Hell

(NICHOLS, *Lit. Anecdotes*, viii. 532, 540).

The proofs that Steevens was guilty of publishing anonymous libels on his boon companions are happily incomplete. In the case of Garrick some allowance must be made for the vanity which detects slander in all criticism that is not unmitigated eulogy. He contributed an appreciative notice of Garrick to Baker's 'Biographia Dramatica,' and the charge made against him by Garrick's biographer, Tom Davies, that he unfairly denounced Garrick's avarice after his death, is untrue; the offender was George Ashby (1724-1808) [q. v.] (NICHOLS, *Anecdotes*, vi. 633). Seward declared that the offensive paragraphs about literary persons that appeared from time to time in the 'St. James's Chronicle,' and were assigned to

Steevens, were by an insignificant journalist, Alexander Bicknell [q. v.]

The suspicion had a *prima facie* justification in the fact that Steevens at one time owned a share in the 'St. James's Chronicle,' and was an occasional contributor to it, as well as to other journals (the 'Critical Review,' the 'Morning Post,' and the 'General Evening Post'). But many of his contributions have been identified, and, although biting enough, do not transgress the bounds of social decency. His journalistic achievements mainly consisted of epigrams and parodies suggested by contemporary literary crazes, or of burlesque accounts of alleged antiquarian discoveries. The former were often smart and pointed. The latter, conceived in a spirit of mere mischief, caused inevitable irritation. His skits included 'The Frantic Lover' (reprinted from Dodsley's 'Annual Register' in ALMON's *New Foundling Hospital for Wit*, 1771, iv. 89); 'A Song in the Character of a Stationer' (in the *St. James's Chronicle*, 11 Jan. 1774); 'The Insensible Lover' (*ib.*); a satiric account of the installation of John Rivington as master of the Stationers' Company (*ib.* 8 July 1775; NICHOLS, *Illustrations*, vi. 433-4); 'Elinor Rummin,' an epigram on the 'grangerising' craze, suggested by the excitement among collectors caused by the discovery of an illustrated copy of the so-named poem by Skelton in Lincoln Cathedral Library (NICHOLS, *Anecdotes*, ii. 660); and laughably stinging verses on the birthday odes of the poet laureate, Henry James Pye [q. v.] 'Reasons why it is probable 'that the coffin (usually alleged to) contain the body of Milton' should really contain that of Mrs. Smith (*St. James's Chronicle*, 7 Sept. 1790; reprinted in *European Magazine*, September 1790, p. 208) was a pardonable skit on a dry antiquarian pamphlet on the subject of Milton's burial by Philip Le Neve [q. v.] Steevens's pretended description of the upas tree of Java in the 'London Magazine,' on the authority of a fictitious Dutch traveller, was conceived in a like vein.

Less can be urged in defence of others of his journalistic diversions. He contributed to the 'Theatrical Mirror' a forged letter purporting to be a description by George Peele of a meeting at the Globe with Shakespeare and others. This was unsuspectingly transferred to Birkenhout's 'Biographia Literaria,' and has led later investigators into needless perplexity. A practical joke of a more laboured kind, which does Steevens even less credit, was devised to play off a trivial score against Richard Gough, director of the Society of Antiquaries, who declined

Steevens's proposal to make over four rare plates by Hogarth in exchange for books. Steevens, in 1789, having procured a block of marble, and having engraved upon it by means of aquafortis some Anglo-Saxon letters, placed it in the window of a shop in Southwark, and caused it to be represented to the Society of Antiquaries that it had been dug up in Kennington Lane, and was the tombstone of Hardecanute. Jacob Schnebbelie [q. v.] produced in good faith a drawing, which was engraved by Basire and published in the 'Gentleman's Magazine' (1790, i. 217). Samuel Pegge, falling into the trap, read a paper on the inscription before the Society of Antiquaries on 10 Dec. 1789; but the deception was discovered before the disquisition was printed in the 'Archæologia.' An acrimonious correspondence between Steevens and those he hoped to dupe followed in the daily and monthly journals (*Gent. Mag.* 1790, i. 217, 290–92; *General Evening Post*, 25 Oct. 1790; NICHOLS, *Lit. Illustrations*, v. 430–32). Steevens finally committed the stone to the custody of Sir Joseph Banks, and it was regularly exhibited at his assemblies in Soho Square.

The resumption of his Shakespearean work diverted him from such mischievous sport. It was a needless dispute which he forced on a rival editor, Edmund Malone [q. v.], that led him to resume his editorial functions. Malone had contributed to Reed's edition of 1785 a few notes in which he differed from Steevens. Steevens demanded that Malone should transfer these notes without alteration to the edition of Shakespeare on which Malone was engaged between 1783 and 1790. Malone declined, and when his edition appeared in 1790 Steevens concentrated his energies on an effort to displace it. A new edition was set on foot. Reed aided with suggestions, and Steevens walked daily, late at night or in the early morning, from Hampstead to Reed's rooms in Staple Inn to correct the sheets. Reed was usually in bed. The edition was published in 1793 in fifteen volumes, and is the definitive contribution to Shakespearean exegesis that Steevens published in his lifetime. There were some twenty-five large-paper copies. 'Pericles' was added, at Farmer's suggestion, to the Shakespearean canon, but the sonnets and poems were excluded, for Steevens asserted that 'the strongest act of parliament that could be framed would fail to compel readers into their service' (p. vii). The illustrative notes were throughout replete in recondite learning, but the text was often recklessly altered in order to convict the cautious Ma-

lone of ineptitude. Malone was not the only personal foe on whom Steevens avenged himself. With a malignity that was not without humour he supplied many obscene notes to coarse expressions in the text, and he pretended that he owed his indecencies to one or other of two highly respectable clergymen, Richard Amner [q. v.] and John Collins (1741–1797) [q. v.], whose surnames were in each instance appended. He had known and quarrelled with both. Such proofs of his confirmed perversity justified the title which Gifford applied to him of 'the Puck of Commentators.'

Steevens's fantastic acrimony provoked much retaliation. Tom Davies and Arthur Murphy both published repulsive sketches of him. But the denunciation that he felt most acutely was that in Mathias's 'Pursuits of Literature,' which appeared anonymously in 1794. When Steevens met Mathias, who was reported to deny the authorship of the 'Pursuits,' he remarked that the work could only be from the pen of 'a liar and a blackguard' (CLAYDEN, *Samuel Rogers*, p. 384). Steevens further retorted in a coarse poem in the 'St. James's Chronicle' (1–3 May 1798) (*Notes and Queries*, 1st ser. i. 212). In the controversy respecting the authenticity of the Shakespearean manuscripts forged by young William Henry Ireland [q. v.] he intervened with characteristic asperity. He had previously distrusted the elder Ireland as a rival collector of Hogarth's prints. From 1795 to 1797 he assailed him and his friends with unrelaxing fury (cf. *Gent. Mag.* 1797, ii. 931); and when Gillray published a caricature of Ireland, Steevens prepared the inscription, parodying Dryden's verses on Milton, and crediting Ireland with the combined impudence of Lauder, Macpherson, and Chatterton.

In his last years Steevens was a frequent visitor at the house in Soho Square of Sir Joseph Banks, one of the few acquaintances familiarity with whom did not breed contempt. It is said that he used to present Banks daily with a nosegay which he carried with him from Hampstead, attached to his cane. In 1795 he joined with Bishop Percy in editing Surrey's poems, and those of other earlier practisers of blank verse; a first volume was printed, and Percy sent a second volume to press in 1807, but the whole impression excepting four copies, one of which is in the British Museum, was destroyed in the fire at Nichols's printing office in 1808. The work was not reprinted. In 1796 Steevens subscribed 1,000*l.* to Pitt's loyalty loan, and he held a commission in the Essex militia.

I 2

Steevens died unmarried at his house at Hampstead on 22 Jan. 1800. 'The outlaw is at last dead in his den,' wrote Samuel Rogers four days later (CLAYDEN, *Early Life of Rogers*, p. 393). He was buried in the chapel at Poplar, beside other members of his family. A fine monument by Flaxman, with full-length portrait in bas-relief, still stands in the north aisle. The inscription describes Steevens as having cheerfully employed a considerable portion of his life and fortune in the illustration of Shakespeare. There follow some eulogistic verses by William Hayley (cf. engraving in NICHOLS's *Illustrations*, v. 427; LYSONS, *Environs*, Suppl.) Steevens bequeathed Zoffany's portrait-group of Garrick and Mrs. Cibber to George Keate; his fine collection of Hogarth's prints to the statesman, William Windham; his edition of Shakespeare, illustrated with fifteen hundred drawings or engravings of persons and places mentioned in the text, to Earl Spencer (it is now in the John Rylands Library at Manchester); and a corrected copy of his edition of Shakespeare, with many unprinted notes in manuscript, to his friend Isaac Reed, with two hundred guineas.

Apart from pecuniary bequests of 500*l.* to Charlotte Collins of Graffham Midhurst, and of 300*l.* 'for a ring' to his housekeeper, Mrs. Mary Collinson, all the rest of his property, including his library, passed to his sister, Elizabeth Steevens of Poplar (see will in *Monthly Mirror*, 1800; cf. copy, dated 1788, in Brit. Mus. Addit. MS. 20082, f. 126); she died at his house at Hampstead in March 1801, aged 'about 52' (NICHOLS, *Illustrations*, vii. 53). Her brother's books were sold by the auctioneer King some months before, in May 1800. The 1943 lots brought 2,740*l.* 15*s.* A copy of the second folio of Shakespeare, which had belonged to Charles I, was purchased for 18*l.* on behalf of George III, and it is now in the king's library at the British Museum. Two copies of Langbaine's 'Dramatick Poets,' into which he had transcribed Oldys's and others' notes, are also in the British Museum (cf. Addit. MSS. 22592-5 and c. 45 d. 14-15). A copy of Fuller's 'Worthies,' with his manuscript additions, formed lot 1799 (cf. *Bibliotheca Steevensiana: a Catalogue of the curious and valuable Library of George Steevens, esq.*, 1800, with names of purchasers and prices in manuscript in British Museum; CLARKE, *Repertorium Bibliographicum*, p. 543). Some of Steevens's letters to Thomas Hill, William Cole, and others are among the additional manuscripts at the British Museum. His handwriting was small, neat, and clear.

Isaac Reed [q. v.] brought out in 1803 a new issue of Steevens's edition of Shakespeare in twenty-one volumes, in which he embodied Steevens's unpublished notes. This is usually quoted as 'the first variorum.' The 'second variorum' of 1813 was mainly a reprint. The third and best 'variorum,' which was begun by Malone, was completed by James Boswell the younger in 1821. It was the last edition in which Steevens's valuable and suggestive notes were reproduced in their entirety, but every recent edition of Shakespeare draws from them the aptest of their illustrative extracts from contemporary literature.

According to Cole's account of Steevens in 1780, he was 'well made, black, and tall.' A portrait by Zoffany was engraved at the expense of Sylvester Harding. Another portrait by George Dance, R.A., was engraved by W. Daniell. A reduced copy forms the frontispiece of Nichols's 'Illustrations,' vol. vii. Steevens, with characteristic perversity, destroyed two portraits of himself—a miniature by Meyer, and a painting of him in the character of Barbarossa, a character he assumed in some private theatricals.

[Nichols's Lit. Anecd. ii. 650-63, and Illustrations, v. 440 seq. (Correspondence with Nichols and Gough), vii. 1-3 (Correspondence with Percy); Gent. Mag. 1800, i. 178; Thespian Dict. 1805; Chalmers's Biogr. Dict.; Lysons's Environs, Suppl. 1811, pp. 293-5; Park's Hampstead; D'Israeli's Curiosities of Lit.; Walpole's Letters, ed. Cunningham; Boswell's Life of Johnson, ed. Hill.] S. L.

STEEVENS, RICHARD (1653-1710), Irish physician, and Grizell his sister (1653-1746), were the twin children of John Steevens, an English royalist clergyman who settled in Ireland in the middle of the seventeenth century, and was rector of Athlone from 1660 to 1682. Richard Steevens received his education at the Latin school in Athlone and subsequently at Trinity College, Dublin, where he obtained a scholarship in 1674, graduated B.A. in 1675, and M.A. in 1678. Being intended by his father for the church, he took deacon's orders, but proceeded no further in the ministry, and devoted himself to the medical profession. In 1687 he received the degree of M.D. from his university, and thenceforward practised as a physician in Dublin, where he amassed a large fortune. He was a fellow of the Irish College of Physicians, and in 1710 was elected president of that body. He died before the close of his year of office, on 15 Dec. 1710.

By his will Steevens bequeathed the bulk of his property to his sister Grizell for her life, and directed that upon her death it should vest in trustees to be applied in building, and subsequently in maintaining, a hospital in Dublin, 'for maintaining and curing from time to time such sick and wounded persons whose distempers and wounds are curable.' Grizell Steevens, being 'desirous that the said charitable bequest of her dear brother should begin to take effect in her lifetime,' surrendered her estate to the trustees in 1717, reserving only 100l. a year, out of a rental of 600l., together with apartments in the hospital when built. She also gave 2,000l. towards the cost of building. The hospital, thus founded, and since known as Steevens's hospital, was completed in 1733 at a cost of 16,000l., and was the first public hospital established in Dublin, where it is still one of the foremost institutions of its kind. Dean Swift was one of its earliest governors, and 'Stella' (Esther Johnson) in her will bequeathed 1,000l. towards the maintenance of a chaplain of the hospital, so long as the church of Ireland should remain established. Another benefactor was John Sterne [q. v.], bishop of Clogher. Grizell Steevens survived till 18 March 1746. By her will she bequeathed the residue of her property to the governors of the hospital. Her remains are interred in the hospital chapel. Portraits of Steevens and his sister are in the board-room of the institution.

[Short History of Steevens's Hospital, by Samuel Croker King. 1785; History of Steevens's Hospital, by Cheyne Brady, 1865; Athlone in the Seventeenth Century, by Rev. G. T. Stokes, D.D.; Journal of the Royal Society of Irish Antiquarians; Todd's Graduates of Dublin University.]   C. L. F.

STENHOUSE, JOHN (1809–1880), chemist, was the eldest son of William Stenhouse, calico-printer, Barrhead, Glasgow, and Elizabeth Currie. He was born at Glasgow on 21 Oct. 1809, and was educated at Glasgow grammar school and university, where he devoted himself to chemistry under Dr. Thomas Thomson [q. v.] He continued his studies at Anderson's College under Professor Graham, and at Giessen from 1837 to 1839 under Liebig and with Mr. Lyon (now Lord) Playfair and Robert Angus Smith [q. v.] In 1839 he returned to Glasgow, where, by the failure of the Commercial Exchange, he lost the fortune left him by his father. In 1850 Aberdeen University made him LL.D. In 1851 he went to London as lecturer on chemistry at St. Bartholomew's, but resigned his post in 1857, owing to an attack of paralysis. He then proceeded to Nice, where he resided with his mother till her death in

1860. Returning to London, he fitted up a laboratory and started scientific investigation with great energy. In 1865 he succeeded Dr. A. W. Hofmann as non-resident assayer to the royal mint. That post he held till 1870, when it was abolished by the chancellor of the exchequer, Robert Lowe (afterwards Viscount Sherbrooke) [q. v.] In November 1871 a royal medal was awarded him by the Royal Society for his chemical researches. He was one of the founders of the Chemical Society in 1841, was elected fellow of the Royal Society in 1848, and became a fellow of the Institute of Chemistry in 1877. During the last four years of his life Stenhouse suffered acutely from rheumatism in the eyelids, which compelled him to live in a darkened room. He died on 31 Dec. 1880, and was buried in the High church new cemetery, Glasgow.

Stenhouse, either alone or in conjunction with Mr. C. E. Groves, wrote more than a hundred papers on chemical subjects for the Royal Society, the Chemical Society, 'Philosophical Magazine,' and Liebig's 'Annalen' (cf. *Royal Society's Catalogue of Scientific Papers*). Organic chemistry and the lichens occupied a large share of his attention. He was the discoverer of betorcinol, a homologue of orcinol. He was the author of many ingenious and useful inventions in dyeing (patents 13 Oct. 1855 and 12 June 1856), waterproofing (patents 8 Jan. 1861 and 21 Jan. 1862), sugar manufacture, and tanning; but he will always be known for his application of the absorbent properties of wood charcoal to disinfecting and deodorising purposes in the form of charcoal air-filters and charcoal respirators, which have proved of great value (patents 10 July 1860 and 21 May 1867). Among other patents which he took out was one for the manufacture of glue (7 May 1857) and another for the manufacture or preparation of materials for sizing or dressing yarns and textile fabrics (29 April 1868).

[Chemical Society's Journal, 1881, pp. 185–183; Proceedings of the Royal Society of London, vol. xxxi. pp. xix–xxi; Index to Specifications for Patents, 1854–80.]   G. S–n.

STENHOUSE, WILLIAM (1773?–1827), Scottish antiquary, was a native of Roxburghshire, and was born about 1773 (LAING). He became an accountant in Edinburgh. He published 'Tables of Simple Interest and of Commission Brokerage or Exchange' (Edinburgh, 1806). He died in Edinburgh on 10 Nov. 1827, and was buried in St. Cuthbert's churchyard.

Stenhouse was an antiquary with strong musical leanings. He is best known by his notes in the 1839 (Edinburgh) reprint of Johnson's 'Musical Museum,' which he edited. These notes, valuable yet inaccurate in many particulars, have been extensively quoted by biographers of the poet Burns and by editors of Scottish songs. They were reprinted, with additions, in David Laing's edition of the 'Museum' (Edinburgh, 1853).

[Laing's edition of the Museum as above; Scott Douglas's Burns, i. 255, ii. 135; Rogers's Book of Robert Burns i. 347-8; Baptie's Musical Scotland.] J. C. H.

STENNETT, JOSEPH (1663-1713), seventh-day baptist, second son of Edward Stennett (d. 1690?) by his wife Mary Quelch, was born at Abingdon, Berkshire, in 1663. His father, a Lincolnshire man, was a chaplain in the parliamentary army, and appears to have held a sequestered rectory at Wallingford, Berkshire, where, after the Restoration, he had a seventh-day baptist congregation, and supported himself by the practice of medicine. He published 'The Royal Law' (1658, 4to) and 'The Seventh Day' (1664, 4to).

Joseph was educated at Wallingford grammar school, and by his father and elder brother, Jehudah, both of whom wrote Hebrew grammars. In 1685 he settled in London as a schoolmaster, and joined (28 Sept. 1686) in reviving a seventh-day baptist congregation [see BAMPFIELD, FRANCIS] at Pinners' Hall, Old Broad Street, his father undertaking the pastorate. He was sometime evening lecturer to a seventh-day baptist congregation at Devonshire Square, and on 4 March 1690-1 was ordained pastor at Pinners' Hall by Hanserd Knollys [q. v.] and others. He was also Sunday lecturer (before 1695) to the general baptist congregation, Paul's Alley, Barbican, where his hearers in 1700 remonstrated against his preaching Calvinism. On several public occasions he was the trusted representative of the whole body of baptists. The general baptist association, in 1704, deputed him to write a history of baptism; he collected materials, but his health gave way. He was a fluent preacher with a silvery voice. One of his printed sermons gained him a mark of favour from Queen Anne. He is now best known as a hymn-writer, and is the earliest English baptist whose hymns are still sung. Dr. Julian specifies eight of his hymns as now in common use. Stennett died at Knaphill, near Hughenden, Buckinghamshire, on 11 July 1713, and was buried in Hughenden churchyard. His tombstone bears a Latin inscription by John Ward (1679-1740) [q. v.] His portrait was engraved by Vertue. He married in 1688 Susanna, younger daughter of George Guill,

a Huguenot refugee of distinction, and was thus the brother-in-law of Daniel Williams, D.D. [q. v.], founder of dissenting trusts. He left four children.

Stennett's works, consisting mainly of sermons (nine published separately), were collected, with a 'Life' (1732, 8vo, 4 vols.) The fourth volume contains his hymns (originally published 1697-1712) and his version of Solomon's Song (1700). Not included in his 'Works' are 'An Answer to Mr. David Russen's . . . Picture of the Anabaptists,' 1704, and several translations from the French. He printed anonymously political satires in verse; some are said to be in the 'Poems on State Affairs.'

JOSEPH STENNETT, D.D. (1692-1758), eldest son of the above, born in London in 1692, was baptist minister at Exeter, and (from 1737) at Little Wild Street, Lincoln's Inn Fields, London. He died at Bath, 7 Feb. 1758. He published several single sermons (1738-54).

SAMUEL STENNETT, D.D. (1728-1795), grandson of the elder Joseph Stennett, was born at Exeter in 1728, and educated by Hubbard of Stepney. In 1748 he became his father's assistant at Little Wild Street, succeeding as pastor in 1758. In 1763 he received the diploma of D.D. from Aberdeen. He was a man of broad views and considerable public influence. John Howard (1726?-1790) [q. v.] the philanthropist was a member of his congregation. He was assisted by his son Joseph, the fifth in a succession of ministers from father to son. He died at Muswell Hill on 25 (not 24) Aug. 1795, and was buried in Bunhill Fields. His works, chiefly sermons, were collected in 1824, 3 vols. 8vo, with 'Memoir' by William Jones (a few tracts are not included); his hymns are in vol. iii. (the earliest were printed in 1778), and thirty-eight are in the collection (1787) of John Rippon [q. v.]; they are not equal in merit to those of his grandfather.

[Life of J. Stennett, 1732; Memoir of S. Stennett, 1824; Protestant Dissenter's Mag. 1794, pp. 89 sq., 129 sq., 1795 pp. 352, 367; Universal Theological Mag. Jan. 1803, pp. 3 sq.; Wilson's Dissenting Churches of London, 1808 ii. 592 sq., 1810 iii. 236 sq.; Jones's Bunhill Memorials, 1849, pp. 262 sq.; Evans's Early English Baptists, 1864, ii. 295; Cox's Literature of the Sabbath Question, 1865, i. 267 sq., ii. 10, 60; Sabbath Memorial, January 1883, pp. 382 sq.; Julian's Dict. of Hymnology, 1892, pp. 1091 sq.] A. G.

STEPHANOFF, FRANCIS PHILIP (1790?-1860), painter, was born in Brompton Row, London, about 1790. His father,

Fileter N. Stephanoff, was a Russian who settled in England and found employment in painting ceilings, stage scenery, &c., until he died by his own hand about 1790; his mother, Gertrude Stephanoff, was an accomplished flower-painter, much patronised by Sir Joseph Banks, and died on 7 Jan. 1808. Francis became a popular painter of historical and domestic subjects, working both in oils and watercolours; he exhibited largely at the Royal Academy and British Institution from 1807 to 1845, and with the 'Old Watercolour' Society from 1815 to 1820. His best works were: 'The Trial of Algernon Sidney,' 'Cranmer revoking his Recantation,' 'Poor Relations,' and 'The Reconciliation,' which were well engraved; he also furnished many graceful designs for the 'Keepsake' and other annuals. For Sir George Nayler's sumptuous work on the coronation of George IV he drew in watercolours a series of costume portraits, which is now in the South Kensington Museum. At the Westminster Hall competition in 1843 Stephanoff gained a prize of 100l. for a scene from Milton's 'Comus.' The sudden death of his wife, Selina Roland, seriously affected his health, and he ceased the practice of his art many years before his death, which occurred at West Hanham, near Bristol, on 15 May 1860.

JAMES STEPHANOFF (1788?–1874), elder brother of Francis, was born in Brompton Row about 1788. He worked exclusively in watercolours, and excelled in the representation of public ceremonies and historical incidents which required the skilful grouping of large numbers of figures; among his works of this class were 'The Fair held in Hyde Park in 1814,' 'The Interior of the House of Lords during the important Investigation of 1820' (engraved); 'Interior of the House of Commons during the Reform Era,' and 'Reception of the Queen by the Lord Mayor on 9 Nov. 1837.' He was elected an associate of the 'Old Watercolour' Society in 1819, and contributed constantly to its exhibitions up to 1859, sending chiefly subjects from the poets and novelists, some of which were engraved for the annuals. He executed some of the drawings for Pyne's 'Royal Residences' and Nayler's 'Coronation of George IV,' and in 1830 was appointed historical painter in watercolours to William IV. Stephanoff was one of the founders of the Sketching Society. He was much interested in antiquarian matters, and made drawings of St. Cuthbert's stole at Durham for the Society of Antiquaries. He resigned his membership of the 'Old Watercolour' Society in 1861 and retired to Bristol, where he died in 1874. By his wife, Lucy Allen, he had two sons and two daughters.

[Redgrave's Dict. of Artists; Ottley's Dict. of Painters and Engravers; Graves's Dict. of Artists, 1760–1893; Art Journal, 1860; Roget's Hist. of the 'Old Watercolour' Society.]

F. M. O'D.

STEPHEN (1097?–1154), king of England, was the third son of Stephen Henry, count of Blois and Chartres, and his wife Adela [q. v.], daughter of William the Conqueror. As he had at least one younger brother, he must, from the dates of his father's two crusades and death, have been born either in 1099–1100, or, more probably, not later than the spring of 1097. His uncle, Henry I of England [q. v.], undertook to 'bring him up and promote him,' educated him with his own son, knighted him with his own hand, and granted him broad lands in England, and the county of Mortain in Normandy. In 1118 Henry gave the lordship of Alençon to Stephen's brother Theobald, and Theobald made it over to Stephen in exchange for the latter's share of their patrimony. Stephen treated the townsfolk, whose loyalty he doubted, with a harshness which drove them to the verge of rebellion; then he demanded hostages for their fidelity. In his absence one at least of the hostages was shamefully ill-treated; their relatives laid the blame on Stephen, and avenged themselves by admitting the Count of Anjou into the town and joining him in an attack on the castle. Stephen and his brother hurried to its relief, but were defeated in a battle beneath its walls. Stephen was with King Henry at the siege of Evreux in 1119. A passing attack of illness prevented him from embarking, on 25 Nov. 1120, with his cousin William, Henry's son, in the White Ship, and thus saved him from sharing in its wreck, in which William was drowned. Thenceforth Henry adopted him, as far as he could, into William's place. He kept him constantly at his side, and married him to the heiress of Boulogne, a niece of his queen [see MATILDA OF BOULOGNE]. At Christmas 1126 Stephen took precedence of all the other lay barons in swearing that on Henry's death they would acknowledge his daughter, the Empress Matilda [q. v.], as lady of England and Normandy. In 1127 Henry sent him to Flanders to negotiate a league with the Flemish nobles for preventing William 'the Clito,' the son of Henry's brother and rival, Duke Robert of Normandy, from obtaining possession of the duchy (WALTER OF TÉROUANNE, c. xlv.) Stephen again stood at the head of the English barons when, in 1133, they repeated their oath to Matilda.

and also swore fealty to her infant son, whom his grandfather 'appointed to be king after him' (cf. RALPH DE DICETO, i. 247, and ROG. HOV. i. 187).

Three years later one great baron, at least, asserted that Henry had afterwards absolved his subjects from both these engagements and designated Stephen as his heir. However this may have been, no sooner was Henry dead (1 Dec. 1135) than Stephen sailed from Wissant for England to claim the crown. Repulsed from Dover and Canterbury, he was warmly welcomed in London, and chosen king by its 'aldermen and wise folk.' Winchester, and with it the treasury, was secured for him by his brother, Bishop Henry [see HENRY OF BLOIS], who also, by pledging his own word for the new king's fulfilment of a promise to maintain the liberties of the church, induced Archbishop William of Canterbury to crown him at Westminster, seemingly on 22 or 25 Dec. Stephen then issued a brief charter confirming to his subjects, in general terms, 'all the liberties and good laws which they had under King Henry and King Edward.' On 6 Jan. 1136 he attended his predecessor's funeral at Reading. Normandy had now acknowledged him as its duke, while Matilda had lodged an appeal against him at Rome for his perjury towards her. The appeal was heard early in 1136 (ROUND, Mandeville, app. B). Pope Innocent II gave no formal judgment on it, but practically he decided in Stephen's favour by sending him a letter in which he recognised him as lawful sovereign of England and Normandy. Meanwhile the king of Scots [see DAVID I] had invaded Northumberland in Matilda's behalf. Stephen bought him off by a grant of three English earldoms to his son [see HENRY OF SCOTLAND]. Soon after Easter, at Oxford, all the barons swore fealty to Stephen, and he issued a second charter, dealing chiefly with the rights of the church, but containing also a pledge to surrender all lands afforested since the time of William Rufus, and a general promise to abolish unjust exactions and maintain the good old customs of the realm. A few weeks later, on a report of the king's death, Hugh Bigod [see BIGOD, HUGH, first EARL OF NORFOLK] seized Norwich Castle, Baldwin of Redvers [q.v.] threw himself into Exeter, and Robert of Bampton revolted in Devon. Stephen first dislodged Hugh, then he besieged and took the castle of Bampton, blockaded that of Exeter till thirst drove its garrison to surrender, pursued Baldwin to Southampton, and frightened him into doing the like. He spent 1137 chiefly in Normandy, which its overlord, Louis VI of France, agreed to let him hold on the same terms as his predecessor had held it, viz. his eldest son did homage for it in his stead. Stephen also made a truce with Matilda's husband, Geoffrey of Anjou, who was threatening to invade the duchy. On the king's return to England in December, he was met by a demand from David of the earldom of Northumberland for his son Henry. Its refusal was followed by another Scottish invasion. In February 1138 Stephen drove the Scots back across the Tweed. David retreated upon Roxburgh, and endeavoured to lure the English king after him, hoping to surround him and bring him to ruin. But Stephen turned aside and harried south-western Scotland, till lack of provisions compelled him to retire to his own realm.

By this time Englishmen were finding out how greatly they had been mistaken when, at Stephen's accession, 'they weened that he should be even so as his uncle was.' Brave, generous, high-spirited, warm-hearted, open-handed, courteous and affable towards all classes, Stephen was a man to attract affection, but not to inspire awe or command obedience. Haunted, as he naturally was, by a feeling of insecurity, he had begun by surrounding himself with a host of Flemish mercenaries, whose violence and greed made them an abomination to the people, and taking for his chief counsellor a Flemish adventurer, William of Ypres [q.v.], whose influence over him excited the jealousy of the barons and the old ministers of King Henry. Next, he had 'broken his vow to God and his pledge to the people' by holding, in autumn 1136, a forest court at Brampton (Huntingdonshire), evidently one of the places which he had promised to disafforest. He sought to form a party devoted to himself by creating new earldoms and alienating crown lands to men whose attachment he was anxious to secure. A statement said by William of Malmesbury to have been current a few years later, that Stephen debased the coinage, is not borne out by his extant coins (HOWLETT, preface to Chron. of Stephen, vol. iii. p. lii); but he 'dealt out and scattered soothly' the treasure which Henry had left; and when nothing of his own remained for him to give, he did not scruple to despoil those whom he mistrusted for the benefit of his favourites. For instance, on Christmas eve 1137, without any apparent provocation, he laid siege to Bedford Castle, in order to take it from its commandant, Miles Beauchamp, and transfer it to Hugh le Poor, whom he had created Earl of Bedford (cf. Gesta Steph. pp. 30–32 and

73, with ORD. VIT. v. 103–4, and HEN. HUNT. l. viii. c. 6, who gives the true date). During the year then closing he had quarrelled with the most influential of all the barons, Matilda's half-brother Robert, earl of Gloucester [q. v.]; and in the spring of 1138 Robert sent him a formal defiance, which proved the signal for a rising of the barons in the south and west of England. Geoffrey Talbot had already seized Hereford Castle, which he held against the king in person for nearly five weeks (May–June). While Stephen was in London collecting fresh forces, Talbot was made prisoner by the bishop of Bath, and the bishop was captured in his turn by the garrison of Earl Robert's castle of Bristol, from whom he bought his release by giving Talbot up. At this Stephen was so angry that he marched upon Bath, and was with difficulty restrained from deposing the bishop. He went on to Bristol; but the nature of its site made a siege appear so hopeless that he was persuaded to abandon the idea, and, after a reconnoitring expedition to Castle Cary and Harptree (Somerset), he moved northward to Dudley and Shrewsbury. He 'smoked out' the occupants of Shrewsbury Castle by firing some brushwood in the ditch, captured its commandant's uncle and hanged him with (it is said) over ninety comrades, made a truce with the rebel lord of Dudley, and returned to the south to besiege Robert's fortress of Wareham. There he had no success; but early next year (1139) he took another of Robert's castles—Leeds in Kent—while the queen negotiated a treaty with the Scottish king, which Stephen ratified at Nottingham shortly before Easter. Thence Henry of Scotland accompanied him to an unsuccessful siege of Ludlow, where the rebels nearly captured the Scottish prince by means of an iron hook, but he was 'splendidly rescued' by the king. At midsummer Stephen summoned the justiciar, Bishop Roger of Salisbury [q. v.], to a meeting at Oxford. Though the new king had showered gifts and favours upon the old minister of his predecessor, they had been from the outset suspicious of each other. Both went to the meeting with a train of armed followers; a fray broke out between the latter, and the king made it an excuse for arresting the justiciar, his son Roger the chancellor, and his nephew Alexander, bishop of Lincoln. He then went to besiege the justiciar's castle of Devizes, dragging the two Rogers with him; the elder he lodged in a cowshed, the younger he threatened to hang if the place were not given up; and the chancellor's mother, who held the keep, was thus terrified into sur-

render. After securing Bishop Roger's other castles—Sherborne and Malmesbury—Stephen marched against those of the bishop of Lincoln—Newark and Sleaford—and won them by keeping their owner starving at the gates of each in turn till he bade his people yield. For these outrages upon two bishops the king was cited by his brother Henry, now papal legate, to answer before a church council at Winchester on 29 Aug. Stephen's defence was that he had arrested Roger and Alexander as traitors, and that the castles which he had taken from them were not parts of their episcopal baronies, but private possessions, which by canon law they had no right to hold. On this latter point the council decided in his favour; but it compelled him to do public penance for his violence to the persons of the bishops.

Meanwhile, William of Mohun had revolted at Dunster, and Baldwin of Redvers had seized Corfe. Stephen formed a hurried blockade of the former place, and was besieging the latter when he learned that the empress had landed at Arundel. He hastened to blockade her there, till his brother advised him to let her join Earl Robert, whereupon he gave her a safe-conduct and an escort to Bristol. In a few months she was practically mistress of the western shires. Early in 1140 the bishop of Ely raised the standard of revolt in the east; the king attacked his island fortress with equal skill and energy, and drove him out. At Whitsuntide Stephen held his court in London, but in the Tower instead of at Westminster, and only one bishop, a Norman, attended it. Stephen next marched against Hugh Bigod and took his castle of Bungay; in August he had to make another expedition against the same offender, and came to an agreement with him 'which did not last long' (Ann. Waverley, an. 1140). He also wrested Cornwall from its earl, who had joined Matilda; but this was only a temporary success. Shortly before Christmas he went into Lincolnshire to meet Earl Randulf of Chester [see BLUNDEVILLE, RANULF or RANDULPH, EARL OF CHESTER] and his brother, William of Roumare [q. v.] Scarcely had he returned to London when he learned that they had seized Lincoln Castle. He at once went and laid siege to it; Randulf slipped out alone, to reappear on Candlemas day (1141), not only followed by the men of his own earldom, but accompanied by the whole force of the Angevin party, with the Earl of Gloucester at its head. In the battle that ensued the bulk of Stephen's men 'betrayed him and fled,' and he was left with a mere handful of comrades in the midst of a host of enemies. The little band, all on foot, stood firm against charge after charge of the horsemen; and the life and soul of their resistance was the king himself, who 'stood like a lion,' cutting down every man who came within reach of his sword, or, when that was broken, of a battle-axe which a citizen of Lincoln gave him in its stead. When only four (or three) of his companions were left, he still fought on, with 'the fury of a wild boar' and the courage of a hero, till the axe too broke in his hands, probably from the force of a blow which had laid Randulf of Chester in the mire at his feet (cf. JOHN OF HEXHAM, p. 308, with HEN. HUNT. l. viii. c. 18, ORD. VIT. v. 128, and ROBERT OF TORIGNI, an. 1141). At last he fell, struck on the head by a stone; but even then he shook off a knight who sought to capture him, and would surrender to no one but Earl Robert. He was sent to Matilda at Gloucester, and thence to prison at Bristol. A church council summoned by the legate, 7-10 April, declared him deposed by the manifest judgment of God, and acknowledged Matilda as sovereign in his stead. Stephen himself, as if in despair, had already sanctioned the transfer of the primate's allegiance to his rival.

Matilda's harsh government, however, soon turned the tide against her. In November she released Stephen in exchange for Robert, who had been captured by Stephen's partisans; and on 7 Dec. another legatine council reversed the proceedings of the April one, acknowledged the justice of a plaint which Stephen laid before it against the vassals who had betrayed and imprisoned him, and declared him lawful sovereign of England. On Christmas day, in Canterbury Cathedral, Archbishop Theobald again set the crown on the head of the restored king (GERV. CANT. i. 123; cf. ROUND, Geoffrey de Mandeville, pp. 137-8). It seems to have been during the same winter that Stephen joined with the abbot and convent of Westminster and the legate in a request to the pope for the canonisation of Edward the Confessor (RYMER, i. 18; for date see CLARE, OSBERT DE). In the spring of 1142 he was for many weeks sick at Northampton; either before or after this he went into Yorkshire to break up a tournament which the earls of York and Richmond had arranged between them, and which he apparently suspected to be a pretext for an armed gathering with a more serious purpose. This was a danger which he had brought upon himself, for he was the first king who allowed tournaments in England. Shortly before midsummer he profited by Earl Robert's departure for Anjou to swoop down upon Wareham, so suddenly

that its garrison, taken at unawares, surrendered at once. Thence he moved northward and eastward to break one by one the links of a chain of forts—Cirencester, Bampton, Rateot—which the empress had been constructing to protect the line of communication between her brother's territories in the west and her own headquarters at Oxford. On 27 Sept. he reached Oxford itself, forded the river at the head of his men in the teeth of a volley of arrows from Matilda's troops, took the city by storm, and drove Matilda into the castle. There he blockaded her till near Christmas, when she escaped, and the castle surrendered. Robert meanwhile had come back and recovered Wareham; Stephen attacked it again, but in vain. On 1 July 1143 he was routed in a battle near Wilton, and nothing but headlong flight saved him from being made prisoner a second time. After Michaelmas (Liber de Antiq. Legibus, p. 197) he held a court at St. Albans; there he arrested the worst of all the troublers of the land, Geoffrey de Mandeville, earl of Essex [q. v.], and forced him to purchase his release by the surrender of all his castles. Geoffrey resumed his lawless ways as soon as he was free; a vain effort to reduce him to order, another fruitless siege of Lincoln Castle, and a more successful campaign in the west against Earl Robert, occupied the king during 1144. In 1145 his successes against Hugh Bigod in Norfolk and Turgis of Avranches in Essex, following on the death of Mandeville, which had occurred in the preceding August, brought eastern England for a while under subjection to Stephen, who moreover besieged and took a castle which Earl Robert had just built at Farringdon. Deserters from the Angevin ranks now began to join the king, among them Randulf of Chester, who in 1146 helped him to regain Bedford and to build a fortress at Crowmarsh to hold Wallingford in check. Negotiations were begun between the empress and the king, but they came to nothing. Earl Randulf now asked Stephen for his help against the Welsh, who were making raids into Cheshire. The barons persuaded Stephen to let them answer in his name that he would grant the request only if Randulf would surrender Lincoln and some other royal castles, which he still held without licence. Randulf refused; whereupon, as the English chronicler says, 'the king took him in Hampton' (i.e. Northampton) 'through wicked rede, and did him in prison; and soon after, he let him out again through worse rede, with the precaution that he swore to give up all his castles; and some gave he up and some gave he not up.' Among those which he did give up was Lincoln, and there Stephen kept Christmas (1146) with a splendour unexampled for many years past.

In spring 1148 Matilda withdrew oversea, and her husband proposed another trial of the claims of the rival sovereigns in the papal court, and called upon Stephen to lay down his regal authority pending its decision. This Stephen refused to do, unless Geoffrey would likewise surrender the Norman duchy which he had conquered four years before. Hereupon Geoffrey and Matilda transferred to their son Henry [see HENRY II] the task of vindicating his claim to his grandfather's throne; and in spring 1149 Henry came with a small force to England. According to one contemporary writer, finding himself short of money to pay his troops, he appealed to the generosity of his royal cousin and rival, and Stephen sent him the needed sum. The story fits well enough with Stephen's character, but scarcely with that of Henry; and its details require somewhat violent handling to bring them into harmony with ascertained facts (see HOWLETT, Pref. to Chron. of Stephen, vol. iii. pp. xvi-xx, and Round in Engl. Hist. Rev. v. 747–50). Stephen had just put down a new revolt of the earls of Chester and Pembroke when Henry was knighted by the Scottish king at Carlisle on 22 May. Stephen hurried with all his forces to York; but Henry and David retreated to Scotland, and Henry soon returned to Normandy. Next year (1150) Stephen attacked Worcester, which was held by the Count of Meulan, one of Henry's chief partisans. He burned and plundered the town, but failed to win the castle. In 1151 he tried again, but lacked leisure or perseverance to maintain the siege in person; on his withdrawal his siege-works were destroyed by the Earl of Leicester, Meulan's brother, and 'so the king's care and labour perished and came to nought.'

Stephen had now been for four years at strife with the church. First, he had refused to recognise the papal deposition (1147) of his nephew William [see FITZHERBERT, WILLIAM] from the see of York, and to acknowledge Henry Murdac [q. v.], whom Eugenius III had consecrated as archbishop in William's stead. Next, he had forbidden Theobald of Canterbury to obey the pope's summons to a council at Reims in Lent 1148, and vowed that if the primate did go he should not be allowed to come home again. Theobald went nevertheless; and, although his intercession saved the king from the excommunication with which Eugenius proposed to punish these insults to the church, Stephen banished

him on his return. An interdict soon compelled him to withdraw the sentence; but so strongly did he suspect both primate and pope of being in league with the Angevins against him that in 1149 he forbade the great lawyer Vacarius [q. v.], who had come to England at Theobald's invitation, to lecture at Oxford on the Roman law (JOHN OF SALISBURY, Polycraticus, l. viii. c. 22; date from ROBERT OF TORIGNI, an. 1149), and in 1150 he refused a safe-conduct to a papal legate who wanted to pass through England to Ireland. Early in 1152, however, he reversed his policy. He was now anxious to secure the succession to the throne for his eldest son Eustace; so he made his peace with Archbishop Henry of York, and sent him to Rome to plead with Eugenius for permission to have the youth crowned. This the pope would not grant. On 6 April ('Ann. Winton. Contin.' in LIEBERMANN'S Ungedruckte anglo-normann. Geschichtsquellen, p. 82) Eustace was acknowledged in a council at London as heir to the throne; but the bishops refused to crown him in face of the papal prohibition. Stephen shut them all up together and tried to frighten them into submission; but the archbishop of Canterbury escaped oversea, and without him no coronation was possible. At the opening of 1153 Stephen was called away from the siege of Wallingford by tidings that Henry of Anjou had returned and was blockading Malmesbury. Beneath the walls of Malmesbury the rivals fronted each other for a moment, with only the Avon between them, and both at the head of their troops drawn up in battle array; but a storm blew up from the west and beat in the faces of the king and his men with such violence that they were compelled to retreat. Henry next besieged Crowmarsh; Stephen followed to relieve it; the barons persuaded them to hold, across a narrow reach of the Thames, a parley, which ended in a truce and a promise on Stephen's part that Crowmarsh should be razed. Within a few months his spirit was broken by the deaths of his wife and his son, and the barons' reluctance to agree to a settlement was overcome by the successes of Henry and the diplomacy of the primate. On 6 Nov. Stephen and Henry made a treaty at Wallingford (date from ROBERT OF TORIGNI, an. 1153; place from ROG. WEND. ed. Coxe, ii. 255), whereby it was agreed that Stephen should remain king for life, that Henry should succeed him, and that meanwhile the actual work of government should be done in his name by Henry as his adoptive son (cf. Engl. Chron. an. 1140, RALPH DE DICETO, i. 290, and ROG. HOV. i. 212).

The treaty was ratified in a great council at Winchester, and proclaimed by Stephen from London (RYMER, i. 18), which he and Henry entered together. On 13 Jan. 1154 they met again at Oxford, and Stephen made the barons do homage to Henry as their future sovereign. At their next meeting, at Dunstable, Henry complained that the king was conniving at the maintenance of some 'adulterine castles' whose demolition had been stipulated in the treaty. Stephen put him off with an excuse, and soon after went with him to Canterbury, and thence to meet the Count of Flanders at Dover. There the king's already shattered nerves received a double shock, from an accident which befell his only surviving son William, and from the discovery of a plot among his own Flemish mercenaries against Henry's life. He hurried the young duke out of the country; then he bravely girded up his failing strength to carry on the work which Henry had begun of bringing the barons to order and reducing the adulterine castles; and in this he met with considerable success. His last exploit was the capture of Drax (Yorkshire). At Michaelmas he was at a council in London; thence he went to Dover for another meeting with the Count of Flanders; here a sudden illness seized him, and he died in St. Martin's priory on 25 Oct. He was buried beside his wife and son in Feversham Abbey, which he had founded. [For his children see MATILDA OF BOULOGNE.]

Stephen's reputation has suffered from his position in the series of English sovereigns between two much greater men. He lacked the gifts of character and intellect which specially fitted both Henry I, his predecessor, and Henry II, his successor, for the task of governing a country in the transitional stage of development which England was passing through in the twelfth century; but he was in some ways a better man than either of them, and under circumstances less unfavourable than those in which he was placed, he might not have been a worse king. His failure as a ruler was in great part due to causes beyond his control; moreover, the failure itself has been considerably exaggerated. The fairest summary of his character is that given incidentally by the English chronicler: 'He was a mild man, soft and good, and did no justice'—in other words, he was neither strong enough nor stern enough to crush the anarchic tendencies of a feudalism which it had taxed the utmost energies of Henry I to keep in check, and which, twenty years after Stephen's death, even Henry II was hardly able to subdue.

[Ordericus Vitalis, ed. Le Prévost (Soc. de l'Hist. de France); William of Newburgh, lib. i., Gesta Stephani, Richard of Hexham, Robert of Torigni (Chronicles of Stephen and Henry II, vols. i. iii. and iv.), with Mr. Howlett's prefaces; William of Malmesbury's Historia Novella, the English Chronicle, Henry of Huntingdon, John of Hexham (in Sym. Dunelm. vol. ii.), Gervase of Canterbury, vol. i. (all in Rolls Ser.); Continuation of Florence of Worcester (Engl. Hist. Soc.); Historia Pontificalis (Pertz's Monum. Germ. Hist. vol. xx.); Stubbs's Select Charters, Constitutional History, vol. i., and Early Plantagenets; Round's Geoffrey de Mandeville. See also J. R. Green's paper on London and her Election of Stephen, in Old London (Roy. Archæolog. Institute, London Congress, 1866).]
K. N.

STEPHEN, usually known as STEPHEN OF WHITBY (d. 1112), abbot of St. Mary's, York, took the monastic habit at Whitby in 1078. The Whitby monastery had been ruined by the Danes, but it had been partly restored by William de Percy, first baron Percy [q. v.], and there were a few monks living there when Stephen entered the house. The monks soon chose him as their prior. Percy's former friendship for the foundation, however, had changed to enmity, and his oppression, together with the depredations of pirates and robbers, reduced the house to such sore straits that Stephen had to appeal to the king. William I gave them land at Lastingham, not far off, and thither they removed. Still Percy's ill-will pursued them, and, though Stephen followed the king into Normandy, he obtained no redress. But Alan, earl of Brittany, an old friend of Stephen, now came to his aid, and persuaded him and his monks to remove once more to the neighbourhood of York. Here he gave them the church of St. Olave's and four acres of land upon which to build offices. This land was, however, claimed by Thomas I [q. v.], archbishop of York. Again Stephen, through Alan, appealed to the king, and the latter promised to make good the loss to the see of York. William Rufus visited the new foundation at York which was named St. Mary's Abbey, and made a fresh grant of land and himself assisted in laying the foundations of a new church. When the prosperity of the house seemed secure, Archbishop Thomas renewed his suit for the original four acres, and Stephen appeased him only by obtaining for the see of York the grant of St. Stephen's Church in the city from the king, and by himself adding a voluntary gift of land. Stephen died in 1112.

Stephen wrote: 'De fundatione Abbatiæ Sanctæ Mariæ Virginis Eboraci anno ab Incarnatione Domini 1088,' which gives an account of his own life also. It was printed from Bodleian MS. 30 in Dugdale's 'Monasticon Anglicanum,' iii. 544 seq., but is there ascribed to Simon of Warwick.

Stephen is also said to have left a record of the difficulties which attended monastic reform in England in the eleventh century in a treatise (which Bale saw at Westminster) called 'De Reparato Monachatu.' There seems, however, good reason to doubt whether this work was distinct from that already mentioned.

[The chief authority for the life of Stephen is his own work (as above), printed in Dugdale's Monast. Angl. iii. 544 seq. See also Pits, De Illustr. Angl. Scriptt. p. 189; Bale's Scriptt. Illustr. Cat. i. 157; Tanner's Bibl. Brit.-Hib. p. 691; Hardy's Descriptive Catalogue, ii. 49 seq.] A. M. C-E.

STEPHEN, SAINT (d. 1134), abbot of Citeaux. [See HARDING.]

STEPHEN OF EXETER (fl. 1265) is the supposed author of the 'Annales Domus Montis Fernandi ab anno XLV usque ad annum MCCLXXIV,' which is contained in a manuscript in the archiepiscopal library at Armagh. He was apparently born in 1246, and entered the Franciscan order at Multyfarnham, Westmeath, in 1263. Other accounts connect him with Strade in Mayo, where there was a house of the Franciscan order, which Jordan of Exeter, lord of Athlethan, or his son Stephen gave to the Dominicans in 1252 (ARCHDALE, Monasticon Hibernicum, p. 509). Stephen of Exeter may have been a member of the family of the lords of Athlethan. The uncertainty as to his identity has caused him to be claimed both by Dominican and Franciscan bibliographers. He is also called Stephen Hibernicus, and, by an obvious error, Stephen of Oxford.

[Tanner's Bibl. Brit.-Hib. p. 692; Hardy's Descript. Cat. Brit. Hist. iii. 207; Quétif and Echard's Scriptt. Ord. Præd. i. 348; Wadding's Scriptt. Ord. Min. p. 218; Sbaralea's Supplementum in Wadding, p. 666.] C. L. K.

STEPHEN DE GRAVESEND (d. 1338), bishop of London. [See GRAVESEND.]

STEPHEN LANGTON (d. 1228), archbishop of Canterbury. [See LANGTON.]

STEPHEN, SIR ALFRED (1802–1894), chief justice of New South Wales, born at Basseterre, St. Christopher's, on 20 Aug. 1802, was the fourth son of John Stephen (1771–1834), youngest brother of James Stephen (1758–1832) [q. v.]. His mother was the daughter of a Mr. Passmore, who

lived to the age of ninety-six, and when above ninety could write the Lord's prayer within the compass of a shilling. John Stephen practised law at St. Christopher's, and came to England about 1808 with a fortune, which he lost by buying land at high prices. He returned to St. Christopher's in 1815, and was in 1824 appointed solicitor-general, and in 1825 judge, in New South Wales, and died in 1834.

Alfred was sent to England in 1804 by his mother. He was for a year (1810) at the Charterhouse, and afterwards at schools in Somerset and Devon. He returned with his father to St. Christopher's, where he was a lieutenant in the militia, and read a little law. In 1818 he was sent to London, entered Lincoln's Inn, and became a pupil successively of his cousins Henry John and James Stephen. He was remarkable for vivacity and good humour, which led him into adventures at Vauxhall and elsewhere, but stuck to his law, and was called to the bar 20 Nov. 1823. On 22 June 1824 he married Virginia, daughter of Matthew Consett, and in August sailed for Van Diemen's Land (now Tasmania). He had been appointed solicitor-general in the colony, which in 1825 was separated from New South Wales. Up to that time it had been mainly a convict settlement under military rule. It was now provided with a legislature, and Stephen took part in framing the new laws and organising courts. The introduction of trial by jury, which he supported, involved a long struggle, but was ultimately effected in 1834. During a visit to England in January 1833 Stephen was appointed attorney-general, and afterwards framed and passed over a hundred statutes, some of which were adopted in other colonies. He was thanked by the lieutenant-governor, (Sir) George Arthur [q. v.], and recommended for advancement. The loss of his wife and a brother in 1837 caused a severe illness, and he resigned his position. He married, in 1838, the daughter of the Rev. W. Bedford, and practised at the bar till in 1839 he was appointed judge of the supreme court of New South Wales. In 1844 he was made chief justice, and held that position until 1873. As a judge he is said to have been distinguished for courtesy and firmness. Though a man of marked humanity, he had a reputation for a severity not undesirable in a population so largely supplied with convicts. He had a main share in impressing a high standard of judicial conduct upon the Australian courts. His retirement was received with strong expressions of sympathy; his colleagues addressed him warmly; he was presented with a purse of one thousand guineas, raised by public subscription, and his bust was placed in the chamber of the legislative council. He was lieutenant-governor from November 1875 till 1891. In this capacity he had on four occasions to discharge the functions of governor in the absence of the incumbent. He was also president of the first legislative council, 1856-7, and again a member of the council from 1875 to 1890. He was on the council of education from November 1873 till its suppression in 1882, and on the senate of the university and the councils of many other public institutions. He received a knighthood in 1846, was made C.B. in 1862, K.C.M.G. in 1874, G.C.M.G. in 1884, and a privy councillor in 1893, being the second Australian upon whom that honour was conferred. He took a very important part in colonial legislation. In 1870 he was president of a commission for revising the statute law of the colony. It recommended three measures, one of which, drafted by the commissioners, was for a consolidation of the criminal law. After various delays, this was finally passed into law in 1883, and a 'Manual' comprising the act was published by Sir Alfred and Mr. A. Oliver in the same year. In 1879 he opposed a divorce bill introduced in the legislature; but observation of the numerous cases of hardship caused by the desertion of wives led him to alter his opinion, and in 1886 he introduced a bill permitting divorce under certain conditions. He replied to Mr. Gladstone upon this question in the 'Contemporary Review' for June 1891. In spite of a strong opposition, especially from the clergy, he finally carried the measure through the legislature in 1890, when beginning his eighty-ninth year.

Stephen visited England in 1860, but otherwise never left the colony, where the vigour of intellect which he retained till the end and his charm of character gave him the position of a venerated patriarch. His frame was spare and very active. It is stated that he would on occasion sit in court till 6 A.M. and begin a summing-up at 4 A.M. with a perfectly fresh memory. In his last years he wrote some interesting 'Jottings from Memory' (privately printed, 1889 and 1891) describing his early life. He kept up his reading, was full of intellectual interests, and welcomed many distinguished visitors to Australia. Robert Lowe (Lord Sherbrooke), when a barrister in Australia, was a friend of Stephen, who afterwards allowed some letters written to him by Lowe from England to appear in the 'National Review' (July 1894). Froude, in 'Oceana,' describes

a visit to Stephen. He kept up a close correspondence to the last with his English relations. He led a retired life in later years, but was still interested in many charities, and especially in an institution for the blind. His strength gradually failed in the last few weeks before his death at Sydney on 15 Oct. 1894. He was buried at St. Jude's churchyard amid many demonstrations of respect.

Stephen had by his first wife five sons and four daughters, and by his second wife, who died before him, four sons and five daughters. His descendants at the time of his death were over a hundred. One of his sons, Alfred, was a canon of the Anglican Cathedral in Sydney, and another, Matthew Henry, is now a judge of the supreme court in the colony.

[Information from the family; Stephen's Jottings from Memory (see above); Obituary notices in the Sydney papers of 1894, and the 'Times,' 16 Oct. 1894; there is also a full notice in the 'Cosmos' for September 1894; Heaton's Australian Dates.]   L. S.

STEPHEN, EDWARD (1822-1885), Welsh musician, generally known as 'Tanymarian,' was the son of Robert and Jane Stephen of Rhydysarn, near Llan Ffestiniog, Merionethshire, where he was born in November 1822. After a few years' attendance at the local national school, he was apprenticed to a tailor, but about 1841 he commenced to preach, and some three years later entered the Independent College at Bala, where he remained three years. In 1847 he was ordained pastor of Horeb (independent) church at Dwygyfylchi, near Penmaenmawr; but in November 1856 he removed to take charge of another pastorate at Llanllechid, Bangor, where he lived at a house called 'Tanymarian,' by which name he was thereafter chiefly known. He died on 10 May 1885, leaving behind him a widow and several children.

In music, Stephen was entirely self-taught. A series of articles on music which he contributed to 'Y Cronicl' in 1848-9 raised him into sudden popularity, which he further increased by delivering lectures on the subject, interspersed with vocal illustrations of his own rendering. In 1851-2 he composed his first important work, which was also the masterpiece of his life, namely, an oratorio entitled 'Ystorm Tiberias' ('The Storm of Tiberias'), which was published at Bethesda in seven parts, the last appearing in 1855. This was the first work of the kind by a Welsh composer, whence Stephen has been styled 'the father of the oratorio in Wales,' but it has no distinctively Welsh characteristic, and chiefly bears the impress of Handel's influence. Its strength lies in its choruses, some of which, especially 'Dyma'r gwyntoedd yn ymosod' ('How the giant winds do wrestle'), are deservedly popular with Welsh choirs. The airs had numerous defects, which Stephen more or less remedied in a revised score; this was published posthumously under the editorship of Mr. D. Emlyn Evans, with improved English words by the Rev. J. H. Johnes (Dolgelly, 1887).

Apart from his oratorio, Stephen's fame chiefly rests on the services he rendered to congregational singing among the independents of Wales, as John Roberts (1822–1877) [q. v.] did among the methodists. He edited, with the exception of the first two or three metres, the musical portion of a Welsh hymnal entitled 'Cerddor y Cyssegr' (Bethesda, 1860, 8vo), which contains several melodies harmonised by himself, but no tunes of his own composition. This was superseded by the publication in 1868 of a new hymnal, 'Llyfr Tonau ac Emynau' (Wrexham, 4to), under the joint editorship of Stephen and Joseph David Jones [q. v.] of Ruthin, the chief burden of the work falling on the latter. This was followed in 1879 by a supplement ('Attodiad'), edited by Stephen alone, containing six tunes of his own, the best known of which bears the title of 'Tany-marian.' The completed hymnal contains over three hundred tunes and nine hundred hymns, and until recently was in universal use among Welsh congregationalists.

He also composed a number of fugitive pieces, none of them being of the first importance, except perhaps a requiem (Bethesda, 1858), on the death of John Jones (1796–1857) [q. v.] of Talsarn. Stephen, who was a fair geologist, wrote several papers in Welsh on geology, and his collection of specimens was presented to the university college of North Wales, Bangor.

The Welsh memoir of Stephen, edited by Mr. W. J. Parry (1886), contains two portraits of Stephen. There is appended a selection of his prose and poetical compositions, together with several anthems and part-songs, the greater number published for the first time.

[A Welsh biography of Stephen, Cofiant Tany-marian (Dolgelly, 1886, 8vo), under the editorship of Mr. W. J. Parry of Bethesda, with an account and criticism of Stephen's musical work by Mr. Emlyn Evans; Jones's Cerddorion Cymreig, pp. 123–7, 135, 160; Hanes Eglwysi Annibynol Cymru, by Rees and Thomas, v. 304–7; Y Geninen, July 1885; Byegones, 1889, p. 102.]   D. Ll. T.

STEPHEN, Sir GEORGE (1794–1879), miscellaneous author, born in 1794, was the fourth son of James Stephen (1758–1832) [q. v.]. He was placed under a surgeon at an early age, with a view to an appointment in the medical department of the army; but upon the peace was sent to Magdalene College, Cambridge. He showed more taste for hunting than for study, and was therefore removed, after two years' residence, by his father, and placed in the office of Mr. Freshfield, solicitor to the bank of England. During the trial of Queen Caroline he was sent to the continent to collect evidence. Having completed his five years' apprenticeship, he set up in business for himself. In 1826 Sir Fowell Buxton applied for an inquiry into the report that a slave trade was being carried on at Mauritius with the connivance of the governor. Stephen was employed to collect evidence. The inquiry was dropped in consequence of the governor's death. Stephen was led by his investigations to form a plan for stimulating the anti-slavery agitation. He applied to O'Connell, who gave him advice as to the proposed organisation, and drew up a scheme, which was rejected by the committee of the Anti-Slavery Society. It was then taken up by James Cropper [q. v.] and others. The 'Agency Committee,' formed in consequence, arranged for public meetings, and for the promotion of petitions throughout the country, and played an important part in the final agitation (a full account in the Anti-Slavery Recollections). About the same time Stephen was requested by Lord Lyndhurst to act as solicitor under a measure for the relief of pauper prisoners for debt. He had no salary, and advanced sums for the repayment of which there was no provision. In recognition of this service or of his anti-slavery labours he received a knighthood upon the queen's accession. Stephen also wrote pamphlets upon the police and the poor laws. He published in 1835 the 'Adventures of a Gentleman in search of a Horse,' which became very popular; and in 1839 the 'Adventures of an Attorney in search of Practice,' an amusing work, which, though no names were given, was supposed to contain indiscreet revelations. He had at an early period started a society for the purchase of reversions, to which he acted as solicitor. A quarrel with the directors led to his dismissal, and involved a considerable loss of money. He then gave up his profession in 1847, and was called to the bar at Gray's Inn in 1849. He settled at Liverpool, where for some time he had a fair practice in bankruptcy cases. His business, however, declined upon a change in the system, and in 1855 he emigrated to Melbourne, where two of his sons had obtained appointments. He formed an extremely unfavourable opinion of his fellow-colonists, which he did not conceal. He led a retired life, but obtained some practice at the bar. He died at Melbourne on 20 June 1879. His wife died in 1869. They had seven children, of whom the eldest son, James Wilberforce, who had been fourth wrangler in 1844, and a fellow of St. John's College, Cambridge, emigrated about the same time, and became a judge in the colony.

Stephen was a man of very considerable abilities and force of character. He was upright and outspoken; but a hot temper and an unfortunate talent for seeing the worst side of his profession and his fellow-creatures involved him in many disputes, and injured his career.

Stephen's works are: 1. 'Practical Suggestions for the Improvement of the Police,' 1829. 2. 'Letter ... on System of Bread-money in Aid of Wages,' 1833. 3. 'Adventures of a Gentleman in search of a Horse,' by 'Caveat Emptor,' 1835; 5th edit., with name, 1841. 4. 'Letter on the probable Increase of Rural Crime,' &c. [1836]. 5. 'The Juryman's Guide,' 1845. 6. 'The Jesuit at Cambridge,' 1847, 2 vols. (a novel). 7. 'The Niger Trade and the African Blockade,' 1849. 8. 'Letter to Sir F. Buxton on the Revival of the English Slave Trade,' 1849. 9. 'The Royal Pardon vindicated in the Case of W. H. Barber,' &c. 1851. 10. 'Bankruptcy and the Credit Trade,' 1852. 11. 'The Principles of Commercial Law explained in a Course of Lectures,' 1853. 12. 'Digest of County Court Cases,' &c. 1853. 13. 'Anti-Slavery Recollections, in a Series of Letters to Mrs. Beecher Stowe, written at her request,' 1854. 14. 'Magisterial Reform,' 1854. 15. 'Insolvency Reform,' 1863. 16. 'Life of Christ,' 1871. 17. 'Memoir of the late James Stephen,' 1875. Stephen wrote some other pamphlets, and contributed the 'Clerk,' the 'Governess,' and the 'Groom' to Knight's series of 'Guides to Trade' in 1838.

[The above Memoir of James Stephen; family papers; Stephen's Life of Sir J. F. Stephen.]

L. S.

STEPHEN, HENRY JOHN (1787–1864), serjeant-at-law, born at St. Christopher's in the West Indies on 18 Jan. 1787, was the second son of James Stephen (1758–1832) [q. v.] He was for a time at St. John's College, Cambridge, but did not graduate. He was called to the bar on 24 Nov. 1815. He had in 1814 married his cousin, Mary Morison, and, after his stepmother's death,

from 1815 till 1832, kept house for his father in Kensington Gore. He was a man of nervous and retiring disposition, and, though an accomplished lawyer, obtained no great professional success. He became known, however, by a treatise on pleading, published in 1824. There was no want of practical treatises on the subject. The aim of Stephen's book was to develop systematically the principles of the 'science' and exhibit them as part of a general scheme (Preface). 'Stephen,' says Professor Dicey, 'by a stroke of something like genius, at once and precisely accomplished his aim; he exhibited the whole theory in scientific form, arranged the principles in logical order, and expressed them in a series of rules of unequalled clearness and brevity. Though the law has become obsolete, the book is still interesting as a model of lucid exposition. The attempt to reduce an intricate branch of law to a series of well-digested principles was then to a great extent a novelty. Stephen founded a school, but none of his many followers have surpassed him in mastery of the subject, logical power, and terseness of expression.' The merits of the treatise were recognised both in England and America, and gave him a claim to promotion. Stephen became a serjeant-at-law in 1828, and was a member of the common-law commission appointed in that year. His fellow-commissioners all became judges; and it is said, upon doubtful authority, that a judgeship was offered to Stephen by Lyndhurst, and declined upon the ground that he could never bear to pass a capital sentence (SIR G. STEPHEN, *Life of James Stephen*, p. 40). In 1834 he published a 'Summary of the Criminal Law,' which was translated into German. In 1841 appeared the first edition of his 'Commentaries.' It was described on the title-page as 'partly founded upon Blackstone,' and contains much of his predecessor's work, with large interpolations and additions of his own, the distinction being clearly indicated in the text.

'In reality,' says Professor Dicey, ' it was an original production, differing essentially in character and in merit from his predecessor. Blackstone was a consummate man of letters. Stephen showed the qualities in which Blackstone was comparatively deficient—consummate logical power and singular precision and accuracy of style. Had the work been published as an original treatise, it would have stood upon a level with Blackstone's work.' In later editions the name of Blackstone is dropped, as larger additions became necessary in order to keep up with the alterations in the law. The book enjoyed a high reputation from the first, and became, as it still is, the standard work of the kind; new editions have been published at regular intervals. In 1842 Stephen was placed on a commission for inquiring into the forgery of exchequer bills, and in the same year became commissioner of bankruptcy at Bristol; Matthew Davenport Hill [q. v.] was his colleague. He lived at Cleevewood, near Bristol, till his retirement from this post in 1854, and afterwards lived at Clifton until his death on 28 Nov. 1864. He amused his later years by speculating on the prophecies and the theory of music, and, though courteous and kindly, saw little at any time of society. His diffidence prevented him from obtaining the reputation as a writer or the position in his profession which he might have fairly claimed.

His wife and a daughter died before him. He left two children. His daughter Sarah, born 28 June 1816, was author of a religious story called 'Anna; or the Daughter at Home,' which went through several editions, and one of the founders of the Metropolitan Association for befriending Young Servants. She died, aged 79, on 5 Jan. 1895. His son James, born 16 Sept. 1820, was recorder of Poole, professor of law in King's College, London, and afterwards judge of the county court at Lincoln. He edited later editions of the 'Commentaries' and 'Questions for Law Students' upon the same. He died 25 Nov. 1894.

Stephen's works are: 1. 'A Treatise on the Principles of Pleading in Civil Actions: comprising a Summary of the whole Proceedings in a Suit of Law,' 1824, 1827, 1834, 1838, 1843, 1860 (by J. Stephen and F. F. Pender); and 1866 (by F. F. Pender); eight American editions from 1824 to 1859. 2. 'Summary of the Criminal Law,' 1834; translated as 'Handbuch des englischen Strafrechts,'&c., by E. Mühry, 1843. 3. 'New Commentaries on the Laws of England' (partly founded on Blackstone), 1841–5, 4 vols. 8vo; later editions, edited by his son, James Stephen, and his grandson, H. St. James Stephen; the tenth appeared in 1895. The book was reprinted in America in 1843–1846.

[Life of Sir J. F. Stephen, by L. Stephen; family papers.]   L. S.

STEPHEN, JAMES (1758–1832), master in chancery, born on 30 June 1758 at Poole in Dorset, was the son of James Stephen, born about 1733. The elder Stephen came from Aberdeenshire, and was supercargo of a ship wrecked about 1752 on Purbeck Island. Stephen was hospitably received by

Mr. Milner, collector of customs at Poole, and soon afterwards privately married to Milner's youngest daughter, Sibella. He was reconciled to her family and taken into partnership by her brother, but, after some unfortunate speculations at Poole, got into the king's bench prison. He there obtained some notoriety by writing pamphlets to show that imprisonment for debt was contrary to Magna Charta and by organising an agitation in the prison. The benchers of the Middle Temple refused afterwards to call him to the bar, and he was employed in the business of a solicitor. He fell into difficulties, lost his wife in 1775, and died in poverty in 1779.

The younger James had a desultory education during his father's struggles. He was a precocious lad, and when fourteen fell in love with Anne Stent, sister of a schoolfellow. Their correspondence was forbidden, and, with the help of an uncle, he was in 1773 sent for a short time to Winchester school. The help of other relatives enabled him to pass two sessions, in 1775–6 and 1777–8, at Marischal College, Aberdeen. He returned to London, helped his father's last struggles, and supported himself for a time as reporter to the 'Morning Post.' He now persuaded Miss Stent to accept him and throw over another engagement, in spite of her father's disapproval. A simultaneous love affair with another girl brought him into serious perplexities, which caused a breach with Miss Stent. Meanwhile a brother of his father, who had settled as a physician and planter at St. Christopher's, had taken his elder brother, William, into partnership. The uncle died in 1781, leaving all his property to William. William hereupon sent funds which enabled James to be called to the bar (26 Jan. 1782), and next year to sail for St. Christopher's. Miss Stent had finally relented, in spite of the other young woman, and married him before his departure.

Stephen touched at Barbados on his way out, and was shocked at the brutality shown to some negroes on their trial for murder. He made and kept a vow that he would have nothing to do with slavery. Later incidents strengthened the impression. At St. Christopher's he practised at the bar. There was a good deal of legal business arising from the regulation of the trade between the West Indies and the United States. He earned enough to be able to visit England in the winter of 1788–9. He put himself in communication with Wilberforce, who was starting the agitation against the slave trade, and, after returning to the West Indies, sent

M

private information to support the cause. In 1794 he returned to England and obtained practice at the prize appeal court of the privy council, where for some years he had a large share of the leading business.

Stephen had upon his return openly identified himself with the agitation against the slave trade. His wife died in 1796; and Wilberforce's kindness upon the occasion brought the two into closer familiarity, which was increased by Stephen's marriage in 1800 to Wilberforce's sister, widow of the Rev. Dr. Clarke of Hull. Stephen had also accepted the religious views of his allies, and was henceforward one of the most active of Wilberforce's supporters. His ardent temperament led him to regard the abolition of the slave trade as the one great aim of his life, and he was inclined to reproach his leader for attending to anything else. He made his chief mark, however, by a pamphlet called 'War in Disguise,' published in 1805, to denounce the evasions of our regulations by neutral traders. His experience at the English and colonial bar had made him familiar with the facts. The pamphlet produced a great effect, and was supposed to have suggested the orders in council, the first of which were made in 1807. Brougham calls him the 'father' of the system thus adopted. Perceval, with whom he sympathised on religious and political grounds, wished to bring him into parliament to support the government policy. He was elected for Tralee on 21 Feb. 1808, and in the parliament of 1812 sat for East Grinstead.

In parliament Stephen was chiefly known as defender of the orders in council. His want of education and his fiery temper prevented him from doing justice to considerable natural powers of eloquence. He spoke, however, occasionally with much effect, especially (12 March 1810) upon a proposal which had been made by the benchers of Lincoln's Inn to exclude from the bar any one who had written in a newspaper. Stephen excited admiration by frankly confessing that he had himself been guilty of journalism, and the rule was withdrawn. He steadily defended the government against Brougham's attack in the matter of the orders in council. He never lost sight of the slavery question, and spoke with great energy upon various points which arose after the abolition of the slave trade. The refusal of government to take up a measure for the registration of slaves induced him to retire from parliament; and, in spite of many entreaties, he accepted the Chiltern Hundreds on 14 April 1815.

Stephen had been appointed master in chancery in 1811, having, it was said, a claim in consequence of the diminution of his practice due to the orders in council. He lived for many years in Kensington Gore, where Wilberforce was his neighbour; and from 1819 had a small house at Missenden, Buckinghamshire, where the name 'Wilberforce's Walk' commemorates the visits of his brother-in-law. The second Mrs. Stephen died in 1816. Her widower and brother kept up their intimacy to the end; and Stephen to the last took a prominent part in the agitation for the abolition of slavery. He wrote an elaborate treatise upon West Indian laws and practice, and was a leading member of the society which carried on the agitation. Failure of health forced him to resign his mastership in 1831, and he died at Bath on 10 Oct. 1832. He was buried at Newington Green, by the side of his parents and his first wife. Wilberforce had promised to be buried there too, but was claimed by Westminster Abbey.

Stephen was a handsome man, and a very active worker till his last years. In early years he had been a liberal, and thought of joining Washington. In later life he became a tory and an evangelical; and he was one of the most ardent and devoted adherents of the party which became known as the 'Clapham Sect.' He left six children by his first wife: William, for nearly sixty years vicar of Bledlow, Buckinghamshire, who died on 8 Jan. 1867; Henry John [q. v.]; Sir James (1789–1859) [q. v.]; Sibella (1792–1869), who married W. A. Garratt, barrister; Sir George [q. v.]; and Anne Mary (1796–1878), who married Thomas Edward Dicey, and was mother of Mr. Edward Dicey and Professor Albert Venn Dicey.

James Stephen's chief works are 'War in Disguise' (1805, several editions) and 'Slavery in the British West India Colonies delineated' (vol. i. 1824, and vol. ii. 1830). He wrote also a number of pamphlets, the first of which, called 'The Crisis of the Sugar Colonies,' appeared in 1802. In 1815 he published 'Reasons for establishing a Registry of Slaves . . .,' a report drawn by him of a committee of the African Institution, and, it is said, three other pamphlets. A series of letters addressed to the allied sovereigns at Aix-la-Chapelle, and published in the 'New Times,' was translated into French and published in 1818. Another pamphlet (n.d.) about 1821 is 'Strictures on the Charge of Cannibalism on the African Race,' and in 1826 he published 'England enslaved by her own Slave Colonies.' Others were apparently anonymous, and cannot now be identified.

[Family papers; L. Stephen's Life of Sir J. F. Stephen, pp. 1–24; Life of the late James Stephen, by his son, Sir George Stephen, 1875; Jottings from Memory, by Sir Alfred Stephen (privately printed, 1889 and 1891); Wilberforce's Life and Letters, and Colquhoun's Wilberforce: his Friends and his Times, 1886, pp. 180–96; Robert's Hannah More (letters); Brougham's Speeches, 1838, i. 402–14, quoted also in Sir J. Stephen's essay 'The Clapham Sect;' Henry Adams's History of the United States, 1891, iii. 50–2, &c.; Walpole's Life of Perceval.] L. S.

STEPHEN, Sir JAMES (1789–1859), colonial under-secretary, born at Lambeth on 3 Jan. 1789, was third son of James Stephen (1758–1832) [q. v.] An attack of small-pox during his infancy caused a permanent weakness of eyesight. He was under various schoolmasters, including John Prior Estlin [q. v.] and the Rev. Henry Jowett of Little Dunham, Norfolk. In 1806 he entered Trinity Hall, Cambridge, where he learnt as little as if he had passed the time 'at the Clarendon Hotel in Bond Street.' He took the LL.B. degree in 1812, having been called to the bar at Lincoln's Inn on 11 Nov. 1811. His father, who was just leaving the bar, transferred some practice to his son, who also began to make a digest of colonial laws. The third Lord Bathurst, who was in sympathy with the 'Clapham Sect,' allowed him to inspect official records for the digest, and in 1813 appointed him counsel to the colonial department. His duty was to report upon all acts of the colonial legislatures. The work increased, but he was also allowed to practise privately, and in a few years was making 3,000*l.* a year, and in a fair way to the honours of the profession.

On 22 Dec. 1814 he married Jane Catherine, daughter of John Venn, rector of Clapham, one of the founders of the Church Missionary Society. In 1822 Stephen's serious illness caused by overwork. As he was now a father, he decided in 1825 to accept the offer of the post of permanent counsel to the colonial office and to the board of trade, abandoning his private practice. In 1834 he was appointed assistant under-secretary of state for the colonies, and in 1836 under-secretary, giving up his position in the board of trade. The duties became exceedingly onerous, and he devoted himself to them unstintedly. For many years he never left London for a month, and, though afterwards forced to make longer absences, he took a clerk into the country and did business as regularly as in town. He had a very high reputation for his wide knowledge of constitutional law, and was a rapid and decided

administrator. His energy gave him great influence with his superiors, and his colleague, Sir Henry Taylor, says that for many years he 'literally ruled the colonial empire.' The impression of his influence gained him the nicknames of 'King Stephen' and 'Mr. Over-secretary Stephen;' and he was frequently made the scapegoat for real and supposed errors of the colonial office. He had accepted his position partly with a hope of influencing the slavery question. His success in this endeavour raised, according to Taylor, the 'first outcry' against him. When abolition became inevitable, he was called upon to prepare the measure passed in 1833. Unless it could be drawn at once the abolition might be postponed for a year. He therefore on this occasion (and on one other only) broke the Sabbath; and between the noons of Saturday and Monday dictated an elaborate bill of sixty-six sections. At this time he would often dictate as much as ten pages of the 'Edinburgh Review' before breakfast. This effort, however, cost him a severe nervous illness. In later years he was especially concerned in the establishment of responsible government in Canada; and his views are said to have been more liberal than those of the government. He was highly esteemed by his official superiors, but incurred unpopularity in other quarters. A hard worker, he tried to exact hard work from others. He covered a sensitive nature by a formality which kept others at a distance. He was as shy, says Taylor, 'as a wild duck,' but often showed it oddly by talking so continuously as to leave no opening for an answer. In private, as Taylor testifies, his conversation was equally abundant and singularly rich and forcible. Though living in London for many years, he went little into society. The delicacy of his youngest son induced him in 1840 to take a house at Brighton for his family, to which he could make only weekly visits. From 1842 to 1846 he lived at Windsor, in order to send his sons to Eton. The daily journeys to his office made an additional strain. In 1846 he was summoned to Dresden by the illness of his eldest son, who died before his parents could reach him. The shock had serious effects upon his health; and a bad attack in 1847 induced him to resign his office. He was made a K.C.B. and a privy councillor.

Stephen had meanwhile become known as a writer by a series of articles in the 'Edinburgh Review,' the first of which (upon Wilberforce) appeared in April 1838. They were written in the intervals of his official work, generally in the early morning. He carefully disavowed any pretence to profound

M 2

research. The articles had, however, shown considerable historical knowledge as well as literary power. He had partly recovered strength, and was anxious for employment. In June 1849 he was appointed to the regius professorship of modern history at Cambridge, vacant by the death of William Smyth (1765-1849) [q. v.] He delivered a course of lectures upon the history of France during the summers of 1850 and 1851, which were published in 1852, and were warmly praised by De Tocqueville and other competent persons. Another severe illness in the summer of 1850 had forced him to spend a winter abroad; and these lectures were the last work to which he could apply his full power. From 1855 to 1857 he held a professorship at the East India College, Haileybury, which had been sentenced to extinction. He continued to lecture at Cambridge, but the history school then held a very low position; and residence was superfluous. He passed the last years of his life chiefly in London. In 1859 his health showed serious symptoms, and he was ordered to Homburg. Becoming worse, he started homewards, but died at Coblentz on 14 Sept. 1859. He was buried at Kensal Green. Sir James Stephen's widow died in 1875. They had five children: Herbert Venn (1822-1846), Frances Wilberforce (1824-1825), Sir James Fitzjames [q. v.], Leslie, and Caroline Emelia.

Stephen spent his best years and highest powers in work of which it is impossible that any estimate should be formed. He was a most conscientious and energetic official, but the credit or discredit of the policy which he carried out belongs to those whom he advised. In domestic life he impressed all who knew him by his loftiness of principle. He was a man of the strongest family affections. He sacrificed his own comforts for the benefit of his children, and set before them a constant example of absolute devotion to duty. He began life as a strong evangelical, and never avowedly changed; but his experience of the world, his sympathy with other forms of belief, and his interest in the great churchmen of the middle ages led to his holding the inherited doctrine in a latitudinarian sense. He was accused of heresy, when appointed professor at Cambridge, for an 'Epilogue' to his 'Essays,' in which he suggested doubts as to the eternity of hell-fire. The 'Essays' are the work by which he is best known, and show a literary faculty to which he could never give full play. The autobiography of Sir Henry Taylor gives an interesting account of his personal character. Taylor, James Spedding, Mr. Aubrey de Vere, and Nassau Senior were his most intimate friends; but he led a recluse and rather ascetic life, and seldom went into society. A bust by Marochetti is in the National Portrait Gallery.

His works are: 1. 'Essays in Ecclesiastical Biography,' 1849, 2 vols. 8vo; 5th edit. in 1 vol. 1867 (with life, by his son, J. F. Stephen). 2. 'Lectures on the History of France,' 1852, 2 vols. 8vo.

[Family papers; Life by James Fitzjames Stephen prefixed to later editions of Essays; Life of Sir J. F. Stephen, by Leslie Stephen. See also Sir H. Taylor's Autobiography, 1885; Taylor's Correspondence, 1888, ed. Dowden; Macvey Napier's Correspondence, 1879.]   L. S.

STEPHEN, SIR JAMES FITZJAMES (1829-1894), judge, born at Kensington on 3 March 1829, was the second son of Sir James Stephen (1789-1859) [q. v.] He was sent in November 1836 to the school of the Rev. Benjamin Guest at Brighton, and in April 1842 to Eton, which he attended from his father's house in Windsor. He showed from infancy remarkable thoughtfulness and independence of character, though he was not brilliant as a scholar. At Eton he was much bullied and learnt the lesson of taking his own part and resenting injustice. His dislike to the place led to his being entered at King's College, London. He lived with his uncle, Henry Venn (1796-1873) [q. v.], did well in examinations, spoke at a debating society, and was interested by F. D. Maurice's lectures. In 1847 he entered Trinity College, Cambridge. Want of accurate scholarship and of mathematical aptitude made his academical career unsuccessful. He became, however, well known at the Union, where his great rival was the present Sir W. Harcourt, and where his downright oratory earned him the nickname of the 'British Lion.' He was also a member of the 'Apostles,' where he read many papers and formed a close friendship with (Sir) Henry James Sumner Maine [q. v.], then professor of civil law. Failing to win a scholarship, he went abroad with his father in October 1850, abandoning the honours competition. At Paris he attended law courts and became interested in the contrast between French and English procedure. He took an ordinary B.A. degree in the summer of 1851. He now decided to go to the bar, in spite of his father's preference for a clerical career. He entered the Inner Temple, and was called to the bar on 26 Jan. 1854. He found the more technical part of his legal studies uncongenial, but was deeply interested in general principles of jurisprudence. At this time he formed a close friendship with

Henry John Stephen Smith [q. v.], the mathematician, and (Sir) M. E. Grant Duff.

On 19 April 1855 he married Mary Richenda, daughter of the Rev. John William Cunningham [q. v.] Stephen had grown to great physical strength, though he cared little for any athletic exercise except walking, and in mind as in body showed much more strength than flexibility. He had accused himself of sluggishness, and, though he had been a steady worker, had not liked his studies enough to reconcile him to drudgery. From the time of his marriage, however, he became a most energetic worker. He had no connections at the bar when he joined the midland circuit. Business came slowly, though he was engaged in some conspicuous criminal cases. Meanwhile he found it desirable to earn money by journalism. Earlier attempts had brought little success, but at the end of 1855 he began to write for the 'Saturday Review,' then just started. There he found a thoroughly congenial employment in writing social and moral articles, and became very intimate with other contributors, especially George Stovin Venables and Thomas Collett Sandars [q. v.] While occupied with this and other literary work, he was appointed in 1858 secretary to the education commission of that year. The Rev. William Rogers, one of the commissioners, says (Reminiscences, 1888, pp. 129-30) that the success of the commission in 'laying down the future lines of popular education' was due more to their secretary than to any one else. The commission lasted till 1861. In August 1859 his improved position on circuit was shown by his appointment as recorder of Newark. He held the position, worth only 40l. a year, till 1869. In December 1861 he was employed as counsel for Dr. Rowland Williams [q. v.], charged in the court of arches with expressing heretical opinions in one of the 'Essays and Reviews.' His client was convicted upon two counts, but acquitted upon them on appeal to the privy council. On the appeal Williams defended himself. Stephen published his argument in 1862. The case was out of the regular way of business, and his employment was due to his sympathy with the general position of the 'Broadchurch party.' He was a friend of Jowett and Dean Stanley, and at this time had much sympathy for their opinions. He wrote some articles in 'Fraser' upon theological controversies at this time, and sharply criticised Newman's 'Grammar of Assent.' Froude, who was the editor, was a very intimate friend, and Stephen, after Froude, was also one of the warmest friends of Carlyle.

Carlyle's respect was afterwards shown by his appointment of Stephen as his executor. Stephen had also during this period (1860-1863) contributed many articles to the 'Cornhill Magazine,' under Thackeray's editorship. In 1863 Stephen returned to more professional work by publishing his 'General View of the Criminal Law.' He had been long greatly interested in the subject, and published the germ of his book in the 'Cambridge Essays' for 1857.

In 1865 the 'Pall Mall Gazette' was started, and Stephen was invited to become a contributor. For five years he was the chief writer. He wrote sometimes as many as six articles in a week, and in 1868 wrote two-thirds of the articles published. His services were highly valued by the editor, Mr. Frederick Greenwood, and he had a freer hand than elsewhere for the expression of his strongest convictions. Few journalists have succeeded in stamping a paper more distinctly with their personal characteristics, and the paper held a very high and independent position. He was at the same time writing a series of articles upon standard authors in the 'Saturday Review.' His labours were interrupted, though less often than he could have wished, by some important professional employment. His most conspicuous case was in 1867, when he was employed by the 'Jamaica Committee' to apply for the committal of Governor Eyre and other officers charged with excessive severity. He took silk in 1868. In 1869 he received the offer of succeeding Maine as legal member of council in India. He accepted it after some hesitation, caused by his reluctance to leave his family, and the danger to improving prospects at the bar.

Stephen was in India from December 1869 till April 1872. He spent the time in exceedingly hard work, interrupted only by a short illness. His chief duty was to carry on the work of codification, which had been taken up after the suppression of the mutiny. The penal code, drawn by Macaulay in 1834, had been finally enacted in 1860; and other measures had been passed during Maine's tenure of office (1862-9). Several measures of great importance were passed by Stephen, with the co-operation of his colleagues, that which was most exclusively his own being the Evidence Act (passed 12 March 1872). He had, however, to take the chief part in preparing many other acts, some of them of great complexity and involving delicate questions of policy. He had done in two years and a half work which might well have filled five, and thought that the process of codification had been pushed within measurable distance of completion. Some critics held that the work thus rapidly done might be improved in elegance and accuracy, but its value on the whole has been generally admitted. Stephen was profoundly impressed by the great work achieved by the English in India, and the comparatively slovenly nature of English administration and legislation at home. He began during the home voyage to write a series of letters, expressing these conclusions, which appeared in the 'Pall Mall Gazette' in the winter of 1872-3, and were collected as 'Liberty, Equality, Fraternity,' a very forcible protest against some popular opinions. The book shows that in philosophy he was a disciple of Mill and the utilitarians, but in the application to political questions rather followed Hobbes, and was in sympathy with Carlyle's approval of strong government. He agreed, too, with Carlyle in retaining much of the old puritan sentiment, while abandoning the dogmas as indefensible. In spite of this he considered himself to be still on the liberal side, and in the summer of 1873 stood for Dundee as a supporter of Mr. Gladstone's government. He was defeated by a large majority, and his want of sympathy for the popular sentiment led him to see that, although differing on many important points, he was less averse to the conservatives. He had been strongly opposed to democracy since the impression made upon him in 1848.

After his return from India he was much employed in attempts to carry out codification in England. He prepared an Evidence Act with the approval of Sir John Duke (afterwards Lord Coleridge), and a homicide bill with Russell Gurney [q. v.] These, and a bill consolidating the acts relating to the government of India, cost much labour in 1873-4, but never passed into law. He was appointed professor of common law at the inns of court in December 1875, and lectured upon the law of evidence, which led to a 'digest' of that law, published in 1876. In 1877 he published a digest of the criminal law, to which he had been led when preparing a new edition of his 'General View.' His suggestion that this might be converted into a code was favourably received by government, and he was instructed to prepare a measure, which was in 1878 carefully considered by a commission including himself and three judges. A bill to give effect to the code was dropped on a change of government, but again announced in the Queen's speech in 1882. It was never brought before parliament.

Stephen had been employed in some important cases before the judicial committee of the privy council, though his practice was always irregular. He was a member of a commission upon fugitive slaves (1876), a commission upon extradition (1878), and a copyright commission (1878). When he undertook the criminal code he received a virtual promise of a judgeship, and he was accordingly appointed on the first vacancy (3 Jan. 1879). He had been elected a member of the 'Metaphysical Society' on his return from India, and published a few articles which were partly the result of debates in that body upon theological questions. He had by this time entirely abandoned his belief in the orthodox dogmas, though he felt strongly the impracticability of dispensing with the old 'sanctions.' Some letters which he wrote to the 'Times' in 1877-8 in defence of Lord Lytton's policy in India against Lord Lawrence and others also attracted some notice. Lord Lytton, on the eve of his departure as governor-general (March 1876), had made Stephen's acquaintance; they became exceedingly warm friends, maintained a close correspondence, and Stephen heartily admired his friend's general conduct of Indian affairs. Soon after his return from India he took a house at Anaverna, near Ravensdale in Ireland, where he spent his vacations till near the end of his life, and employed much of his leisure upon literary labours.

On becoming a judge Stephen set himself to work upon the new edition of his 'General View,' which gradually developed into the 'History of the Criminal Law,' a much larger book, in which very little of the original remains. It was published in 1883, and represents a great amount of original inquiry. The labour superadded to his judicial duties sensibly tried his strength. He turned for relief to an historical inquiry, and his interest in India led him to contemplate an account of Warren Hastings's impeachment. He began, by way of experiment, to write upon the Nuncomar incident, and in 1885 published an investigation which involves a very searching criticism of Macaulay's famous article. The publication was followed by a serious illness (April 1885), which had to be met by careful regimen and by limited indulgence in hard work. He was, however, fully up to his regular work, and in the autumn of 1886 became chairman of a commission to inquire into the ordnance department. A disease which had been slowly developing began to affect his mental powers. Upon hearing that public notice had been taken of supposed failure, he consulted his physician, and by his advice at once resigned in April

1891. He received a baronetcy in recognition of his services. From this period he gradually declined, though he was still able to collect some of his old 'Saturday Review' articles for publication. He died at the Red House Park, Ipswich, on 11 March 1894.

In January 1877 Stephen was made K.C.S.I. He received the honorary degree of D.C.L. at Oxford in 1878, and of LL.D. at Edinburgh in 1884. He was made an honorary fellow of Trinity College, Cambridge, in 1885, and corresponding member of the French Institute in 1888.

Stephen was pre-eminently a man of masculine or, as his friends often said, Johnsonian power of mind. His massive common-sense implied some want of subtlety. His energy enabled him to turn out an immense quantity of valuable work, marred in some ways by want of finish and done at high pressure. In codifying he was carrying out the theories of his teachers, Austin and Bentham, and his failure to get his schemes adopted in England strengthened his predilection for strong government. His position, both in political and theological matters, made him an assailant of popular views, and he always expressed himself as vigorously and frankly as possible. As a judge his dislike of technicalities and subtleties was some disqualification in the nicer matters of the law, but he was respected for his downright force, and in criminal cases had the highest authority from his wide knowledge and unmistakable love of fairplay. A hatred of brutality gave him the reputation for severity; but no one was more anxious to avoid every chance of hasty and unjust judgments. In private life he was conspicuous not only for domestic affection, but for the warmth of his friendships and his generous support of the unfortunate.

Sir James Fitzjames Stephen's works are: 1. 'Essays by a Barrister' (anon. from the 'Saturday Review'), 1862, 8vo. 2. 'Defence of the Rev. Rowland Williams,' 1862, 8vo. 3. 'A general View of the Criminal Law of England,' 1863, 8vo. A so-called second edition of this published in 1890 is really a distinct book. 4. 'Liberty, Equality, Fraternity,' 1873; 2nd edit. (with additions), 1874, 8vo. 5. 'A Digest of the Law of Evidence,' 1876; reprinted with alterations in 1876 (twice) and 1877; 2nd edit. 1881; 3rd edit. 1887; 4th edit. 1893. 6. 'A Digest of the Criminal Law (Crimes and Punishments),' 1877, 1879, 1883, 1887 and 1896, 8vo. 7. 'A Digest of the Law of Criminal Procedure in Indictable Offences,' 1883, 8vo, by Sir J. F. Stephen and Herbert (now Sir Herbert) Stephen. 8. 'A History of the Criminal Law of England,' 1883, 3 vols. 8vo. 9. 'The Story of Nuncomar and Sir Elijah Impey,' 1885, 2 vols. 8vo. 10. 'Horæ Sabaticæ: a reprint of articles contributed to the "Saturday Review,"' 1892, three series. Stephen contributed many articles to magazines, of which a list is given in the life by Mr. Leslie Stephen (pp. 484–6).

Stephen left a wife, two sons, and four daughters. His eldest son is now Sir Herbert Stephen. His second son, JAMES KENNETH STEPHEN (1859–1892), was born 25 Feb. 1859. He showed great promise and won a foundation scholarship at Eton in 1871. He did well in examinations, but was better known for the intellectual ability displayed in a school periodical, the 'Etonian.' He was famous at the game of football 'at the wall,' and always retained the warmest affection for his school. He became a scholar of King's College, Cambridge, in 1878, won prizes and the Whewell scholarship (1881), and was in the first class of the historical tripos, and the second class of the law tripos, in 1881. He was elected fellow of his college in 1885. A dissertation upon 'International Law,' written as an exercise for this, was published in 1884. At Cambridge he was known as an 'apostle,' and was president of the Union (1882), where he won an unusual reputation for oratory. He appeared as Ajax in a Greek play, a part for which he was fitted by a massive frame and striking face. In 1883 he was for a short time at Sandringham as tutor to the future Duke of Clarence, who died in 1892. He was called to the bar in 1884, but devoted most of his energy to journalism. His high reputation as a speaker led his friends to anticipate for him a career of parliamentary success, and his singular sweetness and frankness gained him innumerable friends. An accidental blow upon the head at the end of 1886 inflicted injuries not perceived for some time. In the early part of 1888 he brought out a weekly paper called 'The Reflector,' chiefly written by himself. He now wished to devote himself chiefly to literature, and was appointed by his father to a clerkship of assize on the South Wales circuit. Meanwhile it became evident that the accident was affecting his brain. He gave up his place, and resolved in October 1890 to settle at Cambridge. He gave lectures, spoke at the Union, and was much beloved by many companions. In 1891 he wrote an able pamphlet, 'Living Languages,' in defence of the compulsory study of Greek at the universities. In the same year he published two little volumes of verse, 'Lapsus Calami,'

and 'Quo Musa tendis,' chiefly collections of previous essays. The first went through five editions, and both were republished as 'Lapsus Calami, and other verses,' with a life by his brother Herbert, and one or two additions in 1896. In November 1891 his disease suddenly took a dangerous form, and he died 3 Feb. 1892. He was buried at Kensal Green, where his father and his grandparents, Sir James and Lady Stephen, are also buried. A brass has been placed in King's College Chapel to his memory; another is in the ante-chapel at Eton.

[Family papers; Leslie Stephen's Life of Sir James Fitzjames Stephen, 1895, 8vo.]   L. S.

STEPHENS. [See also STEEVENS and STEVENS.]

STEPHENS, ALEXANDER (1757–1821), biographical writer, born in 1757, was son of Thomas Stephens, provost of Elgin. His mother's maiden name was Fordyce. At the age of eighteen he left Aberdeen University for the West Indies, and stayed some time in Jamaica. On his return to England he bought a commission in the 84th regiment, but never joined it. At twenty-one he entered the Middle Temple, but gave more time to literature than to law, though he for some time conducted a legal journal called 'The Templar,' and is said to have pleaded successfully before the House of Lords the claim of the Duke of Roxburgh (a distant relative) to the title [see KER, JAMES INNES-, fifth DUKE OF ROXBURGH]. Stephens's first essay in literature was a poem on Jamaica. In 1803 he published in two quarto volumes, with maps and appendices, a 'History of the Wars which arose out of the French Revolution.' The narrative is clear and impartial, but somewhat diffuse. In 1813 appeared his chief work, the 'Memoirs of John Horne Tooke,' 2 vols. 8vo, founded on original letters and papers, as well as upon an acquaintance of several years. The quarrel between Tooke and Wilkes and the controversy with 'Junius' are dealt with in great detail, and the latter part of the book contains reports of conversations with Tooke at Wimbledon. Stephens's book had been preceded only by the wretched compilation of W. Hamilton Reid. It remains the best life of Horne Tooke.

Stephens was a frequent contributor to the 'Analytical Review' and the 'Monthly Magazine' of literary and biographical articles. The 'Monthly Magazine' published after his death (October 1821–August 1824) 'Stephensinna,' a series of articles consisting of anecdotes of his contemporaries collected by him. Stephens edited the first five volumes of the 'Annual Biography and Obituary,'

and contributed most of the contents of the first nine volumes of 'Public Characters' issued by Sir Richard Phillips in 1823. He published numerous anonymous pamphlets, including a brief memoir of Curran (1817). As a biographer he was painstaking, accurate, and scrupulously fair. This is the more to his credit inasmuch as he was a strong whig. He lived at first near Primrose Hill, but afterwards built for himself Park House in Upper Church Lane, Chelsea. Stephens died at his house in Chelsea on 24 Feb. 1821, and was buried 'in the new burial-ground south of the new church.' By his marriage in 1792 with Miss Lewin, daughter of Samuel Lewin of Broadfield House, Hertfordshire, he had three children. One of his sons, Thomas Algernon, was wounded at Waterloo, where he carried the colours of the 3rd battalion of royal Scots.

[Ann. Biogr. and Obituary, 1822, pp. 412–22 (with list of works); Faulkner's Chelsea, i. 151, 254, 273–4; Ann. Reg. 1821 (App. to Chron.), p. 231; Notes and Queries, 2nd ser. xii. 71; Allibone's Dict. of Engl. Lit. ii. 2237; Brit. Mus. Cat.; Dict. of Living Authors.]   G. LE G. N.

STEPHENS, CATHERINE, COUNTESS OF ESSEX (1794–1882), vocalist and actress, the daughter of Edward Stephens, a carver and gilder in Park Street, Grosvenor Square, was born on 18 Sept. 1794. Having shown, like her elder sisters (for one of whom see below), musical capacity, she was placed in 1807 under the charge of Gesualdo Lanza [q. v.], with whom she remained five years. Under his care she sang in Bath, Bristol, Southampton, Ramsgate, Margate, and other places, appearing early in 1812 in subordinate parts at the Pantheon as member of an Italian opera company, headed by Madame Bertinotti Radicati. At the close, in 1812, of her engagement with Lanza, her father placed her under Thomas Welsh [q. v.], as whose pupil she sang anonymously on 17 and 19 Nov. in Manchester. On 23 Sept. 1813 she appeared at Covent Garden as Mandane in 'Artaxerxes,' obtaining a conspicuous success, especially in the airs 'Checked by duty, racked by love,' and 'The soldier tired of war's alarms,' and being compared to Catalani and Mrs. Billington (cf. Theatrical Inquisitor, 23 Sept.). She was depicted as rather above middle size, and 'inclinable to the embonpoint,' looking older and graver than her years, and was credited with pathos, tenderness, and sweetness. On 22 Oct. she sang as Polly in the 'Beggar's Opera,' and on 12 Nov. as Clara in the 'Duenna.' Rosetta in 'Love in a Village' was also taken. Her marked success evoked a fierce polemic between Lanza and Welsh, who both claimed the honour of instructing her. At the concert of ancient music in March 1814 she was assigned the principal soprano songs, and she sang later in the year in the festivals in Norwich and Birmingham.

At Covent Garden, where she remained with but few interruptions from her first appearance in 1813 down to 1822, she at first received 12l. a week; this was successively advanced to 20l. and 25l. a week. On 1 Feb. 1814 she was the original Mrs. Cornflower in the 'Farmer's Wife' of Charles Dibdin, jun. She played Ophelia to the Hamlet of Young and that of Kemble, and was injudicious enough on the first occasion (21 March) to introduce into the character the song of 'Mad Bess,' for which she was hissed. She played Matilda in 'Richard Cœur de Lion,' and on 31 May, as Desdemona to Young's Othello, sang the original air of 'My mother had a maid called Barbara.' On 1 Feb. 1815 she was the original Donna Isidora in Dimond's 'Brother and Sister;' on 7 April Donna Orynthia in the 'Noble Outlaw,' founded on the 'Pilgrim' of Beaumont and Fletcher; and on 7 June Eucharis in 'Telemachus.' Next season she was Sylvia in 'Cymon,' Hermia in 'Midsummer Night's Dream,' Imogen, Cora in 'Columbus,' and on 12 March 1816 the first Lucy Bertram in Terry's adaptation 'Guy Mannering.' On 23 Sept. she was the original Sophia Fidget in Tobin's posthumous 'Yours or Mine,' on 12 Nov. the first Zelinda in Morton's 'Slave,' on 27 Feb. 1817 Laurina in the 'Heir of Vironi,' on 15 April Rosalind in Dimond's 'Conquest of Taranto,' on 20 May Zerlina in the 'Libertine' of Pocock, and she played Eudocia in the 'Humorous Lieutenant' and Peggy in the 'Gentle Shepherd.' Among many original parts of no importance in the next season stands conspicuous Diana Vernon in Pocock's 'Rob Roy Macgregor.' She also played Cowslip in the 'Agreeable Surprise.' On the first production of the 'Marriage of Figaro' on 6 March 1819 she was Susanna to the Figaro of Liston, and in that of the 'Heart of Midlothian,' by Terry, on 17 April, she was Effie Deans. On 14 Dec. she played Adriana in the 'Comedy of Errors,' converted by Reynolds into an opera. In Terry's 'Antiquary' on 25 Jan. 1820 she was the first Isabella Wardour, and in an adaptation of 'Ivanhoe,' which followed on 2 March, she was Rowena. Morton's 'Henri Quatre, or Paris in the Olden Time,' on 22 April, furnished her with a part as Florence St. Leon. In 'Don John, or the Two Violettas,' 20 Feb. 1821, an opera founded by Reynolds on the 'Chances,' altered from Fletcher by the Duke of Buckingham, she was the second

Violetta. She also played Dorinda in Dryden's 'Tempest.' On 14 Feb. 1822 she was the first Annot Lyle in Pocock's adaptation 'Montrose or the Children of the Mist,' and on 11 May Nourjadee on the production of Colman's 'Law of Java.'

The following season she joined Elliston at Drury Lane, and was purposely, it is said, kept in the background. Curious alleged instances of Elliston's behaviour are preserved, such as his fining her for not coming to the rehearsal of the pantomime, not in order to play, which was outside her contract, but to swell with her voice the chorus. For her benefit on 27 April 1823 she played Annette in the 'Lord of the Manor.' In Beazley's 'Philandering,' on 13 Jan. 1824, she was the first Emile, and in Reynolds's operatic version of the 'Merry Wives of Windsor,' on 20 Feb., Mrs. Ford. On the production of an anonymous version of 'Faustus' on 16 May 1825 she was the Adine (Margaret). Malvina in Macfarren's 'Malvina' was seen on 28 Jan. 1826; Edith Plantagenet in 'Knights of the Cross' followed on 29 May. Gulnare in Dimond's 'Englishmen in India' was seen on 27 Jan. 1827. In the following season she was again at Covent Garden, where she played Blanch Mackay in 'Carron Side, or the Fête Champêtre,' on 27 May 1828. High as was the reputation Miss Stephens had made in opera, it was still higher as a concert singer. She was playing with Duruset in Dublin in July 1821 and again in 1825, and in Edinburgh in 1814. She also visited Liverpool and other places. Until her retirement in 1835 she occupied the highest position at the best concerts and festivals. On 19 April 1838 Miss Stephens married, at 9 Belgrave Square, George Capell Coningsby, fifth earl of Essex, an octogenarian widower, who died on 23 April 1839. Lady Essex survived him forty-three years, taking until near the end an interest in theatrical matters. She died on 22 Feb. 1882 in the house in which she was married, and was buried at Kensal Green.

Miss Stephens was held to have the sweetest soprano voice of her time—'full, rich, round, lovely'—a natural manner, a simple style, disfigured by no affectation. In oratorio she lacked passion, but was always pure, sensible, and graceful. As a ballad singer she was unequalled, and her rendering of 'Auld Robin Gray,' 'Savourneen Deelish,' 'W'are a' Noddin',' 'A Highland Lad,' and a hundred others, and of songs such as 'Angels ever bright and fair' and 'If guiltless blood,' has not been surpassed. Hazlitt, who spoke of her and Kean as the only theatrical favourites he had, wrote his first theatrical criticism on her in the 'Morning Chronicle.' Mrs. Billington told him his idol would never make a singer, but, after hearing her as Polly and as Mandane, arrived at the conclusion that she sang some things as they could never be sung again. Of the same performances Leigh Hunt said that they 'are like nothing else on the stage, and leave all competition far behind;' adding that 'the graceful awkwardness and *naïveté* of her manner, more captivating than the most finished elegance, complete the charm.' Talfourd recalled the days when he heard her send forth 'a stream of such delicious sound as he had never found proceeding from human lips.' That first impression was never changed. Oxberry bestows more unmixed eulogy upon her than upon any other actress with whom he deals. On her retirement from professional life she carried with her a character for virtue, kindness, and generosity such as few actresses have enjoyed.

A portrait painted by John Jackson hangs in the National Portrait Gallery, London; another by Dewilde, as Mandane in 'Artaxerxes,' is in the Mathews collection of the Garrick Club, which contains also an anonymous portrait. A portrait of her as Rosetta in 'Love in a Village,' showing a bright, sparkling, intelligent face, accompanies the memoir in Oxberry's 'Dramatic Biography.' Other portraits of her were painted by Linnell and Sir William John Newton (cf. *Cat. Victorian Exhib.* Nos. 414, 427).

A Miss Stephens, possibly an elder sister, made, as Polly in the 'Beggar's Opera,' a very successful first appearance on the stage on 29 Nov. 1799, and played in 1800 and 1801 Sophia in 'Of Age To-morrow,' Violetta in the 'Egyptian Festival,' Blanche in Mrs. Plowden's 'Virginia,' Rosetta in 'Love in a Village,' and other parts.

[Genest's Account of the English Stage; Oxberry's Dramatic Biography, vol. ii.; Dramatic Essays by Hazlitt; Clark Russell's Representative Actors; Theatrical Inquisitor, various years; Grove's Dict. of Music; Georgian Era; Dibdin's Edinburgh Stage; Biography of the British Stage, 1824; New Monthly Mag. various years; History of the Theatre Royal, Dublin; Liverpool Dramatic Censor; Burke's Peerage; Notes and Queries, 5th ser. xii. 329, 357, 417.]

J. K.

STEPHENS, CHARLES EDWARD (1821–1892), musician, who was born at 12 Portman Place (now Edgware Road) on 18 March 1821, was nephew to Catherine Stephens, countess of Essex [q. v.] He studied the pianoforte and violin under J. M. Rost, Cipriani Potter, F. Smith, and H.

Blagrove, and theory under James Alexander Hamilton [q. v.] After the completion of his school career, he was organist successively to St. Mark's, Myddelton Square; Holy Trinity, Paddington; St. John's, Hampstead; St. Clement Danes and St. Saviour's, Paddington. The last-named post he resigned in 1875. Stephens was a fellow or member of most of the English musical institutions, an original member of the Musical Association in 1874 and treasurer of the Philharmonic in 1880, and of the South-Eastern Section of the National Society of Professional Musicians. He died in London on 13 July 1892, and was buried at Kensal Green.

Stephens was an accomplished musician, a good teacher, an excellent pianist, and in his younger days a capable violinist. His compositions, which are numerous, include a symphony in G minor, played at the Philharmonic in 1891, and a quantity of pianoforte and chamber music. In 1860 Stephens gained both the first and second prizes for string quartets offered by Trinity College, London. He was a clever speaker and writer, as his papers read before the Musical Association bear witness.

[Overture, iii. 86; Brown's Dict. of Musicians furnishes a list of Stephens's compositions; British Musical Biography; Musical Times; Grove's Dict. of Music and Musicians.]

R. H. L.

STEPHENS, EDWARD (d. 1706), pamphleteer, was son of Edward Stephens of Norton and Cherington, Gloucestershire, by Mary, daughter of John Raynerford of Staverton, Northamptonshire. He practised for some time at the common-law bar, but afterwards took holy orders. Probably he held no benefice. He published a great number of pamphlets on political and theological subjects, displaying great candour and embodying much valuable research. His friend, Thomas Barlow [q. v.], bishop of Lincoln, considered him an honest and learned lawyer, an Thomas Hearne, the antiquary, says tha he was 'a good common lawyer, great with Judge Hale.' The only record of Stephens's legal ability is a pamphlet published in 1687, with dedication to Jeffreys, entitled 'Relief of Apprentices wronged by their Masters, how by our law it may effectually be given and obtained.' He welcomed the Revolution in 'The True English Government and Misgovernment of the four last Kings, with the ill consequence thereof briefly noted in two little Tracts,' 1689, 4to (the first of which appeared under the pseudonym Socrates Christianus). But Stephens animadverted upon the early conduct of the new government in 'Reflections upon the Occurrences of the last Year' (1689), attributing the want of success in Ireland to division of counsel; complaining that James II's advisers remained unpunished; and denouncing the 'scuffling for preferments in the church.' A Dutch version of the 'Reflections' appeared in 1690. It produced a reply, to which Stephens rejoined in 'Authority abused in the Vindication of the last Year's Transactions, and the Abuses detected' (1690). In the last-named brochure Stephens says that he had joined King William at Sherborne, and assures him of the devotion of himself and his five sons. In 1690 he also published 'A plain Relation of the late Action at Sea between the English and French Fleets from 22 June to 5 July . . . with Reflections.' This was drawn up from information given by 'an honest volunteer seaman' on board the English fleet, and has subjoined to it a copy of a letter written by a Frenchman serving in De Tourville's squadron. It was translated into Dutch the same year, and was followed by 'Reasons for the Tryal of the Earl of Torrington by Impeachment,' an account of his conduct in the battle described.

Stephens devoted most of his later years to theological controversy. As early as 1674 he had written against the Romanists a tract entitled 'Popish Policies and Practices. . . . Translated out of the famous Thuanus and other writers of the Roman Communion.' In the year of his death he says he has been engaged more than twelve years in contests with the papists, who were 'so gravell'd with one or two little papers' as to be obliged to fall back upon 'little tricks, feigned excuses, forgeries, needless charges at law, bribing and corrupting witnesses, &c., and at last forfeiture of no less than 3,000l.' The 'little papers' referred to are probably 'A True Account of the unaccountable Dealings of some Roman Catholic Missioners of this Nation,' 1703, and some other pamphlets on the same subject, one of which was addressed to the Right Rev. Bishop G[ifford], and the rest of the English bishops of the Roman communion.' Stephens also attacked the quakers. George Keith and other leaders had a friendly conference with him, and consented to circulate one of his tracts at their annual meeting, but declined further controversy. 'Achan and Elymas; or the Troublers of Israel . . . detected among the leaders and managers of three dangerous Sects,' 1704, is mainly directed against the quakers, though 'Roman Catholic Missioners' and 'Church and State Deists' are coupled with them. In spite of his con-

troversial publications, Stephens himself propounded plans for conciliating both Romanists and dissenters. His own religious views appear to have been eclectic. He disliked Erastianism even more than Romanism or the quakers, and assailed it in 'The Spirit of the Church Faction detected,' 1691, and other writings. Hearne says that he 'was for the Greek rather than the Western church,' and thinks he died a member of the former.

Stephens's 'The Liturgy of the Ancients represented' was originally published in 1696. It was reprinted in 1848 in Peter Hall's 'Fragmenta Liturgica.' His repute as a theologian is indicated by the appellation 'Father Stephens' or 'Abbat Stephens,' and by his correspondence with Johann Ernst Grabe.

Stephens died in April 1706, and was buried at Enfield by the care of his son-in-law, Dr. Udall, who lived there. He married Mary, daughter of Lord-chief-justice Sir Matthew Hale [q. v.] In 1676 he wrote prefaces to Hale's 'Contemplations, Moral and Divine.'

Besides the works mentioned Stephens published: 1. 'Observations upon a Treatise of Humane Reason,' 1675, 12mo. 2. 'The Apology of Socrates Christianus,' 1700. 3. 'A Collection of Modern Relations concerning Witches and Witchcraft,' prefaced by Hale's 'Meditations concerning the Mercy of God in preserving us from the Malice and Power of Evil Angels,' and 'Questions concerning Witchcraft,' 1693, 4to. 4. 'A Choice Collection of Papers relating to State Affairs during the late Revolution,' 1703, 8vo; a second volume was promised, but not issued. 5. 'A Wonder of the Bishop of Meaux [Bossuet] upon the Perusal of Dr. Bull's Books considered and answered,' 1704. In 1702 he printed a general title and a preface to be bound up with a selection from his tracts (of which very few copies were printed), and gave a copy to the Bodleian.

[Reliquiæ Hearnianæ, ed. Bliss, i. 63 n. (complete list of works), iii. 36, 37; Fosbroke's Gloucestershire, i. 320; Stephens's Works; Brit. Mus. Cat.]   G. Le G. N.

STEPHENS, EDWARD BOWRING (1815–1882), sculptor, son of James Stephens, a statuary, was born at Exeter on 10 Dec. 1815. His artistic training was begun under the guidance of John Gendall [q. v.], a local draughtsman and landscape-painter, but in 1835 he was sent to London and became a pupil of Edward Hodges Baily [q. v.], the sculptor. He was admitted a student of the Royal Academy in 1836, and in 1837 he gained a silver medal at the Society of Arts for a small original model of 'Ajax defying the Gods.' His earliest exhibited works were at the Royal Academy in 1838, when he sent 'Narcissus,' 'An Arcadian Nymph,' 'Maternal Love,' and a bust, and these were followed in 1839 by 'Diana' and another bust. Early in the latter year he went to Italy, and worked for some time in Rome. After an absence of nearly three years he returned to England, and lived for a time in Exeter, where he executed a life-size statue in marble of Lord Rolle. He removed to London in 1842, and in 1843 was awarded the gold medal of the Royal Academy for a small relievo representing 'The Battle of the Centaurs and Lapithæ.' In 1845 he assisted in the decoration of the summer pavilion at Buckingham Palace. Two groups, 'Satan Vanquished' and 'Satan tempting Eve,' attracted some notice in the Great Exhibition of 1851. Apart from his busts, among which were those of Lord Palmerston, Bishop Phillpotts, the Earl of Devon, Earl Fortescue, Viscount Ebrington, and other persons of note, he contributed to the exhibitions of the Royal Academy many groups and statues— 'Eve contemplating Death' in 1853; 'The Angel,' and 'Evening: Going to the Bath,' in 1861; the Earl of Lonsdale (now at Lowther Castle) in 1863; 'Euphrosyne and Cupid' in 1865; 'Cupid's Cruise' in 1867; 'Blackberry Picking: the Thorn' in 1870; 'Zingari' in 1871; 'Eve's Dream' in 1873; 'The Bathers' in 1877; statuettes of 'Ophelia' and 'Lady Godiva' in 1879; and 'Shielding the Helpless' in 1883.

Besides these works he executed in 1862 a colossal marble statue of Sir Thomas Dyke Acland, placed on Northernhay, Exeter, where is also a seated statue in marble of John Dinham. His native city further possesses by him a colossal marble statue of Earl Fortescue, erected in the Castle Yard; a statue of the Earl of Devon in Bedford Circus, and one of the prince consort in the Albert Memorial Museum. His group in bronze of 'The Deerstalker,' exhibited at the Royal Academy in 1876, and generally regarded as his finest work, was purchased by public subscription and placed at the entrance to Northernhay. He produced also statues of Alfred the Great, for the Egyptian Hall of the Mansion House, London; the Duke of Bedford, for Tavistock; General Lord Saltoun, for Fraserburgh; Alfred Rooker, for Guildhall Square, Plymouth; Sir John Cordy Burrows, for Brighton; and a recumbent figure of Elizabeth, countess of Devon, for her monument in Powderham church, Devonshire. These were very successful works, and greatly increased his reputation.

Stephens was elected an associate of the Royal Academy in 1864, but it was generally believed that his election was due to his having been confounded with Alfred Stevens [q. v.], the sculptor of the Wellington monument in St. Paul's Cathedral. He died at 110 Buckingham Palace Road, London, on 10 Nov. 1882.

[Architect, 1882, ii. 315; Builder, 1882, ii. 669; Art Journal, 1882, p. 379; Pycroft's Art in Devonshire, 1883; Men of the Time, 1879; Royal Academy Exhibition Catalogues, 1838–83.]

R. E. G.

STEPHENS, GEORGE (1800–1851), dramatist, was born at Chelsea on 8 March 1800. In 1835 he published 'The Manuscript of Erdély,' a romance, 3 vols. This was followed by 'The Voice of the Pulpit, being Sermons on various subjects,' 1839 (preface dated Bromley Hall, Herts, 28 Nov. 1838); 'Gertrude and Beatrice, or the Queen of Hungary: a tragedy in five acts,' 1839; and 'Père La Chaise, or the Confessor,' 1840, 3 vols.

On 26 Aug. 1841 his tragedy 'Martinuzzi, or the Hungarian Daughter,' was produced at the English Opera House (now the Lyceum Theatre). By the introduction of songs it was speciously converted into a musical drama, and brought out in evasion of the law which limited the performance of five-act dramas to the patent houses and the Haymarket. Samuel Phelps and Mrs. Warner took the chief rôles, and the piece kept the stage for a month, although the critics thought little of its merits. In 1846 he wrote 'Dramas for the Stage,' two privately printed volumes containing 'Nero,' 'Forgery,' 'Sensibility,' and 'Philip Basil, or a Poet's Fate,' four tragedies; 'Self-Glorification,' a Chinese play; and 'Rebecca and her Daughter,' a comedy. He also wrote the introduction to the 'Church of England Quarterly Review,' 1837 (i. 1–34), besides an article, 'The Slumber of the Pulpit.' His further works were 'The Patriot, a tragedy,' 1849; and 'The Justification of War as the Medium of Civilisation,' 1850. In later life he suffered reverses of fortune. He died at Pratt Terrace, Camden Town, London, on 15 Oct. 1851. His widow Ellen died on 11 Aug. 1866, aged 56. By her he had a son and daughter.

To Stephens have been attributed three works published under the pseudonym of 'St. John Dorset.' Two of them, however, 'The Vampire: a tragedy,' 1821, and 'Montezuma: a tragedy,' 1822, appear to have been written by Hugo John Belfour [q. v.]; while the third, a volume of poems, was the joint production of Belfour and Stephens.

[Tallis's Dramatic Mag. May 1851, p. 197; Gent. Mag. 1851 ii. 661, 1852 i. 2.]   G. C. B.

STEPHENS, GEORGE (1813–1895), runic archæologist, son of John Stephens of Ongar, Wesleyan minister, by his wife, Rebecca Eliza Rayner, was born at Liverpool on 13 Dec. 1813. Joseph Rayner Stephens [q. v.] was his brother. George was educated at private schools and at University College, London, of which he was one of the earliest students. At an early age he became deeply interested in the study of English dialects. His brother settled at Stockholm in 1826, and directed his attention to Scandinavian languages and literature. Finding that the Scandinavian languages afforded valuable aid in the elucidation of dialectal etymology, he was led to the erroneous conclusion that English was essentially a Scandinavian and not a German language. This paradox he never abandoned, and in his later years he maintained it with a zeal which owed something of its intensity to his anti-German political prejudices. He contributed several articles on church establishments and similar questions to the 'Christian Advocate' in 1832 and 1833. In 1834 he married Maria, daughter of Edward Bennett of Brentwood, and in the same year took up his residence in Stockholm, where he found employment as a teacher of English. His first separate publication, 'An Outline Sketch of Shakspere's "Tempest," with Remarks,' appeared in 1836, and was followed in 1837 by 'Conversational Outlines of English Grammar,' and an edition of Washington Irving's 'Voyages and Discoveries of the Companions of Columbus,' intended as a reading-book for Swedish students of English. In 1841 he published an English poetical version of Tegner's 'Frithiof,' a translation of Mellin's 'Guide-book to Stockholm,' and a pocket dictionary of English and Swedish. He was one of the founders of the Society for the Publication of Ancient Swedish Texts (Svenska Fornskriftsällskapet), established in 1843, for which in succeeding years he edited from the manuscripts several important works of early Swedish literature. In 1844 he was associated with G. O. Hylten-Cavallius in the publication of a valuable work on Swedish popular tales. His translation of the Anglo-Saxon poem on 'The Phœnix,' in the alliterative metre of the original, published in the thirtieth volume of the 'Archæologia' (1844), attracted attention by its extreme ingenuity, though in other respects it is deserving of little commendation, being written in a pseudo-archaic dialect almost unintelligible to ordinary English readers. The jargon adopted in this translation was still further developed in Stephens's later English writings, which abound in anglicised Scandinavian words such as 'mole' for language, and in foreign idioms. His last considerable publication before leaving Sweden was a catalogue of the most important English and French manuscripts in the royal library at Stockholm ('Förteckning öfver de förnämsta Brittiska och Fransyska handskrifterna uti Kongl. Biblioteket i Stockholm.' Stockholm, 1847, 8vo), which is a work of great merit and usefulness, though disfigured by some curious mistakes. An admirable scheme which he drew up for an organised investigation into the popular antiquities of Iceland was adopted by the Northern Antiquarian Society of Copenhagen in 1845, and printed in the 'Antiquarisk Tidsskrift,' 1843–5, pp. 191–2.

In 1851 Stephens was appointed lector in English language and literature at the university of Copenhagen, and in the following year he was in addition appointed lector in Anglo-Saxon. A collection of the historical and legendary ballads of Sweden, prepared by him in collaboration with G. O. Hylten-Cavallius, appeared in 1853. In 1855, having previously become naturalised as a Danish subject, he was made professor of English and Anglo-Saxon in the university. During the next few years he published several poetical works, including a 'melodrama' in five acts, entitled 'Revenge, or Woman's Love' (1857), which was accompanied by a volume containing the music to the songs introduced in the piece, most of the airs being composed by himself. In 1860 he published, for the first time, a fragment of the Anglo-Saxon poem of 'Waldere,' discovered by Professor E. C. Werlauff in the university library.

In 1866 appeared the first volume of the work on which Stephens's claim to remembrance principally rests, 'The Old Northern Runic Monuments of Scandinavia and England, now first collected and deciphered.' The second volume was published in 1868, and the third in 1884. A fourth volume is stated to have been in an advanced state of preparation at the time of his death, but has not yet (1898) appeared. An abridgment of the first three volumes, containing copies of the most important inscriptions, was published in 1884, under the title of 'A Handbook to the Old Northern Runic Monuments.' The conscientious labour which Stephens devoted to securing accurate copies of the inscriptions is deserving of the highest praise, and as a storehouse of materials for runic studies, his work is invaluable. On the other hand, his own contributions to the interpretation of the inscriptions are almost worthless, owing to his want of accurate philological knowledge. His method of translation consisted in identifying the words of the inscriptions with any words of similar appearance that he could discover in the dictionaries of ancient or modern Scandinavian languages, and then forcing them into some plausible meaning without regard to grammar. Even with respect to the transliteration of the characters, he rejected some of the most securely established results of former investigations, assigning, for instance, the value of A to the rune which is well known to have represented the R sound derived from an earlier Z. His unscientific procedure was criticised with severity by philologists trained in a more rigorous school, and for some years after the publication of the first volume of his work he was engaged in a fierce controversy with one of the ablest runic scholars of the time, Professor L. Wimmer. Although at a later period he showed more respect for sound scholarship, he never abandoned his loose and arbitrary methods of translation. A ludicrous illustration of the worthlessness of his principles of decipherment is afforded by his treatment of the inscription found at Brough in Westmoreland, which he declared to be written in Anglian runes, and translated in accordance with that supposition. When it was pointed out that the inscription consisted of five Greek hexameters, Stephens frankly acknowledged his blunder, though the acknowledgment involved the condemnation of nearly all that he had done in the decipherment of the inscriptions.

The bibliography of Stephens's writings in Erslev's 'Forfatterlexicon,' which extends only to the year 1868, fills eight closely printed pages. He was a constant contributor to many periodicals, both Scandinavian and English, including the 'Gentleman's Magazine' and 'Notes and Queries.' Many of his articles and pamphlets relate to questions of political controversy, in which he was passionately interested, his antipathy to English radicalism being extremely violent. He furnished a large number of quotations, principally from the literature of the sixteenth and seventeenth centuries, to the materials for the 'New English Dictionary.' It is stated that during the last years of his life he was engaged on a glossary to the old Northumbrian gospels, which has not yet (1898) been published.

Stephens was a fellow of the Society of Antiquaries, and a member of many learned societies in Scandinavia and England. In 1877 he received the degree of Ph.D. from the university of Upsala, and he was a knight of the orders of the Northern Star, the Dannebrog, and St. Olaf. He resigned his professorship in 1893, and died at Copenhagen on 9 Aug. 1895.

[Erslev's Forfatterlexicon, 3rd Suppl.; Nordisk Familjebok, vol. xv.; Hofberg's Svenskt Biogr. Handlexicon; Hodgkin in Archæologia Æliana, xviii. 50 ff.; Times 10 and 12 Aug. 1895; Gent. Mag. 1852, i 162-3.] H. B.

STEPHENS, HENRY (1795–1874), agricultural writer, born at Keerpoy in Bengal on 25 July 1795, was the son of Andrew Stephens, a surgeon in the service of the East India Company, who died at Calcutta on 26 Aug. 1806. Henry returned to Scotland at an early age, and was educated at the parochial and grammar schools of Dundee and at the academy there, under Thomas Duncan, subsequently professor of mathematics at St. Andrews. After spending some time at the university of Edinburgh, he in 1815 boarded himself with a Berwickshire agriculturist, 'one of the best farmers of that well-farmed county,' George Brown of Whitsome Hill. Here he gained that thorough and practical knowledge of agriculture which characterises his writings. After three years at Whitsome Hill, Stephens made for about a year (1818–19) an agricultural tour of the continent. In many places, he says, he was the first Briton to visit the district since the outbreak of the revolutionary wars. Shortly after his return home, in 1820, he came into possession of a farm of three hundred acres at Balmadies in Forfarshire. It was in a dilapidated condition, with no dwelling-house, and only a ruined steading. Stephens thoroughly put it in order, and introduced several improvements hitherto unknown in the district; the feeding of cattle, in small numbers, in separate hammels, and from troughs; the enclosing of sheep upon turnips by means of nets instead of hurdles; and the growing of Swedish turnips in larger proportion than other varieties. He also made use of furrow drains, filled with small stones, several years before the Deanston plan was made public by James Smith (1789–1850) [q. v.]

After managing the farm at Balmadies for some ten years, Stephens removed to the neighbourhood of Edinburgh, ultimately settling at Redbraes Cottage, Bonnington. Here at first alone, and afterwards in conjunction with other writers, James Slight, Robert Scott Burn, and William Seller, he produced that series of agricultural works of which the 'Book of the Farm' (Stephens's unaided work) is the best known. These books soon became popular abroad; they were translated into many continental languages and pirated in American editions. Stephens received a gold medal from the emperor of Russia.

In 1832 Stephens became editor of the 'Quarterly Journal of Agriculture,' and he continued till 1852 to edit the 'Transactions of the Highland and Agricultural Society of Scotland,' of which he had been a member since 1826. In his later years he sat for a long period on the society's council. He was a corresponding member of the Société Centrale et Impériale d'Agriculture de France and of the Royal Agricultural Society of Galicia. Stephens died on 5 July 1874 at Bonnington.

He wrote: 1. 'The Book of the Farm,' 3 vols. 1842–4, which soon achieved a recognised position as the standard work on practical agriculture. Several editions of it have appeared, the fourth edition, by Mr. James Macdonald, being published at Edinburgh in 3 vols., 1889–91. It was reprinted in America (New York, 1846–7, 1851), and again in 1858, under the title of 'The Farmer's Guide to Scientific and Practical Agriculture,' with an appendix by John Pitkin Norton, the first professor of agricultural chemistry in Yale College. 2. 'A Manual of Practical Draining,' 1846 (3rd edit. 1848), in which the views of thorough draining, first popularised by James Smith of Deanston, were explained at length, and other systems, including that of Elkington, discussed. 3. 'The Yester deep Land-culture,' 1855, giving an account of the improvements which had been carried on since 1832 by the Marquis of Tweeddale on his estates at Yester, by means of thorough draining, subsoil, and steam ploughing. 4. 'A Catechism of Practical Agriculture,' 1856, written for the instruction of children, and founded on the 'Book of the Farm.' 5. 'The Book of Farm Implements and Machines,' 1858, by Stephens, in conjunction with Scott Burn and James Slight. 6. 'The Book of Farm Buildings,' 1861, in conjunction with Scott Burn. 7. 'Physiology at the Farm,' 1867, the general plan and arrangement of which rested with Stephens, though 'the execution of that plan in all its details, with the exception of such as were of a purely practical nature,' was performed by Dr. William Seller. 8. 'On Non-nitrogenised Food, in a physiological point of view,' 1867; a small pamphlet, the joint work of Seller and Stephens, defending from an attack in the 'Field' certain statements which had been made in 'Physiology at the Farm' concerning the nutritive powers of nitrogen.

[Autobiographical preface to the second edition (1849–51) of the Book of the Farm; Va-

pereau's Dictionnaire Univ. des Contemp. 5th edit. 1880; Obituaries in Agricultural Gazette, 11 July 1874; Mark Lane Express, 13 July 1874; Bell's Weekly Messenger, 13 July 1874; Edinburgh Courant, 5 July 1874. See also Gardeners' Chron. 6 Jan. 1872; Allibone's Dict. 1870, vol. ii. For reviews and notices of his works, &c. see Quarterly Review, March 1849, p. 389; Blackwood, lviii. (1845), 769, lxix. (1851), 590; Athenæum (1861), ii. 405–6.] E. C--R.

STEPHENS, JAMES FRANCIS (1792–1852), entomologist, the only son of Captain William James Stephens, R.N. (d. August 1799), and his wife, Mary Peck Stephens (afterwards Mrs. Dallinger), was born at Shoreham, Sussex, on 16 Sept. 1792. He was educated at the Bluecoat school at Hertford and at Christ's Hospital, to which he was presented by Shute Barrington [q. v.], bishop of Durham. He entered the school on 15 May 1800, and quitted it on 16 Sept. 1807, when he was placed by his uncle, Admiral Stephens, at the admiralty office, Somerset House. His love for entomology showed itself in his schooldays, his attention being divided between it and natural philosophy and electricity until the winter of 1809. At that date he began a 'Catalogue of British Animals,' that was carried up to 1812 in manuscript. From 1815 to 1825 his spare time was mainly given to ornithology, and vols. ix. to xiv. of the 'General Zoology,' which had been begun by Dr. George Shaw [q. v.], or the greater part of the class Aves, were written by him.

In 1818, at the request of the trustees of the British Museum, Stephens was granted leave from his office to assist Dr. William Elford Leach [q. v.] in arranging the insect collection. From that time forth he devoted himself more especially to British insects, and prepared a catalogue and a descriptive account of them. In May 1827 the first part of his 'Illustrations of British Entomology' (4to, London) appeared, followed in August 1829 by 'A systematic Catalogue of British Insects' (8vo, London). In 1832 he was induced to take proceedings in chancery for the protection of his copyright against James Rennie [q. v.], whose 'Conspectus of British Butterflies and Moths' was to a great extent an abstract of his volumes on Lepidoptera; but he lost his case. The feeling, however, of his scientific friends was so strongly in his favour that a subscription was raised towards defraying his legal expenses. The 'Illustrations' were persevered with up to 1837, when eleven volumes had been completed, and a supplement was issued in 1846. After his retirement from the admiralty in 1845 Stephens busied himself at the British Museum, and was engaged to catalogue the British Lepidoptera. He had been elected a fellow of the Linnean Society on 17 Feb. 1815, and of the Zoological Society in 1826. He was also a member of the entomological societies of London and of France.

He died at Kennington on 22 Dec. 1852. Stephens married in 1822 Sarah, daughter of Captain Roberts, who survived him: all their children died young.

Besides the works already named, and twenty-three papers on entomological subjects published in various scientific journals, Stephens was author of: 1. 'The Nomenclature of British Insects,' 12mo, London, 1829; 2nd edit. 1833. 2. 'An Abstract of the indigenous Lepidoptera contained in the Verzeichniss bekannter Schmetterlinge, by Hübner,' 8vo, London, 1835. 3. 'A Manual of British Coleoptera,' 8vo, London, 1839. 4. 'Catalogue of British Lepidoptera' [in the British Museum], 12mo, London, 1850-2; 2nd edit. 1856. He also wrote the entomological articles in the 'Encyclopædia Metropolitana.' His library was purchased by Henry Tibbats Stainton [q. v.], who published a catalogue of it.

[Proc. Entom. Soc. London, new ser. ii. 46-50; Stainton's Bibliotheca Stephensiana; information kindly supplied by R. L. Franks, clerk of the Bluecoat School, and by the secretaries of the Linnean and Zoological Societies; Brit. Mus. Cat.; Brit. Mus. (Nat. Hist.) Cat.; Royal Soc. Cat.] B. B. W.

STEPHENS, JANE (1813?-1896), actress, born about 1813, seems to have kept a tobacconist's shop at 39 Liverpool Road, Islington, previous to her 'first appearance,' which took place on 8 Feb. 1840 at the Olympic Theatre, then under the management of Samuel Butler, as Betty in 'Mr. and Mrs. Grubb.' After playing other soubrette parts she went into the country for three years, and on her return to London was engaged for 'boys and walking ladies' by Phelps at Sadler's Wells. Here, with the exception of one season with Mrs. Warner at the Marylebone, she remained until 1852. In 1853, as Miss Stephens, she joined the company of Charles Mathews at the Lyceum, then in 1858, as Mrs. Stephens, that of Alfred Wigan at the Olympic, where under four different managements she remained many years. Not until she began to assume grandmotherly parts did she make any great hit. In June 1854 in a revival of 'Hush Money' she was Mrs. Crab, and in March 1857 supported Robson as a country servant in 'Daddy Hardacre,' Palgrave Simpson's rendering of 'La Fille de l'Avare.' On

27 May 1863 she won her first great success as Mrs. Willoughby in the 'Ticket of Leave,' Taylor's adaptation of 'Leonard.' On 31 Aug. 1867 she played, at the Adelphi, the Nurse in 'Romeo and Juliet,' on the occasion of Miss Kate Terry's retirement. At the Holborn in October 1867 she enacted a part in Robertson's unsuccessful 'For Love.' On the opening of the Globe Theatre on 28 Nov. 1865 she was the original Miss Pamela Grannet (a schoolmistress) in Byron's 'Cyril's Success.' On 23 Oct. 1869 she was, at the same house, Mrs. Mould in Byron's 'Not such a Fool as he looks.' On the opening of the Court Theatre on 25 Jan. 1871 she was the original Mrs. Scantlebury in Mr. Gilbert's 'Randall's Thumb.' Here also on 27 March 1872 she was Madame Valamour in 'Broken Spelling,' by Westland Marston and William G. Wills. Returning to the Olympic, she was on 4 Oct. 1875 Mrs. Daw in Albery's 'Scrivener's Daughter.' In Mr. Burnand's 'Betsy' ('Bébé'), at the Criterion on 6 Aug. 1879, she was Mrs. Dirkett. At the Princess's on 10 Sept. 1881 she was Mrs. Jarvis in Mr. Sims's 'Lights of London,' and at the Prince's Theatre on 29 March 1884 was Miss Ashford in the 'Private Secretary,' Mr. C. H. Hawtrey's adaptation of 'Der Bibliothekar' of Von Moser. She played many other parts mostly of a similar nature. Her farewell to the stage was taken on 9 July 1889, at an afternoon performance at the Shaftesbury Theatre, in which she appeared as Mrs. Stonehenge Tattle in 'Truth.' She died of bronchitis at her residence on Clapham Common on 15 Jan. 1896, and was cremated on the following Monday at Woking. She was in her latter days a bright, cheery, amiable old lady, who seemed born to play the class of parts into which she drifted.

[Personal knowledge; Pascoe's Dramatic List; Scott and Howard's Blanchard; Era, 18 Jan. 1896; Daily Telegraph, 18 Jan. 1896; Daily News, 20 Jan. 1896; Dramatic Notes; Sunday Times, various years; Notes and Queries, 8th ser. vol. x. passim.] J. K.

STEPHENS, JEREMIAH (1591-1665), coadjutor of Sir Henry Spelman [q. v.], was son of Walter Stephens, vicar of Bishop's Castle, Shropshire, where he was born, and baptised 17 Oct. 1591. He entered Brasenose College, Oxford, on 29 March 1609-10, and matriculated 19 June 1610; graduated B.A. 1 July 1612, proceeded M.A. 3 May 1615, and B.D. 11 Nov. 1628. In December 1615 he was ordained deacon, and on 26 May 1616 priest, being appointed about the same time chaplain of All Souls' College. On 11 Oct. 1624 he was made clerk of the market, Oxford, and 17 Dec. 1628 was licensed to preach. He was presented to the rectory of Quinton, Northamptonshire, on 25 Jan. 1621-2 by Charles I, and to that of Wootton in the same county on 13 July 1626, also by the king.

Stephens is best known as the literary coadjutor of Sir Henry Spelman, to whom he rendered very great assistance in the compilation of the first volume of his 'Concilia, Decreta, Leges, Constitutiones in re Ecclesiarum orbis Britannici,' which was published in 1639. Spelman and Stephens were seven years engaged in preparing this volume. In the preface Spelman acknowledges the help rendered to him by Stephens, 'a man born for the public good, by whose assistance this my first volume comes out, and on whom the hope of the rest is founded.' As a reward for the assistance he had given to Spelman, he was nominated by Laud to the prebend of Biggleswade in Lincoln Cathedral on 29 June 1639, and installed on 10 July following, vice Lambert Osbaldeston, who had been deprived; but Osbaldeston seems to have been collated a second time in 1641, so that Stephens could not have held this preferment for long. During the Commonwealth he was deprived of his livings by a parliamentary committee sitting at Northampton in 1644, and was 'plundered, imprisoned, barbarously used, and silenced' (WOOD). On the accession of Charles II he was reinstated in his livings, and was made prebendary of Ilfracombe in the church of Sarum on 20 Aug. 1660, and again collated to the same prebend on 8 Oct. 1662. He died at Wootton on 9 Jan. 1664-5, and was buried in the chancel of Wootton church.

Besides the help given to Spelman in the 'Councils,' Stephens edited Spelman's 'Apologia pro tractatu de non temerandis ecclesiis' (1647) and 'Tithes too hot to be touched,' 3 parts, 1646, which subsequently appeared as 'The Larger Treatise on Tithes' (1647). He also published on his own account: 1. 'B. Gregorii Magni, episcopi Romani, de Curâ Pastorali liber vere aureus, accurate emendatus, et restitutus e vet. MSS. cum Romanâ editione collatia,' 1629. 2. 'Notæ in D. Cyprian, de Unitate Ecclesiæ,' 1632. 3. 'Notæ in D. Cyprian, de Bono Patientiæ,' 1633. 4. 'An Apology for the Ancient Right and Power of the Bishops to sit and vote in Parliaments,' 1661.

He wrote some polemical tracts, which were not published owing to the Restoration, including 'A Comparison between the Belgic, Gallic, Bohemian, and Scotch with the English Covenant;' 'Account of the Principles and Practices of the Presbyterians;' 'The

VOL. LIV.

Sequestration of the Clergy, by Joh. Pym and Joh. White.'

Stephens also wrote two works, the publication of which was prevented by his death, 'Treatise of the Laws of England,' and 'The Design of the Cormorants upon the Church Lands defeated in the Time of King Henry V, effected in the Days of King Henry VIII.'

[Wood's Athenæ Oxon. iii. 670; Walker's Sufferings of the Clergy, pp. 45-6; Foster's Alumni Oxon. 1500-1714; Clark's Register of the Univ. of Oxford, passim; Le Neve's Fasti, ii. 112, 656-7; Chalmers's Biogr. Dict. xxviii. 385; Hook's Eccl. Biogr. viii. 478. The notices in Chalmers and Hook are mainly taken from Wood.]   W. G. D. F.

STEPHENS, JOHN (fl. 1615), satirist, son and heir of John Stephens of Gloucester, came of a numerous Gloucester family, which took an active part in municipal politics during the seventeenth century, James Stephens being its mayor in 1650-1, and member of parliament 1659-60 (FOSBROOKE, Gloucester, pp. 200, 205, 209; WASHBOURN, Bibliotheca Gloucestrensis, passim). He must be distinguished from John Stephens (d. 1613), who was attorney-general to Henry, prince of Wales, an ancestor of the Stephens of Over Lypiat, Gloucestershire (Visit. Gloucestershire; ATKYNS, Gloucestershire; BURKE, Landed Gentry), and also from John Stephens of Minsterley, Herefordshire (Visit. Herefordshire, 1623). On 11 Nov. 1611 he was admitted member of Lincoln's Inn, where he practised common law; but he held no office there (DUGDALE, Origines Jurid. and Chronica Ser.), and attained to no eminence in his profession (cf. Cal. State Papers, Dom.) His sole claim to remembrance is his authorship of 'Satyrical Essayes, Characters, and Others, or accurate and quick descriptions fitted to the life of their subjects,' London 1615, 8vo. A second edition, entitled 'Essayes and Characters ... with a new Satyre in defence of Common Law and Lawyers,' appeared in the same year, and in 1631 appeared a third, which is a reprint of the second edition with the exception of the title 'New Essayes and Characters' (BRYDGES, Restituta, iv. 503 et seq.) Some of these were reprinted by Halliwell-Phillipps in his 'Books of Characters,' 1857, 4to, and the 'Essay on a Worthy Poet' has been considered, on no very conclusive grounds, to be a sketch of Shakespeare (Notes and Queries, 4th ser. iii. 550). Stephens was also author of 'Cynthia's Revenge, or Menander's Extasy,' London, 1613, which was not entered in the 'Stationers' Register,' but was published surreptitiously, with commendatory verses by Jon-

N

son. It is a long and tedious play, founded on Lucan's 'Pharsalia' and Ovid's 'Metamorphoses' (FLEAY, *Biogr. Hist.* ii. 252-3). Stephens has three copies of commendatory verses in 'Certaine Elegies,' 1617, by Henry Fitzgeffrey [q. v.], also a member of Lincoln's Inn.

[Authorities cited; Works in Brit. Mus. Libr.; Lincoln's Inn Reg.; Baker's Biogr. Dram.; Lowndes's Bibl. Man. ed. Bohn.]   A. F. P.

STEPHENS, JOSEPH RAYNER (1805-1879), social reformer, sixth child of John Stephens (1772-1841), by his wife, Rebecca Eliza Rayner, of Wethersfield, Essex, was born at Edinburgh on 8 March 1805. His father, a native of St. Dennis, Cornwall, became a methodist preacher in 1792, and was president of the Wesleyan conference in 1827. George Stephens (1813-1895) [q. v.] was his brother. Joseph entered Manchester grammar school in 1819, where he made friends with William Harrison Ainsworth [q.v.] and Samuel Warren (1807-1877) [q.v.] He was also at the methodist school, Woodhouse Grove, near Leeds, and in 1823 taught in a school at Cottingham, East Riding. In July 1825 he became a methodist preacher, and was appointed in 1826 to a mission station at Stockholm. He was soon able to preach in Swedish, and acquired a taste for Scandinavian literature, which he communicated to his younger brother, George. He attracted the notice of Benjamin Bloomfield, first baron Bloomfield [q. v.], then plenipotentiary at Stockholm, who made him his domestic chaplain. He also enjoyed a brief but ardent friendship with Montalembert, who spent some time at Stockholm in 1829. Stephens was ordained as a Wesleyan minister in 1829, and stationed at Cheltenham in 1830.

His Wesleyan career ended in 1834, when he resigned under suspension for attending disestablishment meetings in Ashton-under-Lyne circuit. He had joined, under Richard Oastler [q. v.], the movement for improving the conditions of factory labour, and thought establishment checked the popular sympathies of the clergy. Francis Place (1771-1854) [q. v.] says of Stephens that he 'professed himself a tory, but acted the part of a democrat.' The opposition of leading liberals to the 'Ten Hours Bill' confirmed him as a 'tory radical,' a name first given by O'Connell to Feargus O'Connor [q. v.] He threw himself with more zeal than discretion into the agitation for the 'people's charter' (8 May 1838), drafted by William Lovett [q. v.] Lovett reckoned O'Connor and Stephens among the 'physical force chartists' with

James [Bronterre] O'Brien [q. v.], and though Stephens repudiated even the name of 'chartist,' and maintained that his views were 'strictly constitutional,' his impassioned language gave colour to another interpretation. As an orator he possessed unusual gifts; he was distinctly heard by twenty thousand people in the open air; his energy of expression and his mastery of homely sentiment were alike remarkable. His brother George designates him (1839) 'the tribune of the poor;' but his sympathy with popular needs was in excess of his political sagacity. His weekly sermons were for some time published as 'The Political Pulpit.' He contributed to the 'Christian Advocate,' edited by his brother John.

On 27 Dec. 1838 he was arrested at Ashton-under-Lyne on the charge of 'attending an unlawful meeting at Hyde' on 14 Nov. He was tried at Chester on 15 Aug. 1839, the attorney-general, Sir John Campbell, prosecuting. Stephens defended himself, and was sentenced by Mr. Justice Pattison to find sureties for good behaviour for five years, after suffering imprisonment for eighteen months in the house of correction at Knutsford; for this Chester Castle was substituted. He writes that his confinement was made 'as little irksome and unpleasant as possible,' adding, 'To a man who has slept soundly with a sod for his bed, and a portmanteau for his pillow, within a stone's throw of the North Cape, and who has made himself quite at home among Laplanders and Russians, there is nothing so very, very frightful in a moderately good gaol, as gaols now go' (unpublished letter, 9 Sept. 1839). On the expiration of his five years' bail a presentation of plate was made to him (10 Feb. 1846).

He settled in 1840 at Ashton-under-Lyne, where he preached at a chapel in Wellington Road, and conducted several journalistic efforts: 'Stephens's Monthly Magazine' (1840), the 'Ashton Chronicle' (1848-9), the 'Champion' (1850-1). In 1852 he removed to Stalybridge. In 1856 he sold his Ashton chapel to Roman catholics (opened as St. Mary's, April 1856, rebuilt 1868), but still continued to preach at a chapel which he rented in King Street, Stalybridge, till 1875. He took part in various local agitations, retaining his power and popularity as a speaker, and being the recipient of various testimonials from his friends. For some time he was a member of the Stalybridge school board. He took no lead in politics, and claimed to stand aloof from parties. During his long career he published many pamphlets, not equal to his speeches, though he was an admirable letter-writer. In his later years he suffered from gout and bronchitis. He died at Stalybridge on 18 Feb. 1879, and was buried on 22 Feb. in the churchyard of St. John's, Dukinfield, where his tombstone is the font from his King Street chapel. He married, first, in 1835, Elizabeth Henwood (d. 1852); secondly, in May 1857, Susanna, daughter of Samuel Shaw of Derby, and had issue by both marriages. On 19 May 1888 a granite obelisk to his memory was unveiled in Stamford Park, Stalybridge.

[Life, by Holyoake (1881), portrait; Glover and Andrews's Hist. of Ashton-under-Lyne, 1884, pp. 317 sq. (portrait), 342; Stalybridge Herald, 24 May 1888; unpublished letters.]   A. G.

STEPHENS, NATHANIEL (1606?–1678), nonconformist divine, son of Richard Stephens, vicar from 1604 of Stanton St. Bernard, Wiltshire, was born in Wiltshire about 1606. On 14 March 1623, at the age of sixteen, he entered Magdalen Hall, Oxford, as a batler, graduating B.A. 14 Feb. 1626, M.A. 25 June 1628. He was a hard student, giving sixteen hours a day to study. On leaving the university he appears to have become curate at Fenny Drayton, Leicestershire, of which Robert Mason was rector. He probably was in sole charge from 1638. Driven from Drayton by the outbreak of the war in 1642, he took refuge in Coventry, where he subscribed the 'league and covenant' and became morning preacher at St. Michael's. He returned to Drayton in 1645, and had among his hearers George Fox (1624–1691) [q. v.], who was then at a critical stage in his religious history. Stephens thought highly of Fox, discussed religion with him, and preached on the topics of their discourse, a proceeding which, in Fox's sensitive state, made him conceive a dislike to him as his pastor. In 1649, while Stephens was conducting a lecture at Market Bosworth, Fox interposed. Stephens cried out that he was mad, and Fox, stoned out of the town by a rabble, set down the 'deceitful priest' as his 'great persecutor.' A discussion between them at Drayton in 1654 is graphically narrated in Fox's 'Journal.' 'Neighbours,' said Stephens, 'this is the business: George Fox is come to the light of the sun, and now he thinks to put out my starlight.' With anabaptists, and with Gerard Winstanley [q. v.] the universalist, Stephens had similar discussions, when they invaded his parish. His allusions in print to his various antagonists are marked by good sense and good feeling. In controversy he was moderate and fair, aiming neither 'to please nor to displease any party;' even of the Roman church he writes without bitterness. His chief work (1656), on the

Apocalypse, is notable for its rejection of fanciful speculations; his exegesis is highly praised and generally followed by Matthew Poole or Pole [q. v.] in the fifth volume (1676) of his 'Synopsis Criticorum.'

In 1659 Stephens was presented by Colonel Purefey to the rectory of Drayton, which he held till 1662, when he resigned under the Uniformity Act. He continued to preach privately, but his services were often interrupted. Having seven times been driven from Drayton, he at length removed to Stoke Golding, three miles off, and preached there till lameness confined him to his chair. His studies made him absent-minded, but he was not wanting in a playful humour. He was buried on 24 Feb. 1678 in the churchyard of Stoke Golding.

He published: 1. 'A Precept for the Baptisme of Infants...vindicated...from... Mr. Robert Everard,' 1651, 4to (preface by John Bryan, D.D. [q. v.], and Obadiah Grew [q. v.]) 2. 'A Plain and Easie Calculation of the Name...of the Beast,' 1656, 4to (preface by Edmund Calamy the elder [q. v.]) 3. 'Vindiciæ Fundamenti, or a threefold defence of the Doctrine of Original Sin,' 1658, 4to (against the Arminian positions of Everard, Jeremy Taylor, and others). Calamy gives a specimen of his unpublished notes on the Apocalypse, used by Poole, and afterwards in the possession of Sir Charles Wolseley (d. 1714) [q. v.]

[Wood's Athenæ Oxon. (Bliss), iii. 1148 sq.; Wood's Fasti (Bliss), i. 422, 439; Foster's Alumni Oxon. 1500–1714, iv. 1419; Calamy's Account, 1713, pp. 419 sq.; Calamy's Continuation, 1727, ii. 1 sq.; Theological Review, 1874, pp. 51 sq.; extracts taken in 1873 from the parish registers of Stanton St. Bernard, Fenny Drayton, and Stoke Golding.]   A. G.

STEPHENS, Sir PHILIP (1725–1809), secretary of the admiralty, one of a family settled for many generations at Eastington in Gloucestershire, was the youngest son of Nathaniel Stephens, rector of Alphamstone in Essex, and was born there. He was educated at the free school at Harwich (Gent. Mag. 1810, i. 128), and at an early age obtained an appointment as clerk in the navy victualling office, as his eldest brother, Tyringham Stephens, had previously done. After his return from his voyage round the world, Rear-admiral George Anson (afterwards Lord Anson) [q. v.] took notice of young Stephens, and had him moved to the admiralty. Stephens afterwards served as Anson's secretary, and was appointed assistant secretary of the admiralty. In 1763 he became secretary, and so continued for upwards of thirty years. He was elected

F.R.S. on 6 June 1771, and from 1768 to 1806 he represented Sandwich in the House of Commons. In 1795 he applied for permission to resign his office at the admiralty, and was then, 17 March, created a baronet and appointed one of the lords of the admiralty. By a special recommendation on 15 Oct. 1806 (*Orders in Council*, vol. lxvi.) Stephens, at the age of eighty-one, was granted a pension of 1,500*l.*, which he enjoyed till his death on 20 Nov. 1809. He was buried in Fulham church. His only son, Captain Thomas Stephens, was killed in a duel at Margate in 1790; and his nephew, Colonel Stephens Howe, who was included in the patent of baronetcy, predeceased him. The baronetcy thus became extinct. An elder brother, Nathaniel Stephens, died a captain in the navy in 1747; and two nephews, also captains in the navy, William and Tyringham Howe, died in 1760 and 1783 respectively.

[Burke's Extinct Baronetcies and Landed Gentry; Gent. Mag. 1809, ii. 1180, 1234; Faulkner's Fulham, pp. 272-3; Thomson's Royal Society; Official Returns of Members of Parliament. Stephens's name is very prominent in the admiralty correspondence of the last half of the eighteenth century.] J. K. L.

STEPHENS, ROBERT (1665-1732), historiographer-royal, born in 1665, was the fourth son of Richard Stephens of the elder house of that name at Eastington, Gloucestershire, by his wife Anne, eldest daughter of Sir Hugh Cholmeley, bart. His first education was at Wotton school, whence he removed to Lincoln College, Oxford, matriculating on 19 May 1681, but he left the university without taking a degree (FOSTER, *Alumni Oxon.* 1500-1714, iv. 1420). He was called to the bar at the Middle Temple in 1689, and was one of the founders of the Society of Antiquaries in 1717 (*Archæologia*, vol. i. p. xxxvii). Being a relative of Robert Harley, earl of Oxford, whose mother, Abigail, was daughter of Nathaniel Stephens of Eastington, he was preferred by him to be chief solicitor of the customs, in which employment he continued till 1726, when he was appointed to succeed Thomas Madox [q. v.] in the place of historiographer-royal. He died at Gravesend, near Thornbury, Gloucestershire, on 9 Nov. 1732 (*Gent. Mag.* 1732, p. 1082), and was buried at Eastington, where a monument with an English inscription was erected to his memory by his widow, Mary Stephens, daughter of Sir Hugh Cholmeley, bart. (BIGLAND, *Gloucestershire*, i. 541).

Stephens began about 1690 to transcribe and collect unpublished 'letters and memoirs' of Francis Bacon, chiefly in private collections. The first result of his labours was 'Letters of Sr Francis Bacon ... written during the Reign of King James the First. Now collected and augmented with several Letters and Memoires ... never before published. The whole being illustrated by an Historical Introduction,' London, 1702, 4to. After this volume had appeared Harley' was pleased to put into my hands some neglected manuscripts and loose papers, to see whether any of the Lord Bacon's compositions lay concealed there that were fit to be published.' His investigation induced Stephens to prepare another volume, the 'Letters and Remains of the Lord Chancellor Bacon,' London, 1734, 4to. The first 231 pages of this volume (it consists of 515), with a preface and introductory memoir, were sent to press by Stephens. The rest were selected from his papers by his friend John Locker, and the whole volume was edited by Stephens's widow. This work was reissued in 1736 as: 'Letters, Memoirs, Parliamentary Affairs, State Papers, &c., with some Curious Pieces in Law and Philosophy. Published from the Originals. . . . With an Account of the Life of Lord Bacon.'

Among Stephens's collection in the British Museum (*Addit. MS.* 4259) is a catalogue of letters and papers connected with Bacon. Many of these documents cannot now be found, and a list of the missing papers is printed in Spedding, Ellis, and Heath's edition of Bacon's 'Works,' 1874, xiv. 590. It is possible that they are still in existence, and may yet be recovered. All the letters and papers described in Stephens's 'Catalogue' were most probably in the hands of Archbishop Tenison at Lambeth as late as December 1682.

[Lowndes's Bibl. Man. (Bohn) i. 96, 97; Spedding's Bacon. viii. 16, 119, ix. 2, 3, 18, xi. 3, xii. 349, 356, 372, xiii. and xiv. passim; Nichols's Lit. Anecd. ii. 51, 700, iii. 616, v. 373; Ayscough's Cat. of MSS. p. 784; Watt's Bibl. Brit.] T. C.

STEPHENS, THOMAS (1821-1875), Welsh historian and critic, born at Pont Nedd Fechan, Glamorganshire, on 21 April 1821, was the son of Evan Stephens, shoemaker, by Margaret, daughter of William Williams, minister of the unitarian church at Blaengwrach. Stephens was educated at a grammar school at Neath. About the commencement of 1835 he was apprenticed to a chemist at Merthyr Tydfil, where subsequently, on his own account, he successfully carried on the business until his death.

From his earliest days Stephens devoted himself to the study of Welsh history. His taste was first stimulated by Eisteddfod competitions, in which, from 1840 onwards, he was awarded prizes for historical essays. In 1848 he produced 'An Essay on the Literature of Wales during the Twelfth and Succeeding Centuries,' which won him the prize offered in the name of the Prince of Wales at the Abergavenny Eisteddfod, thereby defeating Thomas Price (1787-1848) [q.v.], a Welsh historian of repute. The essay was published at the expense of Sir John Guest, under the title of 'The Literature of the Kymry' (Llandovery, 1849, 8vo), and was enthusiastically received by the best Celtic scholars, including Count Villemarqué, Henri Martin, and Professor Schulz, who thereafter corresponded regularly with Stephens. In later years Matthew Arnold praised this 'excellent book' (*Celtic Literature*, p. vi). Schulz, under his *nom de guerre* of San Marte, brought out in 1864 a German translation of the work, entitled 'Geschichte der walschen Literatur vom xii bis zum xiv Jahrhundert' (Halle, 8vo). A second edition, with the author's additions and corrections, so far as they could be utilised, was posthumously published, under the editorship of the Rev. D. Silvan Evans, in 1876 (London, 8vo), with a biography by B. T. Williams, and a portrait from a bust executed by Joseph Edwards for presentation to Stephens on behalf of the committee of the Merthyr library.

After 1848 Stephens won prizes for historical essays at every Eisteddfod at which he chose to compete, being, for example, awarded three prizes at the Abergavenny Eisteddfod in 1853. One of these was for an essay on 'The History of Trial by Jury in Wales,' which received the encomiums of the Chevalier Bunsen, who acted as adjudicator. For the Eisteddfod held at Llangollen in 1858 he wrote an essay in which he proved the unhistorical character of the Welsh claim to the discovery of America by Madoc ap Owen Gwynedd; but the Eisteddfod committee, influenced by John Williams ab Ithel, withheld the prize from Stephens on the quibbling pretext that he had written on the non-discovery instead of the discovery by Madoc. This essay was published in 1893 under the title 'Madoc: an Essay on the Discovery of America by Madoc ap Owen Gwynedd in the Twelfth Century,' edited by Mr. Llywarch Reynolds (London, 8vo). Stephens did not again compete at the Eisteddfod, though, at the request of that institution, he subsequently drew up a report, along with R. J. Pryse (Gweirydd ab Rhys), on a standard of Welsh orthography, 'Orgraff yr Iaith Gymraeg' (1859, 12mo). Stephens contributed a series of valuable articles in Welsh on the Triads to 'Y Beirniad' for 1861-3, in which he established their mediæval as opposed to their prehistoric origin; and in the course of seven articles in 'Archæologia Cambrensis' for 1851-3 he critically examined the poems traditionally ascribed to Taliesin. He left unpublished at his death a large number of manuscript essays, one of which, probably the most important, was edited by Professor Thomas Powel of Cardiff for the Cymmrodorion Society, and published in 1888 under the title 'The Gododin of Aneurin Gwawdrydd: an English Translation, with copious Explanatory Notes, a Life of Aneurin, and several lengthy Dissertations illustrative of the Gododin and the Battle of Cattraeth' (London, 8vo).

Stephens was almost the first native Welsh scholar of this century to apply a rigidly scientific method to the study of Welsh history and literature. His tendency was sceptical and iconoclastic, on which account he became highly unpopular with Welsh enthusiasts, though he enjoyed the confidence of competent critics. His opinions in other respects were also often unpopular. He evoked the hostility of dissenters by advocating, from 1847 onwards, a state-aided system of secular education. In politics he was a philosophical reformer. Among other institutions at Merthyr which largely owed their origin to him was the public library, of which he acted for twenty-five years as honorary secretary, and to which he bequeathed a valuable collection of books. He was high constable of the town for 1858, and in 1864 undertook the management of the 'Merthyr Express.'

In 1870 overwork brought on paralysis, which, after repeated attacks, ended in his death on 4 Jan. 1875, when he was buried at the Cefn cemetery. He married, on 11 Sept. 1866, his cousin, Margaret Davis, a granddaughter of William Williams of Penrheolgerrig, who survives him (1898), but there was no issue. A bust by Joseph Edwards is at the University College of Wales, Aberystwyth.

[The chief authority is the Life by B. T. Williams, Q.C., prefixed to the second edition of the Literature of the Kymry. To this is added a list of the manuscript essays and writings which Stephens left unpublished at his death. See also Archæologia Cambrensis, 4th ser. vi. 87, 196; Academy, January, 1875, vii. 62; Red Dragon, 1882, i. 3-18 (with portrait); Yr Ymofynydd, June 1895 (with portrait); Wilkins's History of Merthyr Tydfil, pp. 258-60.]
D. Ll. T.

STEPHENS, WILLIAM (1647?-1718), divine, eldest son of Richard Stephens, a 'dealer,' of Worcester, was born probably on

27 March 1647, in the parish of All Hallows, Lombard Street. From Merchant Taylors' school he matriculated at St. Edmund Hall, Oxford, as a batler on 1 July 1664. He graduated B.A. in 1668, M.A. in 1671, being incorporated at Cambridge the same year, and B.D. in 1678. He was for some time preacher at St. Lawrence, Hincksey, near Oxford, ' where, by his sedulous endeavours, he caused the tower to be re-edified,' says Wood, and at St. Martin's, Carfax. On 26 July 1690 he became rector of Sutton, Surrey, and archdeacon. He soon became known for his strong whig principles.

Being appointed to preach before the House of Commons on 30 Jan. 1700, Stephens not only omitted the prayer for the king and royal family, but suggested the propriety of discontinuing the observance of the anniversary of the execution of Charles I; while he further offended a tory house by insisting upon the whig doctrine of the foundation of government on consent (cf. EVELYN, Diary, 25 Jan. 1699-1700). The result was that not only was the usual vote of thanks withheld, but a resolution was passed that for the future 'no one be recommended to preach before the house who is under the degree of a dean or hath not taken his degree of doctor of divinity' (Journals of the House of Commons). The sermon was published in 1700, with an apologetic advertisement, stating that 'since it had stolen incorrectly into the world without his privity,' the author 'hoped it would not be imputed as a crime that he amended the errata of the press.' A reply by 'H. E.' (probably Edward Hawarden), entitled 'A Sermon vindicating King Charles the Martyr,' appeared the same year. Stephens's sermon was reprinted in vol. ii. of R. Barron's 'Pillars of Priestcraft shaken,' 1752.

On 6 May 1706, chiefly on the ground that he refused to give evidence against Thomas Rawlins, the reputed author of a libellous 'Letter to the Author of the Memorial of the State of England' (in reality by Toland), Stephens was himself indicted as the writer. He was sentenced to a fine of one hundred marks, to stand twice in the pillory, and to find sureties for his good behaviour for twelve months. Though the more ignominious part of the sentence was remitted, Stephens had to go to a public-house at Charing Cross and see the scaffold and the gathering spectators (BOYER). Stephens's reticence also led to his being coupled with the leading deists in the satirical 'Apparition' of Abel Evans [q. v.] He died on 30 Jan. 1717-18.

Stephens also published, besides sermons: 1. 'An Account of the Growth of Deism in England,' 1696, 4to. 2. 'A Letter to King William III, showing (1) the original foundation of the English Monarchy; (2) the means by which it was removed from that foundation; (3) the expedients by which it has been supported since that removal; (4) its present constitution; (5) the best means by which its grandeur may be for ever maintained' (in Collection of State Tracts, 1705-7, vol. ii.) 3. 'Bishop Hacket's Memoirs of the Life of Archbishop Williams, abridged,' 1715, 8vo.

[C. J. Robinson's Register of Merchant Taylors' School, i. 252; Wood's Athenæ Oxon. (Bliss), iv. 790; Foster's Alumni Oxon.; Nichols's Lit. Anecd. i. 46, viii. 301; Wilson's Memoirs of Defoe, i. 311-12, ii. 377-80, 425; Brit. Mus. Cat.; Allibone's Dict. Engl. Lit. ii. 2241; J. Hunt's Relig. Thought in England, iii. 98 n.; Manning and Bray's Surrey, ii. 487.]

G. LE G. N.

STEPHENS, WILLIAM (1671-1753), colonist, son of Sir William Stephens (d. 1697), lieutenant-governor of the Isle of Wight (where his family, originally of Cornish origin, had settled), by his wife Elizabeth, was born at Bowcombe, Isle of Wight, on 28 Jan. 1671, and educated at Winchester and King's College, Cambridge, graduating B.A. in 1684 and M.A. in 1688. Upon leaving Cambridge he was admitted at the Middle Temple. He entered parliament for Newport, Isle of Wight, in 1702, became an officer in the island militia, and before 1706 rose to the rank of colonel; in 1712 he was appointed a commissioner for the victualling of the force. His lavish expenditure made him popular, and he represented Newport down to 1722, when he was unseated, and had promptly to quit his seat at Barton, near Cowes, and seek refuge from his creditors.

In 1728 Stephens found employment in Scotland as agent for the York Building Company, with a salary of 200l. a year. Arriving at Findhorn on 28 March 1729, he devoted himself to the timber trade, in which the company was interested, and declined an invitation to stand again for Newport in 1732. Three years later he had to quit Scotland, leaving the company's affairs in confusion.

After a short residence in Penrith, Stephens was asked by one Colonel Horsey in 1736 to execute a survey in South Carolina. There he made the acquaintance of James Edward Oglethorpe [q. v.], and returned with him to England. In August 1737, taking one of his sons with him, he went back to Georgia in the Mary Anne via Charlestown, and arrived on 1 Nov. 1737.

He found the settlement distracted by social quarrels and jealousies, in which he acted the part of a mediator. He met with success, at first as a planter and fruit cultivator, and he was appointed secretary to the trustees in Georgia in April 1741. He was shortly afterwards made president of the county of Savannah, and of the entire colony in 1743. He held this post until 1750, when he gave such evidence of mental and physical decline that he was requested to resign. He was voted a pension of 80*l.*, but appears to have sunk into poverty before his death, upon his plantation of Bewlie (named after Beaulieu in the New Forest), at the mouth of the Vernon River, in August 1753.

He married, in 1697, Mary, second daughter of Sir Richard Newdigate, bart., of Arbury, by Mary, daughter of Sir Edward Bagot. They had issue seven sons and two daughters. The eldest son, Thomas, was the author of a curious memoir of his father, entitled 'The Castle-builder; or, the History of William Stephens of the Isle of Wight, Esq.' (2nd ed. London, 1759, 8vo).

William Stephens was author of 'A Journal of the Proceedings in Georgia, beginning October 20, 1737: to which is added a State of that Province, as attested upon Oath in the Court of Savannah, Nov. 10, 1740,' 3 vols. London, 1742, 8vo. Of this work a limited edition was published by the trustees, and complete copies are very rare (the British Museum copy lacks the third volume). While encumbered with many trivial and irrelevant matters, the 'Journal' is remarkable for accuracy and minuteness of detail. Stephens also possessed some manuscript records of the colony, accumulated during his tenure of office as secretary, and these, having passed to his family, formed part of Sir Thomas Phillipps's library at Thirlestane House, Cheltenham (cf. H. Stevens, in *Collections of the Georgia Hist. Society*, i. 34).

[Graduati Cantabr.; Official Ret. of Members of Parliament; Winsor's History of America, v. 386, 395–7, 400; Appleton's Cyclop. of Amer. Biography; Woodward's Hampshire, vol. iii. Suppl. p. 56; Collins's English Baronetage, vol. iii. pt. ii. p. 626; Brit. Mus. Cat.]

C. A. H.

STEPHENSON, GEORGE (1781–1848), inventor and founder of railways, second son of Robert Stephenson, fireman at the Wylam colliery, was born at Wylam, eight miles from Newcastle, on 9 June 1781. His mother, Mabel, was the daughter of Richard Carr, a dyer of Ovingham, and his paternal grandfather is said to have come from Scotland as a gentleman's servant. His father was a

steady, honest workman, very fond of children, and with a great love for birds, a trait of his character inherited by his famous son.

Stephenson's first employment was herding cows; then he became a driver to the horses working the colliery gin, and at the age of fourteen was an assistant fireman to his father at the Dewley colliery. At fifteen he became fireman, and at seventeen 'plugman,' at the colliery where his father was fireman. While in this post, during his eighteenth year, he began to learn to read and write at a night school. In 1801 he became a brakesman at Black Callerton, lodging at a farmhouse close by. Anxious to increase his earnings, as he had formed an attachment for Frances Henderson, a servant at the farm, he took to mending boots in his leisure hours, and became very expert at the work.

On 28 Nov. 1802, when twenty-one years of age, he married Frances Henderson at Newburn church, and became engineman at Willington Ballast Hill. Here, owing to the experience gained in repairing his own clock, which had been damaged by a fire, he took up the work of cleaning and repairing clocks and watches, acquiring great skill at it. William (afterwards Sir W.) Fairbairn [q. v.], who was then working as an engineer's apprentice in the neighbourhood, became his intimate friend at this time.

On 16 Oct. 1803 his only son Robert was born, and in 1804 he removed to Killingworth, where his wife died of consumption on 14 May 1806. The greater part of the next year he spent at Montrose, looking after one of Boulton & Watt's engines. After his return his prospects seemed so gloomy that he seriously considered the wisdom of emigrating. During this period his father became incapable of active work; his parents therefore became a charge on his limited resources; he was also drawn for the militia, and had to find the money to pay for a substitute. In 1808 he took, with two other men, a contract to work the engines of the Killingworth pit. While there he took his engine to pieces every Saturday in order that he might become a thorough master of its construction. In consequence of the great skill he showed in putting in order a Newcomen engine which failed to do the pumping work it was designed for, he was in 1812 appointed engine-wright to the colliery at a salary of 100*l.* a year.

Meanwhile he again devoted much of his leisure to improving his scientific knowledge. He also converted his home at Killingworth into a comfortable four-roomed house, putting up a sundial in front of it, with the aid of his son.

Stephenson's inventive genius was first applied to a safety lamp for miners. The constant accidents in the pits at which he was working painfully forced the danger of naked lights on his attention. He made numerous experiments on the combustion of the escaping inflammable gases at Killingworth colliery, and eventually designed a safety lamp, by controlling the entry of the air to support combustion, and the escape of the products of combustion by the use of small tubes for the gases to pass through. On 21 Oct. 1815 the first lamp was actually tried, on 4 Nov. a second improved form, and on 30 Nov. a third still better were tested. On this last occasion he entered with his lamp with perfect safety into parts of the working which were full of gas.

Sir Humphry Davy [q. v.] had, unknown to Stephenson, been working on the same subject, and practically at the same time that Stephenson's long experiments bore fruit in his lamp, Davy brought out his well-known safety lamp. A fierce controversy raged for several years on the question to whom was due the credit of this solution of a problem fraught with life and death to so many thousands of miners. A national testimonial to Davy produced a testimonial to Stephenson, and he was presented with 1,000l. and an address (12 Jan. 1818). There can be little doubt that the two inventions were quite independent of each other, and that both men practically reached the same solution by different methods at the same time (cf. *A Description of the Safety Lamp invented by George Stephenson*, 1817).

Meanwhile Stephenson had turned his attention to the question of steam locomotion, with which his name is permanently associated. Steam locomotion on common roads had been an idea of William Murdock [q. v.], one of Watt's most trusty assistants, and he made a working model of a steam carriage in 1784. Richard Trevithick [q.v.] took up the question in 1802, constructing a carriage which ran in Cornwall, and was shown in London for a few days. In 1811 John Blenkinsop constructed a locomotive for hauling loaded coal wagons at a colliery near Leeds, which ran on rack-rails, but was very cumbersome and unwieldy. Mr. Blacket of Wylam colliery was very anxious to introduce steam-power on his horse tramways. He had two engines made, copies of Blenkinsop's locomotive, but they were failures; then he constructed a third, assisted in the design by William Hedley [q. v.], his viewer.

Stephenson saw these attempts at Wylam in progress; his interest, always keen in the matter of improving the steam-power in colliery working, was aroused, and he set himself to deal with this problem of coal haulage. He eventually, in 1813, brought the matter before the owners of his own colliery, and, receiving financial support from them, his first locomotive was built in the engine-shops at West Moor. It had smooth wheels, an improvement at which Hedley had already arrived by experiments very similar to Stephenson's, and a cylindrical barrel to the boiler thirty-four inches in diameter and eight feet long. It was tried on 25 July 1814, and successfully drew a load of thirty tons up an incline of 1 in 450 at four miles an hour. Stephenson soon recognised means of improving his engine, and in February 1815 he took out a patent for a greatly improved engine, with steam springs for the boiler to rest on. In this locomotive the steam-blast was used by him for the first time.

Trevithick had used the steam-blast in his road engines, but without any notion of its real importance. Davies Gilbert [q. v.], however, who saw it at work, recognised its great value, and wrote a letter to 'Nicholson's Journal' on the subject. William Nicholson (1753-1815) [q. v.] himself took out a patent for its use in 1806, but nothing came of it. Undoubtedly Stephenson was the first to use it practically with a full knowledge of its important influence on the working of the locomotive. Meanwhile he was making experiments on the traction of vehicles on smooth roads, and these experiments materially influenced his development of the crude locomotive of 1814 into the 'Rocket' of 1829. He found that a gradient of 1 in 200, common enough on roads, at once reduced the hauling power of a locomotive 50 per cent., since on a smooth, level road a tractive force of ten pounds would move a ton. Moreover, he found that the friction was practically independent of speed. He came to the decision, therefore, that steam carriages on ordinary roads were of no value, and that railways must be specially designed with the object of avoiding as much as possible changes of gradient. Cuttings, tunnels, and embankments were essential. In 1819 the proprietors of Hetton colliery laid down, under Stephenson's direction, a railroad eight miles in length. It was opened for traffic on 18 Nov. 1822. The traction was carried out partly by fixed engines, partly by locomotives.

On 19 April 1821 the project of connecting Stockton and Darlington by a tramroad was, after many years of discussion, approved by act of parliament. Stephenson offered his services to Edward Pease [q. v.], the chief promoter, and strongly urged the advantages of steam locomotives over horse traction. He was at length appointed engineer to the line at a salary of 300*l.* a year. He surveyed the whole line himself, and early in 1823 a fresh act of parliament was obtained for a new route (*Ann. Reg.* 1823, p. 241). On 23 May 1823 the first rail was laid. Stephenson strongly advocated the use of malleable-iron rails, instead of the cast-iron which had always been used up to that time, and the suggestion was in part adopted. But the character of the locomotives to be used on the line occupied his chief attention. He saw the necessity of getting together a trained staff of workmen if the mechanical construction of his locomotives was to be improved. He induced Pease and his cousin Thomas Richardson (1771–1853) [q. v.] to join him in establishing works at Newcastle. They were started in August 1823, and at these works the engines for the Stockton line were made. The line was opened for traffic, amid a scene of great enthusiasm, on 27 Sept. 1825. The first locomotive that passed over it weighed eight tons and attained a speed of twelve to sixteen miles an hour. It now occupies a pedestal at Darlington station.

Stephenson's next undertaking was the Liverpool and Manchester Railway. The enormous and rapidly increasing trade between these two towns had completely outgrown the canal accommodation, and as early as 1821 schemes were mooted for connecting them by a railroad. In 1824 a company was organised, and Stephenson, after several visits of the chief promoters to the Stockton and Darlington line, then in construction, was employed to make the necessary surveys for the preparation of the plans. The surveyors encountered the fiercest opposition from the farmers and proprietors of the great estates through which the proposed line was to run, and were often subjected to actual personal violence; hence, proper surveys could hardly be made. A bill was introduced into parliament in 1825, and, after a most stubborn fight, was eventually rejected, the rejection being greatly facilitated by the admitted inefficiency of the plans. Stephenson was subjected to the most searching cross-examination by the counsel for the opposers, mainly as to his method of crossing the Chat Moss, and as to the speed he proposed his engines should attain. In 1826, urged by Huskisson, the promoters again introduced a bill. The new plans were drawn on surveys made by the Rennies [see RENNIE, GEORGE, 1791–1866, and RENNIE, SIR JOHN, 1794–1874]. Another long struggle ended in their victory. Stephenson was appointed engineer, and work was at once begun. The most important constructional works on the line were the crossing of Chat Moss and the execution of the great Olive Mount cutting. By distributing the load over a considerable surface of the Moss, Stephenson was enabled, as it were, to float his line over this treacherous bog, and thus overcome the chief difficulty. While the line was being constructed long and anxious consideration was given to the question of motive power; and for a time, influenced by a report given by outside engineering experts, the directors were in favour of haulage by the use of fixed engines distributed along the line. Stephenson fought strenuously for the locomotive, and eventually the directors decided to test the possibility of Stephenson's ideas by means of an open competition, the prize offered being 500*l.* The chief condition insisted on was that a mean speed of ten miles an hour was to be obtained with a steam pressure not exceeding fifty pounds per square inch. There were also certain restrictions as to weight of engine in comparison with the load it hauled, the price of engine, and other details. The trial was fixed for 1 Oct. 1829.

Stephenson saw that, if he was to be successful, he must find some means of increasing the heating surface of the boilers of his locomotives. On the advice of Henry Booth [q. v.], the secretary of the company, he adopted tubes passing through the cylindrical barrel and connecting the fire-box with the smoke-box. Several tubular boilers had been previously made by Trevithick, Sir Goldsworthy Gurney [q. v.], and others; and Seguin in France, in 1828, had applied the tube principle to a locomotive. Stephenson's engine for the great trial, called 'The Rocket,' was built at the Newcastle works under the direct supervision of Stephenson's son, and, after many failures, the problem of securing the tubes to the tube-plates was mastered. The boiler was a cylinder six feet long and forty inches in diameter, with twenty-five three-inch copper tubes, the fire-box being two feet by three feet, secured to the front and surrounded by water; the cylinders were two, and were placed obliquely to the axis; its weight was four and a quarter tons. Three other engines entered for the competition besides the Rocket—the Novelty (the only real competitor) by John Braithwaite (1797–1870) [q. v.] and Ericson, the Sanspareil by Hackworth, and the Perseverance by Burstall. The place of trial, Rainhill, near Liverpool, was a two-mile level piece of line, and each engine was to run at least seventy miles in a day, backwards and forwards on this course, at a mean speed of at least ten miles per hour. The contest, which created extraordinary interest and excitement, began on 6 Oct. 1829. On the opening day the Rocket, the only engine ready to time, ran twelve miles in fifty-three minutes, and was eventually awarded the prize, the Novelty meeting with many mishaps during the various tests.

Stephenson's triumph was complete: his former opponents became his warmest supporters, and the railway system of the world may be said to date from 6 Oct. 1829, when the Rocket, in her trials, showed that genius and mechanical ability of the highest order had swept aside all the difficulties which had hitherto hampered progress in the development of steam locomotion on land. The 'Scotsman,' in commenting on the trials, said: 'The experiments at Liverpool have established principles which will give a greater impulse to civilisation than it has ever received from any single cause since the press first opened the gates of knowledge to the human species at large.'

On 1 Jan. 1830 a trial trip with the Rocket was made over most of the Liverpool and Manchester railway, and on 15 Sept. 1830 the line was officially opened in great state, a procession of eight locomotives, with their attendant carriages, passing over it. The Duke of Wellington, then prime minister, and most of the distinguished men of the day were present. The opening ceremonies were, however, marred by the fatal accident to Huskisson [see HUSKISSON, WILLIAM].

From this time forward till 1845, when he arrived at the decision that he ought to retire completely from active work, Stephenson's life is a history of the railway progress of the country. The locomotive underwent further improvements. When Gurney's steam-jet was applied to the Rocket, that engine attained a speed of twenty-nine miles an hour. Stephenson was chief engineer to the Grand Junction line connecting Birmingham with Liverpool and Manchester, begun in 1833 and finished by Joseph Locke [q. v.], his pupil. Stephenson was also chief engineer to the following railways: Manchester to Leeds, Birmingham to Derby, Normanton to York, and Sheffield to Rotherham, and others, all begun in 1836. The Derby to Leeds railway (afterwards called the North Midland line) was commenced under his supervision in 1837. In fact there was hardly a railway scheme in which he was not consulted, or an important line constructed without his help and advice.

After the completion of the Liverpool and Manchester railway Stephenson removed his home to Alton Grange, near Ashby-de-la-Zouch. He had married again, on 29 March 1820, Elizabeth, daughter of Thomas Hindmarsh, a prosperous farmer at Black Callerton (he had no children by her). He opened large coal-pits in this neighbourhood, and spent much time and energy in developing its mineral resources. During the construction of the Midland line he took a lease of Tapton House, near Chesterfield, and lived there till his death.

In 1838 Stephenson was vice-president of the mechanical science section of the British Association at its Newcastle meeting. He took a keen interest in the foundation and support of mechanics' institutes. During the great railway mania of 1844 he kept aloof from the mad schemes then brought forward, and used all his influence to check the mania. The remarkable development of railways and the locomotive in the fourteen years which elapsed since the Rainhill competition is shown by the fact that he travelled from London to Newcastle in 1844 to attend a railway banquet in the then remarkably short time of nine hours. His last great parliamentary struggle was in 1845 in the battle between the supporters of the locomotive and the upholders of the atmospheric railway system, led by Brunel, which arose in connection with the extension of the railway from Newcastle to Berwick. Though the board of trade were inclined to support Brunel in his heresy, Stephenson's party won a great parliamentary victory, and settled the matter for ever. This was the final attempt to dispute the supremacy of the locomotive. In 1847 Stephenson became president of the Institution of Mechanical Engineers, which was founded by him that year in Birmingham. He paid several visits to Belgium in connection with railway work, and received in 1835 the honour of knighthood from Leopold I. In 1845 he also visited North Spain in connection with a proposed railway. He steadfastly refused all proffered honours in England, and also declined to enter public life as a member of parliament.

His last years were devoted to horticultural pursuits at Tapton House, in which he developed great enthusiasm, making many experiments on the values of various manures. His second wife died in 1845, and on 11 Jan. 1848 he married the daughter of a farmer of Bakewell, named Gregory. But his strength was failing, and he died of intermittent fever at Tapton House on 12 Aug. 1848, in his sixty-seventh year. He was buried at Trinity Church, Chesterfield. The foundation-stone of a fine memorial hall was laid at Chesterfield by Lord Hartington on 17 Oct. 1877, and the building was opened in July 1879. A festival in celebration of the centenary of Stephenson's birth was held at Newcastle on 9 June 1881, when a medal was struck in his honour (W. DUNCAN, *The Stephenson Centenary*).

Several statues have been erected in Stephenson's honour. A fine one by Bailey stands in the great hall of Euston Station. Another by Gibson was placed in St. George's Hall, Liverpool, in 1844, and a third by Lough is at Newcastle near the High Level Bridge. There are two oil paintings of him by John Lucas at the Institution of Civil Engineers; in one he is painted along with his son. A third portrait by Pickersgill is in the National Portrait Gallery, London. Schools were built by way of memorial at Willington, where his son Robert, who is separately noticed, was born.

With his high mental attainments Stephenson possessed great physical strength and powers of endurance. In his younger days he was fond of showing his muscular development by feats of strength, and even when very advanced in life he was a good wrestler. His courage and perfect confidence in his work and judgment were shown by his venturing with his trial safety lamps into parts of the mine purposely rendered dangerous. The services that he rendered to the well-being of mankind by his invention of steam locomotion and railways place him among the world's greatest benefactors.

[The Life of George Stephenson, by Mr. Samuel Smiles, appeared in 1857, and, in a revised shape, formed the third volume of the same writer's Lives of the Engineers. In this form it constitutes the standard authority. See also notices of life and character by J. Scott Russell, Proc. Inst. Mech. Eng. 1849; obituary notice by J. Field, Pres. Inst. Civ. Eng. Proc. Inst. Civ. Eng. viii. 49; Memoir by Hyde Clarke in Civil Engineer and Architect's Journal, 1845, pp. 297, 329, 361; Tredgold's Steam Engine; R. L. Galloway's Steam Engine and its Inventors; Summerside's Reminiscences of George Stephenson, 1878; cf. Nature, xxiv. 121–3, an article on the centenary of Stephenson's birth.]

T. H. B.

STEPHENSON, HENRY PALFREY (1826–1890), civil engineer, son of Major John Stephenson of the 6th dragoon guards, was born at Portobello, near Edinburgh, on 27 March 1826. He was educated at a private school at Twickenham, and in 1842 became a student at the college of civil engineers, Putney. The then principal was Dean Cowie of Exeter; Sir Guilford Molesworth, and several other well-known engineers were his fellow students. He founded the Putney Club, which was afterwards converted into the Society of Engineers. His early professional work consisted mainly of the design of iron railway bridges, and of arbitration work. In 1858 he turned his attention to gas lighting for towns; he designed and carried out several important gas undertakings on the continent, and was connected as a director with a large number of similar undertakings both in England and abroad. He was elected an associate of the Institution of Civil Engineers in 1853, and a full member in 1864. About 1882 his health began to fail, and he gradually retired from active professional pursuits; he died on 30 April 1890.

[Obituary Notices in Proc. Inst. Civil Eng. ci. 303.]

T. H. B.

STEPHENSON, JAMES (1808–1886), engraver, born at Manchester on 26 Nov. 1808, was the son of Thomas Stephenson, boot and shoe maker, of Stable Street, near Oldham Street, in that town. James was educated at a school kept by Thomas Rain, adjoining Oldham Street chapel, and before the end of his schooldays was apprenticed to John Fothergill, an engraver, of Prince's Court, Market Street. While there he made the acquaintance of the artist, Henry Liverseege [q. v.], and, probably by his advice, he came to London at the expiry of his apprenticeship and entered the studio of William Finden [q. v.] While there he gained the silver medal of the Society of Arts for an original design of a figure engraved in line.

About 1838 he returned to Manchester and established himself as an historical and landscape engraver in Ridgefield, and afterwards in a studio in St. Ann Street. Besides furnishing illustrations for 'Manchester as it is' (1839), for Charles Swain's 'Mind and other Poems,' and for other books, he engraved the members' card for the Anti-Corn-law League, and executed for Agnew & Sons portraits of prominent members, among others of Sir John Bowring [q. v.], Edward Baines [q. v.], and John Heyworth. During this period he also engraved Du Val's portrait of Richard Cobden, George Patten's portrait of John Frederick Foster, and John Boston's portrait of Daniel Grant, one of the original 'Cheeryble Brothers.' In 1842, for the British Association, which met in that year in Manchester, he executed a portrait of John Dalton (1766–1844) [q. v.], the chemist.

About 1847 Stephenson took up his permanent abode in London, and from 1850 exhibited regularly at the Royal Academy. Among his later engravings were 'The Day of Wrath,' 'The Last Judgment,' and 'The

Plains of Heaven,' after John Morton; 'The Highland Whiskey Still,' the 'Taming of the Shrew,' and 'The Queen at Osborne,' after Landseer; 'Ophelia,' after Millais; and the 'Portrait of Lord Tennyson,' after George Frederick Watts. He also engraved pictures by Maclise, Gilbert Stuart Newton, Thomas Faed, and Sir John Watson Gordon. Stephenson died at his residence in Dartmouth Park Road, London, on 28 May 1886. Among his contemporaries he was regarded as one of the finest line engravers in the country, and in vignette engraving he was probably unsurpassed.

[Manchester Guardian, 4 June 1886; Times, 5 June 1886; Athenæum, 1886, i. 787; Bryan's Dict. of Engravers, supplement.] E. I. C.

STEPHENSON, ROBERT (1803–1859), civil engineer, only son of George Stephenson (q. v.], was born at Willington Quay, near Newcastle, on 16 Oct. (not November) 1803 (cf. *Register*). The following year his father removed to Killingworth, where on 14 May 1806 his mother died of consumption. His first elements of education were acquired in the village school of Long Benton. In 1814 his father, whose circumstances were now improving, and who felt keenly his own want of a sound education, sent him to Bruce's academy at Newcastle, and made him a member of the Newcastle Literary and Philosophical Society. Leaving school in 1819, he was apprenticed to Nicholas Wood (M.I.C.E.), viewer of Killingworth colliery. In 1821 he assisted his father in the survey of Stockton and Darlington Railway, and then in 1822 spent six months studying at Edinburgh University. There he met, as a fellow student, his lifelong friend, George Parker Bidder [q. v.], with whom he afterwards carried on much of his professional work. On leaving the university he settled down in Newcastle to manage the locomotive factory which his father established there in 1823, but his health soon broke down, and he accepted an offer to go abroad to Columbia in South America to superintend the working of some gold and silver mines. He left England in June 1824, and was absent three years. Difficulties in the working of the locomotive factory led to a request for him to return; on the return journey he met Richard Trevithick [q. v.], then on his way back to England, a penniless, broken man. Stephenson reached England in 1827, in the thick of the controversy as to the most suitable system of traction for use on the Liverpool and Manchester line. The famous Rocket was eventually built under his direction at

the Newcastle works, the securing of the tubes in their plates giving him great trouble before the difficulty was overcome. Most of the subsequent improvements in the details of the locomotive were due to his skill. From 1827 to 1833 besides this work he assisted his father generally in the Liverpool and Manchester line, in the Leicester and Swannington line, and in other minor lines.

In 1833 the act for the London and Birmingham line was passed; Stephenson became engineer, and was solely responsible for its success. The work is a memorable one, not only from the great difficulties encountered in its construction—as, for example, in the Blisworth cutting and in the long Kilsby tunnel—but also because it was the first railway into London. It was completed in 1838. He took an active part in the great 'battle of the gauges' which was fought out in parliament, and also in the great struggle between the rival advocates of the locomotive and of the atmospheric system, in both contests supporting with all the strength of his powerful and clear intellect the causes which the judgment of experience has shown to be the right ones. From 1838 till the close of his life he was engaged on railway work, not only in Great Britain, but all over the world: railways were constructed either under his own direct supervision or under his advice which have since become the trunk lines of the countries in which they were laid down.

The greatest works he carried out, or at any rate those by which he will be best known to posterity, were his bridges. The splendid high-level bridge over the Tyne at Newcastle and the Victoria bridge at Berwick were two of his earliest and most successful examples of this branch of engineering. When the act was passed in 1844 for the Chester and Holyhead line, Stephenson gave long and anxious consideration to the best type of bridge for crossing the Conway and the Menai Straits. Eventually he decided upon the tubular girder form, the type of railway bridge which will always remain inseparably connected with his name. Assisted by Hodgkinson, Fairbairn, and Clarke, his schemes were carefully worked out, every step being tested by experiment, and his labours were eventually crowned with success when the Menai bridge was opened for traffic on 5 March 1850. He constructed on similar lines the great Victoria bridge over the St. Lawrence at Montreal, which was begun in 1854 and completed in 1859, and was for many years the longest bridge in the world, and also two others in Egypt. For his invention of the system of tubular-plate railway bridges he was awarded by the council of the French Exhibition of 1855 their great gold medal of honour.

On 30 July 1847 Stephenson was returned to parliament as member for Whitby, which town he represented till his death, being re-elected on 10 July 1852, 27 March 1857, and 29 April 1859. He was a conservative and protectionist. He rarely spoke except on engineering matters; he was an opponent in the house of the Suez Canal scheme. In 1830 he became a member of the Institution of Civil Engineers, and eventually became president, occupying the chair during 1856 and 1857. He received numerous distinctions—the Order of Leopold from the King of the Belgians in 1841, the grand cross of St. Olaff of Norway in 1848, he was elected F.R.S. on 7 June 1849, and on 24 June 1857 he was created a D.C.L. of Oxford University. He married, on 17 June 1829, Frances, daughter of John Sanderson of London. She died without issue at Hampstead on 4 Oct. 1842, aged thirty-nine (*Gent. Mag.* 1842, ii. 553). His health had long been very unsatisfactory, and early in 1859 he was advised to stop all work and take a yachting cruise (the only recreation he indulged in). Eventually, in September 1859, he left for Norway; but after a temporary rally he rapidly grew worse, and was brought back in great haste to die at his own home, No. 34 Gloucester Square on 12 Oct. 1859. He was buried on 22 Oct. in Westminster Abbey, by the side of Telford, amid signs of general mourning throughout the engineering world.

Apart from his numerous reports on professional matters, Stephenson undertook little literary work, his only important work being the article on 'Iron Bridges' he wrote for the 'Encyclopædia Britannica' (8th ed.)

There are three portraits at the Institution of Civil Engineers—one by H. Phillips, one by J. Lucas, and a third, with his father, also by Lucas. A portrait by George Richmond (1849) was engraved for Mr. Jeaffreson's 'Life.' There is also a bronze statue by Marochetti, and a memorial brass in Westminster Abbey.

[Smiles's Life of George and Robert Stephenson; Obituary Notices in Proc. Inst. Civil Eng. xix. 176; The Life of Robert Stephenson, F.R.S., by J. C. Jeaffreson, with descriptive chapters on his professional works by William Pole, F.R.S., London, 1864, 2 vols., with two portraits.]

T. H. B.

STEPHENSON, SAMUEL MARTIN, M.D. (1742–1833), Irish presbyterian divine and physician, youngest son of James Stephenson, by his wife Margaret (Martin), was born in 1742 at Straidballymorris, parish of Templepatrick, co. Antrim. From the school of John Rankin, presbyterian minister at Antrim, he went to Glasgow University, where he was a pupil of William Leechman [q. v.] After being licensed in 1767 by Templepatrick presbytery he became master in the diocesan school at Monaghan, where for two years he lodged with Braddock, an apothecary. This gave him a taste for medicine, which he studied in Dublin and in Edinburgh (1773–6). Meanwhile he received a call in August 1773 from the congregation of Greyabbey, co. Down. His trial sermon, preached on 19 April 1774, was of doubtful orthodoxy, and he declined to subscribe the Westminster confession of faith. By a majority of one he was admitted on 31 May to ordination, and ordained by Bangor presbytery on 21 June (the date, 20 June, in report to synod, is wrong) 1774, reading a written declaration of his faith. On 12 June 1776 he graduated M.D. at Edinburgh, and practised gratuitously at Greyabbey, where his salary was 50l. besides *regium donum.* On 1 Aug. 1785 he resigned his charge, and was succeeded by James Porter [q. v.] Settling as a physician in Belfast, he obtained great distinction in his profession, revolutionising the treatment of fever cases. He founded, in conjunction with James McDonnell, M.D., the dispensary in 1792 and the fever hospital in 1797. He was also a zealous promoter of the (now Royal) Academical Institution which was opened 1 Feb. 1814. In recognition of his high character for public spirit and private charity, the general synod of Ulster in 1818 replaced his name on the ministerial roll, though he had exercised no clerical duties for over thirty years. In 1821 he resigned his public appointments in favour of his son, Robert Stephenson, M.D. (d. 1860). Latterly he amused himself with farming. He died on 13 Jan. 1833. He married Mary, daughter of James Armstrong, presbyterian minister of Portaferry, co. Down, and had a numerous family.

He published: 1. 'The Declaration of Faith,' Belfast, 1774, 8vo; 2 edits. same year; reprinted, with title 'Of Articles of Faith,' [1822?], 8vo. 2. 'A Review of the Reasons . . . and . . . Remarks upon a late Declaration of Faith,' Belfast, 1775, 8vo. 3. 'De Typho,' Edinburgh, 1776, 8vo (graduation thesis). 4. 'On the Linen and Hempen Manufactures of . . . Ulster,' Belfast, 1808, 4to. 5. 'An Historical Essay on the Parish . . . of Templepatrick,' Belfast, 1825, 8vo. 6. 'An Historical Essay on the Parish . . .

of Greyabbey,' Belfast, 1828, 8vo. The last two works are somewhat miscellaneous in character, but deserve credit as early examples of attention to Irish local antiquities.

[Bible Christian (Belfast), 1833, pp. 46 sq.; Irish Unitarian Mag. 1847, pp. 288 sq.; Reid's Hist. of Presbyterian Church in Ireland (Killen), 1867, iii. 337 sq.; Killen's Hist. of Congregational Presbyterian Church in Ireland, 1880, pp. 157, 215; Benn's Hist. of Belfast, 1880, ii. 161 sq.; Witherow's Hist. and Lit. Memorials of Presbyterianism in Ireland, 1886, ii. 187 sq.; Records of Gen. Synod of Ulster, 1897, ii. 507. 561.] A. G.

STEPHENSON, THOMAS (1552-1624), jesuit, was born in 1552 of catholic parents at Windlestone in the parish of St. Andrews, Auckland, Durham. He studied his humanities in England, and went through the higher course at the English College of Douay, then temporarily settled at Rheims, where he arrived on 22 June 1581. He was ordained priest there on 21 Dec. 1581, and was sent to the English mission on 13 April 1583. He was arrested on 13 Feb. 1583–4, committed to the Tower of London, and tried for high treason, but made so bold a defence that his life was spared, and after a year's confinement in the Tower he was sent into banishment, arriving at Rheims with seventy-one fellow-priests on 3 March 1584–1585. On seeking admission to the Society of Jesus he was sent to the novitiate at Brünn in Moravia on 11 Dec. 1585, and he was made a spiritual condjutor on 3 June 1597. He spent twelve years at Prague and Olmütz as professor of Hebrew and Greek, and then became secretary to Robert Parsons [q. v.] in Rome. He was again sent to the English mission in 1605, being stationed for some time in the Suffolk district. He retired to Liège in 1621, and died at Watten on 23 March 1624.

He has been credited with the authorship of translations into Latin of several of Father Parsons's works, as well as of: 1. 'A large Catechism for the Instruction of the Ignorant.' 2. 'Historia Sacra ab Orbe Condito usque ad Christi Salvatoris Adventum,' St. Omer, 1622. 3. 'The Life of Thomas Pounde.' None of his works are in either the British Museum or the Bodleian library.

[De Backer's Bibl. des Écrivains de la Compagnie de Jésus (1876), iii. 940; Dodd's Church History, ii. 418; Douay Diaries; Foley's Records, i. 471, vii. 739; More's Hist. Prov. Anglican. Soc. Jesu, p. 19; Oliver's Jesuit Collections, p. 198; Sochero's Hist. Prov. Austriæ Soc. Jesu, viii. 355; Southwell's Bibl. Scriptorum Soc. Jesu, p. 768; Tanner's Societas Jesu Apostolorum Imitatrix.] T. C.

STEPNEY, CATHERINE, LADY (d. 1845), novelist, daughter of Thomas Pollok, LL.D. (d. 1801), rector of Grittleton, Wiltshire, by his wife Susannah (d. 1802), daughter of Charlton Palmer of London, was first married to Russell Manners, and under that name published two novels, 'Castle Nuovier, or Henry and Adelina,' 1806, and 'The Lords of Erith,' 1809. On 8 June 1813 she married, at Edinburgh, Sir Thomas Stepney, ninth and last baronet, groom of the bedchamber to H.R.H. the Duke of York. He had succeeded his brother, Sir John Stepney, in the baronetcy in October 1811. Sir Thomas died on 12 Sept. 1825 (Gent. Mag. 1825, ii. 277). His widow, who was pretty, accomplished, and fashionable, and made her house the rendezvous of authors and artists, died at Henrietta Street, Cavendish Square, London, on 14 April 1845.

She wrote in later life four novels: 'The New Road to Ruin,' 1833; 'The Heir Presumptive, 1835; 'The Courtier's Daughter,' 1838, 1841; and 'The Three Peers,' 1841, all in 3 vols. They show careful observation of London society. Lady Stepney also contributed to the fashionable annuals; but Miss Mitford declared that everything under Lady Stepney's name was rewritten by Miss Landon, 'or the grammar and spelling would have disgraced a lady's maid' (L'ESTRANGE, Life of M. R. Mitford, iii. 94).

[Allibone's Dict. iii. 1214, 2241; Gent. Mag. 1845, ii. 86; Literary Gazette, 1845, pt. cclvii.; Jackson's History of Grittleton (Wiltshire Topographical Soc.), 1843, p. 22; Burke's Extinct Baronetage, p. 508.] E. L.

STEPNEY, GEORGE (1663-1707), poet and envoy, descended from the Stepneys of Prendergast in Pembrokeshire, was the son of George Stepney, groom of the chamber to Charles II, and grandson of Sir Thomas Stepney, knt., cupbearer to Charles I, by his wife, Mary, eldest daughter and coheiress of Sir Bernard Whetstone, knt., of Woodford, Essex. He was born at Westminster in 1663, and was educated at Westminster School, where he was admitted on the foundation at Whitsuntide 1676, and formed his lifelong friendship with Charles Montagu (afterwards Earl of Halifax) [q. v.] After passing the unusual time of six years as a king's scholar at Westminster, he was elected a scholar of Trinity College, Cambridge, at Whitsuntide 1682. At Cambridge Stepney appears to have acquired a great reputation as a writer of Latin verse, and his ode on the marriage of the Princess Anne to Prince George of Denmark was published in the 'Hymenæus Cantabrigiensis' (Cambridge, 1683, 4to). He graduated B.A. in 1685,

M.A. in 1689, and on 12 Sept. 1687 was elected a major fellow of his college without passing through the intermediate step of a minor fellowship. Though Stepney wrote some fulsome lines on the death of Charles II, in which he compared James II to Hercules, he joined the winning side at the Revolution, and, with the aid of his friend Montagu, entered upon a successful diplomatic career. He became secretary to Sir Cyril Wych at Hamburg, and subsequently to Mr. Johnson at Vienna (*Addit. MS.* 5881, f. 24). In 1692 he was sent as envoy to the elector of Brandenburg, in 1693 to the emperor of Germany, in 1695 to the elector of Saxony, and in 1696–7 to the electors of Mayence, Treves, and Cologne, the elector palatine, the landgrave of Hesse, and the congress at Frankfort. In June 1697 he was appointed a commissioner of trade and plantations, a post which, in spite of his diplomatic work, he retained until his death. In 1698 he was again sent to Brandenburg, and subsequently to Warsaw. In March 1702 he went a second time as envoy to Vienna. In 1705 a misunderstanding arose between him and Count Wratislaw, the imperial minister, which became so serious that Prince Eugène insisted upon Stepney's recall, and presented a formal complaint from the emperor against Stepney's supposed partiality to the cause of the Hungarian insurgents. The Duke of Marlborough, who placed the fullest confidence in Stepney, succeeded in persuading Eugène to withdraw the demand, though he afterwards 'privately engaged to remove Mr. Stepney from the embassy' (COXE, *Memoirs of John, Duke of Marlborough*, 1818–19, i. 382–3, 498). In May 1706 Stepney was sent to take possession of the lordship of Mindelheim, which had been conferred on Marlborough by the emperor (*ib.* pp. 529–42). In October following he was transferred from Vienna to The Hague, where he succeeded Stanhope as envoy. He was taken seriously ill 'of the bloody flux' in August 1707, and returned to England in the vain hope that the change might benefit him (LUTTRELL, *A Brief Historical Relation of State Affairs*, 1857, vi. 200). He died unmarried in Paradise Row, Chelsea, on 15 Sept. 1707, and was buried in great state on the 22nd in Westminster Abbey, the pall being carried by two dukes, two earls, and two barons (*ib.* vi. 215). An elaborate monument, with a long and complimentary epitaph, surmounted by his bust, was subsequently erected to his memory in the south aisle of the Abbey.

Stepney was more successful as a diplomatist than as a poet. Though his juvenile compositions are said to have made 'grey authors blush' (*Works of Samuel Johnson*, 1810–11, ix. 293), his poems are few and of little merit. He was 'a very licentious translator,' and did not, as Johnson remarks, 'recompense his neglect of the author by beauties of his own' (*ib.*) Macky declares that 'no Englishman ever understood the affairs of Germany so well, and few Germans better.' According to the same authority, Stepney spoke 'all the modern languages, as well as antient, perfectly well,' was 'a thorough statesman,' and 'of very good, diverting conversation' (*Secret Services of John Macky*, 1733, p. 142). Stepney was also a bright and perspicuous letter-writer. Extensive collections of his correspondence are preserved in the British Museum and in the Public Record Office. Another large and important collection is in the possession of the Earl of Macclesfield (*Hist. MSS. Comm.* 1st Rep. p. ix, app. pp. 34–40).

Stepney was a member of the Kit-Cat Club. His portrait, by Sir Godfrey Kneller, was engraved in mezzotint by Faber.

Stepney contributed a translation of Ovid's elegy on the death of Tibullus to Dryden's 'Miscellany Poems' (1684), and of the eighth satire of Juvenal to 'The Satires of Decimus Junius Juvenalis translated into English verse by Mr. Dryden and several other eminent hands' (1693). His poems have been reprinted in Chalmers's 'English Poets' and similar collections. He published: 1. 'An Epistle to Charles Montagu, esq., on his Majesty's Voyage to Holland,' London, 1691, fol. 2. 'A Poem dedicated to the Blessed Memory of her late Gracious Majesty Queen Mary,' London, 1695, fol. 3. 'An Essay upon the Present Interest of England. To which are added the Proceedings of the House of Commons in 1677 upon the French King's Progress in Flanders' (anon.), London, 1701, 4to; reprinted in the 'Somers Collection of Tracts,' 2nd edit. xi. 195–227.

[Authorities quoted in text; Harrison's Notices of the Stepney Family, 1870, pp. 9, 22–8; Memoir of the Celebrated Persons comprising the Kit-Cat Club, 1821, pp. 205–6 (with portrait); Alumni Westmon. 1852; Chester's Westminster Abbey Registers (Harl. Soc.), 1875, x. 259–60, 299 n., 311 n., 385 n.; Addit. MSS. (Brit. Mus.) 5881 f. 24, 5846 ff. 123, 167, 9387; Dart's Westmonasterium, 1742, ii. 82, 83–4; Cantabr. Grad. 1800, p. 400; Cibber's Lives of the Poets, 1753, iv. 72–6; Nichols's Select Collection of Poems, 1780–2, iv. 133; Burnet's History of his Own Time, 1833, iv. 501, v. 239, vi. 293; Swift's Works, 1814, x. 313; Granger's Biogr. Hist. of England, 1804, ii. 396 n.; Noble's Continuation of Granger,

1806, ii. 174–5; Faulkner's Chelsea, 1829, ii. 201–2, 321; Notes and Queries, 2nd ser. xi. 225; Brit. Mus. Cat. Some of his correspondence has been printed in Abraham Hill's Familiar Letters (1767), Lord Hardwicke's Miscellaneous State Papers (1778), Rebecca Ward's Epistolary Curiosities, 2nd ser. (1818), Coxe's Memoirs of the Duke of Marlborough (1818–19), Gentleman's Magazine for 1837 (ii. 362–5), James's Letters illustrative of the Reign of William III (1841), The Lexington Papers (1851), Kemble's State Papers (1851), and Angol Diplomatiai Iratok II. Rákóczi Ferencz Korám: Angol Levéltárakból Közli Simonyi Ernő in the Archivum Rákócziánum published by the Hungarian Academy of Sciences.]

G. F. R. B.

STERLING. [See also STIRLING.]

STERLING, Sir ANTHONY CONINGHAM (1805–1871), author of 'The Highland Brigade in the Crimea,' eldest son of Captain Edward Sterling, by Hester, daughter of John Coningham of Londonderry, was born at Dundalk in 1805. John Sterling [q. v.] was a younger brother. After keeping some terms at Trinity College, Cambridge, he was on 18 Feb. 1826 gazetted an ensign in the 24th foot. From 21 March 1834 to 5 Dec. 1843 he was a captain in the 73rd foot, and was then placed on half-pay. He was on active service during the Crimean campaign of 1854–5, first as brigade major and afterwards as assistant adjutant-general to the Highland division, including the battles of the Alma, Balaklava, and Inkerman, and the siege of Sebastopol. He received the medal with four clasps, the order of the Legion of Honour, the Turkish medal, and the fourth class of the Medjidie. On 17 Oct. 1857 he sold his commission, retiring with the rank of colonel; but during 1858–9 he was again employed as military secretary to Sir Colin Campbell, lord Clyde [q. v.], in the suppression of the Indian mutiny, and received a medal with clasp. In 1861 Lord Clyde accused Sterling of wilfully neglecting to insert the name of Colonel Pakenham in a list of persons recommended for reward by the bestowal of the K.C.B. at the close of the mutiny. This led to many letters, which are given in 'Correspondence concerning Charges made by Lord Clyde against Sir Anthony Sterling,' March 1861 (privately printed 1863). He was gazetted C.B. on 5 July 1855, and K.C.B. on 21 July 1860. He died at 3 South Place, Knightsbridge, London, on 1 March 1871, having married in 1829 Charlotte, daughter of Major-general Joseph Baird; she died on 10 April 1863.

Sterling was the author of 'Russia under

Nicholas I,' a translation, 1841; 'Letters from the Army in the Crimea, written by a Staff Officer,' 1857; 'The Story of the Highland Brigade in the Crimea, founded on Letters written during 1854, 1855, and 1856 by Lieut.-Col. A. Sterling, a Staff Officer who was there,' 1895.

[Hart's Annual Army List, 1870, pp. 96, 106; Dodd's Peerage, 1871, p. 585; Ann. Reg. 1871, p. 147; Illustrated London News, 1871, lviii. 267, 315; Carlyle's Life of John Sterling.]

G. C. B.

STERLING, JAMES (fl. 1718–1755), playwright, a native of Ireland, son of James Sterling, entered Trinity College, Dublin, as a scholar in 1718, and graduated B.A. in 1720 and M.A. in 1733. In that year he came to London with his friend Matthew Concanen [q. v.], and it is stated that on their arrival, having come to the conclusion that political writing alone would prove remunerative, they settled by the toss of a halfpenny that Concanen should defend and Sterling abuse the ministry. Sterling caused to be printed in London his weak tragedy 'The Rival Generals, as it was acted at the Theatre Royal, Dublin' (five acts, verse, London, 8vo and 12mo), but he failed to get it accepted by a London manager. In 1724 he made three contributions to Concanen's 'Poems,' signed 'J. S.' In 1728 he issued a version of 'The Loves of Hero and Leander' from the Greek of Musæus, and this was reissued with a few minor pieces as 'Poetical Works of the Rev. James Sterling' (Dublin, 1734, 8vo); and in 1736 he published 'The Parricide: a tragedy' (London, 8vo, five acts, verse). This wretched production was given five times at Goodman's Fields in December 1735. Sterling's work as a journalist and pamphleteer seems to have likewise proved a failure, and about 1740 he migrated to Maryland, where he settled as a preacher in Kent County. One of his sermons on 'Zeal against the enemies of our country' was printed at the Annapolis press in 1755, small 4to.

[Cibber's Lives of the Poets, v. 27; Trinity College (Dublin) Register; O'Donoghue's Poets of Ireland, p. 236; Baker's Biogr. Dram. 1812, i. 687; Genest's Hist. of the Stage, iii. 484; Notes and Queries, 8th ser. ix. 23, 193, 286.]

T. S.

STERLING, JOHN (1806–1844), author, born at Kames Castle in the island of Bute, 20 July 1806, was the son of Edward Sterling by his wife Hester, only daughter of John Coningham, merchant, of Londonderry. He was consequently Irish on both sides of the house, although his father's family was originally Scottish.

The father, EDWARD STERLING (1773–1847), traced descent from William, younger brother of Sir Robert Sterling, who had served under Gustavus Adolphus, and, subsequently attaching himself to James Butler, first duke of Ormonde [q. v.], was knighted in 1649 and exiled until 1660, when he returned and settled in Munster. Edward, born at Waterford on 27 Feb. 1773, was educated at Trinity College, Dublin, and was called to the Irish bar. He fought as a loyal volunteer at Vinegar Hill, and, having attained the rank of a captain of militia, contemplated a military career, and was for a short time attached to the ' eighth batallion of reserve.' Shortly after his marriage, on 5 April 1804, his regiment was ' broke,' and he migrated to Kames Castle and then to Llanblethian, near Cowbridge, Glamorganshire. In 1811 he issued a pamphlet on ' Military Reform,' which led to his becoming a regular correspondent of the ' Times ' newspaper, under the signature ' Vetus,' later exchanged for ' Magus.' Some of his letters were reprinted. During the peace interval in 1814–15 he was at Paris, and on his return to England he became a regular and important member of the ' Times ' staff. Between 1830 and 1840 the paper became, says Carlyle, his ' express emblem,' and his opinions were specially identified with ' The Thunderer's ' admiration for Wellington and Peel and detestation of O'Connell. He retired from active journalism soon after 1840, and died on 3 Sept. 1847 at South Place, Knightsbridge, at the house of his elder son, Sir Anthony Coningham Sterling [q. v.] (*Gent. Mag.* 1847, ii. 440).

John's infancy owed much to Wales, some of his most abiding impressions having been formed when his family were domiciled at Llanblethian. After his father's return from Paris in 1814, he permanently settled in England. He received most of his schooling at Dr. Burney's establishment at Greenwich, and, after a short trial of the university of Glasgow, proceeded to Trinity College, Cambridge, in October 1824. Here his tutor was Julius Charles Hare [q. v.], a circumstance which may be said to have determined his intellectual course for life, not so much from Hare's immediate influence upon him, as from the acquaintances, literary and personal, which he was thus led to form. His opinions had hitherto been radical and utilitarian, but the study of Niebuhr, to which Hare must have introduced him, effected a complete revolution ; he became a leading member of the ' Apostles'' club ; he was the most distinguished speaker at the Union ; and formed friendships with

Frederick Denison Maurice [q. v.] and Richard Chenevix Trench [q. v.] which had the most powerful effect upon his mind and character. It was most probably through Hare that he became acquainted with Coleridge, at whose feet he sat whenever possible, and through whom he came to know Wordsworth and Edward Irving. He migrated along with Maurice to Trinity Hall, with the intention of taking a legal degree, but left the university in 1827 without any, and disappointed his family by declining to study for the bar, ' because,' as he afterwards told Caroline Fox, ' he knew how specially dangerous to his temperament would be the snare of it.' A secretaryship to a political association was found for him. The object of the society was believed by Carlyle to have been the abolition of the East India Company's trading monopoly, a reform eagerly promoted at the time. If so, it would account for Sterling's acquaintance with James Silk Buckingham [q. v.], from whom in July 1828 he, with other friends, purchased the 'Athenæum.' This journal for a half-year was principally conducted by him and Maurice. Both had been regular writers while it was under Buckingham's management, and General Maurice shows in his life of his father that ignorance of the fact that they were not then its conductors has led Carlyle to mistake their sentiments, which were by no means ultra-liberal in politics, although daringly original in literature. Maurice's essay on Shelley, for instance, is a perfect dithyrambic, and either he or his colleague is found seriously exhorting University College to make the opium-eater its professor of logic. With much crudity there was a right spirit in the journal. Some of the little fanciful tales and sketches contributed by Sterling were especially charming. Financial considerations, however, soon made it imperative to transfer the paper to more practical and experienced hands. Sterling occupied the leisure thus gained in trying to fathom Coleridge, whose ' Confessions of an Inquiring Spirit ' he transcribed, and in the composition of his suggestive but unsatisfying novel of ' Arthur Coningsby,' though this did not appear until 1833 (London, 3 vols. 8vo, published anonymously). The best thing in it is the beautiful ballad ' A maiden came gliding over the sea,' which alone would prove Sterling a poet. Another novel, ' Fitzgeorge,' brought out by the publisher of ' Arthur Coningsby ' in 1832, has been attributed to Sterling, but it is impossible that he should have written it.

In 1830 Sterling married under romantic circumstances. He had become connected

o

with General Torrijos and other Spanish refugees who were planning an expedition to Spain to overthrow the tyranny of Ferdinand VII, and it was at his suggestion that an Irish cousin, Lieutenant Boyd, formerly of the East India service (' My victim,' he remorsefully says in a letter to Trench), found funds, a ship, and arms, for this generous but wild undertaking. Sterling himself was to have accompanied it, but upon the point of departure discovered that he had inspired a strong interest in Susannah, eldest daughter of Lieutenant-general Barton of the life-guards, and that the ' stately blooming black-eyed young woman, full of gay softness' (CARLYLE), would by no means let him go. He therefore stayed behind and married her, 2 Nov. 1830, thus escaping the disastrous fate which overtook Boyd, Torrijos himself, and most of the other associates in the unfortunate enterprise. Trench and Mitchell Kemble, who had actually accompanied the expedition, fortunately returned before its catastrophe. Almost immediately after his marriage he had a dangerous pulmonary attack, which decided him to accept a proposal to go out to St. Vincent, and undertake the management of a sugar estate which had belonged to a deceased uncle of his mother's, and in which he himself had an interest. Sugar-planting in the West Indies failed to prove congenial to a man born for the intellectual life, and as the state of his own health had sent him out, the state of his wife's served to send him back in August 1832. A son had been born to him in St. Vincent in October 1831, and in the previous August he had had experience of a tremendous hurricane, graphically described in a letter printed by Carlyle.

His return to England seems to have been vaguely connected in his own mind with a project for the government education of the negroes, now on the eve of emancipation. This was promptly extinguished by the colonial office, and Sterling had for the time nothing else to do than to resume the train of thought into which he had been directed by Coleridge. This led him to Germany to study German philosophy at its source, and at Bonn, in July 1833, an encounter with his former tutor, Julius Hare, now rector of Hurstmonceaux in Sussex, gave definite shape to an idea which had been dimly growing up in his mind of the church as a possible sphere for him. Hare's cordial encouragement clenched the matter, and on Trinity Sunday 1834 Sterling received deacon's orders and became Hare's curate at Hurstmonceaux, where he remained, fulfilling his professional duties in the most exemplary

manner, until ill-health compelled, or was supposed to compel, his retirement in February 1835. Carlyle is no doubt correct in deeming the real reason to have been Sterling's perception that he was out of place, and his ordination was without question an ill-judged and precipitate step.

Yet Sterling certainly did not meditate forsaking the clerical profession when he resigned his curacy. He wished to edit Coleridge's theological works, and would have taken the English chaplaincy at Rome if he could have got it. He continued to reside at Hurstmonceaux until the autumn, when he settled at Bayswater, and constant intercourse with Carlyle, whose acquaintance he had made in the previous February, greatly influenced him. He nevertheless remained constant to the study of German divinity as long as he was in England. Not until his arrival in Bordeaux, whither ill-health drove him in the autumn of 1836, are there indications of his conviction that literature was his vocation.

Upon his return in 1837 he wrote his poem of 'The Sexton's Daughter,' much in the style of Wordsworth, which was published in 1839 with miscellaneous' Poems (London, 12mo; Philadelphia, 1842). At the same time he formed a connection with ' Blackwood,' in which appeared prose pieces more distinctively original. Chief among them in merit is ' The Palace of Morgana,' one of the most beautiful of prose poems. The most elaborate is ' The Onyx Ring' (Blackwood, vols. xliv. xlv.; separately published, Boston, 1856, 16mo), a romance showing decided German influence, and perhaps on this account acceptable to Carlyle, who is apparently idealised in it as 'Collins,' while Hare figures as ' Musgrave.' The connection with ' Blackwood' continued during 1837–8, despite friction caused by the neglect of the contributors' notes and the mislaying of his manuscripts by the erratic ' Christopher North' (MRS. OLIPHANT, William Blackwood and his Sons, ii. 186–92). During these years appeared in ' Maga' the detached thoughts entitled ' Crystals from a Cavern.' To the ' London and Westminster Review,' conducted by Stuart Mill, now a very intimate friend, Sterling contributed an essay on Montaigne, evincing more clearly than heretofore his detachment from theology; and another on Simonides, with translations exhibiting his poetical talent at its best.

In the autumn of 1837 Sterling, again driven abroad by ill-health, repaired to Madeira, where he made the acquaintance of Dr. Calvert, another invalid exile. On his return in 1838 the Sterling Club was instituted, and named after him. A list of the members signed 'James Spedding, secretary,' and dated 8 Aug. 1838, is printed in Carlyle's 'Life of Sterling' (pt. ii. chap. vi.) The winter of 1838-9 was spent at Rome, a pilgrimage disparaged by Carlyle, but justly considered by Hare as momentous in its effect on Sterling's mental development. It was now hoped that he might be able to reside entirely in England, and with this view he took a house at Clifton, where he gained the friendship of Francis Newman, to whom he afterwards bequeathed the guardianship of his son. Here Sterling wrote his article on Carlyle in the 'Westminster,' which went far to complete his intellectual estrangement (there never was any other) from his old friends. This was further promoted by the assent which he found himself no longer able to refuse to some of the propositions of Strauss. He was beginning his tragedy of 'Strafford,' when, in November, a violent attack of hæmorrhage drove him to Falmouth, where he was introduced by his friend Calvert to the amiable and accomplished quaker family of Fox. Stuart Mill was also there, tending his dying brother Henry, and the social intercourse of the visitors and their Cornish entertainers is delightfully depicted in the diary of Caroline Fox [q. v.], which entirely confirms the testimony of Sterling's older friends to his amiability and charm.

The rest of Sterling's life was a hopeless struggle against consumption. On 18 April 1843 his mother and his wife both died within a few hours of each other, but he pursued his literary work in the face of every discouragement. 'The Election: a Poem in seven books' (London, 12mo), analysed and on the whole not dispraised by Carlyle, appeared in 1841; it is a pleasant exhibition of the humours of an election, somewhat in the manner of Crabbe, comic but not farcical, and linked to a pretty story. 'Strafford: a Tragedy' (London, 8vo), published in 1843, with a graceful dedication to Emerson, has much beautiful writing, but is undramatic. Of the eight cantos of 'Richard Cœur de Lion,' an 'Orlandish or Odyssean serio-comic poem' in octaves, after the pattern of Berni, only three have been published. They appeared in 'Fraser' after the author's death, and by their humour and narrative faculty deserve the praise Carlyle bestows upon them. The writer in the 'Prospective Review'—doubtless Francis Newman—however, states that nearly all the part specially commended by Carlyle was afterwards cancelled and rewritten by Sterling, one proof among many that his judgment was not in such bondage

to his friend's as has been stated. One of his last efforts was his review in the 'Quarterly' of Tennyson's 'Poems' (September 1842), in which, after an apology for the paucity of poetic power in England at the time, praise is lavished upon the homely and domestic at the expense of the more purely imaginative poems. He died on 18 Sept. 1844 at Ventnor, where he had dwelt since June 1843, and was interred in the old churchyard at Bonchurch. His writings were edited in 1848 by Julius Hare ('Essays and Tales by John Sterling,' 2 vols. London, 8vo), with a memoir in many respects most admirable, but its inadequacy, inevitable from the writer's point of view, stimulated Carlyle to the composition in 1851 of the biography which has made Sterling almost as widely and intimately known as Carlyle himself. The book is remarkable for its inversion of the usual proportion between biographer and hero. Johnson for once writes upon Boswell. Sterling is a remarkable instance of a man of letters of no ordinary talent and desert who nevertheless owes his reputation to a genius, not for literature, but for friendship.

A fine sculptured head, engraved by J. Brown, is prefixed to Hare's issue of Sterling's 'Essays and Tales,' and a portrait of 1830, after Delacour, by the same engraver, to Carlyle's 'Life' (1851).

[Of all sources of information respecting Sterling, Carlyle's biography is infinitely the most important; next are to be named Archdeacon Hare's memoir, prefixed to Essays and Tales in 1848; the invaluable notices in Caroline Fox's diary, and the article in the Prospective Review, vol. viii. General Maurice's biography of his father and Froude's publications on Carlyle and Mrs. Carlyle also afford many interesting notices. Numerous letters are published in the Letters and Memorials of Archbishop Trench; and the correspondence between Sterling and Emerson appeared in the Atlantic Monthly for July 1897, and was republished in book form 'with a sketch of Sterling's life by Edward Waldo Emerson,' Boston, 1897. Twelve letters on religious subjects to Sterling's cousin, William Coningham, afterwards M.P. for Brighton, were printed in 1851.]   R. G.

STERN, HENRY AARON (1820-1885), missionary and captive in Abyssinia, youngest son of Aaron Stern, a Jew, and Hannah his wife, was born at Unterreichenbach, near Gelnhausen in the Duchy of Hesse-Cassel in Germany, on 11 April 1820. He received his education at a school in Frankfort-on-the-Maine, to which place his parents had removed when he was young. His father destined him for the medical profession, but, at his son's special request, sent him when seventeen years old to Hamburg to be trained for a commercial life. In 1839 Stern received the offer of a good appointment in London, but presently the firm failed, and he found himself unsuccessful in obtaining employment. While in London he was taken to the Palestine Place chapel, where, through the influence of Dr. McCaul, he became a Christian, and was baptised on 15 March 1840. He was then placed in the Operative Jewish Converts' Institution, where he learned the trade of a printer. In August 1842 he was admitted into the Hebrew College of the London Jews' Society, with the ultimate intention of becoming a missionary to the Jews.

Early in 1844 Stern was appointed a missionary to the Jews in Asia Minor, and sailed for Palestine. On 14 July 1844 he was ordained deacon by the Anglican bishop of Jerusalem (Bishop Alexander) in St. James's Chapel at Jerusalem, and the same year began to work as a missionary to the Jews in Bagdad, as well as at Hillah and Bussorah. In 1847 he made a tour through the cities of Persia, labouring among Moslems as well as Jews. In 1849 he returned to England, and was ordained priest in the Chapel Royal at Whitehall on 23 Dec. 1849 by the bishop of London. He returned to Bagdad in June 1850, and remained there until 1853, when he was sent by the society to take charge of their mission at Constantinople. Here he remained for three years, and in 1856, at his own request, went on an itinerary among the Caraite Jews in the Crimea. In July 1856 he made a missionary tour among the Jews who live in the interior of Arabia, returning in the following January to Constantinople, where he stayed until 1859.

The state of the Falashas, or Abyssinian Jews, had attracted the notice of the London Jews' Society, and Stern, at their request, travelled to Cairo, whence, in December 1859, he proceeded southwards to Abyssinia. King Theodore and the Abúna gave him permission to preach to the Falashas, which he did, visiting the various Jewish villages and settlements, and fixing his headquarters at Genda. He paid a visit to England in 1860, but returned to Abyssinia at the close of 1861. Theodore, desiring closer relations between his country and England, forwarded a letter to the queen in November 1862 by Consul Cameron, stating his wish to send ambassadors to England. This communication reached the foreign office on 12 Feb. 1863, but was pigeonholed by Lord John Russell and never answered. Serious troubles followed. Stern was summoned to appear before Theodore in October 1863 at Gondar, was knocked down and beaten by the king's orders and put in chains, together with Mr. Rosenthal, a fellow-missionary. They were first incarcerated at Gondar, then at Assasso, and finally at Amba Magdala, which they reached in November 1864. Consul Cameron and other Europeans were also manacled and cast into prison. Stern was subjected to especially cruel tortures and indignities, for he was charged by the king with having reflected, in his book (see below) entitled 'Wanderings among the Falashas,' on the king's ferocity, and with having stated that his mother was a vendor of Kosso.

In July 1864 Mr. Hormuzd Rassam, first assistant to the political resident at Aden, accompanied by Dr. Blanc and Lieutenant Prideaux, arrived at Massowa, bearing a letter from the queen to Theodore, which he delivered to him at Ashfa on 28 Jan. 1866. On 24 Feb. the hand and foot chains were taken off the prisoners, whose liberation was then announced, and on 12 March they arrived, eight in number, at Korata, where Mr. Rassam was encamped. The 13th of April was the day fixed for the departure of the Europeans, but Theodore changed his mind, and again seized them, and, after a mock trial, sent the envoy and his companions, together with Stern, to Amba Magdala, where they arrived on 12 July. Four days later they were all put in foot-chains. The prisoners were guarded by soldiers day and night. They were, however, enabled to communicate with England, a system of coast messengers having been organised by Mr. Rassam.

On 13 Dec. 1867 Stern and his fellow-prisoners heard that Colonel Merewether and his band of pioneers were at Annesley Bay, preparing for the expedition upon which the government had resolved. Soon the army, which consisted of twelve thousand men, under the command of Sir Robert Cornelis Napier (afterwards Lord Napier of Magdala) [q. v.], reached Mulkutto, and, after a three months' march, crossed the Bashilo river on 10 April 1868, and defeated Theodore's troops. On the following day Stern and the other Europeans were liberated and sent to the British camp. On the 13th Amba Magdala was stormed and captured, Theodore shot himself, all the state prisoners were released, and on the 17th the fortress was burnt, and the troops marched back.

Stern at once returned to England, and (at the request and for the benefit of the London Jews' Society) told the story of his captivity to large audiences. On 1 Jan. 1871 he was appointed senior missionary of the

London Jews' Society in the metropolis, and took up his residence at Palestine Place, working among the Jews and superintending the 'Wanderers' Home.' He was made D.D. by the archbishop of Canterbury in 1881. He died at 5 Cambridge Lodge Villas, Mare Street, Hackney, on 13 May 1885, and was buried on the 18th in the City of London cemetery at Ilford. He married: first, on 2 April 1850, Charlotte Elizabeth, second daughter of Charles Henry Purday, of Hunter Street, Brunswick Square; her health compelled her to remain in England during his captivity, and she died on 1 Jan. 1874. He married, secondly, on 3 March 1883, Rebecca Davis, daughter of S. D. Goff, of Horetown, co. Wexford.

His works are: 1. 'Dawnings of Light in the East: with Biblical, Historical, and Statistical Notices of Persons and Places in Persia, Coordistan, and Mesopotamia,' 1854. 2. 'Journal of a Missionary Journey into Arabia Felix,' 1858. 3. 'Wanderings among the Falashas in Abyssinia: together with a description of the Country and its various Inhabitants,' 1862. 4. 'The Captive Missionary: being an Account of the Country and People of Abyssinia,' 1868. A number of Stern's letters were included in 'Letters from the Captive Missionaries in Abyssinia' (1866).

[Biography of the Rev. Henry Aaron Stern, D.D. by A. A. Isaacs, 1886; History of the Abyssinian Expedition, by Clements R. Markham, 1869; Abyssinian Captives: recent intelligence from H. A. Stern, edited by C. H. Purday, 1866; Times, 15 May 1885; information supplied by Colonel Prideaux, one of the captives.]   W. G. D. F.

STERNE or **STEARNE**, JOHN (1624–1669), founder of the Irish College of Physicians, was born on 26 Nov. 1624 at Ardbraccan, the episcopal palace of his granduncle, James Ussher [q. v.], then bishop of Meath. His father, John Stearne, of Cambridge, who settled in co. Down and married Mabel Bermingham, a niece of Primate Ussher, was distantly connected with the family of Archbishop Richard Sterne [q. v.] Stearne entered Trinity College, Dublin, at the age of fifteen, in 1639, and obtained a scholarship in 1641. On the outbreak of the great Irish rebellion, Stearne fled to England, and in 1643 proceeded to Cambridge, where he studied medicine at Sidney-Sussex College, and collected material for his first work, 'Animi Medela.' He remained at Cambridge about seven years, and then spent some time at Oxford, where he was welcomed by Seth Ward [q. v.], then fellow of Wadham. Prior to his departure for England he had been elected a fellow of Trinity College (1643), a position from which he was ejected by order of the Rump. On his return to Ireland in 1651 he was restored to his fellowship by direction of Henry Cromwell, with whom he was on terms of friendship, and to whom he dedicated one of his books. In 1656 he was appointed the first Hebrew lecturer in the university, receiving the degree of M.D. in 1658, and that of LL.D. in 1660. In 1659 he resigned his fellowship (probably as a necessary preliminary to his marriage in that year to Dorothy, daughter of Charles Ityves), but was appointed to a senior fellowship in 1660, after the Restoration, receiving a dispensation from the statutes of the university respecting celibacy. He became in the same year professor of law. During his tenure of these various offices, Stearne practised as a physician in Dublin, obtaining special permission to reside outside the walls of the college.

Stearne is chiefly noticeable as the founder of the Irish College of Physicians. In 1660 he proposed to the university that Trinity Hall, situated in Back Lane, Dublin, then a college or hall affiliated to the university, of which he had been constituted president in 1654, should be set apart for ever as a college of physicians. The arrangement was sanctioned, and Stearne, on the nomination of the provost and senior fellows of Trinity College, in whom the appointment was vested, became its first president. No students were to be admitted who did not belong to Trinity College. The connection between the College of Physicians and Dublin University may still be traced in the gown of the officials of the former body, which is the same as that formerly worn by fellows of Trinity College. In 1662 Stearne was appointed for life professor of medicine in the university. In 1667 a charter was granted to the College of Physicians, under which a governing body of fourteen fellows was constituted—of whom Sir William Petty [q. v.] was one—with Stearne at their head as president for life. Stearne died in Dublin on 18 Nov. 1669 in his forty-fourth year, having done and written much in his comparatively short but active life. He was buried, by his own request, in the chapel of Trinity College, where his epitaph, by his friend Henry Dodwell the elder [q. v.], in which he is described as 'Philosophus, Medicus, summusque Theologus idem,' may still be read. He had issue three daughters and one son, John Sterne (1660–1745) [q. v.], afterwards bishop of Clogher, who presented a set of his father's works to Archbishop Marsh's library at Dublin.

Few men in the academic sphere have accomplished more than Stearne. Ware says of him 'he was a very learned man, and more fond of the study of divinity than of his own profession, in which nevertheless he had great knowledge.' That he was also a man of the world is shown by the success with which he contrived to stand well both with the Cromwellian and the royalist parties. There is a fine portrait of Stearne in the College of Physicians, Dublin.

The following is a list of his works, all of which were published in Dublin: 1. 'Animi Medela,' dedicated to Henry Cromwell, 1653. 2. 'Θανατολογία,' 1656. 3. 'Adriani Heerboordii disputationum de concursu examen,' 1660. 4. 'De Electione et Reprobatione,'1662. 5. 'Aphorismi de Felicitate,' 1664. 6. 'De Destinatione,' posthumously published and edited by Henry Dodwell, his pupil and literary executor, 1672.

[Chalmers's Biogr. Dict.; Ware's Irish Writers, ed. Harris, p. 159; Stubbs's Hist. of Dublin University; Hist. of Irish Coll. of Phys.; Dublin Quarterly Journal of Medical Science, xix. (paper by Aquilla Smith on the Early Hist. of the Irish College of Physicians) ; Journ. of Medical Science, May 1865 (reprinted as 'A Memoir of Stearne,' by Dr. T. W. Belcher); Todd's List of Graduates of Dublin University.]

C. L. F.

STERNE or **STEARNE**, JOHN (1660–1745), bishop of Clogher, only son of Dr. John Sterne or Stearne (1624–1669) [q. v.], by his wife Dorothy, daughter of Charles Ryves (d. 1700), examiner in the chancery of Ireland, was born in Dublin in 1660. He was educated at the cathedral school under 'Mr. Ryder,' and entered Trinity College, Dublin, on 2 April 1674, his tutor being Philip Barbour. He graduated B.A. 11 Feb. 1677, M.A. 12 July 1681, and D.D. in July 1705. Having been ordained deacon in October 1682 by Anthony Dopping, bishop of Meath, he served for a time as domestic chaplain to that prelate. About 1688 he was made vicar of Trim ; in October 1692 he was instituted to the rectory of Clonmacduffe, and in June 1703 to that of Killary, both in the diocese of Meath. On 11 Sept. 1702 he was installed chancellor in St. Patrick's Cathedral. Upon the death of his mother's kinsman, Dean Jerome Ryves, Sterne was elected dean of St. Patrick's, Dublin, by the chapter, largely, it was said, owing to the exertions of Jonathan Swift, then prebendary of Dunlavin. Sterne retained with the deanery the curacy of St. Nicholas Without, which Swift afterwards maintained he had promised to make over

to him as a guerdon for his support. In July 1707 Sterne was instrumental in the election of Swift to represent the chapter in convocation. Soon afterwards he joined a small social club to which belonged Swift, Stella, and their common friends, the Walls and the Stoytes, who met on Saturdays for cards and other diversions. Sterne had ample means, and was liberal to the verge of profusion in his private expenditure. Swift fully appreciated his house, his library, and his dinners, with which he often compared unfavourably the dinners of his titled friends in London during 1711. Swift's letters during this period are full of allusions to Dean Sterne; he followed with interest the building operations at the deanery, tendered advice as to the laying out of the garden, and exhorted the dean to set an example to the Irish bishops by opposing the repeal of the Test.

As Sterne was assisted in his elevation to the deanery, so likewise he owed his promotion to the episcopate to Swift. On 28 Oct. 1712 the latter wrote to Stella that if he were asked who would make a good bishop, he would name Sterne before anybody. When the vacancy of Dromore occurred, before he had any idea of the deanery for himself, Swift accordingly named the dean to Bolingbroke and Ormonde, and he says 'I did it heartily.' Ormonde raised difficulties; but when the tory leaders, despairing of surmounting Anne's objection to elevating Swift to the bench, determined to provide for him at St. Patrick's, Ormonde had to give way, though he declared that he would have done it for 'no man else' than Swift. Swift was held to have achieved a great diplomatic triumph, for, in spite of the hospitalities of which the deanery was the centre, Sterne had a host of enemies among the protestant clergy in Ireland. He was consecrated bishop of Dromore on 10 May 1713, and in March 1717, upon the removal of St. George Ashe [q. v.] to Derry, he was translated to Clogher. There, as at Dublin and Dromore, he kept up hospitalities which Jonathan Smedley [q. v.] described as the redeeming feature of a forlorn district, while of the bishop himself he rhymed :

> He has a purse to keep a table
> And eke a soul as hospitable

(*Gulliveriana*, 1728, p. 111). In 1721 Sterne was appointed vice-chancellor of Dublin University, to which in 1726 he presented a sum of 1,000l. for the purpose of erecting a university printing-house (cf. BURDY, *Life of Skelton*, 1792).

In 1732 Sterne put his name upon the back of two bills—one for subdividing large preferments, the other for enforcing residence. Nothing came of the bills, but Sterne's action elicited a terrible letter from Swift to his old friend, dated July 1733. To the startling candour of this epistle the bishop answered, after a very long interval, with a suavity and a tact which give the reader a high opinion of him as a courtier. Sterne died at Clogher, unmarried, on 6 June 1745. No one enjoyed more of the confidence of Archbishop William King [q. v.], who about 1728 (that is, a year before his death) wrote to Sterne: 'It would be a comfort to me, if I were dying, to think that you would be my successor, because I am persuaded that you would prosecute right methods for the good of the church.'

By his will, dated 13 May 1741, Sterne munificently endowed a large number of local charities, especially Steevens's Hospital [see STEEVENS, RICHARD] and the Blue Coat Hospital, Dublin. He also left 600l. to Dean Swift's hospital for lunatics. He rebuilt the episcopal mansions at Dromore and Clogher, as well as St. Patrick's deanery, and he bequeathed 1,000l. to build a granite spire to St. Patrick's Cathedral, in addition to 1,500l. or 2,000l., at the discretion of his executors, towards finishing the cathedral of Clogher. He left 50l. per annum in exhibitions to Trinity College, Dublin, poor scholars of the diocese of Clogher to have the preference. The rarer books in his library he gave to Archbishop Marsh's library in Dublin. The remainder of his books (many of them purchased at John Dunton's auction in Dublin) were packed in oaken chests, and distributed by lot among the poor curates of the diocese. His manuscripts, of which he had a most valuable collection, he bequeathed to Trinity College, Dublin; among them are the well-known depositions of the sufferers in the rebellion of 1641.

Sterne's only work of importance was his admirable 'Tractatus de Visitatione Infirmorum' (Dublin, 1697, 12mo; London, 1700, several editions). This was translated in 1840 as 'The Curate's Manual' (London, 8vo). The 'Tractatus' was reprinted in the 'Clergyman's Instructor' of 1807 and 1813; but in the 1843 edition it was replaced by Bishop Wilson's 'Parochialia' (cf. DARLING, Cyclop. Bibl. p. 2827).

A portrait of the bishop by the Dublin artist, Thomas Carlton, is in the provost's house at Trinity College, and a replica is at Clogher. A mezzotint engraving was executed by Beard (EVANS, Cat. of Engraved Portraits, No. 9940).

[Cotton's Fasti Eccles. Hibern. iii. 80-1; Taylor's Univ. of Dublin, p. 380; Stubbs's Hist. of Dublin University, pp. 178, 180; Monck Mason's Hist. of St. Patrick's; Mant's Church of Ireland, ii. 245, 315, 545, 587; Ware's Irish Bishops, ed. Harris, p. 191; Ware's Irish Writers, ii. 263; Wills's Irish Nation; Nichols's Lit. Anecd. iv. 170; Dunton's Life and Errors, p. 517; Burdy's Life of Skelton, 1792; Noble's Contin. of Granger, iii. 94; Craik's Life of Swift, p. 149; Swift's Journal to Stella, ed. Ryland, passim.]   T. S.

STERNE, LAURENCE (1713–1768), humourist and sentimentalist, was great-grandson of Richard Sterne [q. v.], archbishop of York, and grandson of Simon Sterne, the archbishop's third son. Laurence's grandfather married Mary, a Yorkshire heiress, daughter of Sir Roger Jaques, and she inherited her father's estate of Elvington. She bore her husband, who died at Halifax in 1703, three sons and three daughters (THORESBY, Ducatus Leodiensis, ed. Whitaker, p. 214). The eldest son, Richard (1680–1732), succeeded to Elvington, married twice, and left a son Richard and many daughters. The third son, Jaques (the humourist's uncle), pursued a successful career in the church.

Roger, the humourist's father, was the second son, and, despite the wealth of his mother, was left to make his own way in the world. He entered the army, but never rose to high rank. His son described him in an autobiographic fragment as 'a little smart man, active to the last degree in all exercises—most patient of fatigue and disappointments, of which it pleased God to give him full measure; he was in his temper somewhat rapid and hasty, but of kindly disposition, void of all design, and so innocent in his own intentions that he suspected no one.' About 1710 he was appointed ensign in the regiment (now the 34th foot) which, at the date of his joining it, was known as Colonel Hans Hamilton's, and next year as Colonel Chudleigh's. With it Roger Sterne served in Flanders. On 25 Sept. 1711, when he was quartered at Dunkirk, he married Agnes, widow of a brother officer, Captain Hebert, 'of a good family.' She was herself of humble Irish origin, and either daughter or stepdaughter of one Nuttle, 'a noted sutler in Flanders in Queen Anne's wars.' Ensign Roger owed Nuttle money when he took her off his hands, and 'she brought not one sixpence into the family' (FITZGERALD, i. 78–9). Her husband's kindred regarded her as of inferior social station, and she failed to inspire her son with respect or affection. Her first child—a daughter Mary—was born at Lille on 10 July 1712. Late in the autumn of the following year Roger's regiment was ordered to Clonmel in Tipperary; and Laurence was born there on 24 Nov. 1713, within a few days of the family's arrival. Chudleigh's regiment was reduced the same day, and the father, thus placed on half-pay, carried his wife and children to his mother's house at Elvington. There for nearly two years they subsisted on her bounty. In May 1715 the regiment was re-formed, and Roger resumed active service (CANNON, *Records of 34th Foot*). Wife and children followed him to Dublin, and thence, moving in the track of the regiment, to Exeter. In 1719 Ensign Roger left his family in the Isle of Wight while he served in the expedition to Vigo, but in 1720 they rejoined him at the barracks at Wicklow. At the end of a year Mrs. Sterne took the children on a half-year's visit to a relative, one Fetherston, parson of the neighbouring parish of Animo. There Laurence had 'a wonderful escape in falling through the mill-race whilst the mill was going, and of being taken up unhurt.' Like sojourns (each of about a year's duration) followed in barracks or with pitying kinsfolk—at Dublin (where, in the course of 1721, Laurence learned to write), at Mullingar, and at Carrickfergus. Meanwhile the family was growing, but most of Sterne's brothers and sisters were 'of a fine delicate frame,' 'not made to last long.' Four children—two sons and two daughters—who were born between 1715 and 1722, died before completing their fourth year. Only two children besides Laurence survived infancy: his sisters—Mary, the eldest of the family, and Catherine, the youngest (born at Londonderry in 1724).

In the autumn of 1723, when he was ten years old, Sterne's father 'got leave of his colonel to fix him at a school at Halifax.' Thus Sterne's wanderings for the time ceased, but the deep impression that soldiers and barrack life made on him was attested in his portraits of Uncle Toby, Corporal Trim, and Lieutenant Le Fever. At school he spent 'eight long years or more' chafing at the tedium of 'rowowing it at Latin and Greek.' 'He would learn when he pleased,' but was 'inquisitive after all kinds of knowledge,' and spent his slender store of pocket money on chap-books. An exceptional sensitiveness to pain and pleasure soon declared itself, and in the class-room the stories of the 'Iliad' moved him to uncontrollable tears or laughter (cf. *Tristram Shandy*, bk. vi. chap. 32). Though of delicate constitution, he liked the open air and field sports, and was on occasion whimsically mischievous. When the schoolroom had been newly whitewashed,

he mounted the workmen's ladder and 'wrote with a brush in large capital letters " Lau. Sterne," for which the usher severely whipped' him. But the master, according to Sterne's account, took a different view of his freak, and declared that 'that name should never be effaced, for [the lad] was a boy of genius and sure to come to preferment.'

Meanwhile in 1727 his father played a part in the defence of Gibraltar, and there 'was run through the body by Captain [Christopher] Phillips in a duel: the quarrel began about a goose. His health was permanently injured, and when he subsequently went with his regiment to Jamaica in 1729, an attack of 'the country fever' 'made a child of him.' He died suddenly at Port Antonio in March 1731, holding the rank of lieutenant. All that he left his widow and children was a pension of 20*l*. a year. Mrs. Sterne, with her two daughters, was at the time of her husband's death with her relatives in Ireland. Her husband's family were unwilling to aid her, and she opened an embroidery school in her native land—probably at Clonmel. For eleven years her son heard little of her.

Sterne left school soon after his father's death, 'without a shilling in the world.' For two years he lived in idleness, apparently at Elvington, on the bounty of his first cousin, Richard Sterne—who alone of his father's kindred showed much disposition to help him. In 1733 this cousin, who became, he says, 'a father to' him, offered him 30*l*. a year wherewith to go to the university. Of Jesus College, Cambridge, his great-grandfather, the archbishop, had been a master and benefactor, and his uncle Jaques a scholar. Accordingly, on 6 July 1733, when nearly twenty—an unusually late age—Laurence was admitted a sizar of the college. A year later, on 30 July 1734, he was promoted to an exhibition on the foundation of the archbishop. He did not matriculate in the university till 29 March 1735. The long break in his educational career between leaving school and going to Cambridge reinforced his natural impatience of disciplinary restraint, and the educational system in vogue in the university excited his abhorrence. For mathematics he had an inherent incapacity, and he discovered only matter for jesting in the terminology of formal logic and the writings of Aristotle, to which his tutors mainly directed his attention. But his time at Cambridge was not wasted. The classics he read with appreciation in a desultory fashion, and one academic text-book—Locke's 'Essay on the Human Understanding'—which had recently been accorded a place in the university curriculum, awoke in him enthusiasm (cf. *Tristram*, i. 11, 86, 194, 203–4). Locke's perspicuity exerted a permanent influence on his mind, and evoked his intolerance of mock-learning and scholastic pedantry.

Sterne was of too volatile a temperament to make many friends at college, but at the close of his third year there entered Jesus College, as a fellow-commoner, John Hall, afterwards John Hall-Stevenson [q. v.], a precocious lad of seventeen, whose main delight was in coarse jesting and the perusal of obscene literature. With Hall-Stevenson, Sterne, despite his seniority, formed a close intimacy, which was only interrupted by death. They claimed to be distant cousins, but knew little of each other till they met at Cambridge. The tradition of their friendship during the only year (1735–6) that they were at college together was long current. 'They used to study together under a large wallnutt tree in the inner court, where one of 'em wrote underneath these lines:

This shou'd be the Tree of Knowledge,
As it stands in so very wise a colledge'

(CROFT, *Anecdotes in Whitefoord's Papers*, p. 229). In January 1736 Sterne graduated B.A., and he proceeded M.A. in due course in 1740. But he did not quit the university under the best auspices. Despite the allowances made him while an undergraduate by the college and by his cousin, he ran into debt, which long embarrassed him. In his last year at the university, too, an attack of hæmorrhage of the lungs bore witness to a permanent weakness of constitution.

His start in life he owed to his uncle Jaques, who, as precentor and canon of York, the holder of two rectories (Rise and Hornsea-cum-Ritson), and an active whig politician, possessed much influence in clerical and political circles. Acting under his uncle's advice, Laurence took holy orders. He had no fitness for the vocation, but at the time the church was regarded, in the north especially, as a whig fortress against Jacobitism and toryism. Spiritual fervour was the last qualification expected in an aspirant to ecclesiastical preferment. Sterne was ordained deacon by Richard Reynolds [q. v.], bishop of Lincoln, on 6 March 1736, at Buckden, and appears to have served a curacy there. On 20 Aug. 1738 he was ordained priest by Samuel Peploe, bishop of Chester, and four days later, on 24 Aug. 1738, he was collated by the patron, the archbishop of York, on the recommendation of his uncle Jaques, to the vicarage of Sutton-in-the-Forest (of Galtres). This village, which was

'in the forest' only in name, lay on low ground, within eight miles north of York. The parish included the hamlet of Huby, more than a mile distant, and covered an area of 10,650 acres. Entries in Sterne's handwriting in the registers date from 1739. But Sterne kept a curate from 1740, and passed much time at York. His uncle added to his emoluments and duties by procuring his appointment, on 15 Jan. 1740–1, to the prebendal stall of Givendale in York Cathedral. About the same time he was appointed commissary of the court of Pickering and Pocklington, a sinecure office, which entitled him to a share of the fees on the issue of marriage licenses in those parishes. The prebend was worth about 40*l.* a year. Sterne thenceforth took his turn as a preacher in the cathedral; but he never acquired much fame in that capacity at York. It was reported that as soon as he mounted the pulpit 'half of the congregation usually left the church, as his delivery and voice [were] so very disagreeable' (CROFT).

In 1739 there was living, in solitary seclusion in Little Alice Lane, under the shadow of the minster, a lady under thirty years of age named Elizabeth or Eliza Lumley. Both her parents were dead. Her father, Richard Lumley, held from 1721 to 1732 the rich rectory of Bedale, and brought up his family 'in style.' Her mother, Lydia, daughter of Anthony Light of Durham, had married the rector of Bedale, after the death in 1709 of a first husband, Thomas Kirke of Cookridge, near Leeds, 'a great virtuoso in all sorts of learning.' 'Though Miss Lumley was but a homely woman, still she had many admirers, as she was reported to have a fortune, and she possessed a first-rate understanding' (CROFT). For two years Sterne courted her. 'She owned,' he wrote, ' she liked me, but thought herself not rich enough or me too poor to be joined together.' At the end of two years the lady paid a prolonged visit to a sister who lived in rural retreat in Staffordshire, and Sterne wrote to her of his desolation. These letters are the earliest extant examples of that tendency to lachrymose emotion or nervous sensibility which Sterne turned later to account in his literary work. In reminding the absent Miss Lumley in 1740 of 'the sentimental repasts' which he and she had enjoyed together, Sterne, for the first time in the known history of the language, used the epithet which was, under his auspices, to designate all time a definite condition of the tender emotions.

On Miss Lumley's return to York, Sterne resumed his visits. The lady soon fell into what appeared to be a consumption. Thereupon she confided to her leisurely lover that she had bequeathed him all her property. 'This generosity,' Sterne confessed, 'overpowered me. It pleased God she recovered.' He married her in York Minster on Easter Monday (30 March) 1741, Richard Osbaldeston, the dean, officiating (*Yorkshire Archæological Journal*, iii. 93). Mrs. Sterne refused to have her fortune of some 40*l.* a year settled on her, wishing 'for no better security' than her husband's honour (FITZGERALD, i. 75).

Sterne supplied much autobiographic detail in his account of Parson Yorick in 'Tristram Shandy,' and he there credited Yorick with making a hasty journey through Europe in 1741 as governor to 'Mr. Noddy's eldest son' (bk. i. chap. xi.) It is quite possible that Sterne travelled abroad soon after his marriage, and that his pupil was related to Charles Gordon, fourth earl of Aboyne (1726–1794), as whose chaplain he was officially described two years later. In any case he improved his position at home early in 1742 by contriving to exchange his prebend of Givendale for that of North Newbald, which was of greater value (5 Jan. 1741–2), and gave him a house in Stonegate; the lease was at one time held by the York bookseller, Thomas Gent [q. v.], who recorded Sterne's succession to the property in his autobiography (GENT, *Life*, 1832, pp. 194–5). A year later, on 13 March 1742–3, Sterne was instituted to the living of Stillington—the parish adjoining Sutton—which he was permitted to hold in conjunction with his other preferments. The dispensation described him as chaplain to the Earl of Aboyne. Sterne owed Stillington to his wife's influence. 'A friend of hers in the south,' Sterne wrote, 'had promised her that if she married a clergyman in Yorkshire, when the living became vacant he would make her a compliment of it.' The actual patron who presented Sterne was Richard Levett, prebendary of Stillington in York Cathedral. The parsonage-house at Stillington he never occupied (cf. Brit. Mus. Addit. MSS. 16158–66, comprising Sterne's certificates of ordination and of his institution to benefices).

For more than twenty years (1738–59) Sterne resided at Sutton, and followed the ordinary pursuits of a rural parson who enjoyed substantial preferment. His income amounted to some 200*l.* a year. When he was not officiating in York, he preached each Sunday morning at Sutton and every Sunday afternoon at Stillington, walking thither across the fields from Sutton. But parochial duties were irksome to him. His parishioners did not understand the light-hearted indifference with which he viewed them and his sacred functions. He was a good shot, and the story is told that one Sunday, when 'his pointer dog' sprang a covey of partridges on his way to Stillington, he went home for his gun, and his congregation waited for him in vain (CROFT). In the winter he skated, and was once nearly drowned by the breaking of the ice at Stillington and the unreadiness of his parishioners to rescue him. Following the example of other rural parsons, he endeavoured to increase his income by farming. With his wife's money he purchased some land in Sutton parish, and established a dairy farm. He kept seven milch cows, but his and his wife's only notion of business was to sell their butter cheaper than their neighbours, with the result that they lost money and increased their local unpopularity. Frequently Sterne recorded in his registers his planting of fruit-trees in his garden, and his extant correspondence (before 1760) contains many references to the annual yields of his barley and oats. But his agricultural experiments rarely ended successfully. 'The following up of that affair (I mean farming),' he wrote to a friend on 19 Sept. 1767 (*Letter* 107), 'made me lose my temper, and a cart-load of turnips was (I thought) very dear at two hundred pounds.' In his later years at Sutton he tried to 'clear his hands and head of all country entanglements' by finding tenants for his glebe and freehold, and by letting out his tithes (FITZGERALD, i. 92). His dealings in land were not unsuccessful. With characteristic disregard of the rights of his poor parishioners, he, in his capacity, not of clergyman, but of owner of land outside his glebe, actively supported Lord Fauconberg, the lord of the manor of Sutton, and his neighbour, Philip Harland, in securing the passage through parliament in 1756 of a private act 'for dividing and enclosing several fields, meadows, and commons in the township of Sutton upon the Forest.' The act recites how Laurence Sterne was 'seized in his own right of a messuage and certain lands in the said township,' and how, by arrangement with his two fellow-beneficiaries, he was granted various parcels of land in addition to his former holding, amounting in the aggregate to sixty acres, two roods, and ten perches (cf. Sutton Enclosure Act, 29 Geo. II). At a later date (in 1766) he interested himself in a similar act of enclosure in his parish of Stillington, when a share in the common land was bestowed on him in consideration of his surrender of 'the tythes of wool and lamb' (cf. Stillington Enclosure Act, 6 Geo. III).

While in the country Sterne sought relaxation within doors, 'according as the fly stung,' in 'books, painting, and fiddling.' He describes his proficiency on the bass-viol in 'Tristram Shandy,' and used familiarly the technical terms of harmony and counterpoint (cf. *Tristram*, i. 59, ii. 231; *Sentimental Journey*, pp. 36, 99, 104). As an amateur artist 'he chiefly copied portraits; he had a good idea of drawing, but not the least of mixing his colours' (Croft). Some designs by him were engraved in Woodhull's poems (1772). At the end of the eighteenth century many of his pictures were in private hands at York. James Atkinson, the author of 'Medical Bibliography,' showed to Thomas Frognall Dibdin [q. v.], when on a visit to York in 1820, a coarse painting in oils in which Sterne figured as a mountebank at a fair, and a friend, Thomas Brydges, as a quack doctor. The latter figure was by Sterne and the former by Brydges (see print in Dibdin's *Bibliographical Tour*, 1838, i. 212). An offensive caricature-sketch of Mrs. Sterne, signed 'Pigrich fecit,' and engraved in M. Paul Stapfer's 'Life,' is also assigned to Sterne's pencil. But it was on books and society that he chiefly depended to relieve the monotony of rural existence. His reading while at Sutton was multifarious and incessant. He rarely rode about the parish without a book in his hand. Rabelais and Cervantes he was constantly quoting, and he pored over romances in French and English, medical and military treatises, and collections of facetiæ. He was a book-collector, but the purchase of works in his favourite lines of study was often beyond his means. His friend, John Hall-Stevenson, on marrying an heiress, had, however, settled down at Skelton Hall in Cleveland, and acquired a large and curious library, which was freely at Sterne's disposal.

Congenial society was not wholly out of Sterne's reach at Sutton. If the farmers pitied his levity as proof of a cracked brain, Stephen Croft, the squire of Stillington, delighted in Sterne's whimsical vein of humour, and showed him 'every kindness.' With Philip Harland, the squire of Sutton, he was never 'on a friendly footing,' although he made various efforts to ingratiate himself with him. But at Newburgh Priory, near Coxwold, within nine or ten miles of Sutton, lived Lord Fauconberg, the lord of the manor of Sutton, who extended a profuse hospitality to Sterne and his wife. At York they regularly frequented concerts and balls. Sterne spent many an afternoon

in jesting to an admiring audience at the coffee-house which served him as a club, or in visiting the booksellers. A week or two was occasionally spent at Scarborough or London. Outside his immediate neighbourhood he found his most boisterous recreation in sojourns with Hall-Stevenson at Skelton. Hall-Stevenson gathered there at certain seasons of the year a crew of kindred spirits drawn from the clergy and squirearchy of the county, whom he christened the club of 'Demoniacks.' It is said that Sterne was never formally enrolled a member, but he often joined in the orgies of drink and coarse merriment with which the 'Demoniacks' celebrated their meetings.

Throughout his career Sterne's health was a frequent source of anxiety. His lungs were always weak, and the wet climate and low-lying situation of Sutton encouraged a tendency to asthma. His love of social festivities was not salutary, but after a midnight debauch he usually dosed himself religiously with Bishop Berkeley's tar-water. He had his share of domestic worries, and, although they were largely of his own making, he was not on that account the less oppressed by them. The commonly accepted notion that Sterne drew his wife's portrait in Mrs. Shandy—both were named Elizabeth—has little to support it. Mrs. Sterne had none of Mrs. Shandy's placidity, taciturnity, or stupidity. She was of excitable and bustling temperament, and, while frugal in trifles, lacked capacity for orderly or economical housekeeping. But her husband was never blind to her intellectual ability. Even when smarting under her voluble rebukes and abusing her ill-humour to his friends, he admitted that 'in point of understanding and finished address' few of her sex rivalled her (*Addit. MS.* 34527, f. 50). She is said to have aided him in composing his sermons (Croft). Nor, in an irresponsible fashion, was he indifferent to her happiness. He claimed to be 'easy' with her, and he convinced himself that if he left her at liberty to go her own way, he might fairly go his undisturbed. But he never viewed his marital obligations seriously, and his immoral and self-indulgent temperament rendered sustained felicity impossible. He used no figurative language in his often repeated confession that it was his unhappy lot to be 'always miserably in love with some one' outside the domestic circle. There were, however, seasons of calm in the conjugal atmosphere. As parents both husband and wife appear in a favourable light. Their first child—a daughter—who was born on 1 Oct. 1745, was christened Lydia, after Mrs. Sterne's mother, within an hour or two of her birth, and died next day. On 1 Dec. 1747 a second child, again a daughter, was born, and was also baptised in the name of Lydia on the same day. There were no other children of the marriage. The second Lydia reached maturity, and the genuine affection that Sterne lavished until his death on his only child forms the pleasantest feature of his domestic life. A proof of the amity existing on occasion in the household during Lydia's early girlhood is extant in the register of marriages celebrated by Sterne among his poor parishioners at Sutton between 1755 and 1757. Mrs. Sterne more than once signed her name as a witness of the ceremony, and from the age of nine Lydia, who grew into a frolicsome girl, frequently served in the same capacity, on the first occasion signing her name beneath her mother's (31 Jan. 1757).

With others of his kinsfolk Sterne's relations were far less harmonious. His elder sister, Mary, was, as he wrote, 'most unfortunate. She married one Weemans in Dublin, who used her most unmercifully, spent his substance, became a bankrupt, and left my poor sister to shift for herself, which she was able to do but for a few months, for she went to a friend's house in the country and died of a broken heart.' His mother and younger sister (Catherine), of whom he apparently lost sight between his father's death and his marriage, proved sources of graver embarrassment. Soon after his marriage the news reached them in Ireland that his wife was a woman of fortune. They straightway crossed to Liverpool with a view to subsisting at Chester or York on Sterne's or his wife's bounty. His mother visited Sutton, was dismissed with difficulty with 20l. and a gift of clothes, and, in spite of Laurence's remonstrances, took up her residence with her daughter at Chester. In 1744 Sterne's sister Catherine travelled to Sutton to announce their pecuniary distress. His wife offered to set Catherine up as a mantua-maker or milliner in London, and actually secured for her a situation in a nobleman's family, but the arrangement was treated with scorn. Between 1743 and 1750 Sterne reckoned that he forwarded to his mother and sister sums amounting to 90l. Just before the second Lydia was born, in November 1747, the elder Mrs. Sterne again swooped down on Sutton, and, while accepting ten guineas, declined an offer of an annuity of 8l. unless it was legally settled on her. From Sutton she passed to York to complain to Sterne's uncle of her son's neglect. Much of her story was false, and in 1751 Sterne, after defending himself

from her charges in a long letter to his uncle, with whom he was then involved in a bitter quarrel, declared that her pension of 20l. was adequate for her needs, and that he could not rob his wife and daughter in her interest (Brit. Mus. Addit. MS. 25479, f. 12). His mother remained at York, and in 1750 he wrote of paying her and other friends a visit, as if he were on tolerable terms with her (FITZGERALD, i. 91). Some years later she died an insolvent debtor in 'a wretched condition' either in the common gaol at York 'or soon after she was released' (CROFT). In her last days it is said that a subscription was set on foot to relieve her, and that Sterne made no sign (ib.) He was sensitive to public opinion, and it seems incredible that, had he known of her extremity, he should not have come to her rescue. His relations with her were passably amicable in 1759. After that date he was often absent from York, and the chances are that the news of her tragic end reached him when all was over. That he shirked his responsibilities in this as in other relations of life is possible; and in view of his published avowals of sensibility to all forms of distress, Byron's epigrammatic denunciation of him as the man who could whine over a dead ass while he let his mother starve has apparent justification. But allowance must be made for his early efforts to aid her, for her difficult temper, and for her malevolence in widening the breach between him and his influential uncle by retailing fanciful statements of his neglect of her when the quarrel was at its height.

For Sterne's alienation from his uncle, which began after 1745, two causes have been assigned. Jaques Sterne was an active whig politician. He corresponded with the Duke of Newcastle (cf. his manuscript letters in the Newcastle Correspondence in the British Museum), and his nephew, although he had no interest in politics, for a time deemed it wise to propitiate him by sending paragraphs to a York newspaper in the whig interest. When in 1745 a defence fund was raised in York at the outbreak of the Jacobite rebellion, Laurence subscribed 10l., while his uncle subscribed 50l.; and Laurence wrote soon after for 'Lloyd's Evening Post' a congratulatory article on the arrest of Dr. Burton, a York physician, who, as a suspected Jacobite, had incurred his uncle's enmity. Sterne afterwards immortalised Burton as 'Dr. Slop.' In 1747 the elder Sterne, who was archdeacon of Cleveland in 1735 and of the East Riding from 1750, printed a charge to the clergy entitled 'The Danger arising to our Civil and Religious Liberty from the great increase of Papists,' and at the same time helped to inaugurate a new whig electioneering journal, 'The York Journal, or the Protestant Courant.' Sterne at first contributed, but suddenly informed his uncle that he would write for the whigs no more (ROBERT DAVIES, *Memoir of the York Press*, 1868, p. 324). 'Though my uncle was a party man,' Sterne declared, ' I was not, and detested such dirty work, thinking it beneath me. From that period he became my bitterest enemy.' This is Sterne's version of the quarrel. Coffee-house gossip, on the other hand, traced it to a less respectable origin. Laurence was said to have displaced his uncle in the affections of a lady who was living under Dr. Sterne's protection, with the result that Laurence became by her the father of a natural daughter; the girl was stated to be alive in 1796, and to closely resemble her reputed father (CROFT). Uncle and nephew were never reconciled. When in December 1750 Sterne sought to add to his income by offering to take the turns of such appointed preachers in the minster as might be accidentally prevented from fulfilling their engagements, Dr. Sterne intervened and wrote that on no account was extra employment to be given to 'the one person unacceptable to me in the whole church, an ungrateful and unworthy nephew of my own.' When Dr. Sterne died in 1759 no mention was made of his nephew in his will, at which Laurence 'was so offended that he did not put on mourning, though he had it ready, and, on the contrary, showed all possible marks of disrespect to his uncle's memory' (*ib.*)

Despite such difficulties, Sterne maintained his position in York. In 1747 he first appeared in print under his own name, publishing, at the price of sixpence, 'The Case of Elijah and the Widow Zerephath consider'd. A charity sermon, preach'd on Good Friday, April 17, 1747, in the parish church of St. Michael-le-Belfry, before the Right Honourable the Lord Mayor, by Laurence Sterne, M.A., Prebendary of York' (York, 1747). It was printed for John Hildyard, bookseller in Stonegate, but was sold, according to the title-page, by London booksellers. The dedication was addressed to Dean Richard Osbaldeston [q.v.] A presentation copy, inscribed by Sterne to the squire of Sutton, Philip Harland, is in the minster library at York. It was reissued in Sterne's collected sermons (vol. i. No. v.) Although this effort was, on its first publication, 'read by very few,' Sterne soon printed a second sermon, 'The Abuses of Conscience, set forth in a Sermon preached in the Cathedral Church of

St. Peter's, York, at the Summer Assizes, before the Hon. Mr. Baron Clive and the Hon. Mr. Baron Smythe on Sunday, July 29, 1750.' This was stated to be 'published at the request of the High Sheriff [Sir William Pennyman] and Grand Jury,' to whom it was dedicated. This performance, like its forerunner, was little noticed at the time, but it acquired worldwide celebrity on being incorporated at a later date in 'Tristram Shandy' (bk. ii. chap. xvii.), and again in the collected 'Sermons' (vol. iv. No. xii.) The only literary effort, besides sermons and political paragraphs, with which Sterne has been credited in his early years is some fanciful reflections on problems of natural science, which were obviously suggested by Fontenelle's 'Plurality of Worlds.' These reflections were first published from a manuscript by M. Paul Stapfer in his 'Vie de Sterne' (pp. xvi-xlix); but their authenticity is by no means established.

On 29 Oct. 1760 Dean Fountayne, who succeeded Osbaldeston in 1747, bestowed on Sterne, despite his uncle's hostility, a second commissaryship—that of the peculiar court of Alne and Totteston. The emoluments were insignificant, and, although a deputy exercised most of the slight functions, Sterne thenceforth made an annual visitation of the parishes which were subject to the commissary's court. They included Skelton (with Alne and Wigginton).

Soon after the issue of his second sermon a quarrel among the cathedral officials suggested to Sterne a literary effort in a different style. About 1748 Dr. Topham, a lawyer, who held many ecclesiastico-legal offices in the diocese, obtained for his son from Matthew Hutton, archbishop of York (since 1747), a promise of the reversion of one of his patent places. Dean Fountayne complained that Topham had misrepresented the matter, and the archbishop revoked his assent to the arrangement. Topham declared open war on Fountayne, and Sterne supported the dean. Subsequently Topham laid claim to the commissaryship of Pocklington and Pickering, which Sterne himself enjoyed. The dispute lingered on for many years, and Sterne amused himself by humorously satirising in a pretended letter to a friend the ferment in cathedral circles which Topham's greed aroused. He represented York as a village of which Trim (i.e. Topham) was sexton and whipper-in; the archbishop was the parson, the dean the parish clerk, and himself, Lorry Slim, an insignificant parishioner. According to Sterne's sketch, Trim was detected in carrying home 'the warm watch-coat' which was parish property, and was held by him in right only of his office of sexton. But the parish clerk came upon Trim just in time to prevent him from cutting out of the parochial garment an under-petticoat for his wife and a jerkin for himself. Thereupon Trim, thwarted in one direction, endeavoured to rob his neighbour Lorry Slim, 'an unlucky wight,' of a thread-bare pair of black plush breeches. The sketch ends with Trim's signal humiliation. Much of the jesting is coarse, but throughout Sterne gave proofs of his capacity as a literary artist in humour. In its general tone it adumbrates many characteristic features of 'Tristram Shandy.' The name Trim Sterne transferred to his novel unaltered. The sketch was fur-tively circulated among Sterne's friends—doubtless in manuscript—but was deemed unfit for publication. It was first published in 1769, in the year after Sterne's death, under the title of 'A Political Romance ad-dressed to ——, esq. of York,' with a list of dramatis personæ and the names of the persons they were intended to represent. The advertisement vaguely described the piece as 'written in 1759,' but it doubtless dated further back. The edition of 1769 is of some rarity. There are copies in York min-ster and the British Museum libraries. It was subsequently appended to Sterne's 'Cor-respondence,' and often reprinted under the title of 'The History of a Warm Watch Coat.'

This skit indicated Sterne's vocation, and in fantastic accord with his irresponsible tem-perament, a crisis which he disreputably pro-voked in his domestic affairs gave him, at the mature age of forty-six, an opportunity of pursuing it. Writing in Latin during 1758 to his friend Hall-Stevenson, he ex-pressed himself weary of his wife's society, and announced a visit to London on an adulterous errand (this letter is often mis-dated 1767). Within a few months of its composition, in 1758, Sterne's wife was stricken by an attack of insanity. The im-mediate cause was a fit of anger occasioned by her discovery of her husband in compro-mising relations with a maid-servant (CROFT, *Anecdotes*). Sterne suffered for a time such remorse as was possible to his disposition, and in the early stages of the illness took whimsical pains to humour his wife's diseased imaginings. 'She fancied herself the queen of Bohemia. He treated her as such, with all the supposed respect due to a crowned head.' 'To induce her to take the air, he proposed coursing in the way practised in Bohemia. For that purpose he procured bladders and filled them with beans and tied them to the wheels of a single horse-chair, when he drove madam into a stubble field. With the motion of the carriage and

the bladders' rattle it alarmed the hares, and the greyhounds were ready to take them' (CROFT, *Scrapeana*, p. 22). But such reme-dies proved of little avail, and Mrs. Sterne was at length placed in 'confinement under a lunatic doctor in a private house at York' (CROFT, *Anecdotes*). In his wife's absence Sterne lived at first much alone. His daughter's health seemed failing, and his spirits declined. It was then that he turned for solace to literary work, and by way of relieving his melancholy wrote the opening books of 'Tristram Shandy.' He laboured with a rare zest. Although he corrected his manuscript liberally, he had com-pleted fourteen chapters in six weeks (bk. i. chap. xiv.), and reached his twenty-first chap-ter on 26 March 1759. The employment dissipated most of his cares. He was so de-lighted with his facility that he jestingly pro-mised to write two volumes every year for the rest of his days (cf. bk. i. chap. xxii.)

Meanwhile his yearning for feminine sym-pathy revived, and happening to meet at York a very young and intelligent French lady of unblemished reputation, who was lodging with her mother, Madame Fourmantelle, in the Stonegate, he, with indefensible disre-gard of his domestic position, amused him-self with a flirtation. During the year (1759) that he was shaping his *magnum opus*, a playful correspondence and a series of inter-views with Mlle. Fourmantelle, his 'dear, dear Kitty,' formed his main source of re-creation. In the book he refers to the lady as his 'dear, dear Jenny,' between whom and himself there subsisted 'that twice tender and delicious sentiment which ever mixes in friendship where there is a difference of sex.' He sent her sweetmeats and honey, and de-clared himself hers 'to eternity' (the corre-spondence was published from the originals in the possession of Mr. John Murray by the Philobiblon Society in 1855-6, vol. ii.)

When Sterne had gone some way with 'Tristram Shandy,' his friend Croft assembled a select company at Stillington Hall after dinner to hear portions read by the author ; but the company fell asleep, and Sterne is said to have flung the manuscript in anger into the fire. Luckily his host rescued the scorched papers from the flames (CROFT). Other friends who examined it declared it to be laughable. The rumour spread that it would prove 'extraordinary,' and when by the autumn of 1759 two books were completed, Sterne offered them to Dodsley, the great London publisher, for 50l. with much self-satisfaction. The offer was declined. A friend, Arthur Lee, lent him 100l., and he printed at York a small edition of two or three hundred copies, which John Hinxham, the successor of Hildrop, the publisher of his sermons, agreed to publish for him. Dodsley was one of Hinxham's London agents, and took a few copies with many misgivings. On 1 Jan. 1760 advertisements in the 'Publick Advertiser' announced that the work was on sale. The York public at once recognised its attraction; but it was more gratifying to its author, who declared that he wrote 'not to be fed but to be famous,' to learn within a few weeks that it had startled London. Garrick was one of its earliest admirers. Bishop Warburton read it and recommended it to all 'the best company in town.' In March Horace Walpole wrote that nothing else was talked of or admired. A wager was laid in London that a letter addressed to 'Tristram Shandy in Europe' would reach Sterne at Sutton, and the letter was safely delivered (ib.) Sterne's first genuine experiment in literature brought him in an instant a worldwide reputation.

Mrs. Sterne's health was meanwhile improving, and in November 1759 he took a house in the minster yard for her and her daughter, whom he was resolved to educate thoroughly. Anxiety on his wife's account in 1760 made him hesitate to accept Stephen Croft's offer to carry him to London and thus enable him the better to estimate the extent of 'Tristram's' triumph. But Croft pointed out that his presence did his wife no good. In the first week of March they hurried south and put up with a common friend, Cholmley, in Chapel Street, Mayfair. Sterne was welcomed by Dodsley, who accepted without hesitation Sterne's offer of a collected edition of his sermons. One on conscience had already figured in 'Tristram' (bk. ii.) For the sermons and a new edition of 'Tristram' Dodsley paid down 480l. At the same time he commissioned Sterne to supply a fresh volume of 'Tristram' every remaining year of his life. Sterne, although he had asked Dodsley for 650l., skipped back to Cholmley's rooms, declaring that 'he was the richest man in Europe,' and, resolving to prolong his stay in London, took lodgings in St. Alban's Street, not far from Dodsley's shop in Pall Mall. News of his presence there was soon abroad, visitors thronged his rooms, and invitations to fashionable dinners and receptions abounded. Almost every hour of his day and night was straightway engaged for a month in advance. At his suggestion Mlle. Fourmantelle and her mother arrived in Soho to see the town under his auspices, but his social preoccupations left him little time for dalliance

with humble admirers. Although, with repellent levity, he hinted to the young lady at what might befall them if 'an obstacle to their happiness' (i.e. Mrs. Sterne) were removed, their interviews in London were brief and rare. That Sterne's neglect drove Mlle. Fourmantelle mad, and that a chance meeting with her later in France suggested to him his portrait of Maria, are stupid fables. The sentimental passion with which he inspired a bewilderingly rapid succession of Dulcineas in London was not treated very seriously on either side. But he flattered himself that his gallantries were admired (ib.) His witty talk in society was applauded on all hands. According to the poet Gray, the man proved as great an object of admiration as the book (Letters, ed. Gosse, iii. 36). Lord Ossory commissioned Reynolds to paint his portrait. Old Earl Bathurst treated him with all the deference he had extended in early life to Pope and Addison. Lord Rockingham took him to Windsor in his suite on 6 May. Garrick's attentions were incessant.

A large second edition of 'Tristram' was published in April, with a dedication addressed to Pitt and a frontispiece by Hogarth. In the same month there appeared fifteen 'Sermons of Mr. Yorick' in two 12mo volumes. The preliminary list of subscribers numbered over five hundred, and included a long array of noblemen. An engraving by Ravenet of Reynolds's portrait—'his own comic figure'—formed the frontispiece. Admirers of 'Tristram' were not disappointed. Gray declared the 'Sermons' to be 'most proper for the pulpit,' and indicative of 'strong imagination and a sensible heart.' But their main recommendation was that the preacher was 'often tottering on the verge of laughter and ready to throw his periwig in the face of his audience' (ib. iii. 53; cf. MRS. DELANY, Autobiography, 1st ser. iii. 602).

But Sterne's triumph was not unalloyed. In private and in public 'Tristram' excited much adverse criticism. Every character and locality mentioned in the work seemed identifiable by York readers, and Sterne was freely charged there with vilifying his neighbours alive and dead (cf. Letter vi). The man-midwife, Dr. Slop, was Dr. John Burton [q. v.], the leading accoucheur of York, and the minutely described scene of Slop's farcical tumble in the mire at the sudden turn in the road is still recognisable by any traveller approaching Sutton vicarage from York. Parson Yorick was without disguise Sterne himself, and Yorick's large parish, Sutton-in-the-Forest. The account of Mr.

Shandy's ancestor, Sir Roger Shandy, who fought at Marston Moor, bore an obvious relation to an ancestor of the unamiable squire of Sutton, who had set forth his ancestor's prowess at Marston Moor in an epitaph that he caused to be inscribed in the church while Sterne was vicar. Ox Lane and Ox Close are still names of fields in Sutton parish, and Oxmoor figures largely in the conversation of Yorick with the Shandy brothers.

In London 'Tristram' was denounced on wider grounds. Dr. Johnson was offended by its indecent innuendo, and always spoke with scorn of 'the man Sterne.' They met only once, and then Sterne further outraged his censor by displaying to the company an obscene drawing. Richardson declared Sterne's book 'execrable.' Horace Walpole found the digressions insupportable, and the whole 'a very insipid and tedious performance.' Dr. Farmer warned the undergraduates at Emmanuel College, Cambridge, who rated it highly, that, 'however much it may be talked about at present, in the course of twenty years, should any one wish to refer to it, he will be obliged to go to an antiquary to refer to it' (cf. MRS. DELANY, 1st ser. iii. 588, 593). Professional critics in the press, who envied Sterne's reception by the world of fashion, pursued him with unremitting hostility. Goldsmith wrote of him in the 'Citizen of the World' (No. 74): 'In England, if a bawdy blockhead thus breaks in on the community, he sets his whole fraternity [of brother-authors] in a roar, nor can he escape, even though he should fly to the nobility for shelter.' Smollett in the 'Critical Review,' and Griffith in the 'Monthly Review,' made furious onslaughts. A report got abroad in the newspapers that Sterne designed to introduce Warburton into a later volume as Tristram's tutor, and was bought off. Sterne hotly denied the rumour in a letter to Garrick (*Letter* vii.) It seems due to the fact that soon after his arrival in town Warburton, who recognised his genius, sent for him, and sought to obtain a promise that he would restrain his tendency to obscenity in future volumes. On parting Warburton gave him a purse of money and sent him books. Sterne corresponded amicably with the bishop later in the year; but subsequent volumes of 'Tristram' were not purged of indecency, and Warburton, while acknowledging their wit, expressed a fear that Sterne was 'an irrecoverable scoundrel' (cf. J. S. WATSON, *Life of Warburton*, 1863; KILVERT, *Warburton Papers*, pp. 239–46; NICHOLS, *Lit. Anecdotes*, v. 616–18; STERNE, *Letters*, vii.

x. xi.) When in 1760 Sterne's friend, Hall-Stevenson, published a vapid adulatory ode on his 'Cousin Shandy's' visit to town, which disgusted many of Sterne's supporters, the newspapers bespattered Hall-Stevenson as well as his hero. The attack was developed in separately issued pamphlets. 'The Clockmaker's Outcry against the Author of "Tristram Shandy"' was soon followed by 'A Methodist Preacher's Letter to Sterne,' 1760, and 'Explanatory Remarks upon the Life and Opinions of Tristram Shandy, by Jeremiah Kunastrokius, M.D.,' 1760. 'A Funeral Discourse occasioned by the much lamented death of Mr. Yorick ... by Christopher Flagellan, A.M.' (1761), was a well-sustained piece of irony. A more impudent attack was the issue, late in 1760, of a spurious third volume of 'Tristram' by a hack-writer named John Carr [q. v.] Sterne at first bore such blows good-humouredly. 'The scribblers use me ill,' he wrote to Warburton on 9 June 1760, 'but they have used my betters much worse.' Subsequently he complained of 'the cant of criticism' with a good deal of heat.

In the middle of May (1760) he returned to Yorkshire, travelling in unwonted state, as befitted in his opinion his newly acquired fame. He preached in the cathedral on the 18th before the judges of the assizes. At the same date he had the good fortune to receive from his old friend Lord Fauconberg an offer of the perpetual curacy of Coxwold, worth 100l. a year. The village was admirably situated upon high ground on the Thirsk road, some twenty-two miles from York, and lay within easy reach of the moors. Newburgh Priory, the patron's house, was a mile off. Sterne accepted the benefice with alacrity, receiving permission to retain the livings of Sutton and Stillington, which were thenceforth served solely by curates. After a twenty-two years' settlement at Sutton, the climate of which he always found unhealthy, Sterne accordingly moved in the summer of 1760 to the invigorating elevation of Coxwold. There seems to have been no parsonage, but Sterne lived on the Thirsk road, near the church, in a large cottage, which he christened Shandy Hall. The house, which he was constantly extending and improving, has been recently renovated, and is now adorned by a tablet attesting Sterne's occupancy. The change reconciled him for a time to the contrast between the dull monotony of country life and the brilliant variety of his metropolitan experiences. But he had, as Garrick wrote, 'degenerated in London like an ill-transplanted shrub; the incense of the great spoiled his

head as their ragouts had done his stomach' (cf. HORACE WALPOLE, *Letters*, iii. 298). He spent wastefully the money that his books brought him, and resented his wife's biting rebukes of his extravagance. But he found some compensations at Coxwold for Mrs. Sterne's increased and well-justified mistrust —in the society of his daughter, in the hospitable attentions of Lord Fauconberg, and in the delights of literary work. By August he had finished a third book of 'Tristram,' which he believed to contain 'more laughable humour' than its forerunners, with 'an equal degree of Cervantic satire' (*Letter* xii.) By October a fourth book was ready for the press, and before Christmas he hurried to London to superintend the issue of the two new volumes. They appeared at the beginning of the new year with a second plate by Hogarth, and met with mingled cries of abuse and applause. Fashionable society heartily welcomed him back, and for another three months he was immersed in social gaieties. The wits, Foote and Delavall, courted him; Wilkes found him a companion after his own heart. He associated on even terms with politicians like Lord Rockingham, Shelburne, Charles Spencer, and Charles Townshend, and retailed political gossip, with an increasing sense of his own importance, in letters to Yorkshire acquaintances. John, first viscount and afterwards first earl Spencer, sent him a silver ink standish, and offered him repeated hospitalities. On 3 May he preached at the Foundling Hospital, when the collection amounted to 55*l*. 9s.

Next month he cursed anew the churlish fate which rendered resumption of residence at Coxwold needful. His wife, 'in pure, sober good sense, built on sound experience,' declared herself happier in his absence, and suggested that he should cure his discontent by leading 'a bear round Europe.' But he resolved to make the best of his situation, bought seven hundred books, 'dog cheap and many good,' and found all his old satisfaction in working at a fifth volume of 'Tristram.' An unusually amiable impulse led him to read the chapters to his wife as they were finished, while, despite their improprieties, his daughter helped him to copy them (*Letter* xix.) On 6 Sept. 1761 he wrote a paper (still in York Minster Library) promising the dean and chapter to pay the Rev. Marmaduke Collier 16*l*. a year for taking entire charge of his parish of Sutton, and subsequently engaged a curate for Stillington, it is said, at 40*l*. a year. On the day that George III was crowned (22 Sept.) there were extended festivities at Coxwold. Sterne preached extemporarily in

the morning 'an excellent sermon,' which 'gave great content' to a crowded congregation; he published the text in the London and York newspapers (Letter to Lord Fauconberg from his Coxwold agent, Richard Chapman, 25 Sept. 1761; cf. *Sermons*, No. 21). By December he completed the fifth and sixth volumes of 'Tristram,' including the beautiful story of 'Le Fever,' and, while dedicating them to Lord Spencer, inscribed 'the story of Le Fever to' the name of Lady Spencer. A manuscript draft of that story, partly in his autograph, which he sent to his patrons before its publication, is still preserved among Earl Spencer's archives (*Hist. MSS. Comm.* 2nd Rep. p. 20). Becket took Dodsley's place as the publisher, and to Becket Sterne remained faithful to the end.

While supervising the publication of these books in London Sterne fell violently ill, and a journey to the south of France was judged imperative by the physicians. Obtaining a year's absence of leave from the archbishop of York, and hastily borrowing from Garrick 20*l*., which he never repaid, he left for Paris in January 1762. His fame had preceded him in the French capital, and his health improved sufficiently to enable him to plunge with enthusiasm into the whirl of social dissipation that was offered him. Politicians and men of letters alike welcomed him. The Duc d'Orléans added his portrait to his collection of 'odd men;' Diderot gave him a commission to buy English books. He was a familiar figure in the salons of Choiseul, Crébillon fils, Holbach, Suard, and the Comte de Bissy. He visited the theatres, and was introduced as Garrick's friend to the leading actresses. Charles James Fox, who was also visiting Paris, carried him off to spend a week with him at St. Germain in February (*Wombwell MS.*) In March he wrote to his wife of his rapid progress in the French tongue (*Notes and Queries*, 6th ser. v. 254); but, although he spoke and wrote it fluently, he never did either well. In May he sent for Mrs. Sterne and Lydia, who was suffering from asthma; and he forwarded detailed instructions for the journey which would have done credit to the most pragmatic paterfamilias. On 4 June 1762 —George III's birthday—he dined with a distinguished company at the English ambassador's (Lord Tavistock's), and allowed himself to be tricked by some fellow-guests into giving an imaginary sketch of the Abbé Dutens, the French envoy at Turin, in ignorance of the fact that the abbé, who was personally unknown to him, was his neighbour at the table (DUTENS, *Mémoires d'un Voyageur*, i. 165–7). Later in the month another attack of hæmorrhage of the lungs proved the unwisdom of further indulgence in Parisian gaieties. Mrs. Sterne and Lydia joined him in July, and within two weeks they all went south to Toulouse, where he had hired a house at a rental of 30*l*. a year. Although he often talked of returning to Paris, he stayed with them at Toulouse for more than twelve months. Lydia was soon 'hard at it with music, dancing, and French speaking.' Mrs. Sterne, 'a great economist,' was 'charmed' by the cheapness of provisions, but would never let her husband out of her sight, following him everywhere so persistently as to excite pity for him among his friends (COOPER, p. 5). Sterne tried to relieve ennui by fabricating a seventh volume of 'Tristram,' in which he embodied his recent experience of foreign travel. He had originally intended, he told his political friends, to conduct his hero to various European courts so as to give himself the opportunity of comparing the political constitutions of foreign countries to their disadvantage with the government of England (CROFT). But this design was very imperfectly executed. At Christmas he took part with other English visitors in private theatricals, playing in the 'Busy Body' or 'The Journey to London.' Life at Toulouse grew more irksome in the spring. Sterne suffered from ague, and things at home were not promising. Becket wrote that the sale of the last books of 'Tristram' was slackening. Of the four thousand copies, nearly a thousand hung fire (*Morrison MS.*) In July 1763 they removed to Bagnères de Bigorre in the Pyrenees. Thence they visited Aix and Marseilles, and in September settled down at Montpellier for the winter. On 30 Sept. Sterne wrote to Lord Fauconberg offering to purchase for him a hogshead of claret, and expressing his longing to be back at Coxwold (*Wombwell MS.*) In February 1764 he was 'heartily tired of France,' and next month he set his face homewards.

Mrs. Sterne did not share her husband's yearning for home. She declared her intention of staying behind at Montauban. Their daughter, she argued, ought to complete her education abroad, and they could save as much money in a year in France as would keep them in clothes for seven in England. 'My system,' Sterne wrote to Lord Fauconberg of his wife, 'is to let her please herself;' and although he deplored a long separation from his daughter, he accepted Mrs. Sterne's arguments. Her expenditure was to be restricted to two hundred guineas a year. Malicious friends treated the arrangement as a formal separation, suggested by Sterne. But Mrs. Sterne was wholly responsible for Sterne's return to England alone, and it was

very unwillingly that he reconciled himself to the maintenance by his wife and daughter of a separate establishment.

On quitting his family Sterne remained a month (April–May) in Paris, and renewed his intimacy with French society (cf. *Morrison MS.*) Wilkes wrote to Churchill from Paris (10 April 1764) that Sterne and he were often in each other's company (Wilkes MS. in British Museum). He preached at the English ambassador's chapel on Hezekiah to 'a concourse of all nations and religions' (*Sermons*, No. 17), and sent his daughter books and a guitar. The summer was mainly spent in London, and in the early autumn he went to Scarborough to drink the waters. In August he settled down at Coxwold, after an absence of more than two and a half years. He was soon immersed in a further instalment of 'Tristram,' which was to narrate Uncle Toby's amour with the Widow Wadman. In December he had completed books vii. and viii., and took them to London. They were published on 26 Jan. 1765. Dinner engagements set in 'a fortnight deep.' Garrick and his wife were assiduous in their attentions, and he began a flirtation with a fashionable admirer, Lady Percy, a daughter of Lord Bute. His lungs gave him trouble, and he withdrew in April to Bath, where Gainsborough painted his portrait in a single sitting. He returned to his solitude at Coxwold in May, and in the autumn a second expedition abroad was recommended. In October 1765 he set out on a seven months' tour through France and Italy, which he immortalised in his 'Sentimental Journey.'

At Calais he put up at M. Dessein's hotel (now pulled down), which gained so wide a reputation from the account Sterne gave of it that for more than half a century it was a place of pilgrimage for French and English travellers. At his next stopping-place, Montreuil, he engaged the drummer-boy La Fleur as his valet. A few weeks were spent with friends in Paris before a start was made for Lyons. There Sterne enjoyed the society of Wilkes's friend, Horne Tooke. Eight days were required for the journey through the mountain passes of Savoy, and at a wayside inn on the road to Modane, in the plains beyond, occurred, according to the 'Sentimental Journey,' the notorious incident with which that work abruptly closes. But there seems little doubt that this episode never came within the author's experience. It was borrowed from the lips of a fashionable London friend, John Crawford of Errol, who declared that the adventure befell him at an inn between Verviers and Aix-la-Chapelle.

By 15 Nov. Sterne joined Sir James Macdonald, a cultivated young man, at Turin, and together they passed through Milan, Parma, and Florence to Rome. There he was well received in both English and Italian society, and met his censor Smollett, whom he depicted in his 'Journey' as the type of the grumbling traveller under the sobriquet of 'Smelfungus.' In February 1766 he arrived at Naples, still in company of Sir James Macdonald. On the return journey he turned aside while in the south of France to pay a hasty visit to his wife and daughter. They had long since left Montauban, and Sterne sought them in five or six different towns before running them to earth in 'Franche-compté' in May. His wife was 'very cordial,' but begged to stay abroad another year. Lydia was greatly improved in everything her father wished. On parting with them towards the end of May, he wrote to Hall-Stevenson from Dijon in the highest spirits. He was 'most unaccountably well and most unaccountably nonsensical.' He was back in Yorkshire in time to dine with Hall-Stevenson at Skelton on the king's birthday (4 June 1766). In the autumn he completed in his 'peaceful retreat' of Coxwold the ninth and last volume of 'Tristram,' and planned in four volumes his 'Sentimental Journey' (*Letter* lxxi.)

Sterne suffered much depression at the close of 1766. Money was not abundant. He had spent most of his literary profits on his foreign tours. His wife, who, it is obvious, wofully mismanaged her finances, found two hundred guineas an inadequate allowance, and, with a fuller sense of responsibility than was habitual to him, Sterne made every effort to supply her growing needs. Numberless appeals are extant from him to his agents and bankers in Paris (Mr. Foley and M. Panchaud) to forward money instantly to Mrs. Sterne in the south of France, and all give practical proof of Sterne's anxiety to study her and his daughter's material comfort. 'Whilst I have a shilling,' he wrote to his daughter (*Letter* lxxix), 'shall not you both have ninepence of it ?' In 1764 the parsonage at Sutton had been accidentally burnt down while in charge of the curate, and Sterne became responsible for the cost of rebuilding, an obligation which he tried to evade. At Stillington the Enclosure Act required his attention, and at the end of 1766 letters from Lydia announced that his wife was seriously ill at Avignon. But the danger passed, and in December 1766 he was once more in London, hoping to retrieve his position by the issue of the last volume of 'Tristram' and of two new volumes of sermons. The three volumes appeared in January

1767. The ninth and last book of 'Tristram' was dedicated to the patron of the first, the Earl of Chatham, who was reminded that 'honours, like impressions upon coin, may give an ideal and local value to a bit of base metal, but not to gold and silver'—a sentence whence Burns, a warm admirer of 'Tristram,' is credited with deriving his notion of 'the guinea-stamp;' Sterne probably borrowed his simile from a passage in Thomas Tenison's preface to 'Baconiana' (1679), although it could be matched in Thomas Carew's 'Poems' and Wycherley's 'Plain Dealer.' To the 'Sermons' (vols. iii. and iv.) was prefixed a list of over six hundred subscribers, including, besides '*toute la noblesse*,' Voltaire, Holbach, and other French authors. The winter's campaign proved lucrative. 'Shandy' sold well, and 300*l*. fell to Sterne from the subscriptions to the 'Sermons' apart from payment for the copy. The last volume of 'Tristram' was not more refined than its predecessors, and in March 1767 the archbishop of York (Robert Hay Drummond [q. v.]) was the recipient of an anonymous petition from London inviting his attention to the scandalous contrast between the indecent tone of Sterne's writing and his sacred vocation.

On this his penultimate visit to London (December 1766-May 1767) Sterne occupied new lodgings at 41 Old Bond Street, above a silk-bagwig-maker's. He spent much time at the house of Sir William James [q. v.], a retired Indian commodore, who lived in fashionable style in Gerrard Street, Soho. He had met James casually in society, and James's wife and little daughter attracted him. In the repeated hospitalities they offered him he took a genuine delight. Visitors from India were often his fellow-guests at James's table, and there late in December 1766 Sterne first met Mrs. Eliza (or more properly Elizabeth) Draper, a visitor from Bombay, who was to play an important part in what remained of his life. She was a daughter of May Sclater (*b.* 1719), a member of a good west-country family, who had gone out to India in 1736 [see under SCLATER, WILLIAM, 1575-1626]. In India her father married a lady named Whitehill, and apparently settled at Anjengo on the Malabar coast, where Eliza was born on 5 April 1744. After being educated in England, she reached Bombay on the return voyage on 27 Dec. 1757, and when little more than fourteen she married, at Bombay on 28 July 1758, Daniel Draper, at the time a writer in the East India Company's service, who next year became secretary to the government at Bombay. Draper was a dull official, fully twenty years his wife's senior. A boy was born in 1759, and a daughter

(Elizabeth or Betsy) in October 1761. In 1765 Mrs. Draper and her husband paid a visit to England with a view to placing their children at school. Draper soon returned alone to his post at Bombay, and left his wife to follow him later.

Mrs. Draper, when Sterne met her, was no more than a coquettish schoolgirl, who had read widely, and aped the ethical theories of the blue-stocking school. She chattered of 'the rights of women' in matters of education and marriage. But there was no doubt of the reality of her conviction that a wrong had been done her by yoking her in immature years to a husband of formal manner and illiterate tastes, who rendered conjugal life detestable to her. Sterne was not slow in winning her confidence. The sympathy of a distinguished man of letters flattered her vanity. She knew him as the 'mild, generous, and good Yorick,' and became a whole-hearted 'idolater of his worth.' He opened a correspondence with her in his customary vein, calling her his 'Bramine,' in allusion to her Indian connections. He cursed fate that both were married already, sent her his books, and having had her portrait painted, wore it round his neck. But within a month or two of their first meeting Draper summoned his wife home. Eliza fell ill at the thought of leaving her children and relatives. Sterne assigned her melancholy to the coming separation from him. On 3 April 1767 Eliza sailed from Deal for Bombay in the Earl of Chatham, East Indiaman. Sterne and she never met again. Her health and spirits recovered on the voyage. New admirers were forthcoming, and most of the impression Sterne had made on her passed away.

But Sterne had no wish to close the episode hastily. He recognised in Eliza a young woman of intellectual capacity and emotional temperament not unlike his own, and he determined to maintain relations with her in her absence after the manner in which Swift had maintained relations with Stella. He was to keep a journal addressed to Eliza while she was in India. In the fifth of his extant letters written to Mrs. Draper while she was in England he told her 'the journal is as it should be all but its contents.' 'I began a new journal this morning,' he writes in his next letter; 'you shall see it, for if I live not till your return to England I will leave it you as a legacy; 'tis a sorrowful page, but I will write cheerful ones.' On the day they parted Eliza agreed to keep a journal too. At the moment of her sailing Sterne forwarded to her all that he had yet written. Of that effort of Sterne nothing is known. On

9 April, six days after the Earl of Chatham set sail, he wrote in desperation to his daughter (Letter xci.) of his loneliness now that his 'dear friend' had left him and his family was at a distance. 'For God's sake, persuade [thy mother],' he added, 'to come and fix in England. . . I want thee near me, thou child and darling of my heart.' On 13 April Sterne sought relief from his melancholy by applying himself to a continuation of his 'Journal to Eliza.' He carried it on regularly till 2 Aug. A fragmentary entry dated 1 Nov. brings it to a conclusion. The whole still survives in manuscript at the British Museum (Addit. MS. 34527), and has not been printed. Sterne called it 'The Bramine's Journal,' and described it as 'a diary of the miserable feelings of a person separated from a lady for whose society he languished.' It is mainly a mawkish record of his yearning for Eliza's society, of his vague hope of making her his wife, of his antipathy to Mrs. Sterne, of his declining health, and of his social diversions in London and Coxwold. Signs are apparent throughout of the decay of physical strength. One curious feature of the 'Journal' is its frequent plagiarism of his own letters which are extant elsewhere. The sense of desolation with which Eliza's departure fills him is expressed in almost the same language that is applied in his published correspondence to the grief caused by his wife's absence in their courting days, twenty-seven years before. It is just possible that his daughter, who recklessly edited his correspondence, foisted some passages from the 'Journal' on her mother's love-letters. It is barely credible that the close resemblance should be due to an accidental freak of memory on Sterne's part, or that he should have copied his old letters, even in the improbable case that he had access to them. The accounts he gives in the 'Journal' of his illness in London in April, and of the rural charms of life at Coxwold in July, both figure with little verbal change in letters that he sent at the time to other friends. But this accorded with his common epistolary practice.

For the first five weeks after Eliza's departure (13 April-22 May) Sterne lay seriously ill in his lodgings in New Bond Street. But as soon as he was convalescent the old routine of gaiety recommenced. He imprudently ventured on visits by night to Ranelagh or to Madame Cornelys's concerts in Soho Square. He breakfasted or dined with Lord and Lady Spencer, and flirted with female admirers in Hyde Park. At the end of May he travelled down to Coxwold 'like a bale of cadaverous goods consigned to

Pluto and company,' and stayed with the archbishop of York before reaching Coxwold. There his health improved, and he began in earnest his 'Sentimental Journey;' but a letter on 2 June from Lydia and her mother confirmed an earlier threat that they were about to pay him a visit. Mrs. Sterne demanded a new financial settlement, and Sterne's equanimity completely failed him. But with characteristic inconsistency he was distressed to learn that some recent letters to his wife had miscarried. The mishap wore, he lamented, the aspect of unkindness, which his wife by no means merited from him. The threatened meeting threw him, as the appointed date approached, into paroxysms of hysteria. In July visits to Skelton Castle and Harrogate raised his drooping spirits, and friends sympathised with him in his twofold grief—the home-coming of Mrs. Sterne and his vain passion for Eliza. The bishop of Cork and Ross (Jemmet Brown) offered him preferment in Ireland, and there was talk of his exchanging his York livings for a benefice in Surrey worth 350l. a year.

At the end of August his wife and 'dear girl' arrived. Lydia had developed into an elegant and unprincipled coquette, but her father thanked Heaven for her brilliant endowments. Mrs. Sterne kept her temper. After a stay of two months she and Lydia left Coxwold on 1 Nov. to winter in a hired house at York. It was then formally agreed that in the ensuing spring Mrs. Sterne was to return to the south of France with an annual allowance of three hundred guineas, and not to stir again till death. She was well satisfied. The climate of England made life insupportable to her, she said, and she vowed, if her husband would only maintain her at a distance from him, never to give him another sorrowful or discontented hour. 'She leaves me,' Sterne wrote to Eliza, 'more than half in love with me.' To his daughter he gave 2,000l., which his wife, despite his objection, insisted on investing in the French funds. But he assented to permanent separation from Lydia in genuine sorrow. 'This dear part of me must be torn from my arms,' he lamented, 'to follow her mother.' 'My heart bleeds,' he wrote to his friend Lee, 'when I think of parting with my child; 'twill be like the separation of body and soul.'

In November the 'Sentimental Journey' was resumed, and relieved its author's feelings. He designed 'it to teach us to love the world and our fellow-creatures better than we do,' and he enjoyed dwelling on 'those gentler passions and affections which aid so much to' general goodwill. Many references to Eliza—to the little portrait of

her that he wore round his neck, and to his vows of eternal fidelity—figured in the 'Sentimental Journey' (pp. 48, 85, 113, 129). His wife's return had compelled the abandonment of the 'Journal to Eliza,' and it was not resumed. Nevertheless Sterne continued to pen sprightly *billets-doux* to other ladies of his acquaintance in London, and one at least was despatched while his wife was under his roof.

By December 1767 two books of the 'Sentimental Journey' were completed, and, taking leave of his family in the hired house in York, Sterne set out with his friend Hall-Stevenson for London to superintend the publication. It proved his last journey. His lodgings in Bond Street were soon filled with visitors, and hospitalities were offered him in profusion. His weak health depressed him, but he was gratified by the receipt of a curiously carved walking-stick from Dr. Eustace, an American admirer, who was personally a stranger to him. He saw much of Mr. and Mrs. James in Gerrard Street, and strained all his social influence to procure for Mrs. James a ticket of admission to Mrs. Cornelys's fashionable entertainments in Soho Square, to which he had omitted to take out a subscription. On 27 Feb. the 'Sentimental Journey' was published in two 12mo volumes, and added greatly to his reputation. Even Horace Walpole, who could never get through three volumes of the 'tiresome' 'Shandy,' admitted that the new book was 'very pleasing though too much dilated,' and was marked by 'great good-nature and strokes of delicacy' (*Letters*, ed. Cunningham, v. 91). In March Sterne wrote to his daughter that a vile influenza was bowing him down, but he hoped to get the better of it. He repudiated with much heat a rumour which Lydia had brought to his notice, that he intended to bequeath her as a legacy to Mrs. Draper. 'I wish I had thee to nurse me,' he concludes; 'but I am denied that. Write to me twice a week at least. God bless thee, my child, and believe me ever, ever, thy affectionate father.' He rapidly grew worse; pleurisy set in; he was bled and blistered, and his strength waned. On 15 March he took up his pen for the last time, and wrote a touching note to Mrs. James, confiding his daughter to her care in case he should be vanquished in 'this wrestling.' 'My spirits are fled,' he wrote; ''tis a bad omen.' Four days later, at four o'clock in the afternoon of Friday, 18 March, he died. At the moment of his death his friend John Crawford of Errol was entertaining a distinguished party, including many of Sterne's acquaintances, at his house in Clifford Street. The Dukes of Grafton and Roxburghe were there, with the Earls of March and Ossory, Garrick, Hume, and James. Crawford's Scottish footman, James Macdonald, who afterwards published memoirs, was sent by the company to Old Bond Street to make inquiries. Macdonald was told by the landlady to go to Sterne's bedroom. As he approached the bedside he heard the dying man mutter, 'Now it has come,' and a few moments later life was extinct. According to Dr. Ferriar, the lodging-house servant, who was his sole attendant, tore the gold buttons from the sleeves of the garment he was wearing while he was uttering his last breath. Croft says that many compromising letters from ladies of rank were found in his rooms and were burnt by a friendly hand. There seems little ground for crediting Sterne's London hosts and patrons with neglect in his last hours. James was constantly with him in his last days. Late in the evening of his death lady Mary Coke met some of his titled friends. 'Lord Ossory told us,' she wrote, 'that the famous Dr. Sterne dyed that morning; he seem'd to lament him very much. Lord Eglinton said (but not in a ludicrous manner) that he had taken his "Sentimental Journey"' (LADY MARY COKE, *Letters and Journal*, ii. 216).

Sterne was buried on the 22nd in the St. George's burial-ground in the Bayswater Road. According to a ghastly story that seems authentic, on 24 March, two days after the burial, the body was 'resurrected' and sold for purposes of dissection to Charles Collignon [q. v.], the professor of anatomy at Cambridge. The features are said to have been recognised by a friend who stood beside the dissecting table. The skeleton, it is stated, was long preserved at Cambridge. A monumental stone, with an inscription (inaccurate as to the date of death), was afterwards erected near the site of his grave in the St. George's burial-ground by 'two brother masons,' a disinterested act of reverence which they assigned to Sterne's possession of all the qualities that freemasonry honoured, although Sterne himself was not of the fraternity. The burial-ground, long neglected, has lately been put in good order, and the stone has been recut and placed in the mortuary chapel.

Sterne left no will, and his widow took out letters of administration on 4 June. His books were sold to Messrs. Sotheran & Todd, booksellers, of York, and many of them figured among the 5,500 entries in the catalogue published by Todd in 1775, 'of several libraries and parcels of books lately purchased, containing upwards of ten thousand volumes' (copy in Hailstone Library in York Minster). Sterne's debts amounted to 1,100*l.*, and his assets to 400*l.* Mrs. Sterne, with an income of only 40*l.* a year in her own right, was not in a position either to pay the creditors or to provide for herself satisfactorily. Sterne's vicarage at Sutton, which had been burnt down, was still in ruins, and when a suit was instituted against his widow to recover damages, she made an oath of insolvency, but subsequently tendered 60*l.* which was accepted, although the cost of rebuilding amounted to near 600*l.* (*Sutton Parish Reg.*) In August, under Hall-Stevenson's auspices, 800*l.* was collected for her and her daughter at the York races. Early next year three further volumes of sermons were issued for their benefit, and subscribers were numerous (cf. *Brit. Mus. Addit. MS.* 22261, f. 48, receipt by Mrs. Sterne of a payment by Lady Strafford). Resolving to dispose of the rest of Sterne's manuscripts to the best advantage, widow and daughter travelled to London, and took lodgings in Gerrard Street. But they rapidly alienated most of Sterne's friends by the reckless indifference to either his or their own reputation which they displayed in their efforts to make money out of Sterne's literary remains. Mrs. Draper, on learning of Sterne's death from Mrs. James, and of his wife's and daughter's distress, collected six hundred rupees herself in their behalf, and induced a friend, Colonel Donald Campbell, to collect an equal sum among his fellow officers. Campbell brought the money to Miss Sterne with an introduction from Mrs. Draper, who thought he might prove an eligible suitor. In any case, Mrs. Draper offered to provide for Lydia if she would join her in India. Lydia wrote resenting Mrs. Draper's patronage, and defending her mother's character from the aspersions her father had cast on it. With less excuse she joined her mother in a threat to publish, from copies in their possession, Sterne's letters to Mrs. Draper unless a heavy sum of money was at once remitted to them. Mrs. Draper, violently perturbed, wrote to Becket the bookseller, promising any reasonable recompense if he would secure the letters in case they were offered for sale, and hand them to Mrs. James. Mrs. Sterne was better than her word, and the letters did not at the time pass out of her hands. Meanwhile Lydia applied to Wilkes to write a full biography of her father (cf. *Brit. Mus. Addit. MSS. Wilkes MS.* 30877, ff. 70–8). Wilkes assented, and Hall-Stevenson promised his co-operation. In the summer of 1769 Lydia and her mother left England and settled at Angoulême. Thence she wrote repeatedly to Wilkes and Hall-Stevenson, begging them to proceed with her father's biography. But they had no serious intention of gratifying her wish, and her letters remained unanswered. About 1771 mother and daughter removed to Alby on the Tarn in Languedoc. Mrs. Sterne was in bad health, probably suffering from a recurrence of her mental malady. Lydia made the acquaintance of Alexander Anne Medalle, son of a 'receveur des décimes' in the custom-house, who was a year her junior. On 28 April 1772 she abjured the protestant religion in the private chapel of the provost's house at Alby, and was married to the young man on the same day. The registers of Alby state that the marriage was 'forcé, urgent,' epithets to which the gloss is appended: 'car alors la loi autorisait la recherche de la paternité' (Inventaire des Archives Communales d'Alby). The words seem to cast a slur on Lydia's chastity. A son was born soon after the marriage. Lydia's mother, who, owing to continued illness, was absent from the wedding ceremony, died at Alby in the house of a doctor named Lionières (No. 9 Rue St.-Antoine) in January 1773. Lydia's husband did not long survive (CROFT). In June 1775 the widowed Madame de Medalle arrived in London, and published, as a substitute for a biography, her father's letters to her and his friends, with a portrait of herself bending over a bust of her father. She then returned to the south of France, and soon died. On 19 Sept. 1783 her son, her only known child, died in the school of the Benedictines at Sorèze, and it was stated at the time that the boy's mother predeceased him (Athenæum, 18 June and 2 July 1870). The legend that Madame de Medalle was, with her husband, a victim of the French revolution is apocryphal.

The later history of Sterne's Eliza was followed with interest by Sterne's admirers. On arriving at Bombay at the end of 1767, she made the best of the situation, and in 1769 removed with her husband to Tellichery, where he had been appointed chief of the factory. She acted as his amanuensis, and was not, despite the death of her son in England, unhappy there. She described the town as the Montpellier of India, and enjoyed the social distinction accorded her by both English settlers and natives (cf. Magazine of Indian Art, January 1891, vol. iv. No. 33, letter from Mrs. Draper from Tellichery, April 1769, edited by Sir George Birdwood). Her main anxiety at Tellichery was due to

the malicious conduct of Sterne's wife and daughter in threatening to publish her correspondence with Sterne. Every member of the family, including Sterne himself, whom she now declared to have been tainted with the 'vices of injustice, meanness, and folly,' became the subject of Mrs. Draper's warm denunciation. In 1771 Draper removed from Tellichery to fill the same post of chief of the factory at Surat. But intrigues at Bombay jeopardised his prospects. He was recalled thither in 1772, and was for a time without remunerative employment. Life in Bombay was increasingly irksome to Mrs. Draper as the chance of returning to England with a competency grew more remote. On 15 April 1772, in a long rambling letter to Mrs James, she defended the attitude she had maintained to Sterne's family, and set forth in elaborate detail her impatience with her husband and Indian society, as well as her views on life and literature. At length, driven to desperation by her renewed antipathy to her husband, she fled on 12 Jan. 1773 from his house—called both Marine House and Belvidere House—at Mazagon, which overlooked Bombay Harbour (see her farewell letters in Times of India, 24 Feb. 1894). It is said that she was aided in her escape by Captain Sir John Clark, and let herself down to his ship by a rope from a window. But she denied, in letters to her friends at home, that she compromised herself in any other way. Mrs. Draper's disappearance created a sensation throughout India. Writs were taken out against Clark in the mayor's court at Bombay, but he eluded them successfully (DAVID PRICE, Memoirs, 1839). Mrs. Draper retired to the residence of her maternal uncle, Thomas Whitehill, at Rajahmundry, eighty miles from Masulipatam, and wrote home with composure of her contentment there, and of her intention to retaliate if Draper proceeded to extremities. A year later she returned to England. There she met Wilkes, William Combe [q. v.], and other literary men, and exercised over them some of her old fascination (cf. ROGERS, Table Talk, ed. Dyce, p. 117). Her pride in her relations with Sterne revived, and in 1775—the year in which Sterne's daughter published some of his correspondence without making any reference to her—she authorised the publication, under the title of 'Letters of Yorick to Eliza,' of ten letters that Sterne had addressed to her between December 1766 and April 1767. The volume was dedicated to Lord-chancellor Apsley by an anonymous editor, who said he had copied the letters with Eliza's permission from the originals in her possession. Her replies were not given. 'Letters from Eliza to Yorick' (1775, 'printed for the editor') and William Combe's 'Letters, supposed to have been written by Yorick and Eliza' (1779, 2 vols.), were forgeries, some of which were foisted on reprints of the genuine collection. That volume gave 'Sterne's Eliza' a reputation little less universal than Sterne's. But she did not long enjoy the equivocal distinction. Dying at Bristol on 3 Aug. 1778, before she had completed her thirty-fifth year, she was buried in the cloisters of the cathedral there on 6 Aug. A sculptured monument still stands there to her memory. Eliza's husband, who was the object of much sympathy both in India and England, attained the first place in the Bombay council, and finally returned to England on 10 Oct. 1782. His and Eliza's daughter, their only surviving child, married, on 10 Jan. 1785, one Thomas Nevill, esq. (*Gent. Mag.* 1785, i. 75). Draper died in St. James's Street in March 1805.

Eliza's fame died hard (cf. JAMES DOUGLAS, *Bombay and West India*). L'Abbé Raynal, who met her in India, gave it new vigour when, in the second edition of his 'Histoire des Indes' (1779), he rapturously and at great length apostrophised her in his account of Anjengo, her birthplace. In 1813 James Forbes, in his 'Oriental Memoirs' (i. 338–9), wrote of 'Abbé Raynal's rhapsody of Anjengo' that, 'however insignificant the settlement may be in itself, it will be for ever celebrated as the birthplace of his and Sterne's Eliza, a lady with whom I had the pleasure of being acquainted at Bombay, whose refined taste and elegant accomplishments require no encomium from my pen.' A tree at Masulipatam, where she stayed for a time with her uncle Whitehill, was known, until it was swept away in 1864, as 'Eliza's Tree;' and the house that she had occupied in Bombay was, until its demolition in 1874, regarded as a literary shrine. A picture of it formed in 1831 a scene in Burford's famous panorama in London (cf. *Mirror of Literature*, 1831, xviii. 17, with view of house and an apocryphal account of the later life of Sterne's Eliza).

The fine portrait of Sterne (two-thirds length) by Sir Joshua Reynolds belongs to the Marquis of Lansdowne. The expression is slyly humorous, but far less roguish than it appears in the numerous engravings that have been made from it. Sterne wears a clerical gown. A second portrait (half length), painted by Gainsborough at Bath in a single sitting in April 1765, formerly belonged to Thomas Turton, bishop of Ely (FULCHER, *Life of Gainsborough*, p. 223). It

is now at the Peel Park Museum, Salford, to which it was presented by Mr. Thomas Agnew. The expression of countenance is far less distinctive than in Reynolds's portrait. Sterne holds an open illustrated volume in his right hand. It is not known to have been engraved. A watercolour drawing (full length) by Carmontelle is in the Duc d'Aumale's collection at Chantilly. A few copies were reproduced by Messrs. Colnaghi in 1890. Of the rough oil-painting in which Sterne was introduced by his friend Bridges as a mountebank, the original is lost; an engraving appears in Dibdin's 'Bibliographical Tour,' 1838 (i. 213). The bust by Nollekens, executed on Sterne's visit to Rome in 1766, passed to the Yarborough collection. A marble replica is at Skelton Castle in the possession of J. T. Wharton, esq. The bust is reckoned one of Nollekens's finest performances, and it is figured in Dance's portrait of the sculptor.

Sterne's reasoning faculty was incapable of controlling his constitutional sensitiveness to pain and pleasure. His deficiency in self-control induced a condition of moral apathy, and was the cause alike of the indecency and of the sentimentality which abound in 'Tristram Shandy' and the 'Sentimental Journey.' Both the indecency and the sentimentality faithfully and without artifice reflected Sterne's emotional nature. The indelicate innuendoes which he foists on sedate words and situations, and the tears that he represented himself as shedding over dead asses and caged starlings, had an equally spontaneous origin in what was in him the normal state of his nerves.

In itself—with the slightest possible reference to the exciting object—his sensibility evoked a pleasurable nervous excitement, and the fulness of the gratification that it generated in his own being discouraged him from seeking to translate its suggestions into act. The divorce of sensibility from practical benevolence will always justify charges of insincerity. All that can be pleaded in extenuation in Sterne's case is that he made no secret that his conduct was the sport of his emotional impulses, and, obeying no other promptings, was guided by no active moral sentiment. Gravity, he warned his readers, was foreign to his nature. Morality, which ordinarily checks the free play of feeling and passion by the exercise of virtuous reason, lay, he admitted, outside his sphere. Such infirmities signally unfitted him for the vocation of a teacher of religion, but his confessions remove hypocrisy from the list of his offences. His declared temperament renders it matter for surprise not that he so often disfigured his career as a husband and author by a wanton defiance of the accepted moral canons, but that he achieved so indisputable a nobility of sentiment as in his creation of Uncle Toby, and so unselfish a devotion as in his relations with his daughter. He was no 'scamp' in any accepted use of the term, as Thackeray designates him. He was a volatile, self-centred, morally apathetic man of genius, who was not destitute of generous instincts.

In portraying sympathetically the hysterical working of the tender emotions Sterne was an innovator. He knew little of his greater contemporary Rousseau, who was similarly constituted to himself; and there is no ground for tracing Sterne's sentimentality to any spring outside his natural temperament. But, like Rousseau, Sterne unconsciously represented the reaction which was in the air of western Europe against those dominant principles of thought and action, both in politics and religion, which ignored the emotions altogether. Sterne's sentimentality was not militant, like Rousseau's, but its mildness rendered it even more contagious in both England and France. This characteristic was not altogether disadvantageous. Even in its most mawkish manifestations Sterne's sentimentality had the saving grace of running directly counter to inhuman prejudices of long standing. The exaggerated sympathy that Sterne expressed for dumb animals (even flies) helped to create a new and humanising relation between man and animals. His tearful references to the evils of slavery and to the right of slaves to recognition as human beings helped to set the negroes free (cf. *Letters*, lxxv–vi.; *Tristram*, iii. 185; *Journey*, p. 80; art. SANCHO, IGNATIUS). The worst result that may be traced to Sterne's sentimentality is the vogue of mawkishness and unreality that it introduced for a time into English literature, and the hypocrisy that, according to Coleridge, it long encouraged in English life (*Aids to Reflection*, 1839, p. 27). Henry Mackenzie's 'Man of Feeling' (1771) illustrates its immediate effect on literature. For three years —from 1773 to 1775—worshippers of Sterne concocted month by month in the 'Sentimental Magazine' imbecile imitations of his characteristic style and feeling. A little later his sentimentality was responsible for the affectations of Burns's epistolary style. The persistence of its influence may be estimated by the circumstance that it inspired much of the emotional writing of Dickens and Lytton only half a century ago. Seriously minded bystanders could not stem the tide which made Sterne's sentimentality fashionable in thought and speech. Wesley wrote

in his 'Journal' on 11 Feb. 1772, after looking at the 'Sentimental Journey:' ''Sentimental! What is that? It is not English; he might as well say Continental. It is not sense. It conveys no determinate idea; yet one fool makes many. And this nonsensical word (who would believe it?) is become a fashionable one!' In France the 'Sentimental Journey,' mainly on account of its emotional extravagances, enjoyed a popularity even greater than that it could claim in the country of its birth. 'Sterne à Paris: ou le Voyageur Sentimental,' by Révoil and Forbin, was a popular vaudeville on the Parisian stage. Saintine's 'Picciola' was written largely under Sterne's inspiration. In Germany his sentimentality was avowedly imitated by the novelist Hippel in his 'Die Lebensläufe' (1778–81), and more subtly by Wieland and Jean Paul Richter; while its influence has been detected as far afield as in Russian novels of the close of the eighteenth century (DUNLOP, *Hist. of Fiction*, ii. 049).

One proof of Sterne's popularity lies in the many spurious works published under his name, and in the many barefaced imitations of his efforts that appeared before or immediately after his death. The fraudulent third volume of 'Tristram Shandy' (1760), by the impudent hack-writer John Carr (1732–1807) [q. v.], was followed by Samuel Paterson's 'Another Traveller' (1767–9), and by John Hall-Stevenson's more mendacious continuation of the 'Sentimental Journey' in 1769. These heralded a very long series of contemptible imitations of Sterne's travels. 'La Quinzaine Angloise à Paris, ou l'art de s'y ruiner en peu de tems, ouvrage posthume du Docteur Stearne traduit de l'anglois par un observateur' (London, 1776), was an original work in French by James Rutledge [q. v.] William Combe, Samuel Jackson Pratt, Martin Sherlock, and Samuel Ireland showed varying degrees of adroitness in the same direction. Probably the most impudent of the deliberate forgeries undertaken by literary hacks was a volume entitled 'The Posthumous Works of a late Celebrated Genius, deceased, A.M.' (1770, 2 vols.), which consisted of a work in two parts called 'The Koran, or the Life, Character, and Sentiments of Tria Juncta in Uno, M.N.A., or Master of No Arts!' It was by Richard Griffith (d. 1788) [q. v.] There was some clever parodying of the style of thought and language of 'Tristram Shandy.' Reprints were frequent. It was included in the first collected edition of Sterne's works (Dublin, 1770), and it was translated into French by A. Hédouin in 1853. In 1783 Leonard McNally [q. v.] plagiarised for dramatic purposes, with better justification, many passages from Sterne in 'Tristram Shandy: A Sentimental, Shandean Bagatelle in Two Acts;' McNally dedicated it to Sterne's patron, Lord Fauconberg. In 1779 William Combe fathered on Sterne a spurious collection of 'Letters between Yorick and Eliza.' 'Letters from Eliza to Yorick' (1775; printed for the editor) and 'Original Letters of the late Rev. Laurence Sterne,' 1788, came from similar manufactories of fraud.

But writers of position and ability have shown little less hesitation than the denizens of Grub Street in emulating Sterne. Travellers of literary genius like Heine and Robert Louis Stevenson have, as recorders of their impressions of travel, marched under Sterne's banner. On fiction dealing with domestic life his influence has been no less pronounced. Dickens often reflected his humour as distinctly as his sentimentality. Marryat in 'Midshipman Easy,' and more notably Lytton in the 'Caxtons,' levied ampler loans on Sterne's pictures of Mr. Shandy and his household than a stern sense of probity might justify. Conscious mimicry of Sterne's tricks of style—his use of ' 'tis' and ' 'twas,' his picturesque abruptness, his quaint paradoxes—is apparent in much modern essay writing. 'That's another story' fell originally—in the sense that Mr. Rudyard Kipling has made it his own—from the lips of Mr. Shandy in bk. ii. chap. xvii. of his son Tristram's 'Life and Opinions' (ed. Saintsbury, i. 141).

But the plagiarism of which Sterne has been the victim is retributive justice. Hundreds of writers of all ages and nations are quoted in 'Tristram Shandy,' and attest the width of Sterne's reading. 'My dear Rabelais and dearer Cervantes' were, with Montaigne, the authors he declared that he loved the best, and their influence is very obvious throughout 'Tristram.' In Shakespeare and Lucian he also avowed delight. But he did not always confess his debts to his predecessors, and his plagiarisms, although they fail to detract from the literary interest of his achievement, convict him of effrontery, if not of downright dishonesty. Many impressive phrases did he borrow direct and without acknowledgment from Burton's 'Anatomy of Melancholy.' Whole paragraphs in his 'Sermons' come from the published works of Bishop Hall and Wollaston. The story of the dwarf at the theatre in the 'Sentimental Journey' is largely a translation from a chapter of Scarron's 'Roman Comique.' Nor was the general scheme of 'Tristram' more original than many of its details.

John Dunton's 'A Voyage round the World, or Pocket Library divided into several volumes: the first of which contains the rare adventures of Don Kainophilus from his cradle to his fifteenth year,' London [1720?], was beyond reasonable doubt the parent of 'Tristram Shandy's Life and Opinions,' with the whimsical and perverse digressions on which the author prided himself. The resemblance between Tristram's and Don Kainophilus's fortunes has been overlooked by later critics, but it led to the publication in 1762 of an adaptation of Dunton's novel under the title of 'The Life, Travels, and Adventures of Christopher Wagstaffe, Gentleman, grandfather to Tristram Shandy, adapted by the editor' (London, 8vo). He was clearly acquainted, too, with Arbuthnot's 'Memoirs of Martin Scriblerus.' Sterne told the Crofts that many of the ludicrous discussions of the brothers Shandy were due to the less brilliant conferences reported in Béroalde's 'Moyen de Parvenir' (1599). Others were clearly suggested by Bouchet's 'Serées' (Paris, 1608). Sterne's disquisition on noses was adapted from Bruscambille's 'Pensées Facetieuses' (1623). Copies of these three French books were in Sterne's library, and his copy of Béroalde, which bore the inscription 'L. Sterne à Paris, viii livres,' afterwards belonged to Heber. It is notable that his sentimental episodes owed on the whole less to his reading than his humorous episodes. But he knew thoroughly the so-called pathetic romance of 'Le Doyen de Coleraine,' and he assimilated some of the wearisome sentiment of Marivaux's 'Le Paysan Parvenu' which was popular in Mrs. Eliza Haywood's English translation (1735). Sterne's most widely known apophthegm, 'God tempers the wind to the shorn lamb' (*Sentimental Journey*), was a Languedoc proverb which had often been in print in France (cf. JOHN FERRIAR, *Illustrations of Sterne*, London, 1798 ; Warrington, 1812, 2 vols.). Doubt is admissible whether Uncle Toby owes much (as has been suggested) to the Commodore Trunnion of Smollett's 'Peregrine Pickle' (cf. ANNA SEWARD, *Letters*, ii. 30 Oct. 1788). Another tradition represents Uncle Toby as a portrait of one Captain Hinde of Preston Castle, Hertfordshire, a neighbour of Lord Dacre, who occasionally entertained Sterne (*Macmillan's Mag.* July 1873, p. 238). But after all Sterne's thefts have been admitted, it is clear that his wealth alike of humour, sensibility, and dramatic instinct enabled him to steal material from all quarters without obscuring his individuality. His style was his own. At its best it is, in Hazlitt's words, 'the most rapid, the most happy, the most idiomatic of any that is to be found. It is the pure essence of English conversational style. It is seen to best advantage throughout the 'Sentimental Journey.' In 'Tristram Shandy' he at times descends into the rambling incoherence of the buffoon. But his habit of abrupt transition from one topic to another maintains the interest of patient readers. In both books his impertinent grossness occasionally causes irritation. In spite of his trick of masking his predilection for double-entendre by a free use of aposiopesis, his words are often as indecent as his thoughts.

Sterne's sermons are as a rule professional efforts on common-sense lines, and mainly interest the literary critic by the perspicuity, orderliness, and restrained eloquence of which they prove his literary style to be capable. He claimed that they were 'dramatic' (*Tristram*, ii. 231), and admitted that passages were stolen. His careless philosophy of life and his impatience of gravity led him into other incongruities which tend to profanity. The parable of the prodigal son suggests to him remarks on the advantages of foreign travel, and the desirability of confiding one's son when on the grand tour to a tutor of gentlemanly habits and worldly experience. Cardinal Newman admitted Sterne's eloquence when quoting from his sermon (xlii) on the literary value of the bible (NEWMAN, *Idea of a University*, 1889, pp. 270–2).

But after full account has been taken of Sterne's numerous deflections from the paths of literary rectitude—of his indecency, his buffoonery, his mawkishness, his plagiarisms, his wanton digressiveness—he remains, as the author of 'Tristram Shandy,' a delineator of the comedy of human life before whom only three or four humorous writers, in any tongue or of any age, can justly claim precedence. Uncle Toby, Corporal Trim, Dr. Slop, Mr. and Mrs. Shandy, Obadiah, and the Widow Wadman are of the kin—however the degrees of kinship may be estimated—of Pantagruel and Don Quixote, of Falstaff and Juliet's Nurse, of Monsieur Jourdain and Tartuffe. For the guerilla warfare that he incidentally waged in his own freakish fashion throughout the novel on the pedantries and pretences of learning he deserves many of the honours that have been paid to Pope and Swift. No modern writer has shown a more certain touch in transferring to his canvas commonplace domestic scenes which only a master's hand can invest with point or interest. It is this kind of power especially that glorifies 'A Sentimental Journey.' Defects due to the author's overstrained sensi-

bility practically count for nothing against the artistic and finished beauty of the series of vignettes which Sterne, by his sureness of insight and descriptive faculty, created in 'A Sentimental Journey' out of the simplest and most pedestrian episodes of travel.

Apart from 'The Case of Elijah, a charity sermon,' 1747; 'The Abuses of Conscience,' 1750; and 'The Political Romance,' 1769; Sterne's authentic works (with eighteenth-century reprints) are: 1. 'The Life and Opinions of Tristram Shandy,' vols. i. and ii. York, 1759 (2nd edit. London, 1760, with plate by Hogarth); vols. iii. and iv. 1761, with a second plate by Hogarth; vols. v. and vi. 1762; vols. vii. and viii. 1765; vol. ix. 1767. The volumes of the original edition numbered v. vii. and ix. often bear Sterne's genuine autograph on the title-page. The first collective edition, in nine 12mo volumes, appeared in 1767, and the second in 1768. Other editions were, 1777, 6 vols.; 1779, 2 vols. 2. 'Sermons of Mr. Yorick,' London, 1760, vols. i. and ii. 12mo (2nd edit. 1763, Dublin, 1761); vols. iii. and iv. 1766; vols. v. vi. and vii. 1769. Reissues appeared in 1775 and 1777, 6 vols.; 1779, 2 vols.; 1784, and 1787. 3. 'A Sentimental Journey,' 1768, 2 vols. 12mo; 1778, 2 vols. 12mo; 1792, with six plates after Stothard. 4. 'Letters of the Late Reverend Laurence Sterne to his most intimate friends, with a fragment in the manner of Rabelais [apparently a first draft of a projected scene in 'Tristram'], to which are prefixed memoirs of his life and family, written by himself, published by his daughter, Lydia Sterne de Medalle.' 1775. 5. 'Letters from Yorick to Eliza,' 1775. 6. 'Twelve Letters to his Friends on various occasions, to which is added his history of a watch-coat, with explanatory notes,' London, 1775 (letters numbered iv-xi are of very doubtful authenticity). 7. 'Seven Letters written by Sterne and his Friends [one only by Sterne'], edited by W. Durrant Cooper, 1844 (privately printed).

Several volumes of extracts appeared under such titles as 'Sterne's Witticisms' or 'The Beauties of Sterne' (1783). The latter reached a tenth edition in 1787, and was often reissued.

The first collected edition of Sterne's works appeared in Dublin in 7 vols. in 1779. It was dedicated to Eugenius [i.e. John Hall-Stevenson], and includes the spurious 'Koran,' but no letters were admitted. A fifth Dublin edition in five 12mo volumes, 'with additions,' omitted the 'Koran' and included Madame de Medalle's letters. The best early collected edition appeared in London, with all the genuine letters and a few (Nos.

129-31) of doubtful authenticity, in 10 vols. in 1780, with plates by Hogarth: the 'Sentimental Journey' has plates by E. Edwards. Another issue in 1780, in 5 vols., included Eugenius's continuation of the 'Journey.' Other early collected editions of authenticity are dated 1788, 1793, 1803, and 1810. A complete edition in two volumes, edited by Dr. J. P. Browne, appeared in 1873, in 2 vols., with much of the newly recovered correspondence. A useful edition in six volumes, with a selection only of the sermons, and without any of the newly recovered letters, was edited by Mr. George Saintsbury in 1894 (the paged references to 'Tristram' and the 'Journey' in this article are to the reprints in this edition).

A French translation of the complete works, by F. Michel, appeared at Paris in 1835. The 'Sentimental Journey' was translated by Frénais (Liège, 1770, often reprinted), by J. Janin (Paris, 1854), by A. Hédouin (Paris, 1895), and by E. Blémont (with Leloir's illustrations, 1884). 'Tristram' appeared in French by Frénais (London, 1784), by L. de Wailly (Paris, 1842), and by A. Hédouin (1890-1). The 'Sentimental Journey' has also appeared in German, Italian, Spanish, Polish, and Russian versions. A German translation of 'Tristram' appeared at Leipzig in 1801. An Italian translation of the 'Sermons' by Campagnona appeared at Milan in 1833. The 'Letters' have also been rendered into German (Leipzig, 1776).

Of Sterne's manuscripts, the British Museum owns the first half (vol. i.) of the 'Sentimental Journey,' with autograph corrections (Egerton MS. 1610), and the whole of the 'Journal to Eliza' (Addit. MS. 34527). The draft of the story of Le Fever in 'Tristram Shandy,' which Sterne sent to Lord Spencer, has notes in his handwriting; it is still at Spencer House. A copy of the 'Sentimental Journey,' in the same hand as Lord Spencer's transcript from 'Tristram Shandy,' belongs to Sir Andrew Agnew, bart., of Lochnaw Castle, Stranraer. An autograph manuscript of Sterne's sermon on 'The temporal advantages of religion' (vol. v. No. 1), which formerly belonged to Henry Fauntleroy [q. v.], is now the property of Mr. Locker-Lampson at Rowfant. The original copy of only one of Sterne's letters to Eliza has been preserved — the first in the series; it belongs to Lord Basing, and is now at Hoddington. Several letters in Sterne's autograph are in the British Museum; others belong to Sir George Wombwell, or are in the Alfred Morrison collection.

[Unpublished material which contains much new information has been utilised for this article. John Croft, who was brought up under Sterne at Stillington, and was a younger brother of Stephen Croft, Sterne's intimate friend there, collected from the humourist's acquaintances about York a series of anecdotes respecting his career in the north, which he forwarded to Caleb Whitefoord in letters dated from York in August 1795 and June 1796. These letters remain in manuscript among the archives of the Whitefoord family, and are about to be published in the Whitefoord Papers which Mr. W. A. S. Hewins is editing for the Clarendon Press. Three slight anecdotes of Sterne, which have been neglected by Sterne's biographers, also figure in John Croft's Scrapeana, 1792, pp. 22, 25, 33. The parochial registers of Sutton, Stillington, and Coxwold have been perused by the present writer. Two long unpublished letters from Sterne to Lord Fauconberg, one dated Paris, 10 April 1762, and the other Montpellier, 30 Sept. 1763, with a letter respecting Sterne's life at Coxwold, from Lord Fauconberg's agent, Richard Chapman, dated 25 Sept. 1761, have been copied by kind permission of their owner, Sir George Wombwell of Newburgh Priory. Two other unpublished letters to Becket the bookseller, one dated Toulouse, 12 March 1763, and the other Paris, 20 March 1764, are in the Alfred Morrison collection. The unpublished Journal to Eliza was for many years in the possession of Mr. Thomas Washbourne Gibbs of Bath, who lent it to Thackeray in 1851 when he was lecturing on Sterne. Thackeray made no use of it. On Mr. Gibbs's death, in 1894, it passed under his will to the British Museum. It is now numbered Addit. 34527, ff. 1-40; draft letters from Sterne to Daniel Draper and to the Jameses are attached to it (ff. 45-6). The former is printed by Mr. Fitzgerald, apparently from a description of Mr. Gibbs's Sterne MSS. supplied to the Athenæum on 30 March 1878; the latter appears somewhat abbreviated in Sterne's published correspondence. A letter from Mrs. Draper to her friend Mrs. James, dated Bombay, 15 April 1772, covering twenty-four folios, is also bound up with the unpublished Journal at the British Museum (Addit. MS. 34527, ff. 47-70). Other unpublished sources for Mrs. Draper's career are thirteen letters from her to members of her father's family, belonging to Lord Basing, who descends from Richard Sclater, a brother of May Sclater, Mrs. Draper's father; Lord Basing has kindly supplied copies for the purposes of this article. The first, dated Bombay, 13 March 1758, was written before her marriage, and is signed Eliza Sclater; the latest is dated from Rajahmundry, 20 Jan. 1774. The letter from Mrs. Draper from Tellicherry in 1769, which was printed in the Magazine of Indian Art, is now in the British Museum. Those printed in the Times of India in 1894, which are in private hands in Bombay, were communicated by Mr. James Douglas of Bombay.

The earliest biographical notice of Sterne is that by his friend Hall-Stevenson prefixed to the spurious continuation of the Sentimental Journey (1769). Sterne's daughter, Madame Medalle, supplied in her collection of Sterne's letters (1775) a brief autobiographic fragment of great value. Besides his correspondence and the autobiographic fragment, both Tristram Shandy and the Sentimental Journey abound in autobiographic material. Thomas Gill's Vallis Eboracensis collects local information from Coxwold and the neighbourhood.

The only full life of Sterne is by Mr. Percy Fitzgerald, which was published in 1864 (2 vols.), and was reissued somewhat condensed, but with much new information—mainly derived from manuscript letters in the British Museum—in 1896 (2 vols.) Not all the old errors are corrected in the new edition. Laurence Sterne, sa personne et ses ouvrages, étude précédée d'un Fragment inédit de Sterne (Paris, 1870), is a valuable piece of expository criticism and biography by M. Paul Stapfer. Mr. H. D. Traill's Life of Sterne, in the Men of Letters series, supplies no new information, but some sensible criticism. The chief English critical notices are Thackeray's lecture in his Lectures on the Humourists, an essay by the Rev. Whitwell Elwin in the Quarterly Review, 1854, xciv. 303–53, and Mr. Leslie Stephen's essay in his Hours in a Library, 1892, iii. 139–74. Among French critics it is worth noting that Voltaire devoted the whole of section iii., entitled De la Conscience trompeuse, of his article on conscience in his Dictionnaire Philosophique (ed. 1765), to an appreciative account of Shandy and of Sterne's insight into the character of David (Œuvres Complètes, Paris, 1838, vii. 369). In the Journal de Politique et de la Littérature, 25 April 1777, Voltaire condemned Sterne's 'bouffonnerie continuelle dans le goût de Scarron.' Notices by Montégut, Essais sur la Littérature Anglaise, p. 281; Scherer, Etudes Critiques, 1876, pp. 195–221; and Texte, Cosmopolitisme Littéraire, pp. 337–354, are also suggestive.]

S. L.

STERNE, RICHARD (1596?–1683), archbishop of York and alleged author of the 'Whole Duty of Man,' born about 1596, was son of Simon Sterne of Mansfield, Nottinghamshire. Simon, son of William Sterne, who is said to have migrated to Mansfield from Suffolk, where the name is common, married Margery, daughter of Gregory Walker of Mansfield. The future archbishop was educated at the free school at Mansfield, and on 8 July 1611 was matriculated from Trinity College, Cambridge. He was admitted a scholar on 6 May 1614, graduated B.A. in 1614–15, M.A. in 1618, and B.D. in 1625. He was elected fellow of Benet or Corpus Christi College in 1620, and was incorporated B.D. at Oxford on 10 July 1627 (Wood, Fasti, i. 433). He became chaplain to Archbishop Laud, probably in 1633, and on 17 Nov. in that year was selected by him to preach at St. Paul's Cross (Laud, Works, vii. 47). On 7 March 1633–4 he was elected master of Jesus College, Cambridge, and in the same month was collated by Laud to the rectory of Yelverton, Somerset. About the same time he received the rectory of Harleton, Cambridgeshire, and in 1635 he graduated D.D.

On the outbreak of the civil war, Sterne zealously adopted the royalist cause, and in August 1642 he arranged for the despatch of large quantities of college plate to the king. Cromwell, however, who, as one of the burgesses of Cambridge, was engaged in securing that town for parliament, had Sterne arrested on 11 Aug. with Dr. John Barwick (1612–1664) [q. v.] and Dr. William Beale (d. 1651) [q. v.] They were brought up to London, being subject to hostile demonstrations on the journey, and, on the order of the House of Commons, were committed to the Tower (Barwick, Querela Cantabrigiensis, 1644). Sterne remained there nineteen weeks until 12 Jan. 1642–3, when he was ordered to confine himself to Lord Petre's house in Aldersgate Street; after seven months' imprisonment he was placed on board an Ipswich coalship in the Thames. Being shut down beneath hatches he suffered great privation, and his enemies were credited with the intention of selling him into slavery. After ten days, however, he was put on shore and confined in Ely House. Meanwhile he was sequestered from his livings, and in March 1643–4 he was ejected by the Earl of Manchester from the mastership of Jesus College. On 7 Jan. 1644–5, at Laud's request, Sterne was permitted by parliament to attend the archbishop in the Tower, and he was with him from the 8th until his execution on the 10th. Some notes of Sterne's conversations with Laud during this time are printed in Laud's 'Works' (vii. 600–1), and the written address which Laud read to the people on the scaffold on 10 Jan. was handed by him to Sterne, under whose supervision it was printed in 1677 (Oxford, reprinted in Laud, Works, iv. 430 et sqq.) Soon afterwards Sterne regained his liberty, and during the Commonwealth and Protectorate he maintained himself by keeping a school at Stevenage, Hertfordshire.

At the Restoration he was at once singled out for preferment. He was reinstated in the mastership of Jesus College, but a few months later was made bishop of Carlisle. The congé d'élire was dated 9 Oct. 1660, the royal assent was given on 28 Nov., the temporalities were restored on 19 Dec., and he was enthroned on 4 Jan. 1660–1. From

April to July 1661 he attended the Savoy conference. 'Among all the bishops,' wrote Baxter, 'there was none who had so promising a face as Dr. Sterne, the Bishop of Carlisle. He look'd so honestly, and gravely, and soberly, that I scarce thought such a face could have deceived me; and when I was intreating them not to cast out so many of their brethren through the nation, as scrupuled a ceremony which they confessed indifferent, he turn'd to the rest of the Reverent Bishops and noted me for saying "in the nation." "He will not say in the kingdom," saith he, "lest he own a king." This was all I ever heard that worthy bishop say. But with grief I told him that half the charity which became so grave a bishop might have sufficed to have helpt him to a better exposition of the word' (*Reliquiæ Baxterianæ*, 1696, ii. 305). On 5 March 1661–2 convocation is said to have entrusted the revision of the Book of Common Prayer to Sterne, George Griffith [q. v.], bishop of St. Asaph, and Brian Walton [q. v.], bishop of Chester (LE NEVE, *Protestant Archbishops*; but cf. LUCKOCK, *Studies in Hist. of the Common Prayer*).

Sterne is said to have left his bishopric in an impoverished state to his successor, Edward Rainbowe [q. v.], with whom he had a lawsuit (HUTCHINSON, *Cumberland*, ii. 632–633). In 1664 he was translated to the archbishopric of York, being elected on 28 April and confirmed on 10 June following. In that capacity, according to Burnet, he 'minded chiefly the enriching of his family' (*Own Time*, ii. 427). He was a regular attendant at parliament (cf. *Tanner MSS.* xlii. 46), and, according to Burnet, was 'more than ordinarily compliant in all things to the court, and was very zealous for the duke' of York. He was also suspected for this reason of inclinations towards popery. He died at Bishopsthorpe, aged 87, on 18 June 1683 (cf. letter of his son Richard to Sancroft, 20 June 1683, in *Tanner MSS.* xxxiv. 47), and was buried in St. Stephen's Chapel, York Minster, where there is an inscription to his memory. He gave 1,850*l*. towards the rebuilding of St. Paul's Cathedral, and left 40*l*. a year to found four scholarships at Jesus College, and 20*l*. a year to found two at Corpus Christi College.

Sterne married Elizabeth, daughter of Edward Dickinson, lord of the manor of Farnborough. She died in London on 6 March 1673–4, aged 57, and was buried at Farnborough, where there is an inscription to her memory. By her Sterne had thirteen children. The eldest son, Richard, died at York in 1700; another son, Simon, was grandfather of Laurence Sterne [q. v.], the author of 'Tristram Shandy' (THORESBY, *Ducatus Leodiensis*, ed. Whitaker, i. 214). An anonymous portrait of the archbishop was engraved by F. Place.

Sterne published 'A Comment on Psalm ciii' (London, 1649, 8vo), and a work on logic entitled 'Summa Logicæ' (London, 1685, 8vo). He has verses in the 'Genethliacon Caroli et Mariæ' (1631) and in 'Irenodia Cantabrigiensis ob paciferum Caroli e Scotia reditum' (1641). He also assisted in the preparation of Walton's Polyglot Bible [see WALTON, BRIAN].

Sterne has also been claimed as the author of the 'Whole Duty of Man' and the six works published anonymously as by that writer (cf. *The Whole Duty of Man*, ed. W. B. Hawkins, 1842, pp. xiii–xxiii; *Bibliographer*, 1882, ii. 73–9, 94, 164). The claim was based solely on the assertion that the manuscript of the work was once in Sterne's possession (EVELYN, *Diary*, ed. Bray, ii. 321). But Sterne, who was, according to Burnet, 'a sour ill-tempered man,' possessed worldly characteristics quite incompatible with Bishop Fell's account of the author of the 'Whole Duty.' The latter, moreover, in the seventh tract of the series, 'The Christian's Birthright' (sect. vii. paragraph 2), states that he had been driven abroad during the troubles, whereas Sterne never left England. There can indeed be little doubt that the 'Whole Duty of Man' was written by Richard Allestree [q. v.], though severely edited by Bishop John Fell (1625–1686) [q. v.], his biographer and literary executor (Mr. C. E. Doble in *Academy*, 1882, ii. 348, 364, 382; cf. art. PAKINGTON, DOROTHY, LADY).

[Tanner MS. xxxvi. 73, xxxviii. 130, xl. 42, xlii. 46, lxx. 79, cxliv. 130; Rawlinson MSS. A. 290, 20, C. 983. 11; Harl. MS. 3784, arts. 2, 3; Lords' and Commons' Journals; Cal. State Papers, Dom. 1660–71; A True Relation of the Taking . . . of Dr. Sterne, London, 1642, 4to; Baillie's Letters and Journals, ii. 148; Evelyn's Diary, ii. 321, 389; Luttrell's Brief Relation; Burnet's Own Time, i. 312, ii. 427; Walker's Sufferings of the Clergy, ii. 146–7; Peter Barwick's Life of John Barwick, 1724, pp. 41, 42, 281; Le Neve's Protestant Archbishops, 1720, pp. 241–57, and Fasti Eccl. Angl. ed. Hardy; Wood's Fasti Oxon. ed. Bliss, i. 433–4, ii. 336; Laud's Works, iv. 423–4, 430, vii. 47, 660–1; Masters's Hist. Corpus Christi Coll. Cambridge; Worthington's Diary (Camden Soc.); Baker's Hist. St. John's Coll. Cambridge, ed. Mayor, i. 219, ii. 633, 638, 647; Cooper's Annals of Cambridge, iii. 328–30; Granger's Biogr. Hist.; Nichols's Lit. Illustrations, ii. 603–4; Nicholson and Burn's Cumberland and Westmoreland;

Hutchinson's Cumberland, ii. 632–3; Thoroton's Nottinghamshire, ii. 311; Hook's Eccl. Biogr. viii. 479–83; Brown's Nottinghamshire Worthies, pp. 230–1; Foster's Alumni Oxon. 1500–1714.]   A. F. P.

STERNHOLD, THOMAS (d. 1549), joint versifier of the Psalms with John Hopkins (d. 1570) [q. v.], was, according to Holinshed, born at Southampton. Bale (Scriptt. Illust. 1557) styles him 'Suthamptonensis,' which may only mean that he was, as Fuller and Anthony à Wood designate him, 'a Hampshire man.' In conflict with these authorities, Atkyns (Hist. of Gloucestershire) says that he was born at Awre on the Severn, and that his posterity, turning papists, left the place. An inhabitant of the name of Sternhold lived at Lydney, not far from Awre (Visitation of Gloucestershire, 1623, s.v. 'Bond'). An entry in a later hand and printed characters on a blank page after the baptisms of 1572 in the parish register at Awre asserts that he lived on an estate called the Hayfield in that parish with his colleague, John Hopkins, as a neighbour, and that 'from Awre first sounded out the Psalms of David by Thomas Ste[r]nhold and John Hopkins.' The fact that Hopkins was concerned in the posthumous edition of Sternhold's Psalms, and apparently responsible for adding three others of Sternhold's translations to the version in 1561, makes the story in the register probable. The property in his will, however, lies entirely in Hampshire and Cornwall.

Wood says that Sternhold entered Christ Church, Oxford, but did not take a degree. The first ascertained date in his life is 1538, when the name of Thomas Sternhold appears in Cromwell's accounts (Letters and Papers Henry VIII, ed. Gairdner, vol. xiii. pt. ii.) in a list of 'gentlemen most mete to be daily waiters on my said lorde' (the king). He had probably been known to Cromwell previously. He became one of the grooms of the robes to Henry, and was evidently a favourite, since a legacy of a hundred marks was bequeathed him by the king's will. He is probably the Thomas Sternell or Sternoll who was elected for Plymouth to the parliament that met on 30 Jan. 1544–5, and was dissolved by Henry VIII's death in January 1546–7 (Official Return, App. p. xxx). His earliest metrical versions of the Psalms may have been composed in Henry's reign (Coverdale had published his 'Goostly Psalmes,' a translation of Luther's psalm versions, as early as 1539. In 1540 the earliest Psalms by Marot, valet de chambre to Francis I, were the rage at the French court, and soon afterwards passed into protestant worship

at Geneva). In the opinion of learned men of the time metrical versions more nearly represented the structure of the Hebrew psalms than prose, and for singing metre was a necessity. Sternhold, Marot, and Coverdale alike wished to substitute the Psalms of David for the 'obscene' ballads of the court and people. The close parallel in position at their masters' courts naturally suggests comparison between the work of Marot and Sternhold; but there is no similarity discernible. In contrast with the French poet's lyrical variety Sternhold (with the exception of Ps. cxx) used only one metre, and this the simplest of all ballad measures, the metre of 'Chevy Chace.' This choice of metre was really of infinitely wider consequence than the psalms he set to it; for either in this form, which has two rhymes, or that of Hopkins, which has four, it became the predominant metre (C. M.) not only of the old and new versions of England and Scotland, but of countless metrical psalters and English hymns in general. The rapid spread of psalm-singing in Elizabeth's reign was made possible by the easiness of tune and metre, and in the decay of music under the puritans the simplicity of the metre alone kept psalm-singing alive. Sternhold is said to have sung his psalms to his organ for his own 'godly solace' (STRYPE). They won the ear of Edward VI. The only edition which Sternhold lived to publish he dedicated to the young king. In this dedication he thanks God for giving them a king 'that forbiddeth not laymen to gather and lease [i.e. glean] in the lordes harvest,' and trusts as his 'grace taketh pleasure to hear them song sometimes, so he wyll also delighte to see and read them and command them to be song by others.' He expresses a hope also of 'travayling further,' and 'performing the residue' of the Psalter. This, however, was not to be, as his total contribution to the old version consists of only forty psalms.

Sternhold died on 23 Aug. 1549 (Inquisitiones post mortem, 3 Edward VI, Nos. 12, 146). His will, dated August 1549, was proved on 12 Sept. following. Among the witnesses to his will was Edward Whitchurch [q. v.], probably his publisher. He left his property to his wife Agnes and his two daughters, Judith and Philippa, aged respectively three years and one. His property consisted of land in Hampshire and at Bodmin in Cornwall. Part of the Hampshire property might have been inherited. Slackstead, however, had been purchased recently, as it had been granted, as part of the possessions of Hyde Abbey, to Sir Ralph Sadler [q. v.] in 1547. The Bodmin property also he had purchased from the crown in 1543, as part of the possessions of the dissolved priory of St. Petrock there. The total was of the annual value of 10l. 13s. 1½d.

Sternhold is solely remembered as the originator of the first metrical version of the Psalms which obtained general currency alike in England and Scotland. The 'Versification of Certain Chapters of the Proverbs of Solomon' has only been attributed to him by error (cf. COTTON's *Editions of the Bible*). Sternhold and Hopkins's version has had a larger circulation than any work in the language, except the authorised version of the Bible and the Book of Common Prayer (for an account of its evolution, authors, and merits see art. HOPKINS, JOHN, *d.* 1570). Sternhold's work forms its base. His first edition undated, but, as being dedicated to Edward VI, not earlier than 1547, contains nineteen psalms (i–v, xx, xxv, xxviii, xxix, xxxii, xxxiv, xli, xlix, lxxiii, lxxviii, ciii, cxx, cxxiii, cxxviii). It was printed by Edward Whitchurch, and is entitled 'Certayne Psalmes chosē out of the Psalter of Dauid and drawē into Englishē Metre by Thomas Sternhold, grome of ye Kynges Maiesties Roobes' (Brit. Museum). The second edition, printed after his death—apparently by John Hopkins, who adds seven psalms of his own in order to fill in a blank space, deprecating comparison with Sternhold's 'most exquisite doynges'—added to those of the former edition eighteen new psalms (vi–xvii, xix, xxi, xliii, xliv, lxiii, lxviii). It is entitled 'Al such Psalmes of Dauid as Thomas Sternhold, late grome of the Kinges maiesties robes, did in his lyfetime drawe into English Metre,' and is printed by Edward Whitcurche in 1549 (Cambridge University Library). Three more psalms (xviii, xxii, xxiii) are added to these in a very rare edition of the growing Psalter printed by John Daye in 1561, and the complete number (40) appears in the full editions of 1562, 1563, and all subsequent ones. The only one of his psalms which remains current is the simple rendering of Psalm xxiii ('My Shepherd is the Living Lord'). The text of his psalms, as found in all editions subsequent to 1556, follows the Genevan revision of that year.

[Julian's Dict. of Hymnology. See also authorities under HOPKINS, JOHN, and The Scottish Psalter, by Neil Livingstone.] H. L. B.

STERRY, PETER (*d.* 1672), Cromwell's chaplain, born in Surrey, entered Emmanuel College, Cambridge, on 21 Oct. 1629, and graduated B.A. in 1633, and M.A. 1637. He was elected a fellow in 1636. He became a preacher in London, and was one of the

fourteen divines nominated for the Westminster assembly by the House of Lords in May 1642. The omission of his name from the ordinance of June 1643 is probably accidental, as Sterry was serving on a committee of the assembly in August 1645.

Sterry had been known at Cambridge as one of the platonists, and in London he was characterised by Sir Benjamin Rudyerd [q.v.] and others as mystical and obscure. He was intimate with Sir Henry Vane, the younger [q. v.], and Baxter, who calls Vane's followers 'Vanists,' puns on their friendship, asking 'whether vanity and sterility had ever been more happily conjoined.' On 24 Jan. 1644, while he was chaplain to Lady Brooke, Sterry was examined concerning some supposed plot of Vane, which Lord Lovelace was sent by the king to investigate (*Hist. MSS. Comm.* 6th Rep. p. 3). Immediately after the execution of the king, Sterry was voted a preacher to the council of state (16 Feb. 1649). A salary of 100l. a year was settled upon him, and he was ordered to commence Sunday sermons at Whitehall in November of the same year. By that time he had been granted lodgings at Whitehall, and the allowance was doubled. His duties were to preach on Sundays before Cromwell either at Whitehall or Hampton Court, on every other Thursday morning at the former, and frequently before the lords and commons. He was employed to make an inventory of the state records for the Commonwealth, 'so that they may not be embezzled,' to certify of the fitness of ministers, and to report on some works in manuscript which the council decided to print (*Cal. State Papers*, 1653–4, p. 225). He was also commissioned (in 1656) to examine Archbishop Ussher's library, and advise what books should be bought by the state (*ib.* 1655–6, p. 370).

He may have been the 'Mr. Sterry' appointed on 8 Sept. 1657 to assist Milton as Latin secretary when Sir Philip Meadows [q. v.] went on a mission to Denmark; but there was a secretary to the Danish embassy in 1660 also of the name of Sterry (*Cal. State Papers*, Dom. 1657–8, p. 89; cf. MASSON, *Milton*, v. 71; PEPYS, *Diary*, i. 43).

Sterry's attachment to the Protector was sincere, if at times somewhat fulsomely expressed. On the news of Cromwell's death being brought to the chaplains assembled to pray for him, he assured them it was good news, for if he had been so useful in a mortal state, how much more so would he be when translated! His prayer for Richard Cromwell that he might be made the 'brightness of his father's glory and the express image of his person' was regarded by Burnet as nothing short of blasphemy (*Hist. of his Own Time*, i. 141). Baillie (*Letters*, ii. 429) says that after Cromwell's death he was out of favour, and regarded as a parasite. He continued to live in London, took pupils, for whom he prepared a catechism (Preface to his *Appearance of God to Man*), and after the Restoration held a conventicle. Apparently his later years were occupied with literary work. He paraphrased the Canticles, and dictated from his sick-bed a 'Discourse on the Mystery of Love and Wrath.' He died, after a long illness, on 19 Nov. 1672.

Sterry's sermons and books are excellent both in matter and style. Some of his prose has been held worthy of comparison with Milton's. His religion was a pure and lofty platonism. Holding entirely aloof from the polemical spirit of his time, he strongly disagreed with the presbyterian system, whose 'constitutions, methods, and discipline,' he said, 'laboured to hedge in the wind, and to bind up the sweet influences of the spirit.' The very mystical qualities which rendered him unacceptable to Baxter were those that attracted Cromwell. Unlike the majority of the puritans by whom he was surrounded, Sterry was keenly alive to the influences of poetry, music, and art, and speaks with admiration of the works of Virgil, Titian, and Vandyck (*Freedom of the Will*, p. 28). He is satirised in Butler's 'Hudibras' (bk. iii. canto ii. ll. 215, &c.)

Besides many other sermons preached before the lords and commons, in St. Paul's, Covent Garden, St. Margaret's, and elsewhere, Sterry published: 1. 'The Spirit's Conviction of Sinne,' London, 1645, 4to; another copy of the same date has the title, 'The Spirit Convincing of Sinne.' 2. 'England's Deliverance from the Northern Presbytery compared with its Deliverance from the Roman Papacy,' London (printed at Leith), 1652, 4to. 'A rare Epistle' was sent to him by David Brown of Soho, concerning a disturbance made by a woman while Sterry was preaching at Whitehall, to which a satisfactory answer was returned, and the correspondence published,'Cloathing for the Naked,' 1652, 4to. Posthumously were published: 1. 'Discourse of the Freedom of the Will,' London, 1675, fol. 2. 'The Rise, Race, and Royalty of the Kingdom of God in the Soul of Man,' London, 1683, 4to. 3. 'The Appearance of God to Man in the Gospel and Gospel Change,' London, 1710, 4to. This contained miscellaneous works, and an announcement that part ii. (which does not seem to have been published) would contain 'A Discourse of Vertue.' That an Eternity of

Duration having a beginning without end is expos'd to Difficulties. Of the state of the Wicked after Death and of the Divine Wrath and of the Devil. Short essays on A Spirit, Memory, A Plant, the Consort of Musick,' &c. 'Prayers selected from Thomas à Kempis, Everard, Law, and (chiefly) Peter Sterry,' appeared 1785, 8vo, and a sermon of Sterry's was republished in 'Fourteen Sermons,' 1831, 12mo. Some unpublished manuscripts are in the possession of a descendant, Mrs. Wynter, residing at Wodville, Taunton. They consist chiefly of papers and sermons treating of philosophical and metaphysical subjects, together with a number of letters and autobiographical fragments.

NATHANIEL STERRY (*d.* 1698), of Surrey, Peter's younger brother, entered Emmanuel College, Cambridge, on 19 July 1644, graduated B.A. 1648, became a fellow of Merton College, Oxford, in 1649, proceeded M.A. on 31 May 1651, and B.D. on 24 March 1675. He was appointed rector of Stuston, Suffolk, in 1662, and on 8 Sept. 1674 rector and dean of Bocking, Essex. He was, like Peter, an ardent Cromwellian. He died before 10 Nov. 1698, when his successor was appointed (FOSTER, *Alumni Oxon.* 1500-1714, p. 1422; BURROWS, *Visitation of Oxford*, pp. 178, 265, 313, 525; BRODRICK, *Memorials of Merton College, Oxford*, pp. 104, 290, 291, 383; NEWCOURT, *Eccles. Repert.* ii. 68, 69).

[Brook's Lives of the Puritans, iii. 347; Neal's Hist. of the Puritans, iv. 180 n.; Edwards's Gangræna. pt. ii. p. 145; Thurloe's State Papers, p. 621; Wood's Athenæ Oxon. iii. 197, 912, 1170; Cal. State Papers, Dom., Committee for Compounding, p. 2077, and from 1649-50 to 1658-1659 passim; Masson's Life of Milton, passim; Sylvester's Life of Baxter, p. 75; Mitchell's Westminster Assembly, xviii. 112; Minutes of the Westminster Assembly lxxxiv. 121, 134; Cromwelliana, pp. 132, 154, 155; Kennett's Register and Chronicle, p. 555; Hanbury's Hist. Mem. relating to Independents, ii. 217, iii. 423, 590; Notes and Queries, 1st ser. iii. 38, 434, vii. 388, 2nd ser. xii. 271; Walcot's Hist. of St. Margaret's, Westminster, p. 86; Nickolls's Original Letters, p. 18; Sterry's Works; Ludlow's Memoirs, ed. Firth, 1894, ii. 45; Baker MSS. vol. vi. f. 80; information from the master of Emmanuel College, Cambridge, from J. Willis Clark, esq., registrary of the university of Cambridge, and from the Rev. A. B. Grosart.]

C. F. S.

STEUART. [See also STEWARD, STEWART, and STUART.]

STEUART, SIR HENRY SETON (1759-1836), of Allanton, Lanarkshire, author of 'The Planter's Guide,' born on 20 Oct. 1759, was the second but eldest surviving son of James Steuart, tenth of Allanton,

Q

an agriculturist and scholar. His mother was a daughter of Henry Steuart-Barclay, esq. of Collernie, Fifeshire. The family claimed descent from Sir John Steuart of Bonkill, lord high steward of Scotland, who was killed at Falkirk in 1298, and whose sixth son, Sir Robert of Daldowie, was asserted to have been the progenitor of the Stewarts of Lennox, Darnley, and Castlemilk. Sir Henry Steuart supported this claim in a pamphlet issued in 1799, in opposition to Andrew Stuart's 'Genealogy of the Stuarts,' published in the preceding year, and the controversy was afterwards revived on the one side by George Robertson ('Candidus')—who, in his edition of Crawfurd's History of Renfrewshire' (1818), printed the manuscript history of the family, on which the Steuarts of Allanton based their pedigree—and on the other by John Riddell (*Blackwood's Mag.* i. 349–52, 476–83, iii. 439–46).

Steuart completed his education at Hamburg, and returned to Scotland when about seventeen. In 1778 he entered the army as a cornet in the 13th light dragoons. Three years later he exchanged into the 10th light dragoons, and accompanied to Ireland his kinsman, General Sir James Steuart of Coltness, in the capacity of aide-de-camp. In 1787 he retired from the army. He settled at Allanton, and devoted the rest of his life to literary pursuits and the improvement of his estate. His winters he usually spent at Edinburgh, where he enjoyed the society of Erskine, Tytler (Lord Woodhouselee), and Henry Mackenzie, whose father Steuart's mother had married as her second husband. In 1801 Steuart published a pamphlet advocating the construction of a canal from the Lanarkshire coalfields to Edinburgh in order to cheapen and improve the coal supply of that city. He had also projects for supplying Ireland, the Isle of Man, and even some foreign ports with fuel from the same district. In 1806 he obtained some credit for a competent edition of Sallust's works (2 vols. 4to). He was rewarded by the degree of LL.D. from Edinburgh University, and was also elected F.R.S.E. He occasionally contributed to the 'Anti-Jacobin' and other periodicals, and at his death left in manuscript fragments of a 'History of the Rebellion of 1745' and of a history of Scotland. He handed over to Chambers the materials he had collected for a history of the Rebellion.

Owing to bad health Steuart abandoned most of his literary work, and experiments in arboriculture became the chief interest of his life. In September 1823 a deputation from the Highland and Agricultural Society, which included Sir Walter Scott and Lords Belhaven and Corehouse, visited Allanton, and reported on the improvements effected there by Steuart's system of transplanting large trees. Though he had had to contend with an unfavourable soil and an exposed position, he 'attained at no extraordinary expense the power so long desired of anticipating the slow progress of vegetation, and accomplishing within two or three seasons those desirable changes in the face of nature which he who plants in early youth can, in ordinary cases, only hope to witness in advanced life.' From this time Steuart frequently corresponded with Sir Walter, who imitated several of Steuart's experiments at Abbotsford. When, in 1828, Steuart published his 'Planter's Guide; or a practical essay on the best method of giving immediate effect to wood by the removal of large trees and underwood,' Scott reviewed it enthusiastically in the 'Quarterly' (March). When Scott visited Allanton in January 1829, in company with Lockhart, he noted in his journal : 'Sir Henry is a sad coxcomb, and lifted beyond the solid earth by the effect of his book's success. But the book well deserves it.'

'The Planter's Guide' was also favourably reviewed by Southwood Smith in the 'Westminster Review,' by Professor Wilson ('Christopher North') in 'Blackwood's Magazine' (April 1828), and in the 'Edinburgh Review' (March 1829). It had a large circulation in America. In his preface to the second edition Steuart claims to have made the first attempt to apply the principles of physiology to practical arboriculture, and to have created the new science of phytology. W. Billington, formerly of the woods and forests department, asserted, however, that he had anticipated, in a work published in 1825, some of the author's discoveries (*Facts, Observations, &c., being an Exposure of the Misrepresentation of the Author's Treatise on Planting*, 1830). It was also criticised by W. Withers (*Letter to Sir H. Steuart on the Improvement in the quality of Timber by the High Cultivation and Quick Growth of Forest Trees*, 1829). Steuart's method of transplanting was tried with great success on estates in England and Ireland.

A posthumous edition of the 'Planter's Guide' was issued in 1848, with dedication to Queen Victoria. A portrait of the author, engraved by Edward Burton from the painting by Raeburn, is prefixed.

Steuart was created a baronet of Great Britain on 27 Dec. 1814. He died on 11 March 1836, and was buried in the family vault at Camnethan. He married Lilias, daughter and heiress of Hugh Seton, esq. of Touch-Seton, Stirlingshire. His only daughter, Elizabeth, succeeded to her mother's estates in 1835. Her husband, REGINALD MACDONALD STEUART-SETON (1778–1838), originally Reginald Macdonald of Staffa, assumed the name of Steuart, and subsequently that of Steuart-Seton when he succeeded to the baronetcy. He was a friend of Scott, was sheriff of Stirlingshire for twenty-six years, and for thirty-nine acted as ruling elder of the presbytery of Mull in the general assembly. He was for many years secretary of the Highland and Agricultural Society of Scotland. He died in Edinburgh, aged 60, on 15 April 1838. He left three sons and two daughters. The eldest, Sir Henry James Macdonald Steuart-Seton (1812–1884), succeeded to the baronetcy, and was succeeded as fourth baronet by his nephew, Sir Alan Henry Seton-Steuart (b. 1856).

[Burke's Peerage and Baronetage; Memoir (signed R.) prefixed to 3rd edit. of the Planter's Guide; Lockhart's Scott, 1845, pp. 510, 511, 694; Scott's Journal, ii. 40, 90, 221; Biogr. Dict. of Living Authors, 1816 (which attributes to Steuart a history of Catiline's conspiracy, with the four orations of Cicero, published under pseudonym Geo. Fred. Sydney in 1795); Quarterly Rev. March 1855; Irving's Dict. of Eminent Scotsmen; Gent. Mag. 1838. i. 658.]   G. Le G. N.

STEUART or STEWART, SIR JAMES (1635–1715), lord advocate of Scotland, fourth son of Sir James Steuart of Kirkfield and Coltness, by Anne Hope, niece of Sir Thomas Hope (d. 1646) [q. v.], lord advocate, was born in 1635. His father, a banker in Edinburgh, born in 1608, was elected lord provost of Edinburgh in 1648, and also held office under Cromwell. He was in office at the time of the Restoration, but was dismissed, and arrested under a charge of having embezzled money while receiver-general for the army in Scotland, but finally obtained his liberty in 1670, on payment of 1,000l.

The son, who was called to the bar on 20 Nov. 1661, did his best on his father's behalf, but on that account lost almost all his practice. Having also in 1669, in reply to Bishop Honeyman's 'Survey of Naphtali,' published a political pamphlet, entitled 'Jus Populi Vindicatum, or the People's Right to defend themselves, and their Covenanted Reign vindicated,' he found it necessary to leave the country, and went to Rouen, where he became a merchant under the name of Graham. Some years afterwards he returned to Scotland, but being suspected of having had a hand in a political pamphlet, 'An Account of Scotlands Grievances by reason of the Duke of Lauderdale's Ministry,'

1675, an order was issued for his apprehension. He, however, escaped, and lived in different places in England under the name of Lawson. In 1678 he opened a small office in London, where he gave legal advice at half fees, his clerk meeting the clients and transmitting their statements to the invisible Steuart. Returning to Scotland in 1679, he again got into trouble in 1681, from the accidental discovery among the Argyll papers of a memorandum in his hand reflecting on the government, but, as usual, made his escape, and this time took refuge in The Hague. He was present at the meeting at Amsterdam in 1685, when the expedition of Argyll was resolved on, and, having prepared Argyll's declaration of war, was accused of treasonably consulting and contriving Argyll's rebellion, was found guilty in his absence, and was sentenced to be executed whenever he could be found. He, however, received a free pardon from the Prince of Orange, and, on account of his supposed influence with the presbyterian party, was received into favour, and employed to conduct the crown cases along with Mackenzie. In 1692 he was appointed lord advocate, and during his term of office he introduced many legal reforms. He resigned office in 1709, and, dying in 1715, was buried in the church of Old Grey Friars. His only son, Sir James Steuart of Goodtrees and Coltness, became solicitor-general and was father of Sir James Steuart-Denham the elder [see DENHAM].

[Coltness Collections; Wodrow's Analecta; Omond's Lord Advocates of Scotland.]
     T. F. H.

STEUART, SIR JAMES, afterwards DENHAM (1712–1780), political economist. [See DENHAM.]

STEUART, formerly DENHAM, SIR JAMES (1744–1839), general. [See DENHAM.]

STEVENS, ALFRED (1818–1875), artist, baptised on 28 Jan. 1818 at Blandford in Dorset, was the younger son of George Stevens, house-painter, by his wife Susan, daughter of a neighbouring farmer. Alfred claimed relationship with George Steevens [q. v.], the editor of Shakespeare, asserting that his father had dropped the second 'e' of his surname.

Alfred was educated at the village school, and after the summer of 1828 assisted his father in his trade, devoting his leisure to copying pictures. In 1833, through the assistance of Samuel Best, rector of Blandford St. Mary, who was attracted by his artistic promise, he was able to proceed to Italy, where he studied for nine years at Naples, Rome, Florence, Milan, and Venice. From an early period he was a strong advocate of the unity of art; painting, sculpture, architecture, and decorative design all shared in his unremitting application. He received his entire artistic training during his stay in Italy, and never studied in an English school. Even in Italy only a small part of his time was spent in studios, most of it being devoted to the independent study of Italian works of art; and it is said that he was well acquainted with every monument in the country. In 1841 he was employed in Rome by Thorwaldsen, and, after working for him for more than a year, left Italy at the same time as the Danish sculptor in 1842. After two years' residence at Blandford he came to London, and on 7 Oct. 1845 obtained a post in the School of Design as teacher of architectural drawing, perspective, and modelling. He resigned his appointment in 1847, when extensive changes were made in the staff; but even in two years he exercised considerable influence on younger English artists. Among his pupils were Richard Beavis and Godfrey Sykes [q. v.] His chief work at this time was the design of the doors and doorways of the School of Mines in Jermyn Street, which, however, was never carried into execution. The drawing is preserved at South Kensington Museum. Most of his time was devoted to the conception and execution of decorative designs. In February 1850 he obtained the position of chief artist to H. E. Hoole & Co. of Green Lane Works, Sheffield, workers in bronze and metal. His designs, some of which are still in use, secured the first place for his firm at the Great Exhibition in Hyde Park in the following year (cf. WYATT, *Industrial Arts of the Nineteenth Century*). During his stay at Sheffield he exercised a profound influence on the higher branches of metal working, raising the artistic character of the trade. Previously manufacturers had depended on impure rococo ornamentation introduced by secondrate foreigners. Returning to London in 1852, he designed among other things the vases on the top of the railings in front of the British Museum, and the lions sejant on the dwarf posts in front of the grille. The lions have since been placed within the museum.

In 1856 he entered into the competition for the Wellington monument to be erected under one of the great arches of St. Paul's Cathedral, at the cost of 20,000l. On 7 Aug. 1857 Stevens's design was awarded a premium of 100l. and placed sixth in order of merit. On proceeding, however, to consider the fitness of the selected models for the site it became evident that Stevens's was the only design in any way suitable, and, in consequence, the execution of the monument was entrusted to him, 6,000l. being deducted from the amount placed at his disposal, and devoted to other commemorative work in order to compensate unsuccessful artists. Partly through his own procrastination, but chiefly through the hindrances thrown in his way by officials and the inadequacy of the money placed at his disposal, the work was not entirely finished at the time of his death. For many years the monument was suffered to stand in an unfavourable position in the consistory court of St. Paul's, but in 1892, owing to the emphatic recommendation of Sir Frederic (afterwards Lord) Leighton, who raised and contributed to a fund for the purpose, it was placed in the position originally intended for it. The monument has been characterised as 'probably the finest plastic work of modern times,' and consists of 'a sarcophagus supporting a recumbent bronze effigy of the duke, over which is an arched canopy of late Renaissance style on delicately enriched shafts. At each end of the upper part of the canopy is a large bronze group, one representing "Truth tearing out the Tongue of Falsehood," and the other "Valour trampling Cowardice under foot."' The beauty and vigour of these groups alone are sufficient to place their maker among the foremost of modern sculptors. An equestrian statue of the duke, which was designed to surmount the canopy, was never executed.

Stevens died unmarried at his house on Haverstock Hill, London, on 1 May 1875. During his lifetime his merits remained almost unappreciated by the public, and even now the greatness of his genius is not fully realised. His exclusively Italian training and his exemption from English influence help to explain his excellence at a time when English sculpture was at a low ebb. Although the Wellington monument afforded him his only adequate opportunity, his other work was highly meritorious. Some of the best of it may be found in Dorchester House, Park Lane, the residence of Captain George Lindsay Holford, and includes painting on panels and ceiling, ornamental metal work, and especially a noble mantelpiece in the dining-room supported by nude caryatids in a crouching attitude. Among conceptions which remained unexecuted were a scheme of decorations for the reading-room of the British Museum, the model of which is preserved at the South Kensington Museum, and designs for the decorations of the Houses of Parliament, including a fresco painting of incidents from the life of Alfred the Great. 'He designed in all materials, in silver, bronze, iron, marble, and for many purposes—for furniture, churches, porcelain, and mantelpieces.' He was also a painter, though he produced few pictures, owing to his habit of destroying his own work; portraits of Mr. and Mrs. Leonard Collman are among those that survive. A portrait of Stevens, painted by himself at the age of fourteen, was in 1891 in the possession of Mr Alfred Pegler of Southampton. Another portrait of him in later life is prefixed to Hugh Stannus's 'Memoir.'

[Stannus's Alfred Stevens and his Work, 1891, fol.; Armstrong's Alfred Stevens, a biographical study, 1881; Encyclopædia Britannica, 9th ed. xxi. 561; Athenæum, 1875, i. 630; Academy, 1875, p. 487; Bryan's Dict. of Painters and Engravers; Redgrave's Dict. of English Artists; Ward's Men of the Reign; Chambers's Encyclopædia.]   E. I. C.

STEVENS, FRANCIS (1781–1823), landscape-painter, was born, probably at Exeter, on 21 Nov. 1781. He was a pupil of Paul Sandby Munn [q. v.], and became a skilful painter of landscape and cottage architecture, working chiefly in watercolours. He exhibited at the Royal Academy in 1804 and 1805, and in the latter year was elected an associate of the newly founded Watercolour Society; he was promoted to full membership in 1809. Stevens was one of the originators of the Sketching Society in 1808. In 1815 he etched and published a series of views of farmhouses and cottages from drawings by Munn, Varley, Prout, and others. Later he settled at Exeter, whence he sent works to the Royal Academy in 1819 and 1822. He died of apoplexy at Exeter in 1823. His 'Lustleigh Cleeve' is in the Devon and Exeter Institution.

[Redgrave's Dict. of Artists; Roget's Hist. of the 'Old Watercolour' Soc.; Pycroft's Devonshire Artists; Exhibition Catalogues.]
                                      F. M. O'D.

STEVENS, GEORGE ALEXANDER (1710–1784), author of 'A Lecture upon Heads,' was born in the parish of St. Andrew's, Holborn, in 1710. His father was a London tradesman, who apprenticed him to a trade; but the occupation soon proved uncongenial to Stevens, who joined a troupe of strolling players. He showed little talent, but his convivial temper made him popular with his fellow-actors, and the stage afforded him a subsistence. In 1750 he was playing at Lincoln. Next year he had a severe attack of illness, and published a dismal rhapsody called 'Religion, or The

Libertine Repentant' (1751, 8vo). But the libertine was not repentant for long. In 1752 he was playing in Dublin, where he became intimate with a dissolute humorist, known as 'Lord Chief Joker [Isaac] Sparks.' With his co-operation he founded a jovial club called 'Nassau Court,' where mock trials and other buffooneries were enacted. At the same time he published pseudonymously, 'Distress upon Distress . . . A Heroi-Comi-Parodi-Tragedi-Farci-cal Burlesque in two acts . . .' by Sir Henry Humm, with notes by Paulus Purgantius Pedasculus, a nonsensical piece; the line 'And common sense stood trembling at the door' Churchill thought worthy of transference to his 'Rosciad.'

In 1754 Stevens arrived in London to fulfil an engagement at Covent Garden Theatre. He had no success as an actor, but he met with some recognition as a wit, began an imitation of the 'Dunciad' called 'The Birthday of Folly' (1754), and was admitted to several convivial clubs, including 'The Choice Spirits,' near Covent Garden, for which he wrote a number of songs. He also wrote songs and benefit speeches for Edward Shuter [q. v.] and other performers. Some of his ditties were published in 1754 as 'The Choice Spirit's Feast.' There followed a concealed autobiography, 'The History of Tom Fool' (1760), and a short-lived periodical (in anticipation of the 'Review of Reviews') called 'The Beauties of all the Magazines Selected,' of which three volumes appeared (1762–4). Baker credits him with the authorship in 1762 of an interlude entitled 'Hearts of Oak,' consisting of 'little more than a song and dances for sailors,' but this statement is doubtful. The well-known sea song 'Hearts of Oak' (originally 'Heart of Oak') was first given in 'Harlequin's Invasion,' a Christmas pantomime of 1759, and has generally been attributed to David Garrick. It is quite certain that Stevens would have included it among his 'Songs' if he had had any claim to it (cf. FITZGERALD, Stories of Famous Songs, p. 173). In 1763 he gave to the world 'The Dramatic History of Master Edward, Miss Anne, and others, the extraordinaries of these times' (London, 8vo). This volume, which is of some rarity, although it is solely remarkable for its quaint cuts, is a curious libel in the form of a dialogue upon Shuter and Nancy Dawson. Shuter's offence was the refusal of a dramatic sketch upon which Stevens had lavished special pains. The rough draft of this sketch was the germ of Stevens's 'Lecture on Heads,' a skit, in the form of a series of characterisations, upon the reigning follies of the day. He enlarged his original plan, improved the details, and, having provided himself with the necessary properties, commenced operations in April 1764 by a lecture at the Haymarket, which he repeated in the provinces with great success and unprecedented profit. Despite his incompetence on the stage, his animation and quick perception apparently gave the entertainment a character for humorous extravagance which is not perceptible in the published words of the 'Lecture.' At the end of July he reappeared for a short while in London, lecturing in the 'Long Room opposite to Sadler Wells,' and soon afterwards he went for an extended tour in America, meeting with a very fair reception, especially in Boston and Philadelphia. This pioneer of the monologue entertainment is said to have amassed over 10,000l. by his lecture. In February 1766 he essayed a 'Supplement, being a new Lecture on Heads, Portraits, and Whole Lengths,' but this enjoyed little favour. In 1774 he disposed of his original 'Lecture' for a moderate sum to the actor, Charles Lee Lewes [q. v.], who 'improved' it from time to time, but failed to reproduce the full success of the inventor. A spurious edition of the 'Lecture' appeared as early as 1770 (London, 8vo), and of this there were several reissues with varying title-pages: a quarto version appeared in 1784. The first authentic edition is dated 1785 (London, 8vo), 'with additions by Pilon, the whole edited by Lewes, with an Essay on Satire.' Other editions include 1787, 8vo; 1788 (two editions); 1799, with twenty-four heads by Charlton Nesbit [q.v.], from designs by Thurston; Cooke's edition, with alterations and additions, 1800; 1800, 12mo, with forty-seven heads by Nesbit; 1808, 12mo, with twenty-five prints from drawings by G. M. Woodward; Baltimore, 1820, 16mo; 1821, 12mo, with forty-seven heads by Nesbit.

In the meantime Stevens had composed several feeble dramas. 'The French Flogged, or English Tars in America,' was produced at Covent Garden on 30 March 1761, with Shuter as Macfinin the Irish hero, and the author in a minor part, as a sailor; but it was a signal failure, and Stevens did not print it until 1767, when he had won fame by his 'Lecture.' In the same year Stevens was performing at Whitehaven, where a bookseller showed him a manuscript collection of popular songs by various writers and begged him to mark those of the greatest merit, and where possible to affix the names of the authors. Four years later the bookseller, without making any further commu-

nication with Stevens, issued the songs thus indicated under the title of 'The Choice Spirits' Chaplet' (Whitehaven, 8vo), and represented them as a selection by Stevens. The latter responded by issuing an authentic selection entitled 'Songs, Comic and Satyrical' (Oxford, 1772, 8vo; Dublin, 1773; 1801, with cuts by Bewick, and numerous subsequent editions). In this anthology the song 'Hearts of Oak' is definitely ascribed to 'Mr. Garrick.'

Stevens was responsible for at least one fine song, 'Cease, rude Boreas, blustering railer,' which was adapted to the tune of 'Old Hewson the cobbler' (ap. the ballad opera 'The Jovial Crew' of 1731), and soon supplanted the rivals that were already in possession of that popular air. Another once popular ballad, 'The Vicar and Moses,' was suggested by the 'Vicar of Wakefield.' These and others of Stevens's songs were separately printed and hawked by chapmen (cf. *Roxburghe Ballads*, vol. iii. British Museum).

Stevens had already tried his hand at opera without success, and in 1773, in order to exploit such a popular topic as 'the late naval review,' he patched together in five days a number of detached scenes and called them 'The Trip to Portsmouth.' The piece was given at the Haymarket on 11 Aug. 1773, and, with Bannister and Weston in the leading rôles, had a certain success. In 1780 there appeared in his name a volume of selections entitled 'The Cabinet of Fancy,' but it is doubtful if he had any hand in the publication; so-called 'Humorous Miscellanies' were issued in his name as late as 1804. Before 1780 Stevens seems to have retired to Hampstead upon what little remained of his savings. About the same time his intellect began to decay, and he died in a state of imbecility at Baldock in Hertfordshire on 6 Sept. 1784. There appeared posthumously 'The Adventures of a Speculist, or a Journey through London, by G. A. S.' (London, 1788, 8vo). Stevens was an authority on city topics, and wrote a humorous poem on 'The Stocks' inscribed to 'Bulls and Bears.' The manuscript was found among Stevens's papers, having probably been written in 1782.

Stevens's rough and ready wit often found expression in reckless practical jokes, as when he threw a waiter out of window and told the host to put him down in the bill.

[Stevens's Works in the British Museum Library; English Cyclopædia; Baker's Biographia Dramatica, 1812, i. 690; Genest's Hist. of the Stage, iv. 627, v. 378, x. 177; Timbs's Anecdote Lives of Later Wits and Humourists;

Lowe's Theatrical Literature, p. 324; Gent. Mag. 1784 ii. 717, 795; Chappell's Popular Music of the Olden Times, ii. 166; Halliwell's Cat. of Ballads, 187 sq.; Notes and Queries, 1st ser. iv. 196, 277; cf. Anthony Pasquin's [see WILLIAMS, JOHN, *fl.* 1785–1810] Children of Thespis, iii. 32.]

T. S.

STEVENS or STEPHENS, JOHN (d. 1726), Spanish scholar and translator, was a Roman catholic, and probably an Irishman. He is said to have accompanied James II in his Irish campaigns, and to have been employed in other services by him. He is probably to be identified with the Lieutenant John Stephens mentioned by D'Alton (*King James's Irish Army List*, p. 485). He was not attainted, and before 1695 had settled in London. From that time till his death he was busily engaged in translations and historical and antiquarian compilations. He says nothing of himself in any of his numerous works, which are almost always inscribed 'Captain Stevens.' The intimate knowledge of Portuguese and of the Spanish language and literature displayed in his prefaces points to a residence in Spain or Portugal. Miscellaneous as Stevens's work was, he deserves special recognition as a predecessor of Southey, Stirling-Maxwell, and Ticknor in the exploration of the rich mine of Spanish literature, and his translations of Quevedo and of the historians Mariana and Sandoval are of real value. He died on 27 Oct. 1726.

Stevens's first publication, an abridged translation in three octavo volumes of Faria y Sousa's 'Portuguesa Asia,' appeared in 1695, with a dedication to Catharine, queen dowager of England, and daughter of King John of Portugal. In 1698 he produced a translation and continuation from 1640 of the same author's 'History of Portugal.' His English version of Don Francisco Manuel da Mello's 'The Government of a Wife' was issued in 1697. It was dedicated to Don Luis da Cunha, the Portuguese envoy. In the same year Stevens published a version of Quevedo's 'Fortune in her Wits, or the Hour of all Men.' He issued in 1707 a translation of the collected comedies of Quevedo, which was republished in 1709 and in 1742. A collection of Spanish works translated and adapted by him appeared in the same year under the title of 'The Spanish Libertines.' It consisted of Perez's 'Justina, the Country Jilt;' 'Celestina, the Bawd of Madrid,' by F. de Rojas; 'Gonzales, the most arch and comical of scoundrels, by himself;' and D'Avila's comedy, 'An Evening's Intrigue,' adapted by the translator.

Some years previously Stevens had essayed a 'revision' of Shelton's English version of 'Don Quixote' (second edition, 'further revised and amended,' London, 1706, in 2 vols. 8vo). It was dedicated to Sir Thomas Hanmer [q. v.], and was illustrated by thirty-three copperplates, 'curiously engraved from the Brussels edition.' Stevens also translated in 1705 the so-called 'continuation' of 'Don Quixote' made by 'the licentiate, Alonzo Fernandez de Avellaneda,' which had never before appeared in English. The version was prepared from the French of Le Sage.

A rendering by Stevens of Quevedo's 'Pablo de Segovia the Spanish Sharper' formed the basis of the Edinburgh version of 1798, and was reprinted in vol. ii. of 'The Romancist and Novelist's Library,' edited by Mr. W. C. Hazlitt in 1841. Mr. H. E. Watts, who utilised it for the edition prepared by him in 1892, says that it is still the best English version. Stevens also translated from the Spanish many works of history and travel, as well as Quintana's 'The most Entertaining History of Hippolyto and Aminta;' 2nd edit. 1729, 12mo. His rendering of Mariana's 'History of Spain' appeared in 1699, fol.; and of Sandoval's 'History of Charles V' in 1703, 8vo. In 1715 he englished Texeira's Spanish version of Mirkhänd's 'History of Persia.' His translation of Herrera's 'General History of the Vast Continent and Islands of America, commonly called the West Indies,' issued in 6 vols. 8vo, 1725-6, and reprinted in 1740, has been pronounced too free. From Spanish authors Stevens also mainly compiled his 'New Collection of Voyages and Travels,' published in two quarto volume in 1711 (having originally appeared in monthly parts), and republished in 1719.

Stevens was also a learned and industrious antiquary. In 1718 he published anonymously a folio translation and abridgment of Dugdale's 'Monasticon Anglicanum.' Ralph Thoresby, who afterwards corresponded with Stevens, attributed it to a Spanish priest. He terms it 'an useful book in its kind, tho' there are both typographical errors and others, besides some reflections upon the revolution' (*Diary*, ed. Hunter, 12 Nov. 1719, 7 Jan. 1721). In 1722 Stevens published a continuation of the 'Monasticon' in 2 vols., entitled 'The History of the Ancient Abbeys, Monasteries, Hospitals, Cathedrals, &c., illustrated with copperplates. As a further continuation of the 'Monasticon Anglicanum' Stevens issued anonymously in 1722, 8vo, his 'Monasticon Hibernicum.' This is a translation, with additions and alterations, of Alemand's 'Histoire Monastique d'Irlande,' 1690 (cf. THORESBY, *Diary*, 5 Sept. 1723, ed. Hunter).

Stevens also translated Bæda's 'Ecclesiastical History of Britain.' The work is scarce, and the rendering so literal as to be obscure in places. Some of the notes were embodied in W. Hurst's version, published in 1814. Stevens's translation formed the basis of that of Dr. Giles (1840), and of that issued in Bohn's 'Antiquarian Library' (1847).

From the French he translated in 1712 for Lintot 'parts of Dupin' (NICHOLS, *Lit. Anecd.* viii. 298), probably Louis Ellies Dupin's 'Bibliothèque Universelle des Historiens;' and Book iii. of P. J. D'Orléans's 'Histoire des Révolutions en Angleterre sous la Famille des Stuarts,' 1722, 8vo.

He also compiled: 1. 'A Brief History of Spain,' 1701, 8vo. 2. 'The Ancient and Present State of Portugal,' 1701, 8vo (founded on Faria y Sousa's 'Europa Portuguesa'). 3. 'The Lives and Actions of all the Sovereigns of Bavaria,' 1706, 8vo. 4. 'A Spanish-English and English-Spanish Dictionary, with Grammar,'1706, fol.; 1726, 4to. 5. 'The Royal Treasury of England; or an Historical Account of Taxes,' 1725, 8vo; 2nd edit., 1733. Defoe's 'History of the Wars of Charles XII' is wrongly ascribed to him by Watt.

[Baker's Biogr. Dramatica, i. 691, ii. 203; Boyer's Polit. State of Great Britain, xxxii. 411; Hist. Reg. 1726 (Chronol. Diary); Notes and Queries, 1st ser. ii. 359, iii. 306; Watt's Bibl. Brit. i. 880; Lowndes's Bibl. Manual. vol. v.; H. E. Watts's Essay on Quevedo prefixed to Pablo de Segovia 1892; Advertisement to Hurst's Translation of Bæda's Eccles. Hist. 1814; Works in Brit. Mus.] G. LE G. N.

STEVENS, RICHARD JOHN SAMUEL (1757–1837), musician, was born in London, 27 March 1757, and was a choirboy at St. Paul's under Richard Savage. At an early age he formed a friendship with Samuel Birch [q. v.], which lasted all his life, and was of great service to him. On the breaking of his voice Stevens studied the organ, and soon distinguished himself as a glee-composer, winning one of the Catch Club's prizes in 1782 with the serious glee, 'See what horrid Tempests rise.' In 1786 Stevens again took the prize for a serious glee, with his setting of 'It was a Lover and his Lass.' In the same year he was appointed organist at the Temple Church, in succession to John Stanley [q. v.], and published three sonatas for the harpsichord. These sonatas are in two movements, and are bright, spirited, and effective music, with not much invention. During the next few years were composed most of Stevens's glees, in the selection of words for which he was much

helped by Birch. Stevens published three sets of glees, and in Warren's collections there are nine glees and a catch by him. In 1796 he became organist at the Charterhouse, and in 1801, by Birch's influence, he was appointed Gresham professor. These two posts he retained till his death. In 1802 he edited a collection of sacred music, in three volumes folio, intended for private performance, and dedicated to the archbishop of Canterbury. It was mainly drawn from Handel, Greene, Purcell, and Italian composers of the eighteenth century, and was an admirable selection, but the compositions are somewhat freely arranged. Stevens was for sixty years a member of the Royal Society of Musicians. He died, after a long illness, at Peckham, on 23 Sept. 1837. His valuable library, containing a collection of glees in sixteen volumes, and a quantity of rare old English musical literature, he bequeathed to the Royal Academy of Music.

Many of Stevens's glees retain their popularity, but they exhibit a feature (new in the composer's own day) which ultimately destroyed glee-writing. Instead of using the style practised by Webbe and his contemporaries, in which there is quite independent work for each individual voice, Stevens composed a melody for one voice accompanied in simple harmony by the others, thus approximating to the modern part-song. In one case he even added an obbligato accompaniment for the harp. Occasionally he followed the true glee style, but all his best known works, 'From Oberon in Fairy Land,' 'Sigh no more, Ladies,' 'The cloud-capt Towers,' 'Crabbed Age and Youth,' 'Blow, blow, thou wintry Wind,' show the tendency to a harmonised melody, to homophony rather than polyphony. In 'Ye spotted Snakes,' Stevens very cleverly adapted sonataform to vocal music. Excellent remarks upon 'Blow, blow, thou wintry Wind' may be seen in G. F. Waagen's 'Kunstwerke und Künstler in England' (English translation, 1838, p. 71). Several of Stevens's glees have been arranged by Hullah and others for a mixed chorus, for which they are well adapted.

[Ann. Reg. 1837; Times, 27 Sept. 1837; Musical World, 29 Sept. 1837, p. 45; C. F. Pohl's Haydn in London, p. 19; Barrett's Glee and Madrigal Writers, pp. 282-5; Baptie's Sketches of the English Glee Composers, pp. 41, 211; Ouseley's Contributions to Naumann's Illustrirte Geschichte der Musik, English edit. p. 1276; Grove's Dict. of Music and Musicians ii. 420, iii. 712, iv. 796; Davey's Hist. of English Music, p. 416; Stevens's compositions.] H. D.

STEVENS, WILLIAM (1732-1807), biographer and editor of the works of Jones of Nayland, born in the parish of St. Saviour's, Southwark, on 2 March 1732, was son of a tradesman. His mother was sister of the Rev. Samuel Horne of Otham, Kent. He was educated at Maidstone with his cousin, George Horne [q. v.], afterwards bishop of Norwich. In August 1746 he was apprenticed to a hosier in Old Broad Street, named Hookham, whose partner he afterwards became. Hookham's daughter married John Frere [q. v.], and was mother of John Hookham Frere [q. v.] After Hookham's death Stevens became the senior partner, but in 1801 he gave up a large share of his interest in the business, and a few years later retired altogether.

From the first Stevens devoted his leisure to literary studies, and soon acquired a good knowledge of French, Hebrew, and the classics. His chief study was theology. He kept up a constant correspondence with Bishop Horne, to whom he suggested the plan of his 'Letters on Infidelity,' which, when published, were dedicated to him. On Horne's death, Stevens published three volumes of his sermons, and supplied William Jones [q. v.] of Nayland with materials for his life. In 1772 Stevens made his first public appearance as a writer with 'A new and faithful Translation of Letters from M. l'Abbé de ——, Hebrew Professor in the University of ——, to the Rev. Benjamin Kennicott' [q. v.] In this anonymous brochure he followed up Horne's attack upon Kennicott's project of a revised Hebrew text of the Old Testament. In the next year he published, in opposition to the recent effort to get rid of subscription to the thirty-nine articles, 'An Essay on the Nature and Constitution of the Christian Church, wherein are set forth the form of its government, the extent of its powers, and the limits of our obedience, by a Layman.' A new edition of Stevens's 'Essay' appeared in 1799, and it was reissued by the S.P.C.K. in vol. iv. of their 'Religious Tracts' in 1800, in 1807, and in 1833. In 1776 he published 'A Discourse on the English Revolution, extracted from a late eminent writer, and applied to the present time;' and in the following year attacked Richard Watson [q. v.], then regius professor of divinity at Cambridge, in 'Strictures on a Sermon entitled the Principles of the Revolution vindicated.' Daniel Wray [q. v.] described Stevens as 'a tory of the old Filmer stamp' (NICHOLS, Lit. Illustrations, i. 160–1).

Stevens identified himself with that section of churchmen who acknowledged William Jones of Nayland as their leader, and formed a link between the nonjurors and the Oxford tractarians. He joined with Jones and others in forming a 'Society for the Reformation of Principles,' to counteract the influence of the French revolution. The society published a collection of tracts for the younger clergy, and originated the 'British Critic.' In 1795 Jones dedicated to Stevens his 'Life of Bishop Horne.' In 1800, in a 'Review of the Review of a new Preface to the Second Edition of Mr. Jones's Life of Bishop Horne,' Stevens defended his cousin from an attack in the 'British Critic.' It was signed 'Ain' (Hebrew for 'Nobody'), and suggested the title of a collection of Stevens's pamphlets issued in 1805 as 'Οὐδενὸς ἔργα, Nobody's Works.' A club was also founded in his honour under this name about 1800. It met three times a year. Sir Richard Richards [q. v.] was the first president, and it contained many well-known clergymen, barristers, and doctors. It continued many years after Stevens's death under the name 'Nobody's Friends.'

Stevens's last publication was his edition of Jones's works published in 1801 in twelve octavo volumes. Prefixed to it was a life of Jones after the manner of Izaak Walton (part of this had appeared in the 'Anti-Jacobin Review').

Stevens acted for many years as treasurer of Queen Anne's Bounty, liberally aided the work of the chief church societies, and actively interested himself in improving the position of the episcopal church in Scotland. Numberless instances of his benevolence are given by his biographer. Stevens died on 7 Feb. 1807 at his house in Old Broad Street, and was buried in Otham churchyard. He left the bulk of his property to his cousin, William Horne, the rector of Otham.

[A memoir of Stevens by Sir James Allan Park was published in 1812. The substance of it had already been given in an obituary notice in the Gent. Mag. 1807, i. 173–5. A second edition appeared in 1814, and a third in 1823. On these is founded the article in Chalmers's Biogr. Dict. The present article is mainly based upon the revised and enlarged edition of 1859, among the appendices to which are a list of books drawn up by Stevens for Jane Hookham (afterwards the wife of John Frere, the antiquary), and a description of Nobody's Friends. See also Watt's Bibl. Britannica; Lowndes's Bibliogr. Manual; Brit. Mus. Cat.; art. JONES, WILLIAM; HORNE, GEORGE; and KENNICOTT, BENJAMIN.] G. Le G. N.

STEVENS, WILLIAM BAGSHAW (1756-1800), poet, son of William Stevens, apothecary and surgeon, of Abingdon, Berk-

shire, was born there on 15 March 1756.
He was educated at the grammar school of
his native town and at Magdalen College,
Oxford, where he matriculated on 29 July
1772, and held a demyship from 1772 to
1794. He graduated B.A. 2 July 1776,
M.A. 2 June 1779, and D.D. 26 Jan. 1797.
For a short period in 1794 and 1795 he was
a fellow of his college, and he held in 1795
the post of prælector of moral philosophy.

About 1778 Stevens accepted the place of
second master, under Dr. William Prior, at
Repton school, and took holy orders in the
English church. In July 1779 he succeeded
as headmaster, and remained in that position until his death. But the school did not
prosper in his hands. He was naturally of
an indolent and abstracted disposition, and
as years increased he lapsed into idleness and
neglect of his duties, until at the end only
one or two boys remained in his charge. His
most distinguished pupils were Joseph Bosworth [q. v.], Lieutenant-colonel Hans Francis Hastings, eleventh earl of Huntingdon
[q. v.], and Stebbing Shaw [q. v.]

The pre-eminence of Stevens as a scholar
and talker made him a frequent guest with
the family of Burdett at their seat of Fore-
mark, near Repton, where he officiated as
domestic chaplain. Early in 1799 he was
presented by Sir Francis Burdett [q. v.] to
the rectory of Seckington in Warwickshire,
and through the interest of Thomas Coutts
[q. v.], father-in-law of Sir Francis, he was
appointed by the crown to the adjacent
vicarage of Kingsbury. But he did not live
long to enjoy this improvement in his resources. He died, unmarried, at Repton on
28 May 1800 from apoplexy, which was said
to have been caused by an immoderate fit of
laughter, and was buried near other members of his family, on the west side of the
churchyard. A tablet in the chancel bears
an epitaph by Anna Seward [q. v.]

In 1775, while an undergraduate, Stevens
published ' Poems, consisting of Indian Odes
and Miscellaneous Pieces.' Most of the pieces
were in imitation of Collins, who was also a
demy of Magdalen College. His second and
last volume of ' Poems,' including ' Retirement,' came out in 1782 and met with a very
severe reception in the ' Critical Review'
(June 1782).

Translations by Stevens subsequently appeared in the 'Gentleman's Magazine' for
1786 (i. 426–7), and for years he was a frequent correspondent, with the initials of
M. C. S. (i.e. 'Magdalen College Semi-
socius'), of that periodical on subjects
poetical and critical. Stanzas by him ' to
the author of the poem on the loves of the

plants' were prefixed to the first book of
Darwin's ' Botanic Garden,' and a sonnet,
first printed in the ' Gentleman's Magazine'
1783 (ii. 784), is in Shaw's 'Staffordshire'
(i. 343–4). Three idylls written by him at
Anchor Church, Derbyshire, appeared in
' The Topographer' (ii. 39–41), and were reprinted in the ' Poetical Register' (ii. 387–8).
Some others of his compositions were included in the ' Register.' Stevens had some
descriptive talent, but his verse lacks freedom
and energy.

An epistle in verse to Stevens is in Miss
Seward's ' Poems' (1810, ii. 165–71), and
letters to him are in that lady's collected
correspondence (i. 278–81, ii. 47–50, iv.
198–202).

[Foster's Alumni Oxon.; Bloxam's Magdalen
College, vii. 39–43; Hipkins's Repton School
Reg. xvi. xviii. 44; Gent. Mag. 1786 ii. 1109–
1110, 1792 i. 506, 1800 ii. 699, 897, 1801 i.
106–9 (by Sir S. E. Brydges), 316; Brydges's
Censura Literaria, v. 387–98.]   W. P. C.

STEVENSON. [See also STEPHENSON.]

STEVENSON, LORD. [See SINCLAIR,
SIR ROBERT, 1640?–1713.]

STEVENSON, ALAN (1807–1865),
civil engineer, eldest son of Robert Stevenson [q. v.], and brother of David Stevenson
[q. v.] and Thomas Stevenson [q. v.], was
born at Edinburgh in 1807. Educated at
the high school and university of Edinburgh,
where he greatly distinguished himself, he
graduated M.A. on 30 March 1826, and obtained, under Sir John Leslie (1766–1832)
[q. v.], the Fellowes prize as an advanced
student in natural philosophy. With the
view of entering the church, he continued
his studies under a clergyman at Twickenham, but eventually resolved to follow his
father's profession, and became a pupil in his
father's office, at the same time gaining
experience in practical engineering. After
entering into partnership with his father, he
was engaged in general engineering practice,
especially in connection with marine works,
such as piers, harbours, and river and estuarial improvements. He was also engaged on
work for the Scottish lighthouse board, and
in 1843 succeeded his father as engineer to
the commissioners. He designed and carried
out ten lighthouses, including Skerryvore
lighthouse tower, the finest example for mass,
combined with elegance of outline, of any
extant rock tower. This tower, which is exposed to the full fetch of the Atlantic, is built
on a rock fourteen miles from the nearest land,
the island of Tyree. The work was begun in
July 1838, but a storm swept away the tem-

porary barrack, and another had to be erected in its place. The foundations of the tower involved the excavation of two thousand tons of material. The first stone was laid in July 1840, and the light exhibited in 1843. The rearing of this structure, containing upwards of 4,300 tons of granite, occupied three seasons, each extending to about two months, and was personally superintended by its author. The tower rises to a height of 138 ft., is 42 ft. in diameter at the base, gradually decreasing to 16 ft. at the top. The 'solid' or monolithic part extends to 26 ft. above the rock, the cubic contents of which are double the entire contents of Smeaton's Eddystone tower. The walls, as they spring from the solid, are 9½ ft. in thickness, gradually diminishing to 2 ft. The interior is divided into ten floors, including the light-room, each 12 ft. in diameter. The optical apparatus is dioptric revolving, the most complete which had hitherto been constructed; the height of the eight central lenses was extended to 3 ft. 3 in., and, instead of Fresnel silvered mirrors below the lenses, Stevenson designed prismatic rings, which were introduced for the first time in this apparatus. Stevenson designed and carried out some notable improvements on dioptric apparatus used in lighthouses. For the central portion of the fixed apparatus he converted Fresnel's narrow lenses into a truly cylindrical drum, which he divided into sections with helical joints; and he introduced prismatic rings above and below the central belts, thus securing equal distribution of light all round, and extending dioptric action throughout the whole height of the apparatus. He also suggested the spherical mirrors placed on the landward arcs of dioptric apparatus.

In 1830 Stevenson became a member of the Institution of Civil Engineers, and in 1838 a fellow of the Royal Society of Edinburgh, acting as a member of its council from 1843 to 1845. In 1840 the university of Glasgow conferred on him the honorary degree of LL.B. The emperor of Russia and the kings of Prussia and Holland presented him with medals in acknowledgment of his merit as a lighthouse engineer. In 1848 was published his 'Account of the Skerryvore Lighthouse, with Notes on the Illumination of Lighthouses,' 4to. It still remains a standard book. The notes on lighthouse illumination were subsequently extended and published in 1850 under the title of 'A Rudimentary Treatise on the History, Construction, and Illumination of Lighthouses.'

Stevenson had fine literary tastes. He knew Italian, Spanish, French, Greek, and Latin literatures thoroughly. In 1852 he

was seized with paralysis, and thenceforth beguiled his suffering by translating the ten hymns of Synesius, bishop of Cyrene. These translations, along with other poems, were printed for private circulation the year before his death. He wrote articles for the 'Encyclopædia Britannica' (8th edit.) on lighthouses and other subjects. Stevenson died at Portobello on 23 Dec. 1865. On 3 Jan. 1866 the commissioners of northern lighthouses recorded in their minutes 'their deep and abiding regrets for the loss of a man whose services had been to them invaluable,' and whose works combined profound science and practical skill.

[Private information.]   D. A. S.

STEVENSON, DAVID (1815-1886), civil engineer, born at Edinburgh on 11 Jan. 1815, was third son of Robert Stevenson [q. v.], and was brother of Alan Stevenson [q. v.] and of Thomas Stevenson [q. v.] He was educated at the high school and university of Edinburgh, but spent some time in youth in the workshops of millwrights, where he acquired much manual skill. While a pupil he conducted extensive land and marine surveys, in the almost entire absence of trustworthy charts and maps, and made tidal and other hydrometric observations for lighthouses, piers, harbours, docks, and for river and estuarial improvements. His results he published in 'The Application of Marine Surveying and Hydrometry to the Practice of Civil Engineering,' the first book of its kind (1842). On completing his apprenticeship he was engaged with Mr. Mackenzie, the contractor on the Liverpool and Manchester railway, and gave a description of the railway in 1835 to the Royal Scottish Society of Arts. A paper on the 'Dublin and Kingston Railway' followed in 1836. In 1837 Stevenson made a professional tour in Canada and the United States, and published on his return next year a 'Sketch of the Civil Engineering of North America' (republished in 1859 with additions, and now forming one of Weale's 'Engineering Series'). On the outward and homeward voyages he made daily observations on the temperature of the sea and air. In 1838 Stevenson entered into partnership with his father and brother Alan. His father then gave little attention to business, and Alan confined himself to the lighthouse department; the entire management of the general business of the firm consequently devolved on David. He soon was a recognised authority in reference to the improvement of rivers and estuaries, harbours, the construction of docks, and other marine works. He was called on to report on, or to execute works for, the improvement of the rivers Dee, Lune, Ribble, Wear, and Wyre, and the restoration and enlargement of the Fossdyke navigation in England; the Earn and Foyle in Ireland; and the Forth, Tay, Ness, Nith, and Clyde in Scotland. His 'Remarks on the Improvement of Tidal Rivers,' laid before the Royal Society of Edinburgh (published in London separately in 1845; 2nd ed. 1850), describe the works specially necessary for the improvement of the three parts, 'sea proper,' 'tidal,' and river proper, into which he showed that rivers must be divided. Fuller results of his practice in river engineering were given in the article 'Inland Navigation' in the 'Encyclopædia Britannica' (8th ed.), and further enlarged in 'Canal and River Engineering' (Edinburgh, 1858, 8vo, 3rd ed.) In 1877 Stevenson gave a course of four lectures on 'Canal and River Engineering' to the students of the Chatham School of Military Engineering.

In 1846 Stevenson was appointed by the admiralty and the department of woods and forests under the Preliminary Inquiries Act, to hold courts of inquiry and to report on a large number of railway, harbour, sanitary, and other schemes in Scotland, England, and Ireland. In all cases save one his suggestions were carried out. This exception was the proposal to cross the Clyde with a railway bridge, which he reported could be done without injury to the navigation; the admiralty, however, refused its sanction. The scheme has since been adopted with the consent of the board of trade and parliament.

In 1853 Stevenson succeeded his brother Alan as engineer to the northern lighthouse board, and along with his brother Thomas, who, at his request, was at a subsequent date joined with him in the engineership, he designed and executed no fewer than twenty-eight beacons and thirty lighthouses. Three of the lighthouses — North Unst, Dhu Heartach, and the Chickens—were works of great difficulty. The optical apparatus for these thirty lighthouses was in almost every case of novel design. His lighthouse practice was not limited to Scotland, but extended to India, Newfoundland, New Zealand, and Japan. In connection with the lighting of the Japanese coast where earthquakes are frequent, he devised the 'aseismatic arrangement' to mitigate the effect of earthquake shocks on the somewhat delicate optical apparatus used in lighthouses. He took a leading part in introducing paraffin as an illuminant for lighthouses, instead of the expensive colza oil. His report of 1870 settled the relative merits of colza and

paraffin for lighthouse purposes, and all British and many European and foreign lighthouse authorities now use paraffin, with increased luminous intensity, and at decreased cost.

In 1844 Stevenson was elected a member of the Royal Society of Edinburgh, acted as a member of council, and as one of its vice-presidents from 1873 to 1877, and frequently contributed to its proceedings. He was elected a member of the Institution of Civil Engineers in 1844, and acted as a member of council from 1877 to 1883. He contributed to the 'Proceedings' of the institution 'a description of a cofferdam adapted to a hard bottom,' being a cofferdam he designed and used in improving the Ribble; and other papers. He was also member of the Société des Ingénieurs Civils, Paris, and of other learned societies. In 1869, when president of the Royal Scottish Society of Arts, he delivered a valuable address on 'Altered Relations of British and Foreign Industries and Manufactures.'

Stevenson took a warm interest in the better endowment of Edinburgh University chairs, and was a lover and critic of art. He died at North Berwick on 17 July 1886.

Stevenson's books have taken a permanent place in engineering literature. Besides those already mentioned, he wrote 'Our Lighthouses' (from 'Good Words'), 1864, 'Reclamation and Protection of Agricultural Land' (1874), and a life of his father (Edinburgh, 1878). He also contributed the articles 'Canal,' 'Cofferdam,' 'Diving,' 'Dredging,' to the 'Encyclopædia Britannica' (8th edit.)

[Private information.]   D. A. S.

STEVENSON, GEORGE (1799–1856), 'father of the South Australian press,' born at Berwick-on-Tweed on 13 April 1799, was son of a country gentleman who died when the boy was twelve years old. Destined for the merchant service, he was sent to sea with his uncle, the captain of an East Indiaman, but soon threw up his berth, and began to study medicine in Scotland. About 1820 he emigrated to Canada, and for some years lived as a backwoodsman; he travelled through Central America and the West Indies, finally returning to London in 1830. There he commenced literary work, and obtained employment on the 'Globe' newspaper, of which he became editor in 1835.

Stevenson was greatly interested in the Wakefield scheme for the colonisation of South Australia, and was induced in 1836 to resign his editorship in order to emigrate to South Australia as private secretary to

John Hindmarsh [q. v.], the first governor. He was present at the proclamation of the new colony on 28 Dec. 1836. He was first clerk of the legislative council, and one of the first coroners and magistrates in the colony.

Before leaving England Stevenson had arranged with one Thomas Robinson for the issue of the first colonial newspaper, to be called the 'South Australian Gazette and Colonial Register.' In 1838, resigning his office under the crown, he devoted himself to the paper, which then became the 'South Australian Register.' But in 1840 he lost the government contract for printing, and in 1842, in consequence partly of the general financial crisis in the colony, partly of the actions brought against the paper by Sir George Stephens, he relinquished his work, and gave himself to the study of viticulture. In 1845 the discovery of the Burra Burra mines made a new demand for journalism, and he started his paper again as the 'South Australian Gazette and Mining Journal.' In 1851 he went to the diggings in Victoria, with the view of running a mining journal; but his success was not great, and in 1853 he returned to Adelaide, and for a short time acted on the staff of the 'Adelaide Times.' After this he only occasionally contributed articles to the press, and those chiefly non-political.

As a horticulturist Stevenson seems to have been most in his element. His vineyard was one of the first in South Australia, and the colony owes him much for the practical impetus given to its vineyards by his personal example in planting, writing, and lecturing. On agricultural experiment generally he spent large sums of money.

Stevenson was coroner of Adelaide and a J.P. at the time of his death, which took place on 19 Oct. 1856 at his residence in North Adelaide. He married, in 1836, Margaret, daughter of John Gorton (of the 'Globe'), who, with three children, survived him.

Stevenson aided Sir William Henry Lytton Earle Bulwer (Lord Dalling) [q. v.] in his 'France, Social, Literary, Political' (1834, 12mo, 2 vols.)

[Logan's Representative Men of South Australia, Adelaide, 1883; Adelaide Times, 20 Oct. 1856.] C. A. H.

STEVENSON, GEORGE JOHN (1818–1888), author and hymnologist, born at Chesterfield on 7 July 1818, was the son of John George Stevenson (1792–1866) of Chesterfield, by his wife Jane, daughter of John Aldred. George was educated at Duttoris grammar school, Chesterfield. From an early age until 1844 he was employed in the printing and bookselling business. In 1844 he entered St. John's College, Battersea, to be trained for an organising mastership under the National Society. In 1846 a reformatory school was established in the Philanthropic Institute, Southwark, for the benefit of the better conducted criminals from the convict prisons, and Stevenson was appointed first headmaster. In 1848 he became headmaster of the endowed parochial school at Lambeth Green, but in 1855 he resigned his post and established himself in Paternoster Row as a bookseller and publisher, a business which he continued until a few years before his death. From 1861 to 1867 he was editor and proprietor of the 'Wesleyan Times,' and in 1882 he edited the 'Union Review.' He died on 16 Aug. 1888.

After joining the methodists in 1831, Stevenson took the keenest interest in their history and literature, and brought out several publications embodying the results of his researches. One of the most important of these is the 'Methodist Hymn Book and its Associations,' 1869, which was published in an enlarged form in 1883 as 'The Methodist Hymn Book, illustrated with Biography, Incident, and Anecdote.' According to the Rev. John Julian, this is 'the most complete account of methodist hymnody extant.'

Besides the works mentioned, Stevenson wrote: 1. 'The Origin of Alphabetical Characters,' London, 1853, 8vo. 2. 'Sketch of the Life of C. H. Spurgeon,' London, 1857, 12mo; new edit. 1887. 3. 'The American Evangelist,' London, 1860, 12mo. 4. 'The Prince of Preachers, C. H. Spurgeon,' London, 1867, 8vo. 5. 'City Road Chapel, London, and its Associations,' Edinburgh, 1872, 8vo. 6. 'Memorials of the Wesley Family,' London, 1876, 8vo; now edit. 1883. 7. 'Sir Charles Reed: a Life Sketch,' London, 1884, 4to. 8. 'Historical Records of the Young Men's Christian Association,' London, 1884, 8vo. 9. 'Methodist Worthies,' London, 1884, &c., 8vo. 10. 'Memorial Sketch of May Stevenson,' London, 1886, 8vo. He also edited 'A Historical Sketch of the Christian Community, 1818–1826,' London, 1868, 8vo, and 'Samuel Wesley's Memorials of Elizabeth Ann Wesley,' London, 1887, 8vo.

[Julian's Dict. of Hymnology, p. 1093; Boase and Courtney's Bibl. Cornub. ii. 689.] E. I. C.

STEVENSON, JOHN (1778–1846?), surgeon, son of Joseph and Deborah Stevenson, was baptised at Kegworth on the borders of Leicestershire and Derbyshire, on 13 March 1778. He was educated privately, and was apprenticed to his father, a surgeon, at the age of sixteen. Three years later he was sent to the united hospitals (St. Thomas's and Guy's) in the Borough, where he stayed until 1800. It is probable that his medical studies were much interrupted by ill-health, for he was not admitted a member of the College of Surgeons of England until 20 Nov. 1807. On account of his ill-health he determined to devote himself to the ophthalmic side of surgery. After studying for some time under John Cunningham Saunders [q. v.], the oculist, he settled in or near Nottingham. The death of Saunders in 1810 led Stevenson to return to London, where he commenced to practise.

In 1813 he was oculist and aurist to the Princess of Wales, and to Leopold, duke of Saxe-Coburg; he was then living in Great Russell Street, Bloomsbury. He delivered the anniversary oration at the Medical Society of London in March 1817, taking as his subject the treatment of gutta serena. He founded in 1830, at 13 Little Portland Street, Cavendish Square, 'The Royal Infirmary for Cataract,' and he was soon afterwards appointed oculist and aurist to William IV. In 1841 he became oculist and aurist to Leopold I, king of the Belgians, and in 1844 he was living in Conduit Street and at Norwood Park, Middlesex. All trace of him is lost after this year.

Stevenson undertook to operate upon cases of cataract at an earlier period than was thought advisable by other surgeons, and his infirmary was founded with the express design of carrying out his mode of treatment. His works are: 1. 'On the Morbid Sensibility of the Eye, commonly called Weakness of Sight,' London, 1810, 8vo; reprinted at Hartford, America, 1815; 3rd edit., London, 1819; 4th edit. 1841. 2. 'A Practical Treatise on Cataract,' London 1813, 8vo; 2nd edit. 1814; a new edit. 1824, and again in 1834; 5th edit. 1839, 12mo: 7th edit. 1843. 3. 'On the Nature of ... Gutta Serena,' London, 1821, 8vo; an expansion of his anniversary address delivered at the Medical Society in 1817. 4. 'Deafness, its Causes, Prevention, and Cure,' London 1828, 8vo; 7th edit. 1842. 5. 'On Throat Deafness,' London, 12mo; 4th edit. 1843.

[The New Pantheon of the Age, 2nd edit. vol. iii. 1825; Callisen's Schriftsteller-Lexicon, Basel 32, Nachtrag, 1844, p. 436, No. 1187*; additional information kindly given by the Rev. H. M. Stephenson, M.A., vicar of Kegworth.]

D'A. P.

STEVENSON, SIR JOHN ANDREW (1760?-1833), musical composer, born at Dublin about 1760, was the son of John Stevenson, a native of Glasgow, who became a violinist in the state band in Dublin. He was a chorister in Christ Church, Dublin, from 1771 to 1775, receiving his first instruction from Dr. Woodward, and he was in St. Patrick's Cathedral choir from 1775 to 1780. He became a vicar-choral in St. Patrick's in 1783, and in Christ Church in 1800. He was created Mus. Doc. of Trinity College, Dublin, in 1791, and in 1803 was knighted by the lord lieutenant (Lord Hardwicke). He married a daughter of Mr. Morton of the custom-house, Dublin, and widow of Mr. Singleton, and died on 14 Sept. 1833 at Headfort House, Kells, co. Meath, the seat of Thomas Taylour, second marquis of Headfort, whose second wife was Olivia (d. 1834), Stevenson's second daughter. A memorial monument was placed in St. Patrick's Cathedral, and was restored in December 1896.

Stevenson is best known by his symphonies and accompaniments to the collection of Irish melodies, the words for which were written by Thomas Moore [q.v.] He wrote a good deal for the Irish stage, including the operas of 'The Contract' (1783), 'Love in a Blaze' (1800), 'The Patriot,' and 'The Burning of Moscow;' and furnished new music for O'Keeffe's farces, 'The Son-in-law' and 'The Agreeable Surprise.' A collection of services and anthems, with his portrait, was published in 1825 (London, 2 vols. 4to); and numerous glees, duets, songs, &c., were issued at various times. He also published an oratorio, 'The Thanksgiving,' a series of 'Sacred Songs, Duets, and Trios, the Words by T. Moore' (London, n.d.), and 'A Selection of Popular National Airs, with Symphonies and Accompaniments,' 2 vols., London, 1818.

[Grove's Dictionary; Gent. Mag. 1833, ii. 542-4; Baptie's English Glee Composers; Biographical Dictionary of Musicians, 1824; Love's Scottish Church Music; O'Keeffe's Recollections; Brown and Stratton's Biographical Dict. of Musicians.]

J. C. H.

STEVENSON, JOHN HALL-, originally JOHN HALL (1718-1785), country gentleman and poetaster, born in 1718, was son of Joseph Hall of Durham, by his wife Catherine, sister and heiress of Lawson Trotter of Skelton Castle in Cleveland, Yorkshire. On 16 June 1735 he was admitted a fellow-commoner of Jesus College, Cambridge. At the time Laurence Sterne, an exhibitioner of the college and Hall-Stevenson's senior by five years, was nearing the end of his second year at the university. With Sterne Hall-Stevenson formed at once a close intimacy, which lasted till death separated them. They called each other cousin, but the blood-relationship was very distant, if not imaginary. Hall-Stevenson was a precocious under-graduate, delighting in Rabelaisian literature and coarse jesting. Such tastes dominated his life. On leaving the university about 1738, without a degree, he made the grand tour, and on his return he married a lady of property, Anne, daughter of Ambrose Stevenson of the Manor House, Durham, by his wife Ann, daughter of Anthony Wharton of Gillingwood, near Richmond, Yorkshire. He assumed his wife's surname in addition to his own. In 1745 his uncle, Trotter, an avowed Jacobite, fled the country, and Trotter's residence, Skelton Castle, passed to his sister, Hall-Stevenson's mother. Hall-Stevenson inherited it on her death. It dated from the fifteenth century, and was in a half-ruinous condition while Hall-Stevenson occupied it.

Hall-Stevenson's sole aim in life was, he repeatedly declared, to amuse himself. He had no liking for field sports, and divided his energies at Skelton between literature and hospitality. He collected a library, largely consisting of facetiæ, and wrote with fatal fluency verse in imitation chiefly of La Fontaine, whose 'Contes' attracted him by their obscenity. At the same time he gathered round him a crew of kindred spirits, drawn chiefly from the squirearchy and clergy of Yorkshire, whom he formed into 'a club of demoniacks.' The members met under his roof at Skelton several times a year, and indulged by night in heavy drinking and obscene jesting. The chief of these were a clergyman, Robert Lascelles (a connection of the Earl of Harewood), who was nick-named Pantagruel or Panty, Colonel Hall, Colonel Lee, one Zachary Moore, an architect named Pringle, and a schoolmaster, Andrew Irvine of Kirkleatham. Their orgies seem to have been pale reflections of those practised by Wilkes and his friends at Medmenham. An annual trip to London, where he usually lodged in the neighbourhood of Berkeley Square, brought Hall-Stevenson the acquaintance of a few men of literary or political consequence, including Wilkes and Horace Walpole. Three familiar letters from him to Wilkes, dated in 1762, are among the Wilkes manuscripts in the British Museum (*Addit. MS.* 30867, ff. 181, 188, 199). Occasionally he seems to have visited the continent. He claimed friendship with Rousseau, but he may have made Rousseau's acquaintance in England. Each summer or autumn he usually spent a few days at York or Scarborough.

Hall-Stevenson gained some notoriety by his small pamphlets of licentious but tedious and unimpressive verse, which he issued in quarto form with ample margins at frequent intervals. In 1760 he published a 'Lyric Epistle' to his friend Sterne, on his triumphal reception in London after the publication of 'Tristram Shandy' (two lyric epistles, 'To my Cousin Shandy on his coming to Town,' and 'To the Grown Gentlewomen the Misses of ****'). Gray justly described the verses as 'absolute nonsense' (*Letters*, iii. 37). There followed 'Fables for Grown Gentlemen' (1761 and 1770), and in 1762 Hall-Stevenson's best-known publication, 'Crazy Tales' (other edits. 1764 and 1780). An engraving of Skelton Castle forms the frontispiece. Hall-Stevenson and his friends had nick-named it Crazy Castle, and in 'Crazy Tales' he described the merry meetings of his friends there. Into the mouth of each of the members he put a more or less obscene tale, and he appended a few adaptations of Horace's 'Odes' to current events.

Horace Walpole affected to detect in Hall-Stevenson's compositions 'a vast deal of original humour and wit.' But Smollett and the writers in the 'Critical Review' showed truer insight in treating his efforts with caustic contempt. By way of retaliation Hall-Stevenson poured floods of vulgar abuse on the head of Smollett and his Scottish associates in such lucubrations as 'A Nosegay and a Simile for the Reviewers,' 1760, and 'Two Lyrical Epistles, or Margery the Cook Maid, to the Critical Reviewers,' 1760.

Hall-Stevenson's acquaintance with Wilkes turned his attention to politics. In much the same vein as he addressed himself to the reviewers, he denounced Bute and all professional politicians, whether whig or tory. The titles of his political effusions ran: 'A Pastoral Cordial; or an Anodyne Sermon, preached before their Graces Newcastle and Devonshire,' 1763; 'A Pastoral Puke; a second Sermon preached before the people called Whigs; by an Independent,' 1764; 'Makarony Fables, with the new Fable of the Bees,' 1767; 'Lyric Consolations, with the Speech of Alderman Wilkes delivered in a Dream,' 1768; and 'An Essay upon the King's Friends,' addressed to Dr. Johnson, 1776.

Hall-Stevenson's relations with Sterne give his career its only genuine interest. Sterne introduces him into both 'Tristram Shandy' and the 'Sentimental Journey' under the name of Eugenius. He represented him as a prudent counsellor, and gratefully acknowledged the readiness with which Hall-Stevenson often put his purse at a friend's service. Hall-Stevenson returned the compliment by flattering references to Sterne as 'Cousin Shandy,' and often signed himself 'Anthony Shandy.' Sterne was a frequent visitor at Skelton, and from the books in the library drew many hints.

In the summer of 1767, a few months before Sterne's death, Hall-Stevenson stayed with him at Coxwold, and carried him back to Skelton. They amused themselves on the seashore of the neighbouring Saltburn by racing each other in chariots over the sands. But even in his association with Sterne Hall-Stevenson illustrated his lack of decency. He tried to imitate Sterne's style. Hall-Stevenson's 'A Sentimental Dialogue between two Souls in the palpable Bodies of an English Lady of Quality and an Irish Gentleman,' 1768, was a very lame parody of 'Tristram Shandy.' Less defensible was Hall-Stevenson's endeavour to complete the 'Sentimental Journey.' In 1769, within a year of Sterne's death, he issued, with a brief biographical preface, a disreputable continuation. Although in his character of an author Hall-Stevenson had nothing to lose, this achievement is discreditable to him in the character of a friend. After Sterne's death Hall-Stevenson promised Sterne's daughter to write his life, but was too indolent to make serious effort to carry out the promise.

Hall-Stevenson's careless mode of life, which involved very liberal potations, gradually induced chronic hypochondria. In the 'Sentimental Journey' Sterne wrote that Eugenius 'blamed the weather for the disorder of his nerves.' The story is told that Hall-Stevenson took to his bed and regarded himself as *in extremis* whenever there was an east wind, and that one day when the wind came from the east Sterne cured him by tying up the weathercock, and thus led Hall-Stevenson to believe that the wind had changed. He was harassed, too, by pecuniary difficulties, while his relations with his wife were never good. In 1765 he re-opened at Selby Hagg, near Skelton, some alum works which had been discontinued for near fifty years; but he failed to make them pay, and gave them up in 1776. On 17 Feb. 1785 he wrote to his grandson that he had been obliged to raise 2,000*l.* to pay his brother, who had a mortgage on the estate. At the same time he declared that the chief advantages of life had been denied him by premature marriage, and that the scantiness of his fortune had forced him to vegetate in the country, and precluded him from every laudable pursuit suggested by ambition (W. D. COOPER, *Seven Letters by Sterne and his Friends*, 1844. p. 17). He died at Skelton next month (March 1785).

By his wife, who died in 1790, Hall-Stevenson had two sons, of whom one, John,

died unmarried. The surviving son, Joseph William Hall-Stevenson (1741-1786), died within a year of his father, and was succeeded at Skelton Castle by his son, John Hall-Stevenson (1766-1843). The latter, who rebuilt Skelton Castle, assumed in 1788 by royal sign manual the sole surname of Wharton. He was descended from the Wharton family of Gillingwood, Yorkshire, in the female line through Ann Wharton, wife of Ambrose Stevenson and mother of the poetaster's wife. He contested the parliamentary representation of Beverley in the whig interest nine times between 1790 and 1826, and was seven times successful between 1790 and 1820. But the expense of the struggle ruined him, and in 1820 he took refuge within the rules of the queen's bench in Lambeth, where he died on 28 May 1843 (*Gent. Mag.* 1843, ii. 207). Skelton Castle is now the property of this John Wharton's nephew, John Thomas Wharton, esq.

Hall-Stevenson's works, with some unpublished translations and other pieces, were collected and published in three volumes in 1795. An engraving of Skelton Castle (Crazy Castle) formed the frontispiece. 'Seven Letters written by Sterne and his Friends,' hitherto unpublished, were edited from Hall-Stevenson's manuscripts by W. Durrant Cooper, and printed for private circulation in 1844. An edition of the 'Crazy Tales,' dated 1825, was absurdly assigned on the title-page to Richard Brinsley Sheridan [q. v.] 'Crazy Tales' was reprinted privately in 1894.

[George Young's Hist. of Whitby, 1817, ii. ch. ii. iv. v.; Nichols's Lit. Anecdotes; Burke's Landed Gentry, s.v. 'Wharton of Skelton Castle;' Cooper's Seven Letters as above; Sterne's Works and Correspondence; and art. STERNE. LAURENCE.]   S. L.

STEVENSON, JOSEPH (1806-1895), historian and archivist, born at Berwick-upon-Tweed on 27 Nov. 1806, was the eldest son of Robert Stevenson, surgeon, of that town, by his wife, Elizabeth Wilson. His first schooldays were passed at Wooten-le-Wear, and thence he was removed to Durham, where he was placed under the charge of the Rev. James Raine [q. v.] He next studied in the university of Glasgow, but does not appear to have graduated. In 1829 he returned to Berwick, with the intention of entering the presbyterian ministry. He became a licentiate of that body, and preached a trial sermon at Hutton, Berwickshire, where he resided for the period necessary to qualify himself for service in the kirk of Scotland. However, he turned his attention to antiquarian and literary pursuits, and for more than sixty years from 1831 his pen was never idle. Coming to London, he first found employment in arranging the public records, then kept in St. John's Chapel in the Tower, and about midsummer 1831 he was appointed to a permanent situation in the manuscript department of the British Museum. On 19 Sept. in the same year he married Mary Ann, daughter of John Craig of Mount Florida, Glasgow. His post at the Museum brought him into contact with the leading students of British history and antiquities, and he became a member of several learned societies. After his appointment as a sub-commissioner of the public records in 1834, he worked at the proposed new edition of Rymer's 'Fœdera,' and he drew up in 1836 the appendix (vol. E) to Charles Purton Cooper's report on that subject.

In London Stevenson gradually dropped his connection with the presbyterian body, and had his children baptised in the established church. On the death of his eldest son, Robert, on 5 Nov. 1839, he resigned his post on the Record commission, returned to Durham, and was ordained priest by Bishop Maltby. In 1841 he was appointed librarian and keeper of records to the dean and chapter in succession to his old schoolmaster, James Raine, and for the next seven years he was engaged in drawing up a catalogue of the charters and deeds preserved in the treasury. In acknowledgment of his services the university conferred upon him the honorary degree of M.A. He was appointed curate of the parish of St. Giles, Durham, in 1847 (*Clergy List*, 1848, p. 229); and in January 1849 he was instituted to the parish of Leighton Buzzard, Bedfordshire.

In 1856 Stevenson undertook to bring out for the Clarendon Press at Oxford a work which, if completed, would have been of a monumental character. This was a chronological list of English historians of all ages, with a critical account of their works, whether in print or manuscript. Eventually he presented the whole of his collections to Sir Thomas Duffus Hardy [q. v.] for his well-known 'Descriptive Catalogue of Manuscripts relating to the History of Great Britain and Ireland.' When many plans for continuing the work of the Record commission had fallen through, Stevenson's representation in 1856 induced the government to undertake in the following year the splendid Rolls Series of historical works, under the title of 'Chronicles and Memorials of Great Britain and Ireland.' He was himself appointed one of the editors, and in the prosecution of his researches he visited Paris,

Rheims, Chartres, Rouen, and Lille. He resigned his living in 1862, and undertook the work of calendaring at the Public Record Office that William Barclay Turnbull [q. v.] had resigned. His study of the history of the Reformation period led him, like his predecessor, to withdraw from the Anglican communion, and on 24 June 1863 he was received into the Roman catholic church. In consequence of the pressure brought to bear upon him, he resigned his post as calendarer, though he continued to be employed as an editor of the Rolls Series. He retired to Nelly Park, near Birmingham, and assisted Canon Estcourt in composing his book on Anglican orders. The historical manuscripts commission opened for him a further field for congenial labour, and he examined and reported upon no fewer than twenty-four manuscript collections in the possession of various corporations or private families.

After the death of his wife (11 July 1869) he entered St. Mary's College, Oscott. In 1872 he was ordained priest by Bishop Ullathorne, and in the same year he not only received from Mr. Gladstone a pension in recognition of his valuable services to historical literature, but was deputed by the government, after consent had been obtained from the pope, to make a detailed examination of the Vatican archives. This task occupied him about four years, and the results of his labours are contained in thirteen folio volumes of transcripts now deposited in the Public Record Office. In November 1877 he entered Roehampton College as a novice of the Society of Jesus. In 1878 his headquarters were at Oxford, and after that, until his decease, he resided in the 'House of Writers' at 31 Farm Street, Berkeley Square, London. On 25 March 1885 he was professed of the three vows, and when he was eighty-six years old, the honorary degree of Doctor of Laws was bestowed upon him by the university of St. Andrews. He died at Farm Street on 8 Feb. 1895, and was buried in the cemetery of St. Thomas's Church, Fulham.

For the Maitland Club Stevenson edited: 1. 'Illustrations of Scottish History,' 1834. 2. 'Scalachronica, by Sir Thomas Gray of Heton,' 1836. 3. 'The Life and Death of King James I of Scotland,' 1837. 4. 'Selections from unpublished Manuscripts illustrating the reign of Mary, queen of Scotland,' 1837. 5. 'Chronicon de Lanercost,' 1839 (printed also for the Bannatyne Club). 6. 'The Scottish Metrical Romance of Lancelot du Lak,' 1839. 7. 'Documents illustrative of Sir William Wallace, his Life and Times,' 1841. 8. 'Notices of original unprinted Documents . . . illustrative of the History of Scotland,' 1842.

For the Bannatyne Club he edited: 9. 'Chronica de Mailros,' 1835. 10. 'Chronicon de Lanercost,' 1839.

For the English Historical Society he edited: 11. 'Chronicon Ricardi Divisiensis de Gestis Ricardi I,' 1838. 12. 'Gildas de Excidio Britanniæ,' 1838. 13. 'Nennii Historia Britonum,' 1838. 14. 'Venerabilis Bedæ Historia Ecclesiastica . . . et Opera Historica Minora,' 1838-41.

For the Roxburghe Club he edited: 15. 'The Owl and the Nightingale,' 1838. 16. 'Correspondence of Sir Henry Unton,' 1847. 17. 'The Alliterative Romance of Alexander,' 1849. 18. Dan Michel's 'The Ayenbite of Inwyt,' 1855.

For the Surtees Society he edited: 19. 'Rituale Ecclesiæ Dunelmensis,' 1840. 20. 'Liber Vitæ Ecclesiæ Dunelmensis,' 1841. 21. 'The Correspondence of Robert Bowes of Ask,' 1842. 22. 'Anglo-Saxon and Early English Psalter,' 2 vols. 1843-4. 23. 'Libellus de Vita et Miraculis S. Godrici,' 1845. 24. 'Latin Hymns of the Anglo-Saxon Church,' 1851. 25. 'The Gospel of St. Matthew, from the . . . Lindisfarne and Rushworth Gospels,' 1854.

For the collection of 'The Church Historians of England' he edited: 26. 'The Historical Works of the Venerable Beda,' 1853. 27. 'The Anglo-Saxon Chronicle; the Chronicle of Florence of Worcester, with a continuation and appendix,' 1853. 28. 'The History of the Kings of England, and of his own Times, by William of Malmesbury,' 1854. 29. 'The Chronicle of Fabius Ethelwerd; Asser's "Annals of King Alfred;" the Book of Hyde; the Chronicles of John Wallinford; the History of Ingulf; Gaimar,' 1854. 30. 'The Historical Works of Simeon of Durham,' 1855. 31. 'The History of William of Newburgh; the Chronicles of Robert de Monte,' 1856. 32. 'The Chronicles of John and Richard of Hexham; the Chronicle of Holyrood; the Chronicle of Melrose; Jordan Fantosme's Chronicle,' 1856.

For the Rolls Series he edited: 33. 'Chronicon Monasterii de Abingdon,' 2 vols. 1858. 34. 'Letters and Papers illustrative of the Wars of the English in France during the Reign of Henry VI,' 2 vols., 1861-4. 35. 'Narratives of the Expulsion of the English from Normandy, 1449-50,' 1863. 36. 'Radulphi de Coggeshall Chronicon Anglicanum,' 1875.

His other works are: 37. 'Comparison between certain Statements in the Evidence by Messrs. S. Hardy and Cole before the select committee upon the Record Commission,' 1837. 38. 'Calendar of State Papers, Foreign Series, of the Reign of Elizabeth,' vols. i. to vii., 1863, &c. 39. 'Documents illustrative of the History of Scotland from the Death of King Alexander III to the Accession of Robert Bruce,' 2 vols., Edinburgh, 1870, 8vo. 40. 'The History of Mary Stewart. . . . By Claude Nau, her Secretary, now first printed from the original Manuscripts, with illustrative Papers from the secret Archives of the Vatican, and other Collections in Rome,' Edinburgh, 1883, 8vo. 41. 'The Truth about John Wyclif, his Life, Writings, and Opinions, chiefly from the evidence of his Contemporaries,' London, 1885, 8vo. 42. 'Marie Stuart: a narrative of the first eighteen years of her Life, principally from original Documents,' Edinburgh, 1886, 8vo. 43. 'The Life of St. Cuthbert,' translated from the Latin of the Venerable Bede, London, 1887, 8vo. 44. An edition of H. Clifford's 'Life of Jane Dormer, duchess of Feria,' London, 1887, 8vo, forming vol. lxii. of the 'Quarterly Series.' 45. 'Cranmer and Anne Boleyn,' London [1892], 8vo.

He also assisted Mr. James Paton in editing the 'Scottish National Memorials,' 1890.

[Memoir by Rev. J. H. Pollen in the Month, March 1895 p. 331, and April p. 509; Lowndes's Bibl. Man. (Bohn), Suppl. pp. 5, 6, 22-5, 33-5, 131; Times, 12 Feb. 1895, p. 11, col. 5; Tablet, 16 Feb. 1895, p. 243; Athenæum, 16 Feb. 1895, p. 220; Notes and Queries, 2nd ser, iii. 221.]

T. C.

STEVENSON, MATTHEW (fl. 1654-1685), minor poet, was probably of Yorkshire origin, and a resident for the greater part of his life in Norfolk. He was occasionally seen in London, moving in a circle of minor wits of royalist tendencies, who haunted the law courts in the years following the Restoration. The coterie was dominated by such faint luminaries as Henry Bold, Valentine Oldys, Alexander Brome, and Edward Baynard (all of whom are separately noticed). Stevenson's publications were: 1. 'Occasion's Offspring. Or Poems upon Severall Occasions. By Mathew Stevenson. London, for Nathaniell Ekins,' 1654; dedicated 'To my best friend & courteous cousin Mr. Benjamin Cook' and adorned by a portrait of the author by R. Gaywood. 2. 'The Twelve Moneths, or a pleasant and profitable discourse of every action, whether of Labour or Recreation, proper to each particular Moneth, branched into directions relating to Husbandry, as Plowing, Sowing, Gardening, Planting, Transplanting, Plashing of Fences, felling of Timber, ordering of Cattle and Bees & of Malt &c. As also of Recreations, as Hunting, Hawking, Fishing, Fowling, Coursing, Cockfighting. To which is likewise added a necessary advise touching Physick, when it may and when not be taken. Lastly every Moneth is shut up with an Epigrame,' with the fairs of every month; London for Thomas Jenner, Royal Exchange,' 1661. A quaint woodcut illustrates the occupations of each month. Donaldson (*Agricult. Biogr.* p. 29) remarks upon the singularity of the work, which is evidently based less upon research than upon oral tradition and current folklore (BRYDGES, *Censura*, iv. 410). 3. 'Bellum Presbyteriale. Or as much said for the Presbyter as may be. Together with their Covenants Catastrophe. Held forth in an Heroic Poem,' London, 1661, 4to. The catastrophe refers to the burning of the covenant by the common hangman on 22 May 1661 and the consequent confusion of the 'Phanaticks,' at which the author rejoices. 4. 'Florus Britannicus; or an exact Epitome of the History of England From William the Conquerour to the Twelfth Year of the Reign of his Sacred Majesty Charls the Second now flourishing. Illustrated with their perfect Portraictures in exact Copper Plates very delightfull to the reader: as also, every King and Queens Elegie, with a Panegyrick upon his Maiesties Happy Returne. London for Thos Jenner, Royal Exchange,' 1662, 4to. The volume, which is very rare in a perfect state, was dedicated to the writer's cousin 'Mrs. Grace Killingbeck of Baroughby Grange, near Wentherby in Yorkshire,' and dated 'from my study in F. Street,' London, 12 March 1661. The letterpress, amounting to a page and a half for each monarch, was evidently written to accompany the plates, which are by Elstrack. 5. 'Poems by Matthew Stevenson. London for Lodowick Lloyd,' 1665. The work, again preceded by Gaywood's portrait, is inscribed to 'Edward Somerset] Lord Marquess of Worcester,' upon whose 'inimitable Water-Commanding Engine' there is an elaborate panegyrick, and it is recommended by 'Val.' Oldis, Henry Bold, Edw. Baynard, and E. Bostocke.' Many of the poems, as the author avows, had seen the light before. 6. 'Norfolk Drollery. Or, a compleat Collection of the Newest Songs, Jovial Poems, and Catches, &c. By the author, M. Stevenson,' London, 1673, 12mo. Two dedicatory letters are addressed respectively to 'Madam Mary Hunt of Sharington Hall' and 'My Very noble Friend Thos. Brown of Elsing Hall.' There are commendatory verses by 'Arth. Tichborne.' There are several reissues, with fresh title-pages. In one of 1673 the work is

styled simply 'Poems;' in another of 1685 it is headed 'The Wits.' Many of the verses had already done duty before, and the additions are mostly of a frivolous nature. The author celebrates the East Anglian labourer's practice of demanding 'largesse' from fieldfarers; but there is little distinctive of Norfolk about the various collections, which are remarkable chiefly for their quaint originality of manner.

[Hunter's Chorus Vatum, vol. i. in Add. MS. 24487, f. 68; Gent. Mag. 1835, i. 277; Granger's Biogr. Hist. of Engl. iv. 56; Ellis's Specimens, iii. 336; Nichols's Select Poems, ii. 141; Colman's Bibliotheca Norfolciensis, p. 505; Walpole's Cat. of Engravers, s.v. 'Gaywood'; Hazlitt's Handbook, p. 578; Brit. Mus. Cat.]

T. S.

STEVENSON, ROBERT (1772–1850), civil engineer, born at Glasgow on 8 June 1772, was only child of Alan Stevenson, a West India merchant, who died at St. Christopher on 26 May 1774, when Robert was an infant. The father came of a family whose members were originally settled as cultivators at Nether Carswell in the parish of Neilston, Renfrewshire, and afterwards, in the eighteenth century, engaged in business first as maltsters and later as West India merchants at Glasgow. Jean, Robert Stevenson's mother, was the daughter of David Lillie, a builder in Glasgow. After her husband's death she was for a time in straitened circumstances, and Robert began his education in a charity school. It was intended that he should enter the church, but before he had attained his sixteenth year his mother married Thomas Smith, engineer to the recently (1786) constituted northern lighthouse board, and he entered his stepfather's office. He studied civil engineering at the winter sessions of the Andersonian Institute, Glasgow, and afterwards at the university of Edinburgh. Smith showed his confidence in him by entrusting to him, while still in his teens, the superintendence of the erection of lighthouse buildings, lanterns, and optical apparatus, and the formation of 'macadam' roads of access to lighthouse stations. Communication with headquarters was difficult, as the stations were often situated on uninhabited islands or headlands, to which the materials were brought in smacks. In 1796 Smith took him into partnership, and he married Jean, Smith's eldest daughter by a former marriage.

A few years later Stevenson succeeded Smith as engineer to the Scottish lighthouse board, and held the office for about half a century. He practically inaugurated the Scottish lighthouse system, which is still

R 2

[text illegible] ... who concurred in Stevenson's opinion. Both Stevenson and Rennie gave evidence before a new parliamentary committee, and the act was passed on 21 July 1806. Active operations were begun on the reef in August 1807. Rennie was appointed nominally chief or consulting engineer, to whom Stevenson in any case of difficulty could apply. Rennie, who had no experience of lighthouse construction, suggested various alterations of the design, but to none of them Stevenson gave effect. After five years of arduous labour the lighthouse was in working order. Stevenson described its construction in 1824 in his 'Account of the Bell Rock Lighthouse.' The tower, which, as in all Stevenson's lighthouses, is free from architectural adornment, rises to the height of 100 ft.; the diameter at the base is 42 ft., diminishing to 15 ft. at the top. Above the solid, which is 30 ft. in height, is the entrance doorway, the interior being divided into six stories. Smeaton in his Eddystone tower adopted an arched form of floor, rendering it necessary to insert chains embedded in the masonry to counteract the outward thrust; but in the Bell Rock tower, by an

[text illegible] ... The Northern lighthouse board directed a bust of Stevenson, by Samuel Joseph, to be placed in the tower, and at his death placed in their minutes their regret at the loss of him 'to whom is due the honour of conceiving and executing the great work of the Bell Rock Lighthouse.'

Not only was the tower itself novel in design, but the implements used in its erection had to be invented. The balance and movable jib cranes were for the first time used at the Bell Rock. The latter is now in universal use. Ball-bearings were also introduced into the cranes at the Bell Rock for the first time. Stevenson further designed for the temporary lightship moored off the Bell Rock tower during its construction—the first lightship placed in so deep water—a lantern to surround the mast, instead of small lanterns hung from the yard-arms or frames. This improvement is now universally adopted.

In 1814 Sir Walter Scott made his celebrated voyage round Scotland with Stevenson and the lighthouse commissioners, starting from Leith on 29 July and reaching Greenock on 8 Sept. On 30 July he visited the Bell Rock, and inscribed some appreciative lines in the lighthouse album. Speaking of Stevenson in his journal, he says: 'The official chief of the expedition is Mr. Stevenson the surveyor—viceroy over the commissioners—a most gentlemanlike and modest man, and well known by his scientific skill.'

Stevenson's practice was not confined to

lighthouses, but covered the whole field of general engineering. He designed many bridges. His Hutchison Bridge 'is one of the best specimens of the segmental arch.' He also designed a new form of suspension bridge, in which the roadway passes above the chains, and the necessity of tall piers is avoided; many bridges have since, especially on the continent, been constructed on this principle. He also suggested the modern rail used on railways. George Stephenson acknowledged that it was from Stevenson's description that he adopted malleable iron rails. He was the first to discover and point out that the salt waters of the ocean flow up the beds of rivers in a stream quite distinct from the overflowing fresh water; and he invented the hydrophore for procuring specimens of sea and river water, so largely used in estuarial and oceanic observations. Stevenson designed the magnificent eastern road approaches to Edinburgh; of one of the eastern approaches Cockburn wrote: 'The effect was like drawing up the curtain of a theatre.'

His experiments on the destruction of timber by the *Limnoria terebrans* led to the universal adoption of greenheart oak for structures in the sea. He took a great interest in the promotion of the fisheries, and suggested and urged the use of the barometer by fishermen. He was one of the originators of the Royal Observatory of Edinburgh, and strongly advocated the importance to navigation of trustworthy charts founded on careful marine surveys and soundings. He was a fellow of the Royal, the Antiquarian, and Wernerian societies of Edinburgh; the Geological and Astronomical societies of London; and a member of the Institution of Civil Engineers (1828). Stevenson died at Edinburgh on 12 July 1850, and was buried in the New Calton cemetery, close to one of the approaches to Edinburgh which he designed. Joseph's marble bust of Stevenson is in the Bell Rock lighthouse. The original model is in the Museum of Science and Art, Edinburgh. A portrait painted from it is in the National Portrait Gallery, Edinburgh, and has been engraved for David Stevenson's 'Life of Robert Stevenson,' 1878.

Alan, his eldest, David his third son, and his youngest son, Thomas, are noticed separately.

Stevenson contributed many articles on engineering to the 'Edinburgh Encyclopædia' and the 'Encyclopædia Britannica,' such as bridges, blasting, dredging, roads, lighthouses, railways. Among the papers he contributed to scientific societies, that contributed to the Wernerian Society on the

'Alveus of the German Ocean' is frequently quoted by geologists.

[Private information; David Stevenson's Life of Robert Stevenson, Edinburgh, 1878; Robert Louis Stevenson's Family of Engineers, in Edinburgh edition of his Works, 1896, vol. xviii.]

D. A. S.

STEVENSON, ROBERT LOUIS (1850–1894), novelist, essayist, poet, and traveller, was born at 8 Howard Place, Edinburgh, on 13 Nov. 1850. He was baptised Robert Lewis Balfour, but from about his eighteenth year dropped the use of the third christian name and changed the spelling of the second to Louis; signing thereafter Robert Louis in full, and being called always Louis by his family and intimate friends. On both sides of the house he was sprung from capable and cultivated stock. His father, Thomas Stevenson [q. v.], was a member of the distinguished Edinburgh firm of civil engineers [see under STEVENSON, ROBERT; STEVENSON, DAVID; and STEVENSON, ALAN]. His mother was Margaret Isabella (d. 14 May 1897), youngest daughter of James Balfour, for many years minister of the parish of Colinton in Midlothian, and grandson to James Balfour (1705–1795) [q. v.], professor at Edinburgh first of moral philosophy and afterwards of the law of nature and of nations. His mother's father was described by his grandson in the essay called 'The Manse.' Robert Louis was his parents' only child. His mother was subject in early and middle life to chest and nerve troubles, and her son may have inherited from her some o. his constitutional weakness as well as of his intellectual vivacity and taste for letters. His health was infirm from the first. He suffered from frequent bronchial affections and acute nervous excitability, and in the autumn of 1858 was near dying of a gastric fever. In January 1853 his parents moved to No. 1 Inverleith Terrace, and in May 1857 to 17 Heriot Row, which continued to be their Edinburgh home until the father's death in 1887. Much of his time was also spent in the manse at Colinton on the water of Leith, the home of his maternal grandfather. If he suffered much as a child from the distresses, he also enjoyed to the full the pleasures, of imagination. He was eager in every kind of play, and made the most of all the amusements natural to an only child kept much indoors by ill-health. The child in him never died; and the zest with which in after life he would throw himself into the pursuits of children and young boys was on his own account as much as on theirs. This spirit is illustrated in the pieces which he wrote and published under the title 'A Child's

Garden of Verses,' as well as in a number of retrospective essays and fragments referring with peculiar insight and freshness of memory to that period of life ('Child's Play,' 'Notes of Childhood,' 'Rosa quo locorum,' and others unpublished).

Such a child was naturally a greedy reader, or rather listener to reading; for it was not until his eighth year that he learned to read easily or habitually to himself. He began early to take pleasure in attempts at composition: a 'History of Moses,' dictated in his sixth year, and an account of 'Travels in Perth,' in his ninth, are still extant. Ill-health prevented his getting much regular or continuous schooling. He attended first (1858–61) a preparatory school kept by a Mr. Henderson in India Street; and next (at intervals for some time after the autumn of 1861) the Edinburgh Academy. For a few months in the autumn of 1863 he was at a boarding-school kept by a Mr. Wyatt at Spring Grove, near London; from 1864 to 1867 his education was conducted chiefly at Mr. Thompson's private school in Frederick Street, Edinburgh, and by private tutors in various places to which he travelled for his own or his parents' health. Such travels included frequent visits to health resorts in Scotland; occasional excursions with his father on his nearer professional rounds, e.g. to the coasts and lighthouses of Fife in 1864; and also longer journeys—to Germany and Holland in 1862, to Italy in 1863, to the Riviera in the spring of 1864, and to Torquay in 1865 and 1866. From 1867 the family life became more settled between Edinburgh and Swanston cottage, a country home in the Pentlands which Thomas Stevenson first rented in that year, and the scenery and associations of which inspired not a little of his son's work in literature (see especially *A Pastoral* and *St. Ives*).

In November of the same year, 1867, Louis Stevenson was entered as a student at the Edinburgh University, and for several winters attended classes there with such regularity as his health and inclinations permitted. According to his own account (essay on *A College Magazine*; *Life of Fleeming Jenkin*, &c.), he was alike at school and college an incorrigible idler and truant. But outside the field of school and college routine he showed eager curiosity and activity of mind. 'He was of a conversable temper,' so he says of himself, 'and insatiably curious in the aspects of life; and spent much of his time scraping acquaintance with all classes of man and woman kind.' At the same time he read precociously and omnivorously in the *belles-lettres*, including a very wide range of English poetry, fiction, and essays, and a fairly wide range of French; and was a genuine student of Scottish history, and to some extent of history in general. He had been intended as a matter of course to follow the family profession of engineering; and from 1868 his summer excursions took a professional turn. In that and the two following years he went to watch the works of the firm in progress at various points on the mainland and in the northern and western islands. He was a favourite, though a very irregular, pupil of the professor of engineering, Fleeming Jenkin [q. v.]; and must have shown some aptitude for the calling hereditary in his family, inasmuch as in 1871 he received the silver medal of the Edinburgh Society of Arts for a paper on a suggested improvement in lighthouse apparatus. The outdoor and seafaring parts of the profession were in fact wholly to his taste, as in spite of his frail health he had a passion for open-air exercise and adventure (though not for sports). Office work, on the other hand, was his aversion, and his physical powers were unequal to the workshop training necessary to the practical engineer. Accordingly in this year, 1871, it was agreed that he should give up the hereditary profession and read for the bar.

For several ensuing years Stevenson attended law classes in the university, giving to the subject some serious although fitful attention, until he was called to the bar in 1875. But it was on another side that this 'pattern of an idler,' to use his own words, was gradually developing himself into a model of unsparing industry. From childhood he had never ceased to practise writing, and on all his truantries went pencil and copybook in hand. Family and school magazines in manuscript are extant of which, between his thirteenth and sixteenth years, he was editor, chief contributor, and illustrator. In his sixteenth year he wrote a serious essay on the 'Pentland Rising of 1666' (having already tried his hand at an historical romance on the same subject). This was printed as a pamphlet, and is now a rarity in request among collectors. For the following four or five years, though always writing both in prose and verse, he kept his efforts to himself, and generally destroyed the more ambitious of them. Among these were a romance on the life of Hackston of Rathillet, a poetical play of 'Semiramis' written in imitation of Webster, and 'Voces Fidelium,' a series of dramatic dialogues in verse. A few manuscript essays and notes of travel that have been preserved from 1868 to 1870, together with his letters to his mother of the same period, show almost as good a gift of observation and expression as his published work of five or six years later. Less promising and less personal are a series of six papers which he contributed in 1871 to the 'Edinburgh University Magazine,' a short-lived periodical started by him in conjunction with one or two college friends and fellow-members of the Speculative Society.

With high social spirits and a brilliant, somewhat fantastic, gaiety of bearing, Stevenson was no stranger to the storms and perplexities of youth. A restless and inquiring conscience, perhaps inherited from covenanting ancestors, kept him inwardly calling in question the grounds of conduct and the accepted codes of society. At the same time his reading had shaken his belief in Christian dogma; the harsher forms of Scottish Calvinistic Christianity being indeed at all times repugnant to his nature. From the last circumstance arose for a time troubles with his father, the more trying while they lasted because of the deep attachment and pride in each other which always subsisted between father and son. He loved the aspects of his native city, but neither its physical nor its social atmosphere was congenial to him. Amid the biting winds and rigid social conventions of Edinburgh he craved for Bohemian freedom and the joy of life, and for a while seemed in danger of a fate like that of the boy-poet, Robert Fergusson [q. v.], with whom he always owned a strong sense of spiritual affinity.

But his innate sanity of mind and disposition prevailed. In the summer of 1873 he made new friends, who encouraged him strongly to the career of letters. His first contribution to regular periodical literature, a little paper on 'Roads,' appeared in the 'Portfolio' (edited by Philip Gilbert Hamerton) for December 1873. In the meantime his health had suffered a serious breakdown. In consequence of acute nervous exhaustion, combined with threatening lung symptoms, he was ordered to the Riviera, where he spent (chiefly at Mentone) the winter of 1873-4. Returning with a certain measure of recovered health in April 1874, he went to live with his parents at Edinburgh and Swanston, and resumed his reading for the bar. He attended classes for Scots law and conveyancing, and for constitutional law and history. He worked also for a time in the office of Messrs. Skene, Edwards, & Bilton, of which the antiquary and historian, William Forbes Skene [q. v.], was senior partner. On 14 July 1875 he passed his final examination with credit, and

was called to the bar on the 16th, but never practised. Since abandoning the engineering profession he had resumed the habit of frequent miscellaneous excursions in Scotland, England, or abroad. Now, in 1875, began the first of a series of visits to the artistic settlements in the neighbourhood of Fontainebleau, where his cousin, Mr. R. A. M. Stevenson, was for the time established. He found the forest climate restorative to his health, and the life and company of Barbizon and the other student resorts congenial. In the winter of 1874-5 he made in Edinburgh the acquaintance of Mr. W. E. Henley, which quickly ripened into a close and stimulating literary friendship. In London he avoided all formal and dress-coated society; and at the Savile Club (his favourite haunt) and elsewhere his own Bohemian oddities of dress and appearance would sometimes repel at first sight persons to whom on acquaintance he soon became endeared by the charm of his conversation. Among his friends of these years may be especially mentioned Mr. Leslie Stephen, Mr. James Payn, Dr. Appleton (editor of the 'Academy'), Professor Clifford, Mr. Walter Pollock, Mr. Cosmo Monkhouse, Mr. Andrew Lang, and Mr. Edmund Gosse. In 1876 he went with Sir Walter Simpson on the canoe tour in Belgium and France described in the 'Inland Voyage.' In the spring of 1878 he made friends at Burford Bridge with a senior whom he had long honoured, Mr. George Meredith; and in the summer had a new experience in serving as secretary to Professor Fleeming Jenkin in his capacity of juror on the Paris Exhibition. In the autumn of the same year he spent a month at Monastier in Velay, whence he took the walk through the mountains to Florac narrated in the 'Travels with a Donkey in the Cevennes.'

During these years, 1874-8, his health, though frail, was passable. With his vagrant way of life he combined a steady and growing literary industry. While reading for the bar in 1874-5, much of his work was merely experimental (poems, prose-poems, and tales not published). Much also was in preparation for proposed undertakings on Scottish history. His studies in Highland history, which were diligent and exact, in the end only served to provide the historical background of his Scottish romances. Until the end of 1875 he had only published, in addition to essays in the magazines, an 'Appeal to the Church of Scotland,' written to please his father and published as a pamphlet in 1875. In 1876 he contributed as a journalist, but not frequently, to the 'Academy' and 'Vanity Fair,' and in 1877 more abundantly to 'London,' a weekly review newly founded under the editorship of Mr. Glasgow Brown, an acquaintance of Edinburgh Speculative days. In the former year, 1876, began the brilliant series of essays on life and literature in the 'Cornhill Magazine' which were afterwards collected with others in the volumes called severally 'Virginibus Puerisque' and 'Familiar Studies of Men and Books.' They were continued in 1877, and in greater number throughout 1878. His first published stories were : 'A Lodging for the Night' (*Temple Bar*, October 1877); 'The Sire de Malétroit's Door' (*Temple Bar*, January 1878); and 'Will o' the Mill' (*Cornhill Magazine*, January 1878).

The year 1878 was to Stevenson one of great productiveness. In May was issued his first book, 'The Inland Voyage,' containing the account of his canoe trip, and written in a pleasant fanciful vein of humour and reflection, but with the style a little over-mannered. Besides six or eight characteristic essays of the 'Virginibus Puerisque' series, there appeared in 'London' (edited by Mr. Henley) the set of fantastic modern tales called the 'New Arabian Nights,' conceived in a very spirited and entertaining vein of the realistic-unreal, as well as the story of 'Providence and the Guitar;' and in the 'Portfolio' the 'Picturesque Notes on Edinburgh,' republished at the end of the year in book form. During the autumn and winter of this year he wrote 'Travels with a Donkey in the Cevennes,' and was much engaged in the planning of plays in collaboration with Mr. Henley, of which one, 'Deacon Brodie,' was finished in the spring of 1879. This was also the date of the essay 'On some Aspects of Burns.' In the same spring he drafted in Edinburgh, but afterwards laid by, four chapters on ethics (a study to which he once referred as being always his 'veiled mistress') under the name of 'Lay Morals.' In few men have the faculties been so active on the artistic and the ethical sides at once, and this fragment is of especial interest in the study of its author's mind and character.

By his various published writings Stevenson had made little impression as yet on the general reader. But the critical had recognised in him a new artist of the first promise in English letters, who aimed at, and often achieved, those qualities of sustained precision, lucidity, and grace of style which are characteristic of the best French prose, but in English rare in the extreme. He had known how to stamp all he wrote with the impress of a vivid personal charm; had shown himself a master of the apt and ani-mated phrase : and whether in tale or parable, essay or wayside musing, had touched on vital points of experience and feeling with the observation and insight of a true poet and humourist.

The year 1879 was a critical one in Stevenson's life. In France he had met an American lady, Mrs. Osbourne (*née* Van de Grift), whose domestic circumstances were not fortunate, and who was living with her daughter and young son in the art-student circles of Paris and Fontainebleau. At the beginning of 1879 she returned to California. In June Stevenson determined to follow. He travelled by emigrant ship and train, partly for economy, partly for the sake of the experience. The journey and its discomforts proved disastrous to his health, but did not interrupt his industry. Left entirely to his own resources, he stayed for eight months partly at Monterey and partly at San Francisco. During a part of these months he was at death's door from a complication of pleurisy, malarial fever, and exhaustion of the system, but managed nevertheless to write the story of 'The Pavilion on the Links,' two or three essays for the 'Cornhill Magazine,' the greater part of a Californian story, 'A Vendetta in the West' (never published), a first draft of the romance of 'Prince Otto,' and the two parts of the 'Amateur Emigrant' (not published till some years later). He also tried to get work on the local press, and some contributions were printed in the 'Monterey Independent;' but on the whole his style was not thought up to Californian standards. In the spring of 1880 he was married to Mrs. Osbourne, who had obtained some months before a divorce from her husband. She nursed him through the worst of his illness, and in May they went for the sake of health to lodge at a deserted mining station above Calistoga, in the Californian coast range. The story of this sojourn is told in the 'Silverado Squatters.'

Family and friends, who had at first opposed the marriage, being now fully reconciled to it, Stevenson brought his wife home in August 1880. She was to him a perfect companion, taking part keenly and critically in his work, sharing all his gipsy tastes and love of primitive and natural modes of life, and being, in spite of her own precarious health, the most devoted and efficient of nurses in the anxious times which now ensued. For the next seven or eight years his life seemed to hang by a thread. Chronic lung disease had declared itself, and the slightest exposure or exertion was apt to bring on a prostrating attack of cough, hæmorrhage, and fever. The trial was manfully borne; and in every interval of respite he worked in unremitting pursuit of the standards he had set before himself.

Between 1880 and 1887 he lived the life of an invalid, vainly seeking relief by change of place. After spending six weeks (August and September 1880) with his parents at Blair Athol and Strathpeffer, he went in October, with his wife and stepson, to winter at Davos, where he made fast friends with John Addington Symonds (1840-1893) [q. v.] and his family. He wrote little, but prepared for press the collected essays 'Virginibus Puerisque,' in which he preaches with captivating vigour and grace his gospel of youth, courage, and a contempt for the timidities and petty respectabilities of life. For the rest, he amused himself with verses playful and other, and with supplying humorous text and cuts ('Moral Emblems,' 'Not I,' &c.) for a little private press worked by his young stepson. Returning to Scotland at the end of May with health somewhat improved, he spent four months with his parents at Pitlochry and Braemar. At Pitlochry he wrote 'Thrawn Janet' and the chief part of 'The Merry Men,' two of the strongest short tales in Scottish literature, the one of Satanic possession, the other of a conscience and imagination haunted, to the overthrow of reason, by the terrors of the sea. At Braemar he began 'Treasure Island,' his father helping with suggestions and reminiscences from his own seafaring experiences. At the suggestion of Mr. A. H. Japp, the story was offered to, and accepted by, the editor (Mr. Henderson) of a boys' periodical called 'Young Folks.' In the meantime (August 1881) Stevenson had been a candidate for the vacant chair of history and constitutional law at Edinburgh. In the light of such public reputation as he yet possessed, the candidature must have seemed paradoxical; but it was encouraged by competent advisers, including the retiring professor, Dr. Æneas Mackay. It failed. Had it succeeded, his health would almost certainly have proved unequal to the work. A cold and wet season at Braemar did him much harm; and in October he was ordered off to spend a second winter (1881-2) at Davos. He here finished the tale of 'Treasure Island,' begun, on the suggestion of Mr. George Bentley, a life (never completed) of William Hazlitt, and prepared for press the collection of literary essays 'Familiar Studies of Men and Books.' In the summer of 1882 he again tried Scotland (Stobo Manse in Upper Tweeddale, Lochearnhead, and Kingussie), and again with bad results for his health. As his wife

was never well at Davos, they determined to winter in the south, and settled before Christmas in a cottage near Marseilles (Campagne Defli, St. Marcel). Thence being presently driven by a fever epidemic, they moved in January 1883 to a châlet in a pleasant garden on a hill behind Hyères (Châlet la Solitude). Here Stevenson enjoyed a respite of nearly a year from acute illness, as well as the first breath of popular success on the publication in book form of 'Treasure Island.' In this story the force of invention and vividness of narrative appealed to every reader, including those on whom its other qualities of style and character-drawing would in themselves have been thrown away; and it has taken its place in literature as a classic story of pirate and mutineer adventure. It has been translated into French, Spanish, and other languages. Partly at Marseilles and partly at Hyères he wrote the 'Treasure of Franchard,' a pleasant and ingenious tale of French provincial life; and early in 1883 completed for 'Young Folks' a second boys' tale, 'The Black Arrow.' This story of the wars of the Roses, written in a style founded on the 'Paston Letters,' was preferred to 'Treasure Island' by the audience to whom it was first addressed, but failed to please the critics when published in book form five years later, and was no favourite with its author. Stevenson's other work at Hyères consisted of verses for the 'Child's Garden;' essays for the 'Cornhill Magazine' and the 'Magazine of Art' (edited by Mr. Henley); the 'Silverado Squatters,' first drafted in 1880, and finally 'Prince Otto.' In this tale, or fantasy, certain problems of character and conjugal relation which had occupied him ever since his boyish tragedy of 'Semiramis' are worked out with a lively play of intellect and humour, and (as some think) an excessive refinement and research of style, on a stage of German court life and with a delightful background of German forest scenery. The book, never very popular, is one of those most characteristic of his mind. It was translated into French in 1896 by Mr. Egerton Castle.

In September 1883 Stevenson suffered a great loss in the death of his old friend Mr. James Walter Ferrier (see the essay *Old Mortality*). In the beginning of 1884 his hopes and spirits were rudely dashed by two dangerous attacks of illness, the first occurring at Nice in January, the second at Hyères in May. Travelling slowly homewards by way of Royat, he arrived in England in July in an almost prostrate condition, and in September settled at Bournemouth.

In the autumn and early winter his quarters were at Bonallie Tower, Branksome Park; in February 1885 his father bought and gave him the house at Westbourne which he called (after the famous lighthouse designed by his uncle Alan) Skerryvore. This was for the next two years and a half his home. His health, and on the whole his spirits, remained on a lower plane than before, and he was never free for many weeks together from fits of hæmorrhage and prostration. Nevertheless he was able to form new friendships and to do some of the best of his work of his life.

In 1885 he finished for publication two books which his illness had interrupted, the 'Child's Garden of Verses' and 'Prince Otto,' and began a highway romance called 'The Great North Road,' but relinquished it in order to write a second series of 'New Arabian Nights.' These new tales hinge about the Fenian dynamite conspiracies, of which the public mind was at this time full, and to the old elements of fantastic realism add a new element of witty and scornful criminal psychology. The incidental stories of 'The Destroying Angel' and 'The Fair Cuban' were supplied by Mrs. Stevenson. During the same period he wrote several of the personal and literary essays afterwards collected in the volume 'Memories and Portraits;' a succession of Christmas stories, 'The Body Snatcher' in the 'Pall Mall Gazette,' 1884; 'Olalla' in the 'Court and Society Review,' and 'The Misadventures of John Nicholson' in 'Cassell's Christmas Annual,' both for 1885; and 'Markheim' in 'Unwin's Christmas Annual,' 1886; as well as several plays in collaboration with Mr. Henley, viz. 'Beau Austin,' 'Admiral Guinea,' and 'Robert Macaire.' Stevenson, like almost every other imaginative writer, had built hopes of gain upon dramatic work. His money needs, in spite of help from his father, were still somewhat pressing. Until 1886 he had never earned much more than 300*l.* a year by his pen. But in that year came two successes which greatly increased his reputation, and with it his power to earn. These were 'The Strange Case of Dr. Jekyll and Mr. Hyde' and 'Kidnapped.' The former, founded partly on a dream, is a striking apologue of the double life of man. Published as a 'shilling shocker,' a form at that time in fashion, it became instantly popular; was quoted from a thousand pulpits; was translated into German, French, and Danish; and the names of its two chief characters have passed into the common stock of proverbial allusion. In 'Kidnapped'—a boys' highland story suggested by the historical incident of the Appin

murder—the adventures are scarcely less exciting than those of 'Treasure Island,' the elements of character-drawing subtler and farther carried, while the romance of history and the sentiment of the soil are expressed as they had hardly been expressed since Scott. The success of these two tales, both with the critics and the public, established Stevenson's position at the head of the younger English writers of his day, among whom his example encouraged an increased general attention to technical qualities of style and workmanship, as well as a reaction in favour of the novel of action and romance against the more analytic and less stimulating types of fiction then prevailing.

About this time Stevenson was occupied with studies for a short book on Wellington (after Gordon his favourite hero), intended for a series edited by Mr. Andrew Lang. This was never written, and in the winter and spring 1886-7 his chief task was one of piety to a friend, viz. the writing of a life of Fleeming Jenkin from materials supplied by the widow. In the spring of 1887 he published, under the title 'Underwoods' (borrowed from Ben Jonson), a collection of verses, partly English and partly Scottish, selected from the chance production of a good many years. Stevenson's poetry, written chiefly when he was too tired to write anything else, expresses as a rule the charm and power of his nature with a more slippered grace, a far less studious and perfect art, than his prose. He also prepared for publication in 1887, under the title 'Memories and Portraits,' a collection of essays personal and other, including an effective exposition of his own theories of romance, which he had contributed to various periodicals during preceding years.

His father's death in May 1887 broke the strongest tie which bound him to this country. His own health showed no signs of improvement; and the doctors, as a last chance of recovery, recommended some complete change of climate and mode of life. His wife's connections pointing to the west, he thought of Colorado, persuaded his mother to join them, and with his whole household —mother, wife, and stepson—sailed for New York on 17 Aug. 1887. After a short stay under the hospitable care of friends at Newport, he was persuaded, instead of going farther west, to try the climate of the Adirondack mountains for the winter. At the beginning of October the family moved accordingly to a house on Saranac Lake, and remained there until April 1888. Here he wrote for 'Scribner's Magazine' a series of twelve essays (published January-December

1888 and partly reprinted in 'Across the Plains'). Some of these ('Dreams,' 'Lantern Bearers,' 'Random Memories') contain his best work in the mixed vein of autobiography and criticism; others ('Pulvis et Umbra,' 'A Christmas Sermon') his strongest, if not his most buoyant or inspiriting, in the ethical vein. For the same publishers he also wrote the ballad of 'Ticonderoga' and began the romance of 'The Master of Ballantrae,' of which the scene is partly laid in the country of his winter sojourn. This tragic story of fraternal hate is thought by many to take the first place among its author's romances, alike by vividness of presentment and by psychologic insight. In April Stevenson came to New York, but, soon wearying of the city, went for some weeks' boating to Manasquan on the New Jersey coast. At this time (March–May 1888), by way of 'a little judicious levity,' he revised and partly rewrote a farcical story drafted in the winter by his stepson, Mr. Lloyd Osbourne, 'The Wrong Box,' which was published in the course of the year under their joint names. The fact that the farce turns on the misadventures of a corpse caused most readers to think the levity more apparent than the judgment; but the book cannot be read without laughter.

In the meantime the family had entertained the idea of a yachting excursion in the South Seas. The romance of the Pacific had attracted Stevenson from a boy. The enterprise held out hopes of relief to his health; an American publisher (Mr. S. S. McClure) provided the means of undertaking it by an offer of 2,000l. for letters in which its course should be narrated. The result was that on 26 June 1888 the whole family set out from San Francisco on board the schooner yacht Casco (Captain Otis). They first sailed to the Marquesas, where they spent six weeks; thence to the Paumotus or Dangerous Archipelago; thence to the Tahitian group, where they again rested for several weeks, and whence they sailed northward for Hawaii. Arriving at Honolulu about the new year of 1889, they made a stay of nearly six months, during which Stevenson made several excursions, including one, which profoundly impressed him, to the leper settlement at Molokai. His journey so far having proved a source of infinite interest and enjoyment, as well as greatly improved health, Stevenson determined to prolong it. He and his party started afresh from Honolulu in June 1889 on a rough trading schooner, the Equator. Their destination was the Gilberts, a remote coral group in the western Pacific. At two of its

petty capitals, Apemama and Butaritari, they made stays of about six weeks each, and at Christmas 1889 found their way again into semi-civilisation at Apia in the Samoan group. After a month or two's stay in Samoa, where the beauty of the scenery and the charm of the native population delighted them, the party went on to Sydney, where Stevenson immediately fell ill, the life of the city seeming to undo the good he had got at sea. This experience set him voyaging again, and determined him to make his home in the South Seas. In April 1890 a fresh start was made, this time on a trading steamer, the Janet Nicoll. Touching first at Samoa, where he had bought a property of about four hundred acres on the mountain above Apia, to which he gave the name Vailima (five rivers), he left instructions for clearing and building operations to be begun while he continued his voyage. The course of the Janet Nicoll took him during the summer to many remote islands, from Penhryn to the Marshalls, and landed him in September in New Caledonia. Returning the same month to Samoa, he found the small house already existing at Vailima to be roughly habitable, and installed himself there to superintend the further operations of clearing, planting, and building. The family belongings from Bournemouth were sent out, and his mother, who had left him at Honolulu, rejoined him at Vailima in the spring of 1891.

During these Pacific voyages he had finished the 'Master of Ballantrae,' besides writing many occasional verses, and two long, not very effective, ballads on themes of Polynesian legend, the 'Song of Rahero' and the 'Feast of Famine.' He had also planned and begun at sea, in collaboration with Mr. Lloyd Osbourne, his one attempt at a long and sustained story of modern life, 'The Wrecker.' At Samoa he had written the first of his Pacific stories in prose, 'The Bottle Imp.' This little tale of morals and of magic appealed strongly to the native readers to whom (in a missionary translation) it was first addressed (published in English in 'Black and White,' 1891, and reprinted in 'Island Nights' Entertainments'). At Sydney he had written in a heat of indignation, and published in pamphlet form, the striking 'Letter to Dr. Hyde' in vindication of the memory of Father Damien. Lastly, on board the Janet Nicoll, 'under the most ungodly circumstances,' he had begun the work of composing the letters relating his travels, which were due under the original contract to the Messrs. McClure. This and 'The Wrecker' were the two tasks unfinished on his hands when he entered (November 1890) on the four years' residence at Vailima which forms the closing period of his life.

In his new Samoan home Stevenson soon began to exercise a hospitality and an influence which increased with every year. Among the natives he was known by the name of Tusitala (teller of tales), and was supposed to be master of an inexhaustible store of wealth, perhaps even to be the holder of the magic bottle of his own tale. He gathered about him a kind of feudal clan of servants and retainers, whom he ruled in a spirit of affectionate kindness tempered with firm justice; and presently got drawn, as a man so forward in action and so impatient of injustice could not fail to do, into the entanglements of local politics and government. In health he seemed to have become a new man. Frail in comparison with the strong, he was yet able to ride and boat with little restriction, and to take part freely in local festivities, both white and native. The chief interruptions were an occasional trip to Sydney or Auckland, from which he generally came back the worse. From the middle of 1891 to the spring of 1893 his intromissions in politics embroiled him more or less seriously with most of the white officials in the island, especially the chief justice, Mr. Cedercrantz, and the president of the council, Baron Senfft von Pilsach. The proceedings of these gentlemen were exposed by him in a series of striking letters to the 'Times,' and the three treaty powers (Germany, Great Britain, and the United States) ultimately decided to dispense with their services. At one period of the struggle he believed himself threatened with deportation. Whether all his own steps on that petty but extremely complicated political scene were judicious is more than can be said; but impartial witnesses agree that he had a considerable moderating influence with the natives, and that his efforts were all in the direction of peace and concord.

His literary industry during these years was more strenuous than ever. His habit was to begin work at six in the morning or earlier, continue without interruption until the midday meal, and often to resume again until four or five in the afternoon. In addition to his literary labours he kept up an active correspondence both with old friends and new acquaintances, especially with writers of the younger generation in England, who had been drawn to him either by admiration for his work or by his ever ready and generous recognition of their own. He had suffered for some time from scrivener's cramp, and in the last three years of his life was much helped by the affectionate services as amanuensis of his stepdaughter, Mrs.

Strong, who had become a member of the household since 1889. In 1894 the plan devised by his business adviser and lifelong friend, Mr. Charles Baxter, of a limited édition de luxe of his collected works, under the title of the 'Edinburgh Edition,' afforded him much pleasure, together with a prospect of considerable gain. This experiment, without precedent during the lifetime of an author, proved a great success, but Stevenson did not live long enough to enjoy the opportunity of rest which its results were calculated to bring him.

Of his writings during the Samoan period, 'The Wrecker' was finished in collaboration with Mr. Lloyd Osbourne in the winter 1890-1. Throughout 1891 he had a heavy task with the promised letters relating his Pacific voyages. Work undertaken to order seldom prospered with him, and these 'Letters,' having cost him more labour than anything he ever wrote, have less of his characteristic charm, despite the interest and strangeness of the matters of which they tell. They were published periodically in the New York 'Sun' and in 'Black and White,' and have been in part reprinted in the 'Edinburgh Edition.' A far more effective result of his South Sea experiences is the tale of the 'Beach of Falesà,' written in the same year and first published under the title 'Uma' in the 'Illustrated London News' (reprinted in 'Island Nights' Entertainments'). In 1892 he was much occupied with a task from which he could expect neither fame nor profit, but to which he was urged by a sense of duty and the hope of influencing the treaty powers in favour of what he thought a wiser policy in Samoa. This was the 'Footnote to History,' an account, composed with an intentional plainness of style, of the intricate local politics of the preceding years, including a description of the famous hurricane of 1888. The same spring (1892) he took up again, after six years, the unfinished history of David Balfour at the point where ill-health had compelled him to break it off in 'Kidnapped.' This sequel (published first in 'Atalanta' under the title 'David Balfour,' and then in book form as 'Catriona') contains some of the author's best work, especially in the closing scenes at Leyden and Dunkerque. The comedy of boy and girl passion has been hardly anywhere more glowingly or more delicately expressed. In the same year (1892) was published 'Across the Plains,' a volume of collected essays, to which was prefixed the account of his emigrant journey from New York to San Francisco, much revised and compressed from the original draft of 1879; and in the spring of 1893 'Island Nights' Entertainments,' containing with 'The Beach of Falesá,' and 'The Bottle Imp,' a new tale of magic, 'The Isle of Voices,' first published in the 'National Observer.'

In the same year (1892) Stevenson made beginnings on a great variety of new work, some of it inspired by his Pacific experiences, and some by the memories and associations of Scotland, the power of which on his mind seemed only to be intensified by exile. To the former class belonged 'Sophia Scarlet,' a sentimental novel of planters' life in the South Seas, and 'The Ebb-Tide,' a darker story of South Sea crime and adventure, planned some time before under the title of the 'Pearl-Fisher' in collaboration with Mr. Lloyd Osbourne. Of the latter class were 'Heathercat,' a tale of covenanting times and of the Darien adventure; 'The Young Chevalier,' an historical romance partly founded on facts supplied to him by Mr. Andrew Lang; 'Weir of Hermiston,' a tragic story of the Scottish border, in which the chief character was founded on that of the famous judge Lord Braxfield; and 'A Family of Engineers,' being an account of the lives and work of his grandfather, uncles, and father. Some progress had been made with all of these when a fit of influenza in January 1893 diverted him to a lighter task, that of dictating (partly, when forbidden to speak, in the deaf-and-dumb alphabet) a tale of manners and the road called 'St. Ives,' dealing with the escape from Edinburgh Castle and subsequent adventures of a French prisoner of war in 1814. Of these various writings, the 'Ebb-Tide' was alone completed; it was published in 'To-day,' November 1893 to January 1894, and in book form in September 1894. The family history was carried as far as the construction of the Bell Rock lighthouse. 'Sophia Scarlet,' 'Heathercat,' and the 'Young Chevalier' never got beyond a chapter or two each. 'St. Ives' had been brought to within a little of completion when the author, feeling himself getting out of vein with it, turned again to 'Weir of Hermiston.' This, so far as it goes, is his strongest work. The few chapters which he lived to complete, taken as separate blocks of narrative and character presentment, are of the highest imaginative and emotional power.

Despite the habitual gaiety which Stevenson had continued to show before his family and friends, and his expressed confidence in his own improved health, there had not been wanting in his later correspondence from Vailima signs of inward despondency and distress. At moments, even, it is evident that he himself had presentiments that the end was near. It came in such a manner as he would himself have wished. On the afternoon of 4 Dec. 1894, he was talking gaily with his wife, when the sudden rupture of a blood-vessel in the brain laid him at her feet, and within two hours all was over. The next day he was buried on a romantic site of his own selection, whither it took the zealous toil of sixty natives to cut a path and carry him, on a peak of the forest-clad Mount Vaea.

The romance of Stevenson's life and the attraction of his character procured for him a degree of fame and affection disproportionate to the numerical circulation of his works. In this point he was much outstripped by several of his contemporaries. But few writers have during their lifetime commanded so much admiration and regard from their fellow-craftsmen. To attain the mastery of an elastic and harmonious English prose, in which trite and inanimate elements should have no place, and which should be supple to all uses and alive in all its joints and members, was an aim which he pursued with ungrudging, even with heroic, toil. Not always, especially not at the beginning, but in by far the greater part of his mature work, the effect of labour and fastidious selection is lost in the felicity of the result. 'Energy of vision goes hand in hand with magic of presentiment, and both words and things acquire new meaning and a new vitality under his touch.' Next to finish and brilliancy of execution, the most remarkable quality of his work is its variety. Without being the inventor of any new form or mode of literary art (unless, indeed, the verses of the 'Child's Garden' are to be accounted such), he handled with success and freshness nearly all the old forms—the moral, critical, and personal essay, travels sentimental and other, romances and short tales both historical and modern, parables and tales of mystery, boys' stories of adventure, drama, memoir, lyrical and meditative verse both English and Scottish. To some of these forms he gave quite new life: through all alike he expressed vividly his own extremely personal way of seeing and being, his peculiar sense of nature and of romance.

In personal appearance Stevenson was of good stature (about 5 ft. 10 in.) and activity, but very slender, his leanness of body and limb (not of face) having been throughout life abnormal. The head was small; the eyes dark hazel, very wide-set, intent, and beaming; the face of a long oval shape; the expression rich and animated. He had a free and picturesque play of gesture and a voice of full and manly fibre, in which his pulmonary weakness was not at all betrayed. The features are familiar from many photographs and cuts. There exist also two small full-length portraits by Mr. John S. Sargent—one in the possession of the family, the other of Mr. Fairchild of Newport, U.S.A.; an oil sketch, done in one sitting, by Sir W. B. Richmond, now in the National Portrait Gallery; a drawing from life, by an American artist, Mr. Alexander; a large medallion portrait in bronze, in some respects excellent, by Mr. A. St. Gaudens of New York; and a portrait painted in 1893 at Samoa by Signor Nerli, now in private possession in Scotland.

His published writings, in book and pamphlet form, are as follows: 1. 'The Pentland Rising, a Page of History, 1666' (pamphlet), 1866. 2. 'An Appeal to the Church of Scotland' (pamphlet), 1875. 3. 'An Inland Voyage,' 1878. 4. 'Picturesque Notes on Edinburgh,' 1879. 5. 'Travels with a Donkey in the Cevennes,' 1879. 6. 'Virginibus Puerisque,' 1881. 7. 'Familiar Studies of Men and Books,' 1882. 8. 'Treasure Island,' 1882. 9. 'New Arabian Nights,' 1882. 10. 'The Silverado Squatters,' 1883. 11. 'Prince Otto,' 1885. 12. 'The Child's Garden of Verses,' 1885. 13. 'More New Arabian Nights: the Dynamiter,' 1885. 14. 'The Strange Case of Dr. Jekyll and Mr. Hyde,' 1886. 15. 'Kidnapped,' 1886. 16. 'The Merry Men and other Tales,' 1886. 17. 'Underwoods,' 1887. 18. 'Memories and Portraits,' 1887. 19. 'Memoir of Fleeming Jenkin' (prefixed to 'Papers of Fleeming Jenkin,' 2 vols.), 1887. 20. 'The Black Arrow,' 1888. 21. 'The Wrong Box' (in collaboration with Mr. Lloyd Osbourne), 1888. 22. 'The Master of Ballantrae,' 1889. 23. 'Ballads,' 1890. 24. 'Father Damien: an Open Letter' (pamphlet), 1890. 25. 'The Wrecker' (in collaboration with Mr. Lloyd Osbourne), 1892. 26. 'Across the Plains,' 1892. 27. 'A Footnote to History,' 1893. 28. 'Island Nights' Entertainments,' 1893. 29. 'Catriona' (being the sequel to 'Kidnapped'), 1893. 30. 'The Ebb-Tide' (in collaboration with Mr. Lloyd Osbourne), 1894. The above were published during his lifetime; the following have appeared posthumously: 31. 'Vailima Letters,' 1895. 32. 'Fables' (appended to a new edition of 'Jekyll and Hyde'), 1896. 33. 'Weir of Hermiston,' 1896. 34. 'Songs of Travel,' 1896. 35. 'St. Ives,' with the final chapters supplied by Mr. A. T. Quiller Couch, 1897. All the above have been reprinted in the limited 'Edinburgh Edition,' which also contains the 'Amateur Emigrant,' entire for the first time (the title-paper of No. 26, 'Across the Plains,' was the second part of this); the unfinished 'Family of Engineers,' which has not been printed elsewhere; the 'Story of a Lie,' the 'Misadventures of John Nicholson;' and the fragmentary romance, 'The Great North Road'—all here reprinted from periodicals for the first time; the 'South Sea Letters,' not elsewhere reprinted; as well as 'The Pentland Rising,' 'A Letter to the Church of Scotland,' the 'Edinburgh University Magazine Essays,' 'Lay Morals,' 'Prayers written for Family Use at Vailima,' and a number of other papers and fragments, early and late, which have not been collected elsewhere. The edition is in twenty-seven volumes, of which the first series of twenty appeared 15 Nov. 1894-15 June 1896, and the supplementary series of seven December 1896-February 1898.

[Stevenson's autobiographical writings, published and unpublished, of the author; his private correspondence; personal knowledge; information supplied by the members of the family. A biography with a further selection of letters is in preparation by the present writer.]

S. C.

STEVENSON, SETH WILLIAM (1784-1853), antiquary, was born at Norwich in 1784.

His father, WILLIAM STEVENSON (1741-1821), publisher and author, oldest son of the Rev. Seth Ellis Stevenson, rector of Treswell, Nottinghamshire, was born in 1741, and was a printer and publisher in the market-place at Norwich, the firm being Stevenson, Matchett, & Stevenson. For thirty-five years from 1785 or 1786 he was the proprietor of the 'Norfolk Chronicle.' In 1812 he saw through his own press a new edition of James Bentham's 'History of the Church of Ely.' In 1817 he brought out 'A Supplement' to the work. He also edited John Campbell's 'Lives of the British Admirals,' bringing the information down to 1812. To Nichols's 'Literary Anecdotes' and to the 'Gentleman's Magazine' he was a frequent contributor. For many years he was a fellow of the Society of Antiquaries. He died in Surrey Street, Norwich, on 13 May 1821 (Gent. Mag. May 1821, pp. 472-3).

His son, Seth William, was taken into partnership with his father and Jonathan Matchett. From an early period he was connected with the 'Norfolk Chronicle,' of which paper, on the death of his father, he became proprietor, and to a great extent editor to his death. In 1817 he printed for private circulation 'Journal of a Tour through part of France, Flanders, and Holland, including a visit to Paris and a walk over the Field of Waterloo in the summer of 1816.' This work was dedicated to the Society of United Friars of Norwich, a literary society of which he was almost the last survivor. In 1827 he published in two volumes 'A Tour in France, Savoy, Northern Italy, Switzerland, Germany, and the Netherlands,' and in the same year was elected a fellow of the Society of Antiquaries. In 1828 he was nominated a sheriff of the city of Norwich, became an alderman in the same year, and served the office of mayor in 1832. He was elected an associate of the British Archæological Association in 1845, and on the establishment of the Numismatic Society in 1836 he became a member. For many years all his leisure time was engaged in composing a complete dictionary of Roman coins. His idea was to give an explanation of the types, symbols, and devices on consular and imperial coins, biographical notices of the emperors from Julius to Mauricius, and mythological, historical, and geographical notices in elucidation of rare coins. This work, with illustrations by Frederick William Fairholt [q. v.], was left incomplete at the time of his death, as to the last letters U to Z. It was then revised in part by Charles Roach Smith [q. v.], and, being completed by Frederic William Madden, was published, after many delays, in 1889 under the title of 'A Dictionary of Roman Coins, Republican and Imperial,' and remains the standard work on the subject. Stevenson died at Cambridge on 22 Dec. 1853, in the house of his son-in-law, John Deighton, surgeon.

By his wife Mary, he had two sons, of whom Mr. Henry Stevenson, F.L.S., is author of 'The Birds of Norfolk' (1866–90, 3 vols. 8vo).

[Numismatic Chronicle, 1855, vol. xvii., Proceedings, pp. 17–18; Smith's Retrospections, 1883, i. 248–51; Smith's Collectanea Antiqua, 1861, v. 276; Journal British Archæol. Assoc. 1855, x. 124–5; Gent. Mag. 1854, li. 298.]

G. C. B.

· STEVENSON, THOMAS (1818–1887), engineer and meteorologist, born in Edinburgh on 22 July 1818, was youngest son of Robert Stevenson [q. v.], and was brother of Alan Stevenson [q. v.], and of David Stevenson [q. v.] He was educated at the high school of Edinburgh, where he showed an incapacity for arithmetical calculation which remained with him through life. His mathematical faculty was, however, above the average, and he acquired a knowledge of Latin which he cultivated in later years, Lactantius, Lucan, Vossius, and Cardinal Bona becoming favourite authors. In youth he

formed an ardent love of the English classics, and soon developed the habits of a book collector and the faculty of writing English with grace, vigour, and distinction.

In his seventeenth year Stevenson entered his father's office with a view to becoming an engineer. When his apprenticeship was over he in 1842 wrote a paper on the defects of the rain-gauges then in use, with a description of one of an improved form. This was published in the 'Edinburgh New Philosophical Journal,' 1842, xxxiii. 12–21, and was the first of a series of numerous contributions to scientific journals on such subjects as lighthouse and harbour engineering, lighthouse optics, experiments on the force of waves, and meteorology. By 1883 these papers had reached a total of forty-four (see Royal Society's Cat. of Scientific Papers, 1800–63 p. 829, 1864–73 pp. 1014–15, and 1874–83 pp. 495–6). In 1843 Stevenson superintended the construction of the lighthouse on Little Ross Island on the Solway, and wrote a paper on the geology of the island (Edinb. New Phil. Journ. xxxv. 83–8). In 1846 he became a partner in his father's firm, and in 1853 he and his brother David were appointed engineers to the board of northern lighthouses. This position he held till his health failed in 1885.

Stevenson won his chief reputation by his successful pursuit of the experiments in lighthouse illumination, which his brother, Alan Stevenson, began. By his efforts 'the great sea lights in every quarter of the world now shine more brightly.' His crowning invention was his 'azimuthal condensing system of lighthouse illumination.' No attempt had previously been made to allocate the auxiliary light in proportion to the varying lengths of the different ranges and the amplitudes of the arcs to be illuminated, or, where a light had to show all round the horizon, to weaken its intensity in one arc, and with the rays so abstracted to strengthen some other arc, which from its range being longer required to be of greater power. To perfecting this invention he devoted the greater part of his time from 1855 to 1885. Other inventions and improvements he described in his 'Lighthouse Illumination,' 1859 (2nd ed. 1871, expanded into 'Lighthouse Construction and Illumination,' 1881; see SIR DAVID BREWSTER, Reply to Messrs. D. and T. Stevenson's Pamphlet on Lighthouses, 1860), and in his article 'Lighthouse' in the ninth edition of the 'Encyclopædia Britannica.'

Other separately issued works were: 'Design and Construction of Harbours,' 1864, Edinburgh (2nd ed. 1874; 3rd ed. 1886), a reprint of the article in the eighth edition of the 'Encyclopædia Britannica,' and 'Proposal for the Illumination of Beacons and Buoys,' 1870.

Stevenson was elected a fellow of the Royal Society of Edinburgh in 1848, served frequently on its council, and became its president in 1885. He was elected a member of the Institution of Civil Engineers in 1864, and president of the Royal Scottish Society of Arts in 1859-60. His contributions to the transactions of these and other societies were many and varied. Outside his profession his interests were mainly concentrated on meteorology. He was one of the originators of the Scottish Meteorological Society in 1855, was member of council from the commencement, and, on the death of Dr. Keith Johnstone q.v. in 1871, was elected its honorary secretary. Among the original and permanent contributions he made to meteorology were the Stevenson screen for the protection of thermometers, designed in 1864, and now in universal use; the introduction in 1867 into meteorological investigations of the term 'barometric gradient,' which is now commonly employed in the science; and the means of ascertaining, by high and low level observations, the vertical gradients for atmospheric pressure, temperature, and humidity which are fundamental data in meteorology.

In later years Stevenson published 'Christianity confirmed by Jewish and Heathen Testimony, and the Deductions from Physical Science,' Edinburgh, 1877, 2nd edit. 1879. He died at his house, 17 Heriot Row, Edinburgh, on 8 May 1887. By his wife, Margaret Isabella, daughter of the Rev. James Balfour, minister of Colinton, he was father of Robert Louis Stevenson [q. v.] His widow died on 14 May 1897.

[Personal knowledge; Works in Brit. Mus. Libr.; Scotsman, 9 May 1887; Times, 9 May 1887 and 16 May 1897; Proc. Royal Society of Edinburgh, vol. xx. pp. lxi-lxxviii; R. L. Stevenson's Memoirs and Portraits, p. 132.]

A. B.

STEVENSON, WILLIAM (1719?-1783), physician, an Irishman by birth, born about 1719, was first cousin to Andrew Thomas Stewart, sixth baron Stewart of Stewart Castle, co. Tyrone. The Stewarts removed to Scotland in consequence of the troublous times in Ireland at the beginning of the eighteenth century, and it was probably for this reason that Stevenson received his medical education at the university of Edinburgh. Here he studied under Alexander Monro I and Alexander Monro II, John Rutherford (1695-1779) [q. v.], Whytt, and Cullen.

He graduated M.D. with the inaugural thesis 'De Diabete,' and remained in the city two years longer, partly to study medicine further and partly for instruction in divinity. He was one of the earliest members of the Edinburgh Medical Society, founded in 1737, and he appears to have served for a time in the army, for he says that he 'was formerly commander of one of his majesty's forts.' He practised for some time at Coleraine in Ireland, and then moved to Wells in Somerset, where he was practising as a physician in 1779. He lived for a short time at Bath, but moved to Newark at the end of May 1781. Here he died suddenly on 13 April 1783.

A presbyterian in religion and a Jacobite in politics, Stevenson in his later years was constantly at variance with his surroundings. He hated the apothecaries, he despised the College of Physicians, and he abhorred the therapeutic measures adopted by his contemporaries. His pen was venomous, and he spent his life lampooning and being lampooned. He appears to have been a shrewd physician, magnifying his calling, disbelieving in the efficacy of drugs or of bleeding, but with an abiding faith in the curative value of blisters and issues. His contemporaries regarded him as a malignant quack, who endeavoured to destroy their lucrative practice by explaining away the remedial action of the Bath waters in gout.

His works were: 1. 'A Successful Method of treating the Gout by Blistering, with an Introduction consisting of Miscellaneous Matter,' Bath, 1779, 8vo. 2. 'Cases of Medicine interspersed with Strictures occasioned by some late Medical Transactions in the town of Newark,' London, 1782, 8vo. 3. 'Dr. Stevenson's Reply to a Letter addressed to Dr. Stevenson of Newark by Ed. Harrison,' Newark, 1782, 8vo. 4. 'Candid Animadversions on . . . a Singular Gouty Case, to which are prefixed Strictures on Royal Medical Colleges, likewise a summary Opinion of the late Disorder called the Influenza,' Newark, 1782, 8vo. 5. 'Considerations on the Dangerous Effects of Promiscuous Blood-letting and the common Preposterous Administration of Drugs, with other Coincident Subjects, Medical and Moral,' Newark, 1783, 8vo. This work is incomplete, and was published after Stevenson's death.

[Autobiographical details in Stevenson's works; Gent. Mag. 1783, i. 366; Watt's Bibl. Brit.]

D'A. P.

STEVENSON, WILLIAM (1772-1829), keeper of the records in the treasury, son of a captain in the royal navy, was born at Berwick-upon-Tweed on 26 Nov.

1772. He was educated at the grammar school there under Joseph Romney. In 1787 he entered the academy at Daventry as a student for the ministry, and in 1789 the academy was removed to Northampton, where he completed his course of study. After a short sojourn at Bruges as tutor to an English family, the outbreak of the war in 1792 compelled him to return to England, where he obtained the post of classical tutor at Manchester academy. While at Manchester he became an Arian under the influence of Thomas Barnes, D.D. (1747–1810) [q. v.] For a short time he preached at Doblane, near that town, but, becoming convinced of the impropriety of a paid ministry, he resigned his posts and went as a pupil to a farmer in East Lothian. In 1797 he took a farm at Laughton, near Edinburgh; but after four or five years he relinquished farming, and set up a boarding-house for students in Drummond Street, Edinburgh. Shortly after he became editor of the 'Scots Magazine,' to which he contributed numerous essays. In 1806 James Maitland, eighth earl of Lauderdale, who had been offered by Fox the post of governor-general of India, invited Stevenson to accompany him as private secretary. Owing to the strenuous opposition of the East India Company, Lord Lauderdale withdrew his claims to the governor-generalship, but he compensated his secretary by obtaining for him the office of keeper of the records to the treasury. Soon after Stevenson declined the czar's offer of the professorship of technology at the university of Kharkov. He continued to reside in the neighbourhood of London till his death, at his house at Chelsea, on 20 March 1829. He was twice married. By his first wife, Eliza Holland of Sandlebridge in Cheshire, he had two children, a son John and a daughter Elizabeth Cleghorn, who married William Gaskell [q. v.], and became well known as a novelist [see GASKELL, ELIZABETH CLEGHORN]. Stevenson's first wife died in 1810, and in 1814 he married Catherine, daughter of Alexander Thomson of Savannah in Georgia. By her he had a son and daughter.

Stevenson was the author of: 1. 'Remarks on the very inferior Utility of Classical Learning,' London, 1796, 4to. 2. 'A System of Land-Surveying,' 1805, 4to; London, 1810, 4to. 3. 'General View of the Agriculture of the County of Surrey,' London, 1809, 8vo. 4. 'General View of the Agriculture of the County of Dorset,' London, 1812, 8vo. 5. 'Historical Sketch of Discovery, Navigation, and Commerce,' Edinburgh and London, 1824, 8vo. He also contributed the article on chivalry to Dr. Brewster's 'Edin-

burgh Encyclopædia,' wrote the life of Carton and other treatises for the Society for the Diffusion of Useful Knowledge, besides writing numerous articles for the 'Edinburgh Review,' the 'Retrospective Review,' and other magazines, and compiling the greater part of the 'Annual Register' for several years.

[Annual Biography and Obituary, 1830, pp. 208–14; Gent. Mag. 1829, i. 644; Macculloch's Literature of Political Economy, p. 148; Donaldson's Agricultural Biography, p. 97; Allibone's Dict. of Engl. Lit.]   E. I. C.

STEVENSON, W. B. (fl. 1803–1825), writer on South America, landed on the coast of Chili in the Indian district of Araucania about 1803, with the intention of travelling through the country. On proceeding to Arauco he found himself detained a prisoner on the pretext that war had broken out between Spain and England. Thence he was conveyed successively to Concepcion, Callao, and Lima, where he was confined in the gaol for eight months with the most abandoned criminals. His liberty was gradually extended, and he was permitted to reside in the town and to make excursions into the adjoining provinces. In 1808 he became private secretary to Count Ruis de Castilla, president and captain-general of Quito. On the outbreak of the revolution at Quito, where he was stationed, he joined the insurgents. In December 1810 he was appointed governor of the Esmeraldas with the title of lieutenant-colonel, and after the arrival of Lord Cochrane in 1818 he became his secretary and had a share in many of his naval operations [see COCHRANE, THOMAS, tenth EARL OF DUNDONALD]. After twenty years' residence in South America he revisited England about 1824, returning to Peru about the end of 1825. The date of his death is not known.

While in England he published the results of his American experiences in a work entitled 'A Historical and Descriptive Narrative of twenty years' residence in South America,' London, 1825, 8vo. His book is of great value for the period immediately preceding the South American revolution. He used his unique opportunities for observation to advantage. Prescott, in his 'History of the Conquest of Peru,' praised his description of Lima, and made considerable use of his accounts of native manners and customs. Translations into French and German were published at Paris and Weimar respectively in 1826.

[Stevenson's Historical Narrative; Allibone's Dict. of Engl. Lit.; Monthly Review, 1825, iii. 66; Literary Gazette, 1825, p. 627.]   E. I. C.

s

STEVENSON, WILLIAM FLEMING (1832–1886), Irish divine, youngest child of William Stevenson, a merchant in Strabane, co. Tyrone, by Margaret Anne, daughter of Samuel Morton, was born at Strabane on 20 Sept. 1832. After being taught for some time by a private tutor, he was sent in 1844 to the Royal Academical Institution, Belfast, where he remained until in 1848 he entered the university of Glasgow. Here he graduated M.A. in 1851, when he commenced the study of theology at New College, Edinburgh. His course completed, he went in 1854 to Germany, where he studied for some time at the universities of Berlin and Heidelberg, and made his first acquaintance with those forms of Christian activity which he afterwards described in 'Praying and Working.' In 1856 he was licensed to preach by the presbytery of Strabane, and in the autumn of 1857 became a town missionary in Belfast, where a virulent attack of typhus, caught in the discharge of his duties, almost cost him his life. After holding two temporary appointments, one as *locum tenens* in Bonn for William Graham, D.D. (1810–1883) [q. v.], in 1858, and the other as assistant to the Rev. D. McKee in Belfast in 1859, he was ordained on 1 March 1860 as minister of a newly established presbyterian congregation at Rathgar, a suburb of Dublin. Two years later a new church there, built largely through Stevenson's exertions, was opened. So popular were his ministrations that it was soon filled, and was twice enlarged.

Stevenson's literary activity began early. In 1855 he commenced writing in the 'Edinburgh Christian Instructor,' then edited by Dr. Norman Macleod (1812–1872) [q. v.] To 'Good Words' he contributed from the beginning. 'Praying and Working' first appeared in its early numbers. It was published separately in 1862, and was very popular from the first. In 1873 he published a large selection of 'Hymns for the Church and Home,' which had a wide circulation.

Meanwhile, in 1871, Stevenson's deep interest in foreign missions caused him to be appointed colleague to the Rev. James Morgan, D.D. [q. v.], Belfast, in the honorary convenership of the Irish General Assembly's foreign mission. On Morgan's death in 1873 he became sole convener. Much of his time and thought was henceforth devoted to this enterprise. As an auxiliary to it he founded a zenana mission. In 1877, accompanied by his wife, he made, at the request of the general assembly, a journey round the world, visiting mission stations, especially in China and India. In 1879–80 he held the chair of evangelistic theology in New College, Edinburgh, and from 1882 till 1886 he was Duff lecturer on foreign missions. A series of lectures which he delivered in this last capacity was published posthumously in 1887, under the title 'The Dawn of the Modern Mission.' In 1881 he was elected to the lectureship founded in Londonderry in memory of Richard Smyth [q. v.], and lectured on his favourite theme, 'The History and Methods of Christian Missions.'

Many other public duties also devolved upon him. In 1879 he was appointed by the crown one of the first senators of the newly established Royal University of Ireland. In 1881 he was elected moderator of the general assembly, and in the same year received the honorary degree of D.D. from the university of Edinburgh. In 1886 he was appointed chaplain to the lord lieutenant of Ireland (the Earl of Aberdeen), being the first presbyterian clergyman selected for that office. His multiplied activities wore him prematurely out, and he died suddenly on 16 Sept. 1886. He was buried in Mount Jerome cemetery, Dublin. 'The Fleming Stevenson Missionary Training College' was established in his memory at Ahmedabad, and his library, now called 'The Stevenson Memorial Library,' was presented to the Assembly's College, Belfast.

Stevenson married, in 1865, Elizabeth Montgomery, eldest daughter of John Sinclair, esq., Belfast. He left two sons, one of whom became a missionary to India, and three daughters.

[Life and Letters, by his wife, 1886, 2nd edit. 1890; Biographical Sketch prefixed to posthumous edition of Praying and Working, 1886; personal knowledge.]　　　　　T. H.

STEWARD. [See also STEUART, STEWART, and STUART.]

STEWARD, ROBERT THE (1316–1390), king of Scotland. [See ROBERT II.]

STEWARD or STEWART, RICHARD (1593?–1651), dean-designate of St. Paul's and Westminster, and clerk of the closet to Charles I, was baptised at Pateshull, Northamptonshire, on 3 Aug. 1595, probably some two years after his birth. He was third son of Nicholas Steward, esq., of Pateshull. His mother's maiden name was Madox. From Westminster school he matriculated at Magdalen Hall, Oxford, on 1 Dec. 1609. He graduated B.A. in 1612, M.A. in 1615, B.C.L. in 1617, and D.C.L. on 3 July 1624. In 1613 he was elected fellow of All Souls', and in 1622 served the office of proctor. Having taken orders, he became rector of Harrietsham, Kent, in 1626, and on 17 July 1629 was named prebendary of Worcester. In the following year he also became vicar of Aldbourne, and rector of Mildenhall, Norfolk, and of Alton Barnes, Wiltshire. With the last benefice he also held a canonry at Salisbury. He was made a chaplain in ordinary and clerk of the closet to Charles I in 1633, and two years later he received an annuity of 100*l.* from the royal exchequer. On 6 March 1635 he received in addition the deanery of Chichester. In 1638 he resigned his stall at Worcester on becoming prebendary of Westminster (see *Cal. State Papers,* Dom. 1638, p. 305). On 24 Dec. 1639, on the nomination of the king, who dispensed with the statutory obligation requiring membership of the foundation, Steward became provost of Eton in succession to Sir Henry Wotton. In April of the following year he acted as prolocutor of convocation, and was zealous in obtaining the vote of subsidies. He was rewarded by the nomination to the deanery of St. Paul's in 1641, but for some reason was not definitely appointed. On 15 March 1642 he was admitted to the prebend of St. Pancras, and in 1643 he was made dean of the chapel royal. But in the same year he was dispossessed by parliament of the provostship of Eton in favour of Francis Rous [q. v.], and was subsequently deprived of his other preferments. The civil war also prevented him from taking possession of the deanery of Westminster, to which he was nominated in 1645 on the expiry of Archbishop Williams's commendam.

Steward was held in high favour by Charles I. In January 1645 he, together with five other divines, was sent by the king to Uxbridge, 'to attend the commissioners for their devotions and for the other service of the church, as the management of the treaty required' (CLARENDON). He vigorously defended episcopacy. Whitelocke says that Steward 'spake very learnedly (tho' seeming frowardly) against the presbyterian government in the church of England.' After hearing the answers of Henderson and Marshall, he 'thought the disputes to be too various and general, and desired that they might dispute syllogistically as became scholars.' When the discussion was renewed after an interval, he again 'argued very positively.' In August 1646 Charles I, writing from Newcastle, recommended Steward to the Prince of Wales as a trusty servant, and desired him to defer to his opinion 'in all things concerning conscience and church affairs' (*Clarendon State Papers*). From this time Steward seems to have followed the fortunes of Prince Charles. In

1649 he strongly opposed a clause in the proposed royal declaration drawn up by Hyde, to the effect that foreign divines should be admitted to the national synod which was to consult upon the church of England. He protested to the chancellor that he had not slept on account of the 'agony and trouble' caused by his proposal, 'and went from him to the king to beseech him never to approve it.' In the summer of 1650 he was in Jersey, whence, under the name of Nicholson, he corresponded with Sir Edward Nicholas. In August he told Nicholas that he had been received into his highness's (the Duke of York's) favour. He followed the duke from Paris to Brussels, but returned to Paris in 1651, and Evelyn heard him preach at an extraordinary fast on 21 July. While in France he preached several striking sermons. Steward died at Paris on 14 Nov. 1651. He was buried in the protestant cemetery near St. Germain des Prés. Some words in his epitaph summarise his aspirations: 'Qui moriens nihil aliud hic inscribi voluit quam quod vivens assidue oravit pro pace Ecclesiæ' (cf. KENNET, *Register,* 1728; WOOD, *History of the University of Oxford*). Steward married a daughter of Sir William Button of Tokenham, Wiltshire, and left two sons: Charles (1666-1735), and Knightley Steward (1673-1746), both of whom were beneficed clergymen.

Steward's influence over Charles II, who twice visited him on his deathbed, did much to counteract the influence of the presbyterian party. Evelyn described his death as a great loss to the whole church. Wood (who spells the name 'Steuart') says that in the university he was accounted a good poet and orator, and that he was an eloquent preacher with 'a smart fluent stile.' Clarendon characterises him as a very honest and learned gentleman, whose heart was set upon vindicating the dignity and authority of the church 'not without some prejudice to those who thought there was any other object to be more carefully pursued' (*Life,* fol. edit. p. 124). Steward supplied him with some materials for his 'History of the Rebellion,' more especially regarding the Uxbridge conference.

Steward published: 1. 'Three Sermons,' 1656, 12mo; reissued in 1658 with a fourth by Samuel Harsnett, archbishop of York, and an 'Epistle to the Reader,' by T. H. 2. 'Catholique Divinity; or the most solid and sententious expressions of the Primitive Doctors of the Church, with other Ecclesiastical and Civil Authors,' &c., 1657, 8vo (prefatory remarks by H. M.) 3. 'Trias Sacra: a second ternary of Sermons,' 1659,

12mo; reissued as 'Golden Remains, being the last and best Monuments that are likely to be made publick,' 1660. 4. 'A Discourse of Episcopacy and Sacrilege,' 1683; originally printed in 1647 as an answer to a 'Letter to Dr. Samuel Turner' by John Fountaine. 'The Old Puritan detected and defeated,' 1689, is also attributed to him by the printer Sherlock; it was an attempt to prove that the fifty-fifth canon of James I did not favour extempore prayers.

A portrait was engraved by Stow from a picture at Eton. In it he is depicted holding the ribbon, with an augel of gold attached, which was placed round the neck of those who touched for the king's evil.

[The age of Steward as given in his epitaph does not agree with that of his matriculation entry. For his pedigree see Baker's Northamptonshire, ii. 298, 304. See also Welch's Alumni Westmon. pp. 20, 21; Foster's Alumni Oxon.; Wood's Athenæ Oxon. ed. Bliss, iii. 295-8 n., and Fasti Oxon. i. 357, 372, 404, 416; Le Neve's Fasti Eccles. Anglicanæ, i. 258, ii. 315, 425, iii. 79, 344, 348, 352, 492; Cal. State Papers, Dom. 1635 p. 122, 1638 pp. 305, 345, 1639-40 p. 175, 1640 p. 76, 1650 pp. 186, 271, 351, 384, 385, 394, 414-15; Cal. Clarendon State Papers, i. 227, 329, 333, 356, 437, ii. 110; Clarendon's Hist. of the Rebellion, ed. Macray, 1888, iii. 475, 479, 481-3, iv. 341, v. 42, 43, 235; Evelyn's Diary; Whitelocke's Memorials, pp. 128, 132; Stanley's Memorials of Westminster Abbey, 3rd edit. p. 513; Notes and Queries, 6th ser. x. 493, 494, xi. 75, 76, 7th ser. iv. 473; Evans's Cat. Engr. Portraits.] G. Le G. N.

STEWARD, STYWARD, or WELLS, ROBERT (d. 1557), first dean of Ely, born, it is said, at Wells in Norfolk, was the eldest son of Simeon Steward and his wife Joan, daughter and heiress of Edward Ikesteney of Soham, Cambridgeshire. According to a pedigree which the dean says he extracted from the heralds' rolls (it is printed in WHARTON, *Anglia Sacra*, i. 686-8, from a manuscript at Lambeth; cf. TODD, *Cat.* p. 25), the family, of which Elizabeth Steward, Oliver Cromwell's mother, was a later member, descended from a Sir John Steward (d. 1448), a kinsman of the royal house of Scotland, who came to England in Henry V's reign. Apparently, however, the Stewards of Norfolk were settled there long before the arrival of the somewhat fabulous Sir John, who is presumably meant to be Sir John Stuart or Stewart (1365?-1429) [q. v.], and the name was usually spelt Styward (*Genealogist*, 1884, pp. 150-57, where Mr. Walter Rye prints an anonymous pedigree similar to the dean's, with a critical examination of it in *ib.* 1885, pp. 34 et seq.) Among the dean's brothers were Simeon

Steward, grandfather of Sir Simeon Steward [q. v.]; Thomas Steward (d. 1568), who was pastor of the English church at Frankfurt during Mary's reign, and canon of Ely from 1560 till his death; Edmund Steward (d. 1559), who was chancellor of the diocese of Norwich until 1528, and afterwards chancellor and dean of Winchester under Gardiner (COOPER, *Athenæ Cantabr.* i. 205, 263, 555); and Nicholas Steward or Styward (fl. 1560), who was recommended by Andrew Perne (1519?-1589) [q. v.] as his successor in the chancellorship of Norwich (STRYPE, *Parker*, ii. 362, 398, 433, *Whitgift*, ii. 32, iii. 235; *Parker Corresp.*, Parker Soc. pp. 460, 476).

Robert became a monk at Ely, when he adopted as his name the place of his birth. He graduated B.A. at Cambridge in 1516 and M.A. in 1520, but must probably be distinguished from the Dr. Steward who was chaplain to Wolsey, and afterwards a member of Thomas Cromwell's household (*Letters and Papers of Henry VIII*, vol. iv. App. art. 230). About 1522 he was elected prior of Ely, and in that capacity took the chief part in the election of Thomas Goodrich [q. v.] as bishop of that see in 1534. In the convocation of 1529 he maintained the validity of Henry's marriage with Catherine of Aragon; but he found reason to change his views, and became one of Henry's instruments in persuading monasteries to surrender to the king (cf. *Letters and Papers*, XIII. ii. 320; but it is possible that the Dr. Robert Steward there mentioned was not the prior of Ely). In 1536 he was nominated a candidate for the suffragan-bishopric of Colchester, but the king appointed William More (d. 1540) [q. v.] On 18 Nov. 1539 he surrendered the monastery at Ely to the king, and, perhaps as a reward for his compliance, received the considerable pension of 120l., and on 10 Sept. 1541, when the see was refounded, he was appointed its first dean. He then resumed his family name of Steward. He complied with the religious changes under Edward VI and Mary, retaining his deanery until his death on 22 Sept. 1557. He was buried in Ely Cathedral, and his memorial inscription is printed in Bentham's 'Ely' and Cooper's 'Athenæ Cantabrigienses.'

Besides the genealogy mentioned above, Steward continued the 'Historia Eliensis' from 1486 to 1554. The manuscript was formerly preserved at Lambeth, and was printed in Wharton's 'Anglia Sacra' (i. 675-7).

[Todd's Cat. Lambeth MSS. pp. 25, 57; Wharton's Anglia Sacra, vol. i. pp. xlvi-xlvii, 675-7, 686-8; Tanner's Bibl. Brit.-Hib. p. 692; Letters and Papers of Henry VIII; Wright's

Letters relating to Suppression of Monasteries (Camd. Soc.), p. 4; Bentham's Ely, pp. 224 et seq., with Stevenson's Supplement, pp. 121, 143; Dugdale's Mon. Angl. ed. Caley, Ellis, and Bandinel, i. 468–9; Fiddes's Life of Wolsey, p. 202; Egerton MS. 2599, f. 5 (for his nephew Robert's will).]

A. F. P.

STEWARD, Sir SIMEON (d. 1629?), poet, was the son of Sir Mark Steward, by his wife Anna, the daughter of Dr. Robert Huick, one of Queen Elizabeth's physicians. Sir Mark was the son of another Sir Simeon, who was a brother of Robert Steward, dean of Ely [q. v.] According to an untrustworthy family legend recorded on Sir Mark's tomb, an ancestor sailed with James I from his home near Dundee, was captured by the English off Flamborough Head in 1405, married an Englishwoman, and, having transferred his allegiance to Henry V, settled in Cambridgeshire. The poet's father received the honour of knighthood at Whitehall in July 1603. He was then seventy-nine years old, and he died in the following November, when a splendid monument, with a recumbent figure, was erected by his son to his memory in the south aisle of Ely Cathedral.

Simeon Steward was educated at Trinity Hall, Cambridge, and while still in residence was knighted by James I at Whitehall, previous to the coronation, on 23 July 1603. He lived at Trinity Hall for many years, and was known to Robert Herrick and Thomas Fuller, who describes the coat-of-arms which Steward caused to be carved over his chimneypiece. The room was probably the 'chamber under ye Library West,' but the arms have long since disappeared (WARREN, Cat. of Fellows ap. WILLIS's Architect. of Cambr. i. 239). In 1614 he represented Shaftesbury in parliament, and in 1624 he was returned for Cambridgeshire; but his election was declared void upon a petition. In 1627, however, he entered parliament again as member for Aldeburgh. A defaced copy of some elegiac verses upon the death of Sir S. (?) Steward, undated, but probably written in 1629, would refer his death to this year.

Herrick sent Steward some verses as a new year's gift in January 1624, in full confidence of his appreciation; for the knight was the possessor of a small claim to rank as a poet himself. Inspired, it would appear, by Spenser and Shakespeare, he wrote a graceful poem called 'The Faerey King.' This appeared under his name in a volume entitled 'A Description of the King & Queene of Fayries. Their Habit, Fare, their Abode, Pompe, & State' (London, for Richard Harper, 1635, 8vo). Steward's contribution to the volume was reprinted in 'Musarum

Deliciæ' (1656), and in the rare volume of 'Bibliographical Miscellanies' printed at Oxford in 1813 by Dr. Bliss, who made several manuscript notes relating to the 'Faerey King' in his copy, now in the British Museum. The version he prints was discovered by him among the Rawlinson manuscripts in the Bodleian Library (Rawl. MS., Poet. 147), and differs in numerous points from that in the 'Musarum Deliciæ.' Steward's poem reappeared in Mr. A. E. Waite's selection of fairy poems, entitled 'Elfin Music' (London, 1888, 12mo).

[Fuller's Worthies, s. 'Cambridgeshire;' Bentham's History of Ely, pp. 287, App. p. 49; Willis's Architect. History of the University of Cambridge; Noble's Hist. of the House of Cromwell, ii. 339; Cal. State Papers, Dom. 1624–5; Metcalfe's Book of Knights, p. 247; Members of Parliaments; Herrick's Works, 1891, i. 157; Notes and Queries, 8th ser. v. 194; Genealogist, 1885, p. 37.]

T. S.

STEWARD, THOMAS, D.D. (1669?–1753), presbyterian divine, was born about 1669, probably at Norwich. His family was originally of Lackford, Suffolk. He was educated for the ministry by John Collinges, D.D. [q. v.], and in 1689, on the recommendation of John Fairfax (1623–1700) [q. v.], was settled in a congregation at Debenham, Suffolk. In 1706 he succeeded Elias Travers as minister of Cook Street presbyterian congregation, Dublin, on a stipend of 80l. His house rent cost him 20l., and he complains that, funeral sermons being 'quite out of fashion,' he got 'nothing in that way,' and as there was no fee for baptism, 'neither burials nor births are of any advantage to me.' Steward was orthodox, though a nonsubscriber; he attended with Joseph Boyse [q. v.] and others as a deputation from the Dublin presbytery to the general synod of Ulster at Derry (1722), when a vain attempt was made to heal the non-subscription controversy. In 1724 he left Dublin and became minister of the presbyterian congregation at Bury St. Edmund's, Suffolk. He received the diploma of D.D. from Aberdeen in 1738. He was a correspondent of Francis Hutcheson, (1694–1746) [q. v.], Philip Doddridge, D.D. [q. v.], John Leland (1691–1766) [q. v.], and Cromwell Mortimer [q. v.] He died at Bury St. Edmund's on 10 Sept. 1753, aged 84. His wife died in 1749.

Besides one or two tracts, he published 'Sermons,' 1734, 8vo. In the 'Philosophical Transactions Abridged,' 1738, viii. 209, is his paper on a remedy for the bite of a mad dog. A folio volume of manuscript letters in Latin and English, containing about eighty originals addressed to Steward, and twenty copies of his replies, was in 1879 in the possession of Sir Edward Reid of Derry.

[Browne's Hist. of Congregationalism in Norfolk and Suffolk, 1877, pp. 420, 491; Withrow's Hist. and Lit. Memorials of Presbyterianism in Ireland, 1879, i. 175 sq.; Irwin's Hist. of Presbyterianism in Dublin, 1890, p. 322; Records of Gen. Synod of Ulster, 1897, ii. 24 sq.]

A. G.

STEWARDSON, THOMAS (1781–1859), portrait-painter, born at Kendal in August 1781, was son of John and Anne Stewardson of Kendal, who belonged to a quaker family at Ullsmoor, near Shap in Westmoreland. After a short apprenticeship with John Fothergill, a painter at Kendal, Stewardson studied for some years under George Romney [q. v.], who painted a portrait of him, which is stated to have been engraved. After this he came to London, and exhibited for the first time at the Royal Academy in 1804. A portrait was painted of Stewardson in that year by John Opie [q. v.], from whom he is also said to have received instruction; this portrait was engraved in mezzotint by W. W. Barney. Stewardson settled at first in Leadenhall Street, where he soon obtained a considerable practice as a portrait-painter, his portraits being well drawn and the colouring good. He painted members of the family of the Duke of Marlborough, the Marquis of Winchester, and others; and among his sitters were Sir Thomas S. Pasley, bart., the Right. Hon. George Canning (engraved for the National Portrait Gallery, i. 75), Lord Skelmersdale, the Earl of Liverpool, and others. Latterly he resided in Adam Street, Adelphi. A portrait, by Stewardson, of George Grote, the historian, is in the National Portrait Gallery. Many of his portraits were engraved. Stewardson sometimes painted fancy subjects, usually with children in them. One of these, 'The Indian Serpent Charmer,' exhibited at the Royal Academy in 1816, attracted a good deal of attention. He was prevented by illness from practising his profession for the last thirty years of his life, and died, unmarried, at his lodgings in Pall Mall on 28 Aug. 1859. He was buried in Kensal Green cemetery.

[Redgrave's Dict. of Artists; information from Mr. Thomas Stewardson of Philadelphia, U.S.A.; Gent. Mag. 1859, ii. 538; Rogers's Opie and his Works.]

L. C.

STEWART. [See also STEUART, STEWARD, and STUART.]

STEWART, ALEXANDER, EARL OF BUCHAN and LORD OF BADENOCH, called the 'Wolf of Badenoch' (1343?–1405?), born probably before 1344, was the fourth son of King Robert II of Scotland, by his mistress Elizabeth Mure, whom he subsequently married in 1347. He received from his father a grant of the lands of Badenoch on 30 March 1371, with the famous castle of Lochindorb, but he exercised lordship over Badenoch and Strathspey at an earlier date, for in August 1370 he promised Alexander Burr, bishop of Moray, that he would protect the bishop's lands and tenants within the territories named (Registrum Moraviense, p. 171). In 1372 he was king's lieutenant and justiciary north of the Forth. As such he held court at the standing stones of the Rathe of Kingussie and afterwards in his castle of Ruthven in Badenoch on 10 and 11 Oct. 1380, when a serious debate took place between him and the bishop of Moray, who denied the lieutenant's jurisdiction and appealed direct to the crown. The matter ended in favour of the bishop, and the process, with the lieutenant's decree against him, was solemnly burned in presence of the assemblage. This was followed a year later by a declaration from Stewart renouncing jurisdiction over the church lands in the district (ib. pp. 183–9). About 1382 the lord of Badenoch married Euphemia, countess of Ross, daughter of William, earl of Ross, and widow of Sir Walter Lesley, and by this marriage he became, or was created, Earl of Buchan, acquiring also the lordship of Ross and other large possessions (Registrum Magni Sigilli, i. 165 et seq.). He however deserted his wife for another woman, perhaps the mother of his children, and in November 1389 the censure of the church was pronounced upon him by the bishops of Moray and Ross. Resentment for this and other causes of quarrel between him and the bishop of Moray probably led the earl to incite his men, in May 1390, to burn the town of Forres and certain church buildings there; while in the month following he himself in person led a lawless band against Elgin, destroying by fire the hospital there, the houses of the clergy, and the noble and beautiful cathedral, and earning for himself his popular designation, the 'Wolf of Badenoch.' For this offence he was excommunicated, but was afterwards absolved by the bishop of St. Andrews in the presence of Robert III at Perth (Registrum Moraviense, pp. 353, 381).

After this the earl appears to have taken little part in public affairs, and it is usually stated that he died on 24 July 1394. But this is an error first published by Duncan Stewart (History of the Stewarts) in 1739, and repeated by later writers, though there is sufficient evidence to the contrary. Thus, on 3 May 1398, he was ordered by his brother, Robert III, to deliver up the castle of Spynie to William, bishop of Moray (*Registrum Moraviense*, p. 208); and in 1402 the king wrote to him as crown bailie over the earldom of Athole (*Memorials of the Family of Wemyss, &c.*, ed. Fraser, ii. 44). Other evidence, and specially that of the exchequer rolls of Scotland (iii. 600, 634), points to the date of the earl's death as the end of 1404 or beginning of 1405, probably February 1405. The earl had no issue by his wife, but he had several natural children, Alexander (who became Earl of Mar) [q. v.], Duncan, Sir Andrew of Sandhaugh, Walter and James; also a daughter Margaret, who married Robert, earl of Sutherland. The earl's tomb is still to be seen in the church of Dunkeld, though much defaced, having, it is said, been destroyed by the Cameronian regiment stationed in Dunkeld in 1689. His earldom of Buchan fell into the hands of the crown, and was conferred in 1406 on his nephew, John Stewart (1381?-1424) [q. v.]

[The popular view of the 'Wolf of Badenoch' is portrayed in the novel of that name, by Sir Thomas Dick-Lauder; see also authorities quoted under STEWART, ALEXANDER, EARL OF MAR.]   J. A-N.

STEWART, ALEXANDER, EARL OF MAR (1375?-1435), born about 1375, was natural son of Alexander Stewart, earl of Buchan [q. v.], the 'Wolf of Badenoch,' who himself was natural son of Robert II [q. v.] of Scotland. He was brought up to his father's trade as a leader of freebooters, but in 1404, by one of the most daring acts of that lawless age, ' he raised himself from a captain of robbers to be one of the greatest men in Scotland' (*Exchequer Rolls*, 1406-1436, pref. p. lxxiii). This deed was the seizure and marriage of Isabel (1360?-1408), countess of Mar in her own right. She was only daughter and heir of Margaret, countess of Mar, in her own right, by her first husband, William Douglas, first earl of Douglas [q. v.] (her second husband was Sir John Swinton [q. v.]) By the death of her only brother James, second earl of Douglas, in 1388, Isabel had come into the Douglas estates, and in 1390 she succeeded to her mother's earldom of Mar. She had married Sir Malcolm Drummond, the brother of Robert III's wife, Annabella. Alexander Stewart determined to obtain this lady's hand, fortune, and title. His first step was to instigate the murder of

Drummond, which was accomplished in May 1403. In August of the following year, at the head of a body of marauders, he laid siege to the castle of Kildrummy, where the widowed countess resided, and on the 12th he compelled her to make a charter settling on him and his heirs, in default of her own issue, the earldom of Mar. This charter he resigned on 19 Sept. following, when the countess chose him ' in free marriage' for her husband, and settled on him and their issue the earldom of Mar, castle of Kildrummy, and other estates. The marriage took place on 14 Dec. 1404, and the arrangement subsequently received the necessary royal confirmation. From this date Stewart became known as the Earl of Mar. His wife died before 10 Feb. 1407-8, leaving no issue.

This change in his fortunes rendered Stewart in appearance at least a supporter of law and order, and in 1406 he was one of the ambassadors sent to England to treat for peace. On 6 April 1407 he received a safe-conduct until Michaelmas to go to England and tilt with Edmund Holland, fourth earl of Kent [see under HOLLAND, THOMAS, second EARL], and he is said to have distinguished himself in the encounter (*Cal. Doc. relating to Scotland*, 1221-1435, No. 730; WYNTOUN, c. 27). In the following year he led a body of auxiliaries to help William of Bavaria, duke of Burgundy, in restoring his brother John to the bishopric of Liège, from which he had been expelled by a revolt of the citizens. On the way Mar visited Paris, where by his courtesy he endeavoured to secure the favour of the French (MICHEL, *Les Ecossais en France*, i. 109-10). He took part in the storming of 23 Sept. (JUVENAL DES URSINS, *Hist. de Charles VI*, ed. Godefroy, p. 417; WYNTOUN, ii. 421-40; *Mémoires de Pierre de Fenin*, pp. 8-14; MONSTRELET, *Chroniques*, i. 351, ii. 17; MONK OF ST. DENIS, c. 684), and his exploits are recorded in a ballad printed in ' Mémoires pour servir à l'Histoire de France et de Bourgogne,' 1729, i. 373. While in Flanders he married his second wife, Marie, daughter and heir of Willelm van Hoorn of Duffel in Brabant, and widow of Thierry de Lienden (d. 1408), and as a result of this visit he is said to have first introduced Hungarian horses into Scotland (STEWART. *Metrical Version of Hector Boece*, iii. 550). On 4 Oct. 1408 he received a safe-conduct to visit England, probably on his way back, in order to confer with the young king, James I (*Cal. Doc. relating to Scotland*, 1221-1435, No. 772). In 1409 he captured at sea a ship called the

Thomas, belonging to Sir Richard Whittington [q. v.] and other merchants of London (ib. No. 789).

In 1410 Mar was summoned by the regent Albany to concert measures for resisting Donald Macdonald, second lord of the Isles [q. v.], who had invaded Ross to make good his title to that earldom. In 1411 he was placed in command of the royal forces, and on 24 July at Harlaw, in 'one of the fiercest and bloodiest battles ever fought on Scottish soil,' he defeated Donald. His services were amply rewarded; he received a pension of 200l. secured on the customs of Aberdeen, and other sums from those of Dundee, Montrose, and Edinburgh. In the following year he was employed in reconstructing the castle of Inverness, to act as a check on the turbulence of the highlands. In April 1416 he again received a safe-conduct to go to England, and in the same year he furnished ships for service against the islanders. In March 1424 he was appointed conservator of the seven years' truce with England, and was also made warden of the marches. On 16 Nov. 1420 he entered into a curious agreement with the regent Albany [see STEWART, MURDAC], becoming his 'man of speciall feale and retenew,' while Albany bestowed on him half the profits of the office of justiciary of the north, and empowered him to 'infeft' his natural son Thomas in the earldom of Mar. His life rent in the earldom of Mar was thus converted into a fee, defrauding the rightful heir, Robert, lord Erskine, a cousin of the Countess Isabella. This arrangement was confirmed by royal charter in May 1426.

Unlike most of Albany's adherents, Mar remained in favour with James I when in 1424 he left England to take upon himself the government of his kingdom. He died in 1435, when, his only son Thomas having predeceased him, the earldom of Mar reverted to the crown.

[Authorities cited; Cal. Documents relating to Scotland, 1221–1435; Exchequer Rolls of Scotland, 1379–1406 and 1406–36, ed. Burnett, esp. pref. pp. lxxii–vi; Reg. Magni Sigilli Scotiæ, 1424–1513, passim; Rotuli Scotiæ Record, passim; Rymer's Fœdera, viii. 437, 451, &c.; Harl. MS. 4694, f. 22; Wyntoun's Chron.; Bower's Book of Pluscardine; Stewart's Metrical Version of Hector Boece (Rolls Ser.), iii. 496, 548–51; Antiquities of Aberdeen and Banff (Spalding Club), iv. 181; Pinkerton's and Tytler's Histories of Scotland; Wylie's Hist. of England under Henry IV; Wood's Douglas, i. 201–3; Burke's Extinct Peerage, p. 514; G. E. C[okayne]'s Complete Peerage, v. 223.]   A. F. P.

STEWART, ALEXANDER, DUKE OF ALBANY (1454?–1485), born about 1454, was the second son of James II of Scotland [q. v.] and Mary of Gueldres [q. v.] He was created by his father Earl of March and Lord of Annandale in 1455, and payments for his clothes and to his nurse appear in the exchequer rolls between that year and 1457. In the parliament of 1456 his marriage, as well as those of his two brothers, Prince James (afterwards James III), John Stewart, earl of Mar [q. v.], and his sister Mary, was already under consideration. Before 1458 he must have been created Duke of Albany, for in that year he is so styled in the entry of an allowance for horses when he was brought from Stirling to Edinburgh. He had also received a grant of the lordship of the Isle of Man. Such titles in childhood left little for the ambition of youth except the crown. Four years after his father's death at Roxburgh in 1464, he was sent by his mother, on the advice of Bishop James Kennedy [q. v.], to Guelderland, but, in spite of the recently concluded truce and a safe-conduct granted on 20 April 1463, was captured on the voyage by an English vessel [see SPENS, THOMAS DE]. The remonstrances of the Scottish government procured his release, and he appears to have lived in St. Andrews under the care of Bishop Kennedy until the bishop's death on 10 May 1465. Preparations were made for his reception at Berwick between 25 June 1465 and 25 June 1466, so he probably came thither about that time. When only a boy of thirteen, according to the usual date assigned to his birth, he is mentioned as holding a court at Dunbar, no doubt for his vassals in the earldom, where his state as a feudal baron is shown by his having his own justiciar and treasurer, granting fiefs, and collecting customs. For ten years we get only occasional glimpses of Albany, but they show him taking an active part in the defence and government of the kingdom. He was created high admiral of Scotland. As warden of the marches and Earl of March he held Dunbar, and as Lord of Annandale the castle of Lochmaben. While still under age he sat in the parliament of 1471. In 1472 he was appointed governor of Berwick and lieutenant of the kingdom. In April 1474, in expectation of an English raid headed by the Duke of Gloucester (afterwards Richard III) on the west and middle marches, Albany summoned a muster of the lieges at Lauder; but the raid was not made. Privateering had, however, commenced at sea, and Edward IV had to send his almoner, Dr. Alexander Legh [q. v.], as an envoy to Scotland to make reparation for the loss of a royal ship, the Yellow Carvel, which had been taken by the Duke of Gloucester's May Flower, and for another vessel of the laird of Luss taken by Lord Grey.

The last seven years of the life of Albany are crowded with romance and tragedy. The contrast in the character and ambition of the three brothers of the royal house (James III, Albany, and the Earl of Mar) burst into full light; the Scottish court became the scene of fratricidal strife and the country of revolution. Albany's offices and lands on the marches brought him into conflict with the two most powerful barons of the borders, Hepburn and Hume [see HEPBURN, PATRICK, third LORD HAILES and first EARL OF BOTHWELL; HOME or HUME, SIR ALEXANDER, first LORD HOME]. Probably towards the end of 1479 the hostility latent in their character and fomented by their advisers broke out. Both sides attributed the rupture to magical arts. Albany fortified Dunbar against the royal forces, and both he and his brother, the Earl of Mar, were seized by the king's command. Mar, committed to Craigmillar, soon after died [see STEWART, JOHN, EARL OF MAR]. Albany was put in ward in the castle of Edinburgh. His escape was accompanied or magnified by incidents which seized the popular imagination. A French ship in the Forth succeeded in sending him two casks of malmsey which had stowed in them, wrapped in wax, a paper with secret instructions and a 'tow' or rope. Albany invited the captain of the castle to share the wine, and, when he had partaken of it too freely, aided by a chamber child or valet, slew him and three of his guard, whose bodies were cast into the fire. The chamber child let himself down with the rope over the castle wall. It proved too short, and he fell and broke his thigh. Albany, forewarned, used his sheets to lengthen it and, reaching the ground, carried the child on his back to a place of safety, and, himself escaping to Newhaven, near Leith, boarded the French ship, which carried him to France. He arrived in Paris in September 1479, and was received by order of Louis XI at the gate of St. Antoine by M. de Gancourt as royal lieutenant, and lodged at the king's expense at the Sign of the Coq, in the Rue St.-Martin, with a Scottish denizen, Monypenny, seigneur de Concressault, to attend him. His marriage with Anne, daughter of the Comte d'Auvergne et de Boulogne, was celebrated on 10 Feb. 1480. Before May 1482 he crossed to England in the Mickle Carvel, a vessel in the service of Edward IV, and from this time his life was spent in a treasonable alliance

with that king and intrigues with his own countrymen to acquire his brother's crown at the price of the independence of Scotland.

On 10 June 1482 Albany made a treaty with Edward at Fotheringay to do homage and to transfer Berwick to the English king, and fourteen days after he was conducted to Edinburgh. Edward undertook to warrant Scotland to Albany against James, and to give his daughter Cecilia, though already contracted to the infant son of James, in marriage to Albany if he could clear himself 'from all other women,' a curious expression which perhaps indicates that his first marriage required full legal dissolution. The English army, sixty thousand strong, under Gloucester and Albany, was, in execution of the agreement, summoned to Alnwick early in July 1482. Albany assumed the humiliating title, which recalls John Baliol, of 'king' of Scotland by the gift of the king of England, and the nobles who favoured him, headed by Angus Bell-the-Cat [see DOUGLAS, ARCHIBALD, fifth EARL OF ANGUS], met at the kirk of Lauder, hanged Cochrane and other royal favourites over the bridge, and seized the person of the king. Gloucester and Albany now marched through the Merse and Lothian to Edinburgh, burning the villages on their way, and Berwick surrendered to Thomas, lord Stanley (afterwards first Earl of Derby) [q. v.] on 24 Aug.

Meantime a change had taken place at Edinburgh. The Scottish nobles who had possession of the king were willing to acknowledge Albany, but wanted to ignore Gloucester. In the beginning of August Albany and Gloucester, with the English army, lay at Lethington, near Haddington. James was in the castle of Edinburgh under the custody of his uncles, the Earls of Atholl and Buchan. The king's supporters, of whom the chief were Andrew Stewart, Lord Avandale, the chancellor [q. v.], the bishops of St. Andrews and Dunkeld, and the Earl of Argyll, still held the town. On 2 Aug. they agreed to obtain the restoration of Albany to his lands and offices if he would promise to be faithful to King James. Albany accepted the offer, and left Gloucester's camp for Edinburgh on the following day, but before he left took an oath in Gloucester's presence that he would perform all he had promised to King Edward at Fotheringay. A proclamation was at once issued in the name of James in Edinburgh appointing Albany lieutenant-general of the kingdom, and summoning the lieges to meet at Cranshaws, a hamlet and fortress of the Lammermuirs in Berwickshire, and raise the siege both of Edinburgh and Berwick.

Gloucester, not unnaturally, remonstrated, and, after some diplomatic fencing, it was agreed between Gloucester and Albany, on 24 Aug., that there should be a truce till 8 Sept. 1483, and that Berwick should be rendered to the English, which was at once done. Gloucester waived, until he could communicate with his royal master, consideration of a third article that the debatable land should remain *in statu quo*. Meantime the provost and council of Edinburgh had, by Albany's desire, written on 4 Aug. to the English, offering either to stand by the proposal for the marriage of the prince of Scotland to Princess Cecilia, or to repay the instalments of her dowry, already paid in advance. Edward, with apparent hesitation, accepted the latter alternative, and this was announced by Garter king-of-arms, who came to Edinburgh on 27 Oct. James was released from Edinburgh Castle on 29 Sept., and in token of their amity the two brothers rode together from the castle to Holyrood, it was said on the same horse, and slept in the same bed. Albany was not only restored to his estates, but created Earl of Mar and Garioch; and the town of Edinburgh, in return for its services in aiding Albany in liberating James, received a charter, with an ample grant of privileges, on 14 Nov.

In the same month James obtained a safe-conduct from the English king to enable him to make a pilgrimage to Amiens. This was probably a suggestion of Albany's, which the king was prudent enough not to carry out; for had he left the kingdom Albany would have seized the crown. On 2 Dec. a parliament, over which Albany presided in the king's absence, met at Edinburgh, in which new officers of state appear who were all in Albany's interest. It requested the king to ask Albany to act as lieutenant-general of the kingdom, and ordered preparations for its defence, but urged that peace should, if possible, be made with England. About Christmas Albany seems to have attempted to seize the person of the king, but, failing through the king's return to the castle under the protection of some of his nobles, himself went to Dunbar. From Dunbar he sent Angus Gray and Sir James Liddel of Hetherston as his special envoys, on 12 Jan. 1483, to treat with Edward concerning what had been formerly agreed between them, and they, having met the Earl of Northumberland, Lord Grey, and Sir William Parr, Edward's commissioners, entered into a new treaty on 11 Feb. at Westminster, which enlarged the articles of Fotheringay. The Duke agreed, as soon as he obtained the Scottish crown, to become the liegeman of the king of England, to dis-

solve the alliance with France, and assist the king of England in its conquest; to cede Berwick; to aid the Earl of Douglas in recovering his Scottish estates, and to marry a daughter of Edward IV. Two days later a warrant for a safe-conduct to the Earl of Douglas was issued to the chancellor.

Albany, however, whose duplicity at this period exceeded even the limits of the diplomacy of that age, within little more than a month, on 19 March 1483, entered into an indenture at Dunbar with his brother, by which he resigned his office of lieutenant-general of the kingdom, retaining that of warden of the marches; declared false the rumour that there had been an attempt to poison him, and promised not to come within six miles of the king without leave. He received in return a remission of all charges of treasonable intrigue with England. The treasonable plot with England, the full details of which were unknown at the time in Scotland, or by any Scottish historian until last century, was shattered by the death of Edward IV on 9 April 1483, and on 22 June Gloucester, after slaying his nephews in the Tower, seized the English throne. Only five days after, on 27 June, Albany was indicted, and on 8 July condemned in absence for treason, and his life, lands, and offices forfeited. Soon afterwards he returned to England, having given over Dunbar to an English garrison. Next year, on 22 July, along with Douglas, he made a daring raid on Lochmaben with five hundred horse; but the country rose, Douglas was captured and sent to Lindores, where he became a monk. Albany escaped by the swiftness of his horse over the border, but before long returned to France, where he was killed in 1485 by misadventure by a splinter from a lance when a spectator at a tournament between the Duke of Orleans and a knight. He was buried in the choir of the church of the Celestines in Paris, near the tomb of Leo, king of Armenia; the dukes of Orleans and Lorraine and other princes attending his obsequies.

Albany was brave, but equally faithless in love and war. A traitor both to his brother and his country, he does not seem to have deserved the popularity which he had at one time in Scotland and till his death in France. No portrait of him is known, but Pitscottie has described his person in vivid colours: 'For this Alexander was ane man of mid stature, braid scholderit, and weill proportionat in all his memberis, and in special in his face, that is to say, braid facit, raid nosit, great eyit, and verie awful countenance quhen he pleisit to schew himself unto his unfrendis.'

Albany married about 1475 his cousin in the fourth degree, Catharine Sinclair, daughter of William, third earl of Orkney and first earl of Caithness [q. v.], by Margaret Douglas; and three sons and a daughter appear to have been born of the marriage. The daughter Margaret is believed to have married Sir Patrick Hamilton of Kincavel, and to have been the mother of Patrick Hamilton [q. v.] the martyr. One son, Alexander, became bishop of Moray in 1527. This marriage was dissolved on the ground of propinquity by the official of Lothian on 9 March 1478, a dissolution confirmed by parliament on 13 Nov. 1516. This step was taken in order to set at rest doubts as to the legitimacy of Albany's son John, duke of Albany [q. v.], the only child of his second wife, Anne, third daughter of Bertrand, count de la Tour d'Auvergne. Albany married her in France in 1480, and she appears to have died in 1487. The confirmation by parliament raised the doubts of later historians, and its occasion was certainly not above suspicion. Chalmers (*Caledonia*, ii. 268 note *p*) argued with ingenuity that the certificate of the divorce under the hand of George Newton, clerk of the official in 1516, which was laid before parliament, was forged. But the chief ground of his doubt that John of Otterburn, the official by whom the decree was pronounced, was not official at its date has since been removed (*Exchequer Rolls*, vol. ix. p. lvii note 1). The facts that the bishop of Moray did not contest the sentence which declared his own illegitimacy, and that in 1488 a proposal was made by James III for the marriage of Albany to a sister of Edward IV, the Duchess of Burgundy, widow of Charles the Bold, outweigh the doubts of Chalmers, which have not been accepted by other historians. Edward declined the proposed marriage through his envoy, Dr. Legh, then in Scotland, not upon the ground of Albany's being already married, but because, 'after the old usage of our realms, no estate or person honourable communeth of marriage within the year of their dool' (Edward IV to Dr. Legh, *Cotton MS. Vesp.* cxvi. f. 121, printed in PINKERTON, i. 501).

[Acts of Parliament of Scotland, ii.; Exchequer Rolls, vols. viii-ix.; Rymer's Fœdera; the Histories of Leslie and Lindsay of Pitscottie; Michel's Les Écossais en France, les Français en Écosse; Pinkerton's and Tytler's Histories.]

Æ. M.

STEWART, ALEXANDER (1493?-1513), archbishop of St. Andrews, was the natural son of James IV by Margaret, daughter of Archibald Boyd of Bonshaw. In succession to James Stewart (1476-1504) [q. v.], he was before 23 July 1505 appointed archbishop of St. Andrews, being so styled in the Stirling account of that date (*Exchequer Rolls of Scotland*, x. 334). He is usually stated to have obtained the primacy at the age of eighteen; but in a letter of James IV to Julius II regarding the appointment he is referred to as being below the age of puberty (GAIRDNER, *Letters of Richard III and Henry VII*, ii. 179); and as, moreover, Erasmus states that he was twenty years of age when he was killed at Flodden, he was probably born about 1493. In his earlier years his education was entrusted to Dr. Patrick Panter [q. v.]; but he was sent to the continent, probably in 1506, under the guardianship of Sir Thomas Halkerston, and, after visiting the Low Countries and France, he settled in 1508 at Padua, where he studied rhetoric and logic under Erasmus, who in his 'Adagia' highly extols his character and scholarship. 'Heavens,' wrote Erasmus, 'how quick, how attentive, how eager he was, how many things he would undertake together!' In July 1509 James IV wrote a letter of thanks to the pope for reserving to his son, the archbishop of St. Andrews, his primacy and legateship, and confirming the liberties of the chapel royal (*Cal. State Papers, Henry VIII*, i. No. 379), and the same year he also wrote to the pope, proposing that the priory of Coldingham, hitherto attached to Durham, and then vacant, should be annexed and made canonically subject to the abbey of Dunfermline, then held by the archbishop of St. Andrews (*ib.* No. 774). In these and similar schemes of aggrandisement the archbishop himself displayed all the quickness and eagerness which Erasmus noted in the scholar. His ambition was further gratified by his appointment, some time before 2 April 1510, to the office of lord chancellor of Scotland (*Exchequer Rolls of Scotland*, xiii. 358). It is in fact very evident that the youthful archbishop was as resolutely bent on worldly preferment as any churchman of his time, and probably had he lived the reformers would have fared as hardly at his hands as they did at those of Beaton. At the same time he was an enlightened patron of learning. In 1512 he augmented the stipends of the professors of the pedagogium, of the foundation of Bishop Henry Wardlaw [q.v.] (afterwards St. Mary's College), and gave them the fruits of the church of St. Michael of Tarvat, near Cupar, and he also rebuilt the chapel of St. John the Evangelist, in the same pedagogium, after it had fallen. In the same year, along with Prior John Hepburn [q. v.], he was founder of the college of St. Leonard's, endowing it with the tithes of that parish, and of the hospice for pilgrims who came to visit the see at St. Andrews.

The archbishop joined his father in the fatal inroad into England which ended in the disaster at Flodden. While his father dallied in the company of Lady Ford, he is said to have amused himself with an intrigue with the daughter; but the only foundation for the story may have been the fact that he remained in attendance on his father. He was killed at Flodden on 9 Sept. 1513.

[Exchequer Rolls of Scotland; Gairdner's Letters of Richard III and Henry VII; Letters and State Papers of Henry VIII, vol. i.; Martine's Reliquiæ Divi Andreæ; Keith's Scottish Bishops; Crawford's Officers of State.] T. F. H.

STEWART, ALEXANDER, fourth EARL OF MORAY (d. 1701), secretary of state for Scotland, was the second son of James, third earl (who was a grandson of James Stewart, earl of Moray, d. 1592 [q. v.]), by Lady Margaret Home, elder daughter of Alexander, first earl of Home, and coheiress with her sister Anne, duchess of Lauderdale, of her brother James, second earl of Home. He succeeded his father on 4 March 1653. In 1654 he was under Cromwell's act of grace fined 3,500l., which was reduced to 1,166l. 13s. (Cal. State Papers, Dom. 1655, p. 72); but in January 1655-6 he presented a petition for the remission of his fine, because he 'was a child during the late differences,' and because his estate was 'small and much charged' (ib. 1655-6, p. 152). On 22 Jan. 1656-7 it was ordered that, on his giving security to the council of Scotland to pay 500l. before 1 Feb. 1657-8, the residue of his fine should be remitted (ib. 1656-7, p. 248).

He was admitted justice-general on 1 June 1675, appointed a lord of the treasury on 27 Sept. 1678, nominated an extraordinary lord of session on 17 July 1680, and on 2 Nov. of the same year appointed secretary of state in succession to Lauderdale. Previous to his appointment he was known as an active opponent of the covenanters. In 1675 he specially exerted himself in putting down conventicles in Elgin (WODROW, History, ii. 284), and in March 1678 he was deputed by the council to London to encourage the king in his policy of repression (ib. p. 419). Afterwards he co-operated with James II, not only in his unconstitutional procedure, but in his endeavours to introduce Roman catholicism. In 1686, when an attempt was made to obtain toleration for the catholics, he was nominated for this purpose lord high commissioner to the Scottish parliament, and in the following year he was made a knight of the Thistle. At the Revolution he was

deprived of all his offices. He died at Donibristle on 1 Nov. 1701, and was carried to Darnaway and buried in the church of Dyke on 24 Jan. 1701-2. By his wife Emilia, daughter of Sir William Balfour of Pitcullo, lieutenant of the Tower of London, he had four sons: James, lord Doune, who predeceased his father in 1685; Charles, fifth earl, who was created a baronet of Nova Scotia on 23 Sept. 1681, and died on 7 Oct. 1735, aged 75; John; and Francis (d. 1739), who succeeded his brother as sixth earl in 1735.

[Cal. State Papers, Dom. during the Commonwealth; Wodrow's Hist. of the Sufferings of the Kirk of Scotland; Lauder of Fountainhall's Historical Notices; Douglas's Scottish Peerage (Wood), ii. 260.] T. F. H.

STEWART, ALEXANDER, fifth LORD BLANTYRE (d. 1704), was the son of Alexander, fourth lord Blantyre (grandson of Walter Stewart or Stuart, first lord Blantyre [q. v.]), by Margaret, daughter of John Shaw of Greenock. At the Revolution he raised a regiment for the service of King William, which was at Stirling when Mackay was encamped at Killiecrankie (Melville Papers, p. 206). For his loyalty he received from King William a pension. He was one of those who protested against the meeting of the convention of 9 June 1702, and seceded from the meeting. By the seceding members he was sent as a deputy to Queen Anne, who declined to accept their protest, but permitted Blantyre to wait upon her. Blantyre took the oath and his seat in the Scottish parliament on 9 July 1703. On 11 Aug. a complaint was made against him by the lord advocate for having, before witnesses, called the lord high commissioner 'a base and impudent liar' (HUME OF CROSSRIG, Diary, p. 125). He entered the house while the debate was in progress, and having put himself in the lord constable's hands, was placed under arrest in his own chamber. On the 13th a petition from him was read, asking the commissioner and the estates to accept his humble apology. It was agreed that before his liberation he should on his knees crave pardon of the commissioner and the estates, and submit to a fine of 5,000l. Scots; but on his being called in the commissioner dispensed with his making acknowledgments on his knees, and, having promised obedience to the remainder of the sentence, he was dismissed from the bar and reinstated (ib. p. 147). He died on 20 June 1704. He is described by Macky as 'a little active man, very low in stature, short-sighted, fair-complexioned, towards fifty years old' (Memoirs, p. 232). By his first wife, Margaret, eldest daughter of Sir John Henderson of Fordel,

Fifeshire, bart., he had no issue. By his second wife, Anne, daughter of Sir Robert Hamilton, lord Pressmennan, sister of John, second lord Belhaven, he had five sons and four daughters: Walter(d. 1713), sixth lord; Robert (d. 1743), seventh lord; John, James, Hugh; Marion, married to James Stirling of Keir; Frances to Sir James Hamilton of Rosehall, bart.; Helen to John, eleventh lord Gray; and Anne to Alexander Hay of Drummelzie.

[Hume of Crossrig's Diary, and Melville Papers in the Bannatyne Club; Macky's Memoirs; Douglas's Scottish Peerage (Wood), i. 214.]
T. F. H.

STEWART, ALEXANDER (d. 1795), of Invernahyle, Jacobite, was the eighth son of Duncan Stewart, seventh of Invernahyle, by a daughter of Campbell of Barcaldine. He was out with his clan, the Stewarts of Appin, both in 1715 and 1745. On the morning of Prestonpans he took part in a brilliant charge, when they stormed and captured a battery of four field-pieces. Invernahyle engaged in single combat Colonel Whitefoord of Ballochmyle, whose life he spared when it was in his hands, on condition of surrender. At Culloden Stewart was wounded, but made his escape. Colonel Whitefoord endeavoured to obtain his pardon from the Duke of Cumberland, and, when that was refused, asked that protection might at least be granted to his houses, wife, children, and property. This also was refused; but Whitefoord having thereupon requested to lay down his commission, it was finally conceded. Search nevertheless was made for Stewart, but he could not be found, and he was afterwards pardoned under the act of indemnity.

Stewart was a client of Sir Walter Scott's father, and his frequent guest in Edinburgh when Scott was a boy. He happened to be in Edinburgh in 1779 when Paul Jones threatened a descent on the city; he was 'the only person,' says Lockhart, ' who seemed to have retained the possession of his cool senses' at that period of alarm, and offered to the magistrates to collect as many highlanders as would cut off any part of the pirate's crew that might venture into the narrow lanes of the old city (LOCKHART, *Life of Scott*, ed. 1845, p. 39). It was from this old highland warrior that Sir Walter got his earliest lessons in story-telling. His 'tales,' Sir Walter relates, 'were the absolute delight of my childhood. I believe there never was a man who united the ardour of a soldier and tale-teller—a man of "talk," as they call it in Gaelic—in such an excellent degree, and he was as fond of telling as I was of learning; I became a valiant Jacobite at the age of ten years' (*Familiar Letters*, i. 67). At Stewart's request Scott visited him in 1786 or 1787, when he made his first acquaintance with the highlands. Stewart died in 1795. By his wife Katherine, daughter of Robert Stewart, ninth of Appin, he had fifteen children, of whom Dugald succeeded him.

[The Stewarts of Appin, 1880; Lockhart's Life of Scott, chap. v.; Familiar Letters of Sir Walter Scott, 1893.]
T. F. H.

STEWART, ALEXANDER PATRICK, M.D. (1813–1883), physician, son of the Rev. Andrew Stewart (d. 1838), minister of Bolton in East Lothian, by his wife Margaret, daughter of Alexander Stewart, tenth lord Blantyre, was born at Bolton on 28 Aug. 1813. His father had graduated M.D. and practised as a physician before his ordination (SCOTT, *Fasti Eccl. Scoticanæ*, i. i. 323, ii. i. 247). Alexander was educated in the Faculty of Arts of the university of Glasgow, and became a good Greek scholar. He travelled abroad with his family from 1828 to 1830, and thus learnt French thoroughly. On his return he entered the medical faculty, and graduated M.D. at Glasgow in 1838, afterwards making further studies at Paris and Berlin. In 1839 he settled in Grosvenor Street, London, and there practised till his death. In 1850 he was elected assistant physician to the Middlesex Hospital, and became physician there in 1855, in which year he was elected a fellow of the College of Physicians. He was lecturer on materia medica, and afterwards on medicine at the Middlesex Hospital, and retired thence in 1866. From 1850 he was an active member of the British Medical Association. He published in 1849 'Sanitary Economics,' and in 1854 ('Medical Times and Gazette') a paper on cholera, and several other papers, but his title to recollection rests upon ' Some Considerations on the Nature and Pathology of Typhus and Typhoid Fever applied to the Solution of the Question of the Identity or Non-Identity of the two Diseases,' read before the Parisian Medical Society on 16 and 23 April 1840. This paper was reprinted by the New Sydenham Society in 1884. The observations on which it is based were made at the Glasgow Fever Hospital. From the time of Antonius de Haen (1760), a discussion had continued among physicians on the distinction of certain fevers. Johannes Valentinus ab Hildebrand in 1811 regarded the fevers now known as typhus and typhoid, or enteric, as distinct, and P. Bretonneau, a few years later, described exactly the morbid anatomy of typhoid fever. Stewart's experience in the post-mortem room at Glasgow led him to believe firmly in the distinction between the two fevers, and in this essay he states clearly, from his own observation of cases, their differences in origin, cause, course, symptoms, and anatomical lesions, while his remarks against the use of purgatives in typhoid fever entitle him to further distinction as one who has contributed to the saving of many lives by pointing out the danger of what had been a prevalent method of treatment. Sir William Jenner's celebrated papers in 1849, 1850, and 1853 are written on the same lines as Stewart's; but as they were based on a far more extended field of personal observation they had more public effect, and are justly regarded as having finally settled the question. Stewart was an elder in the presbyterian church and wrote in 1843 'Divide and Conquer,' and numerous other pamphlets relating to the church of Scotland. He died unmarried at his house in Grosvenor Street on 17 July 1883. He did not attain to large practice, but both his character and attainments were esteemed by the physicians of his time.

[Memoir by Dr. W. Cayley, New Sydenham Society, vol. cx. 1884; Dr. Norman Moore's Pathological Anatomy of Diseases, 1889; Hilton Fagge's Principles and Practice of Medicine, 2nd edit. 1888; Edinburgh Medical and Surgical Journal, October 1840; obituary notice by John Marshall in an address to the Royal Medical and Chirurgical Society, Transactions. vol. lxvi. 1884; Works.]   N. M.

STEWART, ANDREW, first LORD AVANDALE or AVONDALE (d. 1488), chancellor of Scotland, was, according to the latest authorities, eldest son of Walter, second son of Murdac Stewart, second duke of Albany [q. v.] His mother was apparently a daughter of (Sir Duncan) Campbell of Lochow, ancestor of the Argyll family, but her marriage with Walter Stewart was for some reason considered unlawful. Hence in 1472 and 1479 Andrew obtained from the crown letters of legitimation to himself and two brothers, Arthur and Walter. The date of his birth cannot be stated, but he and a younger brother, Murdach, had both been knighted in England before 12 July 1437 (RYMER, Fœdera, x. 672). It is probable that he was educated in that country and returned to Scotland after the death of James I, as he was a member of the general council held at Stirling in August 1440 (Acts of the Parliaments of Scotland, ii. 56).

Sir Andrew Stewart rose in the favour of the young king, James II, and apparently held office in the royal household. In 1456 he received a grant of the lands of Strathavon, Avondale or Avandale, forfeited by William Douglas, eighth earl of Douglas [q. v.], and was also made warden of the west march and keeper of the castle of Lochmaben. He was created Lord Avandale before 11 June 1457 (RYMER, Fœdera, xi. 397), and appointed to the office of chancellor of Scotland in 1460. He continued to hold this post during the next reign, and was for a time one of the lords of regency during the minority of James III. Stirling Castle was placed in his hands, and he was on more than one embassy to England. He took a very prominent part in the negotiations with the king of Denmark for the hand of his daughter Margaret as wife to the Scottish king (TORFÆUS, Orcades, 1715, p. 193), and was specially successful in obtaining the cession to Scotland of the islands of Orkney and Shetland, then belonging to Denmark.

In May 1471 Avandale obtained a life-rent grant over the earldom of Lennox, and he also got other lands; but little is recorded of him save the duties of his office until 1479, when by order of the king he besieged the castle of Dunbar, rebelliously fortified against the crown by the king's brother, Alexander Stewart, duke of Albany [q. v.] It soon surrendered. In 1482, when James III declared war against England, Avandale is said to have joined those nobles who refused to advance beyond Lauder, and who warded the king in Edinburgh Castle. This is believed to have been done in the interest of Albany. Avandale certainly was one of those who, on 2 Aug. 1482, effected an agreement between James III and Albany (RYMER, Fœdera, xii. 160), and some days later he was deposed from the chancellorship. The reason is involved in obscurity; but as one historian (Lindsay of Pitscottie) expressly names him among the conspirators at Lauder, the king may have been suspicious of his loyalty, or he may have refused to enter into all the plans of those who held the king in durance. Be this as it may, though he was never again chancellor, he took part in public affairs in March 1483, and he sat in the parliaments which deprived Albany of his office of lieutenant-general and pronounced forfeiture against him. Avandale was one of the ambassadors to France in July 1484 who renewed the ancient league with that country, and in the following month he was named as an envoy to England (ib. xii. 230), but did not go. After this he appears to have retired from public life, though he acted as an auditor of exchequer and witnessed a few royal charters, the latest dated

11 March 1488. He died before the following July, when James IV offered 18s. for his 'sawlemess' in the church of Stirling (*Accounts of the Lord High Treasurer of Scotland*, i. 89).

His wife's name is nowhere recorded, and he died without surviving issue. He was succeeded by his nephew, Alexander, son of his brother, Walter Stewart of Morphie, who inherited the lands of Avandale, and, dying before 1500, was succeeded by a younger brother, Andrew, who about that date received the title of Lord Avandale, and in 1543 was created lord Ochiltree (*Registrum Magni Sigilli*, vol. ii. No. 2516, cf. No. 1632). The eldest son of Andrew, third lord Avandale (and first lord Ochiltree), was Andrew Stewart, second lord Ochiltree [q.v.]; the second son was Henry Stewart, first lord Methven [q.v.]; and the third son, Sir James Stewart of Beath, was father of James Stewart of Doune, who was created lord Doune on 24 Nov. 1581, and was ancestor of the Stewarts, earls of Moray.

[Genealogical Sketch of the Stuarts of Castle Stuart, &c., by the Hon. and Rev. A. G. Stuart, M.A., 1854, where the question of the legitimacy of Lord Avandale and his brothers is discussed; The Lennox, by William Fraser, 2 vols. 1874; The Exchequer Rolls of Scotland, vols. iv–ix.; Douglas's Peerage, ed. Wood, i. 158.]   J. A-N.

STEWART, ANDREW, second LORD OCHILTREE (*fl.* 1548–1593), son of Andrew, third lord Avandale and first lord Ochiltree [see under STEWART, ANDREW, (first) LORD AVANDALE], by Margaret Hamilton, only child of James, first earl of Arran, succeeded his father in 1548. On 27 Oct. 1549 he received a grant of the lands of Pennymore, Ayrshire (*Reg. Mag. Sig. Scot.* 1546–80, No. 387), and on 31 Jan. 1556–7 the lands of Barloch-hill, &c. (*ib.* No. 1150). He was one of the lords who in May 1559 came to the relief of the protestants at Perth (KNOX, i. 340), and on the last day of May subscribed the band in defence of the 'Congregation' (*ib.* p. 345). He was one of the commissioners sent in July 1559 by the lords of the congregation to arrange terms with the queen regent (*ib.* p. 367), and he also signed the letter of remonstrance sent to the queen regent in September against the fortification of Leith (*ib.* p. 414). When the lords of the congregation resolved at the close of 1559 to leave Edinburgh, Ochiltree joined the division which occupied Glasgow and the surrounding districts (*ib.* ii. 38). He subscribed the contract between Elizabeth and the lords of the congregation, 10 May 1560 (*ib.* p. 53), and shortly afterwards he, with his followers,

joined at Prestonpans the English army sent to the assistance of the protestants (*ib.* p. 58). He signed the band for defending the 'liberty of the Evangel' and for the expulsion of the French from Scotland (*ib.* p. 63), and his name also appears among the subscribers to the book of discipline, 27 Jan. 1560-1 (*ib.* p. 129). Ochiltree accompanied Knox to Holyrood when in 1563 he went to answer to the queen for railing in his sermon against her proposed marriage to a papist (*ib.* p. 387), and alone bore him company in the outer chamber after the interview (*ib.* p. 389). He joined in the rebellion of Moray against the queen on her marriage to Darnley in 1565, and on 6 Sept. was cited to present himself before the king and queen within six days (*Reg. P. C. Scot.* i. 355). Failing to do so, he was on 1 Dec. declared guilty of *lèse majesté* (*ib.* p. 409). He supported the lords who conspired against Riccio, and also took an active part against the queen after the murder of Darnley. He subscribed the acts of the assembly in July 1567, in which the murder and popery met with the same condemnation (KNOX, ii. 565), and attended the king's coronation on the 29th of the same month (*Reg. P. C. Scot.* i. 537). At the battle of Langside, 13 May 1568, he fought against the queen and was wounded by Lord Herries (CALDERWOOD, *History*, ii. 410). Consistent in his opposition to the queen, he voted against her divorce from Bothwell in 1569 (*Reg. P. C. Scot.* ii. 8), and he was one of the nobles who carried the body of the Regent Moray from Holyrood to St. Giles's church (Randolph to Cecil, 22 Feb. 1569-70, in KNOX's *Works*, vi. 571).

After the death of the Earl of Moray, Ochiltree ceased to take a prominent part in politics; but he was one of the new privy council chosen after Morton's return to power in July 1578 (MOYSIE, *Memoirs*, p. 12). It is probable, however, that he was no special friend of Morton's, for it was his son, Captain James Stewart (afterwards Earl of Arran) [q.v.], who in 1580 accused Morton of the murder of Darnley. On 18 March 1579-80 Ochiltree and his son James received a grant of the lands of Bothwellmuir and of Easter and Wester Moffat (*Reg. Mag. Sig. Scot.* 1546-80, No. 2983). On the slaughter of Ochiltree's son, Sir William, by the Earl of Bothwell in 1588, Ochiltree followed Bothwell persistently from place to place, but did not succeed in capturing him (MOYSIE, *Memoirs*, p. 80). In 1592 Ochiltree agreed to mediate between Huntly and Moray [see STEWART, JAMES, second EARL OF MORAY], who was a partisan of Bothwell, and at his instance Moray came to Donibristle,

Fifeshire, where he was treacherously slain by Huntly (*ib.* pp. 88). Ochiltree made strenuous efforts to be revenged on Huntly for his treachery (*ib.* passim); and in order to achieve his purpose entered into communication with Bothwell and shared in the plot for introducing him to the king in Holyrood (MELVILLE, *Memoirs*, p. 407; CALDERWOOD, v. 256). That the second Lord Ochiltree should have favoured the slayer of his son is improbable, and the most plausible supposition would be that the Lord Ochiltree who did so was the third lord, who was merely the nephew of the slain man, but the second lord was certainly alive until 26 Dec. 1593 (*Reg. Mag. Sig. Scot.* 1593-1608, No. 33). Probably, therefore, it was this same second lord who in the spring of 1594, with Bothwell and the laird of Spot, had a secret meeting, at which they agreed to convene with their forces on 2 April at Dalkeith, and thence proceed to the highlands to join Atholl and Montrose in an attack on Huntly (MOYSIE, p. 113). Their purpose having leaked out, it was frustrated by stopping the boats from sailing to transport the forces across the Firth of Forth, and after encountering and defeating a strong force under Lord Home, they passed south to Kelso and thence into England (*ib.* pp. 115-16). On 26 May Ochiltree was denounced for not appearing to answer for his treasonable attempts (*Reg. P. C. Scotl.* iv. 144); but in the beginning of 1595 the king, who, says Moysie, 'had great favour and liking for the Lord Ochiltree,' induced him to separate himself from Bothwell, and on coming to the king he received a full pardon for all past offences (MOYSIE, p. 122). Lord Ochiltree was in 1598 appointed lieutenant on the borders, and remained for four or five months at Dumfries, holding courts and pacifying the country (*ib.* p. 136). He died some time before 21 March 1601-2 (*Reg. Mag. Sig. Scot.* 1593-1608, No. 1159). By his wife Agnes, daughter of John Cunningham of Caprington, he had five sons and two daughters: Andrew, master of Ochiltree, who died in 1578; Captain James of Bothwellmuir, afterwards Earl of Arran [q. v.]; Sir William of Monkton (*d.* 1588) [q. v.]; Sir Henry of Nether Gogar; Robert of Wester Braco; Isabel, married to Thomas Kennedy of Bargeny; and Margaret, who was the second wife of John Knox the reformer, and afterwards married Sir Andrew Ker of Faldonside. He was succeeded in the peerage by his grandson Andrew, who was gentleman of the bedchamber to James VI, and governor of Edinburgh Castle, and who in 1615 resigned his title to Sir

James Stewart of Killeith, eldest son of James, earl of Arran; Andrew Stewart was subsequently, on 7 Nov. 1619, created Baron Castle Stewart in the peerage of Ireland, and he died in 1632.

[Reg. P. C. Scotl. vols. i-v.; Reg. Mag. Sig. Scot. 1546-80, 1580-93, 1593-1608; Knox's Works; Histories by Calderwood and Spottiswoode; David Moysie's Memoirs and Sir James Melville's Memoirs in the Bannatyne Club; Douglas's Scottish Peerage, ed. Wood.]

T. F. H.

STEWART, ANDREW (*d.* 1671), Irish divine, was one of the four children of the Rev. Andrew Stewart (*d.* 1634) of Donegore, co. Antrim, whom Robert Blair (1590-1666) [q. v.] describes as 'a learned gentleman and fervent in spirit, and a very successful minister of the Word of God.' The story of the father's death is graphically told by Robert Fleming the elder [q. v.] in his 'Fulfilling of the Scriptures' (i. 393).

There is some doubt as to the year of the younger Stewart's birth. The inscription on his tombstone states that at his death in 1671 he was 'of his age the 46;' but as he himself in his 'Short Account' speaks of having witnessed some of the scenes in the religious movement at Oldstone, co. Antrim, which took place in 1625, and his nephew, the Rev. Andrew Crawford, in a letter to Wodrow, dated 7 Sept. 1724, says that Stewart was 'a young man' at the time of this movement, he must certainly have been older than forty-six at death. In 1645 or 1646 he was settled as minister of Donaghadee, co. Down. In 1650 he fled to Scotland, owing to the troubles which arose in Ireland in consequence of the execution of Charles I. He returned to Donaghadee in 1652. In October of that year he appeared with other ministers before the commissioners of the revenue at Belfast to consider how the labours of the presbyterian clergy could be carried on 'without disturbing the peace of the commonwealth,' and in 1654 he was one of a deputation which waited on Fleetwood and the council in Dublin with a view to obtaining a share of the payment given by the government to ministers, a mission in which they were successful. Stewart was assigned a salary of 100*l.* per annum, to be paid by the commissioners of the revenue at Belfast (see R. M. YOUNG, *Historical Notices of Old Belfast and its Vicinity*, 1896, p. 102). In the same year he took part in drawing up 'The Act of Bangor,' intended to prevent the troubles between the resolutioners and protesters in Scotland from spreading to Ireland. In 1661 he was one of the sixty-one presbyterian ministers of Ulster who were ejected from their parishes for nonconformity. In 1663 he was suspected—wrongly, as afterwards appeared—of complicity in Blood's plot [see BLOOD, THOMAS], and was for a time imprisoned first in Carlingford Castle, and afterwards in Dublin. He died on 2 Jan. 1671, and was interred in Donaghadee churchyard.

Stewart compiled a 'Short Account of the Church of Christ as it was (1) among the Irish at first; (2) among and after the English entered; (3) after the entry of the Scots.' A copy of this is among the Wodrow manuscripts in the Advocates' Library, Edinburgh, where it was placed in 1724 by Stewart's nephew, the Rev. Andrew Crawford. It has not been printed in its entirety. The third and most important portion was appended by Dr. W. D. Killen to his edition of Patrick Adair's 'True Narrative' (Belfast, 1866) [see ADAIR, PATRICK]. The work was evidently left unfinished by its author. It ends abruptly with an account of the establishment of the Antrim meeting in 1626.

[Patrick Adair's True Narrative; Killen's prefatory notice to Stewart's Short Account; Witherow's Historical and Literary Memorials of Presbyterianism in Ireland, vol. i.; Reid's Hist. vol. i.] T. H.

STEWART, ANTHONY (1773–1846), miniature-painter, was born at Crieff, Perthshire, in 1773. He received a good education, and while a youth was introduced to the family of General Campbell of Monzie, whose daughters he assisted in painting medallions for the decoration of a summer-house. These ladies were so much pleased with his ability that they proposed to article him at their own expense to Alexander Nasmyth [q. v.] of Edinburgh, the landscape-painter. The offer was accepted, and he made many sketches of Scottish scenery, which display more of the feeling of Richard Wilson and John Cozens than of his master. But before long he gave up this branch of art, and devoted himself to miniature-painting. He practised for a time in Edinburgh, but afterwards removed to London, where he met with considerable success. He was introduced to the royal family, and painted the Princess Charlotte. Subsequently he executed the earliest miniatures of Queen Victoria, who sat to him when a year old, and afterwards for several years in succession. One of these portraits was engraved by Thomas Woolnoth. Between 1807 and 1820 he exhibited a few miniatures at the Royal Academy. He excelled in painting children, and for the last fifteen years of his life he devoted himself almost exclusively to them.

Stewart died at Stockwell, near London,

VOL. LIV.

in December 1846, and was buried in Norwood cemetery.

His daughters, Margaret and Grace Campbell, were instructed by him in miniature-painting. Margaret, the elder, married John Seguier, superintendent of the British Institution [see under SEGUIER, WILLIAM]. Grace Campbell, the younger, practised miniature-painting, and exhibited a few of her works at the Royal Academy between 1843 and 1850. She died in 1863.

[Redgrave's Dict. of Artists of the English School, 1878; Royal Academy Exhibition Catalogues, 1807–56; information from Stewart's grandson, F. P. Seguier, esq.] R. E. G.

STEWART or STUART, LADY ARABELLA (1575–1615). [See ARABELLA.]

STEWART or STUART, ARCHIBALD JAMES EDWARD (1748–1827). [See DOUGLAS, ARCHIBALD JAMES EDWARD, first BARON DOUGLAS OF DOUGLAS.]

STEWART, BALFOUR (1828–1887), physicist and meteorologist, born at Edinburgh on 1 Nov. 1828, was son of William Stewart, a tea merchant of Leith, and his wife Jane, daughter of the Rev. William Clouston, for sixty years minister of Stromness, Orkney. William Stewart belonged to the Stewarts of Brough, Orkney, who at one time owned the Fair Isle and other land. This property was subsequently left by a cousin of Balfour Stewart to charities, and formed 'the Stewart Endowment,' of which Sir Walter Scott was a trustee. According to family tradition, Scott took the characters of Minna and Brenda in the 'Pirate' from Jane Clouston and her sister. A brother, the Rev. Charles Clouston of Sandwick, Orkney, was a meteorologist. Balfour Stewart's grandmother belonged to the family of Balfours of Balfour.

A younger brother, William Clouston Stewart, well known in Scotland as an expert angler, was the author of the 'Practical Angler,' first published in 1857, and of other works on angling, and inventor of the 'Stewart tackle' (see Brit. Mus. Cat.)

Balfour Stewart went to school in Dundee, then for a short time to the university of St. Andrews, and then to Edinburgh, where he attended the class of James David Forbes [q. v.], the professor of natural philosophy, in 1845–6. On leaving the university at the age of 18, he entered the office of a cousin, James Balfour, a Leith merchant. He went to Australia on business about 1855, and his taste for physical science developed. His first two papers—'On the Influence of Gravity on the Physical Condition of the Moon's Surface' and 'On the Adaptations of the Eye to the Rays which emanate from Bodies'—were contributed in 1855 to the Philosophical Society of Victoria (*Transactions*, i. 92, 95). On his return he gave up business, and in February 1856 joined the staff of Kew observatory as assistant observer to John Welsh [q. v.] In October 1856 he became assistant to his former teacher, Forbes, at Edinburgh. Stewart at this time also worked at pure mathematics with Professor Philip Kelland, and in 1856 wrote a paper on a theorem in the theory of numbers (*Trans. Royal Society of Edinburgh*, xxi. 407), his only contribution to mathematics, for which he then showed distinct aptitude (TAIT). In 1857 he published an interesting paper on the relation between the density and composition of sulphuric acid solutions, deducing therefrom the existence of definite compounds of the acid and water (*Proc. Royal Society of Edinburgh*, iii. 482 ; a preliminary abstract appeared in 1855, *Brit. Assoc. Report*, pt. ii. p. 70). Mr. Spencer Umfreville Pickering and others have since employed Stewart's method of research.

It was under Forbes's influence that Stewart undertook the researches on radiant heat which form his most important contribution to physical science, and for which in 1868 he was awarded the Rumford medal by the Royal Society. Stewart extended the 'theory of exchanges' due to Pierre Prevost (1751–1839) of Geneva, and proved, in opposition to the view of Jean Baptiste Joseph Fourier (1768–1830), that radiation is not a surface phenomenon ; that it depends on the thickness of the radiating body, and in general that at any given temperature 'the absorption of a plate equals its radiation, and that for every description of heat' (*Trans. Royal Soc. of Edinburgh*, xxi. 1 sqq., read 15 March 1858) ; and that thus 'the streams of radiant heat crossing any point of an enclosure of uniform temperature are not altered by the interposition of a body, whether opaque or transparent.' It is remarkable, since Forbes had proved the similarity of radiant heat to light, that Stewart did not at once extend his results to optics. He also found out later that, *cæteris paribus*, the internal radiation in different substances varies as the square of the refractive index (*Brit. Assoc. Report*, 1861, i. 107), correcting an erroneous statement made by himself previously. Meanwhile Gustav Robert Kirchhoff (1824–1887) arrived independently at results which included those of Stewart, and led to the explanation of the dark lines in the solar spectrum as due to the absorption by layers of the vapours of various elements, and to the foundation by himself and Robert Wihelm Bunsen of spectrum

analysis—one of the greatest discoveries of the century (*Berichte der preussischen Akad. der Wissenschaften*, 11 Dec. 1859).

Stewart had been pushing on in the same direction, but more slowly. In 1860 he showed by experiments on tourmaline, of which the experimental arrangement was suggested by Professor (afterwards Sir George Gabriel) Stokes, that his law held good for polarised rays of light (*Proc. Royal Soc.* x. 503, read 22 May 1860). In the same year he also showed that red glass, when raised to a sufficiently high temperature to emit light on its own account, gives out greenish light, and similarly that a piece of platinum foil blackened appears, when so heated, brighter in the blackened part than elsewhere (*ib.* x. 385, read 7 Feb. 1860). In May 1861 (*ib.* x. 193) he wrote a paper on the theory of internal radiation in uniaxal crystals, which was developed in the same year by Stokes (*ib.* p. 537). By this time, however, Kirchhoff had practically exhausted the subject for the time being.

On 1 July 1859 Stewart had been appointed director of the Kew observatory in succession to John Welsh, and henceforward he devoted himself mainly to meteorology, and especially to the phenomena of terrestrial magnetism. In 1861 he was appointed additional examiner in mathematics at Edinburgh University for five years, and there made the acquaintance of his future collaborator, Professor Peter Guthrie Tait. In August and September 1859 there had been a great magnetic disturbance, accompanied by auroral displays and by marked changes in sun-spots ; the analysis of the photographic records of the magnetic storm at Kew directed Stewart's attention to the subject. General Edward Sabine [q. v.] had previously shown a connection between the occurrence of sun-spots and magnetic disturbances. Stewart now put forward the view that aurorœ, magnetic storms, and earth-currents are due to variations in a primary electric current in the sun (*Phil. Trans.* 1861, p. 423). In 1862 he was elected F.R.S., and in the same year he suggested that the 'red prominences' are really solar aurorœ (*Phil. Mag.* [4] xxiv. 302). In 1863 he made a careful investigation of the increase of pressure of a given volume of air between $32°$ F. and $212°$ F., his result for this important constant agreeing closely with that of Victor Regnault (1810–1878). In 1866 he redetermined the density of mercury at $32°$ F. with great accuracy. As it could be shown that the law of radiation of Stewart and Kirchhoff does not hold for a moving body in an enclosure of constant temperature, he made, in conjunction with Professor Tait between 1865 and 1873, a number of experiments on the heating of a disc by rapid rotation *in vacuo*, the apparatus for which was designed by R. Beckley, engineer to the Kew observatory. The experiments have been discussed by James Clerk Maxwell [q. v.], Professor Ludwig Boltzmann, and others, but no adequate explanation of the heating effect has yet been given. In 1865-1868 Stewart published, in conjunction with Warren de la Rue [see RUE] and Benjamin Loewy, a long series of investigations on sunspots, the variation of which they attempted, though without decided success, to trace to changes in planetary configuration. Stewart showed, however, that the daily range of magnetic variation appeared to be connected with these changes. He spent much effort from this time until his death on the discovery of certain periodic inequalities in terrestrial and solar phenomena, and attempted to deduce causes for these inequalities; but these deductions, as Stewart knew, can only be regarded as valid when based on an extremely large number of observations (SCHUSTER); and, together with William Dodgson, William Lant Carpenter, and other coadjutors, he spent a large amount of labour on the necessary calculations.

On 1 Jan. 1867 he was appointed secretary to the government meteorological committee, and in this and the following year he supervised the installation of meteorological stations all over the kingdom. He resigned the post in 1869. On 7 July 1870 Stewart was appointed professor of natural philosophy in the Owens College, Manchester, a post which he retained till his death. He continued, however, to act as superintendent of Kew observatory till 1871. In one of his journeys from London, in November 1870, he met with a railway accident in which his thigh was crushed, and for nine months lay ill at Harrow, in the course of which he passed from 'vigorous activity . . . to a grey-headed old age,' although his mental powers remained unimpaired.

In April 1875 was published anonymously a book called 'The Unseen Universe' by Stewart and his friend Professor Tait, in which the authors aimed at deducing from the combination of a number of theological postulates with current scientific doctrines the existence of the soul and of a transcendental universe. The book is written in a popular and picturesque style, and excited much attention, running through fourteen editions in thirteen years. The authors avowed their identity in the fourth edition (April 1876). Professor William Kingdon Clifford (1845-1879) made an attack on the book from the heterodox point of view in the 'Fortnightly

Review' (June 1875), to which a reply was offered in the preface to the second edition. A sequel published in 1878 by the same authors, dedicated to the members of the Paradoxical Society, and entitled 'Paradoxical Philosophy,' portraying in dialogue form the conversion of a cynical and heterodox German mathematician to religious and social orthodoxy, proved less successful.

Stewart, who was a devoted and fervent churchman, was elected by a conference held at Lambeth Palace on 7 Jan. 1881 as member of a committee for promoting interchange of views between scientific men of orthodox views in religious matters. He was also one of the founders of the Society for Psychical Research, in whose investigations he took a deep interest; he made several short contributions to its proceedings, and was president of the society from 1885 till his death.

In February 1887 he was elected president of the Physical Society, and also of the Manchester Literary and Philosophical Society. He died on 19 Dec. 1887 of apoplexy, at Ballymagarvey, a small estate near Drogheda, which he had inherited and whither he had gone to spend his Christmas vacation. He married, on 8 Sept. 1863, Katharine, only daughter of Charles Stevens, a lawyer in London. Two sons and a daughter survived him. Stewart was a man of exceptionally modest, gentle, and kindly nature. A photograph of him is in the common-room of the Owens College.

According to the bibliography by Professor Schuster in the 'Memoirs of the Manchester Literary and Philosophical Society,' Stewart published about sixty-seven papers of his own composition exclusively. In collaboration with others, he published two papers with J. Brito Capello, astronomer at Lisbon, three with W. L. Carpenter, ten with De la Rue and B. Loewy, two with the Rev. Father Walter Sidgreaves of Stonyhurst, two with Professor Tait, four with William Dodgson, one with Morisabro Hiraoka, three with B. Loewy, one with Father Stephen Joseph Perry [q. v.] on the comparison of magnetic observations at Kew and Stonyhurst, and one with (Sir) Henry Enfield Roscoe. He also contributed various reports to the British Association.

In addition to the papers and books already mentioned, Stewart published a number of successful text-books, which are not only in general conscientious and accurate, but show considerable power of picturesque illustration. Their titles are: 1. 'Treatise on Heat,' 1866; 3rd edit. 1866; 5th edit. 1888. 2. 'Lessons in Elementary Physics,' 1870. 3. 'The Conservation of Energy,' 1872, a popular ex-

T 2

position, translated into French, German (1875), and Czech (1885). 4. 'Lessons in ... Practical Physics,' in conjunction with Mr. William Haldane Gee, assistant lecturer in the Owens College, vol. i. 1885 ; vol. ii. 1887 ; 'the most complete exposition of experimental methods in physics which has been written' (SCHUSTER). 5. 'Lessons in Practical Physics for Schools,' 1888, also in conjunction with Mr. Gee. He also contributed an important article on 'Terrestrial Magnetism' to the ninth edition of the 'Encyclopædia Britannica.'

In 1874 Stewart edited, jointly with his colleague, Professor Adolphus William Ward (later principal of the college), a series of 'Essays and Addresses by Professors and Lecturers of the Owens College.' He was joint-editor with Professors Thomas Henry Huxley (1825–1895) and (Sir) Henry Enfield Roscoe of a valuable series of science primers published by Messrs. Macmillan & Co., for which Stewart wrote the 'Primer of Physics' (1872).

[Besides the sources mentioned, see Manchester Guardian, 20 and 24 Dec. 1887 ; Proceedings of the Society for Psychical Research, i. 35, iii. 64, iv. 42, 262, v. 1 ; Thompson's The Owens College, *passim* ; Men and Women of the Time, 12th edit. (from notes by Stewart) ; obituaries in Nature, xxxviii. 202, and Proc. Royal Society, xlvii. p. ix, by P. G. Tait ; Memoirs of Manchester Literary and Philosophical Society [4] i. 253, and Monthly Notices of Royal Astron. Society, xlviii. 166, by Professor Arthur Schuster, F.R.S. ; Proc. of the Physical Society for 1887–8, p. 10, see also p. 6 ; Proc. Roy. Soc. xlv. 85, xxxix. 37 et seq. (Hist. of the Kew Observatory by R. H. Scott, F.R.S.) ; Roscoe and Schuster's Spectrum Analysis, *passim* ; Life and Letters of J. D. Forbes, pp. 367, 391 (a communication from Stewart) ; Brit. Mus. Cat. ; private information from Mrs. Balfour Stewart (his widow) and Professor Schuster ; Stewart's own works, and personal knowledge. Stewart published an historical account of the theory of exchanges (including spectrum analysis) in the Brit. Assoc. Report for 1861, i. 97 &c. Kirchhoff published in Poggendorff's Annalen for 1862 (vol. xviii.) an historical account of the history of spectrum analysis, containing a somewhat grudging estimate of Stewart's work.] P. J. H.

STEWART, BERNARD or BERAULT, third SIEUR D'AUBIGNY (1447?–1508). [See STUART.]

STEWART, BERNARD, titular EARL OF LICHFIELD (1623?–1645). [See STUART.]

STEWART, CHARLES, third DUKE OF LENNOX and third DUKE OF RICHMOND (1640–1672). [See STUART.]

STEWART, CHARLES (1775–1812), lieutenant-colonel, born in 1775, was the eldest son of Thomas Stewart of Drumin, Banffshire, a lieutenant in the 50th foot, by Anne (Gordon). After serving for a short time in the Duke of Gordon's fencibles, he was commissioned as lieutenant in the 71st (highland) regiment on 25 Jan. 1791. He joined the regiment in India, and was wounded in the attack on Tippoo Sahib's camp at Seringapatam on 6–7 Feb. 1792. He was with the light company, and was noticed by Lord Cornwallis. On 3 April 1794 he obtained a company in the 109th, and, when that regiment was reduced in the following year, he was transferred with the men to the 53rd (2 Sept. 1795).

He served several years in the West Indies, and was wounded in storming the Morne Fortuné at St. Lucia in May 1796. He was promoted major in the regiment on 4 April 1800, and came home in command of it about 1804. On 17 Feb. 1805 he was made lieutenant-colonel of the newly raised 2nd battalion of the 50th. Sir Charles James Napier, who was major under him, wrote of him at the time as very pleasant in command and very decided, and afterwards spoke of him as one of the best officers of his rank in the service.

Having been transferred to the 1st battalion, Stewart served with it in the Walcheren expedition, was left in command of the rear-guard when the army withdrew, and was mentioned in despatches. In September 1810 he went to the Peninsula with the 1st battalion, and commanded it throughout the campaigns of 1811–12. It was engaged at Fuentes d'Onoro, and was soon afterwards attached to Hill's corps [see HILL, ROWLAND, first VISCOUNT HILL], and took part in the actions of Arroyo de Molinos, Almaraz, and Alba de Tormes. In the storming of Fort Napoleon, at Almaraz, Stewart led the right wing of his regiment 'in a most gallant and spirited manner.' The hardships of the retreat to Portugal in the autumn of 1812 broke down his health, and he died at Coria on 11 Dec., and was buried with military honours in the Campo Santo. He was unmarried.

[Military Mag. January 1813 ; Fyler's History of the 50th Regiment ; Adventures of Captain J. Paterson, pp. 5, 271 ; Life and Opinions of Sir C. J. Napier, i. 71 ; private information.] E. M. L.

STEWART, CHARLES (1764–1837), orientalist, eldest son of Poyntz Stewart, captain 1st regiment, of Lisburn, co. Antrim, was born in 1764. In 1781 he entered the East India Company's Bengal army as cadet, and left it with the rank of major in

1808. On the foundation of the Fort William College at Calcutta in 1800, he was appointed assistant professor of Persian there, but in 1806 returned to England, and in the following year was appointed to the professorship, which he retained till 1827, of Arabic, Persian, and Hindustani in the Haileybury College. He died at Bath on 19 April 1837. He was a member of the Royal Academy of Sciences of Munich and other learned bodies, and in 1821 received the gold medal of the Oriental Translation Fund.

Stewart married, first, Amelia, daughter of Sir W. Gordon of Embo, bart., and, secondly, in 1828, Anne, daughter of the Rev. Nicholas Holland, rector of Stifford, and widow of J. Reid, esq., of Calcutta, but had no children.

He wrote: 1. 'The Anvari Soohyly of Hussein Vaiz Kashify,' published by Moolvey Hussein and Captain C. S., Calcutta, 1804, fol. 2. 'A Descriptive Catalogue of the Oriental Library of the late Tippoo Sultan of Mysore, to which are prefixed Memoirs of Hyder Aly and his Son, Tippoo Sultan,' Cambridge, 1809, 4to. 3. 'Abu Taleb Khan's Travels in Europe and Asia, edited by his Son, Mirza Hasein Ali, translated,' London, 1810, 2 vols. 8vo; 1814, 3 vols. 12mo. 4. 'The History of Bengal, from the first Mohammedan Invasion until 1757,' London, 1813, 4to. 5. 'An Introduction to the Anvari Soohyly,' London, 1821, 4to. 6. 'Seventh Chapter of Anvari Soohyly, with an English Translation and Analysis of all the Arabic Words,' London, 1821, 4to. 7. 'Original Persian Letters and other Documents, compiled and translated,' London, 1825, 4to. 8. 'The Mulfuzát Timury, or Autobiographical Memoirs of the Moghul Emperor Timur, translated,' London, 1830, 4to (Oriental Translation Fund). 9. 'The Tezkereh al Vakiát, or Private Memoirs of the Moghul Emperor Humayûn,' by Jouher, translated, London, 1832, 4to (Oriental Translation Fund). 10. 'Biographical Sketch of the Emperor Jehángir' (explanatory of a painting presented to the Royal Asiatic Society by C. S.), pamphlet, 8vo, n.d.

[Memorials of the Stewarts of Fothergill, by C. P. Stewart, privately printed, 1879, 4to; Memorials of Old Haileybury College, 1894, 8vo; private information.] T. E. H.

STEWART or **STUART, CHARLES EDWARD** (1720–1788), the Young Pretender. [See CHARLES EDWARD LOUIS PHILIP CASIMIR.]

STEWART, CHARLES JAMES (1775–1837), bishop of Quebec, born on 13 April 1775, was third son of John Stewart, seventh

earl of Galloway, by his second wife, Anne, second daughter of Sir James Dashwood of Kirtlington, bart. General Sir William Stewart (1774–1827) [q. v.] was an elder brother. Charles James was educated by private tutors, and matriculated from Corpus Christi College, Oxford, on 22 May 1792, graduating B.A. in 1795, M.A. in 1799, and B.D. and D.D. in 1816. In 1795 he was elected a fellow of All Souls', and in 1799 he was presented to the rectories of Overton-Longueville and Botolph Bridge in Huntingdonshire. In 1807 he undertook work in Canada on behalf of the Society for the Propagation of the Gospel, and was appointed to the mission of Saint Armand in Misisquoi Bay. From this time he devoted his life and fortune to the work of the church in North America, and as the result of his exertions, and partly of his liberality, twenty-four churches, some no doubt small and primitive, were erected. In 1817, after a visit to England, he removed to Hatley, a district farther east than Saint Armand; in 1819, to meet the needs of the growing number of emigrants, he became a visiting missionary, with the duty of travelling to the more remote parts of the diocese of Quebec.

In 1825 Stewart was selected to succeed Jacob Mountain [q. v.] as bishop of Quebec, and, proceeding to England, was consecrated on 1 Jan. 1826 at Lambeth. As bishop he did not suspend his laborious work, but journeyed incessantly throughout Upper and Lower Canada, seeking to supply by his personal efforts the deficient numbers of his clergy. In 1833 the first steps towards reducing the government grant to the church in North America threw fresh anxiety on him. Notwithstanding frequent visits to England, his labours broke down his constitution, which was not robust. In consequence of his infirmity, George Jehoshaphat Mountain [q. v.] was consecrated coadjutor-bishop of Montreal on 14 Feb. 1836, and later in the year Stewart returned on a visit to England. He died unmarried in London on 10 July 1837, and was buried at Kensal Green cemetery.

He was the author of several published charges and sermons.

[Morgan's Sketches of Celebrated Canadians; Christie's History of Lower Canada, iv. 411; Lives of Missionaries (Soc. for Promoting Christian Knowledge, 1865), North America, pp. 161–205; Waddilove's Stewart Missions (containing a few of Stewart's letters), 1838; Douglas's Peerage, ed. Wood, i. 624; Annals of the Colonial Church, Toronto (Soc. Prom. Chr. Knowl.); Foster's Alumni Oxon. 1715–1886.] C. A. H.

STEWART (afterwards VANE), CHARLES WILLIAM, third MARQUIS OF LONDONDERRY (1778–1854), was the only son of Robert Stewart, first marquis [q. v.], by his second wife, Frances, eldest daughter of Charles Pratt, first earl Camden [q. v.] He was born in Dublin on 18 May 1778, being nine years younger than his half-brother Robert, second marquis, better known as Lord Castlereagh [q.v.] He was educated at Eton, and narrowly escaped drowning there at the age of thirteen in a courageous attempt to save his schoolfellow, Lord Waldegrave. He was commissioned as ensign in a newly raised regiment of foot (Macnamara's) on 11 Oct. 1794, in which he became lieutenant on 30 Oct. and captain on 12 Nov. He obtained a majority in the 106th foot on 31 July 1795, but both this and his former regiment were disbanded in that year. He was employed on the staff of Lord Moira's corps in the campaign of 1794–5 in the Netherlands. He then accompanied Colonel (afterwards Sir Charles Gregan-) Craufurd [q. v.] to the head-quarters of the Austrian army, and served with it in the campaigns of 1795–6 on the Rhine and Upper Danube. In a cavalry affair near Donauwörth he was struck by a bullet under the left eye and his sight injured.

He was aide-de-camp to his uncle, Lord Camden, who was lord-lieutenant of Ireland from 1795 to 1798. On 4 Aug. 1796 he obtained a majority in the 5th dragoons (Royal Irish), and became lieutenant-colonel of it on 1 Jan. 1797. The regiment served in Ireland during the rebellion of 1798; but its discipline became so bad, and so many disloyal men were found to be in its ranks, that it was disbanded on 8 April 1799. Stewart had done his utmost to improve it; his family interest was great, and four days afterwards he was made lieutenant-colonel of the 18th light dragoons.

He served with two squadrons of this regiment in the short campaign of 1799 in Holland. Being attached to Abercrombie's division on 19 Sept., and to Pulteney's on 2 Oct., he had little fighting. He was slightly wounded on outpost duty at Schagenburg on 10 Oct. On 25 Sept. 1803 he was made aide-de-camp to the king and colonel in the army. Shortly afterwards he was appointed under-secretary in Ireland. He had been elected member for Thomastown to the Irish parliament in 1798, and after the union he was member for co. Derry in the imperial parliament till 1814. In 1805, when invasion was threatened, he published 'Suggestions for the Improvement of the Force of the

British Empire.' In 1807 he became under-secretary for war, Castlereagh being the secretary of state. The two brothers were always most warmly attached to each other.

In August 1808 Stewart left his office for a time to command the hussar brigade in the corps sent out to Portugal under Sir John Moore. The brigade consisted of the 18th and the king's German hussars, to which the 10th was afterwards added. It covered the advance of Hope's division upon Madrid and Salamanca in November, and afterwards covered the retreat of the whole army on Coruña. On 12 Dec. Stewart surprised a French post at Rueda and took eighty prisoners; and on the 28th he had a prominent part in the brilliant cavalry action at Benavente, the pickets being furnished by his regiment. He shared with Lord Paget the praise of Moore, that they had put the right spirit into the British cavalry.

He returned to England and to his office in January 1809. He was given the governorship of Fort Charles, Jamaica—a sinecure office worth 650l. a year, which he resigned in favour of Lord Bloomfield in 1822. In April 1809 he went back to Portugal as adjutant-general under Wellesley, with the rank of brigadier-general. At the passage of the Douro he led some charges of squadrons which were specially noticed by Wellesley in general orders, and he also distinguished himself at Talavera. Ill-health obliged him to go to England for the winter, and on 5 Feb. 1810 he received, in his place in parliament, the thanks of the House of Commons. He was promoted major-general on 25 July.

He returned to the Peninsula in March, and served as adjutant-general throughout the campaigns of 1810 and 1811. He was mentioned in despatches for Busaco and Fuentes d'Onoro. In the latter battle he disarmed a colonel of chasseurs and made him prisoner, and at El Bodon he found fresh opportunity of taking part in a cavalry encounter. He was essentially a sabreur, handsome and dashing; in Alison's words, 'his nature was chivalrous rather than administrative;' and he longed to exchange his staff appointment for a cavalry command. But Wellington would not indulge him. On 25 June 1811, in reply to a letter from the Duke of York, he wrote that Stewart was a very gallant and very able officer of cavalry, but, owing to his defective sight and hearing, his gallantry would be apt to lead him into difficulties.

Stewart was at the siege and capture of Ciudad Rodrigo in January 1812, but a return of intermittent fever obliged him to go home in February, and he saw no further service in the Peninsula. He was appointed a groom of the bedchamber on 28 July. At the end of the year he wrote to Wellington to say that it was proposed he should bring out an hussar brigade, and to ask if he could have command of a cavalry division. Wellington replied that he wished to keep all the cavalry in one division under Cotton (*Despatches, Supplementary*, vii. 165, 549, and viii. 413. Stewart's letter is misdated 1813). Disappointed in this, Stewart determined to resign his appointment as adjutant-general, which he had originally accepted with reluctance. Wellington was not sorry to lose him. He harassed the cavalry, and had vexed Wellington by his free comments on the way in which it was handled, and by the pretensions which he set up as adjutant-general. Wellington believed also that he intrigued against him in the army, and preached that no good was to be done in Spain; and this was the more serious because, as Wellington told Croker in 1826, 'Castle-reagh had a real respect for Charles's understanding, and a high opinion of his good sense and discretion. This seems incomprehensible to us who knew the two men' (*Croker Papers*, i. 346; cf. CRAUFURD, *Life of Craufurd*, p. 118). In spite of all this, there were no signs of estrangement in their future relations. Wellington habitually wrote to Stewart in terms of affectionate intimacy, and the latter always showed unstinted admiration for Wellington. An obelisk at Wynyard Park, inscribed 'Wellington, the friend of Londonderry,' commemorated a visit from the duke in 1827.

Stewart was made a K.B. on 1 Feb. 1813, and received the Portuguese order of the Tower and Sword soon afterwards, and the gold medal with one clasp in the following year, for his services in the Peninsula. Castle-reagh had returned to office as foreign secretary in 1812, and on 9 April 1813 Stewart was appointed British minister to the court of Berlin, 'specially charged with the military superintendence, so far as Great Britain is concerned, of the Prussian and Swedish armies.' He reached the head-quarters of the allies at Dresden on 20 April, and signed the formal treaty of alliance between Great Britain, Russia, and Prussia. He was present at Lützen, and was actively engaged at Bautzen; and he took part in Blücher's brilliant cavalry stroke at Haynau on 26 May. He helped to storm one of the redoubts at Dresden, and was severely wounded at Kulm. At Leipzig (16 Oct.) Blücher gave him the command of his reserve

cavalry, and he captured a battery at the head of the Brandenburg hussars.

But it was in bringing pressure upon Bernadotte that he was of most service to the cause of the allies. He at once recognised the prince royal as 'a highly finished actor' who was playing a game of his own, and was not inclined 'to spill Swedish in drawing French blood.' But by strenuous exertions and very plain speaking he brought him to take some share in the battle of Leipzig; and he prevented the completion of a convention under which Davoust, who was in Hamburg with thirty thousand men, would have been allowed to return to France. At the same time he kept on good terms with Bernadotte, and received from him the Swedish order of the Sword. He also received the order of the Black Eagle, and six months later of the Red Eagle, of Prussia, and the Russian order of St. George (fourth class). The latter was accompanied by a letter from the Emperor Alexander, bearing witness to his indefatigable zeal and to the coolness and valour he had shown in the battlefield. On 20 Nov. he was given the colonelcy of the 25th light dragoons.

During the campaign of 1814 Stewart was at the headquarters of the allies with Castle-reagh. He was present at the actions of La Rothière, Fère-Champenoise, and Montmartre, and at the entry into Paris on 31 March. He was promoted lieutenant-general on 4 June, and was raised to the peerage as Baron Stewart on 1 July. He received honorary degrees at Oxford and Cambridge, was sworn of the privy council on 23 July, and made a lord of the bedchamber in August. On the enlargement of the Bath he received the G.C.B., and in 1816 the G.C.H.

On 27 August 1814 he was appointed ambassador at Vienna. He assisted Castle-reagh, and afterwards Wellington, in the negotiations of the congress there, and accompanied the allied sovereigns again to Paris after Waterloo. He represented Great Britain at the congress of Troppau in 1820, and that of Laybach in 1821, and was at Verona with Wellington in 1822. Throughout these affairs he was the zealous instrument of Castlereagh's policy. Among his duties at Vienna was the collection of information about the conduct of Queen Caroline, and he went to England in the autumn of 1820 to advise the government about it. He was a lord of the bedchamber to George IV from his accession to April 1827.

By his brother's death, on 12 Aug. 1822, he became Marquis of Londonderry, and when he found that Canning was to take the foreign office he tendered his resignation ; but at Canning's request he remained till the end of the year to assist Wellington at Verona.

On 8 Aug. 1808 he had married Catherine, daughter of the third Earl of Darnley. She died on 8 Feb. 1812, while he was on his way home from Spain, leaving one son. On 3 April 1819 he married Frances Anne, only daughter of Sir Harry Vane-Tempest, and of Anne, countess of Antrim, and heiress of very large estates in Durham and the north of Ireland. On his marriage he took the surname of Vane, and on 28 March 1823 he was created Earl Vane and Viscount Seaham in the peerage of the United Kingdom, with remainder to the eldest son by his second marriage. After his return from Vienna he and his wife occupied themselves in improving and developing their property, especially the Seaham estate, which he bought from the Milbanke family in 1822. By opening collieries, and making a harbour, docks, and a railway, he created a thriving seaport which have abundantly justified his foresight, and has nearly ten thousand inhabitants. He rebuilt the mansion at Wynyard twice, for it was burnt down in 1841, and he remodelled the park.

In 1835, during Peel's short administration, he was offered and accepted the embassy at St. Petersburg. The support given by France to Mehemet Ali made the British government draw towards Russia, and he was a man who would find favour there. But in England, as a conspicuous opponent of reform, he had incurred so much hostility that he was on one occasion mobbed and dragged off his horse. Always an uncompromising tory, he did not measure his words, and he had shown some want of sympathy with the Poles. The appointment was bitterly attacked in the commons on 13 March, and not very stoutly defended ; and Londonderry, feeling that such a debate would weaken his hands, withdrew his acceptance. The appointment had been recommended by Wellington, who was foreign secretary. He told Greville ' that he was not particularly partial to the man, nor ever had been ; but that he was very fit for that post, was an excellent ambassador, procured more information and obtained more insight into the affairs of a foreign court than anybody, and that he was the best relater of what passed at a conference, and wrote the best account of a conversation, of any man he knew' (GREVILLE, Journals, 15 March 1835).

Londonderry compensated himself by travels in Russia and other parts of eastern and southern Europe in 1836 and subsequent years. He had succeeded the prince regent

as colonel of the 10th hussars on 3 Feb. 1820, and in 1823 he had thought himself bound to accept a challenge from Cornet Battier of that regiment, arising out of a trivial matter brought before him as colonel. This brought him a sharp reprimand from the Horse Guards, while Battier was dismissed from the army. In 1839 he fought another duel with Henry Grattan the younger, owing to an absurd charge which the latter had made against the tories in connection with the bedchamber question. In each case Londonderry received his adversary's fire, and then discharged his own pistol in the air.

On 10 Jan. 1837 he became general, and on 21 June 1843 he was transferred from the 10th hussars to the 2nd life-guards. He had been appointed governor of co. Derry in 1823, and one of the joint-governors of co. Down in 1824 ; and he was made lord-lieutenant of Durham on 27 April 1842. In 1852 he received the Garter made vacant by Wellington's death, and was one of the pall-bearers at his funeral. But he did not long survive his old chief. He died at Holdernesse House, London, on 6 March 1854, from influenza, and was buried on the 10th at Long Newton, near Wynyard Park, co. Durham, where his widow built a ' memorial-room' for the insignia of his orders and other relics of him. She died on 20 Jan. 1865.

Londonderry's only son by his first wife, Frederick William Robert Stewart (1805-1872), succeeded as fourth Marquis of Londonderry. Londonderry had three sons and four daughters by his second marriage. The eldest of these sons, George Henry Robert Charles William Vane-Tempest (1821-1884), succeeded him as Earl Vane, and (by the death of his half-brother) became fifth Marquis of Londonderry on 25 Nov. 1872. The latter's son is the sixth and present marquis.

There is a portrait of him by Sir Thomas Lawrence, painted during the Peninsular war, in hussar uniform, and a later one by Bostock, painted in 1838.

He was the author of several works : 1. ' A Narrative of the Peninsular War from 1808 to 1813,' 2 vols. 4to, London, 1828. This was based upon letters written by him to Castlereagh during the war, and combines freshness of style with much exact information. It did not include the campaigns of 1812 and 1813. 2. ' A Narrative of the War in Germany and France in 1813-14,' 4to, London, 1830. 3. ' Recollections of a Tour in the North of Europe in 1836-7,' 2 vols. 8vo, London, 1838. 4. ' Journal of a Tour in the Southern Parts of Spain, &c.' (privately printed), London, 1840. 5. ' A Steam Voyage to Constantinople by the Rhine and Danube in 1840-1, and to Portugal, Spain, &c. in 1839,' 2 vols. 8vo, London, 1842. A correspondence with Metternich is appended to this work. 6. 'Memoir and Correspondence of Viscount Castlereagh, second Marquess of Londonderry, edited by his brother,' 12 vols. 8vo, London, 1848-53. This grew out of 'a letter to Lord Brougham,' which he published in 1839, in reply to the hostile account given of Castlereagh in the 'Sketches of Statesmen of the Time of George III.'

[Alison's Lives of Lord Castlereagh and Sir Charles Stewart; Gent. Mag. 1854, i. 415; Doyle's Official Baronage; Moore's Life of Sir J. Moore; Napier's War in the Peninsula; Wellington Despatches; Wilson's Private Diary, 1812-14; Liddell's History of the 10th Hussars; Records of the 18th Dragoons.]   E. M. L.

STEWART, DAVID, DUKE OF ROTHESAY (1378?-1402), only surviving son of Robert III of Scotland, by Annabella Drummond, daughter of John Drummond of Stobhall, was born about 1378. After the succession of the father, who was originally called John, earl of Carrick, to the throne as Robert III, the son succeeded to the title of Earl of Carrick. About 1396 he was entrusted with the government or pacification of the northern parts of the kingdom (Chamberlain's Accounts quoted in TYTLER's *History*, ed. 1868, ii. 5). He showed himself able and energetic, but rash, headstrong, and unscrupulous. The bodily defects and mild, if not weak, personality of Robert III unfitting him for the personal duties of government, the management of the affairs of the kingdom had been entrusted to the Earl of Fife, the king's brother [see STEWART, ROBERT, first DUKE OF ALBANY]; but at a meeting of the estates held in January 1398-1399 it was resolved that David, earl of Carrick, as heir to the throne, should be appointed lieutenant of the kingdom with full sovereign powers (*Acta Parl. Scot.* i. 572). About the same time he was created Duke of Rothesay, and his uncle, the Earl of Fife, was created Duke of Albany, these being the earliest examples of the use of the ducal dignity in Scotland. Shortly after his accession to the regency he was betrothed to a daughter of the Earl of March, but the proposed marriage having aroused the jealousy of the Earl of Douglas, he induced Rothesay, by the bribe of a splendid dowry, to prefer his daughter Elizabeth Douglas, to whom Rothesay was hastily married at Bothwell. Determined on revenge, March then proceeded to England, and induced Henry IV as lord superior to undertake an expedition against Scotland to chastise the unfaithful swain. March,

aided by Hotspur and Lord Thomas Talbot, made also a preliminary incursion against Rothesay, but was totally routed near Cockburnspath. Nor did the more formidable array under Henry accomplish anything of a satisfactory nature. Learning its approach, Rothesay, who commanded the castle of Edinburgh, sent Henry a public cartel of defiance. To the challenge he deigned no reply; but his march against Edinburgh failed either to awe Rothesay or to entice him to offer battle; and Henry, baffled of his purpose, withdrew again into England without a blow being struck.

In 1402 the triennial period of Rothesay's government as regent had expired. How far he had misused his power it is impossible to determine, but Albany at least deemed it desirable that he should be removed; and while it was impossible that one of his audacity could be superseded except by force, his successor's tenure of office would have been insecure so long as he remained at large. To effect his purpose, Albany made a paction with Archibald, earl of Douglas—who was offended with Rothesay for his unfaithfulness to his wife, the sister of Douglas—and with Sir William Lindsay of Ramornie, whose sister had been one of Rothesay's victims. It so happened that after the death of Bishop Trail of St. Andrews, Rothesay had arranged, in accordance with royal custom, to occupy the castle of St. Andrews until the bishop's successor should be appointed. As his term of office had expired, his purpose was illegal, and while proceeding to St. Andrews he was intercepted near Strathtyrum, and placed in confinement in the castle which he had hoped to occupy. Thence shortly afterwards he was carried by Albany and Douglas to Falkland, and confined in a dungeon, where according to one story he was starved to death, and according to another died of dysentery (27 March 1402). In any case it is unlikely that he would have regained his liberty while Albany lived. He was buried privately in Lindores Abbey. At a meeting of the council held at Holyrood, 16 May 1402, an inquiry was held into the cause of his death, and Albany and Douglas were formally—but in very equivocal terms—declared innocent (see specially the narrative with authorities quoted in TYTLER's *History*, ed. 1868, ii. 20-22). John Wright, one of his keepers in Falkland, received a special allowance from Albany (*Exchequer Rolls of Scotland*, iv. 135), which he could scarce have been paid had there been nothing that Albany wished concealed. The dukedom was by charter, 22 Nov. 1409, transferred to Rothesay's brother, afterwards James I of Scotland; and by an act of parliament, 22 Nov. 1409, the dukedom of Rothesay, with the earldom of Carrick, &c., was vested in the eldest son and heir-apparent of the sovereign.

[Exchequer Rolls of Scotland; Acta Parl. Scot.; Tytler's Hist. of Scotland and authorities therein quoted. A powerfully dramatic account of Rothesay's death by starvation occupies the thirty-second chapter of Scott's 'Fair Maid of Perth.']   T. F. H.

STEWART, DAVID (1772–1829), major-general, born in 1772, was second son of Robert Stewart of Garth, Perthshire, and was descended from James Stewart (grandson of Robert II) who built the castle of Garth at the end of the fourteenth century. He was given a commission as ensign in the 77th (Atholl highlanders) on 21 April 1783, but that regiment was disbanded soon afterwards. He joined the 42nd highlanders on 10 Aug. 1787, became lieutenant on 8 Aug. 1792, and captain-lieutenant on 24 June 1796. He served with the 42nd in Flanders in 1794, and went with it to the West Indies in October 1795. He took part in the capture of St. Lucia and St. Vincent, and in the prolonged bush-fighting with the Caribs. He was also in the unsuccessful expedition against Porto Rico in 1797.

Stewart returned to Europe with his regiment, was in garrison at Gibraltar, and embarked there with the expedition for the recovery of Minorca in November 1798. But he was taken prisoner at sea, and was detained five months in Spain before he was exchanged. He went to Egypt with Abercromby's expedition, and was severely wounded at the battle of Alexandria on 21 March 1801. Three months before this, on 15 Dec. 1800, he had obtained a company in the 90th (Perthshire volunteers), but he returned to the 42nd on 23 July 1802.

He obtained a majority in the 78th highlanders, on 17 April 1804, by raising recruits for the second battalion which was then being formed, a thing which his popularity in the highlands made easy to him. His men were so much attached to him that, when he was at Shorncliffe in the following year, Sir J. Moore interposed to prevent his being sent to India to join the 1st battalion. He went with the 2nd battalion to the Mediterranean in September 1805, and shared in the descent on Calabria. At Maida, 4 July 1806, he commanded a battalion of light companies, and was again severely wounded. He was appointed lieutenant-colonel of the West India rangers on 21 April 1808, and took part in the capture of Guadaloupe in 1810. He received a medal with one clasp for this and Maida, and in 1815 he was made C.B. He was promoted colonel in the army on 4 June 1814, and in the following year he was placed on half-pay.

In 1817 the officer commanding the 42nd applied to him for information about the history of the regiment, as its records had been lost. The reminiscences and inquiries which were started by this application gradually developed into the 'Sketches of the Character, Manners, and Present State of the Highlanders of Scotland; with details of the Military Service of the Highland Regiments,' which was published in two volumes at Edinburgh in 1822. This book, 'whose excellence shines forth on every page' (J. S. BLACKIE), has been the foundation of all subsequent works on the clans. The first two parts of it, dealing with the country and the people, occupy about half to the first volume; the remainder is devoted to the annals of Scottish regiments. 'Remarks on Colonel Stewart's Sketches of the Highlanders' were published at Edinburgh in 1823, admitting its merits, but objecting to its Jacobite sympathies. Stewart had thoughts of writing a history of the rebellion of 1745, but gave it up.

Soon after publishing his book he succeeded to the estate of Garth by the death of his elder brother. When George IV visited Edinburgh in August 1822, Stewart helped Sir Walter Scott in the reception arrangements, headed the Celtic club in the procession, adjusted the royal plaid for the levée, and pronounced the king 'a vera pretty man' (LOCKHART). He was promoted major-general on 27 May 1825, and in 1829 he went out to St. Lucia as governor. The island was then very unhealthy, and on 18 Dec. he died there, widely regretted.

There are portraits of him by J. M. Scrymgeour and Sir J. Watson Gordon; both have been engraved, and the latter is reproduced by Chambers.

[Gent. Mag. 1830, i. 276; Chambers's Biographical Dictionary of Eminent Scotsmen.]
                                    E. M. L.

STEWART, DUGALD (1753–1828), philosopher, born at Edinburgh on 22 Nov. 1753 in a house attached to the professorship of mathematics, and forming part of the old college buildings, was son of Matthew Stewart (1717–1785) [q. v.] by Marjory, only child of Archibald Stewart of Catrine. Dugald Stewart was sent to the Edinburgh high school in 1761, where he was, in 1764–5, under Alexander Adam [q. v.], then assistant to the rector. Under Adam he is said to have acquired a taste for the classics, and especially for Latin poetry, which he always retained. He was entered as a student of humanity at the university in the session of 1765–6, and completed the usual course in the three following sessions, passing through the Greek class in his second session, the logic class in the third and fourth, and in the fourth attending also the class of natural philosophy under James Russell. He became a good mathematician, and was specially impressed by the teaching of Dr John Stevenson, professor of logic from 1730 to 1775; and of Adam Ferguson [q. v.], professor of moral philosophy. Reid's 'Inquiry' (1764) had been warmly received by both professors, and was mentioned with 'high encomiums' by Russell (STEWART, *Works*, x. 261). Stewart was therefore prepared to accept Reid as the true philosophical prophet. He had thought of obtaining an appointment as an engineer in the service of the East India Company, but afterwards inclined to taking orders in the church of England. He went to Glasgow partly in the hope of going to Oxford as one of the Snell exhibitioners; and partly in order to attend the lectures of Reid, who held the Glasgow chair of moral philosophy. He remained there during the session of 1771–2. He belonged to a literary society at Glasgow, and read before it a paper upon dreaming, afterwards inserted in his 'Elements' (*Works*, ii. 289–305, 490). Its publication there led also to his first acquaintance with Thomas Brown (1778–1820) [q. v.]. Stewart read this and other papers to the Speculative Society of Edinburgh, of which he was an active member from 1772 to 1775. At Glasgow he acquired the personal friendship of his master, Reid, and boarded in the same house with Archibald Alison (1757–1839) [q. v.], who became a lifelong friend, and dedicated the 'Essays on Taste' to him in 1790.

In the autumn of 1772 he was recalled to Edinburgh to take charge of mathematical classes. The elder Stewart was failing, and in 1775 the son was associated with him in his professorship, and thenceforth discharged all the duties of the chair. He is said to have been a very successful teacher. He groaned, however, when he had the prospect of teaching Euclid for the thirteenth time. In the session of 1778–9 Stewart undertook to lecture for Adam Ferguson, who had a temporary appointment in America. He had to give a course upon morality, besides lecturing three hours daily upon mathematics, and giving for the first time a course upon astronomy. He lectured from notes, arranging his ideas while walking in the garden. He afterwards wrote for publication quickly, but altered much while his works were in the press. These early lectures were very successful, and by some hearers preferred to his later efforts. He had to rise at 3 A.M. on five days of the week, and was so exhausted by his labours that he had to be lifted into his carriage for a journey.

In 1783 Stewart visited Paris with his friend, Lord Ancrum (afterwards sixth Marquis of Lothian). On his return he married Helen, daughter of Neil Bannatyne of Glasgow. In 1785 he was transferred to the chair of moral philosophy, upon the resignation of Adam Ferguson. He speedily obtained an influence such as has been enjoyed by few British philosophers. He was, after Reid's death, the only writer of recognised authority upon philosophical topics in the island; and during the exclusion of British subjects from the continent by the war many young men of position were sent to Edinburgh instead of making the 'grand tour.' His character and his eloquence commanded respect, and Edinburgh continued during his life to be scarcely inferior to London as a centre of intellectual activity. His class, during his twenty-four years of active work, increased from 102 in 1785–6 to 196 in 1807–8 and 150 in 1808–9. He also gave summer courses on moral philosophy for a few years, and occasionally lectured for his colleagues upon mathematics, natural philosophy, and logic.

Stewart during the early years of his professorship spent his summers at Catrine on the water of Ayr, in a house inherited from his mother. Burns's farm, Mossgiel, was in the neighbourhood, and the poet was introduced to the philosopher in 1786 [see under BURNS, ROBERT]. Stewart gave an interesting account of their intercourse to Currie, who published it in his life of Burns (also in STEWART's *Works*, vol. x. pp. cxl, &c.). The erection of a cotton mill at Catrine in 1782 diminished the charm of the place.

Stewart's wife died in 1787. He spent the summers of 1788 and 1789 in France, where he made the acquaintance of many eminent men, including Suard, Morellet, Prévost of Geneva, Degérando, and Raynal. He sympathised strongly with the early revolutionary movement, and did not give up his hopes of a satisfactory issue even at the outbreak of the war and the beginning of the Terror (see Letters in Appendix A to *Life*). On 26 July 1790 he married Helen D'Arcy (1765–1838), third daughter of the Hon. George Cranstoun, and sister of Scott's friend, the Countess Purgstall, and of George Cranstoun, lord Corehouse [q. v.] Her mother was Maria, daughter of Thomas Brisbane of Brisbane, Ayrshire. She was a woman of cultivated intellect and great social charm. Burns sent a song by her, 'The tears I shed must ever fall,' to Johnson's 'Museum,' adding to it the first four lines of the last stanza. A set of verses attributed to her in Stanhouse's 'Notes to Johnson's "Museum"' —'Returning spring with lessening ray'—has less merit. Stewart submitted all his writings to her judgment, and she helped materially to make his house the centre of the best society in Edinburgh. His liberal opinions, however, gave some offence to the dominant party. Jeffrey was apparently forbidden by his father to attend the lectures of so dangerous a teacher (COCKBURN, *Jeffrey*, i. 51). Though the young whigs regarded him as the especial glory of their party, Cockburn (*Memorials*, p. 103) says that for some years he was not cordially received elsewhere.

In a chapter of his first book, published in 1792, he had, in the course of remarks upon the use of abstract principles in politics, referred approvingly to some of the French 'philosophes' (*Works*, ii. 219 &c.) Though his remarks were very moderate, two of the lords of session (W. Craig and A. Abercromby), who, he says, 'spent three evenings a week at my house,' suggested to him that he ought, in an 'open and manly manner,' to retract every word he had said on behalf of French philosophy. Stewart, while repudiating any sympathy with revolutionary excesses, declared that he had nothing to retract. He gave a separate course of lectures on political economy, principally following Adam Smith, but with some reference to general politics, in 1800. In 1805 he took an active part in support of John Leslie (1766-1832) [q. v.], who, upon becoming professor of mathematics, was attacked for approving Hume's theory of causation. The whigs took Leslie's side; and Stewart published a pamphlet, and spoke in the general assembly in a 'fine spirit,' according to Cockburn (*Memorials*, p. 200), 'of scorn and eloquence.' In a letter to Horner soon afterwards, he expresses his hope that the Scottish universities will be less 'priestridden' hereafter, and says that the fall of Lord Melville, which was becoming probable, would be 'synonymous with the emancipation and salvation of Scotland.' When the whigs came into power in 1806, Stewart was appointed to the writership of the Edinburgh 'Gazette,' a sinecure of 300*l.* a year. He held it for life, and it was continued to his family after his death. In the summer he accompanied Lord Lauderdale, who, like his pupil, Lord Henry Petty, held

office under the new government, on his diplomatic mission to Paris.

Stewart's health, never very strong, had been failing, and he was much affected by the death of a son in 1809. He requested Brown to act as his substitute in the following session, and finally retired from lecturing. Brown, at the end of the session, was appointed his coadjutor, but was to undertake the whole duty. Stewart canvassed the town council, and used all his influence to obtain his appointment, though he was afterwards greatly dissatisfied with Brown's teaching.

From 1809 Stewart lived in retirement at Kinneil House, Linlithgowshire, lent to him by the Duke of Hamilton. He occupied himself in preparing the substance of his lectures for publication. Upon Brown's death, in 1820, Stewart became again the sole professor. Though invited by some of his friends to lecture, he felt himself too infirm to discharge the duties, and resigned on 20 June. He approved of the candidature of his friend Macvey Napier, and afterwards of Sir William Hamilton. He was unable to take an active part in canvassing, and the election was carried by the tories in favour of John Wilson, 'Christopher North.'

In January 1822 Stewart had a stroke of paralysis. His mind was not seriously affected, and he was able to prepare his work for the press, with the help of his daughter as amanuensis. He died at Edinburgh on 11 June 1828, while on a visit to a friend. Cockburn describes Stewart as slight and feeble, with a large bald forehead, bushy eyebrows, grey, intelligent eyes with very changeable expression, and flexible lips. A portrait, in his seventy-first year, painted by Wilkie, and a bust by Joseph are engraved in the collective edition of his works (vols. i. and x.) A portrait was painted by Raeburn about 1808, for A. Fraser-Tytler, lord Woodhouselee. Soon after his death a meeting was held by his friends, by whom a monument was erected upon the Calton Hill.

Stewart by his first wife had one son Matthew, who entered the army, and went to India in 1807 as aide-de-camp to Lord Minto. He rose to the rank of colonel, and retired on half-pay some years after the peace. There was a strong mutual attachment between him and his father. He had collected many of his father's papers and journals, and had prepared an account of his life and writings. He burnt them all under a delusion, due, it was supposed, to a sunstroke in India (see letter in preface to vol. viii. of STEWART's *Works*). Colonel Stewart died in 1851. Stewart had two children by his second wife, who died at Warrington House, Edinburgh, on 28 July 1838: a son George, who died in 1809, and a daughter Maria d'Arcy, who died unmarried in 1846.

Stewart's lectures produced an extraordinary effect in his own day. James Mill, though opposed to his philosophy, says that neither Pitt nor Fox, whose 'most admired efforts' he had heard, was 'nearly so eloquent' (MACVEY NAPIER, Correspondence, pp. 24, 27). Cockburn speaks of the beauty of his voice and the delicacy of his ear, and adds, ' He was the finest reader I have ever heard.' He was forced to clear his throat by an asthmatic tendency; but there was 'eloquence in his very spitting.' His manner, though slightly formal, became emotional at proper moments. 'To me his lectures were like the opening of the heavens: I felt that I had a soul' (Memorials, pp. 22–6). Cockburn's enthusiasm was shared by others. He remarks that Stewart's high personal character was one cause of the excellence of his oratory. It was clearly one cause of his great influence with the young men who lived in his house. Among the attendants upon Stewart's lectures on political economy were Sydney Smith, Francis Horner, Lord Webb Seymour, Jeffrey, Henry Erskine, Brougham, Sir A. Alison, and Lord Palmerston. Palmerston and J. W. Ward (afterwards Lord Dudley) lived in his house; and Lord Webb Seymour, Lord Henry Petty, and Lord John Russell were pupils, though not living with him (Works, vol. x. pp. liv, lviii). All the young Edinburgh reviewers were admirers. Jeffrey, in a review of his life of Reid, gave a sceptical turn to his argument, to which Stewart replied, to Jeffrey's satisfaction it is said, in the 'Philosophical Essays' (ib. v. 24). Horner was apparently his most reverent admirer. Sydney Smith, at whose country parsonage he was a visitor, speaks in the highest terms of his moral and literary merits, though considering him to be a 'humbug' in metaphysics as compared with Thomas Brown (LADY HOLLAND, Sydney Smith, i. 24, 102, ii. 90, 134, 388). Scott, in spite of his toryism, is as emphatic as others upon Stewart's eloquence (Autobiographical Fragment); was encouraged by Stewart's approval of his early efforts, and, according to Lockhart (ch. vi.), kept up an affectionate intercourse through life.

Stewart's influence owed so much to his personal attractiveness that its decline is not surprising. He was a transmitter of Reid's influence far more than an originator. He held, with Reid, that philosophy depended upon psychology treated as an inductive science. He expounded the doctrine 'common-sense' so as to represent the 'intuitionism' against which the Mills carried on their polemic. He repudiated, however, ontological argument still more emphatically than his master, and was a thorough nominalist. While thus approximating to the purely empirical school, he was the more anxious, as Mackintosh observes (essay on Dugald Stewart in Ethical Philosophy, 1872, pp. 210–27), to mark his disapproval of more thoroughgoing advocates. He speaks with unusual severity of Hartley, Erasmus Darwin, and their English adherents, and of the French disciples of Condillac, while really making concessions to their doctrine. He was annoyed, therefore, by finding that Thomas Brown had attacked Reid most emphatically, and followed, if he had not plagiarised from, the French 'ideologists' Destutt De Tracy and Laromiguière. He spoke with unusual severity of Brown, whose life and lectures had been recently published, in a note to his 'Elements' (Works, iv. 375 &c.) Stewart, therefore, though he constantly shows real power and psychological acuteness, represents rather the decline than the development of a system of philosophy. 'Without derogation from his writings,' says Mackintosh, 'it may be said that his disciples were among his best works.' His 'gentle and persuasive eloquence' stimulated many hearers, and kept up a certain interest in philosophy. Mackintosh's high eulogies upon the eloquence of his style are probably just, as is his intimation that Stewart swells his volumes too freely 'by expedients happily used to allure the young.' Stewart is too much a professor of philosophical department. His reading was wide, but his knowledge of German philosophy stopped at Leibnitz; in his 'Dissertation' he confessed his inability to make anything of Kant, and filled the space with secondhand notices. A curious correspondence between him and Thomas Wirgman may be found in the account of Kant's philosophy published by Wirgman in the 'Encyclopædia Londinensis' in 1823. Wirgman, who was an enthusiastic expounder of Kant, had vainly appealed to Stewart to study the new system (in 1813), and Stewart pathetically apologises on the ground of age and ignorance of German for not undertaking the task.

Stewart's works are: 1. 'Elements of the Philosophy of the Human Mind,' vol. i. 1792 (6th edit. 1818); vol. ii. 1814 (4th edit. in 1822); vol. iii. 1827. The whole in vols. ii. iii. and iv. of 'Works.' 2. 'Outlines of Moral Philosophy,' 1793: 4th edit. in 1813 (a full syllabus of lectures, divided in the 'Works' into three parts, in vols. ii. vi. and viii., prefixed to corresponding lectures). The 'Outlines' were translated by Jouffroy in 1826. 3. 'Account of Life and Writings of William Robertson,' 1801 (originally in 'Transactions' of Royal Society of Edinburgh in 1796). 4. 'Account of Life and Writings of Thomas Reid,' 1802 (originally in 'Transactions' of Royal Society in 1802). 5. These last two, with a 'Life' of Adam Smith, originally in the 'Transactions' of the Royal Society in 1793, were published together, as 'Biographical Memoirs,' in 1811; in vol. x. of 'Works.' 6. 'A Short Statement of Facts relative to the late Election of a Mathematical Professor in the University of Edinburgh . . .' 1805. A 'Postscript' was published in the same year. These are omitted in the 'Works.' 7. 'Philosophical Essays,' 1810; 3rd edit. 1818; vol. v. of 'Works.' 8. 'Dissertation on the Progress of Philosophy and the Revival of Letters,' pt. i. in 'Encyclopædia Metropolitana,' 1815, and pt. ii. in same, 1821; these, with a fragment of pt. iii., then first published, form vol. i. of 'Works.' 9. 'Philosophy of the Active and Moral Powers of Man,' 1828; vol. vi. and vii. of 'Works.' 10. 'Lectures on Political Economy,' first delivered in 1800, and first published in 'Works,' forming vols. viii. and ix. A collective edition of the 'Works' was undertaken by Sir William Hamilton, on condition that they should appear 'without note or comment.' The first nine volumes were published from 1854 to 1856; a tenth, with a 'Life' of Stewart by John Veitch, in 1858; and an eleventh 'supplementary' volume, with index to the whole, in 1860.

[Life by Veitch, as above; a Life by Matthew Stewart (his son) is in Annual Biography and Obituary for 1829, pp. 256–68, and was privately printed in 1838; Cockburn's Memorials, pp. 22–6, 103, 170, 206, 250, 369, 451–3; Macvey Napier's Correspondence, pp. 2–7, 24 &c.; Memoirs of Francis Horner, 1853, i. 29, 130, 467, 470, 474, ii. 10, 158, 166–8, 196, 308, 457; Sir H. Bulwer's Palmerston, 1871, pp. 11, 367; S. Walpole's Lord John Russell, 1889, i. 45; Life of Mackintosh, i. 46, 177, 257, 399; Dalzell's University of Edinburgh, 1862, i. 30, 53, 100, 117, 129, 153, 219, 252, ii. 343, 446, 451; Lady Holland's Sydney Smith, i. 102, 196, ii. 90, 134, 386; Sir A. Alison's Autobiography, 1883, i. 4, 19, 40, 47, 50; Lord Dudley's Letters to Copleston, pp. 3, 21, 168, 186, 326, 329; Parr's Works, vii. 542–53 (Stewart's letters to Parr); McCosh's Scottish Philosophy, 1875, pp. 162–73.]   L. S.

STEWART, ESMÉ, sixth SEIGNEUR D'AUBIGNY and DUKE OF LENNOX (1542?–1585). See STUART.]

STEWART, FRANCES TERESA, DUCHESS OF RICHMOND AND LENNOX (1648–1702). [See STUART.]

STEWART or STUART, FRANCIS, fifth EARL OF BOTHWELL (d. 1624). [See HEPBURN.]

STEWART, HELEN D'ARCY CRANSTOUN (1765–1838), song-writer. [See under STEWART, DUGALD.]

STEWART, HENRY, first LORD METHVEN (1495?–1551?), second son of Andrew, second lord Avandale, by Margaret, daughter of Sir John Kennedy of Blairquhan, was born about 1495 [see under STEWART, ANDREW, first LORD AVANDALE]. He supported in 1524 the revolution, by which, during the absence of Albany in France, the queen-dowager, Margaret, widow of James IV, who had subsequently married Archibald Douglas, sixth earl of Angus [q. v.], got possession of the person of the young king, who then formally assumed the government. Immediately afterwards Stewart was appointed treasurer and lord chancellor, and it was soon evident that his influence with the queen-dowager was paramount. Thus Magnus and Ratcliffe, on 3 Nov., informed Wolsey that her chief, indeed her only, counsellor was 'a young man about her who keeps all the seals and orders everything' (Letters and Papers of Henry VIII, vol. iv. No. 800); and shortly afterwards Norfolk wrote to Magnus that he was not 'surprised at the queen's fickleness, her love to Henry Stewart is so great' (ib. No. 805). Her imprudent conduct led to the return to power of her husband, Archibald, earl of Angus, with whom she was in disagreement; and ultimately he succeeded, notwithstanding her efforts to secure from him a divorce, in compelling her to renounce Stewart's company (ib. No. 2575). But in December 1527 word finally reached her that the divorce had been obtained, and in the following April Stewart became her husband (ib. No. 4134). Not long afterwards Angus compelled her to give him up, and he was placed in temporary imprisonment; but after James V in June made his escape from the tutelage of Angus, Methven and the queen-dowager became the young king's chief advisers. On 17 July he bestowed on them jointly the lands of Methven, Perthshire, and Stewart was raised to the peerage with the title of Lord Methven (Reg. Mag. Sig. Scot. 1513–46, No. 614). He was also made master of the artillery (LESLEY, *History*, in the Scottish Text Society, ii. 200). Subsequently he received other grants of lands, including those of Cockburnspath, Berwickshire, on 20 Sept. 1528 (*Reg. Mag. Sig.* 1513–1540, No. 840); the lands of Ardety, Perthshire, on 5 Jan. 1530–1 (*ib.* No. 982); and the lands of Galashiels and Mossilie, Selkirkshire, on 6 Jan. 1535–6 (*ib.* No. 1535).

In 1537 the queen endeavoured to obtain a divorce from Methven, but the king refused to grant consent (*Letters and Papers of Henry VIII*, xii. No. 920). Methven continued to retain the favour of the king, from whom he obtained, on 25 July 1541, the lands of Gilgerston in Methven (*Reg. Mag. Sig. Scot.* 1513–46, No. 2413). Queen Margaret died on 18 Oct. of the same year; and on 5 June 1546 Methven and his new wife, Janet Stewart, had a grant of a third part of the lands of Nether Gorthy (*ib.* No. 3118), and on 18 Feb. 1547–8 a confirmation of the lands of Methven (*ib.* 1546–80, No. 184). He died some time after 10 Oct. 1551, when the lands and castle of Methven were given to him anew (*ib.* No. 639). He is stated to have had by a first wife, one Lady Leslie, a son, the master of Methven who was killed at Pinkie; but the statement lacks corroboration, as also does another, that by the dowager-queen Margaret he had a daughter who died in infancy. By Lady Janet Stewart, eldest daughter of John, second earl of Atholl, and widow of Alexander, master of Sutherland, he had a son, Henry [see below], and three daughters: Johanna, married to Colin, sixth earl of Argyll; Dorothea, to William, first earl of Gowrie; and Margaret, first to Andrew, master of Ochiltree, and secondly to Uchtred Macdougall of Garthland.

The son, Henry, second lord Methven, was born before his father's marriage, but was legitimated in 1551. He was killed by a cannon-shot from Edinburgh Castle on 3 March 1571–2. By his wife Jean, daughter of his stepfather, Patrick Ruthven, he had one son, Henry, who died without issue about 1595, when the title became extinct. On 24 March 1585–6 the lordship of Methven was granted to Ludovick Stuart, second duke of Lennox and duke of Richmond [q. v.] (*ib.* 1580–93, p. 311).

[Letters and State Papers of Henry VIII; Hamilton State Papers; Reg. Mag. Sig. Scot. 1513–46, and 1546–80; Douglas's Scottish Peerage (Wood), ii. 229–30.]   T. F. H.

STEWART or **STUART**, HENRY, LORD DARNLEY (1545–1567), second but eldest surviving son of Matthew Stewart, fourth or twelfth earl of Lennox [q. v.], and

Lady Margaret Douglas [q. v.], was born on 7 Dec. 1545 at Temple Newsam, Yorkshire. He was educated privately under the direction of John Elder, a Scottish priest, a member of the collegiate church of Dumbarton. From his master he learned to be an accomplished penman, as is attested by a letter of his sent in 1554 to Queen Mary of England (facsimile published in the National MSS. of Scotland, pt. iii. No. xvi.), in which he asked her to accept 'a little plote of my simple penning which I termed Vtopia Noua.' It is further affirmed that he translated Valerius Maximus into English (Montague's Preface to KING JAMES'S *Works*, 1619); and there is even ascribed to him a ballad, 'The Complaint: an Epistle to his Mistress on the Force of Love,' which Allan Ramsay published in the 'Evergreen;' but these instances of literary accomplishment must be regarded with more than suspicion, since it is clear that Darnley's intellectual gifts were quite below the average. On the other hand, his physical endowments were exceptional; like his father, he was an adept in all the manly accomplishments of the time; and he attained no small skill with the lute. But while it is evident that his mother did her utmost to train him worthily to fill the great position which she never ceased to anticipate for him, it is no less certain that, owing it may be to fatal natural defects, he did comparatively little credit to her methods.

Shortly after the coronation of Francis II of France and Mary Stewart in 1559, Darnley was sent by his mother to the French court with letters to the French king, which it can scarce be doubted concerned the restoration of Lennox to the family estates in Scotland. After the death of Francis he again visited France (*Cal. State Papers*, For. 1560–61, No. 88), but on a more important errand. The Spanish ambassador, De Quadra, who was in constant communication with the Lady Margaret, reported to his master in 1560 that it was understood that, should any disaster happen to Elizabeth's life or estate, the catholics would raise Darnley to the throne of England (*ib.* Spanish, 1558–67, p. 135). The hope would therefore be held out to Mary that by marrying Darnley the throne of England as well as Scotland might be hers; and to bring further influence to bear on Mary, the Lady Margaret entered about the same time into communications with the Scottish catholic nobles in view of the marriage (*ib.* For. 1562, No. 26). But Darnley was then a mere boy, and Mary's regards were directed towards Don Carlos of Spain. Negotiations with Spain having come to nothing, Lady Margaret, soon after Queen Mary's return to Scotland, endeavoured to awaken the queen's interest in Darnley by sending his tutor, Arthur Lybart, to Scotland to communicate with her (*ib.*) These intrigues of the Lady Margaret were closely watched by Elizabeth; and in November 1561 she and Darnley were summoned to London and placed in confinement [see under DOUGLAS, LADY MARGARET]. But towards the close of the following year they were set at liberty, and soon afterwards were received, at least nominally, into favour, Darnley being in almost daily attendance on Elizabeth, and frequently playing before her on the lute (*Cal. State Papers*, For. 1563, No. 1027).

After the departure of Lennox for Scotland [see under STEWART, MATTHEW, fourth EARL OF LENNOX], Sir James Melville [q. v.] was secretly commissioned by Mary Queen of Scots to obtain permission from Elizabeth for Darnley to pass to Scotland, that 'he might see the country, and carry the earl his father back again to England.' All the while Elizabeth was ostensibly engaged in the promotion of a marriage between Mary and Leicester; but that she knew perfectly the ulterior purpose of Darnley's visit to Scotland might be assumed, even had there not been the testimony of her own remark to the Scottish ambassador Sir James Melville: 'Ye [that is 'you Scots,' or 'you and your mistress'] like better of yon long lad' (MELVILLE, *Memoirs*, p. 120). True, Melville discreetly answered that 'No woman of spirit would make choice of sic a man, that was liker a woman than a man;' but it is impossible to suppose that the reply was sufficient to deceive Elizabeth. In fact—whatever may have been her motive, and not improbably it was a desire to prevent an arrangement with Leicester, although he was the suitor she herself had selected—Elizabeth virtually sent Darnley to Scotland in order that he might visit Mary.

Leaving London on 3 Feb. 1564-5, he reached Berwick on the 10th. On arriving on the 13th at Edinburgh, he found that the queen was at Wemyss Castle; and on the 18th, at the suggestion of his father who was in Atholl, he went to Wemyss to pay his respects to her, remaining there for two or three days. After visiting his father in Atholl he again returned to Edinburgh, shortly before the queen's arrival there. The two main incidents following his arrival in Edinburgh were his attendance on the preaching of Knox and his dancing a galliard with the queen the same evening, the Earl of Moray looking on. It may be that neither Moray nor Knox at first was

altogether unfavourable to the match, but much depended on Darnley's character and inclinations. Chiefly, if not solely, on the grounds, first, that Mary expressed to Melville the opinion that Darnley 'was the properest and best-proportioned long man that ever she had seen' (*ib.* p. 134), and secondly, that when Darnley fell ill of the measles in Stirling, Mary spent much of her time in his sick room, the theory has been formed that the brilliant and beautiful widow of twenty-two fell violently in love with this girl-faced youth of nineteen. If so, the fact would be little to her credit; for there was nothing in Darnley's character or talents to fascinate any one of average intelligence; and it is at least significant that the queen made no mention to Melville of any special excellence or charm in his disposition.

With regard to Darnley's attitude to Mary there is certainly no evidence of any strong affection. Indeed the vain efforts of Mary to captivate the handsome but headstrong youth are almost pathetic, especially in view of the disastrous sequel. She failed with Darnley almost as wofully as she had done with Knox. Occasionally by adroit flattery she was able to obtain important victories; but all the evidence goes to show that she never had any real hold on his affections, such as they were. On the contrary, their natures seem to have been strongly antagonistic, although neither probably realised their utter incompatibility of temperament until after the marriage. But in the case of both, other considerations were paramount. Darnley had the hope of the joint sovereignty of two kingdoms; Mary, now that the more brilliant prospects of the Spanish alliance had vanished, had concentrated her ambition on winning the sovereignty of England for herself and Britain for Roman catholicism through the Darnley alliance.

On 15 March Darnley was knighted and created Earl of Ross. After his recovery in April from an attack of measles at Stirling, it was announced, but on no tangible evidence [see under MARY QUEEN OF SCOTS], that he had been secretly married to the queen; again, on 16 July, it was reported that the marriage had taken place secretly on the 9th, and that he and the queen had gone to bed at Seton (*Cal. State Papers*, For. 1564-1565, No. 1298). On the 22nd a dispensation for the marriage arrived from the pope, and the same day Darnley was created Duke of Albany (Bedford to Cecil, 23 July, *ib.* No. 1312); finally, on the 29th, the marriage did take place in the chapel of Holyrood. The opposition to it in Scotland is to be traced mainly to Darnley's imprudence.

It was impossible for him to keep a secret, and the queen was forced to adopt a line of action which prematurely disclosed her real aims. Maitland and Moray, when they had fathomed Darnley's character, must have been convinced—even apart from their knowledge of the queen's purposes—that the results of the marriage would be calamitous. Scarcely had Darnley set foot in Scotland when he began to manifest his folly. He chose as his special friends Lord Robert Stewart (afterwards Earl of Orkney [q. v.]) and other nobles notoriously disreputable (Randolph to Cecil, 20 March 1564–5, in KEITH, ii. 272). To those who were not his special friends 'his pride' was 'intolerable,' and 'his words not to be borne, except where no man dare speak again' (Randolph to Leicester, 3 June 1565, Cal. State Papers, For. 1564–5, No. 1221). Moreover he imprudently expressed his surprise at, and disapproval of, the extent of Moray's possessions, and made no secret of his conviction that his power would need to be curbed. It was thus almost inevitable that Moray, since he was backed by Elizabeth, should do his utmost against an alliance which foreboded his ruin.

~Their common dangers and difficulties tended for the time being to foster cordiality between husband and wife; but the essential unhappiness of the union was manifest almost from the beginning. That Darnley was mentally and morally weak was not in itself a fatal objection; but this imbecility was conjoined with reckless courage, strong animal passions, intolerable pride, and fatal obstinacy. In September Randolph reported that he had shown himself altogether unworthy of what the queen had called him to (ib. No. 1519); and this judgment the sequel more than justified. On one occasion when the queen, during a visit to an Edinburgh merchant, tried to dissuade him from drinking too much and encouraging others to do so, he not only declined to listen to her advice, but 'gave her such words that she left the house in tears' (Drury to Cecil, 12 Feb. 1565–6, in KEITH, ii. 403). Other vicious habits are also alluded to (see especially ib. ii. 405); and while it is quite clear that his conduct to the queen was such as rapidly to dissipate any illusion she may at first have cherished, she quickly recognised that he was unfit not merely to aid her with his advice in matters of state, but even to share her political confidence. Thus being compelled to refuse him the matrimonial crown, she found it needful to elevate Riccio to the place in her political counsels which properly belonged to her husband.

Riccio had been the main assistant of the queen in arranging the marriage with Darnley, and he was now engaged with her in a conspiracy for realising its full political fruits. The queen had no reason for ignoring Darnley more than was essential to the success of the scheme; and for its full success it was necessary not merely that the marriage should be maintained in its entirety, but that there should be cordial relations between them. But it was scarcely possible for Darnley to play any other political part than that of dupe; and he never was more a dupe than when he imagined himself engaged in the circumvention of his enemies. Lacking in modesty as in other gifts and graces, he never had a doubt as to his fitness to grapple with the most difficult emergencies; and he seems to have thoroughly convinced himself that his exclusion from the queen's counsels was primarily due to Riccio, and that Riccio's influence with the queen was rooted in his own dishonour. In any case the opponents of Riccio recognised the supreme importance of convincing Darnley of this. It was advisable that he should be utilised as a dupe and tool; and without doubt or misgiving he was, up to a certain point as compliant as could be wished. The conspirators against Riccio were nominally his agents, acting less in their own behalf, or even in behalf of protestantism, than in behalf of an outraged husband. Thus, on 6 March, three days before the murder, Bedford and Randolph wrote to Cecil that Darnley had determined to be present at Riccio's apprehension and execution; and this because the crime of Riccio was that he had done Darnley 'the most dishonour that could be to any man' (Cal. State Papers, For. Ser. 1566–8, No. 162). This meant that the conspirators intended to give such a complexion to the assassination; and in token that they were acting on Darnley's behalf, Darnley's dagger was left by George Douglas sticking in his body [for further details of the plot and its execution see under DOUGLAS, JAMES, fourth EARL OF MORTON; MARY QUEEN OF SCOTS; and RICCIO, DAVID]. But not merely was Darnley bent on revenge; he was resolved on the reality of kingship; and it suited the plotters to flatter his ambition; for they meant, for the time being, to set him up as the nominal head of the government. And thus it was that the chief enemies of Darnley—Moray, Argyll, and others, who had risen in rebellion on account of the marriage—now appeared in the guise of his friends and succourers. These nobles without scruple now engaged to be true subjects to him, to guarantee him the

U

crown matrimonial, and to maintain his right to the crown failing the succession (*ib.* No. 165); and, on the other hand, he did not hesitate to promise them not merely full pardon for their offences, but even the full establishment of the protestant religion (*ib.* No. 164).

But after having been duped so far as to commit himself to the murder, and to play so conspicuous a part in it, Darnley immediately became the dupe of the new circumstances which were thus created, and the new influences they introduced. For one thing, Riccio had ceased to be a rival: for another he had a rooted dislike and dread of Moray; but, more than all, the queen not merely convinced him that they had common interests paramount to all other considerations, but that she would now confer on him the position of trust which he coveted. While concealing from her his own share in the conspiracy, Darnley therefore did not scruple to disclose 'all that he knew of any man' (Randolph to Cecil, 21 May, No. 205); and as he did his utmost to aid her in her escape from Holyrood to Dunbar, their relations became for the time being as cordial as during their days of courtship. But early in April the queen was shown the covenants and bonds between him and the lords, and discovered that his declaration before her and the council of his innocence of the murder was false (*ib.* No. 252). This discovery was fatal to him [see under MARY QUEEN OF SCOTS], and although they nominally became somewhat reconciled in June, before the birth of James VI, there never was a recurrence of real friendship. The favour which the queen now began to show, not merely towards Bothwell, but towards Maitland, Moray, and other avowed enemies of the king, was ominous of how matters were drifting. Left almost without a friend—for even the catholic earls had grown weary of him —and seeing that the queen was more and more favourably disposed towards those whom he had most cause to dread, it is small wonder that he began to find his position almost intolerable. Perhaps, however, it was more in a spirit of sullen resentment and outraged pride than of fear that after the queen's departure on 25 Sept. from Stirling—where he remained —to Edinburgh, he began to form the resolution to leave the kingdom. This resolution he communicated to Le Croc, the French ambassador, who endeavoured to dissuade him, but without effect (Le Croc to Catherine de Medicis, 17 Oct., in TEULET's *Relations Politiques*, ii. 289–93), and on 29 Sept. Lennox informed the queen of his son's resolve and of his inability to change it. The

same day Darnley came to Holyrood with the purpose of bidding the queen farewell; and, although he was induced to stay a night at the palace, he on the following day persisted in his resolve before the council, while admitting that he had no special complaint to make against the queen. He then left for Glasgow on a visit to his father, by whose persuasion, probably, he was induced to have another interview with Le Croc, who was successful in inducing him at least to postpone his departure (*ib.*) From Glasgow, however, he wrote a letter to the queen, in which he informed her that his resolution to depart was unchanged, and assigned as his reasons the refusal of the queen to grant him any real authority, and the fact that the nobility had left him in complete isolation (The Members of the Scottish Privy Council to Catherine de Médicis, 8 Oct. 1566, in TEULET, ii. 288).

During the queen's illness at Jedburgh, Darnley on 28 Oct. paid her a visit, but he left next morning for Glasgow. It was probably his attitude towards the nobles during this short visit that decided them to hold the famous conference at Craigmillar, when it was unanimously resolved that by fair means or foul Darnley should be got rid of. He also visited the queen when she was at Craigmillar, and while there had another interview with Le Croc, who on 2 Dec. expressed to Archbishop Beaton the opinion that he 'did not expect, upon several accounts, any good understanding between them unless God effectually put his hand' (TYTLER, *History*, iii. 230). Le Croc also informed Beaton that he was much assured Darnley would not be present at the baptism at Stirling. His surmise was correct; for, though Darnley went to Stirling, he remained in his own room during the ceremony, and was not even present at the public entertainments—the fact probably being that the ordeal of facing insulting neglect from the queen and the court was more than his pride could brook. Writing from Stirling, Le Croc reported to Beaton that Darnley's 'bad deportment was incurable;' that 'no good could be effected of him;' and that matters could not 'remain long as they are,' without 'sundry bad consequences' (*ib.* iii. 232). On learning that Morton, Lindsay, Ruthven, and other murderers of Riccio had received pardon, he seems to have finally concluded that his cause was hopeless, if not worse, and abruptly left Stirling for Glasgow. His purpose was to have left the country by a ship from the west coast, but a sudden illness rendered this impossible. Knox, Buchanan, and others have attributed the illness to poison; officially it was stated to be small-pox; but some surmise it to have been an infectious malady of a different character. The queen sent her own physician to visit him, and, when she learned that he was convalescent, resolved to go to Glasgow that she might persuade him to come with her to Edinburgh for change of air. A reconciliation took place, and Darnley resolved to accompany her. But coincident with the queen's visit to Glasgow a conspiracy had been formed, which resulted in the blowing up of Darnley's lodging at Kirk o' Field in the early morning of 10 Feb. [see under HEPBURN, JAMES, EARL OF BOTHWELL, and MARY QUEEN OF SCOTS]. Darnley and his servant were, after the explosion, found dead in an adjoining garden some forty yards distant (see engraving in CHALMERS's *Life of Mary Queen of Scots*, from a sketch in the state paper office). There were on them no marks of injury from the explosion, and they were supposed to have been strangled while making their escape some time before the explosion took place; but although a physician examined the bodies, no authentic statement as to the exact cause of death is in existence. The body of Darnley was disembowelled and embalmed, and on 14 Feb. he was buried in the sepulchre of King James V, in the south-east corner of the chapel of Holyrood.

There are two portraits by Lucas de Heere at Holyrood and a third at Hampton Court. There are also portraits at Newbattle Abbey and Wemyss Castle (cf. *Cat. First Loan Exhib.* Nos. 322, 323, 326).

[There is a biography of Darnley in Chalmers's Life of Mary, and in Sir William Fraser's Lennox (privately printed); see also under MARY QUEEN OF SCOTS, and the authorities there referred to.]   T. F. H.

STEWART, HENRY, DUKE OF GLOUCESTER (1639–1660). [See HENRY.]

STEWART or STUART, HENRY BENEDICT MARIA CLEMENT (1725–1807), Cardinal York, and styled by the Jacobites Henry IX. [See HENRY.]

STEWART, SIR HERBERT (1843–1885), major-general, born on 30 Jan. 1843, was the eldest son of the Rev. Edward Stewart, rector of Sparsholt, Hampshire, by Louisa, daughter of C. J. Herbert of Muckross, co. Kerry. His father was grandson of the seventh Earl of Galloway. He entered Winchester College in 1854, went into commons as a prefect in 1861, and was captain of the eleven in 1862. He was backward as a scholar, but his schoolfellows describe him

as pre-eminently a leader. He entered the army as ensign in the 37th foot on 24 Nov. 1863. He became lieutenant on 18 July 1865, and was adjutant from 17 July 1866 to 11 April 1868, when he was promoted captain. The regiment was then serving in Bengal, and from 15 Aug. 1868 to 28 Nov. 1870 Stewart was aide-de-camp to Major-general Beatson, who commanded the Allahabad division. He also acted as deputy assistant quartermaster-general in Bengal from 27 Jan. 1872 to 18 Oct. 1873.

In the summer of 1870 there was an outbreak of cholera, and Stewart, who happened to be alone at headquarters, at once issued orders for the dispersion of the troops into camps. The measures taken were specially commended by Lord Napier, the commander-in-chief, and, having learnt that they were due to Stewart's judgment and promptitude, he employed him in the quartermaster-general's department in 1872–3. During this time Stewart explored some of the country on the north-west frontier.

He returned to England towards the end of 1873, having exchanged into the 3rd dragoon guards on 18 Oct. He had become keenly interested in his profession. He entered the staff college in 1877, and in April of that year, to qualify himself the better for staff employment, he was admitted a student of the Inner Temple, where he kept twelve terms. At the end of 1878 he left the staff college, before the final examination, to go out to South Africa as a special-service officer.

On 26 Feb. 1879 he was appointed brigade-major of cavalry in Natal, and he served in the latter part of the Zulu war. He advocated a cavalry raid on Ulundi instead of the slow advance in force which was actually made. He did not take part in this advance, as his brigadier, General Crealock, was left behind to guard the frontier and the line of communications. Seeing little prospect of promotion, he was seriously meditating retirement from the army; but on Sir Garnet Wolseley's arrival the outlook improved. Through the instrumentality of General Colley, who had heard of him in India, Stewart was attached to Wolseley's staff, and found in him a fast friend. He was mentioned in despatches and received the medal with clasp and a brevet majority dated 28 Oct. 1879.

He afterwards took part in the operations against Sekukuni, as principal staff officer to the Transvaal field force. Colonel Baker Russell, who commanded it, reported that 'the energy and power of hard work displayed by him were marvellous, and the skill, tact,

U 2

and temper he showed in dealing with the very various and conflicting elements of which the force under my command was composed, were beyond praise' (*London Gazette*, 16 Jan. 1880). From 7 Feb. to 25 May 1880 he acted as military secretary to Sir Garnet (afterwards Lord) Wolseley in Natal and the Transvaal. He was made brevet lieutenant-colonel on 24 July 1880.

He thereupon returned to England, but went back to South Africa in the beginning of 1881, when the Boers of the Transvaal, with some of whom he had been serving twelve months before, had risen to recover their independence. He was appointed assistant adjutant and quartermaster-general on 7 Jan., and joined the force under Sir George Pomeroy Colley [q. v.] at Mount Prospect about 20 Feb. as chief staff officer. He shared in the disaster on Majuba Hill on the 27th, and attributed it to the neglect to make some simple entrenchment upon which the men might have formed. He proposed this, but it was thought the men were too tired, and no collision with the Boers was anticipated. In the rush that took place he was knocked over, fell down the side of the hill, and lay hid in a wood till night. He then tried to make his way back to the British camp, but failed, and he was discovered next day and made prisoner by a Boer patrol. He was well treated, and was released with the rest of the prisoners at the end of March (*London Gazette*, 3 May and 10 June).

Stewart was promoted major in his regiment on 1 July 1881. He was appointed aide-de-camp to Lord Spencer, as lord-lieutenant of Ireland, from 9 May 1882, but left Ireland on 4 Aug. following to take part in the Egyptian campaign which followed the rising of Arabi Pasha. He was brigade major of the cavalry brigade sent out from England, and when a second brigade arrived from India he was made assistant adjutant-general of the cavalry division. After the victory of Tel-el-Kebir on 13 Sept. 1882, the cavalry was pushed on rapidly to within a few miles of Cairo, largely owing to Stewart's energy, and he was sent forward with fifty men to the Abbasiyeh barracks, outside Cairo. The troops in those barracks at once surrendered, and Stewart sent for the governor of Cairo, the chief of police, and the officer in charge of the citadel, and told them to arrange immediately to hand over the town and citadel. That same night, the 14th, the citadel was occupied by a detachment sent in under Captain Watson, R.E., and next day Lord Wolseley telegraphed home that the war in Egypt was over. Stewart was three times mentioned in despatches (*London Gazette*,

8 Sept., 6 Oct., and 2 Nov.), and was described by Lord Wolseley as 'one of the best staff officers I have ever known.' He was made brevet colonel, C.B., and aide-de-camp to the queen (18 Nov.), and received the medal for Egypt, with clasp and bronze star and the Osmanieh order (third class).

At the close of the war (on 3 Nov. 1882) he resumed his post as aide-de-camp to Lord Spencer in Ireland. He remained there till 17 Jan. 1884, when he was selected for the command of the cavalry in the force sent to Suakim under Sir Gerald Graham. As brigadier from 12 Feb. to 17 April he was at the action of El Teb (29 Feb.), in which the cavalry made some dashing charges, the relief of Tokar which followed it, the action at Tamai, and the advance to Tamanib. He had made a reconnaissance on the Berber road on 22 March, and was convinced that the mounted troops could push through to Berber. At Graham's request he prepared a scheme for the advance, which he was eager to carry out, but the government thought the risk too great. He was mentioned in despatches (*London Gazette*, 27 March, 3 April, 6 May), received two additional clasps, and was made K.C.B. on 21 May.

He was assistant adjutant and quartermaster-general in the south-eastern district in England from 18 April to 1 Sept. 1884, when he went back to Egypt with Lord Wolseley, to take part in the expedition for the relief of Khartoum. He was sent up the Nile to Dongola to command the troops there, obtain supplies, and organise the camel corps. He arrived there on 29 Sept., and did what he could with the shifty mudir of Dongola. In December the news from Gordon made Wolseley decide to push part of his force across the desert to Metemmeh, while the remainder continued its advance up the river. Stewart was chosen to command the desert column. He was appointed brigadier on 24 Nov., and reached Korti with part of the camel corps on 15 Dec.

As the number of transport camels was insufficient for the stores thought necessary, it was decided to form in the first place an intermediate depot halfway across the desert, at the wells of Jakdul. On 29 Dec. Stewart started from Korti with about eleven hundred men and two thousand two hundred camels. He reached Jakdul on 2 Jan. 1885, having marched ninety-eight miles in sixty-four hours. Leaving a guard there for his stores, he returned at once to Korti. The exhaustion of the camels and the want of food for them delayed his movements, but on the 12th he was again at Jakdul with a larger force. On the 14th he set out for

Metemmeh, with about eighteen hundred men, of whom nearly two-thirds belonged to the camel regiments and 135 were cavalry. He had three guns and 2,888 camels. His orders were to occupy Metemmeh, leave a garrison there, and return to Jakdul. A small detachment was to be sent up from Metemmeh with Sir Charles Wilson in Gordon's steamers to Khartoum, not to remain there, but to encourage the garrison by the sight of British troops.

On 16 Jan., while Stewart was marching from Jakdul, the enemy were found to be in force near the wells of Abu Klea. Stewart formed a zereba and encamped for the night, and next morning advanced in square. The ground was undulating, giving a good deal of cover to the Arabs, and fifteen hundred or more of them made a sudden charge upon the left and rear faces of the square. Owing to the lagging of the camels, which were inside the square, the rear face had bulged out, and the men were not in such close order as elsewhere. The Arabs broke in here, and by the time those of them who were in front were killed and those behind driven off, the British force had lost 168 officers and men.

A small post was made at Abu Klea to shelter the wounded, and on the afternoon of the 18th the column resumed its march. Metemmeh was twenty-three miles off, and Stewart hoped to reach the Nile a little above that place before daybreak. But the night was dark, a belt of acacia bush had to be traversed, men and beasts were fatigued, and next morning he was still some miles from the river. Seeing that the Arabs meant to resist his further advance, he ordered a zereba to be formed for the baggage. While this was being done the enemy gathered round and kept up a hot fire, and about 10 A.M. on the 19th Stewart received a wound which obliged him to hand over the command to Sir Charles Wilson. He lingered for nearly a month, and strong hopes were entertained of his recovery, but he himself recognised from the first that the wound was mortal. He died on the way back from Khartoum to Korti, on 16 Feb., and was buried near the wells at Jakdul.

He lived long enough to learn that the expedition had been too late to save Khartoum, though by no fault of his. He also learnt that he had been promoted major-general for distinguished service, and he received with special pleasure, shortly before his death, a telegram of congratulation from the boys and masters of Winchester. In the telegram reporting his death, Lord Wolseley said: 'No braver soldier or more brilliant leader of men ever wore the Queen's uniform.'

On 19 Dec. 1877 he married Georgiana Janet, daughter of Admiral Sir James Stirling [q. v.], and widow of Major-general Sir H. Tombs, V.C., and he left one son.

There is a mural monument to Stewart in St. Paul's Cathedral, by Boehm, appropriately placed behind the recumbent figure of Gordon in the north aisle of the nave. It is in three panels, the centre containing a medallion of him in high relief. There is also a memorial to him at Winchester, a gateway into the cloisters from the school quadrangle bearing his arms and the college arms, and inscribed, 'In Memoriam Herberti Stewart.' His portrait was painted by Frank Holl, R.A., and engraved by D. Wahrschmidt.

[Times, 21 Feb. 1885; Royal Engineers' Journal, 1881, p. 125; Maurice's Campaign of 1882; Colvile's Sudan Campaign; Wilson's From Korti to Khartoum; Cooper King's Story of the British Army, 1897, pp. 390-3; private information.]

E. M. L.

STEWART, Sir HOUSTON (1791-1875), admiral of the fleet, third son of Sir Michael Shaw Stewart of Ardgowan, sixth baronet, by his cousin Catharine, youngest daughter of Sir William Maxwell, bart., was born on 2 Aug. 1791. He entered the navy in February 1805 on board the Medusa with Sir John Gore [q. v.], and in her went out to Calcutta. On his return he followed Gore to the Revenge, and in October 1806 was moved to the Impérieuse, then commanded by Lord Cochrane [see COCHRANE, THOMAS, tenth EARL OF DUNDONALD], under whom he shared in the many incidents of that remarkable commission, including the defence of Rosas, till in December 1808 he was put in command of an armed xebec, which he himself had assisted in cutting out from under the batteries of Port Vendres, and was sent on an independent cruise in the Mediterranean. He did not return to Gibraltar till the Impérieuse had sailed for England, and was unable to join her till after the affair in Basque roads. He was, however, in her in the expedition to Walcheren, after which he was borne, during the winter, on the books of the flagship at Leith. Through the summer of 1810 he was in the Hussar in the Baltic, and during the following year was again in the Leith flagship, till promoted to be lieutenant on 1 Aug. 1811.

On 16 Aug. he was appointed to the Tigre, 74, in which ship, under Captain John Halliday, he served off Rochefort, and in the two following years he was Keith's signal lieutenant in the Channel, at first in the San Josef and afterwards in the Queen Charlotte.

On 3 March 1814 he was appointed acting captain of the Clarence, of 74 guns, off Brest, but returned to the Queen Charlotte in the end of April. On 9 June he was appointed commander of the Podargus, 14, and was confirmed in the rank on 13 Aug. During the next three years he commanded various sloops on the Jamaica station; in March 1817 he was acting captain of the Pique, and in May of the Salisbury, to which he was confirmed on 10 June 1817, and remained in her as flag-captain to Rear-admiral John Erskine Douglas till April 1818.

From October 1823 to December 1826 he commanded the Menai, frigate, on the North American station, and for two winters had charge of Halifax dockyard. In 1839 he went to the Mediterranean in the Benbow, which in the following year he commanded on the coast of Syria and at the reduction of St. Jean d'Acre, under Admiral Sir Robert Stopford [q. v.] For his services in this campaign he was nominated a C.B. on 18 Dec. 1840. In 1840 he was for a few months superintendent of Woolwich dockyard, and in November was appointed controller-general of the coastguard. This post he held till 1850, when he was appointed a lord of the admiralty. From February 1850 to December 1852 he continued at the admiralty, and during the latter part of the time was M.P. for Greenwich. On 16 June 1851 he was promoted to the rank of rear-admiral, and in the spring of 1853 went out to the Mediterranean as third in command and superintendent of Malta dockyard, where he remained till January 1855, when he became second in command in the Black Sea under Sir Edmund (afterwards Lord) Lyons [q. v.], and commanded the squadron at the reduction of Kinburn. He was nominated a K.C.B. on 5 July 1855; he also received the grand cross of the legion of honour, and the first class of the Medjidie. For some months in 1856 he was superintendent of Devonshire dockyard; and from November 1856 to January 1860 was commander-in-chief on the North American station. He became a vice-admiral on 30 July 1857. From October 1860 to October 1863 he was commander-in-chief at Devonport; became admiral on 10 Nov. 1862; G.C.B. on 28 March 1865; and admiral of the fleet on 20 Oct. 1872. He died on 10 Dec. 1875. He married, in 1819, Martha, youngest daughter of Lord Glenlee, and had three sons, the eldest of whom is the present Admiral Sir William Houston Stewart, G.C.B.

[O'Byrne's Nav. Biogr. Dict.; Navy Lists; information from Sir W. Houston Stewart.]
J. K. L.

STEWART, JAMES (d. 1309), high steward of Scotland, was the son of Alexander, high steward, by Jean, daughter and heiress of James, son of Angus Macrory or Roderick, lord of Bute. He succeeded his father in 1283, and the same year was present in the assembly which acknowledged the maid of Norway as heir to the throne (Acta Parl. Scot. i. 424). After the death of Alexander III on 9 March 1286, he was on 11 April chosen one of the six guardians of the kingdom under Queen Margaret (Chronicles of Fordun and Wyntoun). The same year he signed the band of Robert Bruce and other nobles for mutual defence (Documents illustrative of the History of Scotland, i. 22). In the war which followed between Balliol and Bruce he took part on the side of Bruce. He attended in 1290 the parliament at Brigham at which a marriage was arranged between Prince Edward of England and the Maid of Norway; but her death in Orkney in October of the same year completely altered the political outlook. Being continued one of the guardians of the kingdom after her death, he agreed with the other guardians to submit the rival claims of the competitors for the Scottish throne to the arbitration of Edward I of England; but he afterwards joined with the party who resolved at all hazards to break with Edward, and his seal as a baron is appended to the ratification of the treaty with France in 1295 (Acta Parl. Scot. i. 453). On 7 July 1297 he, however, came to terms with Edward (Cal. Documents relating to the History of Scotland, 1272–1307, No. 908), and, having on 9 July confessed his rebellion and placed himself at Edward's disposal (ib. No. 909), he became a guarantor for the loyalty of the Earl of Carrick, until he delivered up his daughter Marjory as hostage (ib. No. 910). The service he had rendered to Edward, in inducing many barons to submit, caused Edward to place considerable confidence in his loyalty; but this confidence was soon belied. On the outbreak shortly afterwards of the rebellion under Wallace, he pretended to side with the English, and before the battle of Stirling was, along with the Earl of Lennox, sent by Surrey, the English commander, to treat with Wallace; but probably his main purpose was rather to supply Wallace with information than induce him to make submission. At any rate the negotiations failed, and as soon as the tide of battle turned in favour of the Scots he joined in the pursuit. Consequently, on 31 Aug. 1298, he was deprived of his lands, which were granted by Edward to Alexander de Lindsay (ib. No. 1006). In 1302 he was, with six other commissioners, sent to Paris to endeavour to secure that the interests of Scotland would be respected in the proposed treaty between England and France, but the mission was unsuccessful. On 17 Feb. 1303–4 he had a safe-conduct to go to England to treat of peace; and having submitted himself absolutely to the king's will in November 1305 (*ib.* No. 1713), he on 23 Oct. 1306 subscribed an oath of submission and fealty (*ib.* No. 1843). Nevertheless he was one of the Scots barons who on 16 March 1309 wrote to Philip, king of France, recognising Bruce's right to the Scottish throne. He died on 16 July 1309, and was buried at Paisley. By his wife Cecilia, daughter of Patrick, earl of Dunbar, he had three sons and a daughter: Walter (see below); Sir John, killed at the battle of Dundalk with Edward Bruce, earl of Carrick, in 1318; Sir James of Durisdeer; and Egidia, married to Alexander de Menyers or Menzies.

WALTER STEWART (1293–1326), the eldest son, who succeeded his father as high steward, distinguished himself under Bruce in the English wars. At the battle of Bannockburn in 1314, though then, according to Barbour, 'but a beardless hyne,' he, with Sir James Douglas, commanded the left wing. In the following year Robert Bruce gave him his daughter Marjory in marriage, along with the barony of Bathgate, Linlithgowshire, and other lands; and in 1316, during the absence of Bruce in Ireland, he was, with Sir James Douglas, entrusted with the government of the kingdom. On the capture of Berwick from the English, Bruce entrusted the defence of the town and castle to Stewart, who, after repelling all the efforts of Edward to take them by assault, until the defeat of the English at Mitton, eventually compelled Edward to raise the siege. He signed the letter to the pope on 6 April 1320 asserting the independence of Scotland (*Acta Parl. Scotl.* i. 474). In 1322 he was engaged with Douglas and Randolph in the attempt to surprise Edward at Byland Abbey near Melton, Yorkshire, and after the escape of Edward pursued him with five hundred horse to the gates of York. He died on 9 April 1326, and was buried at Paisley. By his wife, Marjory Bruce, who died in 1316, he had a son Robert, who succeeded to the Scottish throne as Robert II [q. v.] After her death he married Isabel, daughter of Sir John Graham of Abercorn, by whom he had two sons, Sir John of Ralston and Sir Andrew. He is also stated to have married as his first wife Alice, daughter of Sir John Erskine, and to have had by her an only child Jean, the first wife of Hugh,

earl of Ross; but this must be regarded as doubtful.

[Documents illustrative of the History of Scotland, ed. Stevenson, vol. i.; Cal. Documents relating to the History of Scotland, 1272–1307 and 1307–1357; Acta Parl. Scot. vol. i.; Barbour's Bruce; Chronicles of Fordun and Wyntoun; Andrew Stuart's Genealogical History of the Stewarts; Douglas's Scottish Peerage, ed. Wood, i. 44–7.]   T. F. H.

STEWART, JAMES, DUKE OF ROSS (1476?–1504), archbishop of St. Andrews and lord high chancellor of Scotland, son of James III, by Margaret, daughter of Christian III of Denmark, was born about 1476, and at his baptism was created Marquis of Ormond. On 23 Jan. 1480–1 he obtained a grant of the earldom of Ross, with the castle of Dingwall (*Reg. Mag. Sig. Scot.* 1424–1513, No. 1457), and on 5 April 1481 of the lands of Brechin and Navar (*ib.* No. 1470). On 23 Jan. 1488 he was created Duke of Ross, Marquis of Ormond, Earl of Edirdale, and lord of Brechin and Navar (*Acta Parl. Scot.* ii. 181). A plot was formed in April 1491 by Sir John Ramsay, earl of Bothwell [q. v.], for the deliverance of the Duke of Ross and his brother, James IV, into the hands of Henry VII, but it came to nothing. In 1498 the duke was appointed to the see of St. Andrews, and went to Rome to be confirmed by the pope. There his appearance attracted the admiration of Ariosto, who in 'Orlando Furioso' (canto x.), while describing him as peerless in personal beauty and grace, refers in terms of almost equal but formal eulogy to his dauntless mind. In 1502 he was appointed lord high chancellor of Scotland, and had a grant of the abbacy of Dunfermline. He died in 1504, and was interred in the chancel of the cathedral church of St. Andrews. The title of Duke of Ross was next bestowed on Alexander, posthumous son of James IV, who was born on 30 April 1514, and died on 18 Dec. 1515.

[Reg. Mag. Sig. Scot. 1424–1513; Acta Parl. Scot. vol. ii.; Keith's Scottish Bishops; Crawford's Officers of State.]   T. F. H.

STEWART, JAMES, EARL OF MORAY (1499?–1544), natural son of James IV of Scotland, by Janet, daughter of John, lord Kennedy, was born about 1499, being referred to in a letter of Dacre to Wolsey of 19 Oct. 1519 as 'a springcolde of 20 years of age' (*Letters and Papers of Henry VIII*, ed. Brewer, ii. No. 1480). On 12 June 1501 he was created by his father Earl of Moray, Lord Abernethy and Strathearn, and received a grant of the earldom of Moray (*Reg. Mag. Sig. Scot.* 1424–1513, No. 2586); and on

12 June he obtained the lands of Abernethy (ib. No. 2587). When, in 1517, Lord Home was arrested by the Duke of Albany, the Earl of Moray accused him of having slain James IV after Flodden, there being a rumour that the king 'was seen to return through Tweed, and that he was slain beside Kelso by the Lord Hume's [Home's] friends or defenders' (CALDERWOOD, History of the Kirk of Scotland, i. 59). He remained always strongly hostile to England and to the English party to which Lord Home belonged.

In September 1523 Moray was appointed one of the guardians of the young king James (Abbot of Kelso to Dacre, 8 Sept., in Letters and Papers of Henry VIII, ii. No. 3313), and a little later was made lieutenant-general of the French forces in the kingdom, consisting of four thousand foot and four thousand horse (ib. No. 3414). He was generally adverse to the English influence in Scotland, and was one of those who sat on the forfeiture of Angus in 1528 (ib. iv. No. 4728). In March 1530 he was made lieutenant-general, and sent to the marches to confer with the Earl of Northumberland about a truce; but nothing was concluded, because they were unable to agree as to whether to meet on Scottish or English ground (CALDERWOOD, i. 100). In 1531 he was engaged in suppressing an insurrection in the isles; and on 10 Oct. 1532 he was appointed warden of the east and middle marches, with the promise of having three thousand men under his command (Diurnal of Occurrents, p. 16; Letters and Papers of Henry VIII, v. 1460). In the following year he threatened England with a large force, but did comparatively little (ib. v. No. 1558, and vi. Nos. 163, 230, and 450; CALDERWOOD, i. 105). He was one of the commissioners appointed, 29 Dec. 1535, to conclude a treaty of marriage between James V and Marie de Bourbon, the treaty being signed on 29 March 1536 (Letters and Papers of Henry VIII, x. No. 578). On 13 May 1536 he was discharged of his wardenship of the marches, which was given to Huntly (ib. No. 862).

The Earl of Moray always remained specially hostile to England. On 5 Oct. 1542 Angus reported to Norfolk that there had been words between the king of Scots and the Earl of Moray, who had reproached the king for the gentle offers he had made to Henry VIII (Hamilton Papers, i. 253). He was not present at the disaster of Solway Moss, but lay with a large force in the neighbourhood of Haddington, purposing to invade England should the Scots be successful (ib. p. 315). In the will of James V—supposed

to have been forged in the interests of Beaton—he was named one of the governors of the kingdom during the young queen's nonage (ib. p. 350; CALDERWOOD, History, i. 153). But, although really devoted to the interests of the cardinal and catholicism, he made a pretence of being not wholly unfavourable to an agreement with England. On 13 Feb. 1542-3 he sent a message to Suffolk of his delight that both realms should be under one government (ib. p. 417); but about the same time he attended a convention at Perth, called to take measures to set the cardinal at liberty. On being summoned by a herald to disperse those assembled he obeyed, and a few days afterwards gave in his submission to Arran, the governor, but this was done mainly in the interest of the cardinal. On 27 March Sadler reported that he found him much less frank than Huntly; for 'he is a great beads-man, and noted here to be a good papist, wholly given to the old ceremonies and traditions of Rome' (SADLER, State Papers, i. 98, summarised in Hamilton Papers, i. 492). Sadler further explained that while Moray merely asserted that once the marriage was agreed on the Scots would 'not pass much upon France,' Huntly promised that, this matter settled, he would actually serve against France. On 26 April Sadler reported that Moray appeared well dedicated to the king (SADLER, State Papers, i. 161); but on 1 May he had to confess that though he had endeavoured to win Moray, Argyll, and Marischal to consent to the young queen going to England by 'promising them largely on ' the king's ' behalf in general terms,' it would be impossible to move them, unless certain 'pledges were given' (ib. p. 169). He further reported that Cassilis had told him that money might tempt Moray as he was not rich, 'but that it must be with a greater sum than any of the rest have' (ib. p. 178). On 16 July he was reported as holding aloof from the cardinal (Hamilton Papers, i. 572); but he was present on 3 Sept. at Callender House when a reconciliation took place between the cardinal and Arran (ib. ii. 19); and he was also named one of the new council of state (ib. p. 46). In May 1544 he took the field against Hertford. He died on 12 June of the same year. By his wife, Lady Elizabeth Campbell, only daughter of Colin, third earl of Argyll, he had a daughter, Lady Mary Stewart, wife of John, master of Buchan. The earldom, having reverted to the crown, was on 13 Feb. 1549 conferred on George Gordon, fourth earl of Huntly [q. v.]

[Authorities quoted in the text: Douglas's Scottish Peerage (Wood), ii. 254.]   T. F. H.

STEWART, LORD JAMES, EARL OF MAR, and afterwards EARL OF MORAY (1531?-1570), regent of Scotland (often called by English historians the 'Regent Murray'), was natural son of James V of Scotland by Lady Margaret Erskine—younger daughter of John Erskine, fifth earl of Mar of that name, and afterwards married to Sir Robert Douglas of Lochleven [see under JAMES V]. Queen Mary Stuart was his half-sister. He is in the peerages and other books usually stated to have been born in 1533 or 1534, but in a papal dispensation of 1534 he is stated to be in his third year (*Hist. MSS. Comm.* 6th Rep. p. 670). On 20 Oct. 1534 he was designated heir to his elder natural brother in the lands of Douglas, which were then conferred on his brother by the king (*Reg. Mag. Sig. Scot.* 1513-46, No. 1425); and on 31 Aug. 1536 he himself received a grant of the lands and famous stronghold of Tantallon, Haddingtonshire (*ib.* No. 1620). In 1538 he obtained the priory of St. Andrews, and he was also prior of Mâcon in France. In 1541 he entered the university of St. Andrews, and he remained at the university until 1544, but there is no evidence that he graduated. He accompanied the young Princess Mary to France in 1548 (LINDSAY OF PITSCOTTIE'S *Chronicle*, ed. 1814, p. 506; LORD HERRIES, *Memoirs*, p. 23). Chalmers (ii. 277) quotes the terms of his pass, 9 July 1548, which gave him license to go to France 'to the sculis and to study, and to do other his lawful business.' He had, however, returned, according to Lord Herries, 'but newly' (*Memoirs*, p. 24) by September 1549, when he collected the levies of Fife, and repelled a strong force of English raiders under Lord Clinton, driving them to their ships, with a loss of six hundred killed and wounded and one hundred prisoners (*ib.*) In October of the same year he sat as prior of St. Andrews in the provincial council held at Edinburgh (WILKINS, *Concilia*, iv. 46). On 16 Jan. 1549-50 he was contracted in marriage to Christian, countess of Buchan, infant daughter of the master of Buchan, but the contract was never fulfilled. On 6 Sept. 1550 he had a license to pass to France for 'dressing some affairs of the queen' (CHALMERS, iii. 279), and on 7 Feb. 1550-1 he obtained from the queen of Scots letters of legitimation (*Reg. Mag. Sig. Scot.* 1546-80, No. 565). In 1552 he again visited France, going by way of England (CHALMERS, ii. 280), and in the register of the English privy council for 1550 and 1552 are entries of sums of money paid to James Stewart, among other Scots, on four separate occasions. On this account it has

been inferred that while in France he acted as a spy in the interests of England; but there is no proof that the James Stewart referred to was Lord James, nor, if there were, is it known that he was paid as a spy. But without doubt Lord James at a comparatively early period was a sympathiser with the reformed doctrines, and therefore inclined to the English alliance. He is included by Knox among the persons of rank who after Knox's return to Scotland in 1555 resorted to his teaching at the house of the laird of Dun (*Works*, i. 250), and his resorting thither implied previous dissatisfaction with the old doctrines. Knox afterwards returned to Geneva, but in March 1556 Lord James, with four others, signed a letter inviting him to return to Scotland (*ib.* p. 268).

Appointed, with other commissioners, by the parliament of 14 Dec. 1557 to go to France to witness the marriage of Queen Mary to the dauphin, Lord James was equally with the commissioners most careful to guard the independence of Scotland. Like most of the commissioners, he was also attacked on the way home by a sudden illness, and, although in his case life does not seem to have been seriously imperilled, he ever afterwards felt its ill effects (*ib.* p. 265). According to Bishop Lesley, Lord James while in France intimated to Queen Mary that he had renounced the ecclesiastical life, and craved from her the earldom of Moray, which she declined to grant him, on the ground that he ought to remain in the kind of life to which his father had consecrated him. She, however, expressed her willingness, should he return to the ecclesiastical life, to place him in a bishopric, and to grant him various other preferments in France and Scotland; but, according to Lesley, Lord James was obstinate in his determination not to accede to her desire, and, disappointed in his ambition to obtain the earldom of Moray, resolved strenuously to oppose Mary of Guise, the queen regent (*History*, Scottish Text Soc. ii. 280). There is just enough of truth in Lesley's accusation to render it efficacious as a calumny. It may be that originally secular ambition did induce Lord James to renounce the ecclesiastical life and embrace protestantism, though the choice was most hazardous; but in any case, from whatever motives, he had already made his choice before he visited France in 1557, and this implied opposition to the queen regent, should she endeavour to hinder the progress of the Reformation. Had she been disposed to favour the reformed doctrines, he would have given her his warm support. We must in fact begin with conceding that Lord James had become as strenuous a Calvinist as Knox himself. His faith seems to have fitted him like a glove. It was conjoined probably with a powerful secular ambition, but this rather strengthened than impaired it. How far this ambition was an inheritance from his royal ancestors, and how far it was imposed on him by circumstances and the instinct of self-preservation, are questions which can be answered, if at all, only after a very careful sifting of facts. Frank and even bluff of speech, he possessed marvellous self-control, and no one was less dominated by impulse. Thus there is no statesman of his time who reveals to us less of his personality. He is ever outwardly calm, passionless, imperturbable. Moreover, with all his bluntness, he is not only peculiarly reticent, he seems to delight in self-effacement. If he contrives it is mainly through others. His favourite rôle is that of the national delegate, responding at the last, and merely at the call of duty, to save his religion or his country from disaster when all other help has failed.

In November 1558 the Scottish crown matrimonial was voted by parliament to the dauphin (*Acta Parl. Scot.* ii. 500-7). Knox asserts that Lord James favoured the proposal, and that it was through him that the act of parliament was passed (*Works*, i. 294); but be this as it may, though nominated by the queen to bring over the sword, sceptre, and crown of Scotland to the dauphin, he did not do so: and Lord Herries states that he had determined in no case to proceed to France, and delayed setting out under various pretexts (*Memoirs of Mary*, p. 38). Other events also occurred to hinder his journey, for the dispute with the queen regent on religious matters was rapidly nearing a crisis. From the time of the meeting of parliament in November it was foreseen that a conflict of some kind was at hand; but Lord James had at first determined to appear rather as a supporter than an opponent of the queen regent. When in May, after the spoiling of the monasteries at Perth and elsewhere, the queen regent gathered a force to prevent further excesses, Lord James joined her, and, undertaking the office of mediator, was sent by her as commissioner to the protestants who had assembled to defend Perth (KNOX, i. 337), and on the 28th succeeded in effecting an agreement between the two parties (*ib.* p. 343), but he secretly left her on discovering that she did not mean to keep the agreement.

Immediately afterwards Lord James stepped to the front as the leader of the lords of the congregation. Not merely his birth, but his abilities and education, ensured him a certain predominance over the unlettered Scottish nobles; and henceforth, until his death, whether acting avowedly as leader or remaining carefully in the background, he was the dominant political personality in Scotland. Along with Argyll, though summoned by the queen regent to return to allegiance, he openly defied her, and proceeded to St. Andrews, whither they invited the gentlemen of Fife and Forfar to meet them to concert measures for defence (*ib.* p. 347). How far he was directly responsible for the destruction of the cathedral of St. Andrews which followed the preaching of Knox cannot be ascertained; but there is at least no evidence that he interposed to prevent it; and since prompt and stern opposition on his part could scarce have failed to be effectual, it is probable that if he did not incite or countenance the vandalism, he was not averse to it, and realised its sensational value in impressing the popular imagination. When the queen regent resolved to march on St. Andrews to revenge the outrage, he and Argyll with great celerity gathered a powerful force, with which they barred her approach in a strong position on Cupar Muir (*ib.* i. 351-2). Baulked of her purpose, she agreed to a truce of eight days; but it being discovered that she was now taking advantage of the truce to strengthen her forces, it was resolved to march on Perth and drive the French garrison from the city, which was accomplished on 25 June (*ib.* p. 359). This was followed by an attack on the palace and church of Scone, which Lord James and Argyll for that day succeeded in saving from the fury of the multitude (*ib.* p. 360), but being at nightfall compelled to make a forced march, so as to anticipate the French in holding the passes of the Forth at Stirling, they were unable to prevent the multitude from working their will on the morrow.

As to this forced march, not only was it successful in its special object, but the promptitude of Lord James and Argyll so alarmed the queen regent that she hastily evacuated Edinburgh and fled to Dunbar, the reformers, with Lord James at their head, entering Edinburgh in triumph on 29 June. The inevitable result of such a bold and decisive step was to put Lord James forward as the rival of the queen regent. Indeed, as soon as the reformers took up arms the queen regent seems to have taken for granted that the main purpose of Lord James was to seize the crown for himself (MELVILLE, *Memoirs*, i. 78). On account of his representations Melville was sent by the king of France to sound Lord James as to his real intentions. To his inquiries Lord James replied, with at least perfectly conclusive logic, that, so far from desiring the crown, he was prepared, if toleration to the protestants were guaranteed, to accept for himself perpetual banishment from Scotland, provided only that his rents were sent to him in France. He succeeded in convincing Melville of his disinterestedness; but he could scarcely expect to be taken at his word, and he was not.

If the conduct of the queen regent rendered a change of government necessary, it was as likely as not that Lord James would be chosen regent in her stead. On 27 Jan. 1558-9 Throgmorton wrote to Cecil regarding secret information that a party was being formed to place Lord James in supreme power (*Cal. State Papers*, For. 1558-9, No. 1080), and there are various contemporary rumours to a like effect. Nevertheless Lord James acted throughout with perfect fairness and prudence, and his position is logically unassailable. Whether it was that he judged that the time had not yet come, or that he cherished no such ambitions as were ascribed to him, he never, so far as is known, gave the slightest encouragement to the notion that personally he was the rival of the queen regent. On the contrary, it was probably at his suggestion that James Hamilton, second earl of Arran and duke of Châtelherault [q. v.], was induced in September 1559 formally to join the protestant party as its recognised head. But again there is no proof that in supporting the duke he was entirely disinterested; the introduction of the duke may or may not have been a device to divert suspicion from himself. The issues were complicated and uncertain, and in any case his accession to the regency was as yet probably not regarded by him as within the range of practical politics. The two urgent essentials were to strengthen the hands of the reformed party in Scotland, and to secure the active support of Elizabeth. Therefore, while replying to the remonstrances of the king of France, Queen Mary, and the queen regent with the same emphatic expression of his desire for 'the quietness of the realm,' and with the assurance that if the queen regent would accede to the reasonable demands of the reformers, he would do his utmost to support her authority, Lord James was doing his utmost to obtain the help of Elizabeth to expel the French from Scotland, and thus leave the queen regent without the only support that could maintain her in power. Moreover, as

Mary Stuart since 10 July 1559 had been queen of France, the expulsion from Scotland of her own troops was clearly in open defiance of her authority, and practically amounted to a renunciation of her sovereignty.

A contest of the most momentous nature thus seemed imminent, and that the sovereignty of the young queen was not overthrown was mainly due to unforeseen accidents. The queen regent resolved to proceed with the fortification of Leith, and when, on 12 Oct., the reformers entered Edinburgh with a force of twelve thousand men, she retired within her fortifications. On the 28th she was formally suspended from the regency. Lord James, a bold and skilful soldier, took an active part in the skirmishes which broke the monotony of the siege, but without much success. On 21 Oct. he and Argyll vainly endeavoured with a party of horse to capture the Earl of Bothwell, who had seized from the laird of Ormiston the money sent by Elizabeth to the help of the reformers (KNOX, i. 456). On 5 Nov. a force under Lord James and James Hamilton, third earl of Arran q. v.], was severely defeated by the French near Restalrig, and the misfortune so dismayed the reformers that 'men did so steal away that the wit of man could not stay them' (*ib.* p. 464). It was therefore determined that a special appeal should be made to Elizabeth for assistance, and that meanwhile, Edinburgh being evacuated, the forces of the congregation should divide into two parties, one proceeding to the west and the other, under Arran and Lord James, occupying Fife. Learning that the French were moving eastwards from Stirling, Arran and Lord James assembled their forces at Cupar Muir, whence they proceeded to defend the towns on the south coast of Fife. Here, though much inferior in numbers to the enemy, they maintained not unequally a desperate struggle, until the appearance of English ships in the Firth of Forth caused the French to retreat hastily again towards Stirling (*ib.* ii. 9-13; SADLER, *State Papers*, i. 684). In February 1559-60 he was, with several other leaders, delegated to negotiate at Berwick a treaty with the English commissioners by which Elizabeth agreed to assist the Scots in expelling the French from Scotland, the Scots undertaking, in accordance with Elizabeth's jealous regard for sovereign rights, to remain loyal to the queen of Scotland and her husband, so far as was consistent with the ancient laws and liberties of the kingdom (treaty in KNOX, ii. 46-52). The English army entered

Scotland on 2 April 1560, and was joined by Moray and other lords, with their followers, at Prestonpans, whence the combined force proceeded towards Edinburgh (*ib.* p. 58). In subsequent negotiations with the queen regent Lord James took a prominent part, insisting specially on French evacuation, which the queen regent would probably have agreed to, had not her death, on 10 June, taken place before the negotiations could be completed.

The death of the queen regent was a happy deliverance, probably for her, and certainly for Lord James and the protestants. It left the catholics without a recognised head, and thus rendered possible the very one-sided treaty of Edinburgh on 8 July 1560. The cardinal provision of the treaty was that against the employment of foreign troops in Scotland; for although the sovereignty of Mary Stuart was also formally recognised, this formal recognition was virtually little more than a mockery—a circumstance made clear by the fact that, without taking counsel with their sovereign, the estates sent commissioners to Elizabeth to propose a marriage between Elizabeth and Arran. The intention to supersede Mary by a joint sovereignty of Arran and Elizabeth is self-evident. To this proposal Lord James was by his silence a party; but he could scarce have desired its success, even had he regarded his own sovereignty as impossible or improbable; for Arran's promotion would mean his own political extinction. Still, even had he been disposed so far to favour his sister's rights, he probably knew that any objection on his part would be attributed to jealousy of Arran, and would therefore do more harm than good. As Lord James perhaps anticipated, Elizabeth rejected the proposal; and hardly had she done so when news reached Scotland of the death of Mary's husband, Francis II, on 5 Dec. 1560. No event could have been more unwelcome to Elizabeth; nor could it have been welcome to the reformers and Lord James. It brought matters to a sudden crisis, a crisis full of difficulty and peril. Either Mary's rights to the Scottish throne had to be recognised by her recall to Scotland or formal deposition would be necessary.

But here again Lord James was equal to the occasion, though Elizabeth was not. He was equal to it in spite of, and almost in direct opposition to, Elizabeth. If selfishness was his main motive, it was selfishness under thorough discipline, and the selfishness of a consummate statesman or at least politician. It was a great opportunity for himself, and he probably made the most of

it; but it must be placed to his credit that the path he decided to tread was also seemingly—that is, so far as acts are a key to motives—one of the strictest integrity and honour. Compelled by almost inevitable destiny to assume overwhelming responsibilities, he acquitted himself to admiration. Fully recognising the personal danger to himself in Mary's return, he was yet persuaded that her return ought not to be prevented, and, except at the risk of greater evils, could not. From the beginning, therefore, he sought to win her confidence; but he did not attempt to do so by disguising his opinions or aims. On 15 Jan. 1560-1 he was by the Scottish parliament appointed deputy to her, the main object of his visit being to 'grope her mind.' While he was in France every attempt was made to win him to catholicism; but not for an instant did he even pretend to waver. On the contrary, he aimed to impress on her the impossibility of reimposing catholicism on Scotland; and on 10 June 1560, after his return to Scotland, he, with perfect candour, advised her, 'for the love of God,' not to 'press matters of religion, not for any man's advice on earth;' and stated that he gave her this advice not merely in her own interest, but for the affection he bore the religion which he himself confessed (Letter in Addit. MS. Brit. Mus. 32091, fol. 189, printed in full in PHILIPPSON, *Marie Stuart*, iii. 434-43). To Throgmorton, the English ambassador in Paris, Lord James revealed the whole tenor of his interview with his sister, concealing absolutely nothing. For doing so he has been denounced as a traitor of the blackest kind, influenced mainly by a desire to prejudice his sister in the eyes of Elizabeth. But only the most superficial acquaintance with facts could originate such a theory. It is not a question of his disinterestedness. It was absolutely necessary for his own sake that he should retain Elizabeth's confidence, and he could only succeed in doing so by perfect frankness. That he did succeed is evident from the letters of Throgmorton, who on 1 May wrote to the queen that Lord James deserved to 'be well entertained and made of by the Queen of England' (*Cal. State Papers*, For. 1561-2, No. 158), and expressed the opinion that Elizabeth could not bestow 'too much favour and benefits on him' (*ib.* p. 159); and on 4 May described him as 'one of the most virtuous noblemen, and one in whom religion, sincerity, and magnanimity as much reign as ever he knew in any man in any nation' (*ib.* p. 167). But, though it was doubtless of the highest importance to him personally to stand well with Elizabeth, this was not the main motive of his frankness, for he was bound in honour to reveal to Elizabeth, who was in close alliance with the Scottish protestants, the tenor of his communications with his sister; he was bent on effecting a reconciliation between the two sovereigns; and he was ready to dare Elizabeth's displeasure by insisting that his sister should return to Scotland. It is, in truth, as clear as noonday that Lord James, so far from endeavouring to prejudice his sister in the eyes of Elizabeth, had an entirely opposite purpose in view. His main aim seems to have been to impress Elizabeth with the necessity of securing the friendship of the Queen of Scots. Thus, when Throgmorton learned that Elizabeth was proposing to intercept Mary on her voyage from France, he wrote on 26 July that he marvelled at Elizabeth's resolution, because Lord James, during his visit to France, had done what he could to persuade his sister to come home (*ib.* No. 337); and on 6 Aug. Lord James himself opined to Elizabeth that 'the chief glory of both' queens stood 'in a peaceable reign, which is apt to conciliate a mutual love between them,' and made this very definite proposal: 'What if your title did remain untouched, as well for yourself as for the issue of your body? Inconvenient were it to provide that the Queen, my sovereign, her own place were reserved in the succession to the crown of England, which your majesty will pardon me if I take to be next by the law of all nations, as she is the next in lawful descent of the right line of Henry VII, and in this meantime this isle to be united in a perpetual friendship' (*ib.* p. 384).

Indeed, in nothing does Lord James appear to such advantage as in his conduct to his sister in this dubious crisis; and it is simply inconceivable that his main aim was her ruin. He did his utmost to smooth her difficulties and reconcile the protestants to her rule; defended her, notwithstanding the denunciations of Knox, against the attempt to deprive her of the mass (KNOX, *Works*, ii. 271); and exercised all his skill to promote a close friendship between Elizabeth and her. Granted that he was striving mainly for the retention of his own authority, still it remains that he regarded his interests as compatible with his sister's sovereignty. It was naturally of prime importance to him and Maitland that they should win her confidence, but they endeavoured to win it by means not merely perfectly honourable, but highly praiseworthy: by effecting a reconciliation between the two queens, their hope being that if Elizabeth forgot the past and recognised

the Queen of Scots' right of succession to the throne of England, the Queen of Scots might be led to forget even her devotion to catholicism. How far they were wrong in their calculation as regards the Queen of Scots it is difficult and unnecessary to decide; it suffices that in circumstances of great peril and difficulty they chose what was undoubtedly the path of honour, and that they are wholly free from the blame of failure, which must be shared, in whatever proportion, between the two queens. Nevertheless the conduct of Lord James was quite compatible with enlightened selfishness; for though by promoting this alliance he was extinguishing any hopes he himself might have cherished of succeeding to the Scottish throne, the success of his diplomacy would almost certainly assure him a position of exceptional power and splendour. Moreover, besides staving off immediate danger, he was creating an opportunity for rendering himself secure against the future.

No special office was assigned to Lord James beyond that of member in the new privy council chosen on 6 Sept. 1561. He was merely the friend and informal adviser of the queen, but the internal administration of the kingdom was virtually committed to him; Maitland, as secretary, being employed in all important diplomatic business. On 30 June 1561-2 he had a grant under the privy seal of the earldom of Moray, and on 7 Feb. he obtained the earldom of Mar, and publicly assumed that title: apparently because it was deemed inexpedient that he should assume that of Moray, the earldom of Moray being then held informally by Huntly under the crown. On 8 Feb. he was married by Knox, in the church of St. Giles, to Agnes Keith, eldest daughter of William, earl Marischal, when, according to Knox—then much exercised about Lord James—'the greatness of the banquet and the vanity used thereat offended many godly' (ii. 314). But Knox's alarms were not justified. Never for a moment does Lord James seem to have contemplated the possibility of turning traitor to protestantism; rather was he bent on obtaining guarantees for his continuance in power, should his devotion to protestantism finally compel him to break with the queen. He was utilising the queen somewhat unscrupulously perhaps, but honestly, according to his lights, for the advantage of protestantism plus himself. For mere self-protection it was essential that he should either cripple his chief rivals among the nobility or attain to a special position of ascendency. His most powerful rivals were Bothwell, Châtelherault, and Huntly.

By an expedition against the thieves of Liddesdale in July 1562 (*Cal. State Papers, For.* 1562, Nos. 290, 320), he prevented Bothwell, a fugitive from justice, from re-establishing himself in the south of Scotland, and compelled him to leave the country. As for Châtelherault, though his place in the succession constituted him a direct rival, his indecisive character rendered him comparatively innocuous, especially since his influence had been discounted by the curious escapade of his son Arran. The most formidable and avowed of Moray's enemies was Huntly; and it was of vital importance even for protestantism that his power in the north of Scotland should be crippled. A convenient and plausible method of doing so was by the transference of the earldom of Moray to Lord James; and Lord James, having obtained a private grant of it from the queen, persuaded her to make an expedition to the north in order that he might, by force if necessary, enter into possession. Apparently anxious to stand well both with her brother and Elizabeth, Mary made no objection. Also, as good luck would have it, Huntly was foolish enough to resist; and thus Lord James, formally created on 18 Sept. Earl of Moray, had the opportunity not merely of deducting from Huntly's possessions that earldom, but of effecting the forfeiture of all Huntly's estates, Huntly himself being also a victim of the battle which resulted in the total defeat of his followers.

But it was from the date of this signal triumph that Moray's difficulties really began. Probably his sister had been induced to sanction the expedition against Huntly mainly by a consideration of the favourable impression it would produce on Elizabeth. She may have even calculated that it would remove the last doubts of Elizabeth as to the expediency of formally recognising her right to the English succession. But the news that when Elizabeth in October was at the point of death, only a single voice was raised in behalf of the Queen of Scots as her successor, necessarily awakened both Moray and his sister from their day dreams. Once the Queen of Scots was robbed of the hope of recognition as Elizabeth's successor, Moray's position became one of supreme danger; and it is plain that the hope of the Queen of Scots at this time received a crushing blow. She was almost constrained to look out definitely for a catholic alliance; whereupon she and Moray necessarily became distrustful of each other. Perhaps her one objection to him was, as she said, that he was so 'precise' in matters of religion; but he never pretended that he could modify this

precision. Indeed about this time Randolph relates a really ludicrous instance of what she must have regarded as his impracticable fanaticism. 'There is,' so he wrote from Dunbar on 30 Dec. 1562, 'thrice in the week an ordinary sermon in the Earl of Moray's lodgings in the queen's house so near to the mass that two so mortal enemies cannot be nearer joined without some deadly blow given either upon the one side or the other' (*Cal. State Papers, For.* 1562, No. 1375). But, though uncompromising as regards his own faith, Moray was quite disposed to make allowance for his sister's disappointment. Moreover he was anxious to discover some *via media* which would enable him to remain in power; and, like all the other Scots, he was disposed to resent the insult to them implied in Elizabeth's refusal to recognise their queen's right to the English succession. How far he was sincere in his approval of the Don Carlos marriage project cannot be determined; but that he did formally approve is beyond doubt. Maitland, who then enjoyed his confidence, was employed in the negotiations; and De Quadra, the Spanish ambassador in London, in his long letter to the King of Spain on 18 March 1563, referred to Lord James as a party to the proposal (*Cal. State Papers,* Spanish, 1558–1567, pp. 305–12), and on 3 April informed him, on the authority of Mary's French secretary Raulet, that Lord James was extremely desirous of the marriage (*ib.* p. 318). It has been supposed that Moray —who expected that in Scotland protestantism would, as heretofore, be tolerated —calculated on being appointed regent during his sister's absence in Spain; and had such an arrangement been possible or compatible with the more ambitious purposes of the Queen of Scots, it would have been a not unsatisfactory solution, at least from Moray's point of view, of a most puzzling problem. But the Don Carlos proposal, having come to nothing, was succeeded by Elizabeth's pretended ultimatum, the absurd, and apparently insincere, offer to Mary of the hand of her own favourite, Dudley, earl of Leicester. The intolerable patronage implied in such an offer, especially when coupled with no guarantee of Mary's right to the English succession, was probably as distasteful to Moray as to his sister. His attitude was quite unequivocal: he plainly told the English ambassadors that Elizabeth's offer, unless conjoined with parliamentary recognition of Mary's right to the English succession, was little better than mockery; that if, however, her right were conceded, he would do his best, provided Elizabeth really

wished it, to persuade his sister to accept
Dudley; but that if after all these years he
failed to win for Mary this recognition of her
right, he knew perfectly well both that she
would feel bound to ally herself with Elizabeth's enemies, and that he himself would
cease to share her confidence (Bedford and
Randolph to Cecil, 23 Nov. 1564, in *Cal.
State Papers*, For. 1564-5, No. 813). The
Dudley proposal having also failed, Mary
almost immediately began to indicate a
desire to accept the proposals of Darnley.
Indeed, she had contemplated such a possibility when she proposed the recall of Lennox, who had arrived in Scotland in September 1564; and Moray was no doubt aware
that she did so. Nor probably was he altogether hostile to the arrangement. At any
rate, he declined to be a party to prevent
Lennox's recall, and informed Cecil not
only that he could not labour for the stay
of Lennox, but that he thought it could not
stand with Elizabeth's honour to be the
occasion thereof (*Cal. State Papers*, For.
1564-5, No. 556). Maitland also further
reminded Cecil that Moray and Lennox were
both of one name, then regarded in Scotland as one of the strongest bonds of unity
(*ib.* No. 557). It is therefore likely that
Moray was originally disposed to favour the
Darnley marriage provided he could trust
Darnley and his father, and especially if
Elizabeth could be induced to sanction the
marriage and conjoin with this the recognition of Mary's right to the succession. No
other match was in truth more desirable
in the abstract as insuring the permanent
union of the two kingdoms. But any hopes
of salvation by such an alliance were dashed
by his knowledge of the dispositions and
purposes of Darnley and his father, and
by Elizabeth's hostility to the marriage.
The very fact that Darnley was next lineal
heir to the throne of England after Mary
rendered all the more dangerous a marriage
unsanctioned by Elizabeth; for it tempted
Mary and Darnley to seek to make good their
joint rights by force and by catholic aid.
His strenuous opposition to the marriage
can thus be fully accounted for by his complete comprehension of the political situation: selfish motives probably mingled with
patriotic ones, but had the protestants understood the case as he did, they would have
given him their unanimous support.

As early as 3 Feb. Randolph wrote to Cecil
that both Moray and Maitland in their hearts
disliked Lennox (*Cal. State Papers*, For.
1564-5, No. 958); on 7 April he reported
that Moray had retired in disgust from the
court (*ib.* No. 1085); on 29 April he informed

Cecil that when Moray came to the court of
the queen at Stirling he had worse countenance than he looked for (*ib.* No. 1125); and
on 8 May he wrote that Moray having declined to give a written promise to support the
marriage, the queen had given him 'many
sore words' (*ib.* No. 1151). As soon in fact
as the queen had resolved to marry Darnley,
friendship with her brother became impossible. A significant indication of Moray's
impending doom was given in the sudden
arrival of his enemy Bothwell from France.
But Bothwell was a little premature; on
Moray demanding justice on him for his
previous conspiracy with Arran, the queen
dared not give a positive refusal; and when
on 1 May Moray came with six thousand
men to Edinburgh to keep the law against
him, Bothwell failed to appear (Randolph to
Cecil, 3 May, in *Cal. State Papers*, For.
1564-5, No. 1140).

Moray was perfectly frank with his sister
as to his motives for refusing assent to
the Darnley marriage: it was because he had
little hope that Darnley 'would be a
favourer of Christ's true religion.' But
having once informed her of his decision,
and his reasons for it, his frankness ceased;
not only did he forbear to intimidate her by
threats or warnings, but he carefully masked
his preparations to defeat her purpose. At
a meeting of the nobles held at Stirling on
15 May he kept silence, and permitted a
resolution in favour of the marriage to pass
without dissent. As far as the queen could
gather, he might have intended to make the
best of it. Nevertheless, along with Knox,
he was concerting plans to frustrate it.
He excused himself from attending a convention at Perth on the ground of concern
for his own safety, but about the same
date an assembly of the kirk was held
at Edinburgh, at which resolutions were
passed against popery and the mass. From
a letter sent by Arygll and Moray to Randolph on 1 July (*Illustrations of the Reign
of Mary*, p. 118), it seems certain that
Moray did form a plan for the capture of
the queen and Darnley on the journey from
Perth to Callendar. For this he has been
severely reprehended; but it must be
reckoned rather to his credit than not that,
instead of delaying to oppose the queen
until the marriage had taken place, he did
his utmost to prevent her committing herself to a course of action which he saw
would entail either her own ruin or the
ruin of protestantism in Scotland. He
failed in this particular stratagem, nor was
he successful in preventing the marriage by
force of arms: partly by reason of Mary's

promptitude, partly because of Elizabeth's deception, partly because he was unable to convince the bulk of the nation that the quarrel was more than a personal one. There was no general belief that protestantism was in danger; for the queen maintained that it was not; and she had as yet given no adequate cause for doubting the sincerity of her assurances. Therefore Moray, though backed by Knox, was mainly supported by nobles, such as Châtelherault and Argyll, who had a personal grudge against Lennox, while Morton and other protestant nobles were from motives of kinship ranged on the side of Darnley and the queen.

Having failed to prevent the marriage, Moray's position became much more hazardous; for he found himself committed to a direct attempt to overthrow his sister's sovereignty; and as yet the bulk of those who sympathised with protestantism, even although they realised more and more that protestantism was in danger, were not disposed to support even such a trusted leader in so momentous an enterprise. Only by the substantial aid of Elizabeth could Moray have triumphed, and Elizabeth carefully limited her aid to incitement and small doles of money. Thus the result [for particulars see under MARY QUEEN OF SCOTS] was that Moray on 18 Oct. crossed into England; and since an urgent request on the 14th for reinforcements to be sent to him at Carlisle met with no response from Elizabeth, he discovered too late how grossly Elizabeth had beguiled him. Not only so, but he found that Elizabeth, after using him as her tool, had resolved, at least ostensibly, to disown him, and treat him in a fashion as a criminal. On learning that Moray was proceeding to the court at London, she ostentatiously despatched a message to forbid his approach. He was therefore stayed at Ware, but some time after he received a private message that Elizabeth would receive him. It is scarce conceivable that he was not secretly informed of the ignominious part he was expected to play in the farce which was in contemplation, else how could Elizabeth be certain that he would agree to play it? Be this as it may, she invited him to come to the court only that she might publicly insult him before the ambassadors of France and Spain; compel him to deny in her presence that in his rebellion he had received aid or countenance from her; and bid him to leave her presence as an unworthy traitor to his sovereign (the queen's speech quoted in TYTLER's *History*, ed. 1868, iii. 219; MELVILLE, *Memoirs*, p. 212). Still, Elizabeth not only gave this traitor an asylum in Eng-

land, but continued confidential communications with him with a view to contriving a new method of circumventing the purposes of the Queen of Scots.

Moray, who on 7 Aug. had been put to the horn in Scotland (*Reg. P. C. Scotl.* i. 349), made an attempt through Cecil to obtain the pardon of his sovereign and permission to return to Scotland; and, according to Sir James Melville (*Memoirs*, p. 147), he even sought the intercession of Riccio, 'more humbly than any one would have believed, with the present of a fair diamond enclosed within a letter full of repentance, and fair promises from that time forth to be his friend and protector.' He probably had some hopes of success when he learned that the queen and Darnley were not on good terms; but discovering that Riccio was a more formidable enemy than Darnley, and being threatened with the forfeiture of his estates at a parliament to be held in Edinburgh in February, he became a party to the plot against Riccio's life. No doubt to effect Riccio's overthrow was to render an important service to protestantism; but this was to be conjoined with Moray's return to power. Nor, even had Moray's aims been wholly unselfish and religious, would they have justified the means. The expedients to which he had recourse to insure his final return to power were even more humiliating than the average Scottish noble would have stooped to. After taking the preliminary resolve to do away with Riccio, he not only without hesitation supported, if he did not suggest, the charge of conjugal infidelity against the queen, but he condescended to enter into a special compact with Darnley, whom but lately he had endeavoured to ruin with such disastrous consequences to himself, and he even signed a solemn obligation to be a 'loyal servant' to Darnley as king (*Cal. State Papers*, For. 1566-1568, No. 165). Moreover, while utilising Darnley, he was all the while intending to deceive him; for his faith in Darnley's character and intentions was as slight as ever, and in truth the intention was that not Darnley but Moray should have the supreme power. Thus on arriving at Holyrood on the morrow after Riccio's assassination, Moray had to pretend to the queen that he knew nothing of and abhorred the plot; and while condoling with her on the outrage, he at once set himself to utilise it so as to deprive her of her sovereignty. Frustrated in this attempt by her flight to Dunbar, he had to disguise as best he could his deep disappointment; and while accepting 3,000l. from Elizabeth (*ib.* 1566-8, No. 193) as a bribe to do his utmost for the restoration of English influence, he was compelled from mere motives of personal safety to pretend friendship with his sworn enemy Bothwell, and effectively, if obscurely and indirectly, to aid him in his ambition to win the queen's hand. At first merely tolerated by Mary, because for the time being she deemed it inexpedient to punish him, he was formally reconciled to her before her accouchement, and on 11 July he wrote to Cecil that he was restored to his sovereign's favour, and would do all in his power to maintain the unity between her and Elizabeth (*ib.* No. 567); but 'the utmost of his power' amounted to less than nothing. Any influence he possessed over the queen he had lost for ever; he was simply not to be interfered with, and he knew it, so long as his aims coincided with those of Bothwell and the queen: so long, that is, as he could be utilised for furthering the marriage on which the queen and Bothwell were both equally bent. A necessary preliminary was to get rid of Darnley, and they certainly had in some fashion assurance of Moray's consent to this. That the subject of assassination was directly mooted in Moray's presence at the Craigmillar conference is unlikely; and probably he kept quite clear of the special conspiracy against Darnley. But if he did so it was not to save Darnley but himself; for he must have known that murder was afoot. He was plainly determined not to be made a scapegoat or a martyr, and therefore, instead of either encouraging or discouraging the assassins, he contrived to be at St. Andrews when the assassination occurred. But Bothwell and Mary must have understood that the assassination had his sanction. The tacit bargain—for bargain there was, else Morton and other banished lords would not have been recalled—was apparently that Bothwell was to have a free hand [see Douglas, James, fourth Earl of Morton]. But the stipulation for Morton's recall shows that Moray had further purposes in view, and he no doubt wished to give Bothwell and the queen full facilities for accomplishing their own ruin. Even after the assassination not a word escaped his lips against Bothwell, not a syllable of warning or remonstrance to his sister; but he took care—for his life even was at stake—to obtain license to leave the country and go to France before the marriage took place.

Having thus saved himself from direct contamination with the assassination and the marriage, Moray awaited the developments of a situation which, partly by mere passivity, partly by subtle and indirect suggestion, he had done so much to create. Even when protestants and catholics combined against the queen and Bothwell, he gave no sign. It has been supposed that Morton and others were acting by his advice; but no trace of communications with him has been discovered. He remained in his foreign retreat, and conscientiously abstained from any participation in this second and successful rebellion. He was neither consulted as to the terms of the queen's surrender at Carberry Hill, nor did he give his sanction to her imprisonment in Lochleven. It was only after she had been induced to resign the crown, and to sign on 24 July an act nominating him regent (*Reg. P. C. Scotl.* i. 539-40), that he consented to return to Scotland. Even then he declined to have anything to do with the regency, until during an interview with the queen at Lochleven he so forcibly impressed on her her own folly and danger that she entreated him to accept the regency as a special act of kindness to herself. When also on 22 Aug. he was formally installed, he professed to consent even at the last with the greatest reluctance, and only did so after special pressure of the lord justice clerk in the name of the queen and king, seconded by the intercession of the assembled lords (Throgmorton to Elizabeth, 23 Aug. 1567, in *Illustrations of the Reign of Mary*, p. 289). One of his main reasons for this show of reluctance was that he wished to appear in the eyes of Elizabeth as merely the protector and guardian of the queen, who had proved herself unfit to be entrusted with the government; and nothing could have been more pleasing to Elizabeth than such an interpretation of the arrangement.

Once he had accepted the government, Moray undoubtedly displayed great firmness and courage, or, as Throgmorton expressed it, he seemed resolved to imitate 'rather some who led the people of Israel than any captaine of our age' (Throgmorton writing about 20 Aug. 1567, *ib.* p. 282). But at the same time he manifested an unscrupulous adroitness worthy of the worst of the Israelitish kings. While he showed no trace of vindictiveness against his sister, he determined that her return to power should be rendered impossible. Therefore without trial she was declared by the parliament of 15 Dec. to have been herself 'privie art and part of the actual device and deed of the murder of the king,' and thus virtually incapacitated from ever again occupying the throne. Further, though himself indirectly involved in the Darnley murder, he did not scruple, in order to silence popular clamour and prevent inconvenient revelations, to do his utmost to secure the conviction and death of the mere tools of the conspiracy, while the principals were allowed to go scot free. Sir James Balfour (d. 1583) [q. v.], the closest of Bothwell's associates, not merely remained unaccused, but obtained the gift of the priory of Pittenweem.

The escape of the queen from Lochleven made still greater demands on Moray's courage and address. Though completely taken by surprise, he rejected the offers of reconciliation, and rallied his followers with such rapidity as wholly upset the calculations of her supporters. But with her defeat at Langside and flight to England the situation became still more complicated. He had to protect himself and Scotland against Elizabeth as well as Mary; he had to circumvent the intrigues of Maitland and other secret favourers of the dethroned queen; he had to save his own reputation from the possibilities of damage by searching inquiry into the circumstances of the murder. All this he accomplished with consummate ability and address, but also by means of unscrupulous deception wherever this was deemed necessary. Thus his original consent to the Norfolk marriage scheme was a mere ruse either to throw Maitland off his guard or to prevent a full inquiry; it is not even impossible that he himself revealed the scheme to Elizabeth. Though induced finally to commit himself to a public accusation of the queen of Scots, he made it manifest that he did so on compulsion, and he even succeeded in obtaining the formal sanction of Elizabeth for his continuance in the regency. Also when confronted on his way to Scotland by a plot for his assassination, in revenge for his treachery to Norfolk, he unblushingly asserted that he was as devoted as ever to the Norfolk marriage project, that his accusation of the queen of Scots had been compulsory, and that he would do all that he could to promote the marriage. Yet no sooner had he arrived in Scotland than he procured the formal ratification of all his proceedings against the queen in England. Further, after inducing some of her leading supporters to attend a convention on 10 April 1568 at Edinburgh to consider the terms of a pacification, he ordered the Duke of Châtelherault and Lord Herries, on their refusing to sign an acknowledgment of the king's authority, to be apprehended and thrown into prison. Thus summarily deprived of their most powerful allies, both Argyll and Huntly soon afterwards gave in their submission. All the while Moray, partly it may be with a view to being accurately informed of his sister's intrigues, partly to promote pacifica-

tion in Scotland, kept up the pretence of favouring the Norfolk marriage. At the convention held at Perth on 28 July he, however, voted against the divorce from Bothwell, and as soon as the intrigues of Norfolk were discovered by Elizabeth he revealed to her all that he knew, excusing himself for giving the project his seeming approval by his desire to escape assassination, and by his uncertainty as to her attitude towards himself and the Queen of Scots. But, either to protect himself against a most dangerous enemy or to save his credit with Elizabeth, he now deemed it advisable to proceed against Maitland of Lethington, and did so by contriving that Maitland should be formally accused by Captain Crawford, a dependent of Lennox, of the murder of Darnley. Maitland, however, was rescued from prison by Kirkcaldy of Grange; and even his trial, fixed for 22 Nov., was indefinitely postponed owing to the concourse of his friends in Edinburgh. Shortly after this, Moray, having secured the special approbation of Elizabeth by the capture of the rebel Earl of Northumberland and his imprisonment in Lochleven, made a proposal for the deliverance of Mary into his hands. 'There is no more likely means of remedy,' so runs the bond of Moray and others, 'and for the quiet of both the realms, than that the said queen's person were again in Scotland, and so be something further from foreign realms and daily practice with the princes thereof.' She was of course to be detained, but was to be 'provided for in competent state like unto a queen,' and no 'sinister means' were to be taken 'to shorten her life' (Cal. State Papers, For. 1569-71, No. 580). That Elizabeth would have agreed to a bona fide arrangement of this kind is unlikely, but the negotiations were suddenly cut short by the assassination of Moray at Linlithgow by James Hamilton (fl. 1566-1580) [q. v.] of Bothwellhaugh, on 21 Jan. 1569-70. His body was removed to the abbey of Holyrood, and on 14 Feb. was carried thence to St. Giles', where it was buried in the south aisle. Knox, according to Calderwood, making a sermon in which 'he moved three thousand persons to shed tears for the loss of such a good and godly governor.' The following Latin epitaph by George Buchanan was engraven in brass and set above his tomb: 'Jacobo Stewarto, Moraviæ comiti, Scotiæ proregi, viro ætatis suæ longe optimo, ab inimicis, omnis memoriæ deterrimis, ex insidiis extincto, ceu patri communi, patria mœrens posuit.'

Moray by his own party was canonised as the 'good regent;' but the epithet 'good' can only be allowed of him in its strict puritanic sense; his goodness was essentially that of a cold temperament. His house, says Calderwood, was 'like a sanctuary;' his solemnity was indeed too preternatural to be wholesome even if it were wholly sincere. And if strictly good and honourable in his private relations, he allowed himself a very wide latitude in politics; while it is certain that here he was even less generous than he was just. No doubt he professed, and probably believed, that he was influenced by the highest possible motives, but these for the most part harmonised with his own advancement; and to suppose that one of his overmastering temperament was destitute of personal ambition would be absurd. Still his task was one of supreme difficulty, and his opponents were at least as unscrupulous as himself. Judged by the political standards of his time, he cannot be charged with conduct that was exceptionally unprincipled, and his career was suddenly cut short before his abilities and aims as a ruler could be so tested as to enable us to pronounce a full and decisive opinion on his character and motives.

By his wife, Agnes Keith, Moray had two daughters: Elizabeth, married in 1580 to James Stewart or Stuart, afterwards earl of Moray (d. 1592) [q. v.], son of James, first lord Doune; and Margaret, married to Francis, earl of Errol. Moray's widow married, as her second husband, Colin Campbell, sixth earl of Argyll, whom she predeceased in July 1583.

[In addition to the authorities quoted in the text, reference may be made to the bibliography appended to Mary Queen of Scots.] T. F. H.

STEWART or STUART, JAMES, Earl of Moray of a new line (d. 1592), was the elder son of James Stewart (d. 20 July 1590), abbot of St. Colme, who was on 24 Nov. 1581 created Lord Doune, by Lady Margaret Campbell, eldest daughter of Archibald, fourth earl of Argyll. From James VI he received in 1580 a gift of the ward and marriage of the two daughters of the regent Moray, and a few days thereafter married Elizabeth, the elder one, and assumed, *jure uxoris*, the title of the Earl of Moray. His personal beauty and accomplishments gained him the name of 'the bonny earl.' On 1 Aug. 1588 he was appointed a commissioner for executing the act against the Spanish armada (*Reg. P. C. Scotl.* iv. 307), and on 5 March 1589-90 a commissioner for executing the acts against the Jesuits (*ib.* p. 468). In 1590, along with the Earl of Atholl, he assisted the laird of Grant when his house was besieged by Huntly (Moysie, *Memoirs*, p. 85); and Huntly having on

23 Jan. 1590-1 presented a supplication against his having taken part with the malefactors in the north (*Reg. P. C. Scotl.* iv. 569), both earls were on 15 March commanded to proceed to Edinburgh and sign bands to keep the peace (*ib.* p. 597). Afterwards Huntly obtained a special commission to pursue the Earl of Bothwell and his associates. To prevent Bothwell obtaining shelter from the Earl of Moray, who was his cousin-german, Moray was induced by Lord Ochiltree, specially deputed by the king, to come south on condition of receiving the king's pardon (Moysie, *Memoirs*, p. 88; Spotiswood, *History*, ii. 419). According to Spotiswood, after this had been agreed on, a rumour arose that Moray had been seen in Holyrood Palace along with Bothwell, and Huntly therefore received from the king a warrant to apprehend him (*ib.*) But even if this were so, such a proceeding was unjustifiable after Moray had been enticed south on a promise of pardon; and it was strangely unwise, if not worse, to entrust his apprehension to Huntly, who was the hereditary enemy of his house. Besides, there was no need to apprehend him before the king had questioned him on the new charge. The inference seems therefore almost inevitable that the king was influenced by private motives, and these probably were, as was rumoured and as is set forth in the traditionary ballad, that he was jealous of Moray's favour with the queen. Moray, in expectation of a summons to the court, had arrived at Donibristle, a house of his mother on the Fifeshire coast, when on 7 Feb. 1591-2 it was suddenly beset by the followers of Huntly, who called upon him to surrender. To suppose that Moray would quietly put himself into the hands of his enemy was to credit him either with abject cowardice or incredible simplicity. He declined to do so, and Huntly, without scruple, set fire to the house. After every one in the house had rushed out, Moray stayed for a time within, and, suddenly dashing out, he broke through the cordon surrounding the house, and, outpacing his enemies, made for the rocks on the seashore. The burning of the top of his headpiece, however, betrayed him, and he was followed to his place of concealment and slain—a quite unnecessary precaution, since there is no evidence that he even sought to make further resistance. The corpses of the earl and of Dunbar, sheriff of Moray, who had also been slain by Huntly's followers, were brought over by the earl's mother to Leith, to be placed in the tomb of the regent Moray in St. Giles's church; but for some months they remained in their coffins unburied,

x 2

their friends refusing to bury them until 'the slaughter was punished' (ib. p. 420). Captain Gordon, one of Huntly's followers, who being wounded was unable to escape to the north, was brought to Edinburgh and executed; but this did not assuage the indignation of the people, and the king deemed it prudent to retire from Edinburgh to Glasgow, until Huntly entered himself in ward in Blackness. This Huntly did on 12 March, but on the 20th he was released on giving surety that on six days' notice he would appear and stand his trial whenever called on to do so. The murder of Moray is the theme of a short traditional ballad or song, the simple pathos of which is evidence that the tragedy powerfully affected popular feeling.

By his wife, Elizabeth Stewart, who died three months before him, he had two sons and three daughters: James, second earl of Moray; Sir Francis Stewart, knight of the Bath, who was well known in London literary society, and is said to have frequented the literary meetings at the Mermaid tavern; Margaret, married first to Charles Howard, earl of Nottingham, lord high admiral of England, and secondly to William, viscount Monson; May, married to John, eighth lord Abernethy of Saltoun; and Grizel, to Robert Innes of Innes.

[Reg. P. C. Scotl. iv.; Moysie's Memoirs and History of James the Sext in the Bannatyne Club; Histories by Spotiswood and Calderwood; Douglas's Scottish Peerage (Wood), ii. 258-9.]

T. F. H.

STEWART, JAMES, of Bothwellmuir, EARL OF ARRAN (d. 1596), was second son of Andrew Stewart, second lord Ochiltree [q. v.], father-in-law of Knox, by Agnes, daughter of John Cunningham of Capringston. Sir William Stewart (d. 1588) [q. v.] was his younger brother. He was well educated, probably with the intention of entering the church, but, preferring an adventurous life, he became a soldier of fortune, and for some time served in the army of the states of Holland against the Spaniards. Plausible, able, and accomplished, he was at the same time quite unscrupulous in the choice of methods to attain his ambitious hopes, while in impudent audacity he probably had no equal even among the Scottish courtiers. Returning to Scotland in 1579, he was on 15 Oct. 1580 appointed a gentleman of the chamber (Reg. P. C. Scotl. iii. 323). He was also made captain of the guard and tutor to his cousin, the insane Earl of Arran [see HAMILTON, JAMES, third EARL OF ARRAN]. In December 1580 he was made use of by Esmé Stuart, duke of Lennox [q. v.],

to accuse Morton before the council of the murder of Darnley (CALDERWOOD, iii. 481; SPOTISWOOD, ii. 271; MOYSIE, Memoirs, p. 28). On 7 Feb. 1580-1 he was admitted a member of the privy council (Reg. P. C. Scotl. iii. 356). The reward for his bold and dangerous coup against Morton was his recognition as the legitimate head of the Hamiltons. On 22 April 1581 he obtained a grant of the earldom of Arran in Bute, of the lands and barony of Hamilton in Lanark, and of other lands in Lanark, Berwickshire, and Linlithgow (Reg. Mag. Sig. Scot. 1580-1593, No. 167); and under the pretence that he was the lawful heir of the family (his father's mother being only child of the first Earl of Arran), he had, on 28 Oct., a letter of confirmation under the great seal, ratifying anew the old erection of the earldom of Arran, and creating him and his heirs male earls of Arran and lords of Avane and Hamilton (ib. No. 262). After the execution of Morton a special act was passed by the privy council approving his services in accusing Morton of Darnley's murder (Reg. P. C. Scotl. iii. 389); and the reason for passing the act, according to Spotiswood, was to acquit him for putting some of Morton's servants to the torture, although, according to the same authority, the object of applying torture was 'to find out where his gold and money was hidden, and for no purpose else' (History, ii. 280). After his accession to the earldom of Arran he did not scruple to manifest his jealousy of the Duke of Lennox, and 'spared not to affront him on all occasions' (ib.). On the ground that his 'house was nearest the king,' he protested against the duke bearing the sword at the parliament held in October (CALDERWOOD, iii. 592). Thereupon, in consequence of Arran's insolence, the duke declined to attend the parliament; and the king, taking the duke with him to Dalkeith, forbad Arran to come to court (Spotiswood, ii. 281). Arran gave out that the quarrel was 'on account of religion;' but finding that he was gaining nothing by this open hostility, he resolved to bide his time. Some time in December they therefore were reconciled; but on 1 Feb. 1581-2 Arran demitted the office of captain of the guard (Reg. P. C. Scotl. iii. 439).

Shortly after being created earl, Arran married, on 6 July 1581, Elizabeth, eldest daughter of John Stewart, fourth earl of Atholl [q. v.] Arran was her third husband. Her first husband was Hugh, sixth lord Lovat, on whose death she became the wife of Robert Stewart, earl of Lennox and March. Subsequently Arran seduced her, and after she was with child by him she obtained a divorce from the Earl of Lennox on account of his impotency. Her child by Arran, according to Calderwood, was 'born a quarter of a year before' he married her; and before baptism could be granted 'he and his lady had to underlie the discipline of the kirk' (CALDERWOOD, iii. 596). For some time he and Lennox had been in collision with the kirk for the 'intrusion' of Robert Montgomerie [q. v.] into the bishopric in Glasgow, and on 9 May he and Lennox 'fell out in outrageous words' against the commissioners of the kirk sent to the king on the subject (ib. p. 619). Also when certain articles on the subject were presented to the king and nobility at Perth in July, Arran asked, 'with a thrawn face and in boasting manner, who dare subscribe these treasonable articles' (ib. p. 631). It was especially the attitude of Arran and Lennox towards the kirk in the Montgomerie case that led to the raid of Ruthven on 22 Aug., when the king was seized by the protestant lords [see RUTHVEN, WILLIAM, first EARL OF GOWRIE]. As soon as he knew what had happened, Arran, who was at Kinneil, hastened to Ruthven, trusting by the Earl of Gowrie's friendship to obtain access to the king. Learning that Mar was guarding the approaches, he sent his brother, Sir William Stewart, to attack Mar and divert his attention, and while Mar was engaged with Stewart he succeeded in gaining access to the castle unperceived; but instead of obtaining an interview with the king, he 'was put in a close chamber and afterwards transported to Dupplin' (ib. iii. 637). Finally he was placed under the charge of Gowrie, first in Stirling and afterwards at Ruthven. While at Ruthven he offered, on condition of being placed at liberty, to reveal as much as would cost Lennox his head. No doubt the offer was made con amore, nor was it a vain boast ; but Lennox's head was not desired, his banishment being deemed sufficient. The offer, therefore, was not accepted ; on the contrary, an order was made on 19 Oct. for his continued detention in custody of the Earl of Gowrie at Ruthven Castle until it was definitely known that Lennox had left the kingdom, after which Arran was to be at liberty to reside anywhere 'benorth the Earn' (Reg. P. C. Scotl. iii. 519). 'Gowrie, however,' says Calderwood, 'was drawn by the king to be a friend of Arran ;' and the council, at the king's request, agreed on 15 Nov. to set Arran at liberty, which would have been done but for the remonstrance of Bowes, the English ambassador (CALDERWOOD, iii. 690). In May 1583 Colonel Sir William Stewart (fl. 1575-1603) [q. v.]

informed Queen Elizabeth of the king of Scots' desire that Arran should return to court, he having given a promise not to return without her consent (ib. iii. 714); but the request was refused. Neverthless, after the king's escape from the Ruthven raiders, Arran on 5 Aug. came to the king at Falkland and was well received (ib. iii. 722). In September he was made provost of Stirling, and was entrusted with the keeping of the important fortress and royal residence of Stirling Castle. Although described by Calderwood with some justice as 'a profound mocker of all religion, more fit to be the executioner of some Nero nor counsellor to a Christian prince, let be sole guide and commander of the commonwealth' (ib. iv. 47), he now began to wield an influence over the king quite as paramount as that formerly exercised by Lennox. On 15 May 1584 —the Earl of Argyll having fallen into ill-health—he had a gift of the survivancy of the chancellorship, with the power to act in the absence of Argyll, and on the death of Argyll he was placed in full possession of the chancellorship. The failure of a plot of the protestant nobles for the overthrow of his ascendency, due to the capture of the Earl of Gowrie by Colonel Stewart, established his supremacy on a more secure basis than ever. Gowrie, at whose trial Arran was one of the jury, was executed at Stirling on 2 Aug.; and the other protestant lords who had engaged in the conspiracy fled into England. On the ground of having, whether truly or falsely, discovered a plot for the capture of the castle of Edinburgh through the treachery of the constable, Arran on 8 Aug. obtained the charge of this fortress as well as of Stirling (ib. iv. 170). Still further to consolidate his authority, he entered into private communication with Elizabeth, who, resolving to make use of him so far as suited her own purposes, appointed Lord Hunsdon to hold a conference with him at Berwick (see specially CALDERWOOD, iv. 171-97); and at the conference, if Arran did not succeed in impressing the ambassador with his entire devotedness to Elizabeth, he induced her to believe that there was no immediate necessity for his overthrow. Having thus succeeded in staving off any design for the immediate return of the banished lords, he resolved to make the best use of the breathing space afforded him, and set himself to crush his more prominent enemies in Scotland by wholesale forfeitures, among those on whom such sentences were passed being the Earl of Angus, the Earl and Countess of Mar, the Master of Glammis, and others (ib. iv. 190). During the procession of the king to the parliament, the Countess of Gowrie went down on her knees to petition the king for grace to her and her house, but was rudely thrust away by Arran, and, falling into a swoon, lay in the streets until the procession passed into the Tolbooth. At the same parliament 'all ministers, readers, and members of colleges' were ordered within forty days to subscribe the act of parliament acknowledging the supreme authority of the king in matters temporal as well as spiritual. On 6 Oct. Arran was chosen provost of Edinburgh, and he had now reached the acme of his influence. But the more secure he felt, the more he endangered his position by his reckless use of power. 'Supposing all things to be right,' says Spotiswood, 'he went on in his accustomed manner, not caring what enmity he drew upon himself' (*History*, ii. 325). The Earl of Atholl, the Lord Home, and the master of Cassilis he committed to prison simply because he had a private grudge against them. Thus when the crisis came he was left practically without a supporter. It was not long in coming. Just when he supposed that negotiations with Elizabeth were reaching a stage which would render his lease of power almost for ever secure, his influence with Elizabeth was being undermined by the very agent employed to conduct the negotiations. This was Patrick, master of Gray [see PATRICK, sixth LORD GRAY, d. 1612], who, either in secret dread of Arran's supremacy or from the more ambitious resolve to supplant him, professed, and with some justification, to reveal to Elizabeth that no trust could be placed either in Arran's intentions or in the stability of his authority, and offered, if she would support him, to do his utmost to effect his ruin and secure an indissoluble league between the two countries.

In the following spring Wotton, the English ambassador, endeavoured to contrive a plot for Arran's assassination (see specially TYTLER, *History of Scotland*, ed. 1868, iv. 99–100), but did not quite succeed in completing arrangements before an event happened which rendered the execution of the plot unnecessary. This was the slaughter, on 27 July 1585, of Francis, lord Russell (son of Francis Russell, second earl of Bedford [q. v.]), in a border affray between Sir John Forster and Kerr of Ferniehirst. Elizabeth complained to the king through her ambassador, asserting that Russell had been slain at the instance of Arran; and as the ambassador offered further to prove that Arran and Kerr had been art and part in the murder, the king had no choice but

meanwhile to send Arran into ward in the castle of St. Andrews (CALDERWOOD, iv. 379). But strangely enough a saviour now appeared to Arran in the person of the master of Gray, who, either because he had become doubtful of Elizabeth's regard for himself or wished to conceal his intrigues with her, arranged with the king, on the receipt of certain bribes from Arran, that Arran should be sent to nominal confinement in Kinneil. Nevertheless, the master knew that he could not trust Arran, and immediately set on foot a new plot for his overthrow by the recall of the banished lords. About the middle of October 1585 rumours reached Scotland of the advance of the banished lords, and Arran, escaping from Kinneil, hurried to the king at Stirling to announce that he was being betrayed by the master of Gray. But learning this, the master returned also to court, and Arran, frustrated in a design for the master's assassination by the rapid approach of the lords, secretly left the castle (*Relation of the Master of Gray* in the Bannatyne Club, pp. 59, 60; CALDERWOOD, iv. 389–90). Soon after their entrance into the castle Arran was proclaimed a traitor at the market-place, and fled to the west coast. About the end of March 1586 he was commanded to depart out of the country before 6 April, and obeyed, going either to Cantyre or Ireland (CALDERWOOD, iv. 547). Afterwards he returned to Scotland, where he resided as merely Captain James Stewart. On 27 Nov. 1592 he came to court at the request of the king, 'to give articles' against the chancellor and Lord Hamilton (CALDERWOOD, v. 186). While in Edinburgh he made an attempt to get reinstated in the favour of the kirk; but it was concluded that he had shown no such offers of repentance as the kirk looked for, and he was dismissed with the general answer: 'Ye must give us as good proofs of your well-doing as ye have given of your evil-doing before we can credit you much' (*ib.* p. 190; MOYSIE, *Memoirs*, p. 89). 'And so Captain James,' says Calderwood, 'finding so great opposition, went home, and came not to court again' (*ib.*) Various intrigues were set on foot for his return to power, but they were unsuccessful. Towards the close of 1596, while riding homewards through Symington in Clydesdale, he was attacked and slain by Sir James Douglas of Parkhead, nephew of Morton, in revenge of Morton's death. His body was left where he fell, a prey to dogs and swine, and his head, having been fixed on the point of a spear, was carried by Douglas through the country in triumph.

By his wife, Lady Elizabeth, he had two sons—Sir James Stewart of Killeith, fourth lord Ochiltree, and Henry. For bringing a charge of treason against the Marquis of Hamilton that, in pretending in 1631 to raise troops for the aid of Gustavus Adolphus, he was aiming to secure his right to the Scottish crown, Lord Ochiltree was convicted of lease-making, and sentenced to imprisonment for life in Blackness Castle, where he remained until 1652, when he was released by the English after the battle of Worcester.

[Histories by Calderwood and Spotiswood; Reg. P. C. Scotl.; Reg. Mag. Sig. Scot.; Melville's Memoirs; Papers of the Master of Gray; Moysie's Memoirs; History of James the Sext in the Bannatyne Club; Calendar of Scottish State Papers; Bowes Correspondence in the Surtees Society; Douglas's Scottish Peerage (Wood), i. 121–4; G. E. C[okayne]'s Complete Peerage.]   T. F. H.

STEWART, JAMES, fourth DUKE OF LENNOX and DUKE OF RICHMOND (1612–1655). [See STUART.]

STEWART, JAMES (1791–1863), engraver, was born at Edinburgh in October or November 1791. He was articled to Robert Scott [q. v.] the engraver, and had as his fellow pupil John Burnet [q. v.], from whom he received much assistance; he also studied drawing in the Trustees' Academy, and became a very able line engraver. Stewart's first independent plate was from Sir William Allan's 'Tartar Robbers dividing the Spoil,' which was followed by 'Circassian Captives,' 1820; 'The Murder of Archbishop Sharpe,' 1824; and 'Queen Mary signing her Abdication,' all from paintings by Allan. He then became associated with David Wilkie, for whom he executed, with several minor works, an admirable plate of the 'Penny Wedding.' On the foundation of the Royal Scottish Academy in 1826 he became an original member. In 1830 Stewart removed to London, where he engraved 'The Pedlar,' after Wilkie, and 'Hide and Seek,' from a picture painted by himself in the style of Wilkie, which was exhibited at the British Institution in 1829. In 1833 he was induced by financial embarrassment to abandon his profession and emigrate to Cape Colony; there he settled as a farmer, but within a year lost everything through the outbreak of the Kaffir war. He then went to reside in the town of Somerset, where, by teaching and portrait-painting, he earned the means of purchasing another property. He subsequently became a magistrate and a member of the legislature, and died in the colony in May 1863.

[Art Journal, August 1863; Redgrave's Dict. of Artists.]   F. M. O'D.

STEWART or STUART, JAMES FRANCIS EDWARD (1688–1766), the Old Pretender. [See JAMES FRANCIS EDWARD STUART.]

STEWART, JOHN, EARL OF BUCHAN (1381?–1424), born about 1381, was the eldest son of the second marriage of Robert Stewart, first duke of Albany [q. v.] The first notice of him is in a grant made before 1399 to him and his younger brothers, Andrew and Robert, of the lands of Coull and O'Neil in Aberdeenshire (Exchequer Rolls, vol. iv. p. clxxxi), and in later years, it is said, his valour obtained for him the popular epithet of 'brave John O'Coul.' He held only the rank of 'squire' in 1406, but on 20 Sept. of that year (DUNCAN STEWART, History of the Stewarts, p. 114) he received from his father, then governor of Scotland, the earldom of Buchan, which had fallen to the crown by the death of his uncle, Alexander Stewart (1343?–1405?) [q. v.] In 1407 he was appointed chamberlain of Scotland, an office which he held till his death, and in 1415 he succeeded his niece, Euphemia Lesley, in the earldom of Ross.

The events which gained fame for the earl began in 1418, when an embassy arrived from France earnestly pleading for Scottish aid to assist the dauphin (afterwards Charles VII) against the English. In answer the earl led a force of six thousand Scots by sea to Rochelle in Spanish and other ships provided, and arrived at the French court in October 1419. He and the other Scottish leaders were well received, but no special occasion arose for distinguishing themselves, and the earl appears to have returned to Scotland on a mission for more money and more men. He was again in France in the early part of 1421, when the Scots and their allies under his command completely defeated the English at Beaugé. The English leader, the Duke of Clarence, was slain, and his death has been ascribed to Buchan's own hand, but this is doubtful; in a letter announcing the victory to the dauphin the earl only states that the duke had been killed [see THOMAS, DUKE OF CLARENCE, d. 1421]. This success won for the earl the office of constable of France, and he also received the remarkable gift of the person of an astrologer, who is said to have predicted the deaths of Charles VI and Henry V. The earl marched into Normandy, took Avranches and laid siege to Alençon, while he also gained other places for the dauphin. About this time overtures were made to him by his native prince, James I, then in France with the English king, but he and the other Scots refused to lay down their arms.

The earl was not present at the battle of Crevant, where the Scots were defeated, as he had returned to Scotland for reinforcements. He induced Archibald Douglas, fourth earl of Douglas [q. v.], his father-in-law, to engage in the French service, and a force of ten thousand well-equipped Scots landed in France in the beginning of 1424. Their warlike career, however, was brief, as on 17 Aug. of that year the Scots and French under the two earls were defeated with great slaughter by the English near the town of Verneuil [see JOHN OF LANCASTER, DUKE OF BEDFORD]. Buchan commanded the centre, chiefly composed of Scots, and when at a critical moment they were deprived of their supports, they fought so bravely and stubbornly, refusing all quarter, that nearly nine thousand were left dead on the field. Among these was Buchan, who fell covered with wounds, and was buried at Tours on 24 Aug. in the same tomb with the Earl of Douglas.

The earl married, about 1413, Elizabeth, daughter of Archibald, fourth earl of Douglas, by whom he had a daughter Margaret, who became the wife of George, lord Seton. Elizabeth Douglas afterwards became the wife successively of Thomas Stewart, master of Mar, and William Sinclair, third earl of Orkney [q. v.]

A portrait is given in Pinkerton's 'Iconographia Scotica,' 1797. The original is said to be at Chambord in France. Another bearing his name is shown at Amondell, Linlithgowshire, the seat of the present Earl of Buchan. Their authenticity, however, cannot be positively asserted.

[Exchequer Rolls of Scotland, vol. iv.; The Scots Guards in France, 2 vols., by William Forbes-Leith, S. J.; Fordun's Scotichronicon, ed. Goodall, ii. 459-64; Michel's Les Écossais en France, vol. i.] J. A-N.

STEWART, SIR JOHN (1365?-1429), of Darnley, first SEIGNEUR OF AUBIGNY. [See STUART.]

STEWART, JOHN, EARL OF MAR (1457?-1479?), third and youngest son of James II of Scotland, by Mary of Gueldres, was born after October 1456, his name not occurring in the list of the king's sons in the comptroller's account of that date. James III [q. v.] and Alexander Stewart, duke of Albany [q. v.], were his elder brothers. Between 21 June 1458 and 23 June 1459 he was created Earl of Mar and Garioch (Exchequer Rolls of Scotland, vi. 516). He sat in the parliament of March 1478-9 (Acta Parl. Scot. ii. 120), but between that date

and October 1479—for he was not present at the parliament which met in the latter month (ib. p. 124)—was arrested by James III at the instance of Cochrane, the king's favourite. The traditional story is that he was accused by Cochrane of using magical arts against the king; but the probability is that Cochrane and the king dreaded a combination against them. Mar was confined in Craigmillar Castle, and, according to one story, an incision being made in one of his veins, he was allowed to bleed to death; while those who desired to absolve the king of blame asserted that his death was the result of misadventure while he was being bled by a physician for fever. 'The Earl of Mar,' says Lindsay of Pitscottie, 'was ane fair lustie man, of ane great and weill proportioned stature, weill faced and comelie in all his behaviours who knew nothing but nobilitie. He used meikle hunting and hawking, with other gentlemanlie exercise, and delighted also in interteaming of great and stout hors and meares, that thair offspring micht florisch, so that he might be served thairwith in tyme of warres' (Chronicle, p. 178). He was unmarried, and his honours became extinct.

[Exchequer Rolls of Scotland; Acta Parl. Scot.; Histories of Lesley and Buchanan; Lindsay of Pitscottie's Chronicle.] T. F. H.

STEWART or STUART, SIR JOHN, LORD DARNLEY and first (or ninth) EARL OF LENNOX (d. 1495) of the Stewart line, was eldest son of Sir Alan Stewart, second son of Sir John Stuart of Darnley, first seigneur of Aubigny [q. v.]. Sir Alan was treacherously slain by Sir Thomas Boyd at Linlithgow in 1439. His mother was Catherine Seton, probably a daughter of Sir William Seton, killed at Verneuil in 1424. On 16 May 1450 he granted to his brother, Alexander Stewart, a charter of the lands of Dreghorn, Ayrshire (Reg. Mag. Sig. Scot. 1424-1513, No. 350), and on 17 July 1460 he had a charter of the lands of Tarbolton, Ayrshire, to be held in a free barony (DOUGLAS, ii. 94). On the death in 1460 of Isabel, duchess of Albany [see STEWART, MURDAC, second DUKE OF ALBANY], and daughter of Duncan, earl of Lennox (d. 1425), Sir John Stewart, by virtue of his descent from Duncan's daughter, Elizabeth Lennox, wife of Sir John Stewart, seigneur of Aubigny, laid claim to a share in the earldom of Lennox (Hist. MSS. Comm. 3rd Rep. p. 389). To prove his claim he relied on a charter, dated 8 Nov. 1392, of which there exists a notarial transcript, dated 21 Jan. 1460, granted by King Robert III 'to Duncan, earl of Lennox, of the whole earldom of

Lennox and lordship thereof' to be held by him 'and the lawful heirs male of his body, whom failing, by Murdac Stewart and Isabella, daughter of the said earl, and lawful heirs of their bodies, whom failing, by the nearest and lawful heirs of the said Duncan, whomsoever, of the king and his heirs, for rendering the services due and worthy' (ib.) By authority of this charter Sir John Stewart laid claim to one half of the earldom of Lennox, equal parts of the other half being claimed by two sisters, daughters of another daughter of Earl Duncan: Agnes Menteith, married to Sir John Haldane of Gleneagles, and Elizabeth Menteith to John Napier of Merchiston. As the lord chancellor—Andrew Stewart, lord Avandale [q. v.], grandson of Isabella, Earl Duncan's eldest daughter and suo jure Countess of Lennox [see under STEWART, MURDAC, second DUKE OF ALBANY', and desirous himself of succeeding to the earldom—took no action in Sir John Stewart's behalf, Stewart, on 12 Oct. 1463, presented a petition to parliament, praying that his majesty would direct breves to be issued from chancery for serving him heir to the lands of half the earldom of Lennox, for which he bound himself to maintain at his own expense for one year a hundred spears and fifty bows, and to find caution that his occupation of one half of the earldom should not prejudice any claim his majesty might have thereto when he attained his majority (ib.) No proceedings, however, were adopted to place Stewart in possession of his share in the earldom, the position assumed by the lord chancellor being probably that the king had a claim on it by virtue of the last clause of the charter of 1392. Meanwhile Stewart had been created a lord of parliament, with the title of Lord Darnley, some time between 17 July 1460, when he is mentioned as Sir John Stewart, and 24 July 1461, when, as Lord Darnley, he obtained certain grants of land from James III (ib.) On 4 Feb. 1465 he had a charter appointing him governor of Rothesay, in the Isle of Bute, until the king reached the age of fifteen (ib. p. 388), and in 1466 he served heir to his grandfather Alan, who fell at Orleans in 1429, of various lands in the barony of Avandale.

On 10 May 1471 Andrew Stewart, lord Avandale, succeeded in obtaining a life-rent grant of the whole earldom of Lennox (Reg. Mag. Sig. Scot. 1424–1513, No. 1018), and his permanent possession of it was further guaranteed by letters of legitimation on 28 Aug. 1472; nevertheless Lord Darnley immediately began to make strenuous efforts not merely to obtain recognition of his right to his share in the earldom, but to make

good a claim to the title. To obtain his purpose he endeavoured to induce the other claimants to forego their claims, and in September 1472 he obtained from Elizabeth, wife of John, lord Napier, letters of renunciation of her share (i.e. a fourth part) of the earldom (Hist. MSS. Comm. 3rd Rep. p. 388). Darnley also entered into an agreement with Sir John Haldane to submit to the arbitration of the bishops of Aberdeen and Orkney, and of the earls of Avandale and Argyll, regarding the satisfaction to be made by Darnley to Haldane and his spouse for giving over to him the claim they had to the earldom of Lennox (ib. p. 389); but no arrangement was come to. Haldane was sent on an embassy to Denmark in 1473, and Darnley on 27 July of the same year (after guaranteeing to Avandale undisturbed possession of the life rent) obtained an instrument of sasin in his favour, as heir of his great-grandfather Duncan, earl of Lennox, of the principal messuage and half of the lands of the earldom of Lennox and superiority of the same (ib. p. 390).

On being infefted in the principal messuage Darnley assumed the title of Earl of Lennox; but Sir John Haldane, on his return to Scotland in 1475, contested his claims to the principal messuage and title. On 12 Jan. 1475–6 letters were given by the king under the privy seal revoking and annulling the breves and service to John, lord Darnley, as heir to Duncan, earl of Lennox, as being unjustly deduced against Sir John Haldane. Darnley had claimed descent from the elder daughter of Earl Duncan (Retour of Service, ib.), and it is probable that herein consisted the injustice of his claim, for he endeavoured to set aside the claims of Sir John Haldane to the principal messuage by, in July 1476, contesting the legitimacy of Agnes Menteith, Haldane's wife (FRASER, Lennox, i. 302). No decision, however, seems to have been given on this latter point, or at least no decision against Haldane, and matters rested in statu quo, Avandale continuing to enjoy the life rent, Darnley ceasing to use the title of Earl of Lennox, and the claims of him and other coheirs remaining in abeyance.

On 8 May 1477 Darnley was reappointed keeper of Rothesay (Hist. MSS. Comm. 3rd Rep. p. 390). Having everything to hope from a change of government, he joined the conspiracy against James III in 1482, when Cochrane, the king's favourite, was hanged over the bridge of Lauder. He remained with James during his confinement in Edinburgh Castle, and on 18 Oct. obtained a signature from him, affirming that the king owed his life to the constant watch of Darnley and others over him day and night, and on that account declaring them innocent of the king's detention in Edinburgh Castle, and absolving them of all blame (*ib.* p. 391); but the document must be taken to represent rather the opinions of Darnley than the king. On 17 July 1484 Darnley was appointed keeper of Bute for seven years (*ib.*), and on 20 Oct. 1488—both James III and Lord Avandale having meanwhile passed away — he was appointed, as Earl of Lennox, keeper of the castle of Dumbarton (*Reg. Mag. Sig. Scot.* 1424–1513, No. 1794), and he also sat as Earl of Lennox in parliament. But his succession was not the consequence either of a new creation or of a legal decision in his favour as against Sir John Haldane; it was merely a case of appropriation sanctioned by those who had usurped the government. Nevertheless this did not content him, and, disappointed by being overlooked in the distribution of the more important offices, he suddenly determined to rouse the country against those in authority, and in behalf of the young king, James IV, who, he asserted, was detained in captivity against his will by the murderers of his father. Several of the discontented nobles joined him, and Lord Forbes paraded the country with the king's bloody shirt displayed as a beacon; but the nation as a whole was apathetic, and the rising was soon at an end. After the strongholds of Duchal and Crookston, which were held for Lennox, had been carried by assault, the forces of the king marched to the aid of Argyll, who was besieging Dumbarton, held by Lord Lyle and Matthew Stewart, eldest son of Lennox. Meanwhile Lennox himself, who had gone to the highlands to raise reinforcements, was marching to its relief, when a highland deserter brought word to the king's camp, and advised that he should be surprised by a night attack. The advice was adopted with success, Lennox being taken unawares, and sustaining a complete defeat at Tallymoss, on the south side of the Forth. As his followers either were slain or taken prisoners, or had dispersed to their homes, the defenders of Dumbarton, despairing of succour, soon afterwards surrendered, and Lennox succeeded in making his peace, the act of forfeiture against him being rescinded on 5 Feb. 1489–90 (*Acta Parl. Scot.* ii. 213). Lennox being now in favour with the king, the two rival claimants made a virtue of necessity and came to terms with him. On 18 May 1490 Elizabeth Menteith, wife of John Napier, with consent of her son, resigned for ever all right she had to the superiority of Lennox, on condition of being left in possession of a fourth part of the estate (*Hist. MSS. Comm. 3rd Rep.* p. 390),

and a similar agreement was come to with Sir John Haldane on 3 July 1493 (*ib.*) Lennox died some time before 1 Aug. 1495.

By his wife Margaret, eldest daughter of Alexander Montgomerie Knight, lord of Ardrossan, he had five sons and four daughters: Matthew (see below); Robert, seigneur of Aubigny (see below); William, seigneur d'Oizon (*d.* 1502); Alexander; John of Hermeston, sometimes stated to have been rector of Kirkconner in Galloway, but who succeeded his brother as seigneur d'Oizon, and died without issue in 1512; Elizabeth, married to Archibald, second earl of Argyll; Marion, to Robert Crighton of Kinnoul; Janet to Norman, lord Ross; and Elizabeth, to John Colquhoun of Luss.

The earl's eldest son, MATTHEW STEWART, second or tenth EARL OF LENNOX (*d.* 1513), joined his father in 1488 in the conspiracy against James IV; after the death of his father received from James IV a grant of the sheriffdom of Dumbarton which was united to the earldom of Lennox and made hereditary in the family; and, with the Earl of Argyll, commanded the right wing of the Scots army at Flodden, where he and the greater part of his followers were slain on 9 Sept. 1513. By his wife Elizabeth, daughter of James, first lord Hamilton [q.v.], and niece of James III, he was father of John Stewart, third (or eleventh) earl of Lennox.

The earl's second son, ROBERT STUART or STEWART, SEIGNEUR OF AUBIGNY (1470?–1543), was born about 1470, took service under Bernard Stewart, seigneur of Aubigny [q. v.], and was enrolled in 1498 as lieutenant of the Scots men-at-arms to his brother William: served with great distinction in the Italian wars, 1500–13; was chosen a marshal of France in 1515, and the same year defeated General Prospero Colonna at Villa Franca; fought at Marignano; was appointed one of the judges to act for France at the tournament of the Cloth of Gold in July 1522; was taken prisoner at Pavia, and died without issue in 1543.

[Lennox Muniments in Hist. MSS. Comm. 3rd Rep.; Sir William Fraser's Lennox (privately printed); Napier's Partition of the Lennox, and the same author's Lennox of Auld; Reg. Mag. Sig. Scot. 1424–1513; Exchequer Rolls of Scotland, vols. vii–x.; Histories by Buchanan, Leslie, and Lindsay; Lady Elizabeth Cust's Stuarts of Aubigny (privately printed, 1891); Douglas's Scottish Peerage (Wood), ii. 94–6.]

T. F. H.

STEWART, SIR JOHN, of Balveny, first EARL OF ATHOLL of a new Stewart line (1440?–1512), eldest son of Sir James

Stewart, the black knight of Lorne, by Jane or Johanna [q. v.], queen dowager of James I, was born about 1440. The father, according to Lesley, was in close alliance with the Douglases (*History*, Bannatyne ed., p. 14); and while he and Douglas, shortly after Stewart's marriage to the queen dowager, were plotting the overthrow of Sir Alexander Livingstone [q. v.], the governor, Livingstone suddenly seized Stewart and his brother Sir William. 'The Auchinleck Chronicle' (p. 34) states that he put 'thaim in pittis and bollit them,' whatever that may mean; but anyhow Stewart was subsequently liberated as Lesley affirms, for on 22 Nov. 1445 he and his son John had a safe-conduct for a year in England (*Cal. Documents relating to Scotland*, 1357–1509, No. 1181), and in November 1447 he and his sons had a safe-conduct for four years abroad (*ib.* No. 1203). The son was created Earl of Atholl in or shortly before 1457 (*Rot. Scot.* ii. 383), and on 25 March 1460 the king conceded to him the lands of Balveny, Banffshire (*Reg. Mag. Sig. Scot.* 1424–1513, No. 750), and on 20 March 1473–4 the lands of easter and wester Duncaveloch, Perthshire (*ib.* No. 1159).

About 1462 Donald Balloch, the famous general of John Macdonald, fourth and last lord of the Isles and eleventh earl of Ross [q. v.], made a great raid in Atholl, and, having stormed the castle of Blair, dragged the Earl and Countess of Atholl from the chapel of St. Bridget, where they had taken refuge, and took them prisoners to Isla. After plundering the chapel he endeavoured to set fire to it, but the flames refused to do their work; and on his voyage home a terrible storm of thunder and lightning overtook him, during which several of his galleys loaded with booty foundered and were lost. This so preyed upon his mind that, besides doing penance before the altar of the desecrated chapel, he released the Earl and Countess of Atholl from prison (see especially TYTLER, *History of Scotland*, ed. 1868, ii. 192). On 8 May 1468 Atholl had a safe-conduct for six months to pass into England (*Cal. Documents relating to Scotland*, 1357–1509, No. 1375). In 1475 he was appointed, along with David Lindsay, fifth earl of Crawford [q. v.], to the command of a powerful combined land and naval force for the reduction of the Earl of Ross, who, however, surrendered himself to the king's mercy before he was attacked. In 1480 he assisted in the subjugation of Angus of the Isles, and on 12 March 1481–2 he received a new charter of the earldom of Atholl to him and his heirs male with remainder to the crown. The reason of this regrant is supposed to have been that the dower of Mary of Gueldres had been secured on it, and that its alienation by the crown during her lifetime was a questionable proceeding. Atholl, with Huntly, in 1480 commanded the first division of the army of James III against the prince (afterwards James IV) and the rebel lords; and on that account he was, on the accession of James IV, imprisoned for a time in the fortress of Dunbar. On 2 July 1502 the king confirmed to him his charter of the thanedom of Glentilt (*Reg. Mag. Sig. Scot.* 1424–1513, No. 2655), and on 5 June 1506 granted him and his wife Eleanor Sinclair the lands of Buchquhairn, Banffshire. He died on 19 Sept. 1512, and was buried in Dunkeld Cathedral.

By his first wife, Margaret, dowager countess of Douglas, only daughter of Archibald Douglas, fifth earl of Douglas [q. v.], called the Fair Maid of Galloway, he had two daughters. By his second wife, Eleonora Sinclair, daughter of Sir William, third earl of Orkney and first earl of Caithness [q. v.], he had two sons, of whom John, who succeeded as second earl, was killed at Flodden, 9 Sept. 1513; and nine daughters, of whom Anne was mother of Matthew Stewart, fourth (or twelfth) earl of Lennox [q. v.] By his wife Lady Mary, third daughter of Archibald Campbell, second earl of Argyll [q. v.], the second earl had a son John (third earl) and five daughters.

JOHN STEWART, third EARL OF ATHOLL (d. 1542), entertained James V and the French ambassador at a great hunting match in Atholl in 1529. For this purpose he built a curious palace of wood in the midst of a 'green meadow,' while the table was supplied with 'all sich delicious and sumptuous meats as was to be had in Scotland, for fleschis, fischis, and all kinds of fine wine, and spyces, requisit for ane prince,' at the daily expense, according to Pitscottie, of 'ane thousand poundes' (Scots). The third earl died in 1542, leaving by his first wife, Grizel, daughter of Sir John Rattray, two sons and five daughters, of whom John [q. v.], the eldest son, became fourth earl of Atholl, and by his second wife, Jean, youngest daughter of John, sixth lord Forbes, two daughters.

[Bishop Lesley's Hist. of Scotland, Auchinleck Chronicle; Lindsay of Pitscottie's Chronicle; Calendar of Documents relating to Scotland, 1351–1509; Reg. Mag. Sig. Scot. 1424–1513; Douglas's Scottish Peerage (Wood), ii. 140–1.] T. F. H.

STEWART, JOHN, third or eleventh EARL OF LENNOX (d. 1526), was the son of Matthew, second (or tenth) earl of Lennox, by Elizabeth, daughter of James, lord Hamilton, and a niece of James III [see under STEWART, SIR JOHN, first (or ninth) EARL OF LENNOX]. On 2 Feb. 1511–12 he had a charter of the lands of Tarbolton (*Reg. Mag. Sig. Scot.* 1424–1513, No. 369), and on 23 Sept. 1513 he was served heir to his father (killed at Flodden) in the lands of Dumbarton. After the marriage of the queen regent to Archibald Douglas, sixth earl of Angus [q. v.], he joined the party of James Hamilton, first earl of Arran [q. v.], and in 1515 seized the castle of Dumbarton, and expelled from it Erskine the governor, who had held it for the queen regent (TYTLER, *Hist. of Scotland*, ed. 1868, ii. 300; *Letters and Papers, Henry VIII*, vol. ii. No. 50). After the arrival of John Stewart, duke of Albany [q. v.], he in August 1515 took part in the blockade of Stirling (*ib.* No. 783), and in the other measures adopted to frustrate the designs of Henry VIII. In 1516 he combined with Arran and other earls against the regent Albany, and on this account was confined in the castle of Edinburgh; but having made his peace for a time became a consistent supporter of Albany. He was present at the capture of Tantallon Castle from Angus in 1522 (*ib.* vol. iii. No. 1976), but took no part in the invasion of England in 1523. After the departure of Albany for France in 1524, he joined in the scheme for proclaiming the young king of age, and formed one of the queen regent's escort from Stirling palace to Holyrood, where the king formally assumed the government. But when the queen regent began to show amorous inclinations towards Henry Stewart (afterwards Lord Methven) [q. v.], he left Edinburgh and associated himself with Angus and the English faction. He was one of those deputed in July to communicate with Thomas (II) Howard, third duke of Norfolk [q. v.] (*ib.* vol. iv. No. 529), and it was deemed fitting that his co-operation with Norfolk should be rewarded (Wolsey to Norfolk, 9 Aug. *ib.* No. 571). Although he signed a special band to the queen's grace on 3 Oct. (*ib.* No. 702), he remained faithful to Angus, and seconded him in surprising Edinburgh on the morning of 23 Nov. by scaling the walls and opening the gates for the entrance of four hundred armed followers, backed by whom they proceeded to the lords of the council and desired them to take the government into their own hands (*ib.* No. 854).

A nominal reconciliation now took place between Angus and the queen regent, the charge of the young king being entrusted to a council of peers; but the queen regent continued to act so imprudently that gradually the real authority became centred in Angus,

with Lennox for the time being as his chief lieutenant; and on 18 June Angus, Lennox, and Argyll ratified their alliance by signing a band for maintaining James V, and for mutual support (FRASER, *Lennox*, i. 355). The conspirators were rewarded by a pension from Henry VIII, Angus, Lennox, Arran, and Argyll receiving 250 marks sterling, with more in ready money (*Letters and Papers, Henry VIII*, vol. iv. No. 1446). Lennox was one of the members of the privy council under the new régime, and also one of the witnesses to the ratification of peace with England, 10 Jan. 1525–6 (*ib.* No. 1873).

The young king having on 26 June 1526 made a bond to Lennox by which he engaged 'to use the counsel of the Earl of Lennox especially and in preference to all others' (*Hist. MSS. Comm.* 3rd. Rep. p. 392), Lennox was induced to enter into a plot for his deliverance from the custody of Angus. In the first instance he arranged that Scott of Buccleuch should attack Angus while returning from a border expedition. During the conflict Lennox, who was in the train of Angus, retired with the young king, accompanied by George Douglas and Lord Maxwell, to a neighbouring hill to watch the result of the contest; but Buccleuch was completely defeated. Failing therefore in this secret device, Lennox finally threw off all disguise, and, having leagued himself with the chancellor Beaton and the queen regent, raised a force of ten thousand men to march to Edinburgh for the king's rescue; but he was completely defeated by the combined forces of Arran and Angus, near Linlithgow, 4 Sept. 1526. Having been wounded and taken prisoner by John Hamilton of Bardowie, he was after the battle seized from those guarding him and slain in cold blood by Sir James Hamilton [q. v.] of Finnart, a natural son of Arran. Not long afterwards Sir Andrew Wood, despatched by the king to take measures for the protection of Lennox if he were alive, found Arran weeping beside his body, saying, 'The hardiest, stoutest, and wisest man that ever Scotland saw lies here slain this day.' Arran also cast over the body his own scarlet cloak, and caused his men to stand guard over it until the king's servants came and buried it (LINDSAY OF PITSCOTTIE, *Chronicle*, ed. 1814, ii. 328).

By his wife, Anne, eighth daughter of John Stewart, first earl of Atholl [q. v.], he had issue: Matthew, fourth (or twelfth) earl of Lennox [q. v.], Robert, sixth (or fourteenth) earl of Lennox, and John, lord Aubigny; and a daughter Helen, who married, first, William, sixth earl of Errol, and, secondly, John, tenth earl of Sutherland.

[Reg. Mag. Sig. Scot. 1424–1513 and 1513–1580; Cal. State Papers, Henry VIII, vols. iii. iv.; Lennox Muniments in Hist. MSS. Comm. 3rd Rep.; Sir William Fraser's Lennox (privately printed); Histories by Buchanan, Leslie, and Lindsay; Douglas's Scottish Peerage (Wood), i. 97.]

T. F. H.

STEWART, JOHN, DUKE OF ALBANY (1481–1536), regent of Scotland, was the only son of Alexander Stewart, duke of Albany [q. v.], by his second wife, Anne de la Tour d'Auvergne, third daughter of Bertrand II, comte d'Auvergne et de Boulogne. Early left an orphan by the death of his father in 1485, Albany was brought up by his mother in France, and continued through life to consider France his native country, its king his master, and to sign his name Jehan. He held the office of admiral of France, and was a knight of St. Michel, the tutelary saint of France. He married, on 8 June 1505, his cousin, Anne de la Tour, comtesse de la Tour d'Auvergne, elder child and heiress of his mother's brother, Jehan III, comte d'Auvergne, whose younger sister married, ten years later, Lorenzo de' Medici, duke of Urbino, nephew of Leo X, and was mother of Catherine de' Medici.

The Scots, however, treated him as a Scot, described him as John, duke of Albany, and their parliament not only elected him regent, but declared him next heir to the crown. Before the first parliament or general council met after Flodden at Perth, on 26 Nov. 1513, a request was sent by Cumming, the Lyon king, to Louis XII, that Albany might come and assume the government of Scotland. He was unable or unwilling, but sent Antony d'Arcy de la Bastie as his representative. With De la Bastie came James Ogilvy (afterwards abbot of Dryburgh) as ambassador of Louis XII, and at the meeting of the general council at Perth they expressed the desire of the French king to renew the old alliance with Scotland, and that Scottish ambassadors should visit France with full powers. The French king, they said, was willing, if the Scots desired it, to send Albany to Scotland for its defence. The lords of council declared their consent to the renewal of the alliance, and their wish that Albany should be sent with Robert Stuart, seigneur d'Aubigny, the captain of the bodyguard of Scottish archers, and all other Scotsmen who could get license from the French king, to protect their country against the English [see under STEWART, JOHN, first (or ninth) EARL OF LENNOX]. The influence of Henry VIII, who then supported his sister, Margaret Tudor, in the regency of Scotland, and was carrying on the negotiations which resulted in the marriage of his sister Mary to Louis XII, was sufficient to prevent Albany's departure until after the accession of Francis I, at whose consecration, on 25 Jan. 1515, Albany was present. While still in France he acted as the representative of Scotland, and on 2 April 1514 sold in Paris to the French king for forty thousand crowns of Tours the Great St. Michael, the pride of the Scottish fleet, which had been built by James IV.

It was not till May 1515 that Albany sailed from St. Malo to the west coast, to avoid English cruisers. Landing at Dumbarton on 18 May, he at once went to Glasgow, where, on the 22nd, he wrote as regent of Scotland to Francis I signifying his assent to the treaty between France and England, in which Scotland was to be included. On the 26th he was received with acclamation in Edinburgh, and comedies, says Leslie, were acted to welcome him. Parliament met on 12 July, when Albany was declared tutor and governor both of the kingdom and the king, the queen mother having forfeited her right of guardianship and regency by her marriage to the young Earl of Angus [see DOUGLAS, ARCHIBALD, sixth EARL OF ANGUS]. Early in August she was forced to surrender Stirling and her children to Albany. Though closely watched, she escaped to Tantallon, and thence on 23 Sept. to Harbottle, where she gave birth on 30 Oct. to Lady Margaret Douglas [q. v.], afterwards Countess of Lennox and mother of Darnley. Albany resided at Holyrood. Among the nobles who had urged his coming to Scotland was Lord Hume or Home, the chamberlain [see HOME, ALEXANDER, third LORD HOME]; but an imprudent remark Albany made when he first saw Hume, who was a little man, 'Minuit præsentia famam,' alienated the proud border chief. He and his clan rebelled, and towards the end of August Albany assembled a large army on the Borough Muir, with which he marched to the borders, visited on his way De la Bastie at Dunbar, and seized Hume Castle and the chamberlain before 12 Sept. Hume was put in charge of James Hamilton, first earl of Arran [q. v.]; but that feeble noble liberated Hume, and entered into a band or league with him and Angus against Albany, which was abetted by Lord Dacre of the north, the English warden of the marches. Albany returned north and seized Arran's estates; but at Hamilton Castle, the chief seat of Arran, terms were made. Arran was pardoned and detached from the league. Albany also endeavoured by conciliatory language to induce Margaret, who had fled to England, to return to Scotland, but without success. The sudden death of her infant son, the Duke of Ross, led to suspicion of poison, with which Margaret did not hesitate to charge Albany. In February 1516 he was at Linlithgow, and from 19 April to 20 June at Falkland. Between these dates he appears to have come to the north of England and to have made an offer to visit Henry VIII, which Wolsey declined. Henry addressed a letter to the Scottish estates, asking them to dismiss Albany, but the parliament of Edinburgh, on 1 July 1516, sent an emphatic and spirited refusal. On 24 July 1516 Albany agreed with Wolsey to prolong the truce with England to St. Andrew's day, 1517, and this was ratified in January 1517 by the commissioners of the estates.

Parliament again met at Edinburgh in the end of September 1516 (24th according to Buchanan), but its record has not been preserved. Albany was present, and Hume, the chamberlain, and his brother were condemned to death for treason, and executed on 8 and 9 Oct. Immediately after these executions Albany went to the borders and took possession of their estates. Returning early in November, on the 12th of that month parliament confirmed the divorce of his father from his first wife, Catherine Sinclair, daughter of the Earl of Orkney [see STEWART, ALEXANDER, DUKE OF ALBANY], and declared Albany next heir to the kingdom and only heir of his father, thus bastardising his elder brother Alexander, who, in compensation, was made bishop of Morny and abbot of Scone. At the same time he got the reluctant consent of the estates to his return for six months to France. Before he left a regency, consisting of the two archbishops and the earls of Huntly, Argyll, Angus, and Arran, was appointed. Lord Erskine and the earl marshal were named guardians of the king, De la Bastie warden of the marches, and Lord Fleming of Cumbernauld chamberlain. The fortresses of Dunbar, Inchgarvie, and Dumbarton were placed in the hands of French garrisons. On 6 June 1517 Albany sailed from Dumbarton to France, taking with him as hostages the sons of several leading nobles. During this first period of his regency Albany had been singularly successful. He had removed or conciliated his chief adversaries, baffled Henry VIII, and restored peace on the borders. His expenditure had been lavish, as the exchequer accounts show; but it was repaid by the tranquillity of the realm. So far from being 'a coward and a wilful and furious fool,' as Wolsey called him, he had proved an active commander and a prudent governor. His weakness was that his heart was not in Scotland, and he returned to France with his work only half accomplished.

The attempt to conduct the government in Albany's absence by dividing the power between the chief Scottish nobles and De la Bastie and the French commanders failed. No sooner had the duke left Scotland than the old dissensions broke out among the nobles. On 15 June Queen Margaret returned to Scotland, little more than a week after Albany's departure. Towards the end of July or beginning of August De la Bastie was slain by David Hume of Wedderburn in revenge for Albany having put his chief to death. There was a surcease both of the courts and parliament, and the nobles soon became jealous of the growing influence of Angus.

Albany had full power while absent to represent Scotland in foreign affairs, and did not neglect his commission. He promoted the interests of the Scottish merchants who traded with France, and negotiated the treaty of Rouen on 26 Aug. 1517, by which France and Scotland entered into an offensive and defensive alliance against England; and Francis I promised his eldest daughter in marriage to James V if the marriage to the king of Spain or his brother did not take place; or failing her, his second daughter, if he had another. In the spring of 1518 his sister-in-law, Madeline de la Tour d'Auvergne, was married to Lorenzo, duke of Urbino, the nephew of Leo X, who wrote to Francis I he could deny Albany nothing. Through the influence of France and his affinity with the pope, Albany procured on 5 March 1518 from Leo X a confirmation of all the privileges already granted to the kings and kingdom of Scotland by the Holy See. In 1519 a writer called Gremond or Dremond Dornat translated into French for Albany's use the chronicles of Fordun and Bower, a proof of his desire to become acquainted with the history of Scotland. In June 1519 the Scottish estates wrote to the pope, requesting him to use his influence with Francis I to procure the return of Albany to Scotland, and Lord Fleming of Cumbernauld was sent to France as ambassador of James V to solicit the French king's permission; but Francis had, by a secret article of his treaty with England, promised not to allow Albany to leave France while James V was a minor.

Meantime the quarrel between Margaret Tudor and her husband Angus had reached a crisis, and the rivalry between Arran and Angus led to a contest for the possession of Edinburgh. Angus gained the upper hand in April 1520. Arran fled to France, and probably returned with Albany in the following year. The distracted state of Scotland, which made the Scots more than ever anxious to have Albany back, is reflected in two poems of William Dunbar: one, 'When the Governor passed to France,' prays God to 'help this pure realm in partys all divýdit,' and the other, written in 1520 or early in 1521, speaking in the name of the nobles, entreats him 'to return and not to absent himself for the sake of " worldly gear."'

At last, in November, or perhaps not till 3 Dec. 1521, Albany returned to Scotland. He remained less than a year, till 27 Oct. 1522, but the short period was a time of busy intrigues. Already, in November 1521, it had been bruited that Albany was aiding Margaret at the court of Rome in her suit for divorce from Angus, which was true, with the object of marrying her himself, which was certainly false. The first trace in the voluminous correspondence of Henry VIII of the latter rumour is in a letter by Wolsey to his master from Calais, in which he says he has done what he could with the pope's ambassador to prevent the divorce, 'which shall not proceed when the pope shall be informed that the same is procured only for marriage betwixt the Duke of Albany and the queen, whereby the destruction of the young king shall ensue.' It is probable that Wolsey was himself the originator of the calumny. There is no proof that either Albany or Margaret had designs on the life of her son, James V. As to the divorce, there was a serious obstacle: Albany had a wife still living. There were plausible grounds for a divorce between Margaret and Angus, which was in fact procured in 1527, mainly by the influence and money of Albany. But there is no proof that Albany wished, or could have obtained, a divorce from Anne de la Tour d'Auvergne, whose sister was married to the pope's nephew. Nor, though the rumour was persistently spread, is there any reason to believe there were amatory relations between them. Their temporary reconciliation and mutual support were entirely politic, and on Margaret's part, as soon appeared, insincere. Albany aided her in procuring the payment of part of her dowry, which had been withheld, as well as her divorce. In the balance of parties in Scotland and in his conflict with England it was important for him to have the queen dowager and the sister of the English king as his ally. At a meeting at Kirk of Steele on 14 Dec. 1521 between Angus, Hume, and John, third lord Somerville, they drew up a series of charges against Albany, in which they accused him of having been too intimate with the queen on his return to Scotland. Dacre, who forwarded it to Henry VIII, followed it up by a letter of 20 Dec., in which he

magnified the scandal, alleging that 'aid must be given to the Scotch lords, or the young king will be destroyed, and a Frenchman will be king and marry the king's sister.' There were many meetings between Albany and Margaret in the end of 1521 and beginning of 1522; but they had quite enough legitimate business to transact without the invention of so nefarious a plot. Charles V, to whom its alleged existence had been communicated by Wolsey, shrewdly remarked that 'he did not think any pope would have given the duke the dispensation he would require [for marrying Margaret], especially as he has children by his present wife;' though, if this latter statement was not an error, the children died young, for none survived their mother.

Henry VIII and Wolsey were not, however, to be stayed in prosecuting the charge which was formally made in a letter brought by the Clarencieux herald to the Scottish estates, accusing Albany with 'endangering the life of the young king and working the perdition of his sister' by procuring the divorce of Margaret and marrying her himself. Albany, Margaret, and the estates in separate answers indignantly repudiated the accusation. Albany privately informed Clarencieux that he preferred his French estates to the crown of Scotland, and that one wife was enough for him. The lords in parliament on Monday, 8 Feb. 1522, unanimously assured Clarencieux, who brought Henry's letter, that they had invited Albany and would not dismiss him. The truce between England and Scotland expired on 2 Feb., and both sides prepared for war. Hostilities began by seven vessels which Henry sent early in April to the Forth. They seized Scottish ships and ravaged the villages on the coast. In July a raid was made across the western border and Kelso partially burnt. On 18 July the Scottish parliament in Edinburgh, at which Albany was present, agreed that the king should be sent for safe custody to Stirling, under the custody of Lord Erskine, and a muster for the invasion of England in September was sanctioned.

The queen, though apparently still acting in concert with Albany, had now entered into a secret correspondence with Dacre, in which she not only betrayed Albany's plans, but undertook to do her best to prevent the invasion of England and procure peace. Albany advanced from Edinburgh on 2 Sept. towards Carlisle with one of the largest armies ever collected in Scotland; it was said to number eighty thousand men, but this is probably an exaggeration. An attempt to conclude a truce was made on 6 Sept. Albany rejected the proposal to grant even a delay for twelve days to ascertain Henry's approval of its terms, and marched to Lauder on the 7th, to Annan on the 9th, and on the 11th pitched his tents on the debatable ground near the Chapel of Solan, within four miles of Carlisle. The situation was critical for England. Up to this point Albany had wisely rejected every dilatory proposal. But in a private interview, where only interpreters were present—for Albany could not speak English, nor Dacre French—an abstinence or truce was agreed on between Albany and Dacre for one month, and without waiting for its expiry Albany disbanded his army and returned to Edinburgh before the end of the month. Perhaps it would be more correct to say the army disbanded itself, for, according to Leslie, the Scots absolutely refused to fight out of Scotland. On the 27th he despatched his secretary, Jehan de Barron, to England to request the extension of the truce till midsummer, and that France should be included. This condition was of course impossible. After appointing a new council of regency, the chancellor, Huntly, Argyll, and Arran, with Gonzolles, a French officer (called Grosellis or Grosillis by Scottish writers and records), he sailed, on a galley with oars, from Dumbarton to France on 25 Oct., promising to return before 15 Aug. 1523 on pain of forfeiting the regency. The conduct of Albany at this juncture has been variously judged. France was still his first interest; Scotland was to him only a means to promote the interest of France. He declared in his letters to Francis that he was absolutely at the disposal of Francis, his master. He pointed out the increasing influence of England in the Scottish parliament, now the queen dowager had gone over to it, and the reluctance of the Scots to fight. He concluded by asking the French king to say whether he was to go or stay in Scotland, but hinted that he was tired of the country and its customs. Supplies were not sent. No orders came to stay. The Scots lords refused to fight, and practically no course was open but to retreat, and it is unreasonable to accuse him of personal cowardice or pusillanimity. But his diplomatic skill may be reasonably impugned. To allow his whole army to disperse and leave the borders open to new English raids was to throw up the game. His hasty return to France without receiving positive orders was evidently prompted by personal desire. Possibly another private reason combined with this. His wife was already ill of the disease of which she died in 1524. Even if there was, as seems likely, no great affection between

them, her will had not yet been made, and after her death Albany was engaged in discussions as to her inheritance, which was left to her niece, Catherine de' Medici.

Albany remained in France till the middle of September 1523, taking an active part in the scheme by which Richard de la Pole [q. v.] was to invade England with the aid of Christian, duke of Holstein, afterwards king of Denmark. Meanwhile the queen dowager was corresponding with her brother and Dacre, and endeavouring to bring over the Scottish lords to the English side; while the English, under Surrey, were constantly wasting the Scottish borders. On 25 Sept., the day when Jedburgh was burnt by them, Albany, who had again evaded the English cruisers, landed in the Clyde. He brought with him four thousand French infantry, one hundred knights, and eighty cavalry, as well as artillery, provisions, and gold. The gold was freely used to influence the needy Scottish barons. The queen wished to retreat to England, but Wolsey and Henry declined to receive her, and she now tried to play off Albany and the French against the English, ready to take part with whichever would help her most.

In the beginning of October the Scottish parliament sanctioned a muster at Edinburgh on the 20th, with provisions for twenty days. On 22 Oct. Albany started from Edinburgh by the road to Lauder, and, despatching Robert, fifth lord Maxwell [q. v.], with five thousand men to the west border, advanced himself with the main body of his troops by way of Melrose, which he reached on the 24th. But after a fruitless attack on Wark, which failed partly because the Scots refused to second the assault by the French troops, Albany on 3 Nov. made a precipitate retreat.

The English ministers and generals, and Skelton, the poet-laureate, scoffed at Albany who, 'void of all brain, shamefully retreated back to his great lack when he heard tell that my Lord Amirell [Admiral] was coming down to make him frown.' His prestige in Scotland, which had survived the misfortunes of the former year, was now lost. It did not help his popularity that while he was always running away to France when he was most wanted in Scotland, he left Frenchmen in some of the most important posts, and was for them, as for himself, always exigent about money. He received upwards of 1,200l. for his personal expenses at Wark, made a demand that royal domains should be sold to pay for the bootless campaign, and for forty thousand crowns of the Sun for the cost of his voyage to France (though this was to be repaid at Dieppe). The parliament in

Edinburgh, on 17 Nov., rejected this proposal, and new guardians, one the Frenchman Gonzolles, now captain of Dunbar, were appointed for the king. The king was to remain at Stirling, where his mother's visits were carefully regulated. Leave of absence was readily granted to Albany on condition that if he did not return in four months he should forfeit the regency. Gonzolles was nominated treasurer, but it is doubtful whether he ever exercised the office.

Albany sailed from Dumbarton on 20 May 1524, and never saw Scotland again. On 30 July, before the expiry of the four months, James V, now a boy of twelve, was, in Scottish phrase, erected king at Holyrood, and an instrument signed by the leading nobles and prelates which annulled Albany's regency. The parliament which met on 14 Nov. passed an act declaring that he had broken his promise to return, and thereby forfeited the office of tutor and governor. Albany lived for twelve years after his departure from Scotland. Though he continued a not unimportant factor in continental politics, he never attained the same position as when governor of Scotland. Shortly after his return he accompanied Francis I in the campaign of Italy against Charles V which ended in the disaster of Pavia on 24 Feb. 1525, where Francis was taken prisoner. He had been detached at Milan from the main army, and sent with two hundred lances, six hundred light horse, and eight thousand infantry to make a diversion against the Spaniards in Naples. In the middle of February he was stopped by an illness, and the capture of Francis I put an end to the expedition. Albany retreated to the papal territory, where his presence in Rome led to fights between the faction of the Colonna who favoured the emperor, and the papal faction of the Orsini. Albany and his troops went to the coast, and were soon after recalled by the queen regent, in June 1525. His appointment to this important command shows that in the opinion of Francis I he was not an incompetent general. The French ambassador in England at this time engaged that Albany should not return to Scotland during the minority of James V, but he had no wish to go thither. Through his influence with Clement VII he was instrumental in obtaining, on 11 March 1527, the decree for Margaret's divorce from Angus. He paid the cost of the divorce, which her agent, Duncan, at Rome assured him would amount to not less than six hundred ducats. The English court and Henry VIII himself in 1527 revived the rumour that Margaret desired to marry Albany, but in March 1528 she declared her secret marriage to Henry Stewart, brother of

Lord Avandale, with whom she had already had an illicit amour.

Between 1530 and 1533 Albany, as we learn from the Spanish state papers, several times visited Rome as French ambassador. He was narrowly watched by the envoys of the emperor, who suspected, not without reason, that the chief object of his diplomatic activity was to get a footing again for the French in Italy, and renew the league against the emperor. But the only result achieved was the marriage of his wife's niece Catherine to the Duke of Orleans, which gave the pope a family interest in the French royal succession. When absent from Italy Albany carried on an active correspondence with M. d'Inteville, the French ambassador who succeeded him at Rome; Strozzi, the pope's ambassador in France, and more than one cardinal. This correspondence, which is in the French archives, has not yet been published. It probably related to the expenses of the divorce, and to the marriage of his wife's niece, Catherine de' Medici, with Henry, duke of Orleans, the second son of Francis I, which was celebrated at Marseilles by the pope on 28 Oct. 1534, and the arrangements prior to this marriage as to the inheritance of Auvergne and Boulogne between Albany, the Duke of Orleans, and Catherine de' Medici. Albany was selected by Francis I to conduct Catherine to France, probably on account of his office as high admiral as well as his relationship. When in Italy he obtained a cardinal's hat for his uterine brother, Philip de la Chambre.

Another matter in which Albany took a leading part was the institution of the court of session in Scotland, and the endowment of its judges out of the revenues of the Scottish bishops, which required the sanction of the pope. He had started this project while regent, but the bull of Clement VII was not issued till 15 Sept. 1531, the court was not instituted till 1532, and the bull for its endowment was not procured till 1535. Albany was also largely concerned in the negotiations for the marriage of James V. The marriage of James to a French princess had been agreed to by the treaty of Rouen, which Albany had negotiated in 1517. It was naturally renewed when James became of a marriageable age, and the bride first selected was Madeline, daughter of Francis I. Eventually, however, in 1534 the choice of the Scottish ambassadors, David Beaton and John, lord Erskine, fell on Marie de Bourbon, daughter of the Duc de Vendôme, with whom a contract of marriage was entered into at Crémieux in Dauphiné on 6 March 1536.

Albany was named one of the proxies for James in a procuratory dated 29 Jan. 1535, and being unable to attend the signature of the contract through ill-health, the notaries went to his house and read it to him, where he added his signature on 29 March 1530. It was his last public act, for he died on 2 June of that year. Among the unpublished documents in the French archives there is a significant commission to Jean Doutet to verify the debts of the late Duke of Albany, and a decree against him for a small debt has also been preserved. There is some evidence that James V claimed his succession, but no proof that he recovered any estate. He had always been lavish in expenditure, and not improbably died bankrupt. He left no legitimate issue, and contracted no second marriage, acting on his saying that one wife was enough. An illegitimate daughter by Jean Abernethy, his mistress in Scotland, perhaps married Jean de l'Hospital, comte de Choisy, in 1547.

The character of Albany, notwithstanding the different views taken of it both by contemporaries and by historians, does not seem difficult to understand. He was no general, but he was an able negotiator, succeeding in almost all he undertook—the treaty of Rouen, the divorce of Margaret, the protection of the Scots both in France and at Rome, the institution of the court of session, and the marriage of James to a French princess, though after his death Madeline of France was substituted by James's personal choice for Marie de Bourbon. His services were valued equally by James V and Francis I, with whom he was so great a favourite as to have the entry to the royal bedchamber, a privilege not so common as it afterwards became. The miscarriage of his Scottish regency was due to the inherent difficulties of the situation, but his dislike of a life in Scotland, and strong bias in favour of France contributed to it. The history of his relations with Queen Margaret and her son, when fairly examined, refutes the calumnies of Wolsey and Henry VIII. His straightforward manner contrasts favourably with the duplicity of the English ministers and diplomatists, and with the plotting of the Scottish nobles. He was a Frenchman in Scotland, but retained a good deal of the Scot when abroad, and this explains much of his conduct. It is probable that he was passionate; according to Dacre, when displeased he threw hat after hat into the fire. He was certainly superstitious, carrying a relic in an ornament suspended to his neck, and his habit was to swear by it as his favourite oath. There are many signs that he

was extravagant, but his conduct to Queen Margaret and to his French followers shows that he was generous, though not particular whether the money he expended was his own or drawn from the French or Scottish revenues; it is probable he spent more than he received.

There is a good portrait of his broad face, dark beard, and handsome features in the enigmatical group now in Lord Bute's collection at Cardiff, in which he is represented as receiving a paper from Margaret, to whom he is making a payment, probably of her dowry, in 1522, as recorded in the exchequer rolls, with the figure of a herald pointing to a butterfly floating in the air between them, which perhaps represents this payment. The picture has been attributed to Holbein, but must have been painted before he came to England, and there is no likelihood that the painter ever saw Albany.

[Acts of Parliament of Scotland, ii., Exchequer Rolls, vol. xiv., where an attempt is made by the present writer to explain the Cardiff picture; State Papers of Henry VIII; Cal. State Papers, Spanish, 1531-5; Teulet's Relations Politiques de la France et de l'Espagne avec l'Écosse, 1862, tome i.; Contemporary Histories of Buchanan, Leslie, and Lindsay of Pitscottie; Michel's Les Écossais en France, les Français en Écosse give many minute details as to Albany, and a print of his coat of arms. Of modern historians Pinkerton and Tytler are the best; Burton is meagre. Brewer, in his History of Henry VIII, has much information, but views Albany too much with the eyes of Wolsey.] Æ. M.

STEWART, LORD JOHN (1531–1563), prior of Coldingham, was a natural son of James V of Scotland by Elizabeth, daughter of John, lord Carmichael, and half-brother of Lord James Stewart [q. v.], 'the regent Moray,' and of Lord Robert Stewart, earl of Orkney [q. v.] In a dispensation of Clement VII to James V, dated in 1534, dispensing with 'the defects of birth' of the king's three natural sons, on the king's desire that they should 'be enlisted in the spiritual army,' John Stewart is stated to be in his third year (Hist. MSS. Comm. 6th Rep. p. 670). On 6 Dec. 1546 the queen regent bestowed on him and his convent the lands of Greigston (Reg. Mag. Sig. Scot. 1546-80, No. 41). He received letters of legitimation from Queen Mary at the same time as his brother, Lord James Stewart, 7 Feb. 1551-2 (ib. No. 565). In the answer of Maitland to the English privy council, 10 Dec. 1559, he is mentioned as one of the neutrals (Cal. State Papers, For. 1559-60, No. 392), but Knox includes him among those who before the meeting of parliament in August 1560 had renounced popery (KNOX, *Works*, ii. 88). After the celebration of the queen's first mass in Scotland the priests were committed to the protection of Lord John Stewart and his brother, Lord Robert, who, Knox states, 'were both protestants, and had communicated at the table of the Lord' (*Works*, ii. 271). Shortly afterwards the stronghold of Dunbar was committed to his custody (Randolph to Throgmorton, 26 Aug. 1561; *Cal. State Papers*, For. 1561–2, No. 455). Writing to Cecil, 24 Aug. 1561, Randolph remarks that 'Lord John of Coldingham bath not least favour' at court 'by his leaping and dancing,' and that he was 'like to marry the Earl of Bothwell's sister' (KEITH, *History of Scotland*, ii. 94; *Cal. State Papers*, For. 1561–2, p. 377). The marriage took place in the following January at Seton, 'with good sport and many pastimes' (Randolph to Cecil, 15 Jan. 1561–2, *ib.* No. 802). Indeed it is very evident that Lord John, though he had 'communicated at the table of the Lord,' was a protestant of a very different complexion from his brother, Lord James. Thus in December 1561 he, along with his brother-in-law Bothwell, headed an unseemly riot, which 'highly commoved all godly hearts,' when an attempt was made to get hold of one Alison Craik, who, it was supposed, was the mistress of the Earl of Arran (KNOX, *Works*, ii. 315). On 30 Dec. 1562 Randolph also reports to Cecil that 'this day' the queen had gone 'to Dunbar to be merry with the Lord John' (*Cal. State Papers*, For. 1562, No. 1375). While holding justice courts in the north of Scotland, he died at Inverness, probably in December 1563. Throgmorton stated (letter to Cecil, 9 Dec. 1563, in *Cal. State Papers*, For. 1563, No. 1470) he was to have been made captain of a thousand Scots men of arms, which the cardinal of Guise was raising, had he not died. According to Knox it was affirmed that he 'asked God mercy that he had so far borne with' the queen 'in her impiety, and maintained her in her wickedness against God and his servants.' Knox further expressed the opinion that he had good cause to lament his wickedness, the more especially as he was reputed to have expressed the desirability of sticking Knox in his pulpit, rather than that he should trouble the queen as he was doing' (*Works*, ii. 392). By his wife, Lady Jane Hepburn, daughter of Patrick, third earl of Bothwell, he had two sons: Francis Stewart Hepburn, fifth earl of Bothwell [q. v.]; and Hercules.

[Reg. Mag. Sig. Scot. 1546–80; Hist. MSS. Comm. 6th Rep.; Knox's Works; Cal. State Papers, Foreign, reign of Elizabeth.] T. F. H.

STEWART, JOHN, fourth EARL OF ATHOLL (d. 1578), eldest son of John, third earl of Atholl [see under STEWART, JOHN, first EARL] by Grizel, daughter of Sir John Rattray of that ilk, succeeded his father in 1542. He was one of those nobles who in 1554 supported the queen dowager in her claims to the regency (KEITH, *History*, i. 140). In the following year he was sent to the north of Scotland to chastise a Highland chief, called by Bishop Lesley John Mudyard, and succeeded in capturing him (LESLEY, *History*, Scottish Text Society, ii. 360; CALDERWOOD, *History*, i. 318). He supported the queen regent in her contest with the lords of the congregation in 1559, and although referred to on 8 June as an enemy of Huntly, and as expected to join the lords (*Cal. State Papers*, For. 1560–1, No. 172), he was one of the three lords of the temporal estate who at the parliament of 17 July voted against the confession of faith and affirmed that they would believe as their forefathers believed (CALDERWOOD, ii. 37). Nevertheless, on 8 Sept. Randolph reported to Cecil that Atholl had met with Argyll and Lord James at a tryst to bridle Huntly (*Cal. State Papers*, For. 1560–1, No. 501), and on 23 Sept. that he had joined with them in a perpetual league against Huntly (*ib.* No. 559). His support of the protestant party was further shown in his adherence to the movement in favour of Queen Elizabeth's marriage to Arran (KEITH, ii. 8); but, according to Knox, while Lord James Stewart was in France, on a mission to Mary Queen of Scots, Atholl joined with Huntly and others in a scheme for the capture of Edinburgh in the interests of the papists, which was unsuccessful (*Works*, ii. 156).

After the return of Queen Mary to Scotland in 1561, Atholl was appointed one of her new privy council of twelve (*Reg. P. C. Scotl.* i. 157), and for a time worked in perfect harmony with Lord James Stewart (afterwards the regent Moray), whom he accompanied in 1562 in the expedition to the north against Huntly (*Cal. State Papers*, For. 1562, Nos. 718 and 919). But he was always on more intimate terms with Maitland of Lethington than with Moray. According to Knox, Maitland even 'set forward' Atholl as Moray's rival in the court, and thus it was that Moray began to 'be defaced' (*Works*, ii. 391). The true explanation is, however, that Atholl was a favourite at court not because of Maitland, but because he was a catholic, and that Moray was 'defaced' because he was a protestant, while Maitland, who was probably neither catholic nor protestant, wished to avoid being defaced along with Moray. The 'setting forward' of Atholl properly dates from the arrival of Lennox in Scotland. Lennox spent much of his time in Atholl, and, there can scarcely be a doubt, was fully apprised of all the ulterior purposes dependent on the proposed marriage of the queen to Darnley. Huntly having been forfeited, Atholl was now the leader of the Scottish catholic nobles, and the 'singular trust' (Randolph to Cecil, 24 Oct. 1564, in *Cal. State Papers, For.* 1564–5, No. 757) which Lennox placed in him was fully justified. As soon as the queen had decided on marrying Darnley, Atholl and Maitland superseded Moray and Maitland respectively as the queen's chief counsellors, and towards the close of April 1565 the queen virtually placed herself under the protection of Lennox, Atholl, and Ruthven.

Before the queen's marriage to Darnley Argyll was rumoured to have purposed the invasion of Atholl with a powerful force; but a proclamation from the queen was apparently effectual in preventing hostilities (KNOX, ii. 491–2). Atholl was present with the queen in her journey from the parliament of Perth to Callander, and assisted to protect her and Darnley against the plot of Moray for their capture. On the outbreak of Moray's rebellion after the marriage, he was on 23 Aug. named lieutenant in the north (*Reg. P. C. Scotl.* i. 357), and on 10 Oct. he was appointed to lead the rearguard in the force raised for the suppression of Moray (*ib.* p. 379).

Knox states that after the marriage Atholl went openly to the mass in the queen's chapel (*Works*, ii. 514). When the queen, with Riccio, began to prepare for a catholic revolution, she bestowed on Atholl the stronghold of Tantallon, which was taken from Morton (LORD HERRIES, *Memoirs*, p. 73). Atholl had no connection with the plot against Riccio, and possibly Lennox and Darnley did not even make known to him their special grievances against the queen. On the evening of the assassination he was at supper in an apartment of the palace with Huntly, Bothwell, and other lords in attendance on the queen. Attempting to make their escape by a back way, they were intercepted and forced to return (*ib.* p. 77); but they afterwards got out by a window (MELVILLE, *Memoirs*, p. 147), and they left Edinburgh before the queen's escape to Dunbar (KNOX, ii. 523). It was with Atholl that Maitland took refuge after Riccio's assassination, and therefore Atholl, like the majority of even the catholic nobles, was probably by no means grieved that Riccio had been 'taken away.' Through Atholl's interposition Maitland was again

permitted to come to court (Randolph to Cecil, 2 April 1566, *Cal. State Papers, For.* 1566–8, No. 242, and Randolph to Cecil, 20 Aug. *ib.* No. 677); but Atholl was undoubtedly kept in the dark as to the plot against Darnley, with whom and with Lennox he would seem to have remained on friendly terms; and, in common with other catholic nobles, he probably witnessed with dismay the increasing predominance of Bothwell. So much, indeed, was he shocked by the assassination of Darnley, and by the queen's association with the principal assassin, that he did not scruple to join the protestant lords in taking up arms against her. He was reputed to have held, not long after the murder, a private conference with Moray and Morton at Dunkeld for concerting measures for avenging it (Darnley to Cecil, February 1566–7, *Cal. State Papers, For.* 1566–8, No. 977); and on 8 May he also entered with other lords into the bond at Stirling for this purpose (*ib.* No. 1161; KNOX, ii. 156; LORD HERRIES, *Memoirs*, p. 93). An attempt to capture Bothwell and the queen at Borthwick Castle failed, mainly because Atholl did not arrive in time to enable the lords to surround it; but shortly afterwards he joined them along with Lethington, and he was one of the leaders against the queen when she surrendered at Carberry Hill. In Morton's declaration regarding the discovery of the casket containing the alleged letters of Mary to Bothwell, he is mentioned as one of those present when the casket was opened and the letters were first read. He approved of her removal to Lochleven Castle, received her demission of the government (*Reg. P. C. Scotl.* i. 533), was present at the young king's coronation at Stirling (*ib.* p. 537), and consented to act as one of the council of regency until the return of Moray from France (*ib.* p. 540). Gradually, however, his sympathies veered again towards the queen, especially after her escape from Lochleven. At first he did not openly support her; but he was in secret communication with Maitland, and privy to the designs for her restoration. With a view to this he in 1569 voted in support of her divorce from Bothwell (*ib.* ii. 8).

After the assassination of the regent Moray, Atholl, 'inspired,' according to Calderwood, 'by the secretary,' advised that the council should delay taking active measures against those concerned in it 'until there were a fuller assembly of the nobility' (*History*, ii. 527). Shortly afterwards he, with Huntly, Lethington, and others, openly joined the Hamiltons in a league against the king's party. On 4 March the heads of both parties held a convention in Edinburgh to consult on their common affairs, but were unable to arrive at an agreement as to the arrangements for the government (*ib.* pp. 544-5); and about the end of March 1570 Atholl and others sent a letter to Elizabeth asking her to enter 'in conditions with the queen of Scotland, whereat the different claims betwixt her highness and her son may cease from henceforth' (*ib.* p. 549). On 13 April they came to Edinburgh, but were unable to persuade the magistrates to deliver up the keys of the town and ports (*ib.* p. 554). Atholl then attempted to induce the lords of the opposite party to attend a convention at Edinburgh, but they declined to come to Edinburgh before 1 May, the day fixed for the meeting of parliament (*ib.* p. 557); and on 20 April he and others left Edinburgh for Linlithgow, where they held an opposition convention to that held by the king's lords at Edinburgh (*ib.* p. 560). The election of Lennox as regent in the protestant interest was entirely displeasing to Atholl, his former confidant; and at a great council of the nobility held at Atholl in August it was definitely resolved to combine in support of the cause of the queen (*ib.* iii. 11).

Atholl sought to prevent the election of Morton to the regency on 24 Nov. 1572 by sending, along with Lord Gray, 'a bill to desire the election to be stayed for the present' (*ib.* p. 243), but seems to have refrained from active opposition either to Morton's predecessors or to himself. In 1574 proceedings were taken against him as a papist; and for not executing the sentence of excommunication against him and his lady James Paton [q. v.], bishop of Dunkeld, was, at an assembly of the kirk held at Edinburgh on 6 March, ordained to confess his fault in his own cathedral kirk, and to undertake to execute the sentence within forty days thereafter (*ib.* p. 331). Notwithstanding this and other injunctions, Paton still refrained from taking action, and, being finally asked to explain his remissness to the assembly, stated that the earl desired a conference with the ministers for the resolution of his doubts. This was granted, and it was reported that as yet he was 'not fully resolved upon sundry heads of religion;' whereupon the assembly gave him until midsummer to be resolved (*ib.* p. 341), with apparently satisfactory results.

In the spring of 1577-8 Atholl joined with Argyll in a coalition for ousting Morton from the regency. The scheme succeeded, a council of regency being appointed, of which Atholl was one, and Atholl was also, on 28 March, appointed chancellor (*Reg. P. C. Scotl.* ii. 679). When Morton shortly afterwards obtained entrance into Stirling Castle, and resumed his custody of the young king, Argyll and Atholl took up arms against him, and marched towards Stirling with seven thousand men. But before the two parties came to blows they were pacified through the intervention of Bowes, the English ambassador, Atholl and Argyll being added to the new council, which was to assist Morton in the government. After attending a banquet given by Morton at Stirling to celebrate the reconciliation, Atholl, on his way home, was seized with a sudden illness, of which he died on 24 or 25 April 1579 at Kincardine Castle, a stronghold of Montrose near Auchterarder. At once the rumour spread that he had been poisoned; and, according to Calderwood, after a post-mortem examination, all the doctors affirmed so except Dr. Preston, who having, in token of his confidence in his own opinion, rashly touched with his tongue a portion of the contents of the stomach, 'almost had died, and was after, so long as he lived, sickly' (*History*, iii. 443). At a convention of the friends of Atholl held at Dunkeld on 3 May it was resolved to bring the matter before the king (TYTLER, *History*, ed. 1808, vol. iv. app. No. iv.); but nothing was done. The suspicion, of course, was that Morton was the instigator of the supposed crime; but even the evidence of poisoning is vague, and probably it was with perfect sincerity that Morton, in his 'confession,' expressed his detestation of such a method of revenge. Atholl was buried on 4 July in the cathedral church of St. Giles, Edinburgh.

By his first wife, Elizabeth Gordon, daughter of George, fourth earl of Huntly, he had two daughters: Elizabeth—whose third husband was James Stewart, earl of Arran [q. v.] —and Margaret, married to George, seventh lord Abernethy of Saltoun. By his second wife, Margaret, widow of Thomas Erskine, and daughter of Malcolm Fleming, third lord Fleming, he had a son, John, fifth earl of Atholl, on whose death in 1595 the earldom reverted to the crown. By his second wife Atholl also had three daughters—Grizel, married to David, tenth earl of Crawford; Jean, to Duncan Campbell of Glenurchy; and Anne, to Francis, ninth earl of Errol. The second wife of Atholl was reputed to possess magical powers; and, when Queen Mary was confined with the child afterwards James VI, she was said to have cast the pains of childbirth on Lady Rires.

[Knox's Works; Histories by Buchanan, Calderwood, Keith, and Leslie; Diurnal of Occurrents, Melville's Memoirs, Moysie's Memoirs, and Hist. of James the Sext (Bannatyne Club); Herries's Memoirs (Abbotsford Club); Register of the Privy Council of Scotland, vols. i-iii.; Reg. Mag. Sig. Scot. 1546-80; Cal. State Papers, Foreign, Elizabeth; Douglas's Scottish Peerage (Wood), ii. 141-2.]   T. F. H.

STEWART, Sir JOHN, first EARL OF TRAQUAIR (d. 1659), lord high treasurer of Scotland, was the son of John Stewart the younger of Traquair, by Margaret, daughter of Andrew, master of Ochiltree: he was thus fifth in descent from James Stewart, a natural son of James Stewart, earl of Buchan, who was the second son of Sir James Stewart, the Black Knight of Lorne [see under STEWART, SIR JOHN, of Balveny, first EARL OF ATHOLL], by Jane or Johanna Beaufort, queen dowager of James I. On 20 Feb. 1489 this James Stewart obtained from his father an act of legitimation under the great seal, and also a charter of the lands of Traquair, Peeblesshire. His son, William Stewart of Traquair, had four sons, of whom the elder, Robert, died in 1548; the second, Sir John, was knighted by Queen Mary on 20 July 1565, was chosen a captain of her guards, and also fought for her after her escape from Lochleven in 1568; and the third, Sir William, was gentleman of the bedchamber to James VI, and governor of Dumbarton Castle. These three sons were successively lairds of Traquair, and, all dying without issue, the estate fell in 1605 to the youngest, James, who died in the following year, and, being predeceased by his eldest son, was succeeded by his grandson, afterwards first Earl of Traquair.

John Stewart received his early education under Thomas Sydserf [q. v.], bishop of Galloway, and afterwards spent some time abroad. In 1621 he was elected commissioner for Tweeddale in the Scottish parliament; he was also sworn a member of the privy council, and was knighted. On 19 April 1628 he was raised to the peerage by the title of Lord Stewart of Traquair, to him and his heirs male. In 1630 he was appointed treasurer depute, and on 18 Nov. of the same year an extraordinary lord of session. During the visit of Charles I to Scotland, in 1633, he was on 23 June created Earl of Traquair, Lord Linton and Caberston, to him and his heirs male whatever, bearing the title and arms of Stewart.

In 1634 Traquair was chancellor of the jury at the trial of Lord Balmerino [see ELPHINSTONE, JOHN, second LORD BALMERINO] and, it is said, lest he should offend the bishops and the court (BALFOUR, Annals, ii. 210), gave the casting vote against him: but finding that the sentence was extremely unpopular, he went up to London, and, after fully explaining the case to the king, obtained his pardon. The attitude of Traquair on the Balmerino case is a sample of his attitude throughout the covenanting struggle; he always succumbed to the policy of the king when necessity compelled him to do so, but at the same time did his utmost both to temper that policy and to reconcile the nation to obedience to it when there was no other option than open resistance. Having gone to London in 1636, he returned in June as lord high treasurer, in succession to the Earl of Morton (SPALDING, Memorialls, i. 71). Probably, before receiving office, he gave the king to understand that he would do his best to aid him in introducing the liturgy into Scotland. Indeed, according to Bishop Guthry, Traquair, being a secret enemy of the bishops, encouraged the king to proceed with the imposition of the liturgy in order to accomplish their ruin (Memoirs, pp. 17, 20). Spalding, who also describes him as 'a great enemy of the bishops,' states that in July 1637, before the liturgy was introduced, he and other nobles, with 'various miscontented puritans, held a meeting, at which they began to regret their dangerous estate with the pride and avarice of the prelates' (Memorialls, i. 78-9). Spalding does not hesitate even to suggest that Traquair, although taking an active part in the arrangements for the introduction of the liturgy into Scotland, secretly encouraged the tumult of the serving-women against the service in St. Giles (ib.); but of this there is, of course, no proof. The probability is that Traquair personally cared little either for presbyterianism or episcopacy, and would have been satisfied with any kind of peaceful settlement of the question. He therefore did his utmost to assuage the anger of the king against the offenders, representing that 'the flame kindled was of little danger for its consequence' (GORDON, Scots Affairs, i. 14); and he further endeavoured to impress him with the necessity of acting with caution by signing, with others, the letter of 25 Aug., representing that the opposition to the liturgy was so vehement and general that they could not take further steps for enforcing its introduction until they received fresh instructions (BALFOUR, Annals, ii. 229-31). In October following he had an unpleasant reminder of the excitable temper of the people; for in a tumult against the bishop of Galloway he was himself thrown down, and had his hat, cloak, and white wand of office pulled from him (GORDON, *Scots Affairs*, i. 23–4). Traquair represented to the king that it would be vain to demand observance of the liturgy unless he was prepared to enforce compliance with forty thousand men. But he by no means desired the latter alternative. In a private conference with John Leslie, sixth earl of Rothes [q. v.], he stated that he was himself opposed to the liturgy, but advised that some kind of acknowledgment should be made by the city of Edinburgh of the lawlessness of the citizens' procedure, in order that the 'king might be righted in the eyes of the world for the contempt which appeared to proceed from this people to his authority' (*Relation*, p. 52). In answer to a letter of the council to the king, Traquair was asked to proceed to court. While there he was, according to Guthry, accused of treachery to the bishops; but the king, says Guthry, 'would not be induced to take any hard course against him, to the grief of all that were loyal, and the encouragement of rogues and traitors' (*Memoirs*, p. 55). In what way Traquair represented matters to the king is of course unknown; but if he advised him, meanwhile, to let the matter drop, he was unsuccessful, for in February 1638 he was sent down—according to his own account 'with great unwillingness' (Traquair to Hamilton, 15 March, in *Hardwicke State Papers*, ii. 101)—with a proclamation commanding obedience to the service, and forbidding all meetings convened in opposition to it under pain of treason. The proclamation was, however, met at all the principal towns with a protestation against it (GORDON, i. 33–6), and a movement at once commenced for a renewal of the national covenant.

To be prepared against eventualities, the king resolved to place the castle of Edinburgh in a state of defence; but the covenanters forbade the landing of a cargo of arms and ammunition sent by sea for this purpose. Thereupon Traquair secretly provided a boat at night, and conveyed the arms and ammunition to Dalkeith Palace (GORDON, i. 66). He found it, however, impossible to transfer them to Edinburgh Castle. After the capture of the castle by the covenanters, on 19 March 1639, a force of one thousand musketeers was sent by them under the command of the Earl of Rothes and other noblemen to Dalkeith. They compelled Traquair to deliver up the palace, and brought the arms and ammunition, as well as the royal ensigns, to Edinburgh Castle (*ib.* ii. 208; BALFOUR, ii. 322). After this surrender Traquair joined the king at York, but was regarded

for some time with suspicion and ordered to keep his chamber. After the treaty of Berwick, in June he was appointed, in place of Hamilton, the king's commissioner to the assembly which met at Edinburgh on 12 Aug., when an act was passed abolishing episcopacy. Not only did Traquair give his verbal assent to this act: he promised both to give a written declaration of his approval of it and to ratify it in the ensuing parliament, to which he was also the king's commissioner (GORDON, iii. 48; BALFOUR, ii. 353). He did sign the declaration of assent (GORDON, *ib.*), and he also, as a subject, consented to subscribe the covenant, with an explanation of his reasons for doing so (*ib.* iii. 54); but, instead of arranging for the ratification of the act by parliament, he adjourned the opening of parliament from 14 Nov. 1639 to 2 July 1640. On his return to London he is said, in order to excuse his own conduct, to have given in a report strongly representing the obstinacy of the covenanters; and if he did not, as Gordon suggests, seek to 'play with both parties,' the result probably was, as Gordon affirms, that he 'was trusted of neither' (*ib.* iii. 83). In any case, his inconsistency was so strongly resented by the covenanters that the Scots commissioners for the treaty of Ripon had private instructions to object to him should he be one of those appointed to treat with them (BALFOUR, ii. 410). In 1641 also an act was passed by the Scottish parliament against him as one of the chief incendiaries, and a warrant was directed to the Scots commissioners in London to have him sent home for trial (*ib.* iii. 3). He failed to appear, but in his absence he was sentenced to execution; and although at the instance of the king the sentence was revoked, he was deprived of the office of treasurer, and the king also undertook that he should not be employed in any office of court or state without the consent of parliament (*Acta Parl. Scot.* v. 495). In 1644, for having repaired to the court, and for having indicated his opposition to the covenant, he was declared an enemy to religion, and his goods were ordered to be confiscated. To avert further evil consequences, he therefore offered to the parliament a sum of forty thousand merks, whereupon he was formally fined in that sum, and ordained to confine himself within the sheriffdoms of Roxburgh, Tweeddale, and Peebles—all the former acts made against him in the parliament of 1641 to stand 'in force and vigour' (BALFOUR, iii. 286). In 1645 he sent his son, Lord Linton, with a troop of horse to join Montrose, and, according to Bishop Guthry, undertook to inform Montrose of General Leslie's movements (*Memoirs*, p. 201); but as Lord Linton secretly withdrew with his troop on the night before the battle of Philiphaugh, it has been supposed that Traquair was in communication with Leslie, and gave him private information as to Montrose's position (*ib.* p. 202; WISHART, *Memoirs of Montrose*, ed. Murdoch and Simpson, 1893, p. 143). In November 1646 Charles addressed a letter to William Hamilton, earl of Lanark (afterwards second Duke of Hamilton) [q. v.], Scottish secretary of state, particularly recommending that Traquair should be admitted to his place in parliament; and this was accordingly done. In 1648 he raised a troop of horse for the engagement, and with his son, Lord Linton, was taken prisoner at Preston. He was confined in Warwick Castle, but at different periods was allowed to go to Berwick and Scotland for several months on parole (*Cal. State Papers*, Dom. 1651–4, passim). While a prisoner in England he was, in May 1650, discharged to enter the kingdom (NICOLL, *Diary*, p. 14; BALFOUR, *Annals*, iv. 42). He was set at liberty by Cromwell in 1654, and returned to Scotland. In August 1655 he was panelled and accused before the criminal court for perjury at the instance of his son-in-law (NICOLL, p. 156), but the result is not stated. If, however, the story of the kidnapping at his instance of Lord Durie by Willie Armstrong (1602?–1658?) [q. v.] be true, it would at least appear that he had no very scrupulous regard for legal tribunals. He died on 27 March 1659, 'sitting in his chair in his own house, without any sickness preceding' (*ib.* p. 228). By his wife, Lady Catherine, third daughter of Sir David Carnegie, first earl of Southesk [q. v.], he had, with four daughters (of whom Margaret married James Douglas, second earl of Queensberry [q. v.]), a son John, lord Linton (1622–1666), who succeeded as second earl of Traquair.

[Gordon's Scots Affairs and Spalding's Memorials (Spalding Club); Rothes's Short Relation, Baillie's Letters and Journals, and Nicoll's Diary (Bannatyne Club); Wishart's Memoirs of Montrose; Bishop Guthry's Memoirs; Balfour's Annals; Hardwicke State Papers; Cal. State Papers, Dom. Charles I.] T. F. H.

STEWART, JOHN, called JOHN ROY (Gaelic *ruadh* = red) (1700–1752), Jacobite, was son of Donald Stewart by his second wife, Barbara Shaw. He belonged to the Stewarts of Kincardine, Inverness-shire, the first of whom, Walter, third son of Alexander Stewart, earl of Buchan [q. v.], was knighted for his valour at Harlaw (24 July 1411), and obtained the barony by charter from Robert III in 1400. The property continued in the family till 1683, when it was sold to the Duke of Gordon.

'John Roy' was born at Knock, Kincardine, in 1700, when his mother was fifty-two years of age. He served for some time as lieutenant and quartermaster in the Scots greys, but, being refused a commission in the Black Watch, he resigned. Subsequently he was employed as a Jacobite agent, and, on being arrested, he broke out of Inverness gaol by the connivance of Simon Fraser, lord Lovat [q. v.], 1736 (*State Trials*, vol. xviii.) Retiring to France, then a sort of Cave of Adullam for discontented Scots, he was next sent on a mission to Rome. He fought in the French army at Fontenoy (30 April 1745). At the opening of the Jacobite rebellion in the summer of 1745 he joined Prince Charles at Blair in Atholl, and was placed in command of the 'Edinburgh regiment.' His regiment was actively employed in all the engagements from Prestonpans (21 Sept. 1745) to Culloden. Scott calls him 'a most excellent partisan officer,' and Chambers says he was 'the beau ideal of a clever highland soldier.' His courage and devotion, his gift of song, and the knowledge and culture which he had acquired by service at home and in France, made him a great favourite with the Prince, who called him 'the Body' ('Lyon in Mourning'). The highland chiefs had such confidence in his skill and resource that it was at one time proposed to make him commander in place of Lord George Murray (1700?–1760) [q. v.]. After Culloden a price was set on his head, but, though he had many hairbreadth escapes, he was never betrayed. He described his immunity in a poem which he called 'John Roy's Psalm.' After biding for some weeks on Speyside, he joined the prince in Lochaber and accompanied him to France, where he died in 1752.

John Roy was noted as a poet as well as a soldier. His Gaelic songs and laments are marked by strength and ardour, with fine touches of humour and pathos. They are still popular in the highlands.

[Duncan Stewart's History of the Stewarts, 1739; Old Statistical Account; Chambers's History of the Rebellion; The Beauties of Gaelic Poetry.] W. F.

STEWART, JOHN (1749–1822), 'Walking Stewart,' born in Bond Street, London, in 1749, was the only child of Scottish parents, his father being a linendraper. He was born, to use his own phrase, 'of the most animated and passionate parents' (*Opus*

Maximum, 1803), from whom he often in childhood wandered away. At the age of six he was sent to a school in the country, but freed himself from it by inventing a falsehood to discredit the establishment. He went, at the age of ten, to Harrow school, where he broke all rules and refused all lessons. Two or three years later he was placed at Charterhouse school, and again made himself conspicuous by refusing all tasks except the composition of English themes.

Through the interest of Lord Bute he obtained in 1763 the post of writer under the East India Company at Madras. He very soon discovered that enormous abuses flourished in its administration, and wrote to the court of directors pointing them out. As they were unchecked, he sent the court, two years after his arrival in India, a letter, which was entered on its minutes as a curious specimen of 'juvenile insolence and audacity,' resigning his place from his love of travel and through the possession of a soul above copying 'invoices and bills of lading to a company of grocers, haberdashers, and cheesemongers.' He then obtained employment as interpreter to Hyder Ali, but soon abandoned it for more active life, becoming finally a general in Hyder's army. In this service he received several wounds from sword and bullet (the crown of his head being indented to the depth of nearly an inch), and applied for leave of absence in order that he might consult a surgeon on a European settlement. It was granted, but the escort, so runs one narrative, was instructed by Hyder Ali to murder him. Stewart, however, escaped by swimming a river and outrunning his guards (*Life*, 1822). It should be added that this remarkable story does not agree with the simpler statement of Colonel Mark Wilks in his 'Sketches of the South of India' (*Quarterly Review*, October 1817, p. 51).

Stewart next entered the service of the nabob of Arcot, and ultimately rose to the position of prime minister. In this position he expended large sums of money in official entertainments, which were not repaid for many years. His savings as interpreter amounted to 3,000*l.*, and with that sum he quitted the nabob's court and travelled 'into the interior parts of India,' emerging on the Persian Gulf.

After a hazardous passage across the gulf, Stewart visited Persepolis and other parts of Persia, and completely mastered the language. He also travelled through Ethiopia and Abyssinia, remarking the most curious customs of their inhabitants. Although, as he said, he was afflicted by 'a muscular

debility contracted by the pernicious use of tobacco in smoking,' by means of a strict temperance and a peculiar hygienic method of his own he acquired perfect health. He seems effectually to have adopted the Persian proverb, 'Human energy increases in the ratio of travels.' He was often urged in after years to describe what he had seen, but persistently refused on the ground that the object of his walking expeditions was the study of man.

About 1783 a longing for Europe seized upon Stewart. He 'crossed the desert of Arabia and arrived at Marseilles,' after which he walked through France and Spain, and ultimately arrived in England. In 1784 he purchased with his savings of 3,000*l.* an annuity of 300*l.* a year on the French funds, and set off on his travels once again. Michael Kelly [q. v.] met him at Vienna in that year, and described him as, 'though a great oddity, a well-informed, accomplished man, a true lover of the arts and sciences and of a most retentive memory.' He had walked thither from Calais, and in a few days was going on to Constantinople (*Reminiscences*, i. 251-2). At that date he lived entirely upon vegetables.

On his return to London Stewart frequented 'the most noted promenades and resorts of the people,' and wore the Armenian habit until it was threadbare; a coloured print of him in this attire was long conspicuous in the shop-windows. The story of his wanderings and adventures was generally received with incredulity.

At the close of July 1791 Stewart arrived at Albany, New York, and the same evening he set off for Canada (*Notes and Queries*, 2nd ser. viii. 247). He returned to Ireland and then crossed to Scotland, and while crossing was in danger of shipwreck, whereupon he begged the crew, if they escaped, to take care of the book 'Opus Maximum,' which he had written. Wordsworth met him at Paris about 1792, and was captivated by his eloquence. The disturbances in that city caused him to beat a speedy retreat to England with the loss of the greater portion of his property. An application to the English government for an appointment as 'oriental interpreter'—he is said to have known eight languages—was unsuccessful, and he settled down to poverty with resignation. For a time he was helped by 'a humane and respectable tradesman in the borough of Southwark, who had married his sister' (TAYLOR, *Records of my Life*, i. 284 &c.), and he then revisited America, where he eked out his existence by lecturing. He returned to find that his sister was dead, but his brother-in-law again gave him assistance; his advances were afterwards repaid.

De Quincey made the acquaintance of Stewart at Bath in 1798-9, when he frequented the Pump Room and all public places, walking up and down persistently and distributing to the right and left papers containing his philosophical opinions. Details of his appearance about 1802 and of his opinions are set out in Mrs. Bray's 'Devonshire bordering on the Tamar and the Tavy' (1836, iii. 210-14, 304). In March 1803 he announced his intention of giving a course of twelve lectures on 'the human mind and the study of man' for two guineas at 40 Brewer Street, Golden Square. Somewhere about this time he obtained from the French government a settlement restoring to him a part of his property. De Quincey came up to London about 1808 and sought for Stewart at a coffee-house in Piccadilly, where he read his papers every day. He was still in comparative poverty, and lodged in Sherrard Street, Golden Square. A few years later, probably about 1813, the East India Company paid 10,000l. in satisfaction of his claims against the nabob of Arcot. He purchased an annuity and went to lodge in more luxurious rooms in Cockspur Street, for he loved to be 'in the full tide of human existence.'

In these 'Epicurean apartments,' brilliantly decorated with mirrors and Chinese pictures, Stewart gave dinners every Sunday to a few select friends, such as Colton, Robert Owen, Thomas 'Clio' Rickman, and John Taylor, and before the wine was removed lectured on his own doctrines. These discourses were not appreciated, and evening parties of both sexes, with music and whist, were substituted for them. He was, says De Quincey, 'a man of great genius, and, with reference to his conversation, of great eloquence.' His language was remarkable for the aptness and variety of his illustrations; he possessed much humour, and he showed great skill in imitating 'the tone and manner of foreigners.' So frequently was he to be seen in the thoroughfares of London that more than one observer has pronounced him ubiquitous. On fine mornings he would seat himself on Westminster Bridge to contemplate the passers-by. At other times he reposed in 'trance-like reverie among the cows of St. James's Park, inhaling their balmy breath and pursuing his philosophical speculations' (DE QUINCEY).

Stewart was much troubled by the riots in connection with Queen Caroline, and meditated a flight to America. In 1821 his health declined, and a visit to Margate proved

of small avail. In January 1822 he became worse, and on the morning of 20 Feb. 1822 he was found dead in his rooms in Northumberland Street, London. He always carried with him a sufficient quantity of poison to put an end to his existence if he tired of it, and a bottle which had contained laudanum was found in the room; but he probably did not commit suicide. He is said to have left 1,000l. to the university of Edinburgh, and the rest of his property to James Maitland Dods of Lincoln's Inn. He stood fully six feet in height; was handsome, with Roman features, and of great strength. A portrait of him by T. T. C. Kendrick was engraved by E. Wheatley.

Learned himself, Stewart boasted of being a 'man of nature,' and argued against over-learning and excessive training of the memory. He contended, amid much that was beyond comprehension, for such wholesome practices as temperance, cleanliness, and exercise in fresh air. In the middle of his disquisitions in the 'Roll of a Tennis Ball through the Moral World' he inserts a page on the dangers of damp beds and sheets, and to the 'moral or intellectual last will and testament' he appends a codicil lauding 'earth-bathing, or a warm mud-bath.' He was a good-hearted man, and all his doctrines aimed at inducing men to promote the happiness of their fellows.

Henry George Bohn, who used in company with Thomas Taylor, the Platonist, to attend the soirées of Stewart, inserted in his edition of Lowndes's 'Bibliographer's Manual' (ii. 2515-17) a good list of Stewart's writings, many of which were anonymous and were printed for private distribution. A set of those printed before 1810 was published in that year in three volumes. The chief pieces included were: 1. 'Travels to discover the Source of Moral Motion' [1789?]. 2. 'Opus Maximum, or the great essay to reduce the World from Contingency to System' [1803]. 3. 'The Apocalypse of Human Perfectibility' [1808]. Fearing lest these important volumes might perish, he wished his friends to bury some copies of them and to transmit to posterity the particulars of their resting-places; while in order to provide against the extinction of the English tongue, he asked De Quincey to translate them into Latin.

[Gent. Mag. 1822, i. 279-80; Annual Biogr. and Obituary, vii. 101-9; Timbs's Eccentrics, pp. 300-4; Notes and Queries, 8th ser. xi. 485, xii. 35, 178-9; Temple Bar (by H. S. Salt), xciii. 573-8; Life of Alaric Watts by his son, ii. 280-7; Taylor's Records of my Life, i. 284-94; London Mag. November 1822, pp. 410-11, and

September 1823 (by De Quincey), pp. 253–60; Tait's Mag. October 1840 (also by De Quincey). The last two articles are included in De Quincey's Collected Writings (1890), iii. 93–117, and an editorial note by Prof. Masson is added (pp. 118–20). A slight life of him, price sixpence, was published in 1822 by a relative, possibly W. T. Brande (says the catalogue of the British Museum Library), and another sketch, by J. W. C., was the first of a series of twopenny tracts on Materialism (1861). The statements in these authorities are vague and contradictory.] W. P. C.

STEWART or STUART, LOUISA, COUNTESS OF ALBANY (1753–1824), wife of the Young Pretender. [See ALBANY.]

STEWART, LUDOVICK, second DUKE OF LENNOX and DUKE OF RICHMOND (1574–1624). [See STUART.]

STEWART or STUART, MARIA CLEMENTINA (1702–1735), wife of the Old Pretender. [See under JAMES FRANCIS EDWARD.]

STEWART or STUART, MARY (1542–1587), queen of Scots. [See MARY.]

STEWART, MATTHEW, fourth or twelfth EARL OF LENNOX (1516–1571), regent of Scotland, son of John, third earl of Lennox [q. v.], by Anne, eighth daughter of John Stewart, first earl of Atholl [q. v.], was born in Dumbarton Castle 21 Sept. 1516 (FRASER, Lennox, i. 364). He succeeded his father in 1526, and on 13 Feb. 1530–1 came to an agreement with Sir James Hamilton of Finnart on behalf of James Hamilton, second earl of Arran [q. v.], whereby 'for the removal of suspicion and hatred' conceived by him against 'the said James, earl of Arran, for the slaughter of the deceased John, earl of Lennox, committed beside Linlithgow,' Sir James Hamilton became bound to fee six chaplains to 'do suffrage for the soul of the said deceased earl for seven years; three of them to sing continually in the college kirk of Hamilton, and the other three to sing continually in the Blackfriars, Glasgow' (Hist. MSS. Comm. 3rd Rep. iii. 393). On 21 April 1531 he had letters under the privy seal appointing him and his heirs keepers of the castle of Dumbarton (ib.). He was present as a peer in parliament on 26 April 1531 and 17 May 1532; but shortly after the latter date he went to France, and obtaining a command of Scots men-at-arms, accompanied his uncle Robert, seigneur of Aubigny, in the campaign in Provence in 1536 [see under STEWART, JOHN, first (or ninth) EARL OF LENNOX]. In January 1537 he was naturalised as a French subject.

After the death of James V in 1542 Lennox was induced by Cardinal Beaton and the French party to return to Scotland to assist in the overthrow of Arran. On the ground of Arran's illegitimacy (Hamilton Papers, i. 409–10) Lennox was put forward as next heir to the throne after the Princess Mary, and therefore entitled to act as governor in place of Arran; and the hope was also held out to him of a marriage with the queen dowager, Mary of Guise (q. v.) (Privy Council to Angus and his brother, 10 Feb. 1542–3, ib.). Escaping the English vessels which had instructions for his capture, he landed at Dumbarton, 3 March 1543, with only two ships and a small company (ib. p. 510), but according to repute, 'with much French gold' (ib. p. 511), with which he is said to have boasted he would fill the Scottish purses (ib.), although, according to Sadler, it amounted to no more than five thousand crowns (ib. p. 519). In April he had an interview with Arran, to whom he delivered a flattering message from the French king, with the offer of troops and money to maintain him against an English invasion (SADLER, State Papers, i. 102–3). Later he was reputed to have expressed his willingness 'to remain a prisoner' if the 'French king did not accomplish such things as he offered' (ib. p. 173). Finding, however, that the governor had no mind to accept his offers, he refused to subscribe the act acknowledging his authority (ib. p. 185), and thereupon was required to deliver up the castle of Dumbarton on pain of treason (ib. p. 197). He excused himself for declining to do so on the ground that Stirling of Glorat, the captain, refused to deliver it up (ib. p. 201); and after promising to submit himself to Arran and 'confess him to be governor and second person of the realm,' he, on Arran's approach with a strong force, fled to the highlands (ib. p. 202). A little later, however, he secretly returned to Lennox, and having gathered a body of followers, on 21 July joined with other lords in an attempt to rescue the queen dowager and the infant princess from the power of Arran. With a force of ten thousand men they marched towards Edinburgh, and compelled the governor to deliver up his charge, whereupon Lennox escorted the queen dowager and the infant princess back to Stirling (Diurnal of Occurrents, p. 28). Thereafter, according to David Lindsay, the 'Cardinal' (Beaton), who had now persuaded Arran—in dread of his rival, Lennox—to come to terms with him, caused the queen dowager 'to entertain him very tenderly and put him in hope of marriage,' that she 'might pacify him by her love:' i.e. reconcile him to the unlooked-for new alliance of the cardinal with Arran. There was a rival suitor in the Earl of Bothwell, but, according to Lindsay, Lennox far excelled Bothwell in personal grace and strength, as well as in knightly accomplishments, for he 'was ane strong man, of personage weill proportioned in all his members, with lustie and manlie visage, and vent verrie atrecht up in his passage: quhairfoir he appeired verrie pleasant in the sight of gentlewomen' (Chronicles, pp. 422-3). But Lindsay also records that she gave to both 'nothing but fair words;' and Lennox (suspecting that the cardinal was using him merely for his own aggrandisement, and had no desire, but the opposite, that he should be successful in his suit) began to look out for a new alliance. Of necessity it could be found only among the cardinal's enemies, and without any scruple or the least consideration either for France or Scotland, he gave Henry VIII, through the Earl of Glencairn, to understand that his services might be bought by the hand of Henry's niece, Lady Margaret Douglas [q. v.], daughter of Angus, and by Henry's help to recover 'his right and title to this realm (Scotland), which he sayeth the governor now usurpeth' (Hamilton Papers, ii. 56).

Than this offer of Lennox nothing at this crisis could have been more welcome to Henry. He could now make Lennox his trump card in place of Arran, who, in fear of Lennox's rivalry, had succumbed to the cardinal. That Lennox was next heir to the Scottish throne after Arran would have been sufficient for Henry's purpose; but the fact that his claims to be the rightful heir instead of Arran had already been backed by the cardinal and the catholics elevated him into an almost heaven-sent instrument. His pretensions to the hand of the Lady Margaret, far from being objected to, were merely an additional commendation, since his marriage with her would bind up his interests more completely with England. But both as an earnest of his good faith and as a most important step towards the attainment of Henry's purpose, it was deemed advisable to ask him, before negotiations proceeded further, to give up to England Dumbarton Castle, regarded as the key to the west of Scotland (the Privy Council to Sadler, 11 Oct. ib. p. 98). The difficulty was that Lennox supposed this to be his main trump card, and that to give it up would place him in Henry's power. He therefore point blank refused, Sadler reporting that Lennox would sooner part with his life, and that if Henry pressed him to give it up he would join the French

party (Hamilton Papers, ii. 108; SADLER, State Papers, i. 308). Failing thus to obtain definite assurances from England, he broke his promise to attend a convention of Angus and other lords of the English party held in Douglas Castle about the end of October (ib. i. 325); but although the cardinal, alive to the danger of his alliance with England, made every endeavour to reconcile him to Arran's governorship, he failed, and on the arrival of a French fleet with a supply of stores, artillery, and treasures for the Scots against England, Lennox, to make sure of what in any case would be of vital assistance to himself, secured it in Dumbarton Castle (Diurnal, p. 29).

Profoundly distrusting the cardinal, Lennox in January 1544 definitely joined Angus and the English party, and united with them in an advance against Edinburgh. Their forces numbered over four thousand, but Arran being prepared to give battle with a much more powerful array, they were forced to pretend to come to terms (Hamilton Papers, i. 250; Diurnal, p. 30). An agreement was therefore signed, 23 Jan. 1543-4, between commissioners of Arran on the one side, and of Angus and Lennox on the other, for mutual obedience to the queen of Scotland (Cal. State Papers, Scot. i. 45); but, this notwithstanding, Lennox did not scruple to continue his negotiations with England, and on 17 March he and Glencairn agreed to put the king of England in possession of several of the strongest fortresses in Scotland, including Dumbarton, and to promote the marriage of the young Princess Mary of Scotland to Prince Edward. For reward Lennox was to obtain the hand of the Lady Margaret and to be appointed governor in place of Arran on the ground of Arran's illegitimacy, while Glencairn was immediately rewarded for his services in the negotiation by a grant of one thousand crowns per annum (ib. p. 46). Further, Lennox undertook to become a protestant and promote the preaching of 'the word of God' in Scotland.

Having thus broken his allegiance to his religion and his country, Lennox, on 28 May, set sail from Dumbarton to England (Hamilton Papers, ii. 399; Diurnal, p. 33), landing at Chester on 6 June (Hamilton Papers, i. 403). Proceeding to London, he there on 26 June signed a treaty with Henry's commissioners for his marriage to the Lady Margaret. On the one hand he not merely agreed to surrender to Henry the castle of Dumbarton and the Isle of Bute, but to give up to him what title he had to the Scottish throne, and to support him in his claim to be supreme lord of Scotland;

and in return Henry confirmed his agreement of 17 March consenting to the marriage with Lady Margaret, and also granted him lands in England to the annual value of 1,700 marks (*Cal. State Papers*, Scot. Ser. i. 47). In the final ratification of the bargain there was small delay: obtaining letters of naturalisation on 10 July 1544, Lennox was married the same day to the Lady Margaret.

Although the specially momentous results of this unscrupulous faction could scarcely have been foreseen by either party, it is no matter of wonder that Lennox now regarded his interests as mainly bound up with those of Henry VIII, and that, recreant to his country and his faith, he was steadfastly true to his new master. He had little to hope for elsewhere. Moreover his own intellectual mediocrity and lack of personal stamina were now atoned for by his partnership with the Lady Margaret. Never had any one, some moral considerations apart, a more admirable helpmeet, and never was there a partnership more cordial and complete. Uniting to the dominant will and resolute ambition of the Tudors the subtle cunning of the Douglases, she gradually took the reins, with the admiring consent of her lord and master, into her own hands. With more than willing devotion he allowed himself to be finally guided by her judgment in every important purpose of his career, while she with sleepless activity and great feminine cleverness set herself to make the utmost of every political opportunity, and to win for her house all that was within the range of possible attainment. Nor did Henry allow Lennox to dally in the performance of his part of the bargain. Before his honeymoon was over he had to undertake an expedition against the west of Scotland, with eighteen ships and about six hundred men. On 8 Aug. he was proclaimed by the English king lieutenant for the north of England and south of Scotland (*Cal. State Papers*, Henry VIII, No. 449), and on the 10th he arrived at Dumbarton (*Diurnal*, p. 35). Stirling of Glorat, the captain of the castle, cordially welcomed Lennox its owner, but when Lennox proceeded to hint of its delivery to the English, captain and garrison at once took up arms, and Lennox and his retinue, in dread of their lives or of captivity, fled precipitately to their ships. Proceeding down the Clyde, Lennox was fired upon by Argyll while passing Dunoon, but landed and defeated Argyll's followers, and, continuing his voyage, invaded Cantyre and also plundered the Ayrshire coasts. But he nevertheless returned to Bristol without

having achieved anything of the least practical value to the king of England. In December following he received instructions to go to Carlisle, and from thence to treat with the Earl of Angus and bring him to the interests of England (*Cal. State Papers*, Scot. Ser. p. 48). In 1545 he was again appointed to the command of an expedition against the west coast of Scotland; but before anything was accomplished he was called away to assist Hertford [see SEYMOUR, EDWARD, first DUKE OF SOMERSET] in his invasion of Scotland from the south. After Hertford's retreat towards the end of September he passed over to Ireland, and on 17 Nov. sailed with a large armament from Dublin to attempt the capture of Dumbarton, but arrived only in time to discover that it had passed into the hands of his rival. On 1 Oct. of the same year he was pronounced guilty of treason by the Scottish parliament, and sentence of forfeiture was passed against him (*Acta Parl. Scot.* ii. 456), his lands being parcelled out among various noblemen.

After the death of Henry VIII, Lennox in September 1547, while Somerset advanced by the east coast and routed the Scots at Pinkie Cleugh, made a diversion by invading the west marches with Lord Wharton at the head of five thousand men; and, having blown up the church and steeple of Annan and razed the town to the ground, he obtained the submission of the whole of Annandale, compelling the inhabitants to give pledges for their fidelity (*Cal. State Papers*, Scot. p. 68). He also took part in an invasion of Scotland in the following year (*ib.* p. 79). With the accession of Mary Tudor to the English throne, his star was in the ascendant, for his wife and he were special friends of the queen; but with Elizabeth on the throne the Lennox fortunes seemed to have reached their lowest ebb. Nothing was to be obtained through Elizabeth in the way of satisfying his main ambition—the recognition of his wife's eventual right to the succession to the English and Scottish crowns. Necessarily as regards England the main hope of Lennox and his wife was in the catholics; and without the same aid their chances in Scotland appeared still more hopeless than in England. Consequently their house at Temple Newsam, in Yorkshire, became more and more the centre of catholic intrigue in Britain. For the fulfilment of their main ambition, their hopes, especially after the death of Francis II of France, the husband of Mary Stuart, became concentrated on their eldest son, Henry Stewart, lord Darnley [q. v.]; for by his marriage to the young widowed queen of Scots, who also claimed to be rightful queen of England, he might secure to his and their descendants the unexampled honour of succession to both crowns.

When Arran in 1559 became a convert to protestantism, it was thought that the French party would do their utmost to win Lennox (ib. For. 1558-9, No. 1111), and in truth Lennox was only too willing to be won. On the death of Francis, he sent his servant Nesbitt to Scotland to treat regarding his return (ib. 1559-60, Nos. 467-8); and he afterwards defended himself to Elizabeth for doing so, on the ground that he was simply 'travelling for his right' (ib. No. 579) —that is, for the repeal of the sentence of forfeiture and restoration to his estates. With Mary in Scotland, his return thither became to him a still more engrossing object of desire; and although the mere thought of it so provoked and alarmed Elizabeth that in 1562 she sent him to the Tower, she in 1564 allowed herself to be persuaded— either through the flattery of the Lady Margaret, or by the influence of intrigues which it is now impossible to trace, or from a special freak or purpose of her own, which now baffles full explanation—to grant his request. An important point in his favour was probably the fact that both Moray and Maitland 'were disposed rather to further than hinder his coming' (ib. For. 1564-5, No. 557). Their reasons are not quite clear, but their lack of love for Châtelherault was one; and no doubt also Lennox had had private communication with them. They must have been well aware that his main purpose was to promote a marriage between Darnley and Mary. This they may have imagined beyond his attainment, at least without their sanction; and besides they had no personal knowledge either of Lennox or of Darnley, and, until they knew them, may have thought Darnley an eligible suitor for Mary.

Lennox arrived in Scotland in September 1564, and shortly afterwards, on the 22nd, he was released from the horn by open proclamation at the market cross of Edinburgh (Diurnal, p. 77). After this necessary preliminary, he on the 23rd rode with his attendants in gaudy style to Holyrood Palace, where he had an interview with the queen, and gave presents to her and the principal nobles (ib.) On 9 Oct. proclamation was made of his restoration to his lands and of the repeal of the doom of forfailture (ib. p. 78); and on the 27th he and Châtelherault were formally—but only formally—reconciled at Holyrood Palace. With the permission of Elizabeth, Darnley was soon afterwards permitted to come to Scotland; but

when Elizabeth learned that the Queen of Scots had determined to marry Darnley, she on 10 June 1565 sent a belated and impotent summons to Lennox and Darnley to return to England (ib. p. 125).

After the marriage of Mary and Darnley, Lennox on 6 Sept. 1565 was appointed lieutenant over all the western counties (Reg. P. C. Scotl. i. 366); and on 10 Oct. he was named leader of the vanguard of the army against Moray and the rebel protestants (ib. p. 379); but during the remainder of his son's life he, although of necessity continuing to reside in Scotland, was little more than a political cipher. Notwithstanding his fervent attendance at mass in the queen's chapel (Knox, ii. 514), he probably lost the queen's regard even before his son did; and in fact there was a dispute between Mary and her husband as to whether Lennox or Bothwell should be commander of her forces against the rebels. His haughty manners provoked the resentment of most of the nobility, while, like his son, he lacked the qualities necessary to secure even toleration of his pretensions. Worst of all, he was neither wise enough nor in character strong enough to be a proper mentor to his son, over whom he speedily lost all control. His wife, who could have exercised a salutary influence over both son and husband, was detained a captive by Elizabeth, and could not hold free communication with them even from a distance.

Lennox was privy to the plot for the murder of Riccio; but it was of course without his knowledge that Darnley treacherously conspired with the queen for her escape; and thereanent he was reported to be 'much offended with his son,' as he well might be (Randolph to Cecil, 21 March 1566, Cal. State Papers, For. Ser. 1566-8, No. 205). Despised almost from the beginning by the queen, and almost equally with his son the object of her wrath, for his part in the plot against Riccio, Lennox was helpless to prevent the estrangement becoming a public scandal, but he had sufficient good sense to warn the queen in October of Darnley's purpose to leave the kingdom, and to inform her that it was not in his power to turn him from it (Le Croc to Bethune, 15 Oct. 1566, in Keith's History, ii. 450). He proved equally impotent to protect Darnley from the inevitable dangers that attended his stay in Scotland. Not only so, but it may have been through his unwise and blind advice that Darnley was lured into the toils which ended in his murder. After its occurrence, Lennox adopted an attitude at once prudent and determined. His wise restraint was probably due to the advice of others; his courage was always adequate for any demand upon it.

On 20 Feb. 1566-7 he addressed a letter to the queen begging her to call a meeting of the estates, that prompt measures might be taken for the discovery of the murderer (KEITH, ii. 525); and it was only when he found that appeals to her were vain that, on 24 March, he formally accused Bothwell of the crime and demanded that he should be brought to trial. This demand it was impossible to pass by; but matters were so arranged that Lennox was unable to appear at the trial as Bothwell's accuser. Bothwell having filled the city with his own supporters, Lennox deemed it necessary to bring with him a force adequate for his protection; but when the queen learned that he was approaching the city with three thousand followers, she sent her commands to him at Linlithgow not to enter Edinburgh with more than six in his company (*Cal. State Papers*, For. 1566-8, No. 1097; *Diurnal*, p. 108). Not daring to place himself under the protection of Bothwell and the queen, Lennox sent his servant, Robert Cunningham, 'to pursue in his name' (*ib.*), but the substitute was not accepted, and, on the ground that no accuser had appeared, Bothwell was formally acquitted of the charge of murder and declared not guilty. On 29 April Lennox, deeming a longer stay in Scotland not only useless but unsafe, set sail from the west coast for England (*ib.* p. 109); but after the queen's surrender at Carberry Hill and imprisonment in Lochleven, he was on 23 June nominated regent provisionally (*Reg. P. C. Scotl.* i. 541), and he returned to Scotland in July. On the escape of Mary from Lochleven, he joined the lords who defeated her at Langside; and at the Westminster conference in November 1568 he appeared and delivered a paper in which he accused the Queen of Scots of conspiracy against the life of his son.

After the assassination of Moray, Lennox was on 16 June 1570 appointed lieutenant-general of the kingdom; and on 12 July he was on the recommendation of Elizabeth—who, however, resolved to detain the Lady Margaret in England—chosen regent. With no party in Scotland was his election popular; and it so provoked the queen's sympathisers that in a parliament held at Linlithgow on 10 Aug., they declared their intention never to acknowledge him as regent, while Kirkaldy of Grange resolved openly to espouse the cause of the queen, and to hold the castle of Edinburgh on her behalf. Huntly also assembled his forces and

marched south to Brechin, but was on 18 Aug. surprised by Lennox, who was at least a good soldier, and completely defeated. Shortly afterwards he issued a proclamation against 'the Earl of Huntly's calumnies,' that he 'was a sworn Englishman' (summarised in CALDERWOOD's *History*, iii. 9); and, proceeding westwards, he besieged the castle of Doune, which surrendered within three days. Elizabeth now sought to interpose to bring about an arrangement between the two parties, and on 14 Jan. 1571 an abstinence for two months was agreed upon; but during its continuance the Hamiltons seized the house of Paisley from Lord Sempill's servants, and Lennox, having appointed the lieges to meet him at Glasgow, defeated Hamilton and obtained its surrender on 12 Feb. On 2 April one of his followers, Captain Thomas Crawford [q. v.], by a daring feat of climbing, succeeded in capturing the all but impregnable stronghold of Dumbarton; and thus established the authority of the regent over all the west of Scotland. On 13 April Kirkcaldy published at the market cross of Edinburgh a public cartel against Lennox, and as a counter-move Lennox, having on 11 May arrived at Leith with a large force, on the 14th fortified a space at the head of the Canongate to enable him to hold a parliament within the freedom of Edinburgh. After various decrees of forfaulture had been passed, the parliament was adjourned until August at Stirling, and while the chief nobility of the regent's party were assembled there, the town early on the morning of 4 Sept. was surprised by an armed party sent by Grange from Edinburgh. Many of the nobility, including the regent, were taken prisoners; but while a portion of the raiders had dispersed in quest of plunder, a rescue was effected by Mar, and the party put to flight, although not before the regent had been stabbed in the back by Captain Calder.

Mortally wounded, Lennox rode back to the castle, and died at four o'clock in the afternoon (4 Sept. 1571) after commending the young king to the care of the assembled lords, and beseeching Mar to carry a last message of love to his wife. He was buried in the chapel royal of Stirling. George Buchanan, who had so warmly espoused the cause of the murdered son, commemorated the father in a Latin epitaph. By Lady Margaret Douglas, Lennox had four sons and four daughters; but of these only two sons survived infancy: Henry, lord Darnley [q. v.], and Charles, who, the earldom of Lennox being on the death of the regent vested in James VI, succeeded to the lordship of Darnley with all the family estates and heritable jurisdictions. He married, in 1574, Elizabeth, daughter of Sir William Cavendish [q. v.] (and sister of William, first earl of Devonshire), by whom he had an only daughter, Lady Arabella Stuart [see ARABELLA]: the fifth earl died in London in 1576, aged 20, and was buried in Henry VII's chapel in Westminster Abbey.

[Letters and Papers, Henry VIII; Cal. State Papers, temp. Eliz. Domestic, Foreign, Spanish, and Venetian Series; Hamilton Papers; Sadler Papers; Reg. P. C. Scotl. vols. i-ii.; Reg. Mag. Sig. Scot. 1543-80; Histories by Knox, Lindsay of Pitscottie, Bishop Leslie, Buchanan, Calderwood, Keith, and Spotiswoole; Diurnal of Occurrents; History of James the Sext, Sir James Melville's Memoirs and Richard Bannatyne Memorials (all in the Bannatyne Club); Lord Herries's Memoirs in the Abbotsford Club; Sir William Fraser's Lennox; see also under LADY MARGARET DOUGLAS.] T. F. H.

STEWART, MATTHEW (1717–1785), mathematician, born at Rothesay in Bute in 1717, was the second son of Dugald Stewart (d. 1753), minister of Rothesay, by his wife, Janet Bannatyne (d. 1761). He was educated at the town grammar school, and entered Glasgow University in 1734. There he enjoyed the friendship of Francis Hutcheson (1694–1746) [q. v.] and of Robert Simson [q. v.], the mathematician, to whom he owed his marked predilection for the Greek geometricians. In 1741 he proceeded to Edinburgh University, and studied under Colin Maclaurin [q. v.], but regularly corresponded with Simson on the subject of ancient geometrical methods. Simson was at that time engaged in restoring Euclid's porisms, and Stewart pursued the same subject in a different direction. In 1746 he published 'General Theorems of considerable use in the higher parts of Mathematics,' Edinburgh, 8vo. Several of these theorems were in fact porisms, but Stewart avoided the name through fear of seeming to anticipate his friend. Though given without the demonstrations, they placed 'their discoverer at once among the geometers of the first rank.'

On 6 May 1744 Stewart was licensed to preach by the presbytery of Dunoon, and on 9 May 1745, on the presentation of the Duke of Argyll, he was ordained minister of Roseneath, Dumbartonshire, which charge, however, he resigned on being elected professor of mathematics at Edinburgh University in the beginning of September 1747. In 1756 he published in the 'Essays' of the Philosophical Society of Edinburgh (vol. ii.) a solution of the problem involved in Kepler's second law of planetary motion,

remarkable as the first which avoided the use of infinitesimals and employed only elementary geometrical principles. In 1761 Stewart, pursuing his plan of introducing the simplicity of ancient geometrical demonstrations into astronomic investigations, published 'Tracts, Physical and Mathematical, containing an Explication of several points in Physical Astronomy,' Edinburgh, 8vo. In these tracts, after laying down the doctrine of centripetal forces in a series of propositions requiring only a knowledge of the elements of plane geometry and of conic sections, he proceeded to determine in the same manner 'the effect of those forces which disturb the motions of a secondary planet.' A theorem in which he deduced the motion of the moon's apsides attained an accuracy far surpassing that reached by Newton. The result confirmed that arrived at through algebraical methods by Charles Walmesley [q. v.] in 1749. In 1763 Stewart issued a supplement entitled 'The Distance of the Sun from the Earth determined by the Theory of Gravity' (Edinburgh, 8vo), in which he computed the distance at nearly 119 millions of miles. The inaccuracy of this result was due to the difficulty of treating so complex a subject geometrically, Stewart being obliged to neglect so many small quantities in his calculation that the total error seriously affected the result. The nature of his fault was first pointed out in 1769 by John Dawson [q. v.] in a pamphlet entitled 'Four Propositions' (Newcastle, 8vo). In 1771 John Landen [q. v.] published an independent refutation of Stewart's conclusions.

On 21 June 1764 Stewart was elected a fellow of the Royal Society. In 1772 the failing state of his health compelled him to retire to his estate at Catrine in Ayrshire, and from 1775 the duties of his mathematical professorship were performed by his son Dugald. He died on 23 Jan. 1785. By his wife Marjory (d. 1771), only daughter of Archibald Stewart, writer to the signet, he was father of Dugald Stewart [q. v.]

Besides the works mentioned, Stewart was the author of 'Propositiones Geometricæ more veterum demonstratæ,' Edinburgh, 1763, 8vo; translated in 1801. He also published four propositions extending a theorem in the fourth book of Pappus, in the first volume of the 'Essays and Observations' of the Edinburgh Philosophical Society (1754).

[Memoir of Matthew Stewart, by John Playfair [q. v.], in the Transactions of the Royal Society of Edinburgh, i. 57–76; Memoir of Dugald Stewart, by Colonel Matthew Stewart, 1838; Thomson's Hist. of the Royal Society.

App. p. li; Encyl. Britannica, 8th ed. i. 695, iv. 104; Bower's Hist. of Edinburgh University, ii. 357; Anderson's Biogr. Dict. of Eminent Scotsmen.]

E. I. C.

STEWART, MURDAC or MURDOCH, second DUKE OF ALBANY (d. 1425), was the eldest son of Robert, first duke of Albany [q. v.], by Margaret, countess of Menteith. During the lifetime of his father he was known as the Earl of Fife. He is mentioned, 30 July 1390, as a conservator of a truce on the marches (Cal. Documents relating to Scotland, 1357–1509, No. 416), and in 1392 as justiciary north of the Forth (Exchequer Rolls, iii. 316). At the battle of Homildon in 1402 he was taken prisoner by Sir John Skelton, who on that account received from Henry IV a grant of one hundred marks (Cal. Documents relating to Scotland, 1357–1509, No. 723). He remained a prisoner in the Tower, with occasional liberty on parole, until, on 4 May 1415, the constable of the Tower was ordered to deliver him up to the king's esquires (ib. No. 859). On 6 July direction was given that his capture and abduction should be inquired into by a Yorkshire jury (ib. No. 863); but no further information is obtainable in regard to the incident. Early in August he was exchanged for Henry Percy, second earl of Northumberland [q. v.] (ib. Nos. 895, 900). On the death of his father on 3 Sept. 1420 he, in the absence of James I in England, succeeded him as governor, but whether by usurpation or by consent of the nobility in parliament there is no evidence to show. In any case, there can be no doubt as to either the incompetence or the corruption of his rule, and the majority of the nation became more than ever anxious for the return of the king. In 1423 a commission was given to Albany by parliament to treat of his liberation, and the negotiations were successful, the king returning to Scotland, amid general rejoicing, on 24 April 1424.

Upon James's coronation at Scone, Albany —in accordance with the privilege which the earls of Fife claimed as successors of Macduff, the conqueror of Macbeth—performed the ceremony of installing him on the throne. But after he had established himself in power, James, either because he believed that his imprisonment in England had been prolonged by the Albany faction, or because of their endeavours to frustrate acts passed for the recovery of crown lands, or because he saw that they constituted a serious possibility of danger, resolved at all hazards to render them impotent. At a parliament held at Perth on 25 March 1425 he suddenly ordered the arrest of Albany, of his younger son, Lord Alexander Stewart, and of twenty of the

principal nobility and barons. Previously to this, Walter, the eldest son of Albany, had been arrested and imprisoned on the Bass Rock. Albany himself was sent first to St. Andrews and then to the castle of Dunbar, and his wife Isabella, daughter of the Earl of Lennox—whom the king found in Albany's castle of Doune—was sent to Tantallon. Of the charge against Albany and his sons there is no record. It is usual to assume that as Albany had succeeded to the regency without the sanction of the estates, he had been guilty of treason; but even if he were chargeable with this crime, his sons were not. No doubt Albany and his sons must have been convicted, justly or not, of acts which warranted the death sentence; but the main reason for associating his sons with him probably was that, if spared, they were certain to do their utmost to revenge his death. Walter Stewart (said to have been father of Andrew Stewart, lord Avandale [q. v.]), the eldest son, was tried at a court held at Stirling on 24 May, and, being found guilty, was instantly executed before the castle. A similar fate on the next day (25 May 1425) befell Albany himself, his son Alexander, and the aged Earl of Lennox. Albany was buried at Stirling. The titles (Earl of Fife and Duke of Albany) and estates were forfeited and annexed to the crown. Albany's eldest son Robert, earl of Fife, died about 1420; the youngest son James escaped to the highlands, collected a band of freebooters, and attacked the burgh of Dumbarton, which he sacked and gave to the sword, killing, among others, the king's uncle, Sir John Stewart of Dundonald, known as 'the Red Stewart.' He then retired to the highlands, but, being hard pressed, made his escape to Ireland, where he married one of the Macdonalds, and had a son James, ancestor of the Stewarts of Ardvoirlech. On those of his followers who were captured in Scotland James took signal vengeance, causing them, while alive, to be torn limb from limb by horses. Some time after her husband's execution Albany's widow received her liberty, and she was permitted to enjoy the estates of the Earl of Lennox, of which she was sole heiress. In 1450 she founded the collegiate church of Dumbarton, and she died in 1460.

[Cal. Documents illustrative of the Hist. of Scotland, 1350–1507; Exchequer Rolls of Scotland, vol. iii.; Chron. by Fordun and Bower; Douglas's Scottish Peerage (Wood). i. 58–9; G. E. C[okayne]'s Complete Peerage.]

T. F. H.

STEWART, PATRICK, second EARL OF ORKNEY (d. 1614), the second but eldest surviving son of Robert, first earl of Orkney [q.v.], by Janet Kennedy, eldest daughter of Gilbert, third earl of Cassilis, succeeded his father in 1502. On 11 July 1594 he was summoned before the council at the instance of the inhabitants of Danzig for the spoliation of a ship belonging to that town (*Reg. P. C. Scotl.* v. 153), but on 24 Dec. was absolved (*ib.* p. 195). While in Edinburgh he served the king as sewer at the great banquet on the occasion of Prince Henry's baptism on 23 Aug. (CALDERWOOD, *History,* v. 342). On 1 March 1600 he had a charter of the earldom of Orkney and the lordship of Zetland (*Reg. Mag. Sig. Scot.* 1593-1608, No. 1022), and he was served heir to his brother Henry, master of Orkney, on 2 Oct. 1606. Already, however, he had, as Spotiswood states, 'undone his estate by riot and prodigality' (*History,* iii. 213); and in order to secure an income he had resort to the imposition of fines within his jurisdiction for a great variety of trivial or fictitious offences, among his enactments being the specially inhuman one which forbade the supply of relief to vessels in distress (*ib.*) Gradually he assumed a kind of independent sovereignty, with all its external formalities. While observing in his household the ceremonial of a prince, he never went abroad without a guard of fifty musketeers (*History of James the Sext,* p. 386), probably intended less as a mark of royal dignity than as a precaution against the ill-will aroused by his oppressions.

Various complaints having been made to the privy council against his cruelty and tyranny without any action being taken against him, the king on 18 Sept. 1608 wrote a letter of expostulation on their remissness to the privy council, who excused their passivity from 'want of forces;' but added that if the king himself 'put his hand thereto,' they would gladly 'follow' (*Reg. P. C. Scotl.* viii. 531). Finally, on 27 Dec. 1608, Orkney was charged to appear before the council (*ib.* p. 214), and, having been denounced on 2 March 1609 for not appearing (*ib.* p. 255), did at last come to Edinburgh, when on 6 June David, earl of Crawford, became surety in 20,000*l.* that he should keep ward in Edinburgh and the Canongate until relieved (*ib.* p. 292). In 1609 he was committed to ward in the castle of Edinburgh on general evidence, the final sentence being postponed until special evidence was obtained (*ib.* pp. 312-13). On 18 July he was relaxed on finding sureties in 20,000*l.* and giving his great oath not to escape (*ib.* pp. 322-3); but on 7 Nov. a warrant was issued for keeping him a close prisoner (*ib.* p. 371), to be ready for his trial, which took place on 11 Dec., and resulted in his being detained a prisoner,

while in May 1611 he was discharged of his office of justiciar within Orkney (*ib.* ix. 185). On 31 Aug. he was released on a band of 50,000*l.* to remain within four miles of Edinburgh; but in October he was again committed to ward for having sent a commission of justiciary within the bounds of Orkney to his natural son, Robert Stewart (*ib.* p. 257); and on 27 Feb. 1612 his ward was changed to Dumbarton Castle (*ib.* p. 340). On 11 June 1612 he was charged to give orders for the surrender of his castles of Orkney and Shetland (*ib.* p. 388); but although various endeavours were made to induce him to come to terms (*ib.* vol. x. passim), he utterly declined to do so. In June 1613 a more favourable method of treatment was adopted towards him, his allowance in prison being fixed at 4*l.* a day (*ib.* p. 90); but this proving of no avail, he was on 17 May 1614 transported again to Dumbarton (*ib.* p. 239). Learning that his principal castles had been surrendered to the sheriff, he resolved on measures to re-establish his power; and for this purpose despatched his natural son, Robert, to Orkney, who, gathering a band of the more adventurous spirits, succeeded in recapturing the castle of Orkney and other strongholds, but was finally defeated and taken prisoner by the Earl of Caithness. With five of his accomplices Robert was, on 6 Jan. 1613-14, hanged for rebellion at the market cross of Edinburgh, much 'pitied,' says Calderwood, 'of the people for his tall stature and comely countenance' (*History,* vii. 194). In October the earl himself had been brought back from Edinburgh (*Reg. P. C. Scotl.* x. 274), and on 1 Feb. he was put upon his trial for having instigated his son's rebellion. The main evidence was the confession of his son, who, however, also stated that Orkney had afterwards countermanded the order; but as Orkney himself had twenty days before his own trial confessed that he had instigated the rebellion, and had placed himself in the king's mercy, he was found guilty, and sentenced to be beheaded at the market cross. The ministers sent to wait on him, 'finding him,' says Calderwood, 'so ignorant that he could scarce rehearse the Lord's prayer, entreated the council to delay the execution some few days till he were better informed, and received the Lord's supper' (*Hist.* vii. 194). Their petition having been granted, he communicated on Sunday the 5th, and was executed on Monday the 6th. By his wife, Margaret, daughter of William, lord Livingstone, relict of Sir Lewis Bellenden of Auchinoull, lord justice clerk, he left no issue.

[Reg. Mag. Sig. Scot.; Reg. P. C. Scotl. vols.
v.-x.; Hist. of James the Sext (Bannatyne
Club); Histories of Scotland by Calderwood
and Spotiswood; Pitcairn's Criminal Trials;
Douglas's Scottish Peerage, ed. Wood, i. 216.]
T. F. H.

STEWART, ROBERT, first DUKE OF
ALBANY (1340?–1420), regent of Scotland,
born about 1340, was third son of Robert,
earl of Strathearn (afterwards Robert II
[q. v.]), by Elizabeth, daughter of Sir Robert
Mure of Rowallan. His parents' marriage
took place some years after his birth.
Robert III [q. v.] and Alexander Stewart,
earl of Buchan [q. v.], were his brothers. In
1360 he was sent to England as hostage for
David II. After his marriage, by papal
license (THEINER, Vet. Mon. p. 317), 9 Sept.
1361, to Margaret, countess of Menteith,
daughter of the Countess Mary and Sir John
Graham, he was known as Lord of Menteith, and he was present, as a baron, at parliaments held at Scone in 1367, 1368, and 1369.
On 28 Feb. 1371, the day after his father's
coronation, he swore fealty as Earl of Menteith (Acta Parl. Scot. i. 545). On 30 March
following an indenture was made between
him and Isabel, countess of Fife, widow of
his brother Walter, who died in 1360, by
which the countess agreed to acknowledge
him as her heir-apparent (Harl. MS. 4604,
f. 8, part published in SIR ROBERT SIBBALD's
History of Fife, and printed in SIR WILLIAM
FRASER's Red Book of Menteith, ii. 251–4).
Henceforth, therefore, he held the style and
designation of Earl of Fife and Menteith,
the earldom of Fife being the older creation.

In 1371 and 1372 the Earl of Fife and
Menteith was, along with his elder brother,
John, earl of Carrick (afterwards Robert III),
engaged in presiding in the courts of redress
on the borders (WYNTOUN, Chronicle, bk. ix.
chap. i. line 31). On 7 Feb. 1373 he had a
charter from the king making him and his
heirs male hereditary governors of the castle
of Stirling, with the power to appoint and
dismiss the constables and janitors of the
castle; and during his term of office he did
much to improve and strengthen its defences.
At a meeting of the parliament held at Scone
on 4 April of the same year it was declared
that, failing the king's eldest son and his
heirs, the succession should devolve on the
Earl of Fife and Menteith and his heirs
(Acta Parl. Scot. i. 549).

On the death of Sir John Lyon of Glammis,
high chamberlain of Scotland (4 Nov. 1382),
the Earl of Fife and Menteith was chosen
to succeed him, and he held this office until
1407, when he resigned it in favour of his
son John Stewart, earl of Buchan [q. v.]

The Earl of Fife was one of the leaders of
the expedition into England in 1385 in concert with the French admiral, John de
Vienne, when after a reconnaissance of Roxburgh Castle, then held by the English, but
deemed too strong to be carried by assault,
the joint Scots and French force proceeded
to Berwick, and crossing into Northumberland captured Wark Castle, and ravaged
the country to the gates of Newcastle. Information then reaching them of the approach of a large force under the Duke of
Lancaster, they fell back on Berwick, and,
while permitting the English army to march
by Liddesdale and Teviotdale to Edinburgh,
they again entered England by the western
marches and devastated Cumberland (WYN-
TOUN, bk. ix. chap. vi. lines 54 &c.); FORDUN,
ed. Goodall, ii. 401; FROISSART, ed. Buchon,
ix. 144–55). After the departure of the
French, whose assistance the Scots deemed
too dearly purchased by the expense incurred
in supporting them, the Earl of Fife and
Menteith accompanied the Douglases on
another great plundering raid; entering England by the Solway Sands, they ravaged
the fruitful western borders as far as
Cockermouth, whence they returned with
great store of booty (WYNTOUN, bk. ix.
chap. vii. lines 31 &c.; FORDUN, ii. 402–3).
By these successful raids the earl had won
such renown among the Scots that, when in
1388 the council decided on an expedition
into England under his leadership, no less
than twelve hundred men at arms and forty
thousand infantry assembled under his
standard on the day of tryst at Yetholm.
Having so large a force at his disposal, and
obtaining information that the English
wardens had determined to invade Scotland
as soon as they learned in what direction
the Scots intended to advance, the earl determined to baffle them by forming his army
into two separate divisions, and himself
with the larger division, comprising two-
thirds of the troops, entered the western
marches by Liddesdale and Carlisle, while
the Earl of Douglas with the remainder
proceeded to ravage Northumberland and
Durham. Of the doings of the western
raiders there is no definite information, their
achievements being overshadowed by the
glorious feat of the other division, which,
though at the cost of the Earl of Douglas's
life, won the great historic victory of Otterburn (WYNTOUN, bk. ix. chap. viii.; FORDUN,
ii. 404).

The earl had now attained a position of
commanding importance in Scotland, and
his father being old and infirm, while his
elder brother John, earl of Carrick, had been

z 2

severely weakened in health by the kick of a horse, which rendered him unfit for active exertion, it was agreed at a meeting of the estates in 1389 that he should be elected guardian of the kingdom until the Earl of Carrick should recover from his weakness, or until the latter's eldest son David should be able to assume the government (*Acta Parl. Scot.* i. 555). Immediately afterwards the Earl of Fife and Menteith set out with a large force for England to meet a challenge of the Earl of Nottingham, marshal of England and warden of the eastern marches, who had declared his readiness to engage in fair fight any Scottish force, though double in numbers to his own; but finding Nottingham entrenched in a position of great strength, from which he declined to move out, the earl returned immediately to Scotland (WYNTOUN, bk. ix. chap. ix. lines 33 &c.; FORDUN, ii. 414). Shortly afterwards the French, having concluded a three years' truce with England, induced the Scots to agree to a suspension of hostilities.

On the death of Robert II, 13 May 1390, and the succession of his eldest son, John, earl of Carrick, who took the title of Robert III, the Earl of Fife and Menteith, in accordance with the previous agreement, retained the office of governor, and continued to be entrusted with the chief administration of affairs. In 1397 he was sent with his nephew, David, earl of Carrick, to compose the distractions in the north of Scotland, and on 16 March 1397–8 he was appointed, along with the Earl of Carrick, a commissioner to meet with John of Gaunt, duke of Lancaster, and other English commissioners at Hawdenstank to arrange their mutual differences (RYMER, *Fœdera*, viii. 35; *Cal. Documents relating to Scotland*, 1359–1507, No. 502). At a parliament held at Perth on 28 April following he was created Duke of Albany—from Albania, the ancient name of the country between the Forth and the Spey—his nephew David, earl of Carrick [see STEWART, DAVID, DUKE OF ROTHESAY], being created Duke of Rothesay (WYNTOUN, bk. ix. chap. ix. lines 65 &c.; FORDUN, ii. 423). This, the first introduction of the ducal title into Scotland, is supposed to have been occasioned by certain prerogatives claimed, on account of his ducal rank, by the Duke of Lancaster at the recent conference at Hawdenstank.

In January 1398–9, in accordance with the previous understanding, Albany was succeeded in the governorship of the kingdom by the heir to the crown, the Duke of Rothesay, who was elected for three years, and was to act with the advice of a council,

of which Albany was one of the principal members (*Acta Parl. Scot.* i. 572). Whether or how far Albany was jealous of this transference of power to Rothesay is matter of dispute. When Rothesay in 1400 was besieged by Henry IV in Edinburgh Castle, Albany collected a numerous force for his relief, but contented himself with lying encamped on Calder Moor until the approach of colder weather and the lack of provisions compelled the English to raise the siege and proceed southwards (FORDUN, ii. 430). This passiveness of Albany has been attributed to indifference as to Rothesay's fate; but there is no evidence that Rothesay was in extremities, and the result fully justified Albany's watchful inactivity, which, moreover, entirely accorded with the usual methods of Scottish strategy. As regards Albany's responsibility for the imprisonment and death of Rothesay in 1402 [see under STEWART, DAVID, DUKE OF ROTHESAY], at a meeting of the parliament held on 16 May 1402 it was declared that Rothesay had died from natural causes, and Albany and Douglas, who acknowledged their share in his arrest, were formally pardoned for any breach of the law which that act might have involved (*Acta Parl. Scot.* i. 582). Albany was further reinstated in the office of governor of the kingdom. Immediately afterwards he sent a force into England, which was routed at Nesbit Moor on 22 June; and another force despatched by him under Douglas, to take revenge by ravaging Northumberland, was on 14 Sept. almost decimated by the English archers under Hotspur, Murdac, eldest son of Albany, being taken prisoner.

During the rebellion of Hotspur against Henry IV, Albany is supposed to have acted in concert with him by undertaking an invasion of England. Hotspur, having collected a large army, made a pretence of advancing into Scotland, where he surrounded the insignificant tower of Cocklaws, and, having entered into an agreement with its commander to capitulate unless relieved within six weeks, immediately retired southwards. This seems to have been intended as a signal for Albany, who, on the pretence of avenging the supposed insult, called a meeting of the nobility and proposed an immediate expedition into England. At first they deemed the affair too insignificant for further notice; but when Albany vowed that he would be at Cocklaws on the appointed day though only his page-boy should accompany them, they at once agreed to collect their vassals. Hardly, however, had Albany set out with an immense army when news reached him of the defeat and death of Hotspur on 21 July at Shrewsbury, and after proceeding to Cocklaws and formally relieving the garrison by proclaiming the death of Hotspur, he returned without entering England, and disbanded his forces (FORDUN, ii. 435–6). The Earl of Northumberland and Lord Bardolf having after the death of Hotspur obtained refuge in Scotland, Albany has been accused of having entered into an arrangement to deliver them up in order to procure the liberty of his son Murdac and other Scottish captives in England; but it would appear that they returned to England at the king of England's invitation (WYNTOUN, bk. ix. chap. xviii. lines 135 &c.; FORDUN, ii. 441). Shortly afterwards the young Prince James was captured off Flamborough Head on his way to France, and, being brought to London, was sent by Henry to the Tower. His capture and detention broke down the enfeebled health of the king, who died on 4 April 1406. At a meeting of the estates held shortly afterwards at Perth the captive James was declared to be their lawful king, and Albany was chosen regent of the kingdom.

The regency of Albany, possibly on the ground that the king was in the hands of Henry, a hostile monarch, assumed an entirely independent character. Charters ran in his name and were dated in the year of his regency, and in a letter to Henry IV he calls himself governor Dei Gratia (BURNET, Preface to Exchequer Rolls, iv. p. xlviii). It has been usual to assert that Albany connived at the captivity of the young Scottish king, but there is no evidence of this; nor if there were is there any reason to suppose that his connivance or non-connivance had much effect on the resolution of Henry, whose main aim in detaining the young king seems to have been to bring him under the domination of English influence. What is certain is that Albany—at least formally—sent different embassies to England to negotiate both for the deliverance of the king and his own son Murdoch (RYMER, passim), and that until 1415, when his son was exchanged for Hotspur's son, Henry Percy (afterwards second Earl of Northumberland), they were all equally unsuccessful.

The earlier years of Albany's regency were uneventful, the main occurrence being the burning of the English reformer Reseby at Perth in 1407. The university of St. Andrews was founded in 1410, and the following year was notable for the rebellion of Donald, lord of the Isles [see under MACDONALD, DONALD, second LORD OF THE ISLES and ninth

EARL OF ROSS], who, claiming the earldom of Ross in opposition to Albany, to whom the government of the earldom had been granted by his granddaughter Euphemia of Ross on her entering a nunnery, formed an alliance with Henry IV of England, and invaded the earldom with a force of ten thousand men, but was defeated by Alexander Stewart, earl of Mar [q. v.], nephew of the regent, at the famous battle of Harlaw on 24 July. Following up this success, Albany, having collected a strong force, marched into the earldom of Ross, and, after seizing the castle of Dingwall, compelled Donald to retreat to the Isles. The contention was renewed in the following summer, but Donald found it necessary to give in his submission; and Albany, with a view to consolidating the influence of the government in the north, caused the castle of Inverness to be erected under Mar's direction.

After the release of his son Murdac by Henry V in 1415, Albany in 1416 sent his second son, John, earl of Buchan, on a special embassy to England with the avowed aim of securing the release of the king, but the negotiations were without result. The sincerity of Albany has been called in question, but mainly on the ground that he could not possibly desire to put an end to his own regency. There is no evidence available for either his exculpation or his inculpation; but it is perhaps worth noting that all the while he was protecting the impostor, Thomas Warde, as the exiled Richard II, and that on Warde's death in 1419 he caused to be inscribed on his tomb in the church of the Dominican friars, Stirling, 'Angliæ Ricardus jacet hic Rex ipse sepultus.'

In 1417 Albany sought to take advantage of the absence of Henry V in France to recapture Roxburgh, but news reaching him of the approach of the Duke of Bedford, he immediately abandoned the siege and retreated northwards. In this he only manifested that 'discretion which is the better part of valour;' but, on account of its inglorious result, the expedition obtained from the people the name of the foul (i.e. fool or foolish) raid (FORDUN, ii. 449). Shortly after Albany's retirement the English entered Scotland by the eastern marches, and ravaged the country, burning many towns and villages. Albany took his revenge by sending in 1419 a force of seven thousand picked troops under the Earl of Buchan to the aid of the French against the English. Albany died at Stirling Castle in 1420. The date given by Bowyer is 3 Sept. 1419, but Albany granted a charter at Falkland as late as 4 Aug. 1420; and the probability is that Bowyer simply made a mistake in regard to the year. Albany was buried in Dunfermline Abbey between the choir and the chapel of our Lady. A eulogistic Latin epitaph was inscribed on his tomb (FORDUN, ii. 460).

Albany's conduct may be assigned with almost equal facility to lofty and patriotic or to base and selfish motives. But of his strong personality and great ability his remarkable ascendency over the turbulent nobility is sufficient proof; and if that ascendency was won partly by winking at their extortions and oppressions, it must be remembered that while this does not in itself sufficiently account for it, it was almost impossible for one who was only a regent to retain his position otherwise. Moreover he is to be judged by the standards of the time; and the chroniclers of the period, while they bear witness to his imposing presence, are almost equally unanimous in extolling his affability, temperance, justice, fortitude, and wisdom.

By his first wife, Margaret, countess of Menteith, Albany left a son Murdac or Murdoch Stewart, second duke of Albany [q. v.] By his second wife, Muriella (d. 1449), daughter of Sir William Keith (d. 1407) [q.v.], marischal of Scotland, he had three sons: John, earl of Buchan, Andrew, and Robert. He had also six daughters: Janet, betrothed to David, infant son of Bartholomew de Loen; Mary, married to Sir William Abernethy of Saltoun; Margaret, married first to Sir John Swinton of Swinton, and afterwards, probably, to Robert Stewart of Lorne; Isabel, married to Alexander, earl of Ross, and secondly to Walter Haliburton of Dirleton; Marjory, married to Duncan Campbell of Lochow; and Elizabeth, married to Malcolm Fleming of Biggar and Cumbernauld.

[Chronicles of Wyntoun, Fordun, Froissart, and Walsingham; Rymer's Fœdera; Cal. Documents relating to Scotland, 1359-1507; Accounts of the Great Chamberlain of Scotland; Exchequer Rolls of Scotland, vol. ii-iv.; Acta Parl. Scot. vol. i.; Sir William Fraser's Red Book of Menteith; notes collected by the late William Galloway.] T. F. H.

STEWART, LORD ROBERT, afterwards EARL OF ORKNEY (d. 1592), was a natural son of James V of Scotland by Euphemia, daughter of Alexander Elphinstone, first lord Elphinstone. He was a half-brother of Mary Queen of Scots, of James Stewart, the regent Moray, and Lord John Stewart (1531-1563) [q. v.]. In 1539 he had from the king a grant of the abbacy of Holyrood. His name first appears as a member of the privy council, 20 March 1551-2 (Reg. P. C. Scotl. i. 119). He early joined the lords of the congregation against the queen regent, and Knox states that in 1559 he was present during the surprise attack of the French on the Canongate, and on their withdrawal was one of the first to follow in pursuit of them (Works, i. 458). He subscribed the treaty of Berwick between the lords of the congregation and Queen Elizabeth on 10 May 1560 (ib. ii. 53), and he is included by Knox among those attending the parliament of July-August of this year, who 'had renounced l'apistry and openly professed Jesus Christ' (ib. p. 88). No doubt, like his half-brother Lord John, he was in his political conduct mainly guided by Lord James (afterwards Earl of Moray), whose force of character secured him the loyal devotion of both. Thus on the arrival of Queen Mary in Scotland both Lord Robert and Lord John placed themselves at the disposal of Lord James in regard to the queen's celebration of her first mass, and after the ceremony protected the priest and conveyed him to his chamber (ib. p. 271). In 1561 he also with Lord John kept watch at Holyrood Palace when, during the absence of Lord James on the borders, a rumour arose of a projected night attack (ib. p. 293).

On 3 Nov. 1566 Lord Robert received from the queen a pension of 990l. and several chalders of different kinds of grain out of the temporalities of Holyrood for the maintenance of his legitimate and natural children; and the grant was confirmed on 19 April 1567 by act of parliament. The grant, as well as the confirmation, may have been intended as a bribe in connection with the murder of Darnley. Though he took no active part in the murder, he would appear to have had a more or less intimate knowledge of the plot. After Darnley's arrival at Kirk o' Field he was reported to have warned him that mischief against him was intended. Darnley, it is further stated, informed the queen of what Lord Robert had told him; but Lord Robert denying that 'he had spoken any such thing,' they put their hands to their weapons, and the Earl of Moray had to be called in to separate them (CALDERWOOD, History, ii. 343). In 1569 Lord Robert exchanged the temporalities of Holyrood House for the temporal estates of the see of Orkney with Adam Bothwell, bishop of Orkney; but in 1570 the bishop of Orkney explained that Lord Robert had 'violently intruded himself on his whole living with bloodshed and hurt of his servants;' that 'after he had craved justice, his and his servants' lives were 'sought in the very eye of justice in Edinburgh;' and that he was 'then constrained, of mere necessity, to take the abbacy of Holyrood by advice of sundry godly men' (*ib.* p. 531). On 18 July 1574 a letter passed the great seal in favour of Lord Robert, confirming the letter of pensions to his three legitimate and two natural sons out of the abbacy of Holyrood, reserving 800*l.* to the ministers and readers (*Reg. Mag. Sig. Scot.* 1546–80, No. 2283). Having, however, been accused in the following year of treason in offering the Isles of Orkney to the king of Denmark, he was in August imprisoned by the orders of the regent Morton in the castle of Orkney (*Hist. of James the Sext*, p. 157); and although he made large offers to obtain his freedom, he was retained in prison until Morton's resignation of the regency (*ib.* p. 182). On being set free he became one of the chief conspirers of Morton's ruin (MELVILLE, *Memoirs*, p. 206); and he was one of those who, on 18 Jan. 1580–1, conveyed Morton to imprisonment in Dumbarton Castle (MOYSIE, *Memoirs*, p. 29; CALDERWOOD, iii. 484). On 21 Oct. 1581 he was created by the king Earl of Orkney, when his lands of Orkney and Zetland were erected into an earldom (*Reg. Mag. Sig. Scot.* 1580–1593, No. 263); and on 18 Dec. he had a grant of the island of Caned in Orkney (*ib.* No. 307). He died in 1592. By his wife, Lady Janet Kennedy, eldest daughter of Gilbert, third earl of Cassilis, he had five sons and four daughters: Henry, who died before his father; Patrick, second earl of Orkney [q. v.]; John, earl of Carrick; Sir James, gentleman of the bedchamber to James VI; Sir Robert; Mary, married to Patrick, seventh lord Gray; Jean, married first to Patrick Leslie, commendator of Lindores, by whom she was mother of David Leslie, first lord Newark [q. v.], the general; and secondly to Robert, lord Melville of Raith; Elizabeth, married to Sir John Sinclair of Murchil, brother of George, fifth earl of Caithness; and Barbara.

[*Reg. P. C. Scot.* vols. i.–v.; *Reg. Mag. Sig. Scot.* 1546–80 and 1580–93; Knox's Works; Calderwood's Hist. of Scotland; Moysie's Memoirs, and Hist. of James the Sext (Bannatyne Club); Douglas's Scottish Peerage, ed. Wood, ii. 341.]   T. F. H.

STEWART, Sir ROBERT (*d.* 1670?), governor of Londonderry, reputed to have been the younger brother of Sir William Stewart (*d.* 1662) [see under STEWART, SIR WILLIAM, first VISCOUNT MOUNTJOY], in which case he was the third son of Archibald Stewart of Bardye, and other places in the parish of Whithorn, Wigtonshire (cf.

LODGE, *Peerage*, vi. 243; M'KERLIE, *Lands and Owners in Galloway*, i. 481–4); but the grounds of identification are insufficient, and there is reason to connect him with Patrick Stewart, second earl of Orkney [q. v.] He apparently accompanied James I, to whom, if this latter conjecture is correct, he was not very distantly related, to England in 1603, and was granted letters of denization on 3 July 1604 (*Cal. State Papers*, Dom. 1603–10, p. 127). In 1609 he was appointed to conduct eight hundred swordsmen, followers of the fugitive Hugh O'Neill, second earl of Tyrone [q. v.]—whose presence in Ulster was deemed by the government likely to interfere with the success of the plantation of that province—out of Ireland into Sweden. He sailed from Lough Swilly with three vessels in October; but whether he reached his destination is doubtful, for towards the end of November he was arrested in London for debt, at the instance of one Lesly, executor of Lord Lindores. Salisbury, in notifying the fact to Sir Thomas Lake, adds that three vessels, with Irishmen on board, had arrived at Newcastle (*ib.* p. 564). The debt amounted to the considerable sum of 2,500*l.*, and notwithstanding the personal exertions of the king, who was himself involved in the matter, and a grant to Stewart of 'tops and lops' in the royal parks, the matter was still unsettled in July 1611, when James, acting on the advice of Sir Alexander Hay, allowed Stewart to enter the service of Gustavus Adolphus. He left England early in August, and, proceeding through Denmark, endeavoured, though unsuccessfully, to enlist James's intervention in the settlement of the differences existing between that kingdom and Sweden (*ib.* 1611–13, pp. 51, 66, 98).

Stewart remained abroad apparently till about 1617, in which year, on 24 July, he received, as a recompense for his faithful and acceptable services, a grant of lands in the counties of Leitrim, Cavan, and Fermanagh, to the value of 100*l.* a year. After a time, however, being of an adventurous spirit, he again repaired abroad, serving this time apparently under Sigismund III, king of Poland, in whose interest he undertook in 1623 to raise eight thousand volunteers in Scotland (*Register of the Privy Council Scotland*, xiii. 364). That his promise did not remain altogether a dead letter appears from some correspondence between Secretary Conway and Viscount Annandale in March 1624 (*Cal. State Papers*, Dom. 1623–5, pp. 183, 192); but of his career abroad information is restricted to incidental reference (*Monro his Expedition*, pt. ii. p. 13) to the effect that a certain Captain Robert Stewart came over to Germany as lieutenant-colonel in a regiment of Scots volunteers commanded by Colonel James Lumsden [q. v.], 'having served at first as ensign and lieutenant to Captain Mackenzie under this regiment, and then after came again unto Spruce, captain under Sir John Hamilton's regiment, in May 1629. And was preferred after the intaking of Virtzberg, having been before at the battle of Leipsigh' (cf. also GRANT, *Memoirs of Sir John Hepburn*, p. 154). On 26 April 1636 Chancellor Oxenstjerna applied to Charles I for permission for Stewart to enlist troops in England for service in Germany (*Clarendon State Papers*, i. 516), and on 15 May 1637 Charles granted him a warrant to take up in Ireland and transport four hundred volunteers for the service of the crown of Sweden (LODGE, *Peerage*).

On 11 April 1638 Stewart was appointed governor of Culmore Castle on Lough Foyle, commanding the approach by sea to Londonderry, of which city he was on 25 Feb. returned a member to the Irish parliament which met in 1639. After the outbreak of the rebellion of 1641 he received a commission, dated 16 Nov., from Charles I to raise and command a thousand foot and a troop of horse for his majesty's service. But before the commission arrived he and Sir William Stewart had got together a thousand men, with which they managed to relieve Captain Audley Mervyn at Augher, and, though they were unable to prevent Strabane falling into the hands of Sir Phelim O'Neill [q. v.], their efforts were entirely successful in securing the barony of Raphoe, 'in which the safety of the city of Londonderry was highly concerned' (MERVYN, *Relation*). Not, however, receiving any support either from England or the government at Dublin, Stewart was forced to exhaust his own resources, and in the following spring his men were reduced to great extremities. Nevertheless he and Sir William Stewart on 16 June inflicted a severe defeat, 'after the sharpest action that had been fought in the north,' on Sir Phelim O'Neill at Glenmaquin, near Raphoe, though want of provisions disabled them from profiting by their victory. The merit of the action seems to have rested mainly with Stewart.

Early in the following year, 1643, Stewart was, on the death of Sir John Vaughan, appointed governor of Londonderry, in addition to his charge at Culmore. He was superseded next year by Colonel Audley Mervyn: but in the meanwhile the appointment did not prevent him acting, so far as circumstances allowed, on the offensive. In May he made an excursion as far as the borders of co. Mona-

ghan, capturing a number of prisoners, and burning the enemy's quarters. Returning in June, he surprised Owen Roe O'Neill [q. v.], at the head of about sixteen hundred men, in the neighbourhood of Clones. His force greatly outnumbered that of O'Neill, but the conflict was a desperate one. The Irish were defeated with serious loss, 'most of their arms being taken, and the greatest part of the foreign officers which came with Owen O'Neill killed or taken prisoners.' Want of provisions and ammunition, however, again prevented Stewart improving his victory, and, after capturing the castle of Denge and ravaging the country round about Dungannon, Charlemont, and Kinard, he returned to his headquarters. His position, always one of great difficulty, became extremely uncomfortable after the arrival of orders for the Scots army under Robert Monro (d. 1680?) [q. v.]—called the New Scots, in order to distinguish them from the army of the Scottish planters—to take the covenant and the proclamation of the lords justices of 18 Dec. condemning it. Unwilling at first to cut themselves off from all assistance from Scotland, Stewart and the other royalist commanders refrained from publishing the proclamation; but, after meeting at Belfast on 2 Jan. 1644 to consider the situation, they agreed not to accept the covenant. Matters after this remained in an uncertain state till the beginning of April, when a number of kirk ministers arrived with instructions to enforce the taking of the covenant. Stewart continued obdurately opposed to it, and, though most of his officers were seduced by Sir Frederick Hamilton, he bravely read the lords justices' proclamation against it at the head of his regiment. But after the appointment of Monro with a commission from the parliament of England on 27 April to the chief command of all the English as well as Scottish forces in Ulster, he gave way, and at a meeting of ministers at Coleraine publicly took the covenant, saying, 'Now I will be as arrant a covenanter as any of you' (ADAIR, *True Narrative*, pp. 113-17).

After this step his difficulties perceptibly diminished. On 7 Feb. 1645 the committee of both kingdoms ordered provisions to be at once despatched to Lough Swilly for him and Sir William Stewart, and on 8 Oct., in consequence of his capture of Sligo Castle, of which he was in June appointed governor, passed him a vote of thanks for his good services. As a result of Monro's precipitancy in fighting Owen O'Neill, Stewart arrived too late on the scene of action to take part in the battle of Benburb on 5 June 1646. He had reached Augher when he heard of O'Neill's advance after the victory, and, immediately decamping in the night, made good his retreat to Derry, leaving 'Mac Art but an old drum and two or three muskets.' When Sir Charles Coote (afterwards Earl of Mountrath) [q. v.] in 1648 succeeded to the government of Londonderry, Stewart, who loyally adhered to Charles, refused to obey him, and from his position at Culmore seriously obstructed the approaches to the city. On 28 Feb. Warwick, writing to Michael Jones [q. v.] in the name of the committee, warned him to observe him narrowly, as his behaviour 'looked with a face of danger,' and on 4 Nov. Coote and Monck were instructed to take measures to secure him and certain others 'who, we are informed, will certainly serve the king's interest.' Coote laid his plan well, and immediately on receiving his instructions inveigled him to Londonderry, arrested him, and sent him prisoner to London. He was committed on parole to the custody of Mr. Morgan at the 'Wheatsheaf,' and on 8 Jan. 1649 it was resolved to try him by a council of war; but a week or two later he managed to escape. On 14 May he received a royal commission appointing him, in the event of Viscount Montgomery of the Ardes declining the charge, to the command of the five regiments in the north of Ireland, and twelve days later he joined the besieging army before Londonderry. In obedience to his instructions Sligo Castle surrendered on 7 July to the Marquis of Clanricarde, and on 23 Aug. he gave his vote at a council of war for defending Drogheda.

After the collapse of the royalist cause in Ireland Stewart seems to have retired to Scotland. He was excepted from pardon for life and estate by the act of 12 Aug. 1652 for the settlement of Ireland. At the Restoration he was on 6 Feb. 1660 given a company of foot, and six days later reappointed governor of Londonderry, city and county, 'in consideration of his many services performed to King Charles I, and the good affection expressed by him in the late troubles in Ireland, in his arming and maintaining a regiment of foot and a troop of horse at his own charge in the service of the said king.' He resigned or was superseded on 17 Sept. 1661 by Colonel John Gorges. On 22 May 1662 he was appointed a trustee for the '49 officers, and seems to have retained his position as governor of the fort of Culmore till the close of 1670, in which year he is conjectured to have died.

There seems reason to believe that he never married; but if Lodge is correct in making him the brother of Sir William Stewart, he married Helen M'Kie, daughter of John M'Kie of Palgown, by whom he had issue George, who succeeded him, and married Elizabeth, daughter of James Blair of Dunskey; and Agnes, who married William Houston of Cutreoch.

[Lodge's Peerage, ed. Archdall, vi. 213–5; McKerlie's Hist. of Lands and their Owners in Galloway, i. 481–4; Cal. State Papers, Dom. (in addition to references already given), 1645 p. 183, 1647–8 pp. 22, 318, 327, 1649–50 p. 526; Cal. State Papers, Ireland, James I, iii. 272, 292, 296; Carte's Life of Ormonde, i. 188, 309–10, 350, 366–7, 433–4, 487, 491, 493, 530, 535, ii. 59–60; Gilbert's Contemporary Hist. of Affairs, i. 111, 471, 565, 672, 686, 763–4, ii. 230, iii. 157, 199, 342; Hill's Montgomery MSS. pp. 157, 182; Cal. Clarendon State Papers, ii. 11; Gilbert's Hist. of the Confederation, iv. 353, vii. 120, 224; Manuscripts of Marquis of Ormonde, i. 89, 92–5; Hempton's Siege and Hist. of Londonderry, p. 342; Larcom's Survey of the County of Londonderry, pp. 44, 45, 79, 81, 240; Official Return of Members of Parliament, Ireland.]   R. D.

STEWART, ROBERT, first MARQUIS OF LONDONDERRY (1739–1821), eldest son of Alexander Stewart of Ballylawn Castle, co. Donegal, and Mount Stewart, co. Down, M.P. for Londonderry, who died in 1781, by his wife Mary, sister and heir of Sir Robert Cowan, governor of Bombay, was born on 27 Sept. 1739. His family was very influential in the county Down; in 1769 he was elected one of the county members for the Irish parliament, and was re-elected in 1776, but lost the seat in 1783, and was a peer before the next election. He was undoubtedly a sagacious though never a prominent public man. During the Irish volunteer movement he was one of the delegates sent to the second Dungannon convention in 1783, and was one of its leading spirits. He was advanced to the peerage as Baron Londonderry on 20 Sept. 1789, having been previously sworn of the Irish privy council during Lord Lansdowne's administration, and appointed a trustee of the linen board. He was created Viscount Castlereagh on 6 Oct. 1795, Earl of Londonderry on 8 Aug. 1796, and was made Marquis of Londonderry on 22 Jan. 1816. He was also appointed in 1801 and 1803 governor and custos rotulorum of the county of Down and of Londonderry. His claims to be made a peer of the United Kingdom in 1800, in consideration of his son's services, though not pressed by himself or his son, were not unfavourably considered by the crown, and an assurance was given that if at any future time he or his descendants should desire a British peerage, their wish should be granted (*Cornwallis*

Correspondence, ii. 273, iii. 274). Neither the father, however, nor the son claimed the fulfilment of this promise, probably to prevent Lord Castlereagh's removal from the House of Commons. He died at Castle Stewart on 8 April 1821. He was twice married: first, on 3 June 1766, to Lady Sarah Frances, second daughter of Francis Seymour Conway, marquis of Hertford [q. v.], by whom he had two sons, of whom Robert (1769–1822) [q. v.], the younger and surviving son, succeeded him; and secondly, on 7 June 1775, to Lady Frances, eldest daughter of Lord-chancellor Camden (see PRATT, CHARLES, first EARL CAMDEN), by whom he had three sons and eight daughters. Of his second family, General Charles William Stewart (afterwards Lord Stewart and third Marquis of Londonderry [q. v.], British ambassador at Vienna, was the eldest.

In private life Londonderry was not only a very charitable man, but also enlightened. He resided on his estates almost exclusively, and encouraged tenant-right; he remitted rents; he made work for the unemployed, and brought supplies into the district for the distressed. To his family, and especially to the training and fortunes of his son, Lord Castlereagh, he was deeply devoted.

[Gent. Mag. 1821, i. 373; Alison's Life of Lord Castlereagh and Lord Stewart; Castlereagh's Memoirs and Correspondence; Correspondence of Lord Cornwallis; Froude's English in Ireland, ii. 370.] J. A. H.

STEWART, ROBERT, second MARQUIS OF LONDONDERRY, better known as VISCOUNT CASTLEREAGH (1769–1822), second but eldest surviving son of Robert Stewart, first marquis of Londonderry [q. v.], and of his first wife, Lady Sarah Frances, second daughter of Francis Seymour Conway, marquis of Hertford [q. v.], was born on 18 June 1769. From his childhood he displayed great talent, industry, and resolution of character. His education was begun under Archdeacon Hurrock at a public school in Armagh, and while there he was nearly drowned by the upsetting of a boat on Strangford Lough on 5 Aug. 1788. Shortly afterwards he was placed at St. John's College, Cambridge, where William Pearce (afterwards dean of Ely) was his tutor. He distinguished himself in several college examinations, and was then removed with a view to his entering the Irish House of Commons. He passed portions of 1788 and 1789 in Paris, Geneva, Rome, and Vienna, giving particular attention to political affairs at home and abroad, and on his return to Ireland in 1790 was brought forward on behalf of the independent freeholders of co. Down to wrest one of the county seats from the influence of the Marquis of Downshire. In spite of his youth—for it was only during his canvass that he came of age—his ready speech and pleasing manner secured his election, after a forty-two days' poll; but the expense of the contest, 60,000*l*., nearly ruined his family, and left his father poor for the rest of his life. He then entered one of the regiments which were enrolled on the outbreak of the French war, and on 26 April 1793 became lieutenant-colonel of the Londonderry militia. On 9 June 1794 he married Lady Emily Anne, youngest daughter and coheiress of John Hobart, second earl of Buckinghamshire [q. v.]

His political views at first were not very definite, or even very consistent. On his election he had pledged himself to parliamentary reform in the sense of the extension of the Irish parliamentary franchise to Roman catholic freeholders, and the act of 1793 which removed the disability was warmly supported by him; but this limitation of his disposition to reform exclusively to the case of the Irish franchise had not been clearly expressed in the first instance, and he was often in his later and strong tory days taunted with apostasy on the strength of this pledge. At first he generally voted with the opposition, but, owing to his duty with his regiment, he was frequently absent from parliament; and although he had already formed the opinion, in advance of his contemporaries, that the parliamentary union of England and Ireland and the repeal of catholic disabilities were both necessary and just, and that the French revolution was likely to lead not to the dismemberment but to the consolidation of France, his sympathies were generally of a tory kind. Besides sitting for co. Down in the Irish parliament, he sat for Tregony (1794–6) in the English parliament, and in 1795 he seconded the address in the English House of Commons. From May 1796 to July 1797 he was member for Orford, Suffolk, and then accepted the Chiltern Hundreds on taking office in Ireland. In February 1796 Thomas Pelham, second earl of Chichester [q. v.], chief secretary, returned to England owing to his rupture with Grattan's party, though he did not resign his office till April 1799. Stewart (now Lord Castlereagh by his father's elevation to an earldom in 1796) was on 25 July 1797 appointed by Lord Camden, the lord lieutenant, to the office of keeper of the privy seal, and was entrusted with the duties of the chief secretaryship in Ireland in Pelham's absence, succeeding to the office when Pelham resigned (November 1798). War with France and the outbreak of rebellion at home called for strong and prompt measures, and it fell to him to take many of the necessary steps, the officials of Dublin Castle being unable to deal with such a crisis. He received timely information of the plans of the rebels, and ordered the arrest of the leaders before the day fixed for the outbreak. He was thus largely responsible for the administration during the conspiracy of the United Irishmen, and was frequently accused of encouraging and ordering inhuman punishments. That he was completely guiltless of this charge even Brougham admits; indeed it was his repeated and urgent demands that at length obtained the despatch from England of a proper military force. The substitution of regular troops for the disorderly Irish militia then enabled him in some degree to check the cruelties and excesses which had been perpetrated. The substitution of Lord Cornwallis for Lord Camden in the lord-lieutenancy gave vigour to the administration. The battle of Vinegar Hill broke the strength of the insurgents. Even the landing of the French troops under General Humbert, and his success at Castlebar on 27 Aug. 1798, failed to restore the cause of the rebels. Of Lord Castlereagh's services during this time Lord Cornwallis reported in warm terms of appreciation (*Cornwallis Correspondence*, ii. 359, 439). A liberal amnesty was recommended by Cornwallis and Castlereagh even before the rebellion was at an end; but under pressure from the English government, which thought them unduly lenient, it was granted in a much less generous form.

It was the preparation of a scheme for the union of Great Britain and Ireland, to be followed by a measure of Roman catholic emancipation, which led to the resignation of Pelham, who was hostile to any further concession. Castlereagh's views made him a suitable person to forward the government's policy, and, in spite of the rule that the chief secretary should not be an Irishman, Pitt, on his own knowledge of Castlereagh's talent and recent services, as well as upon Lord Cornwallis's recommendation, made him Pelham's successor. To carry an act of union with the rebellion hardly extinguished was a hard task, but to carry it by protestant votes as the precursor of an emancipation measure was harder still. First the Dublin bar, and then the citizens of Dublin generally, denounced any project of union; the Roman catholics were at best indifferent. But Castlereagh pressed vigorously on. He visited London, and laid his views before the ministry. Having regard

to the aggressive policy of the French republic, Ireland, he argued, must be secured by an incorporating union, and that without the loss of a single session. If the catholics could win over the protestant freeholders to a policy of separation, it would be beyond the power of England to maintain her hold on Ireland. The bill which he was accordingly authorised to introduce was, even in its details, drawn in accordance with his own views; but it gained less and less favour the better it was known. All classes in Dublin feared the personal loss that would follow if the centre of political affairs were removed to London; and the catholics, though they saw a prospect of immediate gain in the substitution of English influence for protestant ascendency, saw also that there could be no hope, after a union, of ultimately securing a similar ascendency for themselves. The best argument for the measure, the rottenness of the existing system of government, was one on which it best beseemed the present members of that government to be silent. The borough proprietors and the members of parliament who had sunk large sums in buying their seats were almost unanimously hostile, and estimated their certain pecuniary loss at an aggregate of 1,500,000*l*. Under these circumstances any course was attended by many evils; none was likely to be an unmixed good. If emancipation was to precede union, the Roman catholics could not be withheld from supporting a separate parliament in order to secure an opportunity of taking vengeance on their opponents; if it accompanied union, all hope of protestant support was gone. If an act of union passed without emancipation, a new crop of difficulties would be sown. Reluctantly Lord Castlereagh was driven to choose the third of these three courses; equally reluctantly Pitt was brought to the same way of thinking. Even so Castlereagh perceived that success was hopeless if the government were either irresolute or scrupulous. He made up his mind and had his way. He secretly asked for money from England, and remittance after remittance was sent him.

The British parliament passed the bill without difficulty; but, much to Castlereagh's disappointment, the Irish House of Commons passed, though only by a majority of two, on 22 Jan. 1799, George Ponsonby's resolution 'that the house would be ready to enter into any measure short of surrendering their free, resident, and independent legislature as established in 1782.' Still he was undeterred. His temper, a happy mixture of suavity and obstinacy, stood him in good stead; he kept his head and persevered, and Lord Cornwallis, though despondent, supported him. The Duke of Portland expressed approval of his tone and conduct. It was announced that the government meant to proceed at all costs.

Now began a traffic most skilfully conducted by Castlereagh, while Cornwallis held aloof. The votes that argument could not win and patriotism could not secure were bought. Though money compensation for extinguished seats was indeed granted irrespective of votes, and money was not directly paid for votes to any considerable extent, pensions and promotions and advancements in the peerage were freely promised. The only justification for such procedure is that, while it did not affect the principle or policy of the union, it secured it. To the difficulties of these negotiations was added the danger of a fresh rising in view of the renewed plans for a French invasion. Some modifications of the bill had also to be arranged with the English cabinet as regarded the adjustment of the public debt of the two countries, the position of the Roman catholic peers, and some other matters, and Castlereagh attended meetings of the English cabinet for this purpose. Thanks to these changes and to the other influences at work, Castlereagh approached the session of 1800 with confidence. An amendment to the address was lost by forty-two votes. There followed a violent agitation outside of parliament and a series of bitter debates within it; and Castlereagh, though his supporters in the House of Commons might vote for him, had to find all the arguments and the eloquence for himself. His speeches were highly praised, and he kept his temper in public; but he was with difficulty dissuaded from challenging Grattan (BROUGHAM, Statesmen, ii. 113). To his dismay he saw his majorities sinking and his supporters flinching from their bargains. The belief that this was due to more open-handed corruption by his opponents was small consolation, but at length, after four months of conflict, the bill passed the Irish House of Commons on 7 June 1800 by a majority of 65, and the House of Lords by 69.

The bill being safe and the country tranquil, the difficult task began of performing the bargains and distributing the rewards. The English ministry declined to recommend to the king more than half of the peerages promised by Cornwallis and Castlereagh, but gave way when they threatened to resign on 17 and 18 June. Places of profit were also given or promised

as rewards for supporting the bill. Castlereagh himself waived any claim for reward, but the king promised that his father should be advanced to the peerage of the United Kingdom whenever he or his son chose. Although Castlereagh had carefully avoided giving any pledges that an emancipation measure should follow the act of union, his opinion as to its justice and necessity was known, and he had written a tract in favour of the Roman catholic claims and planned the establishment of the Roman church in Ireland. He now visited London to press for the introduction of a bill, and the catholic party in Ireland looked for one with confidence. But the king was obdurate; he had only recently heard the views of Pitt and Castlereagh on this point, and he would not accept them. Pitt resigned, and Castlereagh followed his example, holding office, however, till 21 May 1801, when his successor, Charles Abbot (afterwards first Baron Colchester) [q. v.] arrived in Ireland. As a member of the united parliament Castlereagh had removed to London. His recent labours and anxieties brought on severe attacks of fever there, and his health was for some time impaired.

Castlereagh now sat in the imperial parliament for co. Down, and held that seat till July 1805. He was then defeated, and elected for Boroughbridge in Yorkshire in January 1806, for Plympton-Earl in Devonshire in November 1806, and for county Down again in 1812, 1818, and 1820; and on succeeding to the Irish peerage he was elected for Orford in April 1821.

Castlereagh soon came into intimate relations with Pitt again, and adopted his plans and policy, especially in foreign affairs. Though he held no official position, the Addington administration entrusted to him the conduct of its two chief Irish measures in the House of Commons in 1801—the Suppression of Rebellion Act and the Suspension of Habeas Corpus Act. He prepared and submitted to the government elaborate memoirs upon the danger of continuing the exclusion of catholics from parliament in view of a French invasion, and of levying tithes for the protestant clergy in kind. He prepared plans for the commutation of tithes, he recommended the payment of state salaries to the Roman catholic clergy, and the erection of fortifications in different parts of Ireland. His capacity for affairs was so evident that in 1802, in spite of his views on the Roman catholic question, he received, under pressure from Pitt, and accepted the offer of the presidency of the (East India) board of control, with a seat in the cabinet, and kissed hands on 17 July.

From this time he ceased to be specially concerned with Irish affairs, and became chiefly engrossed in foreign concerns. His position in the Addington cabinet was the more important, in that his intimacy with Pitt made him in some degree Pitt's mouthpiece. Within a few months he was almost the leading member of the cabinet on questions of foreign policy, though officially still only connected with India. He was strongly for the retention of Malta after the peace of Amiens, in spite of the pledges given for its evacuation, and his minute stating the grounds for renewing the war was adopted by the ministry as its collective justification of its policy. He formed also a strong friendship and admiration for Lord Wellesley, supported him against the court of directors, and obtained their reluctant sanction for his annexation in the Carnatic and Oudh. He had to mediate between the cabinet, which desired to reduce the Indian army, and the governorgeneral, whose policy urgently demanded its increase, to obtain fresh supplies of silver for the Indian treasury, and at the same time to check the growth of its debt; but he performed his difficult task with skill. Less resolution on his part might have crippled the empire in India, and only his unfailing courtesy and temper could have conciliated so many conflicting powers. He had charge also of the negotiations, then of considerable importance, with the court of Persia. When Pitt succeeded Addington in May 1804, he felt Castlereagh to be too valuable to India to be removed from the board of control, and accordingly, without laying down his other office, Castlereagh in July 1805 succeeded Lord Camden as secretary of state for the war and colonial department. It was on seeking re-election for co. Down that he was defeated, and compelled for several years to sit for an English seat.

As secretary of war he showed himself something of an amateur strategist, and plunged eagerly into the plans for setting fire to the Boulogne flotilla by means of fireships called catamarans, but they did not succeed. He was responsible for the organisation and despatch of the force sent to the Elbe in October 1805, and must bear a large share of the blame for its too tardy arrival. The battle of Austerlitz compelled its return almost as soon as it had landed. Taught, however, by experience, he now grasped the fact that the British army, if it was to lend effective assistance to the continent at all, must be employed in force, and for large and definite objects, and not in scattered and desultory expeditions. He prepared minutes showing that, without endangering home defences, sixty thousand British troops could take the offensive, and, thanks to the command of the sea, could choose their own sphere of operations. Nothing, however, could be done with these objects before Pitt died in January 1806. During Grenville's government which followed Castlereagh was active in opposition, taking foreign affairs as his department, while Perceval attacked the ministry on home questions. When Grenville's ministry fell in March 1807, Castlereagh returned to his former place of secretary at war in the Duke of Portland's ministry, and a more active co-operation with the continental powers at once began. Money and stores were promptly despatched; treaties were entered into for the assistance of Prussia; but again, before anything could be done, the battle of Friedland (14 June 1807) and the treaty of Tilsit detached Russia and left Great Britain isolated. The Copenhagen expedition followed, and the Danish fleet having been secured, Castlereagh transferred the troops which had been employed in Denmark to Gothenburg in Sweden, and prevented the Swedish fleet from falling into the hands of Napoleon. The Russian fleet was thus shut in at Cronstadt; the Baltic remained under the control of Great Britain, and the naval combination which Napoleon had prepared by the secret articles of the treaty of Tilsit was frustrated as far as the north of Europe was concerned. Castlereagh now directed the attention of the ministry to the same objects in southern Europe. The maritime strength of Spain was derived from her connection with her Eastern and American colonies, and, though broken at Trafalgar, might now, unless the attempt were forestalled, be revived by Napoleon. Castlereagh had been in communication with Sir Arthur Wellesley on this subject since November 1806. Canning and Castlereagh anticipated Napoleon's design for seizing the naval force of Portugal by bringing about the prince regent's withdrawal with it and the royal family to Brazil on 27 Nov. 1807.

The recruiting for the army proving now very insufficient to maintain the forces at the height of the establishment authorised by parliament, Castlereagh next devoted himself to a new organisation of the army, by which the regular army was to be fed by volunteering from the militia as well as by recruiting, and kept up to a level of over two hundred thousand men. This plan was adopted by the cabinet and acted on till the end of the war. At the outbreak of the

Spanish war the army was thus both larger and better supplied than at any previous time. In anticipation of this Castlereagh had been preparing transports and disposing troops for prompt embarkation, and, after considering an attack on Boulogne, he prepared the expedition to Portugal. He endeavoured to obtain its command for Sir Arthur Wellesley, whose genius he had quickly divined; but he could only prevail so far with the military authorities as to have him appointed to the command of the detachment from Cork which sailed first, to be superseded in due course as the others, with commanders senior to him, should arrive in Portugal. He approved both of the convention of Cintra and the advance of Sir John Moore. Adopting Wellesley's views rather than Moore's, he determined upon a stubborn defence of Portugal, and had prepared reinforcements, when the news of the disaster at Coruña arrived, and the remains of the force returned home. He now carried the cabinet with him in his determination to persevere in the war, raised the forces at Lisbon to twenty thousand men, and sent Wellesley out again on 14 April 1809. He set himself still further to increase the regular army by dividing every regiment of the line into two battalions, the first of volunteer recruits forming the regular army for service at home and abroad, the second to be raised in the different counties by ballot, forming a militia for service at home only. This raised the total forces to 532,000; the plan was in substance carried out, and during the rest of the war worked admirably. The battalions of the regulars supplied the gaps in the Peninsula army; the regulars were fed by volunteering from the militia; the militia was kept up partly by voluntary recruiting and partly by balloting for service.

The prolonged operation of making the base in Portugal first of all impregnable in itself, and then a starting-point for advance into Spain, had now begun; and Castlereagh's statesmanship, which had seen how Napoleon's naval combination in the Baltic might be thwarted by a moderate but promptly disposable force, had thus with similar means prevented any combination in the south. Castlereagh had proved the superiority of his strategy over that of his contemporaries; he had now to show how he could cope with protracted scarcity of transport, of supplies, and of specie. Of these Portugal itself was practically bare : Great Britain had to supply almost everything. But from this time fortune was against him. To complete his scheme of engaging Napoleon's European front at all available points, he proposed

to despatch an expedition against its centre and to seize the island of Walcheren. Antwerp was Napoleon's great naval establishment, and there he was building a fleet. In addition to the chance of ending the French naval schemes, a blow in the Low Countries might encourage the German states to further efforts. The plans were prepared by Castlereagh even as early as April 1807, and were brought forward again in April 1809; but the cabinet long resisted and delayed till many opportunities had been lost. But no doubt it was a grave proposal to send nearly forty thousand men to Belgium, when there were already twenty thousand in Portugal and the burden of the war was so heavy. Delay was caused also by the scandals which ousted the Duke of York from the commandership-in-chief, and when the expedition set sail at the end of July 1809, the chance of spurring Prussia and north Germany to action had been destroyed at Wagram. Napoleon had, however, been obliged to denude the Low Countries of troops, and Antwerp seemed open to Castlereagh's great force of thirty-five sail of the line, besides frigates, and nearly forty thousand troops of all arms. Knowing that the attack was unexpected, Castlereagh urged speed on Lord Chatham [see PITT, JOHN, second EARL], whom the king's influence had placed in command. His plan was to regard the expedition as a coup de main, and to invest Flushing and Antwerp simultaneously. If this were done, there were still good prospects of success. The board of admiralty, however, insisted that Flushing must be taken before Antwerp could be attacked, and the fourteen days that were spent in taking Flushing gave Napoleon time to mature the defence of Antwerp. Dissensions then broke out between the English military and naval commanders (Chatham and Sir Richard John Strachan [q. v.]); fever decimated the troops, and early in September the expedition ignominiously returned home without achieving any part of the brilliant successes at which Castlereagh had aimed. Still, the French themselves recognised that with proper promptitude the British must have seized Antwerp and the French fleet there, and it was on the fever, soon to break out if the expedition delayed, that Napoleon counted for its defeat.

The Walcheren expedition was known to be Castlereagh's scheme. Canning and Wellesley thought that for its sake he had starved the Peninsula expedition, and had sent to Holland troops that were urgently needed in Portugal. Its failure was conspicuously due to incompetence somewhere, and its disastrous losses lacked even the compensation of brilliant feats of arms. The public was determined to find a scapegoat, and they found one in Castlereagh. His unpopularity was increased by the fact that the British, in spite of the victory of Talavera, had been compelled to retire behind the Tagus, and by the news of extensive sickness and mortality in the Peninsula army. Hence, when he fell through dissensions in the cabinet, he fell unlamented.

The events of 1809, which led to the quarrel between Canning, the foreign secretary, and Castlereagh, are obscure. Whoever was responsible for the way in which Castlereagh's colleagues treated him, he certainly had the right to deem himself ill-used. Canning and he administered departments whose duties overlapped, and for some time there had been friction and probably rivalry between them. Castlereagh had carried the cabinet with him in supporting the convention of Cintra; and Canning, who took the opposite view, was not only overborne, but thought that insufficient regard had been had to his position as foreign secretary. As early as the end of March 1809 Canning had told the prime minister, the Duke of Portland, that rather than go on as the ministry then was going on, he would resign. Apparently he did not name, but certainly he must have indicated, Castlereagh as the difficulty before him. The duke consulted the king, who appears to have suggested that, if Canning would hold his hand, Castlereagh might be removed to another office at the end of the session. Portland, afraid of the shock his ministry must sustain by any change, procrastinated, and by a reticence, which may have been due to misunderstanding but looks very much like treachery, Castlereagh was kept in complete ignorance of what was going on. In the House of Commons he was being attacked as to his disposal of Indian patronage in Lord Clancarty's case (LORD COLCHESTER, *Diaries*, ii. 178) and his intervention in Maddock's election; and Canning naturally thought he had gone too far in the former matter, and would do well to retire. Parliament was prorogued on 21 June, and the Walcheren expedition was then agreed upon. No hint reached Castlereagh that his colleagues, when agreeing to his plan, had already arranged for his removal. Canning chafed and protested against both the secrecy and delay. Perceval, the chancellor of the exchequer, was then for the first time told of what was in contemplation, and pointed out that, after adopting the military plan, the ministry could not honourably drop its author. Matters drifted on. The Wal-

cheren expedition failed; on 2 Sept. was published Chatham's despatch abandoning the attempt on Antwerp. The Duke of Portland was in ill-health, and, as he was on the eve of resignation, there was probably some fishing in troubled waters among his possible successors. At length, almost by accident, dining with Lord Camden, Castlereagh was told that he was to go. An offer was indeed made him of the office of president of the council, but though he consented to resign, he declined any other post. Perceval then showed him the letters that had been written by Canning on the subject, and Castlereagh thus first learnt that for months, during the Talavera campaign and the Walcheren expedition, he had been allowed to go on in ignorance that his colleagues had already resolved to supersede him. Fastening the blame for the whole affair on Canning, he sent him a challenge, and a duel took place on Putney Heath on 21 Sept., in which Canning was slightly wounded in the thigh. Both rivals then quitted the ministry.

During his tenure of the war office, in spite of checks and disasters, Castlereagh, largely by his own exertions and policy, had altered England's position from one of isolation after Tilsit to one in which headway against Napoleon was being made, though slowly, still on a comprehensive scale. He had begun that combination of forces by sea and land which ultimately wore out the power of the Napoleonic empire. The design was, however, too bold to be popular either with his colleagues or with the country. It abandoned alike Fox's policy of holding aloof from continental alliances and Pitt's series of desultory operations; and, though events proved that the offensive abroad was the only successful means of defence at home, nothing but successes at the outset, instead of the failures which were actually met with, would have won for it general support.

Castlereagh remained out of office during the greater part of Perceval's premiership. He assumed no ill-natured attitude to Perceval's ministry, and spoke frequently with effect in the House of Commons. On the regency question, at the end of 1810, he supported the restrictions on the regent's powers, and, in spite of the treatment he had received, defended the ministerial resolve to continue the Peninsular war when it was attacked by the whigs. On 1 Feb. 1810 he warmly praised Lord Wellington's character and conduct of the campaign of Talavera, and again defended the whole policy of the Peninsular war on 4 March 1811. When the difficulty of procuring specie became almost insuperable, and England was drained of gold coin, he was a member of the bullion committee which was appointed to inquire into the question, and when, in spite of his efforts, the committee reported in favour of an early resumption of cash payments, he vigorously defended Vansittart's resolution in favour of continuing the suspension of cash payments till six months after the conclusion of a general peace. The debate took place in May 1811, the report of the committee was rejected, and Vansittart's resolutions adopted, though not by very large majorities, on 9 and 15 May. Whatever may be said of his policy from the point of view of political economy and finance, there can be no doubt that the critical moment of the Peninsular war was no time to select for the great disturbances that the resumption of cash payments was certain to bring about whenever it took place. In the debate on the Roman catholic claims on 4 Feb. 1812 he declared himself favourable to concession if accompanied by adequate securities, though subsequently in March he pronounced, as a minister, against any step being taken for the present.

For some time pressure had been brought to bear on him to accept elevation to the House of Lords, but he resolutely refused, and with good reason. The ministerial changes which followed Wellesley's resignation restored him to office on 28 Feb. 1812. He became foreign secretary, and held that post till he died. To these duties were added, on Perceval's assassination in May 1812, those of leader of the House of Commons, in spite of Canning's claims and objections. Only a man of indomitable industry could have borne such a strain so long continued; undoubtedly it led to his death. On 16 June Brougham moved the repeal of the orders in council, and, in the face of the widespread distress in the country and the loss of the north American trade, Castlereagh found it hard to support their continuance. He defended them historically, and declared that their consequence had been beneficial and in accordance with the design of the ministry responsible for them; but the American Non-intercourse Act had not been foreseen, and had done England immense harm. The orders would therefore be for the present cancelled. This was done on 23 June, but not in time to procure the repeal of that act in the United States, or to prevent the outbreak of war with America. His resolution and tenacity soon made themselves felt in the cabinet, over which his strong will completely asserted itself. The ministry resolved to prosecute the war with vigour, and by the autumn the forces in the Peninsula were increased by twenty thousand men.

Napoleon's offers of terms of peace in April were promptly refused, since they did not provide for the restoration of Ferdinand VII to the throne of Spain. Preparations were made for renewed activity in Sicily and Italy, and Castlereagh set himself to strengthen and assist the Russian emperor, and to overcome his incredulity and distrust of English promises and suggestions. Thanks to his timely revelation to Turkey of the secret articles of the treaty of Tilsit, a peace was signed between Russia and Turkey, 28 May 1812, the Porte preferring an accommodation with Russia to witnessing the complete triumph of Napoleon and his liberation for the prosecution of his designs against the east. A treaty between Russia and Great Britain was concluded on 18 July. Sweden, too, had to be detached from its alliance with Napoleon, though the price demanded—the separation of Norway from Napoleon's ally, Denmark, and its union with Sweden—was felt to be high. Accordingly treaties were concluded in April between Sweden and Russia, with the knowledge and assistance of Lord Castlereagh, though he declined to make Great Britain a formal party to them, and on 12 July peace was concluded between Great Britain and Sweden, and the harbours of Sweden were again thrown open to English ships. Thus by the end of 1812 Castlereagh had placed the struggle with Napoleon, as far as England's share in it went, on a new and extended basis.

Castlereagh's main object was now to maintain in full vigour the coalition of the northern powers. Singly he knew none could make head against France, and during the previous ten years they had severally so often made their own terms, or pursued their own individual objects, that to keep them in line and united was a heavy diplomatic task. Both personally and through his brother Sir Charles William Stewart (afterwards third Marquis of Londonderry) [q. v.] and Lord Cathcart he laboured at this work unceasingly. At his instance the British government raised its subsidies to foreign powers for 1813 to 10,000,000*l.*, though the year's expenditure reached 117,000,000*l.*, and its own troops under arms numbered 155,000 men (*Parl. Debates*, xxvii. 86). A force was despatched under Sir Thomas Graham (afterwards Lord Lynedoch) [q. v.] to the Scheldt. The terms of peace proposed at Frankfort, though Castlereagh had been at first disposed to acquiesce in them in November 1813, were later on vigorously opposed by him through Lord Aberdeen, the British ambassador to the Austrian court at Frankfort, and at length, on 31 Dec., he left England himself for the allied headquarters as British minister plenipotentiary.

He spent some time in Holland, on a mission to the Prince of Orange, and did not reach Basle till 18 Jan. 1814. So great was his personal influence, so important was the course England might take at this juncture, and so unlimited were his powers understood to be, that till his arrival the representatives of the allies would take no steps in negotiation. Nor was it easy to conciliate the jealousies and harmonise the conflicting interests of the different powers. Against the Emperor Alexander and his party, who wished to press on to Paris and make no peace till it had fallen, were ranged the Austrian adherents led by Metternich, who had no mind to complete the destruction of France, especially at the cost of so much exalting Russia. Castlereagh found the alliance almost on the point of breaking up. On 3 Feb. 1814 the congress assembled at Châtillon, but in form Lord Castlereagh was not a member of it. England was formally represented by Lords Cathcart and Aberdeen and by Sir Charles Stewart. The line taken by Lord Castlereagh was that peace ought to be concluded with Napoleon without ulterior dynastic motives, and that a Bourbon restoration must be brought about, if at all, by the force of circumstances, and not by the arms of the allies. His view prevailed with Russia and Prussia, and the negotiations proceeded without the abdication of Napoleon being demanded as a preliminary; and he subsequently carried the powers with him in his plan for the creation of a kingdom of the Low Countries, under the Prince of Orange, the Cape of Good Hope being ceded to Great Britain by way of compensation, and Venice to Austria. France was to be reduced to her dimensions as they existed in 1790, and the sovereigns of Spain and Portugal were to be restored to their thrones. The envoys of the allies were instructed to negotiate on these lines, and Lord Castlereagh at once established his influence by severing himself from all intrigue, and endeavouring to convince Napoleon's plenipotentiary, Caulaincourt, and the representatives of the powers that England was sincerely anxious for peace, and was willing to make great sacrifices to obtain it. These proposals were put forward on the 7th. Caulaincourt succeeded in gaining time for Napoleon to act, and the battle of Champaubert was won on 10 Feb., a victory through which Napoleon expected to force the allies shortly back across the Rhine. His successes on this and the following days did in fact add greatly to the dissensions already exist-

ing among the allies. To prevent open disunion, Castlereagh was obliged to take a firm tone with them. He pressed upon the Austrians a vigorous continuance of the war. He resisted the Russian demands for more money, and temporised with their proposals for a change of dynasty in France; he constrained Bernadotte to a more loyal support of the joint operations. He brought the allies to sign a new treaty of alliance on 1 March, the treaty of Chaumont, and did not shrink from pledging Great Britain to maintain one hundred and fifty thousand men in the field, and to contribute to the resources of the other powers 5,000,000l. sterling per annum. The secret terms of this treaty, as to the territorial rearrangement of Europe beyond the dominions of the allies, subsequently became the basis of the treaty of Vienna, but from this point the negotiations of Châtillon became less and less promising of any conclusion. Each side rejected the other's proposals, and the congress eventually broke up on 18 March. Though the prospects of peace were thus for the time being overcast, and Lord Castlereagh's mission had failed of success, there can be little doubt that but for his presence with the allied sovereigns in Germany in February and March 1814, and his mingled firmness, resource, persuasiveness, and personal influence, the alliance would have broken up, and combined action against Napoleon would have ceased.

When the congress of Châtillon terminated, Castlereagh went to the headquarters of the emperor of Austria at Dijon, and remained there till after Napoleon's abdication at Fontainebleau. He was principally occupied during this time in negotiating the future arrangements of Italy, where matters were complicated, as far as Great Britain's course was concerned, by the unauthorised act of Lord William Bentinck in April in proclaiming the re-establishment of the Genoese constitution, contrary to Castlereagh's instruction from Dijon. He arrived in Paris on 10 April, and on the following day signed the preliminaries of peace of 30 March, but with a reservation that Great Britain answered for its own obligations only, and not for those of other powers. Castlereagh was in fact wholly opposed to the title of emperor and the position in Elba assigned to Napoleon, foreseeing that he must there be a source of danger to Europe. The final adjustment of European questions was reserved to the congress shortly to be held at Vienna. Wellington became British ambassador in Paris, and Castlereagh returned home and received the order of the Garter (installed 28 June 1814).

A A

The congress of Vienna assembled in September 1814, and, with his brother, Sir Charles Stewart (now Lord Stewart), ambassador at Vienna, Lord Castlereagh represented Great Britain. His policy was now to secure the permanence of peace by the restoration of the Bourbon monarchy, by limiting France to its prerevolutionary frontiers, by discouraging the revolutionary elements in Europe, and by checking the growing power of Russia. With the latter object he desired therefore to restore the German confederation and the kingdom of Poland, and so to maintain the balance of power; and in order to consolidate the power of Germany, he was for increasing the resources of the two chief German states, Prussia and Austria, by giving the former Saxony, which had deserved hard treatment by its support of Napoleon, and the latter north Italy, where it was supposed no native state could be permanently established strong enough to resist the neighbouring power of France. For these ends he was prepared to risk the charges of spoliation and disregard of the rights of nationalities. Norway, too, was to be annexed to Sweden, and so with an independent Poland two strong powers would be formed to keep a check over Russia. No doubt this plan wholly disregarded the feelings of the minor peoples of Europe, but it had for its principal object the old ideal of European statesmen, the maintenance of the balance of power as the best security against such a dangerous ascendency of one nation as had been recently seen in the Napoleonic empire.

Castlereagh had not the good fortune to see this policy fully carried out. The czar desired indeed a restored Poland, of which it was to be one of which he should himself be hereditary king. Castlereagh found few supporters of a free Poland, nor did this article of his scheme excite any enthusiasm at home. He secured the admission of France to the congress, but, to his disappointment, Talleyrand gave him little support, and the united Germany he desired seemed as little likely to be created as an independent Poland. Prussia, in return for aid on the Saxon question, sided with the czar, and Austria was alike opposed to any increase of Prussian power and any surrender of the Polish territory. The English people at the moment were chiefly interested in the abolition of the slave trade, and were neither clearly set on territorial gains for Great Britain, nor eager for any particular arrangement of Europe. Castlereagh thus found his hands tied by feeling on this subject at home which demanded the instant abolition of the slave trade as the condition of the retrocession of the Dutch

and French colonies, while to this abolition Talleyrand, whose aid was required elsewhere, offered a steady opposition. The Polish question almost provoked a renewal of the war. The czar occupied Poland with his troops even while the congress was sitting, and handed over Saxony to the king of Prussia. As Great Britain was more concerned in general peace than in particular partitions, Castlereagh was now instructed by the British cabinet to endeavour to bring about a compromise, by which some part of Saxony at least might be retained to its royal family. Having failed after various interviews to shake the resolution of the czar, he set to work to detach Prussia from its Russian alliance by bringing his influence to bear on the Prussian ministers, and through them on the Prussian king. His arguments were supported by Talleyrand and Metternich, but for a considerable time the czar was immovable, and the king of Prussia could not be detached from him. Wellington, as early as the end of September, had formed the opinion that war was inevitable, and now Bavaria and France increased their forces, the Austrian troops were concentrated, and, at Castlereagh's instance, a treaty, offensive and defensive, was agreed to between Great Britain, France, and Austria on 3 Jan. 1815.

This bold act turned the scale, and at this juncture an important point was gained by the conclusion at Ghent of a treaty of peace between Great Britain and the United States, thanks to the conciliatory policy laid down by Lord Castlereagh for the British commissioners. The liberation thus effected of a British army and the discovery by the czar of the treaty of 3 Jan. led at length to a compromise. The Polish question was settled by conceding to Prussia a defensible frontier against Russia, limiting the Russian claims on Austrian Poland, and leaving to the czar Warsaw and its province. Castlereagh so far prevailed for the Poles as to procure for them the grant of a constitution on paper; but as no one else was much concerned for them, he could do no more, and was practically defeated on this point. A settlement of the Saxon and other questions soon followed. Luxembourg was annexed to the Netherlands, as the most feasible, if not the best, mode of preventing a future expansion of France into the Low Countries; and the same paramount necessity of securing Italy against French ambition led Castlereagh, in spite of the British pledges given by Lord William Bentinck to the Genoese, to favour the annexation of the reluctant Genoese to Piedmont. With regard to the abolition of the slave trade, Castlereagh found himself hampered as he had been in regard to the independence of Poland. Outside of England no one greatly desired it, and the colonial interests of France and Spain were ranged in opposition to it. He was himself a believer in the plan of gradually abolishing the trade by the imposition of high import duties, and was accused of having flinched from pressing the total abolition at Vienna as vigorously as he might have done. Probably there was little justice in the charge; at any rate, after much patient negotiation, he was obliged to be content with undertakings for its abolition by France and Spain within a fixed term of years. He quitted Vienna on 15 Feb. 1815, having been urgently pressed from home to return for the meeting of parliament, where the government felt his assistance to be indispensable. On his way he visited Paris, and, thanks to his personal influence with Louis XVIII, successfully negotiated the questions in dispute as to the duchy of Parma. He landed at Dover on 3 March amid demonstrations of welcome, applauded as the negotiator of a European peace. At that moment Napoleon was advancing towards Paris.

Castlereagh, on hearing this new danger, at once apprehended its gravity, and urged on Wellington the promptest action. The treaty of Chaumont of the previous year was put in force, and Castlereagh authorised Lord Clancarty at Vienna to sign a further treaty binding Great Britain to pay 5,000,000l. as a subsidy and over 2,000,000l. in lieu of the contingent which the treaty of Chaumont required her to bring into the field. By his speeches in the House of Commons he awoke public feeling to the necessity of a renewal of the war, though he brought odium on himself, and even a street attack by a mob in June. He laboured to provide men and money for a campaign, and to bring the allied sovereigns into the field. On 8 April, to Napoleon's great indignation, he refused his offers, made through Caulaincourt, for a separate accommodation with England. After Waterloo he returned to Paris, and by his resolute remonstrances moderated Blücher's violent plans for taking vengeance on Paris. On the question of restoring to their former possessors the works of art plundered by the French armies abroad, he succeeded in restraining the allies from making reprisals on native French collections. The treaty of Vienna, substantially embodying the terms settled before his return to England, was finally signed on 9 June 1816. He was much attacked because

in return for the efforts and sacrifices made and the part played by Great Britain so little was secured for her by the peace. Probably he was right in thinking that England was more interested in European peace and security than in particular acquisitions. Still, one term to which he consented he found few defenders: he restored Java to the Dutch, it was said because he could not find it on the map, and therefore did not know what to say about it; in reality he relinquished it in pursuance of his general policy of maintaining the influence of Great Britain in the task of settling the future of Europe by the most complete demonstration possible of her own disinterestedness. The selection of St. Helena as the place of Napoleon's internment was due to him; and he settled the terms of his confinement, if not very magnanimously, still with keen regard to his safekeeping. With regard to the terms to be enforced on France, Castlereagh was in negotiation for some months longer, and did not conclude the agreement with Prince Nesselrode till 20 Nov. 1815. He had considerable difficulty, not only with the German powers, but with his colleagues at home, in preventing France from being treated with a severity which would have made against, and not for, the prospects of future peace; but, supported by Nesselrode and Wellington, he at length succeeded, and France was simply reduced to her position of 1790.

The year 1815 was the zenith of Castlereagh's career; from that time forward his popularity declined, and before long vanished. The social and financial questions that were forced to the front as soon as the war was over were difficult to deal with in any case, but he least of all men could handle them in a manner likely to conciliate public opinion generally. Though not the originator of the home policy of the government, still, as leader of the House of Commons (the home secretary, Lord Sidmouth, being in the House of Lords), he was always its mouthpiece, and was identified with all its acts of domestic as well as of foreign policy. He was fortunate neither in the policy he advocated nor in the arguments he employed. He defended the maintenance of a high income tax on 18 March 1816, and was defeated; but the continuance of the restriction of cash payments by the Bank of England was carried. He introduced the bill for the suspension of the Habeas Corpus Act on 24 Feb. 1817, nor was his reputation restored by his support in 1818 of the ministerial palliative for distress—the bill granting 1,000,000l. for the building of new churches. The extent

The labour of leading the House of Commons was in itself heavy, and after Lord Sidmouth's retirement from office in 1821 he also undertook the duty of superintending the home office, as he had done for Lord Liverpool early in 1800. Throughout June and July of 1822 his mind was visibly overwrought, and he suffered also acutely from gout. His usually neat handwriting was hardly legible; he forgot appointments. It was remarked in the House of Commons that he denied all knowledge of a document which was actually lying before him. On 9 Aug. he had an audience of the king, at which the king was so struck with his manner that he recommended him to consult a physician. Later in the same day the Duke of Wellington thought his case so serious that he wrote privately to Dr. Charles Bankhead (see under BANKHEAD, JOHN), Lord Londonderry's physician, warning him to take precautions (GLEIG, *Life of Wellington*, iii. 118). Dr. Bankhead was summoned to St. James's Square, and advised Lord Londonderry to go down to his country seat, North Cray Place, Kent, and there, having caused his razors to be removed, he remained in attendance. Lord Londonderry's mind continued affected, and on 12 Aug. he cut his throat with a penknife in his dressing-room, and died almost immediately. His death profoundly affected the public. After the inquest, at which a verdict of unsound mind was returned, his body was buried in Westminster Abbey on 20 Aug. between the graves of Pitt and Fox. There were some scandalous demonstrations when the hearse reached the abbey doors, but in the main the expression of public grief was unanimous. He had no children, and was succeeded in the title by his half-brother, Charles William, from whom Stewart. His widow died on 12 Feb. 1829, and eight days later was buried beside her husband in Westminster Abbey.

Few men have taken part in so many important events as did Lord Castlereagh in the quarter of a century that covers his public career; few men have been the victims of such constant and intense unpopularity. Yet the services which he rendered to his country and to Europe were signal. He bore a large part, and often the principal part, in crushing the Irish rebellion of 1798, in effecting the parliamentary union of Great Britain and Ireland, in initiating and in continuing the war in the Peninsula, in combining the great powers of Europe against Napoleon, and in resettling the affairs of Europe at Vienna. In manner he was cold; 'as for my friend Lord Castlereagh,' writes Lord Cornwallis,

'he is so cold that nothing can warm him' (*Correspondence*, iii. 506). This made him many social enemies, especially in Dublin in 1800, and to the end of his life it was a characteristic trait. 'Just and passionless' was Caulaincourt's description of him. He came in turn into collision with almost every party; he had his own way almost always, and was rewarded by being equally feared and hated. He was in collision with the Irish patriots on the union, with the Irish protestants on emancipation, with the whigs on the continuance of the war, with the radicals on popular rights and repressions, with the French legitimists when he was prepared to negotiate with Napoleon in 1814 without first pressing for his abdication, with the Holy Alliance at the time of the congress of Troppau. Even the English tory party looked somewhat askance on a statesman who was not an Englishman himself and was a self-made man. In domestic affairs it must be owned that Castlereagh's repressive system was outworn, and that many of the measures which he supported if he did not originate them, whatever might be said of them in the crisis of the war, were unjustifiable in time of peace. But there must be set to his credit his general comprehension of the strategic principles on which alone Napoleon could be combated, the knowledge of character and of war shown in his selection of Wellington for the Peninsular command, and his steady support of him in Portugal, and the moderation and wise disinterestedness, when, as almost the arbiter of Europe in 1815, he brought about a fairly durable settlement, and at least averted further war. He was no orator, though the stress of circumstances during the debates of 1798 and 1800 made him a fair speaker and a ready debater. His speeches were long, and he had a tendency to be tedious and confused, to mix metaphors, and to fall into indiscreet phrases, such as his well-known 'ignorant impatience of taxation' uttered in 1816; yet he 'never spoke ill,' was sensible and well informed, and could not be daunted or put down. In person he was tall and handsome, and was much admired; his manners were exquisitely and unfailingly courteous; his dress, like his personal bearing, was plain and simple. He spoke French slowly but correctly, and in dealing with kings and ministers possessed an invaluable combination of courtier-like suavity and invincible resolution. Constantly it happened that his strong will and unflinching courage dominated the cabinet (Lord Aberdeen to Bishop Wilberforce, *Life of S. Wilberforce*, ed. 1888, p. 396), and as he was indifferent alike to unpopularity or the reverse, his influence on the English history of the first twenty years of the century was greater even than it would seem to be on the surface. He was always calm and unruffled, punctual in his work, accumulating no arrears. He was neither guilty of nepotism in his appointments nor of corruption, though the expenses of his position exceeded his official salary and appointments, and trenched on a private income never very large. He was religious and charitable, a patron of letters, and one of the founders of the Dublin Gaelic Society; but his knowledge outside his public work was, owing to his exceedingly busy life, very scanty.

His portrait was painted by Sir Thomas Lawrence, and is engraved in the edition of his correspondence published in 1848, and there is also a half-length in the National Portrait Gallery.

[The principal authority for Lord Londonderry's life is his Correspondence, collected by his brother Charles, and published in twelve volumes in 1848-53, with a memoir. Sir Archibald Alison also had access to the family papers in preparing his unduly laudatory Lives of Lord Castlereagh and Sir Charles Stewart, 1861. For other information see Cornwallis's Correspondence: Burghersh's Memoir of the War of 1814; Wilson's Diary; Stanhope's Life of Pitt; Twiss's Life of Eldon; Lord Colchester's Diaries; Yonge's Life of Lord Liverpool; Seeley's Life and Times of Stein; Life of William Wilberforce. For instances of savage attack on him see Byron's Poetical Works, ed. 1855, epigram ii. 406, Dedication to Don Juan v. 275, 276, Preface to cantos 6, 7, and 8, vi. 78. For depreciatory criticism, Brougham's notice of him in Statesmen of George III, and Greville's character of him in Memoirs, 1st ser. i. 53; Scott gives an instance of his humanity in contrast to Blücher's cruelty, which he witnessed in 1815, Lockhart's Scott, iii. 371; and there is a curious anecdote of his courtesy in the Autobiography of Wolfe Tone, ii. 5.]   J. A. H.

STEWART, SIR ROBERT PRESCOTT (1825-1894), musician, born at Dublin on 16 Dec. 1825, was son of Charles Stewart, librarian of the King's Inn, Dublin. He was musically educated in the school attached to Christ Church Cathedral, of which church he became organist in 1844. He was also appointed in the same year organist to Trinity College, and in 1852 to St. Patrick's Cathedral, where he also was a vicar-choral. In 1846 Stewart became conductor of the Dublin University Choral Society, which presented him with his robes and a jewelled bâton when he graduated doctor of music in 1851. Ten years later he was created professor of music in Dublin University. In

1872 he declined an invitation to represent Ireland at the peace festival at Boston, U.S.A. In the same year he became professor of theory at the Royal Irish Academy of Music, and was knighted by Earl Spencer. In 1873 he was appointed conductor of the Dublin Philharmonic. He died at Dublin on 24 March 1894. He married, first, in 1846, Mary Anne, daughter of Peter Browne of Rahurs, Castlebar. She died on 7 Aug. 1887. Stewart married, secondly, on 9 Aug. 1888, Marie, daughter of Joseph Wheeler of Westlands, Queenstown.

Stewart was a remarkable organist and extemporiser, while his memory is said to have been phenomenal. His compositions, many of which gained prizes, are numerous, the most popular being his glees and church music. In 1870 an ode by Stewart was given at the Birmingham festival. The list of his published works includes a number of cantatas, songs, and organ music. Stewart delivered many series of lectures, including one on bagpipes, on which he was an acknowledged authority. To him belongs the credit of requiring candidates at Dublin for musical degrees to pass a literary test, an example followed some years later at Oxford and Cambridge. He was editor of the Irish 'Church Hymnal' (1876).

A portrait, painted by Sir T. A. Jones, belongs to the Royal Irish Academy of Music, and a statue was erected on Leinster Lawn, Dublin.

[Art. by Dr. J. C. Culwick in Musical News, 31 March and 12 May 1894; Brit. Mus. Biogr. 1897; Grove's Dict. of Music and Musicians, passim; manuscript life by O. J. Vignolles.]   R. H. L.

STEWART, WALTER (d. 1177), steward of Malcolm IV. [See under ROBERT II, king of Scotland.]

STEWART, WALTER, EARL OF ATHOLL (d. 1437), was the second son of King Robert II [q. v.], by his second wife, Euphemia Ross. Robert III [q. v.], Robert Stewart, first duke of Albany [q. v.], and Alexander Stewart, earl of Buchan [q. v.], were his half-brothers. Another son of King Robert II, named Walter, by his first wife, was still alive in July 1362, so that possibly the second Walter was born subsequently to this; but in any case as early as 19 Oct. 1378 he married Margaret, only daughter and heiress of Sir David de Barclay, lord of Brechin, with whom he obtained the estate and also the title of lord of Brechin (Reg. Mag. Sig. Scot. pp. 146, 147, quoted in BURNET's Preface to the Exchequer Rolls, vol. iv. p. clx). On 15 Nov. 1391 he had a safe-conduct to go to England with thirty attendants (*Cal. Documents relating to Scotland*, 1357-1509, No. 431), and he had similar safe-conducts on 5 Dec. 1391 (*ib.* No. 433), 10 Jan. 1402-3 (*ib.* No. 627), and 8 June 1404, in the last instance that he might make a pilgrimage to the shrine of Thomas of Canterbury (*ib.* No. 656). In 1398 and 1400 he received a hundred marks as keeper of Edinburgh Castle (*Exchequer Rolls*, iii. 437, 487). He had a charter of the earldom of Caithness, on the resignation of his niece Euphemia, countess palatine of Strathearn, and is so designated in July 1402 (*ib.* iii. 545). In charters of 20 Oct. 1416 and 22 Aug. 1421 he is also mentioned as tutor of Malise, earl of Strathearn [q. v.] (*Hist. MSS.* 7th Rep. p. 706). In the safe-conduct of 8 June 1404 he is designated Earl of Atholl and Caithness, the earldom of Atholl having been previously vested in his father, Robert II. On 22 Sept. 1409 he received from the regent Albany a grant of the barony of Cortachy in Forfarshire. He took a leading part in the movement for the return of James I to Scotland in 1424; was a conservator for Scotland of the truce with England, signed 28 March (*Cal. Documents relating to Scotland*, 1357-1509, No. 949); and at the same time gave surety in twelve hundred marks that his son David would remain a hostage in England for King James's ransom (*ib.* No. 950). He was also one of the jury which after the king's return condemned Murdac Stewart, second duke of Albany [q. v.] On 22 July 1427 he had a grant of the earldom of Strathearn for life (*Reg. Mag. Sig. Scot.* i. No. 93), and on 15 May 1430 he resigned the earldom of Caithness in favour of his son Alexander. In 1437 he engaged in the plot for the assassination of James I, in order that his grandson, Sir Robert Stewart, chamberlain to the king, might succeed to the crown. It was successful so far as the king's assassination was concerned; but the cruel deed in the Blackfriars monastery, on 20 Feb., was approved of by few except those immediately concerned in it. Atholl was captured by the Earl of Angus, and, along with the other conspirators, was put to death in April 1437 after enduring unspeakable tortures. He affirmed that although he had been made aware of the conspiracy, he had used every endeavour to persuade his grandson against it, and believed that he had succeeded. Before execution he was placed on a pillory, and, in bitter mockery of his supposed purpose, his head was encircled with a red-hot iron crown, on which was inscribed 'The king of traitors.' By his wife, Margaret, daughter of Sir David de Barclay, he had two sons: David, who

seems to have died before him in England, leaving a son, Sir Robert, conspirator with his grandfather; and Alan, in whose favour his father resigned the earldom of Caithness in 1430, and who was killed by Donald Balloch in 1431, leaving no issue.

[Exchequer Rolls of Scotland, vols. iii-iv.; Cal. Documents relating to Scotland, 1357-1509; Reg. Mag. Sig. Scot. vol. i.; Douglas's Scottish Peerage (Wood).]   T. F. H.

STEWART or STUART, WALTER, first LORD BLANTYRE (*d.* 1617), was son of Sir John Stewart of Minto (*d.* 1583), provost of Glasgow, by his second wife, Margaret, second daughter of James Stewart of Cardonald. The family descended from Sir Thomas Stewart (*d.* 1500), third son of Sir Thomas Stewart of Dalswinton and Garlies, progenitor of the earls of Galloway, who received from his father the lands of Minto, Sinlaws, and Merbottle, Roxburghshire, on 2 Nov. 1470. The elder Sir Thomas's eldest son, Sir John Stewart of Minto, was killed at the battle of Flodden in 1513, and his second son, William Stewart (1479-1545) [q. v.], was bishop of Aberdeen.

Walter (the great-grandson of Sir John who fell at Flodden) was educated with the young king, James VI, under George Buchanan (CRAWFORD, *Officers of State*, p. 393). He was designated prior of Blantyre in 1580, when he was nominated a gentleman of the bedchamber. On 28 Jan. 1580-1581 he, also as prior of Blantyre, subscribed the second confession of faith (CALDERWOOD, *History*, iii. 501). On 14 Nov. 1582 he was sworn a member of the privy council and appointed keeper of the privy seal. On 29 July 1583 he received a grant of the lands of Calderhall (*Reg. Mag. Sig. Scot.* 1580-93, No. 589), and on 3 Nov. 1587 of the lands and barony of Glasgow (*ib.* No. 1406). On 28 May 1593 he was chosen an extraordinary lord of session; in January 1595-6 he was appointed one of the commissioners of the treasury, known as octavians; and on 6 March 1595-6 he was promoted to the office of lord high treasurer, when he resigned the privy seal. In the same year he went to the west of Scotland to superintend the preparations for an expedition against Cantyre and the isles. On 18 Jan. 1598-9 he received a charter of the barony of Blantyre, Wrightslands, and Cardonald. For interfering on behalf of Robert Bruce in regard to a pension which Bruce had from the abbacy of Arbroath—or rather for interfering to prevent injustice to Bruce—he so incurred the displeasure of the king that, although the lords asserted that he had acted quite legally, the king not only ordered him into ward in the castle of Edinburgh, but desired him to demit the office of treasurer. He refused to do so until the king paid what he owed him; but, after being sent a prisoner to Inverness, he finally demitted his office on 17 April (CALDERWOOD, v. 733; *Reg. P. C. Scotl.* v. 549). After doing so he was, however, released, and on 11 March 1600 an act was passed recognising his long and faithful services (*ib.* vi. 92). In 1604 he was appointed one of the commissioners for the treaty of union between England and Scotland; and on 20 June 1605 he signed the letter commanding the Aberdeen assembly to dissolve (CALDERWOOD, vi. 281). On 10 July 1606 he was created a peer by the title of Lord Blantyre, and the same year he was appointed one of four delegates to reason with the imprisoned ministers and bring them to submission (*ib.* p. 375). He was an assessor at the trial, 12 Aug. 1608, of George Sprott [q. v.], for concealment of the Gowrie conspiracy, and also an assessor at the trial of Lord Balmerino, 4 March 1609. He was reconstituted an extraordinary lord of session, 13 Jan. 1610, and on 15 Nov. of the same year he was appointed an assessor of the treasury. He died on 8 March 1617. By his wife, Nichola (*d.* 1614), daughter of Sir James Somerville of Cambusnethan, he had three sons: William (*d.* 1638), who succeeded him as second Lord Blantyre, and was grandfather of Alexander Stewart, the fifth lord [q. v.]; Sir James, who fought a duel with Sir George Wharton at Islington on 8 Nov. 1609, when both combatants were killed (see *Gent. Mag.* 1800, ii. 1019); Walter, a doctor of medicine and father of Frances Teresa Stewart (la belle Stuart) [see STUART], and a daughter Anne, married to John, eighth lord Abernethy of Salton.

[Reg. P. C. Scotl.; Reg. Mag. Sig. Scot. 1580–93 and 1593–1610; Calderwood's Hist. of Scotland; Crawford's Officers of State; Douglas's Scottish Peerage (Wood), i. 213–14.] T. F. H.

STEWART, SIR WILLIAM (*d.* 1402), of Jedworth, sheriff of Teviotdale, was the son of John de Foresta, mentioned in a safe-conduct on 26 July 1368 (and descended from Sir John Stewart of Bonkyl, killed at Falkirk in 1298), by a daughter of Turnbull of Minto. A charter of the lands of Minto was granted by John Turnbull of Minto to Sir William Stewart his relative ('nepos') 8 Dec. 1380, and ratified by Robert III on 4 July 1390–1. The earls of Galloway trace their descent from this Sir William Stewart of Jedworth, and, on the ground that he is identical with Sir William Stewart of Castlemilk, they have been claimed as the repre-

sentatives of the Darnley line since the death of Cardinal York in 1807 [see HENRY BENEDICT MARIA CLEMENT]; but that the two Sir William Stewarts are different persons is clearly proved by the fact that the mother of Sir William Stewart of Castlemilk was Janet Keith, and by irrefragable evidence of their deaths at widely different dates. Sir William Stewart of Castlemilk, who has been claimed as the father of Sir John Stewart of Jedworth, and who was a son of Alexander Stewart of Darnley, was killed at the siege of Orleans on 12 Feb. 1428–9.

Sir William Stewart of Jedworth is mentioned in 1390 as an auditor of customs (*Exchequer Rolls*, iii. 219), and also, a little later in the same year, as clerk of audit (*ib.* p. 236). On 1 Oct. 1397 he received a command from Robert III to appoint a day for the English commission to meet on the marches for the redress of grievances and negotiation of a truce (*Cal. Documents relating to Scotland*, 1357–1509, No. 491), and in March 1398 he was named a deputy commissioner of the Scots to see to the observance of a truce agreed on until Michaelmas following (*ib.* No. 502). On 27 June of the same year he also received from Robert III a grant of a pension of forty marks annually for his life out of the customs of Edinburgh for loyalty and attachment (*Exchequer Rolls*, iii. 207). On 26 Oct. of the same year his name appears as a 'borow' of the Earl of Douglas for the bounds on the middle marches (*Cal. Documents relating to Scotland*, 1357–1509, No. 570), Sir William of Castlemilk being mentioned in November as 'borow' of Douglas for the west marches (*ib.* No. 512). Having been taken prisoner at Homildon Hill on 14 Sept. 1402, Sir William Stewart of Jedworth was accused by Hotspur of treason for having broken his allegiance to the English king. Two successive juries acquitted him of the charge, but Hotspur summoned a third, from which he succeeded in wringing a verdict in accordance with his wishes, and Stewart, having been sentenced to the death of a traitor, was immediately executed with appropriate tortures, his four quarters being placed on the gates of York. He left a son, Sir John Stewart, who married Marion Stewart, heiress of Garlies.

[Cal. Documents relating to Scotland, 1357–1509; Exchequer Rolls of Scotland, vol. iii.; Andrew Stuart's Genealogical Hist. of the Stewarts; Wynton's Chron.; Douglas's Scottish Peerage (Wood).] T. F. H.

STEWART, WILLIAM (1479–1545), bishop of Aberdeen, was the second son of Sir Thomas Stewart of Minto, of the family of Garlies, by Isabel, second daughter of Sir

Walter Stewart of Arthurlie. His elder brother, Sir John Stewart of Minto, was killed at Flodden on 9 Sept. 1513 [see under STEWART or STUART, WALTER, first LORD BLANTYRE]. He was born in Glasgow in 1479, and educated at the university there, where he took the degree of B.A., being a determinant in 1494, and licentiate in the following year. In accordance with the custom of the period, he probably studied canon law and theology abroad. He was successively parson of Lochmaben, rector of Ayr, and prebendary of Glasgow; and in 1527 he was made dean of Glasgow. On 2 Oct. 1530 he was named lord high treasurer of Scotland, and at the same time he obtained the provostry of Lincluden. On 14 Nov. 1532 he was elected bishop of Aberdeen. On 3 March 1533-4 he left Scotland as principal ambassador, with a large company of attendants, to treat of a peace with England (*Diurnal of Occurrents*, p. 17), and he returned, after a satisfactory embassy, on 3 July (*ib.* p. 18). On 5 Aug. he left on an embassy to France to treat regarding a marriage between James V and Marie de Bourbon (*ib.*) He resigned the treasurership in 1537, and died on 17 April 1545. According to the 'Album Amicorum Collegii Regii Aberdonensis' (*Fasti Aberd.* p. 533), Bishop Stewart built the library of King's College, Aberdeen, and furnished it with a number of books, and also built the jewel- or charter-house, as well as the vestry or chapter-house.

[Keith's Scottish Bishops; Crawford's Officers of State; Diurnal of Occurrents in the Bannatyne Club; Fasti Aberdonenses in the Spalding Club; Turnbull's Pref. to Hector Boece (Rolls Ser.)]

T. F. H.

STEWART, WILLIAM (1481?–1550?), Scots chronicler and verse-writer, born about 1481, was great-grandson of one of the illegitimate sons of Alexander Stewart, earl of Buchan [q. v.], and was thus descended from Robert II, king of Scotland. He was educated like his namesake, William Stewart (1479–1545) [q. v.] (afterwards bishop of Aberdeen), at St. Andrews, where apparently he was a determinant in 1499, and first of the licentiates in 1501. He was destined for the church, and possibly some of the minor preferments assigned to the future bishop were really held by the chronicler. Before 1526 he became a frequenter of the court, and the treasurer's accounts in that and the succeeding years contain entries of various payments and presents to him from James V; in 1527 he held a pension of 20*l.* which was doubled before 1530. The last entry referring to him occurs in 1541, and he was dead before 1560.

Sir David Lyndsay, writing in 1530, mentions Stewart among the poets of James V's court, and John Rolland [q. v.], in his prologue to the 'Seven Sages' (1560), classes him with John Bellenden [q. v.] and Bishop Andrew Durie (*d.* 1558) among his 'masters.' The collections of George Bannatyne (1545–1608?) [q. v.] and Sir Richard Maitland, lord Lethington [q. v.], contain several poems ascribed to Stewart, but only one, beginning 'This hinder nicht, neir by the hour of nyne,' is inscribed with his name. But he had probably written much verse, which has been lost, before 1528, when he was commissioned by James V to prepare a metrical version of the history of Hector Boece [q. v.] This work had been published in Latin at Paris in 1527, and James requested Bellenden to translate it into Scots prose and Stewart into Scots verse. Bellenden's version appeared in 1536, but Stewart's, which was begun in 1531, remained in manuscript until 1858, when it was published in three volumes in the Rolls Series. It was edited by William Barclay Turnbull [q. v.] from a unique manuscript which, after being in the possession of Hew Cranfurd of Cloverhill, Bishop Moore, and George I, was presented by the last-named to Cambridge University library (Kk. ii. 16). Stewart's style is rugged and ungrammatical, but his translation contains some graphic descriptions. He shows an acquaintance with the works of John Mair or Major, Froissart, and Fordun, and he made some notable additions to Boece's original—for example in the account of the siege of Perth by the Danes in 1041, in which he introduces Macbeth and Banquo (TURNBULL, pref. pp. xvi–xxiii). Stewart's account is fuller than that of Boece. Holinshed, who is usually supposed to have been Shakespeare's authority, is far more meagre than either of his predecessors (*Notes and Queries,* 8th ser. xi. 321–2).

[Turnbull's Preface to his edition in Rolls Ser.; Exchequer Rolls of Scotland, vols. xv-xvi.; Sir David Lyndsay's Works, ed. Chalmers, i. 286; Rolland's Seven Sages, 1560.] A. F. P.

STEWART, Sir WILLIAM (*d.* 1588) of Monkton, was the third son of Andrew Stewart, second lord Ochiltree [q. v.], by Agnes, daughter of John Cunningham of Caprington. Captain James Stewart of Bothwellmuir (afterwards Earl of Arran) [q. v.] was his elder brother. After the raid of Ruthven in 1582, Arran left his followers under Sir William when he went alone to Ruthven Castle, and they were routed by the Earl of Mar, Sir William being hurt and mutilated of two fingers (CALDERWOOD, iii.

637; Moysie, *Memoirs*, p. 37). Afterwards he was captured and sent a prisoner to Stirling Castle (*ib.* p. 38), but was released on 25 Oct. on condition that he should remain within the sheriffdom of Ayr (*ib.* p. 41). After the fall of Arran in 1586 he was taken prisoner by Lord Hamilton and sent to Edinburgh, but was there set at liberty (*ib.* p. 56). On 26 March 1587 he was sent to treat of a renewal of the league with France (CALDERWOOD, iv. 612); and on his return he accused the master of Gray of having endeavoured to obtain a knowledge of the letters with which he had been entrusted to France, of having trafficked with France and Spain for the subversion of religion, and of having consented to the death of Queen Mary. Both were thereupon committed to ward in the castle of Edinburgh, but after further hearing of the case Stewart was set at liberty, the master being found guilty (*ib.* p. 613; Moysie, *Memoirs*, p. 63; Spotiswood, ii. 373). In May 1588 he was commissioned to pursue John, lord Maxwell [q. v.], and, after capturing him in a cave on 5 June, obtained the surrender of the castle of Lochmaben on the 9th, when the captain, David, brother of Lord Maxwell, was hanged, with five of his men, before the castle gate (CALDERWOOD, iv. 678; Spotiswood, ii. 384; Moysie, p. 68). On 10 July 1588 he had a controversy, in the king's presence, with Francis Stewart Hepburn, fifth earl of Bothwell [q. v.], when each gave the other the lie; and, after the king crossed the Forth a brawl occurred on 30 July between them in the High Street of Edinburgh. Sir William stabbed one of Bothwell's followers, whereupon he was attacked by Bothwell, and, after being stabbed with a rapier, fled to a hollow cellar in the Blackfriars Wynd, where he was despatched (30 July 1588).

[Histories by Calderwood and Spotiswood; David Moysie's Memoirs and Sir James Melville's Memoirs in the Bannatyne Club.]

T. F. H.

STEWART, Sir WILLIAM (*fl.* 1575–1603) of Houston, soldier and diplomatist, was, according to De Thou, an illegitimate son of some Scottish noble (CHÉRUEL, *Marie Stuart*, p. 100), but Douglas and others make him to be the younger son of Thomas Stewart of Galston by Isabel Henderson, his wife (DUNCAN STEWART, *Genealogy of the Royal Family*). Tytler, David Laing, and others confuse him with Sir William Stewart of Monkton (*d.* 1588) [q. v.] and with Sir William Stewart of Caverstoun, who was captain of Dumbarton castle from 1580 to 1585. According to Calderwood (iv. 448), Sir William of Houston 'was, as is constantly reported,

first a cloutter of old shoes. He went to the Low Countries first as a soldier, then as a captain, and last as a colonel.' He is probably the 'William Stewart, servant to Lady Lennox,' who was reported (13 Oct. 1572) to be passing through Berwick prepared to give Burghley certain information (which he afterwards did give) regarding the proceedings of Du Croc in Scotland (*Cal. State Papers*, For.) He was certainly the Mr. William Stewart who despatched to Burghley from the Low Countries news of military affairs in the summer of 1575, and wrote from Rotterdam in the October of that year that he had received a commission from the Prince of Orange to serve with three hundred Scots, and therefore craved license to transport pikes and corslets from England, as he doubted if arms could be purchased at reasonable prices in his own country. In 1579–80 Colonel Stewart, who was for some time quartered at Brussels, had under his command eight companies (RENON DE FRANCE, *Troubles*, ii. 512, iii. 382). Great efforts were now being made by the Spaniards, in conjunction with Mary Stuart, to entice or bribe the Scots to abandon the service of the Dutch or to betray their fortresses. Balfour was reported to be already wavering; and Stewart, who was said to be much under the influence of Mary's ambassador at Paris (April 1580), was 'to be sounded.' The queen herself wrote (October 1581) to urge her Scottish friends to withdraw, and in particular promised Colonel Stewart a good pension in Scotland (*Cal. State Papers*, Spanish, iii. 27, 184). He had meanwhile married a Flemish wife, the widow of the Count of Manderscheit (LITTENHOVE, *Les Huguenots*, vi. 147). There is no evidence that Stewart accepted the bribe referred to, but within twelve months he made his appearance in Scotland, having for some reason forfeited his wife's dowry, and was acting contrary to expectation with the English and anti-catholic party which came into power after the Ruthven raid. He was appointed one of the commissioners at the general assembly of the kirk in 1582, and captain of the king's guard. In the following April he was sent with John Colville [q. v.] on an embassy to England, where he was well received by Queen Elizabeth, who presented him with a valuable chain. His object was to cement the friendship with England, and to procure, if possible, a large sum of money for James. Mauvissière, in his disgust, described him as 'ung pauvre aventurier escossois,' and discovered in him a passion for money-making. Some divergence in his policy from that of his colleague, Colville, soon made itself felt, and on his return to Scotland the colonel, who enjoyed the confidence of the king, became his chief instrument in effecting the counter-revolution which released James from the control of the Ruthven raiders, and brought back James Stewart, earl of Arran. The earl and the colonel, notwithstanding some jealousy between them, now governed the king and country, and incurred the fierce hostility of the church. Stewart was made a member of the privy council, and (July 1583) received a grant of the priory of Pittenweem. As captain of the guard he vigorously supported the king, besieged and captured the Earl of Gowrie [see RUTHVEN, WILLIAM, first EARL OF GOWRIE], at Dundee, brought him to his trial at Edinburgh, helped to frustrate the attempt of the insurgent lords at Stirling, April 1584, and held Lord Maxwell in check on the south.

Fontenay reported to Mary Stuart that James, according to the king's own account, valued Stewart simply as a fighting man, and had said that the colonel, though devoid of intelligence or gift of speech, was a brave and faithful servant. On one occasion Stewart had forgotten himself, and the king brought him to his knees by threatening to reduce him to the *coquin et bélître* that he once was. Stewart, however, as the king must have soon discovered, possessed considerable diplomatic skill. At this moment he was bent on recovering his Flemish wife's property. He got the king to write on his behalf to Philip II, and he himself sent letters through Fontenay and Mary to Parma and Guise, as well as to the king of Spain; and he even induced Elizabeth to request as a favour from Mary Stuart that she should herself intercede for him with Parma, which Mary did on 13 May 1585 (LABANOFF). Fontenay told Nau that Stewart would be on Mary's side, if not from good will, at least from self-interest: 'this and money rule all the Scots nobles' (*Hatfield MSS.* 15 Aug. 1584).

In November 1585 there occurred another *coup d'état* on the part of the banished lords; and with the help of John, lord Maxwell and earl of Morton [q. v.], who from personal reasons had momentarily joined their party, they made the king a prisoner at Stirling. The Earl of Arran was dismissed; the colonel lost his office of captain of the guard, and was given into the custody of Maxwell, who took him to Dumfries. Stewart quickly accommodated himself to the change of circumstances, made friends with Maxwell, reappeared for a short time at court to the disgust of the church party, and slipped away or was dismissed to the continent with a secret mission from James. He first appeared in Denmark, where he added the Danish king to the list of royal suppliants for the restoration of his wife's dowry; and in December 1586 he was in Paris closeted with Mendoza, to whom he explained that he came as a secret agent from the catholic earls, who were resolved with the aid of Spain to free the king from the hands of the English faction, to secure liberty of conscience for catholics, and finally to restore Scotland to the Roman church. To carry out this enterprise, said Stewart (and in this he was supported by the assurances of another catholic agent, Robert Bruce), it would only be necessary to kill four of the hostile lords—Angus, Boyd, Hamilton, and Mar. In return for aid they offered to molest the queen of England. 'Stewart,' wrote Mendoza to Philip, 'is a catholic himself although a politique.' It is not surprising after this to learn that the colonel was in great credit with Parma, and had at last recovered his wife's possessions. In the same year he was again in Denmark, busy apparently with James's matrimonial projects.

On his return to Scotland on the eve of the armada, Stewart found the king was no longer willing to give countenance to his Spanish intrigues; but Stewart, now bent on claiming from the Dutch the arrears of pay which he declared to be due to him for his former military services, persuaded the king to grant him letters of marque to enable him to extort forcible compensation from the Dutch merchants. The States-General, indignant at the audacity of these proceedings, sent envoys to Scotland with instructions to pass through London on their way. They were stopped by Elizabeth, who undertook to bring James to reason if they would leave the matter in her hands. Thus baffled, the Dutch despatched De Voecht and De Warck on a second mission direct to Leith, where they landed 17 May 1589. The result of the conferences which they held with James and his councillors, partly in the presence of Stewart, was not satisfactory to the Dutch, and a few years later they were compelled to pay to the colonel a large sum of money. No sooner had the envoys re-embarked than Stewart set sail for Aberdeen to join the earl marischal and others who were to complete the king's marriage with the Princess Anne. After many delays and adventures he finally commanded the six ships commissioned to bring back both king and queen from Denmark. His zeal in this matter raised him higher than ever in the king's favour. He became once more a member of the privy council, and in the summer of

1590 was sent as ambassador to the princes of Germany. On his return he was rewarded for his great services to the king in foreign nations with a gift of ten thousand merks and a further grant of lands (*Privy Council Reg.* 12 Jan. 1591). A cloud passed over him for a moment in 1592, when he was warded in the castle of Edinburgh on suspicion of being concerned in one of the mad freaks of Bothwell; but in the following year he was entrusted with an embassy to the Low Countries, having instructions to form an evangelic alliance against the jesuits. He now received a grant of the lands of Houston, and was knighted on the occasion of the baptism of Prince Henry. In December 1594 Sir William Stewart of Houston went again as ambassador to the Low Countries, where he requested a loan of cavalry and infantry to fight against the catholic rebel earls. Two years later he was granted a commission as the king's lieutenant for the Isles and Highlands to establish the royal authority in Kintyre; in 1598 he was once more in Denmark, soliciting the king's goodwill in the prospect of James's accession to the English throne; and in the same year he was one of the 'gentlemen adventurers' who were appointed, at their own cost, to plant policy and civilisation in the hitherto most barbarous Isle of Lewis.

Stewart had meanwhile married, for a second time, a widow, Isabella Hepburn, the lady Pitfirrane, the daughter of Patrick Hepburn of Wauchton, 'not without suspicion of the murder of her former husband,' adds Calderwood (iv. 448). The suspicion may fix approximately the date of the marriage. For in 1585 the laird of Pitfirrane, provost of Edinburgh, having given offence to the clergy, the brethren commended the wrong to God, and 'within a few years after,' adds Calderwood, he was found fallen out of a window of his own house of Pitfirrane. 'Whether he threw himself out of a melancholious despair, casting himself, or by the violence of unkind guests hudgit within,' remarks James Melville, 'God knows' (*Diary*, p. 151). Stewart survived this marriage some eighteen years or more, dying between 1603 and 1606.

By Lady Pitfirrane Stewart had a daughter Anne, born 5 June 1595, and an only son Frederick, in whose favour the lands and baronies of the priory of Pittenweem were erected into a temporal lordship by act of parliament in 1606. Frederick was created a peer, under the title of Lord Pittenweem, on 26 Jan. 1609, but died childless on 16 Dec. 1625 (G. E. C[OKAYNE], *Complete Peerage*, s. v. 'Pittenweem').

[Calderwood's History, iii. 714, iv. 422–50; Tytler, viii. 77, 97, 153, 198, ix. 19, 320; Hatfield MSS. (Hist. Comm.), iii. 52, 57, iv. 600, &c.; Cal. State Papers, Spanish, iii. 26, 183, 458, 471, 488, 681; Border Papers, i. 1583–1588; Hamilton Papers, ii. 649, 697, 703; Privy Council, Scotl. 1583–1606; Reg. Mag. Sig. Scot.; Colville's Letters (Bannatyne Club); Douglas's Peerage; Meteren's Hist. des Pays-Bas, p. 310; Manuscript Reports and Papers relating to the affairs of Colonel Stewart, the embassy of De Voecht, &c., from the public archives at The Hague, now in course of publication by the Scottish History Society.] T. G. L.

STEWART, Sir WILLIAM, first VISCOUNT MOUNTJOY (1653–1692), only son of Sir Alexander Stewart, was born six weeks after the death of his father, who fell fighting against Cromwell at Dunbar on 3 Sept. 1653. His grandfather, Sir William Stewart (d. 1602), was an undertaker for the plantation of Ulster, sat in the Irish parliament for co. Donegal, 1613–15, was created a baronet on 2 May 1623, and served with distinction against the Irish rebels, 1641–2 [cf. art. STEWART, Sir ROBERT]. The grandson was heir to much property in Donegal and Tyrone, and his wardship was given in 1660 to Sir Arthur Forbes, created earl of Granard, who had married his mother. In 1662 he succeeded his grandfather as second baronet. In 1675 he was appointed a commissioner for managing claims under the acts of settlement and explanation by protestant officers who served before 5 June 1649. In 1678 he was made *custos rotulorum* of co. Donegal. Although his father had been a presbyterian, the son was somewhat active against the ministers of that persuasion (REID, *Hist. of Irish Presbyterians*, ed. Killen, ii. 339). By patent dated 19 March 1682–3 he was created Baron of Ramelton and Viscount Mountjoy, and on 9 May 1684 was made master-general of the ordnance for life. He was also colonel of a regiment of foot and a privy councillor (*Hist. MSS. Comm.* 14th Rep. App. vii. 358).

The accession of James II made no immediate difference in Mountjoy's position. Clarendon describes him as 'very industrious in the king's service' (*Clarendon and Rochester Correspondence*, i. 249), and recommends him to Evelyn and others as 'an encourager of ingenuity' (*ib.* p. 251). Mountjoy went to England in 1686, and Clarendon charged him to represent the pitiful state of arms and stores in Ireland. Among other things, the muskets were of many different bores (*ib.* p. 547). Mountjoy intended to return in two months, but was induced to volunteer for foreign service, much to the disgust of Clarendon (*ib.* p. 407), who regarded him as a check on Tyrconnel's growing power [see TALBOT, RICHARD, *d.* 1691]. He was dangerously wounded at the capture of Buda by the imperialists on 2 Sept. 1686.

Returning to Ireland in 1687, Mountjoy was made a brigadier-general, with the pay of 407*l.* 10*s.* a year. Clarendon was gone, and Tyrconnel, as viceroy in his stead, was busy discharging protestant soldiers and replacing them by Roman catholic recruits. Mountjoy's regiment was quartered at Londonderry when William landed in Torbay. It had been less interfered with than others, and still consisted largely of protestants. Had it remained stationary, the famous siege might never have taken place; but Tyrconnel removed it to Dublin, to replace the Irish troops sent to help James in England. Londonderry was thus without a garrison at the critical moment. The anonymous letter to Lord Mount Alexander on 3 Dec. 1688 is now admitted to have been a hoax, but it put the protestants on their guard. Mountjoy was a tory of the passive obedience kind, and was inclined to put up with almost anything from his lawful king; but circumstances were too strong for him as for other protestants. On 7 Dec. the Londonderry apprentices, moved by an uncontrollable impulse, shut their gates against Lord Antrim's men. The graver citizens accepted the situation with many qualms, and invited Mountjoy's intercession in an apologetic letter (WITHEROW, *Derry and Enniskillen*, p. 39). The Roman catholics all left the town, and protestant guards were established.

As soon as the news reached Dublin, Tyrconnel burned his wig in a rage, and despatched Mountjoy and Robert Lundy [q. v.], with six companies, to the scene of action. Mountjoy halted at Omagh, and sent a message to Londonderry. Representatives of the citizens came to him at Raphoe, and afterwards the acting-governor, George Philips [q. v.], and others met him near St. Johnstown with full powers. They demanded a protestant garrison and a full pardon under the great seal. Mountjoy demurred, and it was not without some debate that he was admitted unattended within the walls. Philips resigned the governorship in his favour. On the 21st Mountjoy bound himself by articles with the town to procure a general pardon for the inhabitants of Ulster within fifteen days. Two companies only of his regiment—and these all, or nearly all, protestants—were to be admitted until after 1 March, and even then at least one half of the garrison were to be of the same religion. Mountjoy's two

sons were to remain within the walls as hostages, and the two companies, if withdrawn, were to be replaced by armed citizens (*ib.* App. p. 3). The soldiers were then admitted, and Lundy became governor.

From Londonderry Mountjoy went to Newtown-Stewart, where delegates from Enniskillen met him. He told them that they were too weak to resist, and that they must receive a garrison and trust to the king's protection. Allen Cathcart 'sharply replied that he could not protect himself' (McCABMICK, *Enniskillen*). Mountjoy, after some reflection, said he would go to Enniskillen himself, cautioning the inhabitants to shed no blood in the meantime. Before he could carry out his resolution he was summoned by Tyrconnel to Dublin.

As a trusted leader of the protestants, with some knowledge of war, Mountjoy was in Tyrconnel's way, and he persuaded him to go to France on 10 Jan. 1688-9 with Sir Stephen Rice [q. v.] Mountjoy refused to sail until Tyrconnel promised 'upon his word and honour' that no more levies should be made, no additional troops sent into Ulster, no more arms issued, and no fresh commissions signed until King James's pleasure should be known. Tyrconnel did everything that he had promised not to do. Mountjoy was commissioned to tell James that Ireland was untenable, and that the viceroy considered it so; while Rice had secret orders to denounce his colleague as a traitor. Tyrconnel's admirers considered this 'a wise and seasonable dissimulation' (*Jacobite Narrative*, ed. Gilbert, p. 43).

On his arrival at Paris Mountjoy was thrown into the Bastille. 'If your majesty,' wrote Avaux to Louis XIV, on 23 April 1689, 'had not ordered the arrest of Lord Mountjoy, and had allowed him to leave France, as the king of England wished, the latter would never have been master of Ireland, Lord Mountjoy having great power there throughout the whole north.' Mountjoy's life appointment as master of the ordnance was given to Justin Maccarthy, titular viscount Mountcashel [q. v.], and he was included in James's great act of attainder (7 May 1689) as not appearing in Ireland on the appointed day, although he was in the Bastille, and although he had gone to Paris by the viceroy's orders. After the battle of Newtown-Butler it was proposed to exchange him for Maccarthy, but the latter escaped. Ultimately, but not till 1692, Mountjoy was exchanged for Richard Hamilton [q. v.] He had had enough of passive obedience, joined William's army as a volunteer, and was killed at Steenkirk on 3 Aug. following.

Mountjoy married Mary Coote, daughter of the first Lord Colooney. By her he had several children, of whom the eldest son, William, succeeded him as second Viscount Mountjoy (see LODGE, *Peerage*, vi. 253–4). Clarendon, who was of the same political school, gives Mountjoy a high character (*Correspondence*, ii. 241, 251); and Avaux, who had no prejudices, calls him ' bon officier et homme d'esprit.'

[Lodge's Irish Peerage, ed. Archdall, vol. vi.; Lascelles's Liber Munerum Publicorum Hiberniæ; King's State of the Protestants under James II; Négociations de M. le Comte d'Avaux en Irlande; Burnet's Own Time; Macaulay's Hist. of England, chapters xii. and xix.]

R. B–L.

STEWART, SIR WILLIAM (1774–1827), lieutenant-general, born on 10 Jan. 1774, was second son of John, seventh earl of Galloway, by Anne, daughter of Sir James Dashwood, bart. Charles James Stewart [q. v.] was his younger brother. William received a commission as ensign in the 42nd foot on 8 March 1786, became lieutenant in the 67th foot on 14 Oct. 1787, and captain of an independent company on 24 Jan. 1791. In that year he went with Sir Robert Murray Keith [q. v.] to Vienna and to the congress of Sistova. His company was disbanded in December, and he was appointed to the 22nd foot on 31 Oct. 1792. He served with that regiment in the West Indies in 1793–4, and commanded a company in the grenadier battalion at the capture of Martinique and Guadaloupe. He was wounded in the unsuccessful attempt on Point-à-Pitre on 2 July 1794, when Guadaloupe had been recovered by the French. He returned to England in November, and obtained a majority in the 31st foot.

He was made lieutenant-colonel in the army and assistant adjutant-general to Lord Moira's corps on 14 Jan. 1795, and in June he served on the staff of the expedition to Quiberon. On 1 Sept. he was given command of the 67th foot, and went with it to San Domingo. He was commandant at Mole St. Nicholas, with the local rank of colonel, till it was handed over to Toussaint l'Ouverture in August 1798. Returning to Europe, he obtained leave to serve with the Austrian and Russian armies in the campaign of 1799, and was at the battle of Zurich.

It was probably what he saw of Croats and Tyrolese in this campaign that led him to propose, in concert with Colonel Coote Manningham, that there should be a corps of riflemen in the British army. The proposal was adopted, and an experimental 'corps of riflemen' was formed in January 1800 by detachments from fourteen regiments. This was brought into the line two years afterwards as the 95th, and eventually became the rifle brigade. Manningham was colonel and Stewart lieutenant-colonel of it, his commission being dated 25 Aug. 1800. The organisation and training of the corps fell to Stewart, for Manningham was equerry to the king. The standing orders show how much he was in advance of most soldiers of his time. Medals for good conduct and for valour, lectures, school, library, classification in shooting, and athletic exercises were among the means adopted to heighten the efficiency of the corps. He preferred Irish recruits, as ' perhaps, from being less spoiled and more hardy than British soldiers, better calculated for light troops.' Charles James Napier [q. v.] was a subaltern in the corps in 1802, and wrote of Stewart as open-hearted and honourable in the highest degree, but with much passion, much zeal, and not the least judgment (*Life and Opinions*, i. 25–9).

In August 1800 Stewart went with three companies of his rifles to Ferrol in Pulteney's expedition, and was dangerously wounded in the first skirmish. He commanded the troops which served as marines in the fleet sent to the Baltic in 1801. He was himself on board Nelson's flagship at Copenhagen, and wrote the best account of the battle (in CLARKE and MCARTHUR'S *Life of Nelson*. The journal on which it was based is in the *Cumloden Papers*). Nelson wrote of him to St. Vincent as ' the rising hope of our army,' and there was a cordial and lasting friendship between them. By Nelson's wish Stewart's first son was named Horatio. Stewart was included in the vote of thanks of parliament, and was made colonel from 2 April.

In 1804 he was appointed brigadier of volunteers in the eastern counties, and in 1805 he published ' Outlines of a Plan for the general Reform of the British Land Forces,' in which he recommended for general adoption many of the institutions which he had already introduced into his own corps. In December 1806 he took command of a brigade in Sicily, and three months afterwards went on to Egypt with Fraser's expedition. On 3 April he was sent to Rosetta with 2,500 men to avenge Wauchope's repulse. Though a most ardent soldier, he was afraid of responsibility; he wished that the command had devolved on some one else, and felt ' a sort of inward presentiment that matters would not go well.' In his first reconnaissance he received a bullet-wound in the arm. He invested the town and made batteries, but did not risk an assault. On the 21st the Turks received reinforcements from Cairo, and cut to pieces a detachment of seven hundred men which he had placed at El Hamed, and he had to fight his way back to Alexandria, losing three hundred more on the road.

The expedition returned to Sicily in September, and Stewart was commandant of Syracuse till February 1809, when he came home. He had been promoted major-general on 25 April 1808, and on 31 Aug. 1809 he was made colonel of the 3rd battalion of the corps he had formed, the 95th rifles. He commanded the light brigade in the Walcheren expedition, but was invalided early in September.

In January 1810 he was sent to the Peninsula to command the British and Portuguese troops which were to form part of the garrison of Cadiz. He did well there, but was soon superseded in the chief command by Thomas Graham (afterwards Baron Lynedoch) [q. v.] In July he left Cadiz, and was appointed to the 2nd division of Wellington's army under Hill. He was present at Busaco, but could not obtain the medal, as he was not 'personally and particularly engaged.' In December Hill was invalided, and Stewart commanded his corps for a time, but his self-distrust led Wellington to send Beresford to take Hill's place.

In 1811, after Masséna's retreat, the 2nd division—still forming part of Beresford's corps—shared in the first siege of Badajoz, and bore the brunt of the battle of Albuera. The 1st brigade of it (Colborne's) was nearly destroyed there by a sudden attack of French lancers on its rear as it was advancing to charge the French infantry. According to Napier, this happened because 'Stewart, whose boiling courage generally overlaid his judgment, heedlessly led up in column of companies,' without waiting to deploy, as Colborne wished to do. But the charge was made by three deployed battalions (out of four), and, according to Sir Benjamin d'Urban, Beresford's quartermaster-general, Stewart's fault lay rather in rejecting Colborne's proposal to keep a wing of one regiment in column. There can be no doubt that his impetuosity had something to do with the result; but the urgency of the case and the mist which hid the French cavalry go far to excuse him. Beresford had nothing but praise for him in his despatch, and he was thanked by parliament. In July he went home on account of ill-health, and was employed in the eastern district.

In August 1812 he was again appointed to the army in the Peninsula, with the local rank of lieutenant-general. He joined on 6 Dec., and was given command of the 1st division. It comprised the brigade of guards, and a question of privilege soon arose, as he was not a guardsman. In April 1813 he was transferred to his old division, the 2nd. On 4 June he became lieutenant-general. At Vittoria he was on the right under Hill, who spoke highly of his conduct. He was included in the thanks of parliament, and was made K.B. on 11 Sept. When Soult tried to relieve Pampeluna, the 2nd division was guarding the passes near Maya, and was attacked on 25 July by three divisions of d'Erlon's corps, and forced back. Stewart reached the field late, having been at Elisondo with Hill, and reformed his line. Four Portuguese guns, which were moving by his order to the new position, stuck fast, and were taken by the French. Wellington referred with some asperity to the loss of these guns in a postscript to his despatch. Stewart took part in Hill's action at Buenza on the 30th, and next day he led the attack on the French rearguard at the Dona Maria pass. In this attack he was badly wounded, having been already slightly wounded on the 25th. He was present at the Nivelle, Nive, and Orthes, and had a prominent part in the combat of Aire and a minor part at Toulouse. He was popular with the men of his division, among whom he was known as 'auld grog Willie' on account of the extra allowances of rum which he authorised, and which Wellington made him pay for. For his services in the Peninsula he received the gold cross with two clasps, the Portuguese order of the Tower and Sword, and the Spanish order of San Fernando. On 2 Jan. 1815 (on the enlargement of the order of the Bath) he received the G.C.B.

Stewart had been M.P. for Saltash in 1795, and for Wigtonshire from 1796 onward, and on 24 June 1814 the speaker thanked him in his place, on behalf of the house, for his share in the victories of Vittoria and Orthes, and in the intermediate operations. He saw no further service. His health was broken by seventeen campaigns, in which he had received six wounds and four contusions, and in 1816 he resigned his seat in parliament. In July 1818 he was transferred to the colonelcy of the 1st battalion of what had then become the rifle brigade. He settled at Cumloden on the borders of Wigton and Kirkcudbrightshire, near the family seat. He died there on 7 Jan. 1827, and was buried at Minigaff. In 1804 he married Frances, daughter of the Hon. John Douglas (second son of the Earl of Morton), and he left one son, Horatio, a captain in the rifle brigade, and one daughter, Louisa.

[The Cumloden Papers, printed for private circulation in 1871, containing a memoir, with extracts from his journals, and correspondence with Nelson and Wellington; Cope's Hist. of the Rifle Brigade; Verner's The first British Rifle Corps; Gent. Mag. 1827, i. 175; Royal Military Calendar, ii. 322; Wellington Despatches; Napier's War in the Peninsula; Beresford's Further Strictures on the War in the Peninsula, p. 159.]

E. M. L.

STEWART-MACKENZIE, MARIA ELIZABETH FREDERICA, LADY HOOD (1783-1862), eldest daughter and coheiress of Francis Mackenzie, earl of Seaforth, and Mary, daughter of Baptist Proby, dean of Lichfield, and brother of Lord Carysfort, was born at Tarnadale on 27 March 1783. She married, on 6 Nov. 1804, Sir Samuel Hood (1762-1814) q.v., vice-admiral of the white, whom she accompanied to the East Indies when he commanded on that station. He died on 24 Dec. 1814, and in the following year she succeeded to the family estates on the death of her father, and became the chieftainess of the clan Mackenzie. Scott, who refers to her as having 'the spirit of a chieftainess in every drop of her blood' (LOCKHART, Life of Scott, ed. 1845, p. 306), devotes some lines to her in his poetical 'Farewell to Mackenzie,' as one

Whom brief rolling moons in six changes have left
Of thy husband and father and brothers bereft.

He also describes her 'as an enthusiastic highlander, and deep in all manner of northern tradition' (Familiar Letters, i. 142); and he doubtless profited not a little by the tales with which her memory was stored. On 21 May 1817 she married the Right Hon. James Alexander Stewart of Glasserton, elder son of Admiral Keith Stewart (d. 1795), who was third son of Alexander Stewart, sixth earl of Galloway. On his marriage he added the name Mackenzie to that of Stewart. He was M.P. for Ross and Cromarty from 1831 to 1837. From November 1837 till 1840 he was governor of Ceylon, and from 1840 to 1843 lord high commissioner of the Ionian Islands. He died at Southampton on 24 Sept. 1843. His widow died at Brahan Castle on 28 Nov. 1862. By her second husband she had three sons, of whom the eldest was Keith William Stewart-Mackenzie (1818-1880), and three daughters.

[Gent. Mag. 1862, ii. 379-80; Lockhart's Life of Scott; Sir Walter Scott's Familiar Letters, 1893.]

T. F. H.

STICHIL, ROBERT DE (d. 1274), bishop of Durham, whose name is probably derived from a village in Roxburghshire, was the son of a cleric, possibly William Scot or de Stichil, archdeacon of Worcester, whose election to the bishopric of Durham in 1226, two years after the death of Richard de Mariseo q.v., was quashed by the pope as uncanonical, because it was not made 'per viam inspirationis,' but 'singulariter a singulis' (GRAYSTANES, pp. 36-7). Robert was a monk of Durham, and originally of insubordinate character. He was actually about to apostatise, when he was turned back by a voice in the minster. He then reformed, studied the scriptures 'ad miraculum,' and became prior of Finchale. He is described by the Lanercost chronicler as 'vir prudentiæ secularis et scientiæ admodum tenuis, genere nullus, sed pietatis operibus refertus' (Chron. Lanerc. p. 70); and in 'Flores Historiarum' (p. 455) as 'elegans, discretus, et commendabilis.' On the death of Walter de Kirkham, Robert, for whom his friend the sacrist, Henry de Horncaster, afterwards prior of Coldingham, had secretly procured a papal dispensation, was elected bishop of Durham on 30 Sept. 1260, being the first member of the convent to attain that dignity. He received the temporalities on 5 (or 28) Dec., and was consecrated at Southwell on 13 Feb. 1261 by Godfrey de Ludham, archbishop of York. He gave the monks thirteen hundred acres of woodland, and assisted them in making the church of Howden collegiate; but in December 1272 he quarrelled with them as to the provision to be made for his friend Hugh de Darlington, on resigning the priorate, and he specially complained that they did not 'profess' in his presence, as in other cathedral monasteries. During the vacancy in January 1273 the bishop appointed a layman, William Whitby, constable of Durham, to be custodian of the convent; but he eventually yielded to the monks' protests on this point. In 1274 he attended the council of Lyons, received leave from Gregory X to retire (or, possibly, to resign his see), and died two days after leaving Lyons (4 Aug.) at 'Arbipeyllis,' i.e. l'Arbresle (department of Rhône), and was buried in the neighbouring Benedictine monastery of Savigny (reading Savinyacense, for Wharton's Sayacense, and Raine's Saninyacense), his heart being conveyed to Durham. His seal is engraved by Surtees (vol. i. pl. ii. 2).

In January 1272-3 Bishop Stichil founded a hospital at Greatham, near Stockton, out of the manor of that place, which had been forfeited by Peter de Montfort the younger after the battle of Lewes, and, having been at first granted to Thomas de Clare, was successfully claimed by the bishop in right of his palatinate. The forfeiture, however, is not mentioned in his charter, nor in that which he appears to have obtained from Peter to guard against any possible defect. This hospital, originally for forty poor brethren, survived the Reformation, but the number was reduced to thirteen in 1610. The buildings were entirely renovated by John William Egerton, earl of Bridgewater, who held the mastership 1785-1823. The charters, statutes, &c., are printed by Surtees, Hutchinson, and Dugdale (*Monast.* ed. Ellis, vi. 689-90). The seal, which really belongs to Stephen Payn, dean of Exeter 1415-1419, is figured by Hutchinson.

[All the facts, unless otherwise stated, are given by Graystanes, Hist. Dun. Scriptt. Tres, ed. Raine, pp. 45-56. See also Surtees's Durham, i. xxix, xxx, iii. 134-8, and 389: Hutchinson's Durham, i. 214-23, and iii. 91-103; Ann. Monast. ii. 117, iii. 383, iv. 465; Chron. de Lanercost. p. 96.] H. E. D. B.

STIGAND (*d.* 1072), archbishop of Canterbury, was almost certainly the priest of that name who was appointed in 1020 to the church built by Canute [q. v.] at Assandun, probably Ashington in Essex, to commemorate his victory there (*A.-S. Chron.* sub an., Canterbury; FREEMAN, *Norman Conquest*, i. 473). He was chaplain to Canute and Harold Harefoot, and the chief counsellor of Canute's widow, Emma [q. v.] Florence of Worcester, under 1038, says that he was appointed to the see of Elmham, but lost it because Grimketel, bishop of the South-Saxons, or of Selsey, offered more money for it, and held it along with Selsey; Stigand, however, was reinstated and held the South-Saxon see, and obtained the see of Elmham for his brother Æthelmær (FLOR. WIG. i. 193, followed by WILL. MALM. *Gesta Pontificum*, p. 150). There is some confusion in this account, which probably combines changes that happened some years apart. This much, however, seems certain, that Stigand was appointed to Elmham in 1038, and lost it before he was consecrated, that he obtained it again, and was consecrated to it in 1043 (*A.-S. Chron.* sub an., Abingdon). In that year he lost it again, for as Queen Emma's adviser he shared in her disgrace [see under EMMA]. He was reinstated in 1044, and received the bishopric of Winchester in 1047. Edward the Confessor employed him in 1051 during his quarrel with Earl Godwine, with whom Stigand was in sympathy [see under GODWIN or GODWINE]. He is said to have advised and agreed to the king's appointment of Duke William as his successor (WILLIAM OF POITIERS, p. 129; the story of the appointment probably refers to a promise made by Edward in 1051). On Earl Godwine's return in 1052 he was engaged in the negotiations between him and the king; and Robert of Jumièges [q. v.], the archbishop of Canterbury, having fled and being outlawed, Stigand was appointed to succeed him. The appointment was uncanonical, and the pope ordered the restitution of Robert. While Stigand was acknowledged in all civil matters, his ecclesiastical position was regarded as bad even in England: bishops avoided receiving consecration from him, and even his friend Earl Harold (afterwards king) chose to have the minster that he built at Waltham dedicated in 1060 by the archbishop of York rather than by him (*De Inventione Crucis*, c. 16, where the twelfth-century writer describes the see of Canterbury as vacant in 1060; see also FLOR. WIG. ann. 1062, 1070, and WILL. MALM. *Gesta Regum*, vol. ii. c. 199). He is said to have been cited and excommunicated by five successive popes (*Norman Conquest*, ii. 607), and the schismatical position in which his appointment placed England was evidently urged by the messengers of the Norman duke to Alexander II in 1066, while the injury that it did to Robert is said to have been one of the causes of William's wrath against the English (WILLIAM OF POITIERS, pp. 121-3; HEN. HUNT. p. 199). Stigand made his case worse by retaining the see of Winchester together with that of Canterbury, and he is also said to have held several abbeys, and to have obtained and disposed of church preferments simoniacally (*Gesta Pontificum*, pp. 35, 36, where his ill-doings may be exaggerated, but he certainly held the abbey of Gloucester, *Ecclesiastical Documents*, p. 16, Camden Soc., and for a short time, Ely, *Historia Eliensis*, p. 220; as to other alleged cases, see *Norman Conquest*, iii. 643). For six years he used the pall that Robert had left behind him. In 1058, however, he received a pall from Benedict X, evidently in consequence of a request of Earl Harold, and he then consecrated two English bishops. In 1059 Benedict was declared uncanonical and was deposed, so that Stigand's position was rendered even worse than before. The legates sent to England by Alexander in 1062 seem to have published the papal condemnation of him, and Wulfstan went for consecration to the see of Worcester to Aldred [q. v.], archbishop of York (GREEN, *Conquest of England*, pp. 580-1). He did not dedicate Westminster. He was present at the death of the Confessor, and expressed to Harold his disbelief in the king's visions (*Vita Ædwardi*, p. 431). Norman writers assert that he crowned Harold (WILLIAM OF POITIERS, p. 121; ORDERIC, p. 492; the *Bayeux Tapestry*, so also the author of the

De Inventione, c. 20; on 6 Jan. 1066; but Florence of Worcester (sub an.) says that Harold was crowned by Aldred, which from Harold's conduct in 1053 seems far more probable (*Norman Conquest*, iii. 616–22).

After the defeat and death of Harold, Stigand joined in electing Edgar Atheling (q. v.) to succeed him, but met the Conqueror at Wallingford, and submitted to him (WILLIAM OF POITIERS, p. 141). The story of his leading the men of Kent to meet William in arms and forcing him to confirm their privileges is a mere fable (THORN, col. 1787), and so, too, is the assertion that he refused to crown William (WILL. NEWB. vol. i. c. 1), who was crowned by Aldred, Stigand taking part in the ceremony. Against his will he accompanied William to Normandy in 1067, and was received honourably at the churches and monasteries of the duchy. On his return he consecrated Remigius of Fécamp to the see of Dorchester (*Norman Conquest*, iv. 132; GIR. CAMBR. ed. Dimock, vii. 151). Though this seemed to indicate that his position was stronger, the king must have determined to displace him. No credence is to be given to the statement that he engaged in a widespread revolt (*Gesta Abbatum S. Albani*, i. 45). When, at William's request, the papal legates visited England in 1070, they cited Stigand before them on 11 April. Various charges, including perjuries and homicides, were made against him, and he was condemned on three counts—for usurpation of the archbishopric in the lifetime of Robert and using his pall, for receiving his pall from a schismatical pope, and for holding the see of Winchester in plurality (ORDERIC, p. 516; FLOR. WIG. sub an.) He appealed to the good faith of the king, who had at least treated him as though he acknowledged his claim, but was deprived of both his sees, and placed by the king in custody at Winchester (see *Norman Conquest*, iv. 333), where he remained until his death. Unless he escaped, was retaken and again committed to prison (*ib.* n. 2), which is improbable, he could not, as is alleged (*Historia Eliensis*, p. 227), have been one of the companions of Hereward in the Isle of Ely in 1071.

Part at least of Stigand's property was left to him. William of Malmesbury relates that he received only a small sum from the treasury, and would spend nothing of his own upon himself; that Queen Edith or Eadgyth (d. 1075) (q. v.) and others of his friends tried to persuade him to dress and live more comfortably, and that he swore that he had no means, but that after his death it was discovered that he had a buried treasure, and that a key was found round his neck that opened a case containing a list of his moneys and deeds (*Gesta Pontificum*, p. 37; cf. GERV. CANT. ii. 363). He appears to have died in 1072 (*Annales de Wintonia* sub an.), his obit being 22 Feb. (STUBBS). He was honourably buried in the cathedral abbey of St. Swithun, Winchester. He was covetous and unscrupulous. He is said to have wrongfully held lands belonging to the monasteries of Ely (*Historia Eliensis*, p. 220) and Abingdon (*Chronicon de Abingdon*, i. 462). On the other hand, he gave rich gifts to Ely (u. s), to Winchester a large cross with the figures of St. Mary and St. John with drapery of gold and silver, bought with money that he received from Queen Emma (*Annales de Wintonia*, an. 1047), and to St. Augustine's, Canterbury, among many other benefits, a large cross covered with silver (GERVASE, i. 70; THORN, col. 1785).

[Authorities cited in text.]   W. H.

STILL, JOHN (1543?–1608), bishop of Bath and Wells, and reputed author of 'Gammer Gurton's Needle,' was only son of William Still of Grantham, where he was born about 1543. He matriculated as a pensioner of Christ's College, Cambridge, in 1559, graduated B.A. in 1561–2, M.A. in 1565, B.D. in 1570, and D.D. in 1575. After 1561 he was elected a fellow of the college and took holy orders. He remained an active member of the university for more than thirty years, and at an early period acquired a reputation for learning. He came to know Gabriel Harvey and Edmund Spenser while the former was a fellow and the latter an undergraduate of Pembroke Hall. Harvey credited him with being 'an excellent philosopher, a reasonable good historian, a learned divine, and a wise man' (HARVEY, *Works*). Sir John Harington (q. v.) benefited by his instruction, and wrote that Still had given him 'some helpes, more hopes, all encouragements in my best studies; to whom I never came but I grew more religious, and from whom I never went but I parted better instructed. . . . His breeding was from his childhood in good literature and partly in musique. . . . I hold him a rare man for preaching, for arguing, for learning, for lyving; I could only wish that in all these he would make lesse use of logique and more of rhetoricke' (*Nugæ Antiquæ*).

Church preferment was Still's ambition, and he was not disappointed. On 20 Oct. 1570, after failing to obtain the rectory of St. Martin Outwich, London, from the Merchant Taylors' Company, he was admitted

Margaret preacher in the university, and two months later was nominated Margaret professor of divinity in the place of the puritan Thomas Cartwright. Still had already signed a letter to the chancellor urging that Cartwright's alleged heterodoxy might be dealt with leniently, but he soon proved himself a stalwart supporter of the established church and a relentless foe to nonconformity. Archbishop Parker noticed him favourably, and on 30 July 1571 collated him to the rectory of Hadleigh, Suffolk. There he married a parishioner's daughter, and superintended the education of two youths, John Boys [q. v.] and John Overall [q. v.], who attracted him by their promise. Both became scholars of repute. For Hadleigh he always maintained a great affection, leaving on his death 50l. to buy clothing for the aged poor of the village. On 4 Nov. 1572 Still was appointed joint dean of Bocking with Dr. Thomas Watts, and at the same period became chaplain to the primate. On 18 July 1573 he was nominated vicar of East Markham, Nottinghamshire, and in the same year canon of the seventh stall at Westminster, succeeding, as in the Cambridge professorship, one who had been deprived for nonconformity (Thomas Aldridge). On accepting the Westminster canonry he resigned his professorship at Cambridge. On 15 Nov. following he was recommended to Lord Burghley for the vacant deanery of Norwich, and Archbishop Parker, his patron, then wrote of him by way of testimonial: 'I took him, although so young (he was thirty), to be more mortified than others of forty or fifty.'

Still was recalled to Cambridge next year to become (fourteenth) master of St. John's College. The election took place on 14 July 1574, after a vote in his favour by a majority of the fellows. He was admitted a week later. His rule was chiefly notable for his refusal to countenance puritan practices and his economical management of the college finances. His skill as 'a disputer' on theological topics rose so high that 'the learned'st were even afraid to dispute with him' (HARINGTON). He acted as vice-chancellor for the year beginning 4 Nov. 1575, and on 6 March 1576-7 became archdeacon of Sudbury. On 30 May 1577 he was transferred from the mastership of St. John's to that of Trinity College; there he pursued with prudence and integrity the same policy as at St. John's. In 1578, when the contemplated diet at Schmalkald for the discussion of differences between protestants and catholics was under consideration in England, Still was chosen as delegate for Cambridge to uphold the protestant cause (HARINGTON). A few years later he drew up, conjointly with William Fulke [q. v.], answers to the propositions of one Shales, on the authority of the fathers 'as lately renewed in the writings of the Jesuits' (Cal. State Papers).

Ecclesiastical affairs compelled him to spend much time out of Cambridge. He preached the Latin sermon before the convocation of the Canterbury province on 5 Feb. 1588-9, and was straightway elected prolocutor. In November 1592 he was chosen vice-chancellor of Cambridge for a second time. Next month officers of the court applied to him as vice-chancellor to provide an English comedy for the queen's amusement, owing to professional players' inability to keep their engagements on account of the plague which prevailed in London. Still replied that it might be possible to provide a Latin play, but 'Englishe comedies, for that wee never used any, wee presentlie have none; to make or translate one in such shortness of time wee shall not be able' (COLLIER, Annals of the Stage, ii. 293). Before his year of office as vice-chancellor ended he was appointed bishop of Bath and Wells. The congé d'élire was dated 16 Jan. 1592-3, and he was consecrated on 11 Feb. He thenceforth resided in his diocese, and confined himself to the discharge of his episcopal functions. In November 1597 he made proposals in convocation for the better keeping of parish registers (STRYPE, Whitgift, p. 510). He again attended convocation in March 1603-4. He died at the palace at Wells, 26 Feb. 1607-8, and was buried in his cathedral on 4 April. A fine alabaster monument erected by his eldest son, Nathaniel, and containing a recumbent statue of the bishop in canonical attire, now stands in the north aisle. It was engraved by G. Hollis from a drawing by J. Buckler, F.S.A. The Latin inscription was by William Camden. By his will, which was dated 4 Feb. 1607-8, he left, among other charitable bequests, 500l. to Bishop Bubwith's hospital at Wells and one hundred marks for new buildings at Trinity.

Still married, in 1574, his first wife, Anne, daughter of Thomas Alabaster of Hadleigh. By her he had five daughters and four sons. Of the latter, Nathaniel (b. 1579) was fellow of Trinity, and John (b. 1588) graduated M.A. from the same place. His second wife, whom he married after he became bishop, was Jane, daughter of Sir John Horner of Cloford, Somerset. By her he had a son Thomas (b. 1596?).

Portraits of Still are extant in the episcopal palace at Wells, and in the master's lodge at Trinity College, Cambridge. The latter was engraved at George Steevens's expense in 1789 by J. Jones, after a drawing by Silvester Harding. A second engraving was by Henry Meyer (cf. *Cat. Third Loan Exhibition* at South Kensington, No. 637).

The serious-minded Still has been generally claimed as the author of the boisterously merry comedy 'Gammer Gurton's Needle,' but the evidence in his favour proves on examination to be inconclusive. While Still was in residence at Christ's College the books of the bursar show that a play was performed there in 1566, when 20s. was paid 'the carpenters for setting up the scaffold.' It may be inferred (although there is no positive proof) that the play was identical with the one published in 1575 under the title of 'A Ryght Pythy, Pleasaunt, and Merie Comedie: Intytuld Gammer Gurton's Nedle: Played on Stage not longe ago in Christes Colledge in Cambridge. Made by Mr. S. Master of Art' (London, 4to, by Thomas Colwell). It has been argued that the piece was written at an earlier date than 1566, on the ground that a play called 'Dyccon of Bedlam' (not now extant) was, according to the 'Stationers' Register,' licensed for publication to Thomas Colwell, the publisher of 'Gammer Gurton's Needle,' in 1563; and that 'Diccon the Bedlam' (a half-witted itinerant beggar) is a leading character in the extant comedy. But the sobriquet was at the period not uncommonly applied to any half-imbecile mendicant, and in itself offers no proof of the two plays' identity. 'Mr. S. Master of Art,' the author of 'Gammer Gurton's Needle,' was first identified with Still by Isaac Reed in 1782 in his edition of Baker's 'Biographia Dramatica.' Reed's main argument was that Still was the only M.A. of Christ's College whose name began with S. in 1566, when 'Gammer Gurton's Needle' may be assumed to have been first performed. This statement is not accurate, for William Sanderson graduated M.A. from Christ's College in 1555, and was living more than thirty years later, and twelve other masters of arts of the college, all of whose names began with S, proceeded to the degree in or before 1566, and were alive in 1575, when 'Mr. S. Master of Art' was put forth as the author of 'Gammer Gurton's Needle' on the title-page of the first edition. In his lifetime the comedy was not assigned to Still, who is not known to have manifested any interest in the English drama. The only contemporary references to the question of authorship are indeterminate, but they do not point in Still's direction. During the Martin Mar-Prelate controversy of 1588-90

the puritan assailants of the bishops recorded a rumour that 'Gammer Gurton's Needle' was from the pen of their arch foe John Bridges (d. 1618), then dean of Salisbury [q.v.] 'Martin Mar-Prelate' addresses Bridges in his 'Epistle' thus: 'Your first book was a proper Enterlude called "Gammer Gurton's Needle," but I thinke that this trifle, which sheweth the author to haue had some witte and invention in him, was none of your doing: because your bookes seeme to proceede from the braynes of a woodcocke, as having neither wit nor learning.' In 'Martin Mar-Prelate's Epitome' (1589) there are two passing references to the play, and to one is appended a marginal note to the effect that Bridges 'made' it, 'as they say.' These inconclusive statements seem negatived by the fact that Bridges was a graduate of Pembroke Hall, of which he was fellow from 1556, and that on no pretence could 'Mr. S.' do duty for his initials.

A study of the play itself gives no assistance as to its authorship, which must be left undetermined. Its wit is coarse, homely, and boisterous. The main theme is the loss of a needle by Gammer Gurton, a village housewife, while she is engaged in mending her husband's breeches. The plot turns on the search for the needle and the suspicion of theft which falls in turn on each of the members of Gammer Gurton's household and of her gossiping neighbours. The *dénouement* is reached, after much horse-play, when the needle is found by painful experience by Hodge himself in that part of his breeches on which his wife had been exercising her skill. The whole is written in rhyming doggerel, and most of the characters speak in rustic dialect. The only literary feature is a spirited drinking-song, at the opening of the second act, beginning 'Back and side go bare, go bare;' it is adapted, with very slight changes, from a popular song of far earlier date (cf. SKELTON's *Works*, ed. Dyce; BELL, *Songs from the Dramatists*). Historically the piece is of interest as the second extant attempt at comedy in the language—Udall's 'Ralph Roister Doister' being the first—and the first extant play known to have been performed in an English university, while it amply illustrates the phase of merriment which most forcibly appealed to sixteenth-century society. The play was reprinted in 1661; in 'The Ancient British Drama' (1810), edited by Sir Walter Scott, vol. i. pp. 100-31; and again in Dodsley's 'Old Plays,' ed. Hazlitt, iii. 163 seq. (cf. *The Authorship of 'Gammer Gurton's Needle,'* by Charles H. Ross, in *Modern Language Notes*, vii. No. 6, Baltimore, June 1892).

[Cooper's Athenæ Cantabr. ii. 467-9; Pref. to Gammer Gurton's Needle in Dodsley's Old Plays, iii. 165-9; Pigot's Hadleigh; Baker's Hist. of St. John's College, Cambridge, ed. Mayor, i. 168-72; Cussans's Bishops of Bath and Wells; Strype's Works; Harington's Nugæ Antiquæ, i. 135; Warton's English Poetry; Wood's Athenæ Oxon. ed. Bliss, ii. 820; Brit. Mus. Addit. MS. 24487, ff. 33-7.] S. L.

STILLINGFLEET, BENJAMIN (1702-1771), naturalist and dilettante, was born in Norfolk in 1702. His father, Edward Stillingfleet (1660?-1708), eldest son of Edward Stillingfleet, bishop of Worcester [q. v.], was a Lady Margaret scholar of St. John's College, Cambridge (graduating B.A. in 1682, M.A. in 1685, and M.D. in 1692). He was elected F.R.S. in 1688, and Gresham professor of physic. Subsequently he practised as a doctor at King's Lynn, married against the bishop's wishes, got into debt, and further offended his father by his Jacobite opinions; but, on his taking orders, the bishop obtained for him the rectory of Newington Butts, which he exchanged in 1698 for the rectory of Wood Norton and Swanton, Norfolk (cf. BAKER, Hist. of St. John's College, Cambridge, ed. Mayor, ii. 702). On the bishop's death in 1699, however, he left nothing to his son, and accordingly, on the death of the latter in 1708, his widow was in straitened circumstances. Besides Benjamin, she had three daughters, of whom the eldest, Elizabeth, afterwards married John Locker [q. v.], and she herself afterwards married a Mr. Dunch.

Benjamin was educated first at Norwich school, from which he entered Trinity College, Cambridge, as a sub-sizar in 1720, by the advice of Bentley, then master, who had been Bishop Stillingfleet's domestic chaplain. He distinguished himself both in classics and in mathematics, and was chosen scholar in 1723, graduating B.A. in the same year. To this year also belongs his first extant work, 'A Poetical Epistle to a Friend,' printed in the 'Poetical Magazine' for 1764, and in his 'Select Works' (1811). In 1724 he settled at Felbrig, Norfolk, as tutor to Ashe-Windham's only son William, then seven years old, whose mother was a niece of Bishop Stillingfleet. Here Stillingfleet remained for fourteen years, having the entire charge of the boy's education until his coming of age, when he addressed to him an excellent letter of advice (Literary Life, pp. 20-64). In 1726 Stillingfleet was disappointed of a fellowship at his college; the failure was attributed to the influence of Bentley, who is reported to have said that 'it was a pity a gentleman of Mr. Stillingfleet's parts should be buried within the walls of a college.' Though acknowledging his scholarship, Stillingfleet after this bore a grudge against Bentley, which is evinced both in his 'Essay on Conversation' and in his unpublished notes on Bentley's edition of Milton. At Felbrig Stillingfleet became ardently attached to Miss Alice Barnes, granddaughter of Dr. Beck, rector of North Repps and Felbrig, and sister of the Rev. Edward Barnes, who succeeded Dr. Beck; but, after ten years' courtship, she married a richer man named Russel, and Ashe-Windham, to salve the poor tutor's wounded affections, sent him abroad with his pupil in 1737. Before leaving England probably, Stillingfleet wrote the mathematical jeu d'esprit published in 1738, under the pseudonym of Irenæus Krantzovius, as 'Some Thoughts concerning Happiness.'

In Italy and Switzerland the travellers made the acquaintance of Robert Price of Foxley, Herefordshire, the father of Sir Uvedale Price [q. v.]; Richard Aldworth (afterwards Neville) [q. v.], the father of the first Lord Braybrooke; Lord Haddington; his brother, the Hon. George Baillie; and Dr. Dampier, an Eton master (afterwards dean of Durham), and father of Thomas Dampier [q. v.], bishop of Ely. These friends established at Geneva a 'common room' where they read and acted plays and pantomimes, forestalling Garrick in adopting the 'natural' manner and 'improving' 'Macbeth' by substituting magicians for the witches. Stillingfleet acted as 'director of the scenes and machinist,' and, in conjunction with Price, managed the orchestra and composed the airs for the pantomimes. In 1741, in company with Dr. Richard Pococke [q. v.], the party explored the Mer de Glace in the valley of Chamounix. The ascent was described in 'An Account of the Glacieres or Ice Alps in Savoy' (London, 1744, 4to), in which Stillingfleet collaborated with Windham and Price.

In 1743 they returned to England, and Stillingfleet received a pension of a hundred pounds a year from Ashe-Windham until the death of the latter in 1749, when it was continued by his son. He lived mainly in a house in Panton Square, which was rented jointly by William Windham and Price, paying visits to Aldworth Neville at Stanlake in Berkshire, and to his friend Robert Marsham at Stratton in Norfolk. At this period Stillingfleet devoted himself largely to the study of Homer, Plato, and Aristotle, and meditated a reply to Locke on the Understanding, he having espoused Hutcheson's views of ideal beauty as against

Locke's denial of innate ideas. He then made preparations for a critical edition of 'Paradise Lost.' His material he entrusted to his friend Dr. Dampier, but Newton's proposals for his edition under the patronage of Pulteney, earl of Bath, prevented its publication. Dr. Dampier's son, the bishop of Ely, however, communicated Stillingfleet's notes to Henry John Todd [q. v.], who made use of them in his edition of 1801. The original manuscript is interleaved in a copy of Bentley's edition of 1723, now in the library of the British Museum, with which is bound up Stillingfleet's unpublished 'Monody to the Memory of Lord Henry Spencer.'

In 1746 Price married a sister of Lord Barrington, and they persuaded Stillingfleet to make his chief home with them at Foxley, though to maintain his independence he insisted on living in a neighbouring cottage. In 1748 he contributed to Dodsley's 'Collection' 'An Essay on Conversation,' which Dr. Doran styles (*A Lady of the Last Century*, p. 286) his contribution ' towards the social reform commenced by Johnson, Miss Mulso (Mrs. Chapone), and Mrs. Montagu. . . . It rings with echoes of Pope, and lays down some very excellent rules that, implicitly followed, would make conversation impossible.' The poem, which consists of about three hundred rhyming couplets, is addressed to Windham. It was about this time that Mrs. Agmondesham Vesey began at Bath those evening assemblies for rational conversation without card-playing in which she was rivalled by Mrs. Elizabeth Montagu [q. v.], and to which the name 'Blue Stocking' or 'Bas Bleu' afterwards attached. There seems little doubt that this nickname arose from the grey or blue worsted stockings that Stillingfleet habitually wore at these assemblies, which his conversation tended more than anything else to enliven (cf. BOSWELL, *Life of Johnson*, chap. lxxiii.; D'ARBLAY, *Memoirs of Dr. Burney*, ii, 262–3; and see art. MONTAGU, ELIZABETH).

His health being delicate and his eyes becoming subject to inflammation, Stillingfleet, who had refused several offers of travelling tutorships, began to devote himself first to field sports, then to gardening, and then to botany, beginning this last study with the works of Gerard, Parkinson, and Ray, consulting Theophrastus and Dioscorides in the original; and, probably through his friend Robert Marsham, making the acquaintance between 1750 and 1755 of the Linnæan system, of which he became one of the earliest defenders. He was also a proficient performer on the violoncello, and

his intercourse with Price kept up his interest in music. In 'The Letters of Mrs. Montagu' (1813, vol. iv.), is one from Stillingfleet, dated 1757 or 1758, giving an account of the early days of Malvern as a watering-place.

In 1759 Stillingfleet published 'Miscellaneous Tracts relating to Natural History, Husbandry, and Physick; translated from the Latin, with Notes,' being six essays from Linnæus's 'Amœnitates Academicæ,' with a preface of thirty pages and 'Observations on Grasses' by the translator. This preface has been styled 'the first fundamental treatise on the principles of' Linnæus published in England, so that the issue of this work 'may be considered as the æra of the establishment of Linnæan botany in England' (ARCHDEACON COXE, *Life of Stillingfleet*, p. 123). With his friend Price, Stillingfleet made occasional tours, and the journal of one in Wales undertaken in 1759, and printed in Coxe's 'Life' (pp. 126–50), to some extent anticipates such 'tours in search of the picturesque' as those of William Gilpin [q. v.]

In February 1760 he wrote the drama of 'Moses and Zipporah,' intended to be set as an oratorio by his friend, John Christopher Smith [q. v.], the pupil and successor of Handel, and, probably about the same time, those of 'Joseph,' 'David and Bathsheba,' and 'Medea,' two acts of the latter being actually set, though abandoned as too horrible for the stage. These dramas were printed, but never published, only eighteen copies being struck off. 'Paradise Lost,' an oratorio, also set to music by Smith, was performed twice at Covent Garden during 1760, and published with a dedication to Mrs. Montagu, the whole edition of one thousand copies being sold for the author's benefit on the first night. In the same year was published 'The Honour and Dishonour of Agriculture,' translated from the Spanish (of Father Feijoo) 'by a farmer in Cheshire,' which is stated in Nichols's 'Literary Anecdotes' (ii. 336) to have been 'edited, if not translated,' by Stillingfleet, and it is noteworthy that Stillingfleet is stated by Sir James Edward Smith in Rees's 'Cyclopædia' to have directed William Hudson (1730?–1793) [q. v.] to the writings of Linnæus, and persuaded him to write his 'Flora Anglica' (1762).

In 1760 Lord Barrington, then secretary for war, at the instance of his brother-in-law Price, appointed Stillingfleet surveyor of the barracks in the Savoy, and the guard-room at the Tilt-yard, St. James's, and Kensington. This produced an income of about 100l. a year, half of which he gave to the support of an orphan niece and a widowed sister. His poverty prevented his marrying Anne Scudamore of Kentchurch, Herefordshire, whose acquaintance he made in London somewhat late in life. In gratitude to Lord Barrington he dedicated to him 'The Calendar of Flora, Swedish and English, made in the year 1755,' the latter at Stratton, where he had been staying with Marsham. To this was added a similar calendar compiled from Theophrastus, and in the preface Stillingfleet suggests the scheme alluded to by Gray, who wrote in 1761: 'I have lately made an acquaintance with this philosopher [Stillingfleet], who lives in a garret in the winter, that he may support some near relations who depend upon him. He is always employed, consequently (according to my old maxim) always happy, always cheerful, and seems to me a worthy honest man. His present scheme is to send some persons, properly qualified, to reside a year or two in Attica, to make themselves acquainted with the climate, productions, and natural history of the country, that we may understand Aristotle, Theophrastus, &c., who have such heathen Greek to us for so many ages; and this he has got proposed to Lord Bute, no unlikely person to put it in execution, as he himself is a botanist' (MASON, *Memoirs ... of Gray*, iv. 70).

In 1761 Stillingfleet lost both his friends Robert Price and William Windham, the latter appointing him, in conjunction with Dr. Dampier and David Garrick, his executor, with the charge of his only son William Windham (1750–1812) [q.v.], afterwards the politician. This brought with it a slight addition to his income. In 1762 the second edition of the 'Miscellaneous Tracts' was published, with considerable enlargements, including 'The Calendar of Flora' and eleven plates to the 'Observations on Grasses,' drawn by Robert Price. Stillingfleet, who had tested several species of grasses in experimental plots at Foxley, in this work first proposed the English, or, as he termed them, 'trivial' names still used for our commoner species, and subsequently devoted several years to the collection of materials for a 'General History of Husbandry.' Towards this, six volumes of manuscript were found at his death, and published in the 'Select Works.'

His last published work was the anonymous 'Principles and Power of Harmony,' an analysis of and commentary on Tartini's 'Trattato di Musica' (Padua, 1754), which Dr. Burney, though ignorant of its authorship, characterises as 'an elegant, clear, and

masterly performance' (*Present State of Music*, iii. 131). This was published in the year of his death, which took place at his lodgings over a saddler's in Piccadilly on 15 Dec. 1771. He was buried in St. James's, Piccadilly, where his grand-nephew, Edward Hawke Locker, erected a tablet to his memory. The same modesty which caused him to write of himself with a small 'i' made him order all his papers to be burnt; but Pennant, in his 'British Zoology' (vol. iv. pref.) and in his 'London' (3rd ed. p. 138), alludes to his having made an exception of some notes sent to himself.

A portrait of Stillingfleet by Zoffany, formerly in the possession of Edward Hawke Locker (q.v.), was engraved in mezzotint by Valentine Green in 1782, this engraving being copied on a smaller scale in 1810 by James Basire for Nichols's 'Literary Anecdotes' (vol. ii.) and Coxe's 'Life.' Dr. Alexander Garden named the genus of euphorbiaceous plants *Stillingia* in his honour.

Of his works, the 'Thoughts concerning Happiness,' by Irenæus Krantzovius, London, 1738, 8vo, was reprinted in the 'Repository' (1790, vol. iii.), and was translated into French by H. A. Boulanger, as 'Traité Mathématique sur le Bonheur,' Paris, 1791. The 'Essay on Conversation,' in Dodsley's 'Collection,' London, 1748, was reprinted by Foulis, Glasgow, 1783, and in the 'Select Works of Benjamin Stillingfleet,' published by Coxe in 3 vols. in 1811. 'Some Thoughts occasioned by the late Earthquakes: a Poem,' London, 1750, which is very scarce, is also reprinted in the 'Select Works.' The 'Miscellaneous Tracts' went into a third edition in 1775, and a fourth in 1791, and are partly included in the 'Select Works,' the 'Observations on Grasses' being supplemented by Professor Thomas Martyn, and illustrated by sixteen plates by James Sowerby. 'A Discourse concerning the Irritability of some Flowers: a new Discovery, translated from the Italian of Count Giov. dal Colvolo,' London, 1767, 8vo, is also in the 'Select Works.'

[Literary Life and Select Works of Benjamin Stillingfleet, by William Coxe, London, 1811, 3 vols. 8vo; Gent. Mag. 1776, xlvi. 162–4, and xlvii. 440; Nichols's Literary Anecdotes and Literary Illustrations; Fetis's Biographie des Musiciens; and the authorities above quoted.]

G. S. B.

STILLINGFLEET, EDWARD (1635–1699), bishop of Worcester, born on 17 April 1635 at Cranborne, Dorset, was the seventh son of Samuel Stillingfleet (of the ancient family of Stillingfleet of Stillingfleet, Yorkshire) by Susanna, daughter of Edward

Norris of Petworth. After early instruction
from his parents he was sent to Cranborne
grammar school, under Thomas Garden, and
in 1648 to Ringwood, that he might procure
one of the Lynne exhibitions. At Michaelmas 1649 he was admitted to St. John's
College, Cambridge, and obtained a scholarship there on the Earl of Salisbury's nomination on 8 Nov. Immediately after graduating
B.A. he was elected to a fellowship on
31 March 1653. He proceeded M.A. in 1656,
and was incorporated at Oxford on 17 June
1677. In 1654 he went to reside with Sir
Roger Burgoyne at Wroxhall, Warwickshire,
and then became tutor to Mr. Pierrepoint
at Nottingham. During this period he was
ordained by Ralph Brownrig [q. v.], deprived
bishop of Exeter, and wrote his first book,
'The Irenicum' (1659; 2nd ed. 1662), suggesting a compromise between the church
and the presbyterians. This work, from
which its author in later years dissented,
took a prominent place among the writings
of the 'Latitude-men' of the time. It regards the form of church government as im-
material, and as left undecided by the
Apostles; but the argument is directed against
nonconformity, which is regarded as indefensible. It shows clear traces of the influence of Hobbes. Burnet says that 'it took
with many, but was cried out upon by others
as an attempt against the church. Yet the
argument was managed with so much learning and skill that none of either side ever
undertook to answer it.'

In 1657 Stillingfleet received from Sir Robert Burgoyne the rectory of Sutton, and in
1659 he married Andrea, daughter of William Dobyns of Dumbleton (agreement dated
22 Feb. 1659, *Stillingfleet MSS.*) While at
Sutton he wrote his 'Origines Sacrae' (1662),
which would 'have been deservedly esteemed
a most complete performance for one of more
than twice his age' (Bentley's 'Life' in vol. i.
of Stillingfleet's *Works*, 1710). This was an
apologetic work on an historical basis, asserting the divine authority of the Scriptures.
Bishop Robert Sanderson [q. v.] of Lincoln
was greatly struck by it. When he saw
Stillingfleet at a visitation he was astonished
at his youth, and gave him a general license
as preacher in his diocese on 16 Oct. 1662.

Similarly impressed by the learning of the
'Origines,' Bishop Humphrey Henchman
[q. v.] requested the author to answer the
jesuit account of the controversy between
Laud and Fisher (LAUD, *Labyrinth*). This he
did in 'A Rational Account of the Grounds
of the Protestant Religion; being a Vindication of the Lord Archbishop of Canterbury's
"Relation of a Conference between him and

John Fisher the Jesuit," from the Pretended
Answer of T. C.,' London, 1664. This performance, of considerable acuteness and
learning, gave him still wider fame, and
shortly afterwards he was appointed preacher
at the Rolls Chapel. In January 1665 he was
appointed to the rectory of St. Andrew's,
Holborn, which he held till 1689 (instituted
21 March 1665). He retained his preacher-
ship at the Rolls Chapel, and was also made
reader of the Temple.

He now made the acquaintance of many
eminent lawyers, and became the friend of
Sir Matthew Hale and of Chief-justice
Vaughan, whose funeral sermon he afterwards preached. On 9 Feb. 1667 he was
collated to the prebend of Islington in St.
Paul's Cathedral, which he exchanged for
that of Newington on 11 Oct. 1672. On
21 April 1669 he became a 'canon in the
twelfth prebend' in Canterbury Cathedral
(LE NEVE, *Fasti*, 1854, i. 61, ii. 402, 419);
and he graduated B.D. at Cambridge in 1663,
D.D. 1668. He soon became a popular
London preacher. A petition to Bishop
Henchman of London from the parishioners
of St. Andrew's, Holborn (*Stillingfleet MSS.*),
complains that he only 'vouchsafes' to preach,
coming in late, when the reading of prayers
is over. A sermon on the courageous text,
'Fools make a mock of sin,' preached before
Charles II on 13 March 1667, was printed
by the king's command. Having been made
a royal chaplain (see *Cal. State Papers*, Dom.
1667–8, p. 335), Stillingfleet was once asked
by Charles why he always read his sermon
when preaching before him and used no
notes elsewhere. He told the king that 'the
awe of so noble an audience, where he saw
nothing that was not greatly superior to
him, but chiefly the seeing before him so
great and wise a prince, made him afraid to
trust himself.' Stillingfleet in his turn asked
Charles why he always read his speeches
'when you can have none of the same reasons.' The king replied, 'I have asked them
so often and for so much money that I am
ashamed to look them in the face' (*Richard-
soniana*, p. 89).

Pepys, who had known Stillingfleet at
Cambridge, says, when he heard him preach
at Whitehall on 23 April 1665, that 'he did
make a most plain, honest, good, grave sermon, in the most unconcerned and easy, yet
substantial manner that ever I heard in my
life,' and that when he was presented to St.
Andrew's, Holborn, 'the "bishops" of Canterbury, London, and another believed he is
the ablest young man to preach the Gospel of
any since the Apostles.' In 1666, on the fast
day for the fire, he notes that when Stilling-

fleet preached before parliament there was no standing room.

Though now clearly in favour with the court, Stillingfleet remained on good terms with the nonconformists. He was a friend of Matthew Henry, attended the funeral of Fairclough (WOOD, *Life and Times*, ed. A. Clark, iii. 23), and was requested by Charles II, as a moderate man, to argue with William Penn (*Cal. State Papers*, Dom. 1668–9, p. 146). While he was still rector of Sutton he had given a home to one of the ejected ministers, and taken a large house, which he turned into a school, for another.

His literary and controversial activity was prodigious, and his books against the Socinians and Romanists were extremely popular. On 4 May 1677 he was made archdeacon of London, and on 16 Jan. 1678 dean of St. Paul's. He was also prolocutor of the lower house of the convocation of Canterbury. He was no less prolific as an antiquary than as a theologian. His treatise on the jurisdiction of the bishops in capital cases, published on the occasion of Danby's trial, was considered, says Burnet, to 'put an end to the controversy in the opinion of all impartial men' (*Hist. of his own Time*, 1753, ii. 93). Still more important was his elaborate work the 'Origines Britannicæ,' 1685, which was an acute historical investigation of the sources of British church history. His 'Discourse of the True Antiquity of London' (published after his death) shows him also an antiquary of wide learning. He was a great book collector, and formed a very large library of manuscripts and rare works.

At the time of the popish plot 'a manuscript against' him was examined by the committee of investigation (*Hist. MSS. Comm.* 11th Rep. App. ii. 68), and it was said that there was an attempt to entrap and murder him. 'Thereupon on Sunday about forty persons for a guard waited on the doctor to church and home' (*ib.* 14th Rep. App. iv. 108).

During the reign of James II he was in less prominence. Letters show that he was required at different times to attend on the king's ecclesiastical commissioners in the chapter-house of St. Paul's (*Stillingfleet MSS.*) He prepared an elaborate argument against the legality of the commission, which was published in 1689, as the second part of his 'Ecclesiastical Cases,' and reasons against the repeal of the Test Act (20 April 1689, *Stillingfleet MSS.*) At the Revolution he was at once taken into favour. Burnet recommended him to William of Orange as 'the learnedst man of the age in all respects'

(SIDNEY, *Diary*). A letter from Hickes, dean of Worcester, announcing the death of William Thomas (1613–1689) [q. v.], the bishop, shows that it was already known that he would have the next preferment (26 June 1689, *Stillingfleet MSS.*) On 12 Oct. 1689 his election was confirmed in Bow Church (WOOD, *Life and Times*, ed. A. Clark, iii. 312), and next day he was consecrated bishop of Worcester at Fulham. The temporalities were restored to him on 21 Oct. (LE NEVE, *Fasti*, iii. 68; *Cal. State Papers*, Dom. 1689, p. 297). He was at once put on the commission to consider the revision of the prayer-book and the possibility of comprehension.

Stillingfleet was an active and energetic bishop. His charges (1690, 1693, and 1696) were elaborate investigations of the duties and rights of the parochial clergy, and were published in the first part of his 'Ecclesiastical Cases,' 1696. He was a frequent speaker in the House of Lords. He continued his literary labours, his collection of books, and his correspondence with learned men. An interesting letter from Sir William Trumbull [q. v.] shows him keenly interested in the 'wretched state of the Grecian and Armenian churches' (10 June 1688, *Stillingfleet MSS.*) On the death of Tillotson the queen strongly urged his appointment to the archbishopric; but he was already in bad health, and does not appear to have been offered the primacy. It is said that when Tenison, the new archbishop, called upon him he wittily alluded to this by remaining seated, and saying 'I am too old to rise.' He became, however, the constant adviser of Tenison, and, when he was no longer able to attend parliament, was consulted by the bishops on all points of importance (many letters in *Stillingfleet MSS.*)

Despite his infirmity he engaged in a controversy with Locke on the doctrine of the Trinity, which he believed was impugned by some passages in the 'Essay on the Human Understanding.' He published three pamphlets on the subject (1696–7), each of which was answered by Locke. He drew up also an elaborate paper of advice to the bishops in case the king should demand new measures for the suppression of the papists, showing that the existing laws were sufficient (*Stillingfleet MSS.*, undated). The last years of his life were occupied in the revision and publication of sermons, and in the revision of the 'Origines Sacræ,' which he did not live to complete. He also reformed the procedure of his consistory court, and took an active part himself in its work. His second wife, Elizabeth, daughter of Sir Nicholas Pedley, died early in 1697 (letter from the

Duchess of Lauderdale, dated Ham, 20 Feb. 1697, in *Stillingfleet MSS.*), and from that time his health rapidly failed. He had a dangerous fit at Hartlebury early in 1698 (*ib.*, letter from Dr. Stanley, dean of St. Paul's), and died at his house in Park Street, Westminster, on 27 March 1699. He was buried in Worcester Cathedral, and his epitaph is from the pen of his chaplain, Richard Bentley. By his first wife he had one son, Edward (father of Benjamin Stillingfleet [q. v.], and two daughters; by his second, seven children, of whom James became dean of Worcester and rector of Hartlebury.

His valuable library was offered for sale. The historical manuscripts were bought by Robert Harley (afterwards Earl of Oxford), and the books, after lengthy negotiations, by Narcissus Marsh [q. v.], archbishop of Armagh, in 1704 (it is stated that there were over two thousand folios). 'He is supposed to have paid over 6,000*l.* for the books and manuscripts, in the collection of which all over the learned world he spared no cost, . . . and the choiceness of the collection and fewness of common books appears very remarkable and hard to be equalled' (*ib.*)

No bishop of his day was more prominent or more famous than Stillingfleet; but the reputation which his remarkable industry, wide knowledge, and popular gifts gave him among contemporaries was not enduring. Although the publication of his complete works did not enhance his fame (cf. HEARNE, *Diaries*, ed. Doble, ii. 373, iii. 251), his power as a writer and the accuracy of his historical and antiquarian knowledge are unquestionable.

His works were published in 1710 in six volumes, with a 'Life' by Richard Bentley, who had been his chaplain. The most important have been mentioned above. To these may be added his 'Miscellaneous Discourses on Several Occasions,' published by his son in 1735, which show him in his most practical aspect.

He was a handsome man, of a high colour and bright vigorous expression. He was nicknamed 'the beauty of holiness.' Portraits of him are numerous. Among the best are a half-length and a beautiful miniature in the possession of the Stillingfleet family. Engravings exist by R. White and Blooteling, fine copies commanding a high price (EVANS, *Cat.* No. 9935).

[The chief authorities are Bentley's Life of the bishop, Burnet's History of his own Time, Bentley's Correspondence, and the biographical notes by Professor J. E. B. Mayor in his edition of Baker's History of St. John's College, Cambridge, ii. 698–703. The present writer is indebted to Mrs. Stillingfleet, of Grafton Lodge, Hereford, for permission to inspect the interesting family manuscripts.]   W. H. H.

STILLINGTON, ROBERT (*d.* 1491), bishop of Bath and Wells, and lord chancellor, was son of John Stillington, who held property at Nether Acaster, near York (*Rot. Parl.* vi. 256). Stillington was educated at Oxford, and is sometimes alleged to have been a fellow of All Souls' College; but the latter statement seems to be an error, which originated from Stillington having resided at the college during his disgrace (WOOD, *Colleges and Halls*, p. 273). He graduated as doctor of the civil and canon law, and was principal of Deep Hall in 1442 (ANSTEY, *Munimenta Academica*, p. 528). On 2 Aug. 1445 he became canon of Wells, was chancellor of that church on 6 June 1447, and archdeacon of Taunton on 20 April 1450. Stillington had already entered on an official career, having been one of the commissioners to treat with Burgundy on 25 Oct. 1448 (*Fœdera*, xi. 218). Other ecclesiastical preferments quickly followed. He received the prebend of Fenton, York, on 21 March 1450, which he exchanged for that of Wetwang on 28 May 1459; at Southwell he held the prebend of Oxton and Cropwell from 9 July 1457 to 28 May 1459; he became dean of St. Martin's, London, in 1458, archdeacon of Colchester in 1460, of Berkshire on 9 March 1464, and of Wells on 28 Feb. 1465. He had attached himself to the Yorkist party, and through their influence was made keeper of the privy seal on 28 July 1460 (*ib.* xi. 458). After the death of John Phreas or Free [q. v.] in 1465, he was elected bishop of Bath and Wells; his election was confirmed on 11 Jan. 1466, the temporalities were restored on 29 Jan., and on 16 March he was consecrated at Westminster by George Neville [q. v.], archbishop of York (*ib.* xi. 559; *Anglia Sacra*, i. 574).

On 20 June 1467 Stillington was made lord chancellor. The seal was in the king's hands for a short time in March–May 1470 (*Fœdera*, xi. 651). On the Lancastrian restoration Stillington was deprived of his office, but was again made chancellor on the return of Edward IV, receiving a pardon for any past offences on 25 Feb. 1472 (*ib.* xi. 736). He was absent from the parliament of October 1472 through illness, and during 1473 temporary keepers of the seal were appointed to act for him (cf. *Cont. Croyland Chron.* ap. GALE, *Scriptores*, i. 557). Stillington resigned the chancellorship on 25 July 1475. Later in the year he was employed in an unsuccessful attempt to obtain the surrender of Henry of Richmond from the Duke of Brittany. About

March 1478 Stillington was imprisoned in the Tower (BENTLEY, *Excerpta Historica*, p. 354), and on 20 June following received a pardon for some words which he had uttered prejudicial to the king and his state, of which he afterwards cleared himself before the council (*Fœdera*, xii. 66). Commines (v. ch. 18, vi. ch. 9) relates that for some offence Stillington was imprisoned by Edward IV, and had to pay a round sum for his ransom. The same author relates that the bishop had married Edward to a lady before the marriage with Elizabeth Woodville, and afterwards revealed the secret to Richard, duke of Gloucester. Buck, in his 'History of Richard III,' relates the same story, and gives the lady's name as Eleanor Talbot, stating that the bishop, under pressure from the lady's family, informed Gloucester, and hence fell into disgrace with the king (KENNETT, *Hist. of England*, i. 562, 565). There is probably some truth in the story, and Stillington's action may have been due to enmity for the Woodvilles (GAIRDNER, *Richard III*, pp. 113–16).

After the death of Edward IV, Stillington gave his support to Richard of Gloucester, and drew up the bill declaring the invalidity of the marriage of Edward IV to Elizabeth Woodville [see ELIZABETH, 1437?–1492]. It is possible that this circumstance is the basis of Commines' story that Stillington had himself celebrated the previous marriage (RAMSAY, ii. 488). Stillington took part in Richard's coronation, when he performed the ceremony of hallowing the king and queen. On the accession of Henry VII he naturally fell into disgrace, and on 22 Aug. 1485 a warrant was issued for his arrest. Five days later he was already in prison at York, 'sore crased by reason of his trouble and carying' (DRAKE, *Eboracum*, p. 122). He, however, obtained a full pardon on 22 Nov.(CAMPBELL, *Materials for Hist. of Henry VII*, i. 172), and when the act declaring Edward IV's children bastards was repealed, the king refused to call him to account for his share in its composition. Nevertheless, he was deprived of the deanery of St. Martin, mention being made in the act of the 'horrible and haineous offences ymagined and donne' by him against the king (*Rot. Parl.* vi. 292). Stillington took part in the rebellion of Lambert Simnel [q. v.], and on its failure sought refuge at Oxford. At first the university refused to surrender him, but on pressure yielded to the king (MAXWELL-LYTE, *Hist. Univ. Oxford*, pp. 369–71). Stillington was taken to Windsor in October 1487, and kept prisoner there till his death early in May 1491. He was buried at Wells

Cathedral in a chapel which he had built there. During the reign of Edward IV he had founded the college of St. Andrew, Nether Acaster, on property which belonged to his father (*Rot. Parl.* vi. 258). Commines relates that Stillington had a son whom Richard III designed to marry to his niece Elizabeth, afterwards queen of Henry VII; but the young man, being captured off the coast of Normandy by the French, died in prison at Paris (*Memoires*, vi. ch. 9).

[Wharton's Anglia Sacra, i. 574–5; William of Worcester, pp. 783, 787, 792, ap. Letters and Papers illustrative of reign of Henry VI; Le Neve's Fasti Eccl. Angl. i. 141, 160, 167, ii. 340, 635, iii. 185, 223, 451; Foss's Judges of England; Cassan's Lives of Bishops of Bath and Wells; other authorities quoted.]   C. L. K.

STIRLING. [See also STERLING.]

STIRLING, EARL OF. [See ALEXANDER, SIR WILLIAM, 1567?–1640.]

STIRLING, JAMES (1692–1770), mathematician, commonly called 'The Venetian,' born at Garden, Stirlingshire, in 1692, was the third son of Archibald Stirling of Garden by his second wife, Anna, daughter of Sir Alexander Hamilton of Hoggs, near Linlithgow. Stirling was educated at Glasgow University and afterwards proceeded to Balliol College, Oxford, whence he matriculated on 18 Jan. 1710–11. In 1715, however, he was expelled from the university for corresponding with members of the Keir and Garden families who were noted Jacobites, and had been accessory to the 'Gathering of the Brig of Turk' in 1708. He made his way to Venice and employed himself in the study of mathematics. The vicinity of Padua gave him the opportunity of acquiring the friendship of Nicolas Bernoulli (1687–1759), who was mathematical professor in the university there. In 1717 he published 'Lineæ Tertii Ordinis Newtonianæ' (Oxford, 8vo), which was intended to supplement Newton's 'Enumeratio Linearum Tertii Ordinis;' it supplied four additional varieties to Newton's seventy-two forms of the cubic curve. In 1718 he communicated to the Royal Society, through Sir Isaac Newton, a paper entitled 'Methodus Differentialis Newtoniana illustrata' (*Phil. Trans.* xxx. 1050). Having discovered the trade secrets of the glass-makers of Venice, he returned home about 1725 from dread of assassination, and with the help of Sir Isaac Newton established himself in London. In December of the year following he was elected a fellow of the Royal Society, and remained a member until 1754. He lived for ten years in London, corresponding with various mathematicians and enjoying Newton's friendship and hospitality. During the greater part of the time he was connected with an academy in Little Tower Street (cf. a prospectus entitled 'A Course of Mechanical and Experimental Philosophy,' by Mr. James Stirling, F.R.S., &c., London, 1727). In 1730 he published his most important work, 'Methodus Differentialis, sive Tractatus de Summatione et Interpolatione Serierum Infinitarum' (London, 4to; new ed. 1764; translated into English in 1749, by Francis Holliday). In 1735 he was appointed manager to the Scots Mining Company at Leadhills in Lanarkshire, and proved extremely successful as a practical administrator, the condition of the mining company improving vastly owing to his method of employing labour to work the mines. In 1746 he was suggested as a candidate for the mathematical chair at Edinburgh University, vacant by the death of Colin Maclaurin [q. v.], but his Jacobite principles rendered his appointment impossible. At a later time he surveyed the Clyde with a view to rendering it navigable by a series of locks, thus taking the first step towards making Glasgow the commercial capital of Scotland. The citizens were not ungrateful, and in 1752 presented him with a silver tea-kettle 'for his service, pains, and trouble.' He died at Edinburgh on 5 Dec. 1770. By his wife, the daughter of Watson of Thirtyacres, near Stirling, he left one daughter, Christian, who married her cousin, Archibald Stirling of Garden.

Besides the works mentioned Stirling communicated to the Royal Society a paper 'On the Figure of the Earth, and on the Variation of the Force of Gravity at its Surface' in 1735, and in 1745 'A Description of a Machine to blow Fire by the Fall of Water' (Phil. Trans. xxxix. 98, xliii. 315). He also left two volumes in manuscript of a treatise on weights and measures and a number of papers and letters, which are preserved at Garden.

[Fraser's Stirlings of Keir, 1858, p. 85, 91–102, 535; Encycl. Britannica, 9th ed. xxii. 555, 8th ed. i. 711, xviii. 617; Thomson's Hist. of Royal Soc. App. p. xxxvi; English Cycl. Biogr. v. 731; Gent. Mag. 1853, i. 500; Brewster's Memoirs of Sir Isaac Newton, ii. 411, 516.]

E. I. C.

STIRLING, Sir JAMES (1740?–1805), first baronet, lord provost of Edinburgh, born in 1740 or early in 1741, was the son of Alexander Stirling, cloth merchant in Edinburgh, by his wife Jane, daughter of James Muir of Lochfield, Perthshire. In early life he went to the West Indies as clerk to Archibald Stirling of Keir, an extensive planter there, who was great-uncle of Sir William

Stirling-Maxwell [q. v.]; and not long afterwards he was appointed, through Stirling's influence, secretary to Sir Charles Dalling, governor of Jamaica. Having acquired in the West Indies a considerable fortune, he returned to Edinburgh, and became partner in the banking house of Mansfield, Ramsay, & Co., marrying Alison, the daughter of James Mansfield, the senior partner. Having entered the town council of Edinburgh in 1771, he filled the office of treasurer in 1773–4, and was thrice chosen lord provost —in 1790, 1794, and 1798. For his firm yet prudent conduct in connection with the reform riots in 1792 he was on 17 July of the same year created a baronet. He died on 17 Feb. 1805, leaving three sons and two daughters, and was succeeded in the baronetcy by his eldest son, Gilbert, on whose death in 1843 it became extinct.

[Kay's Edinburgh Portraits; Fraser's Stirlings of Keir, 1858, p. 185; Anderson's History of Edinburgh; Anderson's Scottish Nation.]

T. F. H.

STIRLING, Sir JAMES (1791–1865), admiral and first governor of Western Australia, born in 1791, was fifth son of Andrew Stirling of Drumpellier, Lanarkshire, by Anne, daughter of Sir Walter Stirling [q. v.] He entered the navy in August 1803 on board the Camel storeship, in which he went out to the West Indies, where he was moved into the Hercule, of 74 guns, flagship of Sir John Thomas Duckworth. In 1805 he was in the Glory, then flagship of his uncle, Rear-admiral Charles Stirling [see under STIRLING, SIR WALTER], and was in the action off Cape Finisterre on 22 July 1805. He continued with his uncle in the Sampson, and again in the Diadem, in which he served during the operations in the Rio de la Plata in 1807. He was promoted to be lieutenant on 12 Aug. 1809, and in 1811 went out to the West Indies as flag-lieutenant to his uncle; by him he was promoted on 19 June 1812 to the command of the Brazen sloop, in which for some months he cruised successfully off the mouths of the Mississippi. Still in the Brazen, he was afterwards in Hudson's Bay, in the North Sea, on the coast of Ireland, and again in the Gulf of Mexico, and after the peace commanded her in the West Indies till 1818. On the special recommendation of the commander-in-chief, he was promoted to post rank on 7 Dec. 1818.

On 25 Jan. 1826 he was appointed to the Success, and sent to form a settlement in Raffles Bay, Torres Strait. For the successful performance of that duty he was highly complimented by the commander-in-chief and by the government of New South Wales. His report of further explorations in 1827 determined the government to attempt a settlement in Western Australia, and in October 1828 he was appointed to command a party of intending colonists. The expedition sailed in the spring of 1829, and reached its destination in August. The sites of two towns, Freemantle and Perth, were marked out, and within four months of its foundation the colony had a population of thirteen hundred. Stirling remained governor of Western Australia till 1839, when the apparent imminence of a war with France led him to resign the appointment in order to return to active service. From 1840 to 1844 he commanded the Indus, of 78 guns, in the Mediterranean, and from 1847 to 1850 the Howe, of 120 guns, on the same station. On 8 July 1851 he was promoted to be rear-admiral. He was commander-in-chief in China and the East Indies from January 1854 to February 1856, during the war with Russia, which, however, scarcely interfered with the routine of the station. He became vice-admiral on 22 Aug. 1857, and admiral on 22 Nov. 1862. He was a Knight Grand Cross of the Redeemer of Greece, and died on 22 April 1865. He married, in 1823, Ellen, daughter of James Mangles of Woodbridge, and by her had a large family. His daughter, Georgiana Janet, married first Sir Henry Tombs [q. v.], and secondly Sir Herbert Stewart [q. v.]

[O'Byrne's Nav. Biogr. Dict.; Gent. Mag. 1865, i. 801; Jenks's Hist. of the Australasian Colonies, ch. vi.; Foster's Baronetage.]

J. K. L.

STIRLING, Mrs. MARY ANNE, commonly known as FANNY, afterwards LADY GREGORY (1815–1895), actress, the daughter of Captain Kehl, a military secretary at the war office, was born in July 1815 in Queen Street, Mayfair, London, and was, it is said, educated at the catholic seminary, Brook Green House, Hammersmith. Her first appearance was made unobtrusively at the Coburg Theatre, then managed by Davidge, where, under the name of Fanny Clifton, she carried messages and the like. Her first part of importance was Amelia Wildenheim in 'Lovers' Vows,' adapted from Kotzebue. She is said to have been in the ballet at the Surrey in 1827. At the East London Theatre, Commercial Road, she opened early in 1832 in John Stafford's 'Pretender, or the Rose of Alvery,' and Dimond's 'Hunter of the Alps,' her principal business being comedy and 'singing chambermaids.' On Easter Monday 1832, at a salary of 3l. weekly, she opened for leading business at the Pavilion Theatre, under

Farrell, as Susan Oldfield in 'Speed the Plough,' and as Patrick in O'Keeffe's one-act musical farce 'The Poor Soldier.' Here she met Edward Stirling or Lambert (see below), who was playing 'walking gentleman.' Soon afterwards she married him, and went with him to Liverpool, Manchester, and Birmingham, where she became a favourite. Her first appearance in the west-end was at the Adelphi, where, as Mrs. Stirling from Birmingham, she succeeded Mrs. Nisbett, her manager, as Biddy Nutts in Buckstone's 'Dream at Sea.' A prominent position was thus at the outset assigned her. She was a brilliantly pretty woman, with much grace and propriety of style, carriage, and diction. In the 'Ghost Story' by Serle, 'Luke Somerton,' 'Catching an Heiress,' and the 'Dream at Sea' she played soubrette and low-comedy parts, and as Lady Randolph in William Leman Rede's 'Douglas Travestie' essayed burlesque. In May 1836 she played at the St. James's the heroine of a burletta entitled 'Love and Charity.' In Leman Rede's 'A Flight to America, or Ten Hours in New York,' she made, at the Adelphi, a great hit as Sally Snow, singing negro and patter songs, her associates being T. D. Rice, Yates, John Reeve, and Buckstone. Other parts were played at the Adelphi, the St. James's, and elsewhere; and Mrs. Stirling then accompanied W. J. Hammond, the manager of the Strand, to Drury Lane, where he soon beggared himself. Here in November she failed as Beatrice in 'Much Ado about Nothing,' and in December made a success as the heroine of 'A Night in the Bastille,' a translation by T. Archer of Mlle. de Belle-Isle. In 1840, at the Haymarket under Webster, she took Helen Faucit's part of Clara Douglas in 'Money' (in which her 'freshness' was praised by Macready), and in 1841 Mrs. Glover's rôle of Mrs. Franklin in the same piece. In Macready's second season at Drury Lane she was, on 1 Oct. 1842, Celia in 'As you like it.' She played during the season, among other parts, Sophia in Holcroft's 'Road to Ruin,' Mrs. Foresight in Congreve's 'Love for Love,' and acted with Keeley and C. J. Mathews in Selby's 'Eton Boy.' At the Strand, in June 1843, she was the first Mrs. Blandish in Lunn's 'Rights of Woman,' playing other parts. She failed in January 1844 at Drury Lane as Queen Anne in 'Richard III.' Rejoining Macready at the Princess's in 1845, she was a poor Helen in the 'Hunchback,' but made a success as Cordelia to his Lear. In 1846 she was Dot in the version of the 'Cricket on the Hearth' given at the Princess's Theatre, played Julie de Mortemar in a revival of

'Richelieu,' and Mercury in a fantasy called 'The Ruins of Athens.' In April she was the first Ernestine in the piece so named, in May was Cora in 'Pizarro,' played Mrs. Ford in the 'Merry Wives of Windsor,' and was the original Madeleine Weir in White's once famous 'King of the Commons.' On 4 Sept. 1848 she was, at the Olympic, the original Laura Leeson in 'Time tries All.' She was also seen as Juliana in the 'Honeymoon,' Katharine in 'Taming of the Shrew,' and Cousin Cherry in the piece so named. After the burning of the Olympic on 29 March 1849, she joined the Strand under Henry Farren, and was on 10 Oct. the original Adrienne of the 'Reigning Favourite,' Oxenford's adaptation of 'Adrienne Lecouvreur.' Other original parts were Iolanthe in [Sir] Theodore Martin's 'King René's Daughter,' and Olivia in Tom Taylor's adaptation of the 'Vicar of Wakefield.' At the rebuilt Olympic, under William Farren, she played, on 14 Oct. 1850, the heroine of Stirling Coyne's 'My Wife's Daughter' ('La Femme de quarante Ans'), and on 13 Jan. 1851 Martha Gibbs in 'All that glitters is not Gold;' the Widow, in an adaptation of Sir Roger de Coverley, followed. Back at the Haymarket, she was on 21 April 1852 the first Fanny Morrison in Mark Lemon's 'Mind your own Business.' On 20 Nov., at the Haymarket, she obtained her greatest success as Peg Woffington in 'Masks and Faces,' by Taylor and Reade. Mrs. Trotter Southdown, in 'To oblige Benson,' was seen at the Olympic on 6 March 1854. At the height of her powers she played at the Olympic Lady Teazle, Miss Dorrillon in Mrs. Inchbald's 'Wives as they were, and Maids as they are,' and some original parts, among which were: Mrs. Metcalfe in 'Stay at Home,' an adaptation by Slingsby Lawrence (G. H. Lewes); Mrs. Levenson in Troughton's 'Leading Strings,' and Madam Bergmann in Wilkie Collins's 'Red Veil.' In February 1857, at the Lyceum, she had been the heroine in Taylor's 'Wolf in Sheep's Clothing.' At the Haymarket she was, 6 March 1861, the first Joconde in Taylor's 'A Duke in Difficulties;' her daughter Fanny—who had on 25 July 1860 played at Drury Lane Miranda in the burlesque of the 'Enchanted Isle' for a benefit—making as Colombe her first regular appearance on the stage, which she soon quitted.

After the season of 1860–61 Mrs. Stirling seems to have temporarily retired from the stage. On 24 Aug. 1863, however, she was, at the Adelphi, the heroine of a drama called 'Hen and Chickens;' on 29 Aug. 1864 the first Mrs. Hall in 'A Woman of Business,'

attributed to Webster: and on 30 Nov. the first Marguerite in the 'Workman of Paris' ('Les Drames du Cabaret'). At the Princess's, 2 July 1866, as the Duchess, she supported Miss Neilson in Watts Phillips's 'Huguenot Captain.' In Coyne's 'Woman of the World,' Olympic, 18 Feb. 1868, she was the first Mrs. Eddystone. Her last original part was Lady Carvll in Pinero's 'Lords and Commons,' 24 Nov. 1883. On 23 April 1869 she gave at the St. James's Hall a reading of 'A Midsummer Night's Dream.' At Webster's farewell benefit, Drury Lane, 2 March 1874, she played Mrs. Candour, repeating the performance at the same house for Buckstone's benefit, 8 June 1876. At the Imperial (Aquarium), 22 Sept. 1879, she was Lady Bountiful in Miss Litton's revival of the 'Beaux' Stratagem,' where also she was seen as Mrs. Hardcastle. In 1880, at the Haymarket, she was Mrs. Malaprop, and on 8 March 1882, at the Lyceum revival of 'Romeo and Juliet,' was the Nurse, a part she repeated on 1 Nov. 1884 at the same house to Miss Mary Anderson's Juliet. At the Haymarket, 6 Feb. 1883, she played the Marquise de Saint-Maur in a revival of 'Caste.' On 25 March 1885 she and Mrs. Keeley spoke an address at the Criterion, and on 29 Oct. she recited for Creswick's benefit a ballad called 'Our Whaling Fleet.' On 19 Dec. 1885 she was Martha in Wills's Lyceum version of 'Faust,' the last part in which she was seen. Her husband, died from whom she had long been separated, in August 1894, and in the same year she married Sir Charles Hutton Gregory, K.C.M.G., consulting engineer to the crown agents for the colonies, who was one year younger than herself, and with whom she had long been on terms of close intimacy. She died on 31 Dec. 1895. In her will, made in 1891, she speaks of herself as Mary Anne, otherwise Fanny Stirling or Lambert, wife of Edward Stirling or Lambert, formerly of Drury Lane Theatre. Her personal estate sworn under 11,556l., was left by codicil to her second husband.

Mrs. Stirling was an excellent actress, with a breadth of style in her late years drawing close to extravagance. She was almost the last actress to exhibit the grand style in comedy. Her method of receiving a call from the public was in itself a lesson in art. Peg Woffington was her greatest part, and was indeed a fine creation. In later years she had no equal in rôles such as Mrs. Candour, Mrs. Malaprop, and the Nurse. From 1870 her impersonations, though masterly, were rare, and she devoted herself principally to reciting and teaching elocution at the Royal Academy of Music. In her late years she was almost blind.

A portrait of her, in oils, is in the Garrick Club, and pictures from photographs are numerous.

Edward Stirling or Lambert (1809-1894), her first husband, born in April 1809, at Thame in Oxfordshire, was originally a banker's clerk, and took to the stage at the Pavilion in 1828, becoming a favourite in the country. At Birmingham he produced his first play, 'Sadak and Kalasrade,' a spectacular drama, the first of some two hundred pieces that have been seen at various London theatres. He was an actor stage manager under Yates at the Adelphi, and also at Covent Garden (where he produced ' Antigone '), the Surrey, Olympic, Lyceum, and Drury Lane. In addition to patriotic pieces, farces, burlesques, melodramas, and adaptations from Charles Dickens (including versions of 'Nicholas Nickleby,' 'The Cricket on the Hearth,' 'Old Curiosity Shop,' and ' Martin Chuzzlewit'), he is responsible for ' Old Drury Lane—Fifty Years' Recollections,' 2 vols. London, 1881, 8vo.

[Personal knowledge; Stirling's Old Drury Lane; Pascoe's Dramatic List; Theatrical Times; Macready's Reminiscences, ed. Pollock; Dramatic and Musical Review, various years; Scott and Howard's Blanchard; Era Almanack, various years; Clark Russell's Representative Actors. Accounts of Mrs. Stirling's early career are confused and contradictory.] J. K.

STIRLING, ROBERT (1790-1878), divine and inventor, was born in Perthshire in 1790. He was licensed by the presbytery of Dumbarton on 4 July 1815, and, being presented to the second charge at Kilmarnock in Ayrshire by the commissioner for the Duke of Portland, was ordained on 19 Sept. 1816. On 29 Jan. 1824 he was translated to Galston, Ayrshire, where he remained for upwards of fifty-three years. He received the honorary degree of D.D. from the university of St. Andrews on 11 Jan. 1840. On 30 May 1842 he was suspended with nine others by the general assembly from his judicial functions in the presbytery and the other higher courts for holding communion with the deposed ministers of Strathbogie, but was reinstated on 1 March 1843. After two years of failing health he died at Galston on 6 June 1878. He married Jane, eldest daughter of William Rankine, wine merchant, Galston, on 10 July 1819. By her he had three sons, Patrick and William, civil engineers, and David, minister of Craigie in Perthshire.

On 16 Nov. 1816 he took out a patent (No. 4081) for an engine which produced motive power by means of heated air, and on 1 Feb. 1827 and 1 Oct. 1840 he took further patents (Nos. 5456, 8652) of the same nature. One engine of 45-horse power was actually constructed on his model and employed for three years in driving machinery at the Dundee foundry. He also constructed many optical and other scientific instruments.

[Kilmarnock Standard, 8 June 1878; Scott's Fasti Ecclesiæ Scoticanæ, ii. i. 116, 176; Ward's Men of the Reign, p. 852; Woodcroft's Alphabetical List of Patentees.] E. I. C.

STIRLING, SIR THOMAS (1733-1808), bart., general, born on 8 Oct. 1733, was second son of Sir Henry Stirling, bart. (1688-1753) of Ardoch, Perthshire, by Anne, third daughter of Thomas Gordon, admiral of the Russian fleet and governor of Cronstadt. He received a commission from the Prince of Orange on 11 Oct. 1747, and served ten years in the Scots brigade (afterwards the 94th), which was then in the Dutch service. On 24 March 1757 he was made captain in the 42nd highlanders, having raised a company for that regiment. He served with it in the conquest of Canada, the capture of Martinique in 1759, and of the Havannah in 1762. In 1765 he was sent to take possession of the Illinois country ceded to Great Britain by the peace of 1763.

The 42nd returned from North America in 1767, but was sent back thither in 1776, when the war of independence had begun. Stirling had become major on 12 Dec. 1770, and lieutenant-colonel on 7 Sept. 1771, in the regiment; and he raised its strength from 350 to 1,200 men in five months in 1775. Under his command it took a very active part in the war, and was especially distinguished at the storming of Fort Washington on 16 Nov. 1776. Stirling and his men were thanked in general orders. They were again thanked for the capture of a post at Elizabethtown in February 1779. On the 19th of that month Stirling was appointed aide-de-camp to the king and colonel in the army. In the attempt upon Springfield (Massachusetts) in June 1780 he commanded a brigade. His thigh was broken by a shot, but he refused to allow amputation, as it would disable him for active service. Of this, however, he saw no more. He was given the colonelcy of the 71st foot on 13 Feb. 1782, but it was reduced soon afterwards. On 20 Nov. he was promoted major-general, and on 13 Jan. 1790 he was made colonel of the 41st foot. He became lieutenant-general on 3 May 1796, and general on 1 Jan. 1801. In 1794 he had bought the estate of Strowan, Perthshire, and he was made a baronet for his services. By the death of his brother, Sir William

Stirling, on 2d July 1799, he succeeded to the baronetcy of Ardoch, which became extinct at his death. He died unmarried at Strowan on 8 May 1808, leaving his property to his sister's son, Thomas Graham of Airth, with reversion to Graham's second son, who took the additional name of Stirling.

[Fraser's Stirlings of Keir, 1858; Foster's Baronetage; Burke's Landed Gentry; Cannon's Historical Record of the 42nd Highlanders; Stedman's Hist. of the American War; Cust's Annals of the Wars; private information.] E. M. L.

STIRLING, SIR WALTER (1718–1786), captain in the navy, only son of Walter Stirling (1686–1732), of Sherva in Stirlingshire, by Janet, daughter of William Ruthven of Torryburn, was born on 18 May 1718. He was promoted to the rank of lieutenant on 18 Feb. 1745–6; of commander on 26 Feb. 1757; and on 10 Jan. 1759 was posted to the Lynn, which he commanded for two years, and was then moved to the Lowestoft, in which he remained till the peace. From 1764 to 1766 he commanded the Rainbow, of 44 guns, on the North American station, and in 1770 was appointed to the Dunkirk as flagcaptain to the commodore, George Mackenzie, at Jamaica. In 1771 he was moved to the Portland, and in her returned to England. He was then employed for some years on the impress service, and in 1780 was appointed to the Gibraltar, going out to the West Indies with Sir Samuel Hood [see HOOD, SAMUEL, VISCOUNT HOOD]. After the capture of St. Eustatius he was sent home with the despatches and was knighted. In 1782 he was commodore at the Nore. He had no further employment, and died on 24 Nov. 1786. He married, in 1753, Dorothy (d. 1782), daughter of Charles Killing of Philadelphia, and had issue a daughter Anne (who married her cousin, Andrew Stirling of Drumpellier, Lanarkshire, and was mother of Sir James Stirling, 1791–1865 [q. v.]), and two sons, of whom the elder, Walter, was created a baronet in 1800, and died on 26 Aug. 1832.

The younger son, CHARLES STIRLING (1760–1833), vice-admiral, born on 28 April 1760, served as a lieutenant under Sir Edward Hughes [q. v.] in the East Indies. In May 1780 he was promoted to the rank of commander, and on 6 Sept. 1781, being then in the Savage, of 14 guns, 125 men, off Charlestown, fell in with the American privateer Congress, of 20 guns and 215 men, and was captured after a gallant resistance, for which, on the recommendation of Lord Howe, he was advanced to post rank on 25 Jan. 1783. In 1795 he commanded the Jason, frigate,

in the expedition to Quiberon under Sir John Borlase Warren [q. v.]; and on 29 June 1798, in company with the Pique and Mermaid, captured the French frigate La Seine, though with the loss of the Pique [see MILNE, SIR DAVID]. On 11 Oct. 1798, while chasing a French convoy near Brest, the Jason struck on a rock and became a total wreck, Stirling and his ship's company escaping to the shore and surrendering as prisoners of war. Within a few weeks they were exchanged, and in February 1799 Stirling was appointed to the Pompée, of 74 guns, which he commanded in the attack on the French squadron at Algesiras on 6 July 1801 [see SAUMAREZ, JAMES, LORD DE SAUMAREZ], when the ship received so much damage that she had to be left at Gibraltar when Saumarez sailed on the 12th in pursuit of the enemy.

In 1803–4 he was resident commissioner at Jamaica, and became a rear-admiral on 23 April 1804. In 1805, with his flag in the Glory of 98 guns, he commanded the Rochefort squadron, joined Sir Robert Calder [q. v.] on 15 July, and took part in the action off Cape Finisterre on the 22nd. In 1806 he commanded the squadron which convoyed the troops to the Rio de la Plata, and co-operated with them there [see POPHAM, SIR HOME RIGGS; MURRAY, SIR GEORGE, 1759–1819; AUCHMUTY, SIR SAMUEL] till, after the surrender of Lieutenant-general John Whitelocke [q. v.], he was ordered to the Cape of Good Hope as commander-in-chief. He became vice-admiral on 31 July 1810, and in 1811 was appointed to the Jamaica command, but was recalled in 1813 on a charge of corrupt practices. A court-martial, held in May 1814, decided that the charge was partly proved, and Stirling was placed on half-pay and barred from all further promotion. He died at his residence, near Weybridge, Surrey, on 7 Nov. 1833.

He married Charlotte, second daughter of Andreas Grote, banker, of London, and grandfather of George Grote [q. v.] the historian, and left issue.

[Fraser's Stirlings of Keir, p. 183; Charnock's Biogr. Nav. vi. 339; Ralfe's Nav. Biogr. iii. 73; Marshall's Roy. Nav. Biogr. i. 402; Gent. Mag. 1834, i. 330; O'Byrne's Nav. Biogr. Dict. p. 1120.] J. K. L.

STIRLING-MAXWELL, SIR WILLIAM (1818–1878), baronet, Spanish scholar, historian, and virtuoso, born at Kenmure on 8 March 1818, was the only son of Archibald Stirling of Keir, who married, on 1 June 1815, Elizabeth (1793–1822), third daughter of Sir John Maxwell (1768–1844), eighth baronet of Pollok and M.P. for Paisley,

1833-4. The descent of the Stirling family is traced from Walter de Striuelyng (*fl.* 1150), grandfather of Thomas de Striuelyng (*d.* 1227), chancellor of Scotland (see FRASER's *Stirlings of Keir*, 1858, passim). William's father, Archibald Stirling of Keir and Cawder, was born at Cawder on 2 Aug. 1769, and sailed for Montego Bay in 1789, to take charge of the family estates in Jamaica; the property had been built up by his uncle Archibald Stirling (1710-1783). For nearly twenty-five years he continued a planter there. In 1831 he succeeded his brother James in the family estates, and settled at Keir, near Dunblane. A keen agriculturist and breeder of shorthorns, he drained and improved his lands, and, though his West Indian property greatly deteriorated in value, his fortunes were augmented in Scotland by the discovery of coal, iron, and freestone upon his estates. He died on 9 April 1847.

William was educated at the private school of Daniel Baxter Langley, vicar of Olney in Buckinghamshire. He entered Trinity College, Cambridge, in 1835 (pensioner 28 April, fellow-commoner 13 Oct.), graduating B.A. in 1839, M.A. in 1843. His college tutor was Whewell. Upon leaving Cambridge at the close of 1839 he spent some time abroad, visiting Spain and the Levant. He explored Mount Lebanon, stayed with the monks on Mount Carmel, and returned to England from Syria in 1842. The study of the Bible amid the scenery of Palestine prompted him to versify a number of episodes of the Old Testament, and a few copies of his 'Songs of the Holy Land' were printed for private circulation (Edinburgh, 1846; 2nd ser. London, 1847; the two series were united and published in 1848, London, 4to).

Renewed visits to Spain induced a growing interest in Spanish art. The subject was practically unexplored, being represented in English by such perfunctory essays as the dramatist Cumberland's 'Anecdotes of Spanish Painting' and A. O'Neil's 'Dictionary of Spanish Painters,' 1834. Nor was either France or Germany much better off in this respect. Stirling's scholarly work on the subject thus proved to a large extent a revelation. It appeared in 1848 as 'Annals of the Artists of Spain' (London, 3 vols. 8vo; twenty-five copies with extra plates and adornments command high prices—one was sold in 1895 for 17*l.*; a new edition with emendations, 4 vols. 1891, 8vo); and, despite a tendency to discursiveness and over-elaboration of style, the good sense and taste displayed by an author so young were no less remarkable than the amount of precise information which his work embodied. The part relating to Velazquez was afterwards rewritten and published separately as 'Velazquez and his Works' (London, 1855, 8vo; translated into German, Berlin, 1856, and into French by G. Brunet, Paris, 1865). Two articles in 'Fraser's Magazine' for April and May 1851 showed that Spain was about to reveal new subjects and fresh sources of information; and in the following year appeared 'The Cloister Life of the Emperor Charles V' (London, 1852, 8vo; 2nd edit. 1853; 3rd edit. 1853; new edit. 1891, incorporating new materials contributed to 'Philobiblon Miscellanies,' vol. ii. 1856, besides American editions and German and Dutch versions). Stirling's work, which censures somewhat harshly the work of Robertson and other predecessors in the same field, is based mainly upon Siguença's 'History of the Order of St. Jerome' of 1605 and upon the Gonzales manuscript in the archives of the French foreign office. These archives were under the jealous custodianship of Mignet, who was himself meditating a work upon the subject (MIGNET, *Charles V, son abdication*, &c., 1854), and it required all Stirling's pertinacity to effect his object of transcribing the documents. When finished the book was dedicated to Richard Ford [q.v.] as a mark of 'admiration and friendship.' It was warmly praised by Ford, Milman, and the American historians, Prescott, Motley, and Kirk; but its position has necessarily been somewhat impaired by the rivalry of Mignet's book and by the elaborate Belgian monograph of Gachard ('Retraite et Mort de Charles V,' 3 vols., Brussels, 1854-5).

In the meantime (1847) Stirling had succeeded to the family estates, which he disentailed in 1849. Between that date and 1851 he remodelled the mansion at Keir, removing the entrance and turning the old hall into a library. In 1852 he sold the estate of Hampden in Jamaica, which from being a highly lucrative property had ceased to pay expenses. In 1852 he was returned unopposed for the county of Perth as a 'moderate conservative,' and in 1857, 1859, and 1865 he was re-elected without a contest. In 1868 he was unexpectedly defeated, but in 1874 was restored by a large majority. His speeches in Scotland were much appreciated for their point and flavour, but he took a very small part in debate, although he did effective work as a member of several commissions—of the universities commission, 1859, of the historical manuscripts commission, and from 1872 of the Scottish education board.

In addition to his seat at Keir, Stirling

had a mansion with a very fine library in London (128 Park Street, Grosvenor Square), where he exercised a wide hospitality. He was one of the original thirty-five members of the Philobiblon Society in 1854, and was also a member of the Athenæum Club (he was elected in 1849 under rule 2). From 1848 he was a familiar figure in literary society, and was specially friendly with Lord Dufferin and his circle, with the Duc d'Aumale, with Thackeray, Monckton Milnes, Dean Milman, and Peter Cunningham. Prescott during his sojourn in London met him at Lockhart's, and wrote of him afterwards to Ford as 'that prince of good fellows' (October 1850). To the 'Times' of 4 Sept. 1858 Stirling sent an appreciative memoir of Ford, and in 'Fraser's Magazine' for March 1859 he paid a like tribute to Prescott (this was privately printed with additions; both were reprinted in 'Miscellaneous Essays'). On 27 Nov. 1862 he was elected rector of St. Andrews University by 101 votes as against 59 recorded for Lord Dalhousie. His excellent address was not published at the time, though a few copies were struck off (see, however, *Miscellaneous Essays*; cf. KNIGHT's *Rectorial Addresses*, 1894). In 1865, by the death of his uncle, Sir John Maxwell, Stirling succeeded to his baronetcy, and assumed the additional name of Maxwell. In 1870 he was elected rector of Aberdeen University by the casting vote of the chairman, but declined to accept the honour. In 1871 he took an active part in organising a loan exhibition in Edinburgh of pictures, manuscripts, and relics relating to Sir Walter Scott, and in November 1872 he wrote the preface for the quarto catalogue of the exhibition (1872). On 5 Feb. 1872 he was installed rector of Edinburgh University, and on 27 April 1876 chancellor of Glasgow University (both of his addresses are in the 'Collected Works,' vol. vi.) On 21 June 1876 he was created D.C.L. by the university of Oxford, and in the same year he had the exceptional honour for a commoner of being nominated a knight of the Thistle.

These literary and academic distinctions did not prevent Stirling-Maxwell from an energetic discharge of his duties of landed proprietor. On the contrary, he devoted extraordinary care to the breeding of shorthorn cattle, and both in this matter, and more particularly with regard to the breed of Clydesdale horses, he raised the standard which had been attained by his immediate predecessors; in both classes of animals a 'Keir strain' came to be highly valued. He joined the Highland and Agricultural Society in 1841, took a leading part in the direction of the shows at Perth (1861) and

at Stirling (1864), and on 15 Jan. 1868 was elected honorary secretary of the society, a post which he held until his death; he was also president of the Glasgow Agricultural Society.

Meanwhile he indulged with absorbing eagerness in the collection of works of art and vertu and in many other hobbies, which tended to become the serious business of his life. His collection of sixteenth-century engravings and blocks for head and tail pieces was probably unrivalled. He himself acquired no little skill in the designing of initial letters. Other hobbies were the collation and bibliography of proverbs and the application of the bewildering variety of newly invented photographic processes. As an ardent bibliographer he was a regular frequenter of the reading-room at the British Museum, and referred more than once with gratitude to its '420 feet of wall covered to the height of six feet with books of reference.' He was appointed a trustee in 1872, and he was also a trustee of the National Gallery and a member of the senate of London University (1874-8).

Sir William died of a fever at Venice on 15 Jan. 1878, and was buried with his ancestors in Lecropt church. He married first, at Paris, on 20 April 1865, Anna Maria (d. 8 Dec. 1874), third daughter of David Leslie Melville, tenth earl of Leven and Melville, and by her left two sons, Sir John Maxwell Stirling-Maxwell, present baronet and M.P. for the College division of Glasgow, and Archibald, lieutenant in Princess Louise's Argyll highlanders. Sir William married as his second wife, on 1 March 1877, an old and attached friend, Caroline Elizabeth Sarah Norton [q. v.]; she was at the time confined to her room by indisposition, and she died on 15 June following.

There is a watercolour drawing of the historian as a child at Keir, painted by W. Douglas in 1824. A mezzotint was engraved from a photograph by R. B. Parkes as a frontispiece to the sixth volume of the 'Collected Works' in 1891, and there is a copperplate, by the same engraver, from a portrait by George Richmond, R.A., at Keir (prefixed to vol. i. of 'Works' in 1891). A terra-cotta bust, modelled in 1873 by Francis J. Williamson, is in the National Portrait Gallery, London.

It was not until five years after Stirling-Maxwell's death that his most elaborate historical work became available to the public under the title 'Don John of Austria, or Passages from the History of the Sixteenth Century, 1547-1578,' 1883, 2 vols. 8vo. It was edited and prefaced by Sir G. W. Cox, and adorned by cuts from a collection of engravings, &c., formed by the author, with a valuable appendix of documents and authorities (a few copies had been printed for private circulation as early as 1839, and others apparently at later stages of completion; and 115 copies were now issued in folio, with extra plates). The author had been at work upon 'Don John' almost continuously since the conclusion of his 'Cloister Life,' but his fastidious taste and regard for precision conspired to postpone publication. He was happily inspired in his subject; he was never happier than when elaborating a treatise within a treatise, such, for instance, in the present case, as his description of a slave galley, or that of the state of the navies of the Mediterranean in the sixteenth century. His good judgment generally in historical and literary matters is shown very clearly in his 'addresses.' His style gained in lucidity and succinctness with his years, and few scholars have had a wider bibliographical or historical purview of their subjects.

The minor publications of Stirling-Maxwell comprise: 1. 'A Posie of Poesies,' Cambridge, 1839, 8vo (in conjunction with Alexander James Beresford Hope [q. v.]) 2. 'An Essay towards a Collection of Books relating to the Art of Design, being a Catalogue of those at Keir,' London, 1850, 8vo (25 copies; another edit. 1860). 3. 'Lemmata Proverbialia,' London, 1851, 4to (10 copies only, privately printed in red, one on vellum). 4. 'Napoleon's Bequest to Cantillon: a Fragment of International History,' London, 1858, 8vo. 5. 'An Essay towards a Collection of Books relating to Proverbs, Emblems, Apophthegms, Epitaphs, and Ana,' London, 1860, 8vo (75 copies privately printed). The writer enumerates over a century more works than Duplessis in his 'Bibliographie Parémiologique,' Paris, 1847, and by 1870 his collection exceeded twelve hundred works on the subjects indicated. 6. 'Examples of the Ornamental Heraldry of the Sixteenth Century,' London, 1868 (300 copies, folio). 7. 'Arabesques and other Ornaments in Typographical Use at Zurich in 1559,' London, 1868, folio (the impression consists of 50 copies, 25 with red ornaments and black text, 25 vice versa; privately printed). 8. 'The Chief Victories of the Emperor Charles V. Designed by Martin Heemskirk in 1555, and now illustrated with Portraits, Prints, and Notes,' London and Edinburgh, 1870, folio (dedicated to the Duc d'Aumale, patron of the Philobiblon Society). 9. 'Examples of the Engraved Portraiture of the Sixteenth Century,' London, 1872, folio (50

copies privately printed). 10. 'The Turks in 1533: a series of drawings made in that year at Constantinople by Peter Coeck of Aelst, with introduction,' London and Edinburgh, 1873, obl. folio (100 copies privately printed, and bound in emblematic cloth). 11. 'Essay towards a Catalogue of Prints engraved from works of Velazquez and Murillo,' London, 1873, 12mo (100 copies privately printed). 12. 'Andrew Vesalii Tabulæ Anatomicæ Sex,' originally printed at Venice in 1538, London, elephant folio, 1874 (privately printed, 30 copies on paper, one on vellum, and one on parchment; prefixed are a portrait and a life of Andrew Vesalius by Stirling-Maxwell; the 'Tabulæ' are reproduced in facsimile). This choice reprint, like several others of these issues, has a presentation page with a coloured border enclosing Stirling-Maxwell's autograph (Brit. Mus.) 13. 'The Procession of Pope Clement VII and the Emperor Charles V after the Coronation at Bologna on 24 Feb. 1530;' engravings after Nicolas Hogenberg, with historical introduction, Edinburgh, 1875, folio (250 copies).

Stirling-Maxwell contributed some valuable papers to the early 'Miscellanies' of the Philobiblon Society, and several reviews to the 'Examiner,' to 'Fraser's Magazine,' and other periodicals. The life of Prescott in the eighth edition of the 'Encyclopædia Britannica' was by him; and he wrote a number of smaller pieces in prose and verse. A selection of his verses is included in Grant Wilson's 'Poets and Poetry of Scotland' (ii. 406). A six-volume edition of his 'Works,' comprising a new edition of 'The Artists of Spain' (4 vols.), a fourth edition of 'The Cloister Life,' and a volume of 'Essays, Addresses,' &c., appeared in 1891, 8vo (415 large-paper copies, with red initials and rules and duplicate illustrations).

[A very brief 'biographical note' is prefixed to the Collected Works, 1891, vol. vi. See also Fraser's Stirlings of Keir, 1858, and the same author's Maxwells of Pollok, i. 115; Foster's Alumni Oxon. 1715-1886; Foster's Peerage and Baronetage; Athenæum, 1878, i. 89; Academy, 1878, i. 75; Times, 17 Jan. 1878; Scotsman, 17 Jan. 1878; Guardian, 16 Jan. 1878; Foster's Members of Parliament—Scotland; Ticknor's Life of Prescott; Martin's Privately Printed Books, pp. 520, 526, 540; Allibone's Dict. of English Literature; Anderson's Scottish Nation; Stirling-Maxwell's Works in Brit. Mus. Library; information kindly supplied by Dr. Aldis Wright and James Macdonald, esq.]   T. S.

STISTED, Sir HENRY WILLIAM (1817-1875), general, son of Charles Stisted, lieutenant-colonel of the 3rd hussars, who died on 24 July 1842, by his wife Eliza, daughter of Major-general Burn, was born at St. Omer, France, in 1817. After being educated at Sandhurst, he entered the army as an ensign in the 2nd foot on 4 Dec. 1835, and served with his regiment in Afghanistan and Beloochistan, taking part in the storming of Ghuznee, where he was wounded at the gateway, the capture of Khelat, and the occupation of Cabul, for which he received a medal. On 19 April 1850 he was gazetted lieutenant-colonel of the 78th foot, and in the Persian war of 1856 and 1857 commanded a brigade in the night attack and battle of Kooshat, and took charge of his own regiment at the bombardment of Mohamrah, after which he received the thanks of the governor-general as well as a medal and clasps. He commanded the advanced guard of Havelock's force at the relief of Lucknow, 25 Sept. 1857, when (on Brigadier-general James George Smith Neill [q. v.] being killed) he was appointed to command the first brigade. That post he held until the close of the operations, when on 1 Jan. 1858 he was nominated C.B. In that year he served also in Rohilcund, and commanded the second brigade at the battle of Bareilly on 7 May.

He became lieutenant-colonel of the 93rd foot on 30 Sept. 1859, and served with the field force against the mountain tribes on the north-west frontier of India in December 1863. He was nominated to a divisional command in Canada in 1867, and appointed lieutenant-governor of Ontario in June of the same year. For his services in this capacity he received the thanks of the governor-general of Canada, and was nominated a K.C.B. on 20 May 1871. On 5 Feb. 1873 he was appointed a lieutenant-general, and was nominated colonel of the 93rd foot on 28 Sept. 1873. He died at Wood House, Upper Norwood, Surrey, on 10 Dec. 1875, having married in 1845 Maria, daughter of Lieutenant-colonel Burton.

[Illustrated London News, 25 Dec. 1875, p. 635; Dod's Peerage, 1875, p. 618; Hart's Annual Army List, 1874, pp. 8, 339; Kaye and Malleson's Hist. of the Indian Mutiny, iv. 241, 357.]   G. C. B.

STOCK, JOSEPH (1740–1813), bishop of Killala and afterwards of Waterford and Lismore, was the son of Luke Stock, a hosier, in Dublin, and Ann, his wife, and was born at 1 Dame Street, Dublin, on 22 Dec. 1740. He was educated at Mr. Gast's school in his native city and at Trinity College, Dublin, where his career was a distinguished one. He obtained a scholarship in 1759, graduated B.A. in 1761, and gained a fellowship in

1763. In 1776 he published anonymously a life of George Berkeley [q. v.]—subsequently republished in the 'Biographia Britannica'—a work of some value as the only memoir of its subject based on contemporary information. Having taken orders, Stock retired on the college living of Conwall in the diocese of Raphoe. In 1793 he was collated prebendary of Lismore, but resigned this preferment in 1795, on his appointment to the head-mastership of Portora Royal school. In January 1798 he succeeded John Porter as bishop of Killala. Shortly after his consecration, and while holding his first visitation at the castle of Killala, the bishop became a prisoner of the French army under General Humbert (cf. LEVER, Maurice Tiernay). Of his experiences at this time he has left a partial record in his private diary—23 Aug. to 15 Sept. 1798—which has been printed in Maxwell's 'History of the Rebellion of 1798,' and in two letters to his brother Stephen, published in the 'Auckland Correspondence' (iv. 46–51). In 1799 he published a more complete account of the French invasion of Mayo in his 'Narrative of what passed at Killala in the Summer of 1798. By an Eye-witness.' This little work is the most authentic record extant of the episode it describes, and is written with a rare impartiality. Its liberality is said to have been a bar to the bishop's advancement (HOLLAND, Memoirs of the Whig Party). In 1810 Stock was translated to the diocese of Waterford and Lismore, and died at Waterford on 13 Aug. 1813. He was twice married. By his first wife, Mrs. Palmer, a sister of William Newcome [q. v.], he had several children. He married, secondly, in 1795, only ten weeks after his first wife's death, a widow named Mary Obins. Portraits of the bishop are in the possession of two of his descendants, Mr. St. George Stock of Oxford, and the Rev. Henry Palmer, of Killiney, co. Dublin.

Stock was an accomplished classical scholar, an excellent linguist, and a man of much general culture. Besides the works mentioned he wrote: 1. 'The Book of the Prophet Isaiah in Hebrew and English, with Notes,' Bath, 1803. 2. 'The Book of Job metrically arranged and newly translated into English, with Notes,' Bath, 1805. He also published school editions of Tacitus and Demosthenes, and was an active contributor to the controversial theology of his day. He left two manuscript volumes of correspondence which are preserved in the library of Trinity College, Dublin. They consist chiefly of letters written from Killala and Waterford between 1806 and 1813 to his son Henry in Dublin, and give interesting glimpses of life in an episcopal palace in a remote part of Ireland at the beginning of the nineteenth century. A manuscript autobiography belongs to the family of the bishop's second wife.

[Berkeley's Works, vol. i. 1784; Cotton's Fasti Eccles. Hib. i. 134, 191, iv. 77; Mant's Hist. of the Church of Ireland, ii. 472; Ballina Herald, 4 Nov. 1897; Gilbert's Hist. of Dublin, ii. 308; Taylor's Hist. of the University of Dublin, p. 429; Lecky's Hist. of Ireland, v. 42–68; Public Characters, 1807; Stubbs's Hist. of Dublin University.] C. L. F.

STOCK, RICHARD (1569?-1626), puritan divine, was born at York about 1569. He entered St. John's College, Cambridge, in his nineteenth year, was chosen scholar on 10 Nov. 1587, and, after graduating B.A. in 1590 and M.A. in 1594, would have been elected fellow had there been a vacancy. He was a favourite with the master, William Whitaker [q. v.] He began to preach in 1594. On 15 July 1595 he was incorporated M.A. of Oxford. He was to have been one of the original fellows of Sidney-Sussex College, but left the university soon after the college building was begun (20 May 1596). He was rector of Standlake, Oxfordshire, in 1599 (FOSTER). After acting as domestic chaplain successively to Sir Anthony Cope (1548?-1614) [see under COPE, SIR ANTHONY, d. 1551], and to Lady Lane of Bourton-on-the-Water, Gloucestershire, he went up to London, and was appointed lecturer at St. Augustine's, Watling Street. Soon afterwards he became curate to Thomas Early at St. Mildred's, Bread Street, and, on Early's death in 1604, became curate to Thomas Edmonds, B.D., rector of Allhallows, Bread Street. Edmonds was at the time too infirm to do duty; he died in 1610, and on 8 March 1611 Stock succeeded him in the rectory. Brian Walton [q. v.] was his curate in 1623–6. Both as a parochial clergyman and as a public preacher Stock maintained a high reputation. As a young man he had dealt, in a sermon at St. Paul's Cross (1606), with the inequalities in the incidence of the city rates, which pressed heavily on the poor, and was decried as 'a greenhead.' Towards the end of his life he reverted to the topic in a sermon at the election of lord mayor, remarking that 'a grayhead spake now what a greenhead had done formerly.' He was active in promoting the observance of the Lord's day. In preaching he made more use of quotations from the fathers than his puritan hearers were accustomed to. He died on 20 April 1626, and was buried in his church, where a

monument (destroyed in the fire of 1666) was erected to his memory by his parishioners on 28 Jan. 1629. His portrait has three times engraved; he wore a moustache and square beard, and dressed in skullcap and ruff. His wife, by whom he had three daughters, survived him many years.

He published single sermons, 1606–14, including a funeral sermon for John Harington, second lord Harington of Exton [q. v.] Posthumous were: 1. 'A learned ... Commentary upon ... Malachy,' 1641, fol. Appended is an 'Exercitation' on Malachi by Samuel Torshell [q. v.] 2. 'A Stock of Divine Knovvledge. ... Description of the Divine Nature,' 1641, 4to. Brook distinguishes him from a contemporary Richard Stock, rector of Kirk Heaton, Yorkshire, and founder of a school there.

[Funeral Sermon, by Gataker, 1626; Foster's Alumni Oxon. 1500–1714, iv. 1425; Wood's Fasti (Bliss), i. 271, ii. 82; Stow's Survey of London, 1633, p. 821; Fuller's Worthies, 1662 (Yorkshire), p. 231; Clarke's Lives of Thirty-two English Divines, 1677, pp. 61 sq. (portrait); Newcourt's Repertorium, 1708, i. 246, 493; Granger's Biographical Hist. of England, 1779, i. 368; Brook's Lives of the Puritans, 1813, ii. 344 sq., iii. 515.] A. G.

STOCK, ST. SIMEON (1165?-1265), Carmelite. [See SIMEON.]

STOCKDALE, JOHN (1749?-1814), publisher, born in Cumberland about 1749, was brought up, it is said, as a blacksmith, then became valet to John Astley of Dukinfield, Cheshire, and eventually removed, about 1780, to London, where he was engaged as porter to John Almon [q. v.], the publisher. When Almon retired from business in favour of John Debrett [q. v.], Stockdale opened an opposition shop; and, 'being a man of natural parts, he soon became conspicuous in business in spite of much eccentricity of conduct and great coarseness of manners' (Gent. Mag. June 1815). Among the numerous works bearing his name as publisher are: Ferguson's 'Roman Republic,' 1783, an edition of Shakespeare's 'Dramatic Works,' 1784, Edwards's 'History of the West Indies,' Chalmers's edition of Defoe's 'History of the Union,' Phillips's 'Voyage to Botany Bay,' and Dr. Johnson's Works,' 1787 (vols. 12 and 13 of which Stockdale edited). He also issued 'Debates in Parliament,' 1784–90, an edition of 'Robinson Crusoe,' and Aikin's 'Country round Manchester,' 1795, originally intended to be merely an account of the neighbourhood of Mottram-in-Longdendale, with which Stockdale had personal acquaintance. In 1788 he published the Rev. John

Logan's 'Review of the Charges against Warren Hastings,' which was conceived by the government to embody a libellous charge of corruption and injustice against the House of Commons. Stockdale was accordingly prosecuted. The case came before Lord Kenyon in December 1789, and Stockdale was eloquently defended by Erskine (see ERSKINE, *Speeches*, 1847, vol. iii.; *Parl. Hist.* xxvii. 1–7; HOWELL, *State Trials*, xxii. 237). Erskine contended that the defendant was not to be judged by isolated passages, selected and put together in the information, but by the entire context of the publication and its general character and objects. Stockdale was acquitted, and so conspicuous a triumph for the liberty of the press led to the passing of the Libel Act of 1792, which established that a man was not to be punished for a few unguarded expressions, and committed to the judgment of the jury the construction to be placed on an alleged libeller's general purpose and animus in writing.

Stockdale again figured as defendant in an action for libel brought by Joseph Nightingale [q. v.] in 1809, when he was amerced in 200*l.* damages. Towards the end of his career he dealt largely in the surplus printed stock ('remainders') of other publishers, and excited the jealousy of the regular traders by a series of sales of books by auction which he established in various parts of the country. By his earlier speculations he acquired considerable property, but afterwards he was less successful; and the circumstance of having to make an arrangement with his creditors is said to have preyed upon his mind and accelerated his death, which took place, at the age of sixty-five, on 21 June 1814.

He married Mary Ridgway, a native of Roe Cross, Mottram-in-Longdendale, Cheshire, and sister to James Ridgway, a well-known publisher of Piccadilly, London. By her he had several children, including Mary R. Stockdale, who wrote: 1. 'The Effusions of the Heart: Poems,' 1798. 2. 'The Mirror of the Mind: Poems' (with an autobiography), 1810, 2 vols. 3. 'The Life of a Boy,' 1821, 2 vols.; besides translations from Berquin and others, and some minor pieces.

His eldest son, JOHN JOSEPH STOCKDALE (1770–1847), was admitted to the freedom of the Stationers' Company on 3 Aug. 1802, and afterwards took up the livery. He compiled and edited a large number of books, including: Wellesley's 'Events and Transactions in India,' 1805, 'Cevallos's Usurpation of the Crown of Spain,' 1808, and 'Sketches Civil and Military of the Island of Java,' 1811. He was the publisher of the notorious 'Memoirs of Harriette Wilson,' 1826.

During the recess of 1836 Stockdale commenced an action against Messrs. Hansard for the publication of a libel in an official 'Report of the Inspectors of Prisons,' in which certain strictures were made on some obscene books alleged to be published by Stockdale. The verdict went against Stockdale, upon a plea of justification; but Chief-justice Denman, in summing up, made a declaration adverse to the plea of 'privilege' which Messrs. Hansard had set up in their defence. Stockdale thereupon brought another action, and the case was thenceforth tried upon the single issue—whether the printers were justified in printing animadversions on Stockdale by the privilege and order of the House. The latter having ordered the Hansards to plead, the court of queen's bench unanimously decided against them. The costs were paid by the treasury; but it was decided that in case of any future action Messrs. Hansard should not plead at all. Stockdale duly brought another action in the recess of 1839, and judgment went in his favour by default. When, however, the sheriffs of Middlesex proceeded, by order of the court of queen's bench, to put the verdict into effect, the printer fell back upon parliament for protection. Accordingly the sheriffs and other persons who sought to carry out the orders issued by the law court against the Hansards were imprisoned by order of the House of Commons. These protracted and vexatious proceedings were only brought to a close by the passing in 1840 of the 3 & 4 Vict. c. 9, by which it was enacted that proceedings, criminal or civil, against persons for the publication of papers printed by order of either house of parliament shall be stayed upon the production of a certificate to that effect (MAY, *Parliamentary Practice*, 1893, pp. 99, 138 sq.) Stockdale was thus finally defeated, and the printer was indemnified. He died at Bushey on 16 Feb. 1847, aged 70.

[Gent. Mag. 1814 i. 701, 1815 i. 649, 1847 i. 452; Chadwick's Reminiscences of Mottram, pp. 22, 64; Brit. Mus. Cat.; Lowndes's Bibliographer's Manual (Bohn), p. 2942; Dict. of Living Authors, 1816; Bray's Life of Stothard, 1851, pp. 36, 37; Erskine May's Const. Hist. 1865, i. 460, ii. 113; communication from Mr. C. R. Rivington, clerk to the Stationers' Company.]

C. W. S.

STOCKDALE, PERCIVAL (1736–1811), miscellaneous writer, born on 26 Oct. (O. S.) 1736 at Branxton, Northumberland, was the only child of Thomas Stockdale, vicar of that parish and perpetual curate of Cornhill, near the Tweed, by his wife, Dorothy Collingwood of Murton, Northumberland. After spending six years in the grammar school at Alnwick, he was removed in 1751 to the grammar school at Berwick-upon-Tweed. He became intimately acquainted with the Greek and Latin classics, and acquired a taste for poetry. He never harboured a doubt that he was a poetical genius of the highest order, and the indifference of the public to his pretensions embittered his life. In 1754 he proceeded to the university of Aberdeen, having obtained a bursary in the united colleges of St. Leonard and St. Salvador. The death of his father in 1755 left the family in pecuniary difficulties, and he accepted the offer of a lieutenancy in the 22nd or royal Welsh fusiliers. He joined Admiral Byng's fleet, which anchored in the bay of Gibraltar in May 1756. Stockdale, with part of his regiment, was on board the Revenge, in the expedition sent, under the command of Admirals Byng and West, to the relief of the besieged garrison of St. Philip in the island of Minorca. He returned to England in October 1756, and in November 1757 he left the army on the ostensible ground of ill-health.

On his way to his mother's house at Berwick he stayed at Durham, and was introduced to Dr. Thomas Sharp (1693-1758) [q. v.], archdeacon of Northumberland, who persuaded him to take holy orders. At Michaelmas 1759 he was ordained deacon by Dr. Richard Trevor [q. v.], bishop of Durham. Immediately afterwards he came to London as Sharp's substitute in the curacy and lectureship of Duke's Place, near Aldgate. Henceforth he mixed in the best literary society of the metropolis, and became intimate with Garrick, Dr. Johnson, Dr. Browne, Goldsmith, Hawkesworth, and Lord Lyttelton. He published 'A Poetical Address to the Supreme Being' (Berwick [1764]), 4to, and 'The Constituents: a poem,' London, 1765, 4to. In 1767, being without church employment, he visited Italy, and resided for two years at Villafranca, where he read and wrote assiduously. He returned to London in 1769, and in the following year published a translation of Tasso's 'Amyntas.' He succeeded Dr. Guthrie in the management of the 'Critical Review,' edited the 'Universal Magazine' in 1771, and wrote a 'life' of Waller, prefixed to the poet's 'Works' (1772). He also translated the 'Antiquities of Greece' from the Latin of Lambert Bos (1772), and in 1773 he published 'Three Discourses: two against Luxury and Dissipation, one on Universal Benevolence.' In the summer of 1773 his most important work appeared—a poem entitled 'The Poet.'

At this period Lord Sandwich, first lord of the admiralty, appointed him chaplain of the Resolution, guardship, lying at Spithead. He was attached to that vessel for three years. He composed some characteristic minor poems, besides translating into English Sabbathier's 'Institutions, Manners, and Customs of the Ancient Nations,' and publishing 'Six Discourses, to which is prefixed an introduction containing a view of the genuine Ancient Philosophy,' London, 1777, 8vo. Afterwards he wrote 'An Enquiry into the Nature and Genuine Laws of Poetry; including particular defence of the Writings and Genius of Mr. Pope' (London, 1778, 12mo), against the essay by Warton. He published in the same year 'Miscellanies in Prose and Verse' and a translation of Riccoboni's 'Letters from Lord Rivers to Sir C. Cardigan.' In 1779 he contributed to the 'Public Advertiser' political letters under the signature of 'Agricola.' According to his own doubtful story, the principal London booksellers, having resolved to bring out a new edition of the 'English Poets,' with biographies, requested Stockdale to undertake the work. An agreement was made, but, by some 'strange misunderstanding,' Stockdale was deprived of this employment, and Dr. Johnson wrote the 'Lives of the Poets.'

After a brief experience as tutor to the eldest son of Lord Craven, he was presented in 1780 by Sir Adam Gordon to the rectory of Hinxworth, Hertfordshire. While there he took priest's orders—twenty-three years after his admission to the diaconate. In 1782 he wrote 'An Examination of the Important Question whether Education at a Great School or by Private Tuition is preferable,' London, 1782, 8vo. In 1783 Lord-chancellor Thurlow presented him to the vicarage of Lesbury, Northumberland, and to this the Duke of Northumberland added the vicarage of Long Houghton in the same county. There Stockdale composed an 'Essay on Misanthropy,' 1783. On 28 Oct. 1784 Archbishop More conferred upon him the Lambeth degree of M.A. (Gent. Mag. June 1864, p. 770).

His tragedy of 'Ximenes,' in five acts and in verse, was printed in 1788, but was not acted, as the manager of Covent Garden Theatre declined to accept it. After paying a visit to Tangier for the sake of his health, Stockdale returned to Lesbury in 1790. Subsequently he published 'Thirteen Sermons to Seamen, preached on board H.M.S. Leander in the Bay of Gibraltar,' 1791; a 'Letter to Granville Sharp, suggested by the present Insurrection of the Negroes in the Island of St. Domingo,' 1791; 'Observations on the Writings and Conduct of our present

Political and Religious Reformers,' 1792; 'Poetical Thoughts and Views on the Banks of the Wear,' 1792; an amusing correspondence with Shute Barrington, bishop of Durham, 1792; a 'Letter to Mr. Bryant, occasioned by his late Remarks on' Mr. Pope's Universal Prayer,' 1793; an edition of Thomson's 'Seasons,' with biography, 1793; a 'Letter to a Gentleman of the Philanthropic Society on the Liberty of the Press, 1794; 'The Invincible Island: a poem, with introductory Observations on the present War,' 1797; 'A Discourse on the Duties and Advantages of Old Age,' Alnwick, 1801, 4to; 'A Remonstrance against Inhumanity to Animals, and particularly against the Savage Practice of Bull-Baiting,' Alnwick, 1802, 8vo; 'Lectures on the truly eminent English Poets,' 1807, which present a strange combination of good and bad sense, of just and petulant criticism; a selection of his best 'Poems,' 1808; and 'Memoirs of his Life and Writings, containing many interesting Anecdotes of the Illustrious Men with whom he was connected,' 2 vols. 8vo, London, 1809, with his portrait, engraved by Fitter from a painting by Downman. Unbounded egotism, conceit, and yearning for poetical fame are exhibited in these 'Memoirs.' 'I know,' he exclaims, 'that this book will live and escape the havoc that has been made of my literary fame.' He died at Lesbury on 14 Sept. 1811, and was buried at Cornhill-on-the-Tweed.

[Stockdale's Memoirs; Boswell's Life of Johnson, ed. Hill; Baker's Biogr. Dram. 1812, i. 694, ii. 27, iii. 426; Gent. Mag. 1810 ii. 248, 1811 ii. 384, 528, 667; D'Israeli's Calamities of Authors, 1812, ii. 313; Watt's Bibl. Brit.; Nichols's Lit. Anecd. viii. 14, 18.]   T. C.

STOCKER, THOMAS (fl. 1569–1592), translator, is described by Tanner as 'ex generosa familia oriundus,' and may have been connected with the Stockers of Bedfordshire (Harl. Soc. Publications, xix. 143). He translated from the French the following: 1. 'A righte noble History of the Successors of Alexander, taken out of Diodorus Siculus: and some of their lives written by the wise Plutarch,' London, 1569, 4to. This was a translation of C. de Seyssel's 'Histoire des Successeurs d'Alexandre le Graud,' Paris, 1530, fol. 2. 'Two and twentie Sermons of Maister John Calvin. In which sermons is most religiously handled the hundredth and nineteenth Psalme of David,' London, 1580, 8vo. 3. 'An excellent treatise of the Immortalytie of the soule. Set foorth by M. John Calvin and englished from the French by T. Stocker,' London, 1581, 12mo. 4. 'Divers Sermons of Maister John Calvin concerning the Divinitie, Humanitie, and Nativitie of

Our Lord Jesus Christe,' London, 1581, 8vo. 5. 'A Tragicall Historie of the troubles and Civile warres of the lowe Countries,' 8vo. The dedication to Lord Robert Dudley, earl of Essex, is dated 15 March 1583–4. The work is a translation of 'Histoire des Troubles et Guerres Civiles des Pays-Bas,' 1582, 8vo, which is prefaced by a dedication signed 'Théophile D. L.' 6. 'The Second Part of the Demoniacke Worlde, or worlde possessed with Devils,' London, 1583, 8vo (two editions); a translation of the second part of Pierre Viret's 'Monde Demoniacle,' Geneva, 1579, 8vo. 7. 'The Cauteles, Canon, and ceremonies of the most blasphemous, abominable, and monstrous Popish Masse. Togither, the Masse intitled Of the body of Jesus Christ. Fully set downe, both in Latine and Englishe. With annotations set forth by Peter Viret,' London, 1584, 8vo. Dedicated 'To Syr William Cycell, Lord High Treasurer of England.' 9. 'Sermon of Maister John Calvin on the Historie of Melchisedech, also Abraham's Faith, in believing God: comprehending foure sermons. And Abraham's Obedience in offering his sonne Isaak; in three sermons,' London, 1592, 8vo.

The above works are contained in the library of the British Museum. Stocker translated another volume of sermons (London, 1594, 12mo), and published 'A Lamentable Paraphrase on the Lamentations of Jeremiah by Daniell Tousain,' London, 1587.

[Tanner's Bibl. Brit.-Hib. p. 693; British Museum Library Catalogue; Ames's Typogr. Antiq. ed. Herbert, index; Gray's Index to Hazlitt's Collections.]   E. I. C.

STOCKS, LUMB (1812–1892), line-engraver, son of a Yorkshire coal-owner, was born at Lightcliffe, near Halifax, on 30 Nov. 1812. He was educated at Horton, near Bradford, and while there he received instruction in drawing from Charles Cope, the father of Charles West Cope, R.A. At the age of fifteen he came to London, and was articled to Charles Rolls, the line-engraver, and in 1832 he exhibited at the Royal Academy a 'Portrait of a Young Artist.' On the expiration of his articles he began the practice of his art by engraving some excellent plates for the annuals then in vogue, among which were 'The Lace Maker' and 'Going to Service,' after James Inskipp, for the 'Amulet' of 1835. He next engraved for Finden's 'Royal Gallery of British Art' the plates of 'The Procession to the Christening,' after Penry Williams; 'Preparing Moses for the Fair,' from the 'Vicar of Wakefield,' after Maclise; and 'Nell Gwyn,' after Charles Landseer, R.A.

These were followed by 'Raffaelle and the Fornarina,' after Sir Augustus Wall Callcott, R.A., engraved for the Art Union of London, and by three plates—'The Glee Maiden' and 'Ruth,' after Robert Scott Lauder, and 'The Parable of the Ten Virgins,' after James Eckford Lauder—engraved for the Association for the Promotion of the Fine Arts in Scotland. About the same time he produced 'The Dame School' and 'The Rubber,' after Thomas Webster, R.A., and 'Bedtime,' after Mr. W. P. Frith, R.A., as well as several plates for the 'Art Journal' from pictures in the Royal and Vernon collections, which included 'Cupid and Psyche,' after Thomas Uwins, R.A.; 'Uncle Toby and the Widow,' after Charles Robert Leslie, R.A., and 'St. Luke painting the Virgin,' after Steinla.

In 1853 Stocks was elected an associate engraver of the Royal Academy, and in 1855 became an associate engraver of the new class, which rendered him eligible for the higher rank of academician, to which he was elected in 1871. About 1859 he engraved for the Art Union of Glasgow 'Many Happy Returns of the Day,' after Frith, which was followed by a series of plates illustrating 'The Dowie Dens of Yarrow,' after Sir J. Noel Paton, R.S.A., and later on by 'The Gentle Shepherd,' after Wilkie, and 'O Nannie, wilt thou gang wi' me?' after Thomas Faed, R.A., for the Association for the Promotion of the Fine Arts in Scotland. He likewise engraved for the Art Union of London 'Claude Duval,' after Frith; 'The Meeting of Wellington and Blücher after the Battle of Waterloo,' from the painting by Maclise in the House of Lords; 'Dr. Johnson waiting for an Audience of Lord Chesterfield,' after Edward Matthew Ward, R.A.; and 'Stolen by Gipsies: the Rescue,' after J. B. Burgess, R.A., the last of which had been left unfinished by Charles Henry Jeens.

Among other and later brilliant works by Stocks were 'Charlotte Corday in the Conciergerie' and 'Marie Antoinette listening to the Act of Accusation the day before her Trial,' after E. M. Ward, R.A.; 'Detected,' by J. Callcott Horsley, R.A.; 'The Fight interrupted,' after Mulready; 'The Odalisque' and 'The Sister's Kiss,' after Sir Frederic (Lord) Leighton, P.R.A.; 'The Silken Gown,' after Thomas Faed, R.A.; 'Olivia and Viola,' from 'Twelfth Night,' after Sir J. Noel Paton; a 'Souvenir of Velasquez' and 'The Princes in the Tower,' after Sir John Everett Millais, P.R.A.; and 'The Spanish Letter-Writer,' after J. B. Burgess, R.A.

Stocks died at 9 Richmond Villas, Seven Sisters Road, Holloway, London, on 28 April 1892, and was buried in Highgate cemetery. He was the last survivor of the eminent English line-engravers of the nineteenth century. A portrait of him was painted by his son, Arthur Stocks, and exhibited at the Royal Academy in 1885.

ARTHUR STOCKS (1846–1889), third son of Lumb Stocks, was born in London on 9 April 1846, and educated at the Islington Proprietary School. He was at first a pupil of his father, but afterwards gave up engraving and entered the schools of the Royal Academy, where he gained in 1868 a silver medal for painting from the life. His first appearance as a painter was in 1866, when he sent to the Society of British Artists a picture entitled ''Twas a famous Victory.' In 1867 he sent to the Royal Academy 'Christmas Upstairs' and 'The Expected Letter,' and these were followed in subsequent years by 'A Review at Chelsea,' 'Mending the Old Cradle,' 'The Best of Husbands,' 'Her Last Sacrament,' 'Sermon Time,' engraved in mezzotint by his brother, Bernard O. Stocks, 'At Last,' and 'A Friend of Mine, Grandfather,' and 'The Sands of Time.' The last two were at the Royal Academy in 1889. He exhibited also at the Institute of Painters in Oil-Colours and the Dudley Gallery, as well as at the Royal Institute of Painters in Watercolours, of which he was a member. He died at 63 Hanley Road, Hornsey Rise, London, on 12 Oct. 1889, and was buried in Highgate cemetery (*Times*, 28 Oct. 1889).

Walter Fryer Stocks, second son of Lumb Stocks, is known as a painter of landscapes in watercolours, which have appeared at the Royal Academy and elsewhere from 1862 to the present time.

[Sandby's Hist. of the Royal Academy of Arts, 1862, ii. 355; Times, 30 April 1892; Athenæum, 1892 i. 607, 1889 ii. 604 (Arthur Stocks); Royal Academy Exhibition Catalogues, 1832–92.]   R. E. G.

STOCKTON, OWEN (1630–1680), puritan divine, fourth son of Owen Stockton, prebendary of Chester Cathedral, was born at Chester on 31 May 1630. His father traced descent from a younger branch of the Stocktons of Kiddington, Cheshire; his mother was a Tylee of Cambridgeshire. Upon her husband's death in 1637 she removed to Ely, where Owen was educated at William Hitch's grammar school. He was a precocious pupil, and read Foxe's 'Acts and Monuments' instead of playing. At fifteen he entered Christ's College, Cambridge. Henry More, the platonist, was his tutor. Stockton graduated B.A. from Christ's College in 1649, and M.A. from Caius (whither he had migrated) in 1653. He was appointed by the parliamentary commission a junior fellow of Gonville and Caius College in 1651, senior fellow in 1652-8. He was also morning lecturer, 1651; Hebrew lecturer, 1652; steward, 1653; and catechist in 1654. On beginning to study divinity he went to London, read at Sion College, attended the Gresham lectures, and sat under popular preachers. He began to preach in the villages round Cambridge, and after July 1656 he preached fortnightly in St. Andrew's Church, Cambridge, having received presbyterian ordination on 20 Feb. 1655 in London.

He was chosen town lecturer at Colchester by the mayor and aldermen in 1657 (MORANT, *Hist. of Essex*, i. 100), and gave a morning lecture at St. James's Church, as well as an afternoon and week-day lecture elsewhere in the town, until the Act of Uniformity was passed. After 1662 Stockton and Edmund Warren established a dissenting congregation in Colchester, their first meetings being held by consent of Speaker Lenthall, the owner, in the castle (CUTTS, *Colchester*, p. 209). Stockton also preached in his own house until 1665, when on 24 Aug. (St. Bartholomew's Day) he removed with his wife and family to Chattisham, Suffolk, where his wife's brother-in-law, John Meadows [q. v.], was living. Stockton inhabited a large country house with his sister Sarah, occasional pupils, and his brother Thomas Stockton, who managed the land pertaining to it. He often preached in the church, the rector, with whom he was on good terms, having another cure. He frequently revisited Colchester, Manningtree, White Colne, and other places in Essex, and was often in danger of arrest, although more than once at Colchester he was forewarned by the constable, who was one of his hearers.

In 1669 Stockton was reported to Archbishop Sheldon as having a conventicle in Colchester, and in the next year was presented in the ecclesiastical court by one Mr. Maidstone. At the indulgence of 1672 he took out licenses, 16 April, to be an independent teacher at Ipswich, Colchester, and Hadleigh. Having received calls to both Colchester and Ipswich, he decided to preach alternately at both, residing meantime at Ipswich, where he died of fever after a few days' illness on 31 Aug. 1680.

By his will (P. C. C. 'Bath' 156) Stockton left his library and 500*l*. to found a fellowship and scholarship at Gonville and Caius College, an annuity of 20*l*. to Harvard College, Massachusetts, and legacies to his brother William Stockton, his cousin Owen Stockton, and others. A clause desires that his only surviving child, Sarah (*d.* circa 1695), 'attire herself in a sober manner as becometh one professing godliness;' the provisions for the endowment are also thoroughly puritan.

Stockton's wife Elianor, daughter of Roger Hunt of Swaffham Priors, Cambridgeshire, survived him. Her diary, dated 20 June 1695, is in Dr. Williams's library, where is also that of Stockton from 1 April 1665 to Bartholomew's Day, 24 Aug. 1680, a week before his death. It is in a clear but minute hand, largely introspective and self-condemnatory. Extracts from it were printed by T. W. Davids in his 'Annals.' With the diary are the following unpublished manuscripts by Stockton: 'A Treatise of glorifying God,' in three parts, prepared for publication with a revised copy of the introduction dated 16 Aug. 1661; 'Practical Questions concerning the Pestilence;' 'A Treatise concerning an Interest in God;' 'Of Walking with God;' 'On knowing the Plague of one's own Heart;' 'Cases of Conscience.'

Stockton published: 1. 'A Treatise of Family Instruction,' in two parts, London, 1672, 8vo. 2. 'Consolations in Life and Death' (on the death of Mrs. E. Asty), London, 1681, 12mo; 1847, 12mo. 3. 'A Warning to Drunkards,' 1682, 8vo. Nos. 2 and 3 were published posthumously.

[John Fairfax's True Dignity of St. Pauls Elder exemplified in the Life of Owen Stockton, republished in Christian Biography, 1835; Clarke's Lives, 1682, p. 193; Kennett's Register, 1791; Davids's Annals of Evangel. Nonconf. in Essex, p. 365; Browne's Hist. Congregat. in Norfolk and Suffolk, pp. 367, 521; Palmer's Nonconf. Mem. ii. 191; information from Dr. Venn, of Caius College, Cambridge; manuscript diary in Dr. Williams's Library, Gordon Square.]

C. F. S.

STOCKWOOD, JOHN (*d.* 1610), schoolmaster and divine, was a pensioner of St. John's College, Cambridge, when Queen Elizabeth visited that university in August 1564, being matriculated on 4 Oct. in that year, and admitted a scholar on the Lady Margaret's foundation on 10 Nov. following. He graduated B.A. in the university of Heidelberg in 1567, and was incorporated in that degree at Oxford on 10 May 1575, when he stated that he was about to open a 'ludus literarius' at Cambridge. He was admitted M.A. at Oxford on 9 July 1575 (*Oxford Univ. Reg.* ii. i. 376), and was incorporated in that degree at Cambridge in 1579. In 1571 he occurs as minister of Battle, Sussex. In or before 1578 he was appointed headmaster of the free grammar school at Tunbridge, Kent, by the Skinners' Company of London. It is supposed that Sir Robert Heath [q. v.] (afterwards chief justice) was one of his pupils. He was a celebrated and powerful preacher, and obtained the vicarage of Tunbridge, Kent, in 1585 (FOSTER, *Alumni Oxon.* 1500–1714, iv. 1426). At one period he was in great poverty. The records of the corporation of Gravesend show that on 30 Aug. 1594 he received a contribution of forty shillings out of the stock of the chamber of that town, in compliance with a written request from Sir Robert Sidney. He had ceased to be master of Tunbridge school in 1597, when his 'Progymnasma Scholasticum' was published. In the dedication of that work to the Earl of Essex he acknowledges the kindness of that nobleman in relieving his poverty and protecting him from malevolent antagonists. It is believed that he retained the vicarage of Tunbridge till his death. He was buried there on 27 July 1610. Jonathan Stockwood of St. John's College, Cambridge (B.A. 1605–6, M.A. 1609), may have been his son.

His principal works, mainly translations of devotional works by continental reformers, are: 1. 'Common Places of Christian Religion,' London, 1572, 1581, 8vo; translated from the Latin of Henry Bullinger, and dedicated to Henry, earl of Huntingdon. 2. 'The Treasure of Trueth . . . newlie turned into English,' London [1576], 8vo; from the Latin of Theodore Beza; another edition 1581. 3. 'A Shorte . . . Treatize of the Plague,' London, 1580, 8vo; translated from the Latin of Theodore Beza, and dedicated to Sir Henry Sidney. 4. A Short Catechisme for House Houlders. With prayers to the same adjoyning [by E. Dering, B.D.] . . . Gathered by J.S.,' London, 1582 and 1583, 8vo. 5. 'Of the Duetie of a Faithfull and Wise Magistrate, in preserving and delivering of the comon wealth from infection in the time of the Plague or Pestilence,' London, 1583, 8vo; translated from the Latin (1582) of Johann Ewich. 6. 'A verie profitable and necessarie discourse concerning the observation and keeping of the Sabbath day,' London, 1584, 8vo; translated from the Latin of Ursinus. 7. 'A Right Godly . . . discourse upon the book of Ester,' London, 1584, 8vo; from the Latin of John Brentius; dedicated to Sir Francis Walsingham. 8. 'A godlie and learned Commentarie upon the excellent book of Solomon, commonly called Ecclesiastes, or the Preacher,' London, 1585, 8vo; translated from the Latin of John Serranus. 9. 'An exposition of the 51 Psalme, by Wolph. Musculus, translated,' London, 1580, 8vo. 10. 'A Bartholmew Fair-

ing for parentes, to bestow vpon their sonnes and daughters, and for one friend to giue vnto another; shewing that children are not to marie without the consent of their parentes,' London, 1589, 8vo. 11. 'A plaine and easie laying open of the Meaning and Vnderstanding of the Rules of Construction in the English Accidence, appointed by authoritie to be taught in all schooles of hir Maiesties dominions, for the great vse and benefite of young beginners,' London, 1590, 4to; . . . 1703, 8vo. 12. 'A fruitfull Commentarie upon the twelve Small Prophets,' Cambridge, 1594, 4to; translated from the Latin of Lambert Danæus, and dedicated to the Earl and Countess of Huntingdon. 13. 'Progymnasma Scholasticum. Hoc est, Epigrammatum Græcorum ex Anthologia selectorum ab Ho. Stephano duplicique ejusdem interpretatione explicatorum Praxis Grammatica,' London, 1597, 8vo; dedicated to the Earl of Essex. 14. 'Disputatiuncularum grammaticalium libellus, ad puerorum in scholis triuialibus exacuenda ingenia excogitatus,' London, 1598, 12mo; 4th edit. 1619; again 1650.

[Ames's Typogr. Antiq. (Herbert); Dr. Bliss's Sale Catalogue, i. lot 3986; Churton's Life of Nowell, p. 169; Collier's Annals of the Stage, i. 229, iii. 266; Cruden's Gravesend, p. 257; Hallam's Lit. of Europe, i. 513; Hawels's Sketches of the Reformation; Lowndes's Bibl. Man. (Bohn); Watt's Bibl. Brit.]   T. C.

STOCQUELER, JOACHIM HAYWARD (1800–1885), compiler, the son of Joachim Christian Stocqueler, an insurance broker of Hatton Garden, who was of Portuguese extraction, by his wife Elizabeth, second daughter of Dr. Francis Hayward of Hackney, was born in London in 1800. About 1821 he sailed for Calcutta, and spent the next twenty years in India. There, in addition to writing a guide to the overland route, Stocqueler did much journalistic work, editing, among other papers, the 'Bengal Monthly Sporting Magazine,' the 'East Indian United Service Journal' (1833), the 'Indian Racing Calendar' (1838), and some worthless satirical prints, such as the 'Calcutta Englishman' and the 'English Gentleman.' He also compiled several works of at least temporary value, including 'Fifteen Months' Pilgrimage through Khuzistan and Persia' (2 vols. London, 1832), 'The Wellington Manual' (extracted from the Despatches, Calcutta, 1840), and 'Memorials of Affghanistan' (illustrative of the British expedition, 1838–42, Calcutta, 1843). He returned to England in 1841 in order to find a wider market for his Indian experience, and, in addition to lecturing on Indian subjects, established an East Indian institute and a general inquiry office. During 1855-6 he lectured on the Crimean war with a diorama. Shortly after this he left London in debt, and was employed throughout the American war as a newspaper correspondent. Returning to England, he lived to a ripe old age, and died at Brighton in 1885. A book professing to be his 'autobiography' was printed in India about 1873, but was suppressed.

Besides the works mentioned, he wrote: 1. 'Handbook of India,' London, 1844. 2. 'The Oriental Interpreter, and Treasury of East India Knowledge,' London, 1848. 3. 'Alfred the Great: a romance,' 1849. 4. 'The British Officer: his Position, Duties, Emoluments,' London, 1851. 5. 'Life of the Duke of Wellington,' 2 vols. London, 1852-3. 6. 'The Military Encyclopædia,' London, 1853. 7. 'The Old Field Officer, or the Military and Sporting Adventures of Major Worthington' (pseudonym), 1853. 8. 'India: its History, Climate, Productions, and Field Sports,' London, 1853. In a later edition (1857) this was carried down to the mutiny. 9. 'Memoirs and Correspondence of Major-General Sir William Nott,' 2 vols. London, 1854. 10. 'A Familiar History of British India,' London, 1859; another edition, 'brought down to 1865 by J. H. Siddons' (pseudonym), was published in 1865. 11. 'A Familiar History of the United States' (under the above pseudonym), London, 1865. 12. 'A Familiar History of the British Army from 1660,' London, 1871. 13. 'A Personal History of the Horse Guards from 1750,' London, 1873. 14. 'The Shakespearean Referee: a Cyclopædia of 4,200 Words occurring in the Plays of Shakespeare,' Washington, 1880. Two farces also appeared in his name, 'Polkamania' and 'An Object of Interest' (Lacy's edition, vol. xvi.)

[Notes and Queries, 8th ser. xi. 267, 315; details kindly furnished by H. J. Hunter, esq., of Bath; Allibone's Dict. of English Literature; Brit. Mus. Cat.] E. M. L.

STODDART, CHARLES (1806-1842), diplomatist, born at Ipswich on 23 July 1806, was the son of Major Stephen Stoddart (1763-1812), of the 6th dragoons, and his wife Katherine Randal (1773-1824). Major Stoddart was thrown from his horse and killed near Limerick in 1812.

Appointed to the royal staff corps as second lieutenant on 15 March 1823, and lieutenant on 9 Feb. 1826, Stoddart was placed on half-pay on 7 Feb. 1834 with the rank of captain. From 1833 to 1835 he was secretary to the Royal United Service Institution, London; and secretary to the Institute of Civil Engineers. In 1835 he went to Persia as military secretary to the British envoy, Mr. (afterwards Sir Henry) Ellis (1777-1855) [q. v.] When the king of Persia (Mahomed Shah) marched to attack Herat in 1837, Stoddart was ordered to accompany him, and remained in the Persian camp throughout the greater part of the siege. Having left with John (afterwards Sir John) McNeill [q. v.] in June 1838, he was sent back in July with a message to the shah saying that unless the siege was raised England would declare war. This threat, with the news that a British force had reached the Persian Gulf, produced the desired effect, and Herat was saved. Writing on 16 Aug. 1838 to his brother (the Rev. George Stoddart), Stoddart said, 'I cannot tell you how thankful to the Almighty I feel at being the humble means of effecting this happy change from war to peace.' Stoddart's services during this critical period were warmly acknowledged by McNeill in a despatch dated 6 Oct. 1838.

After the retirement of the Persian army, Stoddart, who had been given the local rank of lieutenant-colonel (2 June 1837), joined Eldred Pottinger [q. v.] in Herat, and shortly afterwards left for Bokhára, being instructed by McNeill to negotiate for the release of Russian captives there, and, if possible, to conclude a treaty of friendship with the ameer, Nasrulla Khan (KAYE). Reaching Bokhára on 17 Dec. 1838, he appears to have offended the ameer by riding on horseback in the precincts of the palace, and, according to one account, by striking a court official, though it is more probable that he merely drew his sword when an attempt was made to force him to an obeisance (Edinburgh Review, 1845). According to the account given by Grover, and accepted by Kaye, Ferrier, and later writers, he was seized four days after his arrival at Bokhára, and confined for two months in the Siah Cha or 'Black well,' an underground dungeon infested with vermin. The same authorities state, with some discrepancies, that, worn out by his sufferings, he consented to become a mahomedan [see CONOLLY, ARTHUR]. That Grover, Kaye, and Ferrier were all to some extent misinformed is clear from letters which Stoddart wrote on 14 and 17 March 1839, in which he said that he was still confined, not in the Siah Cha, but in the Zindan, and that he was in good health. Nor do any of the original reports of his alleged conversion support the statement that this event took place within two or even three months after his imprisonment. It was questionable indeed whether it took place at all. That he became a mahomedan at a later period, namely during the latter half of 1839, was asserted by more than one Asiatic witness, including his servant Rujub Beg; and Arthur Conolly [q. v.], who before he left Cabul credited the story, believed it up to the last. Stoddart himself, however, merely wrote that his life was spared and that he was released from prison, on 8 July 1839, on his promising to serve the ameer. 'I argued hard and long with them, till they brought the executioner with spade and pick to dig the grave near the prison. I told them that the ameer must know it was a false pretence, my service to him; but it ended in my release' (Letter to his family on 31 July 1839). There is nothing to show that 'service' included apostasy.

Towards the end of 1839 Stoddart was again placed in more rigorous confinement, from which he was not wholly released till 8 Oct. 1840. What happened during the twelvemonth from September 1839 to September 1840 is uncertain; but in January 1841 he wrote, 'Thank God I have fought my way from imprisonment and insult to the highest favour with the ameer.' On 22 Feb. he became the guest of Abdul Samut Khan, a Persian adventurer in the ameer's service. At this time the ameer was anxious to enter into a treaty with the British government; and at his request Stoddart informed Lord Palmerston of his master's wish to become the ally of England. In the spring of 1841 information reached Russia that, in deference to repeated requests from the Russian authorities, the ameer had given Stoddart leave to proceed to Orenburg, but that he refused to profit by the intercession of a foreign power. Letters he wrote in July intimated his belief that he would shortly be allowed to leave by the way he came. He had also sent messengers to Arthur Conolly, then in Khokand, inviting him in the ameer's name to return via Bokhara; but he hoped to leave before Conolly's arrival (Edinburgh Review, 1845). In August he wrote expressing entire confidence in the ameer's friendliness towards England and himself, and hoped shortly to be allowed to depart with honours (ib.) On 8 Sept. 1841 the Russian envoy, Colonel Buteneff, who had reached Bokhara three weeks before, met Stoddart, who ten days later was allowed to remove to the house occupied by the Russian mission. Buteneff described Stoddart as 'a very clever, well-educated, and agreeable man.' On Conolly's arrival in Bokhara (9 Nov.) Stoddart resided with him at Abdul Samut's house.

On 10 Dec. Stoddart received a despatch from Lord Palmerston, and the ameer is said to have been annoyed at not getting a letter from the queen. More probably his dislike of the English was revived by the news of the rising at Cabul and the murder of Alexander Burnes (2 Nov. 1842). On 20 Dec. Stoddart and Conolly were both imprisoned in the house of Abdul Samut. Writing on 28 March, Conolly said: 'Stoddart is such a friend as a man would desire to have in adversity.' A few letters from Stoddart have been preserved. On 28 Feb. 1842 he wrote to his sister: 'Don't believe all you hear or may hear.' On 28 May he wrote: 'The Russian mission left this toward the end of April. I feel convinced that Colonel Buteneff's kind desire to procure our release failed solely in consequence of the unreasonableness of the ameer.' On 17 June 1842 Stoddart and Conolly were taken to a public square in the city and beheaded (so VÁMBÉRY, and KAYE, ii. 139; FERRIER gives 24 June as the date). According to a statement made to Dr. Wolff, Stoddart, before he was killed, said, 'Tell the ameer I die a disbeliever in Muhammad; that I am a Christian, and a Christian I die.' A miniature portrait of Stoddart by an unknown artist was bequeathed to the National Portrait Gallery, London, by Stoddart's sister, Miss Frances Agnes Stoddart.

[Blue Book, Correspondence relating to Persia and Afghanistan, 1839; The Bokara Victims, by Captain Strover; Records in the Secret and Political Department at the India Office; private information; see art. CONOLLY, ARTHUR.]

S. W.

STODDART, SIR JOHN (1773–1856), journalist, eldest son of John Stoddart, lieutenant in the royal navy, was born at Salisbury on 6 Feb. 1773. His only sister, Sarah, married, on 1 May 1808, William Hazlitt [q. v.] He was educated at Salisbury grammar school, and matriculated on 25 Oct. 1790 from Christ Church, Oxford, where he was elected a student in 1791, and graduated B.A. in 1794, B.C.L. in 1798, and D.C.L. in 1801. He was admitted a member of the College of Advocates in 1801, and from 1803 to 1807 he was the king's and the admiralty advocate at Malta. Returning to England, he practised in Doctors' Commons, and from 1812 to 1816 was a leader-writer on the 'Times.' In February 1817 he had a difference with the 'Times,' and started a rival daily, entitled 'The New Times,' which was soon amalgamated with the 'Day.' For a short time it appeared as the 'Day and New Times,' but dropped the first half of the title in 1818, and survived as the 'New Times' until about 1828. During the period of his editorship he was scurrilously known as 'Dr. Slop,' and was the subject of several satires, of which 'A Slap at Slop' (1820) ran through four editions. His connection with the 'New Times' probably ceased in 1826, when he was appointed chief justice and justice of the vice-admiralty court in Malta, and on 27 July was knighted by George IV at St. James's Palace. Finding that the Maltese complained that former judges were imperfectly acquainted with their language, he made himself master of Italian. He gave entire satisfaction in his office, and the islanders had perfect confidence in his decisions. He published in 1830-2 (3 parts) 'Trial by Jury: a Speech on the opening of a Commission in Malta for establishing a modified Trial by Jury, translated from the Italian.' During an outbreak of cholera in the island he devoted himself to its suppression with great success. Returning to England in 1840, he made progress in an etymological theory, which he believed would supplant that of Horne Tooke, and he embodied it in a work called 'Glossology, or the Historical Relations of Languages.' Of this work he completed the first part only, which was published in 1858 in the 'Encyclopædia Metropolitana.' He died at 13 Brompton Square, London, on 16 Feb. 1856. In 1803 he married Isabella, eldest daughter of the Rev. Sir Henry Moncrieff Wellwood, bart. She died on 2 Feb. 1846, having had, among other children, three sons: Henry Moncrieff, who died while a pupil at the Charterhouse; John Frederick, a member of the Scottish bar in 1827, a judge in Ceylon in 1836, who died of a jungle fever while on circuit on 29 Aug. 1839 (*Gent. Mag.* 1840, i. 110); and William Wellwood, vicar of Charlbury, Oxfordshire, who died at Genoa on 21 Nov. 1856.

Stoddart published in 1801 'Remarks on the Local Scenery and Manners of Scotland,' London, 2 vols. 8vo. Of his writings on legal subjects, the most important was 'A Letter to Lord Brougham,' one in the minority of the law lords by whom the great Irish marriage case, Queen v. Millis, was decided in 1844, and, as Stoddart endeavoured to show, erroneously decided. On this case he also published in 1844 a pamphlet entitled 'Irish Marriage Question: Observations on the Opinions delivered by Lord Cottenham in the Irish Marriage Case,' 1844. His legal acumen was also shown in his article 'The Head of the Church' in the 'Law Review,' February 1851, pp. 418-36. He translated from the French of Joseph Despaze 'The Five Men, or a review of the Proceedings and Principles of the Executive Directory of

France, with the lives of the present Members,' 1797 ; and, with Georg Heinrich Noehden, Schiller's 'Fiesco,' 1796, and 'Don Carlos,' 1798. To the quarto edition of the 'Encyclopædia Metropolitana' he contributed 'Grammar' (i. 1-193), and the introductory chapter on 'The Uses of History as a Study' (ix. 1-80) ; and to the octavo edition, 1850, an introduction to the 'Study of Universal History,' besides 'Glossology' in 1858.

[Law Magazine and Law Review, 1857, iv. 124-30 ; Gent. Mag. 1856, xlv. 524.] G. C. B.

STODDART, THOMAS TOD (1810-1880), angler and poet, was born on 14 Feb. 1810 in Argyle Square, Edinburgh. He was the eldest son of Captain (afterwards Admiral) Pringle Stoddart, a descendant of the Stouthearts of Liddesdale and Ettrick, and his wife Frances, daughter of James Sprot. At the age of ten he was sent to a Moravian school in Lancashire, but soon returned to attend the high school and the university of his native city. One of his professors was John Wilson, the celebrated 'Christopher North,' in whose house young Stoddart met De Quincey, Hartley Coleridge, the Ettrick Shepherd, Aytoun, Ferrier, Henry Glassford Bell, and others. He early began to evince a passion for angling, which afterwards became the chief business of his life. He was a very expert angler, having much delicacy of wrist, and a great knowledge of the haunts and habits of fish, besides being an adept at fly-making. In 1833 he was admitted a member of the faculty of advocates, but never practised. He busied himself with the preparation of papers on the 'Art of Angling,' which appeared in 'Chambers's Journal,' and were published in 1835 in book form—the first treatise of its kind that appeared in Scotland. In 1836 he married and settled in Kelso, where he found the surroundings so congenial for the practice of his art in the rivers Tweed and Teviot that it became his home for life. In 1847 he published 'The Angler's Companion to the Rivers and Lakes of Scotland' (3rd edit. 1852), which still remains an angling classic in Scotland, being distinguished from others by its Waltonian note of appreciation of natural scenery and literary excellence. His later life was devoted to fishing in his home streams, and in the Yarrow and other western rivers. He was much interested in the acts against the pollution of rivers, and several times gave evidence before the Tweed commissioners and parliamentary committees on these and kindred subjects. He died on 21 Nov. 1880, and was buried in Kelso cemetery. By his wife Bessie Macgregor, daughter of a farmer at Contin in Ross-shire, whom he met while on a fishing tour, he had two sons and a daughter Anna. Miss Stoddart became the biographer of her father and also of Professor Blackie. An engraved portrait by Charles Laurie is prefixed to 'Angling Songs' (1889) and a photograph to 'Songs of the Seasons' (1881).

Besides the works mentioned Stoddart was the author of: 1. 'The Death-wake, or Lunacy: a Necromaunt in three chimeras,' 1831, which was surreptitiously published in America in 1842 in 'Graham's Magazine' as 'Agatha, a Necromaunt in three chimeras, by Louis Fitzgerald Tasistro' (new edit. 1895). 2. 'Angling Reminiscences,' 1837. 3. 'Angling Songs,' 1839 and 1889. 4. 'Abel Massinger, or the Aëronaut,' 1846, a romance in prose. 5. 'An Angler's Rambles, and Angling Songs,' 1866. 6. 'Songs of the Seasons,' 1873; new edit. with autobiographical memoir, Kelso, 1881. He was also a contributor to 'Bell's Life,' 'The Field,' and the 'Sporting Gazette.'

[Stoddart's Autobiography; Stoddart's Angling Songs, edited by his daughter with Memoir; Stoddart's Death-wake, with Introduction by Andrew Lang, 1895; personal information.]
W. W. T.

STOGDON, HUBERT (1692–1728), nonconformist divine, born at Bodicote, near Banbury in Oxfordshire, on 9 Jan. 1691–2, was eldest son of Robert Stogdon, presbyterian minister, by his wife, Elizabeth, daughter of Francis Hubert or Hubband, nonconformist minister, who was disinherited by his father for his religious opinions. On the death of his father in 1697, Hubert went to reside with relatives in the neighbourhood of Exeter. He was first educated by the presbyterian minister at Withycombe Raleigh, and afterwards at the free school at Exeter. He entered the presbyterian ministry in 1715, and for a short time was chaplain to Sir John Davy, hart., at Creedy Park, near Crediton, and afterwards preached for two years at Thorverton, a village near Exeter. About this time, under the influence of Nicholas Billingsley [q. v.], he embraced semi-Arian views; and, as this occasioned some differences with his friends at Exeter, he accepted the pastorate of Wookey, near Wells, and was ordained at Shepton Mallett in August 1718. He remained in the neighbourhood preaching at Wookey and Coleford for seven years, and in 1721 married a gentlewoman of the neighbourhood. Towards the close of the period he became convinced of the expediency of baptism by immersion, and was rebaptised at Barbican in London. In spite of this, however, in 1724 he was called to Trow-

bridge in Wiltshire by a congregation of pædobaptists, and remained there until his death on 20 Jan. 1727–8. He was buried in the parish church. His wife survived him.

Stogdon was the author of: 1. 'A Defence of the Caveat against the New Sect of Anabaptists,' Exeter, 1714, 8vo. 2. 'Seasonable Advice respecting the Present Disputes about the Holy Trinity,' London, 1719, 8vo. 3. 'Poems and Letters,' ed. N. Billingsley, London, 1729, 8vo.

[Billingsley's Sermon on the Death of Hubert Stogdon.]
E. I. C.

STOKES, DAVID (1591?–1669), divine, born in 1590 or 1591, was educated at Westminster school, and was elected a queen's scholar, proceeding to Trinity College, Cambridge, in 1610, and graduating B.A. in 1614–15. After becoming a fellow of Peterhouse, he proceeded M.A. in 1618, and in 1624 became a fellow of Eton College. In 1625 he was appointed rector of Brinklow in Warwickshire; he was made canon of Windsor in 1628, precentor of Chichester in 1628, and in 1630 he took the degree of D.D. at Cambridge. He became rector of Binfield in Berkshire in 1631, of Everton in Northamptonshire in 1638, and vicar of Erchfont in Wiltshire in 1644. On the outbreak of the civil war he was, as a royalist, despoiled of all his preferments, and compelled to seek refuge in Oxford, where, in 1645, he was admitted ad eundem. On the Restoration he was reinstated in his livings, and died on 10 May 1669, shortly after resigning his canonry at Windsor. He was buried behind the altar in St. George's Chapel, Windsor. His will is in the Prerogative Office of Canterbury.

He was the author of: 1. 'An Explication of the Twelve Minor Prophets,' to which was prefixed a laudatory preface by John Pearson [q. v.], bishop of Chester, London, 1659, 8vo. 2. 'Verus Christianus, or Directions for Private Devotions,' Oxford, 1668, folio. 3. 'Truth's Champion,' 8vo, not known to be extant; besides two sermons.

[Wood's Fasti Oxon. ed. Bliss, ii. 81; Brit. Mus. Add. MSS. 5858 f. 226, 5880 f. 33; Carter's Hist. of Cambridge, pp. 24, 326; Walker's Sufferings, ii. 93; Le Neve's Fasti, iii. 400; Welch's Alumni Westmonasterienses, p. 81; Foster's Alumni Oxon. 1500–1714.]
E. I. C.

STOKES, HENRY SEWELL (1808–1895), Cornish poet, was the eldest son of Henry Stokes (d. 1832), proctor and notary at Gibraltar, who married in 1807 at Gibraltar Anne Sewell (1787–1857). Born at Gibraltar on 16 June 1808, Henry Sewell came to England in 1815, and was sent in 1817 to

St. Saviour's grammar school, Southwark, and at a later date to the school of a young baptist minister called William Giles at Chatham, where Charles Dickens was his companion. In 1825 he returned to his native place, studied mercantile law in his father's office, and acquired a knowledge of French, Spanish, and Italian. He was then articled to Mr. Bridgman, a solicitor at Tavistock, and was admitted attorney and solicitor in January and February 1832. For a short time he was a student of the Middle Temple.

Stokes dwelt for some weeks at St. Austell in Cornwall, getting up evidence on mining customs in the duchy, and in April 1832 settled at Truro, where he practised as solicitor for many years, and played an active part as a liberal in local politics. He started in that town in July 1833 the 'Cornish Guardian and Western Chronicle' newspaper (afterwards merged in the 'West Briton'), and for three years was its editor, with Charles Buller [q. v.] and Sir William Molesworth [q. v.] as occasional leader writers. He also wrote leaders for the 'Devon Independent,' published at Devonport, but with a large circulation in Cornwall, and was an occasional contributor to the 'West Briton.' In 1856 he was elected mayor of Truro, and in 1859 was appointed its town clerk. On the nomination of Lord Vivian, lord lieutenant of the county, he became in February 1865 clerk of the peace for Cornwall, and continued in that position until his death. The duties of this post forced him to remove to Bodmin, where he spent the rest of his days. He died at Bodmin on 7 April 1895, and was buried in its cemetery on 13 April. He married at Tavistock, on 9 Aug. 1834, Louisa Rachel, daughter of the Rev. William Evans of Parkwood in that town. She died at Bodmin on 15 Feb. 1890, aged 80. They had issue one son, William Evans Stokes, and three daughters.

From the number of his poems on the county, Stokes was sometimes called 'the laureate for Cornwall.' Tennyson spent a week with him at Truro in 1848. His chief works, many of which attest his love of Cornwall, were: 1. 'The Lay of the Desert,' 1830, designed and in part written on Dartmoor; the substance of it was revised and included in the sixth and seventh cantos of 'Memories,' 1872. 2. 'The Song of Albion: a Poem on the Reform Crisis,' 1831. 3. 'Discourses on Opinion,' 1831. 4. 'The Vale of Lanherne,' 1830: new edit. with costly illustrations by Charles Haghe, from designs by James G. Philp, 1853. 5. 'Echoes of War,' 1855. 6. 'Scattered Leaves,' 1862.

7. 'Rhymes from Cornwall,' 1871; reissued in 1884 as 'Voyage of Arundel and other Rhymes from Cornwall.' 8. 'Memories' [anon.], 1872; new edit. [anon.] 1879. 9. 'Poems of later years,' 1873; reissued in 1881 as 'The Chantry Owl and other Verses.' 10. 'Restormel: a Legend of Piers Gaveston,' 1875; republished 1882. 11. 'The Gate of Heaven: the Plaint of Morwenstow,' 1876.

Stokes published numerous flysheets and small poems. He contributed to the 'Mining Almanac' of Henry English (1849, pp. 105–116) an article on the court of the vicewarden of the stannaries, and read before the meeting of the British Archæological Association at Bodmin on 17 Aug. 1876 a paper on books and manuscripts relating to the county, which was printed in its journal (xxxiii. 35–45). An oil portrait which was presented to him, with a cheque for 500l., at a public meeting held at Truro in December 1891, now hangs in the Truro councilchamber.

[Boase and Courtney's Bibliotheca Cornub. i. 204, 227, ii. 691–2, iii. 1340; Boase's Collectanea Cornub. pp. 808, 934, 1367; Times, 9 April 1895, p. 10; The Realm, 26 April 1895 (by T. H. S. Escott); West Briton, 20 Feb. 1890 p. 8, 11 April 1895 p. 4, 18 April p. 7; Foster's Men at the Bar.]   W. P. C.

STOKES, JOHN LORT (1812–1885), admiral, born in 1812, was second son of Henry Stokes of Scotchwell. He entered the navy on 2 Feb. 1826 on board the Beagle, then fitting out under the command of his namesake, Commander Pringle Stokes, for the survey of the southern parts of America, in company with the Adventure, commanded by Captain Philip Parker King [q. v.] On the death of the commander in November 1828, Robert Fitzroy [q. v.] was promoted to the vacancy, and with him young Stokes continued till the return of the Beagle to England in 1830, and again, on the renewed commission of the Beagle, from 1831 to 1836, during which period Charles Darwin was naturalist on board the vessel. On 10 Jan. 1837 he was promoted to the rank of lieutenant, and when in February the Beagle was recommissioned by her former first lieutenant, Commander John Clements Wickham, for the survey of Australia, Stokes was again appointed to her. In March 1841 Wickham was obliged to invalid, and Stokes succeeded to the command, being confirmed in the rank on 16 Aug. following. For the next two years he was principally engaged in the survey of Timor and of New Zealand, and in September 1843 he arrived in England after a service in the Beagle of nearly eighteen years. During the years immediately following he wrote 'Discoveries in Australia, with an Account of the Coasts and Rivers explored and surveyed during the Voyage of the Beagle, 1837–1843' (2 vols. 8vo, 1846). On 4 July 1846 he was advanced to post rank, and on 14 Oct. 1847 he was appointed to the Acheron, steam vessel, employed for the next four years on the survey of New Zealand. In the end of 1851 the Acheron was paid off at Sydney, and for a few years Stokes was on half-pay. From 1860 to 1863 he was employed in surveying the coasts of the Channel. He became a rear-admiral on 9 Feb. 1864, vice-admiral on 14 July 1871, admiral on 1 Aug. 1877, and died on 11 June 1885. He was twice married and left issue.

[O'Byrne's Nav. Biogr. Dict.; Times, 13 June 1885; Proceedings of the Royal Geographical Society, new ser. vol. vii.; Fitzroy's Adventure and Beagle; Navy Lists; Pasco's A Roving Commission, 1897, p. 102, with a portrait at p. 124.]   J. K. L.

STOKES, PETER (d. 1399), Carmelite, became a Carmelite friar at Hitchin, Hertfordshire, and, afterwards proceeding to Oxford, graduated there as doctor of divinity before 1382. During the religious troubles of that year Stokes acted as the representative of Archbishop Courtenay in the university. During Lent he had made an ineffectual complaint against Nicholas Hereford [see Nicholas], and in May he had a statement of Hereford's heresies drawn up by notaries (Fasciculi Zizaniorum, pp. 296, 305). On 28 May the archbishop sent him a list of twenty-four heresies extracted from Wiclif's writings, and directed him to publish it in the university. Robert Rygge [q. v.], the chancellor, opposed Stokes in the matter, and on 5 June, when Philip Repington [q. v.] preached at St. Frideswide's, Stokes was prevented from publication by fear of violence. On 10 June Stokes determined against Repington, but on the following day left Oxford at the summons of the archbishop. He had already reported what had happened in a letter to Courtenay on 6 June, and was now present in the council on 12 June, when Rygge was condemned. The royal letter of 13 July specially forbade Rygge to molest Stokes further. Stokes, however, appears to have withdrawn from Oxford to Hitchin, where he died on 18 July 1399. A contemporary rhymester describes Stokes as

Rufus naturaliter et veste dealbatus,
Omnibus impatiens et nimis elatus.

(Pol. Songs, i. 267, Rolls Ser.) Stokes is credited with various quæstiones, conclusiones,

and lecturæ. He also wrote a work in defence of William Ockham [q. v.], which Leland says was extant in his days, and 'Præconia Sacræ Scripturæ,' which the same writer describes as 'opus non contemnendum.' But the only one of Stokes's writings which seems to have survived is his letter to Archbishop Courtenay on 6 June 1382; it is printed in 'Fasciculi Zizaniorum,' pp. 300–1.

[Fasciculi Zizaniorum; Tanner's Bibl. Brit.-Hib. p. 674; Villiers de St.-Etienne's Bibl. Carmelitana, ii. 601–2; Wood's Hist. and Antiq. of Univ. Oxon. i. 502–5, 508, 510.]   C. L. K.

STOKES, WILLIAM, M.D. (1804–1878), physician, was fifth child of Whitley Stokes, regius professor of medicine in the university of Dublin, and his wife Mary Anne, daughter of Hugh Picknell of Lough Gall, co. Armagh.

WHITLEY STOKES, M.D. (1763–1845), the father, was son of Gabriel Stokes, D.D., fellow of Trinity College, Dublin, prebendary of Elphin, chancellor of Waterford, and rector of Desart Martin in the diocese of Derry, and grandson of Gabriel Stokes, an engineer and deputy surveyor-general of Ireland in 1735, the first of the family to settle in Ireland. Whitley was born in 1763, entered Trinity College, Dublin, in 1779, obtained a scholarship in 1781, and was elected a fellow in his twenty-fifth year. He proceeded to the degree of bachelor of medicine in 1789, and to that of doctor in 1793. As a young man he joined the United Irishmen, and won the admiration of Wolfe Tone, who designated him the fitting ' head of a system of national education' should Ireland become independent (Tone's Autobiography). Although Stokes denied that he had any connection with the Society of United Irishmen after 1792, he was suspended for three years from all functions as a tutor on the ground of his political opinions in 1798, when Lord Clare made his visitation of Trinity College. But Stokes soon regained the confidence of his colleagues. He was elected a senior fellow in 1805 and lecturer in natural history in 1816. He became regius professor of medicine in 1830, resigning in 1843. He died at his residence in Harcourt Street, Dublin, on 13 April 1845. He married, in 1782, Mary Anne, daughter of Hugh Picknell of Lough Gall, co. Armagh, and had nine children.

The son, William, who was born in Dublin in 1804, was educated in classics and mathematics by John Walker, a fellow of Trinity College, Dublin, and in science by his father. He studied medicine and graduated in 1825 at Edinburgh. On his return in the same year to Ireland he became a licentiate of the College of Physicians there, and was immediately elected physician to the Meath hospital. He published in 1825 'An Introduction to the Use of the Stethoscope,' one of the earliest treatises on the subject in English. It is dedicated to William Cullen [q. v.], and shows that the author had done much solid pathological and clinical work. Dr. Robert James Graves [q. v.] was his colleague at Meath Hospital, and they reformed the clinical teaching of Dublin. Stokes at once became famous as a teacher of medicine, and in the great epidemic of typhus in Dublin in 1826 his exertions in the treatment of the poor were conspicuous. He was himself attacked by the fever in 1827. In April 1828 he married. He first lived at 16 Harcourt Street, Dublin, and in 1828 published two lectures on the application of the stethoscope to the diagnosis of thoracic disease. His practice increased, and in 1830 he moved to a larger house in York Street, Dublin. Every Saturday he had an open evening, and the excellent society of his house became a powerful influence in Dublin. He encouraged the labours of George Petrie [q. v.], and stimulated by kindly sympathy the studies of younger men in all branches of learning. Asiatic cholera visited Dublin in 1832, and he reported the first case. He gave clinical lectures at the Meath hospital, and contributed lectures to the 'London Medical and Surgical Journal,' as well as a paper on the curability of phthisis. In 1832 he published 'Clinical Observations on the Use of Opium,' and in 1833 and 1834 papers in the 'London Cyclopædia of Practical Medicine.' He became in 1834 editor of the 'Dublin Journal of Medical Science,' and in 1835 began a work entitled 'A Treatise on the Diagnosis and Treatment of Diseases of the Chest,' which was published in 1837. It is based on his clinical discourses, and is remarkable for the lucid and definite character of its summaries on each of the diseases described. It sets forth and discusses all the views of Laennec and his school, but is most valuable where it is most original, and whatever additions may be made to the information contained in it will always be useful as a model of medical exposition. In 1838 he founded the Pathological Society of Dublin, and in 1839 the university of Dublin conferred upon him the degree of M.D. His foreign travels, which he repeated in 1840, enabled him to add to his already extensive knowledge of art, and in Ireland George Petrie [q. v.] and (Sir) Frederick Burton were his favourite artists and dearest friends. Miss Helen Faucit

(afterwards Lady Martin) visited Ireland, and they became friends. He discharged the duties of regius professor of medicine in the Dublin University from 1843, and on his father's death in 1845 his appointment was confirmed. In that year he visited Icolmkill and the Hebrides, and in 1849 he enjoyed a period of repose and antiquarian study in South Wales. He published in 1854 'Diseases of the Heart and Aorta,' a profound work of the same kind of merit as his treatises on diseases of the chest, and in 1863 he edited 'Studies in Physiology and Medicine' by Robert James Graves. He was made physician in ordinary to the queen in Ireland in 1861, and elected F.R.S. in the same year. His 'lectures on fever,' which are chiefly valuable from the light they throw on Irish epidemics, were edited by Dr. J. W. Moore in 1874.

Meanwhile in 1866-7 he wrote the 'Life and Labours in Art and Archæology of George Petrie.' This was published in 1868. Throughout life he took deep interest in Irish antiquities, visited the isles of Arran twice and many other remote parts of Ireland with his daughter Margaret and the Earl of Dunraven [see QUIN, EDWIN RICHARD WINDHAM WYNDHAM-, third EARL OF DUNRAVEN]. He was elected president of the Royal Irish Academy in 1874.

Stokes owned a house called Carrig Breac on the most remote part of the promontory of Howth, and he retired thither when he gave up practice. In 1876 he was awarded the Prussian order Pour le Mérite in recognition of his medical writings. He had a paralytic stroke in November 1877, and died on 10 Jan. 1878. He was buried at St. Finlan's, Howth.

Besides the works mentioned, he published numerous medical essays and several addresses on medical education, in which he insists on the advantage of a wide general education for students of medicine. His services to his country in encouraging the study of her architecture, artistic work, and music, were very great, and every young man found in him a generous friend. He was long the undoubted head of his profession in Ireland, and Sir George Edward Paget [q. v.], a most capable authority, expressed in 1868 the opinion that Stokes was the greatest physician of that time in Europe. Several of his works were translated into French, German, and Italian.

His portrait, by Sir Frederick Burton, is in the possession of Mr. Whitley Stokes, and has been engraved; and his statue, by John Henry Foley [q. v.], is in the hall of the King's and Queen's College of Physicians of

Ireland. In April 1828 he married Mary, daughter of John Black of Glasgow. His eldest son, Whitley, became a legal member of council in India, and is well known as a Celtic scholar; while another of his sons is the eminent Dublin surgeon Sir William Stokes. One of his daughters, Miss Margaret Stokes, has published several works on Irish art and its history.

[Information from Miss Margaret Stokes; Stokes's works; Ormsby's Medical History of the Meath Hospital, personal knowledge.]

N. M.

STOKESLEY, JOHN (1475?–1539), bishop of London, was born at Collyweston, Northamptonshire, on 8 Sept., probably in 1475. He was doubtless related to the Richard Stokesley, parson of North Luffenham, Rutland, not far from Collyweston, on whose death in 1526 Stokesley was presented to that church. His mother was Margaret, daughter of Edward Spendlove or Spendlowe; the John Spendlove (d. 1581) whom Stokesley in 1534 collated to the prebend of Hoxton and in 1537 to that of Holywell, both in St. Paul's Cathedral, was no doubt his cousin (LE NEVE, Fasti, ii. 398, 402, 408; BRIDGES, Northamptonshire, ii. 606). Stokesley was elected fellow of Magdalen College, Oxford, about 1495, and for a month in 1497 he was usher in Magdalen College school. In 1498 he was appointed prelector in logic and principal of Magdalen Hall, and bursar in 1502. In 1503 he was dean of divinity and northern proctor. He was ordained deacon on 8 March, and priest on 22 March 1504–5, and in the same year was appointed prelector in philosophy and vice-president of Magdalen College. In that capacity Stokesley became involved in the fierce dissensions among the fellows which between 1504 and 1507 reduced the college to a condition of the utmost disorder and laxity. He seems to have been an adherent of the absent president, Richard Mayhew, bishop of Hereford, and the opposite faction accused Stokesley of every sort of offence, from heresy, theft, perjury, and adultery, to witchcraft, neglect of duties, spending the night at Sandford without leave, and christening a cat. Between 28 and 30 Jan. 1506–7 John Dowman, the commissioner of Richard Foxe [q. v.], bishop of Winchester, held a visitation to examine into the condition of the college. On the 27th Stokesley solemnly denied on oath all the charges against him, and, no witnesses appearing to substantiate them, he was admitted to compurgation. Finally the fellows 'in sign of unity all drank of a loving-cup together' (MACRAY,

Register of Magdalen College, i. 37–60; BLOXAM, ii. 20–4).

In February 1505–6 Stokesley was instituted to the vicarage of Willoughby, and soon afterwards to the rectory of Slimbridge, Gloucestershire, both college livings. After Henry VIII's accession, perhaps through Bishop Foxe's influence, he became chaplain and almoner to the king and a member of his council. Writing on 26 July 1518, Erasmus described him as 'well versed in the schoolmen, and intimately acquainted with three languages,' and on 23 July 1519 classed him with More, Linacre, Colet, and Tunstal as men who were a credit to Henry VIII's court (Letters and Papers of Henry VIII, ed. Brewer, ii. 4340, iii. 394). In June 1520 he attended Henry as his chaplain to the Field of the Cloth of Gold, and in the following month was present in a like capacity at the meeting between Henry and Charles V. In the parliament of 1523 he was a trier of petitions from Gascony and parts beyond sea, and on 23 March 1523–4 was collated to the vicarage of Ivychurch, Kent; he was also appointed dean of the chapel royal.

In 1529 Stokesley was sent with George Boleyn (afterwards Viscount Rochford) [q. v.] as ambassador to France in place of Sir Francis Bryan [q. v.] He was instructed to prevent Albany's return to Scotland and the formation of a league between France and Scotland. But the more important part of his mission was to induce Francis I to join Henry in preventing the assembling of a general council 'considering the influence the emperor has over the pope,' and to collect opinions from foreign universities in favour of Henry's divorce. He had already become a prominent advocate of this measure, and before his embassy had, with Edward Fox [q. v.], bishop of Hereford, and Nicholas de Burgo [see NICHOLAS], composed in Latin a book on the subject, which was translated into English with additions and alterations by Cranmer. It was published as 'The Determinations of the most famous and most excellent Universities . . .,' London, 1531, 8vo (Letters and Papers, viii. 1054). In pursuance of this object Stokesley proceeded in 1530 to Italy, spending the spring and summer in attempts to win over the universities of Bologna, Padua, Venice, and others. More than a hundred references to Stokesley in vol. iv. pt. iii. of the 'Letters and Papers' testify to his activity in this matter, and according to his own boast he 'recovered' the king's cause 'when it had slipped through the ambassador's fingers and was despaired of' (ib. vii. 15). His efforts satisfied Henry,

D D 2

and on the translation of Cuthbert Tunstal [q. v.] to Durham. Stokesley was during his absence nominated bishop of London in July 1530. He returned in October, and was consecrated on 27 Nov.

As bishop of London Stokesley shared in the further measures for the completion of the divorce, and concurred in the various enactments which abolished the papal authority in England. He was with Cranmer at Dunstable when the sentence of divorce was pronounced against Catherine, and on 10 Sept. 1533 he christened at the Greyfriars Church, Greenwich, Princess (afterwards Queen) Elizabeth. He took part in the dissolution of monasteries at Reading, Godstow, and others in Lincolnshire (*Cotton MS.* Cleopatra E. iv. ff. 223, 225, 235-7; *Arundel MS.* 249 ff, 82-4), and he induced the Carthusians of London to submit to Henry. Conjointly with Tunstal he wrote in 1537 a remonstrance to Pole on his book, 'Pro Unitatis Ecclesiæ Defensione,' and on his acceptance of the cardinalate; it is printed in Bernard Garter's 'New Year's Gift,' 1571. In August 1531 he was employed to assess for taxation various benefices, a measure which roused the indignation of their holders. They assembled on the 31st in the Greyfriars Church, London, and 'made an assault on the Bishop's palace at Paul's, where they continued an hour and a half, and, from thence returning to the chapter-house, made a new assault on the bishop and his officers, whom they put in fear of their lives' (*Letters and Papers*, v. 387). The ringleaders were brought before the Star-chamber on a charge of attempting to murder the bishop and evade payment of the clerical subsidy (cf. FROUDE, i. 340; DIXON, i. 68-9).

Stokesley, however, was strenuously opposed to all doctrinal changes; even the royal supremacy he accepted only with a proviso safeguarding 'the laws of the church of Christ,' and he became a strenuous persecutor of gospellers. On 3 July 1533 he reported to Henry that he had condemned John Frith [q. v.] for heresy, and handed him over for execution to the lord mayor (*Letters and Papers*, vi. 761; FOXE, v. 16). He attacked Alexander Alesius [q. v.] in the convocation of 1537, and argued against John Lambert (*d.* 1538) [q. v.] According to Foxe he boasted on his deathbed of having been the means of executing over thirty heretics (FOXE, iii. 104; cf. LAURENTIUS HUMFREDUS, *Vita Juelli*, p. 268). Similarly he refused to revise the translation of the 'Acts of the Apostles' which Cranmer had entrusted to him when preparing an English version of the Bible, declaring that reading it in Eng-

lish infected the people with heresy (*Narr. of the Reformation*, Camden Soc. pp. 277-278). He also resisted Cranmer's metro-political visitation of his diocese, and joined with Tunstal in giving as catholic a colour as possible to the 'Institution of a Christian Man,' 1537.

This attitude laid Stokesley open to Cromwell's hostility, and he was subjected to various vexatious proceedings. In 1535 he was required to send the king a written copy of a certain sermon he had preached; he excused himself by saying that he never wrote out his sermons. 'If I were to write my sermons, I could not deliver them as they are written, for much would come to me without premeditation much better than what was premeditated' (*Letters and Papers*, viii. 1054). On 29 May 1538 the attorney-general, Sir John Baker [q. v.], instituted proceedings against Stokesley on the king's behalf, accusing him of infringing statutes 16 Richard II and 28 Henry VIII by executing a bull of Martin V. The bishop, who was brought into court in the marshal's custody, confessed his offence and was admitted to bail; when called upon to receive judgment he produced a pardon from Henry VIII (*ib.* xiii. i. 1095). He also complained bitterly of the way in which the king assumed the right of presenting to prebends in his diocese, and declared that he could have no learned men about him because he had no means of providing for them.

Stokesley died on the anniversary of his birthday, on 8 Sept. 1539, and was buried in St. George's Chapel, St. Paul's Cathedral, on the 14th. A memorial, with a Latin inscription, an English version of which is given in Wood's 'Athenæ,' ii. 749, was erected over his tomb. A portrait, painted by Holbein, is at Windsor, and a copy of it, presented by J. R. Bloxam, hangs in Magdalen College School, Oxford.

[Letters and Papers of Henry VIII. ed. Brewer and Gairdner, vols. iii-xiv.; State Papers, Henry VIII, 1830; Inquisitiones post mortem, 2 Edw. VI, ii. 28, 3 Edw. VI, i. 109; Cotton MSS. Otho C. x. 161, Cleopatra E. iv. 207 b, 223, 225, 237, v. 378; Arundel MS. 249 ff. 82-4; Foxe's Actes and Mon. ed. Townsend; Strype's Works (General Index); Wriothesley's Chronicle; Narratives of the Reformation, Greyfriars' Chronicle, and Pretended Divorce of Catherine of Aragon (Camden Soc.); Wood's Athenæ Oxon. ii. 746-50; Hall's Chron.; Wilkins's Concilia; Le Neve's Fasti, ed. Hardy; Pocock's Records of the Reformation; Burnet's Hist. of the Reformation, ed. Pocock; Fuller's Church Hist. ed. Brewer; Brewer's Reign of Henry VIII; Oxford Univ. Reg.; Foster's Alumni Oxon. 1500-1714; Bloxam's and Macray's Registers

of Magdalen Coll. Oxford; Lingard's History; Froude's Hist. and Divorce of Catharine of Aragon; Dixon's Hist. of the Church of England; First Divorce of Henry VIII, ed. Gasquet, 1894; Dr. Stephan Ehses's Römische Dokumente, 1893.]
A. F. P.

STONE, ALFRED (1840–1878), musician and choir-trainer, born in Bristol 12 Feb. 1840, was educated at the Bristol city school (Queen Elizabeth's Hospital). He displayed an enthusiasm for music in early life, studying under John David Corfe, organist of Bristol Cathedral [see CORFE, ARTHUR THOMAS], and, after a brief experience of commercial life at Messrs. Thomas's Bristol soap works, made music his profession. In 1858, when only eighteen, he became organist of St. Paul's Church, Clifton, and was successively organist of Arley chapel (1862), of Highbury chapel (1863–9), of St. Paul's again (1869–75), of Christ Church, Clifton (1875–8), and by the mayor's appointment of the mayor's chapel (St. Mark, Bristol) (1873–8). He trained his church choirs to a high state of efficiency, notably at St. Paul's.

In 1863 he edited, with Mr. Fred Morgan, the 'Bristol Tune Book,' comprising 342 hymn-tunes and chants; a few were written by himself. The book at once gained popular favour, chiefly among nonconformists. In a third edition, edited by H. Eliot Button, the number of tunes reached nine hundred. The sale exceeded three-quarters of a million copies in England and colonies. No hymn-tune book except 'Hymns Ancient and Modern' has exercised a wider influence on congregational singing. In 1863-4 Stone adopted the tonic sol-fa system for purposes of teaching, although he did not wholly abandon the old notation. His tutorial appointments included that of master of singing at Queen Elizabeth's Hospital, 1867–76, at the Bristol Red Maids School, 1867–78, and at the Blind Asylum, 1876–8. He conducted the Bristol Orpheus Glee Society (founded in 1844) from 1876 till his death, and under his rule the society conspicuously flourished. Stone organised and trained a male-voice choir in 1872 to compete at the national music meetings which were inaugurated that year at the Crystal Palace. He gained the prize (50l.) in that year, and next year obtained honourable mention. In 1873 he organised the first Bristol musical festival. He was secretary, chose and trained the festival choir of three hundred voices, and conducted the preliminary concerts and intermediate Festival Society concerts till his death. The chorus singing won the highest praise from critics, and the choir became a permanent institution.

For preparatory singing classes he edited 'Progressive Exercises for Elementary and Advanced Mixed Choirs,' which are still in use. He wrote a series of papers, 'Hints for Elementary Teaching,' in which he strongly advocated the tonic sol-fa. For a contemplated work on harmony (never completed) he wrote 'The Common Sense of the Minor Scale,' which was published in the 'Tonic Sol-fa Reporter,' August 1878. He adjudicated at the Welsh Eisteddfodau, and travelled in Germany with Mr. J. S. Curwen for the purposes of his profession. His last public appearance was at a festival concert, when he conducted Roeckel's 'Ode in Memory of Titiens' in November 1877. He died at Stoke Bishop, near Bristol, on 3 Jan. 1878, leaving a widow and children. A memorial fund of 2,000l. was raised in behalf of his family. He was a stimulating teacher and conductor, and by his energy improved musical education and taste in the west of England.

[From personal knowledge, also that of his family and friends; biographical notice by W. Critchley in Tonic Sol-fa Reporter, October 1887; Recollections of A. Stone by J. S. Curwen in Western Daily Press, 12 March 1878; notices in musical and Bristol press.]
E. T. W.

STONE, ANDREW (1703–1773), undersecretary of state and tutor to George III, born in 1703, was elder son of Andrew Stone, a banker of Lombard Street, London, by his wife, Anne Holbrooke. George Stone [q.v.], archbishop of Armagh, was his younger brother. The father resided for some time at Winchester, and Andrew was sent to a school there. In 1717 he was admitted scholar at Westminster, whence he was elected to Christ Church, Oxford, matriculating on 6 June 1722. He graduated B.A. in 1726 and M.A. in 1728. He then became private secretary to Thomas Pelham-Holles, duke of Newcastle [q. v.], to whom he was introduced by William Barnard [q. v.] (afterwards bishop of Derry), who married Stone's sister. He became the intimate confidant of Newcastle and his brother Henry Pelham [q.v.] When Horace Walpole was seeking Newcastle's favour, his first step was to present Stone with a snuff-box (WALPOLE, Letters, ed. Cunningham, i. 223, 319), and to his influence was largely due his brother's rapid rise to the primacy of Ireland. According to Horace Walpole, Stone, whom he describes as 'the dark and suspected friend of the Stuarts,' exercised a pernicious influence over the Pelhams. 'From that hour,' he wrote, 'every measure was coloured with a tincture of prerogative; and a foundation was laid for that structure against which the disciples of the Pelhams have so much declaimed since ' (*Memoirs of the Reign of George III*, ed. Barker, iv. 91). The negotiations between Hardwicke, Pulteney, Carteret, and Newcastle for the formation of a ministry on Walpole's fall in 1741 were carried on at Stone's house, and 'during 30 or 40 years no man was more completely behind the scenes of the political stage.'

In 1734 Stone was appointed under-secretary of state to Newcastle, and in 1739 joint collector of papers in the office of the secretary of state. On 5 May 1741 he was returned to parliament for Hastings, for which he sat continuously until 1761, being re-elected on 26 June 1747 and 15 April 1754 (*Official Return*, ii. 94, 106, 119). He was appointed secretary to the island of Barbados in 1712, joint secretary to the lords justices of the regency during George II's absence in 1744, and registrar of chancery, Jamaica, in 1747. In May 1748 he accompanied the king on his visit to Hanover, acting as his private secretary until the arrival of the Duke of Newcastle. According to the latter, the king showed him 'the greatest distinction' and expressed 'the greatest regard and approbation.' From 1749 to 1761 Stone was also a commissioner of trade and plantations, and in 1752 he was elected a trustee of the Busby charities.

When, on the death of Frederick, prince of Wales, in 1751, the household of his son, the future George III, was reconstituted, Stone was appointed sub-governor to the young prince, under the Earl of Harcourt. The whigs regarded his influence over Prince George with fear and suspicion ; he was credited with instilling into his mind those exaggerated ideas of the royal prerogative which were derived from Bolingbroke's ' Patriot King,' and were afterwards put in practice when George became king. Early in 1763 Horace Walpole anonymously circulated a memorial denouncing the establishment in the prince's household of men who were 'the friends and pupils of the late Lord Bolingbroke.' Stone was also accused, with William Murray (afterwards first Earl of Mansfield) [q. v.], of having toasted the Pretender. The question was taken up by Lord Ravensworth, the Duke of Bedford, and others, and caused some sensation. Several cabinet councils were held to discuss the matter in February, and Stone was summoned to answer the charges against him, which he did to the cabinet's satisfaction. These charges were the subject of a lengthy debate in the House of Lords on 22 Feb., but Bedford's motion for further inquiry was finally negatived without a division

(*Parl. Hist.* xiv. 1294-7; WALPOLE, *Mem. of Reign of George II*, i. 289-332 ; *Addit. MS.* 33050, ff. 200-368 ; cf. art. JOHNSON, JAMES, 1705-1774).

Stone retained the entire confidence of the court. In 1755 he conducted the negotiations which led to Henry Fox (afterwards first Baron Holland) [q. v.] taking office, and after the accession of George III he was appointed treasurer to the new queen, Charlotte Sophia [q. v.], on her arrival in England in September 1761. He attached himself to Bute, and was one of the party of 'king's friends' whom Burke denounced (*Thoughts on Present Discontents*, 1769, passim). In 1763 Horace Walpole reported that Bute's private junto met daily at Stone's house in Privy Garden (*Mem. of Reign of George III*, ed. Barker, i. 334). Stone died at his house in Privy Garden on 16 Dec. 1773, and was buried in Westminster Abbey on the 24th (*Gent. Mag.* 1773, p. 622 ; WALPOLE, *Letters*, ed. Cunningham, vi. 34).

Stone married at Tooting, on 7 July 1743, Hannah, daughter of Stephen Mauvillain of Tooting and Morden, Surrey, by his wife, Hannah Gregory. She died on 5 June 1782, aged 72, and was buried in Westminster Abbey. Stone's only son, Thomas, born on 6 Dec. 1749, died on 7 Feb. 1761, and was buried in Westminster Abbey on the 15th (CHESTER, *Reg. West. Abbey*, pp. 397, 433).

According to Walpole, Stone was 'a dark, proud man, very able, but very mercenary,' and probably his high tory views influenced George III's mind in a direction that subsequently proved disastrous. Bishop Newton described him as a man of much reading, great knowledge, and exact memory. A mass of Stone's correspondence, including letters to Sir John Norris, Sir Thomas Robinson, Lord Tyrawley, and other politicians, is among the British Museum Additional MSS. (see *Cat. of Additions*, 1854-75) and forms an important source for the ministerial history of the period.

[Gent. Mag. 1749 p. 475, 1761 p. 44, 1773 p. 622 ; Hist. Reg. xxi. Chron. Diary, p. 22 ; Foster's Alumni Oxon. 1714-1886 ; Welch's Alumni Westmon. pp. 277-9 ; Egerton MS. 2529 ff. 211, 218, 235, 237 ; Parl. Hist. xii. 219, xiv. 84, xv. 318 ; Hervey's Memoirs, ii. 328 ; Walpole's Letters, ed. Cunningham, vols. i-iii. and v-vi.; Walpole's Mem. of the Reign of George II, ed. 1847 i. 283, 289-332, ii. 43, 45, and Memoirs of the Reign of George III, ed. Barker, 4 vols. passim ; Bubb Dodington's Diary, 1784 ; Coxe's Pelham Administration, i. 423, 430, ii. 128, 167, 235-6 ; Bishop Newton's Life, pp. 133-5 ; Lord Waldegrave's Memoirs, pp. 10, 80 ; Torrens's Hist. of Cabinets, 2 vols. 1894, passim.]   A. F. P.

STONE, BENJAMIN (*fl.* 1630–1642), sword-maker, was an enterprising cutler of London who about 1630 established on Hounslow Heath, on the site now occupied by Bedfont powder-mills, the earliest English sword factory of which anything is known. He employed English workmen under the direction of foreigners, probably Flemings, paying by the piece and finding workshops, tools, &c., as usual in the trade until recent times. His grindstones and polishing wheels were turned by a water-wheel, this being in all probability an innovation. His establishment was on a scale that enabled him to produce about a thousand swords a month. His blades were of exceptional quality. On one occasion three of his blades which were falsely represented by a rival cutler to be of Toledo manufacture were purchased by Robert South, formerly cutler by appointment to James I, who, despite fifty years' experience, did not detect the false pretence. Stone's persistent condemnation of the work of contemporary London cutlers converted them into personal and bitter enemies. Their opposition and the remote site of his factory, combined with the popular belief in the superiority of imported blades, served in course of time to ruin Stone's business, and in 1636 he was in danger of arrest for debt. He appealed to the king for protection and assistance, and was appointed blade-maker to the office of ordnance. Subsequently, upon the occasion of a contract for four thousand swords being given to his rivals, Stone attempted to claim a monopoly of supply to the royal stores; but the influence of Captain William Legge [q. v.], master of the armoury, was cast against him, and the attempt failed. The withdrawal of Charles I and the flight from London of the chief officers of ordnance, with the rest of the nobility, left Stone without protectors and with a stigma of 'malignancy' upon him in the midst of enemies. The parliamentary party was too poor to encourage the making of new swords, and when Waller and Hesilrige in 1643–4 appealed for two hundred horsemen's swords of Stone's Hounslow make, the appeal was met by public subscription in kind. After the civil war the factory passed to other hands, and was removed to a point lower down the river. The industry languished and ceased in the eighteenth century. The Duke of Newcastle testified both in his 'Truth of the Sword' and his 'Country Captain' (act i. scene 2) to the surpassing excellence of Hounslow blades, at a time when the mill was probably under Stone's management.

[State Papers, Domestic; Ordnance Office, Declared Accounts and Journal (Harl. MS. 429); Glover's Survey of the Hundred of Isleworth.]

STONE, EDMUND (*d.* 1768), mathematician, was the son of a gardener in the employ of John Campbell, second duke of Argyll [q. v.], at Inveraray. In a letter from Andrew Michael Ramsay [q. v.] in the 'Mémoires de Trévoux' for 1736, it is stated that Stone was eighteen years old before he learned to read, but that afterwards he made extraordinary progress. The Duke of Argyll, one day seeing a copy of Newton's 'Principia' lying upon the grass, supposed it to be his own and directed it to be carried to the library. It was, however, claimed by Stone, and a conversation ensued in which the duke learned to his surprise that the young man without teachers had acquired a considerable knowledge of mathematics, besides having mastered the rudiments of the Latin and French languages. The duke, delighted by his ability and knowledge, placed him in a position which afforded him opportunity to pursue his studies.

In 1723 Stone published a work on 'The Construction and Principal Uses of Mathematical Instruments, translated from the French of M. [Nicolas] Bion, to which are added such instruments as are omitted by Bion, particularly those invented or improved by the English' (London, fol. 2nd edit. with supplement, 1758), and a translation of de L'Hôpital's 'Traité Analytique des Sections Coniques' (1720), entitled 'An Analytick Treatise of Conic Sections' (London, 4to). On 22 April 1725 he was admitted a fellow of the Royal Society (THOMSON, *Hist. of Royal Soc.* App. p. xxxvi), and in the same year he published 'A New Mathematical Dictionary' (London, 8vo; 2nd edit. 1743). In 1730 he issued a treatise on 'The Method of Fluxions, both direct and inverse, the former being a translation from . . . de l'Hôpital's "Analyse des Infinement [sic] petits," and the latter supply'd by the translator, E. Stone' (London, 8vo). The latter part, on the integral calculus, was translated into French in 1735 by 'M. Rondet, Maître de Mathématiques.' In 1736 Stone communicated to the Royal Society 'concerning two species of lines of the third order not mentioned by Sir Isaac Newton nor Mr. Sterling' [see STIRLING, JAMES] (*Phil. Trans.* xli. 318). These two forms complete the seventy-eight different varieties of cubic curves. They had, however, already been discovered—one by Nicole in 1731, and the other by Nicolas Bernoulli about the same time. Stone seems to have suffered by the death of his patron, the second Duke of Argyll, on 4 Oct. 1743, for about that time he withdrew from the Royal Society, and the latter part of his life was spent in poverty. In 1760 a writer in the 'Critical Review' describes him as 'living at an advanced age, unrewarded, except by a mean employment that reflects dishonour on the donors.' He died in 1768. If his last work, 'Some Reflections on the Uncertainty of many Astronomical and Geographical Positions' (London, 1768, 8vo), were intended to be more than an extravaganza, it is a proof that his mind was failing. It consists of a series of propositions attacking the accuracy of the conclusions of astronomers concerning the shape of the earth and other matters of a similar kind.

Besides the works mentioned, Stone was the author of: 1. 'An Essay on Perspective,' London, 1724, 8vo, translated from the French of Willem Jacob Storm van Gravesande. 2. 'Geometrical Lectures,' London, 1735, 8vo, translated from the Latin of Isaac Barrow [q. v.] 3. 'The Whole Doctrine of Parallaxes,' London, 1763, 8vo. He also published two editions of 'Euclid' in 1728 and 1752, and revised 'A New Treatise of the Construction and Use of the Sector by Samuel Cunn,' London, 1729, 8vo.

[Encycl. Britannica, 8th edit. xx. 708; English Cyclopædia Biogr. v. 739; Georgian Era, i. 834, iii. 131; Anderson's Scottish Nation; Chalmers's Biogr. Dict. 1816; Rondet's Discours Préliminaire to his translation of Stone's treatise on Fluxions, 1735; Hutton's Phil. and Math. Dict. 1815.]   E. I. C.

STONE, EDWARD JAMES (1831–1897), astronomer, was born in London on 28 Feb. 1831. His father, Edward Stone, came of a Devonshire family. Having taken a studentship at King's College, London, he went up to Cambridge in 1856, was elected a scholar of Queens' College, and graduated thence as fifth wrangler in 1859, proceeding M.A. in 1862. He held a fellowship of his college 1859–72, and was readmitted as honorary fellow in 1875. Appointed in 1860 chief assistant at the Royal Observatory, Greenwich, he devoted ten laborious years to the improvement of the fundamental constants of astronomy. The thoroughness of his investigations was shown by his early detection of the 'variation of latitude.' From observations of the opposition of Mars in 1862 he deduced a solar parallax of 8″·94 (Monthly Notices, xxiii. 183), while an elaborate discussion of a mass of data relative to the transit of Venus in 1869 afforded him a value of 8″·91, corresponding to a distance of the sun from the earth of 91,700,000 miles (ib. xxviii. 255). The gold medal of the Royal Astronomical Society was awarded to him in 1869 for this work (ib. xxix. 175).

In 1870 Stone succeeded Sir Thomas Maclear [q. v.] as royal astronomer at the Cape of Good Hope. His energies were there mainly devoted to the preparation of the Cape Catalogue of 12,441 stars for the epoch 1880, the standard merit of which was acknowledged by the bestowal of the Lalande prize of the French Academy in 1881. He witnessed at the Cape the memorable aurora of 4 Feb. 1872 (Nature, v. 443), and observed from Klipfontein in Namaqualand the total solar eclipse of 16 April 1874, when he confirmed Young's spectroscopic discovery of the 'reversing layer' (Memoirs Roy. Astr. Society, xlii. 35). A series of magnetic observations made by him on the occasion were printed by the Royal Society (Proceedings, xxiii. 553). At the Cape, too, he watched the transit of Venus on 8 Dec. 1874, and, having returned to England on his nomination in 1879 to the post of Radcliffe observer at Oxford, he ably organised the government expeditions to observe the corresponding event of 1882. In his report, presented in 1887, he carefully examined the baffling phenomena of 'contacts,' and concluded for a solar parallax of 8″·85. In the 'Radcliffe Catalogue for 1890,' published in 1894, he completed his useful survey of the southern heavens. It gives the places of 6,424 stars between the equator and − 25° of declination.

Stone was a fellow of the Royal Society, and presided over the Royal Astronomical Society during the term 1882–4. He received the degree of doctor of science from the university of Padua in 1892. He made successful spectroscopic observations of the eclipsed sun at Novaya Zemlya on 8 Aug. 1896, and planned an expedition to India for the eclipse of 22 Jan. 1898. But his design was frustrated. He died suddenly at Oxford on 9 May 1897, aged 66. He married, in 1866, Grace Tuckett, who survives him with a son and three daughters.

A worthy inheritor of Airy's methods, Stone rendered very considerable services to exact astronomy; yet he fell into a strange misconception regarding mean solar time, which the reiterated arguments of Professors Newcomb and John Couch Adams failed to dissipate. The proper motions of 406 southern stars were determined by him (Memoirs Roy. Astr. Soc. xlii. 129), and, approximately, the relative masses of the components of a Centauri (Monthly Notices, xxxvi. 258). Almost simultaneously with Dr. Huggins he made in 1869 an attempt to measure stellar heat (Proc. Roy. Soc. xvii. 309, xviii. 159).

His communications to the Royal Astronomical Society were very numerous, and they included a painstaking inquiry into the origin of certain errors in the tables of the sun and moon, completed one month before his death (*Monthly Notices*, lvii. 458). The event just preceded the issue of a new edition, revised by Professor H. H. Turner, of his 'Tables for facilitating the Computation of Star-constants.'

[Times, 10 May 1897; Observatory, June 1897; Nature, 20 May 1897; Astronomische Nachrichten, No. 3426; Athenæum, 15 May 1897; Men of the Time, 13th edit.; Royal Society's Catalogue of Scientific Papers.]

A. M. C.

STONE, FRANCIS (1738?–1813), unitarian divine, son of Arthur Stone of the Middle Temple and Fleet Street, London, was born about 1738. His mother was Susanna, second daughter of Francis Fox [q. v.] He was but two years old when his father died. From the Charterhouse school, of which he was captain, he was elected scholar in 1755 at University College, Oxford, where he matriculated on 15 May 1755, aged 16, graduated B.A. 1759, and M.A. 1763. He studied Hebrew under Thomas Hunt (1696–1774) [q. v.] In 1760 he became curate at Crawley, Hampshire, to his mother's brother-in-law, Henry Taylor [q.v.], who made him an Arian. In 1762 he became curate of Worth, Sussex, having as neighbours William Hopkins (1706–1786) [q. v.] and John Bristed, rector of Slaugham, Sussex, both Arians. Bristed, a good Hebraist, of the school of Gregory Sharpe [q. v.], taught him to discard the Massoretic points. In 1765 he was presented by the governors of the Charterhouse to the rectory of Cold Norton, Essex (instituted 11 May).

A pamphlet by Stone, issued in 1768 under the name of 'Tyro-Theologus,' initiated the movement for a petition to parliament for relief from clerical subscription. Stone wrote avowedly in the interest of unitarians; the proposal was renewed on broader grounds (1771) by Francis Blackburne (1705–1787) [q. v.] The petition was promoted (1771–2) by William Robertson, D.D. [q. v.], and Theophilus Lindsey [q. v.] Stone's name was not put forward, but he acted as chairman of the 'society of the petitioning clergy' at the Feathers tavern in the Strand. The large number of names from Essex was greatly due to his activity. By 1784 he had got beyond Arianism, rejecting the doctrine of the miraculous conception. Meantime he was turning his attention to economic and social questions, and became a fellow of the Society of Arts. At length, on 8 July 1806, during a visitation held at Danbury by William Gretton [q. v.], archdeacon of Essex, he put forward his unitarian views in a sermon which he published, with the title 'Jewish Prophecy the sole Criterion to distinguish between genuine and spurious Christian Scripture,' 1806, 8vo (three editions). He offered the profits of the publication to the fund for widows of Essex clergy, but the offer was rejected 'with disdain.' For this sermon he was prosecuted in the bishop of London's consistory court. The trial took place on 13 May 1808 before Sir William Scott (afterwards Lord Stowell) [q. v.], who condemned Stone to deprivation unless he recanted. Failing to do this, he was deprived (20 May) by Beilby Porteus [q. v.], who died on 14 May 1809. Stone made a futile appeal to the court of arches. The loss of his living threw him into debt. The unitarians raised a subscription, from which they paid him 100l. a year, but from Michaelmas 1810 he was confined within the rules of the king's bench. It would appear that his eccentricity alienated his friends. He died at 30 Garden Row, London Road, Southwark, on 1 Nov. 1813. He married in 1761, and must have married a second time, as he left a widow and eight children, several of them young, and one born after 1800.

He published, besides sermons: 1. 'A short and seasonable Application . . . in behalf of . . . a legal redress of . . . religious Grievances, by Tyro-Theologus, M.A.,' 1768, 8vo. 2. 'A New . . . Method of discharging the National Debt,' 1776, 8vo (he suggests the appropriation of church property, after paying to all ecclesiastics a uniform stipend of 200l. a year). 3. 'Political Reformation on a large scale,' 1789, 8vo. 4. 'An Examination of . . . Burke's Reflections on the Revolution in France,' 1792, 8vo. 5. 'Thoughts in favour of the Abolition of the Slave Trade,' 1792, 8vo. 6. 'A Letter to . . . Dr. Beilby Porteus,' 1807, 8vo. 7. 'An Unitarian Christian Minister's Plea for Adherence to the Church of England,' 1808, 8vo. To the 'Monthly Repository,' 1813, he contributed biographical notices of Henry Taylor and William Hopkins. His promised autobiography did not appear.

[Foster's Alumni Oxon. 1888, iv. 1359; Morant's Essex, 1768, i. 350; Monthly Repository, 1806 p. 490, 1807 pp. 528, 565, 1808 pp. 274, 282, 518, 1809 pp. 404, 411, 1812 pp. 447, 752, 1813 pp. 133, 285, 425, 1818 p. 16; Gent. Mag. 1808 i. 455, 1813 ii. 508; P. A. Taylor's Account of the Taylor Family, 1875.]

A. G.

STONE, FRANK (1800–1859), painter, born at Manchester on 22 Aug. 1800, was the son of a cotton-spinner. He was brought up in his father's calling, and did not turn his attention to art until the age of twenty-four. He is said 'never to have studied under any master or even to have received a drawing lesson at school.' After seven years' application he came to London in 1831. His earliest work consisted in making pencil drawings for Charles Heath (1785–1848) [q. v.], at five guineas each, to be engraved by him in the 'Book of Beauty.' On 11 Feb. 1833 he was elected an associate exhibitor of the Watercolour Society, and in 1837 was represented for the first time at the Royal Academy exhibition by a couple of portraits in oil. His early works were extensively engraved. They were distinguished by 'a pretty sentimentality' which made them popular. Among them may be mentioned 'The Last Appeal,' 'Cross Purposes,' 'The Old, Old Story,' and the companion pictures 'Impending Mate' and 'Mated.' In 1841 he was awarded a premium of fifty guineas by the British Institution, and on 13 June 1842 was elected a member of the Water-colour Society, but resigned his membership on 17 July 1846.

Among London writers and artists Stone had many acquaintances. He was the associate of Thackeray, and of the poets Campbell and Rogers, and the intimate friend of Dickens. From 1845 to 1851 he resided at Tavistock House, Tavistock Square (afterwards the dwelling of Dickens). He frequently assisted Dickens in theatricals, and in 1847 he accompanied the novelist in a troupe of amateur players on a tour in the north. Dickens made Sairey Gamp describe Stone as 'a fine-looking, portly gentleman, with a face like an amiable full moon' (FORSTER, Life of Dickens, ii. 353). In November 1848 he assisted in illustrating the 'Haunted Man.' In the same year he exhibited at the Royal Academy 'Christ and the Sisters of Bethany,' and two years later a 'Scene from the Tempest,' the first of several Shakespearean subjects. In 1851 he was chosen an associate of the Royal Academy. During the last five or six years of his life his work acquired more breadth and simplicity and showed less trace of drawing-room sentiment. Among his later productions may be mentioned 'The Gardener's Daughter' and several sea studies. Stone died in London on 18 Nov. 1859, and was buried in Highgate cemetery. He was father of the well-known artist, Mr. Marcus Stone, R.A.

Stone seldom attempted large or compli-

cated compositions, preferring groups of two or three figures which he could paint with careful attention to matters of technique. The characteristics of his art have been described as 'a combination of technical elaboration with a definite predilection for beauty of physical type.' With such tendencies he was necessarily popular, but his most successful work was perhaps not his best.

[Athenæum, 1859, ii. 707; Redgrave's Dict. of English Artists; Bryan's Dict. of Painters and Engravers, ed. Armstrong and Graves; Ward's Men of the Reign; Roget's Hist. of the 'Old Water-colour' Soc. ii. 217–23; Letters of Dickens, 1882, passim; Mrs. Ritchie's Chapters from some Memoirs, 1894, p. 91.]   E. I. C.

STONE, GEORGE (1708?–1764), archbishop of Armagh, born about 1708, was younger son of Andrew Stone, an eminent banker of Lombard Street, London, by his wife, Anne Holbrooke. Andrew Stone [q. v.] was his elder brother. George was educated at Westminster school, where, at the age of thirteen, he was elected a king's scholar at Whitsuntide 1721. Four years later he obtained a Westminster studentship at Christ Church, Oxford, whence he graduated B.A. on 7 May 1729, M.A. on 10 May 1732, and D.D. on 20 May 1740. Stone seems to have first thought of entering the army (NICHOLS, Illustrations of Literary History, 1817–58, v. 383), but ultimately took orders, and, on the appointment of the Duke of Dorset as lord-lieutenant of Ireland, went over to Dublin as one of his chaplains. His rise in the church was remarkably rapid. He was appointed dean of Ferns by patent dated 22 Aug. 1733. On 11 March 1734 he was promoted to the deanery of Derry, and was installed on 3 April following. On 3 Aug. 1740 he was consecrated bishop of Ferns and Leighlin by the archbishop of Dublin, assisted by the bishops of Meath and Derry, in the parish church of Chapelizod, near Dublin. He took his seat in the House of Lords for the first time on 6 Oct. 1741 (Journals of the Irish House of Lords, iii. 497). He was translated to the bishopric of Kildare by patent dated 19 March 1743, and in the same month was installed dean of Christ Church, Dublin. On 11 May 1745 he was translated to the bishopric of Derry, and thereupon resigned the deanery of Christ Church. He was appointed archbishop of Armagh by patent dated 13 March 1747, and took his seat on the archbishops' bench in the Irish House of Lords on 6 Oct. following, but he was not enthroned until 26 Sept. 1752.

Stone was sworn a member of the Irish privy council on 10 April 1747, and on the same day was appointed a lord justice along with Robert Jocelyn, Baron Newport, the lord chancellor, and Henry Boyle, the speaker of the House of Commons. Though Stone had already on several occasions 'signalised himself by a most determined opposition to the Irish interest' (PLOWDEN, *Historical Review of the State of Ireland*, 1803, i. 304), it does not appear that he exercised much influence on the Irish administration during the viceroyalty of Lord Harrington. A rivalry, however, soon sprang up between the young primate and Boyle, who had been for a long time one of the most considerable men in the kingdom. On the reappointment of his old patron, the Duke of Dorset, as lord-lieutenant in 1751, Stone allied himself with Lord George Sackville, the new chief secretary. This alliance, combined with the influence of his elder brother, Andrew Stone, in England, enabled him more effectually to contest the supremacy of his rival in the direction of Irish affairs. The contest between Stone and Boyle was merely for power, but the question nominally at issue in the struggle between them from 1749 to 1753 was whether the Irish House of Commons had or had not the right to dispose of the surplus revenues of the country. Stone supported the claim of the crown, while Boyle, who had been driven into opposition by Lord George Sackville's attempt to induce him to resign the speakership in favour of John Ponsonby, took the popular side. In the session of 1749 heads of a bill for the appropriation of the surplus were sent over to England, but the English authorities insisted that the surplus belonged to the crown, and that the Irish House of Commons had not even the right to entertain any question of the kind without the express consent of the crown. In order to establish this principle Dorset, at the opening of the session in 1751, declared the royal consent to the proposed measure. The house, however, passed the bill without taking any notice of this consent. The bill was returned from England with an alteration in the preamble, signifying that the royal consent had been given. The Irish parliament thereupon gave way, and the bill was passed in its altered form. In the session of 1753 the struggle was renewed. Dorset again signified the king's consent to the appropriation of the new surplus towards the payment of the national debt. As in the previous session, the bill was sent over without any mention of the consent of the crown. It was returned with the same alteration as before; but by this time the opposition had grown stronger, and the bill was rejected by the Irish House of Commons on account of the

alteration by a majority of 122 votes against 117. Hereupon strong measures were taken by the government; Anthony Malone [q. v.] and other servants of the crown who had voted with the majority were dismissed from their places, and a portion of the surplus was by royal authority applied to the liquidation of the national debt (LECKY, *History of Ireland*, 1892, i. 463–5).

Stone was now virtually dictator of Ireland. 'Without this Wolsey's interposition it is vain,' writes Adderley to Lord Charlemont, 'to look after honours or any kind of preferment' (*Hist. MSS. Comm.* 12th Rep. app. x. p. 189). Though Boyle was excluded from the regency of 1754–5, he still continued his active opposition to the government until the Duke of Dorset's dismissal. During the Duke of Devonshire's viceroyalty the tables were turned. Boyle was created Earl of Shannon, and several members of the opposition received places or pensions, while Stone was forced to retire from the direction of affairs. Though he was excluded from the regency in May 1756, he was not struck off the list of Irish privy councillors, as Plowden and others assert. With the object of regaining power, Stone now entered into an alliance with John Ponsonby [q. v.] in opposition to the government. The House of Commons was at this time divided into three parties, of which Stone, John Ponsonby, and the Earl of Kildare were respectively the chiefs. Unable to govern Ireland independently of these factions, the Duke of Bedford, who succeeded the Duke of Devonshire as lord-lieutenant of Ireland in September 1757, attempted to induce Kildare to make up his differences with Stone. Stone had always been a special object of hatred to Kildare, who, in his famous petition to the king in 1754, described the primate as 'a greedy churchman,' affecting to be 'a second Wolsey in the senate' (PLOWDEN, *Historical Review of the State of Ireland*, vol. i. app. pp. 255–257). Though Stone was willing to serve with anybody so long as he was restored to power, Kildare was inexorable. Ultimately Stone's intrigues prevailed, and, having promised to be faithful in future, provided he received a share of the public patronage, he was appointed a lord justice along with the Earl of Shannon and John Ponsonby, by patent dated 29 April 1758. With the aid of his old antagonist Shannon, and the steady assistance of John Ponsonby, Stone was enabled to carry on the government of Ireland during the remainder of his life, but he never regained his former ascendency. Stone died unmarried, at his brother's house in Privy Garden (now known as Whitehall Gardens), on 19 Dec. 1764, aged 50, and, after lying in state in the Jerusalem Chamber, was buried in the north aisle of Westminster Abbey on the 28th of the same month. There is no monument to his memory, and the large marble slab which formerly marked his burial-place has been removed. There is a portrait of Stone by Ramsay in the hall of Christ Church, Oxford.

Stone was an able but somewhat unscrupulous man, with a handsome presence and insinuating manners. His ambition and ostentation were unbounded, and he was much more of a politician than an ecclesiastic. His tact and finesse were alike remarkable. 'No man,' says Cumberland, 'faced difficulties with greater courage, none overcame them with more address; he was formed to hold command over turbulent spirits in tempestuous seasons; for if he could not absolutely rule the passions of men, he could artfully rule men by the medium of their passions' (*Memoirs of Richard Cumberland*, 1806, p. 172). According to Horace Walpole, Stone 'ruined his constitution by indulgence to the style of luxury and drinking established in Ireland, and by conforming to which he had found the means of surmounting the most grievous prejudices, and of gaining popularity, ascendant, power—an instance of abilities seldom to be matched' (*Memoirs of the Reign of King George III*, 1894, ii. 27). The appellation of 'the beauty of holiness,' which was given to Stone, as previously to Bishop Stillingfleet, on account of his good looks, was not confirmed by any singular excellence of his moral character. But though he did not conform to the decencies of his profession, he was probably innocent of the grosser charges which were brought against him by his numerous enemies. Stone was favourably inclined to the toleration of Roman catholics, and strongly opposed a bill for the registration of priests (STUART, *Memoirs of the City of Armagh*, 1819, pp. 438–40). He was one of the very few persons who recognised the merits of Hume's 'History of England' on its first appearance ('Life of David Hume, Esq., written by himself,' 1777, pp. 17–20). Some satirical verses on Stone will be found in the 'Twelfth Report of the Historical Manuscripts Commission' (App. x. pp. 272–273). In 'Baratariana' he figures as 'Cardinal Lapidario' (*Notes and Queries*, 2nd ser. viii. 211–12).

Many of Stone's letters to the Duke of Newcastle and others are preserved in the British Museum and the Public Record Office. A copy of verses by him is printed among the Oxford poems on the death of George I (*Pietas Univ. Oxon. &c.* 1727). Ser-

mons by him were published in 1742, 1751, and 1760 respectively. He is said to have been the author, conjointly with Anthony Malone, of 'The Representation of the L—s J—s of Ireland, touching the Transmission of a Privy Council Money Bill, previous to the calling of a new Parliament,' Dublin, 1770, 8vo.

[Authorities quoted in text; Walpole's Memoirs of the Reign of George II, 1846; A Letter from a Prime Serjeant to a High Priest, 1754; Hist. MSS. Comm. 8th Rep. App. i, pp. 175–81 et seq.; Bedford Correspondence, 1842–6, vol. ii. pp. xii–xiv, 348–52, 355–9, 377–82; Chatham Correspondence, 1838–40, i. 158–9, 229–30, ii. 59–67; Coxe's Memoirs of the Pelham Administration, 1829, ii. 284–8; Hardy's Memoirs of the Earl of Charlemont, 1810, pp. 41–2, 44–52, 80, 85–6, 94–9, 102–5; Mrs. Delany's Autobiogr. 1861–2; Lord E. Fitzmaurice's Life of William, Earl of Shelburne, 1875–6, i. 346–8, ii. 81–91; Campbell's Philosophical Survey of the South of Ireland, 1777, pp. 55–6; Curry's Historical and Critical Review of the Civil Wars in Ireland, &c., 1786, ii. 261–2, 270; Mant's Hist. of the Church of Ireland from the Revolution to the Union, 1840, ii. 580, 600–5, 617, 781, 784, 785, 786; O'Flanagan's Lives of the Lord Chancellors of Ireland, 1870, ii. 86–7, 101–5, 109–10; Froude's Eng. in Ireland, 1872–4, i. 610–12, 617–22, ii. 39, 197, 449; Addit. MS. Brit. Mus. 5808, f. 232; Alumni Westmon. 1852, pp. 240–1, 270, 275, 278, 286, 290, 294; Chester's Westminster Abbey Registers (Harl. Soc. Publ.). x, 49, 405, 410, 418; Neale's Westminster Abbey, 1818–23, ii. 243; Gent. Mag. 1764, p. 603; Wood's Hist. and Antiquities of the Colleges and Halls in the Univ. of Oxford, pp. 205, 446; Cotton's Fasti Ecclesiæ Hibernicæ, 1848–60, ii. 46, 234, 339–40, 351, iii. 26, 324, 333, v. 200; Foster's Alumni Oxon. 1715–1886, iv. 1359; Liber Munerum Publicorum Hiberniæ, vol. i. pt. ii. pp. 12–13; Halkett and Laing's Dict. of Anon. and Pseudon. Lit. 1882–8, iii. 2184.]
G. F. R. B.

STONE, GILBERT (d. 1417?), mediæval letter-writer, born at Stone in Staffordshire, whence he took his name, is said by Brian Twyne [q. v.] to have been educated at Oxford, where he devoted himself to the study of civil law, to have been made chancellor successively to Robert Wyville (d. 1375), bishop of Salisbury; Ralph Ergham (d. 1400), bishop of Bath and Wells; and to Richard Clifford, bishop of Worcester, who was translated to London in 1407. The defective registers afford no confirmation of these statements, but in 1384 Richard II confirmed Stone in possession of the prebend of Buckland Denham in Wells Cathedral, and early in the fifteenth century he held the prebend of Ynge or Eigne in Hereford Cathedral, which he resigned in 1414. On 9 March 1411–12 he was collated to the prebend of Portpoole in St. Paul's Cathedral, and he died probably in 1417, when his successor in that office was appointed (LE NEVE, ed. Hardy, i. 534, ii. 427). Stone is said to have written 123 letters, some of which are extant in the collections of Sir Thomas Bodley and Richard James in the Bodleian Library (BERNARD, *Cat. MSS. Anglia*, p. 261). One addressed while he was chancellor of Worcester to Thomas Arundel [q. v.], archbishop of Canterbury, is extant in Cotton MS. Vitellius E. x. 121. Two others are in Harleian MS. 431, f. 25 *a* b. Richard James, in his 'Iter Lancastre' (Chetham Soc. p. 6), says: 'Gilbert Stone, being for y⁰ time a trimme man of his penne, was sollicited by y⁰ monks there [i.e. at Holywell] to write their founders or saints life; when he requested summe memories of him, they had none at all. Wherefore in a letter of his, he says "tis no matter, for he would write them notwithstanding a fine legend after y⁰ manner of Thomas of Canterburye."'

[Tanner's Bibl. Brit.-Hib. pp. 693–4; Twyne's Antiquitatis Acad. Oxoniensis Apologia, 1620; authorities cited.] A. F. P.

STONE, **JEROME** (1727–1756), linguist and poet, was born in the parish of Sconnie, Fifeshire, in 1727. His father, a seaman, died abroad in 1730, and his mother was left in poverty. He commenced at an early age to earn his living, first as a chapman, and afterwards by selling books at fairs and travelling with them over the country. With no assistance but that of his books he acquired a knowledge of Hebrew and Greek, and, with the aid of a parish schoolmaster, he studied Latin. The professors of St. Andrews, hearing of his abilities, permitted him to attend their classes, and at the end of three years recommended him for the post of usher in the grammar school, Dunkeld. In two or three years afterwards the Duke of Atholl appointed him headmaster. While in his thirtieth year he was seized with fever, and died on 11 June 1756.

Stone's fame as a linguist was wide, but he did not live to complete any large literary work. While at St. Andrews he began to contribute to magazines, and at Dunkeld he studied Gaelic literature, both Scottish and Irish, with a view to translating. His contributions to the 'Scots Magazine' include poems, an allegory, and a preliminary welcome to Dr. Johnson's dictionary. At his death he was engaged on two works: (1) 'An Enquiry into the Original of the Nation and Language of the Ancient Scots;' and (2) 'The Immortality of Authors,' an allegory (*New Statistical Abstract*, 'Fife,' p. 267).

[Encyclopædia Perthensis, xxi. 440 ; Scots Magazine, June 1756.] J. R. M.

STONE, **JOHN HURFORD** (1763–1818), political refugee, was born at Taunton, Somerset, in 1763. Losing his father in childhood, he was sent to his uncle, William Hurford, coal merchant and common councilman in London, and, with his younger brother William, he appears to have succeeded to his uncle's business. Being a unitarian, he became intimate with Price and Priestley, and his radical opinions, coupled with his acquaintance with continental languages and literatures, attracted to his dinner table Fox, Sheridan, the poet Rogers, Talleyrand, and Madame de Genlis. A prominent member of the Society of the Friends of the Revolution (of 1688), he presided in London in October 1790 at the reception of a deputation from Nantes, at which the downfall of French despotism was celebrated. In September 1792 he was in Paris, and was chairman at a dinner of British residents and visitors held to commemorate the French victories in Belgium ; Thomas Paine and Lord Edward Fitzgerald were present. Madame de Genlis, on quitting Paris, entrusted some manuscripts to Stone, which he confided to Helen Maria Williams [q. v.], who, apprehensive of a domiciliary search by Jacobin inspectors, destroyed them. He advanced twelve thousand francs for a scheme for procuring the escape of M. de Genlis from prison, a debt of honour which the widow afterwards refused to discharge. He returned to London in February 1793, but was again in Paris in the following May, when he was a witness in favour of General Miranda. On the arrest of British subjects in the autumn of 1793, in retaliation for the capture of Toulon, he was imprisoned for seventeen days at the Luxembourg. He was again arrested, with his wife, Rachel Coope, in April 1794, probably on account of his Girondin sympathies, but was released on condition of quitting France. He accordingly went to Switzerland, but was speedily allowed to return to Paris, and in June 1794 obtained a divorce. This presumably marks the date of his liaison or secret marriage with Miss Williams. Tone found them living together in 1796. In January of that year Stone's brother William was tried at the Old Bailey for 'treacherously conspiring with John Hurford Stone, now in France, to destroy the life of the king and to raise a rebellion in his realms ;' but being shown to have acted entirely under his brother's influence in harbouring William Jackson (1737?–1795) [q. v.], he was acquitted, whereupon he retired to France and became steward to an Englishman named Parker at Villeneuve St. Georges. Stone himself, who published in Paris a caustic pamphlet on the trial, became agent in Paris for O'Reilly's pottery works at Creil, and subsequently started in business as a printer. He undertook some government contracts, brought out an edition of the Geneva (French Protestant) Bible, and was ruined by a costly Latin edition of Humboldt's 'Cosmos.' He was naturalised as a Frenchman in 1817, simultaneously with Miss Williams. He died in the following year, and his tombstone in Père-Lachaise (beside which Miss Williams was afterwards buried) describes him as an enlightened champion of religion and liberty.

Under the name of Photinus he published in French in 1800 a letter to Du Fossé in advocacy of unitarianism. An intercepted letter from him to Priestley in 1798 was printed by Cobbett in America; it elicited from Priestley a repudiation of Stone's desire for a French invasion of England.

[Gent. Mag. 1796; Life of Tone; Mém. de Madame de Genlis; Early Life of Samuel Rogers; Alger's Englishmen in French Revolution; Fitzpatrick's Secret Service under Pitt (which confuses the two brothers).] J. G. A.

STONE, NICHOLAS (1586–1647), mason, statuary, and architect, born at Woodbury, near Exeter, in 1586, was the son of a quarryman. He came to London early, and was apprenticed for two years to Isaac James, a mason, whom he also served for one year as a journeyman. He then went to Holland, and worked as a stone-mason in Amsterdam under Pieter de Keyser, son of Hendrik de Keyser, the celebrated sculptor. He is recorded to have designed and built a portico to the Westerkerk in Amsterdam, and to have gained thereby the hand of his master's daughter and also a share in a stone-quarry in the Isle of Portland in which De Keyser had a large interest. Stone returned to England before 1614, from which date he had a large practice as a mason and statuary, especially for monuments and similar works. Stone was employed by James I at Holyrood, St. James's Palace, Whitehall, Somerset House, Nonsuch, Theobalds, and Greenwich. He appears to have carried out, as mason, several designs of Inigo Jones, such as the Banqueting House, Whitehall, the watergates of Somerset House, and York House (in which works he was assisted by his brother-in-law, Andreas Kearne [q. v.], and the portico to the old St. Paul's Cathedral. At Oxford he designed and executed the porch of St. Mary's Church and the gates of the Physick Garden. In 1619 he was made master-mason to James I, and in April 1626 he received a patent from Charles I as master-

mason and architect at Windsor Castle (RYMER, Fœdera, xviii. 675). As architect he designed, or rebuilt, Cornbury House, near Oxford, and Tart Hall in St. James's Park.

Stone is best known for his monuments, which are in the late debased Renaissance style, known as Jacobean. In some of them he was associated with Bernard Janssens or Jansen [q. v.], Stone contributing the figures (or 'pictures') only, as in the tomb of Sir Nicholas Bacon and his lady in Redgrave church, Suffolk. Among other tombs made by Stone were those of Henry Howard, earl of Northampton, set up in Dover Castle (1615), and afterwards removed; of Thomas Sutton at the Charterhouse (1615) and Sir Thomas Bodley at Oxford (1615); of Sir Charles Morrison and other members of his family in St. Mary's Church at Watford, Hertfordshire; of Dr. John Donne in a winding-sheet to St. Paul's Cathedral, one of the few tombs which survived the great fire of 1666. For Westminster Abbey Stone made the tombs of Francis Holles, Sir George Holles, Sir Richard Cox, Isaac Casaubon, the Countess of Buckingham, and Dudley Carleton, viscount Dorchester. The well-known tomb of Sir Julius Cæsar in St. Helen's, Bishopsgate, is by Stone; and he made those of Sir Adam Newton at Charlton in Kent, Lord-chief-justice Coke at Tittleshall in Norfolk, Sir Robert Drury at Hawstead, Suffolk, and many others. An account-book of Stone, in which details of many such works are recorded, seems to have been given by his son-in-law, Charles Stoakes, to George Vertue [q. v.], and was purchased, with other manuscripts belonging to Vertue, by Horace Walpole. At the Strawberry Hill sale it was purchased by Sir John Soane, and is now in the Soane Museum, Lincoln's Inn Fields. In 1645 he published 'Enchiridion of Fortification; or, a Handful of Knowledge in Martial Affairs . . .,' London, 1645, 8vo, illustrated by engravings. Stone, whose work was considerably affected by the outbreak of the civil war, resided in Long Acre, and died there on 24 Aug. 1647, aged 61. He was buried on 28 Aug. in the church of St. Martin-in-the-Fields, and was followed thither on 22 Nov. by his wife Mary, by whom he was the father of three sons.

HENRY STONE (d. 1653), the eldest son, went to Holland, France, and Italy to study art, and returned in 1642. After his father's death he and his youngest brother carried on their father's business of mason and statuary. Stone was, however, chiefly known as a painter, and has acquired note as one of the most successful copyists of the works of Vandyck. He also copied Italian pictures with success. A slight work on painting, entitled 'The Third Part of the Art of Painting,' was compiled by him. Stone inherited his father's house and workyard in Long Acre, and died there on 24 Aug. 1653. He was buried on 27 Aug. near his father in St. Martin's Church, and on his inscription it is stated that he had passed the greatest part of thirty-seven years in Holland, France, and Italy. He is usually known as 'Old Stone' to distinguish him from his younger brothers. His portrait was painted by Sir Peter Lely.

NICHOLAS STONE, the younger (d. 1647), second son of Nicholas Stone, practised as a mason and statuary. In 1638 he accompanied his brother Henry to France and Italy, and a journal of his is preserved in the British Museum (Harl. MS. 4049). He worked there for a short time under the celebrated sculptor Bernini, and made many drawings of architecture and sculpture. He died at his father's house on 17 Sept. 1647, a few weeks after his father, and was buried on 20 Sept. in the same grave in St. Martin's Church. A portrait of him was in the possession of Colley Cibber.

JOHN STONE (d. 1667), youngest son of Nicholas Stone the elder, was educated at Westminster school and at Oxford, being intended for the church as a profession. On the outbreak of the civil wars, however, he entered the army on the king's side, and, after a defeat, narrowly escaped being hanged. Having lain concealed for several months in his father's house in Long Acre, he made his escape to France, and eventually succeeded to his father's house and profession in Long Acre, as the last survivor of his family. When the Restoration became imminent he went to Breda to petition the king for a post as master-mason or surveyor, but was seized there with illness, from which he died a few years later in Holy Cross Hospital, near Winchester. He was buried on 11 Sept. 1667, as 'Captain Stone,' with his parents and brothers in St. Martin-in-the-Fields.

Portraits of Nicholas Stone the elder (from a medallion), Nicholas Stone the younger, and Henry Stone (after Sir Peter Lely) were engraved in Walpole's 'Anecdotes of Painting' (ed. 1798).

[Walpole's Anecdotes of Painting, ed. Wornum; Vertue's Diaries (Brit. Mus. Addit. MSS. 23068, &c.); Pycroft's Art in Devonshire; Notes and Queries, 5th ser. ii. 465, 8th ser. xi. 402; Registers of St. Martin-in-the-Fields (by kind permission of the Rev. J. F. Kitto); Papworth's Dict. of Architecture.]   L. C.

STONE, SAMUEL (1602–1663), puritan divine, son of John Stone, a freeholder of Hertford, was born in that town and baptised at All Saints on 30 July 1602. He was educated at Hale's grammar school, and proceeded to Cambridge in 1620 as a pensioner of Emmanuel College, matriculating on 19 April, and graduating B.A. in 1623 and M.A. in 1627. He studied theology at Aspen in Essex, under Richard Blackerby, a non-subscriber. In 1630 he went to Towcester as a private lecturer, and remained there about three years (SHEPARD, Autobiogr.; YOUNG, Massachusetts Chronicles, p. 518).

In 1633 Stone sailed for New England in company with John Cotton and Thomas Hooker [q. v.], as an assistant to the latter. Hooker and Stone arrived in Boston on 4 September and went at once to Newtown (now Cambridge), where, on 11 Oct., they were chosen pastor and teacher respectively. In 1636 Hooker and Stone, with the majority of the inhabitants, removed to a new settlement on the Connecticut, which they called Hartford, after Stone's birthplace. In the following year Stone accompanied the Hartford contingent in the expedition against the Pequot Indians, which broke the power of that tribe.

In 1656 differences arose between Stone and William Goodwin, the ruling elder, concerning the former's method of exercising his functions of teacher. As a consequence Stone resigned his office, but was induced to resume it shortly after. The controversy ended in schism, Goodwin with several church members withdrawing to Hadley in 1659. Stone died at Hartford on 20 July 1663.

Stone was twice married. By his second wife, Elizabeth Allyn, whom he espoused in 1641, he had four surviving children—a son Samuel and four daughters, Elizabeth, Rebecca, Mary, and Sarah.

Stone published 'A Congregational Church, a Catholike Visible Church,' London, 1652, 4to, in answer to Samuel Hudson's 'Visible Catholick Church' (1645, 4to), and left two works in manuscript: a catechism and a confutation of the Antinomians.

[Winthrop's Hist. of New England, ed. 1853, i. 108, 109, 115, 142, 235; Mather's Magnalia, ed. 1853, i. 434–8; Walker's First Church in Hartford, passim; Appleton's Cyclopædia of American Biography, v. 703.]   E. I. C.

STONE, WILLIAM (1603?–1661?), colonist, born in Northamptonshire about 1603, was nephew of Thomas Stone, a London haberdasher. He was a Roman catholic. He emigrated to America, and on 6 Aug. 1648 was appointed governor of Maryland by the proprietor, Cecil Calvert, second lord Baltimore. In 1652 the commissioners who were appointed by parliament to reduce Maryland to obedience to its authority deprived Stone of his office, but in the same year restored him by request of the inhabitants, on the understanding that henceforth writs should run in Maryland as in England in the name of the keepers of the liberties of England, instead of, as hitherto, in that of the crown. Two years later Stone reasserted the authority of the proprietor by requiring the inhabitants to take an oath of fidelity to the proprietor, and to take out their patents in his name, and by ordering that writs should run as before 1652. But before long (May 1654) Stone issued a proclamation accepting, on behalf of Baltimore, the authority of the Commonwealth. Nevertheless, the parliamentary commissioners, Clayborne and Bennet, treated Stone's action as a defiance of their authority. They resumed the government, disfranchised Baltimore's co-religionists, the Roman catholics, and declared Stone's proclamation requiring an oath of fidelity to the proprietor null and void. Armed hostilities followed. Stone was wounded and taken prisoner, and, with some of his associates, condemned to death, but he was afterwards pardoned. In 1659, when Lord Baltimore came to terms with his enemies, and eventually recovered his authority, Stone was again appointed a councillor. He died in 1660 or 1661.

[State Papers; Archives of Maryland (Maryland Hist. Soc.); Pamphlets enumerated in Winsor's History of America, vol. iii.; Bozman's History of Maryland; Neill's Founders of Maryland.]

J. A. D.

STONEHENGE (editor of 'The Field'). [See WALSH, JOHN HENRY, 1810-1888.]

STONFORD, JOHN DE (*fl.* 1360), judge. [See STOWFORD.]

STONEHEWER or **STONHEWER**, RICHARD (1728?-1809), friend of Thomas Gray, born about 1728, was the son of Richard Stonehewer (d. 29 Oct. 1769), rector of Houghton-le-Spring, Durham, from 1727 to 1769. After a rudimentary education at the Kepyer grammar school in Houghton parish, he was admitted pensioner at Trinity College, Cambridge, on 4 Nov. 1745, 'aged 17,' and obtained a scholarship on 2 May 1747. He at once became known to Gray, probably through the introduction of Thomas Wharton, M.D., of Old Park, near Durham, the poet's lifelong friend. He graduated B.A. in 1749-50, being eighth wrangler in the mathematical tripos; was elected a fellow of

Peterhouse on 29 Oct. 1751, and proceeded M.A. in 1753. While residing on his fellowship in Cambridge he was the tutor of Augustus Henry Fitzroy, third duke of Grafton (1735-1811) [q. v.] When the duke threw himself into politics, Stonehewer became his private secretary, and remained throughout life his confidential friend. In April 1761 and until June 1763 he was 'interpreter of oriental languages.' On 19 July 1765 he was the duke's under-secretary of state for the northern department, and on 28 June 1766 he became under-secretary for the southern department to the Duke of Richmond (*Calendars of Home Office Papers*). Through the Duke of Grafton he obtained for Gray the professorship of modern history and languages at Cambridge, and was himself made permanent auditor of the excise. In 1768 he was living at Queen Street, Mayfair, London, where Mason paid him a visit, and he afterwards lived at 14 Curzon Street, a house nearly opposite the chapel (WHEATLEY AND CUNNINGHAM, *London*, i. 486-7). He was elected F.S.A. on 17 May 1787. Gray called him in 1769 his 'best friend,' and left him 500*l.* in his will. William Burke deemed him 'a gentleman of great worth, extreme good understanding, and of the politest manners' (*Cal. Home Office*, 22 April 1766). He was friendly with Horace Walpole, and in 1773 made a trip to the English lakes with Mason (MITFORD, *Correspondence of Walpole and Mason*, ii. 372-5). In May 1782 he was 'very ill of the influenza,' but he lived to a good old age, dying on 30 Jan. 1809, aged 81. His portrait was painted by Sir Joshua Reynolds in 1775 for the Duke of Grafton, and is in the possession of the present duke at Wakefield Lodge, Stony Stratford. A replica of it is at Middleton Park, Bicester, the seat of the Earl of Jersey. They are in excellent preservation, half length; a black fur hangs round his neck, and the costume is dark red.

The manuscripts which Gray left, together with his library, to Mason, were left by Mason to Stonehewer, who bequeathed to Pembroke College, Cambridge, Gray's commonplace books and holograph copies of most of his poems (GRAY, *Works*, ed. Gosse, vol. i. pp. xiii-xiv). The correspondence of Gray and Mason, published by Mitford in 1853, was left by Mason to Stonehewer, and passed from him to his relative, Mr. Bright of Skeffington Hall, Leicestershire. So did a part of Gray's library, the subsequent fate of which is described by Mr. Austin Dobson in 'Eighteenth-century Vignettes' (1892, p. 138). Stonehewer presented a manuscript by Gray on Aristophanes to Mathias. Letters to him are in Mr. Gosse's edition of Gray's 'Works,' ii. 277-9, 373-5, iii. 46-8, 342, 351 (NICHOLS, *Literary Anecdotes*, viii. 568).

[Leslie and Taylor's Sir Joshua Reynolds, ii. 146; Corresp. of Gray and Mason, p. v; Gent. Mag. 1769 p. 559, 1809 pt. i. p. 188; Gray's Works, ed. Gosse, ii. 197-8, 241, 395, iii. 317, 322; Gray's Works, ed. Mathias, pp. 585-6, 589; Walpole's Letters, ed. Cunningham, v. 117, 128, 501, viii. 229; Surtees's Durham, i. 157; information from the Earl of Jersey and Mr. W. Aldis Wright.] W. P. C.

STONHOUSE, SIR JAMES (1716-1795), baronet, physician, and divine, was the eldest son of Richard and Caroline Stonhouse of Tubney, near Abingdon, Berkshire, and was descended from the third baronet of the house. His father died about 1725; the mother lived for many years later. From them he inherited an estate worth about 200l. per annum. Stonhouse was born at Tubney on 20 July 1716. In 1722 he was at Merchant Taylors' school, and he was afterwards at Winchester College. He matriculated from St. John's College, Oxford, on 15 Jan. 1732-3, and graduated B.A. 1736, M.A. 1739, M.B. 1742, and M.D. January 1745-6. His medical teacher was Frank Nicholls [q. v.]; he attended the school at St. Thomas's Hospital, and then went abroad, where he studied medicine at Paris, Lyons, Montpellier, and Marseilles. On his return he settled for a year at Coventry, and while there married, in May 1742, Anne, eldest daughter of John Neale of Allesley, M.P. for Coventry and a maid of honour to Queen Caroline (*Gent. Mag.* 1742, p. 274). In April 1743 he removed to Northampton, and practised there for twenty years. His success was great, and Akenside fruitlessly tried in June 1744 to wrest his practice from him (JOHNSON, *Poets*, ed. Cunningham, iii. 378). This act did not put an end to their friendship, for Akenside, when withdrawing to Hampstead, carried with him an introduction from his rival (*Gent. Mag.* 1793, ii. 885). Though an absolute stranger to the place, Stonhouse succeeded in about four months after his arrival in founding the county infirmary at Northampton. He compiled the statutes for its government, and continued for many years its physician. In 1766 he drew up 'the statutes and rules for the general infirmary at Salisbury,' which were several times printed. In early life he was 'extreamly licentious both in principles and practice,' but soon after coming to Northampton a close friendship with Philip Doddridge and James Hervey led to his conversion. He had published a pamphlet against Christianity which had

VOL. LIV.

passed through two editions; the third he now burnt.

According to one account the change followed the hearing by Stonhouse of a funeral sermon which Doddridge preached on one of Stonhouse's patients. He was favourably influenced by the sermon, and Doddridge's 'Rise and Progress of Religion' was written to complete the good work. There is perhaps better ground for believing that the friendship was originally sought by Doddridge (HUMPHREYS, *Corresp. of Doddridge*, iv. 334-8). The first wife of Stonhouse died in her twenty-fifth year at Northampton on 1 Dec. 1747, leaving two surviving children. Several letters on her loss, which completed her husband's conversion, are printed in Hervey's 'Letters,' 1760, pp. 194-9 (cf. HERVEY, *Meditations*).

Stonhouse now meditated taking orders in the English church, and in October 1748 Doddridge, without his knowledge, wrote to Lord-chancellor Hardwicke asking for some preferment for him should he take that step. The chancellor replied with politeness, but declined to give any pledge (HARRIS, *Life of Hardwicke*, ii. 372-8). By this time he was known to George Whitefield, but was timorous and afraid of being classed among Whitefield's followers. After much hesitation he was ordained deacon in September 1749 by the bishop of Hereford in Hereford Cathedral, and a week later priest by the bishop of Bristol in Bristol Cathedral. For several years after this he remained at Northampton and practised in medicine. In 1758 he attended Hervey in his last illness.

In May 1764 Stonhouse was appointed by Lord Radnor to the rectory of Little Cheverell, near Devizes, Wiltshire, where he made at his own cost considerable improvements to the parsonage-house, and from December 1779 he held with it the adjoining rectory of Great Cheverell. He spent most of the year at Bristol for the sake of its waters. In 1788 he took up his residence permanently at Hotwells. There he preached, without stipend, as lecturer in the church of All Saints, and subsequently for five years at St. Werburgh's. He continued until the year of his death to minister occasionally at Bath and Bristol. Samuel Curwen praised his 'discourse serious and sensible, and his delivery with becoming energy' (*Journal*, p. 154), and Polwhele admired the 'fine inflexion of a voice distinct and sweet' (*English Orator*, bk. iv.); but his egotism and love of flattery were excessive. He was once reproved by Garrick for his faults of manner while ministering in church. Stonhouse advised Hannah More as to her reading, and figures as Mr.

E E

J[own]n in her train.' The Shepherd of Salisbury Plain.'

Stonhouse succeeded a cousin, Sir James, tenth baronet, in the baronetcy on 15 April 17[92]. He lived at Hotwells, Bristol, on a [lac. 174]0, and was buried in Dowry chapel, now the church of St. Andrew the Less, in the same grave with his second wife. She was [Sarah], only child and heiress of Thomas Ekins of Chester-over-Water, near Wellingborough, Northamptonshire, and Doddridge was her guardian. They were married after her father's death in 1754, and the estate came to Stonhouse. She died of consumption at Hotwells, Bristol, on 19 Dec. 1788, aged 35, leaving two sons and a daughter (for metrical epitaphs by Hannah More upon her and her husband see Gent. Mag. 1814, ii. 535). Thomas, the only son of the first marriage, was twelfth baronet, and on his death without issue in 1810 the title passed to his half-brother's son, Sir John Brook Stonhouse (d. 1849), thirteenth baronet.

Most of Stonhouse's tracts were reprinted by his son, the Rev. T. Stonhouse-Vigor, in a volume dated Bath, 1822, 12mo. It contained: 1. 'Friendly Advice to a Patient,' 174[8]. 2. 'Spiritual Instructions,' 1748. 3. 'Faithful and Unfaithful Minister contrasted,' 1768. 4. 'Considerations on some particular Sins,' 1758. 5. 'Sermon before Governors of Salisbury Infirmary,' 1771. 6. 'Admonitions against Swearing.' 7. 'Short Explanation of the Lord's Supper,' 1773. 8. 'Prayers for private Persons,' 1773. 9. 'Hints from a Minister to a Curate,' 1774. 10. 'Religious Instruction of Children recommended,' 1774. 11. 'Most important Truths of Christianity stated,' 1778. 12. 'Address to Parishioners of Great Cheverell,' 1780. 13. 'Materials for Talking familiarly with Children and others on Religion,' 1795. 14. 'Remarks on the Office for the Visitation of the Sick and on the Communion Service.' Many of these tracts went through several editions, and were long included in the 'Religious Tracts of the Society for the Promotion of Christian Knowledge.' Several were anonymous, including the 'Hints from a Minister to a Curate,' i.e. the Rev. Thomas Stedman. Stonhouse was also the author of: 'Universal Restitution' (anon.), 1761 and 1768; 'Every Man's Assistant and the Sick Man's Friend,' 1788 (often republished); and 'On the Importance of keeping a Diary.' Two volumes of letters from Job Orton [q. v.] and from Stonhouse to the Rev. Thomas Stedman were published in 1800, and again in 1805. Stonhouse contributed extensively to the life and letters of James Hervey.

[Gent. Mag. 1758 pp. 17–20, 1795 ii. 1058, 1075, 1796 i. 165, 1801 i. 81, 1815 i. 389; Foster's Alumni Oxon.; Foster's Baronetage; Betham's Baronetage; Burke's Peerage; Berry's Buckinghamshire Genealogies, p. 53; Orton's Letters, 1800, ii. 260–70; Nicholls and Taylor's Bristol, ii. 279; Robinson's Merchant Taylors' School Reg. ii. 60; Tyerman's Whitefield, ii. 195–200, 213, 237, 220; Doddridge's Corresp. iv. 369–73; Nichols's Illustrations of Literature, ii. 843–4, iii. 819; Nichols's Literary Anecdotes, ix. 811; Stanford's Doddridge, pp. 101, 113–21; Jay's Autobiography, pp. 342–3; Roberts's Hannah More, 2nd edit. pp. 303–4, and pref. to 3rd edit. p. xix. A life of Stonhouse, with extracts from his correspondence, said to have been published in 1843, is not at the British Museum.] W. P. C.

STONOR, JOHN DE (d. 1354), judge, was probably born at Stonor, near Sandwich, Kent, for in 1316 he took a release of the lands of Robert de Dumbleton in that county. He was, however, also connected with the manor of Stonor, near Dorchester, Oxfordshire, in the church of which place there is the effigy of a judge bearing his arms. Stonor frequently occurs as an advocate in the yearbooks, and in 1313, as one of the serjeants, was summoned to parliament. In 1316 he had 20l. per annum for his expenses in the king's service, and was about this time frequently employed on judicial commissions. On 16 Oct. 1320 Stonor was appointed one of the justices of the common pleas. Dugdale makes him one of the judges of the king's bench in 1323–4; but, though this seems to be an error, he was perhaps removed for a time from the common pleas, since mention is made of his reappointment to that court on 3 May 1324. Stonor was reappointed after the accession of Edward III, on 31 Jan. 1327, and in the autumn of that year was employed in the inquiries into the disturbances at Bury St. Edmunds and Abingdon Abbey (Cal. Pat. Rolls, Edward III, i. 2, 217, 221–2, 287–9; Memorials of St. Edmunds Abbey, ii. 302, 348, 353). On 22 Feb. 1329 he was made chief baron of the exchequer, and on 3 Sept. of the same year chief justice of the common pleas (Cal. Pat. Rolls, Edward III, i. 365, 439). He was removed from the chief-justiceship on 2 March 1331, and on 1 April appointed to the second place in the same court (ib. ii. 78, 102). He was confirmed in this position on 8 Feb. 1334, but on 16 July following was displaced by Geoffrey le Scrope [q. v.] However, on 7 July 1335 he was once more made chief justice of the common pleas (ib. ii. 510, 565, iii. 151). In this same year he was sent to inquire into the disputes between north and south at Oxford (Wood, Hist. and Antiq. i. 427).

Stonor was one of the judges who were removed from office by the king on his sudden return to England in November 1340, and was for a time imprisoned in the Tower (MURIMUTH, p. 117; AVESBURY, p. 323). He was, however, restored to his office on 9 May 1342, and retained it till his death in 1354. In 1335 the prior of Christchurch, Canterbury, had suggested that Stonor would be a suitable seneschal of the monastery, as being a prudent man, well known and popular among the nobility, and solicited the services of Archbishop Stratford to obtain his consent. Stonor declined the honour, but wrote a letter to the prior recommending John de Hildesley for the post (*Litteræ Cantuarienses*, ii. 84–8, 98, 108). Stonor held lands in nine counties, in which he was succeeded by his son John.

[Authorities quoted; Foss's Judges of England.]
C. L. K.

STOPES, LEONARD (1540?–1587?), priest, born about 1540, probably belonged to the branch of the family of Stopes settled at Much Hadham in Hertfordshire, and may have been brother of James Stopes, whose son James, brother of St. Catharine's by the Tower, was rector of St. Mary Magdalene, Old Fish Street, London, from 1577 till his death in 1624 (cf. his will—a very detailed document—110 Byrde at Somerset House). In 1555 Leonard was chosen one of the four original scholars on the foundation of St. John's College, Oxford, by Sir Thomas White (1492–1560) [q. v.], and afterwards became one of the first four fellows. He graduated B.A. on 23 Oct. 1558, and M.A. on 21 March 1558–9. In 1559, refusing to conform, he was ejected from his fellowship, and went abroad, as Wood conjectures, to Douai. Returning to England as a seminary priest, he was imprisoned for some years in Wisbech Castle. He subsequently was released and exiled. He died before 1588 (BRIDGEWATER, *Concertatio Eccl. Catholicæ in Anglia*).

Stopes was the author of twenty-four verses in praise of Queen Mary, entitled 'Haile Mary, full of grace,' which were printed as a broadside by Richard Lant. The Society of Antiquaries possesses a copy. It is possible that Stopes was also the author of 'An Epitaph on the Death of Queen Mary,' another broadside belonging to the Society of Antiquaries, for printing which without a license Lant was imprisoned in 1559 (AMES, *Typogr. Antiq.* ed. Dibdin, 1814, p. 583; ARBER, *Transcript of the Stationers' Reg.* iv. 237).

[Boase's Reg. Univ. Oxon. i. 234; Wood's Hist. and Antiq. of Oxford Colleges, p. 538; Wood's Hist. and Antiq. of Univ. Oxon. ii. 133,

Annals, ii. 145; Wood's Fasti, ed. Bliss, i. 154; Dodd's Lives of Elizabethan Clergymen, ii. 87; Sanders, De Visibili Monarchia Ecclesiæ, 1592, vii. 674; Much Hadham Registers; Stonyhurst MSS.; Addit. MS. 29489; Chester's Marriage Licences; Antiquary, p. 198, November 1890.]
C. C. S.

STOPES, RICHARD (*fl.* 1521–1544), last abbot of Meaux, studied at St. Bernard's College, Oxford, and graduated B.D. on 7 Dec. 1521. He was appointed abbot of the Cistercian monastery of Meaux or Melsa in Yorkshire before 1526, and drew up an account of the value of the abbey in 1534–5. At the dissolution in 1539–40 he received a pension of 40*l*. As he is not mentioned in the lists of expelled or pensioned priests who were alive in 1555–6, he was probably by that time either dead or abroad.

[Boase's Reg. Univ. Oxon. i. 119; Wood's Fasti Oxon. i. 56; Dugdale's Monast. ed. Caley, v. 397 (where his name appears by error as Draper); Patents 17 Hen. VIII, pt. 2, mems. 2 and 3; Misc. Doc. Aug. Office, vol. 234, f. 362; Uncal. Papers, Hen. VIII, 1537–8; Harl. MS. 600, f 37 b.]
C. C. S.

STOPFORD, JAMES (d. 1759), bishop of Cloyne, born in London, was the son of Joseph Stopford, a captain in the English army. He entered Trinity College, Dublin, in 1710, became a scholar in 1713, graduated B.A. in 1715, was elected a fellow on 25 March 1717, and proceeded M.A. in the following year. He was an intimate friend of Swift, who materially aided his promotion in the church, appointed him one of his executors, and bequeathed him a portrait of Charles I by Vandyck, which Stopford had formerly given him.

In 1727 Stopford resigned his fellowship on being appointed vicar of Finglas, near Dublin, by Lord Carteret, the lord-lieutenant. On 11 July 1730 he was installed provost of Tuam, on 10 July 1736 he was collated archdeacon of Killaloe, and on 8 Jan. 1748 he was instituted dean of Kilmacduagh. He held these preferments until 1753, when, in pursuance of letters patent dated 28 Feb., he was appointed bishop of Cloyne. He died on 23 Aug. 1759, and was buried at St. Anne's, Dublin, where a tablet was erected to his memory on the outside of the south wall of the church. He married, on 16 Dec. 1727, Anne, second daughter of James Stopford of Tara Hill in Meath, and sister of James Stopford, first earl of Courtown. By her he had three sons—William, James, and Joseph—besides other children.

[Brady's Records of Cork, Cloyne, and Ross, 1864, iii. 119–20; Lodge's Irish Peerage, ed.
E E 2

Archdall, 1789, iii. 121 ; Swift's Works, ed. Scott, 1824, index ; Cat. of Dublin Graduates, p. 545 ; Cotton's Fasti Ecclesiæ-Hibernicæ, i. 273, 420, iv. 25, 204.] E. I. C.

STOPFORD, JOSHUA (1636–1675), divine, born in Lancashire in 1636, entered Brasenose College, Oxford, in 1654, and thence migrated in 1656 to Magdalen College, where he was one of the eight clerks on the foundation. He graduated B.A. on 23 Feb. 1657-8 and M.A. and B.D. in 1670. In 1650 he was appointed morning lecturer at the Old Church, Manchester, and in 1659 he took an active part in encouraging the insurrection in Cheshire under Sir George Booth. On 12 Sept. 1660 he was ordained deacon and priest by William Piers [q. v.], bishop of Bath and Wells; and on 7 Nov. 1660 he was collated by Archbishop Frewen to the prebend of Dunnington in the church of York. In 1683 he was presented to the vicarage of Kirkby Stephen, Westmoreland; on 7 Oct. the same year he was instituted to the rectory of All Saints, York, on the presentation of the king; and on 12 Sept. 1667 he was collated by Archbishop Sterne to the vicarage of St. Martin, Coney Street, York. He died at York on 3 Nov. 1675.

His works are: 1. 'The Ways and Method of Rome's Advancement ; or, Whereby the Pope and his Agents have endeavoured to propagate their Doctrines,' York, 1672, 8vo. 2. 'Pagano-Papismus ; or an exact Parallel between Rome-Pagan and Rome-Christian, in their Doctrines and Ceremonies,' London, 1675, 8vo. The copy in the British Museum has copious manuscript notes; the book was re-edited in 1844 (London, 12mo).

[Bloxam's Magd. Coll. Reg. ii. 70; Davies's York Press, p. 81; Drake's Eboracum, pp. 294, 327; Earwaker's East Cheshire, i. 228; Foster's Alumni Oxon. 1500-1714; Kennett's Register, p. 309; Newcome's Autobiogr. and Diary, passim; Palatine Notebook, i. 155; Wood's Athenæ Oxon. ed. Bliss, iii. 1053, and Fasti, ii. 199.] T. C.

STOPFORD, SIR ROBERT (1768–1847), admiral, third son of James Stopford, second earl of Courtown (d. 1810), by his wife Mary, daughter and coheir of Richard Powys of Hintlesham Hall, Suffolk, was born on 5 Feb. 1768. He entered the navy in May 1780 on board the Prince George, the flagship of Vice-admiral George Darby [q. v.], and was in her at the relief of Gibraltar in April 1781. The Prince George afterwards went out to the West Indies, and took part in the action of 12 April 1782. In December Stopford was moved into the Aigle, and afterwards into the Atalanta and Hermione. He was promoted to the rank of lieutenant on 15 July 1785, and, after serving on the Newfoundland station and in the Mediterranean, was made commander on 2 June 1789. On 12 Aug. 1790 he was posted to the Fame, from which he was, a few months later, moved to the Lowestoft, and from her to the Aquilon, in which he remained for three years, and was present in the action of 1 June 1794 ; during the engagement he took in tow the Marlborough when disabled and in a critical situation. From July 1794 to July 1799 he commanded the Phaeton, of 38 guns, which played an important part in the celebrated retreat of Admiral William Cornwallis [q. v.] on 16 and 17 June 1795, and was declared by the admiral to have done the work of three frigates. The Phaeton continued to be employed in the Bay of Biscay, where she captured a great number of the enemy's privateers and small vessels of war, till July 1799, when Stopford was appointed to the Excellent, forming part of the grand fleet under Lord Gardner; in 1802 he was sent to the West Indies under the orders of Rear-admiral Totty ; after Totty's return he was left there, as senior officer, to deliver up the French and Dutch settlements in accordance with the terms of the treaty of Amiens.

Early in 1803 Stopford was obliged by ill-health to return to England. Some months later he was appointed to the Spencer, which through 1804 was one of the fleet off Brest or detached off Ferrol, and, having joined Nelson in the Mediterranean, took part in the celebrated chase to the West Indies. The Spencer was afterwards one of the fleet with Nelson off Cadiz, but was detached with Rear-admiral Thomas Louis [q. v.] a few days before the battle of Trafalgar. She then went to the West Indies with Sir John Thomas Duckworth [q. v.], and took a brilliant part in the battle of San Domingo on 6 Feb. 1806, for which Stopford received the gold medal. Shortly after this he returned to England. Still in the Spencer in November he went out to the Rio de la Plata with Rear-admiral Charles Stirling [see under STIRLING, SIR WALTER], and on his return to England in July 1807 joined the expedition against Copenhagen under the command of Admiral James (afterwards Lord) Gambier [q. v.], when, with other senior captains, he entered a protest against a junior being appointed over his head to the responsible post of captain of the fleet [see POPHAM, SIR HOME RIGGS]. On 28 April 1808 he was promoted to be rear-admiral and appointed to command the blockading squadron off Rochefort with his flag in the Spencer and afterwards in the Cæsar. While on this service he was repeatedly engaged with the French batteries and frigates, several of which he drove ashore and destroyed. In April 1809 he was joined by the main fleet under Lord Gambier off the Basque roads, and was a witness of the attack made on the French shipping by Lord Cochrane in the Impérieuse, and the unsatisfactory results of Gambier's negligence [see COCHRANE, THOMAS, tenth EARL OF DUNDONALD].

In the autumn of 1810 Stopford went out as commander-in-chief at the Cape of Good Hope with instructions to reduce Mauritius, which, however, had fallen before his arrival on the station. In August 1811, on the news of the death of Vice-admiral Drury, he left his station to take command of the expedition against Java, where, in co-operation with the army, he gained a complete success. The extraordinary step of leaving his station to take the command in another naturally excited the indignation of the officer whom he superseded [see BROUGHTON, WILLIAM ROBERT], who applied for a court-martial on Stopford, an application which the admiralty, approving of Stopford's conduct, refused to grant. After the conquest of Java Stopford returned to his own station. On 12 Aug. 1812 he was promoted to be vice-admiral, and shortly afterwards returned to England. He was nominated a K.C.B. on 2 Jan. 1815, became admiral on 27 May 1825, a G.C.B. on 6 June 1831, and a G.C.M.G. on 10 May 1837. From April 1827 to April 1830 he was commander-in-chief at Portsmouth.

In 1837 he went out to the Mediterranean as commander-in-chief, with his flag in the Princess Charlotte, and was still there when the English government deemed it necessary to undertake active measures in support of the sultan against his rebellious subject Mehemet Ali. In August 1840 Stopford was instructed to demand, and if necessary to enforce, the restoration of the Turkish ships which had been treacherously delivered to Mehemet Ali by the Capitan Pasha. The situation was extremely critical, for the French were avowedly in favour of Mehemet Ali's claims, and it was thought not impossible that, as their fleet was in splendid order, they might attack the English, whose ships were manned on what was then known as the 'peace establishment.' In September Stopford was joined on the coast of Syria by a reinforcement under Commodore Charles Napier [q. v.], and the operations against Mehemet Ali were carried out with celerity and vigour. Sidon and Beyrout were successively occupied, and on 3 Nov. Acre was reduced after a few hours' bombardment. This was decisive; Mehemet

Ali evacuated Syria, and the threatening attitude of France was abandoned. The thanks of both houses of parliament were voted to Stopford and to the fleet; Stopford received also the freedom of the city of London, a sword of honour from the sultan, and honours from Austria, Prussia, and Russia; besides which the promotion after Acre was very large. In 1834 Stopford had been appointed rear-admiral of the United Kingdom; on 1 May 1841 he became governor of Greenwich Hospital, a post which he held till his death at Richmond, Surrey, on 25 June 1847. Stopford married, in 1809, Mary, daughter of Captain Robert Fanshawe, commissioner of the navy at Portsmouth, and by her had a large family.

A portrait, by F. Ramsay, is in the Painted Hall at Greenwich.

[O'Byrne's Nav. Biogr. Dict.; Ralfe's Nav. Biogr. ii. 1; James's Nav. Hist.; Jurien de la Gravière's La Marine d'Autrefois; Napier's Hist. of the War in Syria; Letters of Sir H. J. Codrington; Official letters in the Public Record Office; Foster's Peerage.]   J. K. L.

STORACE, ANNA (or ANN) SELINA (1766–1817), vocalist and actress, born in London in 1766, was daughter of Stefano Storace. The father, whose name was originally Sorace, was a musician of Naples; he changed his name to Storace on removing to England, where he was engaged as a double-bass player at the Haymarket Opera-house. Anna's mother belonged to a Bath family named Trusler. Her elder brother, Stephen, is noticed separately. The name was often spelt Storache, for the sake probably of indicating its pronunciation. Instructed in music by her father, she acquired early proficiency, and on 15 April 1774 sang at the Haymarket in a concert given by Evans, a harper. She then became a pupil of Rauzzini, and in 1777 sang in oratorios in Hereford and at Covent Garden, and had a benefit concert at the Tottenham Street Room (subsequently the Prince of Wales Theatre), 27 April 1778. With the money thus obtained she accompanied her father to Naples, where she is said to have sung in oratorios given during Lent at the San Carlo Theatre. She also went to Venice, where she studied under Sacchini, and to Florence. In 1780 she played at the Pergola Theatre, Florence, with much success. Michael Kelly [q. v.] gives a curious account of the circumstances that brought her into renown: 'Bianchi had composed the celebrated cavatina, "Sembianza amabile del mio bel sole," which Marchesi (an eminent tenor) sung with most ravishing taste; in one passage he ran up a voletta of semitone octaves, the last note of which he gave with such exquisite power and strength that it was ever after called "La bomba di Marchesi!" Immediately after . . . [Signora Storace] had to sing. She attempted [a bomba of her own], and executed it to the admiration and astonishment of the audience, but to the dismay of poor Marchesi' (*Reminiscences*, i. 97). Menaced with the resignation of the tenor, and met with a blank refusal by Signora Storace to discontinue her exhibition, Campigli, the manager, dismissed his soprano, who then went to Lucca and Leghorn. In 1781 she sang in Parma, in 1782 at the Scala, Milan, and in 1784, at a salary equivalent to the then large sum of 500l. a year, was engaged in Vienna, where she was the original Susanna in Mozart's ' Nozze di Figaro.' Here she contracted her disastrous marriage with John Abraham Fisher [q. v.], from whom, after undergoing brutal treatment, she separated.

Returning to England, she made her appearance on 24 March 1787 at the King's Theatre as Gesinda in Paisiello's 'Gli Schiavi per amore,' and in other comic operas. Abandoning Italian opera for English, she was seen for the first time at Drury Lane on 24 Nov. 1789, as Signora Storache, playing Adela in the ' Haunted Tower,' by James Cobb. On 16 April 1790 she was the original Margaretta in Hoare's ' No Song no Supper.' In Cobb's 'Siege of Belgrade,'1 Jan. 1791, she was Lilla, and in Hoare's 'Cave of Trophonius,' Daphne, both original parts. In 1791 she sang at the Handel festival in Westminster Abbey, and in 1792 at the Hereford festival. On 21 Nov. 1792, with the Drury Lane company in the King's Theatre, Haymarket, she was the first Fabulina in Cobb's 'Pirates.' For her benefit on 11 March 1793 she played with great success Caroline in Hoare's 'Prize, or 2, 5, 3, 8,' and on 16 Dec. also for her benefit, was Florella in Hoare's 'My Grandmother.' Back at Drury Lane, she played on 29 Dec. 1794 Elinor in Cobb's 'Cherokee,' took a part on 6 May 1795 in Hook's unprinted ' Jack of Newbury,' and played for her benefit Clara in the 'Duenna.' Rosina in the ' Spanish Barber' ('Le Barbier de Seville') she took for the first time on 16 Nov. 1795. In Cobb's 'Shepherdess of Cheapside' she had an original part on 20 Feb. 1796, was on 12 March the first Barbara in Colman's ' Iron Chest,' and on 30 April had an original part in 'Mahmoud, or the Prince of Persia,' an opera by Hoare. The music, by Stephen Storace, left unfinished at his death, was vamped up by her, and the receipts were, it is said, given to the widow, her sister-in-law. At Drury Lane 'Nancy' Storace (as she was

called by her musical friends) met John Braham [q. v.], with whom she long acted, forming close and enduring relations with him, and having by him a son. The following year she accompanied him to Paris, where, under the patronage of Josephine Beauharnais, they gave a series of concerts, remaining in Paris eight months. They arrived in Italy in 1798. Refusing a joint engagement in Naples, they went to Leghorn and Venice, then by Trieste, Vienna, and Hamburg, home to England, where they arrived in the winter of 1801. On 9 Dec. 1801, in 'Chains of the Heart, or the Slave by Choice,' by Hoare, with music by Mazzinghi, apparently an adaptation of the 'Gli Schiavi per amore' previously mentioned, Braham and Signora Storace both appeared at Covent Garden, the latter as Zulima. In Cobb's 'Siege of Belgrade,' on 15 March 1802, she was Lilla to Braham's Seraskier. On 13 Dec. 1803 she was Katherine and Braham Valentine in T. Dibdin's ' English Fleet in 1342,' and on 10 Dec. 1804 was Rosanna to Braham's Foresail in T. Dibdin's ' Thirty Thousand, or Who's the Richest?' On 28 Feb. 1805, in 'Out of Place, or the Lake of Lausanne,' by Reynolds, she was Lauretta to Braham's Captain Valteline. In the summer she sang with Braham for six nights in Brighton. Back at Drury Lane, where she remained until her retirement, she played on 12 Nov. Floretta in the 'Cabinet' to Braham's Orlando. On 22 Jan. 1806, as the Marchioness Merida, she supported Braham as Koyan in Cherry's 'Travellers, or Music's Fascination.' On 12 Jan. 1807 she was the first Susan in ' False Alarms, or My Cousin,' by Kenney, music by Braham and King; on 13 April was, for her benefit, Wowski in 'Inkle and Yarico;' on 11 Feb. 1808 was the first Rozella in Brandon's 'Kais, or Love in the Deserts,' music by Braham; and on 3 May 1808 the first Mammor ain Cumberland's 'Jew of Mogadore.' On 30 May she took a benefit, delivering to the audience a farewell address by Colman, and appearing as Floretta in the 'Cabinet.' She then retired to Herne Hill Cottage, Dulwich. Braham was married in 1816, and Signora Storache died on 24 Aug. 1817, it was hinted through disappointment, and was buried at St. Mary's, Lambeth. By her will, made shortly before her death, she left legacies amounting to 11,000l., including 1,000l. to the Old Musical Fund, Royal Society of Musicians, and 1,000l. to the New Musical Fund. Her personalty was sworn under 50,000l. In her later years the signora increased in bulk, and her features, always strong, became coarse. She persisted to the last in playing parts to which she was unsuited, and her final retirement was accepted with something more than resignation. At her best she was a finished singer and an admirable comic actress.

Her portrait, by Sharpe, is in the Mathews collection in the Garrick Club.

[Genest's Account of the English Stage; Monthly Mirror, various years; Kelly's Reminiscences; Grove's Dict. of Music; Georgian Era; Gilliland's Dramatic Mirror; Thespian Dict.; and see under BRAHAM, JOHN.] J. K.

STORACE, STEPHEN (1763–1796), musical composer, born in London in 1763, was son of Stephano Storace, and brother of Anna Storace [q. v.] Stephen's progress as a violinist was so rapid that at twelve he was placed in the St. Onofrio Conservatorio at Naples, where he studied for several years. Subsequently he travelled on the continent with his sister Anna. In Vienna he became acquainted with Mozart, but was imprisoned owing to a brawl with an officer, and on being released the Storaces returned in 1787 to England. Stephen, finding no opportunity of earning a livelihood as a musician, taught drawing, but was soon engaged by Linley as composer to Drury Lane, and to superintend the production of opera at the King's Theatre. As a theatrical manager he met with some successes, but was driven to Bath by the intrigue and jealousy of his associates. On his return to London he adapted Dittersdorf's opera 'Doktor und Apotheker' for Drury Lane. In 1785 he resumed work for a short time at the King's Theatre, but ultimately devoted himself to Drury Lane, where he produced his first English opera, 'The Haunted Tower,' on 24 Nov. 1789, which was an extraordinary success. On 20 Nov. 1792 he scored another triumph with 'The Pirate' (libretto by Cobb), the finale to which is considered his best musical effort. In this his sister sang. In the same year he brought out 'Dido,' and for the next two and a half years he was constantly engaged in producing new operas, and operas composed of music by himself and others. On 12 March 1796 'The Iron Chest,' by Colman and Storace, was produced, the music making a popular success; but the anxiety and labour attendant on its production at Drury Lane brought to a climax an illness from which Storace had previously suffered. He died in Percy Street, Rathbone Place, on 19 March 1796, leaving a widow, daughter of John Hall (1739–1797) [q. v.] the engraver, and children.

Storace had a good gift for the invention of melody, and many of his compositions enjoyed an enormous vogue at the time of their production. He wrote about twenty operas, and a string quartet, which was played in Vienna by Haydn, Dittersdorf, Mozart, and Vanhall. Sheridan is said to have declared that Storace had a fine literary talent. His ballads are good; one from Hoare's 'No Song, no Supper' (1790), has been often reprinted.

[Harmonicon, vi. 1; Kelly's Reminiscences, passim; Parke's Musical Memoirs, vol. i. passim; Colman's Preface to The Iron Chest; Georgian Era, iv. 266; Baker's Biographia Dramatica; Musical World, 1840, p. 212.] R. H. L.

STORER, ANTHONY MORRIS (1746–1799), collector and man of fashion, born on 12 March 1746, was elder son of Thomas Storer of Westmoreland, Jamaica (d. Golden Square, London, on 21 July 1793, aged 76), who married Helen, daughter of Colonel Guthrie. Anthony was at Eton from about 1760 to 1764 with C. J. Fox and Earl Fitzwilliam, and some sets of Latin verse by him are in the 'Musæ Etonenses.' His 'sense and good nature' while at school are lauded by the fifth Earl of Carlisle in 'Verses on his Schoolfellows,' 1762. About 1765 he proceeded to Cambridge, probably to Corpus Christi College, and was a close friend there and at Eton of Lord Carlisle, but left without taking a degree.

Storer then blossomed in the gay world of London, becoming conspicuous as the best dancer and skater of his time, and beating all his competitors at gymnastics. He excelled, too, as a musician and a conversationalist. Like most of his school friends, he was both a man of fashion and a whig in politics. During 1778 and 1779 he was in America with Lord Carlisle and William Eden (afterwards first Lord Auckland). He visited Carlisle when lord-lieutenant of Ireland in 1781, and, through his interest, succeeded Benjamin L'Anglois as a commissioner of the board of trade on 26 July 1781. Meanwhile he sat in the House of Commons as M.P. for Carlisle from 1774 to 1780, and subsequently—from 1780 to 1784—for Morpeth. Much of his time was passed with the family of Lord North, and in August 1782 he was a medium of communication between that nobleman and Fox. He enlisted under the 'coalition,' and in September 1783, greatly to the indignation of Gibbon, who was also an aspirant to the office, he was sent by Fox to Paris as secretary of the legation. On 13 Dec. 1783, when the ambassador, the Duke of Manchester, came home, he was nominated as minister plenipotentiary, but six days later his friends were ejected from office. His connection with politics then ceased. He had by that time quarrelled with Carlisle, to whom he revoked a bequest of all his property, and did not seek re-election for Carlisle's borough of Morpeth after the dissolution of 1784.

In September 1781, according to Horace Walpole's testimony, Storer was seized with a passion for collecting books and prints. These expensive tastes and the love of cards kept him in comparative poverty until his father's death. In 1786 he was reading the Latin and Greek writers half the day with Dr. Edward Harwood [q. v.], whose 'View of the Classics' was greatly improved, in its fourth edition, from Storer's library. He was desirous in December 1787 of entering the diplomatic service, and in April 1793 he languished for employment; but his father's death in the last year brought him an ample fortune. He purchased Purley Park, between Pangbourne and Reading, and, with the advice of Humphrey Repton [q. v.], expended a considerable sum in improving and ornamenting the grounds. His health was bad; he had been very ill in the winter of 1787-8, and he did not live to complete the house for the estate. But the sum of 20,000*l*. was set apart by his executors for that purpose, and the present mansion, 'a large square stone building,' was erected from the designs of Wyatt (BRITTON AND BRAYLEY, *Beauties of England and Wales*, i. 175). He died 'of a deep decline' at Bristol Hotwells on 28 June 1799, and was buried at Purley, a monument by Nollekens, with a Latin inscription, being erected to his memory in Purley church. His fortune was left to his nephew, Anthony Gilbert, the only son of his brother Thomas James, who had married the Hon. Elizabeth Proby, daughter of the first Lord Carysfort. The only other legacy was the sum of 1,000*l*. to James Hare [q. v.]

Storer was elected F.S.A. on 11 Dec. 1777, and became a member of the Dilettanti Society on 18 April 1790. His library was rich in old classics, rare books of history and travels, and antique bindings, and it contained two undoubted Caxtons and 'Les fais du Jason' (*Life of Caxton*, 1863, ii. 55, 88, 94). Many of his books were illustrated with prints by himself and drawings by various artists, his copy of Granger being amplified into many large folio volumes. He left his complete library, with the exception of such works as they already possessed, to Eton College, and he also gave the college his beautiful collection of prints. Many sprightly letters by Storer are printed in Jesse's 'George Selwyn' (vols. iii. and iv.) and in the 'Correspondence of William Eden, Lord Auckland.' Mathias, among others, praises his literary attainments (*Pursuits of Lit.* Dialogue iv.)

Storer's portrait, a full-length, with an engraving in his left hand, was painted by Sir Martin Archer Shee [q. v.] It remains at Purley, the property of Major Storer. Another portrait of Storer hangs in the college library at Eton.

[Gent. Mag. 1799 ii. 626, 1800 ii. 689; Gibbon's Letters, ed. 1896, ii. 67-8, 86-7; Notices of Soc. of Dilettanti, p. 123; Leslie and Taylor's Sir Joshua Reynolds, ii. 124, 146; Eton Loan Coll. 1891, pp. 3, 5, and 6; Notes and Queries, 6th ser. vol. iii., s. v. Eton Coll. Libr.; Walpole's Letters, viii. 51-2, 125-6; Nichols's Lit. Anecdotes, ii. 660, viii. 657, ix. 508-10; Jesse's Selwyn, ii. 129, iii. 74-6; Rev. J. Richardson's Recollections, ii. 93-4; information from Major Storer of Purley.]   W. P. C.

STORER, JAMES SARGANT (1771-1853), draughtsman and engraver, was born in 1771, and devoted himself to the production of works on topography and ancient architecture, the plates in which, drawn and engraved by himself on a small scale, were distinguished for extreme accuracy and beauty of finish. For some years he was associated with John Greig, another topographical artist, in collaboration with whom he published 'Cowper illustrated by a Series of Views,' 1803; 'Views in North Britain illustrative of the Works of Burns,' 1805; 'Views illustrative of the Works of Robert Bloomfield,' 1806; 'Select Views of London and its Environs,' 1804-5; 'The Antiquarian and Topographical Cabinet,' 10 vols., with five hundred plates, 1807-11; and 'Ancient Reliques,' 1812. He was one of the artists employed upon Britton and Brayley's 'Beauties of England and Wales,' 1801-1816. From 1814 James Storer worked wholly in conjunction with his eldest son (see below), whom he outlived. He died at his house at Islington on 23 Dec. 1853, and was buried beside his son at St. James's Chapel, Pentonville.

The eldest son, HENRY SARGANT STORER (1795-1837), produced with his father 'The Cathedrals of Great Britain,' 4 vols. 1814-19 (pronounced by Pugin to be the most accurate views of those buildings in existence); 'Delineations of Fountains Abbey,' 1820, a work of great excellence; 'Views in Edinburgh and its Vicinity,' 1820; 'The University and City of Oxford displayed,' 1821; 'Delineations of Gloucestershire,' 1824; and 'The Portfolio: a collection of Engravings from Antiquarian, Architectural, and Topographical Subjects,' 4 vols., 1823-4. The letterpress of some of these works is believed to have been written by the elder Storer.

He and his son also engraved the plates to Cromwell's 'History of Clerkenwell,' 1828, and 'Walks through Islington,' 1835, and other similar publications. They resided for some time at Cambridge, where they issued several sets of views of the town and university, the latest being 'Collegiorum Portæ apud Cantabrigiam.' H. S. Storer engraved, independently of his father, the plates to Pierce Egan's 'Walks through Bath,' 1819, and a view of Christ's College for the 'Cambridge Almanack,' 1822. He exhibited drawings at the Royal Academy from 1814 to 1836, and died, at the age of forty-one, on 8 Jan. 1837.

[Gent. Mag. 1854. i. 326; Redgrave's Dict. of Artists; Graves's Dict. of Artists, 1760–1893; Universal Cat. of Books on Art; Willis and Clark's Architectural Hist. of Cambridge.]

F. M. O'D.

STORER, THOMAS (1571–1604), poet, born in 1571, the son of John Storer, a citizen of London, was elected a student of Christ Church, Oxford, in 1587, and graduated B.A. on 27 March 1591, and M.A. on 13 May 1604. At Oxford, says Wood, 'he was had in great renown for his most excellent vein in poesy.' In 1599 appeared 'The Life and Death of Thomas Wolsey, cardinall. ... By Thomas Storer, student of Christ Church in Oxford. At London printed by Thomas Dawson,' 4to. The poem, which is written upon the model of Churchyard's legend on the history of Wolsey in 'The Mirrour for Magistrates,' consists of three parts or cantos, 'Wolseius aspirans,' 'Wolseius triumphans,' and 'Wolseius moriens;' these contain respectively 101, 89, and 51 seven-line stanzas of decasyllabic verse (rhyming ababbcc). The volume is dedicated to John Howson [q. v.], Queen Elizabeth's chaplain, and there are introductory verses by Charles Fitzgeffrey [q. v.] and Thomas and Edward Michelborne [q. v.], and a poem in fifteen eight-line stanzas addressed to the author by his fellow-collegian, John Sprint. The poem is carefully based upon the narratives of Cavendish and Holinshed, and, sententious though it is, contains some happily expressed characterisations, notably that of Richard Foxe [q. v.], bishop of Winchester,

A man made old to teach the worth of age.

It was warmly praised by Dr. Alberic Gentilis in his 'Laudes Academiæ Perusinæ et Oxoniensis' (1605, p. 41), and Aubrey commends its historic veracity (*Letters from the Bodleian Library*, 1813, i. 145). Malone has unconvincingly conjectured that Storer's poem may have suggested the subject of Wolsey's fall to the dramatist when he wrote 'King Henry VIII.' Early in the eighteenth century Thomas Hearne, having long sought in vain for a copy, at length procured one for a shilling. In more recent times the price of a copy of the first edition has ranged from ten to twenty guineas (the British Museum has three copies, and there are also copies at Britwell, in the Huth Library, and in the Malone collection at the Bodleian). The 'Life' was reprinted in Park's 'Heliconia' (1815, vol. ii.), and reissued separately in 1826 from the press of Talboys at Oxford.

According to Wood, in addition to the 'Life of Wolsey,' Storer published some 'Pastoral Aires and Madrigals,' which 'were afterwards remitted into a book called "England's Helicon;"' but this appears to be a mistake. No lyrics by Storer are included in 'England's Helicon,' but in 'England's Parnassus' (1600) are a score or so of specimens of his workmanship; they are derived from the 'Life of Wolsey,' and display the elaborate style of metaphor in which the poet excelled. Some verses by Storer are prefixed to Sir William Vaughan's 'Golden Grove' (1600). He died in London in November 1604, and was buried in the church of St. Michael Bassishaw in the city.

[Wood's Athenæ Oxon. ed. Bliss, i. 751; Foster's Alumni Oxon. 1500–1714; Phillips's Theatrum, pp. 206–7; Addit. MS. 24491 (Hunter's Chorus Vatum), f. 110; Ritson's Bibl. Anglo-Poetica, p. 665; Corser's Collectanea Anglo-Poetica, x. 282; Retrospective Review, v. 275; Drake's Life and Times of Shakespeare, i. 702; Hazlitt's Handbook; Huth Library Cat.; Brit. Mus. Cat.]

T. S.

STORKS, Sir HENRY KNIGHT (1811–1874), lieutenant-general, born in 1811, was eldest son of Mr. Serjeant H. Storks (appointed a county-court judge in 1847), and was educated at the Charterhouse. He was commissioned as ensign in the 61st foot on 10 Jan. 1828, and became lieutenant on 2 March 1832. On 23 March he exchanged into the 14th foot, in which he became captain on 30 Oct. 1835, and from which he exchanged on 30 May 1838 into the 38th foot. He served with that regiment in the Ionian Islands, obtained his majority on 7 Aug. 1840, and went on half-pay from the regiment on 23 May 1845. He was employed as assistant adjutant-general at the Cape of Good Hope during the Kaffir war of 1846–7, and was assistant military secretary at Mauritius from 1849 to 1854. He was given an unattached lieutenant-colonelcy on 15 Sept. 1848, and became colonel on 28 Nov. 1854. During the Crimean war he was placed in charge of the British establishments in Turkey, from the Bosphorus to Smyrna, and received the local rank of major-general on 23 Nov. 1855. He superintended the final withdrawal of the British from Turkey at the end of the war; and was then employed at the war office as secretary for military correspondence from 1857 to 1859. He obtained one of the rewards for distinguished service on 25 Sept. 1856, and was made K.C.B. on 2 Jan. 1857. On 2 Feb. 1859 he was appointed high commissioner of the Ionian Islands, and was the last man to hold that office. In response to a unanimous vote of an Ionian parliament specially summoned, the British protectorate was resigned by treaty on 14 Nov. 1863, the islands were neutralised, and united themselves with Greece. Shortly before this Storks had found it necessary to make some changes in the judicial bench, in consequence of complaints made against the two Ionian judges. Their two English colleagues took their part, and some acrimonious correspondence followed, but Storks's action was upheld by the colonial office. He received the G.C.M.G. in 1860, and was promoted major-general on 12 Nov. 1862. On 1 July 1864 he received the G.C.B.

He was made governor of Malta on 15 Nov. 1864, but at the end of the following year he was sent to Jamaica to inquire into the disturbances which had taken place there and the measures taken to suppress them. A commission was appointed for this purpose on 2 Jan. 1866, on which Russell Gurney [q. v.] and J. B. Maule were associated with him, and at the same time he replaced Mr. Eyre as governor from 12 Dec. 1865. The very strong partisanship which the events in Jamaica had aroused added to the importance and difficulty of the inquiry; but the report was unanimous, and met with general acceptance. The commissioners found that the danger which Mr. Eyre had had to face was a very real one, and praised him for the skill, promptitude, and vigour which he showed during the early stages of the insurrection; but they held that martial law was prolonged unnecessarily, and that the punishments inflicted were excessive.

Storks gave up the governorship of Jamaica on 16 July 1866, and, as a reward for his services, was made a privy councillor in November. On 19 Dec. 1867 he was appointed controller-in-chief and under-secretary at the war office. The control department, of which he was the head, was formed at that time, at the suggestion of Lord Strathnairn's committee, to give unity to the administration of army transport and supply, which had hitherto been dealt with by several independent branches. It was in imitation of the French intendance. But the amalgamation of the different branches caused some heartburnings: the new department encroached on the field of the quartermaster-general, the name 'controller' (scil. of army expenditure) was open to misinterpretation, and was a cause of unpopularity, and the department did not last many years.

There was great difference of opinion as to whether the charge of 'warlike stores' should be committed to it. Eventually it was decided, in 1870, that they should be entrusted to a sub-department under the director of artillery, who (with the director of supplies and transport) should be subordinate to the surveyor-general of the ordnance—an old title revived, the functions of which were fixed by order in council of 23 June 1870. Storks exchanged the controllership-in-chief for this new office, which he continued to hold till his death. One object of the change was to afford more support to the secretary of state for war in parliament; and Storks became M.P. for Ripon on 15 Feb. 1871, and assisted Cardwell in the prolonged debates on the abolition of purchase in the army. He became lieutenant-general on 25 Oct. 1871. He lost his seat at the election of 1874, and died on 6 Sept. in that year. He was 'a man whose varied experience and abilities made him a very valuable administrator and adviser;' not a brilliant speaker or writer, but a man of tact and devotion to the public service. He married, in 1841, the daughter of Cav. Giuseppe Nizzoli of Milan. She died in 1848.

[Times, 8 Sept. 1874; Annual Register for 1865 and 1866; Sir P. de Colquhoun's Letter to Sir H. Storks respecting the Ionian Judges (London, 1864); Reports of Lord Northbrook's Committee on the Army Departments, 1870.]

E. M. L.

STORMONT, first Viscount. [See Murray, David, d. 1631.]

STORY, EDWARD (d. 1503), bishop successively of Carlisle and Chichester, a native of the diocese of York, was admitted a fellow of Pembroke Hall, Cambridge, in or about 1444, and in 1450 was elected master of Michael House in that university. He was chaplain and confessor to Elizabeth, queen of Edward IV, chancellor of the university in 1468, and in the same year became bishop of Carlisle. He was again chancellor of the university from 1471 to 1473, and was translated to the see of Chichester in 1477. He officiated at Edward IV's funeral on 17 April 1485. He died on 29 Jan. 1502-3, and was buried in his cathedral. He is said to have founded the prebendal free school at

Chichester (KNIGHT, *Life of Colet*); but what he really did was 'to procure the annexation to the school, which existed long before, of a canonry and prebend in the cathedral in 1498, and it is therefore still called the prebendal school' (LEACH, *English Schools*, i. 9). Story also erected the magnificent cross yet existing in the centre of that city.

[Cooper's Athenæ Cantabr. i. 5; Gairdner's Letters, &c., of Richard III and Henry VII, and Campbell's Materials (Rolls Ser.); Dallaway and Cartwright's Sussex, i. 67, 145, 168; Godwin, De Præsulibus; Hawes and Loder's Framlingham, p. 214; Jefferson's Carlisle, p. 207; Le Neve's Fasti (Hardy); Documents relating to the University and Colleges of Cambridge, 1852, i. 122, 143.]   T. C.

STORY, GEORGE WARTER (d. 1721), historian, was eldest son of Thomas Story of Justice Town, near Carlisle. Thomas Story [q. v.], the quaker, was a younger brother. In 1688 George Story was chaplain to the Countess-dowager of Carlisle at Castle Howard. He was in London when the army for Ireland was being raised in March and April 1689, and accompanied Meinhard, duke of Schomberg [q. v.], in August as chaplain to Sir Thomas Gower's regiment of foot. Gower died early in 1690, and Henry, third earl of Drogheda, succeeded him in the command (see LODGE, *Peerage*, ed. Archdall, ii. 110), the survivors of two regiments being fused into one. Story was an admirer and apologist of Schomberg, who was much criticised for his unwillingness to risk raw troops in a pitched battle, and for the number of men lost by disease.

Story was at the Boyne [see under SARSFIELD, PATRICK], and served with Lord Drogheda while the war lasted. A younger brother, who was ensign in the same regiment, was killed near Birr in June 1691. 'This officer,' says the chaplain, 'was well and at liberty at nine o'clock in the morning, but before twelve he was not only in the power, but buried by his enemies, and that with great formality. And a man that is at the pains to describe other people's actions may be allowed the liberty to leave one page to the memory of his own brother.' After the surrender of Limerick in November 1691, Story's regiment went to Ulster, 'the poor men enduring a great deal of hunger and hardship in so long a march,' and when the war was quite over they remained in the northern province as part of the standing army.

In December 1694 Story was appointed dean of Connor. Subsequently he sometimes visited Carlisle, where he had a living, his

curate being a deprived Scots episcopal clergyman whom Story's father took into his own house (STORY, *Journal*, p. 51). On 7 April 1705 Story was instituted dean of Limerick and removed from Connor. On 23 Oct. 1714 he preached in London at St. Dunstan's in Fleet Street, being the day appointed by the Irish parliament to give thanks for deliverance from the massacre of 1641. He urged the Irish protestants, who formed his congregation, and who belonged to both political parties, to bury the hatchet in Queen Anne's grave and to unite in support of the Hanover succession. The sermon was published 'at the request of the stewards and several of the gentlemen of Ireland.' Story was careful of the privileges of his church, and in 1715 established his right to swear in the vicars-choral, notwithstanding the usurpation of successive bishops. In June 1716 he entertained his brother Thomas at Limerick. Story died on 19 Nov. 1721. He had inherited Justice Town, and left it to his widow, who sold it to Thomas Story in 1723. She was Catherine, daughter and coheiress of Edward Warter of Bilboa, near Doon, co. Limerick. The Warters' residence had been burned by some of Sarsfield's men, and they estimated their loss by the war at over 13,000*l.* (LENIHAN, *Hist. of Limerick*, p. 283).

Story's 'History,' by far the most important authority for the war in Ireland on the Williamite side, is scarce. The first part, entitled 'An Impartial History,' which goes down to January 1690-1, was licensed in London on 30 April 1691. A second edition was published with the 'Continuation' early in 1693. The 'Continuation' has useful maps—some by Captain Samuel Hobson, 'who drew the most exact map of Londonderry.' Story dedicated the later work to William himself; 'though I'm no soldier, yet four years' conversation with men of that profession has emboldened me to address your sacred Majesty.' His account ends with the official close of the war by proclamation on 23 March 1691-2. Story leaves us in no doubt about his protestant and whig principles, but he is fair on the whole.

[Journal of Thomas Story, the Quaker, Newcastle-on-Tyne, 1747; Cotton's Fasti Ecclesiæ Hibernicæ. Story's movements during the Irish war may be traced in his History.]   R. B-L.

STORY, JOHN (1510?-1571), Roman catholic martyr, born about 1510, was the son of Nicholas Story and Joan, his wife, and may have been a member of the family of that name settled in Northumberland and

Durham (cf. SURTEES, *Durham*, i. 233; other branches were settled in London, cf. *Visit. London*, Harl. Soc.) He became a lay brother of the Greyfriars, and was educated at Oxford at Henxey or Hincksey Hall, whence he graduated B.C.L. on 8 May 1531. When in 1535 Henry VIII's commissioners established a civil law lecture at Oxford, Story, as 'a most noted civilian and canonist of his time,' was appointed to the post. In 1537 he was elected principal of Broadgates Hall, afterwards Pembroke College, but resigned the post in 1539. On 29 July 1538 he graduated D.C.L. (*Reg. Univ. Oxon.* i. 164), and in the following year he was admitted an advocate of Doctors' Commons. In 1544 he is said to have 'performed excellent service at the siege of Bologne in Picardie in the administration of the civil law under the lord marshal there;' but he must be distinguished from the John Story, a knight of the order of St. John (*Letters and Papers*, vols. xi-xiv. passim), and also from the 'Captain Story' who was killed at Boulogne in 1546 (*State Papers*, xi. 4). As a reward for his services he received a fresh patent for his office at Oxford, and, dating from this time, he is reckoned as the first regius professor of civil law at the university (cf. LE NEVE, iii. 511).

Story is one of the instances selected by Nicholas Sanders (*De Origine ac Progressu Schismatis*, ed. 1877, p. 200) to illustrate the persecution of Roman catholics under Edward VI. He recanted his romanist opinions in the first few months of the reign, and on 19 Nov. 1548 the council ordered the continuance of his salary as reader in civil law at Oxford and the payment of his arrears (*Acts P.C.* ed. Dasent, ii. 229). He sat for Hindon, Wiltshire, in the parliament which met in November 1547. During its second session, in November 1548, he created a sensation by his vigorous opposition to the act of uniformity, and by exclaiming, 'Woe unto the land whose king is a child!' For this conduct the house ordered his imprisonment on 21 Nov. and drew up articles of accusation against him. Story remained in the Tower until 2 March 1548-9, when, having made his submission, the house ordered his release. This is the first recorded instance of the House of Commons punishing one of its own members (HALLAM, i. 271). Story now retired to Louvain, where he remained until Mary's accession, spending a large portion of his time, it is said, in prayer and meditation with the Carthusians of that town. On 21 Feb. 1549-50 he made over to Sir William Herbert (afterwards first Earl of Pembroke)

[q. v.] a lease of the prebend of Tottenhall in St. Paul's Cathedral (*Cal. State Papers, Dom.* 1547-81). In 1552 he was excepted from Edward VI's pardon.

Story returned to England about August 1553, and his patent as regius professor was renewed. He resigned it, however, before the end of the year to William Aubrey [q. v.], to become chancellor of the dioceses of London and Oxford and dean of arches. As chancellor to Bonner, Story became a bitter persecutor of the protestants; he was the most active of all the queen's agents in bringing heretics to trial and the stake, and Foxe, who gives many instances of his cruelty, pronounces him even worse than Bonner (*Actes and Mon.* ed. Townsend, passim, esp. viii. 743-5). In 1555 Story was appointed queen's proctor for the trial of Cranmer (STRYPE, *Cranmer*, pp. 534-5 et seqq.), and in February 1556-7 he was placed on a commission to discover a 'severer way of dealing with heretics' (BURNET, ed. Pocock, ii. 556). Nevertheless in parliament (where he represented East Grinstead 25 Sept. 1553; Bramber, March 1553-4; and Ludgershall, 6 Oct. 1555) he opposed, on 20 Nov. 1555, the admission of papal licenses into England; the commons reported this offence to the queen, but Story, on expressing regret, was pardoned in consideration of his zeal for religion (*Commons' Journals*, i. 44-5).

On Elizabeth's accession, however, Story took the oath renouncing all foreign jurisdictions, and was not for the time molested. He was returned to parliament for Downton, Wiltshire, on 17 Jan. 1558-9, but soon fell once more under the displeasure of the House of Commons. On 23 March it was reported to the house that he had appeared before the lords as counsel for Richard White (d. 1584) [q. v.], bishop of Winchester, though a bill depriving the bishop had already passed the commons. Story again acknowledged his fault, and escaped with a reprimand from the speaker. In the same session he made a speech glorying in what he had done in Mary's reign, and regretting only that they had 'laboured only about the young and little twigs, whereas they should have struck at the root' (STRYPE, *Annals*, I. i. 115). On 20 May 1560 he was sent to the Fleet prison (*ib.* p. 220), but seems to have been again at liberty soon afterwards. In April 1563 he was arrested in his barrister's robes in the west of England and imprisoned in the Marshalsea (Parkhurst to Bullinger, 31 May, *Zurich Letters*); before the end of the month a commission was issued for his trial (*Cal. Simancas Papers*, i. 322-3). Story, however, escaped in May to the house of Bishop De Quadra, the Spanish ambassador, whose chaplain sheltered him and enabled him to make his way to Flanders (ib. pp. 323–5). For this proceeding De Quadra was taken to task by the privy council, but denied all knowledge of the affair.

In Flanders Story resumed his activity in persecuting protestants, and it is said to have been largely due to his instigation that the inquisition was established at Antwerp in 1565. He received a pension from Philip II and gained the confidence of the Duke of Alva. When Alva, in order to check the spread of heresy in the Netherlands, determined to exclude all English books, he gave Story a commission to search ships coming into Flemish ports. This commission supplied the English government with a means of kidnapping him. In July 1570 one William Parker obtained the help of three young merchants, Roger Ramsden, Martin Bragge, and Simon Jukes, in carrying out this plan. They hired a vessel commanded by Cornelius de Eycke and sailed into Bergen-op-Zoom. The three merchants then went to Antwerp and brought down Story to overhaul the vessel; while he was examining the cargo Parker shut down the hatches and weighed anchor with Story on board (State Papers, Dom. lxxviii. 51). He was landed at Yarmouth on 11 Aug. and conveyed to the house of Thomas Watts, archdeacon of Middlesex. Thence he was transferred (on 4 Sept.) to Beauchamp's Tower, where an inscription he carved on the wall is still legible. He managed to write several letters to Guerau de Spes, the Spanish ambassador, who sent them on to Philip II, and Alva twice made formal demands for his release on the ground that he was a Spanish subject. Story was indicted in Westminster Hall on 26 May 1571 with Christopher and Francis Norton and Christopher Neville. He was accused of having incited Alva to invade England, and of having been privy to the northern rebellion of 1569 (He must, however, be distinguished from another John Story, 'a servant of Richard Norton' [q. v.], who was in Antwerp in 1572, and was afterwards apparently a captain in the Spanish service: see Cal. State Papers, Dom. Addenda. 1566–1579, pp. 349, 379; ib. For. 1575–7, No. 470). He refused to plead, maintaining that he was a Spanish subject. He was condemned for treason on the following day, and executed with horrible cruelty at Tyburn on 1 June. Story was at once numbered among the saints at Rome, and his life and death became one of the regular themes in the

English College there (ANTHONY MUNDAY, English Romaine Lyfe, 1590, p. 25). This sentiment was recognised by his formal beatification by papal decree dated 29 Dec. 1886 (printed in Tablet, 15 Jan. 1887, p. 81).

Wood attributes to Story four pieces: 'An Oration against Thomas Cranmer, Archbishop of Canterbury' (1556), 'Discourse with John Philpot the Martyr,' 'Answer to Examinations during his Imprisonment,' and 'Speech at his Execution.' These are printed in Foxe, but no separately published copies have been traced.

Story's wife, whom he married before 1548, was named Joan. She survived him and lived at Louvain, where she enjoyed a pension from Philip II (Cal. Simancas Papers, ii. 327). A daughter Ellen married one Weston, who in 1570 was imprisoned in the Fleet as a recusant. A son John became a priest at Douai (Douai Diaries, pp. 120, 123, 126). By his will, which he made in 1552 (printed in STRYPE, Annals, II. ii. 450–2), Story left his daughter Ellen 600 florins, which she was to forfeit on marriage, and 120 florins to any religious order she might enter. His executor was Antonio Bonvisi [q. v.], whom Story calls his 'second father.'

[Cornet's Admonition to Dr. John Story, n.d.; Confession of Dr. John Story, 1571; Declaration of the Life and Death of Dr. John Story, 1571; Welcome Home of Dr. John Story, 1571; News of Dr. John Story, 1571; Cal. of State Papers, Domestic and Addenda, Foreign, Venetian, and Simancas Ser. passim; Commons' Journals, vol. i.; Cal. Hatfield MSS. i. 80; Acts of the Privy Council, ed. Dasent; Off. Return of Members of Parl.; Diego de Yepes, Historia Particular de la Persecucion de Inglaterra, Madrid, 1599, pp. 291–6; Bridgewater's (Aquipontanus) Concertatio Eccl. Catholicæ in Anglia, 1594, pp. 43–4; A Temperate Watchword by N.D. (Robert Parsons), 1599, p. 31; Circignano's Eccl. Anglicanæ Trophæa, pl. 30; Sanders, De Visibili Monarchia, 1570, p. 700, and De Origine ac Progressu Schismatis, ed. 1877, pp. 206 &c.; Camden's Annales, sub annis 1569 and 1571; Stow's Annals; Foxe's Actes and Mon. ed. Townsend; Wood's Athenæ Oxon. ed. Bliss, i. 386–90; Digges's Compleat Ambassador, p. 105; Dodd's Church History; Tanner's Bibliotheca; Strype's Cranmer, Ecclesiastical Memorials, and Annals of the Reformation, passim; Burnet's Hist. of the Reformation, ed. Pocock; Gough's Index to Parker Society Publications; Wright's Elizabeth, i. 373, 374, 378; Stowe's Modern British Martyrology, i. 129; Maitland's Essays on the Reformation; Stanton's Menology, pp. 249–50; R. W. Dixon's Hist. of the Church of England, vols. iii–iv.; Hepworth-Dixon's Tower of London, 4th edit. i. 782–3; Lingard and Froude's Hist. of England; Foster's Alumni Oxon. 1500-1714; Macleane's Hist. of Pembroke Coll. (Oxford Hist. Soc.) 1897.]

A. F. P.

STORY, ROBERT (1790–1859), Scottish writer, was born on 3 March 1790 at Yetholm, Roxburghshire, where his father, George Story, was parish schoolmaster. His mother was Margaret Herbert, of a Northumbrian family. After receiving elementary education at home he entered Edinburgh University in 1805, associating with Thomas Pringle (1789–1834) [q. v.], the son of a neighbouring farmer. He was a good student, earning distinction in the debating societies as well as the class-rooms. From July 1811 to the beginning of 1815 he was tutor in several families, preparing at the same time for entrance into the church of Scotland. One of his tutorial posts was in the family of Lord Dalhousie, his youngest pupil being James Andrew Broun Ramsay [q. v.], afterwards governor-general of India, whose warm friendship he enjoyed through life. Licensed as a preacher in July 1815, Story was in December appointed assistant at Rosneath, Dumbartonshire. In 1817 Carlyle, on a walking tour with a common friend, sojourned with him several days, which days, he says, are 'all very vivid to me and marked in white' (Reminiscences, ii. 50, ed. Norton). Ordained minister of the parish on 26 March 1818, Story was introduced to his congregation by Dr. Chalmers.

Devoting himself mainly to his professional work and the improvement of a somewhat demoralised parish, Story stoutly defended his friend and neighbour, M'Leod Campbell of Row, who was deposed in 1831 by the general assembly for his views on the Atonement. He was himself threatened for a time with trouble on the same grounds, but the prejudice passed, and in both cleric and lay circles he came to be called 'Story the beloved.' In 1830 his parishioner, Mary Campbell, professed to have received the 'gift of tongues;' and, though Story exposed her imposture, she found disciples in London, and was credited by Edward Irving [q. v.], then in the maelstrom of his impassioned fanaticism. On the basis of her pretensions arose the 'Holy Catholic Apostolic Church' (see CARLYLE, Life, ii. 213, and Reminiscences, ed. Norton, ii. 204). Story remained in his charge at the secession in 1843, and in 1853 saw a new parish church erected and a supplementary church placed on his southern borders—the expenses largely defrayed through his own exertions—to meet the needs of a young community when Lochlongside was feued. After a period of weak health, he died on 22 Nov. 1859. He was

buried in Rosneath churchyard, and a monument to his memory, from a design by the sculptor William Brodie [q. v.], was placed on the wall of the chancel in the parish church. Story married, in 1828, Helen Boyle, daughter of Mr. Dunlop of Keppoch, Dumbartonshire, and was survived by her and two children.

In 1811 appeared 'The Institute,' an heroic poem in four cantos, written conjointly by Story and Thomas Pringle. Its youthful satire is direct and pungent, and the couplets display ingenuity and ease. In 1829 he published, under the title of 'Peace in Believing,' a memoir of a devout girl named Isabella Campbell, sister of the Mary Campbell who later professed the 'tongues.' The book ran into three editions in a few weeks. Wilberforce said that the narrative filled him 'with reverence and admiration.' Story wrote on his parish for the 'Statistical Account' of 1841.

[R. H. Story's Memoir of the Life of the Rev. Robert Story, 1862; Mrs. Oliphant's Life of Edward Irving, ii. 128; Memorials of M'Leod Campbell; Hanna's Life of Chalmers.] T. B.

STORY, ROBERT (1795–1860), Northumberland poet, born at Wark on 17 Oct. 1795, was the son of Robin Story (d. 14 May 1809), a Northumbrian peasant, by his wife, Mary Hooliston, a native of Lauder. He was educated at Wark school under Mr. Kinton, with whom he made rapid progress, and then at Crookham, where he was tempted to play truant by a lame fiddler. About 1807 he commenced work as a gardener, but found more congenial service as a shepherd, an occupation commemorated in one of his best lyrics, 'Pours the spring on Howdsden yet.' In the summer of 1810 he began to teach the elements in a school at Humbleton, and studied with ardour the verses of Dr. Watts and Mrs. Barbauld. He subsequently served in various schools, where his accent excited derision. He was ambitious to follow the plough, like Burns, but after some intermittent field labour, in the intervals of which he corrected the proofs of his ill-conceived poem on 'The Harvest' (1816), he returned to teaching. In 1820 he eventually started a successful school on his own account at Gargrave in Yorkshire, his home for over twenty years. There, on 17 May 1823 (having discarded in turn several 'rustic loves' apostrophised in early poems), he married Ellen Ellison, by whom he had a large family. About 1825 he made the acquaintance of John Nicholson [q. v.], the Airedale poet, in emulation of whom he issued a small volume of verse entitled

'Craven Blossoms' (1826, 8vo). He augmented his income by acting as parish clerk and by contributions to the Newcastle papers. But about 1830 his prosperity was rudely interrupted. At the time of the reform agitation Story signalised himself by strong partisanship on the conservative side. His views were obnoxious to the parents of most of his pupils; on various pretexts the children were removed, and the schoolmaster was persecuted in numerous ways. His imprudent attempts at resistance involved him in debt. He met with some success in selling a volume of verse entitled the 'Magic Fountain,' written in 1829, and his hopes were wildly excited by the applause which attended his poetic rallying cry to the conservative party, entitled 'The Isles are Awake' (1834). In 1843 the conservative members of parliament for the West Riding obtained from Sir Robert Peel a small post for Story in the audit office. For two years he had depended mainly upon the help of his friends and the sale among them of his new volume entitled 'The Outlaw' (London, 1839 12mo). In 1842 he issued an autobiographic medley called 'Love and Literature' (London, 8vo), which again had a fair sale, mainly in the West Riding and in Northumberland, where he had found a warm friend in William Gourley, a self-taught mathematician. In London he had a struggle to make ends meet, and suffered greatly by the loss of four of his children; but his literary productiveness went on. In 1845 appeared a volume of 'Songs and Lyrical Poems' (London, 8vo; 3rd edit. 1849), and in 1852 a versified tale of the Heptarchy, 'Guthrum the Dane.' In 1854 he visited Paris and was presented to Napoleon III as a successor of Burns, and in 1857 the Duke of Northumberland issued at his own expense a sumptuous edition of his 'Poetical Works' (Newcastle, 1857, 8vo). The beauty of the volume seems to have disarmed the critics, for not only did Macaulay and Aytoun signify their approbation, but Carlyle in November 1857 detected in it 'a certain rustic vigour of life, breezy freshness, as of the Cheviot Hills.' This is notably the case in a few of the lyrics, intimately inspired by the localities of the poet's youth, such as 'The wild thyme still blossoms in green Homil-heugh;' but, broadly speaking, one is less impressed by the distinctive merit of Story's poems than by the courage and success with which he set about selling them with a view to relieve himself of the debts by which he was at all times encumbered. He died at Battersea on 7 July 1860, and was buried in Brompton cemetery. A short life was prefixed to a selection of his 'Poems' edited by John James in 1861.

[Story's Works, especially his Love and Literature; Memoir by John James, with an engraved portrait after R. Waller, 1861; Gent. Mag. 1860, ii. 313; Leeds Mercury, 10 July 1860; Athenæum, 1858, i. 176; Allibone's Dict. of English Literature.] T. S.

STORY, THOMAS (1670?–1742), quaker, son by his first wife of Thomas Story of Justice Town in the parish of Kirklinton, near Carlisle, and younger brother of George Warter Story [q. v.], was born there about 1670. After being educated at the Carlisle grammar school, and acquiring skill in fencing and music, Story read law under Dr. Richard Gilpin at Scaleby Castle, Cumberland. In 1687 he settled in chambers in Carlisle, and, although till then a good churchman, began to have scruples about the christening of infants and other rites. Many of the influential families around were quakers, and Story experienced on 1 April 1689 a call or 'conversion' to their tenets. He at once 'put off his usual airs, his jovial address, and the sword which he had worn as a modish and manly ornament.' He also burned his musical instruments, and divested himself of the superfluous parts of his apparel. In 1693 he began to preach. That year he first met William Penn (1644–1718) [q. v.], who, on his deciding to settle in London (1695), assisted him to find legal employment among the quakers, in conveyancing and drawing up settlements. He was appointed registrar of the society, and employed to abstract and index the deeds of London quarterly meeting. At this time he paid visits to, and discussed quakerism with, the Countess of Carlisle, Sir John Rhodes of Balbur Hall, Derbyshire; Sir Thomas Liddell of Ravensworth Castle, Northumberland; and the Czar Peter, then on a visit to Greenwich. To the latter he presented the Latin version of Robert Barclay's 'Apology,' which, however, the czar could not read, and other books in Dutch.

Story accompanied Penn to Ireland in 1698, stayed at Shangarry, and visited his brother, George Story, then dean of Limerick. In November of that year he sailed for Pennsylvania, where, at the request of Penn, who shortly followed, he remained sixteen years. He was chosen the first recorder of Philadelphia by a charter of 25 Oct. 1701, was a member of the council of state, keeper of the great seal, master of the rolls, and in 1706 elected mayor of Philadelphia, but paid the fine of 20l. for declining to serve (PROUD, Hist. of Pennsylvania, i. 421, 450, 484, ii. 60, App. p. 45). Story was also treasurer of the Pennsylvania Land Company, to which, about the time he left, he sold his estates. James Hoskins, in the 'Pennsylvania Bubble bubbled by the Treasurer,' 1726, accused him of unfair dealings, but Story was adjudged honest by a court of arbitration appointed in London in 1723 (*Determination of the Case of Mr. T. S.*', &c., London, 1724, 4to). During his residence in Pennsylvania, Story travelled about preaching, and visited Jamaica and Barbados. He married while in America, but lost his wife six years later. On 6 Dec. 1714 he returned to London, and on Sunday, 12 Dec., he preached at Gracechurch Street meeting. He held meetings at Oxford, which were attended by 'scholars and people of fashion;' the former created an unruly disturbance.

On a visit to Holland in 1715 William Sewel [q. v.] acted as his interpreter. Next year he was preaching in Ireland. At Limerick crowds came to see the dean's brother; while his cousin, Charles Story, prebendary of Limerick, also attended his meetings. At Kilkenny Story was arrested, but after a few days the sheriff released him, in spite of the bishop of Ossory having committed him for three months' imprisonment. In 1717 Story was with the Barclays at Ury in Scotland. The next year he attended the deathbed and funeral of William Penn. From this time he paid during the season frequent visits to Bath, where his preaching was so much admired that the afternoon meetings were crowded with people of both sexes, and of 'all ranks and notions.' When he was at Justice Town, which he purchased of his brother's widow about 1723, his favourite pursuit was forestry. He planted nurseries of many English and American trees, and at the time of his death, from paralysis, on 24 June 1742, was building a new house. He was buried in the Friends' burial-ground at Fisher Street, Carlisle, on 26 June. By his wife Anne, daughter of Edward Shippen, first mayor of Philadelphia in 1701, Story had no issue. He devised by his will (337 Tremley, P. C. C.), dated 1741, all his lands in England and Pennsylvania to be sold, the former for the benefit of his sister, Ann Elliot, and her two daughters; the latter for members of the Shippen family. Money was left to poor Friends of Carlisle monthly meeting, and for the education of quaker children in Clerkenwell.

Story's sermons were taken down in shorthand and some were collected as 'Discourses delivered in the Public Assemblies of the People called Quakers,' 1738, 1744, 1764, 8vo. Beside several papers, he published: 1. 'Reasons why those of the . . . Quakers challenged by George Keith [1639?–1716,

q. v.] to meet him . . . refuse,' 1696, fol. 2. 'A Word to the Wise,' also in answer to Keith, 1697, 4to; republished as 'A Word to the Well Inclin'd,' 1698, 4to. His 'Journal,' Newcastle, 1747, fol., contains the account of his missionary labours, and of some remarkable interviews with persons of rank. It was abridged by John Kendall (1726–1815) [q. v.], 1786, 1832, and published in the 'Friends' Library,' Philadelphia, 1846. Among many passages which throw light upon contemporary religious opinions is one of special interest in which Story relates a discussion with the Earl of Lonsdale in 1739 upon 'a people of late appearing in this kingdom to which the name of Methodists is given' (*Journal*, p. 741).

[Story's Journal: Conversations, Discussions, and Anecdotes of Thomas Story, compiled by Nat. Richardson, Phil., 1860; Watson's Annals of Pennsylvania, i. 25, 85, 369, 522; Hutchinson's Hist. of Cumberland, ii. 567; Jollie's Cumberland Guide, 1811, p. 55; London Daily Advertiser for 28 June 1742; Smith's Catalogue, ii. 636–9; Buchanan's Shippen Genealogy (Washington, 1877).]   C. F. S.

STOTHARD, Mrs. ANNA ELIZA (1790–1883), novelist. [See BRAY.]

STOTHARD, CHARLES ALFRED (1786–1821), antiquarian draughtsman, born in London on 5 July 1786, was the second son of Thomas Stothard [q. v.] by his wife, Rebecca Watkins. He was educated in Latin by Robert Burnside [q. v.], and early showed talent for drawing. In 1807 he was admitted a student of the Royal Academy, and in 1811 he exhibited there a picture of the death of Richard II at Pontefract, in which the costumes were depicted with strict historical accuracy. In the same year he published the first number of the 'Monumental Effigies of Great Britain,' a work designed to portray the changes in English costume from the twelfth century to the reign of Henry VIII. The work was issued in twelve parts, of which the first ten were prepared by Stothard himself; but the last two issued after his death were the work of other artists. The letterpress was supplied by his brother-in-law, Alfred John Kempe [q. v.], and the last number appeared in 1832. A new edition, with considerable additions, edited by John Hewitt, was published in 1876.

In 1815 Stothard was employed by Daniel Lysons [q. v.] to make drawings for 'Magna Britannia,' and for this purpose he journeyed through northern England as far as the Picts' wall. During his absence in the north Lysons procured him the appointment of historical draughtsman to the Society of Antiquaries. In 1810 he was deputed by the society to make drawings of the Bayeux tapestry, and during his stay in Normandy discovered in a cellar at the abbey of Fontevrault effigies of several of the Plantagenet sovereigns. In 1818 the drawings of the tapestry were completed, and in the year following Stothard laid them before the Society of Antiquaries together with a valuable paper on the date of the tapestry (see *Archæologia*, xix. 184). In this essay Stothard for the first time pointed out that the tapestry might be contemporary with the events it depicted without being the work of Matilda [q. v.], queen of William of Normandy, with whom it was traditionally associated, and conclusively proved, from the accuracy of the costumes, that it could not be a work of twelfth-century date, as had been contended by the Abbé de la Rue (cf. FREEMAN, *Norman Conquest*, 1869, iii. 367). On 2 July of the same year Stothard was elected a fellow of the Society of Antiquaries, and his drawings were published between 1821 and 1823 in the society's 'Vetusta Monumenta' (vol. vi. plates 1–17). Stothard was killed on 28 May 1821 by a fall from a ladder while he was making drawings of a stained-glass window in the church at Beerferris in Devonshire. He was buried at Beerferris. In February 1818 he married Anna Eliza, daughter of John Kempe, bullion-porter at the mint. She afterwards married Edward Atkyns Bray [q. v.], and was well known as a writer under her name of Anna Eliza Bray [q. v.]

Besides the works mentioned, Stothard illustrated his wife's 'Letters written during a Tour through Normandy,' London, 1820, 8vo. A portrait engraved from a miniature painted by Alfred Chalon is prefixed to Mrs. Stothard's 'Memoirs' of her husband.

[Memoirs of C. A. Stothard, by Mrs. Stothard, 1823; Autobiography of Anna Eliza Bray, 1889; Memoir by A. J. Kempe in Gent. Mag. 1821, i. 643, reprinted in the Annual Biogr. and Obituary, 1822; Gent. Mag. 1830, ii. 497; Blackwood's Mag. xxxix. 764; Quarterly Review, xxv. 115; Redgrave's Dict. of English Artists; Bryan's Dict. of Painters and Engravers, ed. Graves; Encyclopædia Britannica, 9th edit.; Chambers's Encyclopædia, 1895.]

E. I. C.

STOTHARD, THOMAS (1755–1834), painter and book-illustrator, the son of a publican, was born at the Black Horse Inn, Long Acre, London, on 17 Aug. 1755. His father was a native of Stutton, near Tadcaster, and his mother, whose maiden name was Reynolds, came from Shrewsbury. They

removed from Stutton to London in 1760. Being delicate, Stothard was sent to his uncle at York, who placed him with an old lady, named Stainburn, at Acomb, where he copied some prints by Strange and Houbraken. At eight years old he was sent to two old aunts at Stutton, and went to a day school at Tadcaster. When thirteen his father brought him to London and sent him to a boarding-school at Ilford, Essex, where he was half starved, and took dancing lessons from the father of the celebrated clown, Joseph Grimaldi. His father died in 1770, leaving a provision for his mother and 1,200l. to himself. His mother lived at Stepney Green, and Stothard was apprenticed to a draughtsman of patterns for flowered silks in Spital Square, Spitalfields. The fashion for these silks declining, he employed his leisure in making designs from Homer and Spenser, being encouraged thereto by his master, who died before his apprenticeship was out. He appears to have remained with his master's widow after this, as it was at her house that his drawings attracted the attention of Mr. Harrison, the publisher of the 'Novelist's' and the 'Poetical' magazines, who gave him his first commission for an illustration, but he was not regularly engaged by Harrison till about 1779. Meanwhile he gave up the pattern business and entered the schools of the Royal Academy (1777). In this year he exhibited at the Society of Artists two Welsh landscapes, and 'A Battle' from Homer. He was then living at Mr. Somner's (or Sumners) near The Blind Beggar, at Bethnal Green. About this time he formed a friendship with Samuel Shelley [q. v.], with whom he took lodgings in the Strand in 1778, when he commenced to exhibit at the Royal Academy, sending a picture of 'The Holy Family.' He added to his slender income by painting small family portraits, and frequently visited the studio of Sir Joshua Reynolds, from whom and from Richard Wilson, the landscape-painter, he received encouragement and advice.

In 1779 Stothard commenced his career as an illustrator of books, being employed to illustrate 'Ossian' and Hervey's 'Naval History.' But his principal employers were Bell and Harrison, and in this year his numerous designs for Bell's 'Poets' and Harrison's 'Novelist's Magazine' began to be published. The first of the latter was a scene from 'Joseph Andrews' (dated 1 Dec.), and in the following year he made no less than 148 drawings for this publication, for which he was paid a guinea apiece. He also made many drawings for the 'Ladies' Magazine'

F F

in this and the following years, and a number of small but spirited drawings of the famous actors and actresses of the day. Among the prose works illustrated by him were novels by Fielding, Smollett, Richardson, and Sterne, Ridley's 'Tales of the Genii,' Paltock's 'Peter Wilkins,' 'Don Quixote,' 'Gil Blas,' 'Robinson Crusoe,' the 'Arabian Nights,' the 'Vicar of Wakefield,' and 'Gulliver's Travels.' These designs made a new departure in book illustration by their variety of invention, their literary sympathy, their spirit and their grace. Those to 'Peregrine Pickle' and 'Peter Wilkins' have been specially admired, but Stothard never surpassed those to 'Clarissa Harlowe' for elegance, or those to 'Tristram Shandy' for delicate humour. He may be said to have founded the types of Sancho Panza and Uncle Toby, afterwards adopted by his friend Charles Robert Leslie [q. v.] and others. To this period also belong a few charming illustrations to Ritson's 'Songs' (1783). A little later (1788-9) came his illustrations to the 'Pilgrim's Progress,' in which he found a region of pure but very human allegory well suited to his gentle imagination.

Some larger prints published separately about this time included 'The Power of Innocence,' illustrations of 'Cecilia,' the 'Sorrows of Werther,' 'Caroline de Lichtfield,' and a few classical and allegorical pieces, as 'Callisto' and 'Zephyrus and Flora.' The last two were engraved by William Blake [q. v.], at this time a friend of Stothard, and often employed to engrave his designs. To 1790 belong his illustrations to 'Robinson Crusoe,' published by John Stockdale, and engraved by Medland, a series of great beauty (reingraved by C. Heath, and published by Cadell thirty years later); and also a set of six charming groups of children at school and at play. Besides these more important designs, he executed a number of headpieces, tailpieces, frontispieces, and vignettes of all kinds, including some charming miniature drawings of royal festivities. He designed even shop-cards and fashion plates, for, though popular, he was poorly paid, and, having married in 1783, had to provide for an increasing family.

For some years Stothard's contributions to the Royal Academy consisted principally of designs from poets and novelists, and he sent none from 1786 to 1791. In the latter year the exhibition of 'Friars, a Conversation,' and three historical pictures ('Marriage of Henry the Fifth with Catherine of France,' and two from the life of Richard I), was followed by his election as an associate. It is said that after this his contributions to

the academy exhibitions were generally painted in oils. It was at this time that he was employed upon Macklin's bible, for which he painted 'Jacob's Dream,' 'Ruth and Boaz,' and 'St. John preaching in the Wilderness.' In 1792 he exhibited 'A Confirmation,' one of his elegant illustrations of the Book of Common Prayer, which was published by Harding in that year. In 1793, besides six paintings from Telemachus, came the exquisite little picture of 'The Dryads finding Narcissus,' which is now in the National Gallery. Those years, 1792-3, are memorable for the appearance of his designs to Milton, which were engraved by Bartolozzi, and perhaps show more than any other of his works the true limits of his genius. It was far more at home in 'Paradise' than 'Pandemonium,' but his 'Sin' and 'Death' are finely conceived. It was in 1793 also that his first illustrations to Rogers's 'Pleasures of Memory' were executed. The first edition of the poem in the British Museum, illustrated by Stothard, is dated 1794, but there are two engravings in the print-room—one of them the delightful 'Hunt the Slipper'—which are dated 1793.

Stothard was elected an academician in 1794, and removed from Henrietta Street, Covent Garden, to 28 Newman Street, where he remained till his death. He purchased the house and furniture out of the capital left him by his father. About this time he began a series of a dozen or more pictures of historical events for Bowyer's 'Historic Gallery' or illustrated edition of Hume, on which he appears to have been engaged for ten years at least (1795-1805). They range from the 'Suppression of the Monasteries' to the 'Landing of William III at Torbay.' They are of no great merit, but one of them, 'The Smothering of the Princes in the Tower' (dated 1795), is interesting from its likeness to Chantrey's famous 'Sleeping Children' in Lichfield Cathedral (which is said to have been designed by Stothard); the pose of the children had, however, been anticipated in Northcote's 'Murder of the Princes in the Tower,' exhibited in 1786 (cf. Mrs. BRAY, Thomas Stothard, p. 184 n.) In 1796 he exhibited 'A Victory,' which he kept till his death, and regarded as his finest painting, and in this year appeared his illustrations to the 'Fables of Flora,' which are remarkable for the gracefulness of their fancy and the beautiful drawing of the flowers. In 1798 were published his beautiful illustrations to Pope's 'Rape of the Lock,' in 1799 the 'Seven Ages' from Shakespeare, and by the close of the century he may be said to have almost covered his field of illustration, though he often went over the same ground again for different publishers. He illustrated Shakespeare, e.g. for Tegg, Bell, Boydell (three plates only), Kearsley, Heath, and Pickering; the 'Spectator,' and many poets and novelists for John Sharpe; Spenser for Kearsley, Burns for Cadell and Davies (he visited Scotland for the purpose in 1809), Byron for John Murray, a number of poets for the Chiswick Press, some of the 'Waverley' novels, and Rogers over and over again; but, excepting perhaps by the Watteau-like fancy of scenes from the 'Decameron,' a number of which were exhibited at the Royal Academy in 1819 and 1820, he added little to his known accomplishment as a book-illustrator. This was not, however, his only employment. In 1799 he commenced the decoration of the grand staircase at Burghley House, near Stamford, for the Marquis of Exeter. The subjects of his designs are 'War,' 'Intemperance' ('Antony and Cleopatra'), and the 'Descent of Orpheus into Hell,' and the figures are much larger than life. He exhibited sketches for this work in 1806 and 1810, one of which is now in the National Gallery. The execution of this important commission occupied the summers of four years, during which he lost his mother, who lived with him.

In 1806 Stothard received a commission from Cromek the engraver to paint his famous picture of the 'Canterbury Pilgrims setting forth from the Tabard Inn.' The subject had been treated before by Stothard for Ritson, but Cromek had previously offered the commission to William Blake, and hence ensued a lamentable breach between the two old friends which was never healed [see BLAKE, WILLIAM, 1757–1827, and CROMEK, ROBERT HARTLEY]. The picture (now, with many sketches for it, in the National Gallery) was exhibited in 1807 in England, Scotland, and Ireland, and drew crowds. The engraving was entrusted to Luigi Schiavonetti [q. v.], who etched the plate and engraved wholly in part some of the figures. After his death it was being worked upon by Francis Engleheart [q. v.] when Cromek died (1812). It was next given to Niccolò Schiavonetti, who had not finished it at his death in 1813, and it was finally completed by James Heath [q. v.] and published in October 1817, some years after Blake's rival engraving. Its success was enormous, but Stothard had no share in the profits. All he received was 60l. from Cromek for the picture, which Cromek sold to Hart Davis for 300l. Cromek promised

him an extra 40l., but never paid it, and Stothard did not like to press the widow for it. She gave him some copies of the engraving. Stothard made a copy of the picture for Samuel Rogers, and another, lengthened and altered, for Mr. Benson of Doncaster. He is also said to have made a third copy, which was perhaps that exhibited by Lady Marian Alford at the winter exhibition of old masters at the Royal Academy in 1872.

During these years his taste was frequently consulted in the decoration of the houses of his wealthy friends and patrons, of whom Samuel Rogers was the earliest and most constant. Stothard helped in the decoration of Rogers's house in St. James's Place (built 1803), and in the illustration of successive editions of his poems for over forty years. In the most elaborate editions of Rogers's 'Italy' (1830) and the 'Poems' (1834) Stothard joined with Turner in contributing illustrations, which were engraved on steel by Finden and others. The smaller engravings on wood by Luke Clennell (the first of which appeared in Rogers's 'Pleasures of Memory,' 1810) are justly prized for their close imitation of Stothard's beautiful touch with the pen. Less known are the little illustrations of the 'Pleasures of Memory' (1808) and 'Human Life' (1810) in the 'Royal Engagement Pocket Atlas,' an annual for which he provided the headpieces for many years. Other patrons (and friends also) were Robert Markham (archdeacon of York), Thomas Hope, William Beckford of Fonthill, Samuel Boddington, whose children he painted, and Colonel Johnes of Hafod, whose library he decorated (1810) with eight scenes from Froissart and Monstrelet in imitation of sculpture. He also designed the monument (executed by Chantrey) for Johnes's daughter, his own pupil, who died in 1811.

In 1812 he was appointed librarian of the Royal Academy, after acting as deputy for two years. In 1814 he successfully competed for the silver shield to be presented by the merchants and bankers of London to the Duke of Wellington in commemoration of his victories. His design for this elaborate work, well known as the 'Wellington Shield,' was prepared in three weeks, and excited great admiration. He also executed the models for the silversmiths Green, Ward, & Green, and made etchings of the designs. Among his miscellaneous works are many other designs for silver plate, such as salvers, knife-handles, and decanter-tables of much elegance, prepared for Rundle & Bridge; and he designed the reverse of the gold medal of the Royal Academy, and the monument to Garrick in Westminster Abbey. He also designed transparencies on the occasion of the jubilee, and two on the installation of George III [...]

In [...] Stothard went over to Paris with Chantrey and others, and visited the Louvre [...]

The works of art in the painter's possession at his death were sold at Christie's in June 1834. There included a hundred of his pictures in oil and upwards of a thousand sketches, which realised about 1,500l. The enormous number of his designs, which are estimated at five thousand (Mrs. Bray says ten thousand), is enough to prove his industry, and it is recorded that even on his wedding day he attended the academy schools, and casually asked a fellow-student to come home and dine with him and his bride in order to celebrate that event. He was a great reader, and never tired of observing nature; and he was fond of hunting butterflies, whose wings he studied for their beautiful arrangements of colour. Stothard's life appears to have been as pure and blameless as the art to which it was devoted. His disposition was retiring, and he did not seek society; but he was justly esteemed by his fellow-artists and his few intimate friends. He paid visits to Archdeacon Markham and other of his friends; he went once to Paris; but his art supplied him with sufficient pleasure to the end of his life. As Leigh Hunt said of him in his last days, 'an angel dwelt in that tottering house amidst the wintry bowers of white locks, warming it to the last with summer fancies.'

Stothard was not much regarded as a painter in his lifetime; he sent comparatively few pictures to the academy, and most of these were very small; but as a colourist he was always pure, and sometimes lovely. It was as an illustrator and 'embellisher' of books that he attained a place which is second to none for invention and for grace. He followed in the wake of Cipriani and

Angelica Kauffmann, but he raised the prettiness of their school above insipidity and affectation. By constant study of nature and his affinity for all that was pure and beautiful in older art (especially the Elgin marbles and the designs of Raphael and Rubens) he formed a style of his own which, in spite of some mannerism, has exercised an unabated charm from his own day to the present. He illustrated almost the whole range of English literature with a taste that seldom failed and a sympathy that was often remarkable. He was deficient in vigour and passion, but he had an exquisite sense of beauty; and his drawing, if not always accurate in detail, was of exceeding grace. He had a true genius for composition and excelled in tender pathos and gentle humour, and in the rendering of virginal purity, womanly grace, and the charms of childhood he has few rivals.

More than three thousand of Stothard's designs were engraved, and nearly all of them are to be found in the Balmanno collection at the British Museum, where are also other engravings after Stothard and a number of drawings. There are many of his pictures in the National Gallery and at South Kensington Museum, principally from the Vernon and Sheepshanks collections.

There are several portraits of Stothard. He introduced himself, his wife, and his son Alfred into a picture of 'Speech-Day at Christ's Hospital,' exhibited in 1799. There are later portraits by Harlow, Jackson, and Wood, and busts by Chantrey, Baily, and Behnes.

[Mrs. Bray's Life of Thomas Stothard, R.A., 1851 (with lithographed portrait after Harlow), and the same writer's Memoir of Charles A. Stothard; Cunningham's Lives of Painters, ed. Heaton; Magazine of the Fine Arts, 1833; Watt's Bibliotheca Britannica; Redgrave's Dict.; Redgraves' Century; Bryan's Dict. ed. Armstrong; Pilkington's Dict.; Gilchrist's Life of Blake; Letters of James Smetham; Wedmore's Studies in English Art, 1st ser.; Dobson's Eighteenth-Century Vignettes, 1st ser. ('The Quaker of Art'); Colvin's Children in Italian and English Design; Monkhouse's Earlier English Watercolorists; Sandby's Hist. of the Royal Academy; Catalogues of the National Gallery and South Kensington Museum.]   C. M.

STOTHERD, RICHARD HUGH (1828–1895), major-general royal engineers, director-general of the ordnance survey of the United Kingdom, son of General Richard J. Stotherd (1796–1879), colonel commandant royal engineers, by his first wife, Elizabeth Sydney (d. 1853), daughter of Hugh Boyle, of Dungiven, co. Londonderry, was born at Angler Castle, co. Tyrone, on 25 Nov. 1828. His father, who came of a Lincolnshire family, was long employed upon the ordnance survey of Ireland, was commanding royal engineer in succession at Limerick, Halifax, Nova Scotia, and at Dover, and was promoted general 19 June 1872.

Educated at University College school, and at the Royal Military Academy at Woolwich, Stotherd received a commission as second lieutenant in the royal engineers on 2 May 1847, and first lieutenant on 28 Oct. He went through the usual course of professional study at Chatham, and then served at Woolwich and at Gibraltar, and on his return home was posted to the ordnance survey of Great Britain and sent to Dumfries. He was promoted to be second captain on 21 May 1855, and first captain on 17 May 1860. After quitting the ordnance survey in 1861 Stotherd went to Weymouth, and then, in connection with the Trent affair, to North America, where he acted as brigade major and assistant to the commanding royal engineer. He was commended for his services during the four years he served in Canada and New Brunswick.

On Stotherd's return to England on 13 Feb. 1865 he was appointed instructor in electricity, chemistry, and photography at the school of military engineering at Chatham. There he took up the question of the application of electricity to mining and to submarine mining (then in its infancy), and he also organised the first field telegraph. In 1867 he was sent to the Paris Exhibition to report on military telegraph apparatus and engineering exhibits. In 1868 Prince Arthur (afterwards Duke of Connaught) was under his instruction.

While at Chatham Stotherd took great interest in the system of army signalling, of which he was the chief instructor, and the army is indebted to him for his advocacy of the Morse system now in use. He was promoted to be brevet major on 22 Nov. 1870, regimental major on 5 July 1872, and regimental lieutenant-colonel on 3 Aug. 1872.

In 1871 Stotherd accompanied Colonel C. C. Chesney of the royal engineers to the continent to report upon the military operations of the Franco-German war, and of the siege of Paris by Marshal MacMahon during the Communist insurrections. In April 1873 he was appointed to the war office in London, to advise the inspector-general of fortifications on the subject of submarine mines and of military telegraphs. He was from 1873 to 1876 president of the first war office torpedo committee, which became a standing committee and still exists.

In 1876 Stotherd was appointed commanding royal engineer of the Belfast military district, where he remained for five years. He was promoted to be brevet colonel on 3 Aug. 1877, and regimental colonel on 26 April 1882. In September 1881 he was appointed to the charge of the ordnance survey in Ireland, residing at the Mountjoy Barracks, Phœnix Park, Dublin. After the assassination of Lord Frederick Cavendish, Stotherd had extra work thrown upon him as a military justice of the peace for the city of Dublin in charge of troops in aid of the civil power.

On 1 April 1883 Stotherd was appointed director-general of the ordnance survey of the United Kingdom, and went to its headquarters at Southampton. The time was a busy and important one for the survey. Large augmentations of staff had been made under his predecessor, Lieutenant-general A. C. Cooke, and increased work in all branches was in full swing, the result of a recommendation of the parliamentary select committee of 1878, that, in order to facilitate the transfer of land, the original large-scale surveys should be completed in 1890, instead of 1900. There was also the difficult question of the general revision of the national survey, for which, in the case of the large towns and cities—London in particular—the need was most pressing. Stotherd placed before the government a comprehensive scheme with an estimate for many years in advance, and urged strenuously the paramount importance of a systematic organic revision. He pointed out that as the field work of the 'primary detail survey' was all but finished, and the 'trig.' hands running out of work, the time was opportune for making a commencement, and so avoid a wholesale discharge of useful men taken on at a time of pressure. The result was treasury sanction to a tentative commencement.

In 1884 Stotherd prepared at Southampton special maps for the boundary commission in connection with Mr. Gladstone's Redistribution of Seats Bill. By working day and night nearly half a million of maps were prepared. Special thanks were accorded by the government to Stotherd for his promptitude in meeting their requirements, and he was made a C.B. In the adaptation of photography and electricity to the production of maps, Stotherd introduced practical improvements. On 25 Nov. 1886 he was compelled by the age rule to retire from the army and from his appointment, receiving the honorary rank of major-general. He died suddenly, from heart disease, on 1 May 1895 at Camberley, Surrey, where he resided.

Stotherd married first, on 11 June 1861, at St. George's, Hanover Square, London, Caroline Frances Wood (d. 17 Feb. 1872), by whom he had a large family; and secondly, on 29 Sept. 1875, at Edinburgh, Elizabeth Janet Melville, who survived him. He contributed articles to 'The Professional Papers of the Corps of Royal Engineers,' vols. xvii. and xviii., and was the author of the first text-book published in England on submarine mining, entitled 'Notes on Defence by Submarine Mines,' 8vo, Brompton, Kent; the second edition is dated 1873.

[War Office Records; Royal Engineers Records; Royal Engineers Journal, 1879 and 1895 (obituary notices); Minutes of Proceedings of the Institution of Civil Engineers, vol. cxxi. (obituary notice); White's Ordnance Survey of the United Kingdom; Blue Books.]   R. H. V.

STOUGHTON, ISRAEL (d. 1645?), colonist, born in England, emigrated to Massachusetts early in 1630, where he and his companions founded the town of Dorchester, of which he was admitted a freeman on 5 Nov. 1633. He was chosen representative (probably, but not certainly) for Dorchester in the assemblies of 1634 and 1635. But in the latter year, when the colony was disturbed by the antinomian disputes, Stoughton wrote a book which, as it would seem, reflected on the constitution of the colony and was displeasing to the general court. The author somewhat strangely petitioned that the book might be 'forthwith burnt, as being weak and offensive.' No copy is known to exist. In spite of Stoughton's submission, he was declared incapable of holding office for three years. This sentence, however, was remitted in 1636, and Stoughton was chosen assistant in 1637. In the same year he was intrusted with the command of the Massachusetts force against the Pequot Indians, and discharged it with no great credit to himself either for soldiership or humanity. Stoughton was annually chosen as assistant till 1643, and in 1639 he, together with John Endecott [q. v.], acted as a commissioner on behalf of Massachusetts to settle a boundary dispute with Plymouth. He visited England towards the end of 1643 or the beginning of 1644, returned to America, and crossed again towards the end of 1644. He was then appointed a lieutenant-colonel in the parliamentary army, and soon after died at Lincoln.

WILLIAM STOUGHTON (1630?–1701), son of the above, born probably in England about 1630, graduated B.A. at Harvard and was called to the ministry, but soon abandoned it for civil life. He came to England, was incorporated at New College, Oxford, on 28 April 1652, and, after being elected fellow of that society, graduated M.A. on 30 June 1653. After the Restoration he was ejected from New College, and, returning to America, was continuously elected assistant from 1671 to 1686. In 1684, however, and again in 1686, he was so displeased with the general result of the election that he refused to qualify for office by taking the necessary oath. In the politics of his colony he was identified with the moderate party, whose general policy towards the crown was one of concession. In spite of this he seems to have retained the confidence of his fellow-colonists, as he was chosen one of the federal commissioners from 1673 to 1677, and again from 1680 to 1686. In 1677 he was appointed one of two agents to represent the colony in England in a boundary dispute with the proprietors of New Hampshire. In 1692 he was appointed lieutenant-governor under the new charter of Massachusetts, and held that office till his death. In the year of his appointment he presided over the court specially constituted for the trial of the Salem witches, and acted with great severity. He died unmarried at Dorchester, New England, on 7 July 1701. He was a liberal benefactor to Harvard University, founding a hall, called by his name, at a cost of 1,000*l.*, and bequeathing twenty-seven acres of land.

[Hutchinson's History of Massachusetts; Palfrey's History of New England; Sewell's Diary in Mass. Hist. Soc. Coll. 5th ser. vol. vi.; Quincy's History of Harvard University; Hist. of Dorchester (Dorchester Ant. and Hist. Soc.), 1851-8; Collections of Dorchester Ant. and Hist. Soc.]   J. A. D.

STOUGHTON, JOHN (1807-1897), dissenting minister, son of Thomas Stoughton by his wife, Sarah Bullard, daughter of the master of the Norwich lunatic asylum (Bethel Hospital), was born in the parish of St. Michael at Plea, Norwich, on 18 Nov. 1807. His father, son of an admiral in the navy, was a strict churchman. He died when Stoughton was only five years old, and the boy's education was somewhat neglected. His mother, a Friend, taught him to read, and sent him to the Norwich grammar school. While there he saw something of the intellectual coterie which then gave Norwich an exceptional position among provincial cities [see TAYLOR, WILLIAM, 1765-1836]. Placed in the office of a Roman catholic lawyer, Stoughton turned with zest from Blackstone and De Lolme to the study of Milner's 'End of Religious Controversy,' and convinced himself that the independent churches most

nearly corresponded to the primitive type. To this view he adhered through life. Abandoning the law, Stoughton in 1828 entered Highbury College, where the society of his contemporary, Henry Rogers [q. v.], formed a potent intellectual stimulus.

On his ordination in May 1833 Stoughton was called to the co-pastorate of the congregational church at Windsor. This charge he resigned after ten years to succeed to that of Hornton Street church, Kensington. He remained at Hornton Street for more than thirty years. Though he never took rank among the masters of pulpit eloquence, his sermons attracted the more cultivated middle class. His leisure he devoted to organisations for evangelical propaganda and to literary work, chiefly historical, which gained him wide recognition. He enjoyed the respect and friendship of some dignitaries of the church of England, among them Deans Alford, Hook, and Stanley, and Archbishops Tait and Magee. In 1856 he delivered the Congregational Lecture on 'The Ages of Christendom before the Reformation,' and was elected chairman of the Congregational Union.

In 1862 appeared his first important work, 'Church and State Two Hundred Years Ago: a History of Ecclesiastical Affairs in England from 1660 to 1663,' London, 8vo. There followed his elaborate 'Ecclesiastical History of England' (Civil Wars, Commonwealth, and Restoration), London, 1867-70, 4 vols. 8vo, which, though unduly diffuse in style, evinced careful study of original sources and freedom from pedantry and prejudice. With its sequels—'Religion in England under Queen Anne and the Georges,' London, 1878, 2 vols. 8vo, and 'Religion in England from 1800 to 1850,' London, 1884, 2 vols. 8vo—it forms an important contribution to the religious history of England.

At the instance of Lord Ebury, Stoughton compiled an account of nonconformist modes of communicating, which was appended to the fourth report of the ritual commission, 1870 (*Parl. Papers*, 1870, No. xix.) Having accepted in 1872 the chair of historical theology in New College, St. John's Wood, he resigned on 11 April 1874 the Kensington charge. With his professorial and literary work he combined for many years occasional duty as a preacher. In the summer of 1876 he arranged a conference between churchmen and dissenters, which met on 4 July in a room in the House of Lords under the presidency of Archbishop Tait, and discussed, without result, the means to co-operation in Christian effort. In 1877 he delivered in

Westminster Abbey a lecture on missions, part of a series of discourses by eminent nonconformists instituted by Dean Stanley by way of protest against ecclesiastical exclusiveness. He was one of the pall-bearers at the funeral of Dean Stanley on 25 July 1881. He attended the conferences held under the auspices of the evangelical alliance at New York in October 1873, at Basel in September 1879, and at Edinburgh in October 1885. On 27 June 1884 he resigned his chair at New College. His later days were spent in retirement at Ealing, varied by visits to Tunbridge Wells. He died of old age at Ealing on 24 Oct. 1897, and was buried in Ealing cemetery.

Stoughton received from the university of Edinburgh in 1868 the honorary degree of D.D., and from the Athenæum Club in 1874 the distinction of election by the committee on the nomination of Matthew Arnold. He was a man of fine figure and features and robust physique. He married, on 12 May 1835, the daughter of George Cooper of Windsor. She died in 1879. Of his eleven children by her four survive—viz. Mr. T. Wilberforce Stoughton, partner in the firm of Messrs. Hodder & Stoughton, and three married daughters.

Stoughton's culture was liberal, and was improved by much travel not only in France and Germany, but also in Italy—Rome he visited thrice—Spain, and Palestine. His travels furnished him with materials for three popular books of some merit—viz. 'Homes and Haunts of Luther,' London, 1875, 4to ; new edit. 1883, 8vo ; 'Footprints of Italian Reformers,' London, 1881, 8vo ; and 'The Spanish Reformers, their Memories and Dwelling Places,' London, 1883, 8vo.

Stoughton was no systematic theologian, and, after having his say on the Oxford movement (*Lectures on Tractarian Theology*, London, 1843, 12mo), eschewed controversy. His only contribution to apologetics was a lecture on 'The Nature and Value of the Miraculous Testimony to Christianity,' printed in 'Modern Scepticism,' ed. Ellicott, London, 1881, 8vo. Among his minor works, mainly historical, were (all published in London): 1. 'Notices of Windsor in the Olden Time,' 1844, 12mo. 2. 'Spiritual Heroes, or Sketches of the Puritans, their Characters and Times,' 1848, 8vo ; 2nd edit. 1850. 3. 'P. Doddridge: his Life and Labours,' 1851, 8vo ; 2nd edit. 1852. 4. 'Lights of the World, or Illustrations of Character drawn from the Records of the Christian Life,' 1852, 12mo ; new edit. 1876. 5. 'Scenes in other Lands, with their Associations,' 1850, 8vo. 6. 'The Pen, the Palm, and the Pul-

pit,' 1858, 8vo. 7. 'Lessons for Nonconformists,' 1862, 8vo. 8. 'Windsor: its History and Description of the Castle and Town,' 1862, 8vo. 9. 'Shades and Echoes of Old London,' 1864, 16mo: new edit. 1889, 8vo. 10. 'Our English Bible: its Translations and Translators,' 1878, 8vo. 11. 'Worthies of Science,' 1879, 8vo. 12. 'William Wilberforce,' 1880, 8vo. 13. 'Introduction to Historical Theology, being a Sketch of Doctrinal Progress from the Apostolic Era to the Reformation,' London, 1880, 8vo. 14. 'Reminiscences of Congregationalism Fifty Years Ago,' 1881, 8vo. 15. 'W. Penn, the Founder of Pennsylvania,' 1882, 8vo. 16. 'Howard the Philanthropist, and his Friends,' 1884, 8vo. 17. 'Golden Legends of the Olden Time,' 1885, 8vo. 18. 'The Rise and Progress of Congregationalism in the County of Norfolk,' 1886, 8vo. 19. 'The Revolution of 1688 in its bearings on Protestant Nonconformity,' 1888, 8vo. 20. 'Lights and Shadows of Primitive Christendom,' 1891, 8vo. 21. 'Recollections of a Long Life,' 1894, 8vo. 22. 'Lights and Shadows of Church Life,' 1895, 8vo.

[Recollections and Reminiscences above mentioned ; Times, 26 Oct. 1897 ; British Weekly, 28 Oct. 1897 ; Independent, 28 Oct. 1897 ; Christian World, 28 Oct. 1897 ; Men and Women of the Time ; Prothero's Life of Dean Stanley ; Wylie's Book of the Bunyan Festival ; Congregationalist Year-book ; Illustrated London News, 30 Oct. 1897, with portrait.]   J. M. R.

STOVIN, Sir FREDERICK (1783–1865), general, born in 1783, was the son of James Stovin of Whitgift, near Howden, Yorkshire. He was commissioned as ensign in the 52nd foot on 22 March 1800, served with it in Pulteney's expedition to Ferrol, where he was one of the few officers actually engaged, and became lieutenant on 7 Jan. 1801. He obtained a company in the 62nd foot on 24 June 1802, and (after a few months on half-pay) in the 28th foot on 9 July 1803. He served with the latter regiment in Ireland, where he was employed as brigade major, in Lord Cathcart's expedition to Bremen in 1805, and in the siege and capture of Copenhagen in 1807. In 1808 he served under Moore in Sweden, and afterwards in Spain in the Coruña campaign. He was aide-de-camp to General Alexander Mackenzie Fraser [q. v.] in the Walcheren expedition in 1809, and was present at the capture of Flushing. In January 1810 he went with the 28th to Gibraltar, and in April to Tarifa, where he distinguished himself in a sortie, driving the French out of an old convent which lay inconveniently close to the walls. He was brigade major at Gibraltar for a few months, but had to return to England in September on account of ill-health.

He went back to the Peninsula in July 1811, and, as aide-de-camp to Picton, he was present at the capture of Ciudad Rodrigo, and Badajoz. He was then appointed assistant adjutant-general to the 3rd (Picton's) division, and served with it in this capacity till the end of the war, without a single day's absence. He was present at Salamanca, Vittoria, Pyrenees, Nivelle, Orthes, and Toulouse, and received the gold cross with two clasps. He was made brevet major on 27 April 1812, and brevet lieutenant-colonel on 26 Aug. 1813.

In 1814 he was appointed deputy adjutant-general to the expeditionary force against the coasts of the United States, and he took part in the unsuccessful attack on New Orleans, and was wounded there. On 2 Jan. 1815 he was made K.C.B. He was promoted major in the 28th on 9 May 1816, and obtained the lieutenant-colonelcy of the 92nd on 2 Sept. 1819. He commanded that regiment in Jamaica from October 1820 to the middle of 1821, when he exchanged (9 Aug.) into the 90th light infantry. He commanded the 90th in the Ionian Islands till 23 April 1829, when he was placed on half-pay. He was made K.C.M.G. for his services there, the order being at that time confined to Malta and the Ionian Islands. He became colonel in the army on 22 July 1830, and major-general on 23 Nov. 1841. He was groom-in-waiting to the queen from 1837 to 1860, when he was made an extra groom. He was given the colonelcy of the 83rd foot on 1 Sept. 1848. He became lieutenant-general on 11 Nov. 1851, and general on 14 Aug. 1859, and received the G.C.B. on 18 May 1860. He died at St. James's Palace on 16 Aug. 1865. In 1815 he married Anne Elizabeth, second daughter of Sir Sitwell Sitwell, bart.; she died at Brighton on 3 April 1856, aged 63.

[Gent. Mag. 1856 i. 550, 1865 ii. 511 ; Cadell's Campaigns of the 28th Regiment ; Wellington Despatches.] E. M. L.

INDEX

TO

THE FIFTY-FOURTH VOLUME.